THE
BONE FLOWER
TRILOGY
COMPLETE AND UNABRIDGED

THE
BONE FLOWER
TRILOGY
COMPLETE AND UNABRIDGED

TL MORGANFIELD

FSB

THE BONE FLOWER TRILOGY
COMPLETE AND UNABRIDGED

Published by Feathered Serpent Books
Thornton, Colorado

Printed in the USA

ISBN 978-0-9909207-6-2

For Jeff

CONTENTS

THE BONE FLOWER THRONE
THE BONE FLOWER QUEEN
THE BONE FLOWER GODDESS

AUTHOR'S NOTE
COMPLETE CHARACTER LIST
FURTHER READING

to the northern desert

Tollan

The Basin of Mexico
10th Century CE

Tultepec

Teotihuacan

Acolman

Lake
Meztliapan

Chapultepec

Culhuacan

Xochimilco

Xico   Chalco

Xochicalco

THE
BONE FLOWER
THRONE

PART ONE
THE YEAR THIRTEEN RABBIT

CHAPTER ONE

In my sister Cualli's love stories, a woman's wedding day is always the happiest day of her life, but none of them had to marry their cousin when they were only seven. Though things could have been far worse; I might have had to marry one of my older brothers, like Itzcoatl, who thought it was funny to blow his snot at my older sisters. My cousin Black Otter at least was well mannered, and my best friend. But none of my sisters had to marry so young.

"It's because your father needs to secure an heir," Mother told me as she finished primping my feathered wedding dress. The handmaidens had finally cleared out of my nursery, leaving us alone with the murals of snakes, birds, and butterflies.

"But why can't he just name someone his heir?" I asked, kicking at the wicker baby basket that hung from the ceiling by a braided rope. No one but my dolls had slept in it since I'd started sleeping on a regular reed mat.

"As the king's only legitimate child, you carry the burden of succession." Though I read the unspoken part in Mother's frown: she too wished this could wait until I was older, and her mood had been just as cloudy as mine for the last two weeks since she'd first told me the news. She fretted over my long braided hair a moment then sighed. "You look beautiful though."

I didn't mind wearing my everyday dresses, but this one went all the way to my feet, and the skirt was stiff with hundreds of red parrot feathers. The handmaidens had covered my face with the traditional yellow tecozauitl paint, which felt like packed clay, and I wore my mother's heavy gold, turquoise, and quetzal-feather necklace. Hopefully I wouldn't always have to wear such smothering finery from now on. I could hardly climb trees and chase lizards dressed like this.

"How am I supposed to go to the calmecac this year, so I can learn to be a priestess like you were? Priestesses can't be married." I tried out some tears, to see if that would change anything.

Mother smiled though. "They'll still let you in, dear. It's a marriage only in name. For now anyway." Though she seemed to be saying it more for herself than me.

I wasn't going to get out of this wedding nonsense, so I held Mother's hand as we left the nursery for the great hall. Still, I pouted the whole way.

"This is a lot for both of us to deal with," Mother said. "The happiest day of my life was the day you were born, and it grieves me to have to give you over to someone else so soon."

I wouldn't have described her as happy on the day I was born. One of my earliest memories: Mother smiling down at me with tears that turned to sobs when a stern, mean woman told her I was the only child she'd ever have. I once told my sister Jade Flower about my memories of that day, but after she told everyone in the play yard about it, and my brothers and sisters spent weeks calling me Princess Lying Butterfly, I decided I should keep those memories to myself.

Nor did I want to remind Mother that her barrenness was why I had to marry Black Otter today. She usually hid her burden well, but the last couple of days I'd often walked into her room late at night to find her still awake and crying. If my marrying Black Otter would help her sleep through the night again, then I could live with it.

My uncle Nochuatl greeted us outside the great hall, wearing his best mantle and a headdress of scarlet macaw feathers. He bowed, kissing his fingers before sweeping them across the ground at my sandaled feet. "You look lovely, My Lady. Black Otter is a lucky boy."

I half-hid behind my mother, embarrassed for the delightful attention. I adored Nochuatl; he'd sit me on his shoulders at the festivals, so I could see over my siblings, and he made me necklaces of flowers and bear teeth. If I wasn't marrying Black Otter, Nochuatl would've been my second choice.

"The king awaits you, My Lady." He offered me his arm and we went into the great hall, Mother following a few steps behind.

The great hall was the largest room in the palace, where my father put on the weekly feasts attended by most of Culhuacan's nobility. Red and blue feathered banners hung from the white plaster walls, adorned with the city's symbol: a hilltop with the crest bent to the left, like an old man hunched over his walking stick. A hearth taller than a grown man was built into the wall at one end of the hall, and my father's reed throne—decorated daily with fresh flowers—stood on an elevated platform at the other end. My mother's smaller reed throne sat next to Father's, with stalks of white bone flowers sticking up along the top of the backrest like lovely, delicate spears. I loved sitting in her throne, surrounded by the sweet, vanilla-like fragrance.

My father stood near the hearth, a crowd of nobles around him, though he stood a good head taller than all of them. He wore a green macaw feather mantle, gold-woven sandals, and a jaguar-skin cape with the head draped over his bulging shoulder. In his crown of long, flowing quetzal feathers, he resembled an emerald sun.

My earliest memory of Father: when the midwife brought me to see him for the first time, he'd refused to hold or even look at me. Only Nochuatl convinced him to. *She's as precious as a butterfly, Mixcoatl.* And when Father had finally looked down at me, the disappointment had slowly melted away and he'd taken me into his strong arms with a distant, dreamy smile. *Yes, my precious little Butterfly,* he'd agreed, and that was how I'd gotten my childhood name.

And for six years I'd enjoyed my father's doting attention, the walks in the garden, the rides in the royal canoe, and even getting to sit on his lap in his throne. He used to tickle my nose with the feathers on the royal headdress and tell me stories about the gods, like how the Feathered Serpent Quetzalcoatl stole the jade bones from Lord Death to make us, or how he lured the love goddess Mayahuel down from heaven, enraging her earth monster grandmother.

But when I turned seven, the gods cursed me with the name I'd wear for the rest of my days, and I was no longer my father's beautiful little Butterfly. Instead I became

Quetzalpetlatl, a Feathered Mat, something that everyone slept on and so it wore out quickly. Now the only time I saw him was when he came to my room with lectures about how proper Tolteca women behaved.

Today though, he granted me one of those smiles he used to give me, and my heart swelled. "You're radiant today, Quetzalpetlatl," he said, setting a firm hand on my shoulder. I beamed at him, basking in the warmth of his attention. He directed me to the long reed mat laid out against the north wall. We sat, with me in the middle between him and Mother, "Because today's your special day," he told me.

I was expecting to have fun, with dancers and musicians and maybe some acrobats painted up like the gods to play out stories for me, but instead I spent the next few hours until dark listening to a stream of noblewomen admonishing me to be a good, honest wife. "Keep your loom busy and your husband's house ready for his return, whether he's gone to the temple or off to war." It sounded suspiciously like they were telling me to be my husband's servant—ridiculous since I was a princess, not a commoner working the maize fields from sun-up to sundown. But at least Mother led me through how to reply to all of this the first couple of times.

But by the tenth bored recitation of the same false thanks, one woman snarled at me, "What a spoiled little disgrace to the gods you are! I'd hold you over the chili roaster if you were my daughter!" Her venom scared me, and I clutched at Mother's wrist.

Mother reacted smoothly though, with astonishing poise. "Please forgive Quetzalpetlatl's youthful selfishness, Lady Silver Flower. Rest assured she appreciates your heartfelt words, and she will gift you the first blanket she completes on her own." The old woman nodded curtly then moved off. Mother then whispered to me, "I know it's a long process, but try to keep your spirits up."

Finally the last noblewoman bestowed her "wisdom" upon me, then Father set me onto a litter attended by four serving girls. The young women hefted me up on their shoulders while a fifth girl sounded a pink conch shell, then they carried me out onto the patio. We passed through the garden and up the stairs to the portico where the commoners went to petition the king. The crowd of noblewomen followed as we set out into the torch-lit city.

The only time I ever left the palace was to accompany Mother to the temple, so this was my first time seeing Culhuacan's other quarters. I'd been most looking forward to this part of the wedding ceremony, and as soon as we passed out of the palace gates, I completely forgot the boredom of the great hall.

Paintings of the gods decorated the whitewashed courtyard walls of the houses in the noble quarters while the fragrance of fried corn and spicy meat clung to the air in the merchant quarters. Whereas the houses in the upper class sections of the city were made of stone and stucco, out in the peasant quarters the houses were drab mud huts no bigger than my nursery, topped with thatch roofs, and grubby, naked babies playing in the dirt outside them. The people were cheerful though, many handing small bundles of flowers to my serving girls as we passed. Girls my own age watched with rapt interest, and a few waved to me before their mothers scolded them. I smiled and waved back at them, to tell them I didn't mind their admiration.

Statues of the Feathered Serpent god Quetzalcoatl stood at every intersection, all with garlands of flowers draped in their open mouths, and his temple in the sacred precinct had large, open-mouthed serpents built into the sides of its grand staircase as well. In Culhuacan, Quetzalcoatl held the highest throne.

Eventually the procession wound its way back to the palace and to the great hall. My cousin Black Otter now stood in front of the giant hearth, wearing a red and blue patterned cloak and matching loincloth. His parents stood with him—my mother's sister Eloxochitl, and my father's eldest brother Ihuitimal.

Eloxochitl helped me down from the litter and complimented my dress. "It's missing something, though." She tied a large white Magnolia flower to my wrist with a bit of twine. I whispered a shy thank you before shifting my gaze over to my uncle.

Ihuitimal thankfully never paid me any mind. He wore a perpetual scowl, and his suspicious eyes looked too large for his skull. He'd even filed his teeth to sharp points, "To look ferocious in battle," Nochuatl once told me. On the rare occasion he did smile, the nasty scar on his left cheek—that went from his mouth to his ear—turned him into a grinning caiman and made my insides curl up. Father had scolded me more than once for not showing him proper respect. "War scarred him, and he deserves your attention every time he enters the room." Though why did Father care, since Ihuitimal snapped at him like a hungry dog all the time?

Luckily, Black Otter shared nothing of his father's face, or personality; in fact, he looked just like Nochuatl; hence my affection. He gave me a secretive smile as we knelt together on the reed mat, but when I giggled, Ihuitimal told us to be quiet.

"Let us begin with gifts!" my father announced. Mother set a feathered mantle and loincloth—both big enough to fit my father—in front of Black Otter, while Eloxochitl set a woman's dress in front of me. I'd seen them working on these in the women's hall several months earlier and I'd thought they were for the children of one of my father's allies. *So silly, giving me a dress I can't wear for many years,* I mused.

Father then took the corner of my wedding dress and tied it into a knot with the corner of Black Otter's cape. "From this day forward, the two of you are bound in marriage. Bring forth the wedding cakes!" Father called, the crowd cheering.

A servant brought tamale maize cakes on a gilded plate, and Father set it between Black Otter and I. "Eat your first meal together as husband and wife, and may you enjoy many more in the years to come!"

Black Otter made to eat his, but I elbowed him. "We have to feed them to each other," I whispered.

Black Otter held his out to me, grimacing. "Don't slobber on me."

Grinning, I mashed mine into his chin. He did the same to me until we were both laughing, but we also earned a stern reprimand from Father. "Respect the solemnity of the day," he scolded. Whatever that meant.

The servants soon brought in clay plates, bowls of food, and jugs of drink, filling the great hall with so many exotic aromas I couldn't begin to describe them all. Musicians played flutes, drums, and rattles while young girls danced, and everyone was laughing and talking. Children were rarely allowed at the royal feasts—though Black Otter and I had been caught more than once spying on them from the doorway—so I watched everything with enthusiasm and a giddy feeling that I'd magically become a grown-up by marrying Black Otter.

But just as the celebration was starting to heat up, Mother told us, "Time to go pray." I knew it was too good to be true. I looked back regretfully as she led me out of the hall by the hand.

Black Otter and I followed our mothers down the hall, leaving the laughing and singing behind. "But it's our wedding, so why don't we get to stay to enjoy it?" Black Otter complained as we passed through a curtain decorated with the city's royal crest. Several hallways branched off from there, but we followed the blue-and-red painted one to the royal family quarters. Guards bowed to Mother as we passed between them.

"The wedding couple prays for four days," Eloxochitl told Black Otter.

"Four days! Ayya!"

"Really?" I asked Mother, hoping it was an exaggeration.

Mother nodded. "And on the fourth evening, both of you will lay quetzal feathers and jade stones on your marriage bed, to bring you good luck in having children."

"Is that why you keep those stones and old feathers on your bed?"

She nodded again. "I re-lay them every day."

"But they weren't very lucky for you."

Eloxochitl shot me a startled glance, but Mother said, "They brought me you, and that's enough for me."

I smiled, tickled by her kindness.

Mother took us to a room a few doors away from her own; it used to belong to my grandmother before the Black Dog came for her last year. The hearth's orange glow lit half the room while moonlight from the open door curtain at the back lit the rest. Wooden folding screens stood in the corner, and two prayer mats lay on the floor in front of the fire.

"Now offer prayers to the gods, so they'll bless you both with a long, happy marriage," Eloxochitl told us.

Kneeling on my mat, I shut my eyes and cleared my mind, as Mother had taught me. I then quoted the prayers she said before bed every night:

"I honor you, Xilonen,
For the maize that fills our bellies.
I honor you, Tlaloc,
For the rain that makes the maize strong.
I honor you, Xipe Totec,
For the fertile land that nurtures the seeds of life.
I honor you, Nanahuatzin,
For lighting the days.
I honor you, Metzli,
For bringing light to the darkness."

And, like her, I saved the most important prayers for last. Quetzalcoatl had given us the sacred calendar for counting the days, and writing to record the deeds of our kings; but most important, he'd given us life by bleeding his tepolli—his manhood—upon Cihuacoatl's metlatl grinding stone. "No god deserves our prayers and sacrifices more," Mother always said. She'd been a priestess of Quetzalcoatl long ago, and I often overheard her praying to him for one last child so she could give Father an heir. I'd taken to backing up her request with prayers of my own:

"Oh Great Feathered Serpent,
Watch over Mother and Father,
Over Black Otter,
Over Nochuatl,
And my aunt Eloxochitl,
And my uncle Ihuitimal.
Hear Mother's prayers,
And grant me a brother.
I promise to be a very good sister to him.
I honor you, oh Merciful Quetzalcoatl,

17

For my family,
For my friends,
For my life."

I looked up when Black Otter tossed some pebbles into the hearth. "This is boring," he moaned. "What do they expect us to do in here? One need only pray so much."

I laughed. One could never pray enough.

"I'm hungry," he added.

My stomach rumbled again. "Me too."

At the door, Black Otter called to a passing servant. "My wife and I need dinner."

"The wedding couple must fast the first night, My Lord," the servant replied.

Black Otter glared at him. "The Princess is famished, practically falling over dead of hunger, and you dare argue with me?"

The servant startled at his tone and glanced past the curtain at me, but he backed away when Black Otter pulled out an obsidian dagger.

"I should cut your head off this very moment, you disobedient wretch!" Black Otter growled.

I gasped, appalled. Boys had to be tough, especially when the other boys teased them about their best friend being a girl, but I'd never heard Black Otter speak so nastily to anyone. It wasn't often I saw his father in him.

The servant promised to bring us food, then hurried away.

When Black Otter grinned at me like a pleased ocelot, I demanded, "How could you say that?"

He rolled his eyes. "Father says it all the time when the servants argue with him."

"My father never threatens the servants."

He laughed. "They wouldn't dare argue with the king."

I turned away, arms folded.

He knelt in front of me, giving me pup eyes. "I'm sorry, Papalotl. I'll apologize when he comes back, so please don't be mad at me."

And since he kept his word and muttered an apology to the servant when he came back, I had to forgive him. I liked him more when he acted like Nochuatl rather than Ihuitimal.

After devouring the roast duck stew and the maize-bread tlaxcallis we ate with every meal, we discussed trying to sneak back to the great hall. I pointed out that with the guards standing watch at the head of the hall, we were unlikely to make it far.

"Then let's see what's out there," Black Otter said, pointing to the curtain at the back of the room. I followed, but gave him a shove when he failed to hold the curtain open for me.

We stepped out onto a flagstone patio with a small private bath house off to the side, complete with bathing pit and steam bath, but what lay beyond it was far more interesting. Vine-covered stone walls enclosed a yard twice the size of the room, and a large copal tree stood sentry at the center, its branches spread across the yard. Flowers of every color choked the beds, many of them still droning with bees even at this late hour. "This must be my garden," I whispered.

"Yours? Maybe it's mine. My father has one just like this off his room."

"Father always visits Mother, so this has to be my room, because you're visiting me." I'd never been to Father's room either, so I wondered what he kept in there that he didn't want us women to see.

"My father never invites Mother to his room either," said Black Otter. We wandered the yard for a moment, but when I found a pond at the back, I called him over and we lay on our bellies, watching the tiny fish and frogs swim in the moonlit pool.

"Maybe this can be our garden, to share," I suggested.

Black Otter knocked his shoulder against mine in silent agreement. I splashed him with a fistful of water, which he returned with equal abandon. We wrestled around in the dirt a moment, laughing and cursing before he pinned my arms behind me and I called him the winner. He always won, but someday I'd get the better of him.

A glint in the water caught my eye, so I reached in to find a warm stone among the reeds. I rinsed the silt off as I brought it out.

"What's that?" Black Otter asked.

"A piece of jade." It resembled the stones Mother kept on her bed with the quetzal feathers, except it grew hotter as I held it. How did one of my mother's precious jade stones get out in the pond?

But then suddenly, something bit my wrist.

I squealed and swung my arm around, tossing something long and hissing across the yard. It landed on the flagstone behind Black Otter. "A snake!" I shrieked, clutching my wrist. "It bit me! It bit me!"

Black Otter pushed a rock onto the snake, pinning it down, then cut off its head.

"Get over here!" I held my throbbing hand out, the pain surging up my arm. "You need to suck the poison out for me!"

"I'm not sucking anything out of you," he said, sticking his tongue out.

"At least look at it," I insisted.

He pulled my wounded wrist close to his face and squinted. He glared at me. "You said it bit you."

"It did!"

"No it didn't."

I looked at my wrist, expecting gaping puncture wounds, but instead my sandy-brown skin remained unblemished, not even a scratch. The throbbing continued though.

Black Otter returned his knife to its sheath with an indignant huff. "That wasn't funny."

"It did—I felt it!" I stared at my wrist, flustered. Had the snake merely brushed against me and I'd overreacted? Embarrassment burning my cheeks, I muttered, "I'm sorry. I really thought it did."

Black Otter patted my shoulder. "At least it wasn't poisonous."

My stomach sank when I looked at the snake again. "You shouldn't have killed it. Snakes are sacred to Quetzalcoatl, and now he might curse our marriage."

Black Otter laughed.

"It's not funny! We must make a sacrifice to make amends for this affront." Mother would've scolded me for saying such a thing, for Quetzalcoatl was good-natured and merciful, unlike most of the gods, but she'd also taught me that one should always try to correct one's mistakes.

Black Otter hesitated then said, "My father won't like this." When I asked why, he shook his head. "Never mind. Let's just do this."

We knelt over the snake. Its white body shimmered in Metzli's pale light, but when I touched the scales, they were feathers. *Like Quetzalcoatl*, I thought. I tried to push that silly notion aside, but with my entire arm throbbing, my worry built all over again.

Black Otter scooped up the head. "What do we do with it?"

"We have to burn it..." I poked the body once more, my trepidation growing. "Doesn't it look kind of...strange?"

"It's just a black and white snake."

I laughed. "Did you actually look at it?"

Black Otter looked again. "So?"

"It has feathers."

"No it doesn't."

"It does too, like Quetzalcoatl."

Black Otter blinked. "You think it's Quetzalcoatl?"

My cheeks blazed. "I didn't say that."

"You think it's the Feathered Serpent!" he cackled. Propping the head between his fingers, he moved the lower jaw and spoke in a comically booming voice, "You killed me, Papalotl, and now I will smite you!"

I almost gave him a shove, but then I saw the long emerald feathers drooping like wilted flowers from the snake's severed neck—feathers like those on the statues of Quetzalcoatl around the city. *Oh my gods! It is Quetzalcoatl! Black Otter killed my beloved god!*

I ran screaming back into the palace and down the hallway. I tried to cut between the guards at the curtain, but they grabbed me. "Nantli!" I shouted through hot tears, still yanking to get away. "Nantli! Help! Nantli!"

Both Mother and Father burst from the great hall. Eloxochitl followed, but Ihuitimal remained at the doorway, glaring at me. "What happened?" Mother demanded, scooping me into her arms. "Are you hurt?"

"He killed him, Nantli!" I sobbed.

"Killed who?" Father demanded, fear straining his voice.

"Black Otter killed Quetzalcoatl!"

Ihuitimal finally joined us. "The child's obviously dreaming."

"I am not!" I wiggled from Mother's arms and led her by the hand down the hallway, back to the room. Up both sides of the hallway, my father's concubines and my siblings peered out from behind their door curtains, many asking what was going on, but Father sent all of them scurrying back inside with a gruff order.

Black Otter was still in the garden, the dead snake at his feet. He cowered as his father approached. "I didn't mean to scare her—"

Ihuitimal slapped him aside and looked down at the headless serpent. He narrowed his eyes then snarled at me, "This is your precious Quetzalcoatl?"

The serpent was only a small black and white banded snake.

I would have flung myself at Black Otter with fists flying if my mother didn't have hold of me. "What did you do with it?" I shouted.

"I did nothing with it," Black Otter retorted, tears spilling down his cheeks. "You're the one who thought it wasn't a regular snake."

"You two are supposed to be praying, not playing in the garden," my father rumbled. "And just look at your dress, Quetzalpetlatl! It's covered in dirt and you've crushed all the feathers!"

I cowered behind Mother.

"I'll go and assure everyone that all's fine," Ihuitimal said.

Father turned to me, his expression fierce. "Such behavior is unbecoming of Culhuacan's future queen. You're nearly eight now!"

"Mixcoatl—" Mother started.

But he cut her off. "You coddle her too much, Chimalma. This kind of hysteria could cost people their lives."

"She's a child, not a warrior!" Mother snapped, startling me. I'd never heard her talk back to my father.

"Then it's a good thing you never bore me a son, if that's how you would've raised him too," he replied, then stalked from the garden.

Mother stood red-faced, clenching her fist before hard-fought tears snaked down her cheeks. When Eloxochitl put an arm around her shoulder, she broke into hiccupping sobs. "He didn't mean it, Chimalma. He's just scared," Eloxochitl assured her.

Seeing Mother cry quickly made me do the same. "I'm sorry I got you in trouble, Nantli," I wailed, clutching her dress.

Mother smiled through her tears. "You have nothing to be sorry about, dear. Think about it no more."

The servants laid out bed rolls on opposite sides of the room and set up the wooden screens around them. Once in my nightdress, I watched the servants gather up the remains of the snake. "I thought it bit me, so Black Otter killed it," I told Mother with more tears. "Will Quetzalcoatl curse us?"

"Quetzalcoatl will forgive, so don't worry," Mother assured me.

"Can we take the snake to the temple in the morning and make an offering of it to him, just to be sure?"

"Offerings are always a good idea." She kissed my forehead. Mother always knew how to make me feel better.

As I turned to my bed, I saw the jade stone sitting inside the back doorway, glimmering in the moonlight. It must have landed there when I threw the snake. I picked it up and held it out to Mother. "I'm sorry I made Father mad at you."

"It's all right." She turned the stone over in her hand. "Where did you get this?"

"I found it in the pond."

She frowned. "Are you sure you didn't take it from my room?"

"I'd never take your stones. I know how much you love them."

"Maybe it's Eloxochitl's, though I think she keeps hers in her wedding basket. Maybe Black Otter took it."

"If it's not hers, I want you to have it," I said. "Maybe it'll bring you good luck, and Father won't be mad at you anymore."

She hugged me. "Forget what your father said. He didn't mean any of it."

I couldn't forget, though. I lay in bed, my chest aching with anger and guilt.

"Papalotl?" Black Otter peered at me from the edge of my screen.

"Go away." I pulled the blanket over my head.

But he tugged it down. "I'm sorry."

"I said go away!"

He cringed as my voice carried. "I mean it, I'm sorry. I shouldn't have made fun of you about the snake."

I sat up against the wall, my knees pulled to my chest. "I don't know why I thought all that. I'm sorry I scared you too."

He sat next to me. "We're still friends?"

"Of course. But you must come to the temple with us tomorrow, to make the offering to Quetzalcoatl."

"I doubt my father will let me."

"Why not?"

He hesitated then whispered, "You must promise never to tell anyone."

"I won't."

"No, you have to swear on something important...swear on Quetzalcoatl that you'll never tell anyone."

"I swear on the Feathered Serpent," I said, intrigued.

He checked the hallway then came back.

"What are you doing?" I asked.

"Making sure no one's spying on us."

Sometimes Black Otter was truly silly. "Are you going to tell me or not?"

He took a deep breath, then whispered, "My father hates Quetzalcoatl."

I laughed. "It's impossible to despise the Feathered Serpent—"

"But he does. My father is the high priest of the dark sorcerer god Smoking Mirror, the Feathered Serpent's mortal enemy. Father tells me the god sent him here to spread his worship among the Tolteca."

"I've never heard of any Smoking Mirror."

"My father learned about him when he lived in the northern desert, with the Chichimecs."

I frowned. Everyone said Chichimecs ate their own children, so what must their god be like? "What does he do?"

"Father says I'm too young to know the god's secrets yet. I only know that he makes warriors fierce and fearless, and he feeds on their hearts. Father says the Smoking Mirror will think me weak if I make offerings to Quetzalcoatl, and he even said he'd sacrifice me if he ever caught me worshiping the Feathered Serpent."

"Being a sacrifice is an honor, not a punishment." Or so Mother had told me.

"I don't want to die," Black Otter said. "My father will flog me if he finds out I told you any of this."

My wrist throbbed again and I rubbed it, worried. "You won't make me stop worshiping Quetzalcoatl, now that we're married?"

He smiled and slipped his arm over my shoulder. "Never! We're friends."

We talked of other things, but the worry remained at the back of my mind. *You should tell Mother about this,* I thought, but I'd given my word.

Eventually I leaned against Black Otter's shoulder and drifted off to sleep, dreaming that when he laid me down, he kissed me on the cheek. But he'd never do something so disgusting.

Later, the dream shifted, to laughter out in the garden, and when I went to investigate, I found a boy hunched next to the pond. I liked him immediately; he had my mother's kind eyes. "Will you play boats with me?" he asked, so we sat next to the pond, blowing autumn leaves across the surface, watching them float like canoes on Lake Meztliapan. Whenever I met his gaze, a pleasant heat filled my body, strange as an out-of-reach memory. His smile made my heart soar like a hawk.

When the wind picked up, I looked up to see storm clouds gathering in the north. Thunder rumbled, growling like a jaguar stalking prey in the forest, waiting for the right moment to spring.

CHAPTER TWO

Mother returned in the morning in high spirits. "Did you and Father make up?" I asked as she braided my hair. Black Otter sat sulking against the wall, stewing after his father told him he needn't tag along after us "women folk".

"We made amends." Mother took my hand and I waved goodbye to Black Otter as we left the palace, a few servants following behind.

"I didn't want to say anything in front of Black Otter, but I have exciting news," Mother said once we reached the market, surrounded by shouting merchants and crowds of nobles and peasants shopping at the blankets laid out in lines. The guards kept close ranks around us as we pressed through towards the gates of the sacred precinct.

"What is it?" I asked.

"The Feathered Serpent came to me in a dream last night."

"He did?" I gaped, awestruck. "What did he say?"

"That I'll have a son soon, an heir for your father."

"I'll have a brother—a real blood-brother?"

Mother took the jade stone from her dress pocket. "Remember this, from last night? Quetzalcoatl told me to swallow it, and it'll grow into a baby inside me."

I stared at her, baffled. "In your stomach?"

She laughed. "Well, not in my stomach, but in my abdomen."

"How odd! Black Otter says that the goddess Cihuacoatl leaves newborns in the kitchen pot and that the mothers' bellies swell with milk."

Mother laughed louder. "That's not exactly how things happen."

"You're going to swallow it, aren't you?"

"Of course. I wanted to make offerings first."

"Is Father excited?"

"I haven't told him yet. I don't want to get his hopes up, in case it was just a dream."

Quetzalcoatl's temple sat atop the biggest pyramid in the sacred precinct, and the soothing smell of copalli incense greeted me at the door, covering the pungent smell of decay. I found the latter oddly alluring. Mother claimed it took years to get used to the temple's smell, so surely the fact that it didn't bother me meant I was destined to be a priestess too.

We knelt on the reed prayer mat before the gilded serpent idol and sang a hymn, honoring Quetzalcoatl for everything he gave us. Mother pulled a long gray snake from one of our baskets and slit its throat with her knife. The blade fascinated me, with its stag horn handle carved in the likeness of Quetzalcoatl, and how the blood pooled in its open mouth. She bled the snake over two grass balls in a clay bowl then repeated the process with five more.

When she finished, I held my hand out and she pricked my middle finger with a maguey thorn tied to a rope of more thorns she kept in her pocket. I winced as she squeezed my finger over the grass balls until a single drop fell. I used to dread that part most, but I was tougher now, and it was nothing like what she did to herself.

While I watched, Mother closed her eyes, meditating. She then opened her mouth and stuck the first thorn through her tongue, slowly dragging the string of thorns through, coating the rough maguey fiber with her blood. She never flinched—oh, her tenacity!—and when she finished, she set the rope in the bowl and held it up.

"Oh Great Quetzalcoatl,
I honor you for blessing my family,
For filling me with life once more,
For giving Mixcoatl an heir,
For giving Quetzalpetlatl a blood-brother,
And for giving Culhuacan her future.
Fill my son's head with wisdom,
So he grows to be a great and respected king.
Fill his heart with love,
So he honors you and his family always.
And fill his stomach with courage,
So he will be a great but just warrior."

When she handed me the bowl, I cleared my throat then said:

"Oh Merciful Quetzalcoatl,
Please pardon Black Otter's mistake.
The fault is mine,
I honor you and ask you spare our marriage from disaster,
Accept this blood to undo my dishonor,
Oh Great Feathered Serpent."

I dumped the bloody grass balls into the idol's gaping mouth.
"The high priest will burn the snake's body with the nightly sacrifice and all will be right again," Mother assured me.
But I was eager for more important things. "Now will you swallow the stone?"
"Bring me some water."
I hurried to the jar by the door and returned with a bowl of water. I watched anxiously as she murmured another prayer then put the jade stone on her tongue. Once she drank down the water, she looked woozy. "Do you need more?"
"It was just difficult to swallow." She touched her belly. "I feel like Lord Sun Himself just lit up inside me."
"Does it hurt?"
"It tickles, like magic swelling." She smiled. "He's growing already."
I bounced, too excited to stay still. "Can I carry him home?"
She laughed. "He'll be in there a while yet, Papalotl, thank the gods."
"But how long?"
"At least until winter."
"But that's so long!"
"Nine months isn't all that long, and once he gets here, you'll wish it was still just you."
"I won't." I'd prayed for someone to share the lonely nights in the nursery with for far too long. "Can I tell Father about the baby?"
"You should leave the good news to me," Mother suggested.

◻

But when I saw Father in the portico out front of the palace with Nochuatl and Ihuitimal, I couldn't help myself. "Father! Father! I'm going to be a sister!" I shouted as I ran up the stone steps to him.

"Then you've heard about Lady Tlallixochitl?" Nochuatl asked me with a crooked smile. "I've never seen you so excited about such things."

"No, Mother's going to have a baby!"

Ihuitimal laughed like a coyote. "Your mother's incapable of bearing children anymore, Quetalpetlatl."

Mother put a hand on my shoulder, but I couldn't stop the excited words pouring out of my mouth. "I found a stone in the garden last night and Quetzalcoatl told Mother to swallow it so it could grow into a baby boy, for Father, so he'll have an heir!"

"He already has an heir," Ihuitimal shot back.

When Father turned to Mother, confused, she sighed. "I really wanted to discuss this with your father in private, Papalotl."

"Then she speaks the truth?" Father asked.

She cast a wary gaze at Ihuitimal, but said, "The Feathered Serpent visited me in a dream last night."

Roaring joyously, Father wrapped his arms around her. I tried to stifle giggles as he kissed her passionately in plain view of everyone at the city registrar's office! Father never showed her such affection in public—Mother said they had to be careful to prevent jealousy among Father's other women. Mother's face flushed once Father released her.

"You actually believe this nonsense, Mixcoatl?" Ihuitimal snapped.

"How can't I? I trust Chimalma to know a real vision from the god when she has one." He set a friendly hand on Ihuitimal's shoulder. "Don't worry about Black Otter's position. He's married to my daughter and is still the heir until my own son is old enough, and even then he won't be forgotten. He'll have very high rank in the war council, and I shall still call him my son. In fact, Nochuatl and I will start taking him with us on our weekly hunts, so he can learn to bear a spear. A man must know how to handle men's weapons."

The veins on Ihuitimal's neck stood out. "You think I haven't taught my boy to be a man?"

"Not at all. You're just very busy, and any potential heir should begin his weapons training early. My own boys started sleeping with play swords in their baby baskets."

Ihuitimal still glared at Father. "I assure you that Black Otter won't disappoint you."

"Of course not. He's his father's son," Father said, smiling, but Ihuitimal strode away down the hall. Mother watched him go, a worried expression on her face.

"Why's he so angry?" I asked.

"Don't worry about him," Father said. "Your uncle's just a grouchy old bear."

Hopefully Black Otter took my good news better than his father did.

□

"You made the prayers for me? Quetzalcoatl isn't going to curse me for the snake?" Black Otter asked, anxious.

"Everything will be fine," I said. "But never mind that. I have fantastic news! I'm going to be a sister!"

Black Otter scowled. "That's not so special. You have more brothers and sisters than anyone I know."

"All by Father's concubines, you tamale-head. My mother is having a baby!"

"But she can't have any more. That's why Father said we had to marry."

"The Feathered Serpent blessed her. Remember that piece of jade I found last night?

She swallowed it, and Quetzalcoatl put a baby in her stomach."

"In her stomach?" He looked incredulous. "But won't he drown?"

"Mother said it's not like that."

"Lord Green Water lied to me!"

I nodded. "I bet babies come from their mothers swallowing the jade stones and feathers they get during the marriage ceremony."

"I'm going to ask my mother to swallow one of her jade stones," Black Otter said. "I want a brother too."

Once the servants delivered our early afternoon atole, we drank the bowls under the copal tree, filling our bellies with watery cornmeal mash to settle us until the evening meal. Black Otter then scaled the tree and beckoned me to follow. "You have to see something."

I hiked my skirt up past my knees and followed him up. We sat on one of the branches above the wall, and I could see all the way to the lake. Many walled gardens lay beyond our own, each paired with a room and backing up to a secret passageway watched by guards. I noticed that the vines hid an archway in our outer wall.

"It goes all the way from the lake to the main gardens," Black Otter said.

When I looked down the line of gardens, I spotted Mother and Father in one, holding hands and smiling. "I've never seen my father so happy," I said with a pleased sigh.

"My father's never happy, and he never holds Mother's hand like that." After a pause, Black Otter said, "I don't think they like each other. He never does anything nice for her, and she's always sad." He pursed his lips, looking as if he'd never considered any of this before. "That won't be us, though. We're going to be happy, like your parents."

I'd always pictured Mother and Father being happy together, but after the outburst in the garden last night....

But we didn't have to be like that either. "You promise?" I asked.

"I promise." He then leaned in and kissed me.

It wasn't like the kiss Father gave Mother earlier, but I almost fell backwards out of the tree in surprise. Black Otter pulled me back though, leaving me feeling hot and dizzy and bewildered. "What was that for?" I demanded.

He laughed, his cheeks red. "It's all right. We're married."

Though my parents were busy gazing at each other, I knew that if my father had seen us, we both would have gotten held over the chili roasters in the kitchen. He'd only done that once, when I'd stolen a doll from one of my sisters, and sometimes even now, when I passed by the kitchens, the smell of the roasting chilis brought burning tears to my eyes. "Don't ever do that again!" I punched Black Otter in the shoulder and climbed back down the tree.

Black Otter joined me on the ground again, avoiding my gaze. "Let's just pretend it never happened." I agreed, and we returned to our room where he tossed pebbles while I tried to focus on my silent prayers.

But my mind kept wandering back to the softness of his lips, the warmth of his breath. The memory renewed the strange, hot feeling inside and I couldn't help giggling like a crazy old woman.

Eventually we returned to the garden and watched the minnows swim in the pond. By evening it was as if the kiss had never happened. And I felt sad about it.

◻

On the fourth evening, servants brought in a stack of large reed mats and several armfuls of bear and wolf skins. They laid everything out under my father's watchful gaze, covering the mats with the skins, and the skins with colorful cotton blankets. Then Mother handed me four jade stones, and Eloxochitl gave Black Otter some quetzal feathers. "Having completed your prayers to the gods, we've now laid the marriage bed for you, my son, my daughter," Father said. "Lay upon it the rich plumes and precious stones it will bring you."

Black Otter laid the emerald feathers on the blankets. "These are the daughters you will give to Quetzalpetlatl, so she'll have women-kin to keep her happy when you're away at war," Father said. I then set the jade stones atop the feathers. "These are the sons you will give Black Otter, so his memory and influence don't die with him," he said.

Mother washed the yellow paint from my face and put me in a new dress with red, green, blue, and yellow feathers. "Now you get to celebrate," she said with a smile.

Cheers greeted us in the great hall, and for the rest of the night the nobles gave us so many gifts: jewelry, clothing, blankets, tapestries, statues, and beautiful birds. The high priest of Quetzalcoatl sprinkled us with water and octli, and then we feasted. I sat with Black Otter for a while but climbed in my mother's lap after the meal and fell asleep. I missed her soft skin and the smell of her bone flower perfume.

Eventually Father carried me to bed. He smelled sweet with tobacco—a scent I'd missed much longer than my mother's. I latched my arms around his neck and snuggled against him.

"I wish her to sleep with me tonight," Mother said when we reached her doorway.

"But I was planning to stay with you tonight," Father said.

"I miss my daughter and want her close tonight."

Father sighed, then handed me over to her. "Tomorrow night she goes back to the nursery. She's too old to share her mother's bed."

"But you won't stay with us?"

"I must stay with one of the others."

"Of course," Mother said with a sigh. She wished him good night, and I puzzled over Father's regretful look as the handmaiden closed the door curtain on him.

Someday that will be Black Otter waiting outside your door, I realized, struck with a strange sense of clarity. *And that's supposed to be happiness?*

CHAPTER THREE

 When Mother and I came to the women's hall in the morning, Father's concubines were chattering in a flurry of heated, indignant discussion which fell silent as we walked through the doorway. They watched us as we wound through the many looms spread about the stone floor to our mats on the open patio overlooking the royal gardens, but Mother held her head high in spite of them. Many of my sisters watched us too, though mostly they wore expressions of curiosity.

"She finally deems us worthy of taking breakfast with again," someone whispered.

I looked around—no one spoke nastily about my mother—but Mother pulled me along. Finally we sat next to my sister Jade Flower and her mother Zeltzin in the sunlight stretching under the stone eaves, and a servant brought us bowls of honeyed atole.

When the conversation settled, Zeltzin leaned closer and whispered, "Is it true,

Chimalma? Did the gods grant you another child?"

"A son," my mother confirmed.

Zeltzin smiled. "I'm glad we made that trip to Xochicalco last spring to make offerings to Quetzalcoatl." She cast her gaze around, and some of the other women stiffened and turned away. "Not everyone's pleased though."

"There's no pleasing some of them," Mother answered.

"Why not?" I asked. When I looked to one of my older sisters nearby, the girl sneered at me, so I stuck my tongue out at her.

"Mind your manners," Mother reminded me, but smiled.

Once I finished my atole, I started my daily work. Mother taught me weaving, and the fine art of being a good wife, and I rather liked the first but found the rules of the second annoying. Girls were expected to be proficient at weaving by age seven, but thanks to Mother's teaching, my own skills excelled. We made intricately-patterned rugs and blankets as gifts for Father's allies, though the tapestry of fish and snakes we were working on now would hang in the meditation room of the high priest of the rain god Tlaloc.

Jade Flower's mother was already unraveling most of the work her daughter had done the day before. Shameful, considering Jade Flower was almost two years past her Naming Day, but she didn't seem to care. She preferred gossip to weaving lessons. "What's it like being married?" she whispered, so our mothers wouldn't overhear.

"All right, I guess." Nothing had really changed.

She gave a dreamy sigh. "You're so lucky, Quetzalpetlatl. Black Otter is so handsome."

I snickered. Black Otter *was* handsome, but nothing short of black magic would make me admit so to her. She might be my sister and a friend, but she couldn't keep secrets.

"Does he kiss you?" she asked, breathless. Heat traveled up my face as some my older sisters turned to listen as well.

"Of course we don't!"

They giggled behind their hands and Mother looked up from her weaving, questions in her gaze. "We don't do such foul things," I spouted.

Jade Flower laughed, but her mother said, "Such talk is uncalled for, and inappropriate. I won't have anyone saying I'm raising you to be anything but a proper king's daughter."

"Yes, Mother." Jade Flower grinned at me.

But when Jade Flower and I left the women's hall to join the rest of our siblings for afternoon play in the yard, the other girls followed us, crowding around and tossing out questions: "Does Black Otter come to your room in the middle of the night, like Father comes to my mother's room?" or "Did he give you that flower in your hair?" or, from one of my oldest sisters, "Has he gotten you with child yet?" My face burned so hot I felt dizzy. They all cackled.

I shoved the oldest in the chest, making the others gasp. She gave me a "how dare you!" look, so I put up my fists, just like Black Otter had shown me. I didn't have to take such nonsense.

"What's going on here?" Nochuatl suddenly asked behind me, and the girls scattered.

"They were making fun of Quetzalpetlatl," Jade Flower said, and I broke down into sobs.

He gathered me into his arms and stroked my hair. "They don't mean real harm."

"I hate every one of them!" I sputtered.

"They're just curious."

"And jealous," Jade Flower added.

Nochuatl laughed. "And that. Don't worry about them. They'll tire of it, and everything will get back to normal. You'll see."

The royal play yard was next to the kitchens, so Jade Flower and I picked up a couple of tlaxcallis to eat before going outside. Most of the yard was covered in plastered flagstone so the boys could practice the sacred ball game with their rubber balls while the girls watched and made fun of their mistakes from the shade of the trees at the edge of the patio.

But today, no one was playing tlachtli; instead everyone was gathered in a chanting mob around two boys beating each other up.

I searched for Black Otter—we never missed a fight—but I couldn't find him. The old matrons who usually made sure we behaved were gone, probably finding someone to break up the fight. I squeezed through the crowd, headed for the front. Jade Flower held my dress to keep up.

My oldest brothers crowded the front line, and they elbowed me back when I started worming past them. I prodded a few into looking down at me and they grudgingly stepped aside. Being the Princess of Culhuacan had its advantages.

Jade Flower gasped and pointed. Black Otter was in the center of the crowd, red-faced and swinging fists at my much larger brother, Itzcoatl, who held him back by a fistful of his hair, laughing and taunting. "Your arms are too short, Lake Monster!" Itzcoatl crowed, then rammed his knee into Black Otter's stomach. Black Otter keeled over, heaving, and Itzcoatl leaned over him, laughing. "Next time get into a fight with a girl, so you don't get the piss beaten out of you."

"Princess Black Otter!" my brothers sang.

Incensed, I shoved the nearest one, sending him stumbling from the circle and slamming into Itzcoatl, knocking them both over. Itzcoatl glared until he saw me; then he laughed. "Now your wife must fight your battles for you? Pathetic!"

Black Otter glared at me, filling me with shame, but then he lunged at Itzcoatl, taking the larger boy by surprise. They swung fists and cursed, rolling around on the hard ground, but soon Itzcoatl started howling and kicking. "Get him off me! Get him off me!" he screamed, as he struggled to his feet. Black Otter had got his hands up under his mantle and dangled like a large rock tied between his legs, but when he twisted, Itzcoatl's knees buckled and he collapsed, his high-pitched wail raising the hairs on my neck.

The oldest boys descended on Black Otter, kicking and punching.

Ihuitimal shoved me aside as he broke through the crowd and tossed the boys aside. Black Otter only let go once his father cuffed him on the cheek. Itzcoatl lay in a heap, sobbing. An old woman knelt beside him, stroking his sweaty hair. "You should have broken this up immediately, My Lord. The king will be very angry."

"He should think twice before picking on someone smaller than him," Ihuitimal replied. Black Otter wiped his bloody nose as Ihuitimal pulled him over to one of the doorways.

"Oh, he's so brave!" Jade flower crooned.

I glared at her, then followed them over to the doorway, keeping at a distance as Ihuitimal squatted to talk to Black Otter.

"Always remember there's no such thing as dirty tactics," Ihuitimal said. "The teachers at the House of Warriors will try to fill your head with nonsense about honor and fair fighting, but in the real world—in real battle when the enemy will drag you off to the sacrifice—if you must cut the stones off your enemy to get away, you do it. You're Culhuacan's heir, and that takes precedence over everything else. Understand?"

"Yes, Father," Black Otter said.

"But men also don't accept help from any woman. Quetzalpetlatl's duty is to be silent and follow your orders, and if she fails, deal with her swiftly, just as you would any soldier in your army."

Black Otter flicked his gaze over at me before slowly nodding.

I felt struck through with an arrow. *How could you agree, Black Otter?* I thought, tears threatening. *You promised we'd be nothing like your parents.* The phantom pain in my wrist—where I'd thought the snake had bitten me days ago—returned. When Mother and my aunt came out of the kitchens, I ran and clutched Mother's dress, my insides boiling.

Eloxochitl gasped. "What happened?" she demanded, as she knelt and dabbed at Black Otter's wounds with the hem of her dress.

Ihuitimal swatted her away. "Leave the boy alone. A bloody nose now and then won't hurt him."

Seeing the old matron helping Itzcoatl limp inside, Mother asked, "What happened?"

"Lessons in battle tactics and underestimating your enemy," Ihuitimal said with a creepy smile.

"The play yard isn't the place for teaching battle tactics."

"You have no sons, so I wouldn't expect you to understand."

Mother's face flushed, and I wanted her to say something nasty back, but she held her tongue, like a good Tolteca woman was expected to.

Father and Nochuatl stepped out of the doorway, and Mother bowed in greeting. "What's the matter?" Father asked. "You look upset."

"I'm fine," she murmured.

"I heard there was a brawl but I trust you took care of it, Brother?" When Ihuitimal nodded, Father bent to scrutinize Black Otter's face. "None the worse, I hope?"

"I'm fine, your Majesty," Black Otter replied.

"Good. Today you'll join me and Nochuatl on a hunt."

Black Otter smiled wide.

To me, Father added, "And you'll spend the afternoon with Ihuitimal."

My stomach dropped. An entire afternoon with Ihuitimal? After what he said to Black Otter?

Ihuitimal was as unenthused as me. "Whatever for?"

"You must oversee her spiritual transition into your son's household, to show her what's expected of her as Black Otter's wife," Father replied.

Dear gods! He's going to make me worship that evil Smoking Mirror!

Mother cast a sharp stare at Father.

To my relief, Eloxochitl stepped up. "My husband is very busy, your Excellency, but I'd be honored to tutor Quetzalpetlatl for the afternoon." I wanted to hug her.

Father considered for a moment, and Mother said it was an excellent idea, but after some hesitation, Ihuitimal said, "No, she'll come with me. I won't shun my duty." He cast a spear-like gaze down at me. "I was on my way to the menagerie to feed some of the animals."

That didn't sound so bad. I liked watching the servants feed the tapirs and otters.

"Excellent." To me, Father said, "Be respectful and well-mannered, Quetzalpetlatl."

"Of course, Father." Why did he think he always had to remind me?

Mother lingered a moment after the others left, still worried, but then finally disappeared into the darkened entryway.

Ihuitimal gave me a skeptical frown. "Come." He then strode through the entryway too. I ran to keep up with him. He took a basket from a servant standing in the hallway and shoved it into my hands. "You will carry this." Its weight surprised me, as did the jostling as something inside tried to nudge the lid open. Ropes kept it secure, though. "Now hurry. I'm late."

We cut through the kitchens to the back hallway leading to the portico. Ihuitimal snapped for me to keep up as we descended the stone stairs and headed towards the archway marking the entrance to the royal menagerie. I sweated under the heavy load, trying not to kick the basket. My arms felt like melting wax.

We passed the tapirs and monkeys, and I noticed no servants out feeding the animals. *That's because they feed them in the morning,* I remembered. I followed Ihuitimal past the mangrove trees to where the pumas, jaguars, and ocelots lived. He waited for me at a stone bench next to one of the jaguar pens.

Father had three black and yellow jaguars, but this one was an unusually large, solid black one I hadn't seen before. I eyed it as I set the heavy basket on the stone bench. It stared back, ears twitching and nostrils flaring as it rested on a log in its cage.

"Proper women don't keep their men waiting," Ihuitimal scolded. I almost said I could have kept up better if he'd carried the basket, but that would just get me into trouble. "You have much to learn about being a proper wife, but you're still young and easily molded."

I bowed, hiding my scowl. "Of course, Uncle."

"You will address me as 'My Lord'. I've earned that right."

"Of course, My Lord."

"First, always remember that your husband doesn't need your opinion or actions when it comes to dealing with other men. Like today when you shoved that other boy."

"But he called Black Otter names!"

"That's his dishonor to deal with. You only worsened his humiliation."

"He would've come to my defense." Anger slithered into my voice.

"Because you're a woman...or rather, will be, someday."

"But we're friends...and friends defend each other."

"He's your husband," Ihuitimal corrected me. "The days of you two carrying on any other way are over. Your place is at the loom, not climbing trees and killing snakes."

My wrist started itching and I scratched it behind my back. "Yes, Uncle—I mean, My Lord."

"A proper woman also formally addresses her husband at all times, just as you would address me. Nor will he address you by that childish name you had as a baby."

I felt as if he'd slapped me. With all these stupid rules, I didn't want to be married to Black Otter anymore.

"This is much to take in, but you'll grow used to it," Ihuitimal said. "Embrace your proper role, and all will be fine."

This word "proper" seemed no better than a wooden slave collar. I despised the very sound of it.

"You'll best serve Black Otter when he's king by keeping the perfect image of the supporting wife. It's why correcting your bad habits now is important," Ihuitimal went on.

"But what if Black Otter doesn't become king?" I asked.

Ihuitimal raised an eyebrow. "Why wouldn't he?"

"Quetzalcoatl gave Mother a son." How annoying that I had to state the obvious.

He flashed me a ghastly smile. "It still remains to be seen whether there's truly a son or not."

He still didn't believe? "Quetzalcoatl is a great and powerful god, Uncle—I mean, My

Lord—and he promised Mother a son, so he will give her one."

"Maybe, but the boy must then survive childbirth, no small feat considering that your mother lost many children in the womb even before she had you. Bearing a child is dangerous enough without involving the gods. She should cast it away or she'll never see her own grandchildren."

I frowned, confused. "What do you mean?"

"Your mother nearly died giving birth to you, and having another child will kill her, and the baby. She's foolish to even consider carrying this child."

My heart flopped like a dying fish in my chest. Surely mother didn't wish to die. "But then why is Mother so happy?" I asked, sure he wasn't telling me everything.

"Blind faith can be very dangerous, Quetzalpetlatl. What do mortals truly know about the intentions of the gods?" He removed the lid from the basket and pulled a rabbit out by its ears. When it squealed, he cradled its bottom with his other hand.

The jaguar perked up its ears and twitched its nose, suddenly interested. As Ihuitimal approached the cage, it jumped from its perch, tail swishing. "In my experience, the gods are like jaguars," Ihuitimal said. "They care not whether they kill their keepers; they just want their due." He held the rabbit out through the bars of the cage.

He's crazy! I wanted to look away, just knowing the cat would tear his arm off, but a strange excitement kept me watching.

The jaguar hissed and backed away, but then snatched the rabbit from Ihuitimal's hands. The rabbit's scream jolted me, and I started inexplicably sweating, my heart thudding painfully in my chest. The jaguar quickly silenced the rabbit, but that did little to lessen the alarming distress coursing through me. It was like watching a brother or sister die, rather than an animal. I had to look away.

"Don't ever turn away from the sacrifice, or someday you'll find yourself the one on the sacrificial stone," Ihuitimal warned. "Everyone must eat, even the gods. Your mother's taught you admirable devotion to the Feathered Serpent, but never forget that Quetzalcoatl doesn't rule the heavens alone. Every god must be given due, and I'll properly educate you so you're prepared to serve your husband's chosen god."

But I don't want to worship your Smoking Mirror, I almost said, but bit back the words. *You promised—swore on Quetzalcoatl—and you can't break that.*

"That's all for today." Ihuitimal turned his back on me.

That's when I saw the glimmer of emerald and white from the corner of my eye. I looked towards the bench where I thought it was, but saw nothing. My wrist started throbbing though, and dizziness swept in and words filled my head like a song desperate to burst forth. So I obeyed. "The Feathered Serpent is merciful, but he is also fierce, so beware your meddling lest he crush you in his divine coils." Once the last word left my lips, the dizziness lifted, leaving me feeling very happy.

Ihuitimal stared at me, incredulous for a moment, but then he narrowed his eyes. "What did you say?"

That look killed my peace. "I bade you farewell, My Lord, and thanked you for your wisdom." I swallowed hard.

"Did you?" He sneered. "Beware the words your mother puts in your mouth, little one. You're just like her, and see what befell her? Left barren and telling her only daughter to trust in dreams from the gods." His words rekindled my anger, but before I could snap off at him—and likely get a lashing—he added, "Run along and play. The days will only get shorter now." He didn't turn from me as I walked away this time.

CHAPTER FOUR

 I'd hoped life would go back to normal after the wedding, but soon I wished I'd never married Black Otter. I quickly tired of the adults nagging me, particularly the old matrons who now kept an even closer watch on me in the yard so Black Otter and I could no longer sneak away to the aviary or spy on the servants tending the gardens.

Though with the other boys increasing their torments of him, Black Otter had little time to sneak away anyway. Packs of my brothers tailed him everywhere, goading him into fights he usually lost. Soon he didn't want to talk to me anymore and ran when he saw me. Everything I'd feared came true.

"I wish I was married to Black Otter," Jade Flower often told me. "It's so romantic, like a love story. Do you think he'll have concubines, like Father does? Oh I hope I'm one of them!"

I wanted to punch her, but Mother had told me that jealousy was an ugly beast undeserving of a princess's company. "If marriage was a love story, Black Otter wouldn't hate me now," I told her instead.

But I had my own reasons to hate him too. I could tolerate his ignoring me, but I couldn't stand him moving in on my father's affections. He sat at Father's side in court, listening to the peasants fight over land boundaries and turkeys, and they spent every afternoon in the men's private yard, practicing with swords and spears. He even hunted deer with Father and Nochuatl once a week. Whereas my heart had missed Father before, now it burned with resentment.

"I wish I was a boy," I told Mother as we walked through the market on our way to the Temple of Quetzalcoatl, to make offerings to honor his miracle. I hadn't wanted to come along—already I hated my unborn brother, for he too would enjoy my father's company—but it was better than being spied on by old women. "It's not fair! Why wasn't I born a boy, Mother?"

"Because the gods wished you to be a girl," she said. "Being a woman is difficult, but men go off to war, many to die and never see their loved ones again. Everyone makes sacrifices."

"It's still not fair," I huffed. "Everybody hates me; the old women, Ihuitimal, Black Otter, even Father."

"Your father doesn't hate you."

"If I was a boy, he would love me."

"That's enough, Quetzalpetlatl." Mother only used my proper name when I was in trouble. "Maybe your father's right. I don't wish to send you away to calmecac already, but perhaps you need the school's strict rules to remind you of your place."

I hung my head, seething inside. *Father has turned Mother against me too.*

Mother knelt before me. "I understand how you feel, Papalotl. I didn't understand why my own father distanced himself from me—"

"What did we do wrong?" I cried.

"Nothing. The world has an order: men and women cross paths for certain reasons, but other than that, we all live our own lives."

"I don't want to live apart from Father, or Black Otter, or Uncle Nochuatl. I'm happy when they're around."

"They make me happy, too." Mother smoothed my hair and sighed. "I'm sorry the world is not fairer. The gods know I don't want you to be miserable, and you deserve better than this life your father thinks is best for you." She thought a moment, then smiled and said, "When we finish at the temple, we'll go down to the lake and see if your father will let us watch him and Black Otter spearing ducks."

I smiled and nodded eagerly.

□

We followed the path behind the temple down to the lakeshore. Fishing boats dotted the lake, the afternoon sun shining brightly off the cerulean water and making me squint. Seeing the boats reminded me of the trips Father and I used to make in the royal canoe, and how I loved to stare at his wavering reflection in the surface off the side.

The memory brought a smile to my face, especially when I saw him sitting on a log a little further down the beach. His guards waved us by when we neared them. My happiness melted away, though, when I saw Black Otter sitting next to my father, listening intently as he showed him how to grip an atl-atl stick.

Seeing us approach, Father rose to greet us. "Is something the matter?"

"We're finished making offerings, and Quetzalpetlatl wished to come see you and Black Otter," Mother answered.

Father frowned. "A woman's place isn't out hunting with her husband—"

"She just wants to watch."

"Surely she has weaving that needs doing—"

"I finished my weaving for the day," I said, giving Father a bow.

Father scrunched his brows, but Mother took his hand and led him away a few steps. "Please, let her have this one little favor. She misses you so much."

"It's not appropriate."

"She's not your best friend's wife. She thinks she did something wrong and you're punishing her."

"I am not!"

"Then give her a little of your time."

Father pulled Mother further away so I couldn't hear them anymore, so I turned to Black Otter. He ignored me as he loaded an arrow into a notch at the end of a wooden baton. "What's that?" He said nothing, so I pushed on. "Can I see it?"

He gave me a scathing look before going back to work. I watched, numb with anger. We'd been friends a very long time—for five of my seven years—and for him to so suddenly turn on me stung as if I'd inhaled chili powder. "Why do you hate me so?" My choked voice spoiled my anger.

He turned still further away. "I don't hate you."

"Why don't you talk to me anymore then?"

"You wouldn't understand."

"Yes I would!"

"No, you wouldn't. You don't know anything about being a man—"

"And neither do you."

He turned on me, furious. "You're just a little girl, so shut up."

I had to tolerate such nastiness for my uncle, but I wouldn't abide it from my best friend. Embracing the rage rising inside me, I lunged, knocking him into the wet sand, pummeling him with my fists. I said nothing, just gritted my teeth and bloodied his nose and cut his lip, and I would've bashed both his eyes in if Father hadn't yanked me back.

"Great Feathered Serpent! What are you doing?" Father pinned my arms to my sides. "What demon has possessed you?"

"Who's just a little girl now?" I screamed. Black Otter stared at me, wide-eyed with fright.

My father squeezed, cutting off my breath until I stopped flailing, then he set me down. "What's gotten into you?"

"I hate you!" I shouted over my shoulder at Black Otter.

But then Father smacked me; just a small strike across the face to draw my attention, but hard enough to leave my cheek numb and my heart thrumming like a hummingbird's wings. Concern rather than anger filled my father's eyes; an expression shared by my mother a few steps behind him. "You will go back to the palace and sit in the nursery," Father said, his voice trembling. "In the morning, your mother will take you to the calmecac and the priestesses will teach you to have respect for your parents and your husband." He pushed me away.

Mother reached for my hand, but I wrapped my arms around Father's leg, trying to keep him from leaving. "I'm sorry, Father," I sobbed. "I didn't mean any of it!"

"Remove yourself from my sight or the guard will do it for you," he snarled. "You've dishonored me. Now I must explain to my brother why I bring his son back abused and bloodied at the hands of a girl. Maybe I should give you over to Ihuitimal for punishment."

The thought sent spikes of terror through me. I'd never envied Black Otter for his father; Ihuitimal punished Black Otter harshly for the slightest infraction, so I didn't dare think of what he'd do to me. "Please no, Father! Hold me over the chili roaster or make me help in the kitchen every day for the next year, but please don't hand me over to my uncle! He's the high priest of a demon god who hates Quetzalcoatl and he threatened to kill Black Otter if he worshiped the Feathered Serpent! He will surely feed my heart to his awful Smoking Mirror!"

Father stared me agape but then turned to Black Otter. Black Otter stared back at us, fear and betrayal painted on his face. My stomach dropped. I'd broken my oath on Quetzalcoatl's good name.

"This is true?" Father boomed. When Black Otter didn't answer, Father sprang upon him like a puma, yanking him to his feet by his hair. "Has your father brought that abomination into my city? Does he worship him in my palace?"

"Yes, Your Highness!" Black Otter shouted, tears streaming down his face.

"And what about you?"

"I worship as my father tells me to!"

Father twisted Black Otter's hair. "Then I wedded my favorite daughter to some spineless demon worshiper?" I imagined him gutting my best friend right there next to the lake.

But I wouldn't let him. *Bite his leg, then Black Otter can break free and swim across the lake. You'll get a lashing for sure, but it'll be worth it. This is your fault.*

I made to rush at Father, but Mother grabbed me, clutching me with both arms. I struggled, but her strength held, leaving me only one option. "Please don't hurt him, Father! I'm sorry, Black Otter! I didn't mean to tell, I swear!" With all my fight drained, I wept against Mother's arms while she whispered that everything would be all right.

Father regained his composure, perhaps moved by my sobs. "We're going back to the palace." He shoved Black Otter over to one of his guards, then started up the hill.

The argument raging down the hall was so loud that Father and Ihuitimal might as well have been right outside my nursery's door curtain.

"I warned you not to bring that deceitful Chichimec god into Culhuacan, but you dare flaunt your treachery by setting up an altar to him in my own palace?" Father roared.

"I dare?" Ihuitimal shouted back. "You talk endlessly about your merciful Feathered Serpent, but where was he when I was being tortured by the Chichimecs? Where were *you*, Brother?"

"We're not discussing that now—"

"It's never a discussion for you, because you're afraid of the truth. You owe me, Mixcoatl, for everything you took from me—"

"And I repay that debt now by not executing you and your son for treason. Leave my palace and never darken my lands with your shadow again!"

Everything fell silent. I pulled aside my door curtain, but the guard pushed me back in. "Don't come out again," he warned, so I peered out the crack between the wall and curtain.

Ihuitimal passed by, surrounded by guards. I couldn't see Black Otter, but I heard him pleading, "I'm sorry, Father. Please forgive me!" Ihuitimal said nothing, his face livid. I sank into the corner and wept.

Mother finally came for me and took my hand. "Your father wishes to speak with you."

But I didn't want to go and made the guard carry me down the hall to Father's room.

Nochuatl looked up at me with a sad smile, but my father paced, fists clenched. The walls' murals of bloody battles made me more anxious, especially when Father stalked towards me. Only Mother's supportive hand on my shoulder kept me from bolting. Father said, "What did that traitor's son tell you, about his father and this Smoking Mirror?" I only blinked, startled, so he shook me. "Tell me, Quetzalpetlatl!"

"She's just a child, Mixcoatl," Mother scolded him. "She doesn't know what you're asking for." She knelt and wiped my tears away. "Can you tell me when you first learned of Smoking Mirror?"

"On my wedding night. Black Otter said his father wouldn't let him come to the temple with us because his god was Quetzalcoatl's enemy, and that worshiping the Feathered Serpent made him weak."

"What else?"

"He said Uncle Ihuitimal would bring Smoking Mirror's worship to the Tolteca—"

"I knew it!" Father barked. "How dare he lie through his sharpened teeth?"

"Is there anything else your uncle might have said that upset you?" Mother pressed.

I nodded, eager to tattle on my wicked uncle. "That day, in the menagerie, he blasphemed against Quetzalcoatl and said Black Otter was going to be king after Father, and that keeping the baby was going to kill you. But he just wanted to scare me, didn't he?"

Mother looked ready to say something, but Father interrupted her. "Of course he lies. That's all he knows how to do." To Nochuatl, he added, "You were right, Brother. If I'd died before Black Otter came of age, Ihuitimal would've taken the throne himself, and no doubt killed my son, to ensure Black Otter's claim." He punched the wall, breaking off the plaster, then he turned on me, his eyes dark and accusing. "And you! Why didn't you immediately tell someone about this?"

"Black Otter made me swear on Quetzalcoatl's good name," I sobbed. "He said his father would flog him like a criminal if I told anyone."

"The boy's lucky *I* didn't beat him for keeping such a secret," Father snapped.

"You're being unfair, tossing him to the coyotes like this," Nochuatl said. "If Father had told you to keep a secret, would you have questioned it?"

"Our Father never would've made us privy to dangerous secrets, for our own good. If the boy had come to me, I would've protected him. But he didn't. My brother can do with him as he wishes."

Nochuatl gave him a sharp stare.

"But we're married, Father, so Black Otter is as good as your son, right?" I asked, hopeful.

Father shook his head. "I've dissolved that union and sent his family into exile in the north."

Black Otter was going to live with the barbarian Chichimecs? I trembled, guilt stabbing my heart.

"You should execute Ihuitimal rather than exiling him, Brother," Nochuatl said. "Eloxochitl and Black Otter are innocent in all this—"

"They both knew, so they aren't innocent," Father snapped. "As for Ihuitimal, I owed him a debt and now I've repaid it. I won't discuss it anymore." He scowled when he saw me crying. "Why are you carrying on again?"

"Will I ever get to see Black Otter again? I didn't even get to say goodbye." Or to tell him how sorry I was for betraying his trust.

"Stop being emotional over a demon-worshiper. It's time to send you off to calmecac, so you can learn to control yourself, like a proper woman."

"Brother, have mercy on her," Nochuatl said. "You can't expect her to snuff her feelings out for her best friend like you would blow out a lamp."

"When you've finally let go of the past and taken a wife and sired a few more children, then you may lecture me on how to raise my daughter. Now out, everyone. I need peace after all this nonsense."

Mother and I followed Nochuatl, but he vanished into his room, a wake of anger behind him.

◻

I shared Mother's bed that night so I wouldn't have to be alone, but even her soothing humming couldn't bring me sleep. I pressed my cheek against her belly, staring at the painting of the Feathered Serpent that covered the wall next to her bed and feeling I might never move again. "Close your eyes and try to sleep. We have to get up early to go to the temple," she said.

"Then you're taking me to the calmecac tomorrow?" I choked.

"I think it best you stay here with your sisters a while longer, so I'll speak with your father in the morning, when he's in a more reasonable mood."

That loosened some of the painful knots in my chest. "I'm sorry I disappointed you, Mother. And Father too."

"I'm not disappointed. Your father just forgets what it's like to not live life fearing that people are trying to harm you."

"But why would anyone want to hurt him?"

"It's one of the perils of being king." She kissed my head. "Now try to sleep."

But instead my bitter words to Black Otter repeated over and over in my head. I'd never get to chase him through the gardens again, nor get to tell him that I really hadn't minded the kiss that much. *I wish that statue were really Quetzalcoatl, so he could crush me in his coils,* I thought as I stared at the small stone idol next to the bed. Mother prayed in front of it every night. *It's what I deserve, for breaking a promise I made on his good name.*

I startled when something pushed against my back. I turned, but Mother was asleep. I poked at her dress, wondering if a mouse had crawled up into it, but I felt only her slightly-swollen belly. *You're so tired you're imagining things.*

But then I felt it again, this time where my hand rested against Mother's stomach. "Great Feathered Serpent!" I gasped as a bulge slid under my hand. "What is that?"

"Your brother," Mother whispered.

"Truly?"

She nodded. "He's moving already."

"Is he supposed to?"

"You did the same, just not so soon."

I followed the moving bulge with my hand for a moment then asked, "Did you swallow a piece of jade to put me in your belly, or was it a feather?"

Mother laughed. "How you came to be in there is a discussion for when you're older."

I set my cheek against her stomach, amazed at my brother's movements. It was like seeing a distant light when I'd been sure I'd have to spend the night out in the cold rain. The pain of Black Otter's leaving lessened a bit.

"I'll be your friend, Brother, if you'll be mine," I whispered to him. I smiled as he pressed against my cheek as if in answer. "I think he said yes!"

She smiled. "I hope the two of you grow up to be the best of friends."

CHAPTER FIVE

Father said to forget about Black Otter, but I couldn't. Where was he, and had his father made good on his threats? Hopefully they were exaggerations, like the way my brothers always said they wanted to kill each other but never did. The adults whispered about Ihuitimal's departure while my brothers and sisters made up stories as to why. Even those who'd bullied Black Otter showed surprising concern for his absence.

Jade Flower took a different tack. She refused to talk to me, so I spent my afternoons with my mother in the women's hall, working on my weaving. I passed a few months working on a blanket for my unborn brother, but I tore out more work than I finished as I made mistakes over and over again. Mother offered me advice, but she mostly left me to my work.

But when the weather turned cold and damp with the first signs of fall, Mother came to me with bad news. "You're starting calmecac next week," she said as she tucked me into bed. When I started crying, she said, "I was your age when I started calmecac, and I was very afraid too. This is when we'd planned to send you even before all this mess with your uncle, so we're not punishing you. It's just your time. And you won't live in the dormitories until the beginning of the year. Everything will be fine; you'll make new friends, learn to read and write and keep the calendar, and you'll have a few years as a priestess before your father calls you back to do your duty to the family. Just as I did." Her voice faded with a hint of regret.

"Did you like being a priestess?" I asked.

"I loved being a priestess."

"Do you wish you were still one?"

She sighed. "What I truly wanted was that I could've married Mixcoatl, but also remained a priestess. Unfortunately, I had no choice either way; as my father's eldest daughter, I had duties that superseded anything else." She hugged and held me for a moment. "If the gods would grant me one wish, it would be that life treat you better than it has me."

I thought of Mother's words often over the next three weeks as I spent my days at the Temple of Quetzalcoatl. The priestesses were strict; failing to sweep behind the gold Feathered Serpent idol got me a switch across my palms; if I spoke out of turn, they held me over the chili roasters in the school kitchen; and if I was late for my day's duty, they kept me well after dark with extra chores. I missed the afternoons with Mother in the women's hall, particularly now that she'd opened up a hidden door into her life and showed me what was inside. I wanted to know so much more about her.

I stayed home during the last week of the year, for tradition said no one should work during these dangerous Leftover Days, which were unaccounted for on either our harvest or festival calendars. The Tolteca didn't even wage war on those days, for it might anger the gods. Everyone kept their heads covered so the gods couldn't see them, and they spoke in whispers. Most people remained in their rooms, to be safe.

A few days before the beginning of the new year, Mother came to the women's hall where I was working on the blanket in front of the hearth and told me Father wanted see me in his quarters. Remembering how he'd acted the last time I was there, it struck me through with fear when Mother said she wasn't coming with me. "He wants to speak with you alone," she said. I felt I was walking to my doom as I left the women's hall.

Luckily I met Nochuatl in the hallway, and his cheerful greeting eased my nerves. "Are you enjoying calmecac so far?" he asked, as we walked together.

"Not really."

He laughed. "It's a big change," he admitted.

"I don't like change."

"We've had more than our share of it," he said. "While we must move on, we don't have to forget. I miss Black Otter too."

I swallowed back a spike of anguish. "Do you think he's all right?"

Nochuatl didn't answer right away. "I hope so."

"Do you think we'll get to see him again?"

"I don't know. The bitterness runs deep between Ihuitimal and the king."

"Why?"

"It goes a long way back, before your father became king. Ihuitimal has a right to be angry, but we have to let go of the past, before it completely destroys us."

"Is that why Father told you all that stuff about getting married?" I asked. But seeing the stricken look on Nochuatl's face, I regretted saying anything.

When we arrived at Father's doorway, Nochuatl smiled at me. "Yes, that's why your father told me to move on."

"I'm sorry I upset you, Uncle."

He hugged me. "You haven't anything to be sorry about," he said, then left me to face Father alone. I rang the copper bells on the hem of the door curtain.

Father called me inside. He sat on the floor in front of the hearth, burning copalli incense and wearing a cloak that didn't cover his head. He smiled the way he had on my wedding day, easing my mind a little. "Come sit with me, Quetzalpetlatl."

I sat near the unlit hearth with him; no one lit the house fires during the Leftover

Days. He didn't say anything for a moment, but then asked, "So the big day approaches? Finally moving into the dormitories at the calmecac? I was very frightened my first night in the House of Warriors, but just knowing Ihuitimal was a few beds away made it better. He'd been there two years already, learning the art of war, and he would've rather have shaved his head than have me dogging after him, but still, he was a comfort to have around." The way he spoke about Ihuitimal seemed nostalgic and kind. I found it puzzling. "Remember that you have older sisters at the calmecac, and they'll help you if you need it. You'll do well though. Your faith in Quetzalcoatl is your strength. Your mother did an excellent job of raising you to respect the gods and she's very proud of you. So am I."

I smiled shyly, unused to him praising me anymore.

He paused, taking a deep breath, then said, "I know I've been very hard on you, and that I wasn't any source of comfort or trust for you when Black Otter left, and I'm very sorry for that. I hope you can find the strength to forgive me my faults."

Father's admission shocked me; and though I also knew it took him a great deal to admit this, at first I didn't entirely trust it. I'd spent so long trying to be what he wanted me to be that this sudden change baffled me.

He took my hand in his. "I don't want you thinking I put you in calmecac to get you out from under my feet. Your mother was right. I always showed you more favor than any of my other daughters, so it shouldn't have surprised me that pushing you away hurt you so. But I want to repair the damage I did. I'll visit you twice a week and I'll take you to the market or out in the royal canoe, or we'll just walk the gardens and you can tell me everything you're learning."

"Truly?" I asked, daring to raise my hopes.

He nodded. "And if you haven't anything planned for the rest of this afternoon, you can stay here and I'll teach you to play patolli."

That startled me even more. "But patolli is a man's game."

He leaned forward and whispered, "Just don't tell your mother. She would kill me for teaching you to gamble."

Not caring about decorum or rules, I flung my arms around his neck like a baby monkey and hugged him tight. When he hugged me back instead of pushing me away, I let slip a few tears. I'd finally gotten my Tatli back. "I love you," I whispered.

"And I will always love you, my little Butterfly, no matter what."

□

"How much longer?" I asked Mother when I touched her belly, checking if my brother was moving. He usually touched my hand while I sang him a song, but tonight he sat very still. Mother had grown very round in the few months since I'd first felt him moving around.

"A while still," Mother said, pulling my blanket up to my chin. "He'll come no sooner than his time."

"You'll tell me when he's born, and bring him to see me?"

"I'll summon you when it's time." She smoothed my hair and smiled. "Did you and your father have a nice talk this afternoon? I haven't seen you so happy in months."

"He promised to come and see me at school twice a week. Will you come too?"

"Of course. But now to sleep with you. It wouldn't do for the gods to see us up late whispering during the Leftover Days." And she blew out the flames on the nursery's lamps.

❑

I awoke when my itching wrist flared up again for the first time in months. I tried not to scratch but couldn't help myself. *Maybe washing it will help,* I thought. I pulled a cloak over my shoulders against the evening chill then padded down the hall to the side corridor that led out to the bathhouse.

A small torch burned over the large water jar near the doorway, giving me enough light to examine my wrist. Four ugly red bumps stood out, two on top and two on the bottom, like a snakebite. I poured cold water over them but it did nothing, making my stomach knot. *Wake Mother and have her look at it,* I decided, so I dried my hands then turned to the hallway.

A coughing sound—like the call of the jaguar—echoed from the main corridor, and a shadow moved in the darkness. When yellow eyes flashed at me, my heart jumped into my throat and I stumbled backwards, knocking over the water jar. There was a jaguar in the palace!

But when I looked again, I saw nothing. The sweet smell of tobacco smoke wafted out of the doorway. *It's probably just a guard,* I told myself, but fear held me captive. If it was a jaguar, it had me trapped.

Hot pine pitch dripped off the torch onto my shoulder, scalding my skin. I scratched it off quickly and glared at the torch as I moved away, but then remembered having seen the servants use one to force Father's jaguars into cages so they could clean the pens. Maybe I could use the torch to get past this jaguar. *Better than waiting to get eaten.*

I'd hoped holding the torch would strengthen my confidence, but I shivered like a cold dog as I approached the main hallway. I stuck the torch around the corner but the hall was empty in both directions, not even any guards. Father's doorway stood open, moonlight creeping through; he never kept his curtain open.

I crept to Mother's room, next door to Father's. Her curtain was closed but her bed was empty. I checked her private bathhouse, but she wasn't there either. "Nantli?" I whispered, wandering around the small garden, looking for her. My panic intensified. She was always in her room in the middle of the night, to give me comfort when I woke up from a nightmare.

Wake Father. I'd surely get scolded for it, but what else could I do? I ran into Father's room, praying he'd understand.

But I slid to a stop and gasped when I saw the black-robed monster hunched over Father's bed mat. Its long, matted hair glistened in the moonlight, and it sang in a harsh voice that sounded like bones snapping. I screamed, my heart thudding as if trying to break out of my chest.

The creature whirled on me, so I swung the torch, shouting, "Get back! Stay away!"

"Quetzalpetlatl! Put that down before you hurt someone!" It wasn't a demon's voice, but rather my uncle Ihuitimal's. A painted gold stripe split his face but I recognized his hideous scowl.

I dropped the torch and ran to him, wrapping my arms around him, relieved. "Thank Omeyocan you're here, Uncle!"

He pushed me away and straightened his robe as if I'd mussed it up. I opened my mouth to ask him why he was dressed like a priest of the Sun, but he said, "I said I would come back."

"Is Black Otter back too?"

"Your husband is here," Ihuitimal replied, his voice chilly. "And wiser now."

I didn't like how he said that. "Is he all right?"

"He's fine."

"Can I see him?"

"In time."

Remembering what had driven me to my father's room in the first place, I said, "There's a jaguar loose in the palace, Uncle! I saw it in the hall by the bathhouse." My wrist itched worse than ever, so I rubbed it against my side.

"I didn't see anything," Ihuitimal said. "You were just having a nightmare, child."

"I was not!" I snapped. Why did he always think I was dreaming or imagining things? And why did my wrist constantly itch around him? *You should have known better than to think he'd changed at all,* I thought, so I tried to step around him. Father at least would listen.

But when Ihuitimal blocked me, I blinked up at him, startled. "I must speak with Father."

"He can't talk right now." But then Ihuitimal seemed to reconsider. "Forgive me, fool that I sometimes am, but I forgot he'd asked me to give you a gift."

"A gift?" I asked, excited.

"To let you know how much he loves you. You must close your eyes and hold out your hands, for it's a surprise."

I did as he asked, eager. *I hope it's a necklace he made for me, so I can wear it every day and remember him while I'm away at school.*

But Ihuitimal put something heavy and wet into my hands. *Like a little dog with its skin pulled off,* I thought, then shuddered. *Don't be stupid. Father would never give you something so disgusting.*

"You may look now," Ihuitimal said, amused.

I stared down at my hands with shocked confusion for a moment before realizing what I held: a heart, warm and covered in blood. But why would he give me...?

But even before I looked up to see that Ihuitimal had stepped away from the bed, the truth struck me like a poison arrow: this was my father's heart.

Father lay on his bed, his throat cut so deeply he looked as though he had a second, gaping mouth that drooled blood. His chest was open too, his ribs snapped aside like a butchered animal. I stared, reeling, intense heat filling me. *It has to be a dream. Great Feathered Serpent, don't let this be real, this can't be real this can't be this can't be!*

But my father's sticky heart oozed in my hands. I felt as if someone were squeezing my stomach. I had to get out of there.

Dropping the heart, I turned to flee, but Ihuitimal grabbed me like an eagle seizing a rabbit. I tried to scream, but instead my stomach tossed my dinner all over the front of his robe. He roared, disgusted. My second attempt came out loud as thunder. Ihuitimal tried to clamp his hand over my mouth, but I snapped at him like a crazed dog, screaming and yelling, "Murderer!"

He threw me down on my father's dead body and struck me so hard my jaw popped and tiny stars invaded the corners of my vision. "Be quiet!" he hissed. I would have defied him, but I suddenly faded away into darkness.

But I soon awoke again, my body sluggish, and my nightdress warmly wet and clinging to my legs. Ihuitimal shook me and said something I couldn't hear at first, but like water escaping a broken dam, the sound suddenly rushed back, loud and painful. "Where is she, Quetzalpetlatl? Tell me and I'll spare you further harm," he whispered.

"What?" I muttered, confused.

"Tell me where your mother is and I'll take you to see Black Otter. You want to see him again, don't you?"

I looked over at my father again, surprised to see him; I'd forgotten he was there, what Ihuitimal had done to him, but not anymore. Even if I knew where Mother was, I wouldn't tell him. He'd kill her too.

"Unhand her, Brother, or I'll relieve you of your head," Nochuatl shouted from the doorway, sword drawn.

Ihuitimal yanked me around, twisting my arm behind my back until it threatened to pop loose of my shoulder. I wailed. "Come get me, Brother, or is your heart too soft to kill the girl to get to me?" He put an obsidian blade to my throat. I couldn't breathe.

Nochuatl backed down and my heart failed me. "Please don't leave me, Uncle," I sputtered, my tears spilling fast. "Please!"

"I won't leave you. I promise," Nochuatl said.

"Always so loyal, even in death," Ihuitimal sneered. "But then what choice did you have when Mixcoatl could turn your secrets against you at a moment's notice? Mixcoatl had no honor when it came to women, but did you really think you were clever enough not to get caught? How could I not have noticed your face when I looked at Black Otter?"

"Leave the boy out of this," Nochuatl said, taking a step forward.

"You think I'd harm him, after all the time I've invested in raising him to be *my son*?" Ihuitimal asked, mock hurt in his voice. "Maybe you had something to do with him coming into this world, but I'm the one he calls Father, I'm the one he looks to to learn about being an honorable man, a concept neither you nor Mixcoatl know anything about."

"Using a child as a shield against your enemies isn't honorable," Nochuatl snarled, but he still didn't move. Why all this talk of nonsensical things instead of rescuing me?

"I'm taking back what Mixcoatl stole from me. Step aside and she won't get hurt; fetch me Chimalma and I'll forgive your betrayal and let you live. Accept me as the rightful king of Culhuacan and you can have Eloxochitl," Ihuitimal said.

"I will never kneel before you as the king," Nochuatl said.

Guards burst into Father's room and my heart leapt, until they turned their spears on Nochuatl. They disarmed him and held his hands behind his back.

"I tried dealing fairly with you, Nochuatl, but now you leave me little choice." Ihuitimal shoved my arm up higher, making me squeal and kick. "You will bring Chimalma to me or I'll pull the wings off her precious little Butterfly. Have you ever seen a butterfly with all her wings plucked off, Brother?"

"I'll kill you if you harm her, Ihuitimal!" Nochuatl shouted.

"Then bring me her mother and our deal can still stand."

I squeezed my eyes shut against my stinging tears, but when I opened them again, I saw a flash of emerald and white, this time slithering under the logs in the hearth. My wrist flared hot and suddenly fire erupted in the hearth.

The guards jostled away, startled. Even Ihuitimal stepped back, dragging me with him.

But the flames extinguished as if doused by water and smoke billowed out, forming a giant snake. The guards fled, screaming as it rushed them. The smoke engulfed Nochuatl and his one remaining guard, reducing both men to coughs and gags, then it rushed at me and Ihuitimal, hissing.

Ihuitimal shoved me and I shrieked, but I fell through the smoke. I looked up to see a smaller smoke serpent split off from the larger mass. It swam down to me, its eyes burning orange like hot coals.

Follow me, and it moved towards the garden doorway. Smoke filled the room and I heard scuffles and cries in the dark, so I hurried after it, holding my breath against the pungent cloud around me but not daring to close my eyes even as they burned and watered.

Out in Father's garden, the smoke-serpent disappeared among the vines hanging over the back wall. I pulled aside the thick mat to find an opening into the secret pathway. I looked over my shoulder, hoping to see Nochuatl coming out of Father's room along with the billowing smoke.

Hurry! the nahual whispered beyond the vines, so I swallowed hard and pushed my way through.

The passageway was empty and the smoke-dragon flew to the right. I followed, my wrist itching less the further away we went. "When you bit me...you gave me something that would warn me...you knew my uncle was a bad man, didn't you?" I panted as I jogged after the nahual.

It is one of several gifts the god has given you, it replied. *It will help keep you and those you love safe.*

We ascended a steep set of stairs and I had to stop to catch my breath. We hadn't passed any doorways in the wall for a long time now and by the time we reached the top I had no idea where we were, but ahead the path bent to the left. Hopefully that meant we'd reached the main garden.

You must hurry, the nahual said as it swam over my head. *Your mother is waiting for you.*

"But what about Nochuatl? We can't leave him behind."

Suddenly two guards charged around the corner, their thick bodies scattering the nahual's smoke. "Come along, Princess," one of them said, while the other man grabbed my hand. His touch shot hot pain up my arm from my wrist. I tore free but he grabbed me from behind. "Calm down. We're taking you to your mother," he said.

"Liar!" I wiggled down to my armpits, but he tightened his grip, so I bit his arm.

He bellowed, letting me go, but the other man wrestled me to the ground. "Bloodsucking brat! I should give her a good thrashing for this. That's going to leave a scar."

The other man laughed. "Can't you even handle a child, Calli?"

Suddenly Nochuatl was there. He grabbed the first man from behind and threw him down the stairs, taking his sword in the process. The guard holding me down went to his knees to reach for his sword, but Nochuatl kneed him in the mouth. I huddled on the ground while the men fought, peeking up when I heard one of them gagging. Nochuatl had the guard pinned with his knee across his throat, his sword raised. "Turn away, Papalotl," my uncle warned. I hid my face again and covered my ears until Nochuatl scooped me into his arms. "Keep your eyes closed, lest you see something no child should see," he whispered, so I buried my face in his chest as he ran. Behind my eyelids though, I still saw my father's dead body as if the image was burned into them.

"You can look now," Nochuatl finally said, his breath labored. I opened my eyes to see a dark stain on the side of his mantle.

"You're injured?" I gasped.

He winced with each step but said, "It's nothing. Ihuitimal stuck me with his knife, but don't worry. It's not deep."

I didn't believe him.

We descended another stair to the mouth of a cave. Nochuatl lit a torch in the pine pitch burning in a clay kettle brazier in the alcove. "Where are we?" I asked, gazing uneasily into the darkness ahead.

"These caves run under the city and let out under Quetzalcoatl's temple, but also along the lake shore, under the shadow of the temple."

I held onto him a little tighter as we went inside.

The deeper in we went, the more I was glad Mother had never taken me to the temple this way. Dripping water echoed in the dark, and fang-like rocks on both the ceiling and the floor made it look as if we were moving through a monster's ugly mouth. I shivered, reminded of those nightmares I sometimes had in which I walked down to Mictlan to face judgment before Lord Death. The trail twisted, climbed, and fell, and once Nochuatl had to backtrack when we came to a dead-end.

"Now we're on the right path," he murmured when we came to a pool of water. He put me on his shoulders and I bent low to avoid hitting my head on the teeth sticking out of the low ceiling. Our progress slowed when the water reached Nochuatl's chest, but ahead I saw the gray glow of the cave exit.

Before we reached it, we came to the bow of a canoe. Mother sat inside, looking sick with worry, but her tear-stained face lit up when she saw me. "Oh my dearest Butterfly," she murmured into my hair when Nochuatl put me into her arms. I clutched her, overwhelmed to be holding her again. "I feared he took you from me forever." One of my mother's handmaidens sat with her, shivering while two guards in thick cotton armor stood ready with poles in hand. "Thank you so much for bringing her to me, Nochuatl."

"I wouldn't let you leave without her, but now you must go. The royal litter awaits you on the opposite shore, manned by my closest comrades, and my most trusted friend Lord Blood Wolf leads them. He'll see you safely to Xochicalco. I've already sent word to Cuitlapanton, and he'll take you and the children in without hesitation. May the Feathered Serpent bless your journey, My Lady." He stepped away from the boat.

"You're not coming with us, Uncle?" I cried. "But you must! It's not safe here...and you're hurt—Mother, Ihuitimal stabbed him! We must take care of him. Make him come with us."

He kissed my forehead. "Someone must stay and stand against Ihuitimal."

"But that should be someone who's not injured." I gave him a fierce hug and wiped my tears against his neck. "Please don't stay. I couldn't stand it if Ihuitimal killed you too, Uncle."

"Don't worry about me. You must watch after your mother, and when all's well again, I'll bring you both home—and your brother, if it takes that long."

"You promise?"

"I promise." He gently pried my arms off his neck then set me back in Mother's lap. "But until then, pray to the Feathered Serpent for my health."

"We will, every day," I assured him.

Nochuatl stepped away again and motioned the soldiers to shove off. "I love you, Uncle!" I called back as we approached the cave's open mouth.

He waved back. "I love you too, little Butterfly."

My heart grew anguished as Nochuatl faded from view, as if the shadows of Mictlan itself had swallowed him up.

CHAPTER SIX

While the soldiers pushed us across the dark lake, Mother and I murmured prayers, asking Quetzalcoatl to watch over Nochuatl and our beloved city. My uncle had once told me that invaders usually burned the temple and the palace, but Culhuacan glowed pale, none the wiser that she was without a king, and that her queen now fled to escape death. How had Ihuitimal gotten back into Culhuacan and past my father's guards? Maybe he used the same passageway Nochuatl and I had used to escape? I'd hoped prayers would calm the sick feeling in my stomach, but now I could do nothing but shiver.

"Your dress is wet." Mother touched my stomach with panicked fingers. "You're not hurt, are you?"

My cheeks flared with heat. "When Ihuitimal grabbed me...he scared me so much I...." An embarrassed sob escaped my throat, preventing me from going on.

Mother understood though. "It's all right," she assured me with a tender hug. She stripped my dress off me and cleaned it in the lake water over the side of the boat. I wrapped my naked body in my cloak to keep warm. "We'll say no more about it," she said as she wrung the water out as best she could.

As we neared shore, one soldier mimicked an owl call and someone soon answered with an identical hoot in the distance. When we reached the bank, soldiers hurried to help Mother and me from the boat. "Your litter awaits, My Lady," one of the soldiers—Lord Blood Wolf—told Mother as he helped her up the grassy bank. She held her large belly and winced, looking tired. He hurried us into the canopied litter, and before we'd settled in among the blankets, the soldiers—three to a side—lifted the litter and headed off into the forest.

I sat at the curtains peering out, but the dark left little to see. The forest was alive with shrieking monkeys and chirping insects, but when I heard the coughing growl of a jaguar, I shrank back to Mother's side and snuggled up close to her. The sound of her steady, soothing heartbeat blocked out all the scary sounds outside until I finally fell into welcoming sleep.

But nightmares of Father woke me at dawn. Mother whispered comforting words and slipped my still-damp dress back on me, but when she gasped in pain, I forgot my own woes. "Are you all right?" Noticing how she held her belly, I asked, "Is my brother punching you?"

She smiled. "It's little wonder your brother wishes to make an attempt to come forth now, but he'll calm down. The Leftover Days are a bad time for a baby to be born, so he'll wait until they're over." The worry lines on her face kept my stomach twisted with trepidation, though.

We huddled together all day, stepping outside only to relieve ourselves. Mother mostly slept, waking whenever more pain gripped her.

"How much longer until we're there?" I asked one of the soldiers when we stopped to eat cold, dry tlaxcallis and rest along the side of the dark dirt road. We had no fire, just the moon, which made it feel all the colder. A dampness that smelled of rain hung in the air.

He ignored me though, instead watching Mother's handmaiden speak with Lord Blood Wolf. She twisted her hands together and glanced back at the litter where Mother rested. "Can the men go on through the night?"

"Does the queen's condition demand it?" Lord Blood Wolf asked.

"Her labor has slowed, but she won't make it past morning. If we delay...do any of the men have medical training?"

"Nothing beyond dressing wounds and mixing tonics." He looked past her at the litter too. "Can't you deliver the baby?"

"The queen knows more about delivering children than I do, but when the time comes, she won't be able to direct me." When Mother started moaning again, the handmaiden said, "Please don't leave the life of the king's son in my incapable hands."

She made it all sounds so serious, reminding me of what Ihuitimal had told me that day in the menagerie. *He can't possibly be right,* I thought. *He'd wanted to scare me. Mother's going to be fine.*

Before Lord Blood Wolf could answer, several soldiers called out an alert and everyone came to their feet, weapons ready. A few closed in around me just as a pack of new soldiers jogged around the bend in the road ahead, carrying yellow and white banners. Everyone relaxed but I crawled back to the litter, not trusting these new strangers. I climbed inside and peered cautiously past the curtain as a tall man dressed like a bird stepped up to Lord Blood Wolf and gave a bow.

"I am Lord Spear Fish, war chief to King Cuitlapanton of Xochicalco," the man announced. "We come on behalf of His Highness, to expedite the queen's arrival."

"And none too soon," Lord Blood Wolf said. "She must get to the city as soon as possible, but my men are almost spent."

"And My Lady will give birth before sunrise," the handmaiden added.

"We'll set off immediately." Lord Spear Fish pointed his men towards the litter.

They tossed all but two blankets out of the litter and I rode on one soldier's shoulders from there on. Light rain fell as we set off into the night.

It soon gave way to a downpour. Lord Blood Wolf trotted with us, insisting he must keep his promise to ensure our safe arrival in Xochicalco. His loyalty to Nochuatl warmed me in the cold rain.

Mother's moans soon became cries, and those intensified into screams and sobbing. Unable to see well now that clouds blocked the moon, I imagined monsters ripping her apart, but everyone continued on as if it were completely normal. I tried jumping from my soldier's shoulders to help her myself, but he held me by the ankles. "Calm yourself, child," he rumbled. "We can't afford to slow down."

"But my mother needs me. *Mother!*"

"Be strong, Papalotl," Mother called back. "Trust in Quetzalcoatl; say prayers for me, to take your mind off what you hear."

So I closed my eyes and whispered under my shaking breath:

"Oh Great Feathered Serpent,
Watch over Mother,
Over Black Otter,
Over Nochuatl,
Over Eloxochitl.
Watch over me and give me strength."

We finally tromped out of the woods, and through the haze I saw dim lights in the distance. "Are we there?" I asked, and my soldier nodded. Soon tall white walls coalesced out of the darkness, reaching into the heavens as if dropped there by Lord Sun himself. The soldiers manning the great gates held torches to help us find our way in the darkness of the Leftover Days.

On the last day of the year, people stayed in their houses until the king relit the city's fires, signaling all was well, but my mother's screams brought more than a few people to their doorways. Seeing a few of the women whispering anxiously together, my own fear for Mother came roaring back.

When we reached the large, empty main plaza, the soldiers turned towards a tall, sprawling building surrounded by stone walls.

"Not the palace!" the handmaid shouted. "My lady wishes to go to the Temple of Quetzalcoatl."

"The palace is closer," Blood Wolf said.

"Stop the litter!" Mother called, and the soldiers slowed to a stop. "He must be born in the temple," she panted from the curtain. When Blood Wolf shook his head, she screamed, "Take me to the temple, *now!*" She let out another keening cry that raised the hairs on my neck.

Blood Wolf helped Mother out of the litter, then he and another soldier carried her up a broad stone staircase leading up the darkened hillside off the square.

By the time we reached the top, the clouds had cleared, letting the moon spill light on Xochicalco's sacred precinct. The flat hilltop hosted several stepped pyramids and a long, rectangular building with a stone-ringed cistern out front. Mother's cries brought out still more people, but those at the tallest temple ran down to meet us. Two priestesses in white cotton robes took Mother and carried her up the stairs into the temple. I followed as soon as my soldier let me down.

Priestesses scrambled about inside the temple, preparing a bed of reed prayer mats on the blue stone altar in the middle of the room, in front of the gold Feathered Serpent idol. Still more hurried to light the large clay kettle braziers. "Fetch Nimilitzli," one of the older priestesses ordered as she laid numerous obsidian knives at the foot of the altar.

What in Mictlan are those for? I clutched the handmaiden's dress as she stood next to me, looking around just as bewildered as I felt.

"I'm already here," a new voice spoke from the doorway. "I heard her in the plaza and came from the king as quick as I could." A tall, imposing woman wearing white robes embroidered with two gold feathered serpents on the front strode down the three steps into the temple. She tossed aside her waist-length black braid when she stopped at the foot of the altar.

She's the one I saw the day I was born, I realized. *The nasty woman who made Mother cry by telling her she'd never have another child.* Noticing me, she asked Mother, "Do you wish the child be here, Chimalma?" Who was this haughty woman who thought she could send me away when Mother most needed me?

As the priestesses helped her onto the altar, Mother panted, "She *must* be here when he's born." She broke out into another agonized cry.

I ran to her side, gripping her hand. "I'm here for you, Mother." I tried to keep my voice strong.

Nimilitzli knelt at the foot of the altar and told the handmaiden, "Keep me supplied with clean cloth as needed."

The handmaiden paled but nodded.

One of the priestesses set a blanket over Mother's lap while Nimilitzli pushed her knees up. "The head's crowned, Chimalma," Nimilitzli said. "I need to cut you, so when you feel the need to push, resist it."

Mother nodded but I didn't share her strange calm. "Cut you, Mother? But why?"

In answer, Mother rose into another scream, crushing my hand in hers. I added my cry to the din ringing off the plaster walls. What was happening? "Mother! Mother!" I sobbed, wanting to crawl into her arms so she could hold and comfort me.

"Push!" Nimilitzli shouted. Mother's face reddened, tendons standing out on her neck. I shut my eyes to block out the terrifying vision, trying to remember her beautiful, carefree smile. Only when she fell silent did I dare open my eyes again. She breathed fast, but blissful relaxation painted her face. I let out a gasp of relief. Finally it was over.

"Cloth," Nimilitzli told the handmaiden, and the sickly-looking girl obeyed.

Mother stroked my hair. "I'm so sorry your father's not here for you, Papalotl," she murmured. "He wanted to make up for past wrongs, but Ihuitimal has no honor. What kind of madman attacks and kills his own brother during the Leftover Days? May the gods curse his reign to be short, if it all—"

She suddenly tried to pull her hand away from me, but I held it tighter, refusing to let her go. But her grip turned bone-breaking, renewing my panic and fear. I screamed with her, the pain shooting up my arm, but I didn't try to break free. I'd hold onto her even if Lord Death himself came walking through the doorway.

When a liquid squalling filled the temple, I looked up to see one of the priestesses holding a wiggling infant in a blanket. Mother's handmaiden stared over Nimilitzli's shoulder, wide-eyed. "Is she supposed to bleed that much?"

"Hold your tongue," Nimilitzli scolded her, then glanced up at me. She whispered to another priestess who then hurried out into the night.

The priestess sat my brother in my arms, and he immediately fell silent. "You have the special touch," she said with a smile. My sore hand hurt under the weight of his head, but I forgot all about it when I looked down at him for the first time.

I'd seen many of my younger brothers and sisters when they were only a few hours old, all tiny with wrinkled skin and sleepy eyes. By contrast, my brother was smooth-skinned and plump as a baby that had been nursing a few months already. He gazed up at me with large, alert eyes, and his grip on my fingers was strong, but not as strong as it was on my heart. Would Nimilitzli call his strange appearance a bad omen and try to leave him to die in the woods? *I won't let her, Brother, I promise.*

When I held him out to Mother, she shook her head. "I'm too weak to hold him." She stared at him a moment before her face twisted with sadness. "He's so beautiful," she whispered. Taking my hand in hers, she added, "Take good care of him. He's special, and someday he'll reclaim what your uncle stole, from both of you. But until then, he'll look to you for his strength." She then looked to Nimilitzli. "What day is it?"

"One Reed, My Lady," the girl in the doorway answered. "I saw the king light the fire just as the boy was born."

"Bless you, oh Merciful Feathered Serpent," Mother murmured. She turned to my brother and after a moment's thought, she said, "My Xocoyacatl."

"Are we going to call him Little Reed, Mother?" I asked.

She nodded, her eyes brimming with tears.

Hearing footsteps at the doorway, I looked up to see the young priestess had come back with a priest. His matted hair hung in clumps around his face, his lower jaw painted black.

I'd seen one like him a few days before my grandmother died last year. Mother had called him Tlazotlteotl, the Eater of Filth, who came to listen to the confessions of the dying, so they could journey into Mictlan without the burden of their bad deeds. Sickening heat spread over me. *No! Not Mother too!*

When the priestess took Little Reed back, he burst out crying again. A second priestess took my arm. "Let me go! I'm not leaving! *Mother!*" I screamed, reaching out to her.

"She has only a short time left, child," the priestess said, dragging me away. "She must prepare herself for the journey to paradise in Teteocan. She's earned that right sacrificing herself in the childbed, so be happy for her."

Once we reached the door, I saw Nimilitzli knelt in a pool of blood, the tails of her white robes stained crimson. "No!" I fought loose and ran back to Mother, falling into a sobbing heap at her side. "Please don't leave me too! I need you!"

Mother wept into my hair then held my face in her hands. "You're strong, Papalotl, and you'll take excellent care of your brother for me. The Feathered Serpent trusts you, so trust yourself and all will be fine. I love you so much." She kissed my wet cheeks. "Now go, and don't dwell on what happened here today. And remember that I'll always be here if you need me." She set her hand over my heart.

"Please, Mother, no!" I whimpered. What would I do without her? Who would take care of me and Little Reed? Who would protect us from Ihuitimal if he came after us? How could she leave me when I needed her most?

The priestess gathered me into her arms but I didn't fight her this time. I might as well have been dying too. I stared back with stinging, watery eyes as Mother's pale, ghostly figure remained behind, Tlazotlteotl kneeling next to her.

The next time I saw her would be only in my memories.

□

The priestesses took us to a line of small houses behind the temple and they ducked through the curtained doorway of the one at the end, leaving the copper bells tinkling. My priestess laid me on a bed mat then went about stoking the fire while the other paced the floor, trying to quiet Little Reed with sweet words. But he wailed relentlessly.

Once the fire glowed in the hearth, the room came into focus: a loom stood near the rear window, and jars and baskets lined the shelves above the hearth. A metlatl maize grinding stone sat near the door, next to a basket of shucked maize. Unlike the walls of my father's palace, these were simple, unpainted plaster. If not for the sturdy stone construction, I would've thought it was a peasant's house.

Nimilitzli came in, now wearing a clean robe. "Inform the king of what's happened, and tell him I'll bring the children to the palace at daybreak," she said, taking Little Reed from the priestess. Once the others left, she sat on the mat next to me. "Do you wish to hold your brother again?"

I said nothing, just lay staring at the fire, wishing Lord Death had taken me as well. Nimilitzli tried to stroke my hair but I flinched away and tucked my head under my arms. From this woman who let Mother die, any touch was vile and unwelcome.

"You think you can't feel anything but pain ever again, but that too will pass, little one," she said with a maddeningly understanding voice. "Have faith in the Feathered Serpent to heal your heart's wounds. Your brother needs you."

"I don't want him," I muttered. "This is his fault."

"He's hardly had enough time to have done such evil."

"He killed Mother." I squeezed my eyes shut against the suffocating pain in my chest.

"Don't blame him for another's fate. Many mothers give their lives capturing a baby from the gods. It's an unparalleled honor to die trying, especially for your mother; she sacrificed herself bringing forth the son of the god. I assure you she bore no regret for having answered Quetzalcoatl's call."

I gave her an indignant snort. Who was this woman who presumed to know Mother at all?

"I don't suppose your mother ever spoke about me," Nimilitzli went on. "We were good friends when we were younger; we served together in the priesthood, before she married. She sent me a letter not long ago telling me Quetzalcoatl gave her a great task, and that when you were old enough, she wished me to teach you in the calmecac. Both of your parents have friends in Xochicalco; your father and the king served together in the campaigns against the Chichimecs, and he was a nobleman of Xochicalco before he became king of Culhuacan."

Now that I gave her my full attention, I noticed she was older than I'd first thought; but her posture was relaxed and her demeanor soft. Strands of gray hid in the contours of her long black hair and the wrinkles at her eyes lent her the air of a wise woman. *Mother trusted her as a friend,* I thought, so it felt wrong to continue hating her.

"What's to become of me and Little Reed?"

"The king will place you in the care of one of his women." Nimilitzli looked down at Little Reed again as he continued crying in her arms. "You're sure you don't want to hold him?" She held him out again.

He fell quiet again as soon as I took him to my lap, and just looking down at him, the joy he brought me burned away the terrible grief in my heart. "I'm sorry, Little Reed. I didn't mean what I said about you," I whispered through tears, resting my head against his.

"Of course you didn't," Nimilitzli said. I didn't shrug her off when she hugged me this time, instead leaning against her side for comfort. We sat that way until sunrise.

CHAPTER SEVEN

King Cuitlapanton leaned forward on his war staff and smiled as he presented me with a bundle of flowers when I greeted him on the steps of the palace. He would've been very tall if not for the hump on his back. I found it odd that his parents had allowed him to have such an unfortunate name as "Hunched Shoulder," for we Tolteca were very superstitious when it came to names. I remembered Cuitlapanton from my wedding; he'd sat with Father at the feast, the two of them laughing like old friends.

Like back home, the halls were painted according to the city's colors—yellow and white here in Xochicalco—but everything else seemed so different. There were so many hallways going off in so many different directions, and every door curtain was a different color, with a different symbol woven into the fabric in the middle, and every room we visited was decorated with flowers, both real and painted. Cuitlapanton showed me the women's hall, filled with countless women and girls; he had at least twice the number of concubines my father had had.

The boys were in the huge stone-paved yard, practicing swordplay under the watchful gaze of warriors who corrected their grips and techniques with gruff words and the occasional flick of a switch across the backside. One boy my age stopped to look at me, following me with a piercing stare until his sparring partner whacked him in the shoulder with a feather-covered wooden macuahuitl sword. "Oh! Sorry, Brother!" the other boy squeaked, lowering his practice sword. The first boy responded by shoving him over.

"You've got rocks for brains, Mazatzin," he hissed. I scrambled after Cuitlapanton, hoping to be gone before the boy could look back at me again.

Once we'd finished touring the palace, Cuitlapanton led us to the living quarters and introduced me to his queen, his sister Lady Emerald. She was tending to their newest child, an infant girl named Rain Bird, and by the look of her round belly, she had another baby on the way. Lady Emerald was very tall—taller than her hunched husband—and looked like a lake reed with a bulge. She also exuded coldness the same way my mother had once given off warmth and kindness, and my stomach twisted when Cuitlapanton informed me that Lady Emerald would care for me and Little Reed for now on. "The children of my best friend shall be raised side by side with my own first heir," he said with a proud smile.

It turned out that this first heir, Prince Red Flint, was the boy who had stared at me in the yard, and I soon found out he was mean as the scorpion he put under my blanket in the nursery that first night. He spent the second night spitting wads of cornmeal that he'd hid in his arrow pouch at me. I missed my old nursery with its paintings of butterflies and bees, and when I awoke crying from a nightmare, Red Flint yelled at me, "Stop your bawling or I'll put you in the baskets with the other two criers." I prayed nightly to Quetzalcoatl, begging to go home again.

I feared Nimilitzli had forgotten about me, but a week into my exile, she visited the palace to check on me. She accompanied me up onto the city's west wall; usually one of the servants took me up there so I could watch the road in hopes that Nochuatl would soon rescue me from Red Flint's nastiness. The climb up the long stone stairway was good for letting me stamp out my anger with whatever new awful thing he'd said or done to me.

"You seem unhappy," Nimilitzli said, once we reached the top and I'd leaned against the wall in a huff, dangling my arms over the edge.

"Red Flint is a mangy dog," I said. "One wouldn't know he's a prince, as nasty as he is. But at least I won't have to put up with him much longer, because my uncle Nochuatl will come for me and Little Reed, and I'll never have to see Red Flint ever again." I blew out an exasperated breath. "I'd have rather stayed with you."

"You belong with other children, not with a childless priestess. You'll go into the calmecac soon enough, and then we'll see each other more than you'd care to." She gave me a knowing smile.

In the fields below us, the farmers tended the maize, beans and squash. The sun's rays hadn't yet turned the white walls into cooking stones, and the cool breeze felt like a good omen. I knew today would be important. We passed the time guessing which cities' merchant caravans were coming into the gates below.

"Xochicalco is the trade hub of the whole central valley," Nimilitzli told me. "Goods come in from the south and we sell them to the local trade caravans, and the taxes pay for Xochicalco's many splendid temples and buildings." She pointed to the hilltop behind us.

I only watched the road when I came up here, so I'd taken little notice of just how beautiful Xochicalco was. At twice the size of Culhuacan, it sported three times as many temples, all of them tall and white, like the walls. And flowers grew everywhere, on rooftops and in the many public gardens; they even grew in clay boxes up here on the walls, and their potent fragrance hung in the air like perfume. As its name claimed, Xochicalco was indeed a house of flowers.

"When I return to Culhuacan, I'll plant a huge bed of bone flowers in my mother's honor. She loved them so." I sniffed my wrist, to see if I could still smell the cream she'd let me use the night before we left; but like her, it too was gone.

I glanced back down at the road to see a column of soldiers headed for the city, the front ones holding feathered banners. "Oh! Who's that?"

Nimilitzli shielded her eyes. "They're wearing red and blue—"

"My father's colors! Oh, I knew Nochuatl would come back for me! I must change my dress and fix my hair. Come and help me." I grabbed Nimilitzli's hand and pulled her back down the stairs.

"Don't get ahead of yourself, Quetzalpetlatl," Nimilitzli warned. "You don't know if it's him."

"Of course it's him! He promised."

◻

While Nimilitzli went to speak with Cuitlapanton, I hurried into a blue and white dress Lady Emerald had given me and begged one of the servant girls to braid vines of flowers into my hair. When Red Flint came to fetch his practice sling, he grimaced at me. "Just when I thought you couldn't get any uglier." He laughed, but I tripped him when he started to leave, making the servants gasp as he called me a stupid bitch then ran out, shouting for his mother like a baby.

Yes, all the omens pointed to this turning into a very good day indeed.

Nimilitzli stood outside the great hall with the king and a priest who said, "What's the child doing here?" when I came up next to her.

Nimilitzli glared at him but then told me, "I think you should wait in the nursery, Quetzalpetlatl."

"But I want to see my uncle," I said.

She pursed her lips a moment. "It isn't who you thought it was."

I didn't believe her, until I noticed that my wrist itched. To my shame, I'd ignored it in all the excitement. It seemed I hadn't paid attention to the right omens. I swallowed back tears. "It's not?"

Nimilitzli shook her head. Cuitlapanton and the priest turned to leave us, but I screwed up my resolve and declared, "As the Princess of Culhuacan, and the king's eldest heir, I will sit in court for my brother, just as my mother would have for my father if he couldn't go himself."

Cuitlapanton looked thoughtful.

"Surely you're not giving this ridiculous request consideration?" the priest said.

"What does it matter to you if she attends, Ahexotl?" Nimilitzli asked.

"I'm thinking of the child's well-being. Hasn't she been traumatized enough already?"

I stood straighter. "You needn't worry about me, Lord Ahexotl. I hold my mother's strength in my heart."

"That's *high priest* Ahexotl." He glared at me. "Show respect to Quetzalcoatl's high priest."

Something about the way Ahexotl carried himself bothered me, but the god had chosen him so I bowed and kissed the earth at his feet and begged his pardon. Still grumpy, he followed Cuitlapanton into the great hall.

"You're sure you want to do this?" Nimilitzli asked.

The thought of seeing Ihuitimal again carved a pit in my stomach, but I couldn't afford to be a fearful child anymore. I had to be strong for Little Reed, and for myself. "Someday Little Reed will want to know what was said here today."

◻

Cuitlapanton's great hall was twice as big as my father's but decorated similarly, with large feather-banners depicting the city's sigil—a house with a bundle of three-petal flowers inside the doorway—in the city's colors. The entire left side of the hall opened onto a limestone patio with stone columns holding up the eaves, so there was a clear view into the splendor of the royal gardens. Captive parrots squawked from their tethers in the trees.

I sat next to Nimilitzli on feathered mats while Cuitlapanton took to his reed-woven throne upon a raised platform. He muttered to Ahexotl as servants fitted him with a large quetzal-feathered headdress and adjusted his mantle of yellow and white parrot feathers. The heavy gold jewelry around his neck made him stoop a little, concealing his hump to all but the closest scrutiny; that he wasn't bent double was testament to both his strength and pride. Eventually he told his guards to bring in his visitors.

The guards brought in a group of ten men, led by a tall, fur-clad warrior with black and blue tattoos on his bare chest. He held a head by its hair in his hand, and he tossed it at Cuitlapanton's feet. The whole group bent to their knees, though the man in the middle stood again while the others remained kneeling.

Ihuitimal looked the part of warrior-king, his mantle covering his cotton armor and a headdress of black turkey feathers on his head. In one fist he gripped a spear with a small obsidian mirror tied to it. A shard of jade hung by a string of gold from his nose. "Most Honorable Lord Cuitlapanton, in accordance with our traditions, I've laid the head of the traitor Nochuatl before you as proof that I alone stand as guardian of the city of Culhuacan."

I leaned forward to see if it was truly Nochuatl's head, but Nimilitzli held me back. Ihuitimal gave me a sweet, deceitful smile, and even bowed his head.

Cuitlapanton dropped a cloth over the head and said, his voice cold and formal, "Why do you seek my counsel, Lord Ihuitimal?"

"Now that peace has been restored, I request the return of the queen and my niece."

"Lady Chimalma has left this world."

Ihuitimal frowned. "And what of the child she carried?"

Cuitlapanton hardened his expression. "Mixcoatl's son survived."

"Then I welcome him with open arms. As the children's only living relative, it's my duty to see the boy is raised to manhood and takes his rightful throne."

I'd spent the last week wishing I'd never walked into my father's room that night, but had I not, Ihuitimal's concern for me and Little Reed now would've fooled me. My wrist burned and itched badly, but rather than feeding my fear, it stoked my anger.

"I don't wish to keep kin apart," Cuitlapanton answered, "however, if you think I don't know what transpired in Culhuacan, you must think my hump is filled with stupidity, Lord Ihuitimal. I'd gladly avenge my old friend's murder if not for him now having a son who's claimed that right as his to exercise once he reaches manhood."

Ihuitimal's mask of kindness slipped. "With all due respect, Culhuacan's internal conflicts aren't yours to judge. You never meddled in my brother's affairs and I ask you grant me the same respect. I settled a matter of personal honor with Mixcoatl—and with Nochuatl—and that concerns no one but me."

"I respect that, but Mixcoatl's children aren't prizes of that outcome. I'm not ignorant of the nature of your quarrel with Mixcoatl, and if I gave them to you, you would scatter the boy's brains on my beautiful white walls as you left. There's only one man I'd relinquish them to, and unfortunately his head rests at my feet." Cuitlapanton motioned the servants to take it away.

Ihuitimal's frown deepened. "I understand your reasoning, your Majesty, but surely you see I hold no ill-intent against the girl. She's my son's wife—"

"Black Otter and I aren't married anymore," I said, no longer able to keep quiet. "Father undid it when he sent you away."

"Your father isn't the law in Culhuacan anymore," Ihuitimal snapped. "You're still Black Otter's wife." He softened his sneer then asked, "Wouldn't you like to see your friend again? He's very eager to be reunited with you."

I missed Black Otter, but not enough to trust Ihuitimal. "You put my father's heart in my hands, and you're the high priest of an evil god who hates my beloved Quetzalcoatl. Never again shall I call you my uncle."

Nimilitzli squeezed my hand and Cuitlapanton smiled at me.

Ihuitimal stepped forward, his neck tendons standing out. "You will come home to your husband, girl."

Fear tickled my stomach, but I had to be strong. "No."

"Then I'll drag you by your ear!"

When Cuitlapanton lifted his chin, the guards descended around me. "The Princess stays here with her brother. When the boy comes of age, he'll settle grievances with you personally."

Ihuitimal summoned his own soldiers. "You will turn them over to me or—"

"You'll do what?" Cuitlapanton roared, coming to his feet too. "You dare threaten me in my own court as if I were no better than a Chichimec dog? I'd take your head from your neck this very moment and toss your carcass from the wall if I hadn't sworn that pleasure to Mixcoatl's son, so get out! And if even so much as a merchant bearing Culhuacan's colors darkens the dirt of my land, I'll declare war on you. Bring your pathetic Chichimec army to my gates, for the Feathered Serpent knows no honorable Tolteca would fight in your ranks."

Ihuitimal's soldiers readied their spears, but when more guards rushed forward, Ihuitimal told his soldiers to stand down. "You've made your position clear, and I don't intend to start an incident a mere week into my reign. My men and I will leave peacefully." He cast me a scathing glare before leading his men out, flanked by Cuitlapanton's guards.

"He knows not whom he trifles with," Cuitlapanton growled. To me, he said, "You were very brave, Princess. Your mother would be proud."

The comment left me sad though, and my heart ached for her.

▢

Back in the nursery, I rocked Little Reed after he'd nursed. "I'm sorry, but we have to stay here longer," I told him, my voice breaking. "Our uncle Nochuatl didn't come back for us after all." Saying it aloud brought forth the scorchingly painful memory of that man holding his head in his hand. *He promised me—promised!—but Ihuitimal made him break that,* I thought, the tears wending down my face.

Little Reed stretched his hands to touch my wet cheeks. *Why do you cry, little Butterfly?* his bright eyes seemed to be asking me.

I laughed. "You're lucky you don't know what's going on. I liked it much better when I didn't either." He gave me a laughing smile and I wiped my tears, my heart melting in strange new ways. Had I even known happiness before he was born?

CHAPTER EIGHT

Life in the palace might have been nice if not for Red Flint and his friends following me around, chanting, "Weeping Woman!" anytime they saw me. Cuitlapanton said Red Flint liked me, but that made no sense; Black Otter had never teased me like this.

Red Flint also took to calling me "the freak baby's sister." Within the first few weeks Little Reed doubled in weight and the wet-nurse couldn't keep up with the demands of both him and Princess Rain Bird, so Cuitlapanton brought in a second woman to feed him.

But Little Reed refused her. When she took Rain Bird to her breast, by the end of the day, the little girl lay dying in her basket.

"Poison," Nimilitzli said when she came to examine the baby. "I can smell it on her breath." Rain Bird passed out of the world by morning, leaving Lady Emerald wailing and Cuitlapanton cursing my uncle.

"This is Ihuitimal's doing," he spat, while he paced in the great hall. I sat in the corner, listening, for Nimilitzli said one should know what their enemy is capable of.

"The girl rubbed the poison on her breast, intending to feed Mixcoatl's son," Nimilitzli said. "She tried to refuse to nurse Rain Bird, but the queen threatened her."

"I want her driven through with arrows then beheaded! Oh, my poor little girl! If that dog wants war, I'll give it to him!"

Lady Emerald wanted both Little Reed and I out of the palace, fearing she'd lose her son next, but Cuitlapanton refused to renege on his promise. Instead he put us into the care of one of his concubines, Lady Necuazcatl.

Her only son Mazatzin was just a month younger than Red Flint, but unlike his brother he was kind and serious. I liked him right away. Nimilitzli said he'd someday make a very good priest; he'd believed my story about the jade stone and Little Reed being the god's son with little question, whereas Red Flint had laughed and said I had mud in my head. Like Mother, Mazatzin looked at Little Reed but wouldn't touch him, as if my brother was too awe-inspiring for mortal hands.

After we'd prayed over Little Reed, like we did every night before bed, I lay awake, sleep eluding me. The toy snake on gold wheels sitting near the hearth held me transfixed, and when the green quetzal feathers unfolded from behind its head, I thought I'd fallen asleep and was dreaming. They flowed in the draft coming off the fire. It turned its head, showing me glowing orange eyes. My heart played a drunken beat as the snake slid off the wheels and slithered over to me. It stared back at me a moment before I found the courage to speak. "Are you a nahual?" I whispered.

It flicked its leather tongue at me then spoke in that familiar ethereal voice. *I am the Feathered Serpent's tonal companion,* it confirmed.

I sat up and immediately bowed. "My Lord." Last time we'd spoken I hadn't had time for bows, but I would do it right this time.

I am but a humble servant. It is you I have come to honor.

"Me?"

The nahual bowed, dragging its neck feathers on the stone floor. *The Morning Star has risen, and through my fangs he anoints you guardian of his only son, the future Emperor of the*

Tolteca, and he gives you the power of his counsel when your need is most urgent.

I touched my wrist. "You mean—"

You may call upon the Great Feathered Serpent in body and spirit and he will come to aid you, the nahual answered.

My mouth dropped open. "You mean I can summon the god anytime I want?"

Use the gift wisely, the nahual warned. *The sacrifice only becomes greater the more you use it. The gift is meant to protect his son and yourself from those who would harm you.*

My mood darkened. "You mean like Ihuitimal. He sent someone to poison Little Reed."

And this very night, another assassin walks the palace halls.

I pulled Little Reed's basket to my side. He slept soundly. "What should I do?"

There is no safe haven for the god's blood in this palace, so take Lord Topiltzin to the temple, where his father's powers are strongest.

"Lord Topiltzin?" I asked, confused.

That is the name the god himself has given his son.

Our Prince. Fitting, I supposed, but I liked Little Reed better.

My time here is limited, the nahual said. *I spent too much magic and will soon fade away, but I can provide cover for your escape. You will have to find a way to the temple on your own.*

"But I don't know how to get out of the palace without being seen."

"I know a way," Mazatzin whispered, and I yelped in surprise. He crawled over, keeping his distance from the nahual as he spoke to it. "I'll see that she and the god's son make it to the temple."

The nahual whipped its head around, flicking its tongue. *He comes.*

Mazatzin grabbed a toy sword and peeked around the edge of the curtain while I gathered Little Reed into my arms. "Someone's coming up the hall."

I'll use what magic I have left to confuse him, but then you must run, the nahual said.

"Put your brother in this," Mazatzin suggested, taking a bag from the wicker chest near the door. "My mother used to carry my baby brother in this before Xolotl came for him." I slipped Little Reed inside and Mazatzin helped me put it across my shoulder. "He's not too heavy, is he?" He looked as if he didn't relish the idea but would carry Little Reed for me if necessary.

But I was Little Reed's guardian so it was only right I should carry him. "I'll be fine."

The nahual slipped soundlessly under the door curtain, but we made the copper bells clatter like obsidian spearheads spilled on the stone floor when we stepped out. My breath quickened as my wrist started itching.

A servant came up the hall, carrying a water jar on his shoulder. "What are you two doing out of bed? Don't you know the bloodthirsty civatateos prowl the streets after dark, hunting children out of their beds?"

"I'm taking my sister to the bathhouse," Mazatzin said, taking my hand. He was sweaty and shaking.

The servant smiled. If not for my itching wrist warning me, I would never have suspected this kindly-looking man of evil. "And that requires your sword, young Lord Deer?"

"In case I meet a civatateo," Mazatzin replied.

I didn't like how close the servant was to us. "I must go," I insisted, fidgeting.

The man laughed. "Hurry along, before she bursts her dam and I have to clean it up." Noticing the bag on my shoulder, he asked, "What's in there?"

"My brother's soiled clothes." I prayed Little Reed didn't choose that moment to start fussing about his cramped quarters. "I'm taking them to the laundry basket."

"Now?"

"I didn't take them earlier, so now the nursery stinks."

"The servants can do that."

"I don't mind it." When he looked inside the nursery at Little Reed's basket, revulsion rose inside me. "I'll do anything for my brother, no matter how petty the task."

"Then he's lucky to have a loving sister like you," the servant said. "Along with you already." He stepped into the room and closed the curtain behind him.

Mazatzin ran, dragging me after him. But after only ten steps, the curtain jangled and the servant came charging after us.

He overtook us a few steps away from the bathhouse, yanking me backwards by the bag's strap, whipping me away from Mazatzin. I kicked at him with my bare feet but he pulled harder, tossing me off my feet into the wall with a thud that brought the painted plaster off in chunks. I tasted blood on my tongue.

Suddenly the air turned thick as sap, and over my shoulder a blue, spectral feathered serpent rose from Little Reed's bag. The man backed away, shocked, but when the ghostly snake leaped at him, he shrieked and fell over backwards, swinging a flint knife at it.

Mazatzin grabbed my hand and pulled me into the bathhouse. "Follow me." He climbed atop the adobe-brick steam bath at the back and in three moves reached the top of the courtyard wall, but I struggled to find handholds on the rounded bathhouse roof.

Just as I clambered up, the servant burst out of the hallway and snagged my ankle. I rolled over and kicked him in the face, breaking his nose in a gush of blood. He cursed but still held on, bringing his knife around to slice my leg.

Mazatzin smacked his wrist with the edge of his wooden sword, knocking the blade out of his hand. He chopped at the man's other arm, laying open a deep gash. The servant finally let me go and both Mazatzin and I scrambled up onto the wall.

"Keep hold of my hand," Mazatzin said as we shuffled along the wall past the private gardens. Reaching the end, we jumped onto the kitchen roof and ran across to the tall oak tree overhanging the main garden entrance. We climbed down, then, after checking the path, we hurried into the unlit area of the gardens. We crawled behind some bushes and through a crack in the stone wall, though I had to put Little Reed through first to fit.

"Your brother's a sound sleeper," Mazatzin noted as he helped me re-shoulder the bag. "I can't believe he never woke up in any of that."

I checked on Little Reed but he still slept, bubbles on his smiling lips as he made "ah, ah" sounds. "Maybe the nahual put a sleeping spell on him, to keep him from crying." I stroked his hair then covered him again. "Where are we?"

"The royal ball court," Mazatzin said, leading the way. "Red Flint and I sneak out here all the time. I don't think the guards know there's a hole in the wall back there."

We scampered through some winding corridors decorated with reliefs of ritual ball players locked in battle with the sacred rubber ball—and of some being beheaded for losing the game—then came out onto the sandy court. The sloping side walls stood tall as temples around us, and I caught a glimpse of the outline of a stone ring near the top on one side. I'd never been to the ball court in Culhuacan—Mother had called it a man's sport, bloody and full of gambling, and so we never attended any matches, though all my brothers were always playing it in the yard.

When we reached the main entrance, we crouched in the shadows. Seeing no guards, Mazatzin hurried us across the empty main square and up the stairs to the sacred precinct. I had little breath left once we reached the top.

The precinct was empty but kettle braziers at the doors of the calmecac and temples gave off a warm glow. I breathed a sigh of relief on seeing Quetzalcoatl's temple just a jog away.

"What should we say when we get there?" Mazatzin asked, as we walked towards the temple.

"We'll get someone to wake Nimilitzli and I'll tell her about the nahual, and what it said."

"You think she'll believe you?"

"Of course! She's the god's high priestess, so she'll know all about this kind of thing."

I hadn't been back to the temple since the night Mother died, and now the beauty of the stone carvings along its base stole my breath: noblemen counting the days on calendar carvings, and giant, slithering Feathered Serpents painted white, green, red, and blue. If anywhere was heavy with Quetzalcoatl's protective influence, this was it.

Mazatzin suddenly gagged, and I turned to see the treacherous servant had stuck a knife through his shoulder from behind. When the man pulled it out, Mazatzin fell to his knees, clutching his chest.

I screamed but the air sounded thick in my ears, as if I were swimming in honey. I put my hands up as the servant rushed me, swinging his blade. He sliced my palm in a jagged rip and I almost ran backwards into the wall. But I spun around in time to avoid crushing Little Reed, instead hitting the wall with my wounded hand and splattering blood across Quetzalcoatl's stone face. The assassin swung his knife again but shattered the blade against the stone wall.

"Please save us from this evil, My Lord!" I stumbled backwards and fell hard, gritting my teeth. I clutched Little Reed's sling as the killer advanced, a victorious smile on his face. Behind him, a black jaguar stood in the shadow at the temple's corner, staring back at me with burning yellow eyes. Was it the same one I'd seen in the hallway the night my father was murdered? "I promise to hold no god above you, oh Merciful Quetzalcoatl! Please help us!" I cried.

The wall above me exploded in a shower of gravel and stone. I rolled over to cover Little Reed, and when I looked up, the giant stone serpent peeled off the temple wall. The man screamed and tried to run, but the serpent opened its stone jaws, letting out a burst of wind that took him off his feet and up into the air. The wind howled louder than I'd ever heard it before and I hunched over Little Reed to keep the dirt out of his bag, my hair lashing around in the wind.

It died down just as quickly as it came, and in the time it took me to blink away my astonishment, the stone serpent vanished and the temple wall was back to the way it had been before all this. When I looked at the back of the temple, the jaguar was gone too. Mazatzin looked around, bewildered.

Little Reed suddenly burst into hiccupping cries, and though he was unharmed inside the bag, he was red-faced and angry.

"By the Great Feathered Serpent, what are you doing out here, Quetzalpetlatl?" Nimilitzli stood at the edge of the pyramid. But then she gasped and rushed down the stairs, kneeling next to Mazatzin and putting the tail of her robe over his wound. "What happened? Who did this?"

"One of the palace servants." I crawled to Mazatzin too. "He came after Little Reed and...and...oh, please don't let Mazatzin die, My Lord!"

"Calm yourself. You're all safe."

I nodded, wracked with tears.

"Whatever possessed you to leave the palace in the middle of the night?" Nimilitzli demanded. She turned to Ahexotl, who'd come from the calmecac where many people were standing outside, looking into the sky. "Rouse the king and let him know his son's been injured." The high priest glared at me before heading for the stairs at a jog. Nimilitzli gave me a similar stare. "The darkened world isn't safe for children, and you dare bring your brother out into it? How did you three get out of the palace without being seen?"

"There's a crack in the garden wall, behind the ball court," Mazatzin replied, wincing.

"Lay still." She then asked me again, "What are you doing here?"

Her anger scared me, so I stuttered for a moment, trying to find my words. *She's the god's high priestess, so she'll understand,* I reminded myself. "The nahual told us Little Reed would be safest here because the god's power is greatest near his temple."

Nimilitzli furrowed her eyebrows. "Nahual?"

"Quetzalcoatl's. On my wedding day, when I found Little Reed's jade stone, the nahual bit me, and now my wrist itches whenever my uncle or one of his men is close." I showed her my wrist, but the bumps were gone now. I pressed on anyway. "The nahual helped me escape Father's room that terrible night by making smoke flood the room, then it led me out into the secret corridor. Tonight it came back and told me to bring Little Reed here, to escape the assassin."

"Then Quetzalpetlatl called on the god and he came and swept the servant away in a great wind!" Mazatzin said, excitedly pointing towards the forest in the distance behind the calmecac. "The wind blew him so far I couldn't even see him anymore. It was incredible!"

"I told you to stay still," Nimilitzli reprimanded him. She looked at me again, the doubt plain in her eyes.

How could she not believe me? Surely such things were ordinary in a life of a priestess. *Aren't they?*

The king arrived with a physician and guards. "Where's my son?" he called as he ran to us. While the physician stitched up Mazatzin's shoulder, Nimilitzli took Cuitlapanton aside, speaking in a hushed voice. Their gestures soon became a heated discussion and I turned away, uncomfortable that I'd caused all this trouble.

"You were so very brave Mazatzin," I said, once the physician finished sewing up my hand and had muttered a prayer to Quetzalcoatl over it, to ensure its proper healing. "I'm sorry you got hurt."

"It's a small price to pay to serve the Feathered Serpent," Mazatzin replied. "And you were incredible! With a gift like that, surely you're destined to be someone great—maybe even the god's high priestess."

I liked the idea of someday being a priestess. Mother would have been proud if I were. "I just wish Nimilitzli would believe me about the nahual."

"I think she was just scared about hearing that the god had something to do with it." Mazatzin sat up and looked over at his father and Nimilitzli. "So what if the adults don't believe us? I know what I saw, and I shall never forget it."

◻

Nimilitzli and Cuitlapanton argued until dawn's first bloody streaks peeked over the mountains, then the king pulled Mazatzin along with him back to the stairs, leaving me and Little Reed behind with Nimilitzli. "Come, you look tired," she said, cradling Little Reed in her arms as he slept. I glanced back at Mazatzin once more before he disappeared down the stairs with his father, then I moped after Nimilitzli to her house.

She gave me and Little Reed her bed mat, but instead of sleeping I watched her stare into the fire, her face a mask of concentration. "What did the king say?"

She looked startled but didn't chastise me. "All you need to know is that he fears for his own children if he keeps you and your brother in the palace anymore. And after tonight, I can't blame him." She shook her head.

"You think I'm lying about the nahual," I concluded, holding back angry tears.

"I've been a priestess a long time, and I've never heard of the god coming to his followers like that."

That puzzled me. "You've never spoken with the god, or his nahual?"

"The god speaks to us, not the other way around. And I've always had to use special mushrooms or the sacred octli liquor to accomplish that little bit. His intent can sometimes be read in the patterns of nature, though. Were you feeling sick tonight?"

"I feel fine."

Nimilitzli sat in silence a moment. "What did you talk about with this nahual?"

"It told me Quetzalcoatl had chosen me to be Little Reed's guardian, and that he'd given me the gift to call on him, in body and spirit, and I did! Quetzalcoatl came just as he promised—as the serpent on the side of the temple—and he killed the assassin." Seeing the skepticism again, I glared back at her. "It really did happen."

She held her hands up. "I'm just trying to understand what took place. It's obvious you've had visions of the god, and I'd encourage you to keep an open mind about these experiences. With some study of the priestly arts, I'm sure you can come to understand what it all means."

Not exactly the enthusiastic acceptance I'd hoped for, but least she wasn't calling me a liar.

"Perhaps this is all for the best, for both of you. I believe Little Reed is the god's son; your mother carried him only three months and he was almost too large to be birthed. And he grows so fast.... He'd have been tormented and ostracized by Cuitlapanton's sons for being different, so he'll be better off among priests, who will treat him like the gift he is. And you'll be starting calmecac soon anyway."

"Then we're to live with you?" I squeaked with excitement. Finally I'd be rid of Red Flint.

"As your mother's friend and confidant, it's my duty to see her children brought to adulthood with respect for Quetzalcoatl in their hearts. And I'll need your help with your brother, having never had any children of my own. But we can discuss that later, after you've finally slept. Now to bed with you."

I snuggled around Little Reed, smiling. I hadn't felt this good since that night I first felt him moving in my mother's belly: proof of Quetzalcoatl's greatness. *And I'll keep my promise to love and protect Little Reed always, My Lord,* I prayed, and for the first time since coming to Xochicalco, I fell into deep, dreamless sleep, feeling that finally everything was as it should be.

PART TWO
THE YEAR ELEVEN HOUSE

CHAPTER NINE

 "You think you're ready for war, but battle is never what little boys think it is," Nimilitzli snapped at Little Reed as we sat on reed mats on the floor of her house eating the beans and tlaxcallis I'd prepared for the three of us. The last ten years had left her with streaky, graying hair, knobby knuckles and thinner skin, but her temperament remained fierce as ever. She was a marvel to watch when pitted against Little Reed.

Little Reed laughed heartily. "I'm hardly a 'little boy' anymore, Mother." Indeed, the accelerated growth he'd experienced early in life hadn't let up, and by the time he'd visited the soothsayer to learn his true name at age seven, he and I had looked the same age. Now age ten, he stood a full head taller than me, and looked a bittersweet mix of my mother and father. I hoped he wouldn't grow too much more or he'd end up a giant. He suffered enough ridicule from Red Flint as it was.

Nimilitzli held up a hand when I motioned with the pot of beans. "You don't look like one anymore, but you also don't even have a young man's life experience yet."

"I have more than you think." Little Reed held out his tlaxcalli flatbread for me to fill with stewed beans.

"Your arrogance is speaking again."

"It's not arrogance to state a fact."

"It's arrogance to assume it's a fact."

Little Reed laughed. "I'll miss these discussions, Mother, but we both know that the longer Ihuitimal holds Culhuacan's throne, the harder it'll be to depose him. He's already building alliances against me. And not only did he not give Mixcoatl a proper burial, he's also outlawed Quetzalcoatl's worship. I can't wait around another ten years for everyone else to think I'm ready to do something about it. By then it could be too late."

Meals at Nimilitzli's house were usually quiet, solemn affairs, but ever since two weeks ago when Little Reed had sprung the shocking news on us that he was leaving for the army, they had argued daily about it. I didn't want him to go, but just the thought of talking about it turned my throat to cotton and my chest into a painful, vibrating drum. I couldn't believe he was leaving me behind so soon.

Nimilitzli showed no hesitation about taking him to task about it, though. "Your uncle is disgraceful, but he's trying to bait you into acting before you're ready. Stay here a few more years. You're ready to take the trials to become a full priest, and you need to build grace with Quetzalcoatl before invoking his name in battle—"

"Using the god's name won't get me anything. The army is full of soldiers who'll demand I earn their respect with my actions, not by the name of my father. You see how Red Flint and his lot treat me—"

"You can't judge others by what Red Flint thinks, Brother," I said. "Mazatzin has always shown you the greatest respect."

"But Mazatzin is a priest, or will be soon, although you're right about Red Flint," Little Reed conceded. "He's just a spoiled royal brat. But I have no reputation among the commoners, and no honorable man will follow me in re-conquering Culhuacan until I prove myself in battle. What's the use in being named 'Our Prince' if I'm only ever a priest and not a king?"

"You will be a king when the time is right," Nimilitzli insisted. "Until then, serve the god."

"The best way I can serve the god is on the battlefield."

"And how do you know that?"

Little Reed sighed. "We all knew this day would come, Mother."

"But after only ten years?" I asked, trying hard not to choke into a sob.

"Who knows if I even have another ten years left to me?"

"Don't talk like that." I had to look away so he wouldn't see the wetness gathering at my eyes.

He set his hand on mine. "I can't ignore that I age faster than everyone else. I'd like to stay, but it'll take me years to amass the troops necessary to retake Culhuacan. I want to have time to rule and produce an heir before this rapid aging escorts me to the road to Mictlan."

All the more reason why you should stay here with me, I thought. By the time Little Reed was two, I'd realized that he was the little boy I'd seen in my dream on my wedding night, but it wasn't until I was older that I understood what that strange fluttering he'd made me feel that night meant. Over the last couple of years, that feeling that used to come only when I remembered the dream started happening whenever he spoke to me, or when he held my hand; and by now it had intensified into sweaty palms, and dreams that I'd blush to describe aloud.

I'd hoped Cuitlapanton would marry us, as Father would have if he were still alive—to ensure the royal bloodline—but to my disappointment, nobody said anything about it. I didn't dare bring it up to anyone; Nimilitzli was so proud that I was taking the trials to become a priestess this summer, and as for telling Little Reed.... Many of the girls at calmecac fluttered their eyelashes at him and giggled behind their hands, and a couple had tried to talk me into delivering notes to him. And though he always seemed to ignore them in favor of focusing squarely on his studies, I couldn't help but wonder: was he merely keeping his interest in someone secret from me, as I kept my interest in him secret? Or maybe he had no interest in such things. He was the son of a god after all, and so perhaps found it easy to ignore such human weaknesses.

Not all of us could be so lucky.

"War is nothing like those battle drills you went through last summer at the House of Warriors, Topiltzin," Nimilitzli continued. "Men lose limbs or become crippled, or worse yet they're dragged off to die in honor of foreign gods. You look like a man to everyone, but you're not mentally prepared for that kind of life. Boys your age are busy catching lizards and learning how to use a bow and arrow—"

"I'm not like other boys. The god didn't put me here to sit back and be afraid of being a man."

I couldn't listen anymore. When Little Reed made up his mind, he never gave other options a backward glance. "I wish to go and pray before my temple duties," I muttered, and left the house.

I wished I could be indifferent to everyone else, like Little Reed, so I too could go on with life without feeling terrible pain for losing someone so dear to my heart.

◻

Across from the temple, Mazatzin stood with Red Flint by the cistern outside the calmecac. Seeing them next to each other, one would hardly believe they were brothers; Mazatzin's broad shoulders and face made him look strikingly like Cuitlapanton, while Red Flint had inherited his mother's lithe build and fine features. Red Flint's smile was his own, though; predatory, like a coyote. His gaze wandered over me as I approached, making my face redden with resentment. I hated it when people stared at me, which seemed to be happening with increasing frequency since I'd attained puberty.

From Little Reed, I wouldn't mind it, but I especially didn't want it from Red Flint. He'd finally outgrown the childish taunts against me; but for the last few years, he'd refocused his attention on Little Reed, especially once Little Reed started catching up to him both physically and mentally. For a while it was just verbal sparring, with Little Reed often getting the better of him, but once Little Reed surpassed him in height, it turned violent.

One afternoon, Red Flint and his friends lured Little Reed to the west ball court and pummeled him with hard rubber balls, breaking his nose and knocking him unconscious. I tried summoning the god but ended up with a bloody palm and no Quetzalcoatl. Only a couple of men arriving to practice early stopped the assault. Red Flint did a year of service to the temple for his actions, but I kept close watch over him from then on.

"You're upset," Mazatzin noted when I reached them.

"I'm fine. Nimilitzli and Topiltzin are arguing again. That's all they've done for the last two weeks."

"So he's still leaving with the army?"

When I nodded, Red Flint snorted. "He made the decision so suddenly, I must question his motives."

"You always do, Brother," Mazatzin said.

I too wondered how much Red Flint's impending army service had played into Little Reed's decision. He couldn't resist any opportunity to show up his boyhood nemesis.

"But I thought he was going to be a priest," Red Flint pressed.

"He'll be one," I said. "He's just chosen to be a warrior first."

Red Flint laughed. "He's no different than any of these other weak little calmecac worms; he'll do his minimum service and call himself a warrior."

"There's nothing dishonorable in doing only the required military service, Brother," Mazatzin said. "Priestly duty is just as important as marching about swinging a sword."

"Kings don't do the minimum."

"Why do you care whether or not Topiltzin becomes a warrior? Are you worried he'll out-sparkle you?"

Red Flint glared at him. "Forgive my being concerned about what his untimely death would do to his family. Particularly to Quetzalpetlatl."

"What's that supposed to mean?" I snapped, my cheeks flushing. I thought I was pretty good about hiding my attraction for Little Reed, but was I instead very transparent?

"Let's be honest, Quetzalpetlatl: you've cared for that whelp since the day he came into this world, but he doesn't care at all that he's hurting you."

I hated the idea of Red Flint being right about anything, but it dug a deep wound in my heart to realize that he was more aware of my pain than my own brother. Just more evidence that I was alone in my foolish infatuation.

"If he cared, he wouldn't rush off bent on impressing strangers while his faithful sister worries about whether he's dead or alive," Red Flint insisted.

"Don't say such things." I tried holding back the tears but failed. Soon Red Flint would break out chanting "Weeping Woman!" at me again, and I wasn't sure I could handle that right now.

But to my surprise, he slid a friendly hand over my shoulder. "I'll watch over Topiltzin while we're gone."

"That's my job," I snapped.

"Topiltzin is a man now," Mazatzin spoke up. "And all men must eventually leave their mothers. Someday he'll come back and become a priest, trust in that. Besides, you have your own future to think about, with the trials coming up in a few weeks."

"He's as callous as Topiltzin," Red Flint said. "Telling you what to think and feel, as if you're not entitled to any of your own. Has Topiltzin even asked you whether you really want to be a priestess?"

Little Reed had never asked me one way or the other, though I'd always thought I wanted to follow my mother's path into the priesthood. But I'd been surprised by just how difficult it was. The lessons were easy, but the calmecac's strict rules punished the slightest transgression, and the fire priestess Mothotli had taken a particular dislike to me, perhaps suspecting I might receive special treatment for being the high priestess's charge. I'd grown weary of the constant sweeping, the raps on the knuckles for not paying attention in boring classes, or Mothotli's constantly probing gazes. Sometimes I doubted I was meant for a priestly life—especially when Mothotli knocked me out of my daydreams about Little Reed with a strike of her switch. But if I didn't want to be a priestess, would Little Reed accept that?

"If Topiltzin is old enough to do what he wants, so are you." Red Flint looked past me with a smug smile. "Speaking of the boar...."

Little Reed came to us, his posture reminiscent of an aggressive turkey. He made a perfunctory bow to Red Flint then said to me, "I thought you were going to the temple to pray."

"Perhaps she prefers actual two-way conversation over the endless mumblings to a god who never answers, Crotch Bleeder," Red Flint said with a sneer.

"He wasn't asking you anything," I snarled. I was used to his offensive pet names for my brother, but I wasn't in the mood for it today.

Little Reed merely smiled back at him and said, "She'll find a more sympathetic ear with the god than with you, Impotent Lizard."

Red Flint moved to draw his dagger, but Mazatzin grabbed his arm. He glared at his brother a moment then told Little Reed, "We'd hoped you'd join us on the pilgrimage this year. There'll be war next year."

"Someday I'm going to make that a false statement," Little Reed replied.

Red Flint scoffed, but Mazatzin said, "I'd hoped to have the great honor of becoming a priest at the same time as you, then we'd march together for our first battle next year."

Little Reed clapped his shoulder. "Then I hope to see you in my ranks next year."

"He'll be in *my* ranks," Red Flint retorted.

"I'll go where the god points," Mazatzin stated. "Now we really must go, Brother, before father skins us for being late."

Red Flint gave Little Reed a glare, but slipped on a smile for me. "Your company is always a pleasure, My Lady." He kissed his fingers and swept them across the ground at my feet with a fluid motion that left me inexplicably breathless. *As nasty as he can be, he's still delicious to watch,* I thought, and nearly gasped aloud. Where in Mictlan did *that* come from?

Once Red Flint and Mazatzin were out of earshot, Little Reed growled, "Stupid dog. How dare he speak so disrespectfully to me?"

I glared at him. "It's not as if you've done anything to earn his respect." I tried not to care about the hurt frown on his face, but I hated seeing him upset. "I'm sorry, but I just don't understand why you two have to act like wolves guarding a kill whenever the other comes around. I can't expect better of him, but I do expect better of you."

Little Reed bowed his head. "You're right, Papalotl. A prince should always have respect for others, especially for his enemy. I'll walk with you to the temple."

I'd never told Little Reed about my childhood name, and as far as I knew no one in Xochicalco knew of it either. But when Little Reed wasn't quite six months old he'd sat next to me one day playing with string while I wove and suddenly blurted out his first coherent word: "Papalotl!" I'd looked around for signs of his butterfly outside the window, but he was staring up at me, eyes bright and laughing. "Papalotl!" he shouted with glee, and he'd called me that ever since.

And truthfully I preferred it, just as he liked me to call him Little Reed. Nimilitzli disapproved of us using our child-names, so we only did so in private.

We knelt side by side on the reed prayer mats in front of Quetzalcoatl's idol. The smell of blood and decay oozing out of the idol's open mouth gave my stomach a funny little jerk and gurgle, so I focused my attention on the baskets of grass balls and obsidian blades next to the gilded statue. That was another thing I never told anyone: the smell of sacrifices made me inexplicably hungry, even after I'd eaten a big meal. It seemed a little too bizarre to risk talking about. I closed my eyes and held my breath against the smell, finding my focus for the prayer.

"You're angry with me, about more than just Red Flint," Little Reed said after we'd finished our silent prayers.

His words dredged up bitterness I'd been glad to be free of while praying. I pulled the wooden blood-bowl to my knees so I didn't have to look at him. "I don't want you to go, I don't like you arguing with Nimilitzli, and I don't like you rushing to keep up with Red Flint—"

"My decision has nothing to do with Red Flint."

"We've been lucky the last ten years, Little Reed. Ihuitimal has made no more attempts on your life, but if you go away...." Mazatzin's words came back to me. But what was so wrong with wanting to protect him? Quetzalcoatl appointed me his guardian, after all. But if Little Reed could fend for himself now, didn't that render me completely useless?

"I understand your concern," Little Reed said. "I'd be a fool if I wasn't afraid. But a man doesn't earn his reputation in safety. I can't stay locked up behind these walls forever."

So why must I? But I couldn't say it. Mother said a woman's lot wasn't fair, and Mothotli's stinging switch taught me it was easier to stay silent about this injustice, but I'd never changed my mind about it; I just simmered with anger.

Little Reed took my hand in his, making my heart skip. "I promise to be very careful out there, Papalotl. I'll make you proud, and with the Feathered Serpent's grace, we'll return to Culhuacan with our uncle vanquished and our fathers avenged. We will be where we belong again."

The thrill coursing through me made all the bitterness vanish again, almost bringing me to tears. "I'll pray for it, Little Reed."

"Will you pray for me too?"

"Every day." It was the only protection I could give him anymore.

☐

Mothotli came at midnight, to make sure I wasn't taking any shortcuts with my duties. Her name—"Chipmunk"—was apt: she had beady eyes and puffy cheeks where she stored her mean words, and when upset she'd shriek like a rodent being savaged by a dog. As fire priestess, she was second to Nimilitzli in power, though someday she'd be the high priestess. I dreaded what life under her rule would be like.

"You've already swept there three times, girl," she snapped. "The rest of the room could use your attention too."

I hadn't realized I'd gone back to the altar again until now. I always swept there first, to get it done quickly before memories of Mother resurfaced. Years ago just being in the temple set off panic, but with time I came to fear Mothotli's switch more than the memories.

Nimilitzli understood though, and had taken me on as an apprentice midwife when I was twelve so I could see that things didn't always go wrong in the childbed. Many of the priestesses were also midwives for the noble class, though as high priestess Nimilitzli cared for Lady Emerald and Cuitlapanton's concubines; she'd delivered every child in the palace. The rational detachment necessary for delivering babies helped me focus my fears into one little area of the temple that I could sweep quickly then move on from.

So why am I lingering so long here tonight? I wondered, as I went to sweep behind the gilded Feathered Serpent idol.

Mothotli checked all the corners of the room with her stern, suspicious stare. "I hear Topiltzin isn't taking the trials this year."

"He's joining the army," I said.

Mothotli shook her head. "That boy's not nearly as brilliant as he thinks. Nimilitzli would do well to put him under the lash more often, teach him humility."

Little Reed could use a dousing in the cistern, but I'd never say so to her. Nimilitzli was strict but never cruel, so I respected her far more.

"He's wasting all the training we gave him. Son of the god, indeed! One wouldn't think a god's seed would produce someone so irresponsible."

I almost said something she'd give me the switch for, but Ahexotl came into the temple and reprimanded her. "Don't disparage Topiltzin to her. She has plenty to worry about as it is." He inspected the braziers and tossed more copal wood into the north one, then told me, "Excellent work as always, Quetzalpetlatl. Have a good night."

I bowed and thanked him for his kind words. As I headed up the steps, he added, "I have to fetch something from my meditation room, so I'll walk with you." He took my broom for me, and as we headed out I caught Mothotli glaring at us, the disdain more vehement than usual.

"Pay Mothotli no mind," Ahexotl told me as we crossed the precinct to the calmecac. "I'd hoped Topiltzin would take his vows before embarking on a military career, but I respect his desire to choose his own path."

I nodded halfheartedly.

"I can't imagine this is easy for you; I know the two of you are close. I'm sure he'll think fondly of you while he's gone. Love of family and faith in the god will see him through the difficult times."

I hadn't expected to like Ahexotl after that first meeting ten years ago, when he'd looked at me as if I was a grub feasting on his tomato plants. For the first couple of years he remained distant and cold towards me, but once I took on priestly duties he took more interest in my progress and encouraged me. He even became something of a father figure to me.

"Are you ready for the pilgrimage next month?"

I nodded. "I'm apprehensive about leaving the city for the first time, though."

"The king will provide us with adequate guards. Xochicalco's soldiers are the best in the land."

We crossed the school's courtyard garden and went into the row of storerooms across from the girls' dormitories. Its four rooms each held different materials: laundry, pottery and baskets, brooms and gardening tools, and an entire room full of copal wood for the temple's braziers. I returned the broom to its hook in the tool room and thanked Ahexotl for walking with me.

"I know these are difficult times for you, Quetzalpetlatl. If you need anyone to talk to, I'm at your disposal," he said with a warm smile. "You'll be one of my priestesses soon and you can come to me with your troubles. You're joining a much larger family, and we're here to support you."

The pain and depression that had built slowly over the last two weeks suddenly welled up inside me; I tried to swallow it but couldn't help frowning.

Ahexotl raised an eyebrow. "Do you need to talk now?"

I almost said "yes," but instead the exhaustion hit hard. "I appreciate the kindness, My Lord, but it's late, and I'm very tired."

"Some other time then. You know where to find me." He then departed, leaving me wondering if I should have taken up his offer. *It might make you feel better,* I thought. But I didn't like the idea of possibly breaking down and revealing my feelings for Little Reed to him.

Only the pine-resin torch at the doorway to the dormitory gave light to lead me across the garden, so when the bushes next to the storerooms began rustling, I stopped like a startled deer.

"Quetzalpetlatl!"

"Red Flint?" I gasped when he grabbed my wrist and dragged me into the bushes. "What in Mictlan are you—?"

"I have to talk to you."

If I was caught in the bushes with a boy...I didn't want to think about the flogging I'd get. And if I must be caught with someone, the last person I wanted anyone thinking I'd been doing anything with was a cur like Red Flint. "It's after midnight and I'm headed to bed."

"I have to tell you something," he insisted, not letting go of my arm when I tried to get up.

"Tell me what?" I snapped, trying to tug my arm free. He finally let me go, so I decided to let him say his piece before leaving.

He pushed branches aside to look into the courtyard, then turned to me again. "I'm not good with words, so hopefully my actions can speak for me," he said, and kissed me hard on the lips, pushing me against the storeroom wall.

My first impulse was to shove him off, maybe even punch him, but a strange haze settled over me and I found myself kissing him back, all concerns about being caught mysteriously gone. When we finally separated I was intensely dizzy, and my skin tingled as if lightning had struck nearby. "What was that for?" I panted.

"I can't go off to war without telling you how I feel about you," he said. When I blinked at him, confused, he continued, "I know I was a scoundrel before, calling you ugly and putting poisonous animals under your blankets, but I was a foolish child who knew no other way to express himself. But I'm a man now, and I know better. I love you, Quetzalpetlatl."

I shook my head, wishing the haziness would go away so I could think straight. What was wrong with me?

"Yes I do," he insisted, then kissed me again.

I should have pushed him away, but again my head swam, and it felt so right to pull him closer instead. In my mind, he was Little Reed, moving his hands all over me, seeking out those areas I scarcely dared touch even while bathing.

Voices in the courtyard finally broke through my stupidity. *You're a breath away from being taken before the entire school and flogged for indecency, Quetzalpetlatl.* I pushed Red Flint away and looked out through the bushes in time to see a couple of priestesses disappear into the calmecac. I closed my eyes and took a deep breath before saying, "The door monitor is expecting me, and if I don't show up on time, she'll report me."

Red Flint sighed but stole one more kiss before I slapped him away. "I must see you again, soon. I march for the army camp in a week, and who knows how long it'll be before I return and can ask you to be my wife."

Oh, Little Reed would hate that! I thought with a disturbing spike of pleasure. I immediately felt bad for wanting to hurt him so.

"When can I see you again?" Red Flint asked.

Befuddled, I muttered, "I...I don't know. I have evening temple duty again in six days—"

"That's perfect. I'll meet you back here again." Red Flint glided gentle fingers over my chin, sending intoxicating chills through me. He then pulled aside the branches. "The courtyard's clear now."

I hurried to the dormitory doorway, sparing a glance back in his direction before going in, but I couldn't see him in the dark. As I walked down the hall towards the girls' dormitory and my head cleared, I started to wonder if I'd just imagined it all. Surely Red Flint had no interest in me, and I certainly had none for him.

Or so I tried to convince myself when my heart raced at the thought of his kiss.

CHAPTER TEN

Nimilitzli and Little Reed were already deep in debate when I arrived at her house in the morning, though they must have been at it for a while. Before I even sat down with my atole, Nimilitzli shook her head and declared, "Well, the king calls you a man now, and men will do as they wish. May the Feathered Serpent watch over you out there."

Little Reed frowned. "I'd prefer you understood my decision rather than just accepting it."

"I do understand, Topiltzin, and I trust I raised you to be cleverer than most noblemen, and that that will see you through it."

"You raised me very well, Mother, and I promise to make you proud." He hugged her but she shooed him away, still frowning. I'd never seen her so disconcerted.

Once he finished his breakfast, he left to go hunting with Mazatzin. "I'll bring you a nice fat deer to see you through the summer," he told us on his way out.

"And so he gets his way," I muttered once we were alone.

Nimilitzli sighed. "Have you ever known him not to?"

"Only with Red Flint."

"When the dislike runs that deep, it's little surprise."

A guilty flush heated my cheeks. It was such a betrayal to set up a clandestine meeting with Little Reed's nemesis. *Why do you worry about what he thinks? He doesn't care what you think about him leaving. He's made his choice, so you should make your own too.*

But if life had taught me anything, it was that women didn't get their own choices. Mother married because her father insisted she did, and she had to give me over to Black Otter at Father's behest. And now Little Reed was handing me over to the priesthood so they could protect my virtue until he had political use for me. As a child I'd thought the priesthood was about serving the god, but it turned out to be mostly an outpost for noblewomen waiting for their fathers or brothers to tell them whom to marry.

Nimilitzli gathered up the dishes. "Perhaps it's for the best. He might be the god's son, but he's flesh and blood like the rest of us, and young men are notorious for their susceptibility to temptation. Best he soothe those desires before devoting himself to the celibate life of the priest."

"How can you speak such things about him?" I asked, my cheeks burning. Her words brought images of him "soothing those desires" with me on the altar in Quetzalcoatl's temple.

"You can't lock him away in your head as a perpetual child, Quetzalpetlatl. Sex isn't a dirty act never to be performed. It serves a very sacred, important purpose."

"Then why must priests and priestesses abstain?" *And why can Little Reed go off to satiate his lusts in the army while I must prove my virginity to be a priestess?*

Nimilitzli gave me a curious look. "Because it's a sacrifice to give that up, and it's our sacrifices that make us worthy of serving the god."

"It hardly seems a sacrifice."

Nimilitzli laughed. "It's a bigger one than you know."

I rolled my eyes. She'd been a chaste priestess all her life, so what would she know about it?

"One should be sure they want to make that sacrifice before committing to the priesthood, so I can't blame your brother for hesitating," she said. "Better he not take the vows than break them. But I'll give him a good whipping if he comes back from war with a week's worth of children and angry fathers demanding he do right by their daughters."

I contemplated that conversation all day long. It distracted me so much that Mothotli shrieked at me during calendar studies and sentenced me to kitchen duty. While scrubbing out the clay pots, my mind went back to that meeting with Red Flint later in the week, and from there the scheming began.

If I'm not an unbroken maiden they won't let me into the order, and Little Reed can't do anything about it, I thought. I loved Quetzalcoatl, but was that enough to endure half a lifetime under Mothotli's switch?

It wouldn't be difficult to coax Red Flint into aiding me to my freedom; as Nimilitzli said, young men were prone to temptation. But would I really make a whore of myself to avoid taking priestly vows?

It wouldn't be harlotry. Red Flint's already mentioned marriage, and if he got you with child, he'd have to make good on that promise early. And what more could Little Reed want for you than to be married to Xochicalco's future king? It's not as if he wants you for himself. Though that left me feeling sad. *No matter what he thinks of Red Flint personally, from a purely practical standpoint it's a good match and would ensure a future alliance between Culhuacan and Xochicalco.*

But was I ready to be a mother? I was of marrying age; many noblewomen married at fourteen and bore their first child within a year. Being already seventeen, if I waited too much longer, I'd squander away my best childbearing years, as well as my marriage prospects.

By sundown, my musings turned to planning. When I took a laundry bag to the storeroom, I stood looking around, thinking, *I could bring Red Flint in here.* Laundry day wasn't until the end of the week, so there would be a large pile of robes and blankets I could build up for privacy. Secrecy was of utmost importance: the penalty for being caught in unchaste activities at calmecac was the direst there was, next to committing blasphemy.

But a woman wasn't guaranteed to become with child with just one attempt, and since I would only get one chance, I needed to improve my chances. There was the chipahuacxihuitl root, usually used to keep a woman from begetting, but Nimilitzli had told me that if it was used at the beginning of one's cycle then discontinued for the remainder of the month, then it actually increased one's chances of conceiving. When I checked her wicker midwife basket, I found some, but I hesitated. She kept track of her medicines meticulously—not because she mistrusted me, but because she hated running out of something unexpectedly. If I took this, I'd be breaking her trust....

I'll tell her one of her patients asked for it. I still cringed with guilt as I brewed the chipahuacxihuitl into a strong tea. But I was choosing my own future, and it would be worth it in the end.

◻

A nervous sickness followed me for the next six days, even up to the evening I had temple duty. I'd thought maybe it was a side effect of drinking the chipahuacxihuitl tea each night, but I'd stopped the day before and still my stomach felt like a simmering pot of hot orange chilis.

Little Reed had kept his promise to bring home a deer, but he was invited to the departure feast at the palace and was expected to be there, so Nimilitzli and I prepared beans and venison for ourselves.

"Are you feeling well?" Nimilitzli asked, for I'd hardly eaten any of my meal.

"I'm fine. My afternoon atole just stuck with me longer than I'd expected," I said, avoiding her gaze.

She continued watching me but said nothing, letting me have my peace. Once we finished and I started cleaning out the cooking pot, she told me, "I have to go and check on some of the women at the palace tonight. Do you want to come with me?"

"I have temple duty."

"I forgot. If you'd like one of the other girls to cover it, so you can go to the celebration with your brother, I can arrange that."

My sour gut told me to accept her offer, but this would be my only chance to execute my plan. "It's a men's celebration, and I doubt Topiltzin wants me hovering around him." And I certainly didn't want to see courtesans hanging on him, for there would surely be many at this farewell celebration.

Nimilitzli nodded then went to her wicker midwife basket and dug around inside. My heart stalled as she looked over everything, but eventually she closed the lid. "I'll see you tomorrow morning, then." She gave me a smile before going out through the curtain. I finally breathed again.

I finished scrubbing the cooking pot then went to the bathhouse. I washed in the cold water pit with copalli soap then put on my best dress and slipped my robe over it. I combed my hair and cleaned my teeth with charcoal powder, then chewed some chicle, to catch whatever hadn't rinsed away when I'd swished with water. I finished by rubbing on some bone flower cream Little Reed gave me last year, making me think of him. *If only I were going to meet with him tonight instead of Red Flint!* I pushed aside the spike of guilt and left the bathhouse.

Next I went to the laundry room. I built an alcove out of the towering pile of dirty laundry, stacking the bags to form a sturdy wall tall enough to hide me and Red Flint; Mothotli often patrolled the grounds after midnight, trying to catch girls out of their beds, so we'd have to be especially discreet.

You're really going to do this, I thought as I examined my handiwork. The sickness returned, but I didn't have time to think on it. The sunset bell rang; I was late for my temple duties.

I walked into the temple to find Ahexotl bloodletting. Women bled their tongues, in honor of Cihuacoatl's breath of life, while men bled their tepolli, in honor of the sacrifice Quetzalcoatl made to bring humankind to life. Male and female students learned their rituals separately from each other, but as full priests and priestesses, they performed them together; and though I'd been taught that the ritual was never shameful, seeing Ahexotl's manhood so plainly felt like catching my father naked.

"You're late," he said, not sharing my discomfort. "I'd hoped you might do a sacrifice with me."

The shame struck hard; there was no greater honor than to make a sacrifice with the high priest, and I'd squandered that opportunity preparing for an illicit meeting. "I'm sorry, your grace. I got caught up helping some of the younger girls." Oh how easily the lies flew from my tongue now!

"Next time, then. Will you say the prayer for me?"

I did so, then poured the blood-wetted grass balls into the idol's fanged mouth. When I turned back, Ahexotl had his hand down his loincloth, and for a moment I thought he was rubbing himself—but that was ridiculous. *He's just adjusting. The high priest of Quetzalcoatl doesn't commit lewd acts, especially in the god's holy temple.* He dropped his robe back down around his knees and smiled at me. "Thank you."

"Of course, your grace." But the uneasiness lingered as I watched him leave.

▫

Mothotli did a thorough inspection, making me sweep a third time behind the idol and refill all the copal wood burners, so I didn't leave the temple until well after the midnight bell. I hurried into the storerooms to put away my broom then went out the other side, to the bushes, my stomach knotting up tighter with every breath. *Maybe he won't show up and you won't have to do this.* I pulled aside the branches on the bushes and whispered, "Red Flint!" But still no sign of him.

Suddenly someone grabbed me from behind, clasping a hand over my mouth. My heart took off at a run, but then Red Flint whispered in my ear, "Why would such a lovely maiden be lurking in the shadows after midnight?"

I elbowed him in the gut and he let me go. "That's not funny!" I tried to hold back the tears but failed.

He gave me a stupid grin as he gripped his stomach where I'd hit him. "Are you really crying?" He wiped my tears away with his thumbs. "I'm sorry."

Hearing voices further down the garden path, I grabbed his hand and dragged him up the stairs, ducking into the laundry room. I listened at the curtain for a moment before finally breathing again.

"I'm really sorry," Red Flint said. "I didn't know I'd scare you so much."

"Of course not, because women just love being grabbed from behind as if you were an attacking Chichimec," I snapped.

"I said I was sorry," he growled. He soon calmed though and pulled me to him. "I promise I'll never do it again." He kissed me, pressing me against a tall shelf stacked with clean robes. With him so close in the darkness I couldn't see anything, but he smelled of tobacco and tasted of greasy, spiced meat.

Like before, the pleasant haze settled over me, but this time I pressed back against him, especially when he started moving his hands over the contours of my robe. He kissed me harder, his pressing body starting to crush me. "I want to touch you," he whispered, voice eager. "Can I touch you?"

"Of course," I said, inexplicably impatient. "That *is* why we came here tonight, after all." This bold, demanding voice coming from my own mouth sounded alien to me.

He worked his hands up under my dress, his fingers and palms hot and sweaty against my skin. He reached for my breasts but my dress shackled his hands just short, so he pulled harder, making it cut into my back. When I shifted it, he clamped onto my breasts like a dog seizing a small animal to shake. I gasped in both pain and pleasure.

"Sorry," he muttered and eased his flexing grip. He thrust his groin against mine, and I closed my eyes, my body inflamed with growing intensity. I could so easily get lost in the sensations, the hungry tingling in my lower abdomen. "A man shouldn't go to battle having never known the pleasure of a woman's love," Red Flint said in a throaty whisper. "I could be carried off by Chichimecs or even die of a festering wound, but all I would think about was how much I wished I'd made love to you, Quetzalpetlatl." He kissed me some more, eager and demanding. "Please let me have you. I want you for my wife; I'll even go to my father in the morning and ask him to marry us before I leave, so you'll be cared for while I'm gone. Just please don't deny me...."

All this talk of marriage inexplicably annoyed me, so to shut him up I grabbed his hand and took him over to the little alcove I'd built.

A lascivious grin crossed his face. "You never cease to surprise me." Abandoning all pretenses of seduction, he removed my undergarment and stripped himself down naked, then he pushed me to the floor and lay atop me.

Nimilitzli had been very forthcoming in educating me about sex, so I knew the basic mechanics for both male and female; and though Red Flint sounded very excited, his tepolli remained disappointingly flaccid, even when I took to stroking it with my hand. A dead snake had more rigidity. "Squeeze me tighter—oh yes, just like that," he whispered, but that soon turned to frustration. "Not much longer now. I'm almost ready."

I shared his frustration. "My arm's hurting," I said. He mashed himself between my legs, against my delicate tepilli, thrusting and huffing and puffing and grunting. He tried to push himself inside, but what little stiffness he'd managed melted away.

By now I'd tired of the wearying effort. "Is something wrong?" I asked, impatient.

"Nothing's wrong with me!" he snarled. "You're just rushing everything." He pinned me to the floor and kissed me hard. But when he again tried to force his limp tepolli inside me, I dug a knee into his side. He yelped and pulled away. "What did you do that for?" He rubbed his ribs.

"Just go home, Red Flint," I said, sitting up and looking around for my undergarment. The very sight of him filled me with a disturbing, hot loathing.

"I can do this! Just give me the time—"

Of course you can't, the annoyed voice wanted to say, but I held it back this time. "I don't want to anymore." With the lust subsiding, shame now burrowed deep in my stomach. *I never should have come here. Such foolishness!*

"You can't change your mind," Red Flint shot back. "You already said yes, so you can't back out now!"

"I did, and I will," I replied.

He stared at me as if contemplating striking me—and for a moment I thought he would—but then he snatched up his loincloth. "You're a whore."

"And so are you, Impotent Lizard."

Red Flint started shaking. "If you tell Topiltzin—"

"You think I want him to know that I actually let you *touch* me like that?" I said, disgusted, with him, with myself. Why had I ever thought it was a good idea to strap myself to this reprehensible dog? Of all the stupid, childish things I'd done in my life, this was by far the worst.

"You weren't any pleasure to lay with either. That perfume you're wearing made me shrivel up like a dead root."

I was about to fire off a retort, but then I heard voices out in the hallway. I froze.

"And if you think that marriage proposal is still any good, think again," Red Flint said, trying to tie on his loincloth.

I clamped a hand over his mouth. "Shut up! Someone's coming!"

In the silence, I heard Ahexotl's voice clearly. Red Flint peered over the top of the wall, towards the curtained doorway, but when shadows blotted out the light, he ducked back down. "If I get in trouble, you little whore—"

I covered his mouth again and glared at him, not daring to speak. What did he have to worry about? He was under the jurisdiction of the House of Warriors, where the young men took women to bed with them all the time—some would say it was even expected of them. But if Ahexotl caught me with Red Flint.... I hoped he'd have mercy and let me take my own life rather than making a public spectacle of my disgrace and permanently dishonoring both Little Reed and Nimilitzli. I watched over the top of the wall of clothing, praying Ahexotl would move on. *Please make him go away, My Lord, please. If you demand my loyalty to the priesthood, I'll gladly give it. Just please make him go away.*

But Ahexotl threw aside the curtain, letting in a flood of blinding light.

CHAPTER ELEVEN

I ducked, feeling faint. *Please don't let him see me!* But since Quetzalcoatl ignored my first prayer, I doubted he would show me mercy now. I closed my eyes, trying to calm myself.

But then I heard a woman's voice: the priestess Xocoyotl. She was a year older than me and usually led the youngest girls in evening prayer and made sure they were on their bed mats at night. I hunkered down as she tossed an armful of dirty robes onto my wall, but when she moved away, I breathed finally. Not daring to peek over the wall again, I opened a hole between the bags with my hand, just big enough to see through.

Ahexotl followed Xocoyotl around the small room, holding a ceramic dish of burning pine resin while she took folded robes off the shelves and talked about one of the girls cutting herself. "Nimilitzli stitched it up and reprimanded her for playing with a sacrificial blade," she finished. "So I think she'll be just fine."

"You do a wonderful job with the girls," he said. "Just today, the god expressed admiration for your dedication during this first year in his service. He's very pleased you're one of his priestesses."

Xocoyotl gasped. "He spoke to you? He really said that?"

I shared her surprise. Nimilitzli said she'd never heard of the god coming to anybody in this way.

"He speaks to me all the time, my dear. The high priest is his earthly vessel, after all, charged with carrying out his desires. He also says you're worthy of being one of his wives, and that's what I came to you about tonight." He put the lamp on the shelf and set his hands on her arms, a proud smile on his face. "The god desires that you consummate your marriage to him."

Xocoyotl took a step backwards. "But Nimilitzli told me the marriage is only spiritual, a devotion to the god's teachings as long as I wear the robes. She said it's nothing like a marriage to a mortal man."

"She must say that, for it's secret priestly knowledge." Ahexotl stepped closer again. "Within the first year, all his priestesses must lie with the god as they would a mortal husband."

Xocoyotl hesitated. "But how?"

I wondered too, and the possibilities terrified me. Would Quetzalcoatl himself manifest, as he did on the sacred precinct that night ten years ago? If he did, he'd surely know Red Flint and I were here. Would he reveal us to Ahexotl? I shuddered, panic blooming.

"As the god's earthly vessel, I perform his will," Ahexotl repeated, then leaned in to kiss her.

I itched as though ants were crawling all over me. I would have preferred a manifested god to the thought of Ahexotl touching me like Red Flint had. How could Nimilitzli lie to me about this? *Except Nimilitzli has never lied to you about anything,* I thought. *Even to spare your feelings. She's embarrassingly honest about many things. Something is very wrong about all this.*

"What's happening?" Red Flint whispered next to me. I clamped my hand over his mouth again but when he stayed silent this time, I let him peer through the hole too.

Xocoyotl tried pushing Ahexotl away, but he pushed her into the wall—exactly where Red Flint and I had stood for our passionate embrace—and pressed his bulk against her, smothering her with a crushing kiss. She squeaked behind his lips and he responded by tearing at her robes as if he was possessed of something terrible and hungry. That couldn't be the god Mother taught me to love, the one who saved me from Ihuitimal.

Ahexotl jammed his hand up under Xocoyotl's robe. She tried to turn away from him, but he followed her mouth, insistent. When he finally stopped kissing her long enough to catch his breath, she cried, "Please stop!" Tears wound down her cheeks and her lips curled into a sob.

"Oh, but you're enjoying it so much, my dear." He smeared his fingers across her cheek, leaving a glistening streak behind. "Why else would you be so wet?"

I had to look away for the hairs rising on my neck.

Xocoyotl cried harder. "Please! I can't do this. I want to go to my bed now."

"You're the god's wife and he demands you submit."

"I'm not ready—"

"If you refuse, I'll have no choice but to take back your robe and denounce you as an unfaithful priestess. There's no room in the priesthood for those who won't obey the god's will."

"Your grace, please—"

"Then you're gone from the temple, and don't come back!" He cast her aside as if she were an animal that bit him. She lay on the ground, weeping. "I had such high hopes for you, but instead you disappoint me. After everything I did for you? I championed your education. I made you worth something. Not all commoners' daughters are so lucky. You would've already been burdened with three children and living in squalor in a shack down in the fields, but I made you into a woman any nobleman would deem worthy of being his wife. And this is the thanks you give me? Disgracing my efforts by refusing to obey the god you took your oath to serve?"

By now, anger had burned away all my discomfort. I wouldn't believe the god was so shallow, so cruel. This was all Ahexotl's disgusting talk. *And to think you actually considered going to him about your problems.*

Xocoyotl sobbed. "I'm sorry, your grace. I've never forgotten your kindness to me."

He knelt beside her and raised her chin. "I don't enjoy this duty, but we all answer to the god. It's not too late; Quetzalcoatl understands you're afraid, but he's not a patient god. Don't throw away all you've worked for. It'll only take a few moments and you'll still be a priestess. You can do this. I have faith in you."

Xocoyotl hesitated but then muttered, "If it's the will of the god...."

I couldn't watch anymore and huddled with my head down and knees to my chest. It was bad enough hearing it all; Xocoyotl's gasp of pain mixed with Ahexotl's boorish grunting. Red Flint continued watching though, a half-smile on his face, as if it amused him. *And someday he's going be king.* I hated him; I hated Ahexotl, and Little Reed too, for setting me up to be violated just like poor Xocoyotl. And there was nothing I could do about any of it.

"Now that wasn't so bad, was it?" Ahexotl sounded winded but pleased with himself. "You did very well. The god's pleased."

"I'm bleeding!" Xocoyotl cried.

"Did no one ever tell you that happens the first time? Don't worry. It won't hurt as much the next time."

"Next time?"

"You're the god's lover now, and I'll call on you to do your duty when he demands it."

"But you said it would only be once—"

"I said nothing of the sort. Keep the god happy, and he'll protect you from the other women. You'd do well to keep this to yourself, lest you become a target of jealousy, particularly from Nimilitzli. The god doesn't call on her to pay wifely tribute anymore, so if she finds out, she'll expel you from the order. But it's far past midnight now, and I have sunrise duties." He departed, leaving the curtain jingling.

Xocoyotl remained behind, still weeping. "What did I do, oh what did I do?" she muttered over and over. Eventually she left, shuffling as she went.

Red Flint poked his head up over the laundry wall. "I was sure we'd get caught."

"We need to leave, right now," I stammered. In the lamplight, I finally found my undergarment and clambered out from behind the laundry, knocking most of it over as I did. When I tried to re-tie my undergarment, I saw I stood over a bloodied robe on the floor and I stepped away, chills scurrying up my back like a hairy spider. "I never should have come here."

Red Flint snorted. "At least I got to see something entertaining, so this night wasn't a complete waste of my time."

I stared at him, incredulous. "The high priest forcing himself on one of his priestesses isn't entertaining."

"She didn't tell him to stop."

"Because he threatened to expel her from the order! You should have done something!"

Red Flint laughed. "Like what?"

"You could have defended her!"

"And interrupt a religious ceremony? Are you crazy?"

"That was nothing but lies, so he could have his way with her."

Red Flint shrugged and started tying on his loincloth.

It was all I could do to not sneer at him. "You're completely unworthy of someday being king. You care about no one but yourself." Though was I any better, hunkered down and thinking only of getting caught while Ahexotl made Xocoyotl submit to his lusts?

"And calling you a whore would be an insult to other whores in my kingdom," he replied with a scathing smile.

I raised my hand to slap him, but a sudden gasp made me freeze mid-motion.

Mothotli stood in the open doorway, staring at us. "What is this?" she demanded, advancing. She gasped again when she saw the bloodstained robe. And with me standing there holding my undergarment and Red Flint still naked, I knew exactly what this looked like.

I didn't expect the switch across the face though. I shied away as she swung at me, so she missed my eye, but she laid open the side of my ear and the corner of my cheek, across the bone. It stung like thousands of wasp bites. I clutched at it, cowering for the next blow, but instead she turned on Red Flint, whipping him across the chest and shoulders, shouting, "You filthy little dog! I'll make sure you can never sit again!"

Red Flint dropped his loincloth as he shielded himself, and fell backwards over the wall of laundry, demolishing the rest of my handiwork. Mothotli clambered after him, screaming and whipping at his naked backside as he turned to right himself. He lumbered to his feet, howling at the switch's bite, and he knocked her over as he pushed past and sprinted for the door.

"Your father will hear about this!" Mothotli yelled as she fought her way out of the ruins of my alcove. I tried to help her up, but she whipped my hands away. "As for you, you little whore," she swore as she struggled to her feet, "your days at this school are over!" She snatched up the bloodstained robe in one hand and wrenched me towards the door with the other.

Her shouting roused the priestess who watched the dormitory door, and by the time we reached the school, we'd attracted curious stares from the windows. Mazatzin, who was returning from the palace, ran to us. "What happened? Is everyone all right?"

"Wake Nimilitzli and tell her to come to the Council Room immediately," Mothotli ordered him. "Tell Ahexotl to come too."

Mazatzin turned his questioning gaze to me, but I couldn't meet it. What must he think of me, standing there with a tear-stained face, messy hair, and carrying my undergarment? He headed for Nimilitzli's house at a jog.

Mothotli dragged me down the hall to the Council Room reserved for meetings between the upper-level priests and priestesses. I'd never been there before, but my stomach fell when I saw the array of weapons on display on the walls: obsidian-studded swords, spears, and atl-atl arrow throwers, like the one my father had been showing Black Otter how to use that fateful day ten years ago. Murals of Quetzalcoatl decorated every wall, and he seemed to glower down at me with dark, vengeful eyes. "Sit down!" Mothotli snapped, pointing at the mats in front of the large hearth.

"Can I please finish dressing myself?" I choked through tears.

"So you can conceal your harlotry?" She snatched the cloth from me. "I said *sit down.*"

I knelt on the hearth stones, tucking my dress over my knees. *This is the spot where I'll die tonight,* I thought, trembling and nauseous. No doubt under the blade of one of the weapons hanging on the wall. Gazing up at the atl-atl again brought on a shameful, hollow sickness. *What would Father have thought of what you've done?*

"What in Mictlan is this all about?" Nimilitzli demanded when she arrived. I turned away when she looked at me.

"I'll explain everything once the high priest arrives," Mothotli said. "Suffice it to say this girl flagrantly violated one of the school's highest rules."

Nimilitzli paled, and this time I couldn't turn away from the fear in her eyes. She came towards me, wringing her hands but not speaking, as if imploring me to defend myself against this accusation. *I'm so sorry, Nimilitzli. I was foolish and desperate, but please—oh Great Feathered Serpent please!—help me now, protect me from my own stupidity!* I wanted to say.

But when Ahexotl shuffled into the room, she shifted her gaze away and the wall went up around her heart. At that moment, I was just another student, to be dealt with accordingly. When it came to priestly matters, Nimilitzli never treated me any differently than any other novice.

I felt betrayed.

"What's this about? I have sunrise duties and I was just about to turn in after a very long night," Ahexotl said.

"I was patrolling the grounds," Mothotli started, "when I came across Quetzalpetlatl in the laundry room, in the company of Prince Red Flint, and he was completely naked, and she was without her undergarment. And I found this on the floor between them." She threw down the bloodied robe.

Nimilitzli turned her stern frown on me, but Ahexotl stared down at the robe, his facial muscles twitching. "In the laundry room, you say?" he asked.

Mothotli nodded, and Ahexotl shot me a hard glare. I shifted my own gaze away, unable to breathe. "She broke the chastity rule. She is not fit to be a priestess!"

"You caught them in the act?" Nimilitzli asked.

"They'd already finished by the time I found them, but the evidence—"

"Is a bloodied robe that could have been soiled by a girl's monthly bleeding?"

Mothotli faltered, then said, "The Prince was naked and she was carrying her undergarment. It's obvious what they were doing."

Nimilitzli turned to me. "What *were* you doing in the laundry room with Red Flint?"

I looked from her to Ahexotl. He glared at me.

"Well?" Nimilitzli pressed, losing patience.

It was useless lying to her, and to try now would only make me look guilty of something I didn't do. I couldn't look at her though. "I met with Red Flint after temple duty and we stole away into the laundry room to...must I really say it?"

"If you think yourself woman enough to do such things, you shouldn't be embarrassed to speak frankly about it," she snapped.

I cringed. "We went there to lie together, as husbands and wives do." I didn't dare look up at her. I didn't want to see the disappointment on her face.

"Then you're responsible for the blood on this robe?" She dangled it in front of me.

"It's not my blood," I said.

"Then whose is it?"

I flicked my gaze over at Ahexotl again, unsure what to say. "Answer her right now," he said, the challenge plain in his eyes.

"I don't know whose it is," I finally said, guilt hitting me like an arrow. I was a coward and ashamed of myself, but fear of Ahexotl kept me from admitting what I'd seen.

"She lies!" Mothotli shouted, the vein on her forehead pulsing like a swollen worm.

Nimilitzli held up a hand. "You've admitted your purpose there, but you say you didn't go through with it?"

"We didn't," I said.

"Why not?"

Because Red Flint's limp snake wasn't up to the task, I almost said, but that would only make me sound unrepentant. "I realized the folly of what I was doing and told him to stop."

"This is ridiculous," Mothotli spouted. "We should make her prove her story by physical examination. That will determine not only if she's broken, but if so, if it just happened tonight."

"I'm not lying!" I cried. "I swear on the Feathered Serpent!" *Why would I have been ready to slap Red Flint if I'd just bedded him, you nasty woman?* I managed to bite my tongue though.

Mothotli glared at me, but Ahexotl said, "Her request isn't unreasonable, Quetzalpetlatl. Given what I've heard here, I believe the examination is in order. There's no sense in continuing your studies if you couldn't pass the physical exam necessary to become a priestess." To Mothotli, he said, "Fetch Ixchell and we'll have it done immediately." He put on a smug smile.

Mictlan be damned, I wasn't about to subject myself to a check of my virginity for the sick amusement of this beastly man. Shaking my head, I shrugged past all of them. Mothotli tried to grab my arm but I ran out of the door. "You can't just walk out. You belong to the Temple—" she shouted after me, but I didn't look back as I ran off down the hall, tears blurring my eyes.

CHAPTER TWELVE

 I sat at the top of the stairs descending to the palace square, staring into the darkness and wondering why I'd let all this happen. *What kind of an idiot tries to strap herself to a dog like Red Flint, and all to do what? Defy your brother? Make him jealous when he clearly has no such feelings for you?*

Nimilitzli came up behind me. "She's right, you know. Your mother gave you to the Temple on the day of your birth, and while you're allowed to leave once you've completed your schooling, you can't avoid punishment for what you did as a student."

"So then everyone but me has a say in my future?" I spat.

"If you wanted to marry Lord Red Flint, why didn't you talk to me about it?"

"Red Flint is the last man I'd ever want to marry."

"Then what were you thinking?"

"With Topiltzin leaving...now I'm the child that needs to become a priestess so I'm a desirable commodity for him to trade on in the future."

"He said that to you?" she asked, surprised.

"He doesn't have to. I'm well aware that my worth in this world has nothing to do with what's in my head or my heart."

Nimilitzli sighed. "Our lot is seldom fair, but you assume too much. We both know Topiltzin isn't like other men."

"He's in such a hurry to run off to war and become another empty-headed nobleman," I said.

"You can't run his life for—"

"And he's not going to run mine. I'll determine my own future."

"Even if it means making a whore of yourself?"

She might as well have slapped me. I stood, glaring at her. "My mother never would've called me that."

"Your mother would've been too horrified to say anything at all," Nimilitzli retorted.

"I don't want to talk about this anymore." I pushed past her, tears threatening.

But she followed me. "Your choices don't go away because you don't want to talk about them. You made one, and now you must live with the consequences."

"I didn't give in to him! Why don't you believe me?"

"Then agree to take the test! You only make yourself look guilty by refusing. You made a judgment error, you've admitted as much, but you can still have a future in the priesthood—"

"Just as Topiltzin wants me to."

Nimilitzli sighed, exasperated. "Then what do *you* want?"

We'd reached the temple base, where the Feathered Serpent's relief rested an arm's reach from me. I wiped my tears away then set my hands on the frieze. "I had purpose, given to me by the god himself, but now Topiltzin has taken all that from me."

"You can't build your whole life around someone else, Quetzalpetlatl. People go away; they leave us, whether by choice or not, and then what are we left with? You believed Quetzalcoatl gave you purpose before, so maybe you can find it again, in the priesthood."

Her words made sense, but fear clung to me. "I can't...I can't go through the trials just to throw it all away...to be coerced into breaking my vows to the god."

"Coerce you? Who?" When I didn't answer, she motioned me to follow her to the house. Once she closed the curtain behind us, she said, "Tell me what you saw."

"I can't talk about—"

"It was Ahexotl, wasn't it?"

I stared at her, shocked. She knew?

She went to stoke the dying fire. "I've suspected him of victimizing the young priestesses for some time now but no one's come forward, and not even I would be so foolish as to accuse the second most powerful man in Xochicalco."

"He told her that you would expel her from the order if you knew," I said, relieved to finally be able to speak about it.

"Who?"

I hesitated before telling her; she scowled and tossed wood into the flames. "What else did he say?"

"That Quetzalcoatl demanded she consummate their marriage by lying with him, and that all priestesses had to do it. And when she resisted, he threatened to throw her out of the order. I've never heard such vile blasphemy." I hugged myself. "How could I be such a fool, thinking he cared about me at all?"

"You haven't the benefit of enough years to understand the true shade of his spots," Nimilitzli said. "Even I only had suspicions until tonight."

"But now he knows I saw him," I cried, sitting on one of the reed mats next to the fire.

Nimilitzli sat too. "It's not my intention to tell you how to live your life, Quetzalpetlatl—you're not a little girl, and you should make your own decisions about your life—but you're dismissing what the priesthood can do for you. Your faith and devotion to the god runs deep; deeper than even my own at times, and that's exactly the kind of women we need in the priesthood. We've unfortunately become a place where powerful men send their daughters to make them more appealing as wives, so we need strong women to preserve the little bit of power we still have. Once, long ago, a woman could have been a powerful war-queen…but these days too many men come back from war having adopted the ideals of those they claim to be barbarians. High priestess is the highest position any woman can hold anymore. And why should we relegate all the decisions to men like Ahexotl or Ihuitimal? You're very strong, if you'd just see it, Quetzalpetlatl, and I won't live forever. And though Mothotli is strong, fate has decided that she will never be high priestess. I can't say who will be, but I see great potential in you."

I blinked, surprised. "Me?"

"Your mother had the potential too, but sadly she didn't think she had the choice. *You* have the choice, and I'll beat Topiltzin over the head if he thinks otherwise. I didn't raise him to be wooden-headed."

The notion of someday being high priestess of Quetzalcoatl held surprising appeal, but still…. "What about Ahexotl?"

"You said you wanted to make your own choices, but if even a bit of you wants to be a priestess and you're holding back out of fear, then you're letting him make the decision for you."

She was absolutely right, of course, and I'd be a fool to let Ahexotl make my choices for me. Little Reed at least had my best interests at heart.

"We aren't allowed dreams for long, so don't let him keep you from yours," Nimilitzli said. "You're better equipped to fend him off than the others were; you've seen the true nature of his sweet words. Men like him prey on those they can easily control, but you're not weak. You've seen his tricks, and you can help arm the other girls against him. Together we can keep him from claiming any more victims."

"That would be a worthwhile task," I admitted. "No one should have to suffer like Xocoyotl did."

"And should you find something else that sings to your heart, you can leave the priesthood without fear of angering the god. He will treasure your service as long as you give it." Nimilitzli stood and took a narrow wooden box off one of the shelves above the hearth. "Your mother gave this to me prior to her death. She asked me to give it to you when I thought you were ready. I think now is a good time."

Carved feathered serpents decorated the box's panels, bringing a flash of memory: I'd seen this box sitting at the bottom of my mother's wicker clothing chest and I'd often tried to open it, but the gold latches had been too stiff for my young hands. I'd always wondered what she kept locked in it. My heart drummed as I pulled the delicate gold latches aside and lifted the lid away.

Inside, Mother's sacrificial blade nestled in a bed of graying linen. The carved serpent handle was worn but still beautiful.

"She had only a moment to get away that night in Culhuacan, but she wouldn't leave it behind. It was very important to her that you should have it," Nimilitzli said.

I gripped the handle and ran my fingers over the side of the blade as I sniffed back fresh tears. "Thank you. For this, and for believing me." I hugged her. "I'm sorry for disappointing you."

She hugged me tightly. "I'm not disappointed, Quetzalpetlatl. Even I was young once."

"I suppose I must go submit to that examination."

She nodded. "And again, should you take the trials, but we only grow stronger for facing the consequences of our choices."

◻

The priestess Ixchell—who was also one of Nimilitzli's assistant midwives—performed the examination behind a screen in the Council Room, but as humiliating as it was to have to go through it at all, Ixchell quickly pronounced me unbroken.

"And that settles that," Ahexotl said. "You assumed wrong about her, Mothotli. What have you against her, always accusing her of lying?"

Mothotli scowled at him. "There's still the matter of her conduct. She confessed to engaging in activities unbecoming of a novice, which are grounds for expulsion."

"As foolhardy and disgraceful as her actions were, I don't think expulsion is necessary. She recognized she'd taken a wrong step before taking matters too far, so she's to be commended for that." He turned his steady gaze to Nimilitzli. "What do you think would be a fitting punishment?"

"If she's to stay, a harsh punishment must be rendered. Casual rule-breaking cannot be allowed." Nimilitzli turned to me. "That is, if you still wish to pursue a future in the priesthood."

"I do," I said. "I'll accept whatever punishment you deem appropriate."

Ahexotl nodded. "Ten lashes then, five on each hand. As is customary, the fire priestess will administer them immediately."

That gave me a knot in my throat, but I wouldn't back out just because I was in Mothotli's hands now. *Better than being turned over to Ahexotl.*

Mothotli took my right hand by the fingertips. She struck her switch across the back of it, laying the skin open. I bit my lip to hold back the cries as she hit me over and over, five times on one hand until it was bloody and raw; then she did the same to the other one. "Henceforth look upon your hands and be reminded of how close you came to a far worse fate," she said. I felt faint with pain.

Ahexotl headed for the doorway. "I trust we're done here then? Sunrise is closer than I wish and I've yet to get any sleep."

"I'll be watching you," Mothotli hissed at me, then she raked the curtain aside with a clatter as she followed Ahexotl out.

Back at Nimilitzli's house, I soaked my bloodied hands in the water jar then smeared salve over my wounds. "I don't think I'll ever be able to close my hands again," I said. Just thinking about it made my split skin sting anew.

"You handled it well," Nimilitzli said as she wrapped my hands in linen. "Stay out of the steam bath for a week while this heals."

"Now I wish Topiltzin had already left, so he wouldn't see what a disgrace I've become. What am I to tell him?"

"The truth is always best. And don't leave out your reason for getting yourself in such trouble." She gave me a pointed look.

Little Reed suddenly tore aside the door curtain and stormed into the house, red-faced and panting. "That wretched, foulmouthed little lake leech!" He stopped short when he saw Nimilitzli wrapping my hands. "What happened, Quetzalpetlatl?"

I struggled a moment before saying, "What are you doing back from the palace already?"

"And what brings you cursing into my house before the Sun has even been born?" Nimilitzli added.

"Red Flint." Little Reed spat his name. "I can't repeat what I heard tonight, and it took all my resolve to not challenge him right then and there, but I fear by morning he'll have crowed his drivel to every nobleman in Xochicalco."

Numbness crept up on me. "What's he saying?"

"I can't say it in front of Mother."

"There's little I haven't heard in my life, Topiltzin," Nimilitzli replied.

Little Reed paced a moment, then blurted out to me, "He's telling everyone that you gave yourself to him like some worthless whore, and that they should all come to you so you can make 'men' out of them!"

I gasped, appalled. "How dare he—"

"And you expected better of him?" Nimilitzli asked, not looking at either of us. I sputtered until the shame took over.

Little Reed stood silent a moment before asking again, "What happened to your hands?"

Nimilitzli stood. "I've already said my piece, so I shall leave you two to talk." She took her cloak off the wall peg. "I need to go and speak with Xocoyotl anyway." She slipped out onto the precinct.

Little Reed took the mat next to me. I turned away, unable to hold his worried gaze. "Please tell me what happened, Papalotl. We have no secrets from each other."

I laughed. "No secrets? What about you not telling us about your plans to leave for the army until two weeks ago?"

"I didn't want to burden you—"

"And I don't want to burden you with my troubles, either." I turned from him.

"I want to be burdened. If I can help you—"

"Don't you mean tell me what to do? To pray to Quetzalcoatl for forgiveness for dishonoring you, and to hang my head like a good little girl? Because it's all about what *you* want and what *you* think is best. You don't care what Nimilitzli and I think, what *we* want, for ourselves or for you. You're a man now and must take your rightful place as our guardian, and make sure we don't do anything to embarrass you."

Stricken, Little Reed asked, "What...where does all this come from, Papalotl? Are you feeling all right?"

"I feel horrible and useless, and abandoned, but you neither notice nor care. You can't wait to run off to prove yourself a man and shove me safely away into the priesthood so my maidenhood will be protected and you can someday make a good marriage of me to someone you desperately need for an alliance."

He gasped, looking as though I'd slapped him. "I don't intend to marry you off to anyone. No one means more to me than you—"

"That will change once you've lived among the soldiers and don't have to answer to Nimilitzli. When you come back, the boy who once listened to me—who used to love me—will be gone."

"I do love you, Papalotl," Little Reed insisted.

"Then you wouldn't have dismissed my concerns and I never would've thought to dishonor myself with Red Flint—"

Little Reed's face reddened. "Then what he said—"

"That I'm a worthless whore?" I snapped.

"Don't call yourself that."

"It doesn't matter what I do, I'll be considered one. I'm cursed if I do and cursed if I don't."

Little Reed rubbed his temples and sighed. "Do you love him?"

"Since when does love matter?"

"It matters to me."

"I'd as soon love a dog."

"Then I don't understand why you did this."

Because I wanted to make you jealous, make you hurt like you're hurting me. But that was such a childish, petty, horrible excuse. "It doesn't matter. I was foolish and I should have just accepted my place and what you required of me."

Flustered, Little Reed shook his head. "I want you to choose your own way, Papalotl, just as I will choose mine. I won't force you to become a priestess; real devotion comes only from a true desire to serve, so if your heart calls you elsewhere, then go there." He went to the doorway then looked back. "I'm sorry I hurt you. That wasn't my intention, and I beg your forgiveness."

"If you must have it," I said, indifferent.

He looked ready to say more, but instead he frowned, bowed his head, and left. I lay on Nimilitzli's bed, exhausted like I hadn't been in years. I stared into the fire, wishing I hadn't let my anger get the last word with Little Reed, and I welcomed restless sleep when it finally whisked me away from my troubles.

◻

When I awoke, an extra bedroll lay in front of the hearth and Nimilitzli was gone, but she'd left me a tlaxcalli in a cloth. I ate it, but when I noticed how little sunlight leaked through the front window, I felt sick. The noontime bell at the calmecac chimed too, confirming my fears: Little Reed had left for the army camp at midmorning and I'd slept through it. *Why didn't Nimilitzli wake me?* I thought, despairing as I pulled my priestly robe on. I never should have let him leave before apologizing for my harsh words.

But when I tossed aside the curtain, Little Reed was coming from the calmecac,

87

dressed in his novice robe. "What are you still doing here?" I asked once he was within earshot. "Hasn't the army contingent left already?"

"I didn't go with them."

I waited until he reached me, then asked, "Why not?" Though I already knew the answer: *He can't trust you to behave yourself. And can you really blame him?*

"Because I stayed up all night thinking about what we talked about, and everything Nimilitzli has been telling me these last two weeks, and you're both right. I'm not ready to go, and perhaps I let Red Flint influence my decision. I should be above such pettiness, and I'll be better off becoming a priest first."

I stared at the ground a moment before saying, "Just because I wanted you to stay doesn't mean you have to."

"I can't go to war worried that you think I don't love you anymore—because I do, and dearly." He drew me into a hug.

I hugged him back fiercely, all my anger and distrust dissolving in a moment of imagining he was expressing that same exhilarating emotion he brought out in me. "I love you too, Little Reed," I whispered, wanting the moment to last forever.

"What's one more year?" he asked once we headed for the temple, still holding hands. "That'll give us both time to settle out our futures."

As we passed the calmecac, I noticed several novice priestesses watching us and whispering. Word of my misdeed had already spread, and no doubt seeing me holding Little Reed's hand wasn't helping the rumors. He looked startled when I tore my hand away from him but said nothing as we continued walking.

When we reached the stairs up to the temple I stopped and asked, "Are you disappointed in me, Little Reed?"

He smiled as he shook his head. "You could never disappoint me, Papalotl. One doesn't learn proper sacrificial technique without once or twice cutting too deep."

CHAPTER THIRTEEN

 For the next two weeks, Little Reed and I spent our evenings studying for our upcoming priestly trials and packing for the pilgrimage to Teotihuacan. It would be a long journey, and though we'd have a heavy guard, rumors abounded of Chichimec raiding parties being spotted as far south as Xochimilco just a week before we were to leave.

"Strange that Chichimecs should start pushing into the south end of the valley right when I was about to march with the army," Little Reed noted as we sat in Nimilitzli's house the night before leaving.

Nimilitzli nodded. "Cuitlapanton agreed to increase our escort, but every man should bring a weapon with them. A heavily-armed entourage may discourage any mercenaries we come upon."

Little Reed had also been giving me weapons lessons. "It's nonsense to say women shouldn't handle swords," he told me. "You're no safer from our uncle than I, and I'd rather you put up a defense than be dragged off without a chance." He took me to the exercise field behind the House of Warriors and showed me all the best places to strike an enemy on the fakes made of grass and maguey cloth. Little Reed let me use the sword

Cuitlapanton had given him—it had a mahogany core emblazoned with Little Reed's name symbols—and I broke the obsidian blades multiple times missing the target. I fared little better with the spears, atl-atl, or axes. I was best with my mother's sacrificial blade, and took great joy at slashing at the grass man as if he were Ahexotl.

Before sunrise the next day, all the graduating novices gathered in the calmecac's courtyard with packs on. The men came armed. The king allotted us thirty soldiers and four porters, the latter to carry Ahexotl and Nimilitzli's single-seat litters, bringing our full compliment to forty-five.

We departed under predawn's gray light and took the northern road through the fields where the peasants tended the maize, beans and squash. Fires burned bright in the mud houses and farmers stood in their doorways, eating their morning tlaxcallis before heading out to work.

By dawn, we reached the stepped pit where workers quarried limestone for the city's buildings, and we kept to one side as the men lugged the heavy stones to the city. We passed two trade caravans manned with slaves carrying packs of merchandise on their backs, balanced by cotton straps across their foreheads. Our lead soldier spoke to the first caravan's security detail about the road conditions and any encounters with bandits. As we approached the forest, I whispered a prayer to Quetzalcoatl, imploring him to ensure I'd get to see Xochicalco's beautiful white walls again.

Little Reed fell back a few steps to walk with me. "Don't worry, Papalotl. We're unlikely to be set upon while traveling so well armed, and Quetzalcoatl watches over us." But still the forest shade left me cold and uneasy.

Upon reaching the main trade route we turned west, away from the Teotihuacan side of Lake Meztliapan. "We used to take the eastern road and stay overnight in Culhuacan," Nimilitzli told me as I walked next to her litter. "But that was before the war, when the Feathered Serpent's followers were still welcome there. Ihuitimal executes Quetzalcoatl's followers and displays their mutilated remains along the road. So now we take the longer western road. At Tultepec, we'll take boats across the lake."

"When we reclaim the throne, Culhuacan will again be a haven for Quetzalcoatl's followers," Little Reed replied with staunch conviction.

We reached the tip of the lake by nightfall and made camp. With our close proximity to Culhuacan's territory, we hoped to pass the night unnoticed, and so forewent any fires and ate cold tlaxcallis and spoke in whispers. We departed in the dark of early morning but still no one spoke above a whisper until past noon, when the opposite shore was far from sight.

Two nights later, we came upon the military camp on the outskirts of Tultepec, one of our allied cities. Hundreds of tents crowded the open plain, and bonfires left none of it in darkness. Banners hung from tall poles along the road, denoting where each city's army camped: Chapultepec's blue and white, Xochimilco's green and red, and Tultepec's black and white, among others. We made camp at the far north end, behind an empty pole. Was this where Father's troops would camp when Culhuacan was still an ally?

We pitched our deerskin tents around two separate fires, but we all gathered in the women's camp for dinner, singing, and music. We girls practiced our festival dances while Nimilitzli admonished the men about smiling or whispering to each other. Little Reed sat away from the others, watching me with a proud smile he refused to abandon even when Nimilitzli scowled at him. I smiled back clandestinely, imagining it might mean more. Ahexotl closed off the night with a sacrifice of snakes, thanking Quetzalcoatl for helping us arrive there unharmed.

I woke before dawn and went down to the lake's edge to bathe before the ride across the lake. The morning was quiet save for the occasional soft quacking of ducks floating serenely in the distance, the lake surface smooth as an obsidian mirror. The coolness felt wonderful on my aching blisters as I eased my feet into the water. The smell of fried maize cakes mixed with the brackish breeze blowing softly off the lake.

The other girls came down the path a short while later. Two of them—Malinalli and Iczoxochitl—greeted me with smiles, but the third—Princess Turquoise Bells, one of Red Flint's countless sisters—merely whispered to her companions and laughed. Iczoxochitl giggled at the whisper, but Malinalli shot Turquoise Bells an annoyed look. I went about my business while they undressed then waded into the lake.

"I thought Topiltzin was joining the army this year," Turquoise Bells said. The day after my ill-advised meeting with Red Flint, I heard through rumors that she had been betrothed to him since she was five, and so I'd spent the last two weeks making concerted efforts to avoid her, and any confrontations it might bring.

But with the others here, I knew I couldn't ignore her without seeming rude. "He's going to march next year," I said, and avoided her gaze as I washed myself with copalli soap.

"What could have changed his mind, I wonder?"

"It's not our business," Malinalli said. She was a commoner's daughter, gifted with more brains than most noblewomen, and she'd go far in the priesthood. We got on well in our classes but rarely spoke outside calmecac.

Turquoise Bells continued anyway. "I bet it's so he can make sure you don't disgrace yourself again."

"Again?" Iczoxochitl asked.

"Didn't you hear? Mothotli caught her in the laundry room with Red Flint."

Iczoxochitl gasped. "Doing what?"

"Suffice it to say that my brother left with an ocelot's smile on his face."

"Red Flint's a dishonorable liar," I fired back.

"Then tell us what really happened." Turquoise Bells gave me a nasty smile.

I could have told them about Red Flint's problem—the gods knew he deserved such humiliation—but fear glued my tongue to the roof of my mouth. When it came to sex and reputation, I'd seen too many of the young women become like wolves on a kill. Why we should relish beating and maiming each other's feelings, I didn't know, but many wielded it as if it were the only power they had.

All the same, my silence condemned me. "Just as I thought," Turquoise Bells sneered. "You won't tell the truth because it's already there for everyone to see." She grabbed my hands and held my fresh scars up for the others to see. I wrenched them away and hid both hands in the water, my face burning with embarrassment. "You hide your disgrace now, but you were trying to force a marriage to him. But the best you can ever hope for is to be one of his concubines."

Seeing her bristle over someone who couldn't even perform the most rudimentary of reproductive functions brought me an amused smirk.

She poked me in the chest with her finger. "Stay away from him. I may not be the queen yet, but that doesn't mean I can't make your life miserable." She waded back to shore with Iczoxochitl. They dressed, then hurried back to camp.

"Don't listen to her," Malinalli said. "So you made a mistake; who hasn't? Besides, whatever it was, it's between you and your family and the god, and in the end those are the opinions that matter most."

I gave her a strained smile. "Thank you, Malinalli."

"I smell tlaxcallis cooking. Shall we head back to camp?"

"I still need to put balm on my feet, but I'll see you there."

I waited until she was gone before coming ashore and drying off with my linen. As I slipped my dress back on I thought about what she'd said, and something new occurred to me: what if Quetzalcoatl didn't want me for a priestess because of what I'd done? Would he reject me during the vision ceremony where I was supposed to receive his spiritual guidance? Might he even take back the gift he'd given me? I felt as if a lump of cornmeal were stuck in my throat.

"You look troubled," Ahexotl suddenly spoke up. I whirled to find him watching me with a disarming smile on his face. "What's bothering you, dear?"

My flesh crawled at his closeness but fear kept me from springing away. "I'm fine."

"Malinalli's right, you know. The opinions of women like Turquoise Bells account for nothing. She might be queen of Xochicalco someday, but you will be the high priestess of Quetzalcoatl."

Just how long had the evil dog been spying on us? My cheeks burned at the thought he might have seen me undressed.

"The god made his intentions for you very clear to me long ago," Ahexotl went on. "I made it my top priority to make sure you pursued his wishes, though after that mess with Red Flint, I feared I'd failed. I'm pleased that you were intelligent enough to realize your folly before it was too late."

"I would prefer not to talk about that, Your Grace." I looked past him to the path, wondering if I could get around him.

"I'm glad you saw what you did. The truth can be difficult to accept when one's told lies about her true duties. Obviously Quetzalcoatl wanted you to see the sacred ritual, to keep you from destroying your future."

The creepy smile on his face made the hair on my nape rise. "I should get back to camp."

But when I tried to hurry past him, he grabbed my arm. "It's natural to be afraid. Don't be embarrassed." I tried to yank my arm away, panic setting in, but he held me firm. "Everyone cowers before he who's greater than them, and when the time comes, you will too."

Thankfully the bushes up the hill rattled and Little Reed came down the path, watching where he was stepping. Ahexotl released me before he could see anything though. "It's time to eat, Papalotl. Malinalli told me you were—" He stopped short when he looked up. "Good morning, Your Grace. I didn't know you were down here too."

"I came to wash my feet." Ahexotl slipped off his sandals and sat on a rock at the lake's edge. "You'd better run along, Quetzalpetlatl, before the men eat everything."

I hurried up the hill and once we were away from the clearing, Little Reed asked, "Is everything all right? You're trembling."

Tell him what Ahexotl said, I thought, but what if he said I'd got what I deserved, after what I'd done with Red Flint? "It's nothing I can't handle on my own, Little Reed," I assured him, avoiding his concerned gaze.

"You're sure?"

"It's nothing at all. Now let's hurry. I'm starving." Though as sick as I felt, I doubted I'd be able to eat anything.

▫

We crossed the lake in a small fleet of wooden canoes that dropped us off on the opposite shore, and they'd return for us in seven days. From there, we cut through the woods for several hours. Teotihuacan's giant pyramids became visible once we broke from the forest, standing out against the sky like mountains. We followed a well-worn road running north-south and reached the city limits by noon.

Mostly only the limestone-walled courtyards of the noble quarters remained standing and we women made camp in one off the main road. It was small, forcing us to pitch our tents close together, but flowering trees provided shade against the sun for both us and the plethora of wild flowers and blooming vines. The men pitched camp further down the road from us. Several guards stood watch at our entryway, though any of us could have easily wormed through the hole in the wall behind Turquoise Bells's tent. We spent most of the day setting up camp and preparing the evening meal, and then Nimilitzli sent us to bed early. I fell asleep as soon as I pulled the blanket over my shoulder.

"Time to rise," Nimilitzli called inside my tent after what felt like only a few moments of sleep. "Much to do today."

Not wanting to deal with Turquoise Bells, I waited until the others came back before going to the water yard myself. A large rain jar sat in the back corner, and though the walls of the deep courtyard stood tall, the open doorway had me hurrying to change clothes, wash my feet, and put salve on my blisters before tying my sandals on again.

After bowls of atole and fruit along with the requisite tlaxcallis, we followed Nimilitzli out to a large open precinct bordered by three mountainous pyramids and countless smaller ones. Standing this close to them, it seemed very possible the gods themselves had built them, as the stories said. Teotihuacan was "The Birthplace of the Gods" after all.

"This road we're on now is called 'The Walk of the Dead', for the kings of the past were carried through here on their funeral processions," Nimilitzli told us, her voice small and hollow in the vast openness. She pointed to the largest pyramid ahead of us. "It was on this very spot that the gods gathered to elect the Fifth Sun, where Nanahuatzin threw himself upon the sacred pyre and became Tonantiuh. This is where Quetzalcoatl bled his tepolli on Cihuacoatl's metlatl stone to create the fifth generation of humanity. Back then this was the paradise known as Tamoachan, where Quetzalcoatl and Mayahuel made the Sacred Tree to hide from her grandmother. Later, our ancestors built the city and these magnificent temples."

The pyramid's flat summit had a stone-ringed fire pit in the center. The men were already there, and I joined Little Reed on the southeast side of the pyramid. Lake Meztliapan stretched into the distance, large and greenish-blue in the morning sun.

"Isn't it exciting being here, where the gods themselves were born?" he asked, his face glowing with boyish charm.

"Meditation time, you two," Nimilitzli warned us, so we closed our eyes. I focused on clearing my mind and relaxing my body, though the breeze caressing my skin like a lover's hand made it difficult. I inhaled the fresh scent of flowers and the trees....

Papalotl!

I opened my eyes to find myself in a garden—not any garden I'd ever been in, but still strangely familiar, like a forgotten memory. Little Reed called to me again, but I couldn't see him, so I followed his voice to a tall stone wall covered with ivy. "Little Reed? Where are you?"

You only need to climb the wall to find me, he whispered back. *I'm waiting for you, my love.*

I felt dizzy with joy. "You called me 'my love'," I said, needing to know for sure if it had been a slip of the tongue.

Of course you are my love! But we can only be together once you climb out of your prison.

I tried to climb up the vines, but they snapped under my weight, so I found hand and footholds between the wall's stones and climbed up that way. The wall grew higher the more I climbed, but I knew it was a trick meant to discourage me and so continued on.

My persistence paid off as I clambered up to the top of the wall. But when I looked down, I saw only a jaguar black as smoke but shimmering like obsidian in the sun. It sprang up and grabbed my head in its jaws, pulling me down off the wall.

And now I fell forever, screaming while the jaguar clung to me. *Come meet your destiny, my love,* it laughed in my head. And to my horror, it was still Little Reed's voice....

Feeling a sudden lurch, I snapped my eyes open and looked around, my heart hammering. Little Reed held my arm, but with his laughing voice still fresh in my head, I wanted to tear free. The concern in his eyes brought me back to my senses. "Are you all right?" He held me a moment longer before finally letting go.

Everyone stared at me, their expressions a mixture of curiosity and concern. Nimilitzli came over, frowning. "What's the matter?"

"She almost tipped over the edge," Little Reed said.

I expected a stern reprimand but instead Nimilitzli asked, "Do you need to return to camp and rest some more?"

"No, I'm fine, I was just—"

But when the tall, mangy black dog crested the stairs behind her, I forgot what I was saying. It sniffed the air, fangs bared. "What's that?"

Nimilitzli turned around. "What?"

I pointed at the dog. "That!"

The concern on Nimilitzli's face now changed to annoyance. Turquoise Bells and Iczoxochitl whispered to each other while the men exchanged amused glances. I looked to Mazatzin too, but he gazed back at me, puzzled. *Now everyone thinks me not only a harlot, but a crazy one too.* "Maybe you should go and lie down a while," Nimilitzli suggested.

The dog was now sniffing each person in turn, sometimes lapping its tongue across someone's cheek. So far it was only licking the men, though it sniffed Ahexotl's sandal before moving on around the circle.

"I'll take her, High Priestess." Little Reed pulled me to my feet, but as we descended the stairs, I noticed him watching the dog too.

Once we were out of earshot of the others, I said, "You could see it too?"

"I did."

"What do you think it's doing?"

"You don't recognize it?" When I shook my head, he said, "The Deformed One? The Black Dog?"

"Xolotl?" In our sacred stories, the deformed god Xolotl—so named because of his backwards-pointing feet and hunched back—was Lord Death's servant, the god who led the dead through the nine trials of the underworld, into the land of Mictlan. His nahual was a dog as black as nothingness.

I looked back at the pyramid, stunned. Xolotl's nahual was marking people for death. "But why couldn't anyone else see him?"

"Maybe my being the son of a god gives me special sight, and you've been god-touched."

"But Mazatzin saw Quetzalcoatl's nahual, so why not—" I suddenly gasped. "Did the nahual lick him too?" I started heading back.

"There's nothing you can do for him now," Little Reed said, taking my hand to stop me. "If he's marked for death, then what will happen will happen."

"But we must do something!"

He thought a moment then said, "I doubt Ahexotl would listen to such a warning, but maybe you can convince Nimilitzli."

But given how she hadn't believed me about Quetzalcoatl's nahual or the stone serpent, I doubted she would believe me about this.

□

I retired to my tent but was too anxious to sleep. I watched the shadows creep along my tent wall, waiting to see Xolotl's nahual coming for me, so when Malinalli came to fetch me, I was even more exhausted. I followed her to the Pyramid of the Feathered Serpent—named for the hundreds of stone feathered serpent heads jutting out of its walls.

"Feeling better now?" Nimilitzli asked as I sat among the others. She already sat behind a small slab of bloodstained basalt stone, a thick, folded codex lying partially open across the ground next to her. Fully expanded, it would've easily stretched from one end of the platform to the other, the pages connected together one after the other with hinges made of animal sinew.

"One of the duties of the priesthood is to divine the future using augury," Nimilitzli began. "We help the king make decisions about war, planting, or alliances. The gods leave clues for us to find in the flight of birds or the patterns of falling stars, or in animal entrails." She pulled a small, hairless dog from the basket behind her, broke its neck, then sliced the belly open and dumped the organs onto the stone slab. "Not everyone is gifted with the Sight, but anyone can learn to recognize omens through study." She motioned Iczoxochitl over. "Examine the entrails and tell me what you see."

Iczoxochitl peered down a moment then said, "I don't know what I'm looking for."

"Then consult the book."

We each took a turn examining the mess on the stone, each person seeing something different. I went last and planned on saying the same thing Malinalli had—a difficult winter ahead—but when I stepped up, the image of the skull was as clear as a real one; not just kidneys laying over the liver in just the right way. A wad of sinew glistened in the sun like a blinking eye. The hairs on my neck stood up.

"You see something?" Nimilitzli asked.

After my strange behavior that morning, who'd believe me divining a death omen? *But Nimilitzli believes in omens, so she needs to see this.* "Would you please look at it for me first? I really don't want to read this wrong."

Nimilitzli stood next to me and looked down at the stone, but showed no sign of recognition. *She doesn't see it,* I thought, crestfallen.

But then her demeanor shifted and she looked back at me, worry painting her face.

"What is it?" Turquoise Bells leaned forward for a second look.

"It's nothing." But Nimilitzli's voice trembled.

Malinalli looked again but this time she narrowed her eyes. "Wait. I think I see...I saw something like that in the book...." She flipped through the still-folded sections of the codex. "Yes, that's it."

When the other two girls crowded around, they gasped. "Who's going to die?"

Nimilitzli shooed them away and folded up the book again. "It's very easy to misread patterns when one's new to the art. Death omens are particularly rare and even then they're often confused with the signs for a harsh winter. Now return to camp and get washed up." She kicked the entrails off the stone, but when they landed in a fan, the omen was still there, even more plain than before. As the rest of us turned to leave, she took to smashing the guts against the stone floor, reducing them to mush.

I remained behind on the stairs while the others left. "Then it's what I thought it was?"

Nimilitzli glanced up and nodded. "You have the Sight, just like your mother. I never had it, and I always envied her abilities, but it's especially strong in you." She slapped her sandals together, knocking the muck off.

"I must tell you something, and I know it'll sound crazy, but...this morning, on the Pyramid of the Sun, I saw another nahual. I know nahuals are supposed to be spiritual rather than physical, but I know what I saw; it was a huge, ugly black dog, and it went around the circle sniffing everyone. It licked the cheeks of some of the men, three that I saw. Paired with this omen...something bad is coming."

Nimilitzli closed her eyes. "Quetzalpetlatl, I could excuse this ten years ago, but you're seventeen now—"

"I didn't imagine it. Topiltzin saw it too." I scowled at her. "Why don't you believe me? You're the high priestess; you're supposed to believe in this kind of thing."

"I saw the omen and I believe it—"

"But you don't believe me." Angry tears wound down my face, and I wanted to say more but it all was spiteful. Instead I ran back to camp and hid in my tent.

But I broke down into hiccupping sobs when I realized that I had no idea whether or not the Black Dog had put his mark on Nimilitzli.

CHAPTER FOURTEEN

For two days I waited for the omen to come true, but instead they passed with nerve-racking quiet. We spent most of our time meditating and practicing rituals, and I saw very little of Little Reed or the other men. Nor did I see any more signs of the Black Dog, or death omens. By our fourth day, I started doubting that I'd seen any of it at all, chalking it up to stress from the pilgrimage and the upcoming trials.

Just before sunset on the fourth day, all the novices gathered atop the Pyramid of the Sun and meditated while Ahexotl and Nimilitzli built a bonfire. Once Lord Sun's last light faded from the horizon, Ahexotl called us into a circle around the fire.

"In a matter of weeks, all of you will be initiated into the order of your choosing; the women will become the wives of their chosen god, or handmaidens to their goddess, while the men will become their god's war companion or their goddess's protector. So long as you wear that robe, you swear to forsake the ways of the mortal world; you'll live a purely spiritual life, devoting day and night to interpreting the will and desires of your god."

I stifled a laugh, hearing Ahexotl, of all people, lecturing us about living a pure spiritual life. Too bad the Black Dog passed him by.

"As part of your trials," Ahexotl continued, "you've come to the very place where the gods first came to earth, so you can meditate on the mysteries of their ways. You've learned their stories, and by now they are as familiar as your own mother's voice; but tonight we tell them again, as the first priests and priestesses told them, under the open skies of the bright heavens, with the elixir of the gods opening your minds and bodies to their divine inspiration."

Nimilitzli filled each of our earthen bowls with octli from the clay jars sitting outside the firelight. "Drink up!" Ahexotl shouted, raising his hands at us. "Imbibe the sacred octli and reach out to the gods!"

I'd never had octli before, for only full priests and priestesses were allowed to partake of it, and it was sinful for young men and women to drink it. The thick, sweet liquor burned my tongue and throat, spreading pleasant heat throughout my body.

Ahexotl threw a fistful of copalli incense into the fire, making it burn orange and smoke white, spreading the spicy aroma. "The world has expired four times now, each to a disaster designated by the name of the Sun that ruled it: the Earth, the Wind, the Fire, and the Water. Each Sun crashed and died beyond the horizon, taking all life with it and leaving the gods to begin anew with their creations.

"And so with the death of the Fourth Sun—consumed in floodwaters that extinguished its light and heat—the gods gathered where they were born and decided that one of them must make a sacrifice and become the new Sun.

"Two gods stepped forward: the handsome but selfish Tecuciztecatl, and the leper Nanahuatzin. To decide who should become the Fifth Sun, the others insisted they each offer four days of penance."

I'd heard this story so many times I could tell it while doing calendar calculations, yet I found myself listening with bated breath, as if I knew not what would happen next. Ahexotl's pacing was like a wave, first up, then down, then sideways, and it all seemed funny yet awe-inspiring all at the same time. My empty stomach gurgled—we'd fasted most of the day—so I filled it with the only thing I had to give it.

"Tecuciztecatl gathered costly tools." Ahexotl grabbed a deerskin bag and emptied it on the ground. He held each item up as he named it. "Quetzal feathers for his fir branches, gold for his grass balls, and slivers of green jade and red coral for his sacrificial thorns. And his incense was the best in the land." He threw another fistful of incense into the fire, turning it red and creating a black smoke that smelled of fragrant hardwoods. "But Nanahuatzin, being only a poor leper, gathered green water rushes, bound in threes for a total of nine bundles. He made his grass balls of dried pine needles, and he cut his spines from the sacred maguey, and painted them with his own blood. And for his incense, he picked off his scabs and burned them." Ahexotl threw more copalli into the flames, overpowering the smell of the other incense. I inhaled deep, enjoying the aroma. I watched Ahexotl run around the bonfire, fascinated, like watching a viper swallow a chipmunk.

"And so the two did their penance and fasted while the others built a great fire—the Teotexcalli. When the two gods finished, the others dressed them for the sacrifice. They gave Tecuciztecatl the finest clothes: a long cotton xicolli shirt and a round, forked heron-feather headdress, and they plugged his earlobes with gold spindles and hung more gold around his neck. Then they dressed Nanahuatzin in paper: a paper breechcloth, a paper stole, and a paper headdress. Then the gods gathered around the fire and implored Tecuciztecatl to cast himself into the flames, to make the sun rise again.

"But when he stepped near the fire, the intense flames jumped so high that he hesitated." Everyone gasped in awe when Ahexotl threw something into the bonfire and the orange flames leaped for the heavens. "He tried again, but again he backed away. Four times he tried to cast himself into the Teotexcalli, but four times his courage failed him.

"So the gods called on Nanahuatzin to make the sun rise, and he flung himself into the fire without hesitation. His body turned to ash and the gods sang his praises and danced in his honor.

"Now to your feet, so we too may dance and sing Lord Sun's praises!" Ahexotl shouted.

We sang and danced around the fire, some of us more clumsily than others. I found a spot next to Little Reed and grabbed his hand, laughing and slurring the lyrics of the sacred hymn to Fiery Lord Sun. The smell of copalli made me feel like I was flying. Ahexotl soon told us to return to the circle, but in a moment of madness, I whipped Little Reed closer and whispered, "I love you." I desperately wanted to kiss him, right in front of everyone, but when Nimilitzli admonished us to get back to our mats, I found the will to let him go. Little Reed stumbled backwards, a half smile on his face as he stared back. He almost stepped over the edge of the pyramid, but Mazatzin caught him and helped him sit down again. Little Reed laughed and clapped him on the back, but he didn't take his eyes off me. I hid my smile by drinking more octli.

"And so Nanahuatzin jumped into the fire and became Lord Fifth Sun," Ahexotl went on. "But Nanahuatzin's courage so shamed Tecuciztecatl that he finally flung himself into the flames as well, and he too burned up. The gods gathered at the four directions, to see where the new Sun would rise, and when he rose in the east, he blinded everyone who dared stare upon his brilliance.

"But another Sun rose as well, and the land scorched and the light blinded. Nothing could live there—"

"And Ehecatl said 'This is no good!'" Little Reed yelled, holding his bowl aloft with a laugh. "'There can't be two Suns!' and he threw a rabbit at Tecuciztecatl and hit him in the face, *smack!* and the cowardly Tecuciztecatl became the Moon." He drained his bowl then asked, "But how could there have been a rabbit there when the Fourth Sun took all life with him?"

I giggled, but Ahexotl gave Little Reed a glare. He might not have liked the interruption, but it was a very good observation.

◻

I don't know how late it was when Ahexotl and Nimilitzli extinguished the bonfire and the soldiers came to escort us back to camp, but Little Reed had passed out before Ahexotl finished his telling of Quetzalcoatl's journey into the underworld to rescue the bones of humanity. I'd given up on the octli shortly after he'd passed out; the whole situation was far less interesting without him smiling and winking at me across the circle.

I felt feverish and so thirsty, and when I tried getting to my feet, the whole world seemed to move under me. Two soldiers had to carry Little Reed down off the pyramid.

Back at camp, Nimilitzli made us drink water and eat some tlaxcallis before letting us go to bed. That quenched my parched throat but the sour ache in my stomach remained; soon I felt I was burning up, and not even taking off my blanket helped. I stripped down to my undergarment, but my tent was like a steam bath and my stomach felt as if someone was squeezing it.

Dear gods, I hope no one saw me leering at Little Reed! I thought, adding to the rebellion in my stomach. I couldn't believe I'd actually confessed my love to him like that. Anyone could have seen and read my lips. *Now everyone will say you've earned the title of whore.* How would I ever face Little Reed in the morning?

I finally listened to my abdominal pains and donned my robe and headed for the water yard, hoping I wouldn't vomit in the courtyard. "You want an escort?" one of the guards asked when I hurried by at a run. I only shook my head and ran faster.

I made it a few paces inside the yard before vomiting. I fell to my knees, panting and heaving as my stomach convulsed until there was nothing left to expel. I crawled to the water jar and scooped up handfuls of the cool liquid to rinse my mouth out, my nose stinging. I knelt against the water jar, waiting for the overheating to pass and my legs to feel capable of holding me up again.

"Someone should have told you to slow down with the octli," Ahexotl suddenly said behind me.

I spun around, my senses shocked into high alert. My robe caught on the lip of the jar and I almost de-robed myself as I fell over the side of it. When Ahexotl stood there, grinning at my near nakedness, I covered up clumsily. "What are you doing here?"

"I heard someone getting ill, so I came to see if I could help."

"I don't need your help." I staggered to my feet, my head swimming, making my tongue quick to release my rising temper. "I'm just fine. Nimilitzli is waiting for me—"

But he blocked me. "She would've come down here with you if she was really awake." His eyes roved over me as he added, "You owe me a favor and I think I'll collect on that now."

"I owe you nothing. You forget whom you answer to, Ahexotl, and someday that power you dishonor will make you pay."

He grabbed my arms and shoved me back against the water jar, sending a jolt of pain up my spine. "Your righteous indignation makes me hard, my dear. Just remember that it was by my mercy that you're not a prostitute, pleasuring men for whatever they're willing to pay when they come shaking your door bells." He plastered his lips over mine and forced his tongue into my mouth.

I pushed back, but he was too big, and my dagger sheath had slid around to my back. I snaked my hands up under his robe and clawed his bare belly.

He cursed and smacked me, making my ears ring. "If you want it rough, I'll oblige you." He flipped me around, and when I pushed back he held my neck down so my nose touched the water in the jar. "Fight me or make any noise, and I'll hold your head under. Keep your mouth shut and this will be over soon." My silent tears broke loose as he yanked my robe up past my waist. "And don't worry, I'll leave you virginal enough to pass the physical examination, and you can owe me again for that favor."

This can't be happening, dear gods this can't be happening! I fumbled around again for my knife, hoping it was within my reach now. My fingers found the stag horn handle and I snatched the blade out then drove it backwards into Ahexotl's leg, and twisted it.

It didn't go in very deep, but he howled and let me go. I fell over sideways, yanking the knife out as I went down. I slashed at him again, this time slicing through the tendon on his left heel. He tried to jump away, but instead crashed to the ground, gritting his teeth as he clutched his ankle.

I hurried to my feet, and once out of his reach I stood panting and staring down at him, disgust stamping out my fear. "I told you Quetzalcoatl would make you answer for yourself." I spat on him then left, shaking from the pride pumping through my veins. *Now to wake Nimilitzli. He's finally going to have to answer for himself.*

The moon had gone down over the mountains, leaving the passageway in pitch black save for the dim glow from the courtyard doorway still far away. Hearing a patter of feet behind me, I whirled and stared into the darkness, my mother's sacrificial blade still ready in my hand.

Past the water yard, two guards stood sentry in the dim glow from the men's courtyard. *It's probably just an animal,* I decided, continuing on my way. *Or maybe it's Xolotl's nahual again.* I picked up the pace.

The sudden clatter of weapons on stone made me look back again. The guards were gone. I stared, trying to work out where they'd gone, but then realized I was scratching my wrist. It hadn't bothered me in years, but now it itched so fiercely I could claw it raw. I ran for my own camp as fast as I could.

The guards raised their spears and called for me to halt as I emerged from the darkness. One grabbed me by the arm as I tried to run by. Shouts erupted down the passageway from the men's camp and the guard shoved me into the courtyard. "Rouse the others."

I flung the flaps aside on Nimilitzli's tent. "Wake up! There's trouble!"

She blinked at me, disoriented. "What?"

"The omen." I hurried to wake the others.

By the time everyone came hobbling out of their tents, the shouts had turned to screams. "What in the name of the Feathered Serpent is going on?" Nimilitzli demanded at the courtyard entrance.

Another soldier limped out of the darkness. "A Chichimec raiding party has taken the men's camp. We're trying to hold them back at the water yard, but there are at least a hundred of them! If you put the fire out and stay quiet—"

But an arrow pierced his neck and he gagged. Another buried itself in his back and he collapsed through the entryway, falling into Nimilitzli's arms and knocking her to the ground. Turquoise Bells and Iczoxochitl screamed. One guard charged off into the dark, spear ready as he shouted for blood. The remaining guard took an arrow to the head and slid down the wall.

When Malinalli and I pushed the dead man off Nimilitzli, she look dazed and frightened, making me wonder if she'd hit her head. "Everybody out through the hole in the wall behind Turquoise Bells's tent. *Now!*" I shouted. Malinalli and I put Nimilitzli's arms over our shoulders and helped her limp to the back of the courtyard. The hole wasn't big enough for her, so I kicked out some of the crumbling stonework to make way.

Just as Nimilitzli cleared the hole, two raiders crept into the courtyard, one armed with bow and arrows, the other with a flint ax. I ducked down just as an arrow chinked off the stone above my head then I hurried through the hole and crouched beside the others. When one of the men began climbing through, I kicked him in the head, knocking him unconscious.

"Where to now?" Malinalli whispered.

The courtyard we were in now had crumbling walls in the back corner, so I ordered everyone in that direction. "We'll climb over into the passage then go north."

Nimilitzli nodded. "Our best hope is to head for the temples."

While the others crossed over the wall, I helped Nimilitzli climb up, but—to my horror—when she slid over the top, she lost her balance and hit the ground on the other side with a thud and a cry.

"Nimilitzli! What happened? Is she all right?" I moved a few steps down the wall before climbing over myself.

Malinalli and I tried lifting her to her feet again, but she gripped my arm with painful strength. "I think I broke my hip."

"Are you sure?"

She tried to move again but went over immediately.

The distant shouting grew louder again, no doubt responding to my cry.

Nimilitzli grabbed my sleeve. "You need to lead the others to safety, Quetzalpetlatl."

"I'm not going anywhere without you!"

"You must. I'll only slow you down."

I'd already lost one mother, and I'd rather never find eternal rest in Mictlan than leave Nimilitzli to die too. "Malinalli and I will carry you. No one's getting left behind."

Malinalli grabbed Nimilitzli under the arms and I took her legs, and together we hefted her into the air between us. "Fools! Put me down!" Nimilitzli scolded us between gasps of pain as we took off jogging down the passageway, Turquoise Bells and Iczoxochitl leading the way.

We wound through the passages until we came out onto the sacred precinct. The Pyramid of the Moon stood outlined against the starry sky ahead of us. "Go there," I panted. When we reached its base, Turquoise Bells and Iczoxochitl hurried ahead while Malinalli and I struggled under Nimilitzli's weight. By the time we reached the summit, my legs felt afire and I thought my arms might drop out of their sockets.

"They're everywhere!" Iczoxochitl whispered as she crouched at the edge, staring over the city. Moving spots of torchlight spread out in every direction, and the men's camp was ablaze with bonfires. "Do you think they killed all the men?"

"My brother's out there," Turquoise Bells sobbed. "Oh Merciful Quetzalcoatl, please let him be all right!"

I whispered my own prayer for Little Reed. *You must find a way to call Quetzalcoatl*, I thought.

"Oh no, they're coming!" Iczoxochitl backed away from the edge and tripped over the fire ring. Below us, the spots of orange spread out over the precinct, and a few came in our direction. "What should we do?"

Malinalli picked up a stone from the fire ring. "I'm a pretty decent shot with rocks. My brother taught me to hunt monkeys with them." With Iczoxochitl's help, they moved all the rocks to a pile by the stairs and Malinalli started telling her how to throw straight and hard.

I left them to it and returned to Nimilitzli's side, hoping for a little solitude to work out what I needed to do. *Last time you gave blood and promised devotion, but the nahual said each sacrifice demands more. All sacrifices involve blood, so that must be part of it, but what more is required?* I glanced back out over the city again. *Oh, you must hurry! You don't know how long Little Reed has, so focus! What kinds of sacrifices does Quetzalcoatl ask of us? How do we show our devotion to him?*

"What are you doing?" Nimilitzli asked, pain in her eyes.

"Trying to work something out."

"Work out what?"

I hesitated then said, "What sacrifice to make to call on Quetzalcoatl."

"Quetzalpetlatl—"

"I don't have time to argue about this."

"You'd be wiser to focus on getting through the night—"

"I am! Quetzalcoatl gave me something truly powerful to call on when all else fails, and while we argue this, the men are dying. Your hip is broken and we're surrounded by Chichimecs bent on killing all of us. What else can I do?" I loved Nimilitzli, but it angered me that she still didn't believe me.

"I told you to leave me behind so you all could get away."

"And I'm not leaving you behind!" Hot with anger, I went to the back of the summit and sat with my back to her.

Turquoise Bells came over next and I almost snapped that now wasn't the time for her latest jealous outburst about Red Flint. "You're trying to find a way out for us, right?"

"Of course. But I need quiet. It's hard enough concentrating with Chichimecs bearing down on us—"

"I know, and that blasted octli! My head is throbbing. Why do the gods ask us to suffer so much for them?"

I started to ask her to give me some peace, but suddenly there was the answer: *They ask us to suffer for them.* The gods always suffered in one way or another in the stories, like when Quetzalcoatl climbed a mountain of obsidian blades in his bare feet to reach the underworld and rescue the bones of humanity. And he cut his tepolli to give mankind life. For a man there wasn't a more painful place to cut himself.

"Oh no, they're coming!" Iczoxochitl shouted and Malinalli hissed at her to quiet down. I hurried over.

Two animal-skin-clad Chichimecs came up the steps, one carrying a torch but both carrying obsidian-bladed spears bearing red and blue feathers: Culhuacan's colors.

"Aim for the nose," Malinalli said then she threw the first stone. It caught the lead man on the cheek, leaving a nasty red gash and knocking him backwards, but his companion caught him. Iczoxochitl's weak toss landed on the steps well before the men but it bounced and hit the lead raider in the stomach. He charged up the stairs. Malinalli's next shot hit him between the eyes, and this time he rolled down head over feet, almost knocking over the other man.

The commotion caught the attention of others in the precinct and their flaring torches showed them approaching us fast. Soon we'd have more Chichimecs storming the pyramid than we had rocks to throw. I had to do something now.

But what should I give? I looked around. My gaze eventually fell to my hands. *Maybe a finger,* I thought, but my stomach churned. *No, something else, something less—*

Less painful? Just imagine what Quetzalcoatl's feet must have look like after he came down off the mountain of obsidian blades; he cut his most delicate part so mankind might live, and you shrink from losing a finger? Nothing less than two would be a worthy sacrifice.

I knelt next to the stone slab where the altar once stood. "Turquoise Bells, come over here. I need your help."

She knelt next to me.

"Hold my fingers down for me, keeping the first three fingers together, like this, and don't let go. Understood?"

"I think so, but what's this all about?"

I untied my undergarment and set it on the stone too. "When I'm done, if I haven't the mind to do it myself, you need to wrap this around my hand."

"What are you doing?" Nimilitzli asked behind Turquoise Bells, her voice awash with fresh fear.

"I'm making a sacrifice." I drew my blade. The knife felt awkward in my left hand.

"Quetzalpetlatl, this is foolishness—"

"Hold my hand still," I told Turquoise Bells.

"You're going to cut a finger off?" Turquoise Bells demanded. "What craziness is this?"

"Hold my hand."

"Is this some sick penance over Red Flint—?"

"Forget Red Flint! This is about saving our lives, because who knows what demon gods those Chichimecs will sacrifice us to. Now hold my hand down!"

She complied but turned her head and closed her eyes. I took a deep breath and poised the blade over the knuckle of my small finger.

"Don't do this, Quetzalpetlatl!" Nimilitzli tried to crawl to me but fell over in a wail of agony.

"Trust in the god, Nimilitzli." I gritted my teeth and started sawing into my knuckle.

Little Reed had replaced my blade before we left, so it went right through the flesh and sinew, holding up a bit in the knuckle joint. But soon my little finger lay detached on the stone in a pool of blood. And the pain...it burned like a flame, making my hand pulse with agony and throb with heat. I paused to take deep, calming breaths and then I started into the next finger. Sweat slicked my left hand, making me stop halfway through to wipe it dry on my robe. I felt cold and dizzy, and where I could hear my heart pounding in my ears before, now everything fell quiet, as if I were drifting away. I was taking too long and bleeding too much. I needed to finish before I passed out. With two final sawing motions, I cut the finger loose.

Turquoise Bells grabbed my hand and wrapped my undergarment around it as Nimilitzli gave her hurried directions on how to tie it to staunch the bleeding. I watched, marveling at how much blood pooled on the stone. At the back of my mind I wondered if I'd ever be able to grip my knife with my right hand again.

"Isn't this supposed to do something?" Turquoise Bells shouted, looking from me to the stairs. I looked too, feeling as if I was floating. Malinalli threw the last stone and Chichimecs came thundering up the stairs. I was forgetting something....

Nimilitzli pulled my sleeve. "You need to pray to Quetzalcoatl. That's what you told me you did last time, so focus. Remember why you made the sacrifice."

My wits leaped back at me. *For Little Reed, and for you, Nimilitzli.* I set both hands in the blood then raised them to the sky:

"Merciful Quetzalcoatl,
Hear my plea!
Come aid your son,
For he lies in the hands of his mortal enemy,
And those he loves face certain death.
Help me save him, My Lord!
Help me save us all!"

Hot orange flames engulfed the stone in front of me, and I grabbed Nimilitzi's arm and dragged her away as it grew larger. Turquoise Bells fled shrieking. Iczoxochitl and Malinalli looked back at the fire with wide eyes, and the Chichimecs behind them stared too, their mouths hanging open.

The fire formed a towering column that sprouted a serpent head with tentacles of sunlight radiating from its neck. Through the back of its swirling head red spots burned for eyes, and when it opened its flaming mouth, it roared like a devastating wind.

The Chichimecs fled down the stairs, but the fire serpent leaped after them, turning their yells to death screams. I crawled to the edge to watch the flaming serpent race through the precinct, reducing fleeing Chichimecs to cinders. It squeezed down the main walkway, shooting smaller fire snakes into the outlying courtyards and passageways. In the distance a few torch lights fled, but soon the flames were everywhere.

"Great Feathered Serpent!" Nimilitzli breathed.

"How did you do that?" Iczoxochitl panted, staring at me with both awe and fear.

I stared down at the stone. My sacrifice was gone, the fingers reduced to ash and the blood boiled away. *At least Little Reed is safe,* I thought, dizziness seizing me again. Nimilitzli called to me, but the darkness swooped down on me like a cloud of bats, and I vaguely recalled a dull pain on the side of my head as it struck the stones.

CHAPTER FIFTEEN

I awoke to Malinalli tending to me with a cool rag. My hand throbbed and when I lifted it to look at, it was stitched closed where I'd cut off my fingers. "Nimilitzli showed me how to do it," she said. I sat up, my head swimming and my stomach feeling like I hadn't eaten in days. "Take it slowly. I gave you some tochtetepon to keep you asleep while I stitched you up."

I clutched my forehead with my now three-fingered hand. "Where's Nimilitzli?"

"Over there."

Little Reed sat next to Nimilitzli, who lay on a mat in the corner of the courtyard, a half-burned tent giving her cover from the sun. It brought me to tears to see them both alive. "How are the others? How many people did we lose?"

"None of the women, but we lost every soldier and three of the male novices. Only Topiltzin, Mazatzin, and Lord Talking Serpent remain."

"What about Ahexotl?"

"He's alive, but badly burned."

Of all the indignities...if anyone deserved the god's flaming wrath, it was him. "I should go talk to Topiltzin."

Malinalli helped me to my feet. "I'll get you something to eat. That'll help with the dizziness."

While Malinalli went to the cooking fire, I hobbled over to Nimilitzli. Little Reed sprang to his feet and embraced me with crushing strength. "Thank Omeyocan you're all right," he murmured. He took my hand in his and shook his head. "The god really asked that much of you?"

"He wasn't in a talking mood, and I had to make a quick decision." I touched the skin under the stitched gash on his forehead, examining it.

But he pulled away from me, looking uncomfortable. "It's nothing. I don't even remember getting it. I don't remember much of anything about last night. The octli...."

Then he didn't remember my moment of lustful insanity. *It'll spare you the embarrassment of having to explain yourself,* I thought, relieved.

Nimilitzli examined my hand as well. "With some relearning, you should still be able to wield your knife with just those three fingers." She shook her head, frowning. "I owe you an apology, Quetzalpetlatl, for not trusting your claims before. You had every right to be angry with me."

"I shouldn't have been. I expected you to believe me without any real proof beyond an omen and my word."

"I'll never again doubt what you say concerning the god."

"You really should get some sleep, Mother," Little Reed said. "We have much to do if we're going to carry you and Ahexotl out of here tomorrow."

We left Nimilitzli to rest and Malinalli brought me a couple of hot tlaxcallis. I ate while Little Reed and I walked to the water yard to see Ahexotl.

"We've left him there for now, for he's in too much pain to move," Little Reed said. "Would you take a look at him, to make sure there aren't any immediate concerns? I need to get directions to the nearest city and he's the only one of us who knows anything about this area."

"I suppose we need him for something then," I muttered, disgusted. *But maybe the god spared him because he saw something good in him.* I couldn't imagine what that might be, but I had to respect Quetzalcoatl's decision. When Little Reed gave me a shocked frown, I decided it was time to tell him the truth.

And I left nothing out, from what Red Flint and I witnessed in the laundry room to the attack in the water yard last night. When I finished, Little Reed's face was flushed with rage, and he wouldn't look at me anymore, bringing me to anguished tears. "You think I brought this on myself, don't you?"

"No one brings such things on themselves," Little Reed said. "The man's an abomination and he'll pay for darkening the god's good name." Taking his sword in hand, he walked faster towards the water yard.

I cut him off though. "I share your outrage, Little Reed, but the god spared him."

"Only so I could reap justice myself." He stepped around me.

But I intercepted him again. "The god stopped short of killing him for some reason. We'd do best to respect his decision."

"Quetzalcoatl spared him because he didn't realize the magnitude of the man's crimes."

"Of course he knows; he knows everything, and I won't let you anger him on account of my honor, which is hardly clean to begin with."

Little Reed sighed. "Don't dwell on your mistakes, Papalotl. We all make them." He kissed my forehead and smiled. "I will spare Ahexotl because I cannot bear the thought of disappointing you."

Mazatzin limped out of the entryway of the water yard, looking worn but blessedly alive. I laughed as I wrapped my arms around his neck. "I'm so glad you're all right!"

He hugged me back. "Not that the Chichimecs didn't try to sacrifice me. I killed two before they were able to drag me out of your brother's tent."

Little Reed set a hand on Mazatzin's shoulder. "While I lay passed out, he stood in my defense. The Chichimecs would've cut my heart out to their demon Smoking Mirror if not for him."

Mazatzin blushed and murmured something about how it was his honor to defend him, then he led us to the tent set up where I'd left Ahexotl after I'd cut his heel.

Lord Talking Serpent—who was completely unscathed—knelt praying over Ahexotl in a shaky voice. Ahexotl was undressed but covered from the chest down with a blanket. He groaned when he saw me.

"Has he had any tochtetepon yet?" I asked.

"A little while ago," Lord Talking Serpent answered.

I pulled the blanket back, making sure it didn't stick. The scorched flesh started just above his navel and went all the way down to his feet, with everything in between a mess of blackened skin and colorful oozing.

I sent Talking Serpent and Mazatzin to fetch some water from the creek outside town and I gave Ahexotl some more tochtetepon in octli, to prepare him for his bath. "You'd better question him now, before they get back," I told Little Reed. "He won't be coherent once I start working on him."

I feared Little Reed might take the opportunity to confront Ahexotl with what I'd told him, but he kept his temper and asked only about the nearby cities and how to get to them. He finished by the time the others returned with the water, but he remained in the tent with me while I worked, as if not trusting Ahexotl to be alone with me even in his terrible condition.

I cleaned Ahexotl's blisters and smeared ointment over them while he howled in agony. His tepolli was mangled beyond recognition, but it still gave me the shakes having to touch it. *The god made sure he'll never abuse his priestesses again,* I thought, my pity surprising me. I should have relished his pain, but instead I felt sick and wondered if death would have been more been merciful than this. Once the tochtetepon took hold, he lay drooling and only half aware of what was going on as I wrapped him in bandages. We then moved him to the main camp on a makeshift litter.

Little Reed then called everyone to a meeting around the fire. "Having discussed matters with Ahexotl and Nimilitzli, I've decided that it's not safe to remain here. Our leaders need more medical attention than any of us are fit to provide, and though the fire serpent wiped out the Chichimec raiding party, Ihuitimal will send more to finish what the others failed to. We must leave and find help. Ahexotl recommended we head for Acolman, which is half a day journey from here."

"But who's going to carry Ahexotl and Nimilitzli?" Turquoise Bells asked. "Neither of them can walk."

"We'll have to carry them," I said.

"Impossible!"

"Leaving anyone behind while Topiltzin and Mazatzin go to Acolman is impossible. None of us are prepared to defend ourselves if more Chichimecs come."

"You can protect us—"

"The safest option is for everyone to go together," I insisted, annoyed that she would talk about my ability to call on the god as if it were as easy as ordering food from the royal kitchens. "And all of us will help carry the litters."

Malinalli nodded. "The four of us can easily carry Nimilitzli. Quetzalpetlatl and I carried her up the temple steps last night by ourselves, and this time we'll have a litter for her to sit in."

"This isn't impossible," I said. "If we all work together, we can do anything."

Iczoxochitl nodded, but Turquoise Bells frowned.

"And two men can carry Ahexotl," Little Reed continued. "But we'll need to make a new litter so he can lay flat. I need volunteers to gather wood outside the city."

"I can help with that," Malinalli said. "I've felled trees before."

"Go with Mazatzin. Talking Serpent, take a bow and keep sentry on the southernmost wall. Alert me immediately if you see anyone approaching. And you two—" He gestured to Turquoise Bells and Iczoxochitl. "—I need you to cook tlaxcallis for the trip. Quetzalpetlatl and I will go find weapons for everyone. No one is to go wandering alone." As everyone stood to go to their duties, he called for their attention one last time. "And while we all know we're only alive because Quetzalpetlatl performed a miracle, when we get to Acolman, it is sufficient to say we fought off our Chichimec attackers ourselves. If she wishes to tell others what she did, that's her choice, but I won't have strangers cornering her into answering questions she doesn't want to answer. Whatever you saw here is between yourself and the god." He turned a pointed stare at Turquoise Bells and Iczoxochitl. "Understood?"

Everyone nodded but Turquoise Bells cast me a scornful frown as I followed Little Reed out of the yard.

◻

Little Reed and I scavenged weapons from the dead soldiers then returned to camp to help finish packing. At sunset we made prayers to the god for a safe journey, then we left Teotihuacan and struck out west down the road, back towards Lake Meztliapan. While the rest of us carried the litters, Little Reed walked ahead, sword in hand, making sure the road was clear. The moon rose behind us, lighting our way with soft white light.

Soon my shoulder ached under the litter's weight, and no matter where I held my hand, it was uncomfortable. It throbbed if I dangled it at my side but turned numb if I propped it up on the carrying pole, hurting even worse when I lowered it again. With nothing to keep my mind off the pain, we seemed to creep through the night. I felt lightheaded from the constant pain, and the litter's jerking motion frayed my nerves. None of us women knew anything about carrying a litter and so did a poor job of matching strides.

"Are you feeling all right?" Mazatzin whispered as he walked next to me. He carried the front of Ahexotl's litter with both hands at his sides, the better to keep Ahexotl from rolling off in his delirium.

"Why is everyone always asking me that?" I snapped, annoyed.

"You don't look well, and Turquoise Bells said you lost a lot of blood."

My face heated up. "Please excuse my short temper. You're right; I'm not feeling very well. My hand hurts like nothing else, and now my shoulders are numb." I tried to laugh but it came out pathetic. "This hasn't been a good pilgrimage for me."

"Or for any of us," he said with a smile. "I can't wait to get back home and sleep on my own mat in the dormitories again." He called ahead and Little Reed dropped back to walk between us. "Quetzalpetlatl needs a rest, and I'm sure the other women could use one as well."

Little Reed slipped his shoulder under the pole, freeing me of the weight. "We'll be to the forest soon and we'll stop once we're in the trees. I'll carry this the rest of the way."

I offered to carry his pack, but he refused, so I drew my sword and walked ahead to keep lookout. It felt strange and unwieldy in my left hand, so hopefully I wouldn't have to use it.

When we reached the forest, we followed the narrow trail for a while before venturing off into the trees, slowly maneuvering the litters among the trunks. Once we were far enough off the trail to not be seen, we made hasty camp, forgoing any fire to stay as undetectable as possible.

"We're running out of yauhtli for their pain," I told Little Reed after giving Ahexotl a dose when he started moaning and whimpering on his litter. "If I give some to Nimilitzli, we won't have enough for Ahexotl in the morning and our trying to stay quiet will matter for nothing."

Little Reed looked over at Nimilitzli. "You know she'll refuse more if she knows we're running out, but I'd rather she refuse it than us deny her."

When we told Nimilitzli the situation, she told me not to worry about her. "The pain isn't so bad," she told me. "How's your hand?"

"It's fine. I know you're worried for me, but your hip is far worse than my hand."

"As your mother, it's my prerogative to worry about you," she said. "So stop trying to shield me from that honor."

I laughed and tucked her under the blanket. She'd never called herself my mother before; she'd always been Little Reed's mother, for she was the only one he'd ever known, and no doubt she'd refrained from calling herself mine out of respect for my real mother. But it warmed me to finally hear her acknowledge how I'd always thought of her. "Good night to you too, Mother," I whispered, and kissed her forehead.

Chapter Sixteen

I slept fitfully but after a while I gave up on it. I thought about taking some of the yauhtli, to dull the throbbing in my hand, but both Ahexotl and Nimilitzli needed it more. I sat up and looked around for Little Reed.

"You should be sleeping," he said from behind me, where he sat against a large tree, his obsidian-edged sword balanced on his knees. He turned his head sharply when a jaguar called in the distance, adding its coughing sound to the cacophony of insects and night birds.

I went and sat next to him. "I did sleep."

"Is your hand bothering you?"

"A little."

"I'm sorry."

I laughed. "You have nothing to be sorry about. It saved everyone and that's worth the pain."

He set his hand over mine, giving the good side a gentle squeeze, making my heart soar. "Maybe you should sleep and I can keep watch," I suggested, heat traveling up my body from my belly. Now wasn't the time for such foolishness.

"I can't sleep either. Too much thinking."

"About what?"

"Remember all those reports about Chichimec raiders ambushing the roads along the west side of the lake in the week before we left, when I was supposed to leave for the army? The Chichimecs who came to Teotihuacan were wearing Culhuacan's colors."

"You think there's a spy in Xochicalco?"

He nodded. "Either in Cuitlapanton's court, or in the priesthood. Our uncle had no luck trying to assassinate me inside the city, so it's logical he'd wait until I was setting out on campaign, so he could attack me with actual troops. And he's planted spies once, so who's to say he didn't do it again, to monitor what I'm doing."

"We should alert the king, so he can launch an investigation."

Rustling sounds along the trail brought us both to silence, and Little Reed grabbed his sword. I couldn't see anything in the dark, but the noise grew louder. Soon I heard voices.

"Go wake the men and send them over," Little Reed whispered, then crept to another tree, closer to the trail.

I woke Mazatzin and Talking Serpent and they joined Little Reed at the edge of camp. I also woke the women, in case we needed to leave in a hurry. We huddled around Nimilitzli.

As the voices grew closer, I could distinguish two different ones, but judging from the footfalls there were more people. Mazatzin crept off to the left and Talking Serpent to the right.

"I hope they're friendly," Iczoxochitl whispered next to me. I hoped so too; we deserved a good run of luck.

But my wrist already itched like the previous night. I started to signal Little Reed, but then I heard a bowstring pull tight behind me.

Three men stood over us, all armed with ready arrows. Iczoxochitl squeaked in terror.

Roused by the noise, Little Reed came to his feet and one of the men shot him in the shoulder, flinging him back. I started getting to my feet, but Little Reed held his hand up as more men rushed the camp, swords drawn. Both Mazatzin and Talking Serpent scrambled to stand between them and Little Reed, but the soldiers knocked them aside easily, bloodying Lord Talking Serpent's nose. Mazatzin tried to raise his sword but one of the archers laid an arrow between his shoulder blades.

I reached for my knife, prepared to cut the rest of my fingers off to save us, but the archer nearest me jabbed an arrow at my throat. "Don't," he said.

Still more soldiers gathered around our men. The leader paced in front of them, looking each over by torchlight. None of the soldiers wore Culhuacan's colors, but I trusted my itching wrist.

The leader stopped in front of Little Reed and leaned closer. He then bent over Mazatzin. "Which of you is Topiltzin?"

"I am." Mazatzin ground out the words. Turquoise Bells gasped and he shot her a warning glare but then sat taller, beads of sweat betraying his pain. "I'm Lord Topiltzin, son of Culhuacan's rightful king, Mixcoatl." Beside him, Little Reed watched, shocked.

"Are you now?" The leader knelt in front of Mazatzin. "Are you sure?"

"I know who I am," he panted.

The man grabbed and twisted the arrow, making Mazatzin writhe. I moved my hand towards my knife again, but the soldier poked me again with his arrow.

"Are you still sure?"

Mazatzin nodded, tears flowing down his cheeks.

"Let's just send all their heads back," the torchbearer replied. "Let Ihuitimal sort it out."

An arrow hissed through the air and struck the leader between the shoulders. He whirled, roaring in both pain and astonishment, and was met by two more arrows, one to the shoulder, the other in his eye. He fell atop Little Reed as the torchbearer took an arrow to the neck, and he too collapsed, trapping Little Reed under a pile of death. Still more arrows flew, from both directions.

Shouts and screams filled the night, mostly provided by Turquoise Bells and Iczoxochitl as they clung to each other. I laid low a moment then crawled to help Little Reed claw his way out from under the dead soldiers. Most of the men had gathered at the back of our camp, where the first set of archers had sneaked up on us, and they'd dragged Mazatzin with them.

I grabbed the torchbearer's sparse clothes and pulled him off the pile so Little Reed could finally worm his way out from under the other body. He shoved me behind him and wielded his sword one-handed as a soldier came at us. While he parried the soldier's blows, I snatched up the leader's sword and swung it too, making the man raise his arms and expose his belly. Little Reed swiped him, spilling his guts on the ground. He went down, and Little Reed finished him off with a quick slash to the throat.

Malinalli had found a sword as well and stood guard over Nimilitzli, but the soldiers were too busy dodging arrows or dying to pay her any mind. Soon only two remained, crouched behind a log to shelter from the arrows. She tossed her sword to Mazatzin who crept up behind and felled them one after the other.

More soldiers flooded from the trees and gathered around us, weapons drawn. Mazatzin backed towards Little Reed and me, sword still ready. I refused to drop my sword too when I saw they wore the same green and white as the soldiers who'd beset us.

A man wearing a wooden helmet shaped like an eagle's head and a xicolli covered in brown and white feathers cut through the crowd. "Put your swords down. We're not here to hurt you." Mazatzin refused, so he turned to his men and ordered them to lower their weapons. "We have no disputes with the priesthood of Quetzalcoatl."

"And I protect the god's own flesh," Mazatzin replied.

Little Reed struggled to his feet, gripping onto Mazatzin's arm for support. "Put it away, my friend. Your loyalty is inspiring, and I thank you for it."

Mazatzin lowered his sword but kept his gaze fixed on the man.

The man bowed. "I'm Lord Citlallotoc, son of the rightful king of Acolman. My men and I mutinied when Ihuitimal's spies infiltrated the king's council and assassinated him. One of Ihuitimal's men now sits on my throne, but those loyal to me have joined Xochicalco's allied forces."

"We were on pilgrimage in Teotihuacan when we were beset by Chichimecs bearing Culhuacan's colors," Little Reed replied. "We were on our way to Acolman, seeking aid, but now I must thank you for saving us from my uncle once again."

Citlallotoc squinted at him. "You're Lord Topiltzin?"

Little Reed nodded. "And this is my good friend Lord Mazatzin, son of King Cuitlapanton of Xochicalco, and this is my sister, Lady Quetzalpetlatl."

Citlallotoc nodded to each of us in turn. His gaze lingered on me a moment before he told Little Reed, "It's very good fortune we found you then. We'll take you across the lake to the allied military camp so our surgeons can tend to your wounded. How bad are they?"

"Our high priestess suffered a broken hip and our high priest was severely burned," I said. "And now both my brother and Lord Mazatzin have fresh battle injuries."

Mazatzin looked down at the arrowhead sticking from his chest, then collapsed. Little Reed and Citlallotoc caught and eased him to the ground. "We should tend to both of you before we leave," Citlallotoc suggested. "It'll take until morning to reach our boats at the lake's edge."

"Will you see to Mazatzin?" Little Reed asked me.

"You need your arrow extracted too," I reminded him.

"It barely hurts—"

"For once stop trying to be the big tough warrior and let me help you."

Citlallotoc grinned. "You do need to be tended to. Leave the rest to me."

Little Reed avoided my gaze as Citlallotoc walked away. "We could have discussed this privately, once we were alone," he muttered.

I sighed. "I'm sorry I humiliated you, but a good leader knows when he should see to his own health for the benefit of those he leads, Little Reed."

□

Only three canoes awaited us at the lake's edge, so half of Citlallotoc's men had to stay behind to make room for us. Little Reed offered to stay behind with them, in case more troops came from Acolman, but Citlallotoc insisted he come along. "I won't leave any wounded man behind. It could mean the difference between your arm healing or having to burn your body for the funeral."

I rode with the women during the crossing and it gladdened me to see Little Reed and Citlallotoc deep in conversation the whole time. "And he thought it would be difficult to gain the other men's loyalty," I told Nimilitzli.

"But he also needs friends," Nimilitzli said. "Someone he can talk to about more than just politics and religion." She set her hand on mine and added, "You need someone too, Quetzalpetlatl." She looked over at Malinalli who sat apart from the other two women.

"You two seem to get along best of any of the girls at the calmecac."

Nimilitzli was right. If not for Little Reed, I wouldn't have had any friends at all growing up. Being the high priestess's foster daughter meant most girls didn't trust me not to tell their secrets to Nimilitzli. I hadn't minded it much, but Little Reed wouldn't be around much longer, and without someone to call a friend, I'd grow miserable. *And Malinalli stood up for you to Turquoise Bells that day by the lake....*

Noticing my gaze, Malinalli edged closer to me. "How's the hand?"

"Hardly noticeable anymore." Though now that she'd mentioned it, it started throbbing again. I hoped we'd reach the camp soon so I could get some medicine.

We landed ashore at midmorning and Ahexotl awoke from his drugged sleep shortly after. By the time we reached camp, his wails brought a handful of guards to investigate. They took us to the medical tents and the surgeons immediately divided up among us, most of them hovering around Ahexotl and shaking their heads.

"Did someone torture you?" my surgeon asked when he examined my hand.

"I lost them in the heat of battle." Easier than telling him the truth.

"These seams look pretty ragged, definitely not made by a macuahuitl...." He gave me another questioning gaze but then said, "It should heal well, and once the swelling goes down, you should have normal mobility in the remaining fingers. The tissue looks healthy, but only time will tell whether or not you'll continue having pain. Keep the chapolxiuitl herb on it until it completely heals, and if the pain keeps you awake, take the yauhtli." He put the medicines in a leather pouch and draped it around my neck by a string.

I checked on the others, starting with Nimilitzli. By the time I spoke with Mazatzin and peered over the shoulders of those tending to Ahexotl, the exhaustion struck hard.

Little Reed walked me out of the tent into the day's heat. "You should go and sleep. I don't think you've rested well in days."

"I haven't," I admitted.

He called Talking Serpent over from the nearby cooking fire and asked him to escort me to our tents across camp. "Sleep well," he said, giving my good hand a gentle squeeze.

"Make sure you get some rest too," I said. He smiled and told me he would.

Talking Serpent took me through the heart of camp, into a row of canvas tents painted yellow and white. Turquoise Bells, Iczoxochitl, and Malinalli stood at the communal cooking fire, getting bowls of wonderful-smelling stew from the tattooed woman tending the fire. She gave me a gap-toothed smile when she handed me my bowl.

As we left the fire, Malinalli said, "They gave us tents to share, but if you'd rather share with someone else—"

"I prefer your company, thank you," I said.

Our tent was so small that our bed rolls touched and we had to hunch over to not bump our heads against the slanted canvas ceiling, but the beans were wonderful. We passed the time talking about Nimilitzli's injuries and what they might mean for taking the trials. "Do you think Mothotli will oversee them instead?" Malinalli asked.

"I suspect she will, though I'd rather she didn't."

"She intimidates you too?"

"She's never liked me, but I think she's especially annoyed I wasn't thrown out of calmecac for...well, my poor judgment with the Prince. I'm sure she'll do her best to make my trials too difficult to pass."

"She has seemed unusually hard on you," Malinalli noted. "We could study together, work hard to prepare for whatever silly questions she throws at us."

I smiled. "I'd like that very much."

After we finished eating, we crept under our blankets. I'd hoped to be able to sleep without the yauhtli, but it was impossible to not think about the dull throb in my hand, so I took some from my leather pouch and drank it down with a cup of water.

"I'm glad you're going through with it," Malinalli said, once I lay down again.

"With what?"

"The trials, and becoming a priestess. You have a gift like no other, one the gods don't just give to anybody, and I think you'd regret abandoning that."

"I could never abandon the god, even if I didn't become a priestess."

"Surely the Feathered Serpent has something great in mind for you."

Her words brought my heart to an excited dash. "Maybe," I whispered.

CHAPTER SEVENTEEN

 When I awoke the next afternoon, Malinalli had folded up her bed like we did every morning at calmecac and left me alone to sleep. I lay in bed, trying to gather the strength to get up and find something to eat, but a familiar voice in the next tent soon drew my attention.

"What's this I hear about you taking an arrow for that no-good Topiltzin, Brother?" Red Flint said. I sighed, annoyed. I'd enjoyed not listening to his prattle the last couple of weeks. "My poor brother, always so misled. And that's quite a wound! Maybe you'll die and the gods will grant you paradise for giving your life for that whelp."

"Enough," Mazatzin said. "I don't tell you where to put your heart, so don't lecture me. Just because you doubt he's the god's son doesn't mean I must follow you."

"I thought you the smartest of my brothers, Mazatzin, but instead you've turned into a fool."

"Then leave me to my foolishness and I'll leave you to yours."

"I must admit, as your future king, I worry where your loyalties lie."

I raised an astonished eyebrow.

Mazatzin laughed. "My loyalties are to Father, but when I become a priest, my devotion to the god will supersede everything else."

"You'd listen to some *god* over your king?" Red Flint asked.

"So long as Xochicalco's king—no matter who he is—remains faithful to the god, then the king shall have my loyalty."

That brought a smile to my face.

"Someday you'll take an oath to your people, Red Flint, to be their king and protect them from harm, and I won't feel slighted when you put their needs over mine. Quetzalcoatl is Xochicalco's patron god, not your competition, and a wise king consults his god in all decisions. When you're older and Father has taught you about the duties of the king, then you'll appreciate how pointless your concern is."

Red Flint raised his voice. "Then you think I'm not fit to be king?"

"I'm only saying you still have much to learn, hardly unexpected when you haven't yet gone into your first battle."

"Oh, but you—who won't do his military duty until next year—you know more than me about being king?"

"He knows more about everything than you do," I whispered with a chuckle.

"You know nothing!" Red Flint went on. "Spent your whole life locked up in the calmecac, with the cold baths scrambling your brain and priests whispering lies in your ears. Maybe you desire my throne for yourself, is that it?"

"Don't even jest with such talk, Red Flint," Mazatzin warned. "If you think I'm conniving for your throne, then make the accusation in front of everyone and challenge me to a fight. But don't expect me to put up a defense to your stupidity. I'll let you explain to Father why you felt it necessary to strike me down without a struggle."

Just then someone jingled the bells on my tent. I hurried over to find Little Reed standing outside. "I came by to see how you're doing—"

But I shushed him and pulled him inside the tent. "Red Flint's talking about you," I whispered. We both sat on my bed mat and listened at the tent wall.

"Of course I don't think you want my throne, Mazatzin," Red Flint went on. "But sometimes I fear you favor Topiltzin over me, Brother."

Exasperated, Mazatzin said, "I wish you'd abandon this jealousy of him."

"I'm not jealous!"

I started to mutter, "Yes you are," but Mazatzin said it first. "Your jealousy is readily apparent, and someday it'll be your undoing, so I implore you to forget about him and focus on your own path. He'll be an important ally that you may need to call on for help. Put aside your personal sentiments and do what's right for your people."

Red Flint laughed. "I won't need his help. I'm heir to the valley's most powerful throne and he's an exiled prince who will need my help to regain his own small, pathetic one. And I wouldn't doubt it at all if he preferred a man to a woman in his bed."

I gasped, appalled that he'd stoop to such slander, but when I looked over at Little Reed, he merely rolled his eyes, as if he expected no better.

"There you go not checking your tongue again," Mazatzin warned.

"Why? Because you fear what it might say about you, here sharing his tent and defending him with your very life? I at least had the good sense to fawn over the female of the pair, whore though she may be. You weren't at the palace to hear what wondrous things I got her to perform on me—"

My cheeks flared. A breath later, I heard the tent flap swish and I turned to see the tail of Little Reed's robe just as he disappeared outside. *Oh no!* I scrambled after him.

"Get out here, you louse-ridden dog!" Little Reed shouted at the tent next to mine, his fists balled tight.

After a tense moment in which I heard Mazatzin telling Red Flint to leave, Red Flint finally came outside, seemingly surprised to see Little Reed standing in front of him. He darted his gaze to me, then back to Little Reed. "What do you want?"

"Say what you want about me, Red Flint, but you go too far when you speak dishonorably of those dearest to me!"

All around us the soldiers looked up, some standing for a better view. Red Flint flashed his gaze around, ending with me again; but when he turned back to Little Reed, he gave him a sneer. "I'm sorry your sister promised to make a man out of you then backed out on it. The little whore did the same to me."

Little Reed leaped at him and they went down in a heap, taking down half of Mazatzin's tent with them. Mazatzin fought his way out of the back end and nearly fell over into the tent behind it as he tried to get to his feet.

Somewhere in the brawl, Red Flint pulled a knife and swiped Little Reed with it. Little Reed scrambled away, bleeding from a shallow cut on his cheek. "Drop the blade and fight me like a man, Red Flint," Little Reed panted as Red Flint rose to his feet. "Or are you afraid you can't best me without an advantage?"

Red Flint looked around at the others, but after a tense moment, he handed his weapon to Mazatzin. "I'm not afraid of you, you little pile of jaguar shit." He advanced on Little Reed, body crouched.

Little Reed matched his stance and they circled a few times before Red Flint came at him, both hands out for the grapple. Little Reed stepped aside and grabbed him by the arm and jammed it behind Red Flint's back. Red Flint swung at him with his other fist, first one direction then the other, but Little Reed dodged his flailing blows, swinging him around as he did. A wave of quiet laughter swam through the crowd as they continued spinning in circles.

But when they came to the fire pit, Red Flint scooped up a smoldering log and swung it at Little Reed's head. Little Reed let him go, barely avoiding the blow. Red Flint lunged at him, spilling them both to the ground like squabbling dogs. The soldiers whistled and hooted.

I didn't share their enthusiasm. In the blur of fists, kicks, and tumbles, I couldn't make out who was winning, though neither seemed to have the advantage. Soon the fighting became hair-pulling and wrestling. They locked arms around each others' necks, but eventually they both let go and rolled away, panting. I started to rush to Little Reed's side but stopped. He'd never forgive me for mothering him in front of the soldiers.

Mazatzin glared down at Red Flint. "That was all rather pointless. Neither of you proved anything; you just acted like boys rather than men, and that's hardly becoming of a soldier, or a priest."

Little Reed glared at Red Flint but said nothing as he wiped blood from his nose. Red Flint batted away Mazatzin's hand when he offered to help him up. "There you go lecturing me again." He gritted his teeth as he stood and snatched his obsidian knife back from his brother. He then limped away, clutching his scraped thigh.

But Little Reed accepted Mazatzin's help up. "You're right as usual. I'm sorry about the tent. I'll get it standing up again."

"No, Red Flint started this, so he'll help me. You should go and clean up. Hopefully you didn't tear open your shoulder again."

Little Reed and I went down to the lake's edge and he sat on a rock while I washed the blood off him. "If you ask me, it's unfortunate that Mazatzin's mother isn't Cuitlapanton's legitimate wife," he said between gritted teeth as I wiped the dirt off his scraped knee. "Mazatzin would be a far better king than Red Flint."

"Why are you rising to Red Flint's insults? He was trying to make you look like a fool, and he just might have succeeded."

"I don't know what came over me," he admitted, embarrassed. "When he said those things about you...I just snapped."

"You asked me not to mother you in front of the men, but I ask you not to leap to defend my honor either. It only lends weight to Red Flint's claims. It's my shame to deal with; it'll only go away by my own actions."

Little Reed started to argue but then sighed and hung his head. "Then we don't need each other anymore?"

I raised his chin for him. "I'll always need your love, Little Reed."

He smiled back. "And I'll always need yours, Papalotl."

His steady gaze made me hot and uncomfortable, so I wiped the blood from his nose and declared him finished. "How long until we can leave for Xochicalco?" I asked, averting my eyes in hopes I could stop the blush rising up my neck.

"Nimilitzli won't be ready to travel for several weeks and Ahexotl even longer than that, but she already told me we shouldn't wait on her account. She thinks we're safer behind the city walls."

"Then you haven't told her our suspicions about spies?"

"I don't want to worry her."

I unwound the bandage from my hand and put salve on it. I only felt pain now if I raised my hand above my head.

"Now you must give even more next time," Little Reed said, looking frustrated.

"Then let us hope I never have need of it again."

He shook his head. "I fear far greater dangers lie ahead. Our uncle keeps very dark and powerful company."

"I'll make the necessary sacrifice when the time comes, and I shall do it with a smile on my face."

"I pray that Omeyocan doesn't ask so much of you."

His frown left me disconcerted. "Let's not talk about that anymore. We should be making our preparations for returning home."

"We should, but first let me help you re-wrap that."

I handed him my fresh linen and watched him wind it around my hand, my heart racing. For the first time, I saw in him the man he so desperately wanted me and Nimilitzli to believe he was, and it thrilled me more than any of those shameful moments I'd spent in the laundry room with Red Flint. *He looks so much like Father, but also like Nochuatl—like everyone who's ever meant anything at all to me*, I thought, tears blurring my eyes.

Little Reed paused mid-wrap when he noticed me crying. "Am I hurting you?"

I shook my head. "Not at all."

He finished wrapping my hand then asked again, "Are you sure you're all right?"

"I'm wonderful, really."

He started to say more but stopped, an expression of consternation on his face. We walked back to camp in silence.

Back in my tent, Malinalli was preparing to go down to the lake to bathe but I declined her invitation to join her and the others. I lay staring at the tent wall, thinking about Little Reed and the things I wished I had to courage to tell him.

But once I fell into a fitful sleep, I dreamt I was a tree that towered over the lake, its branches heavy with white flowers whose intoxicating fragrance freed the knots not just in people's tongues, but in their hearts as well.

◻

We stayed an extra day to give Mazatzin's wounds more time to heal and I spent the last day sitting at Nimilitzli's side, writing down her instructions for Mothotli. I could write with both hands, though I mostly used my right; and having to hold the quill in the left felt awkward for a while and my writing was less steady at the start. Little Reed came by a few times to check on her but spent most of his time coordinating our military escort.

"He's really taken to his leadership role well," Nimilitzli noted. "Though I heard he and Red Flint got into a scuffle a couple of days ago."

"They did, and neither came out ahead," I said. "I'm sure Red Flint took a thorough ribbing from the other soldiers for being unable to best an injured man." I chuckled.

"Your brother will outgrow that rashness in times. He has the intelligence and the favor of the gods, neither of which Red Flint has nor can ever hope for. Someday he'll make a very fine king. And you will make a very fine priestess; maybe even a high priestess."

"I wish you were administering the trials instead of Mothotli," I admitted with a sigh.

"You'll do just fine. I have faith in you, and so does the god. After what you did in Teotihuacan, I can't imagine you not doing well. And believe it or not, Mothotli really wants you to succeed."

I smiled wanly. "I'll try to remember that."

Nimilitzli gripped my hand. "Trust yourself. You're much stronger than you think."

◻

The march back proved thankfully uneventful, and seeing the city's great white walls again filled me with elation. When I was younger, I'd longed to get outside the walls and run the fields and forest trails like the boys did, but somewhere along the years I'd grown used to staying inside. Now I wouldn't have minded if I never left the wall's sanctuary ever again.

We went immediately to the palace to discuss what happened with Cuitlapanton. I left the telling to Little Reed though, for as soon as I entered the great hall, my wrist flared up again. I concentrated on each member of the war council, trying to work out who the spy might be. Was it Lord Necalli, who always looked and sounded angry when he spoke, or maybe Lord Tototl, who always opened his mouth to speak but stopped when someone else started speaking first? I couldn't imagine it could be Lord Spear Fish—who had led me and Mother to safety here in Xochicalco so long ago—but it could very well be Lord Xipil, who kept sniffing and looking bored throughout Little Reed's story. But with everyone crowded around so close, it was impossible to tell.

"The spy is on the war council," I told Little Reed as we left the palace, headed for the bathhouse to clean up after the journey.

"You're positive?" But when he saw me scratching my wrist, he said, "Whom do you suspect?"

I shook my head. "I'm not sure yet. I didn't see anyone who seemed surprised or disappointed to see us alive."

"I did bring up the idea of there being a spy, so they'd be extra careful now. We should have met with Cuitlapanton in private."

"We weren't expecting the viper to be among his trusted advisors. If the spy thinks you're onto him, he might take matters into his own hands, so be extra careful."

"Or now that he knows the god's on our side, maybe he'll thank Omeyocan that the Feathered Serpent didn't come after him."

I looked down at my wounded hand still wrapped in bandages. "And if he doesn't, we do have that option again."

He took my hand in his and gave me a grave look. "We have other options too, so let's not be hasty. We'll find out who it is and we'll deal with him—just you, me, and Mazatzin."

"Of course." I watched him disappear behind the gate into the men's bathhouse. *If only my tongue wouldn't stick to the roof of my mouth every time I think about telling you how I feel about you, Little Reed.* I sighed then headed for the calmecac to deliver Nimilitzli's letter to Mothotli.

◻

I found Mothotli in her meditation room, kneeling in front of an incense burner and rubbing at a strange lump on her hand. She promptly tucked it into her robe sleeve when

115

THE BONE FLOWER TRILOGY

I announced myself. "Back so soon?" she asked, avoiding my gaze. "I thought you weren't going to be back for a couple more days."

I told her the story of our troubles while she glanced over the letter. I left out the part about me summoning the god though; she was in a calm mood and I didn't want to stir her up with what she'd surely think was lies.

She furrowed her brow as I finished. "Sounds as if we have a spy." She finally looked up at me, but when she saw my bandaged hand, she grabbed it. "Great Feathered Serpent! What happened here?"

Her concern took me by surprise. "One of the Chichimec warriors cut them off when I tried to get away."

She let me go. "At least you made it out alive. More than we can say for most of the men." She looked down at the letter again. "Do you wish for a personal guard?"

"I think Topiltzin is the true target. I'm nobody, just his sister."

That soured her mood. "Go and clean up and get back here by sunset. Nimilitzli wants me to start training you in the fire priestess duties, so be on time. No excuses."

I stood a little straighter. "Of course."

"Now let me be. I have things to do." Mothotli reached into her sleeve to rub at her hand again.

I watched her a moment, wondering if I should ask if she was all right, but then she barked at me to get going, so I scuttled out of the door. *Why must she always be so nasty?* I wondered, disgusted, as I left for the bathhouse.

CHAPTER EIGHTEEN

Mothotli wasn't in better spirits when I met her in front of the calmecac an hour before sunset. She pushed a lit torch at me, which I fumbled with my wounded hand, and I glared at her back as I followed her to the main temple. "The fire priest's primary duty is to go around the city before dusk and light all the temples' fires," she said when I joined her at the urn outside the Feathered Serpent's temple. "There are thirty-three to light every night, including the ones outside at the rural temples. Each order has its own fire priests and priestesses, and we rotate days. Normally the fire priest would accompany us, but Eztetl has other things to do tonight, so it's just you and me." I didn't relish the idea of an evening stuck with Mothotli, but the frown hit my face before I could stop it. She snapped, "Don't look so disappointed, girl, and get the kettle lit." She shook her head, impatient as I poked the torch into the pile of copal wood in the drum. "Quickly, so we're back before nightfall. Don't dally."

Once I got it lit, Mothotli set off down the stairs, barking at me to keep up. In the lower precinct, we visited each temple and lit the fire kettles outside, Mothotli lecturing me about needing to be quick. "We don't want to be outside the city walls after nightfall. Even two armed priestesses aren't enough to deter some bandits and murderers."

By the time we left the city gates, heading for the first of the three rural temples where the farmers gave their daily offerings, I'd lost patience with her constant snipping. My hand ached and the short nap I'd taken after my bath hadn't lasted me long. I lagged behind, both out of exhaustion and to avoid having to listen to her complaining. But just as we finished up at the first rural temple, I lost my footing on the short set of stairs and dropped the torch into the nearby canal.

"Of all the incompetence!" Mothotli shouted as she stormed back. She grabbed a new torch from the basket inside the door and lit it in the kettle brazier, before thrusting it into my hands, muttering, "Nimilitzli must have gone daft, thinking you're at all worthy of pursuing such important office."

That was enough. I stayed where I was as she started lumbering off towards the east road. "Why do you dislike me so? You've been nothing but mean and spiteful to me since the day we met, but what could I possibly have done to deserve that?"

Mothotli glared at me over her shoulder. "Move it along, girl. Twilight is not that far off now."

I folded my arms. "I demand you answer me."

She looked towards the road again, her temper cooling; but then it suddenly erupted. "Because you're a lazy, self-absorbed wretch who wastes all the potential the gods gave her."

My jaw dropped open. "I've never misquoted a prayer or a sacred story—"

"Oh, you're very good at memorization and repetition, but anybody could do that. Given your royal blood, perhaps it was too much to expect more of you than just another half-witted noble girl."

My cheeks flushed hot. "How dare...who do you...you don't know me at all!"

She strode back, her fists clenched. "I know you haven't the guts to embrace the challenge of living a life of sacrifice for someone whose name will last long after the bones of princes have gone to dust. Instead you'd rather hand your future over to some pretty noble boy who's not even half the man his father is."

I stared at her, too stunned to say anything.

"I see girls like you all the time, doing what they must to please their fathers, just biding their time until they're told to marry, never making the hard decisions for themselves, never grabbing opportunity because they don't dare upset the men. Nimilitzli hoped you would be different, that the god had given you to her for a reason, but that proved foolish. At least she still has your brother to make her proud; he at least has a firm sense of his self-worth and potential. If you believe the only thing you have to offer this world is your womb, then that's all you'll ever contribute, and I'm not going to waste my time trying to make you into something you can't be." She headed down the path again.

You're going to let that slight go unchallenged? I thought, fuming. "And you're just a jealous old woman who can't stand that she's being passed over to be the next high priestess!"

She stopped but didn't turn around.

"Nimilitzli said you'll never be high priestess," I continued, emboldened by her reaction. "That must have really burned, getting her letter telling you to start training me while she's recovering? All those years you spent as fire priestess, and for what?"

Mothotli laughed, softly at first then harder, until it sounded like a deep drum beat. But then that laughter turned to weeping. "You're right that I'm jealous; of everyone who's been spared my fate, who won't die alone in the desert as an outcast from everyone and everything they love because the gods have cursed them for some unknown reason. Who wouldn't be jealous of that?"

At first I didn't understand, but then I remembered how she'd been rubbing her hand then hid it when I'd come to her meditation room. *She was hiding a skin lesion,* I realized, everything suddenly making sense. I'd seen a couple of people with similar ones, all eventually looking like something was eating them from inside, their skin bubbled up into angry blisters that turned black. The priests called it the Divine Sickness because they believed it was a punishment from the gods; though having seen at least one child with the affliction, I had to wonder what one so young could possibly do to incense the gods. Nimilitzli had taught me some remedies for the numbness in the skin splotches, but once they turned to pustules, there was little to be done for them. And based on the size of the one I saw on Mothotli's hand, it could be only a matter of months before they started taking over. Eventually the king would ask her to leave the city, out of fear of spreading it to others.

I felt as though I'd smacked a child and then laughed about it. "I'm sorry. I didn't know—" I said, my voice barely above a whisper.

"But that has nothing to do with why you disgust me," Mothotli said, her anger palpable. "You're an intelligent woman, when you decide to behave like one, but unfortunately you choose to ignore your own potential and look to everyone around you for validation of your worth. You're the cleverest girl I've ever had in calmecac, but you're lazy and consider mere learning good enough. Your brother is brilliant too, but unlike you he looks beyond what the priests tell him. He finds ways to use what he learns to inspire and give others hope, while you look at it as a cage meant to trap you. Being one of the order's leaders is a huge responsibility; you must make sound judgments and be willing to look beyond yourself to make tough decisions that will help everyone. I trust Nimilitzli's judgment, but everything I've seen of your attitude tells me you don't have what it takes to be high priestess."

My shoulders rose like a ruffled bird. "If I don't, then why would the god entrust me with his power on earth?" I held up my bandaged hand. "I didn't lose these to a Chichimec; I cut them off with my own knife to summon the god to defend us. And it wasn't the first time I called on him, either."

Her annoyed skepticism slowly shifted. "The commotion in the precinct that night, when you were just a girl—"

"The god dealt with that treacherous servant," I answered. "Quetzalcoatl has faith in me, and so does Nimilitzli. Why can't you?"

Mothotli scowled. "All the faith of others means nothing when you have none in yourself." She drew her cloak tighter and looked around. "Let's not continue this foolishness any longer and hope we can get back to the city by moonrise." Without another word, she took off down the path at a jog.

I didn't say anything for the rest of the evening as we visited the remaining temples then headed back to the city. Mothotli didn't say anything either but constantly scanned the darkness, keeping close to my side. We still said nothing even as we walked back up to the sacred precinct. At the calmecac we went our separate ways.

As I lay in bed, trying to get to sleep while the younger novices snored around me, her last statement kept dancing around my mind. Nimilitzli and little Reed might have faith in my abilities, but a leader needed to have faith in herself.

So, *Quetzalpetlatl*, I wondered, *do you have what it takes to lead people in the god's name?*

◻

Per Nimilitzli's instructions, I went back to the palace in the morning to check on the three women who were with child. At least one of them was close to her delivery date— Lady Atzi—and she'd begged Nimilitzli not to go on the pilgrimage, in case she went into early labor. So naturally she was near-hysterical when I told her that Nimilitzli wouldn't be back in Xochicalco for a few months.

"Who's going to deliver the baby?" she cried. "What if something goes wrong?

Nimilitzli said the birth could be very difficult at my age."

"She gave me instructions to attend to the birth with Lady Ixchell's help."

"You? But you're just a girl!"

"Nimilitzli trained me herself for the last five years, and she trusted me to be the lead midwife at two other royal births just this year."

Lady Atzi relaxed. "Well, I suppose that's all right. Nimilitzli is a good judge of such things. I suppose you'll do." She still looked askance at me.

Laughter echoed from the hallway as I packed up the medicine bag, and a moment later Lady Atzi's two sons—Obsidian Eagle and Pochotzin—came in, fighting each other with toy swords. Pochotzin, who was the eldest of Cuitlapanton's sons, held his sword low to keep his nine-year-old brother from clipping his knees. He let Obsidian Eagle whack away furiously a moment before suddenly knocking the sword from his brother's hands. He laughed while Obsidian Eagle rubbed his wrist and glared at him.

My own wrist was itching.

"Don't come into my room with all your clatter, you two," Lady Atzi replied, lying down on her side. "I'm very tired and you're vexing me."

"We'll be quieter, Mother." Pochotzin knelt next to his mother to catch his breath while Obsidian Eagle snatched up his sword. "I just wanted to come by and see how you're doing."

She smiled back, proud and loving. "I'm quite all right. Thank you for coming by."

Obsidian Eagle came over and watched me finish packing. "Who are you?"

"I'm the midwife who's going to deliver your new brother or sister." I tied the bag closed, eager to be on my way.

"But what's your name?" he insisted, impatient.

"She's Topiltzin's sister, Quetzalpetlatl," Pochotzin said with a good-natured laugh. He seemed so genuine; I never would've suspected him of spying for Ihuitimal.

A bright smile crept to Obsidian Eagle's face. "Oh! You're the one Red Flint says lets men put snakes in her hole."

I frowned at the boy, more annoyed than angry, but Lady Atzi gasped. Pochotzin shot to his feet and cuffed Obsidian Eagle's ears and hissed, "You dishonor Father by saying such things."

Obsidian Eagle cried and rubbed his ears. To me, Pochotzin said, "Forgive my brother for repeating such rubbish."

I gathered my bag. "I doubt he meant any harm, unlike the one he heard it from." I bowed, then told Lady Atzi, "Get your rest and call for me if you're at all uncomfortable and can't sleep."

She nodded, her face red. As I left, I felt Pochotzin watching me still.

□

I waited until I'd left the palace to break into a run. By the time I reached the calmecac my side ached, but I didn't stop until I reached the doorway to the boys' dormitory. I caught myself at the door and gulped down breaths. "I need to speak to Topiltzin," I told the door monitor once I could speak again. "Right away. Very important."

"He and Prince Mazatzin went out to the exercise yard at the House of Warriors."

And so I raced down the winding stairs to the south gate, where the warrior school was set on the edge of the forest. I found Little Reed and Mazatzin practicing their atl-atl throwing at a set of targets painted on maguey fiber glued to one of the trees. Some of the warriors standing around talking started hooting suggestively as I ran by, but they stopped when Little Reed raised a hand to wave me over. "Forgive their rough manners." He glared at them over his shoulder.

I waved it off. "Pochotzin is the spy!"

Mazatzin startled. "My brother?"

"But he's not on the war council," Little Reed said.

"I think he was listening from a doorway when we were talking with them yesterday," I said.

"But the king's own son?" Mazatzin asked, taken aback. "How could that be?"

"He is the only one of the king's sons who's gone off to war before now, and wasn't he captured briefly last year then escaped?" Little Reed asked.

"He was." After a tense pause, Mazatzin asked me, "How can you be sure, though?"

"The god gave me the ability to sense when the enemy is near, and all the signs point to him," I answered.

Little Reed nodded but said, "The king will need more than just your special sense to convince him, especially when accusing his own blood."

"We could test him," I suggested. "Feed him false information then see if he contacts Ihuitimal."

Little Reed nodded. "We tell the war council that I'm planning on marching out with the next contingent. One leaves at the beginning of next week."

"And I'll keep an eye on Pochotzin, see who he talks to and meets with." Mazatzin sighed. "I still hate to think that a brother would be involved in such treachery."

"I'm sure he didn't do this willingly," I said. "Who knows what he had to agree to in order to save his life."

"And I doubt he's acting alone," Little Reed added. "Perhaps we can draw the rest of the conspirators out as well. We should get started immediately."

Mazatzin followed us out of the exercise yard and back up to the sacred precinct. "It's a good thing you didn't go marching with the army, Topiltzin, for surely the military has been infiltrated as well," he said. "Perhaps Quetzalpetlatl didn't want you to leave because she sensed something would go wrong."

If only it were so selfless, I thought, ashamed. I'd held Little Reed back out of simple selfishness, but I wouldn't make that mistake again. "You can't let Ihuitimal scare you into staying here forever, Topiltzin. I was wrong to not listen to you, and both Nimilitzli and I agree that you're ready. You're a priest in your heart, but only a warrior will win back our throne."

"You're more ready than Red Flint is," Mazatzin added. "I would follow you into battle any time."

Little Reed bowed his head. "Thank you for your confidence. It means a great deal. I can only hope to inspire such loyalty among others as well."

"You will," I said. "And it'll be nothing less than you deserve."

He gave me a warm smile. "I'm still intending to take trials first. It can't hurt to have the god on my side."

Once we reached the calmecac, Mazatzin headed to the palace to speak with his father, and Little Reed and I went to Nimilitzli's house, to make sure there weren't any mice in the meal bags. "There's something I want to talk to you about," I told him as I looked through the sacks of masa and whole maize.

"Is something the matter?"

"Not at all. I'm going to take up the extra studies to become the next high priestess."

"You're sure that's what you want to do?"

I nodded. "I've learned a lot about myself these last couple of weeks, particularly why letting you go has been so very hard. I've spent my life taking care of you, and it scared me to think that you didn't need me anymore—"

"I'll always need you, Papalotl," he insisted.

"And I'll always need you, but neither of us are the kind to sit back and let others rule our lives; we need to lead others, guide them through tough times and get them to the other side, hopefully in one piece."

Little Reed nodded.

"You've always known where you were headed, but my destiny wasn't so clear. Helping people makes me happy and the god is very important to me, so it's only natural I should pursue a future in the priesthood."

He hugged me. "The god will be so very happy to have you in his order. I'm glad you didn't let the difficulties with Mothotli drag you down."

His embrace left me flushed and delighted. "Actually, it was Mothotli who made me realize I was wandering through life, expecting everyone else to tell me what to do. Mother always wanted to be more than she was, wanted a better world for you and me, and she'd want us both to do things that make us happy and bring hope to others. I want to be the high priestess she never could be; I want to be the leader I know I can be."

Smiling, he said, "And you'll do wonderfully."

I kissed his cheek, letting myself linger there a breath this time. "Just promise that you'll write to me often, and that you'll come back home safely. You're taking a piece of me with you, and I need you to bring it back to me."

◻

I spent the rest of the week following Mothotli around the calmecac, observing her while she taught her classes. I hadn't taken much notice of what she did from day to day until now, and having seen the full extent of her duties to the priesthood, I admired her strength to continue on despite her illness. She still hid the lump on her hand, but she was a proud woman who despised rumors, so I neither asked nor said anything about it, not even to Little Reed. I left a jar of medicine in her meditation room though, to help with the numbness, and the next day she let me out of midnight temple duty to attend Little Reed's farewell feast at the palace—part of the ploy to get the spies out into the open.

The war council and Cuitlapanton's sons attended, and I was the only woman there. *Thank the gods there are no courtesans,* I thought. I wouldn't have been able to bear watching them fawn over Little Reed in front of me. There was so much food though, hundreds of dishes ranging from tadpole and tomato casserole to turkey tamales to tlaxcallis made of flour so finely ground that the cooked flatbreads were almost transparent. We ate in courses, starting with tlaxcallis dipped in countless sauces, followed by fruit of every known variety, then the fowl and venison dishes, and finally ended with xocolatl service. I hadn't drunk xocolatl for years, and even then I'd only been allowed to add honey to it, so the sheer selection of ingredients Cuitlapanton had on offer to add was intimidating. I decided on vanilla but kept close watch on Pochotzin while he spiked his with powdered heart flower. He laughed and carried on conversations with everyone around him, including Little Reed, who did a very convincing job of not suspecting anything of him.

I ate until I felt ready to burst; then, after all the speeches and well wishes, Little Reed and I headed back to the sacred precinct, walking close together to keep warm against the wind.

"So are you ready for the trials?" he asked.

"I feel confident I'll do well," I said. "How about you?"

Little Reed smiled. "Not to sound boastful, but I've been ready for this my entire life. I'm ready to start making things happen, and to find out what my father has in mind for me."

I laughed. "Being king of Culhuacan isn't enough for you?"

"It's very important, but sons of mortals don't have a god they have to impress."

I squeezed his hand in mine. "I'm sure he's very proud of you, Little Reed."

We paused at the top of the stairs and stood facing each other, with me still holding his hand. He looked like he wanted to say something but was holding back. I couldn't hear anything over my thudding heart.

But then the itching began on my wrist again, subtle at first but growing quickly. I looked down into the royal square below, searching for signs of Pochotzin or anyone else.

"Are you sensing something?" Little Reed asked.

I nodded, still looking around. I saw no one in the moonlight, but my heart now pounded for entirely different reasons. "We should get inside." I pulled him towards the calmecac.

The itching only grew worse though, and I wondered if we should head to Nimilitzli's house instead. Little Reed had turned down the guards the king had offered him—not wanting to scare off Pochotzin—but now I didn't think that was such a good idea.

I brought us to a stop in the courtyard and looked around, my wrist itching fiercely now. I pulled my mother's sacrificial blade from my belt, taking comfort in the feel of the carved horn handle in my hand.

Little Reed drew his blade as well. "Head for the dormitories. He's after me, not you."

"What if he's brought help? I might not be much use in hand-to-hand combat, but I can call on the god if necessary."

"I'd rather you didn't—"

A shadowy figure leaped down the stairs from the storerooms, an obsidian-studded sword raised above his head. Little Reed shoved me away, almost knocking my blade for my hand, and he ducked into a roll, barely getting out of the way before the sword came down where he'd stood. He sprang to his feet and moved aside as his attacker brought the sword around again. They circled each other, both weapons ready.

I pressed against the wall of the calmecac, looking for an opening, and surprisingly, the man gave it to me, showing me his back. I lunged, my mother's sacrificial knife gripped in both hands, and buried the flint between his shoulder blades.

But when I tried to rip it out, the twist snapped the blade off. The man roared and whirled towards me. Now if I wanted to call on the god, I'd have to let him stab me for the blood.

Little Reed tackled him from behind and they went to the ground in a heap. The assailant tried to buck Little Reed off, but he dissolved into howling pain when Little Reed shoved his knee into the flat side of the blade protruding from his back. "I give up! I give up! Please stop!" he wailed, clawing his fingers into the hard ground.

Shouting from the stairs on the precinct drew my attention, and I saw Mazatzin running towards us, his sacrificial blade drawn as well. By the time he reached us, priests, priestesses and novices were gathered in the courtyard, coming from the dormitories and the bathhouse, some even as far away as the Temple of the Feathered Serpent. "What in Mictlan is going on out here?" Fire Priest Eztetl asked as he cut through the crowd.

Still not letting his attacker up, Little Reed told him, "My sister and I were set upon by this assassin, sent by Ihuitimal."

Mazatzin knelt next to Little Reed. "I've already summoned the guards." He knelt down to frown at Pochotzin, who lay panting and cringing under Little Reed's knee. He frowned. "How could you dishonor father by working for Xochicalco's mortal enemy, Pochotzin?"

Pochotzin shook his head, on the verge of tears. "I'm sorry, Brother. I did what I had to. They were going to sacrifice me—"

"An honorable warrior would've gone to his death rather than betray his family."

Pochotzin let out a loud, sad breath, but said no more as the guards came to take him into custody.

CHAPTER NINETEEN

Cuitlapanton paced before his throne, wringing his hands and shaking his head. "I can't believe this, my own blood conspiring under my nose. If I'd only known...please forgive my ignorance on this matter, Lord Topiltzin. I failed to instill honor in Pochotzin and that nearly cost you your life."

"It's not your fault, your Majesty," Little Reed said. "My treacherous uncle is a master at using fear, and your son was nothing more than a pawn. Hopefully we can uncover the full network of people involved in passing information and we can make the city safer for everyone again. Undoubtedly they are spying on you as well, your Majesty."

Cuitlapanton's face darkened. "Then let's not waste time; I'll interrogate Pochotzin immediately."

"He's being looked at by the royal surgeon right now, your Majesty," I said. "He was injured during the attack."

"Traitors to the crown don't deserve the mercy of the surgeon. He will suffer the pain he's brought on himself." To the guards, he said, "Bring Pochotzin to me immediately. Carry him here if necessary." He sat on his throne and wiped his face with his hand. "We will get to the bottom of this, even if I must cut each finger from his hand to make him speak the truth."

But Pochotzin knelt on the floor before the throne, staring at the floor as he laid out his involvement in the plot to kill my brother. His voice quaked as he recounted the few weeks he spent in captivity in Culhuacan: the daily beatings, the constant starvation, and how eventually Ihuitimal convinced him to be a spy in the royal court. He reported back to him every few months on military plans and trade routes, but mostly on Little Reed's activities. He admitted that he hadn't done it on his own; over the years since returning to Xochicalco, he'd recruited spies in practically every corner of the city. He gave out the names of merchants and artisans, even a priest. The royal scribe recorded them all on a piece of fig-bark paper.

Little Reed said nothing during this, letting Cuitlapanton do the questioning. The king ran the proceedings with a stern frown, and when Pochotzin faltered on details or showed reluctance to answer, Cuitlapanton had one of the guards twist the knife blade in his back, to encourage compliance. By the end of the interrogation, Pochotzin was pale and sweating and could barely stay upon his knees.

I should have hated him, but instead I pitied him. Had I been in the same situation, might I have chosen a similar path? *Never! Death is preferable to betraying my family.*

"I'm disgusted by your betrayal of your king, but I'm most saddened that you should plot against your own people," Cuitlapanton said. "You've not only put your family in jeopardy, you've endangered the very citizens you swore to protect on the day you first marched to war." He stood and glared down at Pochotzin, his bulky form hunched like an angry bear. "It's with this in mind that I pass judgment upon you."

Pochotzin cast a frightened gaze up at his father, but Cuitlapanton remained firm. "I strip you of your noble title; no longer will you be honored when people speak your name. Second, you will pay restitution to Lord Topiltzin for your assault on him; everything you own now belongs to him—your clothes, your jewelry, all your war prizes. And finally, for your crimes against Xochicalco and her people, you will pay with your life. Because you have exposed Ihuitimal's other spies, I'll spare you the days of torture that normally precede this kind of sentence and you'll instead receive a swift public execution. Your blood shall spill in the name of the god, to avenge his priests, for your actions led to the attack at Teotihuacan that sent many of them to the road to Mictlan before their time."

Pochotzin covered his eyes and wept. "Thank you for your mercy, Father. I'm so very sorry I dishonored you, and I hope to earn back some of that lost honor while I stand before the priests to face my fate."

Cuitlapanton stiffened his lower lip, holding back tears, then motioned the guards to take Pochotzin from the room. "Confine him in the prison yard and send the surgeon to finish patching his wounds." Once the guards had taken Pochotzin away, Cuitlapanton set both hands on Little Reed's shoulders. "I'm so sorry to have been a part of all these troubles, even if it is only through my son." He untied the gold and jade necklace from around his neck and put it in Little Reed's hands. "Please accept this as an apology from me for what my son has done against you. As his father, I share his shame."

"I appreciate the gesture, your Majesty," Little Reed said, trying to give him back the necklace. "But your son is his own master, and his mistakes are his alone. You have been like a father to me in many regards and I cannot in good conscience blame the sins of your son upon you."

"At least take the necklace as an offering to Quetzalcoatl's priesthood, in honor of those who lost their lives to this foolishness."

"That I shall do, your Majesty. The god thanks you for your generous gift."

The scribe handed the paper to Cuitlapanton. "Here's the list of co-conspirators Lord Pochotzin named, Your Majesty."

"The guards will bring in every one who's currently in the city and I'll send a runner to my war chief to have him send the accused soldiers back here for trial," Cuitlapanton finished. "This all will take a while to fully deal with, but justice will be meted out swiftly."

◻

The guards brought in ten people overnight and I sat at Little Reed's side as the war council interrogated and passed judgment on each. At daybreak, the conspirators were publicly garroted with the flowery garland in the royal square, and Pochotzin—called only Pochotl now that the king had stripped his title—was beheaded. It was a brutal yet swift death preferred by most warriors, while those dying by the flower garland lived their last minutes in agony and terror.

I felt a distinct discomfort watching the men writhing under the garrote; the brilliantly-colored flowers looked innocent and beautiful at their necks as their lives slipped away. Little Reed held my hand as the executions played out, the grim spectacle turning disturbingly gory when the guards brought out the beheading stone. I knew such things shouldn't bother me; as high priestess, I'd have to perform the yearly sacrifice: slicing the throat of the sacrificial victim and draining his blood into a bowl until he was dead.

But my sensitivity to such gruesomeness had started very early in my life, even before what happened to my father. The few times I'd gone to witness the sacrifices to the Sun, my gut had wriggled at the gasping cries of dying warriors, and my time in the priesthood hadn't helped at all. Piercing tongues and other body parts didn't bother me; it was the taking of lives. Intellectually, I understood the reason for the deaths, but they still hit me like a knife blow. I'd have to overcome this if I was to be the next high priestess of Quetzalcoatl.

It started to rain once all the unpleasant business finished, but I still took my time returning to the sacred precinct. *You don't suppose you'll have to perform a sacrifice at the trials, do you?* I wondered as I headed towards the temple. I'd only ever seen Nimilitzli and Ahexotl performing any actual human sacrifices, and even then only the highest-ranking priests and priestesses did the sacrifices of snakes and butterflies at the daily ceremonies, so it seemed unlikely. *Stop your worrying. You'll have years to come to terms with this.* But I still shuddered.

Hearing commotion over at Nimilitzli's house, I went to investigate. To my surprise, I found Nimilitzli lying in her bed while a small group of soldiers fumbled around the house, two starting the fire while a third moved her weaving supplies next to her bed. She looked up and smiled when I came in. "You look surprised to see me. You haven't been up to mischief, have you?"

I chuckled as I sat on the floor next to her bed. "I thought the surgeons wanted you to stay until your hip healed."

"I couldn't stop thinking about what you told me about spies. I couldn't leave you two to face that on your own, so I got back here as quickly as I could. There hasn't been any trouble, has there?"

"There was plenty," I said, then told Nimilitzli everything. "I was just on my way back from the executions."

"Is that why you're looking so pale?" Nimilitzli asked.

"Things like this bring back memories of what happened to my father. I wonder if I'll ever get over that."

"Some things stay with us all our lives." She patted my hand. "How's Topiltzin dealing with all this nonsense?"

"With kingly poise." I sat down to grind up some flour on the metlatl stone, flicking beetles away from the pile of dried kernels I'd pulled out of the bag. "He's going to join the army after he takes the trials."

"I'm glad. We underestimated his readiness."

"It's the right time for him to go," I admitted. "He leaves with the rest of the contingent two days after the trials."

"It's for the best."

I nodded. "It is." Though I didn't dare tell her why I thought so.

□

I spent the rest of the week dividing my time between classes, temple duties, studying with Malinalli, and taking care of Nimilitzli, even though she insisted that her priestesses could look after her. "You've taken care of me since I was a little girl, so I can at least do the same for you," I told her when she protested again the night before the trials.

"You need to be rested for tomorrow. I won't have you doing poorly because you stayed up late caring for me, so off to bed with you. Malinalli will come by and check on me tonight anyway," Nimilitzli insisted.

I finally gave in and went to the dormitories at the calmecac, where I usually slept. All the girls slept on mats on the floor of one large room, the youngest at the far end and oldest nearest the door. Already I noticed that several of the beds closest to the door were abandoned; Turquoise Bells had decided not to take the trials and had already gone home to the palace, and Ixzoxochitl had taken her trials a few days before and had gone home to celebrate with her mother and father for a few weeks. When she returned, she'd move into one of the houses along the edge of the precinct, where the priests and priestess lived. I was already planning on asking Nimilitzli if I could move back in with her once I'd finished the trials, so I could watch over her recovery.

Anxiety kept me from sleeping well though, and I rose before dawn, my stomach sour with nervousness. Initiates fasted from dusk the night before to the dawn after the trials, but I was too nervous to eat anyway and so headed for the temple to make prayers.

Little Reed sat on the cistern wall, and his smile sent my stomach into a flutter. "Feeling well this morning?" he asked as I sat next to him.

"A little nervous," I admitted. He'd taken his trials the day before, so I asked him, "Were the tests difficult?"

"Nothing you couldn't pass. You'll do fine. Were you headed for the temple?"

I nodded. "Would you join me, make some prayers on my behalf?"

In the temple, we knelt on the reed prayer mats before Quetzalcoatl's idol, praying silently until the sunrise bell, then Little Reed kissed my cheek. "Good luck," he whispered, and left. I cursed myself for fingering my cheek as if caressing a precious stone. I needed a clear head today, but instead I sat in the Feathered Serpent's holy temple, thinking about Little Reed in very un-priestly fashion. I nicked my inner thigh, both for luck and to beg the god's forgiveness for my weakness. Ordinarily I'd put a thorn through my tongue, but I had too much speaking to do today. I extinguished the copalli burner and left.

Quetzalcoatl's sacred star—the Morning Star—twinkled on the pink horizon, at the beginning of its months-long ascension into the sky. Today was a good day to join his order.

Mothotli and Eztetl awaited me in the courtyard. Eztetl was a very tall, nervous-looking man, and Ahexotl's embroidered robe looked comically short on him. "Today you seek to dedicate yourself to the service of Our Most Precious Twin?" he asked, stumbling slightly over the words as if he hadn't quite memorized them yet. When I answered in the affirmative, he went on, "Do you seek to place your life and destiny in the hands of he who's greater than yourself? Are you prepared to forsake the desires of the flesh for as long as you remain in his service? And are you prepared to devote your life to ensuring that the people know the will of the Feathered Serpent?"

"I am, your grace."

"Then prove your worth to him." Eztetl turned to the gate in the stone wall that ran along the back of the courtyard.

Until now, I'd only ever seen priests and priestesses going in and out of this entrance, and we students often whispered about what might be beyond it. Eztetl opened the creaking gate and held it open for Mothotli and me.

Beyond it, a vast garden stretched onto terraces, all the way down into the valley below

Xochicalco. The trees and bushes grew thick and tall, and the flowers bloomed in brilliant color along winding gravel paths. We followed one to a small temple-like building at the heart of the gardens. Inside, the short walkway came to a vestibule that forked into three doorways with curtains decorated with Feathered Serpents, butterflies, and stars. A slab of wood rang hollow on the floor under our feet.

"First, a priestess will examine you, to make sure you're fit to take the trials," Mothotli said, holding the curtain to the right open for me.

Ixchell stood next to a raised slab of stone in the middle of the room. For the longest time, I'd dreaded this part the most, but now that I knew what to expect, my nerves took a rest. When she finished, she handed me a quetzal feather. "Good luck."

The first half of the day, Eztetl and Mothotli tested my knowledge of Quetzalcoatl's stories, the hymns, the dances, the festival dress, calendar calculations, writing symbols, and charting the movements of both the Morning and Evening Star. We then moved to the last room where all the penance instruments were laid out for me; a sacrificial blade, a basket of maguey thorns and grass balls, a prayer mat woven of green lake reeds, and a jar of copalli incense. I explained why we used them in our sacrificial rituals, recounting the story of the Fifth Sun's rise as I demonstrated the proper use of each, piercing my tongue with the thorns and cutting my upper arms with my blade. My still-healing hand made me fumble a bit, but I persevered. I gathered the grass balls and burned incense while reciting prayers. It was surely close to sunset once we gathered in the vestibule.

Eztetl pulled aside the slab of wood on the floor, revealing a dark hole accessible with a ladder. He opened a box of black and brown dried mushrooms and Mothotli took a few and crumbled them up in a cup of octli. He stirred it with a wooden stirring stick then handed it to me with both hands. "Partake of the sacred teonanacatl then descend into the Underworld. There you will enter the Divine Dream and meditate on your future as one of Quetzalcoatl's priestesses."

I drank the concoction down quickly then climbed down into the cave. When I reached bottom, Mothotli lowered down a lamp. "Ixchell will return for you at dawn," she said, and Eztetl slid the wooden plank back over the hole.

Now I'm stuck down here. A wave of fear coursed through me as I showed my lamp around. Ceramic jars of octli sat stacked behind the ladder, stored there for the cool air blowing up the tunnels. The cavern extended for twenty paces before turning into various passageways that I guessed extended under the city and outside somewhere. At least I could find a way out by walking into the wind if I had to.

I sat on the mats next to the octli jars and tried to meditate, but the wind left me shivering. I huddled under the blanket they'd left me, warming up but growing increasingly concerned that I was still lucid. Had I angered Quetzalcoatl with my unholy thoughts in his temple this morning? *Or worse, did you disappoint him with the whole Red Flint ordeal?*

I am not disappointed in you at all, Butterfly, a windy voice whispered in my ear. I turned to see Little Reed sitting behind me, his arms wrapped around me. My blanket had turned into his cloak of quetzal feathers, and more of them grew from his head, mixed in with his long black hair.

I almost asked how he gotten there, but then the pieces snapped together. "My Lord?" I whispered.

He gave me Little Reed's smile, making my insides roll around like a puppy. *You thought I was Topiltzin?*

"You look like him," I pointed out, red-faced.

A son usually has his father's face, does he not? My heart hammered when he leaned closer, his nose nearly touching mine. *You seek guidance about the future, so let me show you the possibilities.* He stood, leaving me cold without his cloak. *Come, I have much to show you.*

I expected us to walk through the caves, but as soon as I lumbered to my feet, we suddenly stood atop the sacred precinct, outside the temple's door. People went about their routines below us, both in the precinct and the city proper. Lord Sun shone bright against a vibrant pink sky, his tongue sticking out of his open mouth like an artist's rendering. A distant walled city hung among the orange clouds, triggering a feeling of familiarity but no memory. Pointing, I asked, "What's that?"

Quetzalcoatl looked up too. *That is Omeyocan, the home of the gods.* On the wind a strange, snow-like substance floated, forming piles where it landed on the stone. It soaked into my skin when it touched me though, and it smelled wonderful, like bone flowers. *And that is the most precious gift in the whole world, next to life itself,* Quetzalcoatl continued, collecting the flakes on his hands. *Pollen from the tree that grew in Tamoachan, the one the goddess Mayahuel and I created when we came together on earth. I assume you know the story.*

"You stole her from her grandmother, so you could bring octli to the people."

Octli! Quetzalcoatl laughed with bitterness rather than boyish charm. *That had little to do with it, but humanity cannot be expected to know the truth of things that happened long before time was kept.*

"Then the stories I learned in calmecac...they're all wrong?" I asked, shocked.

They are not without a grain of truth, but they are also blurred with prejudice. That is why I sired Topiltzin; I am disheartened with what the priesthood has become, and what sacrifice has come to mean. I want him to speak my discontent and reeducate humanity, show them the path back to true sacrifice. But he needs help. You are quick to question such prejudices, and demand explanation for why some must suffer at the hands of others. That is why I granted you the power to call on me; it is why I am glad you have embraced the priesthood, and embraced me by agreeing to be my next high priestess.

The idea of helping Little Reed with a divine mission from the god sent pleasant chills through me. "I shall do my very best to help your son along his path."

Smiling, Quetzalcoatl motioned me to him. I joined him at the back corner of the pyramid. *Look to the north, so you may see what path he's chosen,* he said.

When I looked, my eyesight became good enough to see far over Lake Meztliapan, past the mountainous temples of Teotihuacan, into the deserts of Chichimec territory. On the border between civilized Tolteca lands and the brutal heat of the desert, I saw a city, shining and grand and overflowing with statues of the gods. Giant stone feathered serpents stood atop a high pyramid in the city's heart, their impassive faces gazing over the land where maize of every color grew twice the height of a man. Flowers cascaded on every roof, and the royal gardens spanned half the city itself. It flickered and faded and re-coalesced, like a mirage.

Topiltzin's future is not just to be the king of Culhuacan, but of all the Tolteca. He will be the high priest of all the gods, ushering in a time of great change that will rattle not only the foundations of the priesthood, but of your people's very culture.

Excited, I asked, "What kind of changes?"

An end to human sacrifice, Quetzalcoatl said with a proud smile.

I blinked, startled. This wasn't at all what I'd expected. I didn't even know what to say.

The sacrifices that take place all over the valley are but a mockery of true sacrifice, he went on. *Who dies on the temple tops now? Criminals and slaves, and captured warriors who honor*

foreign gods, who grant the power of their spilled blood to the dark sorcerers they follow.
My mood darkened. "Like Smoking Mirror."

Some believe the time is right for humanity to pay higher sacrificial rites, gods who think themselves the next high deities of the Tolteca. Humanity's lapsed devotion to true sacrifice emboldens them, and they compel men to atrocities through fear. He turned his gaze down to the people below us, fervor in his eyes. *I cannot feel so indifferent about human suffering; my blood flows in them, so I feel their pain and fear. Topiltzin has a difficult task ahead of him; the people will fear the wrath of their gods if they change.*

I chose my next words carefully before speaking. "Forgive my asking, My Lord, but without blood, won't the Sun fall from the sky?"

Quetzalcoatl gave me a patient smile. *We all need blood, but a return to true sacrifice means more powerful offerings. Some among us enjoy the taste of hearts, but a little blood given in earnest is enough to fill anyone's spirit for a very long time. The personal bloodletting performed by the priests and the nobility holds enough power for any god, but these upstarts want to become more powerful than the rest of us. They have manipulated themselves into power among the Chichimecs, and now Smoking Mirror's insidious influence is growing within Tolteca lands, oozing out of Culhuacan. His high priest is sacrificing hundreds of war prisoners every month. Now is the time to act, before he establishes a stronghold and changes the priesthood forever, for the worse. Without this challenge, the day will soon come when it is not hundreds but rather a countless number who die to feed the greedy ambitions of gods who care not a whit about humanity. Seeing my creations brutally killed is more than I could stand.*

Quetzalcoatl was the most merciful of the gods, but hearing this from him startled me. I'd always assumed that, like the others, he found human sacrifice necessary. And the fact that he felt just as I did about human sacrifice pulled my heart closer to him than ever before. "Tell me what I can do to help, My Lord, and it'll be done," I promised.

Quetzalcoatl knelt on the ground and motioned me to do the same. *Stand with Topiltzin against the tyranny of selfish gods. Show humanity the path to true sacrifice and have patience with them when they resist. Even I did not receive the honor of their sacrifices until I had proven myself worthy.*

"I'll do my best, My Lord." I looked at the shower of snow-like flakes floating down from the heavens again and marveled at the warmth it brought me inside as it soaked into my skin. The smell of bone flowers set my heart thudding. "You still haven't told me what this wonderful dust is though."

When he smiled at me with Little Reed's face, I felt I might melt. *It is Omeyocan's most precious gift, of course. Love.*

"Love?" I laughed, turning my chin up and letting it dance down upon me, soaking it up with relish. *I'm covered in love!* When I opened my eyes and looked at Quetzalcoatl again, my heart swelled with longing and desire, stirring my body in ways that even Red Flint's most successful attempts hadn't. He looked so much like Little Reed.... *What must it be like to be his lover?* I wondered.

But to my horror, the words rang out loud. My face burned when he raised an eyebrow and I wished I could end the Divine Dream, so I could escape this mortifying embarrassment.

I have not had a lover since Mayahuel, he said, a thoughtful smile on his face. *The priesthood calls my priestesses my wives, but I have never lain with any of them.*

"Please forgive my uncouth thoughts, My Lord," I stammered. But I forgot how to speak when he set his fingers before my mouth, not quite touching.

Please do not apologize. I would be lying if I did not admit to sharing that same desire. But

it is not my way to force anyone—

"But I want to," I blurted out, reckless excitement and desire commanding my tongue. *Dear gods! Will I next brazenly reach out and touch him—actually touch the god without his permission?* The words didn't come out as loud as before, but they still whispered on the wind.

He laughed. *Then you have my permission.*

I hesitated a moment before finally touching his cheek with my hand. His skin looked like smooth flesh but felt feathery, as did his lips when he kissed me, first on the mouth then on the neck, just below my jaw. My pulse sounded in my ears, lust swallowing fear as his hands melted away my robe and the dress underneath as if they were crumbling wet paper. His feathery-feeling hands raised tiny bumps in their wake as they moved over my bare breasts, down my body, and between my thighs.

Overwhelmed with desire, I moved my hands over his body too. Unsurprisingly his tepolli was feathery, though the feel of feathers came and went with dreamlike laziness, sometimes leaving him feeling like a man. I pulled him atop me, savoring his weight on me, pinning but not crushing. With the Sun watching us up in the sky, I couldn't see his face, but the clouds soon rolled over, letting me gaze longingly into those eyes that made me think of Little Reed. He stroked himself against me until I couldn't take it anymore. "Now?" I dug my fingernails into the nape of his neck.

Now. His voice was as eager as my own.

I expected pain, as Nimilitzli told me there would be for any woman's first time, but I felt only pleasure as he eased inside me. It made sense though; this wasn't real, and even after this, I'd still be a virgin, at least physically.

Quetzalcoatl rocked me back and forth with each thrust. *Someday we will make love in the real world,* he whispered. *I have things I must do first, but someday....*

"Promise?" I moaned, wrapping my legs around him. For the briefest seconds I wondered if there had been some truth to Ahexotl's claims; and that we would make love in the real world through some intermediary—gods, let it be Little Reed!—but overwhelming pleasure mounted into a wave that crashed down on me with such intensity that I felt my body in the real world reacting.

He collapsed atop me, spent. *I promise, my dearest butterfly,* he whispered. *As soon as the time is right.*

He faded slowly away after that, the cave gradually re-coalescing around me. My sweating body still vibrated like a drum after the strike as I stared at the jagged ceiling, unable to stop smiling. The god had chosen me for his first real wife.

But why would he do that?

CHAPTER TWENTY

Ixchell came for me at dawn, and she brought a tlaxcalli which she handed to me one small piece at a time, to make sure I didn't gobble it down in my desperate hunger. Once I finished, we climbed the ladder and went out into the garden, my stomach still rumbling.

I'd hoped to still see Love floating down from the heavens, but the sky bled orange with the day's first light. My head swam and my body shook, so Ixchell held my arm as we went down a stepped path along the terraces to two walled courtyards surrounded by tall oak trees. Inside the north one were numerous bath pits and adobe steam baths. We walked under a thatch awning erected over the bath pits and Ixchell closed the maguey cloth screen around one then lit a fire in the clay drum at the back. The stone-tiled pit was already filled with freezing cold water and once I finished bathing, I dried with a piece of linen while standing next to the fire, shivering in the cool morning air. She then helped me into my dress and a fresh robe.

"Did everything go well in the Divine Dream?" she asked as she brushed my hair. "It can be a very intense experience the first time."

My cheeks burned at the memories. "It was...illuminating."

"Nimilitzli wants to see you right away. I'm sure she'll want to hear all about it."

She probably would, but some things would remain just between me and Quetzalcoatl.

◻

Little Reed sat at the hearth, stirring something savory in a pot over the fire when I arrived at Nimilitzli's house. His face lit with happiness, triggering that intense flame of desire again. I started to smile back but then averted my eyes. *You can't be unfaithful to Quetzalcoatl, even if it's just in your head.*

"I made a dog stew to celebrate finishing the trials," he said. He sniffed his handiwork then added, "I hope it turns out all right. I'm not terribly handy with cooking."

"It smells wonderful," I assured him. "But how did you get a dog for the pot?" Nimilitzli favored an austere, priestly diet of mostly maize, beans and squash, with the occasional treat of venison, so I hadn't had dog since my days as a young girl back in Culhuacan.

Little Reed smiled. "I have my ways." He offered me a spot near the fire. "Did you have a good experience in the Divine Dream?"

My cheeks burned again.

"I'm sure at the very least it answered many of your questions," Nimilitzli ventured from her bed where she was already working at the loom set across her waist.

I told them about seeing the shining city in the north. "Quetzalcoatl wants me and Topiltzin to end human sacrifice, to curb the influence of gods like Smoking Mirror."

"Sounds very much like the vision you had, Topiltzin," Nimilitzli noted. "That's a lot of expectation to carry. Are you sure you're ready for that?"

"It's what I was born to do, Mother," Little Reed said.

Nimilitzli nodded. "Then go to your destiny, and hopefully something I taught you helps you get there."

Little Reed kissed her forehead and stroked her hair. "You taught me so much, and every bit will guide my heart, now and when I'm king."

"Stop being so sentimental." Nimilitzli shooed him away. "Aren't you supposed to go hunting with Cuitlapanton? One doesn't keep the king waiting."

"I didn't want to spend the day wondering what the god said to Quetzalpetlatl," he said. "The king will understand." He gave my hand a squeeze. "I'm happy you've found a future you can embrace."

I pulled my hand from his, feeling dizzy with lust. I'd really hoped my experience with Quetzalcoatl would cool my feelings for Little Reed, but they seemed stronger than ever now. Why could I not control myself? What was this weakness? It felt at times as though something external were possessing me. "You really shouldn't keep the king waiting any longer, Topiltzin."

Nimilitzli watched him go, then muttered, "Probably a good thing he's leaving now anyway." She cleared her throat. "And you seem very happy with your new assignment from the god."

"I am. It's a tremendous honor," I said, ladling out stew for both of us.

"You don't consider yourself too grown up to listen to an old woman anymore, do you?"

I laughed. "You're not old."

"I'm past my childbearing years, which makes me useful only as a priestess or a servant in the palace."

"I'll always listen to your wise words, Nimilitzli."

"Be very careful taking on this task."

I startled. "What do you mean?"

"It's one thing to serve the gods to honor them. Quetzalcoatl has asked you to become involved in the power struggles of the gods themselves."

I struggled with how to respond. "The Feathered Serpent wouldn't...he'd never...this is about ending human sacrifice, Nimilitzli. Quetzalcoatl cares about humanity and he's tired of seeing us die meaningless deaths to feed greedy gods who only want us for our blood—"

"That's most of the gods, Quetzalpetlatl. You know that."

"Yes, they all need our blood, and we owe it to the old ones, but he's talking about gods like Smoking Mirror, who want us to fear them so we will feed them extra and make them stronger than the other gods. I've seen the work of Smoking Mirror's followers, and I want him driven back into the desert hole he crawled out of."

The anger rolling off my tongue surprised me, until I realized it had always been there, cooking with the years. And now that the words came flooding out, they brought unexpected pain and despair with them, leaving me feeling like a dying fish gasping for water.

Nimilitzli sat up, the pain plain on her face, and she leaned forward to set her hand on mine. "This Smoking Mirror had no reason to hurt you before, but do you really want to give him one?"

I fought to control my voice as I said, "My father's heart fed that monster, so the least I can do is make sure Smoking Mirror is banished from the temples in his memory."

"I don't want to see you suffer any more than you already have—"

"It's the price I'm willing to pay for my father, for my mother, for Topiltzin, for you. For everyone." I wiped hot tears from my face.

Nimilitzli bowed her head. "Then I shall say no more about it."

◻

Her words stuck with me all through my first day as a priestess, casting a gloomy cloud over everything, and when I returned to warm the stew for the evening meal, I tried hard not to feel angry at her questioning my judgment. She noticed my grumpiness, but kept her word and didn't mention it, and I didn't want to start a fight.

Little Reed was nervous but chatty, regaling us with the tale of his day hunting with Cuitlapanton and Mazatzin. He brought home not deer or peccary, but rather a marriage proposal for me, by the king on behalf of Red Flint.

"He really asked you to make me Red Flint's concubine?" I asked, stunned.

Little Reed shook his head. "It was definitely to tie your dress to Red Flint's cape."

Turquoise Bells already hated me enough without adding that insult.

"I told the king that I'm not your master, and if Red Flint desires a marriage to you, then he'll have to ask you himself when he returns from war," Little Reed said.

"My answer is no."

Little Reed gave me a smile which he dropped as soon as Nimilitzli asked him, "You're all packed to leave tomorrow?"

With the stress of preparing for my trials and my new god-granted task, I'd forgotten that Little Reed was leaving for the army in the morning. I tried not to feel sick about it, but failed.

"I am packed and ready," he confirmed.

"I won't get to see you off in the morning, so let me say goodbye now," Nimilitzli said.

Little Reed knelt to hug her. She whispered in his ear and he laughed and nodded. "I will, Mother, and I love you too." Nimilitzli kissed his cheek, then he tucked her under the blankets. "I will see you again soon."

Seeing Nimilitzli's tears made my anger at her dissolve away as I shared her pain at seeing Little Reed leaving us, for real this time. This was best for him—and for me. I was Quetzalcoatl's wife now, and it was time that I moved on from this childish infatuation. *He has his future, and you have yours, and someday they'll merge back together again,* I reminded myself as I blinked back tears.

"Will you walk with me?" Little Reed asked. I followed him out of the door onto the darkened precinct.

When we reached the side of the temple, he suddenly stopped and grabbed my hand. "Will you come to see me off tomorrow? I leave quite early, so I understand if you can't—"

"Of course I'll be there."

He averted his gaze, then dashed it back to me. He was trembling. "There's something I must tell you, and tomorrow won't be a good time."

Now I shared his nervousness. "What is it?"

He gathered his resolve then pulled me to him so our bodies touched. "I love you, Papalotl," he whispered, then kissed me, like Red Flint had. Like Quetzalcoatl had.

I should have worried that someone might see us, but the whole world seemed to fall away so it was just me and Little Reed, tangled up in passion and heat, memories of lying with Quetzalcoatl—the god who had Little Reed's face—flooding my thoughts and stoking my desire like a wildfire. Had Little Reed asked to have me just then, I would've let him, right against the side of the Feathered Serpent relief. The desire to ask him grew more intense the longer I held my breath.

Luckily he had better sense than I did. "You should go," he whispered. "I don't want you to get into trouble."

I looked around, dazed and panting. I felt as drunk as that night in Teotihuacan. I checked to see if anyone was watching us, but we were well-concealed in the temple's shadow. "You're right." I separated myself from him and shook my head, trying to clear my thoughts. "People are depending on us; the god is depending on us." *Not to mention that what you've done makes you an unfaithful wife.*

"I'll write to you often," Little Reed said. "You'll write back, to let me know how you are?"

"I will, but we mustn't linger or someone will see us."

I kept at a distance from him as we walked to the calmecac. He wished me good night when we reached the cistern and I mumbled good night too, but didn't look back as I hurried around the corner, towards the girls' dormitories, to get my belongings to take back to Nimilitzli's house.

I lay in my bed next to the fire, trying to sleep while Nimilitzli droned softly in her own bed several arm-lengths from me. But my mind was abuzz as I thought about that moment by the temple again and again. All this time I thought Little Reed hadn't felt anything for me, and now I wanted to cry. He did love me, but I'd already given myself to the god.

ⵔ

Hours before dawn, I was up tidying the house and debating whether or not to go and see Little Reed off. I wouldn't get to see him again for a year at least, but I feared a repeat of last night's madness, so I took my time when I went to the priestesses' steam baths, weighing the decision. By the time I swallowed my fear and decided to go, I had to run to catch up with the soldiers before they left the city.

I skipped down the winding stone stairs behind the houses, into the lower precinct, past the temples to the other gods, then made my way down another set of steps into the Merchant Quarters. I held up my dress's hem as I ran, garnering puzzled looks from the women up early preparing tlaxcallis and atole before their men went to work the market.

I skidded to an unsteady stop when I reached the gates. I looked over the sea of soldiers marching out, the torches hardly shedding enough light to see by. *Am I too late? Curse my indecision!* I should have been at the palace to hug Little Reed goodbye.

But then I saw him, at the end of the marching line. His frown made my heart ache. I waved, trying to get his attention, but his gaze remained fixed on the ground. "Topiltzin!" I called, but when he still didn't look up, I shouted, "Little Reed!"

When he finally saw me, a relieved smile broke across his face. I waved after him as he marched out onto the darkened road, heading away from the safety of Xochicalco. "Goodbye, Little Reed! Please come home safely!"

I continued waving until he disappeared into the darkness, then I leaned against the wall and buried my face in my hands. "And I love you too, Little Reed," I whispered between my tears.

PART THREE
THE YEAR FIVE FLINT

CHAPTER TWENTY-ONE

Two summers after Teotihuacan, Nimilitzli fell on the temple steps and broke her hip all over again, but this time, she didn't recover. I'd moved out briefly, to share a house with Malinalli, but for the next five years I lived with Nimilitzli again, helping her with the daily chores and getting her to the temple for her duties, though in the last year, she did the latter less and less. She developed a cough and soon couldn't leave her bed. I often stayed up late getting her comfortable and fed, but after all the years she'd cared for me, it was the only right thing to do.

Still, someone shaking the bells on the door curtain in the middle of the night irritated me. Nimilitzli woke up murmuring about visitors but I told her, "Go back to sleep. I'll take care of it." I shrugged on my robe as the bells rattled again, more urgent now.

"It's me, Quetzalpetlatl," Mazatzin called from outside. When I opened the curtain, he looked haggard. "I didn't know who else to come to."

"What's wrong?"

"My father collapsed. The physicians are with him now, but I don't even know if he's alive." He rubbed his hands over his face, accentuating the worry. "Will you come to the palace with me?"

I made sure Nimilitzli was settled again then headed for the palace with Mazatzin.

"I'm so sorry for waking you so late," he said as we descended the stairs. "I know you have dawn duties—"

"Please don't apologize," I said. "You were a very good friend when my own life was a mess, so this is the least I can do for you."

Guards stood in the palace halls, whispering in hopes of news while Cuitlapanton's war council gathered in the great hall, debating. Red Flint's continued absence was often the subject of discussion; why had he stayed away for seven years rather than assuming his duties as heir apparent?

Cuitlapanton's concubines stood in the hallway near his room, many crying and holding their young children. Mazatzin's brother Mocnelitzin stood outside the doorway, talking to a guard. When we approached, they both looked up, and inevitably their eyes roved to me like vultures spotting a kill.

I'd endured such attention for so long now that I wanted to dismiss it as just something every woman learned to deal with in men. Yet the older I became, the more intense it seemed: not a man passed me by without his attention shifting to me as if dragged by an invisible net. Cuitlapanton's gaze lingered longer now that it used to, and all the priests stared, the world around them seemingly forgotten. Only Mazatzin showed no interest of that kind for me.

But perhaps most disturbing was that even some women, like Malinalli, sometimes became ensnared too. I once caught her staring at me across the priestly gardens, her gaze distant and dreamy, but when I waved to her, she hurried away and didn't talk to me for three days after that. I valued her friendship too much to ever bring it up.

While nothing untoward came of this bizarre effect I seemed to have, I still felt naked and vulnerable for it. I never ventured into the poorer quarters alone, and when I had to light the fires around the city, I always took Mazatzin with me.

Mocnelitzin blinked away his dazed expression and embraced Mazatzin. "The doctors fear he may be cursed, Brother."

"He's alive then?" Mazatzin asked.

Mocnelitzin nodded. "I was about to send for Ahexotl, but since the fire priestess is here, perhaps she can take a look at Father?" He avoided looking at me while the guard stared as if undressing me in his head.

"I'll look at him," I agreed, eager to be out of the guard's sight. I followed Mocnelitzin and Mazatzin inside.

I'd seen many of the king's women in their rooms over the course of my midwife duties, but this was my first time in the king's quarters. It resembled my father's room, with murals celebrating battles and death. Cuitlapanton lay on his bed surrounded by physicians and guards, covered with blankets and animal skins. One side of his face sagged like melted wax, but he tried to raise a hand to me when I approached the bed. "What happened?" I asked as I knelt next to him.

"He was with one of his concubines when he collapsed and stopped breathing," one of the guards answered. "We got him breathing again, but now he can't speak. The physicians suspect a curse."

Physicians were good at curing common ailments, like festering sores and rotting teeth, but if they couldn't see the cause, they assumed it was the work of a dark sorcerer. Nimilitzli said that most ailments could be cured with prayer mixed with strong medicines and time in the steam bath, but some rare illnesses refused to bow to medication, and those never turned out well. She'd only once encountered an actual curse, on a man who had defiled a statue of Tlaloc after losing his children in a flood.

I felt the king's forehead, looking for any bumps or bruises, but there were none. He closed his eyes and moaned, the still-working side of his face turning up into a smile. I emptied my divination pouch onto the blanket, spreading dried maize kernels across Cuitlapanton's chest then chanted various incantations and waited for any response to them. The kernels remained in place as his chest rose and fell. "There doesn't appear to be a curse," I told Mocnelitzin and Mazatzin. "But I can ask the god."

Mocnelitzin closed his eyes, relieved. "Thank you, Fire Priestess."

"Who was with him when it happened?"

"Lady Atzi."

"I'll speak with her first." To Mazatzin, I said, "Please make sure that no one disturbs me while I'm in the Divine Dream."

"I'll have Malinalli take your morning duties." He gave my hand a grateful squeeze. "Thank you for your help, Quetzalpetlatl."

As I went down the hall towards the women's quarters, practically every gaze followed me and not all of them were friendly, especially as I passed the women. In some ways I preferred the childish nagging I'd endured at Turquoise Bells's hands to the silent loathing I felt now from some women. At least if an accusation was spoken, I could address it. I was relieved to finally leave the hallway.

I found Lady Atzi in her room wailing on her bed while her handmaiden tried to calm her with kind words. They looked up when I cleared my throat, but Lady Atzi looked stricken and cried harder.

I dismissed the servant and sat next to Atzi. We'd had a cool relationship ever since Pochotzin's execution for treason, so she surprised me by burying her face in my robe. I put my arm around her shoulder. "It's all right, My Lady. The king's still alive. Things could have been much worse."

"It's my fault," she sobbed. "All my fault!"

"Surely not."

"It is! He told me he was tired and not feeling well...and now look at him."

"What happened?"

"It was our night to make love, but he told me he didn't feel well. And I told him 'You felt well enough to bed Lady Emerald this afternoon, so don't give me your excuses.' We all deserve our due, right? He shouldn't have gone to her because it wasn't her turn, but then he's always favored her." Lady Atzi wiped her nose on my robe, and as I waited for her to continue, I gave silent thanks to the god that he didn't keep a harem of women like mortal kings did.

"I told him 'no excuses', so he gave in, just to make me stop beating my drum, I'm sure.

"Everything was going fine, but then...then he got this horrible look on his face, as though he had no idea where he was or who I was; and when I asked him what was wrong, he spoke as if he was drunk. Then he just collapsed. I thought he was being dramatic, but then I saw he wasn't breathing...and I called the guards...." She fell against me again and cried so hard her tears soaked through my robe. "I killed him!"

"He's still alive."

"But I did it to him. I should have believed him."

I stayed with her a while longer, offering what comforting words I could, but eventually I sent for her servant to sit with her.

Back out in the hallway, Mazatzin waited for me. "How is she?"

"She blames herself for what happened."

Mazatzin sighed. "Nothing good has happen to her since Pochotzin was executed."

Indeed, the woman seemed to have no luck left to her.

◻

My meditation room in the calmecac had once belonged to Mothotli. She'd been gone five years now; she'd left once the lesions started showing up on her face. She'd said little to either Nimilitzli or I before she departed, but she did leave me a note wishing me good luck in my future and that she was glad she'd been wrong about me. Even now, as I walked in the door, I caught a faint whiff of the incense she used to burn, as if a part of her refused to leave this place.

I kept a wooden box of teonanacatl mushrooms on the shelf above my meditation mat, for consulting the god, which happened more frequently with the years, regardless of whether I needed his guidance or not. It hadn't been very long since I'd last gone into the Divine Dream, but already my desire flared again. *You don't have time for such distractions,* I reminded myself as I drank down the mushroom and octli mixture.

But that was hard to stay focused on when Quetzalcoatl greeted me by pulling me down onto a bed of clouds where he kissed my neck as he undressed me. *I had hoped you would come back soon, my love,* he whispered as he kissed my bare breasts. *I missed you already.*

I stifled my growing arousal. "This isn't a good time, My Lord. I'm here on important business."

But this is *important business,* he said with an all-too-human smile. It surprised me how un-godlike he could be at times, and it drove away my doubts about why I was his lover at all. At times he seemed just like Little Reed.

He dropped the smile when I frowned at him. *Has something happened?*

"The king's ill, and I must know if anything can be done for him."

Quetzalcoatl paused to think. *Ill indeed.* He raised a brow.

"Do you know what's making him ill?"

The blood in his head stopped. He is not a young man, nor was he in the best of health.

"Can we do anything for him?"

The damage cannot be undone, and he will not recover.

I shook my head. "Lady Atzi blames herself for this."

He would have suffered it soon anyway, regardless.

"How long does he have to live?"

A few months, at most. The Deformed One will come when he is ready to collect him. Quetzalcoatl laid his head on my shoulder.

"But Red Flint hasn't returned yet."

It is time he did.

I sighed. "Will he be as good a king as his father?"

Foresight is not one of my gifts, but he will serve his purpose. He kissed me again, trying to coax me back to play.

But I pushed him away gently. "I want to—I always look forward to the time we spend together—but I need to give this news to Mazatzin, and Red Flint must be summoned back immediately."

Of course. Your devotion to duty is why I want you for my high priestess. I will send you back immediately, my love.

His words set my desire aflame and I gave him one last kiss; a promise that I'd come back when we had time to enjoy each other. He stroked my hair, frustrated. *Someday, my beautiful Butterfly. Someday.* He closed my eyes with his fingertips and the Divine Dream melted away around me. I awoke in my meditation room, my heart heavy with its own frustration.

How much longer was someday?

◻

Mazatzin ran to meet me halfway down the palace hallway. "What did the god say?"

I shook my head and he looked like I'd just shot him with an arrow. "Red Flint should be sent for immediately. I'm so sorry, Mazatzin."

Mocnelitzin embraced him around the shoulders a moment before clearing his own throat and saying, "We should inform the Council."

"I'll bring Red Flint back," Mazatzin said. "He should hear the news from a brother."

◻

Mazatzin left at dawn, taking one soldier with him. Even though Chichimec activity had declined since the allied army sent soldiers to every corner of the valley to hunt out the roving camps, I wouldn't want to travel with only one guard; I was moderately skilled with a macauhuitl sword, thanks to Little Reed's training, but little good that would do me against a group of bandits. Men weren't free to have such fears though. I saw Mazatzin off at the gate, giving him a letter for Little Reed, should he see him.

I went back to sleep after eating but Malinalli woke me around noon. "Ahexotl wants to see you."

"What for?" Ahexotl never wanted to see me for anything.

"He didn't say. He's at the palace."

The number of guards had doubled overnight and I felt as if I was walking into an army camp rather than a palace. The guards eyed me when I asked where Ahexotl was, but eventually they pointed me towards the great hall.

Ahexotl sat on the edge of the king's dais, his scarred legs stretched out before him. His bloated yellow- and red-skinned feet barely fit into his leather sandals. It amazed me that he could walk on them at all. He leaned against his wooden staff, listening to the Council members argue, but he shot me a glance when I came in. "You called for me, Your Grace?" I asked him.

"Normally I'd call Nimilitzli for this, but with her illness, you've become as good as high priestess." He never held my gaze anymore. "The king is dead."

I blinked. "So soon?"

Before Ahexotl could answer, Obsidian Eagle shouted for silence. To add to my surprise, he wasn't wearing his novice priest robe but rather dressed up in royal splendor. He was studying to become a priest of Quetzalcoatl—and usually followed Ahexotl everywhere, carrying the high priest's books or bags like a scribe. So long as one was a student, he or she was to forsake frivolity and wear only the black or white robes of their chosen order. Had he decided to leave early because of his father's demise?

"We cannot stand here arguing about the punishment. He poisoned Father, and would've killed Red Flint when he came back," Obsidian Eagle said. "Mocnelitzin deserves beheading for his ambitions, and if the Council is too weak to order it, I'll do it myself, with my father's sword."

The nobles muttered to each other, but stopped when I approached. "Excuse my intrusion, but what happened?" I asked. They didn't answer, their eyes all muddled. Annoyed, I turned to Obsidian Eagle, who was as distracted as the others but managed to shake it when I repeated the question.

"Mocnelitzin poisoned the king. He's already in custody and he'll pay for this heinous crime this very evening." He turned to the nobles. "Agreed?"

The leader of the nobles—Spear Fish—replied, "The real question is, who will rule in Red Flint's stead now that the man second to the throne cannot do so?"

"Mazatzin is third in line," I said. "And he's faithful and trustworthy."

"But he's not here," Ahexotl pointed out.

"And I fear he won't live long either." Obsidian Eagle paced. "We've learned that Mocnelitzin sent assassins out to intercept him, to ensure Red Flint never received the news."

"Then we must dispatch troops to stop them," I said.

"I suggested as much." Obsidian Eagle glared at Spear Fish again.

The indecision on the nobleman's face frustrated me. Couldn't any of them make a decision, or were they content to let Mazatzin die? "Who's fourth in line for the throne?"

"Pochotzin was." Obsidian Eagle didn't look at me.

"This is ridiculous." Ahexotl maneuvered to his feet and Obsidian Eagle hurried to help him, but Ahexotl pushed him away. "While we all stand here arguing succession, my fire priest is about to be set upon by assassins. Obsidian Eagle is an heir and he's prepared to hold the throne in trust until Red Flint returns."

Spear Fish wrinkled his nose. "The boy? But he hasn't even spent a day in the military, and he's tenth in line—"

"I'm seventh," Obsidian Eagle fired back. "I've lost three brothers to war in the last two years, but what would you care about such—"

"You're a child barely old enough to wear a loincloth let alone the crown of a kingdom!" Spear Fish shouted back.

Obsidian Eagle reached for his sword, but Ahexotl grabbed his hand.

And my own wrist started itching for the first time in seven years. It wasn't unbearable, more like a tickle deep in my flesh of my wrist. I continued watching everyone very carefully.

"No one else is here, Lord Spear Fish," Ahexotl said. "Camaxtli and Oquitzin are still doing their military service, and we all know that thanks to that fall he took as a child, Prince Stargazer isn't mentally fit to assume the throne; he can barely dress himself, let alone make informed decisions about the kingdom. Obsidian Eagle is young and untested, but he's also well-versed in the priestly arts, and with the Council's guidance, he'll do fine until Red Flint comes back. The Council hasn't the power to act on its own, so let's stop the bickering. The people need a king, even if he's only to lead them for a few weeks, otherwise we become vulnerable to our enemies. If Ihuitimal knew there was a power gap in Xochicalco, don't think he wouldn't try to grab that opportunity."

Spear Fish stared down Ahexotl while the rest of the Council whispered. He then shifted his gaze to me. "What do you think, Fire Priestess? What would the god wish us to do?"

Ahexotl stiffened at the slight, but to his credit, he kept his mouth shut.

"I'd have to consult the god to tell you what specifically he'd suggest, but I know he wouldn't want his holy city to fall into Ihuitimal's hands," I answered. "A son of the king must fill the empty throne, or a foreigner will claim it."

"But him?" Spear Fish pointed at Obsidian Eagle. "Another nobleman with more military experience—"

"Like you?" Obsidian Eagle pressed closer to him. "Are you really so bold as to levy a claim on my father's throne?"

Spear Fish's face darkened. "I was suggesting nothing of the sort. Your father was a lifelong friend, and my own son is best friends with Lord Red Flint. I care deeply about his family and kingdom, so please forgive my doubts. You will be the one to hold the throne for the Prince until this crisis passes, and you will have my full support." He kissed his fingers and swept them across the ground at Obsidian Eagle's feet.

Obsidian Eagle smiled stiffly as he clasped Spear Fish's shoulder in thanks. "I'll need your wisdom during this tumultuous time."

He accepted the bows and oaths of support from the rest of the Council. When he went to his father's reed throne, he sat carefully upon it. "He sometimes let me sit here when I was a small boy, and he'd pretend I was the king and he was my loyal jaguar knight. I never thought I'd have to sit on his throne as an interim king to protect it while Red Flint played his games in the north." He stiffened his chin a moment, but the anger soon passed. "Mocnelitzin will die tonight in the palace square, beheaded as a traitor. But first, I must assemble soldiers to intercept this band of assassins bent on killing Mazatzin."

"And I'll go to the temple and pray," Ahexotl said.

Obsidian Eagle started to rise, but Ahexotl waved him off with a pointed glare.

Obsidian Eagle bowed his head, as though he'd been caught doing something stupid.

"Quetzalpetlatl, if you could come with me, we have matters to discuss." Ahexotl headed for the entryway at a stilted limp.

I gave Obsidian Eagle a bow then followed Ahexotl out.

Ahexotl huffed and puffed and wheezed as we walked towards the sacred precinct, but he didn't stop until we reached the stairs. He then sat on the lowest step and massaged his knees. "We need to discuss the next step in your future," he mumbled. "With a new king preparing to take the throne, we can't have leadership disorder in the priesthood. Nimilitzli has chosen you to succeed her as high priestess, and it's time you took on the title and duties formally. Given what happened in the last day, it's all the more urgent."

The news should have brought me joy; I'd finally achieved the first step of my ultimate goal, but instead it left me melancholy. The high priestess served for life, so if Nimilitzli thought it was time I took her robe....

Ahexotl frowned. "Don't look so disappointed with your promotion."

"I'm not. It's just unexpected."

He grunted. "That's life. We'll conduct the formal ceremony in three days, so you have time enough to do the appropriate fasting and to give some thought to whom you want to appoint the next fire priestess."

"I think Malinalli would be a good choice."

"That's fine." He struggled to his feet again, and leaned on his walking stick as he limped up the stairs.

Part of me felt a twinge of guilt at seeing him struggle so much. I moved to take his arm, but he jabbed his stick at my right foot, drawing blood. "I can make it just fine on my own, thank you," he growled and continued on his way.

I watched him go, indignant and furious. What right did he have to speak to me like that?

CHAPTER TWENTY-TWO

 When I returned to the palace to make sure none of the king's expectant women had gone into early labor, many of the women still huddled in groups in the corridors, crying. Whatever jealousy had existed before was now forgotten in their shared grief.

As for Lady Atzi, she lay in her room, staring into the hearth, muttering to herself. I tried to explain to her what Quetzalcoatl had told me, but she didn't respond at all. "Watch her closely for the next few days," I warned her handmaiden. "If you see any cause for concern—no matter how minor—fetch Lady Emerald immediately."

The girl paled. "You think she'll hurt herself?"

"I don't know, but it's vital she not be allowed to make decisions for herself right now."

The sun sat low on the mountains when I left the palace in search of Ahexotl. Both the high priest and priestess witnessed state executions, to collect the condemned's blood for the sacrifice, but he hadn't summoned me yet. When I arrived at the temple though, Malinalli told me that Ahexotl had attended the execution without me. "I offered to go and find you, but he said he'd rather spare you the discomfort."

I seethed. True, every time I helped sacrifice a man, I thought about why Quetzalcoatl had chosen me to stand with Little Reed as his high priestess. Watching the victim struggle repulsed me, but I always performed my duty without complaint. The time wasn't yet right to poke that ant hill.

But had I somehow betrayed my real feelings to Ahexotl, or was it a show of contempt and bitterness for not having been able to have me as he'd had so many others?

He brought it on himself, I thought as I headed home. Still, his behavior left me unsettled. *He can hardly walk up stairs, so how can he possibly hurt you anymore?*

While I cooked the sauce for our tlaxcallis, Nimilitzli talked about the few fragments of news she'd heard and I filled in the details; but mostly I sat in melancholy silence, distracted.

"What's on your mind?" Nimilitzli asked, as I set the bowl of sauce between us.

I didn't meet her gaze as I handed her a warm tlaxcalli. "Ahexotl told me it's time I replace you as high priestess."

"It is. I'm not going to get well again, and you're ready."

"I don't feel it."

She patted my hand. "Have faith in the god, and yourself. You'll be a high priestess all will talk about long after you've gone on to Mictlan, just as people will always speak of what Topiltzin does."

Mentioning Little Reed made me long to lie in Quetzalcoatl's arms again and see his son's face. I'd expected my heart to grow forgetful with the years, but instead I longed for him even more, particularly when he signed his letters to me with "Love always." Did he still mean it the way he had the night before he left? I thought about it every time I lay with Quetzalcoatl and imagined he was Little Reed. Having only his letters to hold and touch was no better than having Quetzalcoatl only in the Divine Dream. And the god's constant "someday" had started wearing on me.

Some faithful, pious priestess you are, wishing your divine lover was someone else instead, I scolded myself as I lay awake late into the night. Still, as frustrating as my relationship with the god was, it was all I had, and I craved his feathery touch and airy kisses as much as I needed food and water. *He wouldn't mind me calling on him; he never does.*

Nimilitzli would never abuse the sacred power of the teonanacatl for pleasure. But eventually desire won out. I put extra logs in the fire and slipped my robe on, then woke Nimilitzli to let her know I was leaving. "I have something I forgot to do, but I'll be back soon." Not completely untrue; this particular itch was keeping me awake, but guilt followed me out the door. What if she choked and I wasn't there to help her? I almost went back, but it would only invite questions.

Inside the calmecac, I passed Ahexotl's meditation room. Light glowed beyond the closed curtain. I closed my own curtain silently and forewent a lamp. Better if he didn't know I was there. I cursed softly when I stubbed my toe on my copal burner, but I found the mushroom box up on the shelf.

Hearing footfalls pass my room, I went to the curtain and peeked out. Obsidian Eagle stood at Ahexotl's curtain, tugging it as he looked up and down the hallway. Ahexotl told him to enter and he pulled the curtain closed behind him. "I've dispatched the troops to intercept Mazatzin."

"And you made sure they are all loyal to us?"

"Of course. They're bringing back his head as proof."

I gasped but clapped a hand over my mouth.

"And what about Red Flint?" Ahexotl asked.

"They'll continue to the army camp and bring him away."

"And you made it clear they weren't to mention Cuitlapanton's death?"

"Of course," Obsidian Eagle said, indignant. "I didn't make mistakes with the poison, did I?"

Ahexotl chuckled. "That's because you always do as I tell you, and that's why you find yourself in these fortunate circumstances."

I almost dropped the box of mushrooms, but caught it and set it carefully on the floor, hardly believing what I was hearing. *Mocnelitzin was innocent!* My wrist itched badly and it took all my resolve to not scratch it raw.

"This isn't going to come cheap though," Obsidian Eagle said. "Paying off the soldiers and the palace guards—"

"Who cares? You'll be king."

"Until Camaxtli or Oquitzin challenge me."

"Stop sucking your stones up into your body. Once you have the throne, the army will fall in line and you can openly dispose of them. That's a natural part of succession; you think your own father didn't shed some blood solidifying his power? Ihuitimal will want you to sit unopposed, and once we combine the armies, you can find more than a few honorless Chichimecs who'd gladly bring you their heads."

The god's own high priest conspiring with Ihuitimal to overthrow Xochicalco's royal succession and seize control of the army? The idea of soldiers wearing Xochicalco's own colors falling upon Mazatzin made me sick and furious. *You should summon Quetzalcoatl.*

But my stomach cramped. I'd spent the years since Teotihuacan trying not to think about what I'd have to give to summon him again. I wrung my three-fingered hand, the pain springing back as if I'd just cut those fingers off moments ago. *No, I shouldn't call on Quetzalcoatl if I don't need to.*

"You would be a better king than me," Obsidian Eagle went on. "I've only ever wanted to be a priest."

"Maybe you are as dense as Lord Spear Fish says," Ahexotl growled. "I'm not royal blood, and thanks to Topiltzin's bitch of a sister, I'm a repulsive cripple. The people would never accept me as their king."

My mouth went dry at the venom in his voice.

"She did *that* to you?" Obsidian Eagle asked, his voice tentative.

"Don't worry about being king; you provide the face while I provide the experience. Do what you're told and Ihuitimal will reward you handsomely."

"What's he giving you?"

"Enough." The hardness in Ahexotl's voice raised the hairs on my neck.

Obsidian Eagle pulled the door curtain aside. "I'm still not sure about this. Surely Ihuitimal will outlaw Quetzalcoatl's worship here, just as he did in Culhuacan."

"One god is just as good as any other," Ahexotl said, shuffling out into the hallway. "They're just tools for exercising power."

I clenched my fist so hard my fingernails dug into my palms.

"I worry about Topiltzin, though," Obsidian Eagle said.

"Don't believe half of what you hear about him. He's but a man, just as fragile before the sword as any. Ihuitimal will take care of him."

Obsidian Eagle nodded. "My only regret is that I won't get to see him or Red Flint die like the lake slugs they are."

"You'll honor Pochotzin's sacrifice by fulfilling these plans. Now take me home. I'm very tired."

Even after their footfalls faded, I stayed in my room, leaning against the wall, reeling from all I'd heard. *You can't stay here all night. The kingdom is in danger—Little Reed is in danger—and with Obsidian Eagle buying the loyalty of the soldiers, who can you trust to warn Mazatzin?*

I wasn't safe here anymore either; not with Ahexotl stoking a bonfire of revenge to throw me into. With the god's sacred city under attack from his nemesis, who but his chosen high priestess should act for his interests?

I made sure the hallway was still empty then went to the Council Room. The weapons still hung on the walls; Nimilitzli said they were gifts bequeathed to the temple from warriors who exchanged their weapons for the priestly robe.

My sacrificial blade would be little good against armored soldiers, and was meant for close combat, so I needed a better weapon. The spear was too heavy for me, and I knew nothing about using an atl-atl, so I reached for one particular macuahuitl sword. Little Reed had taught me a bit about how to weild the flat, lightweight wooden sword edged with obsidian blades, so it was my best choice.

But I hesitated. I'd often seen Nimilitzli giving this one extra care, as if it meant something special to her. Would it be disrespectful to take it?

But when I looked closer, it had feathered serpents carved into the wood core, in a design similar to the one on the side of the god's temple. *It's a sign!* I took the sword and headed home.

I crossed the precinct at a sprint then hurried inside the house, trying not to disturb the bells.

I turned to find Nimilitzli awake and sitting up, reading a letter while a man crouched near the hearth. I immediately recognized him as Lord Citlallotoc of Acolman, who had rescued us the night we left Teotihuacan. He looked much the same as he had then, except he'd acquired a lime-white scar on his jaw.

"Good, you're back," Nimilitzli said. "We have news from your brother." But when she spotted the sword in my hand, she asked, "Why do you have that, Quetzalpetlatl?"

Taking a deep breath, I said, "Ahexotl and Obsidian Eagle are moving to seize Red Flint's throne. Obsidian Eagle poisoned the king and now he's sent assassins to kill Mazatzin and Red Flint—"

"Cuitlapanton is dead?" Citlallotoc asked, rising to his feet, alarmed.

"Yes, in a plot concocted by the king of Culhuacan to seize control of Xochicalco." Nimilitzli sat up straighter. "Where did you hear all this?"

"I overheard them talking in Ahexotl's meditation room."

"What's the sword for?"

"Someone must warn Mazatzin."

"And you thought that should be you?" Nimilitzli asked with an uneasy laugh.

Citlallotoc leaned closer and whispered, "You weren't really going to leave the city unescorted, were you?"

"I'm not completely defenseless," I shot back.

Nimilitzli looked into the fire. "Indeed you aren't."

"You should go to the Council with this news," Citlallotoc suggested.

I shook my head. "Lord Spear Fish might listen, but they all took oaths to Obsidian Eagle, and he's bought off the palace guards. And Ihuitimal promised Ahexotl something involving me for his cooperation and I'm not waiting to find out what revenge he has planned for me."

"You're sure?"

"Him saying 'thanks to Topiltzin's bitch of a sister, I'm a repulsive cripple' is evidence enough for me."

Citlallotoc crinkled his brows. "How dare he speak such vile words? Sounds like he needs to be taught some manners with my sword blade."

"I appreciate that, Lord Citlallotoc, but that won't save Mazatzin." Citlallotoc arched his eyebrow, no doubt surprised I remembered his name, but I pressed on. "He knows nothing of this treachery and he and his guard will be helpless as newborn pups when the traitors find them."

"Then we must get to your friend first. And if you truly feel yourself in imminent danger, I could never show my face to your brother again if I left you here." He turned to Nimilitzli. "Topiltzin is back at the camp for a few weeks before setting off to the north again, so she'll be in his care, and I'll gladly lay down my own life to protect her on route."

To me, Nimilitzli said, "If you really feel you must go, then may the god go with you."

"Will you be all right by yourself?"

"I'll be fine. Someone will come looking for you when you don't show up for your sunrise duties and I'll arrange for help then. Worry only about yourself, understood?"

I kissed her forehead. "I'll try, but I can't promise not to worry."

I made tlaxcallis while Citlallotoc went to the cistern to fill some skins for us. When I went to pack the sword, I found Nimilitzli holding it, staring at it wistfully. "I'll leave it here if you'd rather I didn't take it."

She blinked up at me. "What?"

"I can see that the sword means a lot to you, so if you'd rather I didn't take it—"

"No, it should do what it was made for, not hang unused in the Council Room." Nimilitzli handed it to me. "It served its previous owner well, and it'll do the same for you."

I thought to ask who it belonged to, but then Citlallotoc came back. "Are we ready?" he asked as he shouldered the food pack too.

I donned my traveling cloak and strapped on my medicine pouch, just in case. "Ready."

◻

Even with dawn still far off, the merchant quarter was bustling with activity. At least five caravans were setting out before first light, their slaves loaded down with packs, and Citlallotoc and I walked among them, to blend in with the stream of departing people. While the gate guards probably weren't looking for suspicious people leaving the city, we wanted to avoid unnecessary contact with them.

Once we passed the quarry, we jogged off into the trees. "Your friend likely took the road, as will those following him, but if we cut through the forest, we can get ahead of them and hopefully intercept Red Flint's brother before they do," Citlallotoc said. "It's a good thing I arrived when I did, so I could help you."

"What brought you to Xochicalco anyway?" I asked.

"I had letters for you and the high priestess. Unfortunately, in our rush to leave, I left your letter with Nimilitzli."

"Was it important?"

"I don't know, My Lady, but your brother did personally ask me to deliver them rather than leave them with a runner."

Little Reed had never done that before, so it surely was very important. It was too late to turn back now though.

By dawn my lack of sleep caught up with me. My steps turned to sluggish stumbles and Citlallotoc often got well ahead of me and had to wait for me to catch up. "I haven't slept well in a few days," I admitted, when we stopped to rest and eat.

"I imagine not, with the king's death and now this treachery." He sat on a fallen log opposite me, eating his tlaxcalli. "I must say I'm surprised you remembered me, Lady Quetzalpetlatl. We only met briefly seven years ago."

"I'm blessed with an impeccable memory."

Citlallotoc chuckled. "You're like Topiltzin in that regard. I don't think he ever forgets anything."

The thought of seeing Little Reed again sent a giddy rush through me. I couldn't wait to hug him again and kiss his cheek. *Or his lips.* But I scolded myself for the thought. *It's been seven years, and you pretty much rejected him before he left. For all you know, his heart's moved on to someone new.* Trying to steer my mind away from my growing disappointment, I asked, "Have you served long with my brother?"

"Five years now, though I was looking for an opportunity to serve with him sooner than that. The moment I first met him...I knew I was standing in the presence of a great man. I can't explain why, but I felt as if he had the very ear of the gods themselves. Do you think me crazy?"

I laughed. "Didn't Topiltzin tell you who his father is?"

"Everyone knows he's Mixcoatl's son."

"Actually, he's Quetzalcoatl's."

Citlallotoc blinked at me, startled. "You're serious?"

"My mother was unable to have any more children with Mixcoatl after me, but the god came to her in a dream and told her to swallow a jade stone he'd left for her. A few months later, she gave birth to Topiltzin. That was seventeen years ago."

"Topiltzin is only seventeen? Impossible!"

"When it comes to the god, anything is possible. I've seen the god's work firsthand, so bearing a human son would be the least difficult thing he can do."

Citlallotoc rubbed his chin. "Topiltzin does heal extraordinarily fast. He took a sword slash to the face a few years back and a week later it was gone, without even a scar. Some think he went to a witch for a magic salve." He laughed. "I'm more willing to believe he's the god's son than that he visits witches for potions." He finished his tlaxcalli. "Are you a child of the god as well?"

"I'm afraid I'm not so special."

"I think you're more special then you let yourself believe. Like Topiltzin, you have...an aura about you."

"Yes well, I'd prefer not to have that aura, for it's sure to cause me trouble," I said, and blushed. I'd never mentioned it to anyone before now.

"Sometimes our gifts are difficult to live with." Citlallotoc swallowed some water. "We shouldn't linger if we're to catch up with your friend before the others do."

After we'd gotten back underway, I asked Citlallotoc, "Does my brother ever speak about me?"

"No. If I hadn't already met you once, I never would've suspected he had a sister."

At first I felt crestfallen, but then how often did I talk to Malinalli about Little Reed? Rarely. Not because he wasn't ever on my mind—not a day passed that I didn't think about him at least a few times—but because I feared betraying my feelings for him to her. As the next high priestess, I was expected to be an example of unwavering piety. I didn't even mention him to Nimilitzli unless she brought him up first. Maybe Little Reed said nothing about me for the same reasons.

"He's very private," Citlallotoc went on. "He stays silent about what goes on in his heart and in his tent, unlike others. Prince Red Flint crows to everyone about how many women he takes to bed."

I couldn't contain the laugh. "Red Flint?"

"There's no dignified way to put it. He shows no signs of caring for them, or they for him, and he soon gives them to other soldiers to buy their favor. I pity his future wife, for she will surely marry a husk of a man who spilled all his honey carelessly, leaving none for her. Your brother is much more respectful."

A spike of jealousy surged through me. "Then he has lovers?"

"I don't really know. If he does, he's extremely secretive about it, which I suppose makes sense since he's a priest, and aren't priests supposed to live chaste lives?"

"We do take vows of celibacy."

"Your brother is very dedicated to the god, and I dare say he's already a better leader than most kings. He's promised to return my stolen throne to me once he's reclaimed his own, and I know his word is worth every feather in the valley. I'd lay my life down for him without hesitation." To my surprise, he followed this with a heavy sigh.

"But what?" I asked.

Citlallotoc hesitated. "I wish he weren't so closed off. He's very open to listening to his officers and following their advice when he finds it prudent, but...." He averted his eyes as he said, "I consider him my friend, yet I fear he doesn't consider me the same."

The hurt in his voice surprised me, but also made my heart glow. He was unquestioningly loyal to my brother, exactly the kind of man Little Reed needed at his side, and that made me like him all the more. "He never had many friends," I said. "When he was growing up, most of the priests treated him with reverence befitting a god, but he also suffered a great deal of ridicule and hostility from those who didn't believe his divine parentage."

"Some people cannot help being fools," Citlallotoc said with a frown. "I always found his cool demeanor strange though. I thought priests were supposed to be personally involved with the community."

"Yes, but Topiltzin hadn't been a priest more than a few days before he left for the army."

"He does perform the daily sacrifice for the troops, and he's quite the sight to watch. Even the men from the other armies come to hear him talk about Quetzalcoatl. It all makes good sense now that I know his true parentage. He says we should all give a little blood to the god of our choice before a battle, and once I started doing this, my sword fell swifter and I've twice escaped being dragged off by Chichimecs. I wouldn't think to go into battle without honoring Quetzalcoatl with a little of my blood."

Little Reed had told me about such things in his letters. He'd been working hard instilling the idea of bloodletting as a noble and worthwhile practice, especially among the soldiers. *If I can get warriors to believe in the superiority of sacrificing their own blood, converting the general populace will be easy later on,* he'd written in one letter. *They'll be the most difficult group to convert, since they've been trained for so long to shed their enemies' blood in honor of the Sun, not their own.* Over the years such philosophical statements became the staple of his letters, making me wonder if he considered me nothing more than a religious peer he was exchanging notes with.

But he never fails to sign his letters with love, I reminded myself.

CHAPTER TWENTY-THREE

By midday, my legs felt like melting wax, and stopping to take breaks only let my exhaustion pounce on me. When I started feeling dizzy, Citlallotoc had us stop again, but this time he opened the deerskin pouch at his side and took out his pipe and a sleeve of tobacco. "This will help you."

When he handed the stuffed pipe to me and took out his strikers, I pushed it back to him, appalled. "Courtesans smoke, not priestesses."

"You won't be able to go on much further without something to keep you going. You wish to save your priest friend?" When I still didn't pull the pipe back, he added, "I promise to tell no one."

"You won't think me unsavory?"

"Never." He showed me how to hold the pipe. "Take quick, shallow breaths. If you breathe too deeply, it'll add to your exhaustion."

The first inhalation brought me to tears and coughs, but after a few more breaths, I felt the change, like someone had poured glorious sunshine straight into my blood. I could walk all day, perhaps even run some of it. Citlallotoc puffed a bit as well then said, "We need to keep moving. We're probably ahead of the dog-traitor's men now, but they'll travel through the night and so must we."

We stopped only to replenish our water supply in a creek and re-stuff the pipe, to keep us going once the exhaustion peeked in again. We ate while we walked.

Just before nightfall, we came to the road. I waited in the trees while Citlallotoc went to investigate. Now I was jittery and anxious, hopefully from the tobacco, not my intuition. He prowled the road, creeping low to the ground at the opposite edge, bow at the ready. He came back soon. "The road behind us is clear, but I smell smoke, probably from a campfire. We should stay to the shadows until we see who it is. Have your sword ready." We started up the road, but then he stopped to ask, "Do you know anything about using a sword?"

"Topiltzin showed me how before he left for the army."

Citlallotoc chuckled. "That's Topiltzin, never afraid to defy social convention. He'll either change the world or anger everyone by trying."

The cacophony of buzzing insects and monkey shrieks made it difficult to hear much, but Citlallotoc remained alert, arrow nocked and ready. Soon I caught sight of fire flickering through the trees, and Citlallotoc motioned me off the road. "Stay here," he said then went ahead. I lost sight of him when he went down the hill. I waited, my heart thudding as I muttered prayers to Quetzalcoatl. I measured the time by my shaking breaths and pulsing blood.

When Citlallotoc returned, he came with Mazatzin. I wanted to cry out in relief, but allowed myself only a deep sigh. I didn't spare Mazatzin a hug though. "Thank the Feathered Serpent you're all right."

"I'm fine. It's my guard who's not. Last night a jaguar attacked us, and it mauled him."

He led us back to the small camp where the guard lay on a blanket, his head and one arm bandaged up with the remains of Mazatzin's xicolli. I felt his forehead then opened my pouch and took out a small bag of yauhtli. I had nothing for his fever or to keep his wounds from festering, but at least I could relieve his pain. He resisted the bitter medicine but calmed once I sat him up to wash it down with water. "The pain will go away and you can go to sleep soon," I assured him, but he just moaned and rolled his head.

"How is he?" Mazatzin asked.

"I'm not sure he'll make it through the night. He's already in a state of delirium and he's lost a lot of blood."

Mazatzin cursed. "I should have heard the beast, but it came out of nowhere, like a spirit. Perhaps it wouldn't have attacked us if we'd had torches." He rubbed the back of his neck. "Not that I'm displeased with seeing you, but what are you doing out here?" He shot a glance at Citlallotoc, as if to add, *with him?*

"You didn't tell him?" I asked Citlallotoc.

"I thought he might handle the bad news better coming from a friend," Citlallotoc said.

"What bad news?" Mazatzin demanded.

I pulled him back towards the hill, until we were far enough away that we wouldn't be overheard. "Your father died a couple of days ago. Obsidian Eagle poisoned him, then had Mocnelitzin executed for the crime. He's taken the throne and sent assassins out to kill you and Red Flint."

Mazatzin's face flushed dark. "He did?"

I nodded. "And Ahexotl is helping him. They're acting on Ihuitimal's behalf, to secure the army against Topiltzin. I had to warn you and stop this treachery."

Mazatzin clenched his fists, blinking back tears. "Thank you for looking out for me, Quetzalpetlatl. You're a true and loyal friend, and I shall never forget it."

Citlallotoc came over. "We should extinguish the fire so it's not easy for the traitor's men to find us. If we hide near the road and ambush them when they come, we can pick most of them off with arrows before they realize where we are."

We stamped out the fire then did a bloodletting to the god, to bless our weapons. I remained with the guard while Mazatzin and Citlallotoc went back to the road, but I wanted to see what was happening and so crawled up the side of the hill with my sword and lay on my belly near the top. I spotted Mazatzin climbing a large tree while Citlallotoc hurried to the other side of the road and disappeared into the dark forest. Then the waiting began.

I tried to stay alert, but my body turned heavy as a stone. *I'll be better after a moment's rest,* I thought, finally giving in to the desire to close my eyes....

I awoke when someone stepped on me.

It knocked the wind from me and I lunged to the side. A man cried out and tumbled down the hill. Shouting came from the distance, but I returned my attention to the man groaning and cursing at the bottom of the hill. I gripped my sword tighter and stayed still, hoping he couldn't see me in the dim moonlight leaking through the trees.

He stood and backed up a few steps, but then tripped over the guard. He stared at the other man, then, to my repulsion, he drew his knife and cut the guard's throat. He looked around again.

When his gaze stopped on me, I couldn't breathe. We stared each other down a moment.

I sprang to all fours, but when I got to my feet, I only made it a couple of steps before he grabbed me from behind. He clamped a hand over my mouth, holding my arms to my sides with the other and rendering my sword useless. His hard grip sent my mind screaming back to the night in the water yard with Ahexotl and I lashed out, bashing him in the face with the back of my head, breaking his nose. He howled and let me go, but instead of running, I swung the sword and it lodged in his exposed neck. He groped at my hands and I dashed off into the woods, unsure where my panic was taking me.

Someone stepped in front of me and I tried to swerve, but he seized me with strong hands. I went to bite him, but he shouted, "It's me, Quetzalpetlatl!" Mazatzin let me go, backing away.

I flung myself into his arms, my whole body shaking. "Someone came into camp and killed the guard, slit his throat while he slept—"

Citlallotoc jogged to us, his expression hard in the moonlight. "I saw one of the men duck into woods over here."

"She says he came into the camp," Mazatzin said.

Citlallotoc took off through the trees, sneaking from shadow to shadow, but he stopped when he reached the edge of the hill. He pointed his bow at someone on the ground. "Is this him?"

The man lay in the dirt and leaves, my sword sticking out of his neck and blood oozing from his mouth. He blinked up at us. Mazatzin pulled the sword out, letting the blood surge, and the man stiffened and choked, his breath coming quick and shallow. His eyes soon glazed over. I felt sick.

"It was a good blow. Your brother taught you well," Citlallotoc said. He jogged down the hill to check on the guard, but was back in a few moments, shaking his head. "We need to clear the bodies off the road and move on, before the jaguars and bears come following their noses."

Obsidian Eagle's men—ten in all—lay strewn about the road, all driven through with at least one arrow. We carried them back to camp and tossed them on the ground next to the fire where we stripped them of weapons and whatever food, water and medicine they carried. Mazatzin and I muttered prayers over the slain guard, imploring Xolotl to show him mercy and guide him through the trials of the underworld so he might finally find peace.

We set off into the night, following the road north. We walked until the sky turned gray with dawn, then Citlallotoc suggested we fall back into the trees and find a place to rest. The ground was hard with only a blanket to sleep on, but I fell into dreamless sleep as soon as I lay down.

◻

My stomach woke me when I smelled roasting meat. Mazatzin sat next to the fire, tending to a skinned peccary on a spit while he smoked his pipe. Early afternoon sunshine leaked through the canopy. My muscles protested and my stomach gurgled when I sat up. "Where did you get the meat?"

"Citlallotoc shot it a while ago. He's scouting the road, making sure we don't have unexpected visitors."

Citlallotoc came back shortly before the peccary was cooked, looking well rested and ready to march. "We'll be able to make it to the army camp before nightfall," he said as he cut the charred meat into tlaxcallis for each of us. We then got underway, eating as we marched.

I was used to living with little sleep, particularly since becoming fire priestess, but fatigue set in quicker than I'd hoped. The meat lifted me for a while, but after a time I thought only of sleep. I didn't ever go more than two days without a good steady sleep, but I also didn't want to be the reason we didn't make the camp by nightfall. I wished I could smoke a little, but I didn't dare do such things in front of Mazatzin.

I cheered when I saw the first signs of campfire smoke in the distance. We picked up the pace and came to the guard post just as dusk crept over the mountains. My anticipation mounted as we walked through Xochicalco's end of camp; I hardly even noticed the distant, longing stares as I walked by. "I'm going to find Red Flint," Mazatzin told me. "I'm sure you're eager to see Topiltzin, so we'll talk tomorrow." He disappeared into the milling crowd, leaving me with Citlallotoc.

Citlallotoc took me to a large tent near the center of camp. The guard held the flap open for us.

The warm tent smelled of copalli and xocolatl, and cotton armor and weapons decorated a grass man in the back corner. Citlallotoc knelt on the ground then called out, "Are you here, My Lord?"

"Citlallotoc?" Little Reed came through a second flap at the back of the tent, revealing another room behind him as he came out, dressed in a simple white xicolli.

I knew Little Reed didn't age like normal men, and I'd expected him to look older, but I was still shocked by the strands of white snaking through his hair. It was as if those seven years had been fifteen for him. But his smile was the same one I remembered and loved, and he'd grown handsomer with the years.

The smile dropped from his face when he saw me though. "What are you doing here?"

I'd expected a joyful embrace only to get an uncomfortable silence as I tried to gather my thoughts. Citlallotoc rescued me though. "I brought her here to remove her from harm's way, My Lord. Treachery is running rampant in Xochicalco."

Little Reed embraced me, but it was a stiff, formal action. My face burned with resentment. He'd changed much. "Are you all right?" he asked, once he'd made enough space between us again. "What's this all about?"

I told him about Cuitlapanton and Obsidian Eagle, but when I talked of Ahexotl's part, an angry shadow crossed his face. *You should have let him kill Ahexotl back then. You were completely misguided about the god sparing him.*

Little Reed gripped Citlallotoc's shoulders. "Thank you for watching out for my sister. She can take care of herself, but I feel better knowing you could help her if the need arose."

"It's an honor to serve your family, My Lord," Citlallotoc said, bowing his head. "I'm sure you two have much to talk about after so many years, so I'll retire to my tent and catch up on my sleep." He bowed to me as well, and left.

"Your friend is a very good man," I told Little Reed.

"Citlallotoc? Oh yes, a most excellent man." He motioned me to sit down next to the copalli burner, and once we were sitting, he tossed some more incense on the plate. "My first order of business once I've retaken the throne is to send troops to Acolman to punish the traitors who drove him out and return his kingdom to him."

"That will be a fine token of appreciation for his service, but I believe you can still do better for him."

"What do you mean?"

"Far be it for me to divulge a man's heart, but men are loath to admit such things to each other."

"Admit what?"

"He wants your friendship."

Little Reed laughed. "He has it already."

"He wants to be friends like we are." Though I reddened when I thought of Little Reed's last night in Xochicalco and hoped he didn't think Citlallotoc wanted *that* kind of friendship. "What I mean is that he wishes you'd confide in him as you do with me."

"I do confide in him, on every military matter—"

"He wants your ear to talk to you on a personal level, and to offer you his in return. There's more to life than war."

Little Reed smiled. "Indeed there is. I shall do better by him, Papalotl, and thank you for pointing this out to me. I should have true friends, not just loyal followers."

The guard came with a steaming bowl of stew, which Little Reed handed to me. "Could you please bring one more bowl? I wasn't expecting company."

Once the guard left, I said, "You seem to be doing really well for yourself."

"Well enough, though I anticipate a setback once Red Flint takes the throne. I'd hoped to start pushing at Culhuacan next year, while Cuitlapanton was still alive, but I suspect Red Flint won't immediately agree to his father's promise to provide troops."

"Are you two still fighting?"

"We haven't fought in years; we have mutual respect for our differences, but I know Red Flint's heart better than he thinks. He fears appearing subordinate to me, so he won't immediately bow to my request. Maybe in a couple of years...."

The guard returned with another bowl of stew and we began eating.

"He also thinks he holds a strategic advantage over me," Little Reed continued.

"What would that be?"

"You, of course."

"Me?"

"Didn't Citlallotoc deliver my letter?"

"In our hurry to leave, I left it at home with Nimilitzli."

"I'll just tell you what I wrote then. Red Flint was planning to return to Xochicalco next month, to ask you to be his wife. He came to me first, of course, to try to get my permission to have you, but when I told him that you make your own decisions, he called me your little dog and said you always tell me where I can lift my leg."

I rolled my eyes. "You didn't get into a fight, did you?"

"Like I said, we haven't fought in years. I told him I wouldn't grant him permission, but he was free to win your heart on his own."

"I'd have rather you told him to stay away from me," I said.

"Perhaps I should have. I suspect he may try to trick you into believing I was ordering you to marry him, so that's why I sent the letter."

"I would've seen it for the scheme it was," I said. "You already told me how you feel about such arrangements."

"But I also feared he might make threats if you don't accept. Whatever he tells you, Papalotl, I'd rather never get our throne back than see you locked away in a marriage you don't want."

I smiled, feeling achingly warm inside. "Thank you, Little Reed."

He gave me a smile back, making the desire uncoil inside me. "How's Mother doing?" he asked.

The question dampened my lust some. "She hasn't gotten any better, and frankly I doubt she'll last the rest of the year. I'm surprised she's made it this long."

Little Reed watched the white smoke curl off the copalli burner, his expression mirroring some inner conflict.

"I really think you should come home, for a few days anyway," I said.

"We're supposed to cut off a contingent of Chichimecs reinforcements headed for Culhuacan—"

"Nimilitzli didn't give birth to you, but if she'd had milk, she would've fed you at her own breast. She's our mother, and she deserves the honor of us treating her as such."

He tossed more copalli on the plate and sighed. "I should see you safely back to

Xochicalco, and I do have a stake in who takes the throne in all this mess. This way at least I can ensure that I can get both you and Nimilitzli somewhere safe, should Red Flint's bid go wrong."

"There's nowhere safe if Xochicalco falls to Ihuitimal."

"Which is why we must make sure Red Flint takes the throne," Little Reed replied. "Through whatever means necessary." He took my three-fingered hand and gave it a squeeze.

My stomach clenched. "Maybe it won't come to that."

"Let's hope not."

The sudden weight of my responsibility must have shown on my face, for Little Reed said, "You should lie down, get some rest. You may use my bed." He helped me to my feet.

"I don't want to kick you out of your bed—"

"I'll get an extra mat from the supply tent."

Through the flap at the back of the tent was a small room just big enough for a bed of reed mats, animal skins and blankets, and a single wicker clothing chest. He lit a second incense burner near the bed, filling the room with the calming aroma of copalli. He hung my cloak on a peg on one of the tent poles. "I'll be out here if you need anything." He turned to leave.

But I did need something, and I wouldn't be able to sleep without it. I'd spent the last day wondering how to bring it up, or if I even should, and over dinner I'd become even more unsure about it. Was possibly ruining our friendship worth satisfying my curiosity? Maybe not, but one thing was certain: I couldn't go on not knowing the truth. "L-Little Reed!" I stammered.

He turned to me. "Papalotl?"

"I...what I mean to say...about when you left," I finally choked out. "I must speak with you about that night, by the temple."

He looked as uncomfortable as I felt. "Well, that was a while ago...."

My hopes fell. *He's trying to explain it away.*

"I'm sorry I made you uncomfortable that night," he said.

"Then you don't feel that way anymore?" I felt as if I were grasping at the wind, hoping to snag it. When he hesitated to answer, I added, "We promised to always be truthful with each other, so please, tell me the truth. I promise not to criticize." *Though I can't promise not to cry if I turn out to be the lovesick fool in all this.*

He finally said, "My feelings for you are the same as they were then, Papalotl."

My heart stopped. "Then you do still...?"

"Love you? Absolutely. And I always will."

I laughed and wrapped my arms around his neck. "And I've always loved you too, Little Reed, just had no idea how to tell you."

He embraced me back with a contented sigh. "Foolish indecision, on both our parts. But no more." He caressed the side of my face. "I'm glad you didn't get to read the letter, for a marriage proposal really should be done in person."

"Marriage?" I asked, giddy. "But what about our future as priests?"

"Once I've taken back Culhuacan and I'm high priest of Father's order, I'll change the laws so priests and priestesses can marry. There is no good reason for them not to."

"And every king needs an heir," I added.

He smiled then kissed me, bringing the desire roaring up again. I drew him closer, desperate for his touch. I giggled when we tripped onto the bed, my head swimming. He chuckled too, nuzzling my neck, but his expression turned serious when I started loosening the ties on my robe. "Help me?" I asked with a smile. I never knew I could be so bold.

He hesitated but then finished undoing them for me. While he draped my robe over the wicker chest, I slipped my dress off, so I wore only my undergarment when he finally turned back to me. He stripped his xicolli off and cast it aside to embrace me.

I missed the feathery softness of the god's caresses, but the intensity of real flesh against mine kept that secluded at the back of my mind. *Seven years I've waited for something real, and that's too long to wait for a god and his promises of 'someday'.* Or maybe I was just trying to justify why I didn't care that I was well on my way to breaking my priestly vows.

But all contemplation of moral nuances ceased once Little Reed started moving down my body, kissing my collarbone, kissing my breasts. When he slid his fingers down between my thighs, the longing inside me stretched tight as a bowstring. Now all I needed was an arrow. *And no limp lizards here to disappoint us this time,* I thought as I worked my hand inside his loincloth. Stroking him with increasing urgency, I whispered, pleading, "Now?"

He untied my undergarment, and I'd just relieved him of his when the copper bells on the outer tent flap jangled loudly. "Come out here and pay respects to your new king, Topiltzin!" Red Flint called out.

CHAPTER TWENTY-FOUR

For an exhilarating moment, I thought Little Reed was going to go forward as if Red Flint wasn't there, but when Red Flint shouted, "Don't make me come back there and drag you out of bed!" Little Reed cursed under his breath then rolled away from me.

He pulled the blanket over to cover me then whispered, "I'll be back in a moment." He donned his robe then slipped out through the flap, taking extra care to make sure it closed behind him. I desperately wanted to tell Red Flint to go to Mictlan and leave us alone, but I was too breathless to speak. "Just because I have an anteroom doesn't mean you may barge in unannounced," Little Reed snapped.

"As your king, I will barge in wherever I want," Red Flint answered.

"What do you wish of me, Your Majesty?"

"I'm informing you that I'm marching the full army back to Xochicalco in two days, and I require you to return with me."

"I was already planning to go back, but if you require my help, I'm at your disposal."

"I don't require your help, but as your king, I'll demand it if need be."

"I'll of course serve as you see necessary." The patience strained in Little Reed's voice. "And I trust you'll return the favor once I confront my uncle to take back what's mine?"

Red Flint didn't answer immediately. "I'm amicable to it. But have you given further thought to our discussion regarding Quetzalpetlatl?"

"Brother!" Mazatzin muttered, barely audible.

Little Reed's voice now took on a defensive edge. "My sister makes her own decisions. I'm not going to force her, and neither will you."

I smiled, my heart warming all the more.

Red Flint's voice came closer now. "It would be a pity if you lost your chance to reclaim your throne because of a stupid decision concerning a woman."

"Selling her off for a shaky alliance would be far worse. I haven't hundreds of sisters whom I couldn't care less about; I have one who means far too much to me to see her sequestered in a life of misery."

"How dare you say I'd make her miserable—?"

"Then respect her choice, just as I do!"

I imagined them preparing to tear into each other like that time long ago, but thankfully Mazatzin stepped in again. "Brother, there are far more pressing matters we should be concerned about, don't you agree?"

Red Flint huffed, but he sounded calmer now as he moved away. "We'll discuss this once I've taken care of my throne, but in the meantime, you will coordinate the departure. There's much to do and little time to do it, so get dressed and join me outside immediately. Keep me waiting and I'll have you lashed for disobedience." The bells on the tent jangled as he left.

"A thousand apologies for my brother, My Lord," Mazatzin said, then left as well.

Little Reed finally came back, but he didn't look at me. "I'm sorry, but the king needs me tonight."

Draping the blanket over my shoulders, I stood to hug him. "It's all right. Duty before pleasure." I kissed him on the cheek. "We'll have plenty of time for that."

He sighed. "It's best we wait; I'm not in any position to change the rules of the priesthood yet, and if I got you with child...." He sighed. "Someday...."

His choice of words unnerved me. "We do have to think about the future for everyone, not just for us," I said, guilt creeping up.

"I'll do everything I can to make sure we can be together soon. We've waited a long time already."

I handed him his loincloth. "Better get dressed, before Red Flint comes looking for you again."

He kissed me gently for a moment, making the desire geyser up again, clouding my mind, but next thing I knew he was dressed again and on his way out of the flap. "Get some sleep. It's going to be a long trip back to Xochicalco." He smiled, then left.

My heart thudded so hard I felt dizzy and had to sit down. I hadn't felt tired before, but with the desire fading, my exhaustion showed itself. I slipped under the blankets and inhaled the sweet tobacco and copalli scent permeating the fibers; oh, how much I missed Little Reed, and all too soon I'd have to say goodbye all over again.

❑

I slept late, awakening when I heard the bells tinkling on the tent flap outside. I heard Citlallotoc send off the guard; then he said, "If anything good comes of that man finally taking the throne, it's that he'll no longer be strutting around camp like a dog that doesn't know it's going to be dinner. None of the other kings are pleased with his appointment, surely you know?"

"I think they all hoped he'd get himself killed with his recklessness, forcing Mocnelitzin to take his place," Little Reed answered. "Unfortunately, an even less honorable man is sitting on the throne. I never thought Red Flint would ever be the lesser of two evils."

I pulled my dress on over my head and peeked through the tent flap. Little Reed was lighting his copalli burner while Citlallotoc paced the room like an inpatient jaguar.

"If Red Flint fails, Mazatzin could still challenge for the throne," Citlallotoc said. "We should encourage him to remain behind, just in case."

Little Reed nodded. "I shall speak with him about it, but he's not the kind of man to leave Red Flint to do this on his own. His sense of honor is too good for that."

"It just may get him killed." Citlallotoc stared at the tent wall a moment, then said, his voice lowered, "You know, more than half the army would march at your side if you asked—"

"Take care with your words," Little Reed warned. "Now's the time to get behind Red Flint."

"It shall be done, My Lord. Shall I get us some food?"

"I'm eating with Quetzalpetlatl." Little Reed inhaled the white smoke swirling off the copalli burner, and smiled.

Citlallotoc failed to hide his disappointment. "I'll be off then, My Lord."

"When we arrive in Xochicalco, I'd like it if you'd come to eat with my family," Little Reed said. "My mother should know my best friend."

A shadow of a smile crept to Citlallotoc's face. "I'd be honored, My Lord."

Once Citlallotoc left, I pulled aside the flap. "I believe you've made him the happiest he can be without a wife."

Little Reed laughed. "Did we wake you?"

"No, but some food sounds great."

Over fish tamales, Little Reed told me about his day following Red Flint as he spoke with his generals, making plans. They'd also visited the other armies' generals, who all assured Red Flint that he had their kings' full support and that they would march on Xochicalco with him if need be. "Though they all looked relieved when he told them it wasn't necessary," Little Reed said. "He's so sure of himself."

"To a fault," I told him with a laugh.

"At least he's decided Mazatzin should be appointed the new high priest in Ahexotl's place."

I choked. "That's my decision, not his."

"You already told me you wanted Mazatzin to take the position."

"Yes, but the king doesn't have that kind of power over the priesthood. Red Flint is about as versed in the desires of the gods as I am at the art of spitting tobacco."

Little Reed laughed. "Mazatzin will set him straight when the time comes, but for now let it lie."

Little Reed slept the rest of the afternoon, and I passed the time playing patolli by myself. I wished I had some weaving to keep my mind off thoughts of climbing into bed with him, if only to snuggle and see how tired he really was. These were foolish thoughts though; in my heart I was glad that Red Flint had come when he had, before treacherous desire made us do something I would regret later. Yes, I wanted Little Reed badly, but the thought of getting with child terrified me.

I'd thought I was over that fear, but then last month, one of Cuitlapanton's concubines died in the childbed while I was trying to deliver their baby. I still didn't know what had gone wrong; the baby had been safely wrangled from the gods when suddenly the mother started bleeding like a deer at the slaughter. And nothing I did stopped the bleeding. Eventually I had to have Ixchell take over for me as the poor woman slipped away, for the memories of that night with Mother jumped on me like a silent assassin and my own helplessness rendered me dumb and useless. The nightmares I hadn't had since I was girl plagued me for the next couple of weeks, and I couldn't believe I'd once been so foolish as to actually try to get pregnant by Red Flint.

But did I dare tell Little Reed my fears and risk him deciding that he would be a fool for marrying me?

Once Citlallotoc came back at nightfall, I tidied up the tent and packed a change of clothing for Little Reed while he donned his cotton armor and discussed plans with Citlallotoc.

"I can arrange a litter for you," he told me as he tied his sacrificial blade sheath to his belt.

I tied his cape at his shoulder. "I prefer to walk, actually."

"Red Flint wants me to lead the jaguar knights, so I'll have Citlallotoc walk with you. He'll look after you."

I laughed. "Look after me?"

Little Reed blushed, and Citlallotoc said, "Soldiers can be crass, especially when they're more used to the company of courtesans than ladies. Your brother just doesn't want you to feel threatened among them."

With a smile, I told Little Reed, "If it'll put you at ease, then I welcome Citlallotoc's company."

"It would, thank you." Once Citlallotoc stepped outside, Little Reed pulled me into a passionate kiss, and I wondered if now would be a good time to talk to him about my worries; but as happened so often when the desire took hold, the world and all its concerns seemed to melt away. There was no past, no future, just the moment. Nothing else mattered.

The world had never felt more perfect.

◻

Citlallotoc frowned at the large litter in the middle of the staging area. "Red Flint borrowed it from the king of Tultepec," he answered when Little Reed asked where it came from. "He said he can't strain himself walking back to Xochicalco like a common soldier."

Red Flint had accumulated significant plunder over the years, most of it packed into wicker baskets. Seven Chichimec women stood among the bounty, each dressed in little more than loincloths, shown off like jewels and treated no better than turkeys.

Red Flint strutted out of his tent but stopped like a startled deer when he saw me. Little Reed slid in front of me, breaking his line of sight, then swept his fingers across the ground. "All's ready for your departure, My Lord."

"Good." Red Flint stepped around Little Reed to approach me. He bowed. "It's a pleasure to see you again, Lady Quetzalpetlatl. I dare say the love goddess Xochiquetzal paid you a blessed visit, for your beauty exceeds words."

I wanted to sneer but instead smiled back, remaining cordial. He wasn't just a prince anymore. "It's a pleasure to see you again as well, Lord Red Flint. Or should I say Your Majesty?"

"From your lovely lips, I much prefer Red Flint. Please, allow me to help you into your litter."

"I'm not traveling by litter."

"Nonsense! The daughter of my father's best friend won't walk like a commoner. You must ride in the royal litter."

Little Reed stiffened but said nothing. *Nor would it be wise to humiliate Red Flint in front of his men,* I thought. Red Flint was waiting for my answer, looking intense. "Far be it for me to reject the kind offer of my king."

Red Flint smiled and took my hand to help me up into the royal litter. I stole a glance at Little Reed to find him whispering to Citlallotoc, who was nodding. "Make yourself comfortable and I'll join you once we're ready to leave." Red Flint motioned Little Reed to follow him as he went down the line, inspecting the baskets and his soldiers.

"I doubt Lord Red Flint would be foolish enough to try anything unbecoming where everyone could hear him, but I'll be here should you need anything." Citlallotoc looked over at Red Flint, then added, "Don't hesitate to call on me, My Lady."

I smiled. "I can handle the king."

◻

Once Red Flint climbed inside the litter, he tried to close the curtains, but I grabbed his hand. "It's stuffy in here," I said.

Red Flint grinned as he lounged back on the blankets next to me. "You must be happy to see your brother again after so long," he said after we'd ridden in silence for a while. "And as you can see, he's done very well for himself."

"He has," I agreed.

"He does all this for you, you know?"

"Does all what?"

"All this fighting and recruiting. He wants to be king for your benefit, to make sure you're taken care of. It's all that matters to him."

I wrinkled my brow, wondering what possessed him to speak as if he knew—let along respected—Little Reed.

"He'd do anything for you, even throw away his chances at his throne." Red Flint held a bowl out to me. "Fried grasshopper, My Lady?"

I held up my hand, struggling to keep the look of loathing off my face. *He thinks he can use guilt to persuade me to marry him, does he?* Yet when I thought about Little Reed never regaining Culhuacan's throne because Red Flint refused to help him—

Give yourself over to this man you hate and abandon any hope of ever being with Little Reed? I shook away the creeping guilt. Perhaps I shouldn't have accepted Red Flint's hospitality after all.

He spent the day plaguing me with stories of his many battle victories and near-death escapes. "I was in Chichimec hands twice, and once put upon their sacrificial stone, but both times the Feathered Serpent sent men to rescue me. He is the greatest of all the gods."

But the arrogance on his face told a different story. Who did he think he was fooling with his lip service?

The litter's constant bobbing combined with Red Flint's prattle exhausted me, and it took more energy than I had to keep from nodding off.

"You look very tired," he noted after he'd gone through the list of war booty he'd claimed. "I imagine the journey to camp took much out of you."

"It wasn't so bad. Priestesses are tougher than most people would think."

"I wasn't demeaning your physical prowess, My Lady." Red Flint smiled. "I know better."

"I prefer manual labor to lazing around," I replied. "I'm not made for a life of luxury."

"I wouldn't say that, but yes, it must be tiring to be a noblewoman, as my mother can attest. How is she? She and Father were very close, so I imagine his passing hit her hard."

"I haven't seen her in weeks, but I know she'll be glad you're returning. As will Turquoise Bells."

His smile wavered. "I'm sure many of my sisters will be pleased to see me again. I, however, am more looking forward to seeing you again every day, as the next high priestess of Xochicalco. I'm lucky; my father had only an old woman to look upon all these years."

"Nimilitzli is very beautiful," I said, biting back the urge to snarl the words.

His smile turned catlike. "You should rest, for I'd like you to join me for dinner tonight, and it won't do for you to fall asleep in your food." He jumped from the litter after calling for a halt. "Sleep well, My Lady." He bowed, then closed the curtains.

I situated myself under the blankets, glad to finally be able to rest. *And to think you tried to marry yourself to that braggart.* I felt luckier than ever that fate had saved me from that unfortunate future.

□

Over dinner in Red Flint's tent, Little Reed suggested that Red Flint should put away his royal regalia and disguise himself as a common soldier and march with his ranks when we reached Xochicalco. "Let Obsidian Eagle believe the assassins killed both you and Mazatzin," Little Reed said. "We'll send a runner ahead to tell Obsidian Eagle that Camaxtli and Oquitzin haven't been heard from in months and that they're presumed dead. I'll say I'm bringing the army back to pledge loyalty to Obsidian Eagle as the new king. Then the four of you can ambush him when he's feeling relaxed."

"I suppose that's as good a plan as any," Red Flint conceded. He'd been furious when Little Reed rejected his idea of marching into the city with full pomp. And even now it was obvious Red Flint didn't like this plan but had no better suggestions. I wanted to tell him to stop pouting and that he'd get his royal reception eventually, but Little Reed had worked too hard to get him this far just for me to ruin it all with a nasty comment.

"I know you think hiding is dishonorable, but we're dealing with a dishonorable man," Little Reed reminded him. "If he knew you were coming he'd send more assassins, or worse yet force you to lay siege to your own city. Let him believe all went according to his plan, and then you can jump out and challenge him in fair hand-to-hand combat, may the best warrior win. There is nothing dishonorable in that."

Red Flint harrumphed but said nothing more about it. When Little Reed and I stood to leave, Red Flint said, "I would like to speak with you before you retire, Lady Quetzalpetlatl."

"What for?" Little Reed asked.

Red Flint glared at him. "It doesn't concern you, unless you've changed your mind about allowing your sister the freedom to make her own choices?"

Little Reed glared back, but I touched his shoulder. "I'll be fine."

When Little Reed finally turned to go, Red Flint added, "And don't listen outside my tent, or I'll have the guards escort you away."

"Of course I wouldn't, Your Majesty," Little Reed replied with a perfunctory bow. "Good night." He shot me another glance then ducked out the tent flap.

"Brothers can be so overbearing," Red Flint said with a smile.

"I appreciate him looking out for me."

"But also not making your decisions for you."

His small talk grated on me. "You said you wished to speak with me about something?"

Red Flint poured two cups of xocolatl from the small steaming pot. "Yes, about something very important." He held one cup out to me but I declined. "I'm sure your brother has told you by now that I'm intending to ask you to be my wife."

"He mentioned it—"

"Before you say any more, allow me to address some concerns I'm sure you have. First, the little matter of my...poor showing, that evening in the laundry room. I admit I had a problem for a long time, but now I chew roots every day to cure that. It takes a man to accept he needs help with such things and seek out assistance, wouldn't you agree?"

"I wouldn't argue otherwise, Your Majesty."

"And I'm sure you're concerned about my father having betrothed me to Lady Turquoise Bells. You may be surprised to know that your father first intended to betroth you to me, to strengthen his ties with Xochicalco, but he ended up marrying you to Lord Black Otter to mend a disagreement with Ihuitimal. Our own fathers had intended us to marry, and to be frank, I prefer you to my sister. I'm sure she's grown into a beauty, but she's self-absorbed and never quite grasped concepts of cordiality and public image. Not good qualities in Xochicalco's future queen, wouldn't you agree?"

I'd been listening so as to not appear rude, yet he startled me when he asked me to denigrate Turquoise Bells like this. He probably knew something about our mutual hostility when we were younger and thought I'd willingly take the bait. Well, to Mictlan with him. "I haven't spoken to Lady Turquoise Bells in many years, so I don't know anything about her fitness to be queen."

"I know you're more than up to the task," Red Flint replied. "Your extensive priestly training will help me lead the kingdom in a direction pleasing to the god. The people deserve a strong queen who cares about their welfare, don't you agree?"

"Of course, but Red Flint, I'm not—"

"I know I've been like an angry hornet in the past, and I was completely dishonorable to you before I left. I particularly regret the harsh names I called you for showing common sense in the situation. I beg your forgiveness for that."

"Red Flint—"

"I'm a different man now; battle-hardened, but also appreciative of how the company of a good woman can make me a better man. And you're that woman—no, don't shake your head. You're a very good woman and I love you, so—"

"I've already promised myself to someone else!" I shouted, practically breathless. I immediately snapped my mouth shut, my heart pounding. *You shouldn't have told him that.*

Red Flint stared at me, taken aback. "You lie!" When I didn't answer, he roared, "To whom? Topiltzin said you were free of obligation!"

Without waiting for his dismissal, I ran from the tent. *Fool! Now Red Flint will never help Little Reed reclaim Culhuacan's throne.*

◻

I was almost in tears when I reached my tent to find Little Reed waiting for me. He opened his arms to me, the concern plain on his face, but I couldn't accept his comfort. What if Red Flint had followed me? I couldn't risk him finding out Little Reed was my intended.

Little Reed dropped his arms awkwardly. "Are you all right? Did he do something to you?"

I looked over my shoulder before shaking my head. "I'm sorry, Little Reed. I didn't mean to tell him anything...." The tears finally came.

Little Reed looked around as well, then led me into the trees across from my tent. We zigzagged among the shadows until we reached a clearing next to the lake, where the moonlight shone bright as morning on the water's smooth surface. This time when he pulled me into a hug I didn't resist, welcoming the strength of his arms around me, the smell of sweat and tobacco, his breath warm on the top of my head. "What happened?"

I shook my head, keeping my forehead buried in his chest as I cried, "He kept pushing the issue, no matter what I said, and before I knew it, I just blurted it out, to make him stop."

He stroked my hair patiently. "What exactly did you tell him?"

"I said I was already promised to someone else."

I felt the tension in his body as he kept his voice even, unconcerned. "What did he say?"

I rested my cheek against his chest. "He said you promised I was free of commitment, then he demanded to know to whom I'd promised myself. But I ran from his tent before I could say anything more stupid than I already had."

Little Reed chuckled. "You're not stupid, Papalotl."

"If he finds out it's you—"

"He'll find out eventually anyway," he said. "I don't intend to marry you in secret, as if I'm ashamed of it."

Seeing only laughter in his eyes brought a relieved smile to my face. "Then you're not angry with me?"

"If anything, I'm glad that's out of the way. He should worry about his throne, not who he'll marry when he gets it back. Though maybe I haven't the right to talk, since I'm doing the exact same thing."

"I would still marry you even if you never became king of Culhuacan," I said.

He kissed me gently, his grip on my hand light and undemanding, but still the desire welled up like a jaguar preparing to pounce. I imagined pushing him to the ground and making love to him under Lord Metzli's pale light. I pressed up against him, knotting his cape in my fingers, demanding; and when he parted his mouth from mine, I felt as drunk as I had that night in Teotihuacan so long ago...and strangely hungry despite having just eaten. Often when I fasted for more than a meal or two, intimacy with the god helped take my mind off the hunger, at least for a while, so had the years trained my body to inextricably mesh the two desires together? Still, it troubled me how easily I could forget everything and become so focused on ignoring good sense, all for the possibility of pleasure. *Pleasure that could lead to your death,* I reminded myself.

Little Reed's smile melted away, replaced again with concern. "What's wrong?"

I found it too difficult to look him in eye as I said, "Perhaps I'm not a good choice for a wife, Little Reed."

"Why not?"

"A king needs heirs, and I...." My voice broke.

He set his hands on my shoulders. "You're shaking."

"You need someone who wants children, Little Reed."

After a pause, Little Reed said, "You're afraid that what happened to Mother will happen to you?"

"It's foolish, I know—"

"Not at all. I always thought you'd make a wonderful mother, but I understand."

"You should marry someone who isn't afraid to give you a future."

He shook his head. "Children or no children, I want you, Papalotl. I've loved you so long...forever, it seems, and at the risk of sounding more selfish than the god's chosen high Priest should, you're all that matters to me. I've hated only being able to talk to you in letters these last seven years. I can't count how many times I wanted to just up and go home to you. I'm more powerful with a quill in my hand than a sword anyway, and the turmoil of the battlefield...it's insane, Papalotl, and I don't understand why we do these things to each other. I long for the rational discussions with Nimilitzli, where we solve problems with logic and diplomacy rather than brute strength." He laughed dejectedly then added, "She was right that real war is nothing like what they teach you in the House of Warriors. I wasn't created for such pointless violence."

The raw, exposed emotions on his face broke my heart and I pulled him into a hug of my own. He rested his head on my shoulder with a sigh. "If you find it so difficult...then why not come home?" I whispered.

"Because it's gone too far," he said. "I played by our uncle's rules instead of staying in the priesthood and using faith to turn people against him. I've pushed him into going after you, to get at me, and it has cost so many people their lives. I'm sorry, Papalotl."

I looked up at him. "You can't blame yourself for everything, Little Reed. You did what anyone would have done."

"Yes, but I'm not just *anyone*, am I?"

"No, but you're human, like the rest of us, and we all make missteps. Quetzalcoatl didn't make us perfect."

Little Reed chuckled and looked out over the moonlit lake as he muttered, "No, I don't suppose humanity can be any more perfect than he whose blood gave them life."

The slight against Quetzalcoatl unnerved me, but what did I know about their relationship? Years later I still felt ambivalent about my own father, whom I knew to be anything but perfect.

He sighed. "I will get this done soon, Papalotl. I promise. Then we'll have the peace we all need to move forward. No more waiting." He took my face in both hands and for a moment I thought he was going to kiss me again, but he merely set his warm lips against my forehead and whispered, "We should get back. Morning comes all too soon." A heated flush still traveled lazily up my neck at his touch.

It was on the tip of my tongue to ask him to share my tent tonight, so I could keep him close, but when we reached my tent, Citlallotoc called out to him from further down the row. Little Reed squeezed my hand, and just before he turned away a mask seemed to go up over his face: the vulnerability he'd shown me earlier vanished, hidden behind a facade of absolute confidence and staunchness. How had I not noticed it before? I suspected that tonight had been the first time in many years he'd let it slip away, if only for a little while.

CHAPTER TWENTY-FIVE

The next day I walked among the slaves, afraid to go anywhere near Little Reed, fearing Red Flint might realize that he was my intended and perhaps confront him. I also stayed away from both Mazatzin and Citlallotoc, to spare them from being dragged into this stupid mess. Thankfully, Red Flint didn't come looking for me.

It rained the morning we arrived at Xochicalco and Little Reed and I huddled inside the litter, passing the time in nervous silence. The weather broke around midday as we approached the plain outside the walls. Conch shells sounded from the city, and our frontline soldiers answered with a similar tune. The farmers gathered at the edge of their fields, watching us pass.

"Let's hope Red Flint doesn't rush out too soon," Little Reed said as we came into the city. "When we get there, please remain in the litter. You'll be safer in there once the battle begins."

I swallowed hard. I hadn't thought about there being actual fighting.

The caravan wound through town, towards the palace square. People gathered outside their houses, and the many mothers calling out to their sons and crying reminded me of the joy of seeing Little Reed again after so long.

The soldiers filed into the palace square, spreading out to the edges to make room for all. Those carrying the litter marched to the base of the palace stairs, and once there, Little Reed stepped down and ascended to where both Obsidian Eagle and Ahexotl waited at the top. I sat concealed behind the curtains, peering around from the side, my stomach knotted.

Ahexotl looked ill-tempered as usual but Obsidian Eagle smiled, looking regal in his father's quetzal and turkey-feather headdress, gold-woven sandals, and hummingbird-feathered xicolli. Around his neck he wore the heavy gold necklace Cuitlapanton had worn to that fateful council with Ihuitimal. It forever reminded me of what happened to Nochuatl, and seeing Obsidian Eagle wearing it now was a taunting reminder of whom he'd betray us to.

Reaching the third from the top step, Little Reed swept his fingers across the step before him. Obsidian Eagle inclined his head. "Thank you for bringing my army back to me, Lord Topiltzin. Your loyalty to Xochicalco is not only noted, but admired."

"You're most gracious, My Lord," Little Reed said. "Culhuacan was my parents' city, but Xochicalco was and always will be my home." Little Reed turned to the crowd behind him, and when he raised his hands all the soldiers went to their knees. "Xochicalco once again has her king!" He bent to one knee too.

But then the four soldiers standing in front of the litter jumped up, swords drawn, and charged the stairs. They wore concealing wooden helmets—a jaguar, an eagle, and two coyotes—but I instantly recognized Mazatzin's bulky build under the eagle head. Red Flint—who wore the jaguar head—leaped over Little Reed's bent body, sword swinging.

Obsidian Eagle had been taking in the scene beyond the litter and only at the last moment saw Red Flint and his brothers coming at him. By the time he shouted for his guards, Red Flint was almost upon him. Ahexotl stumbled out of his bow and took a slash across his chest from Little Reed, turning the cloth crimson along the cut.

The guards rushed forward, wedging themselves between Obsidian Eagle and Ahexotl and their attackers. Obsidian Eagle retreated into the palace, but the guards had to carry Ahexotl.

"I'm not done with you, you abomination to the Feathered Serpent's good name!" Little Reed shouted after him, but when more guards pushed towards him, spears ready, soldiers flooded up the steps to defend him. The guards retreated back to the palace.

Red Flint paced the top step. "Come out and claim Father's throne like a man! Or are you still that bawling little boy Mocnelitzin and I tied naked to the sacrificial stone on the ball court? Come out and fight me, you cowering woman!"

"I told you to wait until the signal," Little Reed snapped. "And you were supposed to come out and challenge him, not drive him into hiding."

"I don't need your lectures! He's a dishonorable dog who would never agree to a faithful duel. I saw my opportunity and I took it."

Obsidian Eagle strode out of the palace, flanked by guards. Ahexotl hobbled behind him, clutching his chest. "I'm not your little dog to whip, Red Flint," Obsidian Eagle snarled.

"Then step away from your nursemaids, draw your sword, and claim Father's throne honorably, you puddle of dog piss."

Obsidian Eagle laughed. "You're a brute of a man who can't even coax a turkey in from the rain. A king should have more skills at his belt than just his arm muscles."

I chuckled to myself. "You should listen to him on that one, Red Flint."

"You'll see all my skills in action right before I lop your head off," Red Flint said.

"Is that what you'll do when Ihuitimal threatens you? Your problem, Red Flint, is that you only know how to stomp on those smaller than you, but Culhuacan's army outnumbers our own now. That makes you a fool."

Red Flint hunched his shoulders like a bear. "Of course you'd speak that butcher's name since it's him you honor, not our family. You and your treacherous priest chose the wrong place to discuss your sedition; you were overheard by someone loyal to Father. Do your guards know that you—not Mocnelitzin—poisoned Father? Do they know you plan to hand our great city over to Ihuitimal?" To Ahexotl, he added, "And do they know that you—old man who defiles his priestesses for his own gratification—do they know that you betrayed our city's god with plans to hand his temple to the Smoking Mirror?"

Ahexotl grinned. "I at least didn't have troubles rising to my plans, Lord Red Flint."

Red Flint made to spring at him, but Mazatzin held him back.

Ahexotl was enjoying this far too much, so I jumped out of the litter and ran up the steps. "After the god showed you mercy by leaving you only a cripple, I'd think you'd have better respect for his power." I stopped next to Little Reed, who in turn went up a step to stand between me and Ahexotl.

Ahexotl sneered. "You speak about the god as if you're his chosen one, but it was you who set fire to the courtyard that night. You burned down half the sacred city trying to murder me, you bitch."

Little Reed pressed forward again but the guards closed around Ahexotl. "You know not whom you meddle with, priest," Little Reed growled. "Quetzalcoatl won't extend mercy to you a second time."

"Then call on your god to punish me, and he can also settle this sticky matter of royal succession. Red Flint and Obsidian Eagle should meet on the Tlachtli court and battle this out like kings of the past. The man with the god on his side will prevail."

"Excellent idea," I agreed. The gods had passed the ritual ball game down to us precisely to settle disputes of honor, particularly among kings, and with Quetzalcoatl on our side, there was no way we could lose. "Your man against ours; one backed by the Feathered Serpent, the other backed only by your bragging, and we'll see who comes out victorious."

Red Flint flinched, but I ignored him.

"Then it's settled," Ahexotl snapped. "Lord Red Flint and Lord Obsidian Eagle shall match wits and skill on the battlefield of the ball court tomorrow afternoon, and the winner claims Xochicalco's throne. The loser says goodbye to his head, and his brothers swear on their honor and the risk of committing treason to abide by the results."

Obsidian Eagle's grin stretched from ear to ear. "I'm glad we're dealing with this like honorable men, Brother. Aren't you?" Red Flint looked sick, and he laughed. "Feel free to set up camp for yourself and your men in the palace square. I'd invite you to stay inside, but I don't trust you to be as honorable a man as myself." He turned and disappeared back inside.

A din of conversation rose and Red Flint turned to the crowd. He feigned a smile when they started chanting, "Hail the rightful king!" He glared at me before following Mazatzin down the stairs into the throng.

"It's about time Ahexotl understood the power he spits in the face of," Little Reed said, still glaring back at the palace.

"He's had it coming a long time," I agreed.

"It should never have come to this."

I cringed. "I'm sorry I stayed your hand back then, Little Reed—"

He shook his head. "I admire your desire to believe the best in people. We just must be mindful not to show so much mercy that it costs us our own lives." He took my right hand and looked down at it. "You're very brave, sacrificing so much for all of us."

I hadn't thought about that part yet, or that I had to think it through by tomorrow afternoon. My stomach churned.

▢

After camp was set, Little Reed accompanied me up to the sacred precinct. My mood lightened at the sight of the temple turning yellow in the day's aging sun, the colorful Feathered Serpent slithering along its side.

Malinalli was sweeping out the hearth when we arrived home. She squealed in delight as she embraced me. "I was sure something terrible had happened when Ahexotl kicked you out of the order and named me your replacement. Where were you?" When she saw Little Reed standing behind me, her cheeks flushed and she bowed her head. "Welcome home, Lord Topiltzin."

"It's good to see you again too," he told her with a smile that sent a spike of jealousy through me. My envy immediately shamed me though, and I could barely meet Malinalli's eyes when I asked her about Nimilitzli, who was sleeping.

"Her cough hasn't gotten any better, but it hasn't worsened," Malinalli answered. "I've been coming by four times daily."

"I'm sorry to have dropped this responsibility on you like this, but I had to leave quickly."

She gave me an understanding smile then turned to Little Reed, who was kneeling next to Nimilitzli. "You can wake her. It's time for her medicine."

I joined Little Reed at Nimilitzli's side as he gave her shoulder a gentle nudge. "Mother, it's time to wake up," he said.

Nimilitzli stirred and coughed. I eased her up to rub her back and when she saw Little Reed, she broke into tears. He smiled and kissed her cheek, letting her cry on his chest a while before she smiled up at him. "My little boy, all grown up and handsome, and home again!" She fingered a long white strand of his hair, then sighed. "Your aging hasn't slowed much, has it?"

"Don't fret, Mother," Little Reed assured her. "I look older than I feel. I have many good years left in me."

Nimilitzli turned to me. "I'm very glad to see you made your journey safely."

"Citlallotoc was an excellent guide, and your sword served me well." I set the weapon on her lap.

She ran her fingers over the carvings, her mind suddenly distant, then smiled and said, "I'm glad it saw proper service again."

"It's a very fine sword." Little Reed picked it up and slapped the flat side against his palm. "Light but sturdy. Whose is it?"

"It belongs to the order. Do you like it?"

"The carvings are exquisite, and it's a good weight. The one Cuitlapanton gave me is heavier and doesn't fit my hand so well."

"Then it's yours."

"Oh no, I couldn't steal from the order—"

"It's hardly stealing, Topiltzin. As the high priestess, it's mine to give to whomever I wish, and I know the sword's previous owner would want you to have it. It just gathers webs hanging in the Council Room, so better it should be carried at your side, helping you bring Quetzalcoatl's worship back to Culhuacan."

"Then I shall carry it with honor and dignity, Mother."

While Malinalli and I cooked dinner, I told Nimilitzli about what had happened outside the palace that afternoon.

"And Red Flint agreed to it?" Malinalli asked. "Obsidian Eagle is the city's leading Tlachtli player. He's on the royal team and practices every day after his priestly duties."

"I don't keep up with the sport," I admitted.

"That's why Red Flint looked like he'd swallowed a leech," Little Reed said with a grin as he smoked his pipe. "When the men would go to the ball court in Tultepec to practice, Red Flint was always busy making rounds of the camp, "overseeing" his army or indulging in the courtesans; you know, 'princely matters'. I'm sure he's regretting that now."

"It won't matter how good he is," I replied. "The god will see him to victory."

"You're going to summon Quetzalcoatl again?" Malinalli's gaze wandered to my hand.

"I'll do what I have to." I didn't want to ruin the evening with anxious thoughts about that, though.

After Malinalli left for her temple duties, Citlallotoc arrived. Little Reed greeted him with an embrace, and after the meal they stayed late into the evening, sharing stories of their military exploits while Nimilitzli regaled Citlallotoc with stories of Little Reed's childhood rivalry with Red Flint. It felt wonderful to laugh and remember times past.

"We haven't heard much from you tonight, My Lady," Citlallotoc said once he'd finished his last story. "Tell me what happened to your fingers?"

"That's nothing, really. It happened the day before we met you and your men over by Acolman."

"Your group was set upon by Chichimecs, right? Did you lose them in the skirmish?"

"Sort of. They'd killed most of the men and had the women cornered atop the Pyramid of the Moon, so I cut off my fingers as a sacrifice to Quetzalcoatl, to ask for his help."

"And he came as a giant fire serpent," Little Reed continued. "Burned down half the city and killed every Chichimec warrior."

Citlallotoc looked from me to Little Reed then back again. "You can summon the god?" Reverence—or perhaps it was fear—shone in his eyes.

"I haven't in years. It costs a great deal to use the power," I said.

"Will you use it tomorrow, to help Lord Red Flint win the game?"

"It's in the god's best interest that Red Flint take the throne."

"Then you'll cut off some more fingers?"

"I haven't decided yet what I'll do." Seeing the worry on Little Reed's face, I added, "But I'll know by morning."

The guards outside jingled the bells then told Little Reed that Red Flint had sent for him. "My king calls me," he said; he kissed Nimilitzli on the cheek, and once Citlallotoc disappeared through the curtain, he kissed my cheek too, though he lingered at mine.

"Sleep well, my love," he whispered, and left. I watched the curtain swing a moment before turning back to the room, hoping my face had cooled down.

But Nimilitzli was gazing into her cup of medicine, so I set up my weaving next to her bed, so she could watch me work. "Your brother seems to be getting along just fine out there with the other men," she noted as she sipped. "I'm glad he's made a trustworthy friend like Citlallotoc. That can be a difficult task for the heir of any throne."

"Citlallotoc is a good man," I agreed. She had the distant look in her eyes again, and now that we were alone, I said, "Who did the sword belong to?" When she shot me a sharp look, I added, "You needn't answer if you'd rather not."

She sighed. "No, I've kept this to myself long enough, and honestly, I know I haven't much time left."

My chest constricted. "You have longer than you think—"

"I've always embraced the reality of any situation and I'm not afraid of death, Quetzalpetlatl. I spent my time here well, as attested to by both yourself and your brother, but I haven't walked in two years; and honestly, I'm looking forward to facing Death's road, swimming the Black River, navigating the storm of arrowheads, and scaling the mountain of obsidian blades. In death, even women can be warriors, and I've only lingered here to know that you and Topiltzin will be all right. But it's time for me seek council with the Eater of Filth, so I can ready myself for the next leg of my journey."

I was numb. "Perhaps you're ready, but I'm not."

"You are. I taught you everything I know, and the rest you have to learn for yourself. But there is one last thing I want to tell you."

"I'm always ready to learn from your wisdom, Mother." I tried to be the strong woman she thought me to be, but the tears won out.

Nimilitzli closed her eyes. "I've spent most my life preaching the values of the chaste life to all the young priestesses passing through my tutelage—yourself included—but the truth is I'm not going to Mictlan unbroken."

I blinked, caught off guard. She was the woman who never made a false step, who was completely infallible. I should have felt indignant about all those lectures she'd given me about staying true to our priestly vows, but instead all I could think about was Ahexotl cornering her in some remote part of the priestly gardens— "Who?" I sputtered.

My face must have betrayed my thoughts. "Don't worry; it happened before Ahexotl was the high priest. In fact, it was the former high priest who...well, he was my first love, and my only. I've had my share of fluttery hearts and sweaty palms, but what I felt for Xochimecatl...it was unlike anything I'd felt before, or since." A smile slid onto her lips. "He had one blue eye, 'the color of the ocean', he always told me. My heart still skips to think of him."

I smiled. "He must've been very handsome."

"I found his fierce devotion to the god the most endearing; he too had been committed to serving the god since an early age and we both saw it as our greatest duty. We spent hours in deep discussions of the god and devotion, and ironically, that's what brought us together. We resisted taking the physical path for years, but it became torturous to continue denying our love for each other. It was utter weakness, but truthfully I felt closest to the god in those moments I spent in Xochimecatl's arms."

I thought of all the times I'd spent in the god's arms, wishing he were Little Reed. "The god wouldn't consider you weak," I said.

"Priestesses are supposed to make sacrifices for the god, but as high priestess, we make the hardest sacrifice of all. We should be able to devote ourselves to the god alone in spite of what our hearts feel, and in that regard, I was weak and unworthy."

I disliked the change in her tone. "I've always admired your piety and strength, Nimilitzli, but I admire you even more for knowing this. It gives me hope for myself."

Nimilitzli laughed. "You have the ear of the god himself and are his chosen high priestess, but you doubt your worthiness?"

"This whole chosen future...it's a robe that doesn't fit me as well as I'd hoped. I don't think I can devote myself completely to the god alone." Nor did I want to.

Nimilitzli nodded but then pulled a letter from the basket next to her bed. The copal wax seal on it was broken, but she didn't open it, just held it out to me. "If it gives you any comfort, your brother—son of the god though he may be—feels the same way. He has big plans for the priesthood once he becomes king of Culhuacan."

I nodded, avoiding her gaze. "He told me."

"Then you know what's in the letter?"

"He wants us to rule together as both king and queen, and high priest and priestess of his father's order."

"Have you given him an answer yet?"

I ventured my gaze up at her, fearing disappointment on her face, but there was none. "I've loved him all my life, just as I've loved the god." I sighed, frustrated. "It's not right I should have to make a choice between the two. My loving Topiltzin doesn't diminish my love for the god; it makes it stronger. My mother wished she hadn't had to make that choice either, and it wouldn't have made her any less of a priestess or mother for having been both."

Nimilitzli nodded. "I could never imagine leaving the priesthood, but I also couldn't imagine living without Xochimecatl. That's why we conducted our affair in secrecy." Tears formed in her eyes. "But then a fever took him three winters before you and your brother came to live with me."

My gut twisted. "Oh no!"

Nimilitzli shook her head, lips pursed tight. "For years, I thought it was the god's punishment for having broken our vows, but then he'd never have entrusted me with his only son and his chosen high priestess if he truly thought me an oath-breaker."

"I know for a fact that he thinks very highly of you."

She dried her tears on the sleeve of her night robe. "The god put Topiltzin in this world for a reason, so I trust him not to lead us astray. He's going to change the world for the better, for all of us; both of you will. And it's only appropriate that it should be through love and devotion, strengthening each other. My only regret is that I won't live to see the two of you take the steps that neither I nor your mother thought we could."

Tears swelled my throat closed, so I held her hand tight.

She looked very tired but insisted I go to fetch the high priest of Tlazotlteotl. "I'm in a confessing mood, so I should unburden myself now. I doubt I have enough time left to sin too severely against the gods."

▯

I wept all the way down the stairs to the smaller temples, but I dried my eyes before entering the Temple of Tlazotlteotl. I might not wear the robe of the high priestess of Quetzalcoatl yet, but I wanted to appear a wall of great strength. The high priest was meditating, but when I told him the reason for my visit, he agreed to go and see Nimilitzli immediately.

One's final confession was a private time, for what was spoken was for Tlazotlteotl's nourishment only, so I walked through the lower precinct, the guards Little Reed had assigned to me following at a respectful distance. My mind wandered to the sacrifice I had to make by tomorrow afternoon. The conversation with Nimilitzli had given me a clue of what that might be, but how could I abandon my love for Little Reed to make sure that a man who spoke the god's name with a faulty tongue won the throne?

I descended another set of stairs and came upon a ritual ball court. The one where tomorrow's match would take place was next to the palace, while this smaller secondary one was where the peasant teams and young noble boys practiced. It was the very same one where Red Flint and his friends had attacked Little Reed when they were just boys. Paintings of feathered serpents ran the length of both walls in white, red, and green, crushing skulls under their meandering coils. Two stone rings stuck out into the court from the top of both walls. I stood up next to one of them, peering down at the men practicing below.

Red Flint wore his royal Tlachtli gear: a woven yoke to protect his gut and groin; leather elbow and knee pads with a polished curved stone glued to each; and a wooden helmet decorated with white heron feathers. Mazatzin stood next to him, clutching the maroon ball at his side while his brother and Little Reed argued strategy.

"This is stupid," Red Flint snarled as he grabbed the ball from Mazatzin. "You can talk all night about techniques, but I haven't played Tlachtli in seven years. Obsidian Eagle plays every day; that's all he's ever done."

"Had you not tied him naked to the ball court's sacrificial stone when he was just a boy, perhaps he wouldn't have taken such an intense interest in the game," Mazatzin said.

"That was a long time ago!" Red Flint snapped. "We were all just children."

"The deepest wounds never heal, just fester and grow," Little Reed said. "Now continue practicing."

Red Flint grumbled but readied himself. Other men dressed in Tlachtli gear took turns hitting the ball at him, but he only returned one volley before hitting the ground and scraping his chin. He tore his elbow pads off and threw them at the wall, breaking one in half. "I might as well walk to the palace right now and offer my neck to Obsidian Eagle!" When he saw me, he yelled, "You set me up to die so you wouldn't have to marry me!"

"My Lord, rest assured, you're not going to lose," I said, suppressing the urge to laugh at him.

"I had him cornered into accepting my challenge, under my terms, but then you had to go spouting off about the god to Ahexotl."

"Then why didn't you turn down the challenge?"

"And look like a coward? Honorable men don't follow cowards. You gave me no choice and now you've handed my father's throne to his murderer."

How could this pathetic man be worthy of being the next king of Xochicalco? He spewed false faith, always moaning, "Oh Merciful Quetzalcoatl this" and "Thank be the Feathered Serpent that", to look pious, but he had no true belief. He would win tomorrow's match and he would owe it all to Quetzalcoatl, and to me, but he would never acknowledge that. This ungrateful wretch was what I was supposed to sacrifice my future with Little Reed for? It was ridiculous.

But with all his men around, looking uncomfortable, and him looking like a cornered jaguar, this wasn't the time to speak my mind. "Have faith, My Lord," I said, taking great care to moderate my voice. "I was just on my way to the temple to speak with the god, and he will see to the proper victory. I promise you that." I whirled around and left, desperate to be away before my temper got the better of me.

But Little Reed caught up with me. "I don't think you should make any sacrifices right now, Papalotl. You're angry and you might do something you'll regret later."

"I'm fine, Little Reed," I snapped, the rage rising in me. Seeing him flinch, I took a deep breath, ashamed for having let my anger at Red Flint slip out. "I'm not about to do anything stupid on his account." I touched his cheek and whispered, "I'll see you tomorrow, my love." I sealed that promise with a kiss. I expected the usual desire to well up, but instead my insides were boiling with anger.

"Papalotl, please, know what you're doing—"

"I know what I'm doing."

My anger and indignation carried me all the way to the temple and I cleared the two priests out so I could be alone. I cut my palm and bled it into the wooden bowl at my knees, then bowed my head, my anger still bubbling. *Red Flint doesn't deserve to be king, but I said I'd do this. I'll let the god decide what's best, for who should know that better than he?*

"Oh Great Quetzalcoatl,
I need your guidance again.
If Red Flint is truly meant to be king,
Then make him worthy of it.
Protect him tomorrow as he goes into battle for his throne.
Whatever sacrifice you deem necessary,
I will accept.
I trust in you always, My Lord,
And ask you to give me strength."

The anger and tension drained out of me with the words, as if a great weight had been lifted off my chest. I opened my eyes to see the blood gone. *Then he's agreed,* I decided. *But what did I agree to?* For a panicked moment I wondered if he'd frozen my heart, but when I thought of Little Reed, the familiar pleasure raced through my veins. I sighed, relieved. *So long as I still have that, everything will be all right.*

CHAPTER TWENTY-SIX

 Where is he? I watched the door curtain while I boiled the opossum tail for Nimilitzli's medicine, hoping Little Reed had just slept late. *You should have listened to him last night, and gone to the temple this morning instead of letting your temper do your praying.*

I poured the medicine in a cup and held it out to Nimilitzli, but she shook her head. "I'm going to pass on it today."

"But your cough—"

"It's not bothering me." When I started arguing, she said, "Please humor an old woman. Leave it next to my bed and if I feel the need for it, I'll drink it."

I finally agreed, and promised to come back after the match.

"There's no need to hurry back," she said. "I'm sure you'll have much to celebrate after the game."

My stomach still churned as I headed for the stairs down into the city, but I breathed a sigh of relief when I saw Little Reed sitting on the edge of the cistern. I went over and sat next to him. "You didn't come to eat."

"I had things to do this morning." He didn't look at me.

I didn't know what to make of that, so I said, "We should hurry, so we don't miss the opening of the match."

"I'm not going. Red Flint asked me to make sure Ahexotl doesn't get away." He took my hand and clasped it between his. "Whatever happens, just remember that I love you, and I always have."

"I know you do." Though how he said it disturbed me. I watched him leave, headed for the house, and I was on the edge of going after him, but Mazatzin came over from the calmecac.

"Are you all right?" he asked. "You look upset."

"I'm fine," I replied, forcing on a smile. It seemed to help.

"Then everything is ready? You've spoken to the god?"

"I have."

"Good. I made my own sacrifice as well. You saw Red Flint play last night. He needs all the help he can get."

□

The palace square bustled with soldiers, citizens, and merchants. People meandered into the sacred ball court with its yellow and white feathered banners fluttering in the wind while a band played drums and flutes for the waiting crowd. Mazatzin took us in through the royal entrance and out to the stone-paved court. "Red Flint asked me to extend his apologies about last night, and to say that he'd like you to sit on the sidelines to cheer for him and tend to his wounds."

"He couldn't apologize himself?" I asked.

"I was concerned that I wouldn't get the chance to before the game," Red Flint said, coming out of the hallway dressed in his Tlachtli gear. He looked like a man who knew the point of backing out of the battle had passed and now he must do whatever he could to escape capture. That alone softened my anger and I accepted his muttered apology. "It means a great deal to me that you think I can do this," he admitted. "I should have as much confidence in myself."

Now wasn't the time to tell him that I had no confidence in him, but instead was betting on the god saving all of us. I just smiled and bowed, wishing him good luck.

The court was three times larger than the other, with gently-sloping walls decorated with reliefs of feathered serpents, which would make for interesting bounces. The polished stone rings near the top of the walls glimmered in the sunshine.

Mazatzin and I sat on the stone bench where the extra players usually sat. "Where's Topiltzin?" he asked.

"Making sure Ahexotl doesn't run for it when Red Flint wins."

Mazatzin cracked a smile. "As if Ahexotl could run."

I laughed, then searched for Ahexotl in the crowd gathered in the seating overlooking the court, but he wasn't there.

Uproarious cheering came when Obsidian Eagle strode out of the hallway opposite us, wearing his father's yellow and white feathered robe and the enormous quetzal-feathered headdress. Red Flint—who'd been pacing by himself—clenched his fists. Slaves hurried the robe off Obsidian Eagle's shoulders, revealing his elegant, jewel-encrusted Tlachtli gear. They also replaced the headdress with an eagle-head wooden helmet with feather-covered flaps over his cheeks.

Lord Spear Fish came out of the same hallway, carrying a maroon rubber ball under his arm. He called both Red Flint and Obsidian Eagle to center court.

Red Flint flashed me a weak smile then ran out to Lord Spear Fish. Obsidian Eagle strolled out, waving to the cheering crowd.

Lord Spear Fish raised his hand, and when he spoke, the crowd fell silent. "The first player to win five points, or to knock the ball through one of the rings, will be the winner."

"I've put balls through them three times myself," Obsidian Eagle announced, smiling up the crowd. "And I intend to make my fourth today." The audience cheered.

"Today will be my first one," Red Flint said. "Though it shall be done with your head." Some whistles and shouts for Red Flint broke out among the laughter from the crowd.

I'd never attended a ritual ball game before, but I'd picked up some of the basic concepts listening to Little Reed talk about it growing up. From what I gathered, different cities played by different rules, depending on their idea of skill and stamina, but certain rules were universal: you couldn't touch a ball in play with hands or feet, and points were scored when the opponent allowed the heavy solid rubber ball to hit the ground. It could bounce as much as it wished on the walls themselves, but not roll, and one couldn't climb the wall to fetch it either. Bouncing a ball through one of the two rings way up on the wall automatically won the game, though it was a rare occurrence. The fact that Obsidian Eagle had done it three times gave credence to him being the best player in all of Xochicalco.

But this is the favorite game of the gods, so once Quetzalcoatl shows up, all of Obsidian Eagle's skills will mean nothing, I thought with a smile.

Lord Spear Fish implored both men to play fair, then he bounced the ball hard into the ground and dashed out of the way.

Red Flint sprang at it, but Obsidian Eagle knocked him backwards. On the ball's downward fall, Obsidian Eagle slammed it with his glittering elbow pad and Red Flint moved his knee to intercept it. The ball hit the ground next to his foot. The crowd broke into frenzied cheers as Lord Spear Fish called the point for Obsidian Eagle.

Red Flint bounced the ball off his knee pad, sending it high. Obsidian Eagle backed up, repositioning himself, then he struck it with his right knee pad, sending it catapulting at Red Flint. Red Flint dove to return it, scraping his shin, but Obsidian Eagle whipped around and sent it flying back at his head. Red Flint scrambled to block it with his yoke, but the ball clipped his shoulder as he came up. It spun off behind him as he crumpled to his knees, holding his arm and gritting his teeth.

Obsidian Eagle leaned over and said something inaudible over the crowd noise, and Red Flint shoved him away and limped to fetch the ball. When he neared the bench, he gave me another angry look.

Trust in the god, you idiot, I thought.

Red Flint put the ball into play as he ran back towards center court. He and Obsidian Eagle exchanged a couple of volleys before Obsidian Eagle kneed the ball into his chest, sending Red Flint to the ground, writhing. Obsidian Eagle leaned over him. "I think he wants to forfeit," Obsidian Eagle crowed, but Red Flint struggled to his feet. Blood poured from a gouge under his kneecap. He picked up the ball and took a deep, pained breath before sending it back into play.

The high, arching serve brought a triumphant smile to Obsidian Eagle's face. He watched the ball as he took three quick steps then threw his left knee into it, sending it flying towards the ring on the right side of the court. The crowd fell silent as the ball sailed, many rising to their feet. My own heart stopped as I followed the ball's progress.

The ball hit the ring's inner rim and ricocheted into the wall. Obsidian Eagle leapt to put it back into play before it bounced off the wall but it hit the ground at his feet. The crowd exploded with hoots and hisses.

"I gave him that point!" Obsidian Eagle shouted, a sneer on his face. "I didn't want him looking so pathetic that he couldn't score at all!"

The crowd laughed.

"That was too close," Mazatzin said, letting out an anxious breath.

I shared his worry. Where was Quetzalcoatl? *Perhaps he didn't accept your stupid not-a-sacrifice after all.*

Obsidian Eagle set the ball into play off his elbow, and Red Flint took one step to intercept it, but then he collapsed, his whole body shaking. The crowd fell into stunned silence.

Mazatzin sprinted to his brother. I hesitated a moment then followed. Red Flint thrashed on the ground, his mouth foaming and his eyes rolled up inside his head. Mazatzin held him down. "He's having some kind of fit!"

"He's trying to gain pity for himself," Obsidian Eagle accused, keeping his distance. "The point still counts!"

Lord Spear Fish knelt over Red Flint as well. "He's in no condition to play. We'll have to call the game off."

"Then he forfeits, and by the rules, I win."

Lord Spear Fish looked to Mazatzin, but just then Red Flint fell still. He blinked a few times, bewilderment in his watery eyes, but when he saw me, a shadow of a smile crossed his lips. "I'm here, Papalotl," he whispered.

I let out a held breath and bowed my head. "My Lord."

"Are you all right, Lord Red Flint?" Spear Fish asked.

Red Flint blinked a couple of times then sat up. "I just need a moment to gather myself." Mazatzin helped him up; but when they locked gazes, Mazatzin gasped and bowed his head.

Red Flint turned to Obsidian Eagle. "Did you say something about forfeiting?"

Sneering, Obsidian Eagle threw the ball at him, but Red Flint caught it and smiled back. "Whenever you're ready," Obsidian Eagle said.

"You're ready then?"

"More than you'll ever be."

"You're sure?"

"Let's get this over with," Obsidian Eagle insisted.

Red Flint shrugged then played the ball off his knee, right into Obsidian Eagle's face.

The crowd gasped as Obsidian Eagle lay on the ground, holding his bloodied face and moaning.

"You said you were ready," Red Flint pointed out, a whisper of amusement on his face.

Obsidian Eagle rolled to his knees and spat out a couple of teeth with his bloody phlegm. "That's how you want to play?" he snarled, getting to his feet. "Then let's play."

Red Flint backed up and motioned for me and Mazatzin to get out of the way. We both ran back to our bench.

Obsidian Eagle served the ball hard off his knee pad, aiming for Red Flint's crotch, but Red Flint returned it with little effort, sending it sailing high. Obsidian Eagle backpedaled then dove in front of the ball, bouncing it with his knee as he slid sideways. Red Flint jogged backwards a few steps then hit it off his yoke, delivering a light return. Obsidian Eagle scrambled for it, diving belly first to the ground, but it hit the stone in front of his face and bounced off behind him. He lay on the ground, panting as the crowd broke out into ear-piercing cheers of "All hail Lord Red Flint!" starting from the soldiers sitting on the wall behind me.

"I've never seen Red Flint move so fast," Mazatzin said with an excited smile. "I doubt he knew his body could do that."

Obsidian Eagle struggled to his feet, his chest and left leg scraped raw and bleeding. "You need a break to cover your wounds?" Red Flint asked, his voice sincere, but Obsidian Eagle spat at him and snatched up the ball again. He limped halfway to the back of the court then turned and served the ball off his knee. It arched high, towards the right side of the court.

Red Flint moved in the opposite direction, watching it fall towards the wall. It hit and bounced high, and when it came back down, he returned it with his own knee.

Obsidian Eagle stumbled backwards and returned it with his yoke, but when Red Flint headed towards center court for it, Obsidian Eagle ran into him with his shoulder, knocking them both down. The crowd broke out into boos and hisses.

Red Flint never took his eyes off the falling ball though. When it came within reach, he kicked his leg up, striking the ball with his shin. It streaked towards the south wall, towards the ring, bringing the crowd to its feet in a collective gasp. Even Mazatzin leaped off the bench.

The ball hit inside the ring and spun like a leaf in a whirlpool. It eventually fell out the other side, still spinning as it bounced down the wall towards the court. The crowd burst into riotous cheers.

Obsidian Eagle stared at the ball then scrambled to his feet and ran for the exit hallway. But the guards closed ranks across it.

I followed Mazatzin back out to Red Flint, who was lying on the ground, groaning and looking around as if he had no idea where he was. "My Lord, are you all right?" I asked, but when he looked up to me, I saw Quetzalcoatl was gone.

Mazatzin helped Red Flint sit up. "It was the most frightening thing, Brother," Red Flint gasped. "I could see everything, but I couldn't do anything. My very insides burned."

"You'll be fine soon," I said. "The god has left your body."

"The god?" For a moment I thought he was going to vomit, but then shouting distracted him.

Obsidian Eagle was climbing the wall, trying to escape into the crowd, but the people sitting in the front row shoved him back. He struggled against them, but he slipped and fell, rolling and thumping down the wall back to the feet of the waiting guards.

"Seize him immediately!" Red Flint stood up with Mazatzin's help. When Mazatzin handed him his sword, he took off for the guards at a limping run. "Strip him down!" As he came upon the ball, he scooped it up with his free hand.

Obsidian Eagle squirmed as the soldiers tore his equipment off, not even leaving him the dignity of his loincloth. Red Flint broke into a full run the last few lengths, then threw the ball as hard as he could into Obsidian Eagle's chest. Obsidian Eagle gasped and would have crumpled to his knees, but the soldiers held him up, even when Red Flint finished by ramming his stone-padded knee into his crotch. Obsidian Eagle gagged, his mouth hanging open in a silent scream, his eyes bulging and face straining.

I stopped short, keeping a distance from the murmuring crowd around Red Flint. *This is only going to get uglier,* I thought, nausea growing in my stomach. I tried to step backwards but the crowd of soldiers pressed in behind me.

Red Flint shoved Obsidian Eagle to the ground. "Did you really think you'd get away with stealing my throne? Or with killing Father and inviting his greatest enemy to share in the spoils? And did your precious high priest think I'd let him get away with insulting my manhood in front of the entire army?" He whipped around. "Come down here and face your destiny like a real man, Ahexotl! Or did the fire burn that away too?"

"Ahexotl isn't here, Brother," Mazatzin said.

"Coward! Send guards to find that vile excuse for a man immediately!"

"You already sent Topiltzin to do that before the match," Mazatzin reminded him, though Red Flint looked at him as if he spoke a foreign language.

"It's no matter anyway. The true traitor is caught and he shall pay for his crimes now." Red Flint punched Obsidian Eagle across the face then spat on him. "Bring me the sacrificial stone! And some rope," he added with a coyote-like smile.

Two soldiers lugged out a rectangular slab of stone decorated with carvings of ballplayers playing Tlachti with skulls, and when Obsidian Eagle saw it, he broke out into a keening cry that raised the hairs on my neck. It rose louder as the soldiers dragged him to the stone and tied him down, his neck stretched across its concave middle. "Have mercy, Brother! Ahexotl tricked me! I trusted him as a friend but I see now that he wanted the throne for himself! He's the true traitor, Brother! Have mercy, I beg you!"

Red Flint stepped up to him. "I am having mercy on you. I could have my soldiers molest you like a war prize in front of the entire city, but I'll spare you that humiliation." He poised the sword blade over Obsidian Eagle's neck. "And you're no brother of mine, you little maggot." And he brought the blade down.

I flinched, suddenly drowning in that same feeling I had whenever I dreamed of my father's murder, or when I saw the sacrifices dying for the god—sacrifices the god didn't want.

It took two swings to behead Obsidian Eagle—one with each side of the sword, for half the obsidian blades shattered after the first hit—but once it finally fell, Red Flint picked up the head and threw it at the north courtside ring. It hit the wall, splattering gore before rolling back down to the ground.

Everyone fell to their knees around Red Flint, but then Mazatzin rose again and shouted, "Bring forth King Cuitlapanton's royal robe and headdress!" He beckoned me to join him next to Red Flint.

My sense of duty made me obey, but every hair on my neck stood up when Red Flint draped his arm over my shoulder as if we were friends.

Two slaves hurried through the crowd with the pieces of the royal garb. Mazatzin helped Red Flint into the yellow and white robe and I placed the quetzal feather headdress on his brow. The men rose and shouted his name, raising their swords and fists in the air. He smiled and raised his hands too, glorying in their chant, looking every bit the king.

☐

"Why wasn't Topiltzin at the match?" Red Flint asked as he lounged on his reed throne, a dozen serving women washing his wounds and combing his hair. Mazatzin sat on the high priest's mat next to him, smoking his pipe as he scribbled on a piece of parchment. I could have taken the high priestess's mat on Red Flint's other side, but he was still on edge and stared at me as though he thought I'd set the god upon him rather than helped him win the match. "Stop pulling my hair!" he snapped at one of the serving girls, looking ready to hit her.

"He was out finding Ahexotl, just as you'd ordered, your Majesty," I reminded him.

Red Flint thought a moment then said, "Oh yes, I did. Didn't I?" He looked at Mazatzin, who nodded in confirmation. "Well, maybe I did or maybe I didn't. My head is out of sorts right now."

"There's been far too much excitement for all of us," Mazatzin said.

"I'm thinking of putting him on my war council, you know?" Red Flint rambled on. "So I can consult him on important matters. He'll be honored by the offer."

An administrative role would put an indefinite hold on Little Reed's plans to reclaim Culhuacan; surely Red Flint's way of keeping control of when he could march on Ihuitimal. That was the last honor Little Reed needed.

"And of course, my dearest brother will be the next high priest, now that Ahexotl has forfeited his life," Red Flint went on.

I couldn't remain silent about that though. "Traditionally the high priestess chooses the next high priest, Your Grace."

Red Flint ignored me. "You should bring Nimilitzli to pledge loyalty to me and counsel me about these rituals I must perform prior to my coronation."

"I will do that for you, your Majesty—"

"I'd rather the high priestess do it," he interrupted. "Let's maintain tradition."

I bit back the barb on my tongue. *Fine, fetch Nimilitzli and she'll set him straight. He's always been afraid of her.* "I'll go tell her of your wishes, Your Majesty." I bowed, then left the great hall.

Mazatzin jogged out after me and called for me to stop. "Please excuse Red Flint," he whispered. "He's impetuous—we both know that—but I'll speak with him about proper protocol and authority. He'll listen to me; he always has."

"Tell him he'd do well to remember who put him on his throne. He must keep his hands out of the order's concerns, like choosing the next high priest."

"I'll remind him." I turned to leave, but he set a hand on my shoulder. "If you don't believe me to be the right candidate, I'll gladly step aside—"

"You're absolutely the right choice," I assured him. "You were born for the position and I'm glad to see you finally receive what you deserve."

Mazatzin bowed his head. "Thank you for your confidence in me."

"You're the best and most loyal friend, and I'm honored to have you at my side."

"The honor is all mine."

I sighed, exasperated. "Will you let me praise you for once and just accept it?"

"Well, if you insist," he said with a smile.

I headed up to the sacred precinct, to share the good news with Nimilitzli, and hopefully get some even better news from Little Reed. Finally Ahexotl would pay as he should have long ago.

Strange how things just go on as normal, I thought when I reached the summit to find the novices gathered around the cistern, talking over their afternoon break. *That's because priests are strong and they persevere regardless of the circumstances,* I told myself with pride.

"What do you want to eat, Nimilitzli?" I asked as I elbowed aside the curtain. "I'm thinking something celebratory, something with meat...."

But my words trailed off when I saw the blood splashed across the far wall like a red sunset. My stunned gaze immediately fell to Nimilitzli, lying face down on the floor next to her mat. Slashes and deep rents left her looking more like a butchered animal than a human being.

My stomach heaved and I vomited, bringing myself to my knees. I looked up at her again, bewildered, my mouth raw. "Mother?" I whispered.

She didn't answer.

Hearing shuffling behind me, I turned, only to receive a heavy blow to the head that knocked me into darkness.

CHAPTER TWENTY-SEVEN

Pain dragged me awake and I had no idea where I was; my back was hot, but when I tried to move away, intense pain shot up my right leg. I grabbed my thigh and my hand came back covered in blood. I tried again to stand, but my foot dangled lifeless at my heel.

"Difficult to move, isn't it?" Ahexotl asked. Seeing him sitting in the corner behind the doorway, the nightmare rushed back at me: the blood on the walls, Nimilitzli's cloven remains, the reek of death in the air.

My eyes watered. "Topiltzin will kill you for this."

"He's going to kill me anyway, so what does it matter? I've waited seven years for justice, and I'll die with a smile on my face." He hobbled over to me, relish in his eyes.

I tried again to get up but he grabbed my hair and shoved me back down. "Help me!" I screamed, but he clamped his sweaty hand over my mouth.

"Save it for when the flames are eating you," he panted, then shoved me.

I grabbed the hearth's outer lip with both hands and pushed back hard. He punched my stomach, knocking the wind out of me, and I finally fell in, but I caught his robe and dragged him in with me.

"Ayya!" he cried, flailing to catch hold of the hearth's opening. I groped around to pull myself back, but when I finally found solid purchase, he yanked us both out, shrieking, "Get off me, you bitch! Get off me!" I finally let go and he slumped to his knees, holding his groin. "You filthy whore!" He grabbed a flaming log and flung it at me.

It hit the side of my face, but the pain was only a distant cry in my head as I crawled behind Nimilitzli's body. He threw another and it missed me, but the bright tinder set the sleeping mat smoldering. I slapped at it, but tiny flames began jumping up with alarming speed.

Ahexotl lumbered towards me and tripped over Nimilitzli, crushing me under him. I tried to claw my way out but he closed his fists around my neck. I raked him across both cheeks, leaving trails of oozing blood. "I'll see you on the path to Mictlan and I'll bend you over Lord Death's sacrificial stone and have my way with you while he eats your heart!" He started squeezing, euphoria spreading over his face.

Blood pulsed in my head. I went for his eyes, but couldn't reach them, so I beat on his sides. He only seemed to enjoy my struggling. Panic swooped in and I groped around for any part of him I could claw or twist to make him loosen his grip.

By the god's grace, my fingertips found the smooth handle of the sacrificial blade hanging at Ahexotl's belt. I pulled at it until it dislodged from the sheath, then I gripped it tight and plunged it into his ribs.

His eyes bulged in surprise but he didn't loosen his grip, even when I twisted the blade. I took another jab at him, this time going for his neck.

I missed my mark but buried the blade in the fleshy jowls hanging over his jaw. This time he let go to grab the knife, looking half-dazed. Able to breathe finally, I found a second burst of energy and stabbed him again, this time squarely hitting his neck. The next time I impaled his hand as he tried to shield himself from me. With my last strike I opened his jugular, and the shooting blood splattered wide across the wall behind me.

Ahexotl clutched the blade, blood streaming over his hands. He got it halfway out before his fingers slipped off the handle and he stared down at me with astonishment. His gaze wandered up and he flinched.

I turned my head to see the Black Dog standing in the corner, watching us.

"How was one to know?" Ahexotl gasped, and fell over sideways.

The Black Dog peered down at me. *This is what you get for not being strong enough to make the necessary sacrifice,* I thought, closing my eyes and waiting to feel his tongue on my cheek. *It probably feels like a blade of ice, cutting through flesh and severing all mortal bonds. I pray Little Reed isn't the one to find my body.*

◻

When I came to again, I recognized the weapons hanging on the wall of the Council Room in the calmecac. Malinalli leaned over me, her harried expression changing to ecstatic relief. "Quetzalpetlatl? Can you hear me?" She leaned closer.

"Little Reed," I whispered, my mouth tasting like ash. The strong smell of burning flesh stuck in my nose. "Where's Little Reed?"

"Who's Little Reed?" Malinalli asked.

"He's Lord Topiltzin," Ixchell answered. She was tending to my injured foot. "We'll try to find him for you, High Priestess, but for now, rest."

I shook my head and tried to sit up. "We must save Nimilitzli. The house is on fire—"

Malinalli pushed me back down. "It's too late, Quetzalpetlatl," she whispered, tears in her voice. "She was already gone by the time we found you."

I overflowed with tears. "I must see Little Reed. He must know what's happened." And why didn't he get to Ahexotl before that monster could butcher Nimilitzli?

"I'll find him." Malinalli had me choke down some tochtetepon and octli. "Ixchell's going to try to fix your heel. Everything's going to be all right."

"Tell him I must see him immediately," I pleaded, holding onto her hand as she stood to leave.

She gently removed my fingers from her wrist. "I promise I will."

I didn't remember falling back asleep, but Malinalli wasn't at my side again when I awoke much later, and my throbbing heel made the knife wound in my leg seem like an annoying insect bite. Ixchell soon gave me another dose of tochtetepon and I fell back into dreamless sleep.

◻

I stayed asleep most of the next couple of days, hardly aware that time passed. Coming down off high doses of yauhtli took a while, and though Ixchell stopped pouring it down my throat by the second morning, I still slept as if I hadn't rested in days. Dreams slowly returned, fuzzy at first, but then taking on terrible coherence; I came home to find Little Reed as mutilated and dead as Nimilitzli. I awoke with a start, shaking and sweating.

180

"You're all right," Malinalli whispered, gently stroking my back. "It's just a dream."

I looked around, my heart slowing again. I sat in her bed in her house, and she'd laid out an extra mat next to the hearth where she usually kept her weaving. I clutched my stomach as it battled back and forth between nausea and hunger, and she brought me a warm tlaxcalli. "Eat slowly. You've had nothing but yauhtli and water for almost two days."

I gritted my teeth at the stiff pain as I sat up. "I feel like I'll never walk again," I panted, out of breath already.

"Ixchell thinks you'll get most of your foot's mobility back again, but you'll probably have a limp, and some difficulty running. You should move it as much as you can, so the muscles don't freeze."

I did so, despite the extreme pain in my tendon. I felt faint. "Has Topiltzin been by to see me yet today?"

Malinalli's gaze dropped. "About Topiltzin, Quetzalpetlatl...."

I tightened my grip on the tlaxcalli until it was crumbling between my fingers. "Is he all right?"

She hesitated then said, "Mazatzin wanted to talk to you as soon as you were awake, so I'll go and get him." She cast a worried glance back at me before hurrying out the curtain.

I sat in stunned silence the whole time she was gone, thinking about the nightmare. "That's all it is," I assured myself, but already I felt myself dying inside.

When Mazatzin arrived, the pained smile on his face told me everything I needed to know. He kept his hands behind his back as he said, "Feeling better? Make sure you're doing your ankle exercises, even if it hurts."

"What are you hiding?" My own voice sounded distant.

He hesitated. "I hate being the bearer of such news, but...you risked your life to tell me of my father, so it's only right I return the favor." He finally brought his hands around and held a sword out to me.

I immediately recognized it as the sword Nimilitzli had given to Little Reed. It was covered in dried blood. I felt like someone was throttling me all over again as I took it with trembling hands. "What happened?"

"He didn't report to the palace after the match, and no one knew where he was, so Red Flint sent troops out to find him." He struggled to speak before finally continuing. "They found his remains out in the limestone quarry, burned. We caught those who did it—and Red Flint executed all of them, but...I know that's little comfort. If we'd only known earlier...."

Or I could have made the hard decision and none of this would've happened. Now I wished I'd let Ahexotl choke the life from me. *This time it's all my fault.* I doubled over, unable to hold back the tears any longer.

Mazatzin put his arms around me and whispered comforting words, but I didn't deserve any of them.

□

Malinalli cared for me while I recovered from my physical injuries, but the others—the ones I buried deep and showed no one—for now there was no helping them. Losing Mother and Father had taught me that though such wounds healed with time, there would always be the ghost pains, like the ones I sometimes felt in my hand.

For now I focused on putting it out of my thoughts with work. I officiated over

Nimilitzli's funeral, using the strength she'd taught me to encourage my priests and priestesses to trust in the god to lead us through this dark time. Mazatzin and I buried Nimilitzli's ashes under the stone floor of the temple.

He offered to let me officiate over Little Reed's funeral, but everything I wanted to say was private. I suggested that Citlallotoc give the speech, but no one had seen him since the day of the match. I wondered if he even knew.

Red Flint rambled at length to the crowd gathered in the rain about Little Reed's valor and intelligence, but he stared at me when he started talking about my brother's dedication to family. "Everything he did was for the benefit of his poor, orphaned sister, she who meant everything to him, she whom he leaves behind alone. May she find his tremendous strength in herself to take up the mission he leaves unfinished."

I'd been so busy transitioning to being the official high priestess and preparing for the funerals that I hadn't given any thought to what would become of Quetzalcoatl's plans now that his son was dead. Who would overthrow Ihuitimal and bring the Feathered Serpent's worship back to the people?

Long ago war queens did rule the Tolteca, but those times were dead and I was already at the top of what women could achieve. The people demanded a king, but in my carelessness I'd cost them the future they deserved. Would Quetzalcoatl expel me from his priesthood for this? That was all I had left anymore, and the thought that he might take that away from me.... *I can never face him again. My service is the only thing getting me through this now.*

"The king wants to see you," Mazatzin said, interrupting my thoughts. The great hall was mostly empty after the mourning feast, with only a handful of nobles sitting near the hearth, smoking pipes. Red Flint wasn't there though.

I handed my bowl of cold food to one of the servants. "What does he want?"

Mazatzin looked away, grumbling under his breath. "I told him the whole marriage issue is pointless since you're the high priestess now, but he insists on talking to you about it."

"But he's marrying Turquoise Bells at the end of the week."

"Mother said if he could gain your consent, she wouldn't object."

Mazatzin said little as he led me out into the torch-lit garden, down a stone path to a circle of carved wood benches. Red Flint paced between them, muttering, but he stopped when we approached. Mazatzin cast him a hard glare then left.

"Thank you for seeing me, My Lady," Red Flint said. "If I might be so bold, you're looking better these days. You seem to be walking well on that foot now."

"It's getting better," I acknowledged.

"Wonderful, wonderful." He gazed around nervously before saying, "I never did extend my condolences on your loss. Truly tragic, My Lady."

He could ramble all day about my injured leg or the weather, but I wouldn't talk about either Nimilitzli or Little Reed. "Forgive my bluntness, My Lord, but I have temple duties before dawn."

"Of course. I'll get directly to the matter. I know you meant a great deal to your brother and he'd want someone to step up and look after you now that he's gone on to Mictlan—someone who would also look after his affairs here on Earth. I can be that man, Quetzalpetlatl."

His words felt like knives stabbing my throat.

"It makes perfect sense. Ihuitimal wouldn't stand a chance against my army if I ordered a full assault on Culhuacan. Marry me and I'll go to war to reclaim your father's stolen throne; it's my wedding present to you, and when our eldest son comes of age, he can rule Culhuacan until I pass on, then another of our sons will take his place there. I'll finish what Topiltzin started; I will be his replacement."

For all his sincerity, those last words snapped the fragile string holding my mask of politeness in place. "Have you any idea why Topiltzin was here to begin with? Why Quetzalcoatl put him in my mother's belly and gave him life?" Red Flint tried to say something but I cut him off. "Getting Culhuacan's throne back...that's merely a small mark on the battle plan Quetzalcoatl laid out. Topiltzin was going to be the king of all Tolteca and end human sacrifice in the valley, bringing everyone together in peace and prosperity and leading us all into a great new age. And you—who scoff at the god's power as if it's nothing—you believe yourself worthy of being both the people's high king and the god's high priest?"

Red Flint went livid. "Who do you think you are, daring to defy the request of your king?" he snarled.

"I am the high priestess of the god, chosen by the lips of the god himself; the god who put you on your throne. And if you're not careful, he will withdraw support for your reign."

"How dare you threaten me?" He lumbered at me.

I backed a few steps and drew my knife, holding it poised over my palm. "All I have to do is cut, Red Flint, and you can discuss this with Quetzalcoatl himself." My voice quaked.

Anxiety danced in Red Flint's eyes and for a moment I thought he was going to call my bluff, but he stepped back, his face pale as he realized what had almost happened. "Get out of my sight." The rage had drained from his voice, leaving him raw and vulnerable.

I sheathed my sacrificial blade then hobbled off, not looking back.

□

I prayed in front of the Feathered Serpent's idol a long time, waiting for the shakes to wear off. When they finally did, I felt exalted by what I'd told Red Flint. Perhaps Little Reed had left me a bit of his strength after all.

I finally looked up at the shimmering gold idol. I'd given serious consideration to going into the Divine Dream and saying what needed to be said to the god, but dread held me back; not of facing him, for I'd finally found the truth in my heart: no matter how much I might have erred, Quetzalcoatl would always care about me, and he would forgive my faults. But I couldn't handle seeing Little Reed's face in his and feeling the pain and guilt.

But I could stare all day at the serpent idol and think only of Quetzalcoatl. Had the god come to me that first time in the Divine Dream as a feathered serpent, would our relationship have turned in the same the direction it had? *I'd have seen him for the god he is, not as a human being; especially not one I yearned for. It was wrong to treat him as if he were merely one of us.*

I touched the statue's smooth nose. "I've made a complete mess of your battle scheme, My Lord, but rest assured I'm more dedicated than ever to seeing your reforms to victory." I pierced my tongue with a string of maguey thorns and threaded it through, the familiar, comforting pain of sacrifice calming me. "Please forgive my mistakes and trust me to do what's necessary to see human sacrifice ended. Guide me through these dark days, help me grow stronger for them, and give me the faith necessary to help my people find their way to brighter days."

I extinguished the copalli incense in the burner. In the morning, I'd tell Mazatzin and Malinalli everything Quetzalcoatl had told me about his plans, and together we'd see it through.

PART FOUR
THE YEAR SEVEN RABBIT

Chapter Twenty-Eight

 I wanted to start making progress on Quetzalcoatl's plans, but not long after the tragedy on the sacred precinct, everything started falling apart. A mudslide wiped out half the city's crops and later that summer, just before harvest, swarms of grasshoppers devastated the remaining half. Higher numbers of Chichimec traveled the roads with their families, and the royal nursery remained empty. "The god has cursed us all," the peasants whispered. "He's outraged at his high priest having slain the high priestess a hundred paces from his temple."

But the only real curse on Xochicalco was her king. A few months into his reign, Red Flint publicly executed all his concubines, accusing them of sneaking chipahuacxihuitl to keep from begetting his children. The incident outraged several of his allies—all his concubines were royal daughters from cities like Tepenec and Xochimilco and Cholula—and they rumbled about withdrawing their military support, but he threatened to march on their cities if they did.

He also implicated Turquoise Bells, but Mazatzin talked him out of executing her. "They're all trying to sabotage the royal bloodline," Red Flint insisted. "If she doesn't beget a child in the next two months, then I'll use her head for a ball at the next Tlachtli match!" He beat her, usually to shouts of "inadequate whore!" that could be heard even in the royal gardens. How did she manage to live in such an environment?

Soon his strange behavior crept into his political dealings too. He sent his war council north to demand tribute from the Chichimecs and only Spear Fish returned, carrying the others' heads in a bag. He executed Camaxtli and Oquitzin for sedition when he saw them practicing on the ball court, but when he mentioned Mazatzin conspiring with them, I warned him, "Keep your hands off the high priest, or the god will pay you a visit, Your Majesty." He sneered, but said nothing more about it.

But when he set the royal turkeys loose in the market because they'd been "lecturing him", I had no doubt that he'd become deranged.

"He's always been rash," Mazatzin protested as we sat whispering about it in my meditation room. "That's just Red Flint."

"You would be a much better king than him," I said.

"Don't say such things." He looked over his shoulder. "If we're overheard by the wrong people.... I was Red Flint's most loyal supporter, and for me to turn on him—"

"Who's more important? Him, or your city and your people?"

"I can't talk about this anymore." But the look in his eyes said he knew I was right.

Not that I was above Red Flint's scrutiny. He'd abandoned any notion of marrying me, but instead focused on haranguing me into his bed. Sometimes he spoke sweetly, trying to appeal to my "womanly gentleness", but mostly he screamed and raved, calling me a difficult bitch. "You're a rebellious city in need of conquering," he told me with a chilling grin that seemed to reach to his ears. I'd never seen him look crazier.

But then the new morning dawned.

◻

I sat in my meditation room when a young priest tore aside my door curtain, panting. "High Priestess! You must come quickly! The king—!"

Oh, what's he done now? Yesterday he'd ordered the guards to shoot down any birds over the city, because they were spies for Ihuitimal, and their constant singing was keeping him awake.

"He's at the temple and he...he ordered me to fetch you immediately." The priest looked frightened, so I followed him out to the precinct.

Priests and novices were gathered at the foot of the Feathered Serpent's pyramid, a storm of conversation going. I made my way through, aggravating my ankle when I tried to jog up the stairs, so that I had to hobble the last few steps.

Red Flint stood in front of the idol, flanked by guards. He looked around like a harried, nervous deer, so I knew if I lectured him about bringing weapons of war into the god's house, he would set off into a tirade, and might even damage the temple.

His face lit with joy when he saw me. "I'm so glad you hurried! I have such good news!"

"What is it, Your Majesty?" I tried to sound patient but wanted him out of my god's temple now.

"I know why all my women have failed to give me children!"

Not at all what I'd expected. "That's...wonderful, Your Majesty."

"Not so wonderful, since I had all them garroted when it wasn't their fault. But it's not my fault either. The Feathered Serpent cursed my reign; he hates me—"

"Quetzalcoatl doesn't hate you—"

"Of course he does! He's a fertility god, yet no children run the halls of my palace, knocking over my statues, or tromping in my flowerbeds or stealing my armor for play. He blessed my father with countless children but turns his nose up at me. Well, to Mictlan with him!"

The guards gasped. One even muttered, "The king cursed the god in his own temple!"

"Shut up or I'll stuff you inside this foul idol!" Red Flint screamed, pointing at the gilded Feathered Serpent behind him. He then stood very still. "Do you hear that?" He jumped atop the altar and cupped his ear.

The crowd murmured outside, but surely that wasn't what he was talking about. "What do you hear?" Hopefully he'd admit, in front of his own guards, to hearing nonexistent voices, so they could see him for the madman he was.

He smiled that same crazy smile again. "I cursed the name of the supposedly mighty Quetzalcoatl in his temple and he does nothing. Some all-powerful god!"

"You've held the god's power in your body, so you know he's not weak," I snapped.

Red Flint sneered. "All gods have power, but who put that into me? Mazatzin told me how you summoned the god before, as a fire serpent to ravage attacking Chichimecs, and a stone serpent that peeled off the walls of this very temple. You, My Lady, are the one with the real power."

The calculating look in his eyes startled me. "Not at all true, My Lord—"

He leaped off the altar and landed in front of me like a pouncing jaguar. "We've been worshiping the wrong god the whole time. Or should I say, the wrong goddess...."

"This is crazy, My Lord—"

He slashed his hand at me for silence. "I'm outlawing the worship of that weak Feathered Serpent and instead every citizen shall offer sacrifice to you alone! You'll bring prosperity back to Xochicalco!"

I looked imploringly at the guards, but they whispered to each other, watching me warily. Surely they didn't believe this craziness?

"I'm taking this temple for you," Red Flint continued, advancing on me. "I've already commissioned a new idol fashioned after your enormous beauty—" He reached out to me but I moved away. "Once everything is consecrated, I'll make love to you on this altar, and your divine powers will cure my curse and you'll bear me a son rich with the blood of the gods. The whole city will gather to witness the miracle rebirth of Xochicalco's royal line!"

"I won't have sex with you, Red Flint." Why did it always come down that?

He smacked me hard and I fell backwards onto the stairs, sending a shock of pain up my spine. "Or perhaps I should consecrate the temple's altar with the goddess's virgin blood, shed during the forceful planting of the seed."

I looked to the guards for help, but their fervent expressions chilled me. If I ran, would they catch me and hold me down while Red Flint made good on his threat? Did they really think this would help the city?

Screams rose outside.

Red Flint flashed me a smug smile, so I scrambled outside.

Smoke billowed to the east, and down in the lower precincts, soldiers ran from temple to temple, setting them afire while the priests stood outside, shouting and crying. The high priest of Tlaloc tried to stop two soldiers mounting the stairs of his god's temple, but they threw him down and he lay motionless at the bottom of the pyramid, crowded by his priests.

"So beautiful, don't you think?" Red Flint asked beside me. "The glow will light the entire city when night falls."

"We haven't had rain in over a month! A single wind gust could spread it to the rest of the city!"

"Consider this my last effort to persuade you to do what's best for your people," he said, unmoved.

Malinalli rushed up the steps. "They're setting fire to the calmecac, My Lady!"

"Where's Mazatzin?" Only he could talk sense into him.

"Tucked away." Red Flint sighed. "He was unenthusiastic about my idea too; he even dared challenge my fitness for the throne, so I put him away."

My guts twisted. "You killed him?" When he grinned catlike at me, I pulled my blade.

But Red Flint batted the knife away and seized my hair. "Always so stubborn, you stupid woman." He turned to the guards gathered at the doorway, dragging me with him. "Our uncooperative goddess requires a sacrifice. Take torches down to the merchant quarters, lock every man, woman and child inside their homes, then burn them down." To me, he hissed, "I will sacrifice five more people every day you resist taking my royal seed."

A rumble of outrage finally passed among the guards. "Surely you don't mean for us to kill our own citizens—" someone ventured.

"Go or I'll sacrifice the whole lot of you instead!" Red Flint screamed, so they scrambled down the stairs. "Not you!" he shouted at one young man who looked barely old enough to have served a day in the army. The man cringed but stopped.

Red Flint yanked me back to the temple. "I need a witness to the capture and claiming of the goddess."

The guard paled but followed us inside.

I tried to scramble away when Red Flint flung me onto the altar, but he shoved me back, laughing as he started cutting my robe off with his knife. Jerking the blade through the ties at my neck, he nicked my chin, then he grabbed my head and latched onto the wound like a sucking leech. I beat my fists against his head but cut my arm on his blade. "Can't waste any of that divine blood," he panted, then moved his lips to mine, his sweaty, groping hands crushing my breasts. I wiggled like a trapped dog, trying to find some angle that would allow me to slip away, but he knotted his fingers in my hair so tightly I couldn't move my head anymore. He held his blade to my throat. "You don't want me to hurt you, do you?"

Tears finally broke free—not from the searing pain in my scalp but because I realized I could do nothing to stop him. And the intoxicating desire rose up like a hungry cat, growling, *Go ahead, and see what happens to you, fool!* But I bit back the challenge and squeezed my eyes shut, horrified. What was wrong with me?

"I knew you'd see reason." Red Flint smiled at me with a caring expression. "I'm going to make you so happy, Quetzalpetlatl; I'll make you far happier than Topiltzin ever could have."

That broke through the haze building in my head. "What?"

He grinned like a caiman. "Oh, don't think I didn't know. I'm not stupid." He looked up and laughed, as if recalling a fond memory. "He paid for his treason; I won't tolerate anyone trying to steal from me."

My anger raged past my desire like stampeding deer and I spat in his face. He stared at me, astonished. "You really are nothing but an impotent lizard, you murderer," I snarled.

He sat up and wiped the spittle from his eyes with his fist. "You insolent bitch!" he growled and raised the knife to stab me.

Someone shattered a clay censer across the side of his head, and he fell sideways, crying out in surprise. But when he cracked his head on the sharp edge of the altar, he went down the rest of the way in silence.

Malinalli stood with the handle of the broken censer clutched in both hands, her breath hissing between her clenched teeth. Red Flint sprawled on the floor, blood bubbling out of the deep gouge in his forehead.

The guard stared at him, stunned, but once he looked at Malinalli and me, he ran out screaming, "Please don't curse me! Quetzalcoatl is great! Have mercy on me!"

Malinalli dropped the censer handle and gave me a hug. "Thank the god you're all right," she whispered, tears in her voice.

I couldn't hold back my own tears. "Thank you, Malinalli. I owe you my life."

We looked down at Red Flint. "Dear gods, what have I...is he dead?" Malinalli asked, half crying, half laughing.

I felt a faint, erratic pulse at his neck. He gurgled but didn't move. "No, but he hasn't much longer."

Malinalli clutched her sides, breathing rapidly. "Dear gods, I've killed the king!"

I took her shoulders with my hands. "You did what you had to." Still seeing uncertainty on her face, I picked up Red Flint's blade and slid it into his jugular.

"Show mercy on this lost soul,

My beloved Lord,
Hold not the Black Dog from him.
Let him suffer in this world no more."

A few breaths after I pulled the blade out, Red Flint's gurgling fell silent. "You didn't kill him, Malinalli; I did. And it was the merciful thing to do."

We carried Red Flint's body outside and tossed it down the temple stairs, bringing gasps from the crowd. "The god has laid judgment on King Red Flint's reign," I announced. "We're without a mortal king but we still have the gods, and we must do all we can to save their temples. I need our fastest priestesses to spread word of the king's death to the soldiers, so they know they need not follow mad orders anymore. The rest of you, grab anything you can find that'll hold water. We must get this under control." To Malinalli, I said, "Stay here and oversee. I must go and see the war council."

◻

The war council was gathered among a crowd of guards and servants in the great hall, and to my disbelief—and utter joy—Mazatzin sat in the middle of them, nursing a cut head. I smothered him with a hug. "Dear gods, he said he killed you!"

"He would have, if not for Lord Spear Fish," Mazatzin said, his face flushed. "He left ranting that he was going to bring the wrath of the gods down on me." He shook his head. "I should have dealt with him a long time ago."

"We must seize the king and strip him of his headdress, for the people's safety," Spear Fish said.

"The god has already done so," I said. "Lord Red Flint has been struck down by the god's wrath."

"You called on him again?" Mazatzin asked. I'd told him that I'd never again use my powers; it came at too high a price.

"He made his will known through the hands of his servants," I assured him.

"Then matters are settled." Spear Fish went to his knees and the rest of the room followed. "We honor you, Lord Mazatzin, king of Xochicalco." I knelt too.

Mazatzin frowned, uncomfortable. Even as high priest he'd never grown used to the attention his status afforded him.

"But there's more, My Lord," I said. "Red Flint ordered all the temples burned and he sent men to torch the Merchant Quarters. I've already sent people to stop the soldiers, but hearing the news from other soldiers might help this end quicker."

To Spear Fish, he said, "Dispatch messengers immediately. I'm going to the sacred precinct—"

"With all due respect, Your Majesty, I'd rather you didn't," Spear Fish said. "You should evacuate from the city, in case the fires spread."

"We should evacuate the whole city," I added. "Our soldiers don't need to be worrying about rescuing women and children while they're also battling the fires."

Flustered, Mazatzin said, "I can't run out while the gods' temples are threatened."

"You're the king now," I reminded him. "You're no good to anyone if you're dead."

Mazatzin frowned but relented. "I'll take my father's women and children and get a camp established out by the quarry. Lord Spear Fish, will you stay to oversee the evacuation and fire operations?"

"I'd be honored, Your Majesty," Spear Fish said with a bow.

I was about to head back to the sacred precinct when Mazatzin grabbed my hand. "I

191

did as you asked, so please do me the same honor. I want you to come with me."

"I should be with my priests—"

"They'll evacuate along with the rest of the city. Xochicalco needs her spiritual leader just as much as she needs her king, so please, you must come with me to ensure the order's leadership." He lowered his voice before adding, "I promised Topiltzin long ago that I'd do my best to look after you in his absence. Please don't make me break that promise."

I wanted to argue, but the plea in his eyes stilled my objections. "Very well."

□

By noon, Malinalli arrived at the quarry leading a group of soot-covered priestesses and novices, including the youngest male students. The priests and older male novices had remained behind to help fight the fires.

Mazatzin's tent was set up in the middle of a makeshift camp east of the limestone quarry with the rest of the citizenry's tents pitched around it, the classes clustering together like petals of a sunflower. Farmers gathered in their fields to watch the fires rage.

News trickled in slowly; the fires had spread to the artisan quarters, and the merchant quarters had burned down completely. Roofs were now smoldering in the noble quarters.

"There's just not enough water in the cisterns," one soldier reported at dusk. "And it takes so long to get it from the canals."

"I have Tlaloc's priestesses praying and making sacrifices," Mazatzin said. "Let's hope he hears our prayers and responds."

"We haven't had rain in months," I pointed out.

"We have to hope the gods will show us mercy."

Mazatzin spoke little over the evening meal, then we sat outside, watching our city burn down in a glowing inferno. Even when shifting winds brought the smoke into camp, making it difficult to breathe, I sat with him until dawn, not saying anything but staying in case he needed to talk.

In the morning, gray smoke blanketed the land like fog and it was impossible to see whether or not the city was still ablaze; but a steady stream of soot-covered soldiers wandered into camp, all looking shocked and distraught. There was no laughter, only wailing and prayers as the news spread.

Xochicalco was no more.

□

We waited two days before going back into the city to inspect the damage. While Mazatzin checked on the palace, I went to the sacred precinct, praying Quetzalcoatl had protected his temple from the flames.

The temple's basic structure had survived, but the wooden roof supports had collapsed. The fire spared nothing; not the reed mats, the baskets of grass balls and maguey thorns; even the idol had melted into a grotesque parody of the god. I knelt next to the altar, shocked by how warm it still felt. I rested my cheek against it and closed my eyes against the stinging tears.

"Horrifying, isn't it?" Mazatzin stood outside the rubble, looking around like a lost child.

"It's like losing my mother—both of them—all over again."

Mazatzin sat on the altar. "I feel so much worse than when I found out that Obsidian

192

Eagle murdered Father; I stood by and did nothing, and now my family's city is destroyed."

"You weren't a coward for leaving. You had to."

He shook his head. "How many times did you tell me we have to do something about Red Flint? If I'd been stronger and did what I should have, this wouldn't have happened. I was too cowardly to stand up to him, because I loved him." He covered his face. "I wouldn't make the difficult choice and now we're all paying for it. I'm king of a pile of burnt rubble."

His words tore open my old wounds. I knew exactly what he was feeling right now. I joined him on the altar and put my arm around him. "Sometimes things are out of our hands. The god has reasons for everything that happens."

Mazatzin chuckled dejectedly. "Should I be angry that he wanted Xochicalco destroyed? He put Red Flint on the throne after all."

It made sense that Quetzalcoatl would have wanted a power void for his son to fill, if he were still alive, but that struck me as too calculating for the god I loved. *My faith in the god is all I have left,* I thought, shaking off the unsettling thoughts. "Good things can come from tragedy. I lost my mother and father, but it brought me here, to Nimilitzli, to Malinalli, to you, and the god. You're like a brother to me, Mazatzin, as dear as Topiltzin, and I wouldn't trade that for anything."

He nodded. "Neither would I. Still, seeing everything my father and his father built turned to ash...I must trust the god to show me the way forward from here."

"We all must," I said with a smile.

A conch shell alarm sounded in the distance and we looked towards the camp barely visible in the haze. More blew, one after another, the sound travelling toward the city.

Mazatzin's guards emerged from the smoky haze at the temple stairs. "We should return to camp, My Lord." They both held their swords.

But we only made it to the palace square before a runner found us. "Your Majesty," he panted, looking ready to fall over. "Our scouts just came in from the outpost along the north road. Culhuacan's army is marching this way!"

CHAPTER TWENTY-NINE

 "There must be several thousand men, My Lord," the scout gasped between gulps of water. We gathered around him in Mazatzin's tent, anxiety hanging in the air. "They shot the other scout. I barely made it out of there myself."

"What kinds of soldiers?" Spear Fish asked.

"Spearmen and archers mostly. And Lord Black Otter is among them."

Spear Fish stood straighter. "You're sure?"

"The other scout said as much, but I didn't see the man myself."

A tense silence followed. "Is that bad?" I asked.

"Black Otter commands Culhuacan's general army, which is four thousand strong," Spear Fish answered. "Our own is five thousand strong, but it'll take them a week to get here. Red Flint kept only seven hundred and fifty soldiers in Xochicalco, thinking our reputation alone would defend us. Reinforcements are coming in from the outposts, but we only get a couple hundred men every other day, so we might have fifteen hundred by the time Culhuacan's army arrives."

"But surely we have several thousand able-bodied men just in our peasantry."

Spear Fish nodded. "We'll arm them, but they'll be fighting mostly with gardening tools since we managed to only save half the armory's spears. We stand a good chance against the infantry, but a third of Culhuacan's army is archers, and they will wipe us out fast."

"How long until they get here?" Mazatzin asked.

"The first wave will reach us by nightfall, My Lord," the scout said.

"Could the walls withstand a siege until the army gets here?" Mazatzin asked Spear Fish.

"The walls aren't the worry. All the gates suffered massive fire damage. They wouldn't even need scaling ladders to get inside. Our best hope is to leave."

Mazatzin let out an exasperated breath and thought a moment. "We could head for Xochimilco. We've already sent them messengers, letting them know what's happened."

"If the runners had arrived, we would've heard back from King Growling Monkey by now. I think it very likely Ihuitimal's men intercepted our messengers. We've lost countless runners along that road in the last year and a half."

"The north road is already blocked," the runner confirmed.

"Then we must try to go around and meet up with the army on the west side of the lake," Mazatzin replied. "Let's start preparations to move out. Send soldiers through camp and the fields to give the evacuation alert."

As Spear Fish and the other Council members bowed out of the tent, I told Mazatzin, "I'll get the priests and priestesses ready to move out."

"Make sure everyone wears civilian clothing, in case they're captured," Mazatzin said. "Ihuitimal gave standing orders to execute all priests of Quetzalcoatl on sight."

"I'll make sure."

He pulled me into a fierce hug. "Be careful, and good luck."

"I'll do my best, Your Majesty, and you do the same. You're the strong king the people need now; you're the king I need." I kissed his cheek and headed out.

◻

Rumors of the approaching army spread even before the soldiers gave the evacuation order, and as I went through camp men everywhere were arming themselves with whatever weapons they could find or fashion in short order, while the women made tlaxcallis on every cooking stone.

By mid afternoon, the first caravan set off into the northwestern forest, the same direction Citlallotoc and I had taken to intercept Obsidian Eagle's assassins. It buffered the royal caravan, which set off to the west, and my entourage of priests and priestesses followed behind while the longer columns of peasants took up the flank. A member of the war council led each group, to provide military guidance.

"I feel naked without my robe," Malinalli told me as we marched.

I nodded. "And it's cold now that it's getting dark." I wore a dress that Lady Turquoise Bells had given me and it barely covered me compared to my priestly robes.

"I still can't believe any of this happened." Malinalli shook her head. After a pause, she added, "I had the worst dream last night, that we were back at the temple and Red Flint was...well, you know. Except I did nothing; I just stood there with the censer in my hand, watching." Shame filled her eyes. "But that wasn't the worst of it. The drought ended, Lady Turquoise Bells had a whole bundle of children, mostly boys, and the entire city prospered like never before."

I understood her distress. I'd dreamt of that moment myself; except that, in my dream, when Red Flint made good on his threats, my body drank the life completely out of him as if it were sweet, nourishing octli. He'd then fallen onto the temple floor dead, a dried-up husk of a man with an eerie smile on his face, and I'd awoken, flushed with vengeful pleasure. But even thinking of admitting any of this to Malinalli—especially that unsettling desire that had come on during the attack—left me feeling horribly ashamed.

"How could anyone think that what he was going to do would fix anything?" She shook her head. "It could have been any of us, year after year, feeding his delusion. I'm glad he's dead. He would've locked every one of us in the city to die."

I nodded. "You saved us all, not just me."

Ahead of us, our war council member held up a hand. In the distance came shouting followed by conch shells blaring. "Move the women over that way and take cover," he told me, then ordered the priests to arm themselves.

I dragged two of the younger priestesses into the forest and Malinalli followed with several more. We huddled behind trees, waiting in the dark. I couldn't see much, but as the sounds of fighting grew closer, I gripped my sacrificial blade tighter.

Silence fell over the forest, but then a soft *swoosh!* filled the air, followed by *thunk! thunk! thunk!* into the tree I hid behind. *Arrows!* We squeezed closer together as still more arrows came, so fast that the sounds of their strikes blended together into a continuous drone punctuated with cries of agony. "Keep those shields up!" Lord Spear Fish shouted. "And keep moving, no matter what!" I prayed he was getting Mazatzin to safety.

But now we're on our own, I thought. As the cries of battle rushed towards us, I took the two priestesses by the hands and pulled them up with me. I shot a glance over at Malinalli and motioned them to follow, hoping they could see me in the shadows. I struck off into the trees, not looking back to see if they were following.

The others ran while I did my best to keep up at a swift limp despite the growing pain in my bad foot. My lungs burned, but I pressed on until I couldn't hear fighting anymore. I dropped behind some bushes, glad to be off my feet. A breath later Malinalli and her group came as well. "Where's Tayanna and Paper Flower?" I whispered.

Malinalli looked around. "They must've gotten lost."

Soon I heard footfalls crunching leaves. I rubbed my wrist against my side, trying to relieve the vague itch. Dark shapes moved in the trees and one of them stepped into a strand of moonlight falling through the canopy, revealing his muscled, tattooed body. He looked right at me. In the distance Tayanna cried and my stomach clenched.

"Run!" I whispered to the others.

The other women sprinted from the bushes and I tried to follow, but my tender heel hobbled me. I got no more than ten steps before a soldier sent me sprawling to the ground with the handle of his spear. I crawled away but he pounced, pinning me down. I scrambled for my dropped blade but he kicked it away.

Whooping and shouting filled the night as Chichimecs swarmed through the trees. Women screamed. I strained to see what was happening but my captor held my head down with his knee as he bound my hands behind my back. He dragged me to a clearing where the other men had gathered the rest of my priestesses, all bound.

A tall Tolteca nobleman looked us over. His gaze lingered on me, but when he noticed the other men doing the same, he barked, "Don't stand there gawking! Get them ready to take back to camp." He resumed leering while the Chichimecs bound us together with a length of rope.

His expression reminded me all too well of how Red Flint used to stare at me. I prayed to the god that it wouldn't end like that very nearly did.

□

By the time we reached the camp north of Xochicalco—at the crossroads where Ihuitimal's troops were also intercepting the trade caravans—we were all stumbling from exhaustion. The soldiers prodded us along to the center of camp, to two cordoned off areas; stacks of caged prisoners filled the first, while women and children roamed like turkeys in the second. Guards watched the perimeter.

The Tolteca Captain shoved us one after the other into the holding pen after the Chichimecs released our bindings, but when my turn came, he gave my left breast a hard squeeze.

I instantly flashed back to the temple: Red Flint pinning me down to the altar, his crushing grip making my breast feel ready to rupture. And just like then, a strange mixture of overwhelming helplessness and vengeful desire struck me—

Malinalli punched him, knocking him over with a startled cry and breaking my unsettling trance. He stared up at her in disbelief. Even the guards gaped at her with open mouths.

"Don't just stand there, you idiots!" he shouted. As they took hold of her, he lumbered to his feet and wiped blood from his mouth. He slapped her so hard she lost her footing then he hit her again, this time with his fist. "She wants to fight like a man? She can die like one. Throw her in with the sacrifices."

"You shouldn't have done that!" I cried to her as they dragged her away.

"You shouldn't have to put up with such dishonorable behavior, even as a prisoner of war," Malinalli called back.

I wiped tears away. "Keep your spirits high and say your prayers. The gods may yet show us mercy!" Seeing the Captain scrutinizing me anew, I hurried my priestesses away, wanting as much distance from him as possible.

A strange mix of emotions pervaded the crowd; some women wailed while others tended to their children as if nothing had happened. Most sat in shocked silence, looking around like rabbits expecting coyotes to descend. We found Tayanna and Paper Flower, and they both wept to see us. "But where's Lady Malinalli?" Tayanna asked, looking worried.

"She punched a man for disrespecting the high priestess, so they took her to the other pen," one of the young priestesses said.

"Do not speak any of our religious titles," I warned, looking around. "We are among enemies of the god here."

"What will happen to her?" Tayanna asked me.

"She'll be sacrificed, as will the rest of us if we're found out." *Though it should have been me. I should have been strong enough to defend myself against that dog, not stand there like a frightened young girl.*

We sat around, some sleeping while soldiers brought in more prisoners. I could have nodded off at any time, but I made myself stay awake, listening for news about Mazatzin. Once night fell, the guards gave us each half a tlaxcalli—less than even a peasant child would live off per day—and it was gone all too soon. I gave mine to the younger priestesses who were less used to fasting than me, and I did my best to ignore the bouts of desire and hunger that kept swooping in and out on me. Focusing on conversation seemed to help.

"What do you suppose they're going to do with us?" Paper Flower asked as she ate. "Will we become slaves?"

"Some of us will," I said. "But a good number of us will be taken as concubines by the noblemen."

Tayanna shivered. "Mother told me I'd regret joining the priesthood and rejecting Night Snake's proposal."

"I heard that the road into Culhuacan is lined with the corpses of the Feathered Serpent's followers, on display as a warning," one of the younger priestesses whispered.

Paper Flower glared at Tayanna. "Hopefully no one reveals us."

My wrist had itched constantly since we arrived, but it flared now. I looked around to see the Tolteca Captain snapping at everyone to get out of his way as he came towards us. "That's her, right over there," he told the guards behind him.

My priestesses froze, but I whispered, "Keep to yourselves and say nothing."

The guards hauled me to my feet and took me out of the pen, the Tolteca Captain following behind.

"So who are you? One of Red Flint's sisters? One of his concubines? Maybe even his wife Turquoise Bells?" he asked as we approached the large tents circling the center of camp.

"I'm just a servant," I said. Not exactly a lie, since I served Quetzalcoatl.

"Servants don't wear such nice clothing. Not even a top-ranking noblewoman could wear a dress that nice, so either you stole it, which makes you a thief, or you're being dishonest about who you are, which makes you a liar."

"Turquoise Bells gave it to me."

"You're one of Red Flint's sisters then?"

"I'm not related to the royal family, nor have I ever been a guest in any of the princes' beds, or the king's."

"Lord Black Otter will sort out who you really are and whether you're of any use; even if you aren't, I'm sure he can find *some* use for you." He showed me a toothy smile.

My heart crawled up in my throat as the guards pushed me through the flap of the largest tent.

A fire burned in a clay brazier in the center where three men gathered around a wood slab, examining an open roll of paper. "He'll go north, towards Chapultepec," one man said. "We can send soldiers to intercept them, but we should ask your father for reinforcements to cross the lake."

The man who responded could have been my uncle Nochuatl, had I not known he was dead. The resemblance made my heart ache. "We can also pull off part of the contingent fighting near Tultepec and surround them. With Xochicalco's army bogged down in the north, King Mazatzin should be easily captured before reinforcements can rescue him."

At least something was going right today. Mazatzin was still alive, thank the gods.

"I'll send the messengers immediately," the third man said, getting up. He cast me an interested glance as he left.

The Tolteca Captain stepped forward and bowed. "My Lord, here's the woman I told you about earlier." He yanked me forward with his stony grip.

I glared at him before sliding my gaze over to Black Otter again. I didn't see recognition in his eyes; he looked me over with mild interest, perhaps assessing my beauty rather than actually trying to see beyond it. But then his gaze lingered at my eyes.

In his, I saw his mother. Despite my efforts to ignore this, my heart warmed and a tingle built up deep inside me—that same giggling feeling I'd often felt for him when we were children, but more intense. A flush crept up my cheeks and I swallowed hard, unnerved.

Black Otter wagged his finger at me, a smile coming to his face. "I've seen you before," he said, still unsure, but then he clapped his hands. "Quetzalpetlatl!"

CHAPTER THIRTY

The Captain's eyes bulged. "You mean Mixcoatl's daughter?"

Black Otter laughed lightly. "Why didn't you tell me immediately that she'd been captured?"

"I didn't know she was your wife, My Lord. If I had—"

"You wouldn't have treated me like a camp courtesan?" I snapped.

Black Otter sat straighter, dismayed. "You did what?"

"She wouldn't tell anyone who she was, My Lord, not even when asked. I'd never intentionally behave so reprehensibly to your wife, My Lord!" The words came out in a rush.

Black Otter narrowed his eyes. "Return to your post. We'll speak later." To the other remaining man, he added, "Leave us, please."

Alone now, Black Otter came to me with an amused smile. "You really wouldn't tell him who you are?"

"Would you be forthcoming with your identity in an enemy camp?" My pulse jumped as he neared me.

"My enemies would have no trouble identifying me. I make it a habit of looking them in the face before I send them to Mictlan. Though why would you consider me an enemy? I haven't done anything to you."

"We both know why I'd wish to keep my identity secret."

He set a gentle hand on my shoulder. "You'd really risk becoming some stranger's concubine rather than embrace your birthright? Our parents married us. You're the future queen of Culhuacan."

"My father dissolved our marriage," I snarled. The conversation didn't upset me so much as the fact that I'd said little more than a few words and already I was as flush-faced as a young girl. This growling, hungry lust was far more intense than I'd ever experienced before and it scared me; especially since the god wasn't here to soothe it for me. *Someone else is though,* I thought, heat creeping between my legs and my breasts tingling. I felt as lightheaded as after a night of octli and meditation.

Hardness seeped into his eyes, finally showing me a flash of the man who'd raised him. "Mixcoatl doesn't rule Culhuacan anymore and my father calls our marriage binding. But you still haven't answered my question: is the thought of being my wife so horrible that you'd rather end up someone's whore?"

"Of course not," I muttered, tearing my gaze away from him. "I've hardly eaten anything in days and I've slept even less, and with being chased by your soldiers, bound and groped, and seeing my best friend dragged off for defending me against that dog of a Captain of yours...I'm feeling half out of my mind." Which wasn't far from the truth.

Black Otter's expression softened. "Forgive me. You've surely been through a great deal and I shouldn't have pushed the matter. I'll get you something to eat." At the open tent flap, he told someone to bring a fresh plate of food. "And tell Captain Storm House that I want to see him right away too." He then led me to the wood slab. "Make yourself comfortable. My tent is now yours as well."

I sat and focused on the grain of the wood, for that seemed to calm the desire. A servant boy soon came with a plate of food and a pot of xocolatl, and he filled cups while Black Otter stoked his pipe opposite me. I dove into the food as quick as I could while still retaining some dignity, and didn't hear anything Black Otter said until he tapped the wood in front of me, breaking my concentration. "What?" I reddened when half a mouthful of tamale tumbled out of my mouth, and finished chewing more delicately.

Black Otter smirked. "Do you need more to eat?"

My face burned, but at least now the desire didn't resurface. "No, thank you," I murmured.

He chuckled. "I was saying I know another reason you wouldn't want anyone knowing who you are. The high priestess of Quetzalcoatl would make a powerful sacrifice to the Smoking Mirror."

I almost asked him how he knew that, but caught myself. How many times had Ihuitimal's spies infiltrated Xochicalco over the years? *He probably knows how many times you bathe per week. This food you're eating is probably your last meal.* I grimaced.

"You needn't worry though," Black Otter said. "If you forsake your vows to Quetzalcoatl and embrace your duties to me, he'll let you live."

I choked on my food and had to wash it down with a swig of xocolatl. "With all due respect, my devotion to the god goes back to before we were married, and only my faith saw me through the disaster Ihuitimal made of my life. Do you know he put my father's heart in my hands? Told me it was a gift, like it was nothing more than a pretty little bracelet?"

Black Otter pursed his lips. "No, he never told me that."

"He also threatened to kill me, told Nochuatl he was going to pluck off my wings. I had nightmares for years, and only prayer brought me comfort. If you make me choose between Quetzalcoatl and my life...there *is* no choice." *And I'll use my death to call the god down on Culhuacan to put an end to your father's reign,* I thought. *Maybe that's the true path Quetzalcoatl has set out for me.* Unsurprisingly, the notion didn't bother me.

Black Otter stared at me, startled at first, but then amused. "Let's not talk about my father anymore. I understand why you feel as you do, but he's my father and I ask that you respect that."

"And I remember you as a kindhearted boy who once promised he'd never make me forsake the god I love. What happened to him?"

"And I wonder what became of the girl who promised on the god's name that she would keep my secrets," Black Otter fired back.

I felt pierced with an arrow, until I considered what kind of beating he must've gotten for my betrayal; severe enough that almost twenty years later, he still held a grudge?

A guard announced Lord Storm House, and a moment later the Captain knelt, trembling, in the tent. "You wish to see me, My Lord?"

"You took one of my wife's friends to the slave cages," Black Otter said. "Bring her to me immediately." My stomach dropped as he cast his hard gaze back at me. What trouble had I got Malinalli in now?

"Anything else, My Lord?" Storm House asked.

"Just go and fetch the woman." Once Storm House left, Black Otter puffed his pipe and answered my gaze. "You'll need a handmaiden, and just to show you what a bad man

I am, I'll spare your friend's life. I presume she's also a priestess? Call it a wedding present that she's not standing first in line at tonight's sacrifice."

Storm House returned with Malinalli, bruises shining on her swollen face and a wooden slave collar around her neck. I gave her the remainder of my food, and she too ate as if she hadn't had anything in days—which was true.

Once Black Otter finished his pipe, he donned a jaguar cape. "While I'm making my rounds, clean my wife up for bed," he told Malinalli. "Get a basin and soap from the supply tent on the other side of the bonfire, and don't do anything stupid like trying to escape. The guards will kill you on sight if you do." He gave me a pointed glare then stepped outside.

Malinalli gave me a puzzled look. "His wife?"

My cheeks burned. "My father married us when we were very young, before he found out my uncle was plotting against him. Seems Black Otter still considers that binding." I shot a hesitant glance at the tent flap. *Does he intend to exercise his rights as my husband tonight?* The thought made my stomach clench and I felt I might vomit up everything I'd just eaten. I almost wished for the desire to return, if only to feel stronger—it never made me feel weak or afraid.

Malinalli fetched the supplies and we sat down to work. I admired her adaptability, so strong compared to me as I sat shivering next to the fire while she washed my hair and body. "Are you cold, My Lady?" she asked as she combed my hair.

"It's disturbing, suddenly having as much control over myself as a dog being fattened for the king's table," I admitted.

She nodded. "You're scared about tonight."

"I'll do what I must." Fear broke my voice, and I had to clear my throat and sniffle to keep from losing some of the tears I was holding back.

"I'm sure the god won't see it as a violation of your vows. He'd rather you survive."

I nodded, trying to convince myself.

Like Little Reed's army tent, Black Otter's was divided into two rooms, with the sleeping quarters in the back behind another tent flap, but it was four times larger than Little Reed's. Wicker clothes chests cluttered the open areas around the bed of mats and animal skins that could easily accommodate four people. A room befitting a prince.

We went through the baskets looking for something for me to wear for the night, and settled on a long white xicolli that hung past my knees. "Your dress should be dry by morning," Malinalli said as she turned to leave. "Do you need anything else before I go?"

I stared down at the bed. "Maybe a little of your strength?" She smiled back and I added, "Be careful out there."

"You too."

Alone, I knelt and offered murmured prayers to the god.

See me through this difficult night, My Lord,
Show me how best to serve you in these circumstances.
My heart is forever devoted to you and your mercy.

Not wanting Black Otter to catch me at it, I hurried into the bed and stared up at the shadowed ceiling, trying to ignore my irritated wrist. *Do what he wants and he'll have no reason to hurt you.* I fidgeted, listening for Black Otter's return, but I heard only distant laughing and singing, as if the soldiers were celebrating their victory. *I wish I was waiting for Little Reed instead.*

Sadness washed over me and I covered my face with the blanket. *Dear gods I miss you so much, my love.* The pain hit like a lightning strike, leaving me freshly wounded.

◻

I awoke with a start when something tickled my face. I looked around groggily, not recalling where I was until I saw Black Otter peering down at me with a kind smile. "I didn't mean to wake you," he said with a chuckle. He glided fingers over my chin, studying me. "Have you any idea how beautiful you are?"

"My mother was beautiful." I rolled over, eager to get back to sleep.

"You look just like her."

"And you look just like your father." The memory of Nochuatl's head lying at Cuitlapanton's feet made me frown. "I miss him."

"You miss my father?"

With my brain addled with sleep, it took me a moment to realize my mistake. Of course he wouldn't know who I was really talking about—I doubted Ihuitimal would admit to anyone that he'd been cuckolded, least of all by his own brother. Rubbing the sleep from my eyes, I said, "I'm sorry, I'm half-asleep. I meant our uncle Nochuatl."

Black Otter lay next to me, resting his chin on my shoulder. "A lot of people tell me I look like him." He smelled of the same tobacco Little Reed used to smoke, awakening the wanton desire I'd thought I'd finally banished. The dread I'd felt before bed was thankfully absent, replaced by a pleasant fog, like the beginnings of a divine vision descending upon me. His closeness felt so wonderful, so right....

You need more. The voice in my head commanded obedience, so I moved closer, turning to face him when I felt his breath on my ear. He brushed his lips against my cheek, sending tingles racing through me. He continued the tease for a moment before smiling and whispering, "Will you punch and curse me again if I kiss you?"

I stared at him, confused—and vaguely annoyed—but then I remembered: that's what I'd done the first time he'd kissed me. I laughed. "I was just a girl back then, but I'm not anymore, am I?" The suggestion alone should have made me blush, but then I topped it by pressing firmly against his groin. "And I see you're no mere boy anymore," I added, responding to the hardness I felt there.

He kissed me with an earnest, eager passion. He rolled on top of me, his weight stoking my want, so I tore at his loincloth, desperate to have him inside me. He separated his lips from mine long enough to yank my xicolli off and toss it aside, but he had less luck with my undergarment, fumbling with the knots before tugging with bruising ferocity. I finally untied them for him, my patience wearing thin. "Now." An order rather than request.

He coupled with me fast—painful, but not as much as I'd expected—and didn't slow down after. Unlike those long, drawn-out sessions with Quetzalcoatl where I reached climax after a slow, delicious buildup, this time the pleasure rose fast and crashed over me so hard that a surprised moan slipped past my lips. Black Otter jolting inside me brought the wave cresting again and I felt energized, the tips of my toes and fingers tingling. I felt so alive, as if I'd just done what the gods had created me do!

Black Otter collapsed next to me, panting and trembling. "Dear gods! I've never felt so good."

I almost said, *I know what you mean,* but all those thoughts evaporated as I stared at the ceiling. Surely I was imagining this....

The tent cloth looked no thicker than a thin veil, and outside white flakes of Love fell from the sky like snow. And the night sky had that peculiar hue of purple indicative of a vision. *I'm seeing into the Divine Dream!* I realized, amazed.

My awe soon gave way to concern. *What if Quetzalcoatl finds me here like this, naked and flushed with pleasure?* I reached over Black Otter—who was already asleep—to grab up the xicolli.

But when I looked up again, the tent's transparency was fading away, and within a moment, I lost my connection to the Divine Dream completely. With nary a whisper from Quetzalcoatl. I should have been happy, but instead tears welled in my eyes. Two years I'd stayed away, and until now I hadn't realized just how much I'd missed the Divine Dream, and the god.

CHAPTER THIRTY-ONE

It was still dark when I left Black Otter sleeping as still as a dead man and went out into the anteroom to reheat the pot of xocolatl. I kept quiet so as not to wake Malinalli, but the smell of the boiling xocolatl soon roused her. We huddled around the brazier, sipping our drinks.

"You're positively glowing, Quetzalpetlatl," Malinalli said after we'd sat in silence for a while. "I don't think I've ever seen you look so...I don't know if 'happy' is the right word, but maybe contented?"

"I am feeling better than yesterday," I admitted.

"So it wasn't as terrible as you feared?"

I averted my eyes. "It was...nothing like I was expecting. I'm glad it's over though."

Malinalli chuckled. "It certainly sounded like you were enjoying yourself."

I gasped. "You heard us?"

"It woke me up, though if it makes you feel better, he was much louder. I bet half the camp heard him."

Dear gods, how horrifying! I thought, my ears burning. After a moment of awkward silence between us, I asked, "What if I just failed a test of my faith and loyalty, Malinalli? Isn't it a slap in the god's face to enjoy losing my maidenhood to the son of the high priest of his arch enemy?"

She shook her head. "We trust the god to show us the right path, so maybe tonight he showed you yours."

Maybe she was right. After so thoroughly messing everything up, it was my responsibility to see Quetzalcoatl's plans fulfilled through whatever means necessary, so maybe embracing a fruitful marriage to Black Otter could help bring the god back into the temples in Culhuacan and ensure the future of the order. And maybe, with time, I could learn to love Black Otter; not as much as I'd loved Little Reed, but enough to be happy.

□

Black Otter said little when he came out of his room at daybreak, but once Malinalli left to see about my dress, he asked, "Feeling all right this morning?"

"Fine," I said, not meeting his gaze as we sat eating our morning atole at the wooden table. "And you?"

A smile quirked at his mouth. "I can't remember the last time I slept so soundly. I trust the bed was comfortable?"

"Sufficiently." I tried to hold back the blush but failed. I focused on spooning up my atole to keep from looking at him.

"What happened to your fingers?" he asked after taking a few more bites of his own.

I couldn't possibly tell him the truth—if he knew I had the ability to call on Quetzalcoatl, he might kill me immediately. Better to lie and get a better assessment of his intentions first. "I smashed them between some stones and had to have them removed."

He cringed but thankfully didn't press the matter.

Once he'd finished eating, he said, "We're heading home today. A boat from Xico will meet us north of here and we'll be back in Culhuacan before nightfall."

"So soon?" I'd hoped for a few more days to prepare myself for seeing Ihuitimal again.

"The army camp is no place for the future queen," Black Otter said. "And don't worry. The women of my household will make you quite welcome."

I hadn't given any thought to there being others, nor did I want to think about it. I'd seen enough jealous bickering among my father's concubines to know I wanted nothing to do with such drama. *I suppose it can't be much different from running matters in the priesthood,* I thought, but then my priestesses were there because they wanted to be, not because their fathers made an alliance with the god. It was also accepted that some priests and priestesses had a closer relationship with the god than others, and as high priestess I didn't need to make sure the god divided his time equally among all of us, or that my priestesses were caring for themselves while carrying his children.

You could be with child yourself now. And in nine months you could be dead, just like your mother. My stomach twisted.

Black Otter's expression turned to concern. "Are you all right?"

I shook my head, panic cresting. "This is...overnight I've become a prince's wife, and guardian of a group of women I've never met, and I could be with child." I couldn't catch my breath. "My mother died giving birth!"

"That doesn't mean you will. Women give birth all the time and live to have still more children."

"I know they do!" I snapped.

"I understand this is all very sudden, but the others will help you transition; and as for the other thing...it's too soon to worry about that, don't you think? It was just one night—"

"It takes only once!"

He set his jaw. "You're overreacting."

"Overreacting? When I refuse to forsake Quetzalcoatl, your father's going to torture and kill me, and put my body on display with the rest of the corpses decorating the road into Culhuacan. Don't tell me I'm overreacting!"

"You're too valuable to do that—" he said, but then regret crossed his face. "I didn't mean that the way it sounded—"

"Of course you did. I'm well aware of my worth to both you and your father. I sat in Xochicalco's court, not as a meek wife but as a powerful high priestess who commanded respect the same as any nobleman, and I know love and fondness have nothing to do with marriages like ours, so stop trying to sweeten the truth. I prefer knowing exactly where I stand."

Black Otter set his bowl down with a clank that surely left a crack in the pottery. "You want the grim truth, My Lady? Here it is: you're only of use to me so long as you give me an heir of Mixcoatl's blood. And though you were a high priestess in Xochicalco, in Culhuacan no woman sits in on court. You're not your mother, and I'm not a fool like your father was. That doesn't mean I can't make life good for you, but if you'd rather I be the cruel and vile man you believe I am, I can oblige you." He stood, shaking. "Once we reach Culhuacan, you can tell me which you prefer." He slashed aside the tent flap as he left.

"What a fine mess you've gotten yourself into now," I muttered, then kicked aside his bowl.

□

I spent the morning praying and meditating, hoping Quetzalcoatl would show me the way from here, but without teonanacatl, or even a blade to cut myself, the gulf was too large. *You could always seduce the man again,* that other voice suggested with a lurid laugh. *That will get you back into the Divine Dream.* I shoved the notion aside immediately. That other voice was starting to irritate me.

Black Otter returned before noon to take me to the boat, still stone-faced and short with his words. But we went no more than a step outside the tent before he suddenly stuck his arm out in front of me. I looked down to see a black and white banded snake sliding across the path.

When the guards pointed their spears at it, Black Otter snapped, "Leave it be. It's not hurting anyone." The snake disappeared around the corner of the tent.

I gave Black Otter a sideways glance he didn't return. Perhaps I'd misjudged him and the god wanted me to trust him?

The boat was moored against the bank among the reeds, and several polers stood aboard. It wasn't a very large boat, but it had an enclosed area in the middle made of hide-covered reed walls, to provide protection from enemy arrows. I followed Black Otter inside the enclosure, welcoming the shade of the canopy in the already hot afternoon. Malinalli sat outside, at the bow of the boat. We sat on mats on the floor, neither saying anything as the polers pushed us away from shore and out into the lake. Guards stood stolidly at the doorway, no doubt to make sure I didn't attempt to jump overboard to escape.

I stared at the carving marks in the floor, contemplating the snake again. If it was an omen from the god, it would be foolish not to listen; I'd messed up Quetzalcoatl's plans enough already. Perhaps I could turn this situation around to the god's benefit again. *If you embrace being Black Otter's wife and earn his affection, maybe you can convince him to allow Quetzalcoatl's worship back into Culhuacan.*

I glanced up at Black Otter, assessing exactly what kind of man he was. He carried none of his father's hardness; if anything, sadness hung over him like an invisible cloud as he stared out of the doorway. And thinking back on how he'd smiled at me last night in bed....

I'd hoped the memory might spark some affection for this man who'd once been my best friend, but it only brought forth memories of Little Reed. More than once over the last two years I'd wished Red Flint hadn't interrupted us, and that Little Reed had left me with something more than just memories and pain. Though if he'd left me with a child, I'd have more than myself to worry about now, for any son or daughter would have been as much a target as he had been. Feeling both relieved and regretful at the same time left me befuddled.

Despite my fanciful regrets about the past, the truth of here-and-now pressed heavy on me. Accepting my role as Black Otter's wife meant accepting the risk of childbirth. But if this was the path the god wanted me to take.... *I must believe he will protect me so I can accomplish his goals,* I thought. *He's giving me a second chance, and I can't disappoint him.*

I looked up at Black Otter again, then took a deep breath before speaking. "I'm sorry about this morning. I was cruel, and disparaged your good name for no reason, and I let fear take over the conversation. I don't really think you're vile; in fact, you've been kind and shown care for my well-being, and I thank you for that."

His shoulders rose a bit and a shadow of a smile came to his lips. "Can you forgive me for my sharp tongue as well?" he asked. "I realize this is a lot for you to cope with—probably even frightening, now that I'm taking you back home to Culhuacan, but rest assured I only want you to be safe and happy."

"What about your father?"

"I will protect you." His vehemence surprised me, and for the briefest of breaths, he got that strange, intense look in his eyes I'd seen too often in other men. But it disappeared as quickly as it came. "But you needn't worry, Quetzalpetlatl. You're my wife and the legitimate heiress to Culhuacan's throne. He will want you to stay, if only to quiet critics who still think he's an interloper."

He is an interloper, I almost said, but I caught my tongue in time.

He tentatively reached his hand out to me, smiling when I finally accepted it. His grip was gentle yet possessive. "Everything will be all right, I promise."

ロ

Ihuitimal had made Culhuacan's gray basalt walls higher and thicker, filling me with foreboding as we slipped into the docks. Tolteca archers watched the lake front from on high while Chichimec spearmen guarded the street level. The city didn't look bigger than I remembered; in fact, it seemed overcrowded. The Chichimec men were grubby and barely dressed, and the women wore their hair matted, and most had thin, naked children clinging to their hips.

They all vanished once our porters took us through a stepped archway into the Noble Quarters. There hadn't been any walls around it when my father was king, but here the streets were clean-swept and children played behind courtyard walls, the sounds of their laughter giving the only evidence they were even there. Everyone was Tolteca—even the servants—and dressed in fine clothing, looking proud. We even passed a dedicated Tolteca market—another new addition. The stark class division shocked me. Xochicalco's peasants had lived in their own quarters of the city, but no walls warned them to keep out, nor did the nobles have their own market so they didn't have to mingle with the farmers.

At the palace's front steps, three Tolteca women and a number of children and servants awaited us. Black Otter helped me down from the litter and escorted me to the stairs where he kissed each woman. All but one were younger than me, and the latter had a boy of no more than a year old on her hip while a little girl—probably three or four years old—crouched behind her, squashing ants on the stone with her fingers. The woman smiled with veiled hostility. I couldn't shake the sense of familiarity I felt when I looked at her, and after some thought I finally figured it out: she was my sister, Jade Flower.

The next woman in line was heavy with child and looked the youngest, while the last woman held another little girl's hand—this one about five. Next to her stood a girl of twelve or thirteen, but Black Otter addressed her as "My Lady" and kissed her hand. She wasn't too old to be his daughter, but given the flush on her face when he spoke to her, I doubted she was. *A token of some alliance, the poor girl.* But judging from how quickly he let her hand drop, I knew he must not be sleeping with her yet. Moral tradition dictated that consummation of such arrangements be left until the girl had been through a year of monthly cycles, and I respected him for taking that obligation seriously.

Black Otter brought me forward. "Allow me to present Mixcoatl's daughter, Princess Quetzalpetlatl."

A long pause ensued while the younger women exchanged puzzled looks. Jade Flower's expression remained unchanged though; she already knew who I was, which made her hostility all the more alarming. The pregnant woman asked, "Do you mean the same one your father married you to when you were a boy?"

Black Otter nodded. "She's finally returned home."

Jade Flower took my hand with a practiced smile. "Allow me to be the first to welcome you home, Quetzalpetlatl. I don't imagine you'd remember me, not after so many years."

"I do remember you, Jade Flower. Our mothers used to sit together and weave in the women's hall every day, and we spent many pleasant afternoons playing in the gardens." I answered her calculating expression with a careful smile. "You're looking radiant."

Jade Flower replied, "My heart bursts with joy for seeing you again, especially since I was sure I never would." She then introduced me to the others. Lady Corn Flower had the eldest child while Lady Papantzin was swollen with her first, and the girl not yet of age—confirmed by Jade Flower—was Lady Anacoana. While the others' greetings felt perfunctory—and I was sure there would be much whispering between them after I left—Anacoana was the only one who remembered to bow as was proper.

"I must meet with Father, so Jade Flower will help you settle in," Black Otter said. "I'll come for you later." He gave me a gentle kiss then bade us all goodbye before ascending the stairs into the palace.

When I turned to Jade Flower, she was watching him go too, looking melancholy and ready to cry. She put on a brave face when she turned back to me, but I knew that resentful look in her eyes that she couldn't quite cover up. It looked as if I'd just landed in the middle of a domestic quagmire.

□

"I will have the servants bring all your things out of storage," Jade Flower said as we walked down the hall towards the living quarters. Malinalli followed us, looking around with keen interest.

"I don't think my old clothes will fit me anymore," I said with a laugh.

Jade Flower laughed too. "I meant your wedding presents, though I'm sure a good many of them won't fit either. You were supposed to trade them once you were older anyway. The royal seamstress will put something together for you tonight. You can't appear before the king in an ill-fitting dress."

When we reached the living quarters and Jade Flower started down the left-hand hallway, where Father's concubines once lived, I stopped. "Aren't the royal quarters this way?" I asked, pointing to the other curtain decorated with Culhuacan's royal crest.

Jade Flower shook her head. "Only the king and princes live down there. We're not allowed beyond that curtain." She turned into the first doorway on the right side of the left hallway.

Rugs, screens, and wood carvings of animals and various goddesses decorated the room, and a small gold-plated idol of Cihuacoatl—goddess of the childbed—sat next to the bed of mats and blankets.

Malinalli started a fire while Jade Flower took me out on the patio. The garden wasn't as big as the one off the room where Black Otter and I spent those four days after our wedding, and it looked as if it hadn't been properly cared for in months. The pond was small and overgrown with broad-leafed bushes, and gangly flowers overflowed the beds. A copal tree's spiny branches fanned across the yard to all three vine-covered walls. At the back wall, I pulled aside the vines to find the opening into the passage beyond sealed up.

"Isn't it wonderful to be back?" Jade Flower asked.

"It's strange," I said. "Some things haven't changed, yet when you pull aside the curtain, the things that matter most have." I sighed, saddened by the thought.

"I'll leave you to bathe and get some sleep before the feast tonight. I imagine it will be a late night for you and Lord Black Otter," Jade Flower said. "I'll see you tomorrow morning, in the women's hall."

I nodded. "I look forward to it."

Once Jade Flower was gone, the servants arrived carrying basket after wicker basket loaded with clothing and jewelry. I helped Malinalli go through them, sorting out what needed trading and what was worth keeping. Each piece of clothing brought a memory of who'd given it to me and soon I was regaling Malinalli with stories about the people who gave me specific gifts.

"The old woman who gave me this necklace just about boxed my ears when I acted bored at her ritual chastisement before the wedding. My mother promised I'd make her a blanket. And my father's feather-worker gave me this one, though it looks like the feathers could use replacing."

"Your memory astounds me, Quetzalpetlatl," Malinalli said. "I can hardly remember what I ate for dinner last night but you recall things you told me on some lazy afternoon when we were both seventeen. You never forget anything, do you?"

"It's good for some things," I conceded. Like the way I could remember Little Reed with absolute clarity, from the smell of his skin to the tenor of his voice. I hated it for the very same reason.

The dress I found at the top of the last basket brought a smile to my face. "My aunt Eloxochitl made this for me. She and Mother each worked on a piece of it months before I'd heard anything about marrying Black Otter. They used to smile and laugh together all the time, and she'd doted on me even more than my own mother had, for she had no daughters." If anything pleased me now, it was that I'd soon get to see her again. I'd surprise her by finally wearing the dress she'd helped make to dinner tonight.

◻

Everyone who'd ever known my mother always said I looked like her, but I rarely saw it. She'd been far more beautiful than I could ever dream of being.

But after Malinalli braided my freshly-washed hair with feathers and flowers, I finally saw in the obsidian mirror what everyone else had seen, and it overwhelmed me.

"You look very queenly," Malinalli said, awed.

"My mother always did," I whispered through the knot in my throat.

The bells on my door curtain jingled and a moment later Black Otter stood in the bathhouse doorway, wearing a jaguar-pelt loincloth, a handsome cape of turquoise fabric, arm and calf bracelets of black feathers, and a small feathered headdress with two quetzal feathers tucked between brown eagle feathers. He stared as if he were seeing me now for the very first time. "You're ready?" he asked, finding his tongue again.

"As ready as I can be." Noticing he was holding a necklace, I asked, "What have you there?" It was made of feathers and turquoise, a stone reserved for royalty.

"Oh! I forgot," he admitted, blushing. "My father says it was your mother's, and I thought you would want it. Here, let me help you put it on." Black Otter moved behind me and drew it around my neck, smiling in the mirror. "Now you truly look like the future queen."

It was the necklace Mother had let me wear on my wedding day long ago; my favorite of her jewelry. I'd lost my mother's sacrificial blade—the only thing I'd had left of her— so it brought tears to my eyes to have this now. I smiled back at him in the reflection. "Thank you, My Lord."

He squeezed my shoulders and kissed my cheek as if we were old lovers.

□

A sea of noblemen knelt as Black Otter walked me to the head of the great hall, his arm hooked in mine as if it were perfectly natural there. There was only one royal banner now, directly above the dais, but large polished obsidian mirrors hung on the side walls, casting shadowy reflections of ourselves as we went by. Did I only look so frightened and pallid in the mirror or had Culhuacan truly grown so dark in character that the mirrors showed reality?

Ihuitimal rose from my father's reed throne. His skeletal smile made the scar on his cheek turn into a crevice, lending him a sinister, sunken appearance. His sparse silver hair showed off his thinning skin, and he wore a flowing red and black feathered robe, with an obsidian mirror dangling from a cord around his neck. A diamond-shaped jade shard hung from his pierced septum. The sight of him raised the hairs on my neck, and I felt defiled when he embraced me. "My dearest Quetzalpetlatl, the last of my brother's bloodline," he said, his voice like sand between stones. "Welcome home at last." My wrist felt afire. I wished I still had my sacrificial blade so I could have plunged it into his eye, to make the itching finally stop for good.

To my disappointment, the woman next to him, sitting in my mother's throne, wasn't Eloxochitl, but rather someone at least a couple of years younger than myself—and though she smiled, it lacked any true interest. Where was my aunt? And why was my mother's throne devoid of flowers? It looked so naked and small without the stalks of bone flowers crowning it.

"A pity what happened to Xochicalco," Ihuitimal said. "But every great city sees its sunset eventually. We're grateful you're back at your husband's side, to see the rise of the next great city here in Culhuacan."

I knew I would blast him with spiteful words if I said anything, so I merely bent my head.

"Let's conduct the ceremony, so we may celebrate your return." Ihuitimal motioned me and Black Otter to kneel, but I only did so when Black Otter tugged my sleeve. Ihuitimal placed his hands on our heads and pushed me down so my nose touched my knees. I could hardly breathe.

"Oh Mighty Smoking Mirror,
Who knows everything,
Who sees everything!
Bless this union,

208

Grant us your favor,
Make our children know your greatness
And tremble before it.
I bless this marriage with the blood of your enemies!
Most Powerful,
Most Terrible Tezcatlipoca!"

Cold liquid dribbled into my hair and turned the white fabric of my dress red where it dripped. *He's pouring the blood of Quetzalcoatl's priests on me!* I thought, struggling to stand up. But he held my head down with his claw-like hand. *Protect my heart from fear and tyranny, My Lord,* I prayed. *Give me the strength to remain true to your teachings in the den of your nemesis!* When he finally let me go, I nearly launched over backwards. Blood wormed down the side of my face and the back of my dress, leaving my flesh crawling. It ran out of Black Otter's hair too, but he remained calm.

Ihuitimal tied the edge of my dress to Black Otter's cape, giving it a sharp tug. "Let us feast for the restoration of my children's wedding vows!" he announced, then cleaned his hands with a cloth while a black-robed priest took away the empty blood bowl.

Like before, Black Otter and I shared the traditional tamales, though we stayed for the remainder of the feast this time. All night Ihuitimal watched me, his gaze sometimes lingering like a man watching his lover, and at other times as if he were plotting revenge. I avoided his gaze, chilled at the thought of his eyes groping me the way most men's did. He didn't speak to me beyond that opening greeting—thank the gods, for I knew I'd say something that would land me in the prison yard for the night. *Though denigrating him in front of all his allies and noblemen might be worth the flogging,* I thought, but this wasn't the time to be careless with my life. Quetzalcoatl still had better plans for me.

I breathed a sigh of relief when Ihuitimal finally dismissed us for the night. I couldn't wait to wash all the dried blood out of my hair, and get to know Black Otter better; and to see how difficult it would be to implement my goal to get Quetzalcoatl back into Culhuacan.

But a whole new trepidation cropped up when Black Otter followed me into my own bath house and stood stock-still with his arms out at his sides while his two body servants undressed him one bit of clothing at a time. I fussed with my teeth in front of the obsidian mirror, so as not to look at his nakedness. Malinalli waited with her back turned as well, the uneasiness plain on her face.

Once he dismissed his servants, he asked, "Don't you think you've picked your teeth enough yet, my precious flower?"

I risked a glance over my shoulder to find him sitting submerged to his chest in a large tub of hot water next to the steam bath. A hungry smile stretched across his face. "Surely you haven't forgotten how to stand so your handmaiden can undress you?" he teased.

I looked away again, flushed. It was one thing for Malinalli to help me dress when it was just the two of us, but the thought of having her undress me in front of him.... "That will be all for tonight, thank you," I murmured to Malinalli, not meeting her gaze.

"Thank you, My Lady." She quickly disappeared back into the room like a mouse chased by a dog.

I undid the ties at the neck of my dress, but when I noticed Black Otter watching me, I squeezed my eyes shut. "Must you do that?"

"Do what?"

"Look at me like that."

"Like what?"

"Like...like...I don't know what, but I don't like it," I sputtered, glaring at him.

He laughed. "Why so embarrassed? It's not as if we haven't enjoyed each other before now."

The flush burrowed deeper as I recalled last night's frantic lovemaking, and I half-expected the desire to well up again, but instead I felt humiliated, reduced, and trapped. Like that night in the water yard when Ahexotl had stared at me lying half-naked on the ground. "I was raised to be very modest, as priestesses should be," I choked.

Perhaps the stress in my voice bore through the lust, for he muttered, "Sorry I made you uncomfortable. I promise not to look." And to show his seriousness, he moved to the other side of the tub, with his back to me, then proceeded to wash his hair.

I undressed quickly—and clumsily—then scrambled into the tub too, and by the time he finished rinsing his long hair, I'd submerged myself up to my shoulders. The water's heat was dizzying; for years I'd taken mostly cold water baths, and even the few that were hot had been lukewarm compared to this. Already sweat beaded on my forehead.

Black Otter wiped the water from his face then grinned at me boyishly. "How can you wash your hair with all that in it?"

In my hurry to gain the cover of the water, I'd forgotten to take my hair down. I started picking the bits of flowers and feathers out, but he sidled over next to me and insisted, "Please, let me help you with that."

I wanted to elbow him away—what would he know about untangling a woman's intricate hairstyle anyway?—but he worked with surprising gentleness and deliberate slowness, so as not to tug my hair as he removed the gold pins holding it up. He unwound the two braids one at a time, letting my wavy brown hair fall around my shoulders with a rousing sensuality. He then poured water over my hair from a clay jar, carefully tilting my head back so it didn't leak into my eyes.

But when he started washing my hair with the soap, the first hints of haziness settled over my mind. I tried to shake it away, but the caress of fingers on my scalp only made it worse. Desperate to not lose control like last night, I blurted, "Can I ask you something?" My heart throbbed painfully in my chest.

He smiled. "Of course you may."

"How dedicated are you to your father's chosen god?"

Black Otter blinked at me just before an invisible shield went up behind his eyes. "Why?"

"You know where my heart lies, My Lord, but I know little about yours."

He didn't say anything as he continued massaging my head with his soapy fingers. Eventually he said, "My father wants me to take his place as Smoking Mirror's high priest once he's dead, though I don't know why. I have no priestly training, and while he has shown me some things...I'm a soldier, not a priest. He wants me to go north and live in the desert for a year like he did, so I can have a vision and know what the Smoking Mirror expects of me when I'm king."

The haze still clung to my brain, so I focused on his face above me, taking note of the consternation, the indecision, the unhappiness as he rinsed my hair out with a small water jar. "You don't want to do any of that?"

"I oversee the sacrifices on campaign, and I say my prayers before battle, but...shouldn't serving the gods be a life's calling, not something forced on one?"

"True devotion can't be forced, not the kind you'd need to be a high priest. Faith comes with time and experience, not at spear point."

"Must we talk about such things now?" he asked, setting aside the jar then wrapping his arms around me.

As soon as he kissed me, I tried to fight off the intense desire swelling up inside me, but something sprang up and blocked all control of my body. I felt just like that time when I was a girl, when the god had spoken to Ihuitimal with my tongue.

Though when I settled onto Black Otter's lap, I knew this couldn't be Quetzalcoatl controlling me. So then whose magic was this? Panic rose inside me, but then that voice I disliked whispered, *Watch and learn, little girl.*

This time, when Black Otter's gaze fell down to my exposed breasts, a peculiar confidence cut through the anxiety and I felt lulled and content. "Do you plan to continue your father's policies once you're king?" It was the exact question I'd wanted to ask him all day, but I hadn't willed my tongue to form the words now; they just spilled out, unbidden and exerting a strange authority. It was the voice I used with students, but more calculating. The tone demanded truthfulness, and anything less wouldn't be tolerated. I felt awed that I could sound this way.

Black Otter stuttered a moment, distracted by my naked breasts, but then he said, "I don't...I promised my father...."

I leaned closer, our noses almost touching. He reached up to pull me into his arms, but I pushed them away with gentle but firm hands. "You promised you would never make me give up Quetzalcoatl."

"I did," he conceded, breathless. He trembled under me when I moved in to kiss him. But again I held back at the last moment. "Wasn't last night good for you?" I asked.

"Incredible," he whispered, his voice pained. "I've never felt so good.... Was it not so for you too?"

I smiled but said nothing. This other me didn't care about such things. "It can be even better, My Lord, if I knew I could trust you to keep your promise."

"I will," Black Otter insisted.

"Then you will let Quetzalcoatl back into the temples?"

"I will!" He said it so fast I wondered if he even understood the question.

A smile tugged at my cheeks then I finally kissed him. He hugged me so tight I thought he would crush my ribs, but I did nothing to stop him. Instead I laughed and whispered, "Now get to the bed, so I may satisfy your hunger."

Next thing I knew, I sat atop him in my bed as he writhed in ecstasy under me, knotting his fists into the blankets as I squeezed him between my thighs. I didn't care about the quenching pleasure coursing through me as the octli-like haze dissipated. I just wanted to see into the Divine Dream again; see the flakes of Love floating down from Heaven and glimpse the tall stone walls of Omeyocan high among the night clouds.

But most surprising, I longed to see Quetzalcoatl swirling down from his heavenly abode, not even caring that he'd find me still coupled with Black Otter. *What I wouldn't give to see Little Reed's face one last time, even if only in the face of his father!* I searched the sky, trying to will the Divine Dream to last longer, trying to call out to him with my mind, but it faded without any sight of the face I loved.

Hot tears wound down my cheeks. *Your heart will never mend if you keep doing this, Quetzalpetlatl. You must accept that he's dead, and focus on making a new life for yourself.*

Fearing Black Otter might see my tears, I wiped them away quickly, but it didn't matter. He was already asleep.

CHAPTER THIRTY-TWO

Black Otter slept through breakfast, so I left him in my bed, not wanting to wake him from his very sound sleep. I'd hardly slept at all last night, feeling too awake after we'd finished; strange, since I'd always thought such exertions would be exhausting.

I joined the others in the women's hall and we passed the morning weaving while Black Otter's daughters spun our thread for us. Not much had changed in here: the walls were painted with the same floral patterns and there were a lot of women of varying ages at their weaving, all chattering away as they worked. I'd half expected some veiled hostility when I entered the room, like my mother often had to endure, but to my relief most of them just smiled then returned to their work. Even Black Otter's other women gave me pleasant greetings and made room for me at the circle of mats where they gathered.

Jade Flower was the same mediocre weaver she'd been as a girl, but she made up for that lack with her strong leadership of Black Otter's women. They sought her opinion on a multitude of issues, like dealing with a cruel servant calling Lady Corn Flower's daughter "Little Lizard" because the girl's toes splayed too wide, or distinguishing between real and fake labor pains. She even recommended I send Malinalli to the market for a special skin cream for my inflamed wrist, which had been constantly irritated since I'd arrived in Culhuacan.

Only Anacoana seemed out of place in the group. She rarely said anything, but the others didn't pay her much attention either. While they spent more time talking than working, she wove some of the most intricate patterns I'd ever seen, and with incredible speed.

"I think it's the only thing her mother ever taught her," Jade Flower confided to me as we headed to the kitchen to get something to eat that afternoon. "I shudder to think that she might know nothing about sex and I'll have to teach her all too soon. Though I suppose that will be your duty now, as the Prince's wife. But then you're probably just starting to learn about such things yourself."

"The woman who raised me taught me everything I needed to know about that," I said. "She was always forthcoming with answers, regardless of subject matter."

"You were raised by one of Cuitlapanton's wives then?"

"No, the high priestess of Quetzalcoatl. Topiltzin and I were very lucky to have her once Mother was gone." Uncomfortable with the stiffening in my chest, I changed the subject. "Speaking of mothers, I didn't see Eloxochitl at the wedding feast last night."

Jade Flower shook her head. "She died a few months after your mother, in childbirth too, if you can believe it. The baby survived though; Amoxtli is his name, and he and Black Otter are very close."

"Black Otter has a brother?"

She nodded. "The last few months have been especially difficult though, since Amoxtli was taken prisoner. We do know he's still alive and we're hopeful we'll get him back. I pray to the Smoking Mirror every day for it."

You're praying to the wrong god, Jade Flower, I thought, suppressing an ironic smile. *The Smoking Mirror thrives on your pain and fear, so why would he do anything to lessen it?*

I saw the woman who'd been sitting on my mother's throne last night talking with some of the old matrons by the kitchen doorway. "The king's wife looks younger than us."

"She's not his wife, just his latest favorite concubine. He never remarried after Eloxochitl died."

We took our tamales out into the yard where the children ran yelling and laughing. There were far fewer than I remembered when I was a girl, and hardly any boys at all. "Is this all the royal children?"

"Not all of them are royalty. The boys over there are sons of the nobles who live in the palace, but those three girls over in the corner—the older ones—those are the king's daughters."

"The king has only two sons?"

Jade Flower nodded. "Having lots of daughters can buy favor with his allies, and he sends them off to new households as soon as they come of age."

I watched Jade Flower's daughter sitting with Lady Corn Flower's daughter, braiding the maguey fiber hair of their dolls. "Do you worry Black Otter will do the same to your daughter?"

"Why would I worry?" she asked, puzzled. "That's what girls are for."

Her attitude shouldn't have surprised me, but I couldn't suppress the spike of anger. "That's a sad thing to think, Sister."

"Why? Men cannot make more men without us, so that makes us very important and valuable."

"True, but why should we be so narrowly defined? Men can be a multitude of things."

"What men do is insignificant."

I laughed, incredulous. "A city future or its spiritual well-being is hardly insignificant."

Jade Flower stared at me, taken aback. "You don't think being a mother is important?"

"Of course it's important, but what's wrong with wanting everything, for both our daughters and our sons? Wouldn't you rather your daughter marry someone who loves and respects her, and whom she loves too? Do you really want her to end up like you, second best in this farce nobles call marriage?"

Jade Flower's eyes bulged. She stood, face flushed. "How dare you.... Not all women are as fortunate as us, Quetzalpetlatl! Just remember that." She hurried back inside.

□

Jade Flower didn't return to the women's hall after the meal break. Lady Corn Flower and Papantzin talked in hushed whispers while Anacoana focused feverishly on her weaving. My own mind was distracted by what Jade Flower had said, and the fact that I'd left behind my priestesses to be given out as war prizes. *And what could you have done about it? There's no point dwelling on things you have no control over.* Still, I felt I *should* have done something.

Determined to focus on other things, I edged over next to Anacoana where she was working on a tapestry. "That's wonderful work," I whispered.

She gave me a shy smile. "Thank you."

"Your mother taught you?"

She shook her head. "My servant girl, when I was growing up. Mother said I needed to excel in at least one skill if I ever hoped to find a place in someone's house, since I'd inherited my father's rough looks."

I nearly laughed, though such cruelty from a parent was hardly funny. "One doesn't find one's true beauty until one's grown, but I'd wager that you won't be disappointed."

Her smile relaxed into something more natural. "Thank you, My Lady."

"You're certainly the best weaver I've ever seen. Would you mind showing me how you do that exquisite pattern?"

We passed the rest the afternoon talking about weaving and palace life. Anacoana was exceedingly sharp, picking up easily on the tone of conversations around her, but as soon as a man—be it a nobleman or a servant—came into the room, she spoke no further words until they'd left again. Another thing her mother taught her? And when Black Otter came to fetch me for dinner, she hurried to cast aside her weaving, getting herself tangled in her thread, so I helped her up.

"I see you're settling in nicely," he said. "I trust the others have given you a warm welcome?"

Lady Corn Flower and Papantzin fidgeted but I said, "Everyone has been exceedingly kind, My Lord."

Black Otter took my arm. "Please excuse us," he told the others. "We have preparations to make before dinner tonight." I felt Lady Corn Flower and Papantzin's piercing gazes on my back as we left.

"I didn't see Jade flower in there with you," he noted.

I sighed. "I upset her this afternoon at lunch."

Black Otter laughed. "So you girls are right back where you left off twenty years ago?"

I cast him a scathing glare. "What's that supposed to mean?"

Still smiling, he said, "Nothing. I just noticed that your friendship was always...contentious? What did you say to her?"

I shook my head. "Nothing important. Just foolishness. I'm used to speaking my mind, but that isn't going so well anymore. Maybe you can talk to her, let her know that I didn't mean to upset her. I'm not looking to cause grief in your household."

"It's your household now too." He patted my hand. "The others just need to understand it will take time for you to settle into your new position and responsibilities. And speaking of responsibilities, the prisoner caravan has arrived and I must hand out war prizes at the feast tonight. Father also wants us at temple services, for sacrifices to honor our marriage."

"No doubt to sacrifice all the priests of Quetzalcoatl that you captured," I muttered.

"If we had any, I'm sure he would."

So the civilian disguises worked, I thought. *Perhaps you can turn this in your favor.* I thought about how that other me might deal with this opportunity, but the thought of using seduction to get what I wanted felt unbecoming of Quetzalcoatl's high priestess. Besides, if this marriage was to work, sexual blackmail was ill-advised.

But if I could harness that confidence and authority....

"May I request a gift from you, My Lord?" I asked, gripping his hand tighter in mine.

He smiled down at me. "What kind of gift?"

"A wedding gift."

"I thought I already gave you one."

"Am I really only worth one handmaiden to you?"

He fixed his gaze on me again, a grin quirking at the corner of his mouth. "Of course not."

I granted him a smooth smile, pleased at the influence of my mere words. "A woman of my social status should have at least five handmaidens, to help me dress and bathe. And there must be no royal gardeners, for my garden is a shambles. Let me pick some from the prisoners." I thought to add "please", but that other voice never asked, and that worked quite well.

Black Otter contemplated a moment before asking, "These men and women you're planning to pick...they wouldn't be priests and priestesses of Quetzalcoatl, would they?"

I fought back the spike of panic. If they died because I exposed them, I could never forgive myself. "What does it matter if they are or aren't?"

"Of course it matters. My father—"

"And what about the promise you made me last night?" I demanded, the fear nearly taking over, but I gulped a lungful of air. Words alone weren't going to save my priests and priestesses. I put on a sultry smile that made my stomach crawl, then I played the tips of my three fingernails over his chin, gently tracing his lower lip. His whole demeanor changed, like a predator spotting movement in the bushes. "You do this for me, and I return the favor, My Lord," I whispered, and kissed him.

He embraced me hard, pulling me off my feet. I expected the desire to flare up, but my whole body remained steady, in control of itself. When he backed me up against the wall and reached for the hem of my dress, I stopped him. "Not yet. First, my servants; then I promise I'll make it very worth your while."

Black Otter looked me up and down with longing and frustration. "If my father found out about this, he'd hold my face against the cooking stones." I read the rest on his face: *But I don't care at all.*

I felt disgusted with myself.

Don't denigrate the gifts Heaven gave you, the voice suddenly snarled in my head. *It's his fault for being weak.*

◻

Black Otter took me to the palace prison in the north courtyard. I'd never been there before, but Black Otter had told me numerous stories about it when we were children. I'd been too enthralled by the descriptions of the cages and punishment tools to give any thought to why he and his father must have been going there at all. Stacks of cages lined the yard, but the male war prisoners sat in the middle, tied to each other by a rope looped around their necks. They all looked ragged and scared.

"Get some wooden collars ready with my name carved in them. I need workers for my wife's garden," Black Otter told the guard. He took my hand and led me over to the prisoners. "Pick the ones you want, my precious flower."

Now that I stood in front of all these condemned men, I felt horrible. Why were my priests more important than that farmer or that merchant, or that twelve-year-old boy crying for his mother? How could I choose to save some people while leaving the rest behind? I waited for that stronger voice to speak up, but it remained maddeningly silent.

Black Otter gripped my hand tighter then pointed to a man sitting in front of us, dressed in a dirty xicolli. "How about this one?"

He was a merchant who sold beautiful painted pottery I'd bought for the temple once or twice. The plea in his eyes almost had me nodding. *But if you say yes to every desperate look, you might end up saving none of your priests.* It wasn't the voice I'd hoped for, and my own, familiar one was far from certain, but as high priestess, my loyalty above all else was to the god and his servants, even before king and family. I finally shook my head, my eyes stinging at the grave disappointment on the merchant's face. Not even the relieved expressions from my priests could keep the haunted feeling away once I'd finished. Black Otter had the five low-ranking priests fitted with slave collars.

"I want all my wife's flower beds weeded and thinned before nightfall," he told them, as the guard led them out of the courtyard. He then took me back inside. "Are you all right?" he asked.

"I don't think I'll ever be all right again," I whispered. I'd just left two hundred men to die for no good reason. *It's all a needless waste, and some day I'm going to have the power to stop this nonsense.* It was still my familiar voice but this time loaded with confidence, and anger. *No human should have to die for a god who doesn't give a damn about them.*

The women were in one of the small banquet halls off the kitchen. I picked out my priestesses quickly and tried, unsuccessfully, to not dwell on it; by the time we arrived in the great hall for the victory feast, I thought I might throw up if I ate anything. I ventured a glare at Ihuitimal when I caught him watching me. *Someday you'll pay,* I thought. *For what you did to me, my father, to the followers of my beloved god, to those prisoners in the yard, to men and women alike.* He grinned at me as if amused.

And it's going to be sooner rather than later.

Chapter Thirty-Three

I decided that night that I needed to speed Ihuitimal on his way to Mictlan. I watched him very closely after that, observing his habits. He came to the occasional feast, but I never saw him in the hallways, nor did he ever touch a bite of food or drink without it first passing a taster's testing. Guards formed a shield around him, and manned the curtain separating the royal living quarters; and still more came and went from within, no doubt guarding the king's quarters from possible treachery by his own sons. If only Father had been so cautious...

"Why's he never around?" I asked Black Otter as we lay in bed.

Black Otter shrugged. "I'm usually with the army, so I don't spend much time with him. This is the longest I've been home in years." He kissed my bare shoulder.

"The others must miss you if you're never home."

"I imagine they do." He glided calloused hands over me.

And of course his being here with me right now didn't help matters. By the end of my first two weeks in Culhuacan, I'd become a pariah among the others, except for Anacoana. Jade Flower kept a cool distance, speaking to me only when I spoke first, but she kept conversation short and rarely smiled except in a simpering, forced fashion. Initially her rude behavior angered me, but eventually I decided it wasn't unwarranted. Black Otter had spent every single night since I'd arrived with me, and I'd stupidly assumed that he was seeing to his other obligations during the day. I'd failed in my duties to the others and I feared my own sister might start plotting against me soon if I didn't fix things.

I pulled away from Black Otter, annoyed by his touch. "When's the last time you actually spent the night with Jade Flower? Or even Lady Corn Flower, or Lady Papantzin?"

He stared at me, incredulous. "What does it matter?"

"You have duties, My Lord, and you've been neglecting them."

"Says who?"

"No one dares speak a word about it, but they know exactly how much time we spend together, and they compare it with how little you spend with them."

He shook his head, irritated.

"A good man doesn't keep more women than he has time for."

His face darkened. "Now I'm a bad man?"

"Sometimes even good men need reminding that they're making a wrong step. Do something about it before it's too late."

He sighed. "Very well." He tried to move in again, but I stopped him with fingers against his lips.

"Now."

He looked irritated but said, "Fine. I'll go and see Jade Flower."

"And stay the night with her." When he started protesting, I said, "She loves you, you know."

He looked as though I were speaking a foreign language, but then he blinked and nodded, that distant look vanishing from his eyes. "Of course she does." He donned his cape and left.

Finally! I knew men had big appetites when it came to sex, but he hadn't gone a night without bedding me since I'd come here. Not even the arrival of my monthly cycle deterred him—though its arrival right on time both surprised and relieved me; I would be spared pregnancy at least another month. I supposed one had to be insatiable when one kept multiple women, as all kings do. My own father had had over thirty women in his household, most of them keeping track of who he was with on any given night and whispering their disapproval about it in the morning.

But something was odd about Black Otter; in particular, he'd started looking gaunt, even weak at times, as if he couldn't replenish his strength with food, even though he ate like a ravenous wolf. And he slept like a dead man. Was he sick? If illness took him, what would happen to me? If his oldest son died, might my horrid uncle marry me off to this other son of his whom I'd never seen before? Or if he lost that son as well, might he replace that favored concubine of his with me? The thought sent chills racing up my spine like a giant centipede.

When Malinalli answered my summons, she brought a pot of xocolatl and we took it out into the garden. Servants weren't allowed to partake of xocolatl, but whenever we were alone I made sure she got a cup.

"At least he's leaving at the end of the week," I said, as I poured us each a cup.

"Is it really so bad?" she asked.

I chuckled. "Life could be worse. Still, I've been reduced to little more than a toy. I shudder to think that this is how most women must spend their lives. I had it very good."

"And you will again. The king won't live forever."

But I couldn't wait around years for the Black Dog to finally visit Ihuitimal's bed. Growing up, I'd assumed Little Reed would make my uncle pay for his crimes, and so I'd only fantasized about ways of killing him—most of them involving him holding his own heart in his hand—but now that responsibility was mine alone. I couldn't stab him to death with all the guards around, so my attack required stealth, and hopefully would make the death look natural. In his declining health, it shouldn't take much.

"I'm going to need some poison. Like the kind we used in the laundry room to keep the mice from nesting in the clean robes," I said.

Startled, Malinalli looked around a moment before lowering her voice. "What for?"

"Rodents are eating my bone flowers."

Malinalli nodded, understanding. "How much do you need?"

"Just a spoonful or two," I said lightly.

"I can have it for you by morning."

I shook my head. "I need to observe them more. They come and go like phantoms, and I want to make sure it's mice, not insects, otherwise all this is useless."

"And if the poison works too quickly, you might scare off the others," Malinalli said with a pointed look. "It would be better to poison them slowly, so it builds up and they can't smell it on any of the bodies."

Yes, that definitely was a consideration. I needed to spend more time planning this out in better detail.

I heard the bells on my door curtain jingle and I hurried to my feet, my stomach sinking. *We were overheard!* But it was only Black Otter, fresh-faced and excited. I calmed my racing heart. "What are you doing here?"

"I did as you asked, so now I'm back." He tried to take me into his arms.

But I slipped out of his reach. "You're supposed to stay the night with her."

"She's asleep, so what does it matter? And I still must do my duty to you." He tried again to embrace me.

"I don't need that tonight," I said, avoiding him again.

"But I do." He backed me up against the tree so I couldn't escape, and kissed my neck, making my head cloud.

"But you were just with Jade Flower," I murmured, trying to fight back the desire but failing. "How could you possibly need more?"

"Because I saved it all for you." He pushed up against me, sliding his hands all over me.

My resistance began melting faster. I'd completely forgotten Malinalli was still there—watching us with a blank look on her face—and I imagined her bare breasts pressed up against me, Black Otter caressing us both, her delicate fingers raising my flesh as they glided down my hips, over my abdomen, down between my legs....

The voice crawled forward in my mind, ready to ask my best friend to join Black Otter and myself for the rest of the evening, as if it were the most natural thing to do. I often blushed at remembering the things Black Otter convinced me to do while in the throes of passion, but I couldn't take the chance of wrecking my friendship with Malinalli. It was the only relationship I had left that meant anything to me. "You should be off to bed now," I told her, panting and bewildered. "Thank you for the xocolatl."

Malinalli blinked as if waking from a trance and muttered about talking to me in the morning, her cheeks flushed. Black Otter watched her leave, but I grabbed his chin and pulled him back to kiss me.

Afterwards I was sore from scrapes on my back—he took me against the copal tree—but those were just a minor inconvenience. Among the pants and trembles, he'd murmured, "I think I'd die without you, Quetzalpetlatl," in my ear, then collapsed into the grass, too weak to move. I struggled to drag him to my bed on my own—surely the guards would think I'd done something horrible to him if I asked for their help—and eventually I got him there. He groaned and fell immediately into a deep sleep.

But I stood there a long time, staring down at him, my mouth dry and my whole body trembling. I couldn't stop thinking about that dream of Red Flint, dead on the temple floor with an eerily contented smile on his face, as if having me even once was worth dying for.

◻

The week dragged by, and I tensed every time Black Otter came to see me, especially in the women's hall. He'd stare at me as if the rest of the world didn't exist at all, and Jade Flower's attitude had grown worse. She completely ignored me, walking away if I spoke, and I tried every day to get him to spend more time with her—or even one of the others—but he'd disappear for a little while then return to my quarters, eager to indulge himself.

Black Otter even made his farewell ceremony miserable for me by kissing the cheeks of the others while saving his most passionate embrace for me. Only after Ihuitimal cleared his throat did he finally let me go, leaving me half-drunk with lust in front of the disdainful glares of the others.

Ihuitimal whispered something to Black Otter but his son shrugged and snapped back at him, leaving Ihuitimal fuming. "I should have news in the next couple of days, so look for my runner," Black Otter told him, then ventured a smiling gaze back at me. I kept my eyes downcast until he was gone from the courtyard.

"I'm not going to the women's hall," I told Malinalli once we arrived back at my quarters. Everyone else had left ahead of us; Jade Flower had run from the courtyard, sobbing. I couldn't face her after all that.

"You want me to bring your weaving to you?" Malinalli asked as she gathered my laundry.

I shook my head. "It's been far too long since I've had time to meditate and pray."

"I know what you mean. Ihuitimal requires all servants to give prayers to the Smoking Mirror once a day, so I've taken to whispering prayers to the god in the steam bath in the middle of the night so as not to be overheard."

Anger flushed my face. "How are the others handling it?"

"Tayanna nearly lost her life by babbling about refusing to worship her beloved god's mortal enemy. Luckily the head servant chose to have her whipped rather than turning her in to the king for the sacrifice." She finished packing my laundry in a wicker basket then asked, "Do you think the prayers still count, even if I don't mean them?"

"Real prayers are always stronger than fake ones." As Malinalli turned to leave, I said, "Meet me by the pond in the main garden this afternoon and I can hear all the news you've gathered this week."

Malinalli nodded knowingly and left.

I knelt in the morning sunshine in my garden. My priests were doing a wonderful job, and under their care the bone flowers were starting to bloom. The sharp, sweet smell brought memories of childhood; of Mother, of my wedding day, and of Little Reed bringing me bundles of flowers back from palace visits. I plucked one of the waxy white flowers and crushed it between my fingers, releasing a concentrated burst of sweet vanilla aroma. If love had a smell, this would be it.

Someone clearing their throat broke my reverie. Two guards stood behind me, making my heart stop before it took off at a frantic sprint. "Yes?"

"The king requests your presence," said one, motioning me to stand.

I wasn't about to show fear and condemn myself, so I rose and followed them back inside. But when they turned down the men's hallway, I hesitated; not even female servants were allowed in the men's quarters. The guard gave me a gentle push to get me moving again.

There were only four doors beyond the curtain; there'd been at least ten doorways here before, so the missing six had been sealed up and plastered over and decorated with murals of birds and jaguars. As we passed the first doorway, I recognized my old nursery, still painted with birds and butterflies. Black Otter's son sat on the floor, babbling as he pushed a toy jaguar around on its little wooden wheels. An old man smoked a pipe in the corner, watching over him. Two of the remaining three doorways presumably belonged to Black Otter and his lost brother, but both curtains were closed off.

The lead guard held the last door curtain open. Memories of my father's mutilated corpse and death's foul stench made me freeze until he prodded me forward.

The room smelled very different now—sweet with tobacco, incense and xocolatl. Where Father's bed once sat, a servant crouched, tending a bubbling kettle in the middle of a sitting area. New murals of blood sacrifice stretched across every wall, but the weathered wood hearth mantel looked the same. The wall between Mother and Father's rooms was gone and Mother's quarters were now a sanctuary of sorts, devoted to a painting of a giant, strutting god, human-looking save for the small mirrors in his eyes and the large obsidian mirror in place of his left foot. His skin was so black it seemed to suck the light from the room, as if the picture were a constantly shifting cloud of smoke. Hearts poured into his open mouth from the hands of priests, the color of the blood so dark I doubted it was paint.

Ihuitimal knelt in front of the large mirror; but even when he struggled to his feet, he didn't look at me, just wheezed lightly as he walked by. He drank his xocolatl then waved the servant and his guards from the room.

I hadn't expected that. What was he playing at?

"I trust you've settled into palace life again?" he asked, still not looking at me.

I hesitated to answer at first, but when I finally spoke, I kept my tone cool. "It was a little difficult at first."

"And seeing family again is always good. I'm sure you've missed that a great deal since losing both Topiltzin and that woman who raised you."

A storm of emotions stirred inside me: anger that he'd even dare speak about Little Reed and not even take the time to find out Nimilitzli's name; devastation over being reminded yet again that they were gone; and resentment that this demon-worshipping filth even presumed to say anything about the joys of family. I took a deep, calming breath before speaking though. "I'm glad to see Jade Flower again. And Black Otter."

Ihuitimal chuckled. "If only Jade Flower were as happy to see you. She thinks your being here is a very bad thing for Black Otter. And I'm starting to agree with her."

I couldn't help scowling at him. "Black Otter is his own master, and I cannot make him spend any more time with her than he's willing to—"

"She thinks you're poisoning him," Ihuitimal cut in, his gaze like a dagger. "And given how terrible he's looked recently, I have to wonder as well."

I tried to laugh, but part of me wondered if someone was indeed poisoning him. *Maybe you're doing it without even knowing it.* But I pushed that outrageous thought aside. "I'm trying to make a life for us here."

"By tearing down everything I built to bring that weak Feathered Serpent back into the temples?" Ihuitimal grinned at me. "Let's not play games, Quetzalpetlatl. I'm not afraid of losing face to you; I'd have to believe that you're someone of importance for that to happen. And I know you've waited a very long time to have this chance to confront me, so go ahead, speak your mind. Let us deal honestly with each other."

I wavered only a moment before the anger surged enough to loosen my tongue. "You sneer at Quetzalcoatl, but the truth is that the Feathered Serpent loves everyone, even you; yet you chose to reject him for that demon that hates us all. Don't think you're some exception to that; when you fail your dark master, does he pat your head and say 'try again', or does he make you pay a high price? What did he do when you let my mother escape? Or how about all those failed assassination attempts? At first I found it odd that you have so many daughters, but now I think the reason is clear: you failed the Smoking Mirror so he punished you by denying you any blood sons of your own, and you must rely on your brother's illegitimate son to carry on your legacy. This other son is probably no more yours than Black Otter is, is he?" When Ihuitimal stared at me, surprised, I added, "I was in the room when you confronted Nochuatl. Your murderous rage must have been too thick for you to remember."

A smile crept over his scarred face. "I remember telling Nochuatl I was going to pluck your wings off." He chuckled but soon turned serious again. "He was no better than your father; scoundrels, the whole lot of them. They both got the destiny they wrote for themselves."

"My father deserved nothing you handed him that night," I said, my voice shaking. "You have a nerve calling my father a scoundrel. You earned your exile. You broke the law—"

Ihuitimal turned away to contemplate the hearth with his hard gaze. "Your illusions about Mixcoatl are pathetic. Your father did more damage to me than any other man. He was a filthy, lying dog who sneaked his way onto Culhuacan's throne—the throne I was promised by your grandfather. Never knew that, did you?"

His words shocked me into silence.

He smiled coolly at me. "Everyone always talked about how honorable and noble your father was; even as a child, Father gave him just a little more tlaxcallis than he gave the rest of us." He went back to the kettle to pour himself a new cup of xocolatl. "We were on campaign in the north when we were beset by Chichimecs and I was captured. Mixcoatl vowed to return and free me, even if it took the rest of his years. I spent three years in captivity, forced to fight with one ankle bound to my opponent for the amusement of the chief and his allies, half starving and constantly defending my life, and dreaming of the day when Mixcoatl would keep his promise and raze their miserable village to the ground. I dreamed nightly of finally taking my throne and seeing Chimalma's smile again; that kept me from succumbing to the misery of my waking hours," he added, with a surprisingly nostalgic expression.

I blinked, stunned. "My mother?" The thought of him pining for her made my skin crawl.

Ihuitimal frowned as if I'd interrupted a pleasant dream. "Of course your mother. Your grandfather promised her along with the kingdom, and we were to marry when I returned from my last campaign." He gulped down the xocolatl as if it had angered him. "But Mixcoatl never came. Instead the Chichimecs granted me freedom, won with scars uncountable." He pointed to the one on his face. "So I walked home, eager to see my brothers again after so long." He paused as he stared down at the kettle. "Imagine my surprise when I found that Mixcoatl had told our father that I'd died, and claimed Chimalma for his own. And when her father died, he inherited the throne. He'd already reigned for two years, and he never sent anyone to find me; claimed he thought me already sacrificed. But he couldn't hide the shameful truth from me: he'd left me to die so he could claim my throne."

I knew my father was flawed—he'd made me cry too many times for me to not know—but I never would've suspected him capable of such backhanded deception. *You can't believe Ihuitimal's spiteful lies,* I thought, but I'd heard enough from my own father and others to give the claims credence. Nochuatl had told me that Ihuitimal had a right to be angry. "You should have challenged him for the throne back then," I said, my resentment leaking through.

"I should have," Ihuitimal admitted. "But I clung foolishly to Mixcoatl's promises to make things right. He gave me Chimalma's younger sister, but then Nochuatl wanted to fight me for her." He chuckled. "Mixcoatl wouldn't let him. Eloxochitl wasn't half the beauty your mother was, but she had her own charms, and your father promised to betroth the first compatible set of children we each had."

He extinguished the burner, then sighed. "But even then, I couldn't find a shred of happiness for myself, so I left for the north again. I was determined to find that Chichimec village again and burn it to the ground, for all those years they'd made me suffer and kept me from my rightful future. They cost me everything that mattered."

How often had I felt that same, blinding feeling since I'd returned to Culhuacan? The notion unnerved me.

He stood up, his eyebrows raised in surprise. "But to my amazement, the chief remembered me. He welcomed me into his home and called me a son. He gave me a house and all the women I could want for, saying I'd earned them with my bravery and tenacity. I hadn't received anything like such a kind welcome when I returned home from my captivity, and in my confusion, I fell into a dark despair."

He hobbled over to the mural of the black-painted god. "The village shaman told me to seek guidance from the Smoking Mirror, so I lived out in the desert for two months. I was starving and near death before the god finally came to me as an obsidian jaguar. He set his giant paw upon me and said 'You are my high priest, destined to bring my worship out of the desert. Be my voice and I'll reward you with everything your heart has ever desired.' And for the first time in years, I felt I had purpose again; I'd finally found my life's calling." He stared up at the mural with reverence.

Chills rose up my spine. *That sounds like what Quetzalcoatl told me....*

"After a year in the north, I returned to Culhuacan to find my wife pregnant and Nochuatl unable to look me in the eye," Ihuitimal said, amused. "I considered killing the baby and his mother, but the kindness the Chichimecs had shown me stayed my hand. I prayed to the god to decide their fate for me; if the child lived to learn his true name, it was because the god had use for him." He turned away from the mural finally and came back, not meeting my gaze. "So when Black Otter survived, I accepted him as my son, the same way my Chichimec father accepted me. Since he'd come from Eloxochitl, everyone would accept him as my son, so I raised him, molded him as if he were my own blood. And Chimalma had finally carried a daughter to birth after years of failure and the ordeal left her barren. Everything was falling into place finally."

"But then you had to go and ruin it all by worshiping your beloved god in my father's city," I pointed out.

"My only mistake was telling Black Otter anything about Smoking Mirror before he'd earned the right to know," Ihuitimal corrected me. "The final arrow in my heart came when Mixcoatl once again broke his promise, betraying my son. As soon as he discovered Chimalma was carrying the Feathered Serpent's bastard, he pushed Black Otter aside, proving his word was worthless. What I did was the only right thing to do."

I laughed. "To make sure Black Otter got the throne?" When he nodded, I asked, "Then why isn't he king yet? You were the throne's custodian until he was old enough, but yet he's still not king."

"Do not doubt my love for my son," Ihuitimal snarled. "I will see him on the throne I was wrongly denied and I won't let a conniving woman stand in his way."

"How am I standing in his way? You're the one who's still holding onto it like some pet monkey clinging to its master. It would be best for everybody if you just stepped aside for him now."

Ihuitimal flicked his gaze back to the mural again. "He can only take the throne when the god says he's ready, and as long as you're poisoning his mind with whispers of bringing Quetzalcoatl back, that will never happen. He will only take his rightful throne when he's willing to take up my mantle as the next high priest of the Smoking Mirror."

"You and your god do him a disservice by forcing him to be something he doesn't want."

"Kings sometimes have to do things they don't like. If he hasn't the stomach for it, then he won't take the throne, but I trust my son to do what needs doing when his master demands it."

A smirk crept onto my lips. "You give yourself far too much credit when you claim you've molded Black Otter in your image. I see far more of his true father in him—a failure for you, but a victory for the goodness of mankind."

Ihuitimal flashed his sharpened teeth in a grisly smile. "Then why don't you just do it for him then?" He tossed an obsidian knife to me. "I'm sure it's crossed your mind more than once; I see it in your eyes. How many years have you dreamed of this, Quetzalpetlatl? Since the night you stumbled in here to find I'd slain your father? Does it still haunt your dreams, little girl? Do you wake in the middle of the night in a cold sweat, crying for your Tatli?" He laughed, showing off pointy teeth.

I tightened my grip on the knife's wooden handle, my anger surging and my wrist feeling afire. I'd gotten used to the constant itching so I hardly noticed it anymore, until now. *Plunge the blade into his throat, just like you did to Ahexotl; watch his blood splash across the face of his demon god,* I thought, sweating with anticipation. *Oh who will be the one laughing then?*

"The hatred feels good, doesn't it? As comfortable as a worn pair of sandals." Ihuitimal took my hand and put the blade to his throat, the expression in his eyes intense. "You know you want to do it, so do it!" he growled.

But why was he goading me?

Who cares? Slice him from ear to ear and he'll bleed to death in no time. You know how to do it; you learned it for the spring sacrifices. He deserves the same fate as murderers and thieves.

I started pressing the blade.

But he's my uncle, my blood, my family, what little I have left of it, I suddenly thought. *He's nobody! He deserves to feel the pain you've felt all these years!*

Ihuitimal stepped closer still, pushing so hard that the blade cut into his neck's flabby, wrinkled skin. "Do it, Quetzalpetlatl! Resolution will only come from killing me; trust me, I know all about it."

And become just like him, and his demon god? My grip on the knife loosened. I let it slip from my fingers and it clattered on the stone floor between us. *That's not what Quetzalcoatl would want; that's not the person I am.*

Ihuitimal sneered. "And that, dear, is why women have no business in politics; they haven't the loins to do what must be done for the good of their people. That's why Culhuacan has no queen, nor will she ever again. Your usefulness is just about finished, and thankfully I'll soon be rid of you, and Black Otter can regain the good sense you've stolen from him. Jade Flower at least knows her place, something Black Otter's own mother never quite understood either. Don't make me deal with you like I did with her." He turned away and leaned against the hearth, as if the whole discussion had tired him out. "Now get back in your place and don't darken my doorway again."

CHAPTER THIRTY-FOUR

I met Malinalli by the pond and we went to where my father used to keep his exotic birds. Most of the cages were falling apart with disuse, their doors hanging open. We sat under the large oak tree sheltering the remains of the macaw cage and ate our lunch.

"You're upset," Malinalli noted.

I shook my head. "I had the chance to do it, actually had a blade to his throat with no one around...but I just couldn't do it." I sighed.

Malinalli gripped my hand and gave it a gentle, reassuring squeeze. "What did he say?"

"He spent most of the time justifying what he did to my father, but he thinks me meddlesome. And Jade Flower thinks I'm poisoning Black Otter."

"She's just a fool."

"Maybe she's not." I looked up at her after a hesitation. "I'm...I think there's something wrong with me, Malinalli."

Frowning, she asked, "Why would you think that?"

"You've seen how Black Otter has been behaving. He won't stay out of my bed, and I can't get him to spend any time with the others. And the other night, he told me he couldn't live without me. He's becoming obsessive."

"What does that have to do with you though?" Malinalli asked puzzled.

"What if I'm making him like that? What if I drove Red Flint crazy?"

Malinalli shook her head. "Red Flint was a terrible man. You can't blame yourself for the things he chose to do. Nor can you blame yourself for the kind of man Black Otter is."

I bowed my head. "No, I can't. It's just...when we make love...." My face burned to even speak of such embarrassing, private things, but I needed to talk to someone about it, and who could I trust not to judge me if not my best friend? "I'm not myself; I turn into someone else, and this other woman I become...she scares me. I completely lose my head, and I'm afraid of what I might do."

Furrowing her brows, Malinalli asked, "What do you mean what you might do?"

I thought of the dream again, about drinking the very life out of Red Flint in the throes of ecstasy, but I couldn't bring myself to speak of it. How could I possibly talk about the fear that I was slowly killing Black Otter without sounding completely ridiculous, and crazy? *Because it is ridiculous,* I told myself, and shook my head. "I don't know. I feel like I have absolutely no control of the situation."

Malinalli gave my hand another squeeze. "Granted, I don't know much about sex—not from experience anyway—but maybe all this is completely normal."

"I don't think so." I almost blurted out *because it's nothing like it is with the god*, but I bit my tongue in time. It was difficult enough talking about all this without bringing the true nature of my relationship with Quetzalcoatl into it. "My own experience is limited too, but...I just know that this isn't normal, and I'm afraid something bad is going to happen."

She gave me a sympathetic smile. "I know you, Quetzalpetlatl, and whatever it is that's worrying you...maybe it's in fact a good thing? Maybe it's why the god chose you for his high priestess? He gave you that most important task of ending human sacrifice, after all."

"He gave that task to Topiltzin," I corrected her. "It's only fallen to me because I erred and he's dead." Thinking about Little Reed made the ache in my chest intensify, and I couldn't hold back the tears. "What if I mess this up too? What if Black Otter ends up like Red Flint?" *Or worse yet like Little Reed?*

Malinalli's face turned serious—and a bit scared. "Has he threatened you, the way Red Flint always did?"

"Oh no, Black Otter is nothing like that," I insisted, embarrassed for even insinuating it unintentionally. "He's a good man, but Ihuitimal…he's already warned me about remembering my place or he'll kill me, like he did my aunt." I wiped my tears away with a fierce swipe of my fist. "Eloxochitl was a wonderful woman, so kind and generous…." *And an adulteress,* I imagined Ihuitimal hissing. *Don't forget that!*

"Do you think it's dangerous to stay here now?"

"I don't know. He did say that my usefulness was almost over, so maybe he is planning to kill me after all." Though why hadn't he yet, especially now that Black Otter wasn't here to protect me? *Something else is going on, something that requires him to keep me alive. I'm too valuable for him to kill, at least just yet.* The thought gave me a shiver.

Malinalli glanced around, then whispered, "Then I'll make sure he's dead before morning."

I shook my head, adamant. "I can't ask you to do something I couldn't do myself."

"You shouldn't have to live like this, constantly subjected to terror and dishonor. It's an insult to the god's honor; I should do it to defend that."

"The god wouldn't want you to do it either. He despises gaining power by murder, and it was my mistake to forget that. We can't let fear drive us from our convictions."

Malinalli bowed her head. "Of course, My Lady. Forgive my angry outburst."

I shook my head. "I'm grateful for your loyalty, to both myself and the god. We'll find a way out of this without compromising our principles. I trust the Feathered Serpent to show us the way."

"And so do I," Malinalli replied. "I have faith in the god, and in you."

◻

For the next week I made daily appearances in the women's hall if only to avoid looking like a guilty woman hiding away in her quarters. I wouldn't let Ihuitimal's threats deter me.

While I saw little of him after that day, his guards followed me everywhere, even keeping watch outside my quarters. But the most troubling development came when a serving woman I'd never seen before came to bathe and dress me the day after my meeting with Ihuitimal. I asked where Malinalli was, but she refused to answer, and just brushed my hair with a ferocity that made my eyes water. Once a few days passed and Malinalli still didn't return, I began to really worry. *She's been arrested or maybe even sacrificed,* I thought as I lay on my bed crying. *And once again it's your fault. You put those silly schemes into her head.*

"She's been reassigned to one of the noblemen's wives," Paper Flower told me when she brought me my afternoon atole. I cried still more, relieved Malinalli was alive, but shaken that someone had thought she ought to be taken away from me.

Something else was going on, though. Guards were everywhere, and Paper Flower informed me that the city was crawling with soldiers now. "Three times as many archers are on the defensive wall, and packs of Chichimec warriors are patrolling the Noble Quarters." Everyone—particularly the women—whispered about armies coming around the lake. It appeared that war was on its way to Culhuacan's gates.

But why hadn't Black Otter returned yet? He'd promised to return within a few nights, but a week had passed and I'd heard nothing from him. I started fearing that he'd been taken prisoner, or worse yet killed. I dreaded to think what might become of me if that were the case.

Or maybe his father sent him away, to get him away from you, before he does something stupid, I thought as I climbed into bed. *Whatever has been affecting you, Black Otter, please don't bring it back with you.* For the first time since he'd left, the bed felt so empty without him there with me.

◻

A noise woke me in the deep of night and I sat up, alert: I'd been sleeping more and more lightly as the days went on and my anxiety grew. And my cheek felt wet and tingly; but I'd been dreaming about that day in Teotihuacan when I first saw the Black Dog, so maybe it was all in my mind. I shivered as I looked around. "Who's there?"

"Shhhh!" Black Otter stepped out from behind the screen that shielded my bed from the doorway at night, and an overwhelming desire to hug him fell over me. The worry on his face stopped me though. "Get dressed. We have to go," he whispered.

"Go where?"

"No time to explain." He glanced over his shoulder. "Just get dressed."

I put on a dress and sandals while he glanced repeatedly at the door, as if expecting unwelcome company. He draped a black cloak over my shoulders then led me out into the garden, his sweaty grip painfully tight. My heart started racing. He climbed the copal tree then surveyed the walkway behind the wall. He beckoned me to climb up after him.

I froze. I hadn't climbed a tree since I was a girl and I wasn't even sure my bad heel would allow me to. But when he beckoned again, impatient, I hiked up my hem and made my way up unsteadily. I used to run up trees like a monkey, but now I was clumsy and slow as I shimmied up to the branch where Black Otter crouched. Sweat dripped off my brow and I could barely catch my breath before he wanted me to follow him up to the next large branch, which reached out over the garden's back wall. "Where are we going?" I finally choked out, once we reached the top. To my surprise there were no guards behind my wall.

"I'm getting you out of here," Black Otter whispered, then jumped down to the ground. He held his arms out, so I jumped down too, letting him cushion my fall. He looked both ways down the walled passageway then took my hand and pulled me to the left. "It's not safe for you here anymore," he continued as we walked.

"What do you mean?"

He held up a hand for silence. At the bend in the passageway, he pushed me gently against the stone wall and held a finger to his lips. He stepped around the corner. "What are you two still doing back here? We have an invading army on the way and all able-bodied men are to report to the main gate for orders."

A man answered, "The king told us to guard the corridor, My Lord—"

"My father sent me out to make sure everyone was reporting as ordered." When silence followed, Black Otter asked, "Are you deaf and dumb? Your war chief just gave you an order!"

"We'll go immediately, My Lord," another man squeaked. Once the slapping of their sandals on the ground faded away, Black Otter came back, grabbed my wrist and pulled me along after him.

"There's an army coming?" I panted, jogging to keep up.

"It'll be here by sunrise," Black Otter replied. "I was worried I wouldn't make it back in time to get you."

"Which army?"

"Xochicalco and its allies, of course."

Joy quickened my heartbeat. "King Mazatzin is coming?"

He hesitated before saying, "Mazatzin abdicated his throne."

"To whom?"

He didn't answer, so I repeated the question, refusing to go further. Why didn't he want me to know?

We'd reached the mouth of the cave leading out into the lake. Black Otter peered into the dark before finally saying, "To Topiltzin, all right?"

"Topiltzin's dead," I replied; but when he wouldn't meet my gaze, my throat felt tied in a knot. "What are you getting at?"

He tried to pull me along again but I stood firm. He sighed. "Topiltzin's alive."

"You're lying!" I snarled through tears. "Red Flint had him murdered. Mazatzin brought me his sword."

"He escaped."

"If he was alive he would've let me know...he would've written me letters," I insisted, bordering on hysterical.

"He did, but my father intercepted them."

His face was a watery blur behind my tears. I wanted to punch him for telling me such a cruel lie. "I don't believe you!"

After an uncomfortable silence, Black Otter said, "He calls you Papalotl, like I used to, and he signs his letters as Little Reed."

Little Reed! My eyes widened, a smile tugging at my lips. Though my mind was in turmoil, my heart knew it was true. "He's really alive?" *My Little Reed—my love!—he's not dead! He found out Ihuitimal was holding me prisoner and he's come to rescue me!* The pain that had squeezed my heart for so long loosened, letting joy pulse inside me and a relieved laugh escape my lips. "He's really alive!"

Black Otter took my arm. "You must keep your voice down or someone's going to hear you." We advanced into the darkness, taking no torch with us.

Soon I couldn't see my own hand touching my nose. "How do you know where you're going?"

"Just keep hold of me. I've gone through here many times."

My whole body was abuzz. *This is why I'd never convinced my heart to move on, because it always knew Little Reed wasn't dead. Of course he'd outwit Red Flint, and that dog wanted you to believe he was dead, so you'd fall into his arms in despair and look to him for comfort.*

But Black Otter too had known all this time that Little Reed was alive and said nothing, not even when I mentioned him. *So he could impregnate you and solidify his claim to the throne, making Little Reed the interloper.* Anger and betrayal roiled in my chest, and I couldn't stand his sweaty hand shackling my wrist. I tore it away from him.

He stumbled and I moved away as he floundered around in the dark, calling out my name. With at least ten steps between us, I finally spoke. "Where are you taking me?"

"Why didn't you answer when I called for you?" His irritation couldn't conceal the panic underlying his voice.

"Where are you taking me?" I repeated.

I imagined Black Otter muttering to himself, trying to decide what, if anything, to tell me, but finally he said, "Topiltzin captured my brother Amoxtli in battle three months ago and offered to trade him in exchange for our surrendering Culhuacan's throne. And my father—if you can believe it—was on verge of accepting the compromise, to save Amoxtli, but then Xochicalco burned down and I captured you. We'd been intercepting Topiltzin's letters to you for several years already, so I knew he'd be willing to trade my brother and the throne for you."

"Then why lie about Topiltzin being dead if you were just going to trade me away?" I demanded. "Why go through all that trouble of making me your wife and convincing me we were going to build a life together?" When he didn't answer, I thought my insides would collapse under the weight of my fury. "Because you knew he wants to marry me, and you couldn't resist claiming me for yourself just to spite him, right?" I didn't want to cry but tears muddled my voice anyway. "Or maybe you just wanted revenge against me, for that broken promise when we were children?"

"Absolutely not!" Black Otter insisted. "I do love you, Quetzalpetlatl, more than anything. Maybe it started out as a callous deception, but now...I feel horrible and wonder how I could have ever justified it to myself. You're everything to me. You must forgive me—"

"You convinced me to break my vows to the god, you dog! I could be with your child right now!"

"I know, and that's why I can't let my father trade you back to Topiltzin."

I hadn't heard him moving during our conversation, but suddenly his hand closed around my wrist and when I tried to wrench away from him, he held firm. "Let me go! I'm not going anywhere with you!" He dragged me by the wrist but when I kicked him, he pinned my arms behind my back. "You're hurting me!" I snarled as he pushed me onward.

"It's for your own good," he said, his voice regretful. "I can't let Topiltzin hurt you."

"My brother would never hurt me, Black Otter," I insisted as I stumbled in the dark, tripping, but he caught me before I fell.

"You say that now, but I know what men do to secure their own power. My father killed all your brothers, to make sure none of them would avenge your father, and if Topiltzin found you pregnant, he would kill our child."

"Topiltzin is nothing like your father."

"He can't be trusted, and neither can my father, so we must leave Culhuacan. It's the only way I can guarantee your safety."

Usually it was easy to argue against Black Otter—especially given how prone to irrationality he'd become with the passing days—but he sounded downright coherent now. Not that I believed for a moment that Little Reed would kill any child of mine, regardless of who the father was, but I couldn't call Black Otter crazy for fearing it. *And funny how after a week away from you, he seems almost normal again, as if being around you affects his reason.* The thought sent a chill through me.

A glimmer of light eventually appeared ahead, but it still took a long time to reach it. The glow came from a torch held by a guard standing at the bow of a canoe; an eerily reminiscent scene. We climbed into the boat and sat facing each other as the soldier pushed off from the shore, turning the bow towards the mouth of the cave.

"Where are you taking me?" I asked, glowering at him in the moonlight as we moved out onto the open lake.

"I don't know yet," Black Otter admitted. "There won't be any safe haven for us anywhere in the valley, so we'll have to travel past the mountains, to the south. We'll find somewhere where no one knows us."

"Topiltzin won't stop looking for me, Black Otter. We won't be able to hide from him forever."

He stared at me with eerie dispassion. "I'll die before I let him have you."

My heart quickened. So much for the rationality. "But what about Jade Flower and the others? Surely you wouldn't run out on them?"

His expression didn't change. "You said a good man doesn't keep more women than he has time for, and you're right. I have but one wife to devote my heart and soul to, someone I love and am willing to lay my life down for—"

"But what about your children? Why would the son you already have be any safer than one I may or may not be carrying?"

"They don't matter."

His indifference sickened me. "You can't mean that—"

"They aren't your children, so they are meaningless." He frowned, perplexed. "This is what you want too, isn't it? Isn't this how marriage *should* be? Don't you love me?"

I felt so numb with disbelief. "How could you say such things?"

But he shook his head like an obstinate child. "The gods gave you to me for a reason, and who are you to argue with them? Say you love me, Quetzalpetlatl!"

"Enough!" I cried. *It's like Red Flint all over again,* I thought, tears stinging my eyes. *But worse. You actually care for Black Otter.*

A shadow of anger crossed his face, but a soft whistling distracted him. The guard suddenly gagged and tried to stand up, grasping at an arrow piercing his throat, but he tipped over sideways, almost dumping the boat over with him.

"Get down!" Black Otter pushed me to the floor of the canoe and crouched next to me, sword drawn as he scanned the lake over the boat's edge. Eventually he stood up and waved his arms, shouting, "Hold your fire, you fools! You're attacking your war chief's boat!"

But another arrow whizzed by and Black Otter dropped down again.

"I don't think those are your men," I whispered.

"That dog Topiltzin has disguised his men to fool me," he growled.

"Topiltzin isn't an unreasonable man. We should surrender."

"And be taken as a sacrifice?"

Such foolishness. "The god doesn't want the lives of war prisoners; he doesn't want lives at all. The guard dropped the paddles, and they're going to get us anyway, so surrender is the only reasonable option. Don't throw away your life."

Black Otter peered around wild-eyed. "You promise to negotiate with your brother on my behalf?"

"I promise."

He kissed me hurriedly but the excitement of seeing Little Reed again kept any desire gagged. We remained crouched until the approaching canoe neared, then I told Black Otter, "Call out for our surrender."

He sighed, disgruntled, but did so.

Someone called back, "Stand and toss all weapons overboard." We did so, struggling to not capsize the canoe as Black Otter located three blades and dropped them into the dark water.

In the growing dawn, I saw three men in the other canoe, each dressed like Culhuacan's soldiers. One held a drawn bow pointed at Black Otter while the other two paddled. I started crying, trying to keep it quiet. My captivity was nearly over and I could finally be rid of this constant itching that had me clawing ruthlessly at my own wrist....

As the canoe slipped up next to ours, Black Otter dropped his hands. "What is this outrage?" he demanded, the wildness returning. "These are my father's personal guard. How dare you fire on your future king?"

In answer, the man shot Black Otter in the chest, catapulting him backwards into the water. I nearly fell overboard too, but someone grabbed and dragged me into the other canoe. "Let me go!" I searched around in vain for signs of Black Otter, but I saw only waves where he'd fallen in. The man tightened his grip so I sank my teeth into his arm, tasting blood. The metallic tang brought a strange spike of hunger.

The man ripped free of me, but I claimed a chunk of his flesh. Roaring, he shoved my head into the water.

I thrashed, kicking and clawing, holding against the urgent need to inhale. When the man finally hauled me back up after what felt like days, I sucked in deep, panting breaths, my wet hair plastered across my face.

"You almost tipped us over!" another man shouted.

"Look what she did to my arm!"

"I ought to toss you to the caimans. Can't even handle an unarmed woman! Let Tenoch deal with her."

He let me go but I lay on my stomach on the bottom of the canoe, giving no fight while someone bound my hands. I had none left.

As the men paddled back towards Culhuacan, a strange, strangled cry rang out across the lake, making them pause to look back the way they'd come. "Lake monster," the one called Tenoch said, and the leader told the others to pick up the pace. He shook his head and murmured, "Oh, such a bad omen. I fear none of us will live to see Lord Sun set on Meztliapan ever again."

CHAPTER THIRTY-FIVE

The assassins returned me to the palace and took me to the prison yard, leaving me bound in one of the cages. My muddy, wet dress chilled me but I still fell asleep for a while, plagued by dreams of strange, giant lake otters dragging Black Otter to the bottom of Meztliapan. He broke free of them, but when he reached the surface, he'd turned into one of them, shouting in a high, crying voice, "Mine! Mine!"

I awoke when someone kicked the side of my cage, and I squinted up to see Ihuitimal glaring down at me. His face was painted black with gold stripes across his eyes and mouth, and he gripped an obsidian-tipped spear so tight in his right hand that the veins stood out on his surprisingly thick upper arm. I'd taken him for a frail old man under his bulky royal robes, but now—in just a loincloth and feathered arm and calf bands— it was clear he wasn't nearly so weak. He didn't smile; there was no smug gloating; he was livid, and if not for the cage he probably would've throttled me awake.

But with the dreams of Black Otter's murder still fresh in my head, I refused to melt under his fury. "How could you kill your own son? Does no one matter to you?"

"Kings must make difficult decisions, for the good of their people and god...." Anguish choked the anger in his voice. "I should have kept you locked up in the prison yard instead of showing you compassion you don't deserve. Whatever you did to him—" He shuddered, then looked down at his palms. Blood dripped between his fingers where he'd balled his fists too tight. He stared at it a moment before barking at the guards, "Get her ready to take out." The loathing in his glare intensified as he told me, "Someday you will pay for this. What I did to your father will look like a mercy compared to what Amoxtli will do to you when he hears you forced me to kill his brother." He stormed away as the guards dragged me wet and shivering from the cage.

◻

Troops spread out over Culhuacan's eastern plain like swarming ants, blackening the ground as far as I could see. Ihuitimal's infantry stood between them and the walls, all armed with spears or slings. Archers crowded the walkways atop the walls, their bows pulled tight and ready as Ihuitimal and I set out from the gates.

We walked through the ranks down a gap. A pack of well-armored soldiers formed a circle around us, and the lead guard held up a long wooden pole with a feathered banner attached, displaying the city's royal crest.

A group of soldiers split off from the front of the opposing line, the lead man carrying a standard as well; a white feathered serpent with slender green feathers trailing around its neck. The serpentine flag flapped in the cool breeze from the lake behind us.

As we continued out onto the field to meet them, my anxiety soared, but so did my hope. Any moment now, the nightmare of these last two years would finally end and I could hold Little Reed again.

Both groups stopped about a hundred paces apart, but I saw familiar faces now. Mazatzin stood next to Citlallotoc at the front, both of their faces painted white with vertical green stripes running from their hairlines, over their eyes and down to their jawbones. Everyone wore cotton armor under their feathered xicolli shirts. But still no sign of Little Reed in the serried ranks.

Ihuitimal grabbed my arm with his stony grip and pulled me forward. Our group opened up to let us by, and two soldiers broke off to follow us. We stopped a few paces away when the other group parted as well.

Little Reed stepped out, wearing no face paint but a tall crown of white heron feathers and a matching cloak. The xicolli over his cotton armor bore the feathered serpent emblem, done in shimmering jewels. Hardness resided in his eyes. His hair had gone still whiter, so the dark strands were mere accents now.

A young man wearing only a loincloth walked next to him, and I was struck by how much he looked like Ihuitimal; Amoxtli obviously was the king's natural son. They stopped a few paces beyond their group as well.

"I've come here on your terms," Little Reed called across the gap between us. "I'm returning your son and disavowing any claim to Culhuacan's throne, so now return my sister to me, as unharmed as your son is."

Ihuitimal still frowned, but he said nothing, just shoved me in the back to get me moving. I glared back at him before heading off alone towards Little Reed.

Little Reed nodded and Amoxtli started walking as well, towards me. Little Reed kept his gaze focused on me though. I picked up the pace, eventually passing Amoxtli without a word, then I broke into a limping run for the remaining distance, tears blurring everything.

By the time I flung myself into Little Reed's outspread arms, the reality finally hit with painful force: he truly was alive. I sobbed as I crushed him in my arms. He whispered to me, but in my incoherent joy, I didn't understand any of it. It was enough to have his arms around me and feel his pulse thudding against my nose as I buried my face in his neck. *I will never let you go again,* I thought, squeezing him tighter. "I'm sorry, Little Reed," I wept. "You were so close to getting the throne back if not for me—"

231

"You mean more to me than any throne, Papalotl," he whispered. "So long as I have you, everything will be just fine." I smiled at him through tears when he took my face between his hands and leaned in to kiss me.

But shouting from the other side of the field broke the moment. I turned to see Amoxtli running back to us. Ihuitimal still stood where I'd left him, a panicked, bewildered expression on his face.

Amoxtli fell to his knees before Little Reed. "My Lord, I beg you, accept me into your ranks!" he panted. "I have seen the goodness of Quetzalcoatl and I cannot risk going back into the cradle of his enemy. Please do not turn me over to the mercies of such a dark god!" He groped at Little Reed's legs with pleading hands. "You are the rightful king of Culhuacan!"

Little Reed opened his mouth to answer, but Ihuitimal screamed, "You son of a dog! You poisoned my son! You turned him against me! Just like that whore of a sister of yours turned Black Otter against me!" He ran towards us like a charging bear, but his guards cut him off, trying to hold him back. He tussled with them, cursing, and clawing at the atl-atl baton hanging at one of the soldier's belts.

Little Reed's men started yelling too, and everything turned into chaos. "Close in around your king! Now!" Citlallotoc shouted. "Ready your weapons!"

A burning sting hit my chest as the soldiers shuffled me backwards, as if I'd taken an elbow to the sternum, but the pain grew hotter and sharper, radiating deep through my chest as I breathed. I tried to reach for it, but everyone pushed and shouted. Then I couldn't breathe at all. I gasped for air, but it was like inhaling water. My heart pounded, a strange numbness replacing the pain. Dizziness swooped in on me, and I fell backwards against Little Reed. My hand finally reached my chest; a stiff shaft of wood stuck out. I stared dumbly at the red and blue feather fletching for a breath before recognizing it.

An arrow.

In my growing numbness and confusion, I wrapped my hand around it and pulled. I doubted my muscles had the strength left, but it finally came free, and blood gushed out of the open wound, pulsing in time to my frantic heartbeat. The world fell silent even as the men shouted and the jostling continued. All I heard was my own heart, slowing and faltering with each beat until it stopped altogether.

A startling calm spread over me. The sky turned pink and the clouds melted into orange, like in the Divine Dream. I felt no pain, no cold, no heat, just lightness. I watched the clouds laze by. I'd never felt so peaceful. Why had I fought so hard to remain in that terrible world of pain and misery?

But then I saw Little Reed looking down at me, and his anguished expression shattered my contentment. *Go back and comfort him, tell him he needn't worry about you.* I tried to move my lips, but they refused.

Suddenly I stood at a distance, watching him weep over my body while Citlallotoc and Mazatzin crouched over him, shields raised to protect him from the storm of arrows raining from the city walls. His troops surged forward and the enemy readied their weapons. Ihuitimal's men did the same, those closest holding their shields up to protect their king from enemy arrows and spears. I saw the atl-atl baton lying on the ground, the arrow missing from the slot. Ihuitimal had made good on his promise of vengeance.

I looked down to see the Black Dog sat next to me. *Xolotl?* My voice came disembodied, as if it whispered on the wind.

I am the guide for the dead, he confirmed. While I flinched at soldiers rushing past, he remained steady. *I help them earn their eternal rest on the road to Mictlan.*

I touched my cheek, remembering the strange tingling when I'd woken. It was no dream after all. *You marked me, like you did those atop the temple that day in Teotihuacan?*

I came while you slept. Xolotl reached out and licked a passing man's ankle. A few steps later, the man took a spear to his leg and two men pulled him off behind Culhuacan's line. *War is hard work, requiring many nahuals. Most times I enjoy my job, until days like today. Depending on the outcome, I may be marking people well into the night.*

You don't know who will win?

The future is rarely so clear.

But you chose me for death. How can't you know?

He tilted his head quizzically. *I do not choose; Heaven chooses, based on sacrifices, and I obey. Nothing more, nothing less.*

So then you decide how people will die? A strange, disembodied hostility rose around me like a foul mist. *You're the one who decided that Nimilitzli would be hacked up by an evil, god-hated man wanting revenge on me?*

Xolotl laughed like a coyote. *You assign me importance I do not have. You gave the blood and called on Heaven's mercy when you knew not what to do, and Omeyocan showed you compassion. It found someone willing to pay the tax for you, but now you begrudge it?*

Willing? No one would choose to die like she did.

You would not give your life for someone you love? Xolotl asked, startled. *She saw you struggling with your fear, so when Destiny came to her she embraced it, for you and the Feathered Serpent. Whatever another marked man did to her shell afterwards shouldn't overshadow the sacrifice she made for you.*

She was already dead when Ahexotl...?

She is in the Heaven of the Feathered Serpent, who takes excellent care of his sacrifices.

I felt as if he'd rolled a giant rock off my shoulders. What I wouldn't give to see Nimilitzli one last time, to hug and thank her for all she'd given for me. I stared back at my own dead body barely visible behind the line of shields around Little Reed. *What's to become of me?*

You'll walk the road the same as last time, but since you have no heart to pay to Lord Death for your rest, you must sit and wait, until the day when Smoking Mirror finally earns his own heaven.

What do you mean I don't have a heart to pay with? And what does Smoking Mirror have to do with anything?

Your heart fed the Smoking Mirror in sacrifice, Xolotl answered matter-of-factly.

Suddenly, a deep rumbling shattered the preternatural silence and I took a step back. If I could hear it in death, it must not be good. *What is that?*

As if in answer, thunder crashed even louder and Xolotl looked up, ears perked. He sniffed the wind then turned to me, his black eyes gleaming. *Smoking Mirror always underestimates his opponents' strengths. He doesn't understand the true power of sacrifice.*

What's going on?

See for yourself. He tilted his head towards Little Reed.

I looked to see Little Reed clutching me in his arms while my body jolted like I'd just been pulled from the lake after almost drowning.

Xolotl set his front paws on my shoulders. *I haven't much time, and I'm again bound by deals I helped craft, but listen closely and remember: you are the fire in women who won't bow to the whims of men or gods. Quetzalcoatl gave humanity life, but you give them reason to want that gift.*

What do you mean? I asked, but immediately had to cover my ears against the painful roar of battle. The sky flashed, blinding me.

Feeling fingers stroking my hair, I opened my eyes to see Little Reed gazing down at me. My heart beat hard and fast in my chest, and to my amazement, when I gasped, air not blood filled my lungs. "Omeyocan help me, I thought you were gone for good," he wept, resting his head against mine.

My tongue was heavy as stone and my muscles felt as if they were finally getting blood again after being deprived, but I fought past the painful stinging to give him a one-armed hug. "How am I...what happened?" I finally said, my words slurred.

A piercing roar broke over the battlefield and the group of soldiers that had been sheltering Ihuitimal suddenly flew apart, bodies tossed aside as if they were little more than dead leaves in the wind. Smoke roiled up from the ground, followed by the form of a monstrous jaguar, blackness curling off it like vapor on the lake on a cold morning. Hot coals burned for its eyes. When it spotted Little Reed and me, it bared long obsidian-bladed fangs and screamed, spitting soot and singeing-hot air.

"Great Feathered Serpent!" Citlallotoc grabbed Little Reed under the arms, hauling him to his feet while Mazatzin scooped me into his arms. As he got Little Reed's arm around his shoulder, he yelled, "Behind you, Mazatzin!"

The giant smoke jaguar tore into the nearby crowd, scattering men in a pummeling fan of bodies, knocking Mazatzin off his feet. I hit the ground, lighting up my already painful muscles even more, but I only managed an extended gasp. "Get the king back behind the lines!" Mazatzin shouted.

I rolled onto my stomach and searched desperately for Little Reed. He lay dazed while Citlallotoc stood between him and the jaguar, sword drawn. And to my horror, Xolotl was dragging his tongue up the side of his cheek. Little Reed saw him but showed no surprise, only resignation.

"No!" I cried, but the terrible din of battle swallowed it. The jaguar raked up Citlallotoc and Little Reed, as well as ten other men and threw them through the air. The front ranks closed in around Little Reed, sheltering him as the beast came again, clawing through the scrum and scattering the soldiers like sparrows. They launched spears and arrows but everything passed through the smoke as if the beast didn't exist.

Only Quetzalcoatl can save Little Reed. And this time I wouldn't hesitate to do what I must.

I pulled a dagger off one of the dead men near me and cut my hand. I clasped the knife with both hands, pointing it at my heaving chest.

"Lord Quetzalcoatl,
I call on you now!
Save your son,
And I give you my life,
Taken in your name,
By my own hand!"

But Xolotl snapped the blade from my hands and tossed it aside. "What in Mictlan are you doing?" I demanded. "I'm trying to call on Quetzalcoatl to save Topiltzin."

A noble thought, but Heaven has already accepted your life on behalf of another god, so that sacrifice won't bring forth the Feathered Serpent.

"What could possibly be more powerful than giving one's own life?"

Take counsel with your own heart to find your answer. Xolotl trotted off into the melee, marking soldiers as he went.

My heart, I thought. *I can't literally give it anymore, but emotionally....* I raised my hands again.

"Lord Quetzalcoatl,
I promise to love none but you.
Turn my heart to stone for all others—"

But Xolotl still shook his head. Still not good enough? But why?

Because the high priestess makes the hardest sacrifice of all, Nimilitzli's voice spoke to me for memory. *We devote ourselves to the god alone in spite of what our hearts feel.*

Of course! It wasn't a true sacrifice if I didn't feel the loss, didn't suffer on the god's behalf, and didn't keep the path in spite of it.

I raised my hands and closed my eyes, this time confident.

"Lord Quetzalcoatl,
I will follow your path,
I will see your good works to fruition,
And I will give my body and soul to none but you,
For the remainder of my mortal days.
Give me the strength to save your son,
Oh Great Lord!"

Tingles filled my flesh and I opened my eyes to see glowing white feathers sprouting from my skin. My body elongated and coiled like a snake until the agony melted away and I stood taller than the city walls.

Papalotl, my love! the god's familiar voice whispered, making me ruffle my new feathers with a shiver of joy.

Everyone stopped to stare in awe up at me. The jaguar bared his fangs, bringing a deep rumble. Behind him lay Little Reed, unconscious and bleeding from a deep gash across his chest. *He's not breathing,* I thought, panic welling up. *Was I too late?*

He still lives, Quetzalcoatl whispered. *Hope is not lost.*

So you've finally come to face me, have you, Brother! the jaguar said. *And you've brought your most powerful follower. Let's see how strong she really is.* He sprang, obsidian claws outspread, smoke streaming off his body.

I expected Quetzalcoatl to take control but the jaguar crashed into me, snapping at my exposed throat. I thrashed aside, feathers and flesh singeing as I escaped. *You asked for the power to save Topiltzin,* Quetzalcoatl whispered. *I cannot give more than what was asked for.*

Solidifying my resolve, I struck back at the jaguar with my fangs.

But he leaped away and laughed. *Faith proves itself slow and dumb when pitted against fear. I look forward to eating both of your hearts!*

Trust yourself, Papalotl, Quetzalcoatl continued. *He underestimates you. Smoking Mirror's pride would have him abandon his host rather than risk fair defeat.*

I ducked and slithered away as Smoking Mirror sprang again. He crashed into the city wall, leaving a gaping hole, and as he struggled to free himself of the rubble, I sank my fangs into his shoulder and threw him over my head. His enormous body dug a crater where it hit the ground, knocking people off their feet.

He scrambled to his feet again, lips curled back, and this time I met him halfway, slamming into him with all my strength. He ripped into me as I wrapped my coils around him, each swipe opening a gush of gold dust and pain. I squeezed tighter, panicked when he grabbed my throat, but he had neither breath nor bones for me to crush. *Surely this isn't how it ends!*

Keep faith, Papalotl, Quetzalcoatl whispered. *You have more power than you can imagine.*

I suddenly felt re-energized, as if untapped magic now opened to me. *Puff your neck feathers,* the authoritative voice told me, so I did.

Smoking Mirror howled and wrenched free of my coils, turning up a flurry of white feathers in his wake. I slunk away, feeling gutted, but my wounds healed fast, feathers re-growing. He pawed at the long emerald feathers sticking out of his jowls and neck like daggers. Maguey thorns formed the tips of the quills. When Smoking Mirror lunged again, the voice told me to push magic into the ground beneath me, and this time thousands of lime-white roots shot from the dirt and lashed around Smoking Mirror's body, binding him.

Smoking Mirror howled and slashed the ground with his claws as the roots dragged him under the dirt, hind legs first. *My priest's faith can withhold whatever you can hurl at him! When he gives me his heart, you will pay for your trickery, little girl!*

"What would you know about faith, Smoking Mirror?" I panted. "You'll send your most faithful follower to sit on the banks of the Black Lake in Mictlan, never knowing rest nor peace, spending eternity wishing he'd known that before devoting his last breath to you."

Smoking Mirror shuddered, his smoke wavering. *Give it to me now, priest!* he shrieked. *Don't be a fool!*

Behind the smoldering coals, Ihuitimal's own eyes—afraid and unsure—showed, awakening unexpected pity in me. "Resist him, Uncle! It's not too late. Let go of everything that's bound you as his prisoner all these years!"

The smoke jaguar howled then slowly dissipated, leaving my uncle screaming as the roots pulled him further under. *Stop!* I thought, and they obeyed. As I knelt next to him, my human body returned, but magic still pulsed inside me. "Let me help you, Uncle."

Ihuitimal stared at me with wide, frightened eyes. "Why is it only now, with Death's dank breath on my neck, that I finally see the truth?" He shook his head. "My son had no chance against you; no man does."

His words shook me. "What do you mean?"

But he just stared at me, his breath completely gone.

CHAPTER THIRTY-SIX

Citlallotoc had Ihuitimal's body dug up, to show at the gate as proof that the king had fallen. He wanted to leave him for the buzzards to eat, but I refused. "He was family, so he'll get proper burial rites and we'll make sacrifices to honor his passing," I told him as we watched the surgeons gathered around Little Reed's sickbed in the great hall. "We will honor Lord Black Otter too." When Citlallotoc cast me a puzzled look, I said, "He is in the Land of the Drowned."

Hearing a strangled cry, I turned to see Jade Flower standing paralyzed in the doorway beyond the sea of soldiers. When our gazes locked, she fled from sight.

"Who's that?" Citlallotoc asked.

"My sister, Jade Flower." I sighed, feeling horrible. "I must go and talk to her, but let me know immediately when Topiltzin wakes up."

Women poked their heads out of their doorways, whispering as I went down the hall to Jade Flower's quarters. Over the quieter sobbing came my sister's wails, like a dying heron, and when Lady Corn Flower saw me, she ventured out of her room like a frightened mouse. "What's going on?"

"I need you to gather Anacoana and Papantzin and take them to the women's hall," I said. "We must have a meeting."

"What about Jade Flower?"

"She probably won't come, so I'm going to go and talk to her."

I continued past the few doorways, down to my sister's quarters, stopping in front of the curtain. *She's going to blame you, but you owe the truth to her.* I took a steadying breath, then tugged the curtain, jingling the bells.

"Go away!"

"Please, I need to talk to you," I said.

"I don't want to talk to you!"

"Please, Jade Flower." She said nothing this time, so I went inside.

She lay crumpled on her bed, sobbing. The sight made me cringe; that was me two years ago. Blinking back tears, I said, "I'm sorry you found out like that, Jade Flower. I wanted to tell you myself."

She turned to me, her face lit with anger. "So you could rub it in my face?"

The accusation stung but I kept my composure. "Of course not. The king betrayed him, Jade Flower. He sent assassins to kill him."

"That makes no sense. Ihuitimal loved Black Otter; he'd never do that!" Jade Flower sobbed harder into her hands.

Seeing her pain made the old wounds reopen. Sniffing back tears, I sat and hugged her. "I'm truly sorry, Sister."

But she shoved me away and stumbled to her feet. "You ruined everything! We were happy before you came back! He even used to love me!"

"He still loved you, Jade Flower. I understand how you feel right now—"

"You know nothing! You haven't shed a single tear for Black Otter, so how dare you tell me you understand?" She made to leave but then whipped back and cried, "Ihuitimal should have killed you the moment you arrived!"

I flew to my feet, shaking with fury. "I cared about Black Otter too, and don't tell me that I don't understand how it feels to lose someone so dear, how it hurts so deep you can't breathe, how you struggle to drag yourself out of bed every day to face a future that doesn't include them anymore." Hot tears wound down my face.

Jade Flower stared at me, stunned, then ran into her garden. I rushed from the room too, back to the great hall, desperately needing to see Little Reed again with my own eyes, to verify that this day wasn't a dream.

The surgeons still gathered around his bed when I clutched his hand in mine. *I need to tell you how much I missed you and still love you,* I thought, but he was asleep, drugged with tochletepon for his stitches.

"Quetzalpetlatl!" Mazatzin hugged me, holding on tight and laughing. "Isn't today a miracle? Topiltzin has risen from the ashes and we're all alive to see the dawning of the new era."

I gave him a fierce hug. "I'm so glad to see you again too, Mazatzin. I was really worried for you."

"I'm fine." He glanced at Little Reed as he said, "The surgeons think he'll be fine too. He just needs to rest and heal." His expression then turned anguished. "I'm sorry,

Quetzalpetlatl. If I'd known Red Flint lied about Topiltzin—"

"There's nothing to forgive."

He nodded, looking relieved. He cleared his throat. "We should start making plans for cleaning up the road outside Culhuacan. You wouldn't believe all the bodies out there; some must have been lying out there for years."

I nodded. "The god will want them honored for giving their lives to remain faithful to him. We'll need priests and priestesses to help out with that, so if you go to the servant quarters, you'll find some of them there, including Malinalli."

"You hid them right in the belly of the demon?"

"Right in plain sight. Go and see about freeing them. I'm sure they're anxious to be rid of their slave collars."

Mazatzin hurried to find the others, and though I wanted to stay at Little Reed's side, I had to keep my appointment with Lady Corn Flower, Papantzin and Anacoana.

□

The meeting remained thankfully civil. Lady Corn Flower and Lady Papantzin wept while Anacoana sat in stunned silence for a while before asking, "Will your brother take us as concubines now?"

"And what about our children?" Papantzin asked.

"Topiltzin's reign is a bright new beginning for everyone, men and women alike, so you needn't worry. Tell me where you wish to be, and I'll see it done."

Lady Corn Flower and Papantzin both looked skeptical, but Anacoana piped up, "Can I go home to Xico, to live with my sisters again?"

I smiled. "Absolutely. What about the rest of you?"

"I want to take my daughter back to Chimalhuacan," Lady Corn Flower said, trying for hopeful. "My mother misses her grandchild."

"And I'd like to go home too," Papantzin added. Her smile soon faded, though. "What about Jade Flower? She has no family to go home to...and she has a son."

"Topiltzin isn't going kill all the male children, like Ihuitimal did when he took Culhuacan from my father. And as for Jade Flower having no family, that's not true. She's my sister and Culhuacan is her home, and she and her children are welcome to stay. Topiltzin and I are her family."

"You really mean that?" Jade Flower suddenly asked behind me. When I nodded, she rushed to hug me. "I'm so sorry for all those awful things I said, Sister," she whispered. "Can you ever forgive me?"

My tears came again. "Can you ever forgive *me*, for causing you such grief and heartache?"

She hugged me tighter.

□

Jade Flower didn't stay any longer than the others, though. When Papantzin's father came to bring her home, Jade Flower went with them. "Too many ghosts here. I can hardly sleep, and Papantzin will need help with her new bundle when it arrives."

I understood. I too felt the old conflicts haunting the hallways, and I hated visiting the royal quarters but did so to care for Little Reed. Workers had whitewashed the mural of the Smoking Mirror with five layers of paint, but still the god's shadow showed through, persistently lingering.

238

The surgeons had said Little Reed would be fine that first day, but the next day his wounds started festering and medicine did nothing—unsurprising, given they'd been inflicted by a god. But whispers of residual magic still tingled inside me days after the battle, and when I set my hands on his forehead or shoulders, it eased his discomfort and began, slowly, to heal him.

But he wasn't the only one healing. The scars on both my hands and my ankle were gone. I could run again for the first time in two years, and the puckered skin where I'd cut my fingers off had become smooth, as though I'd been born without them. But most notable of all, the itching was gone. Maybe that meant I'd never again need its warning?

I'd expected Amoxtli—having once been a contender for the throne—to follow Jade Flower's example but he insisted on staying. I wanted nothing to do with him though, not even when he visited the temple, asking how one became a priest and offering to help clean up twenty years' worth of blasphemous mess his father had left in Quetzalcoatl's old temple. I let Jade Flower give him the unfortunate news about Black Otter since I knew nothing about Amoxtli and I didn't trust him to not share more than his father's looks.

Little Reed didn't mind his presence though, and even allowed him into his quarters while he was recovering. I had no idea what they talked about, for I couldn't bear being around someone who reminded me of Ihuitimal.

I needed something to help heal that hole in my heart that felt as if it had been raw all my life, so with the bone flowers in my garden now in splendid bloom, I cut off a dozen stalks and inserted them into the hollow reed slots along the back of my mother's old throne, just as the servants used to do when I was a little girl. I could almost see my mother sitting there, regal and proud, but it wasn't Father who sat next to her; it was Little Reed, wearing a crown of emerald quetzal feathers and the robes of the high priest of Quetzalcoatl. And I realized it wasn't really my mother sitting on the bone flower throne next him; it was me.

◻

Little Reed spent most of his first week as king sleeping while Citlallotoc and I oversaw pressing city matters, but by the second week he finally left his bed for short stints, with the help of a wooden staff. As his strength grew, I took him on walks through the palace, showing him where everything was; and once the weather turned nice, I took him out into the gardens and the menagerie.

"Can I ask you something?" I asked as we walked by the tapir cage.

"You may ask me anything you wish, Papalotl," he said with a smile.

"What happened the day of the ballgame? Red Flint said he had you murdered."

"You didn't get any of my letters?"

"Ihuitimal intercepted them."

The look on his face puzzled me—simultaneously frustrated and relieved, but he went on before I could say anything. "Well, I went to find Ahexotl to arrest him, but some of Red Flint's men jumped me and beat me unconscious. I came to in the limestone quarry when they started stabbing me."

I cringed. The thought of what that must have been like...he had no physical scars, but I wondered how often he woke in the night, panicked and thinking he was dying. "I'm so sorry, Little Reed. I never should have said anything to Red Flint," I whispered, my voice cracking with guilt and shame.

He patted my hand. "It's all right. I made it through alive, thanks to Citlallotoc. He dispatched two handfuls of men. I owe him everything."

"How did he find you?"

"He left the match to use the public bathhouse and saw Red Flint's men dragging someone through the city, so he followed them. He not only killed my attackers, but he took me half-dead upon his shoulders and ran from the place, tending to my wounds when we were far enough away to stop. After that he carried me all night to Xochimilco to get me to a surgeon. Red Flint's men continued pursuing us, so we fled again, to Tultepec. The king took me in and offered protection."

"Xochicalco's army could have easily crushed his city trying to get to you," I noted.

Little Reed nodded. "Luckily Ihuitimal started ramping up his attacks in the north, keeping the army distracted and giving me time to heal. And from what I heard, Red Flint was falling apart, so confidence in his leadership was diminishing. That allowed me to come out and negotiate with his generals. I still had a good many allies in the army, so when word of Xochicalco's destruction reached us and Mazatzin abdicated his throne, the army didn't hesitate to declare loyalty to me."

"I suppose it shouldn't surprise me that Mazatzin abdicated his throne. He didn't seem very comfortable in the role the last time I saw him in Xochicalco."

"I didn't ask him to; I didn't want it, but everyone agreed that if we were to move on Culhuacan, the army needed a leader with more military experience. This is probably all for the best, really." Little Reed sat on a bench to catch his breath. "With the drought south of the valley, Xochicalco would have been abandoned eventually anyway."

I sat too. "So we truly never can go home again?"

"You don't like it here?"

I hesitated before answering. "We've been through so much to get Culhuacan back, but...it doesn't feel like home, and I doubt it ever will."

Little Reed nodded. "Father wants us to build that new city and I plan to get started before too long. Amoxtli tells me that he knows where his father buried Mixcoatl's bones, so once he shows us, we can get started building our new city. I just have a few things that need working out first...." He gazed around a moment then took my hand between his. "Some things I've been putting off far too long." His voice shook and he laughed. "I'm nervous as a boy facing his first battle!"

I gave him an encouraging smile.

He sobered, then continued, "I love you deeply, Papalotl; you're the tiny butterflies tickling my heart and you would make me the happiest being in all the Heavens if you would be my wife, the queen at my side, my best friend and partner, the one whose smile makes every day of my life worth living, forever and always. Please marry me."

Leftover magic danced joyfully inside me. Ten years I'd waited for this, and I desperately wanted to tell him, absolutely, without a doubt, *yes*.

I was unprepared for the crushing feeling as I realized, *But you can't*. He looked so eager with that smile I dearly loved, but if not for that sacrifice my heart now cursed, I wouldn't have gotten to ever see it again. *It's only a true sacrifice if you suffer for it*, I thought, close to tears.

But I didn't want him feeling like I did right now. I couldn't even hold his gaze, afraid he'd see the answer in my eyes, so I looked away, scrambling for the kindest way to disappoint him.

My gaze found the pair of lake otters frolicking in the pen behind him. It brought back the dream about Black Otter, of the creatures dragging him under the dark water until he became one of them, screeching, "Mine! Mine! Mine!" *The end I brought him to, just as I pushed Red Flint over the edge. And eventually Little Reed will end up just like them,*

I thought, and before I knew it, tears streamed down my cheeks. Why would I even think that?

Little Reed looked over his shoulder too, and the smile fell from his face. His shoulders sagged as he turned back to me. "Please forgive my thoughtlessness. He's only been gone a few weeks, surely not enough time to properly mourn the loss of a loved one."

I blinked, startled. "Oh, Little Reed—"

"No, it's all right." He cleared his throat then said, "You thought I was dead, so of course your heart moved on. I understand completely. If I'd truly been dead, I wouldn't want you holding onto my memory forever and never finding happiness. I love you too much to wish that upon you. I just...I didn't think, and I'm sorry. Please forgive me."

It's you I cry for, Little Reed, I wanted to say, but stopped myself again. Perhaps it was better if he thought this, so I didn't have to reject him. Maybe then he could move on sooner. "I'm not angry, Little Reed," I said.

"Thank you." He tried to smile.

I hugged him. "No, thank *you*."

"Can I beg you for one thing though?" he asked when I let him go. "Will you still co-rule with me? The god never intended me to do this on my own, and I need your help building the best possible future for our people."

I gave him a smile, and it felt like my first genuine one in years. "I can definitely do that."

THE BONE FLOWER TRILOGY

T. L. MORGANFIELD

THE BONE FLOWER QUEEN

Part One
The Year Seven Rabbit

CHAPTER ONE

 Sickness and fear knotted my stomach as I fumbled with the wash basin in my bath yard, trying to scrub away the chills with some water to my face. I didn't need to look into the obsidian mirror hanging in front of me to know I looked as if I hadn't slept at all last night; I hadn't slept well since moving into my new quarters a month ago—so I could be close to Little Reed while he recovered from his battle wounds—but now I questioned the wisdom of taking over my dead husband's private quarters. When I did sleep, I was plagued with dreams of death, and in my waking time, I felt as if I was being watched.

I flinched when someone rang the bells on my door curtain. "Who is it?" I yelled, so they could hear me from out in the yard.

"It's me, My Lady," my friend Malinalli's voice answered. I called her inside and she soon appeared at the doorway to my bath yard. She cocked her head when she saw me. "Did you just get up?"

"Am I late again?" I splashed some more water on my face then lathered up with some copal soap.

"The king asked me to fetch you." She handed me a scrap of linen to dry my face with once I rinsed. "Are you all right, Quetzalpetlatl?"

I waved her off. "It was a lot of work, handling Topiltzin's business while he was recovering, plus keeping up with my duties as high priestess—"

"I could have taken over your priestly duties while you cared for the king," Malinalli said. "I'll be doing that while you're gone anyway."

I chuckled. "And you will do a fantastic job, I know. But I'm the god's chosen high priestess—"

"That doesn't mean you can't ask for help when you need it." She picked up my brush and started working the tangles out of my long brown hair.

"You aren't my servant anymore, Malinalli," I protested. She might have been forced to act as my handmaiden while we'd been captives of my uncle, but that ordeal was thankfully over. And though I was Culhuacan's queen now, she was Quetzalcoatl's fire priestess, and having her play the part of my servant was demeaning.

But when I reached for the brush, she held it out of my reach. "No, I'm not, but that doesn't matter. My sisters and I used to brush each other's hair, and I've missed doing it."

I'd had many sisters but we'd never brushed each other's hair; that was servants' work, and while I'd brushed Little Reed's hair when he was young, I'd found it a tedious task. Even in school I'd had no female friends to share such bonding with, for most girls avoided me due to my status as the high priestess's ward.

But who was I to deny my best friend a little joy? So I let her continue.

"Besides, we'll get this done much quicker if you let me do it," she said, a smile in her voice. "All those noblewomen hairstyles are impossibly complicated, and a queen must have flair."

"Not this queen," I said with a laugh. "A simple braid right down the back will suffice."

Chuckling, Malinalli shook her head and started separating my hair for braiding. When I stifled a yawn, she said, "Maybe a sleep tonic would help keep you from waking in the middle of the night?"

Maybe, but will it stop the dreams? As a young girl, I'd suffered recurring nightmares of traveling the dangerous road into the underworld to face Lord Death, but now they happened two or three times a week; Lord Death always towering over me, the hollow eye sockets of his skull-face glowing like swamp gas, his grin pulling his thin, transparent skin painfully tight. "Welcome home, my spiny little princess," he hissed as a spider scurried out of the corner of his mouth to take refuge behind his necklace of extruded eyeballs. After dying and coming back to life, dreams of Lord Death seemed fitting.

But there were also the nightmares about Black Otter, my former husband; every night he was shot with arrows and fell into the lake, but instead of dying, he rose from the icy black depths, changed into a horrendous monster with glistening fangs and five hands—where this fifth one came from, I never could see—and he would latch onto me with his claws and drag me into the water with him, all the while shrieking, "Mine! Mine! Mine!"

"I should just move back into my old quarters," I said. "Then maybe I won't be constantly dreaming of Black Otter."

"Maybe you miss being married," Malinalli suggested.

My marriage to Black Otter had been one problem after another: having to care for and oversee his concubines, and making certain he shared his time and attention with everyone equally, something I failed miserably at. But contending with the jealousy and rivalry growing under my own roof had been the worst, and I didn't know how my mother survived so many years in such circumstances; I didn't understand how anybody could really expect us women to. Did I miss being married? "Not at all. I'm glad it's over and I can return to doing the god's important work."

She cast me a puzzled look in the mirror. "You don't miss Black Otter at all?"

That question wasn't so easily answered. Sometimes I woke in the middle of the night missing him when I found no one lying next to me, but how much of that was about Black Otter being dead rather than the cold truth that that side of my bed would always remain empty thanks to that sacrifice I made to save my brother's life? "Sometimes I do," I finally said, a hitch in my voice. "There was a time when we were good friends."

Malinalli finished my braids and pinned them up against the back of my head, then she reached out to give my hand a squeeze. "Let me cut some flowers to put in your hair and we can get on to breakfast."

"Let me pick. I want to see how the garden looks now that the servants have cleaned it up."

Every room in Culhuacan's palace had a private garden off the back, and no one had tended to Black Otter's garden after he died, nor had I bothered to ask for gardeners when I moved in. But yesterday I'd finally decided something needed to be done about the forest of gangly bushes and long grasses just off my bath yard patio.

The palace gardeners had done a wonderful job rejuvenating the foliage and flowers. Yellow marigolds, purple and white jaguar flowers, and bright orange sunflowers bloomed in the beds, shaded by a flowering dogwood. Bees buzzed among the honeysuckle bushes while blue-throated hummingbirds darted from flower to flower. There weren't any bone flowers—my favorite—and I made a mental note to ask that someone plant them for next year. I picked out a couple of newly-blossomed jaguar flowers and Malinalli cut their stems with her sacrificial blade.

Noticing a glimmer from the back corner of the garden, I leaned slightly forward for a better look as Malinalli carefully tucked the flower stems into the back of my hair. A small stone idol the size of my head sat against the back wall, and the grass was matted down in front of it, as if there had been a prayer mat there. Before the bushes had been trimmed, there would have been no clear view of it from my patio. "What is that?" I asked.

Once Malinalli inserted the last flower stalk, she followed me to the statue for a closer look. It was a small stone jaguar, sitting on its haunches with its mouth open in a grotesque grin. The glimmer that had caught my eye came from the sun reflecting off an obsidian mirror it clutched in its claws. A cold loathing welled up in my stomach.

"I think it's the Smoking Mirror," Malinalli replied. "It must have been Black Otter's."

Black Otter was going to be the Smoking Mirror's next high priest after his father—my uncle, my father's murderer, the usurper of my throne—died. He told me he had no desire for the position, but it was no secret that he gave his devotion to this demon god who sat at the core of all my life's pain; this god who despised my beloved Quetzalcoatl and tried to kill my brother, Little Reed. I'd pushed Little Reed to ban Smoking Mirror's worship here in Culhuacan, but he resisted; "We won't do the things our uncle did to Quetzalcoatl." This was something we'd never agree on.

"I'll take it out of here for you," Malinalli offered; but when she moved towards it, I caught her arm.

"Wait for me out in the hallway," I said, not taking my eyes off of the statue. "I'll be out in a moment."

After a hesitation, Malinalli left me alone.

I stared at my own reflection—so dark and grim—in the obsidian mirror as I knelt in front of the statue. The jaguar grinned, laughing at me, just as Smoking Mirror had when we faced off on the battlefield: *faith proves itself slow and dumb when pitted against fear!* it seemed to say. Smoking Mirror and my uncle had smashed my dreams, starting with my father's murder and ending with my having to sacrifice the future I so desperately wanted with Little Reed in order to save him.

Overcome with rage, I took hold of the idol with both hands and yanked on it. It was heavier than I expected, so it didn't move at first, but with a little more might, I wrenched it from its spot. Without a word, I heaved it at the wall, shattering the mirror all over the ground. The statue itself remained intact, and I had to throw it against the wall a few more times before it finally broke in half.

Breathing heavily, my stomach roiling with bile, I squeezed my eyes against the stinging threat of tears. "Someday Quetzalcoatl will make you pay for what you've done, you vile excuse for a god," I muttered. "And I hope I'm there to see it."

The war council was gathered in the great hall, lounging on feathered mats in a circle around the breakfast platters, waiting for me. The smell of fried eggs, chilis, and hot tlaxcallis set my mouth watering. When both my father and then my uncle had been kings, no one took the morning meal in the great hall; Little Reed and I adopted this practice once we took the throne, for meals were times of bonding with friends and family, and we endeavored to treat our council members as if they were such.

Two months into our reign, we'd only just started exerting our personal touch over the royal palace. In my father's day, feathered banners showing the city crest decorated the walls of the great hall; in my uncle's day, it was obsidian mirrors, in honor of the Smoking Mirror, but they were now gone, and artists worked daily on murals of Quetzalcoatl the Feathered Serpent on every wall in the public parts of the palace. The one in the great hall was only partially finished, but it resembled the friezes from Quetzalcoatl's temple in Xochicalco, with paintings of noblemen and calendar dates, and giant, slithering feathered serpents; "A reminder of the home we lost," Little Reed told me, and I couldn't wait to see it finished.

When Citlallotoc saw me and Malinalli, he nudged Little Reed on the shoulder. My earlier melancholy fled with a flush of desire when Little Reed rose to greet me, the smile I dearly loved on his face. Thanks to his divine parentage, he looked closer to forty summers old rather than twenty; white streaked his dark hair and the corners of his eyes crinkled when he smiled, but he'd regained a healthy glow now that he had fully recovered from his battle wounds.

The rest of the council rose as well but I hardly noticed anything but Little Reed as he took my hand in his. "Is everything all right?"

I breathed deep to swallow back the desire; I'd often let it guide me with Black Otter, but I couldn't do the same with Little Reed, no matter how much it howled and protested—and no matter how much my heart wanted him. *You made that sacrifice to save him and you must keep the path no matter what your heart and body feels,* I reminded myself for the thousandth time; I'd turned it into a mantra to repeat in my head every time I started losing control. The desire growled but soon retreated, letting me breathe again. "I'm fine. Just overslept."

He chuckled, ever oblivious to my internal struggles. Someday I'd tell him the truth of what I'd given up to save him, but not today. "I know you keep saying you don't want a handmaiden, but it wouldn't hurt to have someone come by each morning to make certain you rise in timely fashion. You've been working so hard, and there's no shame in asking for help."

"I know," I assured him. "But it's really not necessary. Now that you're well again, I won't have nearly as many duties keeping me up late."

In fact, one of those "late-night duties" was standing with the other men, looking annoyingly smug. For days, Flame Tongue, the king of our new ally, Xico, had been aggressively seeking to join his house with my brother's through a marriage to his youngest daughter Anacoana. A man's mother customarily listened to such requests from the father or suitors, but with our mother long dead that duty fell to me, as Little Reed's closest female relative.

And the temerity of Flame Tongue's request had struck me speechless. Anacoana was a fine young woman—bright and a highly-talented weaver—but she'd been one of my former husband's concubines. Granted, Black Otter hadn't exercised his "husbandly rights" with her—for she hadn't yet bled a full year—but to even suggest that the King of Culhuacan should take his enemy's former concubine as his legitimate wife was insulting.

Flame Tongue had come back last night promising to guarantee Anacoana's virginity and it took every shred of restraint to not have the guards throw him from my palace. Little Reed made it clear to me years earlier that he wouldn't abide arranged marriage for political reasons, and perhaps I should have dismissed the whole stupid ordeal with that reason from the beginning, but I'd worried about how his untraditional approach to traditional practices would be received by his allies, new and old alike.

Seeing Flame Tongue here left me grumpy again—no doubt he'd keep beating his drum—but Little Reed's tender grip on my hand distracted me as he escorted me to our set of reed-woven icpalli thrones. The servants decorated the top of mine with clusters of the sweet-smelling bone flowers, a practice I'd adopted from my mother. The aroma created a zone of calm that made me feel regal when I sat on my throne. Little Reed's was covered with emerald green quetzal feathers, the same ones that his father Quetzalcoatl— the Feathered Serpent—took his name from. Once seated, he motioned the servants to dish up the food.

Traditionally the royal family was served first at any meal or feast, but in our house, the poorest ate first. The servants filled the plate of the war council's single Chichimec member—a man named Ixtlilxochitl, who wore a plethora of blue and red tattoos. Little Reed had welcomed him warmly, but the rest of us showed less enthusiasm for his presence, and so he watched us with the unease of a cornered jaguar, not daring to take the first bite. The servants moved quickly around the circle, filling dishes with fried quail eggs, roasted duck stewed with spicy tomatoes, and flatbread tlaxcallis in at least a dozen different thicknesses and colors.

Our new war chief Blood Wolf shared none of Ixtlilxochitl's hesitation; he immediately dug into his eggs with his knife and chased them down with a swig of chocolate. Long ago, when my mother and I had fled Culhuacan to escape my murderous uncle, he'd personally seen us to safety in Xochicalco. He'd been my other uncle Nochuatl's best friend, and he'd been quite young and fresh-faced back then. The years in between had left him grizzled and serious. His brother Matlacxochitl—whom I'd never met before a few weeks ago—was younger by a few years and looked to have been spared the harsh military life his brother had endured. A handful of high priests and priestesses from the various orders were here as well, but no one from the cult of the Smoking Mirror, thank goodness.

My diplomatic smile slipped ever so slightly when my gaze fell upon my cousin Amoxtli. The sight of him raised my pulse most unpleasantly; he had Ihuitimal's sharp, pointed jaw and hooked nose, reminding me of a bird of prey. And though he lacked the sharpened teeth and ghastly scar on his cheek, he looked every bit as I imagined his father had looked at that age, before life turned him into a murderer. Amoxtli wasn't a member of our war council, and while he'd expressed interest in joining the priesthood of Quetzalcoatl, he still had years of training ahead before he could take the trials to become one of the god's priests. I doubted he could overcome all the years of indoctrination into Smoking Mirror's cult that his father had forced upon him. If I had my way, I'd exile him from Culhuacan before he could turn against us, as my uncle had turned on my father.

But Little Reed had stood firm against that. "We need him. He's promised to show us where he buried your father's bones, so we can start building our new city." This was all true. But still I hoped that once Amoxtli served his purpose, I might convince Little Reed to leave him behind in Culhuacan when we moved to our new seat of power. Until then I'd asked Quetzalcoatl's fire priest Mazatzin to keep an eye on him—and he was doing exactly that from across the circle, so casually that only I noticed.

Once all the guests were served, the servants filled plates for both me and Little Reed.

I'd been very hungry on the way to the great hall, but now that I stared at the eggs wrapped in a hot, transparent tlaxcalli, my stomach rebelled. I started with a cup of frothy chocolate spiced with vanilla, hoping to settle it.

No one discussed city or priestly business, for we considered meals a community-building exercise rather than a political one, so it wasn't until after the servants cleared the dishes that Little Reed turned to Flame Tongue to say, "I must extend my apologies to you. My slow recovery kept us from spending much time together during your visit, but I trust that Lord Citlallotoc kept you well entertained?"

"Quite," Flame Tongue said as he took his pipe when his body servant presented it to him. "I particularly enjoyed the hunt, but it's a shame how few deer are left in the valley anymore. If we're not careful, the Chichimecs will kill every last one and we'll be left with no sport."

Ixtlilxochitl, who sat a few mats away, cast him a scathing glare but said nothing.

"We should all be mindful of how we use the gifts the gods have granted us," Little Reed answered. "You told me there was an urgent matter you needed to discuss with me before you left today."

Flame Tongue nodded. "Important matters concerning the future of your kingdom, Lord Topiltzin." He puffed to get the tobacco burning and continued, "Getting your throne back was no easy feat, and not without a scrape with the Black Dog. My own throne came to me with its share of tragedies: one of my father's concubines attempted to poison me, and her son gave me this." He tipped back his head and pulled aside his heavy gold necklaces to reveal an old scar embedded deep in the loose skin below his jowls. "I spent the first three months of my reign lying in bed, recovering. Facing one's own death makes one worry for the future, don't you agree?"

"I wouldn't argue otherwise," Little Reed said. "The future has been on my mind for a very long time, and that's why Lady Quetzalpetlatl and I are leaving for the north tomorrow."

Flame Tongue took to thumping his chest as he started coughing, his eyes watering. "Leaving? But you reclaimed your throne not even three months ago yet!"

"It's of utmost importance to the kingdom's future," Little Reed assured him.

"Forgive my boldness, but what could possibly be of interest to anyone in the barbarian north?"

"We must recover King Mixcoatl's bones, for a proper burial."

Flame Tongue stammered a moment before saying, "With all due respect, Lord Topiltzin, there is much that needs your attention here in the valley. We have a Chichimec problem."

Ixtlilxochitl's glare turned darker.

Little Reed raised an eyebrow. "Problem?"

"They're crawling all over the countryside, eating up everything and multiplying like rabbits. Your uncle brought them here—over the objections of his allies, mind you—and now is the time to send them back home, before they get restless. We have no wars to keep them occupied anymore."

"I have no intention of sending them back to the desert. Many have lived in the valley as long as I have, and have raised their families here among us, so who am I to tell them they must leave?"

As with Smoking Mirror's cult, Little Reed and I didn't see eye-to-eye when it came to the Chichimecs. He didn't remember anything of that night long ago in Teotihuacan when they'd attacked us, for he'd been so drunk he wouldn't have woken even if they'd chopped him in half. He wasn't the one who'd cut off two of his fingers to call on

Quetzalcoatl to save us all. And now so many dirty, half-naked, heavily-tattooed men roamed our streets that I didn't dare to go to the market or temple without at least four guards. With nothing for these vile dog-men to do besides steal and rape, the murder rate surged and all too many of them became victims themselves when good, honest Toltecas defended their homes and their lives from them. They belonged in the harsh northern desert that spawned their barbaric ways.

"I'm not unsympathetic to your concerns, Lord Flame Tongue," Little Reed went on. "War has been the occupation of most men—Chichimec and Tolteca—for many years now, and finding purpose in a new paradigm can be challenging. We have plans for redirecting their interests; the Chichimecs will not only contribute to the shift from war to peace, but they'll also be architects of it. I ask you give it time to work, and give the Chichimecs time to prove their value and worth."

"And what if while you're gone they decide they want to be warriors, not architects?" Flame Tongue asked, looking annoyed.

Little Reed nodded towards Blood Wolf. "Our new war chief will deal with any trouble that arises while we're gone."

Flame Tongue cast a dubious glance over at Citlallotoc. "I wasn't aware you'd replaced your old war chief."

"Lord Citlallotoc is returning to Acolman to take his rightful throne." Little Reed smiled at his friend, who bowed his head. "We shall miss him tremendously, but our loss is Acolman's gain. And I'm certain he's eager to settle down and secure his own legacy."

"That is always on the mind of the wisest of us," Flame Tongue said, his mood turning hopeful again. "And certainly you're acutely aware of the issues that arise when one doesn't properly secure his legacy as soon he takes the throne. Have you yet had a chance to meet my daughter, Anacoana?"

While his temper had improved, mine immediately flared. How dare he step on my authority? "We already discussed this issue, Lord Flame Tongue. Twice. And I rejected your proposal both times."

Little Reed glanced at me before turning back to Flame Tongue. "What proposal does she speak of?"

"He wishes you to marry Anacoana," I said, "and I informed him that she is an inappropriate candidate."

Flame Tongue's face blazed. "There is nothing wrong with my Anacoana; she is high-born, appropriately tempered, and she's still in possession of her maidenhead—our priests have verified this."

"She's twelve!" I snapped back at him.

Little Reed held up his hand for silence, looking bewildered. He turned to Flame Tongue. "Why in Mictlan would you subject a twelve-year-old girl to a virginity test?"

"Because she was one of Black Otter's concubines," I supplied. "I told him such an offer is inappropriate at this juncture." *Not to mention completely at odds with your personal standard of ethics,* I wanted to add, but already Flame Tongue was furious, and suggesting that he had no morals would only make it worse.

Flame Tongue struggled for words, but Little Reed held up his hand again. "I have no doubt that Lady Anacoana is a fine young woman, Lord Flame Tongue, and I don't hold the past against her—a past she had no say in nor control over—but there is something you should know; I've already discussed this with my other allies, many of them even before I took the throne, but due to my illness I hadn't yet had the chance to discuss it with Lady Quetzalpetlatl." He patted my hand apologetically then went on, "As Quetzalcoatl's high priest, the god has set out a specific path for me to follow, and at this point, taking a wife is not part of that plan. When the god wishes me to marry, he will tell me, not only when, but to whom. And she will know it in her heart as well; this may not be the traditional way of men, but it is the way of the god, and as one of his highest servants it is my duty to follow his example and live as he would here on earth."

I might have smirked at Flame Tongue's fluster if this whole discussion hadn't brought the nausea back. He didn't look at me when he said, "I respect your reason, My Lord. Forgive my unfortunate outburst; I am a man of great passions when I feel my family has been slighted for no fault of their own. You understand."

"I do."

Flame Tongue rose from his mat. "Thank you for your hospitality, Lord Topiltzin, but I must be getting back to Xico. I bid you a safe journey." He turned to leave, his personal guards flanking him. But he stopped and looked back when Little Reed called out to him.

"I understand your passion all too well, Lord Flame Tongue, for I feel the same way when someone slights my sister for no reason other than the body the gods gave her," Little Reed said, a careful smile fixed on his face. "In case you were unaware, she is Quetzalcoatl's high priestess, chosen by him personally, which makes her one of his highest servants as well. I say *one of* because that is a position we share, as we share the throne here in Culhuacan; we are equals, in the eyes of the god and in the eyes of our people. I realize this hasn't been the way of kings in the valley for a long time, but that is how it is here now; and when you dismiss my sister's decisions, you dismiss me. I'm quite certain this wasn't your intention, of course, but going forward, let it be known that her words are to be taken with the same respect as mine."

Flame Tongue drew in his breath as if preparing to explode, his cheeks burning bright, but instead he exhaled raggedly. He looked as if he'd swallowed a live leech. "You have my apologies, Lady Quetzalpetlatl," he said, bowing to me. "I intended no disrespect."

I bowed my head in return.

Not long after Flame Tongue left, the rest of the breakfast crowd filtered off to their duties, leaving me and Little Reed alone. "You hardly ate anything," he noted.

I shook my head. "Lord Flame Tongue left me with a sour stomach. You don't think he'll withdraw his alliance with us over this, do you?"

"I'm more worried about how disrespectfully he treated you. There's no excuse."

"It won't be the last time," I said with a laugh. "Our ways are strange to most people, men and women alike."

"They will embrace it when they see it's what the god wants. We must be patient and lead the peasants gently, for they are the ones most open to hope. But some of the nobles will see any attempts to change the status quo as an erosion of their own power, and we'll have to handle them with a firmer grip."

"We must be careful not to get bitten in the process," I warned him.

He laughed, and I melted a little inside. Gods how I adored his smile! The desire rose again, intense and demanding thanks to my nearly empty stomach—hunger always made it worse—but I didn't feel up to fighting it off right now. "I still haven't started packing for the trip, so I should go and do that," I said, rising from my reed-woven throne. "Will there be a feast tonight, to celebrate Citlallotoc's ascension?"

Little Reed sobered and nodded. "I must admit I will miss him greatly."

"He's a good friend, and those can be very hard to come by."

"We're going to a tlachtli match this afternoon. Do you want to join us?"

"I don't care for tlachtli," I said. The last match I attended ended gruesomely, both on and off the court, and I had little desire for reminders of such things. "You two enjoy yourselves."

I started to leave but when I turned, suddenly Amoxtli stood blocking my way. I took a step back, my heart hammering. I didn't keep personal guards within the palace walls—it seemed a bit ridiculous to do so, given that most people considered Little Reed the real person of power in our duo—but at that moment I wished I did if only so he couldn't have sneaked up on me like this. I frowned, embarrassed.

He bowed his head. "I'm sorry, My Lady. I didn't mean to surprise you."

"What do you want?" I snapped before I could think better of it. I really should have made an effort to eat something.

He had started to come out of his bow, but now he winced and kept his head down. "Nothing, My Lady. I wanted to compliment you on your speech during the afternoon services yesterday, about the city moving forward into the future without clinging to the past. I found it personally moving, and I wanted both you and Lord Topiltzin to know that I stand with you completely."

Sure you do, I thought but held it back.

Little Reed clasped Amoxtli on the shoulder. "We're glad to hear that. There will be difficult times as we blaze ahead and we may feel compelled to return to the safety of the past, but our faith and resolve will see us through the conflicts, and eventually to our goal. The rewards will be great."

Amoxtli finally looked up, giving me a furtive glance before focusing on Little Reed with a relaxed smile. "I shall remember that, Your Excellency." He spared me another glance—like a whipped dog—then he hurried from the great hall.

As we watched him go, Little Reed said, "I know he reminds you of his father, but he's truly a good man, Papalotl. He could have remained silent about Mixcoatl's bones, but he didn't hesitate to tell me where they were when I mentioned needing them. He wants to do right, and I hope you can find it in your heart to judge him for the man he is, instead of by the man fate decided would be his father."

I wanted to resist, but if the years had taught me anything, it was that Little Reed was a better judge of character than I. How might things have turned out differently if I'd let him deal with Quetzalcoatl's former high priest as he thought right, rather than staying his hand? My defending Ahexotl seemed disgustingly naïve now; the man had used fear of the god's wrath to have his way with his priestesses with impunity for years, but when he survived being severely burned by the god, I'd taken it as a sign that Quetzalcoatl wanted his life spared—a grave misjudgment that almost cost me my life. I'd learned the hard way it could be dangerous to trust anyone beyond the small handful of people who'd already proven themselves to me.

Little Reed gave my hand a squeeze. "Give him a chance, Papalotl. You won't be sorry. I promise."

I sighed. "I'll think about it."

Motioning me to follow him, Little Reed said, "Come. There's something I want to show you."

I followed him out of the great hall and down the hallway, into the royal living quarters to his room. I always felt a hitch of anxiety when I went in there; it had been my uncle Ihuitimal's quarters, but even before that, it had been my father's, where Ihuitimal had murdered him in his bed and put his heart in my hands when I was only seven, to terrorize me for his own amusement. Little Reed had redecorated the entire room with frescoes of the Feathered Serpent, snakes, and butterflies, but no amount of whitewash could completely banish the shadow of the mural of Smoking Mirror that had loomed on the largest wall when my uncle ruled.

Numerous wicker baskets sat clustered in the corner near the door, waiting for the servants to move them to the staging area in the main courtyard later tonight. Little Reed picked up a large clay urn sitting hidden amongst them and brought it over to me. Deep-etched swirls and flowers decorated the outside, and judging from the fragmented swaths of yellow, white and green, it had been painted at one point. When he handed it to me, I recognized it for a funerary urn, similar to the one Mazatzin and I had put Nimilitzli's ashes in after we'd cremated her. We'd buried it under the temple's stone floor in Xochicalco. "Little Reed...you dug up Nimilitzli's urn?" I asked, uneasy.

"Omeyocan no! Xochicalco was her home, and I wouldn't think of taking her away from there," he assured me.

"Then whose is it?"

He touched my hand gently as he said, "It's Mother's."

I stared at the pottery, finally recognizing it; I'd only seen it for a moment or two before King Cuitlapanton had it committed to the earth under the shade of a copal tree in the royal gardens. Little Reed and I had visited the spot at least once a year to lay flowers, and I'd tell him about Mother, describing her as best as I could so he might know what she looked like; and because for the longest time, before I realized my memory was infallible, I feared that I would forget her face. "You dug it up?"

"Actually, I sent Amoxtli to do it and he got back with it last night," Little Reed said.

"But why?"

"With us going north to find your father's burial site and build the god's sacred city, I thought it would be a kindness to Mother to bring her with us so we can bury her with Mixcoatl; and they will both be near us always."

I clutched the urn tight. "She would like that," I managed to whisper, tears threatening behind my eyes.

"Quetzalcoatl told us to build his temple on the spot where Mixcoatl is buried, to provide a strong foundation for our reign. But it will be even stronger if Mother is a part of that foundation as well." He hugged me, pressing the urn of our mother's ashes between us. "Let us build the future on the deeds of not only great men, but great women too."

"And Amoxtli brought her home to us?"

Little Reed nodded. "And he's going to show us where our new home will be."

Maybe Little Reed was right; perhaps I wasn't giving Amoxtli the chance he deserved.

CHAPTER TWO

Amoxtli knelt in front of the Feathered Serpent's idol in the great temple, his body bent forward, arms stretched out before him, head down. Even from this angle, his resemblance to my uncle unsettled me, but I fought the impulse to turn and leave. I stayed in the doorway, watching him rise to his knees while muttering a prayer. He only saw me once he turned to leave, and it was his turn to jump, startled. "High Priestess." He bowed and swept his fingers across the ground at my feet.

Taking a deep breath, I said, "I wanted to thank you for all you're doing for me and Topiltzin...bringing my mother home, and for coming forward with the location of my father's bones. It's very important to the future that we find them."

"It was the least I could do for our family." He didn't meet my gaze as he spoke. "I know my father hurt you, in ways I can never know, and yet he granted him a proper burial with all the rites. Mixcoatl deserves the same."

I struggled to find words in the storm of emotions tearing through me, leaving me raw and exposed. But finally I found my voice again. "Please excuse my cold demeanor this morning. I don't believe the son should bear the burden of his father's crimes, and yet...I treated you as if you should, and I'm truly sorry."

Amoxtli finally met my gaze. "I understand your difficulty. My father...he was consumed by things he had no control over, things he couldn't change, and it destroyed him, long before that battle outside the city. I'm so sorry for the havoc he caused in your life."

"His obsessions didn't hurt only me—or even Topiltzin. It ended up destroying his entire family, and.... I...I'm sorry I didn't come speak to you personally about Black Otter. It was terribly thoughtless of me."

He glanced around, uncomfortable. "If I might impose upon you...what did happen to my brother? Exactly?"

Black Otter's death was a subject I didn't like to think about, let alone talk about; how could I admit to Amoxtli that his father ordered his own son's execution because he feared I'd poisoned Black Otter's mind and robbed him of his will? Even now my uncle's dying words continued to haunt me: "My son had no chance against you; no man does." I'd worried about what he meant, but with the months, I'd convinced myself that I would be better off not knowing.

My sister Jade Flower had told me Black Otter and Amoxtli had been close, and while I didn't care if the truth destroyed any remaining vestiges of love Amoxtli held for his father, I wasn't keen to tell him how mentally unstable his brother became in his final days. He deserved a better memory than that. "Black Otter feared your father would harm me and he tried to smuggle me out of Culhuacan, but Ihuitimal sent his personal guards to retrieve me, with orders to kill Black Otter as a traitor." I looked out of the door towards Lake Meztliapan, to the spot in the deep emerald waters where Black Otter had died and my nightmares began. The vision of the monster filled my mind, making my heart pulse and my stomach clench. *Mine! Mine! Mine!*

I blushed when I realized Amoxtli had spoken but I hadn't heard any of it. "I'm sorry, what did you say?" I asked, shaking the terrible image from my head.

"I said thank you for telling me the truth," Amoxtli said. "As much as I want to believe my father wasn't capable of ordering my brother's murder, I know better. He told me more than once that Black Otter wasn't strong enough to rule and that I needed to be ready to take his place." He shook his head.

"Power does strange things to people," I said.

He nodded, but before he could say more, footsteps on the temple stairs distracted me. I turned to see a man walking towards us, dressed in the black priestly robes of the Order of the Smoking Mirror. Most priests—besides Quetzalcoatl's—wore their hair matted with blood, but this man was freshly washed, with his long hair pulled back into a tidy knot on top of his head. Still, he bore the telltale scars of daily bloodletting on his arms, legs, and notched ears. He smiled when we locked gazes.

I forced myself to smile back.

He swept his fingers across the ground at my feet—the greeting befitting of a queen. "Glorious day, Lady Quetzalpetlatl."

I arched an eyebrow. "Indeed."

"I've been hoping to meet you for a while, but with the king ill and you so busy caring for city matters, I'm afraid formal introductions had to wait until now." He rose back to his full height. "I'm Ozomatli, the new high priest of Tezcatlipoca."

The day after the Smoking Mirror abandoned my uncle to die on the battlefield, Mazatzin told me some priest of the dark sorcerer god came seeking an audience with me, to discuss the future of the cult. After all I'd been through, I was in no mood to speak to anyone connected to Smoking Mirror, and so I put off the meeting. Besides, at that point I was certain Little Reed and I were going to kick Smoking Mirror's cult out of Culhuacan soon.

Or so I'd thought.

I had no interest in speaking to Ozomatli about his murderous god's cult now, but as the highest of priestesses in Culhuacan, I was obligated to do so. "It's a pleasure to finally meet you," I said, inclining my head. I looked past him before asking, "And where is your order's high priestess?"

"Oh, the Smoking Mirror has no high priestess, My Lady."

"Why not?"

"The Smoking Mirror is a god of warriors, and so women have no use for him." His smile added, *Nor does he have any use for them.*

I stood taller. "Women are warriors in their own right; I'd dare any man to endure the childbed and not beg the gods to end his suffering."

He chuckled, but guardedly. "Some gods are more useful to women than they are to men, and the other way around. It isn't a slight."

"Any god that aspires to the all-encompassing importance that Smoking Mirror did under my uncle's rule cannot afford to ignore half of the city's citizens."

Ozomatli did an admirable job of maintaining his composure; but given how he shifted from foot to foot, I could see this conversation wasn't going the way he'd intended. Good.

"If Smoking Mirror wishes to maintain a presence here in Culhuacan," I said, "he will make himself useful to everyone, and he can start by welcoming women into his cult. Ihuitimal may have granted citizen status to only men during his rule, but Topiltzin and I share the responsibility of power; the throne, as with the gods themselves, reflects the duality of the natural order: one side is incomplete and imperfect without the other— but together, working in harmony, balance and peace is achieved. A city out of balance with the gods risks falling apart; a cult out of balance with reality risks destroying itself. Certainly your Smoking Mirror acknowledges this very basic tenet of our faith in the gods?"

Ozomatli's smile twitched. "Smoking Mirror is all-knowing, My Lady, so trust he will do what is necessary to maintain the proper balance. I shall seek out a high priestess, but I beg your patience while I do so, since I haven't any experienced priestesses to choose from."

"I give you six months to train one, and choose wisely; I won't accept a simple mouthpiece, and I'd hate to see my opinion of you suffer."

He'd kept his smile throughout our discussion, but now his eyes burned. "Absolutely." His gaze flicked away to Amoxtli standing in the doorway behind me. "Good to see you again, Lord Amoxtli. My condolences on the loss of your father and brother."

Where I'd made great efforts to be at least cordial, Amoxtli took no such care. He glared at Ozomatli.

Ozomatli turned his conniving smile on me again, bade me good day, and departed down the stairs, his black robe fluttering behind him.

"You'd do well to not trust him, My Lady," Amoxtli said, watching Ozomatli weave his way through the crowd below.

"Oh?"

He nodded. "When he became the cult's fire priest, my father fell ill all the time."

"You think he was poisoning him?" When Amoxtli nodded again, I asked, "How?" I'd thought of doing the very same thing, but with all the food tasters, I'd decided that wasn't a viable option.

"His mushroom box," Amoxtli said. "My father had already been training me in the priestly arts before Ozomatli became his fire priest, and I had experience with the teonanacatl mushrooms. But six months ago, I became extremely ill while doing a vision ceremony and didn't come out of the Divine Dream for three days. Father thought I'd taken too much, but I hadn't taken any more than normal. The only difference was that I'd gotten the mushrooms from his personal box rather than the community one used by the rest of the priests."

I joined Amoxtli, gazing down at Ozomatli in the crowded precinct below. I didn't care that someone had tried to poison my uncle, but what if Ozomatli's ambitions reached higher than merely being Smoking Mirror's high priest? He required close monitoring. "Did you tell anyone your suspicions?"

"Before I left on my mission to hide Mixcoatl's bones, I mentioned to Ozomatli that I thought someone might have tampered with my father's mushrooms, but I didn't make the connection until Topiltzin told me that he'd been tipped off as to what route I was taking back from the north. Ozomatli probably thought he would execute me and he wouldn't have to worry about being found out."

A twinge of protectiveness surprised me. "Do you think he might still try, given his earlier failure?"

Amoxtli stood straighter. "I'm not afraid of him, My Lady."

"I'm going to have him watched." I glared at the crowd again, but Ozomatli was gone, no doubt to tattle on me to Little Reed. I bade Amoxtli goodbye and started down the stairs, but, suddenly struck with an idea, I stopped. "How would you feel about a ceremony on the lakeshore tonight, before we leave? To honor Black Otter?"

"That would be wonderful," Amoxtli said, his smile sober and a touch sad. "Thank you."

Smiling back, I said, "I think it will be good for both of us."

▯

There'd already been a ceremony honoring Black Otter last month, attended by his former concubines, Amoxtli, and a few close friends. Traditionally the wife of the deceased led the ritual lamentations—where the women wept in grief as loud as they could for a week—but I'd passed that honor on to my sister Jade Flower. She'd been closest to Black Otter and, besides, an uncomfortable tension fell over the room whenever all five of his women came together; I hadn't been a welcome newcomer when he was alive, and when he died, things had been said that couldn't be unsaid between me and Jade Flower. Everyone seemed happier when I stayed away, including myself.

Not that I didn't miss Black Otter; for a while, before everything turned strange and disturbing between us, I'd considered building a life with him. But with my one true love back from the dead and sharing my throne, I found it difficult to ache for him as was expected of a grieving widow. So I let the others have their peaceful ceremony without distraction.

And yet I regretted not having that final goodbye such ceremonies provided for those of us left behind. I was very glad it occurred to me to do this before we left.

I donned my high priestess robe and let Malinalli fix my hair again when she visited after dinner to help me with my last-minute packing. We passed the time chatting since I wouldn't see her tomorrow—our caravan would leave before sunrise and she had dawn temple duties.

"Are you positive you don't want me or Mazatzin to accompany you tonight?" she asked, putting the finishing touches to my hair. "I know Topiltzin has taken Amoxtli into his confidences, but...doesn't he remind you of Ihuitimal?"

"I'm hoping with time I'll learn to see him, not his father," I admitted.

"Mazatzin says he's very intelligent and will make a good priest someday. It's strange how he looks exactly like his father but is the opposite of him, while Black Otter—who looked nothing like Ihuitimal—turned out most like him."

It was on the tip of my tongue to argue with that assessment of Black Otter's character, but I stopped. Where might I be now if Ihuitimal's men hadn't stopped us? Locked up in some distant palace, never allowed to leave or, worse yet, dead? Would he have gone that far to make certain we were together forever? Red Flint had almost taken his obsession with me to that end—I still shuddered at the memory of him raising the flint knife to stab me; if not for Malinalli smashing him across the head with the incense censer....

Might that someday be Little Reed too? I wondered, and my insides curled up like tender vegetation in a cold snap. I'd started asking myself such questions even before Black Otter spiraled down the same road of obsession that Red Flint had. I wanted to believe it was only coincidence, an unnecessary and unfair connection in their behavior; and after Black Otter's end, I tried very hard to tuck that thought away and leave it in the past, while I looked towards the future. This freak occurrence had no bearing on my future with Little Reed. *He is strong where they were dangerously weak. He would never succumb to such...magic.* For lack of a better word.

Malinalli had turned away to look over my bags, so she didn't see the sickly frown on my face. I pushed it away again, replacing it with a smile, willing myself to be cheerful. "Do you realize this is the first time in two years that we'll go more than a couple of weeks without seeing each other?"

"I wish I were going with you," Malinalli admitted. "Promise you'll be careful when you're in the north."

"I promise. And we won't be gone that long, a few months at most. You and Mazatzin will do fine running the priesthood while we're gone."

"The other high priests are already grumbling about the new restrictions on sacrifices," Malinalli said.

"Let them. It's not as if we don't allow them any human sacrifices." At least not yet. Little Reed and I had instituted limits on the number of victims each temple could give to the gods each year, with the idea that we'd eventually narrow it down to a handful of willing sacrifices each year, or better yet none at all.

"Ozomatli has been quite vocal about his displeasure with the new laws."

"And I trust you to deal with him appropriately, even if it means punching him in the face, as you did to Lord Storm House."

She laughed. "Some men are completely baffled when we don't behave as feminine as they think we should, aren't they?"

"They'll learn. We must be patient, and not be afraid to show them what we can do."

Malinalli nodded. "You'd best get going before you're late. And get enough rest while you're traveling. You've been working so hard, you deserve the break."

"I will, and I'll write to you whenever I can."

◻

While I allowed myself to wander the halls unshadowed by guards, when I left the palace, I always took some with me; who knew if any of my uncle's loyal followers still remained in Culhuacan, waiting for the right moment to avenge their fallen leader? Tonight I took my normal four-guard complement with me.

We met Amoxtli at the temple where he was waiting next to the smashed remains of the giant feathered serpent heads that once framed the staircase. Replacing them was on our long list of projects to restore the city to her former glory. He took the basket of butterflies I'd picked up from the priestly menagerie on the way over and we walked behind the temple, through the gate at the edge of the precinct, and made our way down the overgrown path to the sandbar; it was the same place where, as a child, I'd picked the fight with Black Otter that led to him and his family being exiled from Culhuacan. The log I'd knocked him off had long since disintegrated; but with my perfect memory I could still tell exactly where it had been, the place I'd stood when my father slapped me for bloodying Black Otter's nose because he called me "just a little girl"; the spot where I'd thought my father would kill him when I let slip that his father was worshiping Smoking Mirror in the palace. So many phantom memories haunted Culhuacan; I looked forward to escaping it when we built our new city.

Amoxtli set the basket on the sand and looked out over the water. The sun hung low, bathing everything in fading orange light; soon it would disappear beyond the mountains and start its journey through the underworld. "Black Otter used to bring me here to spear ducks," Amoxtli said with a heavy sigh. "He once told me your father and our uncle Nochuatl used to bring him here too, but whenever I asked him to tell me about them, he said he couldn't say any more because I'd tell Father. No one was allowed to talk about either of them in Culhuacan; I didn't even know that the box my father asked me to take north contained Mixcoatl's bones until one of my men let it slip while we buried it."

Memories of Ihuitimal soured my mood, and with the sun sinking below the mountains, we had to hurry if we were to get back into the city before sunset. He nodded when I suggested that we get to the prayer, and we both bowed our heads as I recited the plea to Tlaloc:

"Guardian of the Drowned,
Tonight we honor he who fell into your watery embrace.
May he find happiness in the land of Tlalocan,
May you find nourishment in our tears of sorrow,
And turn our grief into the rain that feeds the living."

I cut my palm with my sacrificial blade and let the blood dribble into the water. Once a cloud of red hung in the water like smoke, I closed my fist and raised my hands to the sky.

"Most merciful Quetzalcoatl,
Lighten the burdens weighing down our hearts,
Show us the path forward without those we've lost,
Show us how to turn grief into hope,

And anger into forgiveness.
Show us how to leave the past behind,
Show us into the future,
Most merciful Feathered Serpent."

Amoxtli opened the basket and a flock of black and orange butterflies sputtered out into the open air. They bobbed out over the lake, spreading out and dispersing in the sunset. The sight brought me a smile, and I felt energized, just as I had for so many days after the god had taken possession of me; the tingle of magic had never quite left after that, but I rarely felt so aware of it anymore.

Papalotl! a soft, child-like voice whispered with awe. I looked around, startled that someone other than me, Amoxtli, and my guards might be watching this ceremony. But I saw no one else. And those who were there stood in silent contemplation; Amoxtli's eyes sparkled with tears. I thought to ask him if he'd been the one to speak, but it felt wrong to interrupt the moment.

And since we walked back to the palace in complete silence, I didn't ask him then either. My mind ticked over the strange coincidence that the voice had sounded startlingly like Little Reed had that first time he'd called me by my childhood name—the name he shouldn't have known since everyone who'd known me by that name had been dead for years before.

CHAPTER THREE

 The caravan left Culhuacan while darkness still shrouded the land. There was no grand send-off, no crowds of noblemen bidding us farewell, no musicians playing drums and flutes; as with trade caravans carrying uncounted riches, we slipped from the city under cover of darkness and secrecy.

As usual I hadn't slept well, and with Little Reed sharing the royal litter with me, sleep remained ever elusive. Last night's dreams had been particularly unpleasant: I was back on the battlefield amidst the confusion as my uncle—possessed by Smoking Mirror—tore through the armies as a giant, smoking jaguar, trying to get at Little Reed. But instead of saving everyone, I floundered over the sacrifice I needed to make to harness Quetzalcoatl's power; I dithered and argued over whether never being with Little Reed the way my heart wanted was truly worth it for either of us, and by the time I'd made the right decision, it was too late—Smoking Mirror had already broken through the crowd of warriors protecting Little Reed and eaten him whole, as if he were nothing more than a fried grasshopper. Then the smoke jaguar had turned its fiery orange eyes on me.

Now, instead of closing my eyes to rest, I lay back among the pillows and blankets, watching Little Reed smoke his pipe in the dark as he looked out the curtain, no doubt thinking I was asleep. But I didn't dare close my eyes, lest I open them again to find he really wasn't with me anymore. Would the dreams ever end or would I live the rest of my days worried that reality was the true dream that someday I'd wake up from?

Once the sun rose newly-birthed over the mountains ahead of us, I finally gave up on sleeping. After a slim breakfast of fried fish and tlaxcallis, we sat with the curtain open, playing patolli. It was one of the few "manly" things my father had taught me—

completely unbeknownst to my mother, who found such games unseemly—and I'd taught it to Little Reed when he was young. We didn't gamble with cacao beans the way most people did; instead we wagered secrets, with the person who lost their treasure divulging something the winner didn't know. My impression was that Little Reed was completely non-competitive about the game; he was as content revealing the bits and pieces of himself as he was to hear mine. I often mused that we never would have known each other so well if not for playing patolli after those weekend meals at Nimilitzli's house.

Though I'd bet he'd become competitive if I suggested switching out telling secrets for wagering bits of our clothing off, I thought with a smirk as I captured his first of six treasures. I expected the growling desire when I looked at him, but I felt only a tingling deep inside. It felt so much more pleasant, so much more natural than that intense, hungry desire that Black Otter used to bring out in me.

Little Reed thought for a moment, then he said, "I always preferred Nimilitzli's tlaxcallis to yours. But only slightly."

I rolled my eyes. "That's hardly a secret, Little Reed. You really think I never noticed that you ate twice as many tlaxcallis when Nimilitzli made them?" I sighed. "I liked them more too."

Laughing, Little Reed said, "Maybe we should wager cacao, since we already know all of each other's secrets."

"Hardly. I'm certain there are a lot of things I don't know about you, as there are a lot of things that you don't know about me."

"For example?"

I shook my head. "No, I won your treasure, so you're the one who must divulge."

He took a swig from his water skin then suggested, "How about this: the winner gets to ask the loser a question to answer, with complete honesty and no embarrassment?" He had a twinkle in his eye that made that tingling intensify.

"All right," I agreed.

"So, ask away."

"Did you take any lovers while you were in the army?" I widened my eyes as soon as I asked it; so much for that insistent desire keeping its mouth shut.

Little Reed raised an eyebrow. "We're answering those kinds of questions, are we?"

My cheeks burned. "I don't know why I asked that. You don't have to—"

"The answer is no," Little Reed went on with a lopsided smile. "Though I came close to breaking my priestly vows once, with an exceptionally beautiful woman; unfortunately, a pompous, loudmouthed royal brat barged in and stopped it. I still resent him for it."

The memory of that night brought a hot flush creeping down my neck and over my breasts. I couldn't hold Little Reed's gaze anymore, my heart thudding in my ears.

Little Reed set the bean dice in my hand. "Your turn." Judging from the intense look in his eyes, he had his own questions and no intention of losing this time. I tossed the beans, feeling suddenly numb. What if he asked me the same question? I couldn't lie to him and say I'd had no lovers besides Black Otter; would it devastate him to know I'd been his father Quetzalcoatl's lover, even if it never went beyond the Divine Dream? *Perhaps it's time to get all this out in the open,* I thought as I moved one of my red pebbles around the cross-shaped board.

Little Reed took his roll and moved his jade pebble, knocking mine off the board by landing on it. Now I had no markers on the board and he had claimed one of my treasures. He grinned at me, almost as if he'd planned all this rather than made a lucky roll of the beans. "My turn to ask a question."

I swallowed, hoping my nervousness wasn't obvious. "Ask away," I said, trying to sound relaxed.

But I didn't expect the question he actually asked. "Do you, on some level, still think of me as you used to, before Black Otter?"

I blinked at him, puzzled at first. "Are you asking if I still love you?"

"In a manner of speaking." His expression was completely calm, but a slight hitch in his voice betrayed his nervousness.

I sighed. "Little Reed, I never stopped loving you, and I never could. I could die and be stuck on the banks of the Black Lake in Mictlan for countless years and I'd still love you."

He didn't speak for a moment, a strange look on his weathered face, as if my answer had somehow surprised him. Could he have really thought I could so completely fall in love with another that I could never love him anymore? "Why...why did you say that, about Mictlan?" he finally asked, an inexplicable excitement in his voice.

Now I was even more puzzled. "I don't know...I suppose because it was on my mind. I died on the battlefield, after all, and Xolotl told me that because Smoking Mirror had no heaven for his sacrifices that I'd have to sit on the Black Lake for who knows how long, until Smoking Mirror actually gained a heaven for me and his other sacrifices to go to."

"And that's it?"

I nodded, but felt something tugging at the back of my mind. I tried to draw it in, to make it form a coherent image in my head, but as quickly as it came on, it vanished, lost again.

Little Reed seemed disappointed by my answer, but he quickly handed me the dice. "Your turn."

I tossed the beans, expecting my rotten luck to continue, but two of my beans showed their white dots, letting me move back onto the board. And knock Little Reed off the board at the same time. "Why would you think I don't love you anymore?" I asked.

He shifted uneasily. "When I asked you to marry me...I upset you," he said. "I know it was too soon after Black Otter died, but—"

"Black Otter had nothing to do with any of that," I said. "The man forced me into his bed, so how could I possibly love him as I've always loved you?"

Little Reed's eyes grew wide and hot. "He forced himself on you?" he growled, his voice quaking with pent-up rage.

"Gods no!" I grabbed his hand and gave it a reassuring squeeze. "No, no, he wasn't that kind of man, Little Reed. Not at all. What I meant is that...I didn't want to be in his bed, but under the circumstances...it was a matter of survival. And maybe for a while, I thought...maybe I might be able to find some happiness with him. But it was never like what we had, Little Reed. Nothing at all."

The rage faded to concern. "What do you mean by *had*?"

I stared at him a moment, uncertain what to say. The moment had come, but I still didn't want to tell him. "It's not your turn to ask a question," I said.

The hurt plain in his eyes, he picked up the beans and rolled them. We went through several silent turns and each landed all six of our markers on the board, working our way towards each other's treasure squares. The longer the silence held up—and the longer it took for one of us to finally capture the other person's treasure—the more my chest ached and my stomach twisted. It was on the tip of my tongue to tell him I didn't want to play anymore when he finally captured one of my treasures. He then looked up at me again, his face carefully controlled now. "What did you mean by *had*?" he asked softly.

I fought back tears. "I'm sorry, Little Reed. The Smoking Mirror was going to kill you, and I knew only the god could save you, and I had only one thing of value left to give in sacrifice...." I choked a moment and paused to regain my composure. "We can't get married, Little Reed. That's the sacrifice I made to save you. I'm sorry."

He sat straighter, his shoulders rising as if my words had lifted a burden off of them. "Is that all?"

Given the intensity of our conversation, his casual dismissal of this news startled—and hurt—me. "You say that as if it's no sacrifice at all," I snapped.

A crestfallen expression came to his face. "Not at all, Papalotl. You saved my life and I can't ever thank you enough for that, but what does it truly matter if we cannot ever marry? Marriage is but a social display, a political alliance for convenience sake. Certainly not something to get so upset about."

I shook my head. "You don't understand, Little Reed. I know I said marriage, but...I was speaking of it in the manner in which *we* intended to practice it—not as a political maneuver, but rather as an expression of our love for each other. All my life I've felt as if you were the string holding my sacrificial blade together, that we were meant to be together, and not merely to fulfill the god's religious plans, but to...and I know this will sound crazy and ludicrous, but...I always thought we'd make love important and vital, the way the gods intended it to be."

As soon as I said it, that same itch of inaccessible memory came upon me. None of what I said was supported by anything I'd learned in the priesthood; none of the countless tales of the gods said anything about love, and yet...it had felt so achingly true when I'd said it. I felt almost divinely inspired, and I was acutely aware again of the tingling in my limbs, in my blood, in my belly—burning sun-like inside me.

Little Reed didn't say anything for a moment but eventually he nodded, the look on his face inscrutable. "I have felt that way too," he admitted.

The pleasant tingling faded as I said, "That is what I gave up, Little Reed, to save you. It was what I wasn't strong enough to sacrifice—no, *refused to sacrifice*—on Red Flint's behalf, so instead Nimilitzli paid the price for me. I would have gladly given my very life to save you, but since Ihuitimal had already given that to Smoking Mirror, I had only my heart left to give. So yes, while I still love you as much as I always have—and always will—I've given up being able to act on that. And I don't regret it in the slightest; I would do it again without hesitation to save your life, Little Reed."

He pulled me into a fierce hug that scattered the pebbles on the patolli board between us. "And I would sit on the banks of the Black Lake in Mictlan until the end of time if it meant saving you," he whispered. He buried his face in my neck, holding me close a moment, then he gave my cheek a soft, warm kiss before pulling away, evidence of tears clouding his eyes. He looked at the board and sighed. "I suppose the game is over then."

"It is," I agreed, my heart heavy.

He looked out the curtain then said, "There's one last secret I want to share with you."

"All right."

"I dread to think of you enduring this sacrifice on your own, on my account, so I'm making the very same one for you, my love. I shall take no other into my heart—or my bed."

I shook my head adamantly. "I cannot ask such a thing of you, Little Reed—"

"You're not asking; I'm giving it, freely and without reservation. You might not have the freedom to act on your love for me, but I don't have that restriction, and this is how I choose to act on my love for you."

A few tears finally came, hot on my cheeks. He smiled at me and wiped them away with his thumbs, his hands warm and comforting. "I'm going to walk for a while, stretch my legs," he said, his voice barely above a whisper. "You should get some more sleep; you look exhausted." He gathered the game pieces and folded up the board made from a reed mat and put them away into his leather carrying bag. He called for the caravan to stop but he didn't say anything more as he left the litter, closing the curtain behind him. A moment later the the litter jostled as the porters got back underway.

I lay staring at the roof. In the dim light creeping in from the curtain's slivered opening, I could barely see the painting of Quetzalcoatl flying in his feathered serpent form among the blue clouds where the rain god Tlaloc poured rain from his sacred jars. He slithered towards the earth below, to the underworld where he traveled death's road to rescue the bones of humanity and bring them back to the world, to give humankind life with his own blood. It was so obvious who Little Reed inherited his self-sacrificing ways from.

Except the sacrifice he made puts him in the same predicament as your own father, I thought with a frown. *With no blood heir to carry on the god's wishes after us, how can any of this matter in the long run?*

I knew what Little Reed would say: trust in the god. And really, what else could I do?

□

We reached the city of Chimalhuacan late in the afternoon, right before dinner time, and King Toztli greeted us in the courtyard along with his daughter Cornflower—another of my former husband's concubines. I was glad to see her looking well, and she greeted me with a hug and chattered earnestly the whole way to the great hall. We hadn't been close at all when she was in Black Otter's household—in fact we'd hardly spoken—but coming home to her family had allowed her to put our mutually painful past behind her and open up.

Toztli had a grand feast waiting for us, with all of Chimalhuacan's nobility in attendance; fewer than fifty people, which was understandable given Chimalhuacan's small size. Toztli's eldest son and heir Nahuacatl greeted us, and it annoyed me that he let his gaze linger on me longer than on Little Reed. When we sat to eat, Cornflower whispered to me, "Don't be surprised if he approaches your brother tonight about you. Father's been saying for weeks that we finally have a real chance at combining the royal families, and Nahuacatl is to make the best possible impression on Topiltzin."

I gave Nahuacatl a curt nod when he cast a furtive glance at me from where he sat next to his father. He was little more than a boy, probably hadn't even done a full year in the army yet. He turned away, his face darkening with a blush, and he looked as if he would get ill any moment. "I wouldn't think the former wife of a minor prince would be a fitting match for the heir to the throne," I told her.

"Ah, but to my father, you're not the former wife of a minor prince: you're the queen of a major city and an opportunity to meld two royal bloodlines. This isn't the first time Chimalhuacan has sought to merge with Culhuacan through marriage. Did you know that my grandfather named the city after your mother?"

"Truly?"

Cornflower nodded. "According to my mother, when your grandfather's only son came down with the Divine Sickness, he turned to his best friends to make a match for his eldest daughter. My grandfather changed his city's name to Chimalhuacan, hoping that would impress your grandfather into betrothing my father to your mother. He didn't know that your mother's father owed a blood-debt to your father's father: he'd saved your grandfather from being captured during the first battle they both fought against the Chichimecs. And even though your grandfather didn't betroth my father to your mother, he kept the city name, to honor their friendship. Or so my mother claims."

"That's fascinating," I told her as I held up a bowl of chile sauce for us to share. "I never knew any of that."

"It is funny to think that we might have been sisters had our parents married," Cornflower said, dipping her tlaxcalli into the sauce. "Of course, if your brother does marry you to Nahuacatl, that would make us sisters of a sort."

"Topiltzin won't marry me to anyone," I said, perhaps a bit more sharply than I'd intended, for Cornflower blinked at me, startled. "As priests of the god Quetzalcoatl, both Topiltzin and I have taken vows of chastity, so a marriage would really be pointless for either of us."

"But what about an heir for the throne?" Cornflower asked, confused. "If neither of you can marry...who will inherit Culhuacan after you're gone?"

"It is a dilemma we'll have to work out with the god," I admitted. "But enough about me. How is your daughter?"

◻

After dinner, Toztli invited us to sit with his war council to discuss political matters during the xocolatl service. Being the only woman present, I felt out of place, but was determined not to show any discomfort despite the not-entirely friendly looks from some of the men. Toztli avoided looking at me entirely, as if my very presence made him nervous, but he spoke with an eager friendliness with Little Reed as they smoked their pipes.

"So, Lord Topiltzin, what takes you into the north?" Toztli asked as he stirred his powdered heart flower into his chocolate with his wooden stirring stick, whipping it into the froth indicative of the best xocolatl.

"We're making a religious pilgrimage on behalf of the god," Little Reed answered.

"He has interests in the north?" Toztli asked, surprised. "Are you by chance looking to drive the Chichimecs farther into the desert? I know a good many good Toltecas would support such a venture."

Little Reed chuckled. "Actually, we're interested in improving our relationship with the Chichimecs. Wars between our peoples came about because life in the desert is difficult and the Chichimecs sought better lives. We, on the other hand, sought to deny them that merely because of their tribal affiliations. They have much to offer and teach us, if we're willing to listen and accept them into our communities and learn from them."

"But certainly the god wouldn't want them here in the valley, not after they outlawed his worship in Culhuacan and tried to conquer everyone in the name of their wretched Smoking Mirror god?" Toztli asked.

"Smoking Mirror may be a Chichimec god, but my uncle was not a Chichimec himself," I said between sips from my cup. Toztli flinched when I first spoke but then put on a strained smile. "So long as the Chichimecs honor Quetzalcoatl alongside their own gods, he considers them his people and will extend his blessings and protections upon them."

"But there's no work for them here," one of the war council members grumbled.

"Oh, but there is." Little Reed held up his hand and our scribe hurried forward with a stack of parchment. "I have a proposition for you, Lord Toztli; one that will put the

267

Chichimecs to work and help them integrate into our society." He set the parchments down one at a time, placing them close together so they formed a large drawing of a precinct. "Now that Xochicalco has fallen, there isn't a market center large enough to handle all the trade coming in from the south. So we build a new one, right here." He pointed to a space of empty land slightly south of the halfway mark between our two kingdoms. "We've already invited the King of Chalco to participate as well and he's agreed to help. Together, our three kingdoms would run the market and share in the profits from the taxation, split equally among us of course. And we hire Chichimecs to do the work."

"But the Chichimecs aren't architects, Lord Topiltzin," Toztli pointed out. "They are a warrior society that lives in tents outside the city limits; they can't even weave cotton into cloth, so how can we expect them to build a market complex from stone?"

"We train them, of course, as the Teotihuacanos trained us hundreds of years ago. Quetzalcoatl's gift of civilization is for all his people, not only those who have already mastered the skills; if anything, it is our obligation to spread the god's teachings to every new people we meet, if only to bring them closer to the god himself. We will teach them that there is more to existence than suffering and warfare, and we too will benefit from the rewards that brings. After a hundred years of nonstop war, we can finally enjoy peace and prosperity."

Toztli gazed at the drawing, chewing his lip. "The last ten years have been grueling, with Toltecas fighting each other," he admitted. "And driving the Chichimecs back into the north would probably take another ten years—"

"And cost us many lives," Little Reed added. "We've already lost so many men to Ihuitimal's war—so many we probably won't ever fully recover. If we turn on the Chichimecs, they'll quickly realize they outnumber us, and with the troubles in the south, we can't rely on our trade partners to come to our aid; in fact, we should fully expect goods from the south to dwindle to a trickle within the next generation."

"Then why waste resources building a new market center?"

"Because while the south falters, the valley will rise and the south will need our trade goods the way we've long depended on theirs. The god has foreseen this."

Toztli looked at his war chief, a frown on his face. He was so easily flustered; it was little wonder my uncle had used him so readily. In contrast, his son Nahuacatl was studying the plans and whispering to one of the other war council members who nodded eagerly and whispered back, pointing out things in the drawings. If Toztli accepted this agreement, his indecisive tendencies would weigh down the construction efforts. I casually whispered to Little Reed, "Suggest that his son lead the construction effort."

Little Reed had been watching the young man as well and gave me a nod before telling Toztli, "And we believe that Chimalhuacan's heir Lord Nahuacatl should lead the project as the chief architect. I understand he's an extremely bright man with an eye for beautiful architecture."

Toztli grinned. "He is indeed, Lord Topiltzin. When he was a boy, he used to complain about having to be the heir to the throne because he wanted to be a stone carver instead. I do indulge him a bit; he helped design Quetzalcoatl's new temple here, since Ihuitimal insisted I tear down the old one and replace it with a temple for the Smoking Mirror." He turned to his son, who was beaming now. "I'm certain he will relish a task of such magnitude."

"Then we have an agreement?" I asked.

Toztli gave me that hesitant look again—which was really starting to annoy me. "Yes, My Lady. I believe we do have an agreement. May I extend my humblest thanks for including Chimalhuacan in this venture?"

"Of course you may, My Lord. Topiltzin and I are very pleased that you wish to help us with this; it's a strong first step to reestablishing the friendship and trust our families enjoyed for generations before my uncle's bid for power."

His smile faltered ever so slightly, exposing an underlying sense of fear—not exactly the reaction I'd expected—but he quickly covered that again. "I'm eager to put the last twenty years behind us as well and to move into a prosperous future together."

"As am I," Little Reed said, rising and helping me up too. "Thank you for the delicious meal and the exquisite chocolate, but we should retire for the night. We're leaving for Acolman before dawn tomorrow."

But we didn't get more than a few steps down the hall before Nahuacatl called out to us. He looked nervous as he approached. "Forgive me for delaying you," he said with a bow. "But I was wondering if I might have a moment of your time, to discuss a...political matter with you, Lord Topiltzin?"

Little Reed's brow creased but I patted his arm, and said, "It would be better if I discussed this matter with him, My Lord, so go on ahead without me."

Nahuacatl looked at me with an expression of horror, as if he hadn't expected me to know what this was all about. Or perhaps that I'd be so bold as to suggest that he should discuss marrying me *with me* instead of with Little Reed.

Little Reed hesitated until I gave him a reassuring smile then he left, taking his guards with him. Mine remained nearby.

Nahuacatl cast his eyes down as he said, "Please forgive me if I've offended you, My Lady. I was only following traditional protocols—"

"I know you were, My Lord, but the fact that Topiltzin and I share the throne has made it necessary to...change the way some things have been done in the past. You understand?"

He nodded, his cheeks flushed with youthful embarrassment. "Then my sister told you of my intentions?"

"She did, and I'm flattered by your interest."

The desire scoffed. *Flattered? About being treated like an empty field in need of planting?* I felt it itching to take over my tongue, but I held it back. There was no need to be unduly harsh on Nahuacatl when he was just doing as his father told him.

"May I ask you something, My Lord?" I went on.

"Please do, My Lady," he said.

"How old are you?"

"Nineteen winters."

"Still so young yet. Forgive my asking, but why ever would you want to marry a woman eight years your senior? I said goodbye to my best childbearing years before you even went into your first battle, and Lord Black Otter never succeeded in begetting children with me—and not for lack of trying." I laughed, trying to sound embarrassed, but the desire seethed. "Surely Chimalhuacan's future king deserves better than his former ally's widow."

Nahuacatl started to speak, but when I added, "And surely this isn't some scheme to attach our kingdoms, at both of our expenses," he snapped his mouth shut.

"I didn't realize...the gap in our ages was so vast." He was suddenly sweating, not wanting to admit his father's ploy. "You appear much younger than twenty-seven."

The desire growled, fighting to take control, and take Nahuacatl to task for his evasion, but I held my ground. "You flatter me, My Lord. But even if not for my advanced age, I couldn't accept a proposal. I've taken a vow of chastity in Quetzalcoatl's name, so even if we did marry, I couldn't give you an heir. I cannot—in good conscience—trick you into an unconsummated marriage. And having already been one of several women in a man's household...well, as the joint ruler of the throne, I'm in a position to say I will not go through that again."

Nahuacatl nodded. "Forgive me, My Lady."

"There is nothing to forgive. These are interesting times, for everyone. We no longer need to mindlessly follow the old ways; not only can we make friends with our former enemies, but we can also determine our own futures, both men and women. Surely there is a lovely young woman that makes your heart ache like no other?" When he blushed, I chuckled and suggested, "She's the one you should be asking to tie your cape to, My Lord. And I can't imagine her saying no to such an intelligent, kind-hearted man such as yourself. Best ask her before someone else does."

The thought so appealed to him he started walking away, excitement on his face, but he paused to tell me, "Thank you for your time, My Lady, and your kind words."

I bowed my head as he hurried off. See? It wasn't always necessary to tear people apart.

No, the desire rumbled. *But if we did, next time he would have thought twice about toeing the same old lines of thinking. We already spent far too much of our life bending to the whims of self-important men.*

CHAPTER FOUR

It took two days to reach Acolman, but I remember little of the journey, for I spent most of the time sleeping in the litter. It was just as well anyway, as Little Reed was able to spend most of his time with his friend. But I wanted some time with Citlallotoc too; we'd developed a friendship while he helped me run the city during Little Reed's recovery, and I'd miss him, but not as much as Little Reed would. With Little Reed having lived far from home in the army for a ten-year stretch, Citlallotoc had likely known him as long as I had.

When I was awake I watched them from a distance, letting them have those final days together without distraction and not pretending that my friendship with Citlallotoc was as important as his with Little Reed. But when we reached Acolman and met Citlallotoc's younger brother, Huemac—who was holding the throne for him—the reality hit me hard. I wept when we gathered in the courtyard to go to Teotihuacan for the next few days while Citlallotoc did the penance and religious rituals necessary to take his rightful throne.

"Are you feeling well, My Lady?" Citlallotoc asked me when my turn came to say goodbye to him.

I nodded, the tears flowing freely. "I'm so happy for you. I know how difficult it is to be denied your rightful throne, and you and Topiltzin fought so long and hard to get it back...I'm so happy for you."

He smiled. "We did fight for it a very long time, didn't we?"

I hugged him tightly—the last time I'd be allowed to do such a thing—and whispered, "Thank you for everything you've done for us, Citlallotoc; for being Topiltzin's loyal friend, and for saving him from Red Flint, and standing for him on the battlefield when he couldn't do it himself. I shall never forget any of it."

He didn't answer at first, merely patted my back, and I imagined him shedding a few tears of his own, but I laughed that off. Citlallotoc wasn't a sentimental creature, and when I pulled away from him to wipe away my tears, he smiled back at me. But his smile looked unusually strained. "It has been an honor to serve you and your brother, My Lady, and I shall take to heart every leadership lesson Topiltzin taught me. And no god will be held above Quetzalcoatl here in Acolman."

I kissed his cheek before finally letting him move off down the line to Little Reed, who had been watching us with a proud yet sad smile. He embraced Citlallotoc as well and murmured his goodbyes while he gripped his arm. "We'll be back in time for the coronation," Little Reed promised. "The gods themselves wouldn't let me miss it."

Citlallotoc nodded but said little as Little Reed helped me up into the litter before following me inside. Little Reed sat at the curtain watching the city fade in the distance as we left, letting the mask he wore for everyone but me slip away. "Strange," he muttered, once he finally closed the curtain.

"What?"

"I'm so very glad for him, and yet...I feel as if I'm losing a piece of myself in all this."

I nodded and put my arm around his shoulder, hugging him. "I know what you mean. If Malinalli ever left...I don't know that I'd ever be all right again. After everything we've been through together...she's family to me."

"Yes, he's that important," he admitted. "I didn't expect that at all."

It took only a couple of hours to reach Teotihuacan, to the northeast of Acolman, and as with the previous journey, I slept for most of it. By the time I woke up, famished and grumpy, our men had already set up camp and Little Reed suggested I get something to eat before retiring for the rest of the day. "Tomorrow we start the fast, so best stock up now," he reminded me, handing me two tlaxcallis as he filled my bowl with stewed beans.

I avoided looking at him while I ate; hunger always brought on the desire, but it waned with the second bowl of beans. I ate yet more after that, finishing off the meal with a third tlaxcalli; I couldn't remember the last time I'd eaten so much and I went to bed feeling very full.

But I woke before sunrise, feeling intensely ill. I stumbled out of my tent and wobbled down the passageway to the water yard.

But once there, memories of the last time I'd been there set me into a panic; the high priest Ahexotl had found me alone, retching after a long night of ritual drinking. I remembered it all with a sickening clarity: his thick body pinning me against the water jars, the horrid taste of sour octli as he forced his tongue into my mouth, my nose touching the water as he held my head down over the water jar, threatening to drown me if I made a sound. *I'll leave you virginal enough,* he'd breathed on my neck. *And you can owe me again for that favor.* The shame and fear shooting through me brought up everything I'd eaten until my stomach couldn't heave anymore.

"Do you need help, My Lady?" someone called, and I nearly fled for the cover of the water jars. At the last moment I recognized my guard's voice, but I still shivered, crouched in the corner next to the water jars, feeling horribly exposed.

No hurt, another voice said—a child's voice, the same one I'd heard by the lake a few days ago. The tingling in my limbs intensified and a twinge of anger roiled inside me. *No hurt,* it repeated. The protectiveness in the voice made my heartbeat slow.

"Are you all right, Lady Quetzalpetlatl?" the guard called again. "Should we come in to help you?"

I finally found my tongue. "I'm fine. I just need a moment, thank you."

"We're waiting out here if you need us," my other guard said.

I rose, still shaking, but now because I felt as if magic were dripping off me. *If only I'd felt so powerful when Ahexotl attacked me,* I thought as I scooped handfuls of water from the rain jar, rinsing the foul taste from my mouth. *I would have set him on fire and watched him burn, to ensure he didn't get away.* My stomach clenched painfully, making me take deep, calming breaths, and I stood there, letting the anger drain from me until the tingling became little more than a background sensation.

We were supposed to start a two-day fast, but my stomach hurt so much that I took a tlaxcalli anyway, to help settle it. Little Reed didn't scold me but instead eyed me with concern. As we walked to the temple of the Feathered Serpent to pray, he said, "Your guards told me you got sick this morning."

"It's nothing," I said. "I think I over-ate last night."

"If you're ill, you shouldn't do a full fast," he insisted. "It's enough to give up chilis and salt."

"I appreciate your concern, but really, I'm fine." I hated the idea of not being as strong as him, especially about something I had years of practice with. True, hunger always aggravated my sexual desire, and I had no legitimate means of satiating that anymore. But if Little Reed could control himself, I could as well.

Except fasting probably doesn't affect him the way it affects you, I thought as we climbed the stairs. It was always on the tip of my tongue to ask Malinalli if she experienced something similar, but anytime I really thought about it, I couldn't bring myself to ask. It sounded so ridiculous that the two should have any connection to each other; they were both appetites, but I could choose to go without the latter while the former was a necessity. I had to blame myself for this conflation, for in my early years as a priestess, rather than feel the true pangs of hunger, I'd sought sexual gratification with the god as a distraction. And it had allowed me to vicariously be with Little Reed, since the god shared his face. My tendency to indulge one appetite to forget the other caused this bodily confusion and I'd have to work at un-training myself.

How amusing. It wasn't the same voice as earlier that morning; I knew the sound of my desire well, and while it often made me feel powerful, it also seemed depraved. *That's the stupid priestly training speaking,* it whispered with a laugh. *Leave it to humans to think it a good thing to feel shame for the gifts the gods give them.*

I'm not ashamed, I fired back, my temper rising.

You can lie to everyone else, but you can't lie to yourself. I'm the reason people listen to you at all; I am the fire burning in the bellies of all women, the flame that men—in their pathetic weakness—fear and try to control with their stupid little rules; they try to crush me and call me evil, and you only validate their stupidity by trying to silence me. Without me, you're only half a being, incomplete—exactly what they want you to be.

Those words reminded me of what Xolotl had told me that day on the battlefield, sending a chill through me: *You are the fire in women who won't bow to the whims of men or gods. Quetzalcoatl gave humanity life, but you give them reason to want that gift.* I felt more confused than ever. What did it all mean?

Stop playing the game by their rules and you'll understand.

◻

For a while I was able to sit with Little Reed, praying silently and meditating, but the single tlaxcalli didn't last long. The internal rumbling and gurgling grew steadily more distracting, but by noontime, it gave way to nervous fidgeting as I tried to quell the tickle of desire building inside me.

The day wasn't particularly hot, with blankets of clouds blotting out the sun, but I felt so hot that I thought—more than once—I should take off my priestly robe, to cool down. I usually didn't notice Little Reed's scent unless we were standing very close, but today it carried on the gentle breeze: spicy copal soap mixed with the pungent flowers he rubbed on to combat odor throughout the day. It was as enticing as the aroma of roasting venison. Soon I couldn't focus long enough to even think about meditating.

But when the voice started whispering that I should forget all this meditation nonsense and lay Little Reed on the stone platform and make him feel manly, I had to get away. Fearing the voice would take over, I tried to leave quietly, hoping Little Reed wouldn't notice, but as soon as I reached the stairs, he called after me.

"Where are you going?"

I didn't dare look back at him despite the concern in his voice. "I'm going somewhere else to pray."

"Really? Why?"

I floundered for an excuse that wouldn't raise more questions.

"Are you all right?" he asked. Hearing his sandals on the stone as he walked up to me, I finally took a deep breath and looked at him.

I expected the desire to roar up and take over as it had always done with Black Otter, but instead a different feeling rose in me; an aching in my heart that made me want to cry. I wanted to be in his arms, with him holding me and reassuring me that there was nothing wrong with me, that everyone fought these internal struggles just as I did, even if in my heart I knew they didn't. And that no matter how different—how abnormal—I was, he would love me regardless.

For a moment I thought of telling him everything. But how does one confess yearnings to sexually devour every man she sees as if they were food instead of people, and not seem a lunatic? I couldn't even convince *myself* that I wasn't sick and crazy. "I need to be alone for a while," I finally said. "The feeling here...it's not right for me, so I'm going to find somewhere where I am attuned to the god." Seeing disappointment cross his face, I asked, "You feel that sometimes, don't you? That having others around you can interfere with your spiritual connection to the god?"

"I do, and I understand. Please, don't let me keep you any longer. Go and find the place you need. I'll see you later tonight."

I kissed his cheek quickly—he seemed to need it as much as I did—then I fled down the stairs, fearing the desire would take over. I caught sight of my guards moving to follow me—*Two of them at once! Now wouldn't that be interesting?*—so I hurried on by, keeping a distance from them as I walked out onto the Avenue of the Dead, hoping I could outrun the incessant voice in my mind.

Uncertain where to go, I let my intuition lead me; to my surprise, it took me all the way to the opposite end of the huge precinct, to the Temple of the Moon. But I didn't want to be there either; that was where I'd cut off two of my fingers to summon Quetzalcoatl, to save us from attacking Chichimecs. The memory made my right hand sting where my two outer fingers used to be, prompting me to squeeze it with my other hand.

But this was where the gods had led me, so I took a deep breath and started up the stairs. After a few steps, I stopped to tell my guards, "Stay here. I'll be fine by myself." They looked ready to argue but nodded and let me go. As I continued up, I heard one of them suggest the other go keep watch on the other side of the pyramid. I was making their jobs harder, but I was afraid what might happen if I let them come with me.

When I reached the summit, I turned to look out at Lake Metzliapan. The clouds had cleared, letting the sun shine on the water's shimmering surface. I couldn't see Culhuacan in the distance, but Tultepec shone mirage-like on the opposite shore. To the northwest of the lake, scrub forest stretched for days before opening onto a grass plain bordering the desert.

As I stared at it, my breath caught. In the vision long ago, Quetzalcoatl had shown me temples, buildings, and a magnificent palace filling that land, but I recognized the underlying topography. *That's where we're to build the god's sacred city,* I realized, excitement igniting a righteous flame in my chest.

Home? the child's voice suddenly whispered in my head, startling me. I tried ignoring it, as I often did with the desire, but it asked again, *Home?*

Feeling foolish, I answered, *Maybe.*

Maybe? It didn't know the word.

If the god wishes it, I answered.

God?

I didn't even try to answer that one. But my mind wandered to memories of sitting in front of Quetzalcoatl on the platform outside the Temple of the Feathered Serpent in the Divine Dream, gazing longingly into his eyes—Little Reed's eyes—as the flakes of Love drifted lazily from the sky upon us, our relationship moments away from changing forever. How his touch had melted away my dress, the feathery tickle as he kissed my neck, and that feeling of excitement that, for a few years at least, had been enough....

Tatli!

I started again, unnerved to be interrupted in such thoughts. I should have been praying, not daydreaming about those bygone days when I'd been shameful enough to treat Quetzalcoatl as if he were no better than a mere mortal. I sat and closed my eyes. I didn't have the patience for whatever stupid game the desire was playing with me now.

Why would you play games with yourself? the familiar voice of my desire asked. The child-voice still babbled incoherently in the background with an occasional familiar word thrown in.

I opened my eyes, my heart faltering.

He is annoying, isn't he? the desire growled.

My mouth went dry. "He?" I looked at the front of my robe, to my abdomen hidden beneath the folds, but when I set my hand over it, I felt as if I'd been struck by lightning. *The exhaustion, the sickness this morning*— "No, no, no," I murmured, struggling to my feet. I hurried down the temple stairs, each step more desperate than the one before. *I must check my calendar journal!*

But I already knew what I'd find in there; my perfect memory made such a journal unnecessary, but Nimilitzli had taught me to keep it religiously and so I always did, out of habit. Still, I needed to see it, in ink, in tangible form, to confirm what my gut already knew: between nursing Little Reed back from his wound, handling city business during his recovery, and restarting Quetzalcoatl's cult in Culhuacan, I'd completely overlooked the fact that I hadn't bled for over two months.

Back at camp, I ducked into my tent and immediately emptied one satchel then a second, until I found the little stack of fig bark papers bound between buckskin covers. I'd made a new one when I first came to Culhuacan, since I'd lost my old one in the fires in Xochicalco. Most of the pages were empty, but when I read over my fine Mayan script on the last page I'd written on, my stomach clenched. "Dear gods, I'm pregnant!" I whispered, lips trembling.

And if the child-voice was to be believed, the god was the father.

I flashed back to that fateful day in Quetzalcoatl's temple in Xochicalco: my mother's face pale and drawn, Nimilitzli kneeling in a pool of her blood, trying to stop my mother from bleeding to death. *Bearing a child is dangerous enough without involving the gods,* my uncle had warned me. *She should cast it away or she'll never see her own grandchildren.* Would that be me too?

But why am I listening to some disembodied voice in my head? I scolded myself. *Who's to say Black Otter isn't the father?* Blinking back tears, I picked up the journal again and reread the notes I'd written on the last day I'd bled.

It was the week Black Otter had left to negotiate my release with Little Reed, and within hours of his return, his father's guards had shot him dead out on the lake. No, there was only one possible father, and I would end up dead like my mother.

I dropped the journal and covered my eyes, unable to breathe. *It must have happened when Quetzalcoatl possessed me on the battlefield,* I thought, shaking with rising anger. *He said we would be together in the real world someday, but who would have thought he was being so esoteric?*

Why angry? the child-voice asked, confused.

"Shut up!" I snarled. To my relief, it fell silent again. What would Little Reed think when I told him? He would think it was Black Otter's, of course, and Black Otter had insisted that Little Reed would kill any child of mine he thought came from my former husband—

That's nonsense. The child isn't Black Otter's, and even if it was...there's no way in Mictlan Little Reed would do something so horrible. He will love any child I gave birth to, regardless of its parentage.

But I didn't want children, and I certainly didn't want to die. I didn't ask for any of this, and Quetzalcoatl hadn't asked me if I accepted this risk; he at least gave my mother the choice, so why hadn't he granted me the same? I turned on my side and pulled my knees to my chest, struggling to hold back the sobs. *How could the god I love so dearly do this to me?*

When I finally left my tent, I went to the cooking fire to get something to eat. There was no use fasting; with a child growing inside me, stealing everything, it was only a matter of time before the desire took over and I broke my vow to heaven. Would it cost Little Reed his life? I didn't want to find out, but I was already eyeing my guards with a savage hunger that disturbed me.

As I sat next to the fire, filling my empty belly with one tlaxcalli after another, a new thought occurred to me. *I could cast it away.* Part of me cried sacrilege, but the other part gritted her teeth and barked about letting gods or men dictate my future. No, this would be my decision, my choice, no one else's. That voice I kept trying to silence was right; no more playing the game by everyone else's rules. This was my life, and I would choose my sacrifices myself, not have them foisted on me.

¤

After three days in Teotihuacan, we went back to Acolman for Citlallotoc's coronation. The kings of our various allied cities were already there, and everyone was atwitter with rumors. "The coronation ceremony has been pushed back two days," King Growling Monkey of Xochimilco told us at the feast the night we arrived. "I tried to get some answers, but no one will even let me talk to Huemac, let alone Citlallotoc."

After dinner, I sat in my private steam bath, soaking up the humidity and contemplating my next step. Nimilitzli had shown me long ago how to mix and administer the medicine for ending a pregnancy, but she'd also told me that the side-effects were troublesome: heavy bleeding, vomiting, and—depending how far along the pregnancy was—intense abdominal pains similar to those experienced during labor. If I took it tonight, by morning I wouldn't be able to leave bed for a least a week and, thinking perhaps I was dying, Little Reed might cancel our trip north, forcing us to wait until next spring before resuming the search for my father's bones. We couldn't afford to wait another year though; Smoking Mirror's cult could rise to power once more and war could break out again. The sooner we started building the god's new city, the better. We had to find my father's bones before the end of summer to keep on the path the god laid out for us.

We would only be gone for a few more months at most, but what if I didn't have even that much time left to act? Three months into her pregnancy with Little Reed, my mother was dead. What if this child was growing just as fast? The possession had happened a little over two months ago....

Except, when I looked at my bare belly, I realized I wasn't even showing yet; at this point, my mother had been very obviously pregnant. I didn't look as if I lived the austere life of most religious leaders—thanks to the daily feasting the last four months—but I didn't look pregnant either. This child wasn't growing at the accelerated rate that Little Reed had, despite their shared paternity.

I'll wait until we get back to Culhuacan, I decided as I dressed in clean clothing. I went to Little Reed's quarters, to walk back to the great hall together and wait for news with all our allies.

But shortly after I arrived at my brother's quarters, Little Reed's guards alerted us that Citlallotoc had sought us out.

To my surprise, he wasn't wearing royal regalia when he came in, but rather his usual cotton armor and eagle-feather shirt. He carried his carved wooden eagle knight helmet under his arm. He immediately went to his knees before Little Reed and bowed in supplication. Before he could say anything, Little Reed took him by the arm. "What are you doing? You don't bow to me, My Lord. You're going to be king in a few days."

Citlallotoc sat up but refused to rise any further. "Forgive me, My Lord, but I have given that honor to my brother."

I gasped. "Why in Mictlan would you do that?"

For a moment, Citlallotoc looked uncomfortable, but he said, "I have served with you a very long time, My Lord, and while I used to have aspirations to my father's throne, I found that, with the years, my heart was calling me elsewhere. Please forgive me for not being forthright about this when I first realized it, but I didn't want to disappoint you, for you kept your promise to return my throne. And I thought maybe if I came here and went through with the fasting and purifying ceremonies, my heart would follow me to the throne, as I thought it should."

"What are you saying?" Little Reed asked, gripping Citlallotoc's shoulder.

"You have taught me to listen to the gods, particularly Quetzalcoatl, and within the last two days, I realized he was telling me I don't belong on Acolman's throne. I belong at your side, defending you and your family, and seeing his good works come to fruition, the same thing I have been doing for nearly ten years."

Little Reed went to his own knees in front of Citlallotoc. "If you do this...it means renouncing any claim at all to your family's throne. You can't go back on it."

"I've already done so in private, to my brother," Citlallotoc said. "He's going through all the ceremonies now, and I'll make the formal abdication at the coronation ceremony in two days." Sensing Little Reed's hesitation, he added, "I'm positive about this,

Topiltzin. The first time I met you...I knew you were a man destined for greatness, a man I could give my devotion to without regret or hesitation. Anybody can be a king, but it takes a special man to serve the son of a god, and I hope in my heart I'm that man."

Little Reed beamed as he rose to his feet and told Citlallotoc to bow his head. He motioned me to his side. "Do you pledge to defend and serve your king and queen with faith and loyalty?"

"With my life," Citlallotoc promised. "I also pledge to protect your children, and to treat them with the same love and respect I would give my own."

His words brought forth a torrent of guilt. Only days ago I'd worried about Little Reed having no heir because of his promise, and here I was planning to cast off a child who could be the next king. *You would throw your life away for some stupid tradition that thinks blood equals the ability to rule intelligently?* the desire asked, disgusted. *And only because the child is male?*

"Do you pledge that same loyalty and faith to Quetzalcoatl?" Little Reed went on.

"I do," Citlallotoc said. "And may the gods curse my tonalli should I fail in any of this."

Little Reed motioned for him to rise and when he did, he embraced him tightly. "From this day forth, I shall call you my brother, for that is what you've always been to me," he said.

CHAPTER FIVE

 We stayed a week in Acolman celebrating Huemac's ascension before traveling north again, following the coast of Lake Metzliapan. I'd never been so far from home. There were no roads to follow anymore, only game trails winding through the forests and meadows. Black and orange birds shrieked constantly from the tall grasses, and we subsisted on rabbits our soldiers shot with their arrows. Occasionally we came upon quail nests or berry bushes to give a welcome reprieve from the steady diet of meat waging war on my bowels.

Since realizing the source of my exhaustion, I'd increased my food intake and found sitting in the litter tedious, and so took to walking with Little Reed and Citlallotoc among the soldiers. At first I struggled to listen to the conversations over the suddenly constant flow of babble in my head; it was especially bad at night, when I lay alone in my tent, staring up at the ceiling with nothing to keep me from listening. Those first few days I thought I might go crazy, but eventually it receded to the background, as with music I'd learned to tolerate if not enjoy; and by a week into our travels north, it had become a lullaby as I crawled under my blankets to fall asleep.

Eventually the forests opened onto a plain of golden grasses sprouting from black fertile earth. "Good for farming," Little Reed noted as he let the moist, black dirt break apart between his fingers. He rose and looked into the north again. "Do you recognize it?"

I nodded. "We're finally here."

"And there's the copal grove where we buried the king's bones," Amoxtli said, pointing to a large cluster of trees a quarter hour's walk away.

"Excellent!" Little Reed slapped his hands together to dust off the dirt. "We can have them dug up before nightfall."

Our caravan wound its way through the tall, golden grass, and once we reached the outskirts of the grove, Little Reed told Citlallotoc to set up camp. From there, Little Reed and I gathered a dozen soldiers, and with their digging sticks upon their shoulders, we set off into the trees, following Amoxtli. We picked our way over fallen logs and around clusters of thorny bushes, the layer of decaying leaves and twigs crunching under our feet.

After what seemed forever, Amoxtli finally stopped and looked around. He approached a gnarled old tree and leaned against it as he swept the mat of leaves and dirt away from its roots. "Right here," he said.

Little Reed motioned to the others and they hurried forward, their digging sticks ready.

The afternoon heat made my head pound as the child's voice babbled joyfully, so I sat on a log and watched, the anticipation of finally finding my father's bones making my stomach cramp. Little Reed brought me a water skin as the men chopped into the damp earth with their wooden blades. "Nervous?"

"A little." I swallowed the water, grateful for how fast it settled my stomach.

Smiling, he gripped my shoulder, reassuring. "I'm anxious too, but everything will be all right."

The moments spilled past in an endless march punctuated with the sounds of chopping through soil. I remained sitting on the log, waiting for the telltale thump of wood against stone; Little Reed paced, occasionally glancing over the men's shoulders to check their progress.

"Are you sure this is the right place, Cousin?" Little Reed asked Amoxtli after they'd been at it for an hour.

"I'm positive, Your Majesty. We should have hit it by now."

"There's nothing here," one of the soldiers grumbled, wiping the sweat from his brow.

I stood up, my legs stiff from sitting. "What's going on?"

"The box isn't here," Little Reed said.

Amoxtli shook his head. "I don't understand. I buried it myself!"

Little Reed set a hand on Amoxtli's shoulder. "I believe you, Cousin. It's just not here anymore."

Frustration vied with fear in my stomach. If we couldn't find my father's bones, how were we to know where to build the god's temple? "What are we to do now?"

Scratching his head, Little Reed said, "Let's go back to camp and regroup. After a good night's sleep, we'll decide our next step."

We traipsed back the way we'd come, following the path we'd made on the way in. But within a few moments, one of the guards hooted in alarm.

I looked to the right to see a group of men lurking among the trees a number of paces away from us. They wore bone jewelry and black tattoos decorated the faces peering at us around the sides of the trunks.

Chichimecs!

When the soldiers rushed to stand between the Chichimecs and me and Little Reed, Little Reed ordered them to halt. Our soldiers held their ground, their grips tight on their digging sticks. The Chichimecs showed us their obsidian-bladed spears.

Little Reed stepped slowly in front of his men. "We won't harm you," he called, holding his hands out in front of him to show he carried no weapons.

The Chichimecs eyed him before casting their gazes around at our soldiers. The tension in the air raised the hairs on my neck; the voice that had been babbling in my head all day had fallen quiet. Birds and locusts filled the nervous silence with their music.

"We intend no harm," Little Reed repeated.

The Chichimecs exchanged puzzled looks and one muttered to the others in a strange dialect I didn't recognize.

Little Reed must have known it though, for he immediately matched it when he spoke next. The Chichimecs' eyes widened, but then they started answering him, speaking at a staccato pace. Slowly their postures relaxed, and eventually the men—ten in all—stepped out from behind the shelter of the trees. After another exchange, they pointed to the north. Little Reed bowed and they returned the gesture, almost as an afterthought; obviously he told them nothing about us being royalty, and because he dressed like an ordinary soldier, his rank wasn't obvious.

Little Reed signaled everyone to lower their weapons. "It seems this area is not uninhabited after all. They've agreed to take us to their chief, Ten Spines."

The god hadn't mentioned anything about having to liberate the land from barbarians before building on it. *But the god didn't show you the entire battle plan, did he?* My hand wandered to my stomach as the child's voice resumed its nonsense in my head, the sound oddly comforting.

As we walked back to our own camp in the company of our new companions, I told Little Reed, "I didn't know you spoke Chichimec."

"It isn't so difficult; it's similar to our language, just different pronunciations. I can teach you sometime."

As soon as we emerged from the trees, the camp guards raised the alert and Citlallotoc hurried out to greet us, a look of concern on his face. Even when Little Reed assured him everything was all right and informed him we were going to see the chief, he still didn't relax and kept a close watch on the group of Chichimecs lingering at the outskirts of our camp. "Are you certain this is a good idea, My Lord? Their kind is prone to treachery."

"No more than our kind, my friend," Little Reed answered, giving him a pat on the shoulder.

"I should come with you."

"No, stay here and make sure our camp is secure. If things do go sour, I need you to get our people out of here quickly."

"If you believe there is danger, then I object to you leaving with them."

"I don't believe there is, but I don't make a habit of not considering all possibilities."

Citlallotoc looked as if he wished to continue arguing, but he knew when to follow orders. He said no more as we left, our personal guards escorting us.

We followed the Chichimecs down a winding game trail to a river. The path opened up onto a camp consisting of at least twenty deer-skin tents circling several cooking fires. The women washing laundry at the riverside looked up from their work, curious, and several children followed us from a distance. When we reached the center of camp, our escorts took us to the largest tent. They signaled us to wait then ducked inside.

I looked around, taking in this strange, primitive setting. The tents were clustered close together, and I caught sight of a few young boys watching us from behind the ones across the central fire. A bent old man sat outside his tent, dressed only in a ragged rabbit-skin loincloth, knapping a large chunk of obsidian into the smaller cores used for spears and arrow tips. He wiped his nose with his wrist when he met my gaze but went back to his work, uninterested. A girl sitting at the fire, though—perhaps fifteen, sixteen years old—watched us with open curiosity while the old woman next to her mended a buckskin shirt. When the girl noticed my gaze, she quickly turned to the woman, whispering; the old woman merely chuckled and pointed at the cooking pot, which the girl took to stirring earnestly while still casting furtive glances in my direction. I cast her a smile, which she returned with cautious friendliness.

The flap on the tent parted and a large, battle-scarred man wearing a bone-and-feather headdress stepped out, a broad smile on his face. The other men followed him out but started when he bowed to Little Reed. "Lord Topiltzin, the Revered Speaker of the Tolteca, it is an honor to finally meet you," the man said in our tongue. The others looked at each other, puzzled, but they soon followed suit, bowing to Little Reed as well.

Little Reed returned the gesture. "You've heard of me, Lord Ten Spines?"

"I may not live in the valley anymore, but I keep apprised of what transpires there. I congratulate you on your ascension to Culhuacan's throne; the stars say your reign will be the beginning of great things for all peoples, so it is an honor to host you here in my humble camp."

"The honor is all mine, and I thank you for taking our audience."

Ten Spines waved his words off with a laugh. "The pleasure is all *mine*." His gaze wandered to me standing behind Little Reed, and that familiar glaze men often got when they looked at me settled over his eyes. "And is this lovely blossom your wife, Your Majesty?"

Little Reed urged me forward by the elbow. "This is my sister, Lady Quetzalpetlatl. We co-rule, sharing the throne in Culhuacan."

I bowed to Ten Spines, and to my relief, he quickly shook off the distraction and gestured to the old woman at the fire. "My wife, Lady Bitter Rabbit, and that is my eldest daughter, Mitotia." He finished introductions by pointing at the girl. To me he added, "They would appreciate whatever help you can give them preparing the noon meal while your brother and I speak business."

Little Reed cleared his throat, his posture tense, but I smiled and said, "I'd be honored to help, My Lord." When Little Reed looked at me, questions in his eyes, I whispered, "We're in his camp, so let's respect his ways. Besides, you can't make any actual treaties or alliances without me, so let's ease him into our way of thinking."

"You will join us once the meal is ready?"

"Of course."

Little Reed and Ten Spines retreated into the large tent, and I went to the cooking fire, my guards remaining nearby. I knelt on one of the ratty mats. "What are we cooking?" I asked Bitter Rabbit as I inhaled the aromatic steam above the boiling pot.

She showed me her gapped smile but said nothing.

"She doesn't understand your language," Mitotia replied as she stirred the pot.

"But you do," I noted, impressed.

Mitotia nodded. "My father spent his formative years traveling around the south."

"You speak it very well. Your father taught it to you?" Given how casually Ten Spines had dismissed me, it surprised me that he would do so.

"Sort of," Mitotia said with a blush. "He was teaching my brother and I asked him to teach me too, but he refused, saying it would ruin my disposition for marriage. So I hid outside his tent and listened in and learned as he taught my brother."

I burst out laughing. "That's something I would have done." I liked Mitotia already.

◻

Ten Spines and Little Reed were deep in discussion when Mitotia and I brought the finished stew into the chief's tent. Little Reed immediately rose to help me with the pot while Ten Spines remained sitting, smoking a long cylindrical pipe. Once Mitotia had filled two tortoise shell bowls for the men, Ten Spines tried to dismiss both of us, but this time Little Reed didn't hesitate.

"Forgive me, and I know this will sound strange and maybe even improper, but when I said that Lady Quetzalpetlatl and I co-rule Culhuacan, I meant that we share power equally. We make all political decisions together, and as the highest priests of the Feathered Serpent's order, we both lead our citizens in their spiritual lives. It's imperative we involve her in all treaty discussions, and I cannot proceed any further if that is an issue for you."

Ten Spines looked from Little Reed to me and back again, an amused expression on his face. It softened though when he saw Little Reed was serious. He cleared his throat before turning to me again. "Forgive my behavior, Lady Quetzalpetlatl. I'd heard that Lord Topiltzin's ways were...different than most, but I didn't realize...." He sat straighter, looking distinctly uncomfortable. "I apologize for insulting you."

I sat next to Little Reed, who ladled out some stew for me. "I was not insulted, My Lord. I'm quite used to these kinds of confusions, for as you said, my brother's ways are strange to many." Would there ever be a time when my worth would be judged by my own actions rather than everyone defining it by how Little Reed did things? *Someday,* I thought. *I'll make certain of it.* "Where are we in the discussions?"

"Lord Topiltzin was attempting to convince me that building a Tolteca city on our ancestral lands would somehow benefit us." Ten Spines set aside his pipe and picked up his bowl. "I'm concerned about the kinds of influences this project would bring to our people. The Tolteca have been in a near-constant state of warfare since before I was born, trying to keep the Chichimecs out of the valley, and yet now you seek to establish a Tolteca stronghold in the north."

I suppressed a smirk. He was worried about Tolteca influence after all the chaos and war his people had brought to us? In the days of my great-grandmother, women could be war queens, but the steady invasion of Chichimecs and their philosophies had worn that tradition away. It was little wonder that men such as Flame Tongue thought it perfectly acceptable to dismiss me. It would take years to undo the negative impact Chichimecs had brought to Tolteca culture.

"The valley is at peace for the first time since the fall of Teotihuacan," Little Reed pointed out.

"With all due respect, Lord Topiltzin, you've been on your throne a mere four months," Ten Spines said.

"That is true, but it's the goal of our new reign to keep it that way."

The tent flap burst open and another man came storming in. The stranger's hair dangled in greasy strands around his red-and-white-stripe-painted face, and bits of bone and string decorated his dingy black robe. He brought a wave of fury with him.

Our guards moved to intercept him. When Ten Spines assured them this new man wasn't a threat, they reluctantly retreated to their stations, but remained on alert.

"This is our shaman, Ueman," Ten Spines told us. "Please forgive his blustery entrance; he tends to the dramatic."

"Vile villains!" Ueman barked at us, his face livid.

"Pardon?" I asked, taken aback.

"They desecrated the sacred grove, My Lord!" Ueman told Ten Spines. "They were digging up the god's earth!"

The smile fell from Ten Spine's face, replaced with incredulity. "Is this true, Lord Topiltzin?"

After a tense pause, Little Reed said, "We were looking for something."

Ten Spines stiffened. "The copal grove is a sanctuary dedicated to the god of the hunt. It is a grave crime to disturb the ground."

"We meant no harm by it, My Lord," I assured him. "You see, we came north to retrieve my father's bones, which my cousin buried in the grove. If we'd known your people were here, and that the site was sacred, we absolutely wouldn't have gone forward with the search without consulting you."

Ueman's face turned even fiercer. "Bones? Bones!" He turned to Ten Spines. "They've come to steal the god's bones!"

"Well, they can't have them!" Ten Spines fired back, rising to his feet.

Little Reed stood too, holding his hands up for calm. "I'm afraid there's been a misunderstanding, My Lord. We seek the remains of a mortal king, not a religious artifact."

"Lies, My Lord!" Ueman hissed. "Tolteca treachery! They've come to take Mixcoatl away from us."

I blinked, startled, and puzzled. "Mixcoatl was my father."

"And now they call themselves children of a god? Blasphemy!"

They think my father's a god? I glanced at Little Reed; obviously bringing up his divine parentage now would be a mistake. To Ten Spines, I said, "My father's name was Mixcoatl, but he was not a god, I assure you. He was the king of Culhuacan, but my uncle Ihuitimal murdered him and usurped the throne. Topiltzin and I fought for nearly ten years to regain our rightful throne."

"We do not name our kings for gods," Ueman snarled. "That is the height of disrespect."

"And neither do we," Little Reed said. "The god Mixcoatl is unknown among the Tolteca. I'm sure there are gods we worship that are unknown to your people too."

"I can't believe you, Lord Topiltzin—of all people—can claim ignorance of who Mixcoatl is," Ten Spines said. "You claim to be Quetzalcoatl's high priest."

"We are the Feathered Serpent's high priests," I countered, my voice colored with growing irritation.

"Then you would know that Mixcoatl is Quetzalcoatl's father, My Lady."

I almost laughed but caught myself before losing control of my tongue. *What do these backwards, uncivilized people know of the gods?*

"At the beginning of summer, the god showed us where his bones were buried—inside the copal grove—and he instructed us to dig them up and take them with us when we left for the winter hunting grounds to the north." Ten Spines looked to Ueman for confirmation, and the shaman nodded firmly.

"That may well be," Little Reed said. "But I assure you that the bones you found were not the bones of any god; they belong to the mortal king of Culhuacan, and we've come to give him a proper burial, with full funerary rites. And Quetzalcoatl has instructed us to build a city upon the site where King Mixcoatl's bones are found—"

"Oh, so now they want our land too?" Ueman spouted. "Typical Tolteca scheming!" He barked something else to Ten Spines in their own language as well.

Little Reed said, "We would never dream of building anything without—"

"Enough!" Ten Spines sliced his hand through the air like a sword. "I'm sorry, Lord Topiltzin, Lady Quetzalpetlatl, but I must insist that you return to the valley immediately and not return."

I started to protest, but Little Reed stopped me with a gentle squeeze to my wrist.

"We shall do as you ask, My Lord, but may I beg your indulgence for just one night?

We've been traveling almost nonstop for several weeks and our camp is already set up. Will you allow us one night to rest? We will leave before dawn tomorrow."

Ten Spines thought a moment, his face hard, but then he said, "We are not a pitiless people, so yes, you may have your one night." Ueman started to protest, but Ten Spines silenced him with a raised hand. "But remember that the gods know of any treachery you might be planning, and we will not hesitate to take every last one of you to the sacrifice if they command it."

"We promise no treachery," Little Reed replied. "And as a show of good faith, I invite you to station a patrol of warriors inside our camp, so you may rest easy with your decision to allow us to remain here tonight.

Nodding stiffly, Ten Spines said, "My men will escort you and your sister back to your camp."

◻

Neither of us spoke as we returned to our own camp where our soldiers were busy working. Citlallotoc greeted us at the improvised fire pit our servants had made in the middle of camp. "How did the negotiations fare?"

"They are still not over. These men will remain in camp tonight—" Little Reed pointed to the Chichimecs who'd come with us—"so please let all of our men know they are to be treated as guests, with the utmost civility. Now, if you'll excuse us, Lady Quetzalpetlatl and I will need privacy for the next hour."

"Of course, Your Majesty." Citlallotoc eyed the Chichimecs though, the distaste plain on his face.

Little Reed and I retired to our tent. As soon as the flap was closed, I said, "I can't believe this! They have no right to take my father's bones like that! And I can't believe you let them!"

"I'm not *letting them*, Papalotl," Little Reed said with a chuckle. "This is where the god wants his city built, and I intend to convince Ten Spines to join us in this venture."

"Then why did you agree to us leaving tomorrow?" Would we return to Culhuacan and raise an army to take these lands by force? And could we even convince the valley's Chichimecs to mobilize against their own people still in the north?

"We won't be leaving. In fact, Ueman will convince Ten Spines that we are their friends."

"How?"

"He told Ten Spines he was going into the Divine Dream to get guidance from the gods on how to deal with us."

"Is that what he told Ten Spines when he started jabbering in their language?"

He nodded. "And we will go into the Divine Dream as well."

I hadn't visited the Divine Dream in almost three years, and much had changed for me since then; the last time I saw the god, we were still lovers, using the divine realm more for sex than religious inspiration, and after I thought I lost Little Reed forever, I swore off going back because it hurt too much seeing him in the god's face. But I was also haunted by how arrogant and disrespectful I'd been to the god, lying with him in the Divine Dream, selfishly using him as a substitute while my heart ached for Little Reed. It embarrassed me that I'd behaved so childishly, so pruriently.... I dreaded facing him again and having to answer questions about why I never came back after promising I would. "Must I go too?" I asked, trying to sound casual even as my stomach roiled. "I'm feeling very tired."

"I think it especially important that you go," Little Reed said. "Quetzalcoatl will assure Ueman of our good intensions, so we must be there to stand with the god, show Ueman we are united in our power and fealty to the god. And to each other."

I chewed my lip a moment before nodding. Little Reed was right. Now wasn't the time for timidity and childish embarrassment. I was the god's high priestess, professional in every regard, and I wouldn't let fear stand in the way of my duties.

I hadn't brought any teonanactl mushrooms with me, but Little Reed provided some from his own personal store which he kept in a plain, undecorated box. He mixed the dried mushrooms into two cups of octli—one for each of us—then we drank. I swallowed mine fast to make certain my fear didn't cause me to back down. My sinuses stung from the alcohol but it didn't quite mask the bitter taste of the mushrooms; my body reacted with heightened arousal, as if suddenly remembering why I'd so often drunk this concoction in the past. I squeezed my thighs together, positive that my desire was plain to see.

"Which mat do you want?" Little Reed asked, motioning to the two feathered prayer mats set up in front of our small idol of Quetzalcoatl. It was such a simple, courteous question and yet it made me sweat.

"Actually, I'm going to go to my room," I said. "I prefer to lie down while in the Divine Dream." I bit my tongue, mortified as soon as I said it, but quickly added, "I've fallen over before and hurt myself, so it's safer for me to lie down." I fumbled with the tent flap separating my sleeping quarters from the large anteroom, my cheeks aflame.

"Very well." Little Reed sat, oblivious to my embarrassment.

I ducked into my quarters and secured the flap behind me, breathing deeply. I stared at my bed, the desire rebounding—and bringing with it memories of the god's feathery touch, on my neck, my breasts, my thighs....

But I shook it off. I wasn't seventeen anymore; I had ten years on that foolish girl, and I was not only the high priestess, but the Queen of Culhuacan. I was stronger than this. I swallowed, calming myself, then lay on my bed and waited for the Divine Dream to take me away.

And waited. And waited. Eventually I drifted off to sleep, my body surrendering to the far greater desire for rest.

CHAPTER SIX

"Are you ready to go?" My eyes flashed open to find Little Reed kneeling next to me.

Except I wasn't in the tent any longer. I was in a room similar to mine in the palace back in Culhuacan, but bigger and more airy. When the breeze shifted the half-open curtains closing off the patio, the air smelled heady with flowers and heat; no hint of the brackish water smell of Lake Meztliapan or the cloying humidity that made the air feel thick in the lungs. "Where are we?" I asked, sitting up.

"The Divine Dream," Little Reed replied, taking my hand to help me to my feet. "We're inside the palace we will build in the god's new city."

"You've been here before?"

"The god has shown it to me often." Little Reed gave my hand a gentle squeeze. "Let's go and find Ueman."

As we went for the door leading out, I noticed movement off to my left, at a secondary doorway covered in a bright blue curtain. Embroidered dancing rabbits decorated the hem, but they moved as if alive, playing reed flutes and banging drums with their forepaws as they pranced and bounced about. The corner of the curtain lifted slightly and a real rabbit—tawny brown with glistening pine-pitch eyes—poked its head out. It peered at me, twitching its nose.

Little Reed and I stepped out of the room into a portico that extended in a square around a cozy garden choked with beds of bone flowers in full bloom. "This is our family garden," he told me as I looked around in awe. "Every council member's extended family shall have one in our palace, with their living quarters clustered around it, just like this; as will the priesthood as well." He pointed out the other doorways off the portico.

Opposite my own doorway, across the garden, the curtain on the doorway was light blue with a large white and green feathered serpent in the center—Little Reed's royal sigil. A walkway connected my side of the garden to his, meeting at a large flagstone patio in the middle. At the north end of the patio, a tall limestone statue of Quetzalcoatl in his feathered serpent form curled in a column up towards Heaven, watching over everything.

I glanced back at my own door curtain to find it was a strange murky grey color, as though smoke clung to it, obscuring its true color and pattern. I puzzled over that for a few moments as we left the garden for a hallway that led into the heart of the palace.

But catching a glimpse of our icpalli thrones in the great hall drove it from my thoughts. They looked so small in the giant room—it was at least three times the size of Culhuacan's great hall, and painted from floor ceiling with maps of our various allied cities. The ceiling itself was an illustration of the divine realm; the underworld loomed over the main doorway, and a winding stone staircase led up onto the mortal plane with its rivers and trees and mountains. That eventually gave way to the sky with Omeyocan hovering above our thrones. The various gods had been painted on the three planes, each doing the things they were known for: Tlaloc dumping pots of rain on the earth from the clouds, the Feathered Serpent moving the winds over the earth, Xipe Totec sowing the maize seeds with the blood dripping from his flayed skin, and Lord Death sitting on his throne of bones in Mictlan, his servant Xolotl sitting at his feet in dog-form. Even Smoking Mirror was in the mural, as a black jaguar rising from the smoke of a burning city.

Outside the great hall was a large vestibule whose roof was supported by columns of stone statues of all the gods. This opened onto a set of stairs overlooking a courtyard filled with boxes of flowers of every color and fragrance. The sacred precinct was also visible from the top of the stairs, and straight across from the palace was a large pyramid with an open-sided temple at the top.

"That's the Temple of the Feathered Serpent," Little Reed told me as we walked down the steps to the long walkway that opened onto the city itself. "That's probably where Ueman is."

And as always in the Divine Dream, fat flakes of Love fell from Omeyocan, covering everything and filling my nose with the sweet smell of bone flowers. It made my heart race with exhilaration.

The city wasn't empty either. The sacred precinct was teeming with people; tattooed Chichimecs walked among Tolteca nobles dressed in the styles unique to the various lake valley cities; some even walked and chatted together as if old friends—remarkably different to the dynamic between Tolteca and Chichimecs back in Culhuacan. No one bothered us as we cut through the crowds and made our way up the stairs of

Quetzalcoatl's temple.

The platform was significantly larger than the ones on the pyramids in both Culhuacan and Xochicalco, but here the temple took up the entire area. As in the palace vestibule, large pillars—similar to the one back in the family garden—supported the roof. A gilded idol of the god—coiled upright with mouth gaping open, for the blood sacrifices—sat in the middle with feathered mats spread out in front of it. There was no altar as in the other temples.

Ueman was wandering around inside, gaping at everything in awe. When he noticed us standing under the roof at the front of the temple, he started. "What *is* all this?" he asked, coming to the front to stare at the city spread out below us.

Before either of us could answer, a familiar voice—deep and yet still so similar to Little Reed's—spoke up behind us. *This is the city I have asked Topiltzin and his queen Quetzalpetlatl to build for me.* When we all turned around, the feathered serpent column behind us began untwisting itself, dust and rubble flaking off as it moved.

Ueman gasped and nearly backed right over the side of the pyramid, but Little Reed grabbed his arm. "It's all right," Little Reed said. "He comes to me in such forms often."

Odd, for the god only came to me in such inhuman forms in the real world; in the Divine Dream, he was always a man, with quetzal feathers growing amongst his long black hair, and a touch that suggested his skin was covered in feathers even though he looked no different than Little Reed. My body ached with pitiful longing for the memory, and I hoped he wouldn't notice me as he slithered soundlessly across the floor to circle us.

But once he reached the stairs, he took to the air. The sleek stone feathers carved into his body ruffled in the wind, and when he fanned his long, glorious quetzal feathers around his head, I couldn't breathe. *He's so beautiful!* I thought, imagining him glowing brilliant white with a shimmering halo of emerald accenting his neck. My heart thudded, so sweetly painful.

Ueman went slowly to his knees, bewildered. "Forgive my reaction, My Lord, but the gods have never spoken so plainly to me."

There is no need for apologies, Quetzalcoatl said, hovering before us. *We gods do not often visit our followers in such ways, but this time I wanted to.*

Prostrating himself on the platform, Ueman said, "I am your humble servant, Most Precious Twin. What message do you wish me to bring back to your people?"

I understand your reticence in trusting Topiltzin, for he is but a mortal; but know that as my son he serves his father's will on earth, and together with Quetzalpetlatl will bring such peace as neither Chichimec nor Tolteca have known before.

Ueman started looking up, surprised, but he caught himself. "Lord Topiltzin...is your son, My Lord?"

Quetzalcoatl bobbed his head. *I placed him in the belly of a mortal woman so I might guide humanity out of the darkness and back into the light. He will bring an end to war, and enemies shall join together as friends and allies, and all shall reap the gift of prosperity and happiness. But they must open their hearts, for only then can they worship as their gods truly deserve.*

Ueman turned to stare up at Little Reed. "Forgive my doubting you, My Lord."

Little Reed shook his head. "It's quite all right."

Turning back to the god—but keeping his eyes downcast—Ueman asked, "Tell us what we must do, My Lord."

The god swam towards us, and for a moment I thought he was going to collide hard with us, stone crushing flesh and bone, but instead he passed among us as if he were wind, the tendrils of his essence reaching inside each of us; Ueman clutched his breast and wept while Little Reed breathed deep, smiling. The god's touch sent a tingling wave of pleasure rushing through me and I bit my lip to keep from moaning in ecstasy.

Build this very temple on the spot where you found the bones of the mortal king that shares the name of your tribal god; every odd stone shall be laid by a free Chichimec with earth upon their hands, for these are their ancestral lands; every even stone shall be laid by the hands of a free Tolteca, consecrated by each worker's own bloodletting, a small gift given in the name of the gods. For without both earth and water, nothing grows. The god's stone body returned inside the temple where it had started and slowly reformed the pillar it had once been. *Every temple to every god, every building erected, every street paved here in my sacred city will follow this same code, and the city will henceforth be known as Tollan.*

"And if we should fail in your task?" Little Reed asked.

Then the world shall fall further into the darkness already clawing for a foothold, Quetzalcoatl replied. *Nations shall rise and fall in endless war, spanning far and wide, and the temple steps will run slippery with the blood of countless victims, murdered to satisfy the hunger and power lusts of a few gods and their mortal allies. The bonds of brotherhood will fray, and when the Fifth Sun sets for the final time, it will be too late to keep them from snapping. A great shaking will reduce the cities and their temples to rubble, unleash plagues that devour my people from the inside out, and shatter all faith in the gods. The world will crumble, as will the memory of all that existed here.*

With those final words, the carved stone feathered serpent fell still, once again only a statue. The god had never been quite so ominous before, and hearing his predictions of the end of the world left me chilled.

"We shall not fail you, My Lord," Ueman promised. He looked around at the city with tears in his eyes.

"The god actually spoke to me!" he whispered. "All my life I've dreamed that Mixcoatl would come to me while I meditated with the peyotl and deem me worthy of providence—"

"But didn't Ten Spines say Mixcoatl told you to take the bones with you when you left for the winter?" I asked, trying to sound more puzzled than annoyed. Now I was certain he'd lied to us.

Ueman bowed his head. "A voice spoke to me in the Divine Dream, telling me to take the bones away, but I never saw the face of the one who said the words. I just assumed it was Mixcoatl himself."

Little Reed and I exchanged glances. I would bet my royal headdress it was Smoking Mirror who ordered the removal of my father's bones, to spoil our plans for the god's city.

"But now Mixcoatl has sent his son to bless me!" Ueman turned to look at Little Reed with eyes wide. "And Quetzalcoatl sent you for all of us!" He started to prostrate himself before Little Reed.

But Little Reed stopped him and instead helped him back up. "I don't seek to be anyone's god; I come to be a bridge between our peoples, to finally bring peace and a prosperous future for us all."

"We must speak with Ten Spines immediately!"

Ueman started down the temple stairs, but when my brother followed him, Little Reed became ghost-like; he walked down the stairs and yet he still stood at the edge of the platform, as if his tonalli had stepped right out of his body. The one still standing there turned to look at me and smiled, green quetzal feathers tucked between the folds of his long black hair. *Papalotl,* he whispered; it was Little Reed's face and his voice, but it was the god.

"My Lord," I whispered, that painful ache resurfacing in my chest. I didn't move to hug him—as I often had when we saw each other—but I didn't resist when he embraced me. Eventually the tension melted away under his feathery warmth and I leaned into him, savoring the feeling of safety and security that had brought me back to him as often as desire and need had. He stroked my cheeks with his feathery hands, sending an eager shiver through me, but rather than kiss me he gazed lovingly into my eyes. The way Little Reed often did.

Topiltzin showed you the city? he asked.

"Some of it." My voice hitched with longing but I cleared my throat, embarrassed. "I saw the palace."

Let me show you the rest. He took my hand and led me down the stairs, into the precinct and out into the broader city.

He showed me the artisan quarters filled with homes decorated with exquisite feathered banners and delicately painted flower boxes. Wind chimes of dried reeds played music in time with the clacking of the obsidian knappers making blades for shaving and the kitchen rather than for macuahuitl swords. He showed me the market overflowing with people selling goods from every corner of the world: cacao beans from the south, pottery and hides from the valley, dried fish from the eastern coasts, and medicinal plants from the northern desert. We walked through the various residential neighborhoods where the whitewashed houses were painted with images of the gods and animals, and Tolteca children ran with Chichimec children, laughing and playing.

Eventually we ended up back in the sacred precinct, and he took me to the calmecac where hundreds of children sat in large classrooms learning to read, write, and keep the calendar.

There's one more place I want to show you, Quetzalcoatl told me with a mysterious smile. We went to a gate that led into a vast garden hidden by high stone walls behind the calmecac. There were no people in here, only trees, flowers and bushes, and the sounds of birds and monkeys and bees. We said nothing as we walked along a gravel path, still holding hands; but when we reached a pond in the shade of an enormous oak tree, we sat in the grass to rest.

"Tollan is going to be magnificent," I said, soaking in the thick, sweet fragrance of bone flowers hanging over everything, setting my heart racing and my desire simmering. The unease and fear I'd felt earlier was forgotten, and when Quetzalcoatl leaned in to kiss me I eagerly welcomed his embrace, even more so when he lowered me gently onto my back, the grass prickling through my dress.

I shivered as he trailed his hand down my neck, the illusory feathers tickling as he rubbed his feathery hands over my exposed breasts; it wasn't unusual for us to skip the whole undressing distraction, particularly when we were impatient. Which one of us had banished our clothing, I wasn't certain, but we were both naked and entwined with each other as if it had only been a few weeks since last indulging in such pleasure, not almost three years.

I bit my bottom lip against the gasp as he eased himself into me, holding one of my legs up against his shoulder as he thrust slow and deep, gazing at me with intense eyes. I stared back, swallowed up by the mesmerizing depths there. Gods were supposedly unfathomable, so different from humans, and yet when I looked into his eyes, I knew he saw my very soul, understood me on that most primal level, as if we were kindred in some regard that I didn't yet know how to articulate. In him I saw everything I cherished; faith, love, Little Reed, all meshed together in a blur of breath and muscle and slow, sweet movement. I gripped fistfuls of grass as the pleasure cascaded over me, delicious and familiar.

Slowly the buzz of gratification wore away and the edges of reality began bleeding through the Divine Dream. The orange sky darkened and the ceiling of the royal tent became gradually visible. The teonanactl would only hold me here a few moments longer, but Quetzalcoatl rested his head against my leg as if we had all afternoon to bask in post-coital bliss. He rubbed his feathery fingers over my belly, reminding me of what he'd put in there—under circumstances far less pleasurable than this—and I wondered what he'd say about that, what explanation he'd give me for why he'd done it, and whether he'd assure me that it was all part of his grand scheme and that I would be all right.

But he merely sighed and kissed my calf before lowering my leg. *I missed you so much, my love,* he whispered. *It feels so good to have you back again.* He leaned over and kissed me, his loose hair a curtain around our heads.

His words brought dueling emotions rampaging through me; was that really all he had to say to me? And were we truly back together again? Now that I was thinking more clearly, the guilt and shame of having yet again treated the god as little better than a mortal man bit down on me.

I opened my eyes to find myself back in the tent, fully clothed, my body slick with sweat underneath my dress and my mouth dry from the heat. I went out into the anteroom to get some water, feeling woozy.

But when Little Reed came out of his own room dressed in the lightweight royal robes he'd brought along to wear to Citlallotoc's coronation, I tried to melt back into my own room. I was too slow though. When he saw me he smiled like a man who'd put a ball through the stone ring to end a highly contested tlachtli game. "A most gratifying afternoon in the Divine Dream, don't you think?" he asked, making my cheeks flare. "Ueman has spoken to Ten Spines and they both wish to meet with us immediately to discuss the terms of our partnership."

"Already?"

"It has been several hours since we went into the Divine Dream, and I was waiting for you to come back from it," Little Reed admitted. "Perhaps I put too much teonanactl into your octli." When I looked away, my face hot, he furrowed his brow. "Is everything all right, Papalotl? You look...." He scrutinized me, struggling to find the right word perhaps.

"I'm fine," I assured him. "The heat is a bit stifling. Let me wash up and changes clothes, and we'll get on our way."

He brought me a rag and a wash basin filled with water. "You're certain you're all right?" he asked again as I took his offerings.

I nodded, putting on a brave smile even though the guilt struck hard now. Here he'd forsaken all others because he loved me, and I'd spent the afternoon indulging in shameful lust with his father. Even now I couldn't believe I'd been so selfish and weak. The god's high priestess should be strong and faithful.

I considered confessing my bad behavior to him, but thinking about the god making love to me in the priestly garden set the wanton desire bubbling inside me. *I can't ever go back into the Divine Dream,* I realized. It felt weak to think it, but Nimilitzli had told me that sometimes the strongest thing we could do was distance ourselves from those things that tempted us most. I would have to find less personal ways to learn the will of the god and guide my people from now on.

He still looked troubled, so I repeated, "I am fine," and gave his hand a gentle, reassuring squeeze. "If you wait for me, I'll be out in a moment, my love."

My words brightened his mood again, and he gave me a curiously seductive smile before ducking out through the main tent flap.

◻

"How soon should we start building?" Ten Spines asked as he and Ueman escorted Little Reed and I around the Chichimec camp. The three men had brought their pipes along, indulging in a bit of smoking as they walked. All around us, men and women alike hurried about, preparing for the evening's celebratory feast.

"We should lay the foundation for the main temple before the end of summer, but work will continue through the winter months, as weather permits," Little Reed replied.

Ten Spines shook his head. "Food is plentiful here in the warm seasons, but we'll starve if we stay the winter."

"We'll have food brought in from the valley, enough to sustain all our workers and your tribe through the winter, and in the spring we'll plant maize, beans, squash, and chile, to stock up our stores for next winter."

"But our people have never farmed, Lord Topiltzin," Ueman pointed out. He'd taken to performing a slight hunch whenever he spoke to Little Reed, as if trying to maintain a bow. "Nor do we know about building the giant stone cities the Tolteca are renowned for."

"We will teach your people these skills," I assured him. To Ten Spines, I said, "Imagine the possibilities for your people in the future, My Lord: if they learn to farm, they can settle in one place, build permanent homes and establish schools where their children can learn a wide variety of skills, such as metallurgy and feather-working; skills they can pass on to their children."

"Having spent nearly ten years in the army, I know how difficult it is living out of a tent and moving all the time," Little Reed added. "Neither men nor women live very long in those circumstances, but once your people begin working the land and reaping the benefits of a settled life, they'll be happier, they'll live longer, and their children will be healthier and have greater opportunities."

"The older I get, the more difficult the winters become," Ten Spines acknowledged. "And I worry what will become of my family once I'm gone. My only son...he ran away to the valley because I didn't approve of the woman he wanted to take to wife, and though Mitotia is as bright as any man...." He shook his head. "I wish she'd been born one, for she has always been a better leader than even her brother. But because she is a woman, when I die, leadership will go to someone outside my family, and frankly, the young men of my tribe dream too ardently of war. I've seen my share, and there is nothing glorious about it."

"Sometimes war is necessary," Little Reed said. "But peace is even more so."

"And I have your assurances that my people will not be relegated to being slaves or persecuted because they were born in the desert?"

"All of our peoples will share in the power and wealth of Tollan, and we shall live in peace," Little Reed promised. "That is the will of the god."

When Ten Spines looked to Ueman, the shaman nodded, conceding the fact.

"And as a token of this promise, I would ask you to take command of the project once Lady Quetzalpetlatl and I return to Culhuacan after we've laid the temple's foundation."

"You aren't staying?" Ten Spines asked, surprised.

"Until Tollan is finished, we have ongoing obligations back in the valley."

"It is just as well, for Mitotia will need to learn the ways of the Tolteca royal court."
Puzzled, I asked, "And why might that be, My Lord?"
"Because she will marry your brother, of course."
Little Reed suddenly choked on his smoke and I had to thump him on the back as he coughed.
"She will make a fine wife, My Lord," Ten Spines added hastily. "She can be willful, but she is loyal, and she turned fifteen in the spring, so she hasn't lost more than a few of her best childbearing years."
Red-faced, Little Reed beckoned to his guards for a water skin and one immediately obliged. He gulped some down, coughing between drinks.
Ten Spines' brow furrowed in irritation. "I know Mitotia is not a beauty—"
"Actually, she is very beautiful," I cut in. "And Topiltzin would be so very lucky to have her at his side; I had the opportunity to speak with her while we prepared the afternoon meal, and she deeply impressed me. I see why you think she would be a great leader if only tradition wasn't standing in her way."
Ten Spines puffed up his chest and let a modest smile capture his lips. "She is so very astute; even more so than I. And yet your brother shows contempt for the thought of marrying her?" His smile vanished as he cast a hard glare at Little Reed.
"You mistake his reaction, My Lord. He is merely nervous about having to reject your proposal; he is already betrothed to another." I expected Little Reed to shoot me a questioning look, but he seemed not to hear me with all his coughing, so I continued on. "And while I'm certain you're aware that most Tolteca royalty keep concubines in their households, he's chosen not to take any himself. We're striving to create a more equal society for everyone, and since many traditions undermine such efforts, we've chosen to set the example ourselves. One set of rules for men and another for women—or one set for Toltecas and a different set for Chichimecs—doesn't promote the changes we aim to make."
Nodding stiffly, Ten Spines said, "There is logic to your words, My Lady, but I must admit disappointment. This is how we Chichimecs cement intertribal pacts, and your brother appears a good healthy match for her. I fear this means her last chance at marriage is over; she is obviously too old to interest anyone."
I nodded. "I understand your concerns, My Lord, but what does Mitotia want?"
"She wants to honor her family, of course."
"There are many ways for us to honor our families. In the past, the only way for most women was to marry and have children, but there was also the priesthood. Based on my brief discussion with her, I think Mitotia would excel in the priesthood, and you spoke earlier of what a good leader she would be. In the priesthood, she can be that, and more; she can help support your people in ways she never could as a king's wife, hidden away behind palace walls, risking childbirth one time after another with the possibility that none of those children will survive, let alone go on to do great things for your people. She can do great things for your people *now;* we Tolteca have no cult honoring the Cloud Serpent, so imagine if she helps establish that in Tollan. Perhaps she even becomes Mixcoatl's high priestess."
"That is compelling," Ten Spines admitted. "But what about having a family?"
"She can have both," I assured him. "That is one of the many reforms Quetzalcoatl seeks with our reign. Priests and priestesses will be allowed to take a spouse if they choose."
By now, Little Reed had finally recovered. "Please accept my apologies for this most inopportune moment to be taken by a coughing fit." He cleared his throat again, as if

still bothered by a little smoke in his airways. "I have no doubts that Mitotia is as brilliant as my sister suggests, and we should encourage her to apply that potential in a way that will honor your family and herself. The priesthood will help her explore that potential to its fullest. So, if I might suggest, rather than sealing this pact with a marriage, let's bind it with a dedication to the priesthood, say until Mitotia reaches her nineteenth year. She'll attend the calmecac in Culhuacan where we'll teach her the art of writing, and reading the sacred calendar, as well as teaching her the stories and philosophies of the various gods. At the end of those four years, Mitotia can either take the trials to continue on in the priesthood, or she may choose to pursue a different lifestyle. Are these terms acceptable to you?"

"They are most adequate, Lord Topiltzin." Ten Spines grinned as he clamped his pipe between his yellowed teeth.

◻

"So, who is this mystery woman I'm supposedly betrothed to?" Little Reed asked when we returned to our tent to don our royal headdresses before the night's feast.

"I'm not the one who coughed up my lung at the suggestion of marrying our new ally's daughter," I said. "I had to say something to get Ten Spines to not grab his spear and avenge his dishonor."

"Yes, but now he'll expect me to marry someone."

What marry? the child's voice suddenly piped up. It had been thankfully quiet all afternoon and it annoyed me that it started bombarding me with stupid questions now.

"Don't worry, Little Reed. It will be several years before he'll start to wonder; plenty of time for you to find someone to fulfill that role."

Little Reed took a deep breath, his fists clenched. "I made a promise—"

"I didn't ask you to, so let's stop this foolishness," I fired back, more angry than I'd intended. I wondered if I would feel even half as guilty about this afternoon in the Divine Dream if he hadn't made that promise.

Seeing the hurt on his face, I sighed and pulled him into a hug. "Things didn't turn out as we'd hoped, but we can't let our feelings for each other trump the needs of our people. I can't give us an heir—" *An heir?* "—so you must marry someone. I won't let you end up like my father, with no one to carry on what we build here. There's more at stake than us, and we must never forget that."

"If only you understood," Little Reed whispered. "I *can't* love another the way I love you."

"This isn't about love; it's about your duty." Seeing the pain in his eyes at this, I sighed and added, "Who's to say you won't find someone you can love. Maybe you already know her; maybe she's even in the priesthood."

"Like Malinalli?"

I looked up at him sharply, a surge of jealousy rising inside me. So many paranoid questions raced through my head—did he mention my best friend because he'd always liked her? Was there something between them and I'd never noticed because I'd been so focused on my own feelings? *There was that look she gave him when he came home to Xochicalco with Red Flint,* I remembered. Her blushing smile had raised my hackles but also shamed me; a feeling that started filling me now again. If they were attracted to each other, who was I to stand in their way? It wasn't as if I had anything real to offer him. And what kind of a friend would I be if I kept Malinalli from being happy because of my own selfish longings?

292

Friend? The voice was infinitely puzzled and I wished it would go away. My tongue felt dry as I asked Little Reed, "Do you like her?"

"I don't see her like that." His expression was unreadable.

Looking away again, I asked, "Well, is there anyone you could *see like that*...aside from me, of course?"

He shook his head, exasperating me.

"Well, you're going to have to make an effort," I said, returning to the flap to my sleeping quarters. "Now get your headdress on. We're going to be late."

By the time I returned to the anteroom with my white heron-feathered headdress in hand, I'd calmed the chaos of emotions fouling my mood. Little Reed appeared in better spirits as well and he gladly helped me with my own headdress when I asked. The silence between us felt oppressive though, so I sought to fill it with meaningless jabber. "What did you make of that story Ten Spines told us? About Mixcoatl?"

"What about it?"

"Do you think it's true, that he's Quetzalcoatl's father and your grandfather?"

"He is not the god's father."

"You've asked Quetzalcoatl this?"

"No," he admitted, amusement in his voice.

"Then how do you know?"

Little Reed didn't say anything for a moment. "Because my father would have mentioned it at some point in our conversations. We speak to each other in the Divine Dream at least once a week, often more."

I bit my lip, those moments in the garden today coming back to me, unwelcome. "What sort of things do you talk about?"

Little Reed moved around in front of me to check if my headdress was straight. "Religion mostly, and the future. We talk about the gods as well, sometimes even Mixcoatl."

"Then there is a Cloud Serpent?"

He nodded, adjusting my headdress with the care of a perfectionist. "But never as Quetzalcoatl's father."

"It is a fascinating coincidence," I remarked, "that the Chichimecs should believe that the two are related and your father chose to put you into the belly of the queen of a mortal king called Mixcoatl."

He chuckled. "It was all part of the god's plan; he knew where we'd build Tollan, and that we would need the help of Ten Spines' people, and that they worship Mixcoatl as Quetzalcoatl's father. It makes it easier to sway them to our plans."

"And it would incline them to see you as a god, by proxy," I said with a smirk.

"I consider that an unfortunate side effect, not a benefit. I'd rather people embrace what we do because it's a good thing, not because they fear divine retribution if they question it."

"I only hope that Ueman doesn't get out of hand with you being Quetzalcoatl's son. I won't abide anyone accusing you of being the kind of person who would elevate himself to the status of a god."

Little Reed caressed my cheek. "And you ask why I could never love another, Papalotl."

I took his hand in mine and gave it a squeeze. "I will always love you too," I whispered, a hitch in my throat.

CHAPTER SEVEN

The celebratory feast lasted well into the night, so we slept late into the morning. But when I woke, the meat I'd eaten last night—coupled with anticipation—left my stomach tied in a painful knot. Ueman had promised to bring us my father's bones this afternoon.

I barely touched my breakfast; given Little Reed's concerned glances, I knew he wanted to ask what was wrong with me, but thankfully our guards soon announced that Ueman and Ten Spines had arrived.

Ueman came into our tent along with two warriors carrying a rough-hewn, unpainted stone box. They placed it carefully at my feet as Ueman bowed low. "I humbly return your father to you, My Lady, and I beg forgiveness for my harsh words to you yesterday."

"It's quite all right." I eyed the box with trepidation; it didn't look nearly big enough to fit the bones of a man of my father's considerable size. "This is the box you dug up in the copal grove?"

"Everything is as we found it."

"That is the box I brought north," Amoxtli confirmed. He stood off to the side at a discreet distance.

Ten Spines stepped forward and pulled the stone lid off. He set it carefully against the side. "And as you can see, the bones are still inside."

Both Little Reed and I leaned in for a closer look.

A nest of disarticulated and broken bones filled the box, resting on a thick bed of decomposed tissue turned to sludge. A stale, rotting smell wafted out; a fragrance similar to the curiously alluring fragrance of a temple. Little Reed knelt to look in the box, a frown on his face as he poked among the bones with his sacrificial blade. "The skull is missing."

"It was probably on the skull rack in the temple," Amoxtli said, a deep frown on his face.

"Which means it's gone for good, since we cremated all those remains." Little Reed pulled away again. "And you're positive these are Mixcoatl's bones?" he asked Amoxtli.

"I can only go on what the guard said my father told him."

I continued staring into the box though, taking in every detail. The long bones of the legs had been snapped in half, to fit crosswise in the box, and an irresistible impulse drove me to move them aside. Under them I found the splintered remains of a ribcage, most of the ribs snapped in half along their midpoints.

The memories of what I'd seen that night in my father's quarters rushed back at me, a nightmare I could never fully escape: him lying on his bed mats, his throat hanging open in a grisly, bleeding frown, his already broad chest even broader than normal and showing off the ribs underneath, gleaming like a jaguar's bloodied fangs in the moonlight.

Though Quetzalcoatl's cult didn't practice heart extraction, I'd learned the method the priests of the Sun used, and it wasn't until now—seeing the snapped ribs again—that I realized that what my uncle had done shared nothing with that practice. Priests of Tonatiuh cut into the flesh at the bottom of the ribs, following their contour; then they reached up into the chest, to grip the heart from below to tear it out. What I'd seen that night in my father's quarters...it had none of the respect for the body of the sacrificial victim. Ihuitimal tore my father open like a mad animal, possessed of hate. It wasn't a sacrifice; it was the quenching of a personal vendetta.

"It's him," I managed before the bile and fear and rage bubbled up my throat. Horrifying images of vomiting all over my father's bones made me spring to my feet. I managed a couple of steps outside our tent before losing control.

A breath later, Little Reed crouched at my side, holding my hair back while I trembled and heaved. When he offered me a water skin to rinse out my mouth, I met his gaze and the desire geysered up inside me. I felt lightheaded and for a moment I thought it would take over, but I squeezed my eyes shut and took deep, calming breaths. *Get a hold of yourself, Quetzalpetlatl.* I got up and moved away from him before swigging several mouthfuls of water and spitting it out into the bushes behind our tent, rinsing away the foul burn. Embarrassment kept me staring into the bushes for a moment before turning back again.

Little Reed watched me, pity and regret on his face. "Feeling better now?"

I nodded. "I didn't expect it to overwhelm me so."

He came over and pulled me into a firm hug. "I'm truly sorry, Papalotl," he whispered.

I hugged him tightly in return, squeezing my eyes shut to keep from breaking down again. "Do you think burying him with full rites will finally let my heart mend?"

"I hope so."

✿

After Ten Spines and Ueman left, I retired to my bed, overwhelmed.

Hurt? the child voice asked.

I usually ignored it, but I desperately wanted to talk to someone, and Little Reed was busy with our new allies. *Very much so,* I thought back.

Why?

Because someone stole my tatli from me. I sniffled. *You're lucky; no one can kill your father as someone did to mine.*

What kill?

What is kill, I corrected him. *We ask, 'what is' when we have a question.*

What is kill?

It's when someone makes you die.

What is die?

It's when you don't live anymore. You stop thinking or speaking or feeling.

The voice fell silent, making me believe it hadn't understood anything I'd said—no surprise—but then it asked, *Why you kill me?*

My heart faltered and that nausea swept over me again. *I haven't killed you.*

Will you?

I stared at the ceiling, my heart hammering in my throat. I had no idea how to answer that. I didn't want to answer it.

Will you? it asked again.

"I don't want to die," I whispered. "If I don't...you might kill me."

I won't.

You can't promise that. My nantli let Little Reed live, and it killed her.

Nantli?

My mother.

You is my nantli, the voice whispered.

Tears wound down my cheeks, a tremendous ache swelling in my heart. What was I thinking, even talking to him? *You* are *my nantli,* I corrected him.

You are my nantli? he asked, puzzled.

I tried to hold in the sob but I couldn't stop it. With one word, he'd changed everything; changed my whole future. No matter how much I feared dying, I knew now that I couldn't go through with it; this wasn't some phantom voice in my head—it was the voice of my son, my flesh and blood, and nothing would ever be the same. I set my hand on my stomach, splaying my fingers, feeling the magic pulsing deep inside me; the magic the god had given me, magic I hadn't asked for but was now mine to grow and nurture. I wiped my tears and whispered, "Yes, I'm your nantli, and I will protect you always; I promise."

▢

I slept late into the evening, waking to the sweet smell of tobacco. Little Reed, Amoxtli, Citlallotoc, and Ten Spines sat around a fire in the anteroom, set up in a small kettle brazier. They smoked their pipes and spoke in hushed voices, but everyone looked up when I came out of my room. "Feeling better?" Little Reed asked, concern on his face.

I smiled back at him. "I finally am feeling better." And it was no exaggeration; I felt as if a huge boulder had been lifted off my shoulders. I had such big news to share with him, but not around the others. "What are you discussing?" Hopefully my personal issues this afternoon hadn't slowed progress on our mission.

"We're going to start clearing the copal grove tomorrow," he said. "That should take a week, maybe two, then we can start laying the temple foundation."

"It will really take that long?"

Ten Spines chuckled. "My Lady is eager to get back to civilization."

I smiled gamely at him. "Not at all. There isn't much for me to do until the burial ceremony and the foundation dedication, but perhaps I could start training Mitotia."

Little Reed nodded. "I've been working with Amoxtli on his training, but we'll need more assistance during the burial ceremony."

"Mitotia is eager to go to Culhuacan with you," Ten Spines said with a sigh. "I've always known in my heart that she wasn't meant for the migrant life, still...it grieves me to let her go."

"We will take very good care of her," I assured him. "And she will come home again once she's finished her training, and she will make you most proud."

Ten Spines nodded. "My wife made a wonderful dinner and she's keeping it warm on the fire outside for you, if you're hungry."

"I'm starving," I admitted, and thanked him before ducking through the tent flap, out into the camp.

Amoxtli followed and called to me once we were outside. He was nervous as he approached.

"Is something the matter?" I asked.

"I wanted to...to tell you how very sorry I am for what my father did to your father," he said, wringing his hands, his head bowed.

"You're not responsible for what he did."

"No, but as his son, I share in his shame, and this afternoon...seeing how deeply his crimes affected you, it feels the right thing to do."

I gripped his shoulder. "You're a very good man, Amoxtli, and I'm so very glad you're my cousin."

"You accept my apology?"

"Whole-heartedly." I hugged him and he returned the gesture awkwardly, as if he didn't know what to do; but when I let him go, he was smiling. He gave me a nod goodbye before retreating back into the royal tent.

Bitter Rabbit and Mitotia sat at our camp's cooking fire, Mitotia mending a buckskin dress while her mother wove a basket from river rushes. The old woman gave me a gap-toothed smile and set her weaving aside to fill a bowl with soup.

"I was hoping I might see you tonight, My Lady," Mitotia remarked when I sat on the mat next to her. "My father says he's sending me south with you and your brother, to become a priestess." When I nodded, she said, "Forgive my asking, but what does a priestess do?"

"The various priesthoods make certain the gods are properly honored through sacrifice and prayer. But we also track the heavens and keep the calendars, both domestic and sacred, so we can tell the farmers when to plant and when to harvest. We also read omens for the king, and we lead the people in the monthly festivals. But most importantly, we share the gods' will with the people, so everyone know how to keep them happy so they will continue showing us mercy rather than destroying the world."

"That sounds very important," Mitotia said.

"It is. If you ask me, it's more important than even being queen, for while royalty comes and goes, the gods are with us always."

"So I will be learning only about the Tolteca gods?"

I shook my head. "We welcome all the Chichimec gods into the temples, so they may too enjoy the benefits of our peoples' shared prosperity." *Even the Smoking Mirror?* I wondered, but kept it to myself. "Actually, would you teach me about the Chichimec gods, particularly Mixcoatl?"

"Mixcoatl? Well, he's the god of hunters; we bless our weapons in his name so they might bring down the deer easily and often. They say he came from the clouds as a great serpent, hence his name."

"Your father mentioned that Mixcoatl is the father of Quetzalcoatl."

Mitotia nodded. "The story goes that he journeyed south to conquer lands for the Chichimec people, and he came upon a savage war-queen who wouldn't bend to his rule. They battled for days, and finally he chased her into a cave and trapped her there. Demanding she submit to his rule, he pierced her with an arrow, impregnating her, and she gave birth to the Feathered Serpent, the one who gives us all life and who imparts knowledge upon us."

I bit my lip, horrified. I didn't know what to say that wouldn't be a complete dismissal of Mixcoatl's worship.

Bitter Rabbit said something in the Chichimec tongue and Mitotia answered, a look of bewilderment on her face. "Is it true my father wishes me to become some kind of priestess of the Cloud Serpent, in the new city you and Lord Topiltzin are building here?"

"That was the plan," I admitted. When she frowned, I added, "But plans can easily change. We will not force you to serve a god you wish not to."

She cast a furtive glance at her mother before leaning closer to me and saying, "Every winter, our shaman dresses as the Cloud Serpent and he picks one of the young women to battle, as Mixcoatl battled the war queen." She lowered her voice as she went on. "He drags her to his tent and sheds her maiden blood, so a child is conceived. The following summer, after the child is born, he sacrifices it, to honor the Feathered Serpent."

Without thinking, I set my hand on my abdomen as if to protect my son. I made myself take it away as soon as I realized what I was doing. "Quetzalcoatl doesn't want the blood of children," I said, unable to contain the outrage.

"The priesthood doesn't practice this kind of ritual?"

"Not at all...well, not anymore...or at least not for much longer. Topiltzin and I are on a mission from Quetzalcoatl, to reform the priesthood and how sacrifice is done. So no, such sacrifices will soon be a thing of the past. Nor will the ritual raping of Tollan's citizens be tolerated."

Mitotia let out a held breath. "Forgive me, for I know it is a sacred ritual, but I am glad to hear that. Ueman always picks older girls who haven't, for whatever reason, gotten married yet, and my mother has told me he's already talked to my father...about me. No one's allowed to marry a woman who's been had by the god, and once I had the baby, I would pretty much be useless to the village."

So that was what Ten Spines had been referring to, about this being her final chance. "I will not allow it," I assured her. "For the next four years you belong to the Temple of Quetzalcoatl, so you needn't worry."

She gave me a relieved smile and spoke to her mother again. Her mother nodded approvingly, reaching over to stroke her daughter's shoulder. "What can I ever do to repay you for saving me from such a fate?"

Smiling back at her, I said, "You needn't do anything, but I very much want to learn to speak your people's language."

She nodded. "I shall teach you."

"Tomorrow I'll begin tutoring you in the priestly arts. I'll need your assistance at the temple dedication ceremony in a few weeks."

❑

It was on the tip of my tongue to tell Little Reed my big news when I returned to the tent after dinner but, even though Ten Spines and Amoxtli had left, Citlallotoc was still with him and I didn't fancy saying anything in front of him either. I sat with them for the remainder of the evening, mostly listening; my mind was elsewhere, going over all the questions Little Reed would ask, and my stomach grew tighter and tighter with dread. How could I explain to him that I hadn't told him until now because I'd been planning to rid myself of the god's son? By bedtime, I didn't want to tell him at all, so I slunk away to my quarters and let my son's babble lull me to sleep. Since talking with him earlier that evening, he'd integrated the few speech rules I'd taught.

Come morning, Little Reed had already gone before I woke. Although we saw each other briefly at dinner, he retired early, exhausted from clearing the copal grove. I still said nothing to him about the baby, not wanting to add a worry on top of his exhaustion.

This became our daily routine. I passed my own days teaching Mitotia about the different gods and telling her the stories I'd learned as a child and perfected during my years in the calmecac. She was a highly attentive student, soaking up everything I told her, always asking questions; she reminded me of Mazatzin in intelligence and temperament, and I mused that someday she could be a very successful high priestess of whatever god she chose to serve. When I wasn't teaching her theology, she was teaching me to speak Chichimec.

And to my surprise—and pride—my son learned it right along with me. He babbled assorted Chichimec words the first few days but they quickly became full sentences. His Tolteca became mostly understandable as well, and I spent the evenings before bed singing the sacred songs for him in my head. By the day before the ceremony to bury my father's bones under the temple's foundation, my son could sing the songs back to me. I'd never thought it possible to feel so proud.

I want to give you a name, I told him. *I've been thinking about it for a few days now, and I've come up with the perfect one.*

What is it, Nantli? he asked, excited. I wished he was big enough for me to feel him moving around. *Can it be Quetzalcoatl?*

I chuckled aloud. *You can't have your father's name; if he were human, that would be fine, but you're not allowed to take the gods' names for your own.*

Why not?

Because the gods are special; they're one of a kind whereas we are many…so very many. And there is power in the gods' names, and to take them for ourselves would dilute that power.

I don't understand, he admitted.

It's all right. Someday you will. But I did get the idea for your name from Quetzalcoatl.

Will I like it?

I hope so.

Well?

Yamehecatl.

Warm Breeze?

Exactly. Because you are a wonderful, warm breeze that Quetzalcoatl blew into my life so unexpectedly, and I couldn't imagine you not being in it.

Yamehecatl was silent, and for a moment, I thought he'd gone to sleep, but he whispered, *Then you love me, Nantli?*

I slid my hand up the side of my dress, to set it against my bare stomach, as if to will myself to feel his hand touching mine the same way Little Reed used to touch my hand through our mother's belly. I felt nothing but my own firm guts underneath. *I do, my precious little breeze. Very much.*

I love you too, Nantli.

◻

In the morning, when I came out into the anteroom, Little Reed and Citlallotoc were on their way out of the flap, dressed for the final day of work. Today the men would lay the first foundation stones, dragged all the way from a limestone quarry Ten Spines' men found on the north end of the grasslands. It had taken them all day to get the dozen stones to the temple construction site, dragging the blocks with ropes and rolling them over logs. Little Reed hadn't bothered to wash up yesterday and still bore the scrapes and dirty smudges of a day of hard labor, but he was as handsome as ever. "Sorry to rush out, but we're already late," he told me, planting a kiss on my cheek that sent the desire simmering and growling. "We'll be back a few hours after noon though, to get ready for the ceremony. Can you put together all the things we'll need for tonight?"

"Of course." I swallowed back the desire, taking a deep breath when he finally turned to leave again. "There's something I need to talk to you about tonight, Topiltzin," I called after him, my stomach knotted with a mixture of anxiety and excitement. "After the ceremony."

He looked back at me, concerned. "Is everything all right?" Citlallotoc wore the same expression.

I nodded. "In fact, it's quite good news, but it can wait until tonight. I wanted to mention it, so I won't forget to talk to you about it."

He gazed at me a moment longer, his expression uncertain, but he said, "I'll see you this afternoon then."

I waved goodbye, the desire growling humorlessly, so I took some of the dried meat Little Reed had left for me on the plate on the floor next to the kettle brazier. I sat and chewed it slowly, my jaw already hurting. It was some kind of lizard, with the bones still in it. How did the Chichimecs survive with no maize to make tlaxcallis, and no beans for their soup? We'd gone through our supply within the first week and I couldn't wait to get back to Culhuacan and enjoy nice hot, fluffy tlaxcallis again.

As I finished eating, my guard rattled the copper bells sewn into the flap of the tent and stuck his head inside. "There's someone here to see you, My Lady."

It annoyed me that he still called Mitotia "someone", having not taken the time to learn her name. Initially it surprised me how many of our men were hostile to our new Chichimec allies—not outright—but now it irritated me. Our guards and soldiers glared at the Chichimecs, a practice the Chichimecs returned with equal vehemence, and a few Toltecas addressed them as "Dog Men" in our tongue. Luckily no conflicts had broken out, though I sensed it was only a matter of time before one of the Chichimec warriors learned enough of our language to confirm they were being insulted and took it as a matter of personal honor.

"Just send her in," I snapped at him, and went to retrieve my priestly robe.

"It's not the Chichimec girl, My Lady." He looked over his shoulder before stepping inside and closing the flap behind him. "He claims to be your husband."

I stared at him, not amused. "My *former* husband is dead."

"I told him as much, but he insists on speaking with you."

Someone was playing a trick on my guard, and I didn't appreciate it. Despite my dreams to the contrary, Black Otter was dead in Tlalocan with all other drowning victims, enjoying a paradise of eternal green and plenty for having fed the Rain God with his death. Whoever thought this was funny would get a flogging. "Send him in," I growled.

My guard opened the tent flap and motioned outside. A breath later, a gaunt, harried-looking man stepped inside followed by my second guard. He walked hunched over, his clothes little better than rags—his cotton loincloth was dingy and tattered, as if he'd fished it from the lake and hadn't washed it since. But when he raised his head to meet my gaze, my breath caught. "Black Otter?"

"Quetzalpetlatl!" He took a step towards me, arms outspread as if to hug me.

But when I recoiled, horrified, the first guard snapped his spear out, blocking Black Otter. "No one touches the queen without her permission."

Black Otter threw a murderous glare at him, but said to me, "I nearly died, and this is the greeting you give me?"

I stared at him, trembling. "How...but I saw you die!" The moment Ihuitimal's guards shot him with an arrow and he fell into the lake played over and over in my head.

"I thought I would die too, but instead I washed up on shore at Xico," Black Otter said.

I hadn't seen him surface, but the guards *had* practically drowned me while trying to subdue me after sending Black Otter into the lake. I'd been in no condition to search for him after that, and for all I knew he'd been alive and they left him to die. "The gods spared you?" I concluded.

He nodded, his eyes teary. "It took me a few months to recover, but I came looking for you as soon as I was able, and so here I am!" He held his arms out again expectantly but when I still made no move to embrace him, he asked, "How can my own wife not be overjoyed to see me still alive?"

"I'm not your wife anymore."

"Says who? Topiltzin?"

"*I* say so," I fired back.

He stared at me, flustered before stammering, "You haven't the power to divorce me. Only a man can ask for that."

"Your father's rules are no longer the law in Culhuacan...or here. As far as I'm concerned, our marriage never existed."

"Never...!" Black Otter flexed his fists. "Your father tied your dress to my cape—"

"He declared that union void when he exiled your father."

"Yet we consummated it our first night together. You consented."

I stood straighter, glaring at him. *Let's devour him,* the desire growled. I pushed the voice aside but allowed the confidence to remain. "Don't mistake self-preservation for consent. Under your father's laws, a woman had no right to say no."

When he pressed forward again, furious, the guard pushed back with his spear. "Yet that never stopped you from moaning my name every time after, did it?"

I flinched. *Who does he think he is?* the desire growled. Images of him lying dead on the floor after I'd ravaged him sprang into my head, so similar to those dreams I had about Red Flint after he attacked me in the Temple of Quetzalcoatl in Xochicalco. *If he wants it so badly, let's give it to him.*

But the guard belted Black Otter in the chest with his wooden spear handle, sending him sprawling at the feet of the second one. Both guards turned their spear points at his chest. "Shall I drive this filthy dog through, My Lady?" The first guard didn't take his intense gaze off Black Otter. When I set a calming hand on his shoulder, he relaxed his grip but kept his spear pointed.

"Try to belittle me all you want," I snarled at Black Otter. "But your words mean nothing."

Black Otter's gaze swung back and forth between me and the guards. "Forgive my cruel tongue, My Lady. These last few months, not knowing if you were even alive...it's been rougher on me than you can know. I survived only by the grace of the gods, and I understand you wishing to move on, thinking you'd lost me, but...the gods gave us a second chance, Quetzalpetlatl."

"They did give us a second chance, Black Otter; to undo the mockery of love and devotion your father thrust us into. I'm back where I belong, as the high priestess of Quetzalcoatl, and you...you have women and children who will rejoice to know you're alive." I almost added "and well", but reconsidered, given his shabby state.

"You...are you not happy I'm alive too?" His voice broke.

I frowned, stung that he'd even ask that. Did he think me an unfeeling monster? "Of course I'm happy you're alive, but I also know that what we had...that was not love, Black Otter, and I will not forsake my duties as high priestess to Quetzalcoatl for anything less than real love. Go home to Jade Flower and your children. They need you, and you need them."

"I don't need her," he spat like a petulant child. "I don't want her. I want you!"

I set my jaw tight, the stolidness creeping up on me again. "Then you leave me no choice." I motioned to the guards to stand him up and they did so. "I want him taken back to the valley and turned over to the King of Chalco, so he may be held accountable for at least one of the women he took an oath to keep and protect."

I turned back to him. "Black Otter, I hereby exile you from the cities of Tollan and Culhuacan. Should you choose to ignore my authority, I will declare you an enemy of the god and the guards will kill you on sight. We were once good friends, but you will forget about me. Go home to your women and make a new beginning with them."

Black Otter stared at me, pleading. "I'm in no condition to take care of four women and their children, Quetzalpetlatl. Look at me; I haven't a home, let alone a kingdom to support them."

"I'm certain if you agree to tie your cape to Papantzin's or Cornflower's dress, their fathers will be quite happy to give you a position in their court and means enough to support your family." I told the guards to escort him out.

"But I love you, Quetzalpetlatl!" he cried as they dragged him from the tent. "Why is that not enough for you?" He continued yelling and crying as they led him away.

Mitotia had appeared at the tent flap, and stood watching the commotion. Amoxtli was with her, staring at his brother as the guards dragged him away. When he turned to me, disbelief in his eyes, I nodded and said, "Go. Maybe you can talk some sense into him."

He hesitated while my words sunk in, but then he hurried after the guards, calling, "Brother!"

"Who was that?" Mitotia asked.

"Nobody important." I frowned, setting my hand over my stomach pensively. It was a good thing I wasn't visibly pregnant or that situation might have turned uglier.

"Are you feeling all right, My Lady?" Mitotia asked, noticing my gesture.

I dropped my hand. "I'm fine." I motioned her inside and fetched my priestly robe and my satchel. "We have a lot to do today, so let's get going."

CHAPTER EIGHT

I tried to put Black Otter out of my mind as Mitotia and I left the camp, but the memory of his wildness followed me down the winding game trail through the tall grasses. I imagined him breaking free of my guards and looking for me again, and several times I contemplated going back, just to be safe; we'd left without my guards, after all. But once we forded the small river, helping each other across the rocks, and made our way along the line of trees, to a ravine that opened onto a plain of scrub brush and hundreds of maguey plants, I decided it was pointless to turn back. *We'll get this done quickly,* I decided, as we picked our way down the steep incline.

When we came to the nearest maguey, whose broad, spongy leaves grew taller than either of us, I cut off one of the smaller leaves growing close to the heart of the plant. "The spines on the larger leaves are too thick for our purposes," I told Mitotia as I handed her the leaf and cut off several more. We sat on the ground, our knives out. "The thorns at the end of the leaves are the best ones, for they are the thinnest. So cut the end off, about this far down—" I demonstrated it on the leaf in front of me and she followed my action—"then you shave off the excess until it resembles a needle." I held up my finished thorn before starting on a second leaf.

"What do you use these for?" Mitotia asked as she worked on her first.

"Bloodletting rituals," I said. "Women pierce their tongues—symbolic of the breath of life—while men pierce their genitals, on the testicles or the foreskin."

Mitotia cringed. "We don't have to pierce ourselves...down there, do we?"

I chuckled. "We already give enough blood from there every month."

"Will I have to do any of this bloodletting at tonight's ritual?"

I shook my head. "You must learn proper technique first, so Topiltzin and I will do the bloodletting tonight."

"Will there be a sacrifice too? Father told me people die at the sacrifice daily back in the valley."

"No human sacrifices," I assured her. "Quetzalcoatl prefers the blood of his priests, given in earnest devotion."

Mitotia nodded. "We sacrifice maybe two or three people a year, in honor of the most important gods. In the winter, we take a chosen warrior out into the desert, away from camp, and dress him as the Cloud Serpent, and all the warriors shoot him with arrows. And in the spring, we appease the Rain God by drowning the weakest child in the river. That happened to my youngest sister; she was older than most of the sacrifices, but she fell out of a tree and hit her head, making her no better than a baby. Father said her sacrifice was a mercy, and she would have been honored to help her people."

I shuddered at the thought of my little Yamehecatl drowning. *But what if he was suffering?* No, I didn't want to think about that. I reached to clasp my stomach but stopped myself.

Are you all right, Nantli? Yamehecatl suddenly asked me, and I nearly jumped.

I took a deep breath before replying, *I'm fine, my little warm breeze. I have a lot to do right now, so go back to sleep and we'll talk later? All right?*

Will you sing me a song, Nantli?

Smiling, I gave in, singing aloud one of the many songs about Quetzalcoatl as I carved out the rest of the thorns. He sang with me a while, but eventually his voice became a sleepy drone. Mitotia listened the first few times then joined in, her voice a nice deep complement to my own. We sang as we packed up our supplies and climbed up the incline to the trees. I was relieved to finally be going back to camp.

Mitotia went first, nimble with youth, but when I went up after her, trying to keep pace, the ground at the top gave way. I yelped and tried to sit as I went down, but instead I bounced off a rock and tumbled head over feet down the side of the ravine. I heard Mitotia's cry but otherwise everything was a blur of colors and sound. When I landed at the bottom, I slammed down belly-first, my breath gushing out of me. I gasped for air, pain radiating through my chest and abdomen. *Yamehecatl! Yamehecatl!* I called in my head but he didn't answer. When my lungs finally filled with air again, my first outbreath came out as an agonized wail.

"Are you all right, My Lady?" Mitotia called as she skidded down into the ravine to me. When she rolled me over, I cringed and grabbed my belly, feeling as if a rock shifted inside of me. "What do I do, My Lady? You're bleeding through your dress!"

I tried to sit up, but dizziness and sharp pains changed my mind. *You got your wish after all.* Tears burned my eyes.

"What should I do?" Mitotia asked again, tears in her voice.

Her panic brought my years of midwife training to the fore. "Run and fetch the first strong man you see."

She blinked at me. "And leave you here?"

"No time to argue. Now go, and hurry back."

She scrambled back up the side of the ravine, slipping a few times before making it to the top. She ran off down the game trail, back the way we'd come.

I shielded my eyes from Lord Sun, cursing myself. *This is what you get for questioning the god's plan. He gave you a child to ease your aching heart, but you thought it was a curse and schemed to rid yourself of it. Are you happy now? You'll never get to hold Yamehecatl; you'll never get to talk to him again.* I broke out into hiccupping sobs.

But tears wouldn't help me. I'd probably broken bones and had internal injuries that I might not survive. I was alone and exposed, and my fears about Black Otter getting free came back to me fresh. What would he do if he found me completely helpless and injured? Why hadn't I waited for my guards to return?

Stop it, immediately! The voice of my desire came without all the usual hunger and embarrassing tingling; it was all confidence and command. *Keep your wits, and don't give in to the fear. Take a deep breath and pull yourself together.* I took several breaths until the sobs stopped. *Now you wait, and stay calm.*

It will help to pray, I told myself. *And make an offering to the god.*

Whatever keeps you strong.

I looked for my bag only to find it tangled in some scrub brush. I tried sliding over, but the pain swelled anew in my abdomen. After catching my breath I stretched my arm as far as I could, but the strap remained beyond my reach. *Just a little farther.* My fingers began tingling deep inside....

Suddenly the ground rumbled under me. I looked around, my calm forgotten. Was it an earthquake?

Behind me, the maguey plant's thick, fleshy leaves waved as if caught in a great wind, yet none of the plants around it moved, and no wind was blowing. The rumbling focused between me and the maguey plant, as if something large and sinister was burrowing towards me—

Despite the intense pain in my gut, when lime-white roots burst from the ground next to me, I yelped and rolled away. They wound towards the bush, wrapped themselves around my satchel and dragged it out, shredding multiple branches. When they moved towards me, I started clawing away, but they dropped the bag right in front of me and then withdrew. I watched—mouth hanging open—as they slithered back into the ground and the maguey plant fell still again.

Did I really see that?

Shouts shattered my awe and I turned on my side to see Amoxtli approaching the ravine at a run. Mitotia followed close behind, panting and sweating.

"Quetzalpetlatl!" he called when he reached the edge. "Stay still. I'm coming down to get you." I clutched my bag, tears of relief welling in my eyes. Thank the gods it wasn't Black Otter.

When he reached me, his eyes widened at the blood on my dress, but he didn't question. He slid his arms under me and lifted me gently, straining under my weight; he wasn't a very large man, built thin and wiry the same as his father. I held onto him tight, afraid he might drop me. "Everything will be all right, Cousin," he whispered, sweating as he struggled back out of the ravine, his own legs shaking under him.

◻

When we reached the royal tent, Amoxtli laid me on my bed. "Fetch the surgeon for her," he told Mitotia, who was pacing like an anxious deer. "He's down by the river, tending to a man who smashed his foot under the foundation stones." He turned to me, his face ruddy from exertion. "I'll fetch Topiltzin." He left, and Mitotia started to follow, but I called her back.

"Forget the surgeon," I told her. "He won't know what to do anyway. I need a midwife."

Her gaze wandered to the bloodstain on the front of my dress. "You're pregnant?"

Who would have thought such a small question could so thoroughly break my heart? When I tried to answer, it came out as a choked sob.

"I'll hurry back," Mitotia assured me.

And so I waited again, staring at the ceiling, preparing for the inevitable.

She returned shortly with her mother. "She knows the most about this," she assured me. "She helps all our women in their childbed, so don't worry. She'll take care of you."

Bitter Rabbit told Mitotia to fetch the water jar as she knelt at my feet and pushed my dress up over my hips. "How long since your last bleeding?"

"Four moons." I returned to staring at the ceiling, horrified. I'd never minded performing my midwife duties for others, but it was frightening being on the other side of the mat.

"This is your first child?"

I nodded, and cringed as the old woman felt my stomach none too gently.

"Any abdominal pains that begin small but grow very painful?"

"No, though it hurts when I move or try to sit up." I gritted my teeth when she bent my knees and checked me for signs of labor.

"You've leaked water," she murmured when she finished.

"And the baby?"

"If the baby died, you will give birth by nightfall, early morning at the latest. Time will answer your question."

Mitotia returned with a deer's bladder of water and a buckskin rag. "Is she going to be all right, Mother?" she asked as she wiped the dirt and blood off my face and arms.

"The gods willing." Bitter Rabbit cut my dress off with a knife and with Mitotia's help put me into a clean one. Gritting my teeth again, I settled in, physically drained and emotionally raw. Bitter Rabbit pulled my blanket up to my chin and tucked me in as if I were her own daughter.

As the numbness started whisking me off to sleep, Little Reed burst into the room, out of breath and wide-eyed. Amoxtli followed him in. "Omeyocan blind me, what happened?" he asked, kneeling next to me.

"I fell down a hill," I said.

"Are you all right?" He turned to Bitter Rabbit. "Did she break anything? Is she going to be all right?"

"She will be fine, but it remains to be seen whether the child will survive the night," she answered.

Little Reed turned to me, bewildered. "You're with child?" Behind him, Amoxtli's eyes widened too.

"I wanted to tell you," I stammered. "But I didn't know how to...."

"You were afraid to tell me?" Shock and hurt played across his face.

As I struggled to find the right words, Bitter Rabbit motioned to Mitotia, and her daughter followed her to the tent flap. "I'll come back later to check on you, but if the pain becomes worse, send for me right away."

Once they left, I asked Amoxtli, "Would you mind letting us talk alone?"

"Of course, My Lady." He looked overwhelmed as he ducked out of the flap as well.

Little Reed stared at his hands. "Was this the good news you wanted to tell me tonight, after the ceremony?"

I nodded. "I'm sorry, Little Reed. I should have told you sooner."

"How long have you known?"

I shrugged, hesitating, but admitted, "I started to suspect it when we were at

Teotihuacan."

"Nearly a month?" Little Reed looked as if I'd struck him through with an arrow. "Why didn't you tell me, Papalotl?"

I covered my face, not wanting him to see how torn up I was. "Because I was planning to end this pregnancy once we returned to Culhuacan."

He didn't say anything, and I was afraid to look at him. But when he finally spoke, his voice was calm. "I know you said you didn't want children, and I understand, but I hope you weren't planning this out of loyalty to me. It doesn't matter that Black Otter is the child's father; I would love your child regardless."

"Black Otter isn't the father."

"But who else's could it—"

"It happened that day on the battlefield."

Little Reed's puzzled look continued only a breath before realization lit his eyes. "You mean the god—"

I nodded. "When he took possession of me. Which makes what I was going to do all the worse."

Little Reed gave my hand a gentle squeeze. "You thought it would mean your death."

"I don't want to die. And I didn't ask for this...and it infuriated me that the god would do this to me, with no warning or explanation. Does he expect me to merely accept it?"

My raw, unfettered emotions left him looking bewildered. "I'm sorry," he said, trembling.

I squeezed his hand back. "I know I sound angry, but I'm not anymore. I realize now it's a blessing I didn't know I wanted, but I was clumsy...and now the gods have truly taken my son away from me."

"We don't know that for certain."

"I know it," I sobbed. "Yamehecatl hasn't spoken to me since I fell."

"Yamehecatl?"

"That's what I named him."

"It's a good name," Little Reed conceded. "But what do you mean by him speaking to you?"

"I can hear him, in my head. That's how I know he's a boy. And he's so clever, Little Reed; I taught him all the sacred songs and he's been learning Chichimec as Mitotia's been teaching it to me. And he calls me Nantli." That last statement completely broke me. Little Reed stroked my hair as I rested my head in his lap. "Do you think I'm crazy, hearing voices in my head?"

"Not at all," he said, with no hesitation.

I peered up at him, hope building inside me. "Maybe I wasn't as strange as I thought. "Do you hear them too?"

"No." For a moment I thought that was all he had to say, but he added, "At least not anymore. There was a time, long ago...but not anymore."

So the insistent desire might someday go away and leave me in peace? I thought to tell him about the other voice but the notion of discussing something so embarrassing, so sexual with him was too much to contemplate; even if we were lovers, I doubted I could. "Yamehecatl hasn't spoken to me since I fell, even when I try to wake him."

"He may be sleeping," Little Reed offered. "Let's see what time tells us, and think positively."

"Thank you, Little Reed." I hoped my smile wasn't actually a frown. "I'm truly sorry for keeping all this from you."

He stroked my hand with his. "I want you to know that you're not alone in this, and I will be with you every step of the way." After making certain I was tucked comfortably under my blankets, he said, "I will speak with Ten Spines about delaying the ceremony a few days while you recover."

But I latched onto his hand, keeping him from standing. "There's something else I must tell you about."

His look of concern returned.

"Black Otter came to see me today."

Little Reed blinked, startled. "But he's dead."

"I thought so too, but somehow he survived."

A new intensity showed in his eyes. "Where's he been all these months?"

"In Xico, I think."

"With Flame Tongue?"

"I don't think so. Flame Tongue would have told us." Xico's king was desperate to please Little Reed, after all. "Black Otter looked as if he'd slept under bushes and hadn't washed his clothes in months. He's a complete ruin, Little Reed."

"Did he threaten you?"

I shook my head. "My guards dealt with him swiftly when he became angry, but mostly he begged me to take him back. It was rather sad."

"Sad is too generous a term," he muttered. "Did you say anything to him about the baby?"

"Of course not. He'd have every reason to believe he was the father, and with the mental state he was in...."

"Where is he now?"

"I sent him to Chalco, to make amends with Jade Flower and Papantzin."

He contemplated the tent wall. "Did he say anything about the throne?"

"Only that he couldn't take care of the others without a kingdom to support them, though it was more an excuse to not go and find them. Come to think about it, he never even mentioned his father, or Amoxtli." I would have to ask Amoxtli about what Black Otter said when he spoke to him.

Little Reed tightened his jaw. "It wasn't a good idea to let him go, Papalotl."

Frowning, I said, "Would you want to be the one to tell Amoxtli that his brother survived, but we executed him because he once was a contender for the throne?"

"Of course not, and we both know that's not what I'm talking about."

"He needs time to heal; I broke him, so I owe him the opportunity to restart his life with the others. I'm surprised Cornflower would talk to me at all after everything that happened."

"Don't blame yourself. He made a decision that a strong, moral man wouldn't have, and now everyone pays the price for that. If anyone owes those women an apology, it's him."

"That may be, but that doesn't change the fact that they need him. And if it makes you feel better, I exiled him from our lands, under penalty of death."

"Very well. But now I really must go and talk to Ten Spines." He kissed my forehead before rising. "Now get some sleep and I'll be back soon." He disappeared through the tent flap.

I pulled the blanket up to my chin, letting the exhaustion wash over me. That was two heavy stones off my conscience, but an even bigger one remained. *Please talk to me, Yamehecatl.* He still didn't answer, so I closed my eyes and muttered a prayer, promising to never again doubt Quetzalcoatl's plan if only he wouldn't take my son from me.

◻

When I woke again it was dark and the smell of food set my stomach gurgling. I tried to sit up, but the pain of bruised muscles made me dizzy, so I lay back again, out of breath.

Little Reed parted the tent flap. "Good, you're awake." He held it open for a young man who brought in a small kettle brazier and set to lighting the branches it contained. The fire cast a pleasant orange glow over my quarters. Little Reed brought me a steaming bowl of soup, and I cringed as I sat up again.

"Let me help you." He sat behind me and let me lean against his chest, providing firm, strong support for my back. "How are you feeling?"

"Very stiff," I said between sips. It tasted wonderful in spite of the lack of salt and chile in it. "But the pain isn't so bad anymore."

"Good. Bitter Rabbit says if you'd lost the baby, you'd be in labor already."

"True, but...he's still showing no signs that he's alive."

"I'm certain he will, Papalotl." Little Reed gave me a gentle squeeze with his elbows—the best hug possible while holding my bowl as I rested between sips. "She also said if you don't lose the baby, you shouldn't travel until after you deliver, so we're staying here for the winter. I've already sent word to Acolman, requesting a hundred stonemasons to build permanent houses before the weather turns cold. I won't have our son born in a drafty tent."

I paused, my heart thudding. "*Our* son?"

He nodded. "I know you said we couldn't marry but—and hear me out first—but maybe we still can. You said that you sacrificed the chance for us to be together, and I think we both can agree that our reasons for wanting to marry aren't traditional."

"No, they aren't."

"So, what if we marry for traditional reasons? This is a stroke of luck for both of us; the people expect me to marry and produce an heir, and you're already carrying a child. If we marry, no one can legally question Yamehecatl's parentage or his status as heir."

I gave him a good-natured scowl. "Not to mention all your allies will stop pestering you to marry their daughters."

He grinned. "An added bonus."

I went back to my soup. "It does make good political sense, but...we can't ever consummate this marriage, Little Reed. You understand that?"

He nodded. "I accept that it's a marriage of convenience, for both of us."

"And you can keep a concubine or two, so you have the things I cannot give you."

Little Reed sighed. "Sex is not so important that I can't be faithful to you, Papalotl, so please stop making such suggestions."

Funny how it didn't pain him at all to give up what felt to me like denying my very nature. "I'm sorry," I murmured. "I'm trying to be fair to you."

"I know, but that doesn't mean being unfair to yourself. We'll face the challenges together, with faith in the god."

Smiling, I let myself recline further back against him. But my pessimism didn't allow me peace for long. "But what if Yamehecatl doesn't survive? We shouldn't even talk about this until we know for certain."

"Or maybe we shouldn't talk about *that* possibility until we know," he suggested, a gentle ribbing in his voice.

"It does feel better to be positive." I set my empty bowl back into his hands, and he put it aside before wrapping me in his arms. "But what about Ten Spines?"

"What about him?"

"I told him you were betrothed."

"You didn't say to whom, so why couldn't it be you?"

"True. But when he discovers I'm pregnant, he'll think badly of us."

"Let's not worry about what he thinks."

I watched the shadows dance on the canvas walls. I couldn't remember the last time I'd felt this content, this safe, and I didn't want it to end.

But when I started drowsing off, Little Reed laid me down and pulled the blanket over me. I felt so cold, so alone, and desperately wanted not to be. "Little Reed?"

"Yes, my love?"

"Please stay with me." When he looked towards the tent flap, an indecisive look on his face, I stammered, "Only until I fall asleep."

Nodding, he stretched out next to me and laid on his side, propped up on his elbow so he could look down at me.

I moved onto my side, hoping it would wake me enough to keep him talking—and stay at my side. "If we can't go back to Culhuacan, who's going to marry us? We're the only priests of Quetzalcoatl here, and we can't perform our own wedding ceremony."

"We could ask Ueman—"

"I will not get married in front of anyone but a priest of Quetzalcoatl, Little Reed." The flint to my voice made him raise an eyebrow, so I said, "It was bad enough enduring a wedding ceremony performed by Ihuitimal; he poured blood on me, Little Reed. I still get sick thinking about it."

"That doesn't mean Ueman will do that. I spoke to Ten Spines about their gods, and they don't worship the Smoking Mirror. He says Tezcatlipoca is a far northern god."

"Yes, well, this Mixcoatl god isn't much better. Mitotia told me Ueman reenacts the vile story of Quetzalcoatl's supposed conception by forcing himself on one of the tribe's young women, and Ten Spines was going to give her to him for the ceremony at the end of summer. I can't even imagine.... Ueman is no better than Ahexotl was."

"It's a very good thing you talked Ten Spines into committing her to the priesthood instead." Little Reed sighed, his brows furrowed. "I know the god talks mostly of stopping human sacrifice, but it's also these kinds of exploitations he aims to stop."

I squeezed his hand with mine. "We will stop it."

Little Reed nodded. "We'll summon a priest of Quetzalcoatl to marry us."

"Let's ask Mazatzin. He's been a good friend to both of us for many years."

"He would be a very good choice." He kneaded my hand gently in his, never taking his gaze off me as silence descended between us.

The look in his eyes reminded me of the first time I'd met Quetzalcoatl in the Divine Dream; we'd gazed at each other as Love drifted down on us from Heaven. Back then, Little Reed and Quetzalcoatl had looked exactly alike—except for the emerald green quetzal feathers that grew amongst the god's long black hair. But while his father remained forever the same, never changing, Little Reed had changed a great deal. His silver hairs outnumbered the black ones, and when he laughed, the crinkled skin at the corners of his eyes didn't smooth out the way it once did. Yet he still turned my heart into a war drum, and when I thought of Quetzalcoatl's kiss, of his feathery touch, of making love in the grass in the Divine Dream, it wasn't the young face of the god I thought of, but rather the one that gazed at me now.

Tatli! Yamehecatl piped up, startling me so much I gasped aloud.

Little Reed sat up, suddenly alert. "Are you all right?"

I could only answer him with tears. Bless the gods, they had spared my son! *Are you all right, Yamehecatl?*

Of course, he laughed. *Why wouldn't I be?*

I wanted to scold him for scaring me so, but the joy of hearing his voice again overwhelmed everything else. All I could do was cry harder.

Little Reed held me close even as he trembled against me. "Should I fetch Lady Bitter Rabbit?"

I shook my head, finally finding my voice. "You were right; our son's fine."

"He's talking to you again?" When I nodded, he asked, "What is he saying?"

Smiling, I said, "He's calling you his tatli." And I was so very glad he did, for that's exactly how I wanted him to think of Little Reed.

CHAPTER NINE

Little Reed spent the entire night lying next to me, and, at some point someone brought him a blanket—my own serving as a buffer between us. When I woke, I savored the warmth of his body against mine in the morning chill, and marveled at how wonderful it was to wake up next to someone again. Neither of us said anything about it when Little Reed woke and went to fetch us breakfast, but as we ate in distracted silence I knew last night's special intimacy wouldn't be repeated. There were some things we couldn't do again because they tempted fate.

After breakfast, Little Reed composed a message to Mazatzin and sent it with a runner to Culhuacan. He spent the day out at the worksite, overseeing the construction of the temple's foundation while I remained in bed, following Bitter Rabbit's orders. At lunch time, I sent for Amoxtli and invited him to eat with me.

"I still can't believe that Black Otter is alive," I said once we were deep into the meal of roasted prickly pear. "Did you get to talk to him before he left for the valley?"

He frowned as he nibbled. "I did."

"And?"

"He's...I don't know that he even recognized me." Amoxtli put down his unfinished food.

"I'm sorry I had to send him away—"

He shook his head. "No, I completely understand. He reminded me of some crazed wild animal. I thank you for sparing his life though, My Lady."

"We've lost too much family as it is. Maybe he can recover and find happiness again with Jade Flower or one of the others."

"Let us hope." After a pause, he said, "But what about the child?"

I knew it was only a matter of time before the question came up, and now I was glad Little Reed had given me an easy means of explaining it without having to reveal Yamehecatl's true parentage. "Actually, the child is Topiltzin's." I bowed my head, avoiding his gaze in a show of embarrassment that wasn't entirely faked. "We're going to marry soon."

Amoxtli nodded, looking relieved. "That's a good thing, for my brother certainly can't handle more responsibility right now. And Topiltzin will take good care of you and the baby; his devotion to you is not only obvious, but refreshing as well."

◻

Once I'd rested for several days, and gotten permission from Bitter Rabbit to leave my bed, Little Reed took me to the construction site in the royal litter. I hadn't been back since that first time, when we'd dug for my father's bones. Much work had been accomplished.

All the trees were cleared, even the giant that had sheltered my father's original burial site. A layer of limestone blocks covered the area, with the middle stone removed to reveal a hole large enough to fit the box of bones inside. Amoxtli held my mother's urn while Little Reed and I scooped her ashes into the box.

We consecrated the grave with prayers, sprinkled octli and waved copal smoke over it with a clay censer. Little Reed slit the throat of a small dog, spilling its blood over my father's bones and our mother's ashes, and he laid its body in the box, murmuring a prayer to Xolotl before sealing it again. Citlallotoc lowered the box into the hole.

"We witness the birth of a new, brighter era, built upon the bones of those who came before us." Little Reed motioned to the men to backfill the hole with dirt, and when that was finished, workers laid the heavy stone over the top. It had been a rainy, dreary day when I'd watched Cuitlapanton lay my mother's ashes under the tree in Xochicalco's royal gardens, but today the sun blazed, casting a stifling heat over the entire ordeal; I didn't even cry, but was merely relieved that it was over at last.

But by the end of the ceremony, the short, dull pains came back. "If you don't wish to lose this baby, you need to stay in bed," Bitter Rabbit warned me when I summoned her. "The fall dislodged the child's tonalli and it's trying to leave. Stay still and it will settle back into place once the child is born."

But that's five months away! But I bit my tongue. How many times did I lecture Cuitlapanton's wives about the things they needed to do if they didn't want to miscarry? I didn't want Yamehecatl's soul to wander off, forever lost after the gods gave me a second chance; if that meant sacrificing months to the childbed, then so be it.

The stonemasons arrived within a week and Little Reed put them to work building permanent houses not only for us, but for the workers staying the winter. Mitotia moved in and set up her sleeping mat in my quarters, to look after me during the night while I continued teaching her during the day. Little Reed made an icpalli for me to recline in bed, so I didn't have to lay on my back or side all the time; a nice gesture, but I missed leaning on him.

By the end of the month the stonemasons finished a small royal villa to house us, Citlallotoc, Ten Spines and his wife, and Ten Spines' war chief. The unit consisted of four domiciles and a large storeroom and kitchen, all sharing a common courtyard. A tall stone wall surrounded it all, ensuring privacy. Each house had three rooms—a large anteroom for eating and entertaining guests, and two cozy sleeping quarters, each with its own hearth. Little Reed built a wooden screen for my room, to block any drafts and lock the heat in around my bed, making my sleeping area an ideal place to pass the winter. He also built me a special bed that could be lifted on poles, so he and Citlallotoc could carry me out into the anteroom.

Within a few days of moving into our new quarters, Mazatzin arrived and we all sat down to a hot meal in the anteroom. He looked concerned when he first saw me reclined on my bed while everyone else sat on their mats, but he waited until the evening pipes came out before leaning over and whispering, "Are you injured?"

I laughed. "In a manner of speaking." To Little Reed, I said, "Perhaps now would be a good time to make our announcement?"

311

Both Citlallotoc and Ten Spines were there as well, stuffing their pipes. "Is it good news, I hope?" Ten Spines asked once he got his tobacco smoldering.

"It's very good news." Little Reed took my hand. "Lady Quetzalpetlatl and I are getting married."

Both Citlallotoc and Mazatzin raised their eyebrows in surprise, but Ten Spines roared with hearty laughter. "You Tolteca are a strange lot, bedding your sisters and all. Is there a shortage of women back in the valley?" After a puff on his pipe, he added, "But a lesser man would have conquered and left. You, My Lord, are an honorable man."

Little Reed had the same look in his eyes as when Red Flint had besmirched me as a whore. He'd taken Red Flint to task for it, but now I set my hand on his and gave it a gentle squeeze, to snap him out of it. I told Ten Spines, "We are but following the path the god laid out for us, My Lord."

Ten Spines nodded. "The gods are mysterious, and we cannot comprehend their ways. I ask you forgive me if my original suggestion for binding our alliance trod on your toes, My Lady, though why did you not tell me then?"

"It was a private matter that we'd chosen to keep such until we returned to Culhuacan, but circumstances necessitate revealing our intent early."

"A wedding is always a welcome occasion. When is the ceremony, so I can set my men to gathering the food supplies necessary?"

Having regained his composure, Little Reed answered, "The tying ceremony will be tomorrow night."

"That's too soon, isn't it? It will be impossible for my hunters to kill enough deer by then."

"Traditional Tolteca wedding ceremonies last four days, so there will be time to gather meat," Little Reed said. "And the stonemasons brought a large supply of maize, squash, beans, and chile with them, so we'll have enough food. Do you think Lady Bitter Rabbit would be willing to coordinate the cooking efforts?"

"She would be most pleased to, though our women know little about cooking with the maize," Ten Spines said.

"We'll train them." Little Reed rose. "Perhaps we can go and speak with your wife and get the details solidified while my fire priest rests from his long journey?"

While Little Reed, Citlallotoc and Ten Spines left I finished my last tlaxcalli, savoring it. After two months of meat, wild roots, and prickly pear, even Mitotia's burnt attempts at tlaxcallis were delicious. As Mazatzin finished his plate, he asked, "What did you mean by 'circumstances'?"

"I am with child."

Mazatzin sat taller. "Really? Congratulations! I had no idea you and Topiltzin were...so close. Though I suppose that explains why the two of you lifted the prohibitions against marriage in the priesthood."

I didn't like the idea of he—or anyone else—thinking Little Reed and I had been secretly breaking our vows of chastity, but that was a small price to pay to make sure no one questioned Yamehecatl's parentage.

◻

Unlike my first wedding, no one paraded me around on a litter, showing me off, nor did hundreds of people attend the tying ceremony in our house; only Ten Spines, his wife and daughter, Citlallotoc, and Amoxtli were present while Mazatzin tied my dress to Little Reed's cape. We didn't exchange gifts of clothing either.

But in other ways the ceremony was exactly the same as when I was a girl; we retired to my quarters for days of prayer, something much easier to accomplish with my priestly training and cultivated patience. I wasn't made to fast during the first evening—Little Reed insisted I was in far too delicate a condition to be expected to do that, but I forewent salt and chile, as ritual practice dictated.

And as with that first wedding, after the final feast, Little Reed and I retired to our separate quarters, leaving the marriage unconsummated. *But I will be far happier in this marriage than I ever was with Black Otter,* I told myself. Yet as I lay alone that night, trying to fall asleep, I couldn't quite escape the bitter knowledge that I was so very close to complete happiness but would never fully hold it.

◻

As the weeks passed, my body began showing signs of its condition, and it grew increasingly difficult to find a comfortable position to sleep in. Yamehecatl stayed awake longer and longer, chattering like a parrot into the early hours of the morning, and he resisted going to sleep as if he were already a toddler.

He'd taken to watching the world through my eyes and asking all sorts of questions, from what were the green things all over the trees, and why did they change colors as the weather changed, to why did the sun and the moon chase each other across the sky. *Is the moon trying to catch the sun and kill it?* I answered everything as best I could and mused that when he was born, he would have an immense vocabulary that would make the young me—who had developed language quite early in life—look plain stupid.

But to my sorrow, his interest in the gods and priestly knowledge quickly dwindled to nothing. He slept whenever I taught Mitotia, and he declared my interest in weaving "boring". He loved it though when Little Reed and I played patolli—the traditional way now, for we'd soured our taste for betting our secrets. He also enjoyed music and would sing along to any song he heard. Sometimes his beautiful singing voice choked me up, and I wished Little Reed could hear our son as I did.

Tonight though he was quiet. I'd let Mitotia have the day off to help her mother mend her father's winter clothing, so Yamehecatl chattered most of the day, letting me go to sleep with little trouble.

But sometime in the middle of the night, I awoke with a start, thinking someone had prodded me. I looked over at Mitotia, but she was fast asleep on her mat, at my feet. I closed my eyes, praying I'd find sleep again soon. Yamehecatl woke me earlier every day.

But I felt it again: a strange, ticklish fluttering traveling from one side of my abdomen to the other. Now wide awake, I set my hand on my belly, my heart pounding. Had I felt my son move for the first time, or was I merely imagining it? Yamehecatl was silent, something he rarely was when awake. I didn't dare wake him up to ask though; I wouldn't get back to sleep for hours if I did.

When it came again, a bulge slid under my hand. My heart skipped. *I must share this with Little Reed!*

I prodded Mitotia with my toe a couple of times until she roused. She looked up at me, barely awake. "Is something the matter, My Lady?"

"Please fetch Topiltzin. I must see him immediately."

She stumbled from the room but didn't return when Little Reed came in a moment later, looking far from awake. "Is something wrong?" he asked, kneeling next to me, blurry-eyed.

"Nothing's wrong," I assured him. I took his hand and slid it up under my night

313

dress, setting it palm-down against my abdomen.

"Umm." He cast me an uncertain glance—undergarments were too difficult to tie around my swollen belly anymore—but when Yamehecatl moved, his face lit. "Is that-?" When I nodded, he whispered, "Ayya!" He moved his hand across my abdomen, following our son's movements. "Amazing!"

"Truly." I seemed incapable of not crying these last few months.

"Are you all right?" he asked, his concern returning.

I nodded. "I feel so...happy."

He leaned his head against mine, smiling. "Me too, my love."

His words, his closeness—his bare skin against mine—sent a shiver of desire through me. I felt as if I were floating when our noses brushed against each other, teasingly, until he moved his mouth to mine and the passion engulfed me. I pulled him down onto the bed, the moment wrapping around me like the delicious heat of the steam bath on a cold day.

He bellied up to me, hand moving lower, creeping, caressing. The desire lurched, desperate and oh so glad to have broken free at last....

What are you doing? Yamehecatl suddenly asked, innocent and curious.

Not now, the desire growled. I wanted to pull away, embarrassed, but the desire was in command. I slid my hand down the front of Little Reed's sleep xicolli, finding him already hard despite the thin layer of fabric between his body and my hand. A hunger food couldn't quell spread inside me—

But a sudden, sharp pain radiated through my lower abdomen, cutting through the desire like an obsidian blade. I gritted my teeth against the tight, knotting sensation in my guts, the pain paralyzing.

Little Reed pulled away. "Are you all right? Did I hurt you?"

I shook my head, cursing myself. How could I have been so stupid to let the desire take over? "I'm sorry, I shouldn't have...we can't let this ever happen, Little Reed."

"No, I'm sorry," he stammered. "It's my fault; I shouldn't have kissed you."

I frowned. "No, I should exercise more control; I'm not a slave to my impulses. I made the sacrifice, not you, so the onus is on me to remain faithful to it."

"And I don't expect you to endure it on your own. You made that sacrifice on my behalf; I'd be dead now if not for you, so the least I can do is help you keep the path."

I smiled at him. "I am thankful to Quetzalcoatl every day for giving you life, Little Reed."

"As am I," he replied with a chuckle. He stared into the hearth a moment, an indecisive look on his face. "You know, when it gets to be too difficult, you can always go and see the god in the Divine Dream."

I stared at him, uncomfortable heat traveling up my neck. "What's that supposed to mean?" Little Reed shrugged, bashful now, and my insides curled up. "He...he told you?"

"He never outright stated anything," Little Reed hastily answered. "It's just...why don't you go see him—"

I tried to sit up, cutting him off as he rushed to help me. "I don't go into the Divine Dream anymore because my relationship with Quetzalcoatl.... This is embarrassing to admit, but it was wrong and I never should have done any of it. I was young, and he looked so much like you...and I feared you would never return. I behaved childishly, and selfishly. I disrespected his power and sacredness, to appease my own lusts. But even worse, I disrespected *you*."

Little Reed shook his head. "You didn't disrespect me—"

"I did, because I wanted you, not him, but I was perfectly willing to use him to that end. Quetzalcoatl isn't like us, Little Reed, and it's hugely arrogant to treat him as if we're his equals, or for me to treat my title of his wife as literal, the way we might treat our own if I'd never made this promise to Heaven. I've sworn to never go down that path again, and that means learning to get along without a direct connection to Quetzalcoatl, the same as everyone else. I love him, but he's an unknowable god, so how could I ever really love him the way I love you?"

Little Reed looked baffled. "You speak your true feelings about this...about the god?" When I nodded, he looked strangely wounded. "He would thank you for your honesty. He values that more than anything." He kissed my forehead and stood. "I hope I didn't upset you with my prying questions."

I shook my head. "It's weighed heavily on me, especially now that Yamehecatl thinks you and Quetzalcoatl are one and the same. I hope I haven't disappointed you, Little Reed."

"You could never disappoint me, Papalotl." He left to return to his own bedroom, a wave of regret following him.

¤

In the morning, Little Reed went next door to Citlallotoc's house for breakfast without me. At dinner, he ate with Ten Spines and the other men, leaving me and Mitotia to eat our meal alone, and he didn't come back to the house until after I'd fallen asleep. I wondered how long he'd known about me and his father; likely not long given his sudden distance. Perhaps he'd hoped I would deny the whole thing.

He stayed home for breakfast the next day and I watched him clandestinely, not wanting to be caught staring at him. I desperately wanted everyone else to leave so I could talk to him.

But halfway through the meal, a runner from Culhuacan arrived with a letter from Blood Wolf.

"King Meconetzin of Chalco has died and his sons are brawling for the throne," Little Reed announced once he finished reading. "Several of them banded together and are intercepting the trade caravans traveling to Culhuacan. Matlacxochitl went to negotiate a peaceful ending, but they took him captive and are threatening to maim him if I don't support their chosen candidate for the throne."

"They've already cut off his ear and sent it along with their demands to Lord Blood Wolf," the runner informed him.

"And what of our other allies?" I asked. "Why aren't they helping in this?"

"No one seems willing to step in without Lord Topiltzin to lead."

Little Reed stared at the letter a moment longer, chewing his lip. "What happened to Meconetzin's legitimate heir?"

"He was executed the same night the king died," the runner explained. "They even killed the queen and her daughters."

I gasped. "What about Lady Papantzin and the baby?"

The runner bowed his head, frowning. "I'm sorry, My Lady."

You should have convinced her to stay in Culhuacan, I thought, my appetite gone. The King of Chalco had become one of our staunchest allies since our claiming Culhuacan's throne; even Meconetzin's heir had declared his dedication to maintaining that alliance once he became king. There'd been no reason to believe her life—or the baby's—would be in jeopardy by going home. "What about Lady Jade Flower and her children? Certainly they were spared, not being blood relatives of the King?"

"I'm sorry, but I have no information on your sister."

I prayed Black Otter had arrived there safely and gotten her and the children out before all this transpired.

Little Reed folded up the letter and motioned to Mazatzin. "We'll leave immediately."

Citlallotoc rose to his feet as well. "Don't you mean me as well, My Lord?"

Little Reed shook his head. "I need you to stay here and oversee my affairs."

"But My Lord—"

"And I need you to guard my wife and son." Little Reed set a firm hand on his shoulder. "I trust only my very best man with such an important task."

Citlallotoc looked sullen, but he nodded.

"And move into my quarters while I'm gone, so you're within easy reach of the queen," Little Reed told him.

Amoxtli rose as well. "I ask permission to accompany you, My Lord. My brother was sent to Chalco and I must know what became of him."

Little Reed nodded. "We welcome you to join us, Cousin."

The rest of the meal passed in a whirlwind of instructions and planning, but once it was over, Little Reed went to his quarters to pack. Citlallotoc lingered and only left once I asked him to go so I could have a private word with Little Reed. Eventually Little Reed emerged from his quarters, wearing cotton armor under his heron-feather xicolli emblazoned with the Feathered Serpent, his macuahuitl sword hanging from his belt. He looked striking in his army uniform.

"Will you hurry back once this is finished?" I tried to keep my voice steady.

"If I could fly back, I would," he assured me. When I looked away, he said, "I know this is really bad timing, with the baby due in a few more months, but things could deteriorate if I wait."

I nodded. "I know you must go, but...I'm afraid I upset you and we haven't made amends, and what if you're not back in time, or something happens in the childbed, and I never get to see you again?"

Little Reed knelt and took me into his arms. "I'm sorry I made you believe I was angry, Papalotl. I was working out my feelings about some things, but I shouldn't have kept you at a distance. Your personal relationship with the god...it isn't my business, and you don't need to explain yourself. I'm sorry I made you believe you had to. Can you forgive me?"

I hugged him tighter. "Of course, Little Reed. Just promise me you'll do your best to get back here before the baby comes."

"I *will* be here," he assured me. "And we'll wrestle Yamehecatl from the gods together." He kissed my cheek then moved his mouth towards mine, but after a hesitation he withdrew, leaving my heart hammering. "And don't worry, Citlallotoc will take care of you, and I'll write to keep you apprised of everything."

"I'll miss you." I held onto his hand a moment longer before finally letting go. "And come home safely to me, and Yamehecatl."

"I promise I will," he said with a smile, before going outside where Mazatzin and Amoxtli waited for him.

I sighed. "The last time someone made that promise to me, I never saw him alive again," I muttered.

Chapter Ten

 The weeks turned into months, punctuated with an occasional letter from Little Reed painting grim pictures of life back in the valley. He'd tried negotiating Matlacxochitl's release, but when the reply consisted only of Matlacxochitl's severed nose, Little Reed sent troops into the countryside where the band of villains had taken refuge, and killed the lot. He marched on Chalco and seized control of the city, allowing the remaining sons to come out of hiding to make their petitions to inherit the throne. He listened to each man's case and picked two of the strongest and brightest candidates to co-rule, then installed his own advisor on the new war council to monitor affairs going forward.

He'd planned to return to Tollan at that point, two months after he'd left, but riots broke out in Culhuacan. A mob of Toltecas attacked and killed a Chichimec woman selling cotton cloth in the market, claiming she'd stolen it from another woman's inventory—for everyone knew that Chichimecs knew nothing about weaving "like civilized people". The woman's death spurred her husband to gather his friends and they hunted down and killed her murderers, though not before cutting out their tongues, gouging out their eyes, and slicing off their ears. From there the violence escalated, with mobs hunting any and all Chichimecs, killing the men and enslaving the women and children. Fear and anger ran rampant, and finding and punishing the ringleaders proved more than a little taxing.

But when Little Reed announced the need for workers to go north to help build Tollan, the Chichimecs—tired of being treated as animals—migrated to Tollan in droves, bringing their wives, their children, and their dreams with them.

"This place was already crawling with too many Chichimecs," Citlallotoc growled as he stood at the doorway overlooking the courtyard, watching the women working around the fire pit. He complained at least once a day about the women cooking outside rather than using the hearths in the kitchen. "A bunch of barbarians, the whole lot of them."

"We all want the same things," I told him as I worked on my weaving in front of the anteroom hearth. I'd become very round the last month and found it difficult to lie down all the time, so I sat as often as I could; occasionally, with Mitotia's help, I walked around the house.

"We won't have enough food to last the entire winter," Citlallotoc grumbled. "I'll have to request more from my brother and hope he has enough to spare. Things will turn ugly if we run out, and we'll be the first ones these Chichimec dogs come to looking for relief. You know what they say about Chichimecs and their own children?"

I pinned him with a glare. "My father used to tell me that if I kept crossing my eyes and making faces at my sisters that the gods would freeze my face. I've never witnessed any of our Chichimec allies feasting on their own children." I was grateful Mitotia wasn't here, though had she been, Citlallotoc never would have said anything; she made him uncomfortable and so he rarely spoke around her. I'd initially thought it attraction but I grew increasingly sure it had more to do with his stubborn distrust of all Chichimecs.

Why does he distrust them, Nantli? Yamehecatl asked.

Because they are different from us in many ways. Differences frighten people.

Do they scare you?

Most men frighten me until I get to know them and realize they're safe. Though even that

317

had proven a mistake on more than one occasion.

Why?

It's complicated, my dear. I don't want to mistrust people immediately, but experience has taught me that it's safer to do so.

You're not scared of me, are you? Yamehecatl asked, concerned.

I chuckled aloud. *No. I love you, and trust you implicitly.*

"What's so funny?" Citlallotoc leaned against the doorway as the rain came down beyond the porch.

"I was talking to myself."

He gave me a silly grin. "You do that a lot these days. Am I insufficient company?"

I grinned back at him. "Quite sufficient, thank you."

He closed the heavy door curtain and sat on one of the reed mats in front of the hearth, next to me. He stared into the fire, knees drawn up, arms across them. "You needn't spare my feelings, My Lady. I know I'm no substitute for Topiltzin. I really thought he would be back by now." His gaze rested on my huge belly, concern painted on his face. "I'm certain he'll be back any day now."

Every day I told myself, *only one more day*; but with few weeks remaining until the birth, I worried. If matters went sour in the childbed, Citlallotoc would sit and guard me from the Black Dog, but it wasn't the same. I had so much to tell Little Reed; private things I couldn't imagine asking Citlallotoc to pass on to him after I was gone.

Why do you think you're going to die, Nantli? Yamehecatl asked, puzzled.

I don't think I'm going to, it's only...the childbed is dangerous. Sometimes things go wrong. That's life.

But what does it matter if you die? You'll come back again, as in the stories you tell me about Tatli and the other gods.

I'm not like your father, Yamehecatl. But I had already died once and come back to life....

Citlallotoc chuckled. "I am definitely not adequate company. You're 'talking' to yourself again."

I blushed. "Sorry."

"My father once told me my mother was so scatterbrained in her last month with me that she couldn't hold a conversation at all."

It wasn't unusual for women to become distracted and forgetful in the final months of their pregnancies; Nimilitzli had said it was because they carry two—sometimes more—tonallis in their bodies at once, and they knocked each other around. Though I suspected that it was because they were constantly distracted by the curious chatter of their unborn children.

Mitotia opened the door curtain, her long hair dripping water. "My Lord, my father asks to see you immediately." She looked agitated.

He glanced at her over his shoulder. "Is something wrong?"

"Strangers have arrived out of the north, and their leader...." She paused, as if reconsidering what to say. "Father asks you come right away."

Citlallotoc donned his cloak and went out into the rain.

"What's wrong with their leader?" I asked.

She glanced back at the doorway before whispering, "Lord Citlallotoc is the tallest man I've ever met, until now. This Chichimec is twice his size, and his face...I shudder to remember it!"

"What was wrong with it?"

"Half of it is blue, and not only his face; the whole left side of his body—arm, leg, and chest. I've never seen that color of paint before."

"Where is he?"

"The guards made him and his men wait at the gate."

Then I could see him from the doorway. I motioned her for help up and she did so. I shuffled to the door and peeked out of the curtain.

Citlallotoc and Ten Spines stood at the gate with several armed guards. Beyond, as Mitotia had said, was a giant of a man—he would have to bend down to step through the corbeled arch, if the guards would let him. And the left side of his body was painted the same shimmering color of the blue-throated hummingbirds that haunted the forests around the valley. The arch blocked any view of his face, but his deep, throaty voice boomed. "This is the illustrious Topiltzin everyone speaks of?"

"This is Lord Topiltzin's war chief, Lord Citlallotoc," Ten Spines answered, a quaver to his voice.

"I said I would speak only to Topiltzin."

Citlallotoc glared up at the other man and asked Ten Spines, "An ally of yours?"

The stranger laughed. "I require no allies."

"This is Lord Mextli of the Mexica," Ten Spines replied.

"I despise repeating myself," Mextli growled. "I demand an audience with Topiltzin."

"It's too late for an official visit," Citlallotoc fired back.

"It's never too late for matters of war. Or does the dark scare you, little lord?"

Citlallotoc stiffened. "If you were hoping for shelter tonight, I'm afraid we haven't room for your kind."

"I have no use for your pathetic stone buildings. I'm here to counsel Topiltzin, but he's too afraid to come out and speak to me."

"The *king* has no use for loudmouthed Chichimec dog-shit, and he'd hand you your own tongue if he weren't such an understanding man. Now, if you're finished preening, I'll gladly toss you out on your asses."

Mextli laughed. "I admire your gall, so I won't crush your skull...yet. But hear this: I won't allow you to build a temple to the Feathered Serpent on Smoking Mirror's lands. Quetzalcoatl kicked Tezcatlipoca out of the lake valley, and now his insidious influence infringes on our brother's territory. You will begin deconstructing the offending buildings immediately and leave here forever."

None of the sacred stories spoke of Quetzalcoatl having any brothers, but Smoking Mirror had called him "brother" when we'd faced off in Culhuacan. And now this Mextli made the very same claim. I could accept that the sacred stories were only part of the truth—Quetzalcoatl had told me as much—but I'd never heard of any god called Mextli.

Citlallotoc laughed. "And why should Topiltzin bend to your bawling?"

"If I told you, it would wipe that smirk off your face," Mextli replied. "Refuse my request, and I will do the work myself—and Omeyocan help you, little man, if you get in my way."

"You're asking me to leave you and your men's bodies as scraps for the coyotes!" Citlallotoc roared.

"Such adorable threats. Pity you're not man enough to fulfill them."

Citlallotoc launched himself at Mextli, but Ten Spines held him back. "Let us not spill blood on Lord Topiltzin's doorstep."

"Oh, the blood will spill," Mextli said. "It's only out of respect for your better judgment, Ten Spines, that I will spare your people when everything turns bad—and trust me, it will. What is happening here in the heart of Smoking Mirror's realm is an affront to the gods, and everyone involved with this sacrilege will pay with their lives."

"Big talk for a man flanked by a mere fifteen warriors!" Citlallotoc shouted at him over Ten Spines' shoulder.

Mextli laughed. "Your superior numbers are meaningless. I could defeat the whole lot of you on my own."

"Then stop your strutting and draw your sword!" Citlallotoc reached for his, but again Ten Spines interrupted him.

"This is not the place, My Lord." Ten Spines cast a discreet glance in my direction. "Think of those we swore to protect."

Citlallotoc didn't follow his gaze but nodded, relaxing finally. To Mextli he said, "You and your men will leave. And if you return, there will be bloodshed."

"I wouldn't have it any other way." Mextli turned to his wet and bedraggled men. "Let us go and allow the little lord to sleep. He will need it." The strangers departed from the gate.

Ten Spines and Citlallotoc kept their place, leaning past the archway to watch them go. "It isn't wise to upset that man," Ten Spines said.

"He's a puffed-up grouse who squawks loudly," Citlallotoc growled.

"Perhaps, but his face...he's a monster."

"I don't care how he decorates himself; I won't tolerate anyone insulting my king at the gate to his own house. And his ludicrous demands that we tear down the temple—"

"What are we going to do?"

"He talks big, but he doesn't realize Quetzalcoatl has his own defenses." He finally looked back at me.

I shut the curtain and went back to my bed mat, feeling as if someone had squeezed my heart. Would duty have me call on Quetzalcoatl's powers again? *But I've already given so much.* As I felt Yamehecatl kicking around, a chill ran through me. *Maybe Mextli will go away,* I thought, determined to stop the rising tide of panic. *He's all bluster and I won't have to sacrifice my son.*

Who's Mextli, Nantli? Yamehecatl asked.

I have no idea, love. I shook my head. *And I hope we don't find out.*

□

Shouts in the courtyard woke me before dawn. Bare feet slapped on the stone floor of the anteroom and I heard Citlallotoc tear aside the curtain of Little Reed's quarters. "What in Mictlan is going on out there?" he demanded.

A guard answered, out of breath. "My Lord, the temple is under attack!"

I tossed aside my blanket and went to the door, Mitotia at my side. I opened the curtain to find Citlallotoc donning his cotton armor while a nervous guard stood at the doorway outside. "It's Mextli's men, isn't it?" I asked, my stomach knotting up.

"Undoubtedly." Citlallotoc threw a cloak over his armor. "He will pay with his life for this." He took a long spear from the corner near the front door and told me, "Stay here for now. If I need you...?"

"I will." I tried to sound brave. "But please, it costs me a great deal."

He nodded and disappeared into the dark.

"I thought we increased patrols around the sacred precinct, to make certain the Mexica didn't come back," Mitotia said.

"Apparently those patrols weren't sufficient."

I looked into the courtyard. Screaming and yelling came from beyond the wall, from men and women alike. Bitter Rabbit lurked in her doorway, looking into the sky and muttering under her breath. "Pack us a bag with some clothes and food, and pack one for your mother as well."

"Why?"

"If Mextli kills your father and Citlallotoc we'll need to leave quickly, so don't hesitate any further."

Mitotia raced across the courtyard to talk to her mother. Bitter Rabbit's worry became distress, but she nodded and disappeared inside. When Mitotia returned, she went immediately to my room while I remained at the doorway, watching the outer walls. Oddly, I felt stronger than I had in ages.

With our bag packed, Mitotia suggested I change out of my night dress into some traveling clothes; but as I turned from the doorway, a flaming arrow stuck into the ground next to the cooking fire. The already terrified servants fled screaming through the gate when a second arrow bounced off the stone wall of Ten Spines' house and skidded across the ground onto the reed mats near the cooking fire.

"No time!" I grabbed a cloak off the peg next to the doorway. "We're leaving now. Get your mother and meet me by the gate."

But five guards stood outside the gate, blocking our way. "Lord Citlallotoc ordered us to keep you here," the lead guard replied, nudging me back with the handle of his spear. "You'll be safer in your house."

"When it's on fire?" I demanded. "The Mexica are shooting flaming arrows over our walls!"

"There's enough mayhem out here without worrying about where you are, My Lady."

Losing patience, I snapped, "Step aside or I'll call on the god to clear the path for us!"

He must have been at the battle for Culhuacan, for he paled and immediately stepped aside. "I'm coming with you, though," he said, keeping pace with me. "If I'm to die for disobeying orders, then let it be because I stepped between you and an enemy spear."

Despite the danger of the moment, I frowned. Evidently the orders of my war chief counted more than my own orders as queen.

After months of virtual captivity, I felt exhilarated at being out among the people again. And even better, no pains hounded my movements; in fact, I felt as energetic and strong as at twenty, when I spent my days running up and down the vast staircases of Xochicalco. The further I walked, the better I felt. Had it been a mistake to spend so many months lying in bed when I was perfectly capable of getting up and walking around without pain?

But that good feeling abandoned me when we reached the sacred precinct, where most of the fighting was concentrated. *What madness leads me here, to the middle of a pitched battle?*

We're exactly where we need to be, the desire answered, so confident and sure.

The guard grabbed my arm. "You can't go in there!"

And yet every fiber of my being screamed that if I didn't, I would regret it for the rest of my life. I pulled away from him and ran into the writhing mass of death, feeling light as a feather.

He fought his way through the crowd, shouting after me, "My Lady! You must come back! It's not safe—"

The din of battle swallowed his words when I spotted Citlallotoc sparring with several Mexica warriors at the foot of the half-built temple. Above him, Mextli—massive and hulking—was ripping up blocks of stone and hurling them into the crowd. Finally seeing his face, I was mesmerized. He wore no cotton armor, no elaborate headdress; if not for the simple white loincloth, he would have been completely naked. Blue paint covered him head to foot on the left side, but none of it rubbed off onto his pristine white loincloth. He carried himself as if a spear-thrust to the gut or taking an arrow to the chest meant nothing. He tore apart the Feathered Serpent's temple as if this were a typical day's work.

At the temple's foot, Citlallotoc dispatched the two remaining warriors then charged up the steps, his spear ready. Ten steps up, he launched it, putting his whole body into the throw. He had magnificent form that spoke of a lifetime of training.

But Mextli batted the zipping spear aside as if it were an annoying insect. "Certainly Topiltzin's best warrior can do better than that!" he roared, laughing. His words brought much of the fighting nearest the temple to a halt as both sides watched their leaders face off.

Citlallotoc drew his sword. "Let us decide this like honorable men. Just you and me, to the death, winner claims these lands; for Topiltzin if I win, for Smoking Mirror if you do."

"When I win, I will sacrifice the whole lot of you and scatter your children to the desert," Mextli said. "But with you, little lord, I shall teach my people the art of making tlaxcallis using your ground-up bones for masa." He beckoned to Citlallotoc with one hand.

Citlallotoc charged up the steps, bellowing like a bear.

Mextli scooped up the spear and swung the butt of it around, bashing Citlallotoc in the face. Citlallotoc rolled down the stairs, dazed, but caught hold of one of the stone steps to stop from tumbling all the way down. Blood gushed from his broken nose.

Snickering, Mextli tossed the spear to him. "I think you'll need this too. Maybe you'll fare better if I'm unarmed."

Citlallotoc snatched up the spear and got to his feet. Wiping blood from his mouth and chin with the back of his hand, he climbed the stairs, leading with the spear.

Mextli didn't move, only stared at him. But when Citlallotoc tried to jab him with the spear, he side-stepped and grabbed it one-handed, lifting Citlallotoc off his feet. He swung him around and let go, flinging him down the stairs. Citlallotoc hit the bottom, landing chest down with a gushing grunt.

Mextli descended the stairs and yanked him up by his cotton armor. "How dare Topiltzin come here to exploit the hard labor of Smoking Mirror's chosen people, and make them forget their gods with false promises of peace and prosperity?"

He threw Citlallotoc back to the ground and faced the crowd. "Their real aim is to exterminate every last Chichimec and expel you from your homelands! Tolteca fathers tell their children that you eat your own sons and rape your daughters; they raise generation after generation to hate and despise your people because they know their time is coming to an end, and they are terrified. The Chichimec people are meant for greatness, so stand strong against your Tolteca enslavers and seize the robes of power for yourselves! You will live in their lavish palaces as kings, with them scraping an existence at your borders, paying you tribute to keep you from crushing them. Someday they'll quake in fear before the very name of your people!"

Cheers rose from Mextli's men, but Ten Spines' men exchanged mistrusting glances with the Toltecas they'd fought next to moments before. A heavy, contentious silence settled over the precinct.

Citlallotoc swiped Mextli's left leg with his sword, and a cloud of blue flakes drifted off the wound, like feathers from a sling-shot bird. *That's not paint at all!* I realized.

Mextli roared in pain, but when Citlallotoc tried to roll away, Mextli stepped his right foot onto his hair, pinning his head to the ground. Citlallotoc swung again, but Mextli kicked the sword away. He stamped hard on Citlallotoc's right forearm with a sickening crunch. Citlallotoc howled in agony.

"Now we'll have our fun, little lord," Mextli snarled, pinning him with his knees, gold dust sputtering from the wound on his leg.

Just as when I injured Smoking Mirror during the battle for Culhuacan, I realized with a gasp. *Great Feathered Serpent, he* is *a god!*

And as if to confirm my conclusion, a flint knife suddenly materialized in Mextli's left hand. *Citlallotoc never had any chance at all against this man.* The only way he would survive—that *any of us* would survive this—if I called on the god.

I set my hand on my swollen belly, thinking of all the things I'd miss: getting to hold Yamehecatl, seeing him with my eyes, not only my heart, to see if he resembled the god as Little Reed did. Had all of it been for nothing? I couldn't breathe, but I'd learned the hard way to have the courage to make the right sacrifice when it mattered most.

I felt physically ill, but I took a deep, calming breath, trying to separate myself from my emotions as I reached for my sacrificial blade at my hip.

Forget the knife, the desire chided. *Remember the maguey.*

I hadn't thought about what I'd done since that day; I'd dismissed it as a hallucination. But now that same tingling returned to my fingers, coursing up my arms, and into my chest, a powerful, rhythmic pulsing begging for release.

Mextli waved the knife in Citlallotoc's face. "I'm going to peel the skin off your face and wear it as a mask," he hissed. "And when you beg me to end your suffering, I shall cut out your heart and eat it while you watch, little lord." Smiling, he traced the tip of the blade across Citlallotoc's forehead. "But we're going to take a while to get to that point."

This is crazy, I thought, bending down and setting my hands on the ground. The magic vibrated inside me, so I flexed my arm muscles and pushed.

As in the field, the ground rumbled, softly but with growing intensity. A murmur rose as everyone looked at each other—even Mextli stood, towering over everyone else.

But when the ground bucked, panic erupted. Men fled, falling over each other. I remained where I was, hands to the ground, focused on the magic surging through my arms. The crowd thinned enough that I saw Citlallotoc dragging himself away from Mextli, his right arm dangling useless at his side.

Mextli looked around, bewildered. "Is that you, Brother? Have you come to face me?"

No, Mextli, I *have come to face you.* I felt powerful, in control in a way I never had before. It was intoxicating.

Suddenly, lime-white roots shot out of the ground under Mextli's feet, striking like rattlesnakes and lashing onto him, cutting like obsidian blades. "*What in Mictlan...?*" He tried to yank them off, but they coiled around his chest like a boa constrictor suffocating a tapir. He slashed at them with his knife, slicing them off, but I willed more to spring from the ground, weaving over him into a net. He ripped through the mesh with his bare hands, spewing gold dust as they laid open his fingers and palms. But he was making headway against my trap.

Oh no you don't! I pushed more tingling magic, imagining thousands more roots spearing out of the hard ground to drag him down into the belly of the earth monster. The ground began swallowing him a bit at a time; first his feet, then his knees. Soon he was up to his hips in dirt, clawing to keep from going under. *Squeeze and crush him,* I thought, an intoxicating thrill coursing through me; not very different than when Black Otter got the desire going.

But when Mextli sank to his chest, the roots went up in flames, engulfing him completely. I jolted from my near-trance-state and fell over onto my rear, staring horror-struck into the flames. He looked right at me through the throbbing yellow and orange, but then the flames went out and he was gone. Only the charred roots remained.

With the sacred precinct nearly empty, the guard who'd followed me finally reached me. He helped me to my feet, but I shrugged him off when I spotted Citlallotoc hunched on the ground, surrounded by several Chichimecs who were either trying to help him up or were calling for help.

I hurried over and gasped when I saw the spears of arm bone piercing the skin. He would never use his sword arm again.

Chapter Eleven

 I held Citlallotoc's hand as our men carried him back to the house on a stretcher. Thankfully the compound had suffered only minor scorching around the courtyard, and I welcomed the quietness after the chaos in the sacred precinct.

A surgeon arrived shortly and shooed everyone from Little Reed's quarters so he and his assistant could tend to Citlallotoc unimpeded. I lingered in the anteroom, pacing to work off the distress that Citlallotoc's cries of agony built inside me. I should have stopped Mextli sooner, before he could so injure him. *I shouldn't have even let the two of them face off.* My abdomen tightened unpleasantly but I ignored it; I was too anxious about Citlallotoc to sit still.

Mitotia and her mother came to the door from the courtyard; both looked relieved to see me. Mitotia rushed to hug me. "I've been searching everywhere for you! When you ran off into the fighting...I was certain you'd be killed."

"I'm fine, but Citlallotoc is badly injured. I fear they might have to amputate one of his arms." I flinched when he started a new bout of agonized howling. This time an intense pain gripped me and I winced, clutching my swollen belly.

"You're having pains?" Bitter Rabbit asked.

"A few, but they aren't that bad."

"Do they all feel the same as that last one?"

"I should get back into bed," I conceded.

I crawled into my bed and tried to sleep once Citlallotoc's cries subsided—no doubt thanks to a healthy dose of yauhtli—but my own pain continued to steadily grow. *No, I'm not ready for this yet,* I thought. *Little Reed isn't here. The baby can't come now. What if things go terribly wrong?* I tried to talk with Yamehecatl, to take my mind off of the pain, but he remained distressingly silent.

The hours melted together as the pains came longer with less respite in between. Bitter Rabbit stayed with me, checking my progress time and again while Mitotia kept damp rags on my forehead. The surgeon came to tell me about Citlallotoc, but his words were gibberish to me. I begged him for yauhtli, so I could sleep and forget the pain for a while, but Bitter Rabbit forbade it, saying, "You must be able to follow my directions when the time comes." I despised her.

With no chance for sleep, I scrambled for ways to make the hours bearable. I focused on my breathing, meditated, ground my teeth down on deer-hide straps, but nothing really helped. I prayed for Little Reed to get here soon. I constantly searched the dark corners of my quarters for signs of the Black Dog, waiting to mark me a second time. *At least if I die again, my soul won't belong to Smoking Mirror,* I thought, as sweat poured off me. *I'll go to Teteocan, where Mother went. Maybe I'll get to see her there?* That thought brought me some comfort.

Shortly before midnight, when the pains grew so bad that I screamed when they squeezed me, the gods answered my prayers. Little Reed was suddenly at my side, holding my hand. "I'm here, Papalotl," he whispered. I thought I was hallucinating, but he caressed my sweaty hair away from my face. "Forgive me for being so late."

"Where were you?" I wailed, overcome with a choking mix of despair and joy.

"One thing after another kept coming up back in Culhuacan. But now is hardly the time to bore you with those details," he said with an anxious laugh. "I came as fast as I could; I wore my men out trying to make the journey in ten days."

"I'm so glad you're here," I said, taking his hand with mine. But another bout of pain attacked and I knew only pressure and agony for an eternity before it finally left me alone again. Lying still was delicious bliss.

"Now you go," Bitter Rabbit told Little Reed. "The childbed is no place for men."

But when he tried pulling his hand from mine, I found the strength to tighten my grip. "No, please stay with me," I begged. "If everything goes wrong, I need you to hold me when the Black Dog comes."

He squeezed my hand reassuringly. "I'm not going anywhere."

Bitter Rabbit glared at him. "If you're staying, you will help. Take her under the arms and hold her up, so she can crouch, and don't dawdle; it's time to battle the gods and claim your son."

Little Reed hurried to follow orders, lifting me up.

The pressure came again with numbing intensity and this time I screamed not from pain but determination; I was a warrior charging into battle, sword drawn. The gods had my son but I would capture him and bring him home. They tried to knock me back with another wave of pressure, but I pushed and pushed back, refusing to retreat.

A sudden rush of relief ended the battle at last and I turned limp in Little Reed's arms. He still held me up though, and I heard no crying. "Is he here?" I panted, feeling drunk after so much struggling. "Is it over?"

"The difficult part is," Bitter Rabbit said. "The baby's head is out. One more good push and you'll have the rest of him."

I wept; I was too exhausted to face the gods again. I could barely move. I couldn't do this.

But when the next wave of pain came on, my body forgot its exhaustion and I bore down harder than ever, too focused even to scream. This time the pain left quickly, taking the intense pressure with it. Little Reed gently lowered me onto my bed and sat behind me, letting me recline against him, and he held me tight as Bitter Rabbit washed the blood and afterbirth off our son.

I expected Yamehecatl to be overly large and fat, as Little Reed had been upon his birth, but he was normal in proportions. He had Little Reed's fine black hair, and once Bitter Rabbit dried him off, the curls on his forehead resembled the pictograph for the word "wind". She wrapped him in a blanket of rabbit furs and laid him in my arms. "Your son, My Lady," she said with a smile.

He didn't make a sound during any of this, and I was terrified that he was in fact dead, but then he yawned, showing off two surprisingly long front teeth. Not entirely unheard of, Nimilitzli had told me, but a rare occurrence I'd never seen in my years as midwife to King Cuitlapanton's wife and concubines.

"He's beautiful." Little Reed's voice was choked with emotion. He fingered one of the curls and laughed. "You gave him a most appropriate name, my love."

"He is beautiful," I agreed, kissing Yamehecatl's forehead. He sighed.

"And the birth went well? Nothing we should worry about?" Little Reed asked Bitter Rabbit.

"It went perfectly; in fact, I've never had a birth go so smoothly—I didn't even have to cut her to help the baby pass, and the afterbirth came out immediately." To me, she said, "You must be truly blessed by the gods."

I gazed down at Yamehecatl, my heart breaking with joy. "Quetzalcoatl has indeed blessed me."

"I shall find a warrior to bury the afterbirth on a battlefield for you," Bitter Rabbit said, drying the placenta and umbilical cord between cotton cloths. "So the prince will grow up to be a brave warrior."

I frowned; not that I didn't appreciate the offer, but when I looked down at Yamehecatl—so tiny, so precious in my arms—imagining him as crushed and injured as Citlallotoc curled my stomach. "Actually, we're going to bury it at the foot of Quetzalcoatl's temple." Nimilitzli had done the same with Little Reed's afterbirth, in a solemn ceremony at the foot of the god's temple in Xochicalco a few days after his birth, so his tonalli would always gravitate towards the temple. As was customary, my mother and father had buried mine under the hearth stones in the great hall in Culhuacan, so my tonalli would remain near the home.

Bitter Rabbit nodded. "There was a battle fought there yesterday, so it will do." She rose to leave. "I'll be back in a moment with a fresh fur for your bed."

"What does she mean by a battle?" Little Reed asked, concern in his voice.

I looked up at him, resting my head against his shoulder. "A man named Mextli came looking for you, and he and his men attacked the temple. You should have seen this Chichimec, Little Reed; he was gigantic and he had glued something blue—feathers, I think—on the entire left side of his body, and...I know this is going to sound crazy, but I don't think he was human."

Little Reed furrowed his brow. "Why not?"

"Citlallotoc cut him, but he bled gold dust, as Smoking Mirror did when I wounded him. He even pulled an obsidian dagger right out of the air and he shattered Citlallotoc's arm with a single stomp. Have you gone to see Citlallotoc yet? The surgeon spoke to me about him earlier but I wasn't in any condition to listen."

"No, I heard you and came here immediately." Little Reed gazed towards the door, fidgeting, so I told him to go and see his friend. "You're certain?"

"Of course. I want to know how he's doing too."

He ran his hand over Yamehecatl's head once more then left, the copper bells on the door curtain tinkling softly in the late night silence.

Bitter Rabbit came back with a blanket of wolf pelts and a basket for Yamehecatl; while he lay quiet in his new bed, she washed me from head to toe. She helped me into a clean night dress and brought in my reed-woven recliner, so I could sit up and nurse. She started to teach me the basics of getting him to latch on, but he did it immediately, as if on instinct; in a matter of a moment, he lay comfortably in the crook of my arm. I'd worried about his long teeth, but he nursed with surprising care, making me wonder why so many women struggled with this most basic task. "I swear you were born for childbirth and motherhood," Bitter Rabbit said with a smile.

I swallowed the bitter compliment. *And to think I'd planned to cast him off....* It felt right and natural cradling him in my arms, feeding him; first time mothers often panicked and worried about everything they did, but I felt no apprehension, only a strange confidence that usually came with the birth of the second child. For the first time, the world felt completely in harmony.

As Yamehecatl fell into milk-drunk sleep, Little Reed returned. He looked pale and worried. "How is he?" I asked.

Little Reed shook his head. "The surgeon says there's no fixing his arm, so we're amputating it tomorrow, once the light is good."

"They can't let it heal as it is?"

"The injury will poison his blood and he could die, so we must remove it." He gave Yamehecatl a sad smile. "He did manage to tell me what happened out on the precinct...about why he's not dead right now."

My heart skipped. "What did he say?"

"That before Mextli could dress him like a deer, some sort of plant roots broke out of the ground and dragged him away; the kind of roots that attacked Ihuitimal and dragged him under the ground."

"How do you know about that?" I asked, startled. "You were knocked out during that battle."

"This was what Citlallotoc told me."

That made sense; Citlallotoc had been at both battles. "What else did he say?"

"That the god saved the city as he did in Culhuacan." Little Reed met my gaze, concern in his eyes. "Did you call on Quetzalcoatl again?"

"I thought about it," I admitted.

"But?"

I breathed deep to slow my heart rate, so I didn't feel so scared. "When I was alone after falling down the hill...I wanted to give the god some blood, but my bag was out of reach, and I...I made one of the nearby maguey plants bring it to me, with its roots...with magic!"

I expected suspicion and disbelief, but instead, Little Reed's face lit up. "Why didn't you mention this months ago?"

"I thought I'd imagined it, having fallen and possibly hit my head. And it sounded crazy. But when I saw Mextli out on the precinct—"

"What were you doing out on the precinct in the middle of a battle?"

"They were shooting flaming arrows over the walls, so I took Mitotia and Bitter Rabbit and we left. The god led me to the sacred precinct, and when I saw Mextli battling Citlallotoc...I thought I would have to call on Quetzalcoatl by giving the only thing I had left to give." I peered down at Yamehecatl, hugging him tighter, ever so grateful I could hold him at all. "But then I remembered the maguey plant and decided it was worth trying."

Little Reed stroked Yamehecatl's head. "I'm so very glad you did. I could never forgive myself for not being here to make certain you didn't have to make such a sacrifice in the first place. I'm sorry I didn't get here sooner."

"It's all right. I'm grateful you're home again."

"It's good to be home."

I watched Yamehecatl sleeping. "At first, I thought I might only have had these abilities because of Yamehecatl, but I can still feel the magic inside me. Maybe Quetzalcoatl gave it to me as a gift, just as he gave me Yamehecatl."

"Or perhaps the possession awakened magic asleep inside you," Little Reed suggested. "We should cultivate it, see the full extent of what you're capable of."

I laughed. "I would have thought if one of the two of us would have magic, it would have been you. You're the one with a god for a father."

"Heaven's ways are unknowable."

Seeing him gaze longingly down at Yamehecatl, I held the baby out to him. "You haven't even held your son yet."

He hesitated, but after I insisted, he took Yamehecatl into his arms. He relaxed when the baby didn't stir or protest. "He is a miracle, isn't he?"

Watching him hold Yamehecatl, I realized we were a family with a shared future, and I ached with joy. Maybe this wasn't how I'd imagined true happiness before I made that sacrifice, but this felt just as real and precious. It settled my bitter heart. "He most definitely is."

۵

Yamehecatl never cried when he was hungry; I instinctively knew it was feeding time and would wake to find him already awake and patiently waiting for me. After being such a chattering monkey all of these months, his silence now startled, and worried me. The first time he woke up for more than a few moments to feed, I tried to talk to him, much as we talked when he was still inside me; but I saw no recognition in his eyes, no evidence that he understood anything I said. He looked completely uninterested in the world—and, most upsetting, in me as well. I'd loved those bedtime conversations, teaching him about language and emotions, but now that was gone, and I missed it terribly. I'd lost the Yamehecatl I'd grown to love these last several months and I feared he'd never come back.

But I kept talking to him always, determined to find my boy again. *He's forgotten everything before he was born but someday he'll remember, and that cheeky, curious boy I knew will return.*

The day after the birth, Little Reed and the surgeon amputated Citlallotoc's arm above the elbow. At Citlallotoc's request, Little Reed wielded the sword. I sang loudly, hoping to drown out Citlallotoc's screams as they cauterized the wound. He remained in bed for a week after that, growing increasingly depressed, so Little Reed and I sat with him often, trying to keep him engaged in conversation.

"I was going to leave him here when we left, to watch over the city's progress for us, but I don't think that's a good idea anymore," Little Reed confided to me as we took a tour of the sacred precinct to assess the full damage of Mextli's attack. "He's taken losing his arm really hard; I can see it on his face."

"Well, he *is* a warrior and now he can't even wield a sword," I pointed out.

"He doesn't need to anymore, for we're going to live in peace from now on."

"Be that as it may, he's spent most of his life in the army, Little Reed, and being a warrior is an integral part of his identity. Imagine if you couldn't ever again perform a proper sacrifice to the god because someone cut off your...." I cast my gaze towards his crotch but promptly met his eyes again, my face burning.

Little Reed grinned at me. "That would indeed be tragic."

"Perhaps it's not quite the same thing as losing an arm, but don't underestimate how devastating this is for him. And saying he doesn't need to wield a sword anymore isn't going to help him feel better."

"No, it won't."

That night, after dinner, as the three of us sat in the anteroom drinking xocolatl, Little Reed told Citlallotoc, "I've sent for Matlacxochitl to come and oversee the city's development, and once he arrives in a few weeks we'll travel back to Culhuacan. The weather's warming up nicely."

"I thought I was staying here to oversee the city's construction," Citlallotoc said, his voice flat. He stared into his cup of xocolatl. "Do you no longer trust me to protect the city?"

"I trust you implicitly, which is why I want to entrust you with something even more precious to me than a mere city."

Citlallotoc finally looked up at him, mild curiosity in his eyes. "What would that be, Your Majesty?"

"You're the most skilled and accomplished military man I've ever met, so I'd be honored if you would oversee my son's weapons training. I want him to learn from the best."

Hope burned in Citlallotoc's eyes, but when he glanced at his missing arm, it dimmed. "But I can't even wield a sword anymore—"

"I will help you relearn with your other arm," Little Reed assured him. "I've seen you use your left hand in battle; you might not be as accurate as with your right, but you're still absolutely deadly with it. The only reason you aren't already ambidextrous is purely the lack of need." He gripped Citlallotoc by the shoulder. "We'll get you back in fighting shape in no time. That is a promise, my friend."

Citlallotoc smiled stiffly. "Thank you for your confidence in me, My Lord. And My Lady."

Smiling, I said, "It's easy to have confidence in a man of your quality, Citlallotoc."

□

Once Matlacxochitl arrived—bringing still more Chichimecs from Culhuacan with him, along with some poorer Toltecas looking for work—we packed up our house and prepared to journey back to Culhuacan. After nearly nine months in Tollan, leaving was bittersweet; while we would be more comfortable in Culhuacan, my son had been born here, and I didn't relish returning to a place where memories of brutality and loss lurked around every corner. I begrudged that my son should have to spend his most formative years in that kind of place. But it wouldn't be safe here for our family until the city and her defenses were finished.

Matlacxochitl greeted us in the courtyard as we gathered to leave. I hadn't seen him since he arrived, so his mask took me by surprise. It was molded fig-bark paper painted the same tone as his skin and it covered the top half of his face, disguising his lack of a nose. He also wore a jaguar skin, with the head for a cap, concealing his missing ear. He smiled, surprising given all he'd been through, and the curious looks Ten Spines' men gave him. "You will take good care of Tollan while we're gone?" I asked him, hoping my own smile didn't look as forced as it felt.

He bowed. "I shall take the very best care of it, My Lady. And allow me to congratulate you on the birth of the prince. I promise when he returns, it shall be to the most luxurious palace you've ever seen, in the most beautiful city in Tolteca lands."

While he spoke with Little Reed, I turned to get inside the royal litter but stopped when I noticed Mitotia saying goodbye to her parents. Her mother—teary-eyed—hugged her tight, but to my pleasant surprise, her father made no effort to hold back his own tears. "I know you will do many great things, not only for our family, but your people as well."

"I promise I will make you proud, Father."

He laughed, his whole belly shifting as he did. "You already make me tremendously proud." He kissed her cheek. "Have a safe journey, and we will see you when you return home."

She waved goodbye and hurried to the line of soldiers and servants waiting to depart. Ten Spines held his wife while she wept.

As I started climbing inside the litter again, Citlallotoc stepped up to help me, offering me his good arm to balance on. When he handed me Yamehecatl in his basket, it warmed me to see him finally smiling again.

Little Reed climbed into the litter after me and we sat at the open curtain, waving as we wound our way through the humble beginnings of our god's city and out into the countryside. It was so small—only two neighborhoods and a sacred precinct with a single temple a quarter finished.

"Glad to finally be going home?" Little Reed asked.

I shook my head. "I won't be home until we're back here, with our days in Culhuacan done and over." Feeling a tug at the back of my attention, I turned to see Yamehecatl rousing, waving his arms around. I asked Little Reed to fetch him while I untied the front of my dress. "Don't you think it's odd that he never cries?" I asked as I put Yamehecatl to my breast. He latched on immediately, sucking boisterously. For all I worried, he never lacked for appetite.

"Well, he *is* the son of a god."

"*You* cried. In fact, for the first few weeks, you would only stop crying if I held you." He laughed. "I remember."

I looked at Yamehecatl, furrowing my brow.

"What is it?"

"I'd hoped that, like us, he would remember all those evenings he kept me awake talking late into the night, but when he looks at me now...he has no idea who I am."

"Yes, but what we remember of those first days is all filtered through our life experience, which gives it meaning it didn't have for us back when we first experienced it. It was all a mystery at the time."

"I suppose. But I miss it."

Little Reed slid over next to me and put his arm around my shoulder. "And I bet he misses it too."

I watched Yamehecatl nurse while Little Reed lay napping before the day's heat caught up with us. I waited for Yamehecatl to fall asleep as well, so I could nap too, but he nursed slowly and methodically, showing no signs of going to sleep. Eventually he decided he'd eaten his fill and looked up at me, blinking as if he hadn't even noticed I was there until now. I smiled at him as I dabbed the milk from his soft lips, and my heart skipped a beat when he smiled back at me. "You remember me now?" I whispered. He smiled again, this time making a small cooing noise that made my heart ache. He laid in my arms a long time, smiling up at me and moving his mouth, as if trying to make the words we used to speak to each other.

Yes, everything was going to be fine.

Part Two
The Year Ten House

CHAPTER TWELVE

I found the silver hair during my morning brushing; it fell into the water bowl on the pedestal in my bath yard, and when I looked at the bristles of my brush, I found a second one. *Has Little Reed been using my brush?* Though how could he, when he wasn't even in Culhuacan right now? When I glanced into the obsidian mirror hanging above the bowl, something caught my eye, so I leaned closer for a better look.

I appeared dark and murky in the mirror, but something was out of place. I reached up and yanked a long, silver hair out of the front of my head. I stared at it, puzzled. I wasn't yet thirty and already I was silvering?

Being the queen of Culhuacan wasn't a relaxing job, and with the move to Tollan less than a month away, there was so much to do and take care of. My mother had been only a few years older than I was now when she died, but she'd had no silver hairs. I took after her in many ways, except this, it seemed. I tossed the hair aside and checked the mirror again, but I found no more.

"What are you doing, Nantli?" Yamehecatl asked, startling me. He wore only wrist and ankle bands with little copper bells on them—we fully dressed him only for the temple or market—but somehow he'd slipped into my bath yard without making a sound.

Taking him into my arms, I said, "Nothing, my dear. But what are you doing here? I put you down for a nap."

"I want to go to the field with you," he said, sweeping back his unruly black hair from his eyes. His curls still reminded me of wind glyphs.

"You know you can't come with me."

He frowned, tears queued. "But I like watching you do magic!"

I sighed. "I know you do, but it's not safe. Nantli doesn't have the best control, and I don't want you to get hurt by accident."

"I'm not scared."

I laughed. "I know. You're a brave warrior, like Citlallotoc."

Yamehecatl grinned. "Yesterday he showed me how to throw an arrow with the atl-atl. I'm really good."

"I know you are, my love." It both amazed and disheartened me to see him growing up so fast, a fact exacerbated by his early language development. For his first few months, he developed at the same rate as normal children, babbling and testing out sounds to hear himself speak, but those soon turned into words, and he progressed quickly after that. He learned new words after just hearing them a few times and moved from two-to-three word sentences to full-blown, complex ones within another few months, just as Little Reed had at that age. Luckily that was the only unusualness they shared. Physically, Yamehecatl was growing at the same rate as any normal child, and he was as clumsy as anyone his age, which meant his perception of his own skills with weapons—or staying far enough back while I practiced my magic—were skewed.

He gave me pup-eyes and I tried to resist, but it was futile. "All right, but only if Citlallotoc comes with us, to watch over you while I practice."

Yamehecatl ran in a circle, squealing, but then he stopped, holding his knees together. His cheeks darkened as a small puddle of urine collected on the flagstone under him—one of the reasons we rarely bothered with his clothing at this age. "I should water your flowers," he whispered and tiptoed out into my garden.

Chuckling, I tossed down some copal ash to soak up the liquid. When he returned, I washed his legs off and he led the way to the nursery across the hall to fetch his toy sword.

My uncle changed many things about the palace during my years in exile—most of them foul and self-serving—but he'd left the royal nursery untouched. The birds and butterflies and snakes still adorned the walls, and the family baby basket hung from the ceiling. Yamehecatl tucked his toy sword in there every night. The room looked smaller than in my girlhood memories, when I'd slept in here alone; maybe because Little Reed and I had stuffed it full of toys for our only child. I was Yamehecatl's age when I started noticing that everyone but me had a brother or sister and I began pestering Mother about correcting that. She'd given me a sad smile but always told me, "Maybe if we pray hard enough...." Yamehecatl seemed content by himself, so hopefully he and I would never have to have that conversation.

He tore into his wicker clothes basket, tossing aside xicollis decorated with feathered serpents or birds or geometric patterns. "This one! This one! This one, Nantli!" He held up the rumpled full-body rabbit suit I'd made for him. "Because I'm going to be a rabbit warrior when I grow up!" he'd informed me when I asked him about the peculiar request. Every time I saw it, I remembered the last time I'd been in the Divine Dream and saw the rabbit poking its head out from under the door curtain, to what I presumed now would be Yamehecatl's nursery in Tollan. He wore the suit around the palace a couple of times, and threw a fit about wanting to wear it to temple services, but I hadn't seen him in it for a few weeks now.

I sniffed it—making certain it was clean enough—then helped him into it and tied the many laces up the back. It came with a rabbit-head hood with ears made from lacquered maize-leaves that stood at crooked angles from his head. He grabbed his play sword from the baby basket and stood expectantly in front of me, his chest puffed out.

"My, what a mighty rabbit warrior we have here."

He beamed and took my hand, leading me from the nursery. "Let's get Citlallotoc and go!"

Citlallotoc sat in the great hall, smoking pipes with the other war council members. Three months ago, Little Reed and Amoxtli went to Tollan to oversee the palace's completion, leaving me and Citlallotoc in charge of Culhuacan. Things were quiet, with most city business finished before noon, so the men often gathered in the afternoon, making jokes and talking over their pipes before begging off the rest of the evening.

But with all the fire priests set to move to Tollan in two days, my own free time was scarce. Yesterday I helped Mazatzin prepare the codices for the journey and tomorrow I would help Malinalli pack up her meditation room. And I had my own packing to do as well. But I always practiced my magic at least once a week; who knew when I might need it again.

Once inside the great hall, Yamehecatl sprinted across the room, yelling for Citlallotoc. Citlallotoc handed his pipe to the servant behind him and started to stand, but my son leaped on him, knocking him over. "Well, if it isn't the illustrious rabbit warrior!" he roared. "You must grow faster than your father, for I swear you weren't so heavy yesterday!"

"I measured myself on the door this morning," Yamehecatl said. "I haven't grown at all."

Citlallotoc gathered him up with his one good arm and rose. "You'll catch up to me someday." He turned to me with a self-deprecating smile. "What brings you here, My Lady?"

I motioned him to follow me away from the others, who went back to their vulgar jokes and laughter. "Are you busy this afternoon?"

"I was going to sit in the steam bath for a while, but otherwise no. What do you have in mind?"

Yamehecatl furrowed his brow crossly. "I want to watch Nantli do her magic, but she won't let me unless you come along. Will you come with us?"

"I can't watch him and practice at the same time," I explained, feeling guilty for asking such a favor.

Citlallotoc set Yamehecatl down and nodded. "I can do that."

Yamehecatl hooted and bounded around the great hall, but when he turned back to us, he slipped and landed bottom-first with a yelp. He glared at the floor, rubbing his behind.

"I see why you'd need help with him," Citlallotoc said with a chuckle. "The boy's feet are quicker than his head."

ロ

"Do you ever dream you're a rabbit, Nantli?" Yamehecatl asked as we followed the path along the lakeside.

"I never have," I admitted. "Is that what you dreamt about last night?"

"I dream it all the time. I'm a giant brown rabbit, big as Tatli, and I run all over the mountains, and everything spins around me, like when I do this—" He spun in circles, giggling, and Citlallotoc grabbed his arm to keep him from falling. He swayed on his feet as if drunk. "If you don't dream about being a rabbit, Nantli, what do you dream about?"

"A lot of different things." I still dreamt of Mictlan and Lord Death, but not as often anymore. But two new ones joined the ranks of the recurring dream; in the first, I was trapped in a garden whose walls I could never reach the top of when I tried climbing them. It reminded me of the vision I'd had in Teotihuacan years ago, before I became a priestess, except that in the dream, Little Reed wasn't there. I was all alone, and scared.

The other dreams were more pleasant. I'd make love with Little Reed on the temple altar in Xochicalco, or under the giant copal tree in the main gardens. Sometimes he was his father instead, though often I wasn't positive which of them I was with at any given time. I'd wake questioning my decision to avoid the Divine Dream rather than indulging my desire for the god's feathery touch. *He's a god and you have no business treating him as a mere mortal,* I always reminded myself. My dreams had other ideas though.

335

The lakeside path veered away from the water and climbed a small incline, up to a tall stone wall with a wooden gate. Citlallotoc and I left our guards there and went inside, sliding the latch shut behind us to make certain no one barged in and saw me performing magic. Only a few people close to me knew of my abilities.

Inside was what Yamehecatl called "the field", though it was hardly large enough to be rightfully called that. Inside the gate grew two large oak trees that shaded a shed filled with tools to care for the thirty-odd maguey plants the priesthood cultivated for ritual use. The plants varied in size and maturity, and the field's position atop the highest hill ensured no one could see over the walls—thus why I chose it for practice.

The rows of maguey started ten paces beyond the shed. The biggest ones—near the back wall—had giant leaves standing taller than Citlallotoc, and a few sported the tall yellow flower stalks marking the last months of their lives. Some of these plants were older than me.

Yamehecatl ran towards the maguey, oblivious to the ultra-hard daggers jutting from the tips of their leaves, but Citlallotoc brought him back. "You don't go near the maguey unless you're holding someone's hand," he lectured. When Yamehecatl frowned, he asked, "Don't we have a duel to finish?" He pulled a digging stick out of the shed, and Yamehecatl squealed, fumbling his tiny play sword in his pudgy hands.

With Yamehecatl occupied, I walked out to the edge of the maguey and knelt in prayer.

Lord Quetzalcoatl,
Protect me while I practice your gift,
Show my head, my heart, my hands the way,
Help me cultivate this power to best serve you.
I'm forever your faithful servant.

Keeping my eyes closed, I focused. With the help of prayers, meditation, and much practice, I'd learned to build the magic's intensity slowly, to feel it move through my belly, my arms, and finally my hands. My flesh tingled as if asleep, but my skin pulsed with heat. I rested my hands flat on the ground in front of me.

The closest maguey plants flexed their leaves like a bird's wings. I changed speeds slowly, regulating the flow of magic through my hands by sheer will. After a few minutes of this, my mind started drifting and the world seemed to flex around me, like the beginnings of octli intoxication. As I worked more with the maguey, I felt a strange, indescribable connection between us, as if they spoke in waves of vision and memory; I'd learned from experience that if I stayed too long, depression would threaten to swallow me. I let the magic flow a while longer but soon broke it off, not wanting to press it.

As I knelt resting, I noticed a group of three rabbits peering at me from between the rows. When our gazes locked, they sat up and stared at me with liquid black eyes. How strange that such normally skittish creatures would dare come so close. They looked so soft, so warm.... *I wish I could touch them.*

Suddenly they loped towards me, stopping within easy reach. I stared at them agape, but froze when one of them came closer still. It set its front paws on my knees, staring back up at me, nose twitching. I couldn't bring myself to speak aloud. *Did you come because I asked?*

Another rabbit bobbed its head and rubbed its nose with its front paws. I gasped. The loud noise should have scattered them, but they stayed. I raised my hand slowly, afraid the one on my knee would bolt, but instead it leaned its head into my hand. I ran my fingers through the soft fur behind its ears, my heart thudding with joy.

We learned in calmecac that everyone has a nahual—an animal spirit that followed us throughout our lives—and having been born on the day-sign of Tochtli, mine would be a rabbit. But in my experience, only the gods had actual, physically-manifested nahuals—

"Rabbits!" I turned to see Yamehecatl running towards me, a look of glee on his face. This time the rabbits bolted back into the maguey.

"No! Wait!" When they didn't stop, I pressed magic into the ground, hoping that would draw their attention.

But instead the maguey whipped their leaves around in a frenzy. Something swiped my cheek, leaving it stinging, and when I reached up, my fingers came back bloody. More sharp pain bit my arm; a maguey spine stuck out of my robe sleeve, a blossom of crimson growing around it.

Yamehecatl's laughs turned to screams, and I didn't think; I turned and leaped at him. Scooping him into my arms and burying my face in his hair, I shielded him from the stinging attack spreading pain over my back, my neck, and my calves. Someone grabbed me from behind and shoved me towards the shed.

I didn't look up until Citlallotoc told me we were safe, but Yamehecatl continued clinging to me like a baby monkey, weeping. Maguey thorns marked the head of hundreds of tiny rivers of blood running down Citlallotoc's bare shoulders and back. "Are you all right?" he panted.

"I'm fine." I was more worried for Yamehecatl, and immediately checked him over. He clutched his knees to his chest, rocking back and forth. Tears shimmered in his eyes when I held his chin up to find a single cut on his cheek, but otherwise he wasn't injured. I finally breathed. I'd gotten to him in time. Overcome with guilt, I pulled him into a desperate hug. "Thank the Feathered Serpent you're all right, my darling little breeze. I'm so sorry."

Citlallotoc knelt next to me. "You're not all right, Quetzalpetlatl. You have at least twenty thorns in your back."

I glanced over my shoulder and cringed. "You've got quite a few of your own." Gritting my teeth, I pulled one from the side of my neck and pressed my thumb against the wound to staunch the bleeding; luckily it had missed anything vital. "Will you help pull these out?"

Citlallotoc extracted my thorns for me and I returned the favor. My dress soaked up most of my blood, leaving only a few stains on the sleeves of my robe; those I could explain away as from my daily bloodletting.

Citlallotoc's back was far messier. "I'm so sorry about this," I murmured as I dabbed the blood with a length of cloth I tore off my dress.

He glanced at me over his shoulder. "What exactly happened?"

"I let go of too much magic and the maguey went crazy." I shook my head. "I should know better than to bring anyone with me. I can't properly control this power."

"Things could have been far worse if you were alone."

"I shouldn't have ever brought Yamehecatl though. He could have been hurt, and I would never forgive myself—" A choke rose in my throat and I peered watery-eyed over at my son where he sat in the corner, knees still drawn to his chest. One of his rabbit ears lay crumpled over the side of his head.

"I shouldn't have let him get so far away from me," Citlallotoc said, following my gaze.

"This isn't your fault. It happened so fast...and you got us out of there. I owe you my life." I hugged him and kissed his cheek.

"Good thing I haven't any children of my own, for I'm completely unfit for the task," he muttered, unconvinced.

"Nonsense! Yamehecatl adores you; he loves his father, but he wants to be like you. And what are good fathers if not inspirations to their children?" I tossed the bloodied linen into the garbage heap in the corner. "Certainly you want to marry someday, right?"

"Of course."

"So why haven't you yet?"

He chuckled. "I'd think it would be obvious."

I furrowed my brow at him. "It isn't."

He sighed, and raised what was left of his right arm.

"Because you're missing your arm?"

"Not many women consider a stump appealing."

I almost laughed and declared him ridiculous, but bit my tongue. Honor was everything to him, so it was no surprise he worried what others thought of him. I'd seen the young noblewomen snicker and whisper at the feasts, and imagining what such women might say—or show—in their most private of moments, when a man was at his most vulnerable.... "They're self-absorbed wretches," I snarled, hot with indignation. "And though they might be beautiful, their tonallis are empty black mirrors."

Citlallotoc contemplated his stump. "Sometimes I still think it's there, and I can actually feel my fingers moving. But every time I look, my arm is still gone."

I looked at my own three-fingered hand. "I know what you mean. Sometimes it still throbs, as it did right after the surgeons sewed me up."

"I often feel as if I'm being burned again." He sat in silence a moment before muttering, "And I wonder how much longer I can stand feeling this way."

My mind reeled with his admission. I wanted to say something to comfort him, to assure him the pain goes away, but I still suffered ghost pains years after losing my fingers. I'd never received more than a superficial burn—and those had all been due to carelessness around a hot cooking stone—so what did I know about his pain?

Before I could find the right words, one of the guards called from beyond the gate. I donned my robe, covering up my blood-stained dress, and left the shed.

The guard bowed when I opened the gate. "My Lady, Lord Toztli of Chimalhuacan is here, and he demands to see you immediately."

CHAPTER THIRTEEN

 I didn't meet with Toztli immediately. If Little Reed were here, he wouldn't have "demanded" anything, but because he must deal with me, he made his irritation clear.

And as the queen, I could make him wait.

Back at the palace, I asked my handmaiden to set a warm bath for me while I took Yamehecatl to his bed. He sucked his fingers while I sang, still clutching me tight with his free hand, but eventually sleep whisked him away. When I left the nursery, I spotted Malinalli in the vestibule down the hall and called to her. "Can you help me with something?"

Usually I preferred to bathe myself, but my back ached so badly I wasn't certain I could do it this time. Nor did I want my handmaiden seeing all my wounds and asking questions. Malinalli knew of my magic, so it was easier explaining it to her as she helped me peel off my dress and get into the bath.

"Is Yamehecatl all right?" she asked, scrubbing off the dried blood between my scabbed-over wounds.

I nodded. "Thank the Feathered Serpent." Though the god proved deaf to my prayers today. "Citlallotoc took the worst of it."

"Some of these hit very close to your spine. You're lucky you can move still." She dabbed my back dry, wiped salve over the wounds, and wrapped me with a roll of cotton cloth, so I wouldn't bleed through my dress again. "Lord Toztli is pacing the great hall like a dog in need of relieving himself," she told me while she fixed my hair and applied makeup to hide the cut on my cheek.

"The man hates talking to me." If Little Reed were here, I'd have worn one of my finer court dresses and my royal diadem, but I decided my high priestess robe and headdress would serve me better today; men took me more seriously when I did. Everyone knew how I'd summoned the god to confront the Smoking Mirror outside of Culhuacan, and it paid to remind men such as Toztli that I was the god's chosen high priestess, capable of harnessing his power. And my robe's silver and emerald embroidered feathered serpents and the headdress's brilliant white heron feathers demanded attention. I needed to feel powerful facing Toztli.

Over the last few years, I'd learned to exercise better control over my often impulsive desire, but I appreciated how powerful I felt when it came on, so I'd devoted effort to nurturing and encouraging that particular aspect of it. The desire enjoyed being let off the rope and it came to relish politics almost as much as sex. It knew precisely how to deal with haughty men such as Toztli, who thought it right and proper to disrespect or dismiss me. I let the desire seep in as I walked to the great hall with my head held high. I took my time settling onto my icpalli while Toztli and his bodyguards stood waiting. My war council remained bowed until I was fully seated.

I breathed deeply, marveling at the calm inside me. "You asked for an audience with me, Lord Toztli?" I began, beckoning him forward.

Chimalhuacan's king came to the dais and granted me a cursory bow. His gaze fell on my robe as he straightened, and when he met my eyes, a careful smile slid to my lips. "Thank you for agreeing to see me, Lady Quetzalpetlatl."

"It's always a pleasure to see you. You look quite well."

"You flatter me, My Lady, but I'm far from well." Indignation tinged his words.

"Is something wrong?"

His face darkened as if I'd flung a crass insult. "Something is indeed wrong. My son is missing."

"Nahuacatl?"

"I haven't any other legitimate sons."

Insolent little man, the desire growled but after a silent warning to remain focused, it went on, "Do you wish me to send men out to help you find him?"

He cast me a scathing glare unseen to the men sitting behind him. "That would be ever so kind of you, My Lady. He was last seen in the market, in the company of Chichimec warriors, so I fear for his safety."

"I shall dispatch search parties immediately."

"I hope he's found before you and Lord Topiltzin abandon Culhuacan next month."

"No one is abandoning Culhuacan," I said, barely holding back the snap. "Lord

Ixtlilxochitl will assume control of the city once we move to Tollan, but Topiltzin and I are still her king and queen."

Toztli took to pacing in a small circle. "It's just very convenient that as you prepare to leave, the Chichimecs start making trouble. If you recall, I asked Topiltzin to send them back north years ago, and now Chimalhuacan and the other lake cities are left to deal with the problem you leave behind."

"Problem?"

"The Chichimecs, of course."

"There is no 'Chichimec problem'. They've adapted well to city life, and they've contributed to the prosperity we all enjoy. We couldn't have built the market without them. They've earned the right to be here."

Toztli laughed. "And now they've earned the right to rule over us? You're leaving a barbarian in charge of Culhuacan when you leave."

A general grumble rose from the men sitting on the floor behind Toztli, and the council member seated next to Ixtlilxochitl muttered something to him, but Ixtlilxochitl maintained his normal scowl, his gaze like thrown arrows at Toztli's back.

"Lord Ixtlilxochitl earned this kingdom's trust through his loyalty and honor, and both Topiltzin and I agree he is the best candidate. Our decision is not open for debate."

"And yet a good ruler is mindful of how his allies view his choices," Toztli fired back. "Or whom he lets influence his decisions."

Now my war council members came to their feet, those grumbles turning to shouts. I motioned for them to sit again. "As I said, I'm happy to send troops to help your men locate your son. Chimalhuacan has always been a close and trusted ally, and because we look forward to a long friendship, if anything tragic has befallen Lord Nahuacatl, I personally promise that the culprits will be put to the sword, be they Chichimec or Tolteca."

Toztli stared me down a moment—a gesture only a man of his status could get away with—and he bowed, sweeping his fingers across the ground at his feet. "I thank you for your assistance, My Lady, and I pray we can find my son in time."

"As do I. I shall have troops out searching within the hour. If you wish to stay the night, I will have quarters prepared for you."

"You are most gracious, but I should return home immediately."

"Good journey to you then."

Toztli swept from the great hall, guards in tow. My tense body ached, and with the tight bindings around my chest and the rising clatter of indignant conversation, I couldn't breathe. The desire wanted me to go after him and make him pay for his insolence, but I shushed it. Before anyone could approach, I departed out the back doors to the garden patio.

I peeled off my headdress and exhaled loudly, the buzz of insects a welcome respite. "If you knew what I was capable of, Toztli...." I growled under my breath, letting the desire spit one last time.

"He'd quake in his sandals." Citlallotoc lurked near the doorway, a smile on his face.

When the anger started giving way to arousal, I shoved the desire back into its box. "I didn't see you inside."

"I had to call on the surgeon about some of these wounds, so I was late. I didn't want to be rude, so I listened from out here." He joined me at the edge of the patio. "I commend you on your patience with that pompous monkey ball-sack."

I sighed. "After three years as queen and ruling equally with Topiltzin, you'd think I'd have earned some respect from our allies."

"Many do respect you, My Lady, and not only because they respect Topiltzin. But others—such as Toztli—feel threatened."

I chuckled, but it was true. When we toured our allies' cities, women came out in droves to see me, bringing their young daughters with them, all smiling with fresh hope. Female enrollment in the calmecac had risen sharply since Little Reed and I took the throne, particularly since lifting the prohibition against marriage in the priesthood. And we'd passed laws restricting the authority of husbands and fathers over their wives and daughters, bringing an end to legal forced marriage in Culhuacan. Kingdoms such as Xochimilco and Tultepec followed our lead.

But a good number of our allies grumbled about destroying the fabric of Tolteca society. It was bad enough we educated barbarians, but allowing women and girls to share power with their husbands or fathers was borderline treasonous. "They'll stop having children, and the Chichimecs will out-breed us! In a generation, the Tolteca world will crumble!" Many noble fathers refused to enroll their daughters in the calmecac in Culhuacan; and in Chimalhuacan, women weren't permitted in the calmecac at all. Their existing priestesses were nothing more than figureheads standing in the shadows of the priests, parroting traditional rules at the behest of the king. I dreaded to think of Cornflower and her daughter living under such restrictions, treated no better than dogs bred for the dinner table.

"Being a ruler is thankless work," Citlallotoc said. "But to also be a woman...I do not envy your struggles, My Lady, but I admire your strength and grace in dealing with them."

I wasn't certain how much longer I—or the desire—could deal gracefully with the likes of Toztli. "Thank you. Would you mind assigning the search teams?" This whole day had left me exhausted, but Nahuacatl was Chimalhuacan's best hope for a good future, so the sooner we found him, the better.

◻

No news came with the dawn, but I welcomed the distraction of packing up Malinalli's meditation room with the help of Ixchell and Mitotia. In a matter of hours, everything was in wicker baskets, ready for the journey north, and all that remained was to clean.

"Why don't you come to Tollan now?" Malinalli asked Mitotia as they swept the floor. "Mazatzin and I can continue your training until the calmecac opens in a few months."

"I have to stay here until I take the trials and become a full priestess," Mitotia said.

"That's not a requirement of our agreement with your father," I pointed out as I ensured all of the basket lids were tied securely.

"No, but if he discovers I'm not taking vows to Mixcoatl, he'll be furious."

"He can't force you to; we never even promised you'd take the trials to become a priestess."

"No, but he'll pressure me, and he's very good at that. Why do you think my brother left in the middle of the night and told no one where he was going?"

"But you're still coming to Tollan after you take your vows?" Malinalli seemed unusually anxious.

"Of course. He is pushy, but he is my father."

Malinalli nodded, pleased.

"It's amazing how quickly times change," Ixchell said as she ran a wet cloth over the face of the hearth, cleaning the dust and soot off. "If I'd had more say in my own future when I was a girl, I probably wouldn't have ended up in the priesthood; my father put me in calmecac to keep me out of trouble."

I laughed. I couldn't imagine Ixchell ever being a misfit. "What trouble could that be?"

She gave me a lopsided smile. "Oh, the kind fathers always worry about. My mother died when I was young, and he knew nothing about raising daughters, so I followed my brothers everywhere instead of learning to weave and cook. But when he caught me kissing the neighbor boy when I was seven, he feared he would be a grandfather much too soon, so off to calmecac I went; we were very poor, but he indentured my older brothers to the king for three years to pay my way. My life probably would have been very, very different if not for that."

"You might not be the next high priestess of Quetzalcoatl in Culhuacan, of all places," I said with a chuckle.

"And you might never have met Tlanextli," Malinalli added. Ixchell blushed.

As soon as we lifted the prohibitions against priests and priestesses marrying, Ixchell and Tlanextli—a priest of Tlaloc—married in the great temple. Neither was young and they looked at each other with a fondness grown of many years together; it filled me with joy to know they needn't keep their love secret anymore. If only Nimilitzli and Mother were here to see the changes we'd made because of them.

Bells jingled behind me and I looked back to see Citlallotoc hovering in the doorway, a grave expression on his face. My stomach dropped. He usually spent the afternoons in the practice yard with Yamehecatl, teaching him about weapons, and now grisly visions of accidents filled my head. "Is everything all right?"

"The search teams found Nahuacatl."

I let slip a sigh of relief. Why was my first instinct always to think something terrible had happened to Yamehecatl? It was silly. "Good news then."

He shook his head. "You should speak with the soldiers who found him."

The room fell silent as I rose and followed Citlallotoc out.

A group of four soldiers stood waiting by the cistern behind the Temple of Quetzalcoatl. They bowed to me, sweeping their fingers across the ground, but I motioned them up, impatient. "You found Nahuacatl?"

The highest-ranking soldier stepped forward. "Yes, My Lady, in the copal grove. Someone had removed his heart."

I gasped. After two years of slowly whittling away at the number of sacrificial victims permitted, Little Reed and I had finally outlawed most human sacrificial practices. We still allowed the sacrificing of willing victims, for who were we to deny a person the right to give their life in the name of the gods if they so wished? But we required they registered their wishes before myself and the king, to make certain it was indeed true willingness, and we completely outlawed the sacrificing of children under the age of sixteen. At first the other high priests grumbled, but that lessened as the city prospered and grew as never before, suggesting the gods approved of the new law. There hadn't been any unauthorized sacrifices in Culhuacan in the last year.

"Any other injuries?" I pressed.

He shook his head. "Lord Toztli's men found him first and were wrapping him up to take back to Chimalhuacan when we arrived, so we didn't get a close look at the prince's body."

I sighed. With Toztli already railing against the Chichimecs, this was the worst possible outcome. I cast a glare over at the temple of the Smoking Mirror—a small, ground-level structure more resembling a house than a temple. Oddly enough, of all the priests I thought would take issue with our dramatic curbing of human sacrifice, Ozomatli had been the most compliant and least argumentative. Was that because he was sacrificing people in secret to his demon god? Only Smoking Mirror's high priest would dare to defy the Feathered Serpent's will.

I dismissed the soldiers and motioned Citlallotoc to follow me towards Smoking Mirror's temple.

□

The odor of burnt tobacco greeted me at the temple doorway, covering a musty, rotting smell that sometimes made my stomach gurgle. All temples shared that smell, from the blood offerings poured into the idols, and I'd rested easy this last year knowing little of it came with death. But in here I swore the stink was more rotten than in any other temple.

The Smoking Mirror's high priestess—a Chichimec woman named Yaretzi—knelt on a reed mat in front of an array of polished obsidian mirrors on the wall, muttering prayers under her breath. Another mirror lay on the floor in front of her, holding the smoldering pile of tobacco leaves that emitted the cloud of gray smoke that gave everything a murky appearance. She looked to be in a trance, but when I turned to leave—obviously Ozomatli wasn't there—she turned and asked, "Can I help you with something, My Lady?" She spoke with a heavy northern accent.

It baffled me that any woman would willingly serve the Smoking Mirror, so when I'd demanded that Ozomatli find a high priestess—and not some docile mouthpiece for himself—I really thought he wouldn't be able to find anyone and I'd have a good reason to convince Little Reed to disband the cult in Culhuacan. But in fact he found someone not only capable but also strong and willful. She shared none of Ozomatli's pandering politeness, and when I spoke with her, she listened with a pointed intensity, assessing and judging for later; a skill she undoubedly picked up during her days as a slave in my uncle's court. I both liked yet feared her the way I used to fear the old matrons who took a switch to my behind for bad behavior when I was little. "Do you know where Ozomatli is?"

"At home, sleeping. He was up late performing a ritual." She inclined her head when I thanked her and went back to her prayers, the smoke swirling around her like a lover's caress. I couldn't leave fast enough.

"Wonder what this *ritual* was," Citlallotoc muttered.

"Let's go ask him." I went across the precinct to the priestly quarters, north of Quetzalcoatl's temple.

In Xochicalco, the only children who ever ran around the priestly quarters had been me and Little Reed, but here quite a few young boys and girls played together in the streets or behind the houses' walled courtyards. A few boys bouncing a rubber ball together paused to watch us pass, and though I usually had smiles for children, today I couldn't muster the will to put on a false face.

Ozomatli's house sat at the end of the main row. Most of the high priests and priestesses lived in the palace, in what had been the nobles' suites when my father and uncle had ruled, but Ozomatli chose to live here among the other priests and priestesses. "I want to be readily available to those in need of assistance at any time of the day," he told me. A noble reason, yet I suspected his true purpose was a need for privacy for forbidden rituals. The house was the largest in the priestly quarters, for it once belonged to the high priest of Tlaloc, and the rain god's statues still dotted the colorful flowerbeds of the courtyard garden. A cord attached to a set of copper bells dangled outside the front doorway curtain.

I momentarily considered not announcing our arrival—the better to catch Ozomatli at whatever evil he practiced in secret—but my better sense prevailed. We were here to find out where he was and what he was doing last night, not to throw around baseless accusations supported only by my gut. I pulled the cord, ringing the copper bells.

A young, soot-covered novice answered the bells and quickly ushered us in, bowing to me the whole time. The house's anteroom was clean, a stark contrast to the boy, who had been cleaning out the hearth, and the air smelled of copalli and sweet tobacco. The whitewashed walls bore murals of the gods—the same ones that came with the house— and cut flowers filled numerous vases.

"I wish to speak with the high priest," I told the boy, and he hurried away into a side room closed off with a plain blue curtain. Citlallotoc moved around the main room while we waited, peeking in to side rooms and examining the religious artifacts on display.

Ozomatli emerged from his room, looking sleepy, his priestly robe tied sloppily closed in the front. "Greetings, My Lady," he said, giving me a sluggish bow.

"Up late last night?"

He nodded. "I was performing a ritual for the Offering of Flowers."

"A ritual requiring the shedding of human blood?" Citlallotoc asked.

Grimacing at him, Ozomatli said, "All rituals require blood, My Lord, but since we have no willing sacrifices at the moment, I fear you're insinuating something illegal."

"As you may have heard, two days ago the heir to Chimalhuacan was kidnapped from the market center," I said. "This morning our soldiers discovered his body in our copal grove."

Ozomatli blinked. "He's dead?"

"Sacrificed, with his heart removed in the fashion practiced by your god's cult."

Citlallotoc stepped right up to Ozomatli so the man had to crane his neck to meet his gaze. "Where were you last night?"

"In the temple, performing a sacrifice to the Smoking Mirror," Ozomatli replied, looking to me rather than meeting Citlallotoc's challenging gaze, "but completely in accordance with the rules and regulations set down by the law. I burned the ritual tobacco leaves, partook of the sacred teonanacatl, and slaughtered a juvenile jaguar. You can ask the ritual game keeper; he provided two slaves to handle the beast in the temple for me."

"What about after the sacrifice?" I asked.

Ozomatli shifted uncomfortably and didn't meet my gaze. "I attempted to commune with the god and gain inspiration, but he didn't oblige me." He stepped away from Citlallotoc to approach me. "My Lady, if any of my people broke the law, I have no knowledge of it or who did it. If I did, I'd immediately turn them over to you to face justice, for they taint the good name of the entire cult."

Your cult's good name is tainted by the very god it honors, the desire growled.

"I trust that you would," I said. "But you must admit that the situation is very concerning. When Tozli learns the circumstances of his son's murder, he will call for heads, and he's going to come first to those cults that still practice heart extraction and other such barbarities."

"We keep all our practices strictly within the boundaries of the law—"

"That you are aware of. Every priesthood has at some point had to contend with an outlaw among its ranks, and how the rest of us deal with those criminals colors the perception of the entire cult."

"We are in agreement about that, My Lady."

"Then you will not object to accompanying me to Chimalhuacan, to assure Lord Tozli that you are doing everything in your power to make sure the culprits are brought to justice."

After a brief hesitation—in which he cast an uneasy glance at Citlallotoc—Ozomatli said, "I'm happy to assist, Lady Quetzalpetlatl."

"Good. Be ready to go by dawn."

As Citlallotoc and I left the house, Citlallotoc strode to keep up with me. "We're going to Chimalhuacan?"

"*I'm* going to Chimalhuacan, for Nahuacatl's funeral," I corrected him. "You're staying here to watch over the kingdom in my absence."

"After how Toztli behaved during his last visit...I'd feel much better if I came with you, to make certain he doesn't forget himself."

"He's not going to forget himself; instead, he'll be overjoyed that I'm bringing him his son's murderer."

"Who?"

"Ozomatli, of course."

"But we have no definitive proof—"

"He might not have done it with his own hands, but that's not his style," I said. "He gets others to bloody their hands for him, so he can deny involvement, which makes him even worse than my uncle."

"Then you think he's been orchestrating murders for his cult?"

"It wouldn't be the first time." When Citlallotoc stopped short, I said, "Let's just say that in the past, he hasn't always acted honorably towards his king and high priest."

"You mean Ihuitimal?"

"Yes, but as you said, I have no definitive proof, just stories and...intuition."

"Nothing I can actually bring charges against then," Citlallotoc finished. "This convinces me all the more that I must come with you. If Ozomatli is dangerous, I must be there to protect you."

"And I'm asking you to stay here and protect the one thing in this world that is most precious to me," I countered. "I know it isn't as glamorous as staring down haughty kings and following around treacherous priests, but I trust no one but you and Topiltzin to watch over my son."

Citlallotoc frowned. "I'm honored by your faith in me, My Lady, but you are as important as the prince—even more so. Someone should go with you, for protection."

"I'll have my guards with me." He started to protest again, but I cut him off. "I appreciate your concern, Citlallotoc, but I'm not some weak noblewoman who's never been outside the palace walls. I have my own means of protection that is stronger than any sword."

Citlallotoc bowed his head. "You are perfectly capable of taking care of yourself," he conceded. "Please forgive my thoughtlessness."

I took his good arm with mine and smiled up at him. "And I thank you for caring enough to worry about me."

CHAPTER FOURTEEN

 "But I want to go with you, Nantli!" Yamehecatl sat on my bed next to my travel bag, and when I tried to place a dress inside, he blocked me with his pudgy little hands. "I want to go with you!"

I gave him a sharp glare before moving his hands. "You can't come, my precious little breeze."

"Why not?" he whined, looking pained.

"Because this isn't a casual visit. The women will cry nonstop for several days, and Lord Nahuacatl's body will be laid out for everyone to see."

He gaped at me. "There's going to be a real dead body?"

"It will be wrapped in paper."

"Ayya! Now I really must go!"

I glared at him. "That's precisely why you're not going. Lord Toztli lost his son and you gawking at the body as if it's some colorful lizard is terribly disrespectful. These are delicate matters, and this isn't the appropriate time or place for small children."

He crawled to me and sat up on his knees, wringing the front of my dress with both hands. "Please, Nantli! Please!"

"No."

He yanked on my dress, nearly pulling me over, then he leaped off the bed and stomped towards the door. "You're so mean!" He disappeared out into the hallway.

I let him go, but once I finished packing, I went to the nursery to find him curled up on his bed, fingers jammed in his mouth, brows furrowed. I pulled him onto my lap. "There will be other times—better times—to go. You'll be happier here with Citlallotoc and you'll have the other children to play with—"

"I hate the other children!" he barked.

"Why?"

He frowned, tears dribbling down his cheeks. "All the ones my age are so stupid—they can barely even talk, but the older ones, who talk as well as me...they say I'm still a baby because I'm so small, and they won't let me play their games."

I hugged him. "Sometimes it's difficult being special."

Yamehecatl snuggled against my breast, wetting my dress with his tears. "I miss Tatli."

"Me too." I kissed the side of his head. "He'll be back soon though."

"But when?"

"A few more weeks, maybe a month at the most."

"And you promise you'll only be gone a couple of days?"

"I'll come back as quick as I can."

He rubbed his tears away. "But who will feed me before bed, and sing to me?"

I still nursed him every night; most noblewomen never nursed their children, hiring out the task so they could resume their normal routines quicker, but I'd chosen to stick with it. Most peasant women nursed as long as possible, especially when they desired no more children, and I hadn't missed the inconvenience of monthly bleeding these last couple of years. I cherished those quiet moments holding my son while he drowsed off to sleep with a milk-drunk smile on his face.

But he'd gain his third summer soon, and there wasn't any real need to continue nursing him; he ate and drank with the rest of us, and if the other children were teasing him....

"Maybe it's time to end the nighttime feedings," I suggested. When he looked ready to cry, I added, "You are getting older, and you said you don't like it when the other boys call you a baby."

He looked away, his jaw set, his brows furrowed again. "I hate them all but...they do say mean things...about you feeding me like that."

"Then the time is right." I hugged him and he clutched onto me.

"Will you still tell me stories before I go to sleep?"

"Of course, my dear sweet breeze."

"Tell me one now?"

I leaned back against the wall and he settled into my arms. "Which one do you want to hear?"

"One about the Feathered Serpent."

"How about how he gave maize to the people?"

Yamehecatl scoffed. "You always tell me that one."

"Then how about the one where Quetzalcoatl journeys into the underworld to bring back the bones of humanity?"

"That's Tatli's favorite, and he does better voices than you."

I chuckled. "He is very good at sounding like a god, isn't he?"

He nodded.

"How about the one about the creation of the Sun and the Moon?"

Yamehecatl screwed up his face into a pout. "Aren't there any new ones? Ones you haven't told me yet?"

I thought a moment. "Well, I haven't told you the one about the Feathered Serpent and the goddess Mayahuel."

"Who's Mayahuel?"

"She was the granddaughter of the Earth Monster Tzitzimitl, who held her captive in Omeyocan."

"Why?"

"Because she had powerful magic the Earth Monster didn't want given to the world, so she guarded Mayahuel jealously. But the other gods wanted to give a gift to humanity, to make them happy and bring them closer to the gods. Quetzalcoatl—in the guise of Ehecatl, the Wind—stole Mayahuel from the Earth Monster's garden and took her to Earth, letting her ride upon his shoulders."

"That was very nice of him," Yamehecatl said. "If someone was holding you prisoner in a garden, I bet Tatli would come rescue you."

"I'm certain he would too." Little Reed pretty much had done as such when Ihuitimal brought me to Culhuacan after Xochicalco's destruction.

"What happened next?"

"Ehecatl and Mayahuel went to the earthly paradise of Tamoachan and they came together to form a tree with two branches; one was called Quetzalhuexotl—the Feathered Tree—and the other was Xochicuahuitl—the Flowering Tree.

"But when the Earth Monster discovered Ehecatl had taken her granddaughter, she was furious, and she flew down to earth to find Mayahuel and destroy her."

Yamehecatl frowned. "But why would she do that?"

"Because Mayahuel defied her and left the garden."

"But you said that Ehecatl stole her, so why didn't the Earth Monster want to destroy him instead?"

When I'd first heard this version of the story in calmecac when I was a handful of years older than Yamehecatl, I'd asked Mothotli the fire priestess several similar questions, which caused her to become more and more flustered and culminated with her rapping me on the knuckles with her switch for daring to question the sacred stories. She convinced me to keep my tongue quiet but my brain had refused to follow suit, and the years in between had taught me an answer to that question. Quetzalcoatl had told me that he and Mayahuel had been lovers—much as he and I had been—so it stood to reason that making this tree was a sly way of saying they'd had sex, and that Tzitzimitl focusing her wrath on Mayahuel was a lesson to young girls that terrible things happened when they gave in to the lusts of men.

But I didn't want to talk so frankly to my three-year-old son, whom we hadn't even mentioned sex to yet. "It's what she chose to do because earth monsters aren't known for their kindness or understanding. When the ground shakes as she stretches, she doesn't care if good boys or girls get hurt with falling rocks, or even die. She's a creature of wrath and chaos."

The look in Yamehecatl's eyes told me my answer didn't satisfy him, but he was eager to get on with the story. "Did Ehecatl fight her when she came?"

I shook my head. "No. The Earth Monster savaged the tree and destroyed the branch that was Mayahuel, killing her. Ehecatl's branch was spared though, and when the Earth Monster left, he changed back into his godly form and buried Mayahuel's remains. And from that grew the maguey plant, which we use not only for cloth and rope, but as our sacrificial thorns. But most importantly, we make the sap of the maguey into the sacred octli, which allows men and women to commune with the gods."

Yamehecatl sat listening for a couple of breaths after I finished, expecting me to go on; when I didn't, he cocked his head and asked, "Is that it?"

"That's it," I confirmed.

He looked downright cross. "That was a terrible story, Nantli! Where's the adventure, the fighting? Where is the Feathered Serpent's trickery, like when he convinced Lord Death he could play a rock like a flute?"

"There wasn't any."

"No wonder no one ever tells this story. There's nothing fun about it."

"The sacred stories aren't meant to be fun. They teach us about the world."

"Don't ever tell me that story again, Nantli. I like stories where Quetzalcoatl is heroic, like Tatli."

I chuckled. "Very well. I won't ever subject you to Mayahuel's sad story again."

He asked me to sing him a song and I did so, letting him curl up against my breast, fingers in his mouth as he sucked his way to sleep, but I couldn't stop thinking about the story. Yamehecatl was right; it was depressing, and my heart couldn't reconcile the Ehecatl of the story with the god who had given humanity life with his own blood, who'd brought us civilization through knowledge and kingship, and who used to make love with me in the Divine Dream with such passion.

It was a terrible story, but not for the reasons Yamehecatl thought it so. For all she went through, no one ever honored Mayahuel. *Though maybe we ought to,* I thought as I tucked Yamehecatl under his blanket and kissed him on the forehead. *If we can make room for Smoking Mirror—of all gods—in our temples, why not Mayahuel too?*

□

Ozomatli was waiting in the courtyard with all the fire priests when I came out of the palace before dawn. I'd spoken to the ritual game keeper yesterday and he confirmed Ozomatli's story about the jaguar, but that didn't exonerate him from ordering

Nahuacatl's murder. I would have to watch him very closely.

To my surprise though, Ixtlilxochitl was there as well, with a pack on his shoulders. When he saw me, he greeted me with his usual grim countenance. If I hadn't seen him laughing and performing slight-of-hand tricks for his daughters once, I would have thought him incapable of smiling. "Did Citlallotoc put you up to this?" I asked, casting an annoyed glare back at Citlallotoc, who was watching from the stairs.

"I rather agree with him that you shouldn't go alone," Ixtlilxochitl replied, his voice gruff.

Pointing to the soldiers assembled for the journey, I said, "I'm hardly going alone."

"Lord Citlallotoc says I'd make the ideal companion since Toztli would rather speak to you than me."

Or he'll think I'm insulting him by bringing my only Chichimec council member with me, I thought but held my tongue. That was unfair to Ixtlilxochitl. And if he was to govern Culhuacan when we moved north, Toztli would have to learn to deal with him on cordial terms.

Still, would there ever be a day when men realized I didn't need their protection unless I asked for it? I let it go and instead thanked Ixtlilxochitl as he helped me into the royal litter.

Once I settled among the pillows, I leaned out of the curtain and waved goodbye to Yamehecatl, who dangled half-asleep in a servant girl's arms. He waved back sleepily and I blew him a kiss as the caravan moved slowly out of the courtyard.

It only took a few hours to reach Chimalhuacan, so I caught up on my sleep while the procession of soldiers and priests moved east along the road. Malinalli stopped by the litter with some cold tlaxcallis for me midmorning, but other than that, I kept to myself, planning out what to say to Toztli, and hoping this dull ache in my breasts wasn't a sign of things to come.

I'd sent a runner ahead the day before, informing Toztli of my impending visit, but only his head steward greeted me when the caravan stopped in the palace courtyard. The mousey little man groveled about how the king was otherwise detained; understandable, but he could have acknowledged the value of our cities' alliance by sending someone important—his war chief perhaps—to greet me. The head steward showed me to the guest quarters and promised to see to accommodations for the rest of my company.

"Lord Toztli wouldn't dare to not personally greet Topiltzin," Ixtlilxochitl growled as he investigated the adjoining rooms, making certain all was safe.

"I'm aware of that." I dropped my bag and flopped down on the bed, my aching breasts leaving me irritable.

"You should make it clear to him that it's unacceptable to treat you differently than he does your husband."

"I know!" He didn't react to my outburst but I still felt bad as soon as I said it. "Forgive my foul mood. I know you're trying to help."

"I'm trying to keep him from treating you like a dog rather than a queen," he corrected me. "Toztli is the kind of man who tests for weaknesses to exploit, and if you show the least bit, he will wring your neck with it. He tried that once with Ihuitimal, and Ihuitimal had his second son killed and warned that his heir would be next if he tried it again."

I scrutinized him more closely now, my throat constricting. "You worked for my uncle?"

"I was one of the king's personal guards. I fell into Topiltzin's hands and instead of sending me to the sacrifice, he asked me to carry peace terms to Culhuacan." He glanced out into the hallway as he finished his survey of my quarters. "He didn't ask me to divulge any of Ihuitimal's secrets or plot against him despite my having direct access to him. He was more interested in suing for peace to free you. That's why I pledged my loyalty to him once the war ended." He turned to me. "If you require nothing further, I should investigate my own quarters. The head steward was giving cowardly looks to the palace guards when we passed by them. They may be lying in wait and will require that I correct their behavior with a few broken noses."

◻

Toztli wasn't at dinner, though Nahuacatl's wife took a break from the ritual lamentations to host the meal. Already she looked as if she'd run out of tears to shed.

Cornflower was there as well and I embraced her when she greeted me with a brave face. She was heavy with child—she'd found a place as a concubine in the household of one of her father's advisors—and I hoped this ordeal wasn't taxing her too much. She offered to sit with me and play hostess, but I insisted she sit with her family and not concern herself with entertaining me. Mazatzin and Malinalli sat with me, as did Ixtlilxochitl. Apparently he hadn't been ambushed when he went to his quarters, but he still watched the room with keen eyes.

"Of course something such as this would happen when we're ready to leave for Tollan," Malinalli noted as she dipped her tlaxcalli into our shared bowl of chile sauce.

"The timing is very suspicious." I cast my gaze over at Ozomatli, who was sitting with his fire priest and those of Tlaloc and Xipe Totec. He looked irritatingly relaxed, and even chuckled at the conversation; inappropriate for a mourning feast. But to priests of the demon Smoking Mirror, death wasn't a serious matter, and people were merely dogs waiting for the cook to pick them.

"If war breaks out, it could be years before the seat of power moves to Tollan," Mazatzin noted, watching Ozomatli as well. "Especially if our allies see this as a warning from the gods about Quetzalcoatl's reforms."

"Which is why it's all the more important we produce the culprits. Let them sacrifice themselves until Smoking Mirror has devoured himself into obscurity."

I didn't sleep well; the women's laments carried as far as the guest quarters, and I lay awake thinking about the last time I'd heard such a ritual. I wondered where Jade Flower was now. When I'd returned to Culhuacan, a letter from her awaited me, thanking me for sending Black Otter back to her and the children, and assuring me that they left Chalco before the struggle for the throne broke out; Papantzin's father kicked them all out when Black Otter refused to marry his daughter, and so they were going to Xico to stay with Flame Tongue and Anacoana. I hadn't heard from her since, and I only knew they'd moved again when Anacoana told Citlallotoc as much on one of his official visits a few years ago. I often joked that she was infatuated with him—for she took every opportunity to talk to him despite her father's lectures about proper ladies not doing such things; but if not for her affinity for Citlallotoc, I wouldn't know much of anything about my sister anymore.

I managed to drowse off once the cries ended, but I woke at dawn soaked in milk, thanks to engorgement. I finagled a clean night dress from one of the servants and wrapped my chest with extra layers of cloth before joining Malinalli and Mazatzin for breakfast before they continued on to Tollan. By the time I returned to my quarters for a nap, my breasts throbbed so badly I wanted to cry, so I asked my servants to draw a hot bath for me. A few moments in the heat worked magic, relieving the pain and pressure so

I could finally relax.

The bath in my quarters in Culhuacan was laid into the ground and tiled with shells imported from the south, but this bath sat aboveground and was lined with beaten bronze, the better to retain the heat. I'd had a similar one in my old quarters, and Black Otter and I had made love in it at least a dozen times....

Those thoughts of Black Otter soon melted into memories of that night so long ago with Little Reed in his tent at the army encampment. I still remembered the taste of salt and chile on his tongue, the callused flesh where his fingers met his palm, the heat and hardness of his tepolli against my belly. I'd sacrificed any possibility of real physical intimacy with him, but I could freely carry on an affair of the imagination. And this time Red Flint wouldn't interrupt us, and there wasn't any chance of Yamehecatl wandering in and asking embarrassing questions....

But the laments started up again, soft at first but growing steadily louder and increasingly mournful. They created a grim litany of devastation and loss that chewed away at the desire until nothing remained. If only it were always so easily quelled. I finished washing and remained there until the heat was sapped, then I dressed in my fresh nightdress for a nap.

I gasped when I came into my quarters to find Toztli standing in front of the hearth, staring into the flames. He turned around at my startled cry, and the look on his face was as dark as any I'd ever seen. In only my nightdress, I felt horribly naked, and I swallowed back the shameful desire that feeling provoked inside me. "Lord Toztli," I stammered. "I realize these are trying times for you, but it's highly inappropriate to barge in on the wife of your closest ally."

He laughed. "Don't flatter yourself, My Lady. I'm not interested."

"I should hope not." Anger and embarrassment heated my cheeks, but I tried to appear strong. "How can I be of assistance?"

"My son's death...." But instead of finishing, he returned to glaring into the hearth.

"I'm deeply sorrowed by your loss. Nahuacatl was an exceptional man, and he would have been a most honorable king. His death is a great loss to all of us." When he said nothing, I pressed on. "When I heard of the circumstances of his death, I immediately knew one of Smoking Mirror's followers was responsible and brought his high priest to account. Ozomatli has pledged to do everything in his power to expose the rogue priests who perpetrated this terrible act, and together, he and I will deliver them to justice for you."

Toztli picked up a small bag resting at his feet and dumped its contents on the floor in front of me: five green quetzal feathers, a desiccated snake carcass, and a handful of dried-up butterflies. He stared back at me, anger seething in his eyes. "Then explain these things my men discovered with my son's body."

I stared at these objects that priests of Quetzalcoatl often used in conjunction with sacrifices, and my jaw set tight. *That demon-worshiping lake scum, trying to frame Quetzalcoatl's cult for this atrocity?* "These were placed with the body to make it look as if the god's priests committed this crime. We don't make human sacrifices; not even willing ones."

"It wasn't always that way," Toztli said. "Even as little as four years ago, criminals still died in the Feathered Serpent's name."

"When they did, the priests never took out their hearts."

"That's your official stance, but you've opened your ranks to heathen Chichimecs, so how can you be sure they aren't bringing their bloody rituals to Quetzalcoatl's worship? You blithely lay the blame at the feet of Smoking Mirror's followers, so why not your own as well? The evidence is right there, at your feet, and as the high priestess, you're responsible for controlling your priests and followers. Even if Smoking Mirror's people did this, the blame lies on you as the queen; you allowed that Chichimec cult to continue in your midst. No matter how you look at it, you and Topiltzin are culpable for my son's death."

I clenched my jaw. *I told Little Reed that tolerating Smoking Mirror's cult would come back to bite us,* but my being right gave me no satisfaction. "We did allow the cult's continuance, so yes, we bear part of the responsibility for what happened. I promise you that I will address this issue with Topiltzin again as soon as he returns from Tollan."

"Not good enough!" Toztli snarled. "The future of my kingdom is now in question!"

"And Topiltzin and I will help you, whether it's assisting you in arbitrating the choice of a new heir from among your other sons, or helping you identify a good candidate from among the city's noble class."

He laughed, incredulous. "I lose my favorite son, whom I raised from birth to be my voice once I die, and this is all you offer me?"

"What do you wish of me, Lord Toztli?"

"Your son, of course, you dimwitted woman!"

I stepped back. "Outrageous! How dare you even—"

He bridged the gap between us in three mighty steps, backing me into the wall. "You cost me my kingdom's future! The only proper reparation is for you to suffer the same fate, and I will accept nothing less!" He pointed to my stack of papers sitting with the jar of ink and a goose quill on the floor next to my bed. "You will write to Lord Citlallotoc, ordering him to bring the prince to me."

"You're delusional if you think I'd let you anywhere near my son!"

My years as the most powerful woman in Culhuacan had trained me to believe no one would dare touch me without my permission, so it took me completely by surprise when Toztli grabbed me by the hair and dragged me across the room to the bed. All his assurances that he had no interest in bedding me screamed, *lies!* as he forced me down on the mats and blankets.

But he picked up the papers and shoved them into my face. "You will write that letter and call him here!" he bellowed.

But then he let me go. When I looked back at him, tears blurring my vision, he stared at me with wide, disbelieving eyes. He ran his fingers through his long hair and muttered, "What have I...?"

Only once my heartbeat slowed did I become aware of the magic pulsing in my fingertips. What good were such powers if I couldn't remember them when they could make a difference? I pulled my hands close to my chest, gathering my magic. I wouldn't make that mistake twice.

He turned away from me, tears in his voice. "I deserve justice, My Lady. I didn't ask for this!"

"Neither did I." I held my breath to keep from screaming at him.

"I begged Topiltzin to drive those animals back into the desert but *you* talked him out of it, and now you've destroyed my kingdom—"

"You've done that by declaring war on Culhuacan, Tollan, and the god," I retorted.

"None of this would have happened if you had done the right thing back then. And only doing the right thing now can make any difference."

I flexed my fingers, the tingling burning, my mind growing distant as the desire supplanted me. "I will devour you before I let you touch my son."

Toztli stared at me, taken aback. "Have it your way. Remember it's your stubbornness that forced my hand." He strode from the room, rattling the bells on the curtain's hem.

I flew after him—*how dare he turn his back on me!*—but two of his guards pushed me back inside. "Ixtlilxochitl!" I shouted.

"Your Chichimec dog can't help you now," one of the men said and ripped the curtain closed. I stared at the fabric, panting as I came back to myself. *I never should have agreed to let Ixtlilxochitl come; I should have known they would hurt him.*

But now I was on my own, which meant saving myself. I hurried out to the bath yard again, tearing aside the vines on the walls, searching for a way out. But there were no secret doorways, only smooth, plaster walls. I tried pulling myself up and over using the vines, but they snapped easily, dried out from the hot weather. I tried again and again, determined to scale it—and not think of my recurring dream of the endless high walls— and I nearly made it to the top at one point, but the vines ripped and I hit the ground with a grunt, my tailbone aching. I sat there stewing, tears of frustration creeping up on me.

"All that magic at your disposal and yet you let him manhandle you," a voice suddenly spoke up behind me.

I scrambled to my feet to find a huge man looming in the doorway to my room, leaning casually against the jamb. He wore an amused smile and a feathered xicolli that hung to his thighs, with the tail of a blue and red loincloth visible under the jagged hem. And his entire left side was painted blue. "Mextli?"

"You remember me? But then it's hard to forget a face like mine, isn't it?" He laughed.

"What are you doing here?"

"Reconnoitering," he answered with a grin.

Already twice in one day I stood practically naked in front of someone I hardly knew. I came back to the patio and snatched up my high priestess robe and slipped it on over my shoulders, relieved to be less exposed. "Why would you be at all interested in Chimalhuacan?"

He raised his one eyebrow—there wasn't one on the left side of his face. "Who says that's the interesting thing here?"

Catching his meaning, I edged away while trying not to be obvious. "What's so interesting about me?"

He laughed. "Let's not play games with each other. We both know what happened that night in Tollan. Personally, I found it very...illuminating."

My heart pulsed fear through my body. "I did what I had to. You were going to kill my friend."

"I was." After a tense silence, his gaze shifted to my quarters, the casualness returning. "Don't worry, I'm not bitter. The element of surprise is a time-honored battle tactic, and it was my own fault for not anticipating that Quetzalcoatl would bring his own powerful allies. You won that round. But you won't fool me again."

I looked away too, attempting to match his nonchalance despite the pit in my stomach. "Are we to battle again then?"

"I haven't decided yet. But I warn you, I'm not someone you want declaring war on you."

His annoying arrogance overrode my fear. "Toztli has already done as much, so what's one more?"

"You really haven't any idea who I am, do you?"

"I don't really care," the desire spat.

That arrow hit a sensitive spot; he maintained his smile but the slight narrowing of his eyes betrayed him. "I am the god of war, and I don't lose."

The desire always drove the fear away, so I let it stay. "Tonatiuh is the god of war; you're a little desert quail who's attached himself to a worthless sorcerer."

This time the whole left side of his body puffed up, like a grouse. *He is covered in feathers!* I realized, unable to help staring at the comical yet gruesome display. "You foolishly dismiss me, but I would be stupid to do the same with you." He smoothed his arm-feathers with his right hand. "I will find out who you really are, so I'm better prepared the next time we match powers."

"You don't already know me? I'm Lady Quetzalpetlatl, Queen of Culhuacan and High Priestess of Quetzalcoatl. That is all you need to know."

He laughed again. "I think you're the one who doesn't know who you really are. The Feathered Serpent has convinced you of your own mediocrity, and it's such a shame; so much potential, and yet you allowed that man to slap you around like a dog. Maybe you aren't the worthy opponent I first thought you were."

His words unexpectedly stung. "No, *you're* not worth *my* time, nor do I need your approval, or even your respect."

"Because it's so much better being the Feathered Serpent's plaything?"

A whirlwind of embarrassment and anger raged inside me. "Quetzalcoatl is twice the god your pathetic Smoking Mirror could ever hope to be," I snarled, "so crawl back into that dung-heap you came out of and leave divine matters to *real* gods, little hummingbird boy." It felt both terrifying and exhilirating to say it, to a god of all things!

Mextli still grinned, amused. "Big words for a little *thorn bush*."

The puzzling insult so took me by surprise—and the desire too—that suddenly I was back in control again. And that comfortable confidence had fled. I choked back the fear though, determined not to show it. "Why...why in Mictlan are you here anyway?"

"As I said, I'm learning more about you, seeing what I'm up against. And I was hungry; fortunately the right meal presented himself and now I get to see you and your magic in action."

I stared at him. "You killed Nahuacatl?"

He shrugged. "I would have preferred a warrior's heart, but delicious nonetheless. He served his purpose; you're here, after all."

"You planted all that...that other stuff? The butterflies and feathers and snake—"

"I'm not exactly proud of that," Mextli admitted, contrite. "I prefer to wage honorable war, but sometimes the rules must bend. A good war chief exploits his enemy's weaknesses; Toztli fears your power—both spiritually and politically—and he desperately wants everything to be as it was before you took the throne." He rubbed his chin. "As for your weaknesses...well, that I cannot say yet; I must know the full spectrum of your magic first. Though given how easily he manhandled you, this probably isn't worth my time."

My cheeks burned. "He took me by surprise."

"I can afford to be taken by surprise; you cannot. Topiltzin can only sacrifice so much to keep you from Lord Death."

"Sacrifice?" I thought back to when Xolotl marked Little Reed for death right after I'd come back from the dead. I'd tried hard—futilely—to forget that image, as well as what the fact of his still being alive meant, but I couldn't run from it forever. Somehow I'd cheated Heaven of its sacrifice, and what price would Little Reed pay for that?

Mextli looked into my room again, distracted. But then suddenly he loomed over me, covering me in his shadow. I cowered. "Human life is a fragile, finite thing, and once it's gone, there's no coming back. Never forget that." He disappeared with a sound like snapping sticks.

Toztli stormed into the bath yard, his guards with him. His men grabbed me by the arms. "Time to do the right thing, My Lady."

CHAPTER FIFTEEN

I expected Toztli to try to make me write the letter again, but instead he and his guards escorted me out of the palace. Curious citizens gathered at the sides of the street, held back by guards as we passed.

Eventually we came to the sacred precinct, to the temple of Quetzalcoatl. Crowds flooded in after us, pressing close to the base of the pyramid as we climbed the steps. To my confusion, Mazatzin and Malinalli were at the top, both bound and gagged. Ixtlilxochitl knelt behind them, only bound and looking unperturbed; he wasn't a man prone to verbal outbursts. Ozomatli was there too, but he was free. I stared him down as the guards pushed me by him.

"Don't blame him for your folly," Toztli said, noticing my vehement gaze. "You tried to push responsibility for my son's death on his cult when all the evidence points to your own priests as the culprits. It's only fitting he should witness justice being properly meted out."

"My priests didn't do this either. We're all being played against each other for a god's amusement—"

"Lies!" Toztli shouted. "The law of the land in Chimalhuacan is a life for a life. Culhuacan swore to uphold the laws of its allies and yet you shun that promise now. Hypocrite!"

"My son did not murder your son—"

"Enough! Will you give me the justice I ask for, Lady Quetzalpetlatl?"

I glared back, carefully articulating each word, "I will kill you before I let you harm my son."

"Then your priests will pay for your arrogance." Toztli nodded to his guards.

They seized Malinalli and wrenched her to her feet.

But Mazatzin launched at one of them, butting him in the side of the head with his own. They both fell to the ground as the other guard dragged Malinalli towards the sacrificial stone. Ozomatli stood watching stupidly but stumbled aside when Ixtlilxochitl—he'd somehow freed himself of his bindings—rushed past him. Ixtlilxochitl grabbed Malinalli's guard by the neck with his arm and squeezed.

Seizing the distraction, I rushed to grab Malinalli and get us out of there, but a third guard intercepted me and tried to wrestle me back. Magic gathered in my fingertips and this time I didn't hesitate. I latched onto his bare arms and let it go.

He stumbled backward, weaving around like a drunkard, shouting incoherently. He shuffled past me, towards the edge of the pyramid and stepped over as if he didn't see it. The crowd below screamed as he fell head over feet to his death.

I stared, baffled. What had I done to him?

Toztli stared over the edge too, the color drained from his face. When he turned back to me, his eyes went wild with panic. "Witch!" He fumbled at the dagger on his belt.

"Don't make me hurt you," I warned, backing away. "Topiltzin will come for you.

Think of your people—do what's best for them. Don't let this devolve into all-out war."
I nearly unleashed my magic when I ran into Malinalli behind me. The guard had let her
go in a last-ditch effort to free himself of Ixtlilxochitl's stranglehold.

"Don't just stand there!" Ixtlilxochitl shouted at Ozomatli. "Defend your queen!"

Ozomatli met my gaze, panicked, then fled down the back steps, abandoning us.

"Coward!" Ixtlilxochitl snapped the guard's neck, ending his struggle; but when he
moved to intercept Toztli, the other guard—whom I'd thought Mazatzin had knocked
out—buried a knife in his ribs. They went down in a heap.

Toztli finally freed his own knife and advanced towards me.

"Go!" I shouted over my shoulder at Malinalli. "Get off the temple!" When she
hesitated, I squawked, "Now!" and she finally ran, disappearing down the steps.

"You're nothing but a filthy witch!" Toztli screamed, and leaped at me.

He knocked me over but I grabbed his upraised arm and pushed magic into him.
Nothing happened, and my arms strained under his superior strength; if anything, he'd
gotten stronger and wilder. I pushed harder, the magic burning in my blood like fire. He
huffed and puffed, red-faced, as he strained to stab me. His breath turned foul and
pungent, making my eyes sting.

Then my strength gave out.

The blade pierced my shoulder, all the way to the hilt. The pain didn't register, but
the look of drunken glee in his eyes did and I pushed out all the magic I had left in one
last attempt to get him off me.

His eyes immediately clouded over, as if he'd gone into the Divine Dream. He let me
go at last and tried to stand, but he stumbled away instead, dropping to his knees again.
He tried again to stand but this time he vomited all over the stone no more than an arm's
length from me. The stench of rancid alcohol stabbed my sinuses, threatening to empty
my own stomach. Toztli broke into violent shakes, falling face first into his own vomit.
He stared back at me with one blank, empty eye as the convulsions slowed, and his
breathing along with it, until he lay dead.

I tried to move, but my body refused to obey. I was a sack of stones, so weak I
couldn't even blink. Screams and drunken shouting came from all around me; people
were throwing stones that buzzed in and out of my field of vision like birds in flight.
What have I done? I wondered as my mind slowly drifted away.

◻

I was back in Xochicalco, right after the confrontation where Ahexotl sliced my heel and
tried to burn me alive. Despite knowing Little Reed was dead, I kept asking everyone
where he was, but no one would answer me; Malinalli behaved as if she didn't hear me
talking at all and instead forced me to drink something that reminded me of chewing on
bronze jewelry. Yet I couldn't get enough of it and I begged for more and more.

After a while I wasn't in Xochicalco anymore, but rather in my own bed in
Culhuacan. Little Reed sat next to me, holding my hand and looking harried. My
muscles took their time waking up too, moving with aching sluggishness. A stale, sticky
residue coated my mouth and tongue, begging for water to wash it away, but when Little
Reed helped me sit up and put a cup to my lips, it was that same taste from my dreams.
An inexplicable eagerness took over and I finished it in one long gulp, warmth and
strength spreading through me. I wiped the corner of my wet mouth with the back of my
hand and started when I saw crimson on it. "What in Mictlan—?"

"It's blood."

My stomach twisted right along with my mind. Why on earth did he feed me blood?

Little Reed took the cup and handed it to Malinalli—who stood behind him, looking tired and worried. "I think she's ready for some water." Once she moved off, he told me, "You used too much magic."

"So you fed me blood?" My stomach threatened to heave.

"It's what the god said to do," Malinalli supplied, stopping at the doorway to the bath yard. "When I found you, you looked half-dead, and you stayed asleep for days. Mazatzin and I feared you would never wake up, so we asked the god for help."

"And he told you to feed me blood?" Now I noticed the cuts on her bare arms from the bloodletting.

"We all took turns feeding you," she said. "Mazatzin, Citlallotoc, myself, even Ozomatli—"

"You told Ozomatli about my powers?" I tried not to sound indignant; she'd saved my life again after all.

She shook her head. "I didn't tell him what it was for; I said he needed to give me some each day, and he did, no questions asked. I think he feels guilty for running away instead of defending you."

The events on the temple top came back to me. "Ixtlilxochitl! Is he—?"

"He's all right," Little Reed assured me. "He's recovering, slowly. It was bad enough he'd been stabbed, but he appeared to have been poisoned too. Mazatzin was very sick for a day or two also."

I clenched my jaw. Had I poisoned them when I'd released all my magic on Toztli? Was that why the city sounded like a drunken revel right before I passed out?

When Malinalli disappeared into the bath yard, I asked Little Reed, "Did you give me blood too?"

"Of course."

"But why blood?"

"Remember how you always needed blood to call on the god? Well, your magic uses your own blood, but the small amounts you typically use don't take a toll on you. This time, you used more in one burst than your blood could sustain; you're lucky you didn't kill yourself."

"I didn't even think about what I was doing. I only wanted to stop Toztli."

"What happened?" Little Reed asked.

"Someone murdered Nahuacatl in ritual fashion in our copal grove, and Toztli blamed us, because we allowed Smoking Mirror's cult to continue. I went to Chimalhuacan to pay our respects and to promise we'd find the culprits, but he demanded I hand Yamehecatl over to him. He was going to kill our son, Little Reed...." I started to choke up but worked my way past it. "When I refused to comply, he took Malinalli, Mazatzin and Ixtlilxochitl hostage, and threatened to sacrifice them. And when Toztli attacked me...I unleashed everything I had at him."

Malinalli returned with my cup of water. "Whatever magic you used was potent. I felt as if I'd drunk three cups of octli instantly. Everyone was out of control after that, throwing rocks, breaking things, setting houses on fire...."

"I must be very careful with this. If Ixtlilxochitl or Mazatzin had been any closer to me when I let it go, they might be dead now."

Little Reed gripped my hand. "They're both fine, but yes, care is needed. You almost killed yourself."

I nodded, guilt eating me as I swallowed the cold water.

"Did we ever find out who actually killed Nahuacatl?" Little Reed asked.

"I don't think so," Malinalli answered. "We rather forgot about the investigation in light of Quetzalpetlatl's condition."

I finished my water and asked her, "Could you fetch Yamehecatl? I'm desperate to see him."

"Of course." She ducked out of the door, leaving the copper bells on my curtain jingling.

"It was Mextli again," I told Little Reed, keeping my voice low. "He came to see me while Toztli held me prisoner."

Little Reed sat up straighter. "What did he say?"

"He wanted Toztli to think the god's priests were responsible, so he left some of our sacrificial items with Nahuacatl's body."

"But why?"

"So Toztli would blame me for his son's death."

"So he'd kill you?"

I shook my head. "Mextli knows I attacked him on the precinct in Tollan, and he...wanted to see 'the full spectrum' of my powers."

"That son of a demon god!" he swore under his breath.

"As terrible as it may sound, I learned a great deal about my magic in all this. And Toztli effectively declared war on us, so he reaped the fate he deserved. He'd wanted an excuse to challenge me for a long time, and Mextli played into his fears to make it happen sooner rather than later."

Little Reed nodded. "I must apologize. I knew Toztli had grown uncomfortable dealing with you these last few years, but he and I always got along very well, and I thought that would keep him from behaving horrendously. I should have been far more mindful of it. I'm so sorry."

"I didn't think he was the kind either, Little Reed." I squeezed his hand. "What will we do about Chimalhuacan now?"

"Blood Wolf will run the city until Toztli's remaining sons come of age and one of them proves himself. But until then, Chimalhuacan will be a tribute state to Tollan."

I embraced him. "I'm glad you're home again. These last few months felt like years."

"The next time I leave for Tollan, you and Yamehecatl are coming with me, and we won't return."

"Then the palace is ready?"

He nodded. "And the city is already ten times larger than when last you were there. This year's crop yield promises to eclipse any here in the valley." He brought me another cup of water when I asked. "Tell me more about what Mextli told you."

I shrugged. "He thought I should have dealt with Toztli when he grabbed me by the hair and threw me down—"

"Toztli put his hands on you?" Little Reed started rising to his feet, but I grabbed his hand.

"It's all right. It's over now, and I'm none the worse for it. But Mextli's right; I need to learn better focus and practice more, so my magic becomes a part of me. I was lucky my hesitation didn't get me killed." I chuckled. "I'm actually quite glad Mextli came to talk to me."

Uncertainty crossed Little Reed's face. "He seems to have impressed you."

"Impressed isn't the right word. It's more...it's so unusual for a man to not only think I'm capable of more, but to actually encourage me—"

"I encourage you," Little Reed said with a hint of hurt.

"Of course you do, and so do Citlallotoc and Mazatzin, but...the first time I go on a solo visit to one of our allies, he thinks he can knock me around and bully me. Not many men outside our small circle of friends take me seriously, either as a leader, or as a threat. I'm that loudmouthed woman married to Lord Topiltzin."

"You're not loudmouthed. And how do you know that I'm not that decrepit old man married to the beautiful Quetzalpetlatl?"

"You're not decrepit." I stared at his hands sitting on the blanket so close to mine. "As for Mextli...it was nice for once to not be underestimated and instead be taken seriously."

"I might think he was being nice if he didn't have such a reputation for ruthlessness," Little Reed admitted.

"Well, we aren't always what we seem, are we?"

He smiled. "That much is true of anyone."

"Can I ask you something?"

"Of course."

"Did you save me that day on the battlefield...by sacrificing your own life?" A sudden rush of fear made me bite off the last word, barely getting it out.

He didn't answer right away, and he didn't meet my gaze when he finally did. "It upsets you that I would do such a thing for you when you'd readily do the same for me?"

"What upsets me is that you're still here...."

"You wish I was already gone?" he asked, confused.

I shook my head. "Of course not, but....this means Heaven may decide any day now to collect on your debt. I lost you once, and I can't bear the thought of losing you again." I dabbed my eyes, trying to catch the tears before they fell.

He hugged me again, stroking my hair. "Rest your heart, my love. Where you see a curse, I see a gift. Yes, my time here will be short—everyone's time is finite—but that means I have every reason to make the most of every moment. And without that sacrifice, Papalotl, I wouldn't have you, and I wouldn't have a son I love more than life itself."

I breathed deep, the heaviness dissolving into relief and acceptance. "I love you so much, Little Reed."

"I've never doubted it for a moment."

"Nantli!" Yamehecatl ran to me from the doorway in a blur and leapt into my arms, almost knocking me over. "Nantli! Nantli! Nantli!" he squealed, squeezing me with his pudgy little arms. "Are you all better now? You're not going away again, are you?"

I laughed and pushed his curls aside to kiss his forehead. "I'm fine, and no, I'm not going anywhere without you."

"You promise?"

"I promise."

He sighed and rested his head on my bosom. "I missed you so much, Nantli. Did you miss *me?*"

"Terribly."

"Oh! Oh! Guess what, Nantli! Citlallotoc taught me a new move with my sword and I can't wait to show you!"

"I can't wait to see it."

Little Reed let me lean back against his shoulder. Yamehecatl moved back and forth between our laps like an ant that had lost its way as he told me about everything I'd missed while I was gone. I sighed and closed my eyes, treasuring this moment with all of us together as a family.

CHAPTER SIXTEEN

 Little Reed insisted I rest some more, but after sleeping for nearly four days, come dinner time I needed real food in my stomach. I stuck to tlaxcallis and water, but ate with a ravenous hunger that would certainly make me sick. Such dire hunger always brought out the desire, but it remained mysteriously quiet, letting me carry on conversations with both Little Reed and Citlallotoc.

The latter seemed unusually withdrawn and nervous. Guilt perhaps for not insisting on accompanying me to Chimalhuacan himself? By the end of dinner, I was too fatigued to approach him about it and instead begged off the after-meal activities in favor of putting Yamehecatl to bed and getting some more sleep.

Yet Yamehecatl proved hyperactive and adamantly opposed to sleeping. He hugged me repeatedly and laughed hysterically during all the songs. He begged me to tell him the story of Mayahuel again, "But make Ehecatl more heroic this time, Nantli! Make him take a sword to the Earth Monster and save Mayahuel." I hadn't the patience to go through with that again, and considered nursing him, for that always worked to get him to sleep. But my milk supply had finally dried up enough that I wasn't uncomfortable anymore, and nursing him now would set back that progress. Eventually he wore himself out and drifted off to sleep.

Back in my quarters, Little Reed was waiting for me with another cup of blood. "Must I really drink more of this?" I grimaced into the cup.

"Just once more, for good measure," he told me as he tried to wrap a tourniquet on his left arm to stifle the bleeding.

Yamehecatl's mention of Mayahuel reminded me about things I wished to discuss with Little Reed. "I have an idea, for a new religious policy," I said, helping him tie on the cloth.

"Oh?"

"What would you think of designating a feast week to honor the goddess Mayahuel?" He blinked at me, surprised.

"Yamehecatl had me tell him the story about her the other day, and it struck me how unfair it is that we don't honor her, despite everything her death gave us; we give all the honor and credit to Quetzalcoatl, as if her part were of no consequence—"

"Her role was far from inconsequential," Little Reed said.

"Exactly, so why don't we honor that by giving her a feast week, where people can make offerings of octli and maguey fiber?" I finished tying the tourniquet and looked up into his bright eyes. "It's the least she deserves, don't you think?"

"I think it's a wonderful idea." As he leaned in closer to me, his warm, tobacco-tinted breath on my cheek set me shivering with longing. "It's a grievous oversight we must correct."

"Very grievous," I murmured, my train of thought drowning in the ebb of desire and want flowing over me.

Someone rang the bells on my door curtain, but Little Reed still didn't move away, perhaps fearful of breaking the moment. "Come in."

Citlallotoc entered, closing the curtain carefully behind him. "Sorry to disturb you, My Lord and Lady, but there's something I need to speak to you about." He was more nervous than at dinner.

Little Reed finally moved away, leaving me disappointed. "Is everything all right?"

Citlallotoc shifted his feet. "I should have brought this to you as soon as you returned from Tollan, but with caring for the queen, you already had so much on your mind...."

His evasiveness scared me. "What's going on?"

My words finally broke his hesitation. He hurried over and prostrated himself at my feet. "Forgive me, My Lady, but I failed you."

"What is that supposed to mean?"

"The day you left...that night...the prince got into some octli."

"Where in Mictlan did he get that?"

"I don't know. I checked your quarters—"

"I don't keep octli in my quarters."

He nodded. "I didn't find any in here, or in Lord Topiltzin's quarters either."

Little Reed furrowed his brow. "Did you ask him?"

"I did, but he denied everything."

"Are you certain he wasn't merely misbehaving?" I asked. "He was very high-strung before bed tonight."

"I smelled it on his breath, My Lady."

I cast a worried gaze over at Little Reed. "You don't think someone tried to poison him, do you?"

"I'll question all the guards and servants," Little Reed assured me, heading for the door as if to go and do it right now. "I don't want you to worry; I'll get to the bottom of this. You still need to rest and recover."

Laughter drifted in from the hallway, followed by bare feet pattering on the stone floors. Yamehecatl tore open my curtain with his hand as he ran by, shrieking in delight.

Citlallotoc poked his head out of the doorway. "What are you doing out of bed, young man? Come back here this instant!" He disappeared through the curtain. Both Little Reed and I followed him.

Yamehecatl stood in the doorway to Little Reed's quarters, grinning at us with the curtain draped over his head like a cloak. It might have been cute were he not swaying on his feet like a drunkard. "I'm a magical rabbit and you can't see me!" He jumped up and down.

Little Reed took him firmly by the arm. "We can see you just fine, Yamehecatl. What are you doing out of bed?" He wrinkled his nose as he lifted our son into his arms. "Who gave you octli?"

"Heaven gave it to me," Yamehecatl said with a screechy laugh. But when he locked gazes with me, his jovial mood darkened. "Why won't you feed me anymore, Nantli? Don't you like me?" Before I could say anything, he suddenly spat, "Of course she doesn't like us; she didn't want us in the first place!"

His words cut me like a knife.

"That is enough!" Little Reed rarely raised his voice—and I'd never heard him do so with our son—so I wasn't the only one to flinch. Yamehecatl stared at him, shocked, but then he buried his face in Little Reed's chest and cried.

I moved to comfort him, but Little Reed held his hand up to stop me. "I will speak with him." He took Yamehecatl back to his nursery.

Citlallotoc shook his head. "I don't understand how this happened. He was sitting with us the whole night, and you put him to bed yourself no more than a handful of moments ago. Even if someone did sneak into the nursery after you left, certainly there wasn't enough time for it to affect him so? Could there be?"

His questions were vital and worthy of serious investigation and discussion, but all I wanted to do was curl up in my bed and cry myself to sleep. Yamehecatl had obviously began remembering conversations we'd had before he was born, things that I thought we'd worked out long ago, but I was wrong. I dreaded our conversation tomorrow morning.

Unable to hold in the tears any longer, I shook my head and retreated back into my quarters.

◻

In the morning I stayed in bed until Little Reed brought me breakfast. "Yamehecatl is still asleep," he told me when he set the tray on my lap. "Are you feeling all right?"

I shrugged, too drained to look him in the eye. "I never expected to hear that from him. How can I ever fully apologize to him?"

"You don't need to apologize. You had your own survival to consider."

"That may be, but that doesn't change the ache in my heart."

"I don't suppose it does," he admitted. "No more than it soothes the one in my heart, knowing that if not for me, our mother would still be alive."

I frowned. "She made that choice of her own free will, Little Reed."

He set a hand on mine. "As did you, and it was only yours to make."

While I ate, Little Reed filled me in on his investigation into who might have tried to poison our son. "No one confessed to giving him anything last night or any other time, so we shouldn't allow anyone access to him until we work this out. It means extra tasks for us, preparing all his meals, but until we find the culprit we shouldn't trust anyone."

"Not even Citlallotoc?" I asked.

Little Reed shook his head. "He wouldn't do such a thing, but the fewer people who have contact with Yamehecatl, the better. Citlallotoc will understand."

I would feel slighted if asked to stay away from one of our allies' children, but Citlallotoc's devotion knew no limits. He accepted his new orders with no question and focused on investigating the servants and guards.

I kept Yamehecatl at my side day and night, preparing all his meals and testing all his drinks before allowing him to partake. At first he relished my sudden constant attention, and didn't mind sitting in my quarters watching me weave instead of playing with his friends. He never mentioned what he'd said to me that night, and I avoided bringing it up; he was as affectionate as ever, curling up in my bed with me at night, sucking his fingers while I sang him to sleep.

That contentment couldn't last forever. After two weeks, it started with whining when I wouldn't let him go play with the other children; four days later, he pushed over and broke the small idol of Quetzalcoatl in my quarters. "You're so mean!" he shrieked, his cheeks glowing brighter with each ragged breath. "Why do you hate me so much?" Already the heady smell of octli oozed off him like too much perfume, as if he'd fallen into a vat of the stuff.

I rose from my loom, my heart pounding. He hadn't eaten or drunk for several hours, but he turned increasingly intoxicated right in front of me, stumbling around the room, punching things with his fists and kicking them with his bare feet. I ran to the door and shouted for Little Reed.

He rushed from the great hall, his guards following, and when he saw Yamehecatl raging, he tried to grab him.

But Yamehecatl lashed out at him, pummeling him with his fists. "It's not fair, Tatli! Why won't she teach me how to talk to rabbits? I'm the one who dreams of being one!" Little Reed took hold of him and he struggled a moment before going limp, passed out.

Little Reed laid him gently on my bed while I stood by the door, shaking. "What in Mictlan is wrong with our son, Little Reed?"

He shook his head. "What happened?"

"He was fine one moment, but the next.... He's had nothing to eat or drink since breakfast, and I wasn't doing any magic. It just came from nowhere. And now he reeks like a drunk—" I gasped when a new idea occurred to me. "Do you think someone put a curse on him?"

"We should check." Little Reed smoothed Yamehecatl's sweaty hair away from his forehead while I fetched my divination pouch from the wicker basket in the corner.

I murmured a prayer to Quetzalcoatl and emptied the bag of maize kernels onto Yamehecatl's chest. We both chanted various incantations that reveal divine curses, watching the kernels closely, but I saw nothing out of the ordinary. I shook my head, frustrated; I could deal with curses, but I had no idea what was wrong with him.

"Maybe you should talk to the god," Little Reed suggested.

I fumbled the kernels back into my pouch, trembling. "I don't want to see him. Going to see him will only invite questions about things I'd rather not talk about."

"The god won't pressure you to talk about anything you don't—"

"I'm not comfortable talking to him, for my own reasons, and I ask you to respect that."

Little Reed bowed his head. "I'm sorry. I will talk to him myself. But we should consider the possibility that there isn't anything wrong with Yamehecatl."

I creased my brow. "Meaning what?"

"He has divine parentage, which comes with a cost. I age fast, so maybe this is his price."

"Spontaneous intoxication? What about his future as king? Who would follow a man who smells like one of those old men who spend all day deep in their cups of octli?"

"It could get better with time; my aging has slowed in recent years. And maybe something triggers it—Citlallotoc told me Yamehecatl was very upset and cried himself to sleep the first time it happened."

I stared at Little Reed, appalled. "Why was he crying?"

"It was the first time you'd been away from him for a whole day."

I swallowed back yet more guilt as I gazed at Yamehecatl sleeping so peacefully on my bed. "He was agitated right before this, but what about the last time? He wasn't upset; if anything, he was overjoyed."

"Maybe it's linked to intense emotions and we need to teach him how to better control them so this doesn't control him." Little Reed took my hand and pulled me closer. "Everything will be all right. We'll do it together, as a family."

◌

With the departure for Tollan imminent, I cleaned out my meditation room and packed everything into wicker baskets. As I set about the cleaning, someone rang the bells on my curtain.

"Forgive my intrusion, My Lady." Ozomatli stood in the doorway, looking remorseful.

"What brings you here?" I asked, focusing on dusting off my shelves to keep from looking at him. Remembering his cowardice in Chimalhuacan made the desire want to tear him apart.

"I wanted to see if you needed help with your packing, but you appear to have everything well in hand."

"I do, thank you. I trust you've packed up your own meditation room?"

He nodded. "Smoking Mirror's priesthood is ready for the move to Tollan, My Lady."

I wished it weren't moving there, but after much discussion with Little Reed, I still didn't have a good excuse to forbid it. And though it made me seeth inside, I was no closer to having evidence that Ozomatli had conspired against Amoxtli. "You and your people are leaving tomorrow morning?" I asked. When he nodded, I said, "May you all have a safe trip," and went back to my work, signaling the end of the discussion.

He lingered in the doorway a moment before turning to leave, but then he turned to face me again. "I must apologize for my behavior that day in Chimalhuacan. You needed my help and I abandoned you."

I cast my gaze back at him, searching for signs of insincerity, but he was exceptionally good at hiding it.

"Some would find it amusing that the high priest of Tezcatlipoca is afraid of violence, but I joined the priesthood to avoid facing battle. Hardly a manly admission, but times are changing, as are the expectations of men and women, and I no longer must hide the truth. I thank both you and Topiltzin for ensuring I never again have to fear being dragged off the battlefield to be sacrificed." He bowed and turned to leave again.

But I called out, "If you're so thankful, why are you still a priest of the Smoking Mirror? Those dragged off in battle feed the very god you serve, and he would have your heart as willingly as any other."

Ozomatli thought a moment. "I've always been a priest of Tezcatlipoca, just as you've always been a priestess of Quetzalcoatl. My father gave me to the temple when I was a baby, and in Culhuacan, no god was more revered for many years. The other cults have adapted, and I aim for Smoking Mirror's cult to adapt as well. Who better to do that than someone who knows the god's ways but was never comfortable with the means?" He smiled and left.

Someday I would get the evidence I needed to wipe that false smile off his face for good.

◻

The morning I'd waited three years for finally arrived. Yamehecatl—dressed in his rabbit outfit—skipped around the servants and soldiers gathered in the courtyard, excited about his first long journey since his infancy. I feared he'd fall over drunk, but he kept his excitement low enough. Citallotoc was to remain behind until Matlacxochitl arrived to replace him as Culhuacan's assistant governor, so he stood with the priests and priestesses and various war council members staying behind.

Normally we started our journeys under cover of darkness—the better to slip out unnoticed—but since we weren't returning, we took our caravan through the streets. We sat at the open curtains of the litter, Yamehecatl in my lap, and we waved to everyone as we passed. I was so glad to leave Culhuacan for good, and yet an unexpected heaviness fell upon me.

Even though painful memories haunted most of the palace halls, with the years the good memories had come back: the days spent in the women's hall where my mother had taught me to weave; sitting on my father's lap on his throne while he laughed and tickled my nose with feathers from his headdress; or running through the gardens with Black Otter. And new memories I treasured stacked upon those too: Yamehecatl taking his first steps in the great hall, walking from me to Little Reed who encouraged him with outspread arms; or sitting with Malinalli in the gardens, talking through the troubles of the day as the stars grew brighter in the night sky; or watching Little Reed and Citlallotoc playing at the ball game like a couple of boys in the exercise yard. Together, we'd made Culhuacan into a home, and I had to admit: I was going to miss it.

PART THREE
THE YEAR THIRTEEN FLINT

THE BONE FLOWER TRILOGY

CHAPTER SEVENTEEN

"You and Tatli have too many houses," Yamehecatl told me as we walked hand-in-hand through Tollan's merchant quarters. Two guards cut a path through the crowd ahead while four more protected our sides and backs. Most people stepped out of our way, but some priests in black robes glared at us as the lead guards forced them to step back against the buildings. It was bad enough seeing those filthy, blood-smeared priests of Smoking Mirror as part of my priestly duties, but they seemed to be everywhere whenever I took my son around the city on my free days.

I ignored their stares and swung my arm in time with Yamehecatl's as he skipped at my side. "We need many houses to hold all of Tollan's riches," I told him. "If we kept all of it inside the palace, we'd have nowhere to sleep."

"Where do we get it all?"

"Some is tribute from the valley, but we found most of it here, while building Tollan."

"You mean like the gold and silver and jade?"

"All from the mines east of the city," I confirmed. "Along with the obsidian and turquoise deposits."

"I like the seashells!" Yamehecatl dragged me ahead, pointing up to the nearest tall, limestone treasure house. "Tatli says Citlallotoc brought them from over the mountains, where there's so much water you could never find the end of it."

"It's called the ocean," I told him. Citlallotoc traveled often, negotiating trade agreements with the peoples beyond Tolteca borders, and he'd told me in detail about the ocean; how in some places it shone like a pool of jade stones, but was royal turquoise in others. I envied his freedom to travel and see such magnificent sights. Maybe someday I would get to see it too.

"When I grow up, I'm going with Citlallotoc on his travels," my son piped up. "And we're going to fight great battles and monsters." He slashed the air with a pretend sword.

"Citlallotoc would welcome your company, but you won't find many battles. Tollan is at peace with its neighbors, and that's good for everyone. That's why our allies declared your father Emperor of the Toltecs." A title extended to me as well by virtue of being his wife, but I preferred the title of Queen.

"Peace is so boring." Yamehecatl pouted, but before I could scold him, his attention shifted again and he pulled me along to the next building. "This is the Serpent House, where we keep the animals for the sacrifice. And over there is the Feather House, filled with birds of all colors!"

369

"How do you know so much?" I asked, inviting him to show off, something he loved doing.

He stood taller. "Tatli brings me here a lot. He says someday it will all be mine."

"Well, you will share it with your queen."

"Why would I do that?"

"Because husbands and wives share with each other."

Yamehecatl stuck his tongue out. "I'm not getting married."

"Why not?"

"Because girls are boring."

I creased my brow at him. "Oh, we are?"

He giggled, suddenly shy. "Well, you're not, Nantli, but most girls aren't like you. They can't talk to rabbits, or make maguey plants shoot their thorns off."

"Neither can most men. If you think girls are so boring, it's because you only learn about them from other boys. Maybe you should try befriending some girls; when I was your age, my best friend was a boy."

He gazed up at me, puzzled. "You're very strange, Nantli."

Laughing, I pulled him back on track for the market. "Now you know where you get it from."

◻

Yamehecatl loved the market almost as much as I did because he knew he could manipulate me into buying him something. I loathed spoiling him—nothing was worse than a self-important prince—but as the only son I'd ever have, I found him difficult to resist. I had strategies though: I bought him a small rubber ball at the first blanket we came to and hoped that would keep him distracted while I shopped.

And it was working well today. While I browsed ceramic blood bowls, he bounced his ball back and forth on his knees, as Little Reed had shown him. Yamehecatl's aspirations weren't only to someday be the greatest warrior alive, but also be the best ritual ball player, though he had a long way to go before being anywhere as good as his father. Little Reed had inherited his own father's preternatural skill but only ever played for fun with our council. He once tried to teach me but I found the whole thing tedious, and my one experience with the game in Xochicalco had forever soured it for me.

Tollan's market was twice the size of any in the empire—even the one we'd built between Culhuacan and Chimalhuacan—and it took half the day to walk the entire thing. Hundreds of vendors hawked wares from in and outside the empire, and the aisles were always crowded. Today was no exception. The smell of roasting meat and fried maize permeated the air, making my mouth water. I bought some honey-glazed maize cakes for us, to make certain the pesky desire wouldn't start nagging me. Every salesman and woman smiled and rushed to help me, and a few even tried to sweet-talk Yamehecatl, knowing he could convince me to buy anything. But he was focused on practicing his ball skills, completely oblivious to them.

But while I was busy examining a particularly pretty bowl painted with serpents, Yamehecatl kneed his ball too hard and it flew past the guards, hitting a man standing nearby. The man yelped and rubbed the back of his head as he turned around.

I scrambled to apologize for my son's clumsiness, but when I locked gazes with the man, I nearly dropped the bowl in my hands, my heart hammering. "Black Otter?"

He stared back at me, panic cresting in his eyes.

Oblivious to having done anything wrong, Yamehecatl slipped past the guards to fetch

370

his ball, running right for Black Otter. My panic boiled over. "Grab him, now!"

The guards immediately brought Yamehecatl back to me while he shouted about his ball. I drew him to me, protecting him with my arms as I continued to glare at Black Otter. "What are you doing here? I told you never come back, under penalty of death!"

When the guards turned their hard stares on him, Black Otter held his hands up, the color draining from his face. "Please let me explain, My Lady!" But two of my guards seized him and forced him to his knees, one holding him at spear-point.

It was on the tip of my tongue to have them run him through right there, but a young girl elbowed her way through the crowd and flung her arms around Black Otter's neck. She couldn't have been more than eight or nine. "Please don't hurt my tatli!" she cried.

This girl reminded me of myself at that age, tossing water on my anger before it could flare up. I nodded, and the guards withdrew their spears but stayed close to him. "Please do explain yourself." The sight of him hugging his daughter made my voice choke with emotion.

Black Otter rose slowly and the girl clung to him, her face buried in his side. "I know you exiled me under threat of death, My Lady, but I didn't know what else to do. Jade Flower was very sick, and no one back in the valley would help her because of me—because of who my father was. In a few of the western shore cities, they forbade us from even entering. So we traveled north, trying to find anyone who would help us. Eventually we came upon a family of Chichimecs moving to Tollan. They took us in and brought us to their shaman once we got here, but it was too late for Jade Flower. They helped me care for her until the Black Dog came for her earlier this summer."

The pain in my chest intensified. "Jade Flower is dead?" My sister had been in Tollan, dying, and no one told me? *Because they feared what you'd do to Black Otter.* I bit my lip when he nodded, and I tried to say more, but I was frozen.

"You're squeezing me too tight," Yamehecatl whined. He gave me a puzzled look when I finally loosened my grip. "Are you all right?"

I smoothed his hair with a faint, reassuring smile, but I dropped it when returning my attention to Black Otter. "I'm very sorry, Black Otter."

He didn't look at me as he nodded, tight-lipped.

"You're alone with the children now?"

The little girl—called Tiny Flower when I'd last seen her, though she'd have a real name now—peered at me with cautious eyes. "Are you going to take my tatli away too?" Her voice trembled.

I gave her a reassuring a smile, but Yamehecatl tugged at my sleeve, whispering, "Can we go? I'm bored." I shushed him, so he folded his arms and pouted.

"I should have left after Jade Flower died," Black Otter finally went on. "But this is the first place we've been in two years where no one seems to care who I am, and my children are treated with respect."

"Some of us do care who you are, Black Otter," I said. "And not because of your parentage."

He nodded. "The last time we talked...I cringe to even think about the nasty things I said to you. I know this changes nothing, but I'm sorry I frightened you. My behavior was inexcusable."

"It was." My gaze wandered back to the girl, now crying against Black Otter's side. Her terror hurt my stomach. "I'm pleased you've embraced your fatherly duties. All children should have the opportunity for a good, safe life."

He took a deep breath and bowed his head. "Yes, My Lady."

If I wasn't going to go through with the death sentence because of the child, how could I exile them instead? The desert was no place for children. But what should I do? "The king and I will call on you, to discuss where we go from here. Where do you live?"

"In the shacks outside the city walls." The poorest people lived out there, where we handed out food rations daily because so many of them were too new to Tollan to have found work yet, or they had disabilities preventing them from working. "You can ask anyone out there and they can show you to my hut."

Turning to the guards, I said, "We should get back to the palace."

We started to leave, but Black Otter picked up Yamehecatl's ball. "Don't forget this, young warrior." He held it out to him.

I tensed as Yamehecatl broke away to snatch the ball. He barely gave Black Otter a sideways glance as he murmured, "Thank you."

"You're the young prince?" Black Otter asked, a kindly smile on his face. "And you're what, three summers old now?"

Yamehecatl cast him an irritated glance and piped up, "I'm going to be five come winter."

"So you were born not too long after your mother became queen."

"I suppose. Who are you anyway?"

I shuffled Yamehecatl back to my side. "We really must get going, my dear. Your father's waiting." I motioned the guards to take Yamehecatl ahead, and once they were out of earshot, I snarled at Black Otter, "Before you get any stupid ideas, you're not his father. He's Topiltzin's son, and yes, I am married to Topiltzin as well. Keep that in mind when we call you to court."

"Of course, My Lady," Black Otter said. "I thank you for your mercy."

I nodded and left, my guards flanking me. I wanted to look back, to see if he was still watching me, but I didn't want him thinking I cared.

◻

When he wasn't dealing with civic matters at the palace, or performing his high priest duties at the temple, Little Reed spent his spare time meditating at the priestly sanctuary behind the sacred precinct. It sat in the middle of the private gardens—the ones Quetzalcoatl had shown me in the Divine Dream—on an island in the middle of the river that fed the canals at the southern end of the city.

The garden walls encompassed vast lands, including the maguey fields where I'd fallen when I was pregnant, and when Citlallotoc wasn't traveling he brought Yamehecatl out here to practice with his sling against the many rabbits living near the walls. A sturdy wooden bridge provided access to the island and its walled compound, which was divided into twenty meditation rooms designated for the high priests and priestesses of the various religious orders. We left our guards at the main garden gates, relishing the bit of freedom we enjoyed here.

When Yamehecatl and I reached the bridge, Ozomatli greeted us on his way out. I wrinkled my nose at the smell of the rotting blood on his body—ignoring the quiet rumbling in my stomach—but Yamehecatl stuck his nose in the air and sniffed like a dog catching a scent. "Good day, My Lady," Ozomatli said with a smile. "I hope all is well with you today."

I gave him a feigned smile. "It's fine, thank you."

Yamehecatl bared his overly large front teeth, looking so much like a rabbit that I could laugh. "Why do you smell like the temple?"

Ozomatli turned his gaze to Yamehecatl, his smile strained for patience. His

372

discomfort with children amused me, and I'd briefly entertained the notion of assigning him to teach the youngest calmecac students, just for amusement. In the end I decided it wasn't worth exposing them to him. "It's the way of Smoking Mirror's priests to wear the blood of his sacrifices," he answered.

"Why?"

"Because he enjoys the smell, I suppose."

Yamehecatl sniffed the air again, an uncertain look on his face, but he shrugged and returned to bouncing his ball, all interest in the conversation lost.

"Your god might enjoy the smell of death, but the people don't," I said. "We've had complaints about your priests smelling like a butcher's refuse pile." Not precisely true, but it was hard to ignore the wide berth and disgusted looks people gave them as they walked through the streets. I wanted to outlaw all grotesque displays—such as the high priest of Xipe Totec wearing the skin of a virgin girl, or the cult of Tlaloc's practice of pinching children to make them cry, to feed their tears to the rain god—but the time still wasn't right for outright bans on such things. "Small steps," Little Reed always said, "lest we look as strident as the despot we dethroned."

Ozomatli stood taller. "My Lady, I have made a great many changes to accommodate our new laws; we sacrifice one warrior a year, as the god's double at the Toxcatl festival, and give only our own blood during the rest of the year, the same as Quetzalcoatl's priests."

It was true that we'd approved only one sacrifice last year—for only one man came forward willing to offer himself in Smoking Mirror's name—but the desert would turn into an ocean before I believed that Smoking Mirror's priesthood wasn't secretly practicing the old ways. The sorcerer god's power-hunger and greed infected all those near him, turning his priesthood into a den of liars and murderers. Someday I would find the evidence to finally bring justice to my family which this terrible god and his cult had torn apart.

"Wearing the sacrificial blood is an ancient tradition—the way the god knows the wearer is not only a follower, but one who does his will on Earth. And so long as there isn't a law forbidding us from wearing our own blood on our arms and legs to show our devotion, the god's cult will continue to honor that," Ozomatli finished.

"Careful, or we will oblige you with a law banishing you and your demon god, priest," I snarled. And immediately snapped my mouth shut, horrified that I'd said it aloud. Usually I was very good at not letting the anger take over, but ever since Chimalhuacan, I'd found it increasingly difficult to do so when dealing with Ozomatli. I often imagined a restless, deadly jaguar lurking within me, waiting to pounce and devour anything it could get hold of. And it had a particular craving for Smoking Mirror's followers.

Ozomatli blinked at me, startled; but rather than speak again, I grabbed Yamehecatl's hand and hurried past him. When I reached the tall wooden doors, I glanced back, expecting to find him glaring at me. But he was already gone.

I'd lived with this frightening voice in my head for much of my adult life—even harnessing its power for my own use when needed—but at times like this, I couldn't help but wonder if I was slowly going crazy.

From the sanctuary doors, we walked down a short hall with storerooms on either side—for wood, gardening tools, and food—out into the central gardens. The meditation rooms formed a circle around it, with a small kitchen near the entrance where each high priest and priestess pair took turns making communal meals for the weekly administrative meetings. Murals of the various gods decorated the plaster walls outside each meditation room, identifying which order the room belonged to. A plethora of

Feathered Serpent statues decorated the flowerbeds, while the stone rain spouts on the roofs were carved in the likeness of the goggle-eyed rain god Tlaloc, the second most worshiped god in Tollan.

Little Reed sat under the large avocado tree at the center of the garden, dressed in a simple white robe and meditating in the shade. When my heart soared at the sight of him, I knew I couldn't be as ill in the head as I feared I was.

"Tatli!" Yamehecatl broke free and sprinted down the path towards his father, and Little Reed laughed when Yamehecatl tackled him with a hug.

"I swear you get stronger by the day." Little Reed set the boy in his lap and swept aside his own fully-silver hair to better see him. "You're what, almost two years now?" he asked with feigned ignorance.

Yamehecatl folded his arms crossly. "You know how old I am, Tatli." He turned to me. "I don't look two, do I, Nantli?"

Stifling a giggle, I said, "You look at least twenty, my little breeze."

Yamehecatl beamed.

Laughing, Little Reed said, "Of course I know how old you are. I could never forget the happiest day of my life."

"What day would that be?" Yamehecatl asked.

"The day you were born, of course." He kissed Yamehecatl on the forehead.

"I remember that day too." It didn't surprise me that Yamehecatl remembered such things—I remembered my own birth as well—but he'd only started talking about it within the last couple of months. Sometimes I pressed him, to see if he remembered any of our conversations before he was born, but thus far that part of his life seemed lost to him. Much as my own was lost to me.

"But who was the woman with no teeth?" he asked me.

"That was Lady Bitter Rabbit, and she did have some teeth," I corrected him. "She was Mitotia's mother."

"The one who died last year?" When I nodded, he asked, "And who was the man we talked to in the market?"

Little Reed looked up at me too, casually curious.

I told Yamehecatl, "Why don't you take your new ball and go over there and practice your knee bounces." I pointed towards the far corner of the gardens.

Yamehecatl scurried away, laughing and bouncing his ball on the grass as he went.

I sat next to Little Reed in the shade. "We ran into Black Otter in the market."

Little Reed tensed. "What's he doing here? Is he in the stockade now?" When I shook my head, he blinked, taken aback. "Why not?"

"He and Jade Flower brought their children here because she was very sick and no one would help them, because of his father. She died a few months ago, and now he's left caring for their children all on his own. You should have seen how terrified his daughter was when the guards grabbed him...." I shook my head. "He did right by his family, as I told him to, and I can't blame him for wanting to stay here; the alternative is living in the desert, and that's no life for children."

"It isn't," Little Reed conceded. "But it's not his children I'm worried about."

"I told him that he will have to come and speak with us soon, so we can decide how to proceed. I will say though that he showed no interest whatsoever in getting me back."

"What about our son?" He watched Yamehecatl jumping up and down, trying to knock low-hanging fruit from the tree. "Did he ask about him?"

"He did, and I assured him you were Yamehecatl's father."

"And he accepted that?"

"I don't know. But it doesn't matter because we married before Yamehecatl was born, so by law you are his father."

"Our laws calls most human sacrifice illegal, but that doesn't necessarily stop it from happening."

"Trying to claim Yamehecatl won't do him any good; he won't suddenly be the rightful king, nor will it get him a job, or bring him out of the shacks outside town."

"You think we should give him another chance?"

"I think we should talk to him and find out what he was doing these last five years, and what his plans are for the future. And then go from there."

Little Reed nodded. "A most excellent idea."

CHAPTER EIGHTEEN

 Little Reed wasted no time waiting to size up Black Otter. When we gathered for dinner with the council in the great hall, the guards ushered Black Otter in, along with his two children. The girl held his hand, taking in the maps all over the walls with apprehension; walking slightly behind them, the boy—who was probably no more than seven—stared up in awe at the ceiling with its paintings of the gods and the divine realms. He looked exactly as Black Otter had at that age.

Amoxtli sat in the council's circle, next to Mazatzin, and he started to rise, but caught himself. When he glanced over at Little Reed, questions in his eyes, Little Reed nodded and motioned him to go and greet his brother.

When Black Otter saw Amoxtli standing among the others, he froze; but the girl cried, "Uncle!" and she ran to Amoxtli, her arms wide. Amoxtli scooped her up, laughing while the boy hung back with his father, curious but unwilling to follow his sister. After he'd hugged her, Amoxtli set the girl down and knelt in front of her, holding her hands in his. "You've grown up so much since I last saw you, Cuicatl, and my, how much you look like your mother." He turned his gaze to the boy and asked, "Your mother used to call you Little Water Bug, but what do the gods call you now?"

"Night Wind," the boy replied, scrutinizing Amoxtli.

"Go and embrace your uncle," Black Otter chastised the boy.

But Amoxtli shook his head. "It's all right. He probably doesn't remember me, he was so young the last time I saw him." He came to Black Otter and stopped a handful of steps away from him. "But it feels even longer since last I saw you, Brother."

Black Otter hesitated, but then bridged the gap between them, pulling Amoxtli into a crushing hug. He squeezed his eyes tight as if holding back tears. "It's so good to see you again, Amoxtli."

Amoxtli hugged him back hard. "Sometimes I was certain I'd lost you forever, especially after that last time we talked."

"I'm sorry, Brother. I wasn't well, but I've gotten better, and I promise I won't let anything come between us again."

In spite of myself, a hitch formed in my chest and I had to clear my throat to be able to breathe properly.

Little Reed left his throne to stand with our cousins, setting a supportive hand on each of their shoulders when they finally separated. "Family is such a wonderful thing; we're all the stronger for it." To Black Otter, he said, "Let me be the first to welcome you to Tollan." When Black Otter started to kneel, Little Reed stopped him. "That isn't necessary, Cousin, for we are family." He motioned to the mat where Citlallotoc normally sat. "Please join us for the evening meal."

Black Otter blinked, but thanked Little Reed as he took his place on the mat. Mazatzin moved to Amoxtli's mat so Amoxtli could sit next to his brother, and the children sat behind Black Otter, the same way Yamehecatl sat on the mats behind my throne. When I glanced back, Yamehecatl chewed thoughtfully on a turkey leg and stared at Night Wind, curious. Night Wind didn't return his attention.

The servants served everyone, saving me and Little Reed for last, as was our way, and we settled into our meals. No one said anything for the first few moments while we ate— and Little Reed held the sauce bowl for him and me—a task usually relegated to a man's wife—but eventually he told Black Otter, "Please accept my condolences on the loss of your wife, Cousin."

Black Otter bowed his head. "Thank you, My Lord." After a tentative bite of his roasted dog, he added, "May I extend my compliments on everything you and Lady Quetzalpetlatl have created here in Tollan? The city is magnificent, and the peace and prosperity are a welcome change from how things were in the valley for so long."

Little Reed smiled. "That's kind of you, but so long as our people must come to us for daily rations to feed their children and elders, our work is still incomplete. Have you been able to secure work for yourself yet?"

Black Otter cast an uncertain glance over at me before answering, "A kindly Chichimec family has been helping me, but I took a position as an apprentice obsidian knapper last week."

Nodding, Little Reed said, "Tollan's Chichimecs are selfless and industrious. We're grateful for their help building this great city and improving the lives of thousands through our mutual respect and friendship."

Half of our royal council was Chichimecs—and half of them women—and they all nodded their heads approvingly.

Little Reed set aside his empty plate and lounged back in his icpalli. "I'm eager to hear all you've been doing these last few years, and about your plans for the future."

Black Otter cleared his throat, looking anxious. "Well, after leaving Tollan that first time, I went to Chalco, and under Jade Flower's care, I recovered from my near-death ordeal." To me he added, "I must again apologize for my rough behavior when I first came to Tollan five years ago, My Lady. I was still a shambles after everything that transpired that day on the lake, but Jade Flower helped me move on. I don't know what I would have done without her. She was so patient...so caring." He turned to poke absently at his food. "Honestly, I don't know what I'll do without her now."

"Know that you have family to lean on in your time of need," I said, feeling guilty for my earlier suspicion. Sometimes my own egotism shamed me.

"I thank you for that, My Lady." Black Otter's strained smile broke into a frown when Amoxtli set a hand on his shoulder. Amoxtli whispered to him and Black Otter nodded, looking ready to break into tears, but he pulled himself together. "As for the future, my only wish is to provide stability for my children, especially during this trying time. I believe Tollan is the ideal setting for that. However, I recognize that my past may make our staying impossible, and if Your Majesty insists we leave, I will do so, without argument, this very night if you ask."

"I appreciate that, Cousin, but I'm not inclined to rush to judgment," Little Reed said. "If I might ask, to what god do you give your prayers these days?"

Black Otter averted his eyes, looking uncomfortable again. "I must admit that, in recent years, I haven't done much praying, and I've fallen away from honoring any particular god. My father's religious issues caused me a great deal of heartache and pain, and I haven't regained any sense of personal faith in the gods. Yet I often wonder if my questioning has led to my children's suffering."

Little Reed nodded solemnly. "It is perhaps the way of other gods to punish a crisis of faith, but the Feathered Serpent understands your reticence. Earned faith is strongest. I hope you'll consider exploring a renewal through the teachings of the Feathered Serpent. And now that you're in Tollan, trust you're under his protection, no matter the current of your heart."

"That is good to know, My Lord."

So it appeared Little Reed was leaning towards letting Black Otter stay. The maelstrom of joy and fear rolling through me left me uneasy, and I found myself staring at Black Otter more than was proper. Sweaty memories of frantic flesh crushing against flesh in the heat of intimacy made the desire purr and laugh. *He was a luxurious feast laid out for us. So delicious, so varied, so willing....* When he caught me staring, he looked away, uncomfortable, and I scolded myself for doing the very same thing so many men did to me that I despised. By the end of the meal, I wanted him gone from my sight, so I could relax again.

But at least the children got along fine. Over the course of the meal, Yamehecatl edged closer to them, until he sat right with them. The girl paid courteous attention but he said little to her, and whereas Night Wind had shown Yamehecatl no interest at all before, now the two talked intently and laughed. I couldn't hear their conversation but Yamehecatl was delighted. It warmed me to see my son enjoying himself so.

But then came time for Night Wind to leave. Yamehecatl hadn't suffered one of his drunken fits in several months now, but when Little Reed said Night Wind needed to go home, Yamehecatl stamped his feet and cried. "But I never get to have any friends stay the night!"

"The other noble boys can stay in the nursery with you anytime you want," I corrected him.

"But they aren't my friends! They don't even like me!"

His concern wasn't easily dismissed. The older he got the bigger the gulf between him and the other boys grew; because he was so clever, Little Reed and I had considered starting him in calmecac already, but his lack of emotional maturity made us hesitate. He might be able to speak as coherently as someone twice his age, but his tonalli was still that of a four-year old. For now Little Reed and I privately tutored him in our spare time, and I worried he'd never be truly ready for the discipline of calmecac. Little Reed had endured years of torment from the likes of Red Flint and his friends, but he'd rarely let it get to him; Yamehecatl, however, felt every invisible dart, and if he became too upset....

Already he began swaying so I summoned one of his guards. "Take him to his room and stay with him until I get there."

The guard hefted Yamehecatl into his arms, and my son started screaming and pounding his fists against the guard's shoulders. The man didn't flinch as he carried him from the great hall, the vague aroma of octli lingering.

My cheeks burned to see Black Otter looking uncomfortable on my behalf. "Please excuse him. He's a highly emotional boy," I murmured.

"Children can be." Black Otter gave me an understanding smile then turned to Little Reed again with a bow. "Thank you for your hospitality tonight, My Lord. And for your mercy, and this opportunity to redeem myself, not only in your eyes, but in those of your wife."

Little Reed set a hand on Black Otter's shoulder. "The Feathered Serpent believes everyone is worthy of a second chance. If this job with the obsidian worker doesn't meet your needs, please let me know and I shall see what I can do to help you find something better." He moved his gaze to the girl, who half-buried her face in Black Otter's side, embarrassed. "Have you enrolled the children in school yet?"

Black Otter shook his head.

"Education is compulsory in Tollan for all children at least eight years of age, though we encourage starting them even younger, so bring them by the palace registrar in the morning and we'll place them into temporary classes at the telpochcalli until they are properly tested for formal placement. An educated population makes for a strong empire."

"Thank you, My Lord. I will bring them by first thing in the morning." Black Otter bade us each good night and left.

Once he was gone, Little Reed asked me, "Your impressions?"

"Well, it is only one meal, but I didn't see anything to raise concerns. He does appear deeply affected by Jade Flower's death."

"And deeply uncomfortable around you," Little Reed noted, frowning. Had he seen me staring at Black Otter with lust in my eyes? Gods I hoped not!

"That's very different than how he was before we exiled him," I admitted.

"Then you believe him a changed man?"

I shrugged. "I'm still not entirely comfortable, if that's what you're asking." Though my own discomfort had more to do with my reactions to him than anything he'd said or done since running into him in the market today. But I didn't want to admit as much to Little Reed.

"You want us to send him away again?"

"Not at all; I think we should give him a chance to prove himself, one way or the other."

Little Reed thought a moment then motioned Amoxtli over to us. "We want to make certain that Black Otter integrates well with our ways here in Tollan. Would you keep watch over his progress and help guide him in the right direction? As a personal favor to myself and Lady Quetzalpetlatl?"

"Of course, Your Majesty," Amoxtli said.

"And if you should have any reservations about his ability to adapt—"

"I shall tell you immediately."

Little Reed clapped him on the shoulder. "Your loyalty to the realm is commendable, Cousin." Once Amoxtli walked away, Little Reed told me, "It's a start. Perhaps we can also find some means of testing Black Otter...give him a chance to prove his new good nature in solid fashion."

"What do you have in mind?" I asked.

He shook his head. "I'm not certain yet, but let us both think on it."

I nodded, but hearing Yamehecatl screaming down the hall, I said, "I should go tend to him."

"Do you need my help?"

I laughed. "Thank you, but you have temple duties tonight, remember?"

He sighed but planted a gentle kiss on my cheek. I returned the gesture but lingered a breath longer, wishing—as so many other times—that it could be more. But as always, it had to end. "Goodnight, my love." I hurried to the nursery, not looking back. No matter how guilty I might feel for gawking at Black Otter all night, I had no business indulging myself when my son was in the grips of one of his episodes.

But when I reached the nursery in the royal quarters, Yamehecatl fell silent. I looked inside to see the guard carefully tucking him under his blankets, fast asleep. When the guard saw me, he said, "He screamed himself out, My Lady."

I knelt to stroke Yamehecatl's sweaty hair back from his forehead. "I'm sorry Night Wind couldn't stay tonight, my darling, but maybe sometime soon," I whispered. *Once I know I can trust his father again.*

❑

Worrying about Yamehecatl kept me up most of the night as I checked on him once an hour. It wasn't a long journey to his nursery—it was right behind that same blue curtain in my quarters that I'd seen in the Divine Dream—but eventually I carried him into my room and laid him in bed next to me, to save myself the trip. The next morning he woke in better spirits and we lay in bed singing songs of Quetzalcoatl until my handmaiden came to warm my bathwater.

"Must you go to the temple, Nantli?" Yamehecatl whined. "Can't we lie in bed all day and you can tell me stories and we can sing songs and eat sweet maize cakes?"

"I'd love nothing more than to do that, but yes, I must go to the temple." I stroked his head soothingly. "I have many responsibilities, not only to you, but to the city and to the god."

"Maybe Tatli will sing with me," he said, petulance in his voice.

"Let your father sleep; he was up all night doing his duties to the god. Leave him be until at least the noon hour."

"But no one's here to play with me, Nantli," Yamehecatl moaned. "They're all gone at school, but even if they weren't, they still wouldn't play with me. When can I go to school too?"

"Well, your father and I have discussed it, and we want to put you into school—so you can make new friends—but...."

"But what?"

I had to tread carefully here. "The teachers at the calmecac have high expectations of their students, especially about behavior. We don't feel you're...ready to handle it."

He furrowed his brow. "What do you mean?"

"You struggle controlling your emotions, like last night, and when you get upset you quickly become out of control. I don't think it's your fault; inside each of us is a voice that tries to get us to do things or behave in ways that aren't in our best interest."

He gasped. "You know about the voice?" When I nodded, he asked, "But how?"

"As I said, all of us have one."

"Mine wants to always have fun. And he gets really upset when you tell me it's time to do something else. And I start feeling really strange."

I nodded. "Growing up means learning to recognize whom we should listen to and how we choose to behave. It's difficult, but with work, we learn to control ourselves, and we don't let the other voice rule us or our lives."

"What does your voice tell you to do?"

To devour and enjoy every mortal in sight! the desire cackled. "Just things I shouldn't."

"I wonder what Tatli's voice tells him."

I'd wondered the same thing ever since Little Reed mentioned having his own at one time, but since he never offered to talk about it, maybe he didn't want to anymore than I wanted to discuss my ferocious desire.

When the handmaiden returned from the bath yard, I asked her to dress Yamehecatl and told him I would see him again at dinner. I feared he might break down again, but he merely sighed and climbed off the bed. As they went out of the door, he scowled and said, "Stop saying that! Why are you always so mean?"

The young woman cast me a startled look—no doubt thinking he was talking to her—but Yamehecatl turned to me and said, "I want to go to school, so I'll work hard on it, Nantli."

I gave him a kiss on his forehead, which he promptly wiped away with the back of his hand, but he still beamed at me. "And I know you will do so very well at it because you're strong."

He leaned in closer and whispered in my ear, "Like you, Nantli."

◻

Yamehecatl's words warmed me more than the bathwater, and that glow followed me out of my quarters, ready to start my day.

Upon reaching the Hall of the Gods—the foyer decorated with the statues of the gods—I met Malinalli, on her way from her quarters in the priestly wing where all the highest-ranking priests lived. She had temple duties as well and wore her long, white fire priestess robe embroidered with feathered serpents breathing flames; they bore a striking similarity to the fire serpent I'd summoned long ago in Teotihuacan, and I wondered how much that incident had influenced her choice of the pattern.

When she reached me, she smiled and hooked her arm with mine as we walked side-by-side. "You're looking very happy this morning," I noted with a smile of my own.

She shrugged. "It was a good night."

After watching her grin for a moment, I worked it out. I stopped short. "Did you meet someone?"

After a brief hesitation, she blurted out, "Maybe."

I laughed and hugged her. "That's wonderful! Who is he? You must tell me everything!"

Her smile wavered. "Well...this is all very new, and I don't know if it's going anywhere...."

"You're not going to tell me?" I asked, teasing her with an offended gasp.

A flush crept into her cheeks. "You never told me about you and Topiltzin."

I hadn't, and now I felt guilty. "No, but I didn't tell anyone...except Nimilitzli, but she'd already presumed as much." After an awkward pause, I added, "I'm sorry."

Malinalli shook her head. "We were supposed to be devoted to the god in body and spirit, so I understand why you wouldn't tell anyone. Which is why I know you'll understand when I say I'm not ready to say more yet."

I nodded. "I respect that." As we walked again, I asked, "But you will tell me eventually, right?"

She hesitated again but soon gave me a smile. "I promise I will, when the time is right."

I patted her arm. "I'm happy that you're happy, Malinalli."

She beamed. "I really am. I hope it lasts."

"Maybe you'll get married and have children, and our children can grow up together."

"Maybe," she murmured, distracted. "Will you and Topiltzin have more children soon?"

Surprisingly, no one had ever asked me that before; it was assumed we would have more, and whenever I fell ill for a few days, rumors circulated that I'd miscarried. But in truth, my body had stopped its monthly bloodletting a year ago, not long after weaning Yamehecatl. Most women remained fertile into their forties, but my childbearing years ended before I'd passed my thirty-second summer.

I'd always thought I'd be happy to be rid of that inconvenience, but when it came far sooner than expected, I felt an acute sense of loss. Did this mean that, like Little Reed, I was aging faster, and I hadn't that many years left? That hadn't been the case for most of my life, and though I'd found my first silvered hair only two years ago, that had been easy enough to dismiss—it took a lot out of a person to run a kingdom. But the end of my monthly cycles seemed a warning that things weren't as they appeared.

After much contemplation, I'd decided there was only one possible cause: the magic coursing through my veins was prematurely aging my body. And here I'd once thought carrying the god's child was the thing that would kill me, when in fact it was the other unexpected gift he'd given me.

But there was a certain peace in knowing that now Little Reed and I could grow old and die together. For years the thought that I would have to sit by and watch him wither away while I remained behind all alone haunted me; the notion that once he was dead I could move on to marry—and be intimate—with someone else held no appeal for me. *Nimilitzli warned you about building your entire life around someone else,* I thought with a bitter laugh under my breath.

It was depressing enough to think about all this let alone speak aloud of it, and though Malinalli let me have peace while I mulled, I felt obligated to give an answer. "I've had all the children my tonalli will allow. Yamehecatl is challenging enough on his own, and this lets me to divide my time between family and the god, so it worked out well, to be honest."

Malinalli patted my arm. "That's good to know."

◻

Malinalli had class to teach at the next hourly bell at the calmecac, so I walked her there, on the north end of the precinct. Neither Little Reed nor I taught any classes, but Little Reed led the yearly pilgrimage to Teotihuacan with the newly-graduating novices. There was enough religious interest in Tollan that each order took their own pilgrimage on different weeks each summer, but it had become common practice that everyone preparing to take their vows to Quetzalcoatl—from all over the empire—would meet in Teotihuacan during the last week of summer, to be tutored by the god's highest priest. Little Reed had returned from this year's pilgrimage just a few week earlier.

As we approached the calmecac's courtyard with its cistern guarded by a statue of Tlaloc submerged in the water, Mazatzin and Mitotia came out of the alleyway that led to the priestly gardens, deep in conversation. As always my eyes were immediately drawn to the black tattoo of a feathered serpent along Mitotia's jawline on the right side of her face. Tradition among her tribesmen dictated that every man—and woman—take a tattoo to mark their entrance into adulthood. "Men get tattooed when they take their first war prisoner, and women on their wedding night," Mitotia had explained to me. "But since I'm never going to marry, and my vows to the god are the closest I'll get, this should be the pattern." It took me quite a few weeks to overcome the urge to stare whenever I saw her.

But I wasn't nearly as shocked as her father, who'd roared at her about taking vows to the wrong god. "You were supposed to lead the cult of Mixcoatl in Tollan!" But when he'd blustered to Little Reed about their "deal", Little Reed had listened patiently and explained he couldn't make anyone join any particular cult.

"Our deal was to educate Mitotia, which we've done. Beyond that, as a citizen of Tollan, she's free to choose her own path." Ten Spines called Little Reed a treacherous little snake and talked of gathering his people and leaving, but Mitotia herself spoke sense into him. He came back to Little Reed with much groveling and tears and Little Reed accepted his apologies without hesitation. Little Reed had a far easier time forgiving slights than I did; a quality I envied in him.

Mazatzin smiled and bowed in greeting. "Good morning, My Lady." I'd told him more than once that such a greeting wasn't necessary, but he was a man of formality, and I doubted I would ever change that. We all walked into the calmecac together, Mazatzin filling me in on the status of the priesthood before he went home for the day. When we reached the main hallway, I asked Malinalli about joining me for lunch, but she stumbled over her words before telling me she'd already made plans with someone else. "Maybe tomorrow?" she offered hopefully, and I told her that would be fine. I bade her and Mazatzin a good day and they set out on their separate ways as the first warning bell rang, sending students scrambling through the halls.

Mitotia followed me into my meditation room and immediately took up a goose quill at my desk. To soften Ten Spines's hurt pride, I'd agreed to take her as my apprentice and train her to replace me as High Priestess when I passed out of this world. I'd worried Malinalli would feel slighted, but when I spoke with her, she confessed that she had no ambitions to the position. "After you being the god's chosen high priestess, I'd be a dismal disappointment. That's too big of an expectation to have to live up to." At least my decision wouldn't challenge our friendship.

"You have the final planning meeting for the festival of the Maguey Goddess with the rest of the high priestesses at noon," Mitotia informed me, reading off the parchment calendar she wrote on every day. "Ozomatli requested funds to commission a new obsidian mirror for Smoking Mirror's temple; apparently one of his priests knocked it off the wall while polishing it last night and broke it."

"I'd like to break his stupid god," I muttered under my breath as I poked among the papers on my desk, seeing if there were any letters needing my attention. "Tell him I'll get his funds from the treasury when he has his priests wash more than once a week."

Mitotia allowed herself an amused smile. "Very well. Several women have come asking for your fertility blessing, to help them conceive this month—" Something I always enjoyed doing "—and several farmers have asked for either you or Lord Topiltzin to come and bless their new fields."

"The high priests of Xipe Totec are supposed to do that."

"I told them as much, but they want the Feathered Serpent's blessing on top of Xipe Totec's. I told them I would give you their request." She counted items on her list silently, pointing to each with the quill. "Oh, and we're also out of snakes for the afternoon sacrifice."

"We should visit the royal game warden then. Let me make my offering and we'll be on our way."

She bowed out of the doorway, closing the curtain to give me privacy.

I pulled my string of maguey thorns from my robe pocket and knelt on the reed mat in front of the wooden Feathered Serpent idol in the back corner of the room.

"My most Great Lord,

Today I give thanks for all you've bestowed upon me;
For the faith you instill in my heart,
For the strength you woke in my blood,
For your son who shares my life,
And for my son who is our future.
May he always know your love,
Your understanding,
And your pride.
I honor you, oh Great Feathered Serpent,
For my family,
For my friends,
For my life."

I poked the thorns through my tongue, one after another, coating the maguey fiber with my blood. I was so used to the practice that I hardly noticed the sting anymore. I set the string into a ceramic blood bowl and held it above my head as I prayed silently. Once finished, I dumped the string of thorns into the idol's open mouth, put a small wad of cotton over my wounded tongue, and closed my mouth to hold it in place while the bleeding stopped, giving more silent prayers.

And I thought of all those times I'd spent with the god in the Divine Dream, of the shared pleasure and feathery touches; no matter how long ago I'd stopped indulging that desire, my mind always went back to it when I prayed. Some great chosen high priestess I was.

"It still baffles me that anyone would willingly shove thorns through their tongue," a voice spoke up behind me, slinging my heart into a run.

I nearly knocked over the idol as I hurried to my feet and spun around. When I saw Mextli grinning at me, hunched over to keep from hitting his head on the ceiling, my fear gave way to anger. "What in Mictlan are you doing here?" I demanded after spitting out the cotton. I hadn't felt the desire take over, but I didn't push it back. Right now it was the best shield to protect me. Especially since he was blocking the only way out of the room.

He gave me a mock frown. "It's a pleasure to see you again too, little thorny one."

"Don't call me that!"

The grin returned. "But it's the perfect name for someone so...prickly."

"If I'm prickly, it's because you're a dog's ass!"

"Oh, am I?"

"You forced me to kill two people the last time I saw you!"

"And that's such a bad thing?"

"Says the the delusional dimwit who fancied himself a war god."

He laughed. "Now I understand why he finds you so fascinating."

"Who?"

He answered only by grinning wider.

"What do you want now, little hummingbird boy?"

"I come on behalf of my Lord Tezcatlipoca, with a proposition for you."

The desire guffawed. "What could he possibly offer me?"

"You might be surprised."

"This is all very precious, but I haven't time for your demon lord and his games. I have an empire to run." I started towards him with grim purpose, expecting him to step aside. A crazy notion yet so very solid in my gut; when the desire took over, I wasn't a woman to be trifled with.

And yet he didn't move. "You mean an empire that won't last another ten years?"

"It will last forever."

"Is that what the Feathered Serpent tells you?"

"It's what I *see* when Tollan's crop yields can feed the entire empire, and the ground spits up gold and turquoise for us to find without even digging. There's no more war, no more hunger. No one lives in fear anymore, because we've shown the people they have nothing to fear."

"No more war?" Mextli laughed. "And you say I'm the delusional one. You and Quetzalcoatl have brought only a temporary peace to these lands. The other gods haven't fallen asleep; they've noticed this power-grab, and they won't sit idly by while the Feathered Serpent grows fat. War is coming, and you're on the wrong side of the conflict, my dear."

His threats brought to mind Nimilitzli's warnings about involving myself in the power struggles of the gods. As usual, she'd been right. But the desire was unperturbed. "I'm not the one on the wrong side. Anyone who follows Smoking Mirror is but a pathetic scoundrel interested only in his own power. I would ban that demon's cult in Tollan—"

"If only you didn't have to bend to Quetzalcoatl's will?"

My face burned. "I *choose* to follow the Feathered Serpent's lead because his way is the right way."

Mextli shook his head. "You're so well-trained. The Feathered Serpent has a special gift for emotional manipulation, but you make it so easy. You must enjoy being manipulated."

Surging anger brought tingling magic to my fingertips, and next thing I knew, I stood a breath away from Mextli, barely containing the impulse to unleash it all at him. "You know nothing about Quetzalcoatl. Or me."

"I've made it a priority to get to know you." His voice was casual but the fluff of his feathers told the real story: I'd scared him. "You should let your inner monster out more often; when you do...you're magnificent."

His breathless whisper brought the flush of lust and longing creeping up on me. *Finally! Someone who appreciates the goddess within!* My gaze wandered over him, taking in every curve of muscle, every flash of feathery iridescence, a fire long dormant suddenly reigniting. His feathers met flesh in a precise line down the center of his body, and even the fingernails of his left hand were covered in miniscule blue feathers. *I bet he's feathered on the left half of his tepolli,* the desire mused, my gaze lingering at his loincloth as the heat threatened to overwhelm me. *And if it's even half as big as the rest of him—*

A shiver of excitement broke the desire's hold and I turned away, disgusted and disturbed. *How can you even think of this evil man—or whatever he is—like that? That's as bad as lusting after...after Smoking Mirror!* My desire recoiled like a severed worm; apparently there were things even it couldn't stand.

"Anyone can be fooled once," Mextli said. "But don't let him fool you twice. You're better than that."

My magic retreated from my limbs, leaving me cold and vulnerable. "What's that supposed to mean?"

"When you're ready for the truth, come and speak with Tezcatlipoca."

"What truth?"

But without another word, he vanished.

Chapter Nineteen

It was on the tip of my tongue to tell Little Reed about Mextli's visit, but when I saw him that evening, helping our son tie on a clean loincloth before dinner, I was overwrought with guilt. This wonderful man loved me and our son, had forsaken all others to share in my sacrifice and build a peaceful family life with me, and I'd spent all afternoon dwelling—and sometimes daydreaming—on a moment of lust for some stranger who plotted against our chosen god. This, on top of my uncouth thoughts about my former husband.... I didn't deserve this loving, faithful man.

Little Reed smiled when he noticed me lurking in the doorway, but my expression must have troubled him. "Is everything all right?"

Before I could say anything, Yamehecatl shoved past him and launched himself at me, latching both arms around my legs in a hug. "You're home, Nantli! I was afraid you wouldn't come back!"

I kissed his cheeks, the joy on his face melting me inside. "I always come home." I swept his bangs aside to kiss his forehead too. "Why would you think I wouldn't?"

"I had a bad dream this afternoon, that you and Tatli left me next to a lake in the dark, and you never came back for me. Promise me you won't ever leave me by a lake."

His words inexplicably troubled me, as if I'd had the same dream once but couldn't draw forth any images, just a suffocating feeling of sadness and fear. I shivered as I said, "I promise never to leave you by any lake, my dear."

Yamehecatl hugged me again then rushed back to Little Reed and grabbed his hand. "Let's go! I'm starving!" He tugged his arms, encouraging him to his feet.

Little Reed obliged but took my hand too. My heart danced, the worries of the day dissolving under his loving gaze. "Is everything all right?" he asked again.

I kissed his cheek and leaned my head against his shoulder, welcoming his embrace. His strong, solid muscle brought on my own body's familiar, reassuring reaction and I smiled, basking in the heat between us. It didn't matter what the desire wanted; I was the stronger one, and I had everything I needed right here, in the arms of this man I loved. "Everything is perfect," I whispered.

¤

Sometime in the middle of the night, I woke up to the sound of bells tinkling. At first I thought they were mine, but when I heard Little Reed's voice followed by Mazatzin's, I rolled out of bed. They stood in Little Reed's doorway across our small family garden. "What's going on?" I asked, stifling a yawn as I crossed the flagstone path to the other side.

"So sorry to wake you at this early hour, My Lady," Mazatzin said with a bow. "But I suppose this should be shared with both of you."

"Let's speak in my quarters, so we don't wake Yamehecatl," Little Reed suggested, holding the curtain open for us. Mazatzin waited for me to go in first before meekly stepping in himself.

Little Reed's quarters differed from my own only in decor; wooden screens carved with images of the Feathered Serpent separated his sleeping area from the main anteroom with its walls painted with frescos of birds, snakes, and butterflies. He gestured for us to sit on the mats in front of the hearth and tossed some new logs on the fire to get better light. He also put some copalli incense on a clay burner before settling down on one of the vacant reed mats. "What do you have for us, Mazatzin?" he asked.

"A man came into the temple with a very disturbing report. His son vanished from the fields this evening, at sunset, but the man tracked him into the woods on the northern end of Tollan. Once there, he witnessed a man in a black priest's robe attempting to sacrifice his son. He tried to stop it, but someone struck him from behind. He awoke a few hours later to find his son's body half-buried in a shallow grave nearby, but when he dug it up, he found other bodies as well. He led soldiers to the grave and they pulled a dozen bodies out."

Every bone in my body shouted this was the handiwork of Smoking Mirror's cult, but I'd been wrong the last time. And Mextli was snooping around, causing trouble again. "This newest victim...was his heart removed?"

Mazatzin nodded.

"Was there sign of ritual sacrifice on the other bodies found?" Little Reed asked.

"Some of them, yes. Others were too decomposed to be able to tell at a glance. I should also tell you that the farmer positively identified Ozomatli as the man he saw in the forest."

Finally! The break I need to stick a thorn through him.

But Little Reed wrinkled his brow. "Was it truly light enough to make such a positive identification? It takes at least a quarter of an hour to reach the forest from the most northern fields, and he said his son disappeared at sunset, so it was dark when he finally found him. Did he bring a torch with him?"

"I didn't think to ask," Mazatzin said.

Little Reed sighed. "If this turns out to be true, I'm highly disappointed. I believed Ozomatli was bringing real change to Smoking Mirror's cult, so we could all coexist peacefully."

"Smoking Mirror isn't interested in peaceful coexistence," I said. "We should arrest Ozomatli immediately."

But Little Reed shook his head. "We must avoid rushing to judgment. An accusation is a place to start, but further investigation is warranted. These are serious charges, and Ozomatli deserves the right to defend himself against them."

I grudgingly nodded. "I have been wrong about him before." *He better not slither his way out of this one too.*

"What is obvious is that someone is murdering people in the name of some god, and has been for a while now," Little Reed went on. "We should look through the missing persons reported to the city registrar; perhaps we can identify some of the dead and alert their families. But first, I want to see this mass grave."

I rose to my feet. "As do I."

Mazatzin rose too—paying respect to my social position—but added, "I should warn you that the scene is quite gruesome, My Lady."

"I can't imagine it's any worse than what we saw in Quetzalcoatl's temple after my uncle spent twenty years defiling it," I said with an unintended snap. Mazatzin bowed his head, looking shamed, but I gave his hand a reassuring squeeze. "But thank you for the warning. I appreciate your concern."

Little Reed rose too. "We'll meet in the Hall of the Gods by the next hourly bell. That should give us ample time to dress and locate someone to watch Yamehecatl while we're gone."

I returned to my quarters and dressed in one of my longer, heavier priestly robes; the nights were getting colder as the winter season approached. I ran a brush through my hair but didn't bother fixing it, opting instead to put on a hooded cloak, to protect my ears from the wind.

Little Reed waited outside on the portico and we walked to the Hall of the Gods together. "We should keep all this quiet for now," he said. "We don't want to scare the culprits into hiding. Let them think we're unaware."

"How are we to keep the farmer quiet?"

"I'll discuss it with him. He won't want his son's murderer disappearing without facing justice."

"We need to make certain we act quickly and decisively."

He nodded. "It would be useful if we had someone trusted inside Smoking Mirror's cult. Do you know the high priestess well?"

"We don't talk much, so no." If anything, I avoided her; inexplicably, she made my skin crawl.

When we reached the Hall of the Gods, Citlallotoc came in through the front gate followed by his guards, looking bedraggled. He'd been away for a month, visiting our allied cities and collecting their issues and concerns to bring before us. He smiled when he saw us. "Greetings, My Lord and Lady." He gave us a sweeping bow.

Little Reed embraced him with a hearty hug. "Welcome back. We weren't expecting you for another week at least." Once Little Reed finished, I granted Citlallotoc the same token, but had to stand on my tiptoes to reach his neck even as he bent over.

Citlallotoc unslung his pack. "You'll be happy to know I bring only good news from our allies. All is well throughout the empire."

"If only I could report the same here." Little Reed quickly filled him in on tonight's grim discovery.

Citlallotoc handed his bag off to one of his guards. "Let us go and see the scene then."

"Certainly you're weary from your journey," I said.

"Justice within the city is my purview, My Lady. And after hearing only domestic cases most days, this is an exciting change."

◻

Crime was rarely an issue in Tollan since we'd started providing free food to anyone who needed it. Theft and crimes of desperation were few and far between these days, and violent crime was almost nonexistent. With the years, Chichimecs and Toltecas slowly learned to live together in a semblance of peace, especially the younger generation who attended school together and learned to speak both Tolteca and Chichimec.

And because of Tollan's decidedly anti-war stance, we didn't have a "war council", and we'd changed Citlallotoc's title to "Justice of the Peace". Instead of planning and strategizing war for us, he now negotiated and maintained peace between our neighbors and allied states, and fostered Tollan's internal peace by acting as the city's magistrate. He listened to cases of land boundary disputes, missing livestock, or issues of offended honor. There hadn't been a murder trial for over a year now; it was so rare an occurrence that both Little Reed and I had sat in on that occasion and had been the ones to hand down the sentence of exile. There were no capital crimes under Tollan's laws.

In light of this newest mystery, Citlallotoc forgot any fatigue from his trip and walked with purpose down the trail leading into the forest. Guards greeted us inside the trees and one of them led us through the underbrush to a small clearing blanketed with leaves, in the middle of which lay a triangular stack of logs. More guards held torches, bringing the scene to late-afternoon brightness.

The royal surgeon hunched in the center of the peculiar log formation, muttering to himself. Behind him, lined up one next to the other, were at least a dozen bodies, all covered with blankets. When Citlallotoc called to the surgeon, he hurried over and bowed, brushing his dirty hands off on his cloak. He took Little Reed and Citlallotoc to see the bodies.

I circled the clearing, taking in the rest of the scene. Tension formed in my shoulders and the hairs on my neck stood upright, as if something powerful lurked nearby. The whole area reeked of dark magic; the ground throbbed with it, much the way Quetzalcoatl's temple in Culhuacan had when I'd first stepped into it after so many years. A dark memory clung to this place, a thousand screams of lives lost, families destroyed; and underneath it all, the ground pulsed with a sinister laugh. I shivered.

But there wasn't any outward signs of ritual sacrifice here; no blood-stained stone, no sacred markings carved into the trees, only leaves, logs, and trees. *Ozomatli must have used the logs in place of the sacrificial stone,* I decided, stepping closer to the log formation. The rounded shape was effective for expanding the chest for the incision. The ground in the middle was muddy and smelled of stale blood mixed with pungent earth. Despite my best efforts to suppress the rumbling in my stomach, I started salivating and had to step away. My reaction to such things had only grown stronger since learning I could rejuvenate my magic by drinking blood.

The feeling of being watched intensified and I squinted into the darkness beyond the torchlight, unsettled. Numerous guards cluttered the periphery, oblivious to the oppressive air. The preternatural whisper of *Mine! Mine! Mine!* played on the breeze. Chills raced up my back.

Someone touched my shoulder and I jumped. "I'm sorry, I didn't mean to frighten you," Little Reed said, looking guilty.

I shook my head and rubbed the raised flesh on my arms under my robe sleeves. "It's all right. This place is...." I looked around a moment, hearing the whispering again. "Do you hear that?"

Little Reed called for silence, but after a moment of listening, he shook his head. "What do you hear?"

I listened again, but I didn't hear it either. In the past we'd shared experiences of the divine in ways unnatural to normal human beings, so if he couldn't hear it, it must have been my imagination. "I thought I heard someone whispering, but it was probably the wind."

He too scanned the dark beyond the trees, letting his gaze linger.

"You examined the bodies?" I asked, eager to change the subject.

He nodded. "It's as we suspected; the hearts are missing. The burying is unusual though; sacrifices are only buried when one intends to construct a temple, to make the ground sacred to a given god."

"Someone's building a temple here?" That idea had Mextli's feathers all over it.

"We'd definitely notice a new temple," Little Reed said. "Instead, they're treating this area as if it's already a temple. Come, look at this."

I followed Little Reed over to the pit where the bodies had been buried. He bent next to one of the logs and pointed to scorch marks in the rotting bark. "Someone burned something here, on a round object."

I bent for a closer look, and when I rubbed the ash between my fingers, I detected the faint odor of burnt tobacco. "Smoking Mirror's followers burn tobacco on an obsidian mirror," I pointed out. When Little Reed nodded, I added, "Ozomatli put in a requisition for a new obsidian mirror this morning. He claims one of his priests broke it, but I'd bet he broke it himself, out here."

"Perhaps, but that's not what concerns me."

I furrowed my brow. "Then what does?"

"There's no idol."

"He takes it with him. It would look suspicious to leave it out here for anyone to find."

"The idol would have to be large enough to place a human heart inside of it, and it would look suspicious lugging a large stone idol back and forth between the city and the forest. Someone would have seen it. And one man alone couldn't carry it on his own. It takes six strong men to move Quetzalcoatl's idol."

"But there was a second person; he knocked out the farmer from behind." Someone Mextli's size could heft a boulder onto his shoulders without sweating.

"All true, but there's no evidence that a heavy stone statue sat on the ground anywhere here, even for a short time; no indentations, no scrapes, nothing."

His determination to chew this bone exasperated me. "What does it matter if there's no idol?"

"The idol is the conduit between this world and the divine realm, to feed the sacrifices to the god it represents. If there's no conduit, one of two things is happening: the god is already in corporeal form and is being fed directly—"

"Smoking Mirror is walking around Tollan as we speak?" The hairs on my neck stood up again.

"It's possible, of course, but I doubt it. What did he do the last time someone summoned him?"

"He came as a giant smoking jaguar and he tried to kill you."

"Exactly. If he was corporeal, he would have attacked already; not to mention that we would have heard it happen. Remember how loud it was whenever you summoned Quetzalcoatl, or when Ihuitimal summoned Smoking Mirror at Culhuacan? This close to the city, we definitely would have heard it."

I nodded. "So what's the other option?"

"Someone is attempting to summon Smoking Mirror, and has failed twelve times."

Visions of that giant smoking jaguar tearing through Tollan, searching for me and Little Reed, made the magic roil in my belly. If Ozomatli succeeded, I'd have to call on Quetzalcoatl to fight Smoking Mirror again.

And the only thing I had left to sacrifice was my son.

I said, "We must stop Ozomatli before he tries a thirteenth time."

◻

I wanted Ozomatli arrested immediately, but Little Reed disagreed. "We need to proceed carefully and discreetly. We don't know that Ozomatli is the one behind this, and if he isn't, we risk sending the real culprit into hiding, and we lose the chance to give justice to the victims' families."

I grudgingly agreed, but I lay awake the rest of the night, thinking of ways to catch Ozomatli at his duplicity.

By dawn, Yamehecatl was up and begging me to dress him in his rabbit suit; he could dress himself, but he'd taken to mimicking the other noble children and insisted a servant do it for him. And for now, that servant was me.

"I'm going to be the king one day, and kings don't dress themselves," he declared.

"Your father does." I'd convinced him to at least slip into the outfit himself, but he still struggled with tying knots so I helped out there.

"That's because he only ever wears that ratty white robe," Yamehecatl insisted. "I'm going to dress so elaborately that I'll need an army of servants to dress me every day."

I laughed. "Why would you want that?"

"So everyone will look at me when I'm talking to them. Everyone ignores me when I talk now."

"I don't ignore you. Nor does your father or Citlallotoc."

He scoffed. "That's because you're my family. I'm talking about all those noble boys who pretend I'm not even there when I ask them questions; someday I'll be their king and I can't have them ignoring me, so I need to wear things that will make them want to pay attention to me."

"If all you worry about is wearing beautiful clothing, they will pay attention only to your dress, not to you," I told him. "If you wish them to truly pay attention to you, speak with wisdom and understanding; give them a good reason to listen to you. Your father dresses plainly and yet when he speaks, everyone listens because what he says is important."

Yamehecatl sighed. "I wish I could speak as well as Tatli, but I can't, so I need better clothing."

"You don't need better clothes; you need time to grow wise, and to find better friends than those noble boys."

This time Yamehecatl nodded. "Like Night Wind. *He* gets me, Nantli. Can you fetch him to the palace, so we can play today?"

"He's in school."

He frowned but nodded. "I want to go to school with him, Nantli."

"Night Wind goes to the telpochcalli, and as the prince, you can't go there."

"Why not?"

"Because a prince needs to know how to read and write, and you'll only learn that in the calmecac."

"I don't want to go to the calmecac!"

"A good king knows how to honor the gods for the good of his kingdom."

"I don't care about honoring the gods," Yamehecatl said, growing increasingly vexed. "Why should I anyway? What makes them so special?"

I suppressed the urge to lecture him about blasphemy and respect. When his own mother used magic, why wouldn't he question the usefulness of gods who exercised their own power in vague ways? "Because we owe them our honor, Yamehecatl. They created the world for us by their own deaths, and Quetzalcoatl made painful sacrifices to give us life. Remember all the trials he endured to rescue the bones of our ancestors from Lord Death?"

"I suppose that's something," Yamehecatl conceded with a grumble. "Still, I want to go to the telpochcalli, not the calmecac. I'm not sticking thorns in my tepolli as Tatli does." He shielded his groin as if I'd threatened to prick him with the rope of thorns I kept in my pocket.

I sighed. "Sometimes we have to do things we don't want to because we have obligations."

He balled his fists and stomped. "I won't go to the calmecac, and you can't make me!" Already I smelled the first hints of octli in the air.

But suddenly Citlallotoc pushed aside the curtain and poked his head in. "What's all this noise I'm hearing?" he asked, innocently surprised; his tactic for defusing Yamehecatl when he began getting out of hand.

Yamehecatl pushed past me and latched himself around Citlallotoc's legs. "You're home!"

Laughing, Citlallotoc hefted him up with his one good arm. "I'm surprised you even noticed I was gone."

"Of course I noticed!" Yamehecatl crowed. "I missed you!"

"Why? Did you throw something at me?" Citlallotoc grinned when Yamehecatl giggled at their private joke. "And I missed you, little man. I look forward to the day when you're old enough to come on these confounded trips with me; everyone else is so average with their swordplay, and I don't find them a challenge at all."

"I've been practicing! Let's go to the exercise yard, so I can show you my new moves!"

"Not until you've filled your belly, little warrior." He set Yamehecatl down and crouched in front of him. "And I have some inquiries to make around town—criminals to investigate, spies to unmask, monsters to slay, those kinds of things—but I will be back before lunch and I'm expecting you to be ready to meet swords at that time. You have until then to prepare yourself. And you'd better prepare well, for I intend to show no mercy."

Yamehecatl bounced up and down, giddy. "I'll be ready, I promise!" He wrapped his small arms around Citlallotoc's neck and squeezed, trying to show off his strength. He always saved his fiercest hugs for him.

Why can't it always be that easy for me? I wondered, frustrated. By comparison, our relationship was rocky and contentious. I knew Yamehecatl loved me, but why did he question everything I told him, while always doing whatever Citlallotoc told him to, no questions asked? I supposed that was the lot of a mother; I'd tested my own mother's patience more than once, and I cringed to think of some of the things I'd said to Nimilitzli in the heat of anger.

But at least Yamehecatl had two good men to admire and learn honor and nobility from.

□

After breakfast, Citlallotoc left to snoop around the sacred precinct and watch some of Smoking Mirror's priests, looking for leads. Little Reed went to speak with Ozomatli; I wanted to go with him, so I could interogate the dog, but Little Reed insisted he conduct the questioning himself. "If I can be frank, my love, when it comes to Ozomatli...you have a hard time keeping an open mind. While I vehemently disapprove of his poisoning Ihuitimal to depose him—if he indeed was doing so—whatever proof we might have had is long gone, and short of him confessing to it, there's nothing we can do about it."

"To Mictlan with Ihuitimal; what about him trying to get you to kill our cousin?" I spat.

"He did put him into my hands, but that was a good thing; even Amoxtli himself says so. Whatever Ozomatli hoped to accomplish by that, he alone knows; and again, short of a confession, what are we to do? Put him on trial for betraying the illegitimate king?"

Arguing such things always fatigued me, but even more so today, after so little sleep. Once Little Reed left, I retired to the patio in our family garden to sit down to some weaving.

Yamehecatl sat on the portico in front of his nursery doorway, half of his toys dragged out onto the flagstones, and his dramatic mutterings and imitations of animal sounds blended well with the drone of bees and cicadas, letting some of the day's worries slowly unwind from my shoulders. A breeding pair of quetzals had carved a nest hole in one of the copal trees, and despite this year's young having already left, the parents had stayed behind, fattening themselves on the fruit the servants left out for them every day. I'd brought some melon from breakfast, hoping they'd come down from the tree so I might watch them eat, but they stayed up in the branches, filling the morning air with their melodious *kyow! Kyow! Kyow!*

I'd finally settled my mind and found my focus, but then one of my personal guards came from the hallway. "Lord Citlallotoc wishes to see you in the great hall, My Lady."

"Citlallotoc is back?" Yamehecatl asked, springing to his feet.

If that was the case, he would have come instead of sending for me. I motioned to Yamehecatl's nurse as I stood, and she stepped out of his doorway where she'd been lurking, in case I needed her. "Nelli will watch you while I'm gone, so be on your best behavior," I told my son.

Yamehecatl kicked aside a wooden coyote on wheels but settled back down, resting his head on one hand while he fiddled with a carved warrior, his maize-leaf rabbit ears dangling over his brow.

I followed the guard to the great hall to find Citlallotoc pacing. Black Otter was with him, surrounded by four guards and looking terrified. He clutched a buckskin bag to his chest. "Forgive my interruption, My Lady, but I was in the sacred precinct and look who I found skulking about near the temple." He grabbed Black Otter by the shoulder then shoved him forward, so he tumbled to his knees on the flagstones. He drew his sword with the ease of someone who always had been left-handed. "Shall I carry out his death sentence now?"

I grabbed the handle of the sword, my heart hammering. "Gods no! It's all right; we know Black Otter is here and we've agreed to waive his exile. Forgive me for not informing you of this right away."

Citlallotoc scowled but put his sword away before helping Black Otter back to his feet. "My apologies for being unduly rough with you," he mumbled.

Black Otter shrugged but kept his eyes downcast, like a dog anticipating his master's whip. "I'm not hurt, My Lord."

Noticing him clutching the bag a little tighter now, I asked him, "What were you doing in the sacred precinct?"

"I went to visit my brother before going to work." He darted a nervous glance at me. "He asked me to meet him for lunch today and I wanted to make certain I knew where to go, since my new employer carefully monitors my time during the day."

"And what's in the bag?"

He looked at it as if he'd forgotten about it. "Oh, it's a gift for the temple. I've decided I should start tithing a portion of my income to the order." He opened the bag and produced an obsidian blade. "I made it myself, at work. I was planning to give it to Amoxtli to give to the Temple of the Smoking Mirror, since he's a priest, after all."

A wave of suspicion swept over me but I reminded myself that here in Tollan we didn't tell anyone which god they should devote themselves to, so long as said worship respected the laws of the city. Still, I couldn't keep the sharpness from my voice as I said, "Amoxtli is a priest of Quetzalcoatl, not of the Smoking Mirror."

Black Otter stood a little straighter, surprised. "Well, he was always the more independently-minded of the two of us...and undoubtedly would have been a better king than I would have." He fidgeted. "Will my choosing to resume worshiping Tezcatlipoca make you reconsider my exile, My Lady? Let me reassure you that I will not engage in any of the prohibited methods of worship; I will give my prayers and burn the tobacco as

I used to, but nothing more. I'm relieved to have finally put those days behind me when I was expected to take my father's place as the next high priest; as I told you before, that was a life I never wanted to begin with."

I nodded. "I'm sorry for your detainment. Topiltzin and I should have made the reversal of your exile public knowledge. I'll make certain that an official announcement is made at this evening's public services, so this never happens again."

"I thank you, My Lady." Black Otter returned the blade to his buckskin bag.

"Let me keep you no further. I'm certain you're eager to deliver that fine obsidian spearhead to the high priest of Smoking Mirror. His name is Ozomatli, and you can probably find him at the calmecac."

Black Otter looked up sharply. "Ozomatli? My father's former fire priest?"

I tilted my head, my interest piqued. "Yes, that's him. Is something the matter?" I tried not to sound overeager.

"I'm surprised; he was quite close with my father, one of his most loyal supporters in the priesthood, but I was never very comfortable with him. My father respected the god's power, but Ozomatli...he constantly pestered my father to train him to be the next high priest of the Smoking Mirror, saying I wasn't made for the job. He begged my father to teach him the secret knowledge the god had taught him in the desert, but my father refused, saying he'd share it only with those the god deemed worthy."

"And what did Ozomatli think of that?"

"He tried to convince me to teach him what I knew, so he could better serve me when I was king. Naturally, I refused. I suppose he also tried to manipulate information from Amoxtli, but my father wasn't far into training him, so he probably didn't know anything useful. Ozomatli continued beating that particular drum all the way up to my father's death, so he got his wish to be the new high priest."

This sounded full of possibilities to help us with our current troubles, but I needed to talk it over with Little Reed before going any further. "Perhaps you should allow me to deliver the blade for you," I suggested.

Black Otter handed me the bag. "Actually, maybe it should go to the Feathered Serpent's cult. I don't know if it's an acceptable gift, but it's what I have to give, and perhaps it's best to put all of the past behind and start over anew, with a new god and a new outlook."

"We don't require that of you at all, Black Otter," I reminded him. "But the god accepts your gift and thanks you." I fingered the obsidian blade through the bag as I watched him go, Citlallotoc leading him out. I hissed when I pressed too hard and the blade sliced through the hide and cut my finger. "But your future might depend on you keeping some of that past in the present, at least for surface appearances, Cousin," I muttered under my breath.

✿

Once Citlallotoc returned to take Yamehecatl to the exercise yard for their afternoon weapons lesson, I went to the sacred precinct looking for Little Reed. I found him in the calmecac courtyard with a group of our youngest students gathered around the cistern, telling them the story of Quetzalcoatl and Mayahuel, for today was the beginning of the Maguey Goddess's festival. Each child wore a rabbit, a monkey, or a maguey flower mask they'd made themselves in class, as part of the celebration.

I'd never heard Little Reed tell the Mayahuel story. He did different voices as usual, but this one lacked the joy and excitement he usually brought to Quetzalcoatl's stories.

The young ones gasped when he described the Earth Monster destroying Mayahuel, and a few even cried when Quetzalcoatl buried her remains. The more times I heard the story, the more it depressed me.

Little Reed knelt and beckoned everyone closer. "Mayahuel's story is tragic, but out of it came something truly important, something that makes us all very happy. Can you tell me what that is?"

"Octli!" the children shouted.

Little Reed shook his head. "Something else."

I shared the children's puzzlement as they looked at each other and whispered. "The maguey plant?" a boy asked.

"Yes, she gave us that, and octli; but most importantly, she gave us love. For on the tree she and Quetzalcoatl created in Tamoachan bloomed flowers whose fragrance brought love into the hearts of everyone. And that is the greatest gift Mayahuel brought to us." When he noticed me listening from the far side of the cistern, he smiled, melting me inside. "For the next week, while we celebrate the Maguey Goddess and honor her for all she's given us, think about how different our world would be if not for her greatest gift."

After the priests and priestesses led the children back inside the calmecac, Little Reed came to me. "I thought you were spending the afternoon with Yamehecatl."

"He'd rather spend it with Citlallotoc, of course," I said with mock offense.

Little Reed laughed. "Well, Citlallotoc has been gone for a whole month." He took my arm and started walking with me.

"Is that always how you tell that story?" I asked as we walked towards the priestly gardens. "That's not exactly how we were taught it in calmecac."

He shrugged. "Perhaps my father has told me a different version."

"Except that it makes it all the more tragic."

"I suppose. But certainly you didn't come here to listen to me tell the children stories."

"No. I had an idea about how we might flush out our renegade priest. Have you met with Ozomatli yet?"

"Not yet."

"Good. I spoke to Black Otter this morning and he told me—"

"You spoke to Black Otter? Why?"

I'd never known Little Reed to be insecure, so the edge to his voice took me by surprise. And irritated me. "We didn't tell Citlallotoc we overturned his exile, so when he saw Black Otter in the sacred precinct this morning, he arrested him and brought him to me for sentencing. I promised Black Otter we'd announce the rescinding of his exile today so that this doesn't happen again."

Little Reed nodded, chastened. "I'll be certain to do so this afternoon at the temple service. So, what did he tell you?"

"When I mentioned that Ozomatli was our high priest of the Smoking Mirror, he had much to say, and not much of it positive. Ozomatli was open about his ambitions to be the next high priest, even going so far as to beg Ihuitimal to tell him the secrets he'd learned about the god in the desert—secrets such as how to summon Smoking Mirror—but Ihuitimal refused to teach such things to anyone but his own sons."

"That would give Ozomatli motive to dispose of Ihuitimal," Little Reed conceded. After we walked through the gate into the privacy of the gardens, he went on, "How do you suggest we use this new information?"

"We have Black Otter join Smoking Mirror's order, and because his father taught him those secrets, maybe he'll be able to draw Ozomatli out with the promise of finally getting the knowledge he needs to actually summon Smoking Mirror."

"We don't know that Ozomatli is the true conspirator," Little Reed reminded me.

I shrugged. "Either way, we dangle Black Otter as bait, and whoever is doing it won't be able to resist, especially after so much failure."

"This could work, and we were searching for a means for him to prove his loyalty." He nodded. "Excellent idea, Papalotl. I shall speak with him about it."

"I should be the one to talk to him. You barely know him whereas he and I spent our earliest years as friends, and we were married and shared a bed...." My cheeks blazed, but I quickly made myself go on. "He will be more comfortable talking to me about it." *And we know how to get him to do what we want,* the desire cackled but I bit my tongue. That wouldn't sound proper at all.

Little Reed hesitated, still uncertain, but eventually he nodded. "Fine. You speak with Black Otter. I will let Ozomatli know that our cousin will be joining his ranks soon."

CHAPTER TWENTY

Little Reed wanted me to summon Black Otter back to the palace later that same day, to discuss the job under the watchful gaze of the guards, but the rebellious part of me scoffed. Besides, Ozomatli might have spies watching the palace and if Black Otter kept showing up, he might suspect deception. Instead, I waited until after the work day's ending bell, then I put on a priestly robe and a festival mask. My formal one was gold and silver, in the shape of a maguey flower, but I didn't want to be recognized out among the people, so I borrowed the paper rabbit mask I made with my son last week.

The palace guards wouldn't let me walk the halls with a mask on, and I didn't want them coming with me, so I packed it into a bag and went out into my private garden. A doorway in the back wall led into an open-air passage, similar to the one in Culhuacan, only this one led to the priestly gardens. Guards still manned the corners—to keep unauthorized persons from coming in from the gardens—but once I closed the final gate behind me, I didn't have to worry. I slipped on the mask and followed the path towards the main gate.

Some way down the winding path through the trees and shrubs, I heard women's voices up ahead, near the large secluded pond where Quetzalcoatl and I had made love in the grass. I hid behind a large oak tree that blocked the view of the path and peered around the side.

Malinalli and Mitotia sat next to the pond, both of their backs to me as they ate tlaxcallis and talked. I knew Malinalli didn't have priestly duties today—it was her rest day—so I found it curious she would be out here, sharing dinner with a lower-ranking priestess. Their idle chatter soon turned into laughter, and they leaned their heads together, giggling like young girls over a secret. But it soon faded into a silence rife with tension as they looked at each other....

Like when you look at Little Reed. Suddenly everything I'd said to Malinalli yesterday punched me in the chest. How many times had I thrown around "he" when asking who was making her so happy? I'd been so careless, so full of assumption. What kind of a best friend was I to not know this about her?

All of those dismissed hints made sense now—how uncomfortable she was when we talked about men and marriage and children, as if that was what women and girls were supposed to talk about. Or those distant looks she used to give me when we were younger—the kind of looks I always garnered from men but chose to ignore as meaningless in my best friend. And there was that time in the garden, with Black Otter, when I'd nearly asked her to join us in my bed....

Even the desire knew, you idiot, I scolded myself. No wonder she was hesitant to tell me. We'd grown up learning that such impulses were unnatural and unlawful; codes in both Xochicalco and Culhuacan had strictly forbidden such relationships, and one could have been sent to the sacrifice as a criminal for acting upon them. And though Tollan had no strict rules against same-sex coupling, the general sentiment in the streets was that it was an abomination against the gods; last year's murder had been of a young man stoned to death by a mob of angry noblemen when his lover's father caught him with his son, so I understood her desire to keep quiet.

But certainly she didn't think I would turn on her for this? *I should have seen it, and been supportive, and maybe she wouldn't have felt it better to hide the truth from me. She's always listened and supported me, but I haven't done the same for her.*

I pushed back my mask to wipe the tears clouding my eyes. For years now Malinalli had seemed unhappy, haunted by an emptiness that I'd always assumed she'd fill once she found the right man, so at least I wasn't completely out of touch with her emotions. And I was exceedingly happy she'd found someone who made her laugh, and feel not so alone.

I slipped the mask back over my face and hurried up the path, treading as quietly as possible so as not to draw their attention.

◻

The smell of frying maize and roasting chile peppers filled the crowded, muddy streets outside the city wall. The noise was loud but joyous, children shrieking in delight as they greeted their fathers or mothers returning from the fields or the market. The old men played patolli and sipped cups of octli—a privilege they'd earned with their many years of life—while mothers barked at their children to come to dinner. Somewhere a flute kept time with a drum. It had been a very long time since I'd been out in the city alone, and the crush of bodies moving every direction unnerved me until I was confident my disguise was effective.

Most of the people living outside the city walls were Chichimec, but what they lacked in wealth they made up for in community. Priests of various Chichimec gods went around to the houses, delivering fabric or food, and neighbors helped mend crumbling stucco facades on each other's homes. A few tussles broke out over patolli games, and young women with their teeth dyed red with cochineal lingered at street corners, their high-cut dresses announcing sexual services for the right price. Definitely not the refined palace culture I was used to, but it also made my daily life seem predictable and shallow.

I wound through the crowd, hoping I'd see Black Otter, but with so many people living in close quarters, I would be there for hours trying to find him. I could ask someone, but what if they recognized my voice?

But then I saw Black Otter's daughter Cuicatl come out of one of the side streets, a duck carcass slung over one shoulder and a bag of masa over the other. I hurried and stepped in front of her, so that she had to stop. "I'm looking for your father."

She stepped back, fear in her eyes until I bent closer and lifted the mask enough to show her my face. "You know who I am?"

"I do, My Lady." She tried to bow, but I stopped her.

"No bowing. I don't want to draw undue attention."

"Sorry, My Lady."

"I need to speak with your father. Will you take me to your house?"

She inclined her head to the right and led the way when I motioned her to do so.

I followed her down several side streets until we were one row of houses away from the fields. The houses this far out were small but still constructed of stone and plaster; we provided warm, sturdy housing built by the city's stonemasons for everyone regardless of economic status, and city workers whitewashed every new house to give residents a clean canvas to decorate their exterior walls with designs and murals of their own choosing. Eagles and coyotes were particularly popular. Black Otter's house was plain white, with a log for beekeeping hung from the eaves over the front door. A heavy reed mat hanging across the door kept the wind and bees outside.

Black Otter sat next to the hearth, tying a new obsidian blade to a worn handle. He smiled, until he saw his daughter wasn't alone. Night Wind sat against the wall, looking bored, but his expression turned to curiosity when he saw my rabbit mask.

"Who have you brought home with you, Cuicatl?" Black Otter gripped the half-finished knife tighter than before.

I pulled off the mask. "It's me, Black Otter."

"What are you doing here?" He looked towards the doorway, as if expecting guards to come in too. "And why are you wearing a mask?"

"I've come on behalf of the kingdom to ask something of you. Can I speak to you in private?"

He hesitated before telling Cuicatl, "Take Night Wind to the cistern and fill the water jars while Lady Quetzalpetlatl and I talk."

Cuicatl rolled her eyes and dropped the bag of masa to the floor. She tossed the duck into her father's lap. "Let's go," she told Night Wind, grabbing his hand and dragging him out of the door.

Black Otter hung the duck from a hook on the wall. "Please forgive Cuicatl's temper. Losing her mother has been hard on her."

That wasn't a road I wanted to explore with him, so I moved immediately to the point of my visit. "Topiltzin and I need you to do something for us."

"Whatever I can do."

"We want you to join Smoking Mirror's cult here in Tollan."

Black Otter blinked at me, taken aback. "But, My Lady—"

"I know that's not the life you wanted, despite your father's insistences, but you know useful things that could help us solve a mystery and bring justice to a dozen murder victims."

"Murder victims?"

"We found a mass burial site not far outside town and it bears all the markings of Smoking Mirror's cult. We believe that one of the priests is trying to summon the Smoking Mirror."

Black Otter went back to tying on his blade, uneasy. "That is serious. Who is your suspect?"

"Ozomatli. And given everything you told me this morning, he's even higher on our list now. So far he hasn't succeeded in summoning anything, but he's certainly not giving up. We must put an end to this, before more people are murdered—or, worse yet, he actually succeeds."

"But how would my joining the priesthood help in any of this?"

"Because he'll want you to share your knowledge of the Smoking Mirror and his secrets, so he can finally complete this ritual properly."

Furrowing his brow, he asked, "You want me to show him the proper ritual for summoning the god to corporeal form?"

"Of course not. We can't let it go so far. But you'll need to earn his trust and convince him that you're open to the possibility of sharing. Tell him you're seeking revenge for your father."

Black Otter chewed his lip, debating. "So you want me to pretend to conspire against you and Topiltzin?" When I nodded, he said, "And I suppose that your coming here today is a courtesy, not a request."

"Let's say that your doing this will go a long way to rebuilding trust between us again," I said.

He stared at me with veiled annoyance. "Then I graciously accept this mission from yourself and the King."

"Topiltzin will be most happy to hear it. Rest assured you're doing the right thing."

"I hope this doesn't see me joining Jade Flower on the road into Mictlan. The children have lost so much already."

Smirking, I said, "It takes more than mere arrows or knives to kill you, Black Otter. It's obvious you have the gods on your side."

He tried to laugh but it came out awkward.

"Do well on this task, and your future will be bright again. It would be nice to have an actual blood relative back on the throne in Culhuacan, don't you think?"

Black Otter wrung his hands. "That's a generous thought, My Lady, but those days are far behind me now. My father's name is a curse in many cities, but none so much as in Culhuacan. If I did return—even with your's and Topiltzin's blessing—many would never accept me as their ruler, even if it's merely as a governor."

"Regardless, know you will be handsomely rewarded for your efforts. That is a promise." I slipped the mask back on and added, "At the very least, you'll get your noble title back and won't have to live out here anymore."

"It's not so bad out here. There's something freeing about not being followed everywhere you go."

"Indeed there is," I muttered. "Tomorrow morning, come by the calmecac and see Topiltzin. He'll officially name a position for you in Smoking Mirror's priesthood." I ducked out of the door, leaving the thick reed mat swaying in the growing dusk.

CHAPTER TWENTY-ONE

Black Otter reported to us every couple of days, filling in the details of his efforts to ingratiate himself with Ozomatli, which seemed to be going well. Within the first week, he'd supplanted the fire priest in Ozomatli's confidences, and by the second week, even the high priestess was pushing for him to take over the position. Several times I caught her watching him from afar with the infatuated look of a young girl; when I teased him about it, he reddened and mumbled about how he had no time for such things.

We always met in Little Reed's quarters, so there was no chance of Ozomatli walking in on us. Black Otter brought Night Wind with him, so he and Yamehecatl could play out in the garden while we talked; our meetings often lasted a couple of hours, and since the boys were inseparable, it was easier to let Yamehecatl run himself to exhaustion. I thought it would be uncomfortable spending so much time with Black Otter again, but instead it felt as if this was how things should be, with family all together again.

But not long after Night Wind and Yamehecatl became friends, I started worrying about the kind of influence Night Wind exerted over my son.

Little Reed and I began to talk again about enrolling Yamehecatl in calmecac, and decided we could start sending him there for a couple of hours a day. But when I told Yamehecatl, he said, "I don't want to go to school anymore, Nantli. Night Wind says it's a waste of time."

That struck me as odd; Black Otter had been quite proud when the teachers at the telpochcalli suggested moving Night Wind up to the calmecac. I heard nothing negative about the boy from the other priests, just that he was intense and quiet but always knew the answers when asked.

"Why would he say such a thing?" I asked, puzzled.

Yamehecatl shrugged. "He says they teach pointless things that I'm not going to need at all when I grow up."

Well, Night Wind must not be as intelligent as I thought. "Or maybe he knows that you're cleverer than him and he doesn't want you showing him up in class. You're going to school, regardless."

"So I will be in school with Night Wind?" When I nodded, he perked up. "Can I start tomorrow? Please, please, please!" My boy's temperament was so fickle.

I suppose every mother worries about her child the first time they go off to school, but I was so nervous I couldn't eat breakfast or lunch. I expected someone to come and tell me that I had to take him home because someone claimed he'd gotten into the sacred octli or that he was uncontrollable. But instead he came home bubbling with stories. He couldn't wait to go back, and asked when he could move into the dormitories with Night Wind and the other boys.

"Everyone eats and sleeps together, and everyone knows so much, Nantli! Much more than those stone-headed noble boys who live here in the palace. And the priests don't talk to me as if I'm a baby. When can I move into the dormitories, Nantli? When? Please!"

I laughed. "It's only your first day, my dear. And you've only attended for a few hours. When you're a full-time student, you have daily duties, such as gathering copal wood from the grove, or trapping snakes and butterflies for the sacrifice. When I was in calmecac, the girls used to do all the sweeping and cleaning, but now the boys do that too, and trust me, there's nothing more mind-numbing than sweeping the temple floor day in and day out."

My warnings had little effect on his opinion though. He begged day after day for us to put him into school full time, but I resisted. A mother got to hold her children close for only so long, and Yamehecatl hadn't even reached his fifth summer yet. He might share Little Reed's accelerated mental growth, but he was still small enough for me to carry in my arms—with some difficulty, admittedly. As long as I could do that, he was still too young to be sent off to school full-time. The day would come when I'd have to let him go—maybe next year—but not now.

◻

At any given time, there were numerous students working in the temples or the kitchens, doing their chores, and while it wasn't often that I had the job of watching over them, I did occasionally find myself in the temple with one or more students. Today, when I walked in, Night Wind was at the Feathered Serpent's idol, cleaning the splattered blood and dirt from around the mouth and base.

He didn't make a sound, as intense in his work as he was in everything else, but eventually he looked over at me, a nominally curious expression on his face. It was customary for others to bow when I entered a room—even in my capacity as High Priestess—but he remained knelt on the floor, still rubbing the cloth over the idol while he casually watched me walk around, determining the cleanliness of the temple. I could have chided him for his lack of attention to protocol, but he'd done an excellent job of cleaning, so I ignored the oversight.

I stepped up next to him, watching him scrub for a moment before saying, "Quite fine work, Night Wind."

"Thank you, My Lady." He bowed this time, still on his knees, but with hands out at his sides, so his head nearly touched the ground. "You're most gracious."

"I believe in pointing out the good wherever I see it. Tell me, how do you find the calmecac? Are you settling in well?"

"Well enough." He went back to work. He was a boy of few words, it seemed.

I asked him to work on the other side of the idol for now, so I could do my daily offering. He moved without argument.

I knelt on the reed mat in front of the idol and did my normal routine, bleeding my tongue with the rope and maguey thorns, praying aloud over the blood bowl before tipping the contents into the idol's open mouth. But as I started settling in for silent prayers, I noticed Night Wind watching me. "Yes?"

"Why do you still honor him, after everything he did?"

Furrowing my brow, I asked, "Why would I...what?"

"Why do you still worship Quetzalcoatl when he killed your mother, and your father?"

I gaped at him, a wave of fury rising inside me. "Why would you ask me such a thing?"

"But isn't it true that the Feathered Serpent put the King in your mother's belly and that killed her?" He gazed at me with innocent curiosity, as if he didn't understand why I was so upset. "Aren't you angry about that?"

Why you slimy little— The magic rushed to my fingers but I caught myself. Would I really strike out at a child? The rage brimmed just inside my consciousness, a kind of pulsing that matched my heartbeat, making the world vibrate. I breathed deep to steady myself. *Be careful lest those powers cause you regrets.* "Did your father tell you that?" I carefully modulated my voice so not to scare the boy.

Night Wind shook his head. "He doesn't talk about grandfather, or the others. Ozomatli said it the other day when I was cleaning the temple of Smoking Mirror. He thinks I don't listen when I'm working, but I always do; it makes the work go faster."

Who would have thought a small boy could be such an effective spy? "What else did he say?"

"That if not for the Feathered Serpent, my grandfather wouldn't have killed your father, and that it would have spared many lives in the war that came after."

"Or maybe even more lives would have been lost, sacrificed in temples in honor of that honorless Smoking Mirror," I countered. "There are many what-if games one can play about many things, but it doesn't mean that what happen wasn't for the best, regardless of the sacrifices that came with it. Everyone makes sacrifices."

"Not the gods," he said.

"Of course the gods make sacrifices. Quetzalcoatl gave his own blood so we might live—"

"Yes, but that was so long ago."

"It's a debt we can never fully repay."

He nodded. "So, the god is like my sister, who once saved me from falling into the lake, and now she makes me do things for her."

"That's not how it is at all. Do you even listen in class?"

"I always listen; but people tell so many lies that it's better to listen to the whispers, since those are things they don't want you to hear."

"Has Ozomatli been whispering about other things?"

Night Wind shook his head. "But Yamehecatl whispers to his invisible friend when he thinks he's alone."

I stiffened. I'd been so happy at the thought that my son finally found a friend who would accept him, but perhaps that was a delusion I embraced because I hated seeing him so alone, as I had been.

Night Wind went back to his work but continued, "I've talked to his friend too."

"When was this?" No one had told me that Yamehecatl had had one of his episodes.

"Last week. Yamehecatl says when his friend gets angry, he scares him, so I made him go away, and he hasn't come back since."

And here I'd thought the worst of Night Wind. "Thank you for helping him." My voice cracked despite my best efforts to stay calm.

Night Wind shrugged. "It's good to be around those that understand you."

I nodded, struggling to keep the tears back; I had to leave—the temple's air was suddenly stifling.

As I leaned against one of the feathered serpent columns at the temple's entrance, I traced my fingers over the stone scales, remembering the last time I'd seen the god, and how when I'd gazed into his eyes, it wasn't like looking into the unfathomable cosmos. I'd seen a kindred soul, one who saw and knew everything about me, and understood, and loved me for it. I'd sought that same look in Black Otter's eyes every time we'd made love, but he'd always been so disconnected—so focused on his own pleasure—as to make me feel that we must not even be in the same place. What transpired between us wasn't the sharing of selves and souls that I desperately missed from those times with the god, but rather something as pedestrian and everyday as eating breakfast.

But I can't go back to the god, I thought, the tears coming fast. *It's sacrilegious to see him like that, or to believe on any level that we are equals; I might have powerful magic, but if I were anything other than a true human woman, the god would have told me so long ago. It's no secret that Little Reed is half-divine, so what reason would he have to keep a similar secret from me? To even entertain such a notion is blasphemous, and that's a step I can't take, no matter how confused my heart might be.*

Citlallotoc crested the stairs. "Oh good, I found you." When he saw my tears, he asked, "Are you all right?"

I wiped them away quickly. "Yes, got some smoke in my eyes, that's all." I motioned to the kettle braziers back in the temple. Clearing my throat, I asked, "What brings you here?"

"Black Otter claims we'll finally have our proof tonight, about Ozomatli."

❑

Citlallotoc didn't want me coming along with the rest of them. "It could be dangerous, My Lady," he warned when Little Reed and I met with him and his men in the palace courtyard at the midnight bell.

"I can be as well," I countered. Little Reed had also been reluctant for me to go, fearing Ozomatli might succeed in summoning Smoking Mirror this time, but when I reminded him that I'd already faced that demon once before and defeated him, he stopped pressing the issue. He implored me to be careful, and I asked the same of him, and we said no more about it.

Citlallotoc wouldn't be so easily swayed. "It's not a good idea for both of you to come. If you're both killed, who will rule until the prince comes of age?"

"You, of course, as our most trusted friend," I said. "But if you're truly concerned, it should be Topiltzin who stays behind, since I have considerable weapons that he doesn't. The more vulnerable of the two of us should be the one to remain behind."

Citlallotoc frowned, taken aback, but Little Reed laughed. "If I weren't a more confident man, I might take exception to that." He slipped an arm around my shoulder, giving me a squeeze, then told Citlallotoc, "I thank you for your concern, but let's go, before we're late." He pulled up the hood of his cloak and started out of the front gate.

At this late hour, the streets were mostly deserted, save for the occasional watch patrol, and a few stopped us, questioning why a band of cloaked figures were out so late. But with Citlallotoc speaking for us, we got back underway quickly.

Things grew livelier once we left the sanctuary of the city walls; most of the Chichimec men were up late, burning tobacco in public fire pits and chanting prayers to Tezcatlipoca over their swords and spears. Tonight was the first night of Teotleco, the Coming of the Gods, and since the Chichimecs believed this month was ruled by Smoking Mirror, his followers made offerings of smoke and prayers. The secret ceremony we hoped to interrupt would have more traditional offerings on hand.

We made our way to the edge of the fields and up the path leading into the woods. Ozomatli certainly was brazen, coming back to the same scene to commit more atrocities, almost daring us to catch him at it. We watched each step to make certain we didn't make too much noise.

When voices drifted out of the dark ahead of us, Citlallotoc signaled his men to break off into the trees and surround the clearing. "Stay close to me." Little Reed took my hand with a grip that broached no arguments. He pulled his sword and led me over to a tree trunk thick enough to shelter both of us, and there we crouched, back to back, looking around opposite sides. Citlallotoc disappeared into the dark.

Three men were in the clearing; two dressed in priest robes stood, while the third— dressed only in a loincloth—knelt on the ground, groveling. "Shut him up, before he attracts attention." Ozomatli's voice.

The second man moved to gag the kneeling man, whose groveling turned frantic. "Please! I'll give you anything you want—" but the rest of it was cut off as the other finally gagged him.

Ozomatli chuckled. "You'll indeed give me exactly what I want." He knocked the man over backwards, and told the second man, "Hold him down." As the other man clambered atop the victim, Ozomatli pulled a knife from his belt and knelt as well. Blade held aloft, he chanted, "Lord Tezcatlipoca, your day of feast is upon you! Accept this humble offering as the first of many courses tonight!"

Why isn't anyone stopping this? I started to rise, but Little Reed grabbed my arm and held me there. "Let them deal with him."

"But—"

Shouts filled the night and our men flooded the clearing. The second man leaped away, holding his hands up in the air, shouting, "He threatened to kill me if I didn't help him!" It was Black Otter.

Citlallotoc knocked him aside as he went for Ozomatli, catching the priest's arm as he swung the blade at the man on the ground. He wrestled Ozomatli back until the rest of our men swarmed over them, knocking the priest over and pinning him to the ground. The bound man rolled away and struggled to his feet to run.

But when he saw Black Otter standing off to the side, he stopped, his eyes wide. Black Otter started to speak, but the bound man went over backwards, a knife stuck in his stomach.

"Out of the way!" A hulking figure batted Black Otter aside, sending him sprawling into the bushes.

A breath later, Mextli wrenched the man up by the arm. The man gasped behind his gag when Mextli yanked up on the knife with his free hand, spilling his guts on the forest floor, then he broke into a keening cry when the giant reached up inside his open cavity and plucked his heart out as if he were picking an avocado from a tree. Mextli dropped the useless body.

"What the—" Citlallotoc called out as he turned around, but he stepped back when he saw Mextli. "You!" The other men brought their spears up, the fear in their eyes palpable even in the pale moonlight.

"Fools!" Mextli laughed, holding up the feebly beating heart. "Did you really think you could stop the Smoking Mirror's incarnation?" When Citlallotoc drew his sword, Mextli chuckled. "Admirable. Even one-armed, you don't give up, do you?"

Citlallotoc waved his sword. "I'm even better with my left."

"Then come show me, little lord."

But before Citlallotoc could rise to the bait, I jumped out from behind the tree and let loose a burst of magic, knocking the heart from Mextli's fist. He shook his hand as if burned, but when he saw me, a sly smile came to his lips.

"Ah, the Feathered Serpent's fool, come to face me again." When Little Reed stepped out from behind the tree too, sword in hand, Mextli's smile curled into a sneer. "And you're here too. That's quite a name you've given yourself: Our Prince, a prince above all other princes, just as the Feathered Serpent believes himself a god above all other gods."

"There's room for all the gods here in Tollan," Little Reed said. "We give space and honor to everyone."

"Only on terms that weaken the rest of us. Make no mistake; this treason hasn't gone unnoticed, nor will it go unchallenged."

"There is nothing to challenge, Mextli. If you and Smoking Mirror weren't so opposed to change, you'd see it doesn't weaken anyone; it's better, especially for gods such as yourself. The others see this, and so allowed Tollan's construction and the passing of the laws. Smoking Mirror is needlessly fighting the future when both of you could be at the fore of it all."

"Oh, we will be, once I'm standing over your rotting corpse." Mextli flicked the fingers of his left hand and a macuahuitl sword materialized in his fist. "Time to die, Nobody's Prince," he sneered, advancing on Little Reed.

Little Reed raised his sword—and from the corner of my eye I saw Citlallotoc leap at Mextli—but I couldn't let Mextli get anywhere near Little Reed. I let loose the magic dripping from my fingers and it crashed across the clearing, knocking everyone aside, even Mextli. When I pulled back, no one moved. The thick, acidic fruit smell of octli clung to the air. Little Reed lay unconscious next to me.

Mextli came to his feet again, his feathers standing on end. "You certainly are brazen. If it didn't tickle so, I might take exception with your defiance."

I poised myself over Little Reed. "Maybe it tickles now, but come any closer and it won't tickle anymore." I felt no need to let the desire speak for me this time; I would see Mextli in Mictlan before I'd let him hurt Little Reed.

"So eager to throw your life away."

"Everyone dies eventually."

Mextli shook his head. "You have so much to learn...and unlearn."

I laughed. "And I suppose you think yourself the one to teach me?"

"He's certainly doing you no favors." He pointed at Little Reed. "War is coming, and Quetzalcoatl will lose; it's not a question of if—for Heaven has already written the future in the stars, and the Feathered Serpent's blasphemy will end with his destruction. And that of those who helped him. That means you as well. But it's not too late yet to correct that mistake."

"And join Smoking Mirror?" I growled.

"He offers you the one thing the Feathered Serpent won't."

"And what's that?"

"The truth."

I sneered, the anger boiling over. "And here's what I think of his offer." I launched another attack, pouring twice as much magic into it as last time. How dare he think I was weak and power-hungry enough to turn against Quetzalcoatl, after all the god had given me? *I'll shut that impertinent mouth of yours.*

Mextli dropped his sword and held his hands out in front of him, as if to push back against my magic, but now his brow creased with concern. His feet slid on the ground and his arm muscles twitched, his feathers standing on end. His eyes went wide just before he suddenly burst into thousands of tiny blue hummingbirds. They flew in every direction, but then dropped from the air, pummeling the earth like hail. I shielded my head from them as they rained down on me.

Once the downpour ended, I picked one of the birds up from the ground. It twitched in my hand a moment before falling still and crumbling into glowing blue dust. As I looked around, the others did the same, covering the ground with a layer of pulsing blue that slowly dimmed. I stared a moment, taking in what I'd seen, what I'd done. "Great Feathered Serpent! I killed him! I killed a god!" And it hadn't even taken all that much out of me to do it. Magic was still pulsing in my blood, ready at a thought.

That's because we're strong, the desire purred, delighted. *Invincible!* I'd never felt so exhilarated.

But when I turned to Little Reed, he was convulsing, his eyes rolled up in his head. "Little Reed!" I rushed to kneel next to him as he twitched and flinched, a mix of spit and watery vomit leaking out of his mouth. I rolled him over onto his side and thumped his back, trying to clear his mouth and throat. *Dear gods, what have I done?* My panic grew as he went limp. *If he dies, I'll never forgive myself.*

But when he started coughing, dazed, I sat him up and hugged him. "I'm so sorry, Little Reed!" I sobbed.

He said nothing, in such a drunken haze that he had no idea where he was. When he started shivering, I draped my cloak over his shoulders and sat with him, waiting for the others to wake up.

CHAPTER TWENTY-TWO

Even with Ozomatli in custody, we delayed the trial while Little Reed recovered. I sat at his bedside for two days, keeping watch over him, and when he asked what happened with Mextli, I was too afraid to tell him the truth. If I had indeed killed Mextli, it was amazing Little Reed was still alive, and I didn't want to admit to him that I had very nearly killed him as well.

None of the men were in good condition; Citlallotoc complained of a constant headache for days after, and Black Otter—who had been farthest from me when I'd released my magic—remembered nothing of that night. "One moment that...thing tore that man's heart out, but then I woke up as if from a long night of drinking." He'd been the first to wake from his stupor and had helped me get Little Reed back to the palace. I was glad he didn't remember me using magic, and hopefully that meant the rest of the men didn't either.

As I sat next to Little Reed's bed, I couldn't stop thinking about my conversation with Mextli, and his claims that Quetzalcoatl was keeping secrets from me. I considered going into the Divine Dream to speak with the god, to get reassurances that it was all a ploy to deceive and turn me against him, but how could I take anything that came out of Mextli's mouth seriously? I felt ashamed for even entertaining the notion.

These thoughts soured my mood for Ozomatli's trial and turned my heart to a statue. Smoking Mirror's high priest attempted to grovel his way out of his crimes, claiming to remember nothing of that night—not even going to the clearing with Black Otter and the victim. A convenient excuse. He denied any involvement in the murders, and Little Reed asked pointed questions that reduced him to tears; I could have asked questions too but I merely glared at him with a raw hatred that burned hot as the sun, especially when he tried pushing the blame onto Black Otter, claiming my cousin kept haranguing him to go back to the old ways.

"Whatever Black Otter suggested to you is irrelevant," Little Reed told him when we sat in judgment. "Ultimately, you chose to ignore the law. While we cannot definitively prove that you killed the men pulled from the ground last month, you were seen by no less than a dozen witnesses raising a knife, poised to kill a man; and so for that reason, we find you guilty of attempted murder. As is the way here in Tollan, by royal proclamation, you are therefore forever exiled from Tolteca lands."

I'd gone along with Little Reed on the sentence when we first discussed it, but my indignation and anger boiled over as we sat for dinner in his quarters afterwards, only the two of us. "He murdered at least twelve people and nearly unleashed that demon god on us. How is only exiling him justice?" I demanded, disgust killing my appetite.

"We can't prove all those murders, and even if we could, Quetzalcoatl's way isn't one life for another," he reminded me. "Capital punishment is still murder, Papalotl. It might alleviate some of the anger in our hearts, but it doesn't heal us where we most need it."

"And neither does exiling him!" I snapped, getting to my feet to pace. I had too much furious energy that needed burning off. Ozomatli was getting away with his treachery yet again.

"We heal by learning to forgive," Little Reed said, maddeningly patient.

"And some things are unforgivable, Little Reed." When he put his arms around me, I wept into his neck. "Some things can't heal," I mumbled, holding him tight.

He held my face between his hands. "I know it seems that way, but love can heal anything. There is no magic more powerful."

I gazed into his eyes, my heart racing. He looked at me with that deep understanding I'd only ever seen in the god's eyes, that love that was the food my soul lived and died for. I wanted so badly to feel something other than this suffocating anger. "Please kiss me," I whispered, my own pleading painful in my throat.

He hesitated but did so, slow and sensual. His hands trailed down my neck, his fingertips raising my flesh so wonderfully, melting away the pain and pressure in my chest. I kissed him back, pressing up against him, the desire swelling, burning bright and delicious. My body did what came naturally; my hands parted his royal robes, exposing his firm bare chest—evidence of his daily workouts in the exercise yard with Citlallotoc. They pushed the robe back further, so it slid from his shoulders, and the knot securing his loincloth posed no challenge.

He followed my example, breaking past the ties of my own robe, fumbling with the ones at the back of my dress until it all puddled around my feet. My skin prickled with the sudden cold, but chills came when his lips left mine to work their way down my neck, my shoulders, my breasts, my belly. I clung to him, ready to float off like a cloud as he moved still lower, his tongue carving an escape path through my pain and straining faith. He knelt before me as if praying before an idol, preparing to give a bit of himself to me in sacrifice, as if I were a goddess he worshiped. Magic tingled all over me, begging for release as I ran my fingers with increasing roughness through his hair....

But memories of him convulsing on the ground...of Mextli bursting apart into thousands of tiny, dying birds, brought me to my senses. *What in Mictlan am I doing?* The desire howled but I shoved it aside. One careless moment was all it took to destroy everything I held dear. I stepped away from him, overcome with regret and shame.

He looked up, worry in his eyes, but before he could say anything, I fled the room, not bothering to grab any of my clothes. I tossed aside the door curtain, and dashed across the empty garden to my own quarters. I threw myself on my bed, huddling up, burying my face in my knees, weeping and shaking.

A moment later, Little Reed's tentative voice came from the door. "Did I do something wrong?"

I shook my head. "Forgive me, Little Reed. You did nothing wrong; it's all me. I'm so sorry. I'm so terribly unfair to you...."

He draped my robe over my naked body and sat next to me, carefully securing his own robe as he did so. "I'm more worried about you. Maybe this whole sacrifice thing...maybe you're over-thinking it, and if we just...once...so much more would make sense."

I laughed. "Nothing will ever make sense, Little Reed. I will never understand why the god chose me to be his high priestess when I'm so weak. Living this life of absolute devotion to him feels as if it's slowly killing me."

"You're not weak, Papalotl," he assured me. "You're exactly the way Heaven made you, and you mustn't be ashamed of that. The priesthood taught us to forsake our physical impulses for the spiritual and mental life, but we can't ignore our deepest needs; we might fast now and then, but it would be crazy to never eat again."

"You can't survive without eating, Little Reed, but you can survive without sex. It's not the same thing."

"No, but that doesn't make it any less important." He lay down next to me and wiped my tears away with the side of his hand. "The god doesn't want you to be miserable."

"It doesn't matter what the god wants. I didn't make my deal with him."

"I know."

Sniffling, I debated whether or not to say more, but my fear had become a rock in my chest, growing heavier the longer I held it inside. I had to tell him. "Even if not for that sacrifice, if we did...dear gods, I almost killed you, Little Reed!"

He furrowed his brow. "What do you mean?"

"That night, out in the forest. I was so angry, so out of control that I kept blasting more and more magic, and...I lied to you, about what happened to Mextli. He didn't merely go away; I threw so much magic at him that he burst into all these tiny birds and they turned to blue dust—"

Little Reed blinked, startled. "He disintegrated?"

I nodded, choking on my own tears. "I killed him, and you were so close to me when I was blasting him.... I nearly killed you too! And now, when we were back in your quarters...what is wrong with me? You give me pleasure, but all I could think about is how much I wanted to release my magic into you." I covered my face with both hands.

"But you didn't."

"No, but had we gone on.... I could have killed you!"

"I doubt it."

His casual denial stung. How could he think my magic so inconsequential, after what I'd done to Mextli? "Why not?"

Caressing my cheek, he smiled warmly. "Because I trust you with every fiber of my tonalli."

His words brought me to fresh tears and I hugged him, so grateful to have his love and trust. He pulled me to him, kissing me gently and taking no precautions to keep our bare flesh from pressing together. I expected the growling desire to jump at this second chance, but it gave me peace. His every careful touch made my stomach flutter and my head swim, and I felt as nervous as a young bride on the fourth night of her wedding, preparing to consummate for the first time—strange since I hadn't felt this vulnerable and scared when Black Otter had taken my maidenhead. Neither was this frantic or demanding; everything moved slowly and deliberately, as it always did with the god—merely one more way to so easily mix them up in my head, confusing what I should and shouldn't do. An unspoken plea lay in his eyes; *Just once*. And if I trusted him as much as he trusted me, why not? Maybe he was right and things would finally start making sense. And maybe it was already too late; I bit my bottom lip hard, trying to suppress the moan as his gently manipulating fingers brought on the first warning waves of pleasure—

But suddenly he jumped away from me, yelping in surprise. From the edge of my bed, Yamehecatl swung his play sword at him, rage boiling on our son's face. Little Reed tried to dodge him, but Yamehecatl clipped his bare leg, sending him limping off, cursing.

"What on earth are you doing?" I yelled at Yamehecatl, scrambling for my robe as he went after Little Reed again, this time swiping his sword at his father's exposed crotch. Little Reed fended him off with both hands until I grabbed Yamehecatl from behind and disarmed him.

"You won't hurt my Nantli!" Yamehecatl shouted as I dragged him over to the bed, so Little Reed could retreat from the corner.

The guards burst into the room, spears ready. They usually stayed posted at the main entrance to our family gardens, to give us privacy, but they must have heard the commotion and come running. "Is everything all right, My Lord?"

Little Reed quickly tied his robe closed and assured them we were fine and ushered them back out onto the portico. He stood facing the closed curtain for a moment before turning his cross expression on Yamehecatl. "Why in Mictlan would you think I'd hurt your mother?"

"You were making her cry!" Yamehecatl retorted. "Lord Green Water made one of the servants cry out in the main garden the other day, and Night Wind wouldn't let me go help her, but I won't let anyone make Nantli cry. Not even you." He glared at Little Reed.

"I wasn't crying, dear," I assured him, laughing if only to not look mortified. How long had he been watching us from his nursery curtain?

"You looked as if you were crying." He still stared down Little Reed. "Citlallotoc says that men who hurt women aren't men at all."

"I wasn't hurting your mother," Little Reed assured him, irritated.

Yamehecatl looked to me and when I nodded in agreement, he pinched his mouth together, tears forming. "I'm sorry I hit you, Tatli," he muttered, his jaw quivering.

Little Reed knelt in front of him. "A good man defends those in trouble, so I applaud your desire to protect your mother...and that other woman. But for now on, it would be better for you to report things that worry you to an adult, who can better assess a situation. It's a good thing Night Wind held you back or Lord Green Water and his...friend would have been very upset with you." Under his breath he added, "Though I must talk with him about spending time with her in the gardens."

Yamehecatl nodded, sniffling. He hugged Little Reed, whispering more apologies that Little Reed accepted with gentle reassurances and chuckles. When Yamehecatl returned to me, he climbed into my lap. "Can I stay with you tonight, Nantli?"

I looked at Little Reed and he nodded, resigned but still smiling. "Very well," I told Yamehecatl, and he scrambled under my blankets, nestling in. As Little Reed turned to leave, I said, "You can stay, if you wish." The three of us hadn't shared a bed since our return trip to Culhuacan, right after Yamehecatl was born.

He thought about it but said, "We'll all be more comfortable if I'm in my own bed." He gave my hand a squeeze and left.

I stared at the curtain for a while, numb with realization. No matter how much I wanted to believe we'd built the perfect marriage and family, no matter how much I wanted to think that sex wasn't important at all—to either of us—it was in fact the invisible wedge keeping us from ever being truly happy.

And a time would come when I couldn't expect his holding out hope for something that would never happen would continue to keep him with me.

◻

With Ozomatli sentenced to exile, we needed to appoint a new high priest of the Smoking Mirror, and Little Reed had the perfect candidate.

"I know you said you had no desire to be a priest, Cousin, but I would consider it a personal favor if you took the position," he told Black Otter as we walked from our family garden towards the great hall. "You already have the appropriate training, and after helping us save Smoking Mirror's priesthood, you're the perfect man to lead the cult into the future. Your father brought Smoking Mirror's worship to the Tolteca, so it's only right that you should reform it and turn it into a strong entity that flourishes throughout the empire."

Black Otter smiled. "There was a time when I wouldn't have considered it my first choice of vocation, but the thought of turning my father's work into something positive does appeal to me."

"A noble endeavor. It's also my honor to return your noble title to you, so you might pass it and all its inherent value down to your children. And as the new high priest, we invite you to move your family into the priestly quarters of the palace, and both of your children will be guaranteed educations in the calmecac."

"That is most gracious of you, My Lord." Black Otter bowed.

"I personally want to thank you for your help with the situation with Ozomatli. You saved Tollan from possible disaster, and we shall never forget that." Little Reed embraced him.

Looking embarrassed, Black Otter embraced him back. "Thank you for your faith in me."

"There are ceremonies and fasts you must do to cleanse yourself before taking your vows as high priest, and Quetzalpetlatl will go over that with you. Now, if you'll excuse me, Lord Flame Tongue arrived last night and I'm taking him deer hunting this afternoon." He departed with a nod to each of us.

Black Otter continued walking with me. "I must thank you as well, My Lady, for this opportunity."

"It's my pleasure," I said.

"If my moving here into the palace makes you at all uncomfortable—"

"It doesn't make me uncomfortable at all, Cousin. The past is over, and you've more than proven your loyalty. If anything, I'm glad to have you back in my life, and highly pleased our sons will grow up together, the way *we* should have been allowed to. Night Wind has been a very good friend to Yamehecatl."

"You honor me, My Lady." We walked in silence a moment before he spoke again. "I never got the chance to apologize to you."

"For what?"

"For everything my father did. For all the shame he's brought upon our family."

I stopped and faced him. "And as I told your brother, you don't bear any of your father's shame, especially when...and I've debated whether or not to tell you this, but...he wasn't your father at all. Nochuatl was. And I know this because he admitted as much to me."

I expected surprise, but instead, he bowed his head and nodded. "I suspected as much, especially given how often people said I looked like our uncle, and how upset my father would get when they did. He forbade anyone from mentioning Nochuatl's name."

"You owe Ihuitimal nothing, and you bear no shame for his crimes. They are his own."

"Perhaps, but I do owe him. He knew the truth and yet...why didn't he kill me when I was a babe? Why did he instead raise me as his own son?"

I sighed. "Maybe because even the most terrible among us are capable of compassion and kindness under the right circumstances."

"Truth be told, I wanted to disbelieve my gut about him, so things would be simpler and I wouldn't feel bad about loving him."

"He was the only father you knew, so you shouldn't feel bad. He loved you, Black Otter, and Amoxtli too, and that counts for something."

"Forgive me, but I'd rather not talk about him anymore," Black Otter said, walking again. "Perhaps you could instead instruct me on what kinds of fasting and ceremonies I need to go through before taking the high priest position?"

I continued walking as well. "In most priesthoods, candidates journey to Teotihuacan to do their cleansing rituals; but as I understand it, the tradition in Smoking Mirror's order is to go into the desert. There's a camp to the north for that very purpose. You'll need to fast for a total of three days and pray for five, then return to take your vows before myself and Topiltzin. You'll leave for the camp tomorrow, so the cult is without a high priest for as few days as possible. We're sending a small regiment of soldiers north to escort Ozomatli out of Tolteca lands, so you can travel with them."

"What of my children? Night Wind is at the calmecac, of course, but Cuicatl comes home from the telpochcalli each night. I don't wish her to be alone while I'm gone."

"We'll move the two of you into the palace today and she will be looked after. And while you're gone, I'll get her properly placed in the calmecac."

"Thank you, My Lady."

We finally reached the Hall of the Gods, where we would part ways—me to the palace steward to see to Black Otter's new quarters, and him to the temple to meet with Smoking Mirror's high priestess and other ranking priests. I'd debated all morning whether or not to tell Black Otter the other secret I had, about Ozomatli; knowing that conniving priest was walking away yet again—and this time only with a slap for his ambitions—enraged me, no matter how Little Reed spoke of the god's ways. The families of the victims deserved better. Black Otter and Amoxtli deserved better.

Black Otter started to bid me goodbye, but I cut him off. "I know you said you don't want to talk about your father anymore, but there's something you should know."

"Oh?"

"Ozomatli was poisoning his ritual mushrooms; that's why your father started looking so sickly those last few months of his life. And Amoxtli nearly died using those poisoned teonanacatl, and when he worked out Ozomatli was trying to kill your father, Ozomatli betrayed him to my brother's men, hoping Topiltzin would kill him. Luckily Topiltzin isn't that kind of man."

Black Otter stared at me with a darkness I'd never before seen in him, momentarily reminding me of Ihuitimal. "Thank you for telling me this, My Lady," he said and walked away.

No matter what conflicts Black Otter felt about Ihuitimal, the man had treated him as a son, and Black Otter would avenge him. I tried to smile, knowing justice would finally be served, but inside a part of me cringed. Was I effectively ordering Ozomatli's execution?

Part of the obligations of a ruler is making certain those who have been wronged are given justice, I reminded myself as I continued walking. But a wave of doubt and regret followed me for many days after that, for who was I to question the rightness of Quetzalcoatl's wishes?

☐

"Can I talk to you?" Malinalli lurked in the doorway of my private meditation room, looking nervous.

I set aside the copalli burner, making a place for her on the mats in front of the hearth. "Of course. What's on your mind?"

She fussed with her hands a moment, then took a deep breath. "Well, if I can't tell you this, we must not really be best friends." She cleared her throat then said, "Remember how we talked last month, about me meeting someone?"

I nodded and before she could speak again, I said, "If it makes it easier, I already know."

She blinked at me. "How—"

410

"I saw the two of you in the garden, and it was quite obvious. You look at her like I look at Topiltzin."

She paused. "It doesn't make you uncomfortable?"

"I'm only embarrassed that I jumped to the wrong conclusions when we first talked about this. I'm sorry."

She let out a breath and smiled. "It's all right. That's a rather normal assumption to make, really. And I've tried to feel differently than I do; for a short while I was a nobleman's lover, while we were in Culhuacan, when Ihuitimal was still king, but that changed nothing; if anything, his taking the choice away from me solidified my predilections; no woman has ever forced me into her bed."

My stomach clenched. "Why didn't you tell me of this?" *I could have done something to stop it,* I almost added, but who was I fooling? Those were the dark days when women couldn't legally complain about such things, and they certainly couldn't demand a nobleman respect their autonomy by actually asking permission.

"You had your own burdens, and besides, it's only now that I can actually speak about it without getting upset. Mitotia has been very supportive and understanding. She's helped me move on."

I hugged her tight. "You amaze me with your strength, Malinalli. You stood up for me to Turquoise Bells when I'd behaved horrendously with Red Flint, took me in when Nimilitzli died and I thought Topiltzin was dead, saved me from Red Flint, and defended me against that horrible Captain Storm House when we were captured and taken to Culhuacan." I sighed. "What have I done to deserve such good friendship?"

Malinalli took my hand in hers. "Before you sat and talked to me on the boat ride back from Teotihuacan...I'd never had any real friends. And I've been thankful for every day since—even the bad ones." She wiped a tear away. "You won't tell Topiltzin, about me and Mitotia?"

"He wouldn't bat an eye, but no, I won't tell him."

We spent the rest of the afternoon eating lunch and reminiscing about our younger days. Oh how I wished I'd talked to her the first time I saw her at calmecac instead of waiting until that disasterous trip to Teotihuacan. So many years of friendship missed because I'd been too shy—and too hurt from life—to return her friendly smile that first time.

PART FOUR
THE YEAR TWO RABBIT

CHAPTER TWENTY-THREE

Most children don't live past the first three years of life. Many succumb to common childhood ailments or drink bad water, leaving them desiccated shells. Out in the fields, where the farmers live, more often than not wily ocelotls steal infants from their baskets in the middle of the night. And even if one survives the infancy illnesses or avoids becoming a predatory cat's dinner, childhood curiosity claims quite a few more; several children drown in the canals each year, or they slip and fall out of tall trees, or they mistake wild dogs for the tame ones the merchants raise for the dinner table.

And just as many dangers lurk in the palace: poisonous snakes and insects live in the gardens, and cruel-hearted servants take their frustrations with their masters out on the vulnerable. The most dangerous of all are the rivalries between a king or nobleman's kept women as they vie for power on behalf of their sons. Luckily neither I nor Little Reed had to worry about such nonsense in our household.

The world—and the gods—was seldom kind to children, hence the reason we Tolteca refrained from bestowing a permanent, sacred name on our children until they'd survived to the age of seven; by then, they'd learned to be careful with their lives.

Despite his fearless determination and bouts of sudden drunkenness, Yamehecatl managed what many children didn't, and he was finally going to learn his real name.

With the years, he'd developed better control of his emotions, so it was rare for him to fall over drunk anymore, but he still didn't spend his nights at the priestly dormitories with the other boys. We'd told him that if he could go six months without an incident, we'd know he was ready to go to school full-time with his friend and cousin Night Wind. The two had grown closer with the years, and Yamehecatl had made it his goal to move into the dorms by his naming day. And he'd succeeded in that too.

He was full of pride and cheer the morning of his naming day. He dressed in an eagle-feather shirt I'd made for him—identical to the one Citlallotoc wore—and I braided jade beads and feathers into his hair, so it looked as if he wore a headdress. I'd feared he'd want to wear his rabbit uniform, since he'd insisted I make him a new one when he outgrew the old, but he'd picked out the eagle shirt instead, along with a set of elbow and ankle bracelets inlaid with shell rattles. He made lots of noise when he moved, "So the gods know I'm coming to talk to them today," he told me, showing off the gap where both of his front baby teeth had fallen out last week. My little boy was growing up so fast!

We went to the Hall of the Gods to wait for Little Reed, but Yamehecatl scampered off into the courtyard when he saw Night Wind playing patolli with one of the older boys. Night Wind had sprouted up tall the last couple of years, his already serious demeanor lending him the air of a much older boy than his mere nine summers. He grinned when Yamehecatl came up and sat next to him, making my son look so little again.

"Thank you for giving him the day off from school, so he could spend it with Yamehecatl on his naming day." I turned to see Black Otter standing a bit behind me, wearing his black high priest robes, and looking tired. He always looked as much these days. He'd been scrawny and underfed when he came to Tollan two years ago and I'd expected him to fatten up once he'd moved into the palace and returned to the luxurious noble life, but he was even thinner now. Perhaps being Smoking Mirror's high priest wasn't as fulfilling as I found being Quetzalcoatl's high priestess was.

"It's my pleasure." I looked back at our boys again with a smile. Night Wind had won the game, leaving the older boy scowling as he scooped up his winnings—little clay disks the children earned in class for doing well on exams or answering difficult questions. They used them to buy extra food at meal times or tobacco from one of the high priests. "Are you coming to the feast tonight too?"

"Do you wish me to?" Black Otter asked, surprised.

I laughed. "Of course I do. Half the empire will be here, so why wouldn't I invite you? You're family."

"Thank you."

"I wish Amoxtli was here too," I added. "I've really missed him since he went back to Culhuacan." He'd taken the fire priest position there, vowing to see Quetzalcoatl's cult fully restored in his home city.

Black Otter nodded, looking sickly.

I turned to grip his arm. "Are you all right?"

"I'm fine."

"You don't look it. You're not sick, are you?"

He chuckled, looking embarrassed. "Thank you for your concern, but really, I'm not sick. It's not as easy being a high priest as I thought it would be. There's so much to do all the time. Frankly, I don't know how either you or Topiltzin do it and also rule the kingdom."

"We don't do everything ourselves. If you need to, lean on your fire priest or Yaretzi some more. The priesthood is a group effort."

"I'd rather avoid Yaretzi," he said. "She's become rather...forward in her attentions the last few months."

"Jade Flower *has* been gone almost three years now, long enough to have gone on to her eternal rest in Mictlan. Maybe it's time to start looking for someone for yourself again. Children need a mother."

"Yes, but not her," he said. "Most definitely not her."

"She's not to your tastes?"

"She's...eerie."

I knew what he spoke of, for she made me uneasy as well.

Voices from the guest wing distracted my attention. Little Reed and Citlallotoc came into the Hall of the Gods, walking with several of our allies from the valley. Flame Tongue of Xico walked at Little Reed's shoulder, speaking loudly of how prosperous Xico had become in the years since adopting Tollan's code of laws. "You wouldn't believe the sheer numbers of fish our small fleet of boats pull out of the waters these days.

Xochimilco has twice as many boats, fishing the very same waters, and yet the fish practically jump into ours. Certainly a sign from the god, since Xochimilco has balked at completely abandoning human sacrifice the way we have."

Little Reed wore his smile like a mask, but I recognized it was strained. Flame Tongue had arrived last night and kept me and Little Reed up late with his incessant chatter; one would think he never got to talk at home.

Seeing me, Little Reed's smile broadened and he took the opportunity to hurry ahead and embrace me. He'd aged quite a bit in the last year; his hair had gone white, and his wrinkles were pronounced cracks. He let the stubble grow on his chin, since he found it painful to grip his obsidian shaving blade, and he would only allow me to shave him, joking that he trusted me alone with a blade to his throat. He also climbed the temple steps more slowly these days. I was dreadfully aware that there were fewer years ahead of us now than there were behind us. He kissed my cheek—leaving me hot and fidgety. "Where's Yamehecatl? Are we ready to go to the soothsayer?"

Yamehecatl tugged at Little Reed's robe. "I'm right here, Tatli!"

With a roaring laugh, he hefted Yamehecatl into his arms. "My, have you gotten heavy!" he said, putting him down slowly. "I'm afraid your tatli isn't as young as he used to be," he added, rubbing his back as he stood up again. "So, are you ready to go and find out your true name?"

"I certainly am! I hope it's something good!"

Little Reed took his hand. "All true names are good ones; even the ones that don't seem good at first, they turn out perfect in the end. The gods know us better than we know ourselves."

"I hope it's something fierce, like Bloody Rabbit or Snarling Coyote."

Little Reed laughed and ruffled his hair. "Let's get going, before we're late." He turned to the crowd stopped behind him. "I will see everyone at the ritual ball game this afternoon, but in the meantime, Lord Citlallotoc will take you on a tour of the city."

Flame Tongue and the other lords followed Citlallotoc down the stairs into the courtyard. A group of women followed behind, and when I waved to Anacoana—looking lovely and regal among her handmaidens—she hurried over to greet me. "It's so good to see you again, My Lady."

I embraced her, making her blush. "I'm so glad you could make the journey. The last time I saw you, you were still so young, but you have blossomed into a stunning woman."

Her blush deepened and she glanced at Black Otter, no recognition in her eyes; but she kept glancing back at him as we exchanged the customary pleasantries. Black Otter paid her no attention, looking out of place instead, so I reintroduced them. "My Lady, I know it's been a number of years now since you last saw him, but certainly you remember Lord Black Otter?"

Anacoana gasped. "I thought that might be you, My Lord." She gave him a courteous bow. "It's a pleasure to see you again after so long."

Black Otter gazed back at her, surprised. "Lady Anacoana? I didn't recognize you. You're so...."

"Grown up," I provided with a knowing smile.

He looked flustered, but before he could say anything, Flame Tongue called for his daughter from the courtyard. She gave me, Black Otter, and Little Reed a hurried bow then ran to catch up with the rest of the group. When she reached her father he barked at her, making her bow her head even lower than usual. He continued glaring at Black Otter as the group departed through the front gate.

"He's not at all happy to see me," Black Otter noted, a worried look on his face. He was right, and that squashed all those newborn thoughts of perhaps trying to get the two back together again now that Anacoana was a good age for marriage.

When Night Wind joined us, Little Reed asked Black Otter, "Will you take your son to the ball game today? Everyone's invited."

Black Otter shook his head, distracted. "I have things I must do this afternoon."

Yamehecatl looked crestfallen until Little Reed suggested, "In that case, if you don't mind, Night Wind can come with me and Yamehecatl and sit in the royal box. I'm certain the boys will have great fun watching the game."

Black Otter cast a questioning gaze at Night Wind, who nodded, all business. "That's most kind of you, My Lord. Thank you."

"Can Night Wind come with us when we go to the soothsayer?" Yamehecatl asked, turning pup eyes on Little Reed.

But Little Reed shook his head. "The soothsayer's house is small and cluttered, so there's barely enough room for you, me, and your mother. You can tell him all about your new name when we get back."

Yamehecatl opened his mouth to argue, but Night Wind told him, "It's all right, Cousin. I promised Blue House that I'd whip him at patolli, and I'm a man of my word."

"Let us get going, before we're truly late." Little Reed took my hand with his free one. Yamehecatl jumped up and down, excited, and ran ahead of us, his guards scurrying after him. When I looked back to wave goodbye to Black Otter, he watched us go with a sad, melancholy expression on his face.

ɑ

"Come on! Hurry up, Nantli! We're going to be late!" Yamehecatl tried pulling me through the sacred precinct, but when I made no move to walk faster, he let me go and ran ahead with the guards, clearing the way. I stayed back with Little Reed, holding his hand.

"In such a hurry to grow up." To Little Reed, I added, "He gets that from you, you know."

Little Reed laughed. "I remember thinking adults intentionally walked slowly just to annoy me. Now I know it's because their bones ache when they move too fast."

I squeezed his hand and smiled, determined not to show that his jest pained me.

The soothsayer's house sat at the north end of the precinct, nestled between the shadows of the temples of Xilonen and the Feathered Serpent. It was a small building made of stone, the same as the surrounding temples, but the inside more resembled a house. The single room's light came from the open door curtain and a small hearth, and there wasn't much room to move around inside; baskets overflowing with cotton cloth took up one side and stacks of maguey-fiber manuscripts filled the other. A man in a black robe sat on a reed mat in front of the smoking hearth, hunched over an open book. But when he looked up at us, he immediately came to his feet. "My Lord and Lady," he said with a flourishing bow, sweeping his fingers across the ground at our feet. "Your visit brings me much joy!"

Little Reed nudged Yamehecatl forward. "Today our son turns the seventh page of his life."

The man smiled at Yamehecatl. "Ah yes, the young prince's naming day! Are you ready to hear your destiny, My Lord?"

"Of course!" Yamehecatl answered with a bright smile. "What must I do?"

The soothsayer beckoned him over to the reed mat and Yamehecatl sat while the man ventured to one of the shelves where he kept a box of the sacred mushrooms. He chewed a small handful of them as he ran his finger over the spines of the manuscripts, counting as he went. Finding the volume he wanted, he brought it back. "Before we get to the actual naming, I shall tell you about your tonalli, so you will know who you are and what your destiny is."

"I already know I'm destined to be the King," Yamehecatl said.

"Yes, but there's more to you than that, my young lord. Reading your tonalli will help you realize your ambitions and become the best king you can be." He sat next to Yamehecatl and opened the book. "You were born on the day Nine Wind, which is the ninth day of the second week of the Tonalamatl. The god Quetzalcoatl rules your soul, for Nine Wind is one of his sacred days."

Yamehecatl looked at the book and read, "Nine Winds are compassionate people who show great sympathy for others."

"You can read the sacred script?" the soothsayer asked, startled.

"My Nantli taught me." Yamehecatl beamed at me. "She's a really good teacher."

"That's very impressive. Maybe you can read the rest to us?"

Yamehecatl dove in, reading each glyph carefully, sometimes pausing to work things out. "Nine Winds are extremely analytical and curious about the world. They want to know how the world works, and why."

"He'll do well in the priesthood," Little Reed noted, proud.

But the soothsayer shook his head. "Actually, Nine Winds tend not to be particularly religious, and they don't flourish in such environments. When it comes to spirituality, they prefer to find their own way."

Little Reed frowned, puzzled, so I offered, "But that's good too. At least he won't blindly follow doctrine. That's what we're trying to teach everyone, right?"

He nodded, conceding the point. "Does this mean we shouldn't put him in the calmecac?"

"Some elements will speak to him while others will aggravate him," the soothsayer said. "But he won't learn all that interests him by going to the telpochcalli either, where they don't teach reading or writing or mathematics."

Yamehecatl stared at us, a look of panic on his face; would we back out on our promise to let him go to school with Night Wind because of this? Hoping to put him at ease, I suggested to Little Reed, "We can put together a special curriculum, one that brings the best of both schools to him."

Little Reed nodded. "A good idea."

The soothsayer returned the book to its stack and sat again. "I think the gods are ready to speak your name now."

Yamehecatl sat cross-legged as the soothsayer sat very still, meditating. When Yamehecatl started fidgeting, the man suddenly opened his eyes and said, "Ehecacone. That is the name the gods have chosen for you, the name you shall carry the remainder of your days."

"Son of the Wind?" Yamehecatl wrinkled his nose. "My tatli is not windy, except when he eats beans!"

The soothsayer stifled a laugh but my own came out as a bray that prompted Little Reed to blush. "That's not what is meant by the Wind," the soothsayer explained. "It refers to Lord Quetzalcoatl, Tollan's most beloved god."

"Oh." Yamehecatl tapped his chin thoughtfully, brow still creased. "But my tatli isn't

Quetzalcoatl." He turned to Little Reed. "Are you?"

The soothsayer said, "Son doesn't mean actual son; we are all sons and daughters of the Feathered Serpent, for it was with his sacrifice that he gave us all life. That is all it means."

Yamehecatl glanced at Little Reed again, who gave him a smile. "Well, I suppose it will do."

I laughed and took Yamehecatl by the hand as Little Reed paid the soothsayer a bolt of fine cloth for his services. "It's a good strong name for a king," I assured him.

□

It was still several hours until the celebratory ball game, so while Yamehecatl went to find Night Wind—to share his new name and do some roughhousing before lunch—I went to the kitchens to check on the menu for tonight's feast. The mixing aromas of roasting venison, caiman, rabbit, fish, and chiles gave the air a heavy feel, and the heat was stifling; I didn't know how the servants spent all day every day in here, preparing meal after meal for the nobles they served.

I was about to sample one of the sweet maize cakes my son loved so dearly when Yamehecatl came into the kitchen, looking cross. "No one knows where Night Wind is. We were supposed to play this morning."

"Maybe he had to help his father with something." When he peered over the edge of the large cooking stone to watch the maize cakes frying, I pushed him away. "Not so close, Yamehecatl. It's very hot."

He puckered up his face. "My name isn't Yamehecatl anymore. It's Ehecacone."

"I know. I'm sorry. To me you've always been Yamehecatl, so please forgive me if I don't immediately call you by your new name." But in my heart, he would always be my little Warm Breeze. I took his hand and led him out of the kitchen; the cooks didn't need a child underfoot.

"Do you like my name, Nantli?"

"I do."

We walked in silence for a moment before Yamehecatl asked, "Tatli isn't Quetzalcoatl, is he?"

If only he were, I thought with a chuckle. My life might have been so much simpler. "No, he's not. He's the god's son, not the god himself."

Yamehecatl nodded. Then, after a hesitation, he asked, "Is Tatli really my tatli?" He gazed up at me with pleading in his eyes.

I'd often debated telling him the truth, and I knew eventually it would come up—for Yamehecatl was intelligent and never forgot anything—but still, seeing the desperation on his face broke my heart. I had to tell him, but how to do it without hurting him?

I thought about that conversation Black Otter and I had several years ago, about his own father, and the answer came to me.

I knelt in front of Yamehecatl and took both of his hands in mine. "You know Black Otter, Night Wind's father?"

"Of course."

"Black Otter was raised by my uncle as his own son even though Ihuitimal was not really his father—someone else was—but that didn't matter because Ihuitimal treated him well and loved him the same as he would his own son; in every way that mattered, he was Black Otter's tatli."

"Then Tatli isn't my father?" he asked, near tears now. "And my name—?"

420

"The god might have put you in my belly, but the king is your tatli in every way that matters, and nothing can take that away from you; he will always be there for you, and he will love you no matter what."

Yamehecatl smiled, wiping his tears away. "Will you do something with me, Nantli?"

"I'd love to, but there's so much to do to prepare for tonight—"

"Please?" Fresh tears rolled down his cheeks.

I hated seeing him cry—especially when I caused it—and really, why shouldn't I give my son an hour or two? He wouldn't be a child forever and I'd regret all those missed opportunities. "Very well, my dear. What do you want to do?"

"Will you teach me how you do magic?" he asked, hopeful. "I told Night Wind that you could do magic, and he bet that I could do magic too because that kind of things gets passed down in families."

I couldn't quite keep the irritation from my voice. "You told Night Wind that I can do magic?"

"Don't worry, I told him he can't tell anyone, not even his tatli, and he promised not to. His word is good, Nantli."

"That may be, but we've discussed this before; I don't want you telling anyone about my magic. People can be uneasy about that kind of thing, and fear undermines my ability to rule."

"If I have magic, Nantli, I'm going to tell everybody because *ayya!* I hope I have it!"

I sighed. He still had so much to learn. "Tell me, do you ever get a tingling in your fingers or your hands?"

He nodded, getting excited. "When I fall asleep on my hand, or sometimes my feet start tingling when Lord Mazatzin makes me sit still for the entire lesson."

Chuckling, I said, "That's not magic. Everyone's hands and feet do that when they lay or sit on them too long. Have you ever made anything move by willing it to do so?"

"No."

"Have you ever spoken to an animal and they understood you?" He started to get excited again, until I added, "A wild animal, I mean, not the tame birds in the menagerie."

He grumbled, "No." He started to sniffle. "Night Wind was wrong."

I sighed. "Just because you don't have magic now doesn't mean you won't in the future. I didn't acquire my magic until almost eight years ago, when I became pregnant with you."

Yamehecatl eyed me, shocked. "Did you steal my magic, Nantli?"

I laughed and hugged him. "Heavens no! I'm certain yours is asleep, as mine was, and when the time's right—when you're ready—it will wake up."

He smiled, still disappointed but putting on a brave face. "Can we go to the priestly gardens and you can tell me about the flowers?"

"Anything you want, dear. It's your special day, after all."

As we passed the great hall on the way to my quarters—so we could take the secret passageway out to the priestly gardens—I spotted Citlallotoc standing with Flame Tongue, trying mightily to not look pained as the older man prattled on about the magnificence of his own great hall back in Xico. Anacoana stood off to the side, glancing clandestinely over at Citlallotoc every now and again. Citlallotoc had long ago laughed at any notion of an attraction between them, but given the flush on her cheeks when she looked at him, he'd be a fool to not notice.

I stepped into the great hall. "Lord Citlallotoc, if you wouldn't mind, I require your assistance."

Citlallotoc hastily bowed to Flame Tongue and begged his forgiveness for the interruption, then he came to me and Yamehecatl. "What is it, My Lady?"

"I'll speak with you on the way, but rest assured it is urgent," I said loudly, making certain Flame Tongue could hear me. I grabbed Citlallotoc's arm with my free hand and led both him and Yamehecatl out of the room.

Once out of earshot of the great hall, Citlallotoc asked, "What is so urgent, My Lady?"

"Getting you away from that braggart," I said with a smile. "I cannot imagine a more tedious job than entertaining Lord Flame Tongue."

He chuckled. "Was I so obvious? Thank you for the rescue."

Yamehecatl broke free of my hand and circled around to grab Citlallotoc's. "Guess what? I have a new name! Can you guess what it is?"

Citlallotoc smiled. "I wouldn't even begin to venture a guess, but judging by the looks of you, it's a good one."

"I'm now Ehecacone! I'm the son of Quetzalcoatl!"

"That is a fantastic name, very strong."

He nodded. "Nantli and I are going to the priestly gardens. Do you want to come with us?"

Glancing between me and Yamehecatl, he said, "I wouldn't want to intrude on your time with your mother—"

"We would welcome your company," I said. "Unless you'd rather go back to Flame Tongue and listen to him talk about how much better his artisans are back in Xico."

"No thank you."

I laughed and led the way.

CHAPTER TWENTY-FOUR

 Once out in the gardens, Yamehecatl ran ahead of us, swinging an invisible sword at the flowers and trees. "Don't worry, Nantli! I'll protect you!" He made his own shooting-arrow sounds and cries of invisible enemies dying.

"He certainly has war in his heart," Citlallotoc noted with a lopsided grin.

"Gods know where he gets it from," I said.

"He'll outgrow it."

"I hope so." I watched Yamehecatl barrel through the flowerbeds, leaving a swath of destruction; I always felt guilty asking the other priests and priestesses to fix the disasters he left everywhere in the garden. "Let's talk about something else," I suggested.

"Very well. What would you like to talk about?"

"Anacoana," I said with a sly smile. As his friend, I considered it not only my duty to rescue him from tedious Flame Tongue, but to also pry information out of him regarding a mutual attraction for the braggart's only unmarried daughter.

He cast me a startled glance. "What about her?"

"I bet she really enjoyed your tour of the city today." The sudden flare of color in his cheeks told me I'd hit the right spot. "I see you're not completely oblivious to that longing look she's always giving you. So, tell me, what are you going to do about it?"

He hesitated. "I'm not going to do anything about it."

"Why ever not? She's very nice and kind, and very beautiful."

He cringed when I said that. Puzzling. "She is."

"But?"

"She's too young."

I laughed. "Many would argue that at nineteen, she's too old."

"Lord Flame Tongue would never agree to a marriage between us."

"Why not?"

"Because what father would marry his only remaining daughter to someone who looks like a monster?"

I laughed again, with a touch of annoyance. "You don't look like a monster."

This time his laugh was hollow. "I know what the women say behind my back, when they think I can't hear them. 'Pity about his arm; he used to be quite handsome before that.'"

"Anyone who says that is an idiot. And we both know Anacoana is not one of them; I see the way she looks at you."

"And what way is that?" he asked, bitter.

"As if you're the moon and the stars and the gods, all wrapped up in one person. I bet even her father notices, and he's waiting for you to ask about tying your cape to her dress."

The scowl slowly vanished, this time replaced with uncertainty. "You really think so?"

"Absolutely. And he'd be a fool to turn you down; you'll make an excellent husband, and a father too—a far better one than he ever thought of being." I took hold of his arm and hugged it to me as we walked. "Don't you think it's time you settled down?"

Citlallotoc put on a distant smile. "She *is* quite stunning."

"Ask her father tonight at dinner. You will make her the happiest woman in the world."

We reached a small grove of trees and I was about to sit, but Yamehecatl came up, looking vexed. "You said you would do something with me."

"I will, when I'm ready," I scolded him. He always expected me to jump and do whatever he wanted, but the long walk left my feet aching and I wanted to rest a little while. Little Reed wasn't the only one with aches.

"We can do something while your mother takes a break," Citlallotoc suggested.

"I want to do something with Nantli!" Yamehecatl spat.

"And we will," I assured him.

He rolled his eyes. "No, you'll keep talking to Citlallotoc about that stupid woman."

I cast him a scathing frown. "That kind of rudeness is unacceptable, Yamehecatl."

One would think I'd shoved him; his eyes grew twice their normal size and he shouted, "That is not my name! Stop calling me that! That's a baby's name and I'm not a baby!"

His overreaction so startled me that I didn't say anything.

Citlallotoc didn't share my reticence; he advanced on Yamehecatl like an angry bear. "You will not speak to your mother that way, little man. You will show her respect at all times."

"I don't have to!" I caught a whiff of octli on the breeze and Yamehecatl started swaying on his feet. "Why should I, when all she wanted to do was get rid of me before I was even born?" He turned to me, anger ebbing from him. "Why did you want to kill me, Nantli? What had I done to make you hate me so?"

Yamehecatl was often nasty when the drunkenness took him, and this wasn't even the first time he'd brought up this particular thorn in my conscience, but to even suggest that I hated him stung so deeply I had no words. I wanted to hug him and apologize for something I knew I could never apologize enough for.

Citlallotoc was having none of it. "I'm putting you over my knee!" He reached out to grab Yamehecatl by the arm.

But my son darted away from him rabbit-fast, shouting all manner of profanities I didn't even know he knew. He ran fast as he could, stumbling but somehow keeping his feet. Citlallotoc moved to follow him, but I grabbed his wrist and held him back.

"Let him go," I said, my voice choked.

"You can't let him disrespect you!"

"Let him run; there's no use wearing ourselves out trying to catch him when he's in that state. He'll tire quickly."

Citlallotoc watched him bound through the tall grass near the garden's back wall. "What on earth triggered him?"

"I don't know." My choke turned to tears and I started shaking.

"He doesn't know what he's saying when he gets like that."

"I'm a terrible mother," I muttered, trying not to completely lose it.

"You're a wonderful mother."

I watched Yamehecatl skipping happily, his anger now forgotten for laughter. He tripped and fell, disappearing in the grass, and when he didn't stand up again, I knew he'd finally passed out. "I so desperately want to help him, but I have no idea how."

"My mother told me once that there's no harder job than being a mother, and she always laughed when Father complained about having to sit around for a few hours listening to his war council. I think I'm inclined to believe her. Let's go and get him, and I'll carry him back to the palace for you and we can put him to bed. Maybe he'll recover in time for dinner."

I doubted that. He would probably sleep until midnight.

We walked out to where Yamehecatl fell, but he wasn't there. Great, he was hiding from us. He knew I hated that. We split up and walked through the grass, looking for him—he certainly couldn't have gone far in his condition. "Ehecacone, enough hiding. You need to go home and sleep this off." Hopefully remembering his proper name this time would help.

But he still didn't answer.

Citlallotoc wove through the grass, moving farther and farther away from me. "Enough games, little man. Show yourself."

But still nothing.

I scoured the grass around me in a wide swath with growing concern. Where was my son? I called out to him over and over again as I moved from place to place, praying he'd suddenly jump out and scare me. "Yamehecatl! Where are you?" My pulse climbed to new, painful heights.

"Come out this instant or I'll tan your backside, Ehecacone!" Citlallotoc yelled, his voice carrying over the gardens. Birds took flight from the nearby trees, but nothing more. He looked so far away now, practically at the palace gate. When we met frantic gazes, he called, "I'll fetch the guards. Keep looking for him."

I nodded and kept stumbling around, not even certain where to search anymore. I was almost to the river, where the grass gave way to bare banks, and there was no sign of footprints on either side. Would I have heard him if he fell into the river?

Suddenly, quail took flight behind me and I turned to see the grass fifty paces away moving, as if someone crawled through it. My heart skipped a beat before finally settling, my panic giving way to anger. "This is going to get you a whipping, little man," I muttered as I followed the moving grass, preparing to cut Yamehecatl off before he reached the wall.

As I got closer, he moved faster through the grass—faster than I'd ever seen him run, let alone crawl on all fours. I picked up the pace, building to a full sprint.

But just as I was about to cut him off, he stopped and I overshot him by a couple of steps. I immediately went back. "Yamehecatl?"

This time, a deep, rumbling growl answered me.

I stumbled backwards, every instinct telling me to run, but my son was somewhere in this long grass, unconscious and vulnerable. *I must protect him!* I pulled my sacrificial blade, gripping it tight in my sweaty hand, and began advancing again.

Suddenly something knocked my legs out from under me. I rolled over to see a monstrous black jaguar glaring at me with smoky obsidian mirrors for eyes. Its body glowed purple, like an apparition. It bared its fangs, drawing my attention to what it clutched in its mouth. My heart stopped.

It was Yamehecatl.

The jaguar had him by the head, a tear of blood leaking from his left eye. When I reached out, unable to breathe, the jaguar ran off into the grass again, taking my son with it.

"No!" I tried to follow but I couldn't move, as if stuck in a vat of honey. I fought it and eventually found my feet, and I dashed after the jaguar, pushing myself faster and harder. My lungs burned with the effort. *It's not too late! I can still save him!*

But the jaguar was so far ahead of me, so close to the wall, out in the open where the rabbits had chewed all the grass to the ground. It could jump the stone wall without trouble and all hope of saving my son would vanish. I had to stop it now, before it was too late.

Magic pulsing in my hands, I dropped to my knees and pushed it and all my desperation into the ground. *Please help me! Someone! Anyone!*

A strange rumbling came from the ground—not under me, but rather near the wall. As the jaguar reached the halfway point, a flood of brown and gray spilled out of the rabbit holes and crashed over it, sucking it under.

When it clawed its way to the surface again, it no longer had Yamehecatl in its mouth. It trod the wave of rabbits, snarling and hissing, dragging the mass of gray and brown fur with it towards the wall. Soon I saw my son lying on the ground, a handful of rabbits standing guard over him as the rest of their brethren battled the demon cat.

I scrambled to my feet and sprinted to him. *Great Feathered Serpent, please let him be alive!* The rabbits backed off as I approached and I scooped my son into my arms. I clutched him to my chest, so limp, so lifeless, and when I put my hand on his head, it was misshapen and wet. I forced that to the back of my mind and stroked his face, trying to draw him awake. "Nantli's here, my dear little Warm Breeze."

He didn't respond.

I checked him for a pulse. Panic numbed me when I found none. He wasn't breathing either, so I pinched his nose and blew air into his lungs, but still he didn't move, didn't rouse. Blood flowed down his neck from puncture wounds at his temples and behind his ears, coating my hands and drying to a dark stain in the day's growing heat.

Not certain what else to do, I pushed my magic into him, focusing my thoughts on healing him, on making his heart pump and his blood flow again. But it did nothing. No matter how much magic I dumped into him, the cloying smell of death clung to him.

"No no no no no!" I whispered, crushing him against my chest in some feeble hope he'd suddenly cry out that he couldn't breathe because of it. "I'm sorry, Yamehecatl," I sobbed. "Please forgive me for failing you!"

Hissing and growling made me look up. The jaguar stood atop the stone wall, out of reach of the rabbits bouncing like fleas below it. It bared its teeth, laughing at me.

I glared right back, my fury growing with each breath, the magic burning like fire in my hands. "You will pay for this, you demon!" I screamed, and released everything I had at it.

The rabbits nearest me dropped over, convulsing, and those at the wall tried to run for cover, but they too dropped to the ground after only a few steps, their bodies shaking violently, their mouths foaming and eyes rolled up into their heads in their death throes.

But the jaguar hissed at me and disappeared over the wall.

"Come back and face me, you coward!" I screamed, letting go of everything I had left. When the roaring in my veins finally gave out, I fell over, like a slab of wet stone, my own heartbeat receding in my ears. I stared at Yamehecatl lying on the ground next to me.

The sky gradually changed colors, as if sunset was falling; the Divine Dream leaking into my consciousness. *Like the other time I died,* I thought. A jolt of fear shot through me, but when I thought about how afraid Yamehecatl must be right now, having to face the trials of the underworld by himself, I let it go. I had failed him in life, but in death, I could walk the road into Mictlan with him, holding his hand as we faced the trials together. I tried to take his hand in mine, but my body refused to move.

The sky grew a deeper orange, and soon I saw Yamehecatl standing off in the distance, resting his arm on the back of the Black Dog standing next to him. He'd been crying but now he smiled, wiping his tears away. *I'm coming, my dear Warm Breeze,* I called out to him, waiting for death to finally release me from my fleshy prison so I could hug him again.

But both Yamehecatl and the Black Dog looked off to the side. The smile melted away from my son's face.

Citlallotoc knelt next to Yamehecatl's body and felt his neck. His face paled but he immediately moved to me next, pressing his fingers hard into my neck under my jaw. My heart still soldiered on, one slow beat after another. He shouted silent orders at the guards who had come with him, and they looked shocked by whatever it was he said, but after he yelled again—brooking no further arguments—one of them pulled his own blade and cut Citlallotoc's arm at his elbow joint, opening the vein. The other man turned me onto my back and held my head while Citlallotoc let the blood dribble into my open mouth.

The first drops brought a tingling, but as he fed me more, the magic surged. The sky's orange-ness faded to blue, and the world came back one sound at a time; Citlallotoc's voice, the guards, the birds, the rustling of the leaves. My heartbeat grew stronger.

But so did my panic. *No! Yamehecatl needs me!* I tried to move, tried to fight them off, but my body refused to obey me. The blood kept coming and the hunger grew more ravenous; I longed to grab hold of Citlallotoc's wounded arm and suck every last drop of blood out of him.

Eventually I gathered enough strength to make my jaw move, but when I tried to speak, it came out as a slurring, sobbing babble. Citlallotoc finally withdrew his arm, pale from more than mere blood loss. He checked my pulse again and let out a deep breath. "One of you carry her; I'll carry the prince."

After one of the guards had bandaged his arm, Citlallotoc gathered up Yamehecatl's body, leaning him against his shoulder as if he were asleep. The larger of the two guards cradled me in his arms and carried me away.

Yamehecatl ran after me, the Black Dog following, but when we reached the gate, he fell to his knees and reached out to me, his own voice lost to my ears. *I'm sorry, my love!* I cried, but he couldn't hear me anymore. His sobbing face was the last thing I saw as the guard closed the gate, and it followed me into the darkness once I closed my eyes.

▢

The darkness lasted forever, haunted by images of Yamehcatl crouched among the reeds around the Black Lake in Mictlan, frozen mid-sob, tears like icicles on his pale, bluish cheeks. I tried to carry him away, but when I touched him, death's cold grasp stung my skin, burrowing deep and threatening to overcome me. I could only escape it by letting him go and leaving him behind.

Eventually, the dreams faded and I swam in blackness, a welcome respite from the nightmares. Soon after that, everything became a blur of colors and shapes and incomprehensible sounds. I recognized voices though: Little Reed, Malinalli, Mazatzin, Citlallotoc, Mitotia. I tasted the tang of blood and after a while the incomprehensible sounds began making sense. But I wanted to go back to not understanding when I realized Little Reed was discussing Yamehecatl's funeral arrangements with Mazatzin and Malinalli. I wanted to fall asleep and never wake up again.

But as with most things in my life, I didn't get what I wanted.

Little Reed was the only one there when I finally woke up, feeling as if I would never sleep again. He sat in bed next to me, smoking his pipe in silence, staring into the hearth, but when I shifted my weight, he gave me a relieved smile. "Welcome back, my love." He stroked my hair.

"Water," I begged. Every muscle in my body ached.

He poured a cup and helped me sit up to drink it. I took in cup after cup until my belly ached, then I leaned back against him, exhausted again. "How long?" I asked, no will to move again.

"Four days, though for a while there, we didn't think you'd ever wake up again; we thought you'd gone too far into the afterlife."

"I wish I had," I muttered.

Little Reed kissed my temple, tension in his arms around me. "I, for one, am very glad you didn't."

I clamped my eyes shut, expecting tears, but I was dry. "He's all alone now, Little Reed."

"Not completely. Xolotl will help him."

"I should have gone with him. You should have seen him when the guards carried me away...." I opened my eyes to stare up at the ceiling. "I failed him."

"I doubt that," Little Reed whispered at my ear. "He knew how devoted you were to him."

"I never should have taken him out to the garden. I should have insisted we do something in the palace, where he would have been safe."

"The garden should have been safe. We set traps to keep the jaguars out."

"Nowhere is safe anymore," I muttered. "Mextli warned me I'd pay for helping Quetzalcoatl, and now Smoking Mirror has made good on that."

Little Reed sat up straighter. "Smoking Mirror?"

I nodded. "He sent his nahual to kill our son, and he would have dragged him over the wall and eaten him if I hadn't sent the rabbits after him." I wished I could cry to relieve the painful stinging behind my eyes. "I never should have let Yamehecatl wander off, but I thought it was better to let him calm down. He was having one of his episodes, and he said hurtful things. Citlallotoc wanted to spank him but I told him to let him be, to let him run until he passed out, so he'd be easier to deal with. I should have let Citlallotoc discipline him. He wouldn't have been alone in the long grass, where we couldn't see him...." I started choking and Little Reed poured me more water.

"You can't blame yourself, Papalotl. You did what you thought best. I might have done the same thing if I'd been out there with him. Give yourself time to heal—"

"And everything will be all right?" I jerked away from him, a deep-seated rage filling me with frightening strength. "I'm never going to be all right again!"

He frowned, the hurt plain on his face. "I know it seems so, my love, but we'll get through this, together. We've been through so much already, and while this hurts the worst of anything, we're strong, and we'll make Smoking Mirror pay for this." A similar flame of fury burned in Little Reed's eyes.

I lay back in his arms again, relieved. He'd seemed so collected, so calm about all this, and it filled me with purpose to see he really wasn't. "What are we going to do?"

He kissed my temple. "Let's not talk about it yet. You need to rest and recoup your strength, and we must bury our son tomorrow."

I squeezed my eyes shut again, the pain and panic swelling in my chest. "Will you stay with me, so I don't have to wake up alone?"

"I will stay however long you need me to, my dearest Butterfly."

CHAPTER TWENTY-FIVE

I felt stronger by morning, though seeing Yamehecatl's body knocked that out of me again. Mazatzin and Malinalli had wrapped him in paper ribbons, according to royal tradition, and I dressed him in his favorite rabbit uniform. Maybe it would give him good luck when he faced the underworld's trials, but the sight of him in it broke my heart. There was a small tear on the right seam that he'd asked me to fix but I hadn't gotten around to it. And now he'd never again ask me to fix it, or anything else. He would never again ask me to sing him a song before bed, nor would he ever spend a single night in the dormitories at the calmecac.

Only Malinalli, Mazatzin, and Citlallotoc attended the funeral ceremony in the great hall, and I was grateful Little Reed kept it a private affair. Malinalli held my hand, her eyes red from crying as the men finished digging out the burial hole the servants had started the night before in front of the enormous hearth. I didn't cry; I'd turned into an empty cavern whose silence was broken only by a distant moaning when the pain turned physical in my chest. I was Mictlan, dark and cold, my breath tense with the misery and fear of the dead clambering down its road in search of a hard-won peace.

Once the men finished digging they washed themselves with water and crushed flowers. Mazatzin and Citlallotoc carried Yamehecatl's body to me, holding him up so I could give him one last kiss on his bandaged forehead. I made the gesture quickly, horrified by how my stomach growled at the scent of decay seeping through the bandages. They set him gently into the hole.

Little Reed carried over a small brown dog that had been tethered in the corner. It wagged its tail and shivered as he whispered soothingly to it; we'd fed it a maize cake filled with yauhtli before we'd started the ceremony, in preparation for its task. Standing in front of the pit, he prayed,

"Lord Xolotl, we gather today to honor you,
To beg your mercy upon our son.
Lend him your guidance as he faces the Black River,
The Cavern of Arrowheads,
The Field of Fiery Flags,
And the Mountain of Obsidian Blades.
Nurture his courage when he reaches the plains of Mictlan,
So he may face Lord Death's judgment with bravery
And resolve.
Show him the way as you showed our Lord Quetzalcoatl.
Counsel him,
Care for him in our absence.
Please accept our gratitude for your work,
For your own sacrifices in the name of humanity."

Little Reed set the little dog in the hole atop Yamehecatl's body and slit its throat. It didn't make a sound as it stumbled, oblivious, showing the yauhtli did its job. It kept its feet, bleeding profusely, but soon collapsed and laid still, the blood staining Yamehecatl's paper bandages.

Malinalli handed me a bundle of bone flowers and I tore the petals off and showered them on my son, the smell of vanilla reminding me of all the love I'd been privileged to know in my short life—my mother, my father, Nimilitzli, Little Reed, my son—all but one of them gone now. Little Reed held me close while Mazatzin recited prayers praising Quetzalcoatl.

I hadn't given the god any thought in days, but hearing Mazatzin's words filled me with questions. Why hadn't Quetzalcoatl protected our son? Certainly Yamehecatl was part of his great plan, for gods didn't make mistakes or do anything unintended. And yet he'd let Smoking Mirror kill Yamehecatl; he'd looked after Little Reed, but not our son, as if he meant nothing at all to him. Bitterness swelled inside me when I imagined the god paying no attention at all to what we did here today.

Once Mazatzin finished, Citlallotoc stepped forward and placed Yamehecatl's play sword in the hole with him. After letting his hand linger a moment, he stepped away, his face haggard.

"Are we ready to cover him?" Little Reed asked, his voice breaking as he did. When Citlallotoc answered with a silent nod, Little Reed handed out the digging sticks and the men scraped the dirt back into the hole. I couldn't breathe and had to leave the room when they reset the hearthstones.

Tradition dictated a week of feasting to honor the deceased, but I hadn't the courage to face the hundreds of nobles who'd come to celebrate my son's naming day; I didn't want them to see how raw and lost I was. Little Reed agreed I should ease myself into the public sphere, so as not to overburden myself. He walked me back to my quarters after lunch then returned to the great hall to play host to our guests while I rested.

But I did very little sleeping; I stared at the curtain over the nursery doorway, the bells tinkling softly in the breeze from my garden patio. I imagined Yamehecatl tearing aside that curtain and running to me to complain of a nightmare, confirming all this was only a terrible dream, and I finally found my tears again. When Little Reed returned later to invite me to eat with him in his quarters, I eagerly accepted. I couldn't stand being so close to the empty nursery.

"But shouldn't one of us be at the feast tonight?" I asked as the servants brought us a modest dinner.

"Citlallotoc is hosting for us," Little Reed said, filling my plate. "It's more important that we be together, only the two of us right now."

Since I'd been unable to sleep the last couple of hours, my thoughts had wandered off to the future and what Yamehecatl's death meant for our kingdom. We had no heir, and I couldn't bear any more children even if I wanted to. *You're just like your mother, and see what befell her?* Ihuitimal derided me from the grave. And Little Reed was like my father. I wasn't certain whether to laugh or cry. "What are we going to do now?"

"About what?" Little Reed asked.

"You have no heir to carry on your legacy."

He fidgeted. "I haven't really given it any thought; it seems too early."

"I know it does, but...this whole tragedy reminds me that time is short, and given how quickly you age...we both know what happened when Mixcoatl had no legitimate heir in place."

He took a bite of tamale and chewed thoughtfully a moment before saying, "I know *we* can't produce a new heir, but perhaps the god would bless you again—"

"I'm barren, Little Reed. And before you get any notions that that doesn't matter, because Mother was barren when she had you...maybe that's the reason she didn't survive. That's not a risk I'm willing to take."

"Nor would I expect you to. But how do you know you're barren?"

"I haven't bled in almost four years."

He furrowed his brows. "But you're still so young."

"I suspect my magic takes a toll on me. I'm surprised you haven't noticed how gray I've gotten the last couple of years."

"Probably because I find you as beautiful as ever," he said with a smile that should have lit up my desire, but it only irritated me. I hoped the desire never came back, so I'd finally be at peace with my lot in life.

"The point is that you can't look to me to provide our future anymore, and we must have a plan going forward."

"Of course, but must we really discuss this right now?" He looked as if I might spring at him like a jaguar at the slightest provocation. "We've only just buried Yamehecatl, and it's been a very sad day, for both of us. I agree our time is not unlimited, but we need room to grieve and heal from this tragedy; I need distance before making any kind of judgment on how to proceed."

I bowed my head, ashamed. "I'm sorry. It was selfish of me to not think about how all this was affecting you; I've been so wrapped up in my own pain, and I feel so lost...." I started sobbing when he moved over to let me lean against him. "I feel as if I'm drowning in a pit of honey, but trying to work out what to do next dulls the pain a bit, if only for a moment. It keeps me from dwelling in dark places."

He nodded. "Continuing with my daily routines has kept me from falling apart at times, so far be it from me to tell you that now isn't the time for such discussions. But may I ask one thing though? Can it wait until tomorrow? Today has been so...strenuous, and I want to eat dinner and...." He hesitated before asking, "And if it isn't too difficult for you, would you consider staying the night with me, here in my quarters? If only to have you nearby...for comfort?"

I wiped my tears away and nodded. "I'd rather not go back to my quarters. It was hard enough being alone in there today."

"Stay here with me as long as you wish." He held my dish out to me, encouraging me to eat.

After dinner, I returned to my quarters to change into my night dress. Even with the hearth filled with fire, the room felt cold and barren. I knelt before my idol of Quetzalcoatl and murmured a short prayer—which I did every night, though tonight it felt so cursory—then I hurried back to Little Reed's warm, friendly quarters.

He was already in bed, dressed in a knee-length xicolli. He held the blankets open for me. "You can have my side of the bed."

I slipped in next to him and once he'd folded the blankets over us, I nestled up against him and let out a deep breath. He hooked one arm around me but rested the other on his stomach, holding me close. I listened to his breathing and heartbeat, a lullaby that soothed my anguish like yauhtli.

I had just dozed off when someone shook the bells on the door curtain. Little Reed roused with a start and looked around blurry-eyed before calling out, "Who is it?"

"It's me, My Lord," Citlallotoc's voice answered from beyond the curtain.

Little Reed sat up slowly, yawning. "Come in."

Citlallotoc opened the curtain, but he stopped short when he saw me lying next to Little Reed. He looked away as if he'd walked in on the two of us naked. "I'm sorry. I thought you were alone."

"No need to apologize. What do you need?"

Citlallotoc cast a furtive glance back at me but approached the bed with purpose. He went to his knees, took out his sword, and set it on the ground. "I've come to surrender myself for your judgment, My Lord and Lady."

Little Reed rubbed his eyes, confused. "What are you talking about?"

"Seven years ago, you and Lady Quetzalpetlatl charged me with protecting your son, but I failed you, and the prince, costing you the heir to the throne. Therefore it is only honorable that I forfeit my life in repayment for my failures."

I snatched the sword and clutched it to my breast, my heart thudding. "You've never once failed in any of your duties to either me or Topiltzin, and most certainly not to our son," I cried. "You're not to blame for his death, and I won't listen to you beg for a punishment you don't deserve! We've already lost one loved one, so don't even think of making us suffer yet another loss. You are a dear, dear friend—practically family—and if I had another child, I wouldn't hesitate to entrust you with their care too." I wiped away angry tears.

Citlallotoc looked up at me with such anguish that I felt bad for yelling at him, even in a fit of despair. "I'm humbled by your forgiveness, My Lady," he murmured, his eyes wet.

"You don't need forgiveness, but if that's the only way to heal your heart, then fine, you have it. And my love and gratitude for everything you gave my son." I handed the sword to Little Reed then hugged Citlallotoc.

Little Reed nodded, saying nothing, but his wet eyes spoke volumes. He escorted Citlallotoc back to the door, murmuring something before handing him his sword. Citlallotoc thanked him and departed.

□

We didn't talk the next morning, for Little Reed left early to entertain our guests and let me sleep in. I finally woke up when Malinalli brought me breakfast. "Hungry?" she asked as she set a steaming tlaxcalli in front of me.

I slowly picked it apart, eating it one small bite at a time. Her expectant gaze asked how I was doing, so I answered, "I'm feeling better today."

She smiled. "I'm glad to hear it."

"What did I miss while I was unconscious?" When she hesitated, I added, "Thinking about work keeps me from dwelling."

She filled me in on the daily mundane news of our order. Classes at the calmecac had been cancelled since Yamehecatl's death, but everyone was back in school today.

"How is Night Wind?" I asked.

Malinalli shrugged. "He hasn't said much. He looks surly but goes about his duties."

"He's a strong one."

"It runs in the family. I've always admired your strength in the face of adversity."

I didn't feel strong, but her words lifted my spirits enough that I attended that night's mourning feast. I steadied my nerves in anticipation of an onslaught of concern and crushing pity, but beyond the customary murmurs of condolences, everyone was in a good mood. At first it took me aback seeing people laugh and smile, but hearing people talking about how Yamehecatl always ran around the great hall in his rabbit suit, swinging his sword and challenging them to duels, I couldn't help but smile too. And remember his smile with his unusually large front teeth, and how he'd tell me jokes that made so little sense that I couldn't help but laugh. He would never leave me—not truly—as long as I carried fragments of him in my heart, memories that could see me into the future.

With the meal finished and the men gathered near the hearth to smoke their pipes and talk, the women gathered around me for the xocolatl service. Anacoana had watched me furtively all night, so I invited her to sit with me.

"Have you enjoyed your visit?" I asked as I stirred the deep red liquid into a froth. When she bumbled over an answer, I added, "It's all right. Our days can't be all gloom and grief. That would be depressing."

Anacoana smiled. "Tollan is very beautiful, and it's so nice being away from home for a change. I just wish circumstances were better."

"As do we all." I poured her cup and handed it to her. "But life must go on eventually." I glanced over at the men, where Citlallotoc sat next to Little Reed. "You know Lord Citlallotoc?"

She flushed but nodded. "He comes to Xico to visit my father. He's a nice, honorable man."

"You like him?"

Her cheeks burned even darker. "Is this an appropriate discussion given the circumstances, My Lady?"

"What better way to honor the dead than by celebrating the joys of life? Such as love?"

She looked over at him too, and the tension left her shoulders. "I've loved him since I was sixteen, but he's not interested in me," she admitted. "Why would he be interested in someone else's scraps?"

"You're not scraps. And I know for a fact he's interested. We've talked about it."

"Really?"

"He's concerned your father will reject his proposal."

"Oh but he won't. Two years ago he was very particular about whom to marry me off to—it had to be someone who would be beneficial to Xico—but now he thinks I'm completely useless. 'All you do is eat my food and get in my way, Anacoana,' he says. A murdering bandit could indicate interest and my father would give me away to him without a second thought."

I gripped my cup tighter, magic building in my tense muscles. "He has no right to speak to you like that."

"What am I to do? He's my father."

I glared at Flame Tongue—who was also sitting next to Little Reed, cozy as a leech on a tasty host. He looked old and a bit wrinkled, but still annoyingly vital in spite of that. She couldn't rely on him dropping dead anytime soon. "I'll speak with Citlallotoc first thing tomorrow morning, and you won't have to worry any longer. He will treat you with the respect and kindness you deserve."

▫

Once the feast ended, Little Reed and I returned to his quarters and prepared ourselves for bed. "I'm glad to see you looking happier today," he noted as he turned down the blankets for us, as if we were an old peasant couple who always shared a bed.

"It felt good to be out among people again," I admitted. "I think I'll go to the temple tomorrow for a few hours, do a little work."

"If it will make you happy, then by all means." He took his new spot in bed and propped himself up on one elbow, waiting for me to join him.

"We still haven't talked," I pointed out, climbing in next to him.

"Must we?"

"I need to."

He sighed. "Then let's talk."

"We can't ignore our lack of an heir much longer, Little Reed."

"I know, and I was thinking about that today. We could designate an heir, perhaps choose one of the noble children from the calmecac—boy or girl, doesn't really matter, so long as they're wise and devoted to the god."

"Such as whom?"

"I don't know; nobody immediately comes to mind, but we could consult with Mazatzin and Malinalli, since they have more exposure to the students than we do."

I shook my head. "I'm not comfortable with that idea, Little Reed. What do we know of any of our students anyway? I know Night Wind rather well, and technically speaking he is family, but I wouldn't consider him a good candidate, given who his father is. And we know next to nothing about his upbringing before he came to Tollan. We haven't taken an active interest in the upbringing of any of the noble children, and to be honest, I think if we start making inquiries, conflicts will break out as fathers scramble to make the case that their child should be the next heir. The throne should go to someone you've raised from birth to honor Quetzalcoatl, whom you've taught to respect his ways from a very young age. The heir must be someone of your blood."

Little Reed sat up, confused. "Don't you mean 'we'?" When I shook my head, he matched me, taken aback. "I vowed to take no concubines—"

"I'm not suggesting you do."

"What *are* you suggesting?"

I swallowed the pain swelling in my chest. "You must take a new wife, Little Reed."

He climbed out of the bed to pace. "I will not set you aside, Papalotl—"

"Nor would my father set my mother aside, and we both know what that got him." I sighed, bowing my head. "We married for political considerations, and unfortunately they don't apply any—"

"I married you for love," he retorted.

"And love isn't going to produce an heir for us." I choked on the words but they

433

needed saying. "You can't permit love to ruin everything we've worked for, Little Reed. Tollan's throne needs an heir of our blood, and unfortunately I cannot provide that any longer, so it makes practical sense that you seek a new wife who can bear your children and give everyone the future they deserve." When he didn't reply, just faced the fire, holding both sides of his head as if he might tear his own hair out, I said, "We both know this is the right thing to do."

He let his hands drop to his sides. "You ask too much of me, Papalotl."

"Far less than the god has asked of me, Little Reed," I said, holding back the indignation rising inside me.

"This means we must get a divorce, in the temple."

"I know."

"And I will have to publicly accuse you of being barren, for the official record."

"It's not an accusation, Little Reed. It's the truth."

"Still...I can't put you through that humiliation."

I hadn't thought about that. We'd intentionally made divorce easy and private in Tollan, so people could move on quickly with their lives; but as King and Queen, we weren't afforded that same luxury. Everything we did had to be out in the public eye, for reasons of legitimacy. "It will only burn for a moment," I tried to assure him.

"And then I must find a wife."

I nodded. "I can do that for you—"

"I would rather you didn't." The edge to his voice stung, but when he looked at me, no anger lurked in his eyes. "This is painful enough for both of us without me inflicting that duty on you. I will find her myself."

"I don't want to do this, Little Reed, but we have to make the hard sacrifices, for the good of everyone else."

"I know." He sniffled. "Feel free to remain here tonight, but I must go walking now." He left without another word.

CHAPTER TWENTY-SIX

I decided to stay, hoping Little Reed would come back and we could share his bed one last time, but when I woke the next morning, he still wasn't there. He came to the great hall at breakfast, looking as if he hadn't slept, and though he returned my hesitant smile when I came in, he didn't speak to me. He listened quietly while our council talked of their plans for the day.

But afterwards, he followed me out into the courtyard on my way to the sacred precinct. "I spoke with Mazatzin, about what we discussed last night," he said, keeping his voice low as we walked. "He's willing to officiate over the untying ceremony whenever you wish."

"I don't wish to do it at all," I muttered.

He took my hand and pulled me to a stop. "Then let's not. Let's find an orphan babe that we can bring home and raise as our own. Nobody needs to know the child is not ours."

"And ask Malinalli or Mitotia to lie and say they were present for a birth that never happened? And am I supposed to pose as if I'm pregnant for the next nine months, tying pillows around my waist to make it look legitimate? I don't want to live a lie, Little Reed, and if that child dies too...I can't, Little Reed. I'm sorry, but I can't go through that again. I've had to sacrifice a great deal—often more than I think is fair—but I will sacrifice no more."

He frowned, a sour look on his face. "Divorcing me is no sacrifice?"

I scowled right back at him. "Of course it's a sacrifice, and how dare you suggest otherwise? But it's the last one I'm willing to make, for the good of fulfilling the god's plans. This is the end of it for me. If the god wants something done so badly, he can come here and do it himself." I needed to get away from him, before I rattled out more things he'd misunderstand, so I wrenched my arm away and marched out of the gate, my guards following me.

ꙮ

I found no peace at the temple. Instead I stared at Quetzalcoatl's idol with growing contempt, thinking about how little he seemed to care anymore. *At least when my mother and father died, I came to Nimilitzli and Mazatzin and Malinalli, but what good has come of Yamehecatl's death? My marriage to Little Reed is over, we're barely on speaking terms anymore, and nothing will ever be the same between us again. And yet you say nothing, you don't listen to my prayers, you don't assure me that this is all for a greater purpose and that I will be rewarded for all my suffering—*

"Forgive my disturbing you, My Lady," Black Otter spoke up behind me. He lurked in the temple entrance, wringing his bony hands, dressed in his black high priest robe.

I stood and smoothed my dress, hoping my cheeks weren't tear-stained. "No, it's quite all right. What can I do for you?"

He came inside, his gait reminding me of a timid mouse. "I wanted to say...to give you my condolences on your loss."

I didn't want to talk to him about Yamehecatl, but I accepted his words with the expected graciousness. "How is your own son? Is he coping all right?"

"Night Wind? Oh, he's doing well, I suppose. He's like obsidian; the more you bang away at him, the sharper he gets."

"He never did strike me as the weak kind."

Smiling, Black Otter said, "No, definitely not weak. But how are you?"

I clenched my jaw, trying to hold myself together. "Life is about as good as can be expected these days."

"I'm sorry. I've upset you."

"No, I'm fine, really."

"And what of the King? Is he handling it well?" Genuine concern on his face.

I stuttered a moment before saying, "Can we talk about something else, please?"

"Of course. Completely insensitive of me, but really, the only reason I came was to see if you were all right." He bowed again and turned to leave.

"Wait!" I called after him, feeling bad for making him slink off. When he turned back to me, I struggled to find something to say before settling on, "Thank you for your concern."

He smiled back. "If you need anything at all, even if it's merely someone to talk to, you know where to find me." He then left.

I found myself smiling in spite of how I'd felt a few moments earlier. I'd forgotten how good a friend Black Otter could be.

I went about my daily work, planning to go back to the palace and apologize to Little

Reed for my harsh tongue, but as I packed up my papers in my meditation room, he came to my door, looking repentant. "I'm sorry about what I said. Of course this is a sacrifice for you, and I shouldn't have said otherwise."

"I'm sorry I made you think it was nothing."

"I know it's not nothing, to either of us. And I've been thinking all morning about this, and the more I do, the more I dread having to go through with it; it gives me the shakes thinking about it." He held his hand out to show me. "So I was thinking—and feel free to tell me if this is completely the wrong way to handle this—but I think it would be better, for both of us, if we got this over with. We ask Mazatzin to do the untying ceremony now, so we won't have time to dwell or second-guess ourselves."

I nodded, numb. "That's probably for the best. The longer we delay, the harder it will be. And our allies are only here a few days longer, and you should already be divorced before approaching any of them about their daughters."

"That too." He pulled me into a crushing hug. "I must make one thing very clear before we do this. I still love you with all my being."

"I know you do, Little Reed." I squeezed him back.

He pulled away, not meeting my gaze. "Shall we go and find Mazatzin then?"

□

The ceremony was uneventful; we both swore on the god's name to give truthful testimony supporting our petition, and I promptly agreed to Little Reed's right to divorce me on grounds that I was barren. Mazatzin wrote the claims in the registry book where we kept record of all the marriages and divorces in Tollan, and with little else added, he declared our marriage finished. Funny how our wedding ceremony lasted four days, yet we'd ended it all before the noon-time bell.

As we returned to the palace, we didn't hold hands as we usually did. "I'd rather put off the formal announcement until tomorrow," Little Reed told me.

"I would be fine with that."

We ate a late lunch and retired to our separate quarters for a nap before the evening's feast. I missed Little Reed lying next to me—his body heat, his smell—but it was a good thing I was alone, for I dreamt of kissing him next to the temple in Xochicalco the night before he left for the army, and those sensual caresses we'd shared in the privacy of his tent; of his hand resting on my belly swollen with our child, and his torturously wonderful tongue winding its way down past my navel. I woke at dusk, the desire raging in my blood. It had never been so strong, so hungry. I feared what I might do if I went to the feast in such a condition, so I drew myself a bath, to drown the lust in cold water and shivers. By the end of it I was so numb my teeth were chattering, but at least the desire was again silenced.

We sat together at dinner as usual, and Little Reed even held my hand once or twice—to keep up appearances. But I focused mostly on Anacoana, who watched Citlallotoc from across the room with wistful eyes. I had a promise to keep.

Once the servants cleared the dinner dishes and the men brought out their pipes, I took Citlallotoc by the arm. "Walk with me, please? I need to talk to you about something." Little Reed overheard me and gave me a questioning glance, but I promised I'd bring Citlallotoc back shortly. Little Reed nodded and returned his attention to Flame Tongue as he regaled everyone with tales of his heroic army days.

And to believe I'm going to convince Citlallotoc to marry himself into that man's family, I mused, exasperated.

Once out in the gardens, in the yellow light of the kettle braziers on the patio, Citlallotoc asked, "Is something the matter, My Lady?"

"You need to approach Flame Tongue about Anacoana tonight."

"Tonight? But certainly there's a more appropriate time for marriage proposals—"

"If you wait any longer, I think poor Anacoana will fall over dead of heartache. She told me last night that her father would be very open to a proposal; he seems to think her a burr in his sandal and he's eager for someone to take her off his hands."

He frowned. "Really?"

I nodded. "If they leave here without a marriage proposal, I wouldn't put it past him to dump her on the side of the road on the way back to Xico."

"Certainly you jest?"

Taking his hand between both of mine, I implored him, "She will make an excellent wife; she's caring and thoughtful, and I've never seen anyone who can weave more beautifully. But best of all, she's absolutely in love with you."

Citlallotoc peered back into the great hall, to where Anacoana sat with her mother. "I would be a fool not to, wouldn't I?"

"And you're no fool."

After another pause, he asked, "And you're certain the timing isn't unseemly?"

"Not at all. I welcome the distraction of planning a wedding for the two of you. So go, talk to Flame Tongue. He's harassed Topiltzin all night, so you'll be helping my brother spend a little more time with our other allies."

Citlallotoc stood straighter and raised his chin. "Very well." He marched back into the great hall, full of purpose.

I hurried back to the circle of women as Citlallotoc wove his way over to Flame Tongue. He bowed, and after an exchange of words Flame Tongue nodded and followed him back out into the garden. Flame Tongue's guards followed but lingered at the doorway to the patio.

Anacoana was watching too, so I gave her a nod and a smile. She smiled back, wringing her hands together until her mother scolded her for fidgeting.

The two men returned a moment later, Flame Tongue smiling like a pleased ocelotl, and Citlallotoc striding tall. He gave me a smile and a nod before joining the rest of the men, and this time Flame Tongue sat next to him, positively beaming.

Well, something good will come out of this after all, I thought with a smile, then turned my attention to the other women sitting around me.

◻

I rose early the next morning and made certain I was first in the great hall, so I could ask Citlallotoc for confirmation of the proposal. He was always the first one to arrive in the morning, but today the rest of the council slowly filtered in, followed by guests two or three at a time. Flame Tongue and his family weren't among them, nor was Citlallotoc; they must have been waiting to arrive at the same time, so they could announce the engagement together.

A few moments after everyone else arrived, Flame Tongue and Anacoana finally walked into the great hall, but with Little Reed instead of Citlallotoc. I looked around for Citlallotoc, but still no sign of him. Anacoana wore her best dress and a brilliant smile; I'd never seen a woman look so happy about getting engaged.

Little Reed motioned Flame Tongue to take the reed mat next to his throne—where Citlallotoc usually sat—and Anacoana sat next to him, smoothing her dress and looking around, for Citlallotoc, no doubt. When Little Reed greeted me with a kiss to the cheek, I whispered, "Where's Citlallotoc?"

"He said he wasn't feeling well, so he begged off breakfast in favor of sleeping in."

That good feeling from last night vanished as I sank onto my own reed throne.

Little Reed called for silence then addressed the crowd gathered in the great hall. "Lady Quetzalpetlatl and I want to thank each and every one of you for your tremendous support during these most trying times for our family. Your strength and friendship has already set us on the road to healing, and to the future."

A somber murmur of approval passed through the crowd.

"I have two pieces of news to share; one is not so good, but the other is joyous.

"First, by mutual agreement, Lady Quetzalpetlatl and I have decided to set our marriage aside. It is not something we decided upon lightly, but circumstances dictated that we do so for the future of Tollan." When those murmurs turned to confusion, he added, "Rest assured that she remains Queen of Tollan, and shall be such till the day the Black Dog relieves her of her royal duties."

Everyone's gaze shifted to me, some filled with astonishment, others with pity, as if expecting me to break down on my throne. I trained my gaze on Little Reed so I didn't feel quite so small.

"As for the second piece of news...." Little Reed motioned to Flame Tongue.

Looking immensely pleased, Flame Tongue rose to his feet and cleared his throat. "I'm pleased to announce that my daughter Anacoana is now betrothed to Lord Topiltzin, strengthening the long-standing alliance between Tollan and Xico." He raised a cup of chocolate to Little Reed and added, "May my daughter give you many, many strong sons to carry on your legacy, My Lord."

Anacoana's nervous smile faded into panicked confusion. She plastered on a smile when Little Reed took her hand though. She darted a pleading look at me.

But I was too stunned to speak; nor would it be prudent to do so now. The betrothal was already announced in front of our allies and the council, and to raise objections now would incite an incident with Xico. As much as I disliked Flame Tongue, our alliance was too important to throw away without first finding some answers.

Breakfast dragged on forever, but eventually Little Reed and Flame Tongue went to the garden with Anacoana and her mother to discuss wedding plans and dowries. Little Reed invited me to come with them, but I begged it off, saying I had other things to do. He nodded morosely—no doubt thinking I wanted nothing to do with planning his wedding to a new woman—but he didn't object, and let me go on my way.

Citlallotoc wasn't in his quarters. After asking around with the servants, I found him in the men's exercise yard, wearing only a loincloth and beating a cotton dummy with a practice sword. When he saw me, he granted me a brief glance before pummeling the target with increased ferocity. I stood to the side, watching him until he finally backed away, chest heaving and arm muscles quivering, sweat pouring off him. "What happened?" I finally asked.

"I don't want to talk about it." He gave the dummy one last blow before retreating to the bench under the eaves. I followed him, saying nothing as he wiped himself down, but eventually he spoke on his own. "Lord Flame Tongue rejected my proposal."

"But you looked so pleased last night, after you talked to him—"

"Yes, well, that was before he found that Anacoana had better prospects." He threw the towel on the bench and glared at me. "What is this nonsense about Topiltzin divorcing you?"

I tensed. "It's not nonsense. And, not that it's your business, but we did it by mutual agreement."

"And so he cast you aside?"

"I stepped aside, for the good of the kingdom. But enough of this. What happened last night, when you talked to Flame Tongue?"

Citlallotoc shrugged. "He said my proposal was a welcome offer, and he was pleased that someone finally wanted to look after Anacoana. But this morning, before dawn, he woke me to tell me the arrangement was off."

I gasped. "He backed out on you?"

He stared at the bench as if it vexed him. "Apparently he got a better offer last night, after we talked."

I balled my fists, shaking. "Who does he think he is? You're Topiltzin's best friend—"

"I'm not going to make an issue of it. Topiltzin is the King whereas I'm merely Justice of the Peace. I'm nobody important."

I glared at him. "You're very important, and Flame Tongue will treat you with respect. You must talk to Topiltzin at once, before this dishonorable agreement goes too far."

"It's already gone too far, My Lady. What's done is done, and I don't want to talk about this anymore." He pulled his xicolli on and disappeared into the palace.

Maybe he didn't want to talk about it, but I had plenty to say to Little Reed.

CHAPTER TWENTY-SEVEN

I marched out into the garden where Little Reed and Flame Tongue were deep in discussion. Anacoana and her mother sat off to the side, saying nothing, letting the men plan Anacoana's future for her. I'd not dared speak up in front of the council and our allies lest Flame Tongue lose face—and we lose his support—but I felt no such compunction now.

Not bothering with decorum, I cut Flame Tongue off mid-sentence. "I need to say something, before you two get too far in all this wedding planning."

Flame Tongue stared at me, outraged, and even Little Reed looked taken aback. "Is something the matter?" Little Reed asked.

"Lord Flame Tongue is trying to deceive you, Brother. Anacoana was already promised to another man when he accepted your proposal."

Flame Tongue shot to his feet with surprising speed for a man of his years. "Absolutely untrue, My Lord! This is a vicious lie!"

Little Reed held up his hand for silence, and though it pained Flame Tongue to bite his words, he did so, face dark with rage. "What do you mean, Quetzalpetlatl?"

"Last night, Citlallotoc asked him for permission to marry Anacoana. Remember when the two of them went out to the garden before everyone sat down to smoke after dinner? At that time, he accepted Citlallotoc's offer—"

"He gave no dowry to legitimize his proposal," Flame Tongue shot back. "And so I had every right to reject his offer when a better prospect asked for Anacoana's hand."

"You mean the more powerful prospect," I fired right back.

Again Little Reed held up his hands, cutting off Flame Tongue before he could hurl further defenses at me. Little Reed glared at him. "This is very disappointing to hear, My Lord. I thought we had a healthy respect for each other."

Flame Tongue stood straighter. "I respect you immensely, My Lord, and because of that respect, when we spoke after last night's feast, I decided your need—and the needs of the kingdom—outweighed Lord Citlallotoc's. And I'm certain, as your honorable subject, he agrees with me."

I started to protest, but Little Reed beckoned to one of his guards. "Fetch Lord Citlallotoc immediately."

The guard bowed and disappeared inside. No one said anything as Little Reed paced, visibly upset, and Flame Tongue glared at me. I glared right back. Anacoana sat next to her mother, looking mortified.

When Citlallotoc arrived, he went straight to Little Reed and bowed in supplication. "You asked for me, My Lord?"

Little Reed motioned him to stand. "I've been told some disturbing news, my friend, and I'm hoping you can shed some light on its veracity. Did you ask Lord Flame Tongue for permission to tie your cape to Lady Anacoana's dress last night?"

Citlallotoc cast me a scathing glare before answering, "I did, My Lord."

"And he accepted your proposal?"

"He did."

Little Reed sighed and set his hands on Citlallotoc's shoulder. "I'm so sorry; if I had known you'd already asked, I would never have made my own offer. You're my best, most loyal friend, and it kills me to think I betrayed that, even unwittingly. Can you ever forgive me?"

"There is nothing to forgive, My Lord."

"On that I beg to differ. I cannot in good conscience move forward with this wedding knowing all this. Your friendship is of utmost importance to me, and I cannot bear to lose it...especially after having lost so much already."

Citlallotoc looked to Anacoana for a moment, but told Little Reed, "I vowed an oath of fealty to you long ago, to defend not only you and Lady Quetzalpetlatl, but your kingdom. Right now, Tollan's future is in jeopardy, and it would be selfish of me to put my own desires before what's best for our people. So please, go forward with this wedding without fear of losing our friendship." He looked again to Anacoana, who peered back at him with sad eyes. "I've known the Lady a number of years, and I know her to be an upstanding woman. She will be good for Tollan, and she will be a good mother to Tollan's heir." He nodded towards Flame Tongue without meeting the other man's gaze and added, "She is a testament to her father's wise parenting."

Some of Flame Tongue's surliness softened and he put on a smug smile.

Little Reed considered this, the conflict clear on his face. "Are you certain you can be at peace with this outcome?"

Citlallotoc nodded. "And you needn't fear for our friendship, My Lord; it is as secure, and strong as ever."

Clearing his throat, Flame Tongue said, "Now that we've put that silliness to rest, perhaps we can get on with putting together the details, Lord Topiltzin?"

That man irritated me to no end. Pulling Little Reed's sleeve, I drew him away from everyone else and whispered, "It's wonderful that Citlallotoc is willing to put his own happiness aside for your benefit, but has anyone thought to ask Anacoana if she's all right with all this? This treads very close to being an illegal forced marriage. She has as much right to a say in this as anyone, regardless of what her father might say."

Little Reed nodded, looking thoroughly chastened. "You're absolutely right. Let us ask her opinion."

"You must ask her alone," I added. "She won't feel safe to be truthful in front of her father."

Nodding again, he turned to Flame Tongue. "I require a private word with Lady Anacoana before we can proceed."

Stiffening, Flame Tongue said, "It would be highly improper for me to allow her to be alone with a man prior to the wedding, even if that man is her future husband."

"Lady Quetzalpetlatl will act as our chaperone, if that makes you feel better," Little Reed said, acid in his voice.

Flame Tongue's wife took her husband's hand and drew him towards the door. "Let them talk, my dear," she whispered. He reluctantly followed her into the great hall.

"I am truly sorry, My Lady," Citlallotoc told Anacoana, and he too disappeared back inside.

Little Reed watched them go, then, with a sigh, he turned to Anacoana. "Firstly, I must apologize, My Lady, for not consulting with you before ever thinking about approaching your father about a marriage between us. I have no explanation for this failure other than my own thoughtlessness. For that I am deeply sorry, and I understand if you hold this flaw against me."

"I do not, My Lord," she answered, her head bowed.

"It is not my desire to make you miserable or keep you from what your heart wants. Tell me that you want to marry Citlallotoc, and I will gladly step aside so you two can be together."

Anacoana looked up, fear in her eyes. "Please don't do that, My Lord. I have done much to disappoint my father in my short life, but that kind of slight is one he could never forgive me for."

"I would be the one delivering the slight, not you."

But she shook her head. "I've learned that no matter who delivers it, I am the one he blames. He blamed me for having to come back home after Ihuitimal's death, and he will blame me again if this proposal falls through."

"But if you marry Citlallotoc instead—" I started, trying to calm her growing distress, but she cut me off.

"He will never let me marry him, not now. His pride is wounded, and he would rather kill me than accept dishonor. Please, if we're to not marry, I beg you; end it all for me now, quickly, for it will be far more merciful than what my father will do."

Little Reed stepped up and grasped her shoulders, the alarm clear on his face. "No one is going to hurt you, My Lady. I won't allow it. We will marry, and you needn't live in fear any longer. I promise. Go and bring your family back, and we will continue discussing plans for the wedding."

"Thank you, My Lord." She hurried into the great hall, carefully wiping tears from her cheeks with her wrist.

Letting out a breath, Little Reed murmured, "What else could I do?"

"It's the right decision," I conceded. I'd always known Flame Tongue was a harsh man but seeing her reaction.... "We're getting her away from her father and she'll be safe. That's what's important right now; the rest we can work out afterwards."

▢

A week later, Little Reed and Anacoana married in the palace's great hall; and as when I'd married Little Reed, Mazatzin officiated. This was a much more luxurious affair, with all our allies in attendance, and all of them brought lavish gifts to celebrate the occasion.

Flame Tongue strutted around the palace as if he were the one marrying the King of

Tollan, not his daughter; and though Little Reed asked me to personally oversee the menus for the various feasts, Flame Tongue constantly questioned my selections and made changes behind my back. He even made jokes about me to our allies, which sometimes garnered a laugh, but were mostly met with awkward silence.

"Tragic how she's fallen barren, but the gods are less lenient when it comes to thinking one's self above their superiors," I overheard him say once. Citlallotoc heard it too, and I had to threaten him with a public lashing to keep him from confronting Flame Tongue right in front of everyone.

"Let him make his rude remarks," I said. "I'd rather he didn't think they bother me." And besides, he'd be gone in a few days and I wouldn't have to deal with him anymore.

On the afternoon of the fourth day, the bride and groom's family gathered in Anacoana's new quarters, which were next door to my own, and we watched the solemn laying of the jade stones and feathers on the marriage bed. Anacoana looked pale and nervous—anxious about the coming wedding night, no doubt—and she fumbled over the recitation of her promises of sons to fulfill Little Reed's legacy. Little Reed recited his part with what I could only describe as the bare minimum of enthusiasm required. Tonight was definitely going to be awkward for them both.

Not that the night was remotely normal for me either. I'd told myself days ago that I wouldn't get upset—had no reason to—but I lay awake late into the night anyway, staring at the ceiling and feeling as if I'd swallowed fish hooks that someone now tried to yank back out. *Little Reed's finally having that wedding night I never could give him.* I told myself it was foolish to cry, but the tears came anyway, and I gave serious consideration to seeking solace in the god's arms again. I even went so far as to prepare the teonanactl and octli concoction, but I ended up dumping it into my flowers outside my bath yard; I couldn't keep my reason for the visit secret from the god. Instead I went into the nursery and lay on Yamehecatl's bed, cradling his toys in my arms, and cried myself to sleep. The illusion that Little Reed and I could ever have been happy together in spite of all those limitations and sacrifices was finally over.

▢

The morning that Anacoana's family left, I slept late and took a leisurely bath rather than get up to see them off. I was glad Flame Tongue was finally leaving, and I doubted he cared whether I was there to bid him goodbye; if anything, he probably enjoyed not having to bow and give me compliments.

After I'd dressed, Anacoana came to my quarters, looking embarrassed. "Forgive my intrusion, My Lady, but I can't seem to find the women's hall."

"There isn't one," I informed her as I finished pinning up my hair in front of the obsidian mirror in the bath yard.

"But where do we do our weaving?"

"Wherever you want. Many of the noblewomen gather in the solarium, but I personally prefer the patio in our garden. Would you like to join me?"

Anacoana smiled. "Very much so."

I instructed my handmaiden to bring Anacoana's weaving supplies out to the patio where she'd already set up mine. "I trust you've settled well into your quarters? You're not missing any necessities, are you?" I asked Anacoana as we sat on the flagstones.

"No, I have everything I need for now, but if I do need something from the market, whom should I speak to about it?"

"Your handmaiden can send someone to buy things for you, but you're also free to visit the market yourself; you need not ask Topiltzin's permission, just always take guards with you for your protection."

She blinked, surprised. "I was never allowed out of the palace back in Xico. Except for temple services, but I had to be in my mother's company. Are there places I'm not allowed to go?"

I laughed. "Hardly. We don't believe in cloistering women behind walls here. If you wish, you may even attend the council meetings. Personally I find them boring—all talk about tribute and crop yields; I wouldn't go if I weren't the queen."

"My father never lets any woman sit in on his war council meetings."

"Yes, well, I think you'll find that Topiltzin does many things differently than everyone else."

"He certainly does," she murmured. She gasped and slapped her hand over her mouth, as if she'd spoken out of turn. When I cast her a quizzical smile, her blush deepened. "Not that there's anything wrong with doing things differently."

Now I wondered if she was talking about her first night with Little Reed, not city policy. I couldn't imagine what might have been so strange about it; granted, he and I had never gone so far as they had, but what we had shared seemed perfectly normal—no, not normal; achingly wonderful. *But you're no model of normal sexual behavior, are you?* I thought with a chuckle.

Once we both started weaving, we talked of other things; the weather, the quetzals singing in the trees, and my duties at the temple. At noon the servants brought our lunch, and while we ate, Citlallotoc came in from the main hallway, looking distracted. When Yamehecatl was younger, he'd spend his afternoons with my son, either practicing sword-play in the exercise yard, or walking through the main garden, discussing honor and fair fighting. Once Yamehecatl started school, my son often mentioned missing those afternoons with Citlallotoc, and I wondered if Citlallotoc missed them as well.

When I glanced at Anacoana, she was watching him too, a wistful look on her face. I bristled, but I caught myself. *It's not her fault; this is her father's dream, not hers.* "I'm sorry things didn't work out for you and Lord Citlallotoc."

Caught, she went back to her food. "It is all right. I've grown used to such disappointments." But when she realized what she had said, she quickly added, "Not that marrying the King is in any way a disappointment—"

"It's allright," I assured her. "I know what you mean. Sometimes it seems the gods are conspiring against us."

"I'm lucky to be here in Tollan, under Lord Topiltzin's care. I'm grateful to both of you for this."

I gave her a smile and went back to finishing my lunch, watching Citlallotoc cross the portico to his quarters next to Little Reed's. When he saw us, he promptly ducked into his room, leaving the door curtain bells tinkling in the warm afternoon air. *He's in need of a wife more than ever,* I thought, *if only to keep his lust from overpowering his honor, having to see Anacoana every day.*

But I was quite certain that any suggestion of a new prospect would be met with staunch refusal, at least for a few months anyway.

As I finished up my lunch, Little Reed came out of the hallway too. Anacoana rushed to stand and bow, but as she was halfway up, he said, "It's quite all right. You don't have to rise every time we meet; in fact, I'd prefer that you didn't."

Looking embarrassed, she lowered herself back to the flagstones.

Turning to me, he said, "If you're not too busy, there's something I'd like to talk to you about."

"Of course, My Lord." I bade Anacoana goodbye and followed him into the portico. "I thought you had temple duties this afternoon."

"I decided to work from here today." He held his door curtain open for me. "And I was hoping you might help me."

He'd set up a small working area in front of the hearth, with a slab of mahogany for a desk; stacks of papers littered the floor. "What's all this about?" I asked.

"Unfinished business." He plucked a piece of paper off one of the stacks and handed it to me. "Tell me what you think."

I read it over twice before asking, "Is this a new law?"

He nodded. "Outlawing Smoking Mirror's worship here in Tollan. It completely dissolves the cult and lays down dire fines upon anyone caught practicing any rituals or prayers related to his worship."

I said no more as I read it yet again, my insides a maelstrom of confusion and contempt. When I finally finished, I sputtered, "That demon murdered our son, Little Reed, and you think the solution is to ban his cult in one tiny corner of the empire?"

"This is what you've been asking me to do for years, isn't it?" he asked, confused. "Isn't this what you've been pushing for?"

I handed the paper back to him. "Maybe there was a time when this was enough, but now.... Little Reed, all this does is punish honest people who've followed our laws—people such as Black Otter, who have worked hard to bring the cult into alignment with our philosophies. There have been no illegal sacrifices in Tollan for two years now, but Smoking Mirror is strong as ever, and you think dissolving the cult will do anything to stop him?"

"We haven't the authority to force our allies to follow our lead," he reminded me. "But rest assured that most of them will adopt this law as well—"

"I don't want some stupid law! I want that demon dead! I want him to never be able to hurt another human being ever again!"

Little Reed blinked, startled. "Destroy him? But how?"

"My magic, of course."

Little Reed took my hand in his. "Don't be foolish, Papalotl. He's an extremely powerful god—"

"And I'm nothing?" I tore my hand away from him.

"I didn't say that."

"I destroyed Mextli—"

"And Mextli was not Smoking Mirror. Mextli was a minor deity, worshipped by one small band of Chichimecs. Smoking Mirror is far more powerful than Mextli could have ever hoped to be, and one doesn't challenge him as if he can be felled with a well-placed arrow. He has magic neither of us has seen—powerful magic—and if you try to fight him—"

"I have fought him, and I won."

"With Quetzalcoatl's help. Think about what you'd have to give to call on him again."

"I have nothing left to give," I said, tears threatening. But I wouldn't let them fall. I grabbed the paper from him and held it up. "This isn't good enough!"

He took my hands again, the paper crumpled in my fists. "I understand your anger—I feel it too—but we can't forget our own ethics. And you're right, this law isn't the right answer; we both believe one should choose Quetzalcoatl not because we've eliminated the competition, but because he deserves it. And you're right that this will hurt everyone but Smoking Mirror. We must keep doing what we've been doing; he feels threatened, but if we stay true to Quetzalcoatl's plans—keep pushing Smoking Mirror's priesthood to embrace a different kind of worship—he'll have to come around to a new way of thinking, if he wants to stay relevant. It will take time, and patience, and sacrifice, but it will all be worth it."

Smoking Mirror is incapable of change. But I held my tongue. The gulf between Little Reed and I was one we could no longer bridge because we'd cut those ties to secure the kingdom's future. He had the possibilities of a family while I had nothing. *Except revenge for Yamehecatl. Just because Little Reed's afraid doesn't mean I have to be too. Let him have his wife and new family, let him give his righteous speeches and toe the same old lines. I owe Yamehecatl justice, and letting Smoking Mirror live is not that.* I would do this without Little Reed and without the god, and I'd make the world safe from Smoking Mirror.

Little Reed anxiously awaited my answer, so I gave him the one he wanted to hear. "We'll keep the course the god laid out for us. Forgive my anger and stupidity; I have a hole in my heart that refuses to heal."

He hugged me tight. "I understand, and please don't call yourself stupid. Pain is not stupidity."

No, stupidity was continuing to do the same thing as always and expecting things to change.

CHAPTER TWENTY-EIGHT

I needed significant work with my magic before I could attempt to face Smoking Mirror again, so I began practicing right away; I had evening temple duties, but on my dinner break I went to the maguey fields in the priestly gardens and worked with my magic. I started slowly and methodically, but as the days added up to months, I found I needed to use more and more magic to keep progressing, so I decided I needed to recruit someone to provide blood, to help replenish my strength after strenuous practices.

Still, it took me a couple of days to build up the courage to approach Malinalli after classes one day. "Can we talk for a minute?"

"Of course," she said, gathering up her codices to take back to her meditation room. "What's on your mind?"

I checked the hallway, making certain we were truly alone, then I said, "I feel strange asking you this, but...I've been working with my magic, trying to teach myself to better control it—so I don't end up killing myself with it, as I nearly did a few months ago—but I can't replenish it with food. I need blood."

I expected uncertainty at this request, but instead, without hesitation, she said, "I'm happy to help!"

I breathed a sigh of relief. "Thank you. You're truly a wonderful friend, Malinalli."

"How often are you practicing?"

"Daily, but I'm planning to limit myself to one strenuous practice a week, and that would be the only time I'd need the blood. Do you think that's too often, with our daily bloodletting rituals?"

She shook her head. "Perhaps we should set up a specific day each week, so I know when to eat more?"

We settled on the middle day, and we met in the priestly gardens, tucked away by the maguey plants. She'd eat her lunch under the oak tree while I stood at a safe distance, working and pushing myself a little further each time. I'd killed all the rabbits when I'd thrown everything I had at Smoking Mirror, so I ordered the royal game keeper to set traps to capture more outside the city. I made efforts to not kill them, but I always recited offering prayers to Quetzalcoatl, in case I failed; at least that way their deaths wouldn't be a waste. When I tired of practicing, Malinalli bled her arm into a cup for me. In exchange, I scheduled her temple duties so she had more free time with Mitotia.

All progressed well, and with a few more months of work, I'd be ready to avenge my sweet Warm Breeze. Or at least die trying.

☐

One afternoon, almost exactly four months after I buried Yamehecatl, our servants came to the family garden to take our lunch orders as usual, and while I dithered over what I wanted, Anacoan knew her preference immediately. "Fried maguey worms in the spiciest chile sauce. And double the portion." She'd eaten the same thing for the last three days, and once the servants left, she confided to me, "This is so strange, because I've always hated maguey worms, no matter how much chile sauce you cook them in, but I can't get enough of them these last couple of days. What on earth is wrong with my stomach?"

I gave her a knowing smile. "You're not late by chance, are you?"

"Late?" she asked, puzzled, but then she gasped. "Well, I've never really kept track of such things, but it has been at least a couple of moons since the last time..." She paled. "Do you think I'm with child?"

"Probably." She wrung her hands together, making me wonder if she too had lost someone dear to the childbed. "You're nervous about that?" I said.

"It's so soon. I thought I'd have at least a year to acclimate to being married before become a mother as well." She wiped her cheeks, taking deep breaths.

I gave her elbow a reassuring squeeze. "I know it's scary, but I'll help you through this. And the king will be very supportive. We should go and tell him."

She looked stricken. "Right now?"

I laughed. "Don't worry, he'll be very excited."

"But shouldn't we wait until I know for certain? I don't want to disappoint him."

"I kept my own pregnancy secret early on, and I nearly lost Yamehecatl because of it. He should know that you at least suspect it, so the servants know to help you and the kitchens can serve the right food."

"I suppose you're right," Anacoana finally agreed.

☐

Little Reed was in the temple with Mazatzin, preparing for the noon-time service. Citlallotoc was there as well, lounging against one of the stone columns, and Anacoana nearly retreated when she saw him. I caught her by the elbow and she murmured, "Sorry!" before moving around to my other side, keeping as far away from Citlallotoc as she could.

Little Reed set down the basket of snakes he held. "Is something the matter, Anacoana? You look ill."

She lowered her head, cheeks bright, so I answered, "My Lady has good news to share with you, My Lord." I nudged her forward.

She looked ready to vomit, but she pulled her nerves together. "I'm with child, My

Lord. Or at least I believe so."

Little Reed looked to me for confirmation so I nodded. Smiling, he closed the gap with Anacoana and I expected him to embrace her—the way he always did with me—but he only took her hand, as if he were a father learning he would be a grandfather soon. "Wonderful news indeed. How long now?"

She looked to me this time, so I answered, "We're not exactly certain right now, but I would suppose at least two months, maybe three."

"So sometime after the rainy season," Little Reed concluded. "Right around the time we take the initiates to Teotihuacan each year."

"Looks as if I'll have to go in your place this year," I noted. A nice stroke of luck. I needed somewhere outside the city to make my challenge against Smoking Mirror, lest innocent people be injured or killed. The sacred city would be the perfect place; it was huge and empty for the most part, visited only by priests.

Mazatzin smiled and congratulated Anacoana on her news. Citlallotoc did as well, but he didn't meet her gaze. After all these months, I'd hoped that he'd moved on, but perhaps that was too much to expect.

Anacoana thanked Mazatzin but ignored Citlallotoc, an unexpected coldness to her now.

"This is such wonderful news. We should share it with our people," Little Reed suggested. "Stay for the afternoon service and I'll make a sacrifice to honor this joyous occasion."

"An excellent idea, My Lord," Anacoana agreed with a perfunctory smile.

"I must return to the palace," Citlallotoc said, wandering to the stairs. "I need to wash up before going to the courts."

"Will you join us for dinner tonight?" Little Reed asked.

"If you wish." Citlallotoc left, and Anacoana watched him, but with a scowl.

"I must go too," I said. "I have things to attend to before my temple duties tonight."

"Will you join us for dinner too?" Little Reed walked around Anacoana to take my hand—a gesture I rarely thought about but now it felt wildly inappropriate in front of his wife. "I'm certain if you asked Malinalli, she would take your shift for you."

Feeling Anacoana's gaze, I withdrew my hand carefully from his. "I wish I could, but she already has plans."

Little Reed nodded, disappointed. "I'll see you tomorrow?"

"Of course." I gave a bow to Anacoana and left too, taking to a jog once I passed out of view of the temple platform. My guards picked up their pace to keep up with me.

Citlallotoc was already at the bottom, but he walked with a heaviness about him. He flinched when I ran up next to him. "Mind if I walk back to the palace with you?" I asked, taking his arm with mine.

He smiled. "Not at all."

We walked arm in arm while my guards cut a path through the morning crowds. "Such good news for the King and Anacoana, don't you think?"

"Wonderful indeed. And Topiltzin seems very excited."

"He does."

"And you're not at all bothered by that?"

I laughed. "Why should I be?"

"Well, you two were married and had a son of your own, but now he has this new child—"

A shiver of bitter anger surged through me. "This is the life the gods handed us, so I'm happy for Topiltzin." I didn't want to talk about this so I immediately steered in a more comfortable direction. "Are you bothered by Anacoana being pregnant?"

Now he laughed. "Why would I be?"

I shrugged. "She was rather cold to you back there. You're not still pining for her, are you?"

"I never *pined* for her, My Lady. As with you and Topiltzin, those are the beans the gods rolled for us, and I'm happy for her."

"But what about you? Don't you deserve to be happy too?"

"I am."

"Really?"

He nodded. "Doing my duty to you and the king makes me happy."

"There's more to life than serving us, Citlallotoc. Just because things didn't work out with Anacoana doesn't mean they won't work out with someone else—"

He stopped and pulled his arm from mine. "You talk all the time about making everyone else happy, but what about you? How can it not burn you that Topiltzin abandoned you to take a new wife and beget a new child?"

"He did not abandon me."

"Two days after burying your son, he unties his cape from your dress and gets betrothed to a new woman. What else should I call that?"

I stared at him, a wave of dizzying fury sweeping over me. "How dare you even speak to me about such things? You know nothing about my marriage to Topiltzin, and he doesn't have to answer to you!"

"No, he doesn't, but he owed you better than that."

I walked away, but when he tried to take my hand, I ripped it away from him. The guards stopped, no doubt wondering if they should intervene, but Citlallotoc didn't try again. "Quetzalpetlatl, please—"

"Don't talk to me!" I shouted. People stopped, whispering and gawking, so I stalked up to him and said, voice low but straining, "Not that it's any of your business, but I'm the one who told Topiltzin we had to divorce, and we've worked too hard building Tollan and bringing about the god's reforms for me to throw it all away in the name of selfishness." I swallowed hard, desperate not to cry. "Sometimes love isn't enough." This time when I strode away, my guards closed ranks around me.

Citlallotoc didn't follow.

□

For the next few days, I took extra temple duties, the better to avoid Citlallotoc in the palace hallways. It had embarrassed me to have spoken of my own inadequacies aloud, but I also didn't want his pity.

But he was determined to give it to me anyway. Malinalli told me he'd come by the temple and the calmecac several times over the last couple of days and became quite frustrated when he didn't find me. "What's going on?" she asked, as she helped me go through the robe supply in the calmecac's storage rooms. "I found him lurking outside your meditation room not more than an hour ago."

"I really don't want to talk to him."

She frowned. "What did he do?"

I sighed as I scribbled on the inventory book she held open for me. "Nothing, to be honest." I'd already talked to Malinalli about the divorce, but I didn't want to rehash it all again.

"Then why not talk to him?"

448

"Because I'll get upset and say things I'd rather not, again."

"What is this about?"

"I probably should have never said anything to him in the first place," I admitted. "It's...I was concerned about him. I think he's still in love with Anacoana."

"It has only been four months. Lost love can take a very long time to get over."

I knew that all too well; I suspected I would never fully get over Little Reed, not even if the gods granted me an eternity to do so. On a deep level, I felt as if Heaven had made us for each other, which made our forced separation all the more difficult. "If he can't let it go, he'll ruin his friendship with Topiltzin." Though given what he'd said about Little Reed, perhaps that city had already been sacked.

"That's not exactly the kind of thing you could tell the king about, is it?" Malinalli said.

I shook my head. "He needs to meet someone new."

"That, or maybe get away from Anacoana for a while. He usually makes those trips to our allied cities at this time of year, doesn't he?"

"We canceled it, since all of our allies were here for the prince's naming day celebration," Citlallotoc suddenly spoke up from the doorway behind us. When Malinalli clutched her chest in surprise, he added, "Sorry. I didn't mean to sneak up on you two." To me, he asked, "Can I have a moment of your time, My Lady? We must speak."

It would be rude to decline in front of Malinalli, but perhaps she would help me beg off, claiming we had somewhere to be....

Malinalli, however, had no such intentions. "I have a class I must go and prepare for." She folded up the book and edged past Citlallotoc to the door. So much for best friends.

Citlallotoc stepped up and held out a small silver bracelet in the shape of a feathered serpent biting its own tail. Rubies gleamed in its eyes and leaves of gold formed the delicate neck feathers. "This is for you."

"Why?"

"An apology, for the other day." He looked chastened. "I had no right to pry into such a painful subject—and make all the wrong assumptions, especially about Topiltzin—and I'm deeply ashamed. What right do I have to call myself his friend after saying such things?"

"It undoubtedly looked that way from the outside," I admitted. "I didn't tell him anything you said."

"I told him; honor dictates I accept responsibility for my words and actions, and he has kindly forgiven me for my mistake. And I'm hoping you can do the same. Please?"

I sighed. "I pestered you just as hard, and I am sorry for that."

"Do you accept my apology?"

"Of course. But a gift is not necessary."

He looked at the piece of jewelry, embarrassed. "I saw it in the market the other day and it made me think of you. It was a silly sentiment."

Now how could I turn down such a thoughtful gift? Taking the bracelet, I slipped it on and smiled. "Thank you. You're such a kind man, and I hate seeing you having no one to share that with."

He chuckled. "We're all right again, then?"

"Absolutely."

◻

Matters remained tense between him and Anacoana. As the months passed, their public interactions grew increasingly chilly, with Anacoana often openly glaring at him while he cheerfully ignored her in favor of engaging me in conversation over meals or in the hallways. Whatever fear I might have had about extramarital infidelities appeared to be completely unfounded.

But I also noticed that Little Reed paid only cursory attention to his wife anymore, even as time made it clear she was carrying his child. Anytime he asked me to join him in his quarters, to talk about city business or a new law we needed to enact, she'd watch us from her doorway, staring with forlorn eyes, only to disappear behind her curtain as soon as she realized I'd seen her. I wished I could assure her that she had nothing to worry about, but I knew it wouldn't help. Little Reed had kept his promise to not stop loving me, at her expense. I hoped that when the child was born, that would bring them closer together.

As for Citlallotoc and Little Reed, they seemed closer than ever.

But then one afternoon in early summer, I passed by the great hall to hear them arguing. When I poked my head inside, Little Reed was pacing, agitated, while Citlallotoc stood by the hearth, fist clenched and eyes intense. "I did what you asked of me, Topiltzin," he said, his voice carefully modulated now. "I've always done everything you've asked of me, no questions asked, so why hold out on me on one simple request?"

"This is no simple request," Little Reed fired back.

"You act as if I ask more of you than you did of me. I risked not only my own honor, but yours as well. You're my best friend, and I thought that meant something to you."

"It means everything to me, Citlallotoc!"

"Then why deny me this?"

Little Reed laughed, exasperated. "You have no idea what you're truly asking for. I won't let you fall into ruin!"

"If people find out what I've done, I'd be ruined anyway, so what does it matter?"

"It matters!"

The escalating tension scared me, so I finally stepped inside and cleared my throat. Little Reed's scowl dropped a fraction when he saw me, but he remained on edge. Citlallotoc stood straighter, looking rebuffed. "Why are you two tearing at each other?" I said.

Citlallotoc looked at Little Reed, expectant.

"It's merely a foolish disagreement, that's all." Little Reed embraced me, kissed my cheek, and smiled; quite the display to convince me. "How are plans for the pilgrimage coming along?"

"Well enough." I looked back and forth between the two; Citlallotoc looked even more vexed as he scraped his sandal over the stone floor, but he said nothing. "Is everything all right?" I asked him.

Citlallotoc gave me a false smile. "All is well, My Lady." Turning to Little Reed, he said, "Forgive my rash tongue, My Lord."

"It's all right, my friend." Little Reed patted him on the shoulder. "I do owe you a kindness and I have an idea that will meet your approval. Perhaps we could talk later?"

"I look forward to it. But if you'll excuse me, I'm late for hunting with the other noblemen." He bowed and left.

"Is everything all right between you two?" I asked Little Reed again.

"Of course," he insisted. "Just a disagreement."

"What is this favor he did for you? He said he risked his honor—"

"It's truly nothing, Papalotl," he said, his words clipped.

I'd never seen him so evasive, and that troubled me.

◻

With the pilgrimage only weeks away, I spent most of my time with temple duties and planning the trip to Teotihuacan. I especially looked forward to spending time with Mazatzin; I didn't see him for more than a few minutes each day, but the little bit we shared was always pleasant. He never stared or gawked in that blank way that other men did, and I could lower my personal shield around him. We'd once been friends in the way most brothers and sisters were—something Little Reed and I never could be—and that was precious to me. I looked forward to rediscovering that connection.

I hadn't led one of these pilgrimages since before the destruction of Xochicalco. My duties as a mother kept me from going in the years since, because Yamehecatl needed nursing for the first three years, and after that, I feared a reversion to his drunken outbursts. But it was bitter medicine knowing that the only reason I was going this year was because my son was dead, and his replacement would be born any day now.

But the thought of vengeance eased that a bit.

As the day pressed closer, my focus became exacting and my worries about being prepared and powerful enough faded away. I'd become so good with my magic that I could turn my evening cup of water into octli with only a small amount of concentration. And the octli was far more potent than anything we brewed in the priesthood. Months ago I would have balked at the idea of comparing myself to a goddess, but now I embraced it; I couldn't face a god like Smoking Mirror without a sense that I was his equal, or maybe even better. I was ready to face him.

There was only one thing left to work out; how to get Smoking Mirror to show up exactly where I wanted him when I wanted him to.

But when Black Otter came to my meditation room to deliver his cult's weekly report, the final bean fell into place on my elaborately planned patolli game.

Once we finished discussing priestly business, I asked him to stay for lunch. He sat fidgeting in front of the hearth as I split up the food between us. "You said that if there was ever anything you could do for me that I shouldn't hesitate to ask," I said.

"Do you need my help with something?"

"Something very important." Lowering my voice, I continued, "I need your help summoning Smoking Mirror."

Black Otter dropped his rolled-up tlaxcalli and spilled its turkey and squash filling all over the floor. "Why ever would you want to do that?" He avoided my gaze, focusing on picking up his dropped food.

"Because I intend to destroy him."

Black Otter stared at me, lost for words. Eventually he found his tongue again. "This is madness, My Lady. He's a god! He'd kill us both!"

"I don't need you to do the ceremony, Black Otter. It's enough that you tell me how to do it."

He frowned. "And you really think I'd let you do this alone? I'm no coward."

"And neither am I."

"If you won't allow me to be there during the summoning, then I won't tell you how to do it." He looked nervous but determined.

I sighed. "Fine. We'll do it together."

Black Otter dusted off his tlaxcalli and set it on his plate. He chewed his lip a moment before asking, "When do you mean to do this?"

"When I'm in Teotihuacan."

451

He nodded. "There will be fewer people around, and the ceremony is dangerous if not done properly.... It will require careful preparation, and a sacrifice."

"We haven't registered any volunteers this year for Smoking Mirror's cult."

"I can get one from one of our allied cities. The cult has a larger following in the valley than here in Tollan, and we brought last year's Toxcatl volunteer from Culhuacan. Once I secure one, I'll bring him to the palace to be registered."

"No!" When he cast me a startled look, I said, "If Topiltzin finds out about this, he'll stop us, and he'll be suspicious if we bring in a sacrifice from Culhuacan six months before the next Toxcatl. I'll question the volunteer and make certain he's willing once you bring him to Teotihuacan, all right?"

Black Otter nodded. "You're certain you want to do this?"

"Positive."

"Forgive my asking, but exactly how do you propose we kill Smoking Mirror?"

I shook my head. "It isn't we; I'll let you help me do the summoning, but once that's done, I want you out of there. This battle is between me and Smoking Mirror, and I can't have him using you against me."

Black Otter blinked. "How could he possibly do that?"

"Don't be silly. You're family, and my friend."

He smiled, grateful. "Thank you, My Lady. But you still haven't told me how you're going to destroy Smoking Mirror."

"I have my ways."

My answer visibly frustrated him, but he let me leave it at that. We ate in silence, but when he rose to leave, he paused at the door and turned back to ask, "Why do you want to destroy Smoking Mirror anyway?"

"Because first he took my uncles from me, then my parents, and now he's taken my son too." I stared into the hearth, crumbling the leftover tlaxcalli in my fist. "It's time someone did something about him."

CHAPTER TWENTY-NINE

Two days out from departure, I met with Little Reed in his quarters for breakfast, and to discuss the security arrangements for the journey. "The scouting reports haven't shown any significant hostile activity north of Culhuacan for several months now, so I think a contingent of twenty men should do the job," Little Reed told me. "I'll assign Icnoyotl to lead the detail."

"Really? Is Citlallotoc ill?" For the last seven years, he'd overseen security on the pilgrimages.

"No."

"Then why isn't he leading this?"

"Icnoyotl is a good soldier—"

"And I know nothing about him," I replied, irritated. "I'm more comfortable with Citlallotoc leading this."

Little Reed sighed. "As you wish, Papalotl." He poked at his breakfast with a curious look of dread.

"Are you two still fighting?"

"We're not fighting."

"You've been friends too long to let petty things get between you."

"Nothing is getting between us."

I still felt uneasy when I left his quarters. *You don't suppose they've been arguing about me?* I wondered, but had to laugh that egotistical thought away. Little Reed wasn't prone to jealousy, and while Citlallotoc and I were close, we were only friends; he'd never shown any interest in me as he had with Anacoana. It had to be about her.

So I watched Little Reed and Citlallotoc carefully whenever they were together, but whatever had gone between them seemed indeed fixed. On the day we left for Teotihuacan, they laughed during their goodbyes. Anacoana ignored them with her usual coldness, and gave me a tired farewell. She was very large now, a good sign for the baby she carried, but all this drama and resentment wasn't good for either of them.

When Little Reed bade me goodbye, I warned him, "Take good care of your wife while I'm gone. Spend some time with her; rub her sore back and give her warm baths. The last month is the most tedious, and she will be grateful for your attention."

"I'll keep that in mind." But already I knew he wouldn't do any of it; I could tell by how long and tight he hugged me. I didn't understand it at all. He couldn't keep his hands off me, yet he balked at simply holding Anacoana's hand even for public appearances. How on earth had they managed to conceive at all? I felt as if I was reliving that moment before Black Otter left to negotiate for Amoxtli, where he'd kissed me as if we were on our way to bed rather than saying goodbye in front of half of the palace. And, just as back then, Anacoana watched us, but without the blindfold of youthful inexperience protecting her.

Yet I might never see Little Reed again, I thought. If the battle with Smoking Mirror went badly, this was the last time I'd ever see him, and I wanted to kiss him more passionately than I ever had before, so I'd have no regrets on the road into Mictlan.

But I couldn't be that cruel to Anacoana. I stole a sisterly kiss to his cheek and whispered, "I love you, Little Reed," and turned away quickly, accepting Citlallotoc's help up into the royal litter. Once behind the safety of the curtains, I peeked back out to find Little Reed looking back at me with a wistful, distant look on his face. I watched him the whole way out of the courtyard, until I couldn't see him—or Anacoana—anymore.

◻

When we reached Teotihuacan, we camped in the same courtyard as we had for that first pilgrimage eighteen years ago. The hole in the courtyard wall—which we women had crawled through to escape hostile Chichimecs—had grown larger with the years, and the wall in the adjacent courtyard, the one Nimilitzli had fallen from and broken her hip, had completely tumbled down. It was an acute reminder of how all things changed and crumbled away with time.

And I noticed, for the first time, that Mazatzin's hair had silvered at his temples, and he'd developed a slight hump on his back. He was older than his father had been when I'd first come to Xochicalco, but whereas Cuitlapanton had fathered over twenty children by then, Mazatzin—his only remaining heir—was unmarried, childless, and devoted to the god. When Mazatzin died, Xochicalco's royal bloodline would end. Just as my father's royal bloodline would die with me, thanks to Yamehecatl's death.

In the morning we gathered on the summit of the Temple of the Sun to meditate, but I watched over the city with a wary eye, for signs of enemies; a habit I'd developed after that first pilgrimage. Even though it had been a long time since I'd last been to Teotihuacan, it was one I couldn't shake. But unlike then, the morning was bright and warm, and the Black Dog wasn't prowling the streets, slathering victims with his deadly tongue.

At least not yet, I thought. During my vigil, I noticed a small field of maguey plants growing just northwest of the city, bordered by a meandering brook. It was too far away to see clearly, but there appeared to be a colony of rabbits there too; many small dark blotches moved among the maguey and the scrub brush. The perfect confluence of everything I needed to make the best possible strike against Smoking Mirror. *A good omen.*

And when I took the young women to the Feathered Serpent's pyramid for an augury demonstration, the entrails reinforced my confidence. The guts showed signs of yet another year of abundant rainfall and plentiful crops: more prosperity for Tollan. A positive sign that I would defeat Smoking Mirror and eliminate the one remaining imperfection in the god's utopia.

Yet, in the corner, some of the entrails pooled into a second omen: self-discovery. It wasn't bad, but it gave me pause. It sat completely apart from everything else, unconnected to the prosperity the rest of the omens promised, and I was the only one to see it.

While my novice women cooked dinner, I wandered down to the men's camp, searching for Black Otter. I found him talking with Mazatzin, but he quickly split off to see me.

"You brought what we need?" I asked, keeping my voice low.

Black Otter motioned to a man standing with the other male servants we'd brought with us. He hurried over and Black Otter took all three of us out into the crumbling corridor, leading us towards the women's camp. "This is Falling Eagle."

Falling Eagle bowed his head and I returned the gesture, as was customary when addressing someone who'd offered themselves as a sacrifice. "You're aware of why you're here before me?" I asked.

He nodded. "I am to honor the Smoking Mirror with my blood and breath."

"You enter into this sacred ritual of your own free will? No one has coerced or tricked you into forfeiting your life on the eagle stone?"

"It is a great honor to give my life to the Smoking Mirror, and I give it without regret or reservation."

I couldn't imagine why anyone would willingly give their life to a demon god, but who was I to tell this man whom he should and shouldn't give it to? As required by the law, I kissed the man's cheeks, placing the royal blessing on his new status as a sacrifice. "I hereby note and permit your final offering in the name of Tezcatlipoca the Smoking Mirror."

Falling Eagle nodded, grim, then returned to the camp.

"When do you want to do this?" Black Otter asked as we continued walking.

"Tomorrow night. Is that enough time for us to prepare?"

"We can do it anytime you want. Do you know where?"

"There's a field off that way, outside the city." I pointed to the northwest.

"The one with all the maguey plants?" When I nodded, he said, "I suppose they'll make good cover in a fight."

I'm not going to use them for cover, I almost said, but the less I had to admit, the better. As we approached the entrance to the women's camp, I said, "Let's meet at midnight tomorrow, behind the Pyramid of the Moon, and you bring everything we need." I bade him goodnight and retired to the courtyard, where the smell of fresh tlaxcallis and stewed beans had my stomach rumbling.

◻

The day dragged by like a snail crossing the northern desert, but eventually the sun set on what could be my last day on earth. All the waiting allowed the doubt to build up, but as the camp wound down and the girls went to their tents one by one, my moment of reckoning was close at hand.

I went to my tent too, but didn't sleep. I thought about praying to Quetzalcoatl for strength and giving him an offering of blood, to ask him to watch over me, but I decided I couldn't afford to go into this battle even remotely depleted. I stared at the ceiling, listening to the night until only the mutterings of the guards disturbed the silence.

Using the pretext of visiting the water yard down the passageway, I left the women's camp, but once alone in the yard, I climbed the back wall and stole into the night, toward the Pyramid of the Moon. Jitters turned my steps light and quick. *Finally I can avenge Yamehecatl and rid this world of an evil monster—or die trying.* I let the magic build in my hands, igniting my confidence and easing my nerves.

Black Otter waited for me behind the pyramid, pacing until he saw me approach. Falling Eagle stood nearby, looking as nervous as my cousin.

"We're ready?" I asked.

Black Otter bowed, but glared at the other man when he didn't follow suit. "Show proper reverence, man. You're standing in the presence of the Empress of the Tolteca."

Few people ever addressed me as the Empress, so hearing Black Otter honor me so made the desire glow inside. *After all of this is done, he deserves some extra recognition, a position on the council perhaps,* I thought, granting him a smile. *And maybe a position in our bed as well.* Normally I would scold the desire for its depravity, but I would need it tonight against Smoking Mirror.

Falling Eagle moved to prostrate himself, but I wanted to hurry. "You two follow me." I led us out into the field.

Walking through the maguey was like walking through a forest, for they towered on every side, their fully-bloomed stalks standing sentry against the full moon. And rabbit holes littered the ground all over. I couldn't have asked for a better location.

When we came to a small clearing with the brook a handful of paces away, I stopped and looked around. "Let's do it here."

Falling Eagle looked around, visibly sweating now. "But where's the eagle stone, My Lady?" His voice shook.

Before I could say anything, Black Otter grabbed Falling Eagle from behind and plunged a blade into his back.

As one of the highest priests of Tollan, it was my duty to oversee every human sacrifice performed, to make certain that anyone who wanted to back out at the last moment could do so. It wasn't unusual for a man's survival instincts to take over and fight back once the sacrifice started, but when Fallen Eagle rounded on Black Otter, he fought back with the ferocity of a man who truly didn't want to die. He grabbed Black Otter by the throat and started throttling him, but Black Otter reached around and twisted the knife, making him roar in agony. Black Otter finally ripped the blade out and tackled him to the ground, dodging Falling Eagle's pummeling fists. "Quick! Pin his arms down!" he called to me.

But I stood frozen, my mind reeling.

"Get over here and help me!" Black Otter panted. "It takes two priests to hold down a sacrifice!"

"But he's not willing!" I cried.

"Too late! Hurry or he'll bleed to death and all this will matter for nothing!"

I hesitated while Black Otter's words sunk in; Falling Eagle was going to die—there was no preventing it now—so there was no use wasting his death. I finally shook off the paralysis and rushed over, pressing my knees against Falling Eagle's arms. I started murmuring a prayer to Quetzalcoatl—begging his forgiveness for what we were about to do—but Black Otter snapped, "Don't do that! You'll give the sacrifice to Quetzalcoatl and we'll have nothing to summon Smoking Mirror!"

He was right, but I still felt as if I were abandoning my scruples when I pressed down harder as Falling Eagle made one last effort to buck both of us off. Black Otter sat on his chest until he laid still, struggling to breathe; but when Black Otter made the incision under his ribcage, Falling Eagle screamed, "Gods save me!"

I clamped a hand over his mouth, stifling his cries. He thrashed, nearly tossing Black Otter off, so I flopped my whole body over his shoulders and head, smothering him under me. I clenched my eyes shut, trying to reassure myself that we weren't committing murder.

When Black Otter thrust the man's feebly-beating heart into my hands, I thought I would vomit—I was seven again, standing in my father's room, my entire world ending. I nearly dropped it, but Black Otter clasped his hands—hot and sticky—around mine. "Repeat everything I say," he panted. I nodded, numb, but did as he said.

"Tezcatlipoca,
Lord of Darkness and Deceit,
I call you forth from the veil.
Come forward and answer for your crimes,
Face me,
Face your reckoning!"

I repeated the invocation over and over, each time with growing conviction and anger until I shouted the challenge. Power vibrated in my limbs as the heart shook, but I didn't even flinch when it burst into purple flame in my hands. When it disappeared—leaving me unscathed—I hurried to my feet, magic throbbing in my hands.

But nobody came.

I turned in a circle, sure he was trying to sneak up on me. "What are you afraid of?" I shouted into the night. "Is the so-called great and powerful Smoking Mirror too afraid to come out and face me?" When no one answered, I unleashed a gush of magic at the nearest maguey plant, letting my frustration and anger flow out with it.

As the plant thrashed in the night air, Black Otter backed away from me, his eyes wide. "How—?"

"You summoned me?" a familiar child's voice suddenly asked, and I whirled to see Night Wind standing with Mextli—*Mextli!*—in the bright moonlight.

I stared at Mextli, dumbstruck. "How...you're still alive? But I destroyed you!"

Mextli laughed. "You think you can destroy me with a smattering of octli magic? My, you're an egotistical one!"

"You...faked all that?"

"I couldn't just leave and let you think I run from fights. It was already embarrassing enough that I had to regroup after our first battle."

I turned my disbelieving gaze to Night Wind. "So you took the boy prisoner?"

"Hardly," Night Wind answered. "You summoned me, and I came."

His response confused me at first, but then the truth struck me like an arrow. "You're Smoking Mirror!"

Night Wind nodded, a broad grin on his young face.

"Cowardly dog! You took over an innocent boy so I'd have to slaughter him to actually face you!"

He shook his head and wagged his finger. "While it's true that my bond with him can only be broken with his death, someone else made that decision years ago. The boy you know as Night Wind has been gone a very long time now."

"But Ozomatli never completed the summoning ceremony—"

"Even years before that."

I couldn't wrap my brain around this. "You...you were in Night Wind all along, and you've been living in my palace, playing with my son...? Dear gods, you were Yamehecatl's best friend; he looked up to you!" My skin crawled.

"Why so shocked? Someone needed to encourage him to find his true nature rather than languish in that weak human form he was born to. Mictlan knows his father has no interest in such things. And why shouldn't I take an interest in my nephew? We're all family."

"And that's why you killed him? Because he's family? Because as Quetzalcoatl's son, he must be some kind of threat to you?" Hot tears spilled down my cheeks.

Smoking Mirror glared back at me. "I am many terrible things—things I take great glee in being—but I didn't kill my nephew. I liked him; sharp and prone to bouts of temper that could put even me to shame. He would have made an excellent ally for my cause when he was older."

"He would never join you! You're evil!"

"You say that as if it's a bad thing. Without death, there is no life, without night there is no day, and without evil, there is no good. Everything exists in a balance, and to rid the world of one throws everything into chaos. Is that what you were intending to do tonight? Throw the world into chaos?"

"You killed my son," I repeated through gritted teeth.

"I didn't do it."

"Liar! You ambushed him in the grass in the garden, and when I sent a horde of rabbits after you, you dropped him and fled over the wall like a coward!"

"Yes, but did I say anything witty to insult you?"

His inane question took me aback. "No, but you already know that."

"Of course I know, because my nahual doesn't speak when I'm not in its head, you silly little girl, and had I been there, I would have taunted you, because that's the kind of god I am. You might not believe it, but I would never hurt Ehecacone. But not all of us share that sentiment, do we, Black Otter?" He glared past me.

When I whirled around, Black Otter shrank away, opening a giant chasm in my heart. "You killed Yamehecatl?" Desperation choked me to a whisper. *Please don't let it be so!*

Looking exceptionally pale in the moonlight, Black Otter pressed closer, filled with resolve. "We are meant to be together, Quetzalpetlatl. The first time we made love...my soul opened up and I heard the gods themselves! But you ran off and married Topiltzin and had his son, and I knew so long as that child tied you to him, you wouldn't come back to me. I did what I had to do."

"You're a monster." I didn't shout or scream, merely stated fact, too numb to feel anything.

He glared at me, his posture tensing. "I made sacrifices for you; I gave my soul to the river goddess for a chance to come back to you; I poisoned Jade Flower so she couldn't stand in our way once I came back to Tollan. I gave Smoking Mirror my son's body so he could walk the earth, and I gave him countless more tonallis in the years since, to ensure our future together—"

"You've been killing people, in Tollan?"

"The god requires constant feeding to keep his essence settled in his host. I've just gotten better about hiding the bodies since you and Topiltzin found the grave."

Dear gods, Ozomatli was innocent! I choked on my own guilt as I sputtered, "And what about Ozomatli? Did you kill him too?"

"What do you care? He was far from inculpable; he was poisoning my father, and he tried to have Amoxtli killed. Granted, he did all that under my orders, to help me secure Culhuacan's throne and eliminate my rivals, but he was an easily manipulated coward too afraid to stand up for himself, even when I was his subordinate. His end wasn't anything he didn't deserve."

I was such a fool; I didn't know Black Otter at all. And neither had his father, or his brother. "But...why summon Smoking Mirror? Why is he here?"

"Because I must eliminate Topiltzin; he's the last thing standing between us, and only a fool would challenge him without divine help on their side." He looked at Smoking Mirror, his brow furrowed. "But I grow impatient with your stalling, and your excuses. Tonight you will finally put an end to him."

Mextli stepped forward, his feathers standing on end. "How dare you order around the Lord of Sorcerers—"

But Smoking Mirror grabbed his hand, stopping him.

Black Otter chuckled. "That's right, Lord Nobody. You can't hurt me; I made certain your slippery friend couldn't turn on me, or set his allies on me either. My father taught me enough to know that one doesn't make deals with the gods—especially the Smoking Mirror—without covering all contigencies. You harm me, and he ends up in Mictlan for breaking a solemn vow before Heaven—and are you prepared to pay a hefty price to Mictlantecuhtli to get him back?"

Mextli balled his fists, but Smoking Mirror chided him, "Patience, Mextli."

"Enough stalling!" Black Otter barked. "You will bring Topiltzin here, right now, so I can watch you destroy him!"

I'd felt as if my mind was slowly floating away, but the mention of Little Reed brought it crashing back in a fury. The magic poured out of my hands, down my legs and into the ground. *Make him pay!* the desire hissed with glee.

Black Otter didn't notice the maguey moving behind him, nor the roots slowly snaking out of the ground beneath him. Only when they crept up his legs, twisting and winding did he suddenly break off ranting at Smoking Mirror. "What—what are you doing, Quetzalpetlatl? You can't—Smoking Mirror! What is the meaning of this?"

Smoking Mirror grinned. "She's not my ally."

Black Otter tried backing away from the twining roots, but they shot up around him, lashing over his shoulders and pulling him to his knees. "Don't you understand that I love you, Quetzalpetlatl?" he cried, struggling. "I did everything for you!"

But when I knelt in front of him—my body no longer under my own control—he stared back in awe, and terror, the way Ahexotl had looked at me before he died; the way my uncle had as well. "Heaven save me," he murmured. "Your radiance...your beauty...so sweet an agony, My Lady. My soul, my very life I shall give to no one but you. Forgive me for not seeing the real you until now...for not seeing the truth, for not worshiping you properly!" He froze when I leaned forward and kissed him.

No demanding arousal accompanied the gesture, not even when he returned the kiss with ferocity, trying to wrestle my tongue into submission. The desire was in complete control, calculating and unmoved by any of it, and when I pulled away, he gave me a drunken smile.

"You should have stayed drowned, Black Otter." I looked past him, to the brook a handful of paces away. "Time to correct that mistake."

He watched me with that drunken smile, oblivious as the roots pulled him away from me, but when the water lapped over his feet, he started fighting again. "No! Please! Don't let her have me! Please, My Lady! I love you! I will give my life for you! I'll give it *to* you!"

I said nothing, just basked in the heat of justice flowing over me as the maguey roots wrestled him into the brook, holding his head under the water. He struggled mightily, but only for a moment. I felt his slowing heartbeat through the roots, and as the life seeped from his body, the energy flowed back through them, into my limbs, and my body drank it up with a savor unlike anything I'd ever experienced. The sky took on the vibrant purple of the Divine Dream and I could see Omeyocan high among the clouds.

But when I looked at my own hands, I finally saw what Ahexotl, Ihuitimal, and now Black Otter had seen. A cloud of pale orange light surrounded me, mist-like, licking the air in silent, vibrating wisps. I turned to Smoking Mirror and Mextli, and they too glowed: Mextli with turquoise and Smoking Mirror a bright violet, as with his nahual.... I gasped. "I'm a goddess?"

Mextli chuckled. "I told you she'd work it out."

"And she convinced someone to sacrifice himself to her before even knowing who she truly was. Impressive indeed!" Smoking Mirror conceded. "But it's still disappointing that it took her thirty-five years to see the obvious."

"Obvious? How could I have possibly known—"

But when I really thought about it, the signs had always been there: my perfect memory, my magic, my bizarre cravings for the rotting smell of the temple, and my strange aura that made men—and some women—completely lose focus. Red Flint's obsession I could dismiss as unfortunate, but Black Otter too?

But which goddess was I?

I was about to ask, but those clues were there too: my ability to control maguey plants and my octli magic—all things associated with the fertility goddess Mayahuel. "But she's dead," I whispered, my heart pounding drunkenly in my chest. "The Earth Monster destroyed her."

"Did you learn nothing in that quaint little priestly school of yours?" Smoking Mirror shook his head. "Gods don't die; they just sleep until they rise again."

"But why didn't I know? And why can't I remember anything even now?"

"Because the mists around the Black Lake feed on memories," Mextli provided. "The longer you sit waiting to be resurrected, the more you lose, and the longer it takes to regain those memories. Give yourself time and you will remember again."

"Why didn't you tell me all this to begin with?"

I turned to Black Otter lying face-down in the brook. Might it have spared my friend the madness I'd inflicted on him?

Smoking Mirror and Mextli exchanged glances, as if conversing silently, but then Smoking Mirror laughed. "Why ever would I? It amused me, watching you go around oblivious, unintentionally harming your friends and loved ones." He giggled and shivered as if remembering something hilarious. "And besides, if not for Mextli, I would have let you languish and die a mortal, which is the only way you can truly destroy a god, my

459

dear. Your weak love and octli magic isn't up to the challenge of turning me mortal."

"I have no words for how...disgusting you are," I snarled.

"I tell you the truth about yourself and I'm the disgusting one? What about your precious Feathered Serpent? He kept you blind and deceived you far longer than I did."

His words punched my chest. *Quetzalcoatl knew?* "You're lying...trying to turn me against—"

"Who do you think brought you back from the dead?"

I snapped my mouth shut, unable to breathe now.

"Of course he knew! And long before me or Mextli worked it out. And yet he chose not to tell you the truth. I wonder why? If you'd died a mortal, you could never come back, and yet he chose to keep you ignorant. Why would the god who claims to love you—to love humanity—why would he condemn you to eternal oblivion by keeping your true identity secret from you?"

My stomach rebelled. Smoking Mirror couldn't be right, but...in those countless hours we spent intimately wrapped up in each other in the Divine Dream, why didn't Quetzalcoatl tell me any of this? How many times had I nearly died over these thirty-five years? *Nearly? You actually did die, and it was Little Reed who saved you from oblivion, not Quetzalcoatl. Black Otter's betrayal is unforgivable; but if not for that, would you have ever found out the truth?*

My voice broke when I finally spoke again. "Why does any of this matter to you anyway? You didn't care until Mextli said you should."

"Because war between the gods is coming," Mextli answered. "And the time for picking sides will end soon, and those who choose wrong will pay the ultimate price. Quetzalcoatl's conduct is shameful; you deserve to know the truth of your divinity, and to realize your full potential. You belong in Omeyocan with your own kind, adding your voice to the discussions of the future—not trapped here as a mortal, ignorant of the anger and discontent your actions send through Heaven. You deserve to make an informed choice about which side you truly want to be on once the war begins."

I laughed bitterly. "It's certainly not your side."

Mextli sneered. "So you would continue fighting for the god who lied to you for the last thirty-five years, who would have seen you disappear forever, completely forgotten a hundred years from now?"

The truth stung so badly. My beloved god *had* betrayed me, and I'd be a fool to continue following him, and yet...I'd always seen such love and devotion in his eyes when we were together. How could I reconcile all of this?

"I don't want anything to do with either side."

"Whether you like it or not, you're already involved, Mayahuel," Smoking Mirror said. "More than a few gods already speak your name as if it is a curse. Join me and Mextli against Quetzalcoatl, and we will protect you from them."

I shook my head, my mind reeling. I needed time to think, to digest this new reality and what it meant for my future. "Go away and leave me alone!" I cried.

Smoking Mirror sighed. "Very well, but having eternal life again doesn't mean you have eternity to make up your mind." To Mextli, he said, "Let's go now. This infernal human host requires rest and its complaining muscles and fuzzy brain annoy me."

As Smoking Mirror turned to leave, Mextli stepped up, towering over me. I shied away.

"I understand this is a lot to take in, and after being fooled by one god it's difficult to trust any other. But when you're ready to embrace who you are and what it means, know you could have an ally in that journey, if you so choose." He gave me a pointed look, then turned and strode back to Smoking Mirror—who shook his head and laughed as they walked away together into the night.

I watched them until they disappeared, then my gaze settled on Falling Eagle, lying on the ground. I clasped my hand over my mouth, stifling the sob in my throat as I crumbled to my knees. What had I done? *I've committed murder, which means exile from everything I know, everyone I love—*

Black Otter murdered him, not you, the growling voice of my desire said. *He pulled the fool's heart out.*

But I told him to!

He didn't have to. He chose to.

I should have listened to Little Reed.

And still not know the truth? That man's death wasn't pointless; it brought you back to immortality.

"Wonderful. Now I have an eternity to feel guilty about it," I muttered.

The maguey roots snaked over Falling Eagle's body and pulled it under the upturned soil. I scrambled to my feet, repulsed as the ground writhed like a nest of feasting maggots. "What in Mictlan—?"

His life was nothing before he met you; now it has meaning. It nourishes the earth, it grows the maguey, and it fills the sap that makes the octli. It feeds the goddess, and she is grateful for his sacrifice.

"And it conveniently hides the body," I noted dryly.

You have so much to relearn, Mayahuel.

I walked over to Black Otter, lying face down in the brook. I tried to conjure some guilt for him, but I couldn't let go of all he'd done. The friend I'd loved had died long before that day on Lake Metzliapan, and what came back in his place was someone I didn't know at all.

What will I tell Cuicatl? I wondered, numbness settling over me. *In one day she loses both her brother and her father—*

Black Otter started to groan.

I yelped and jumped away, my heart racing. He rose to his knees, the front of his priestly robe stained with mud and moss; but when he tried to speak, it came out as a shrieking cry.

To my horror, his body transformed right before me. His hands gnarled into claws and glossy hair sprouted from his arms and legs. He tried to stand but only managed to hunch over, his feet contorting and stretching. His face became elongated, more hair growing from his cheeks and jowls while whiskers sprouted from his snout; dagger-like fangs pushed out his human teeth. His whole body stretched, becoming longer and his robe slid off his narrowing shoulders. A tail with a ghastly hand at the end lashed out like a scorpion's stinger.

The dreams! I realized, backing away slowly. It had been years since I'd last dreamt of him rising from the lake as a monster with a grasping hand on its tail—this very monster—screaming, "Mine! Mine! Mine!"

And he shrieked those very words as he lumbered at me.

I stumbled away, summoning magic to my hands, but he suddenly stopped, hissing and pawing at the ground. "Mine!"

I stared, confused, but then noticed the tail's hand clung to the edge of the brook, keeping him from going any further. *Can he not leave the water?* To test my theory, I moved away a couple more steps and called, "Yes, I'm yours, so come and get me!"

He scowled and bared his fangs. There was nothing human in those ink-black eyes, only a single-minded purpose: possessing me. This must have been his payment to the river goddess Jade Skirt for saving him. He beat his paws on the ground, shrieking, and pity and shame filled me. I was as responsible for him becoming this monster as she was.

"I'm sorry I did this to you, Black Otter," I said, unleashing my magic on him. The least I could do was end this terrible existence.

The magic blasted him backwards, across the brook, but again the hand held him to the bank. He squealed in frustration and scrambled to his feet again, none the worse for my attack. I blasted him again, and this time, he retreated down the brook, hissing and howling at me over his shoulder as he went. I chased him, shooting magic, growing more and more furious that it did nothing but drive him on. But eventually he outran me and disappeared, only his calls of "Mine! Mine! Mine!" giving evidence of his existence, but those too soon faded into the night.

CHAPTER THIRTY

 I intended to go back to camp, but by the time I reached the Pyramid of the Moon, I found it impossible to continue walking, so I sat on the steps, my chest aching under the crush of everything. Where did I go from here? So much fear, confusion, guilt and resistance raced through my mind, tearing me in so many different directions at once, but one thing was clear: I had a lot to answer for.

Gods don't answer to anyone for anything. They aren't held to weak human morality.

It was my own morality I didn't live up to, I retorted.

"Quetzalpetlatl?" Citlallotoc jogged across the precinct to me, worry painting his face. "What are you doing out here alone? Everyone's been looking for you."

I laid my head in my hands, the tears arriving in a flood.

"Your guards woke me when they couldn't find you in the water yard," he went on. "Then we heard screaming, and no one can find Black Otter—"

"Black Otter's dead."

"Dear gods, what happened?"

The pain rose fresh and sharp in my chest. "He killed my son...he set Smoking Mirror's nahual on him...he couldn't let me go.... And I did such terrible things...."

Citlallotoc sat and wrapped his arm around me. "It's all right," he whispered. "We'll work it out. You're safe, and that's what's important."

But rather than calming me, his closeness and warmth ignited the desire festering inside me. I gripped him tighter, trying to force it back, but my resolve crumbled when all the other things I'd learned and done swirled through my mind. I needed a reprieve from the suffocating panic and chaos; I needed to meditate, or sleep it off until I could think more clearly.

But instead I kissed him.

He didn't react at first, stunned perhaps, but soon he returned the gesture with a forcefulness that spoke of hidden longing. The desire took command with silent ease, and I let it; pleasure was as good a liniment as anything—

But what about my sacrifice? I reminded myself, yet still reluctant to resist.

You pledged it for the rest of your mortal life; now, you're immortal, and you're free to do as you want.

I had said *for the remainder of my mortal days*. I was indeed free of that sacrifice. Which meant I was finally free to have the relationship I'd always wanted with Little Reed....

So what was I doing here with Citlallotoc?

You think too much, the desire growled. *You always did*.

To my surprise, Citlallotoc pulled away, panting and bewildered. "We can't do this," he muttered, and started to stand.

But I grabbed his xicolli and held him down. "Why not?" the desire purred, pressing my body closer to his.

He gazed at me with a blankness I knew too well, but he shook it off and looked away, fidgeting. After contemplating the precinct in silence, he muttered, "I still can't believe Topiltzin divorced you. If I were married to you, nothing would convince me to let you go."

I laughed. "You want to marry me?"

He shrugged in lieu of an answer.

My arm hooked itself with his and I leaned in and whispered, "How long have you felt this way?"

"Far longer than an honorable man should."

"What has honor to do with anything?"

"You were my best friend's wife."

"But not anymore, so why the dilemma?" I slid my hand across his thigh, and his leg muscle twitched under my splayed fingers.

He cleared his throat before speaking again. "Because I promised Topiltzin I wouldn't pursue you."

"Topiltzin doesn't own me; even when we were married, I wasn't his property, and now I'm free to share my bed with whomever I wish." He tensed when I straddled him, but he couldn't hide his arousal once I settled onto his lap. "And I want to share it with you," I whispered and moved in to kiss him again.

But he blocked me with a firm hand against my sternum. "I think he still loves you, Quetzalpetlatl."

The desire growled jaguar-like in my head but kept my voice sweet when it asked, "Why would you think that?"

He hesitated a moment, debating something before blurting, "I'm the father of Anacoana's child."

I drew back, startled, but also amused. "You cuckolded the King?"

"I didn't do anything he didn't ask me to," he insisted. "He refused to bed her, and he needed an heir, so he begged a favor of me. And being his best friend...I did it."

So this was the mysterious favor that could cost both of them their reputations and honor. A smug satisfaction nestled in my belly; Little Reed did still love me, and so much so he couldn't bear to bed another woman. "What has this to do with us, right now?" the desire asked, impatient. "Did you ask him for permission to court me after the divorce?" When he looked away, embarrassed, I stifled a laugh. "And he denied you? You speak of precious friendship, but what kind of friend denies you happiness for his own selfishness?"

Citlallotoc started to speak, but stopped.

"That's what I thought." I leaned in again, our touching noses sending a shiver through him. "You want me, and I want you, so let's stop playing games and see where this goes." I leaned in all the way and kissed him again.

Again he silently wrestled with his honor, but only for a breath. He kissed me back, gently at first then with growing ferocity, as if an animal had awoken inside him. The desire relished it, kissing him back harder, encouraging him. His initial fumbling with my robe ties turned to pawing and yanking—a task made all the more difficult by his lack of a second hand, and I had to pull away to help him. He watched me with the look of a drunk as I abandoned my clothes and relieved him of his loincloth, and when I eased myself back down on his lap, enveloping him, he fell back against the stone steps as if it were too much to take. "Not so fast!" he moaned, making me laugh, for within a few moves it changed to desperate pleas of "Faster! Faster!"

Even after seven years of celibacy, my body hadn't forgotten anything; every move was perfectly timed and measured, as if I instinctively knew exactly what Citlallotoc liked, and how much. As I'd known with Black Otter, too. Only with Quetzalcoatl had it been a mystery in need of solving. *But then he had been my very first lover....*

And with that one thought, the stone walls imprisoning all my lost memories crumbled down, as did the world around me.

I was back in the garden in Omeyocan. The Earth Monster, with her caiman-head and bat wings—Tzitzimitl, my grandmother, whom I took after in every way but my heart—slept in her cave. I lazed among the flowers, staring up into the blue sky overhead, dreaming of how the world looked beyond the monumental stone walls surrounding me. Were there others like us? How did the clouds move overhead while everything inside the garden stood still, never changing, never growing....

I was watching bees visiting the flowers next to the wall when I first heard the mysterious whisper. *Climb the wall, little goddess. Let me show you all the beauty of the world! You deserve to know more than centuries trapped behind these walls. You deserve companionship and freedom, the same as the rest of us.*

The words—they were a man's—excited a strange buzzing in my chest and belly, and with each passing day, my heart grew braver and stronger. I had no idea how he looked—or even what his name was—but already I ached for him so badly that, by the third day, I couldn't contain it anymore. I had to climb that wall; I had to see him.

And so I climbed and climbed and climbed. The magic imbued in the walls tried to frustrate me and turn me back, as it had so many times before, but this time I refused. I would see what lay beyond these walls, and who lived there. Or else I would spend eternity trying.

When I finally reached the top, he was waiting for me, all shimmering feathers and sharp fangs and fathomless eyes. I'd never seen a snake or a bird, and so had no vocabulary to describe him except a single word my heart provided, with no definition and no reference: Love. And when we flew together to earth, he showed me everything and gave it all names; the mountains, the oceans, the valleys where the deer roamed. He even gave me a name of my own, one so soft and yet so filled with yearning that when he spoke it, my heart cried for joy. He showed me all the gifts the gods had granted the world, every one of them precious and beautiful.

Every god gives at least one gift to the world, he told me. *Isn't it time you shared yours? But how do I do that?* I asked.

He whispered, *Close your eyes and I'll show you.*

After that everything was softness: his feathers on my scaly skin as he twined around me; the stretching and melting into each other as he taught me the secrets of creation one slow, sensual movement at a time; the years spent knowing only the throb of his magic, the sound of his thoughts swimming with mine, when the physical acts fed the emotional ache in an endless cycle, and sex became more than mere pleasure—it became lovemaking, it became new life, it became the future. We became the tree that bloomed Love from its branches and shed its gift upon the world.

The memory brought on the familiar rush of pleasure, filling me from toes to fingertips. My limbs throbbed with magic, and my head buzzed. I followed my old habit of staring up at the sky and watching the Divine Dream leak into my consciousness like water breaking free of a dam. I was flying again, the wind whipping through my hair—

Suddenly I stood on the platform outside the Temple of Quetzalcoatl in Tollan. The face on the sun blazing overhead blinked down at me, its tongue jutting out in a perpetual smirk, but as always, it said nothing. Around me the city was empty.

But inside the temple, a man knelt in the middle of the floor, meditating. As I pressed closer, my stomach knotted: he had the god's green quetzal feathers in his hair. It had been years since I'd last seen Quetzalcoatl.

With Smoking Mirror's accusations plaguing me, my first impulse was to run away, but I stopped. *There has to be a reason he didn't tell me the truth.*

A cry rose outside the temple, as if a monstrous beast had woken to a terrible wound. The sky blackened as something blotted out the sun. *Who has stolen my granddaughter?* a chillingly familiar voice rang. I went to the edge of the platform and looked up to see Tzitzimitl plunging from Omeyocan like an arrow, focused on the tree in Tamoanchan where Quetzalcoatl and I had bound our bodies in love....

I'd felt no fear when I'd heard her coming, for I was with Quetzalcoatl and our love would protect us. Except that as her shadow descended over us, I felt the bonds between us loosen and snap. Suddenly I was alone and vulnerable.

She tore me apart like starving wild dogs; even now I felt her claws ripping into me, her teeth tearing my flesh into chunks, my life leaking away like an offering from a blood bowl.

Eventually Quetzalcoatl did come back, and he showed the humans how to bury my scattered parts so something new and useful would grow. *Your real gift to humanity is not Love, but your death,* he'd whispered over my grave. *For when the people drink your tears, they will know how to serve their gods.* And he'd laughed. And laughed. And laughed.

I turned to see Quetzalcoatl still kneeling, oblivious to everything. I'd misread everything about him, from the moment I first saw him atop the wall in Omeyocan to the last time we'd made love in the Divine Dream. Everything he did was a manipulation, a lie.

He stood up and turned to leave, but started when he saw me. *Papalotl!* His face lit with joy and he reached to embrace me.

I stepped away, shaking with fury and magic. He stopped mid-step. A piece of my heart crumbled at the confusion and fear in his eyes. *What if I'm misremembering?* Unlikely given my divine origins, but still.... Should I give him a chance to explain himself?

Give him the perfect opportunity to tell you the truth and see what he does.

"My Lord," I replied with a careful bow. I didn't return his smile.

After an awkward pause, he said, *I'm glad to see you again. It's been a while now.*

"I had some...issues I needed to work out."

Then you have done so? he asked, hopeful.

I shook my head. "I'm more hopelessly confused than ever. But I thought perhaps coming here and speaking with you...maybe you will give me some answers."

He folded his arms behind him. *I will give you whatever answers I can.*

I paced the floor between the stone columns; I didn't have to fake wringing my hands, for the fear coursed hard through me. "My entire life is falling apart. Nothing makes sense anymore, and I think there's something...different about me."

Tell me.

I laid it out piece by piece for him: my magic, my perfect memory, and the strange, unsettling affect I had on people. He listened but said nothing, making me angrier by the breath. "And there's you!"

Me?

I nodded. "Here I am, a supposedly normal human being and yet I spent years in a relationship—a sexual relationship—with you. Why would you even be interested in me? It's not as if I'm a goddess or something!" I couldn't possibly give him a better reason to tell me the truth right there.

Yet Quetzalcoatl sat there, a contemplative look on his face, as if weighing something.

Stamping my foot, I yelled, "For Heaven's sake! Tell me what I need to know! Why am I like this? Why do you even care?"

He looked at me, sadness in his eyes. *I wish I could help you—you have no idea how badly I want to—but some things are not mine to tell. Some things one…must discover for oneself. And I care because I love you, Papalotl.*

I stared at him as if he'd shot me with a poison-tipped arrow. "You love me, but the truth isn't something you can help me with? I have to find it out on my own? Is that all you have to say for yourself? Or maybe you want to lecture me about how my real gift to the world isn't love, but my death?"

He dropped his arms to his sides, alarm on his face. *You know?*

"Who I really am? Yes, but no thanks to you. I had to find out from Smoking Mirror, of all people!"

He furrowed his brow. *Smoking Mirror told you?*

"Do you know how awful it is to know that the god who killed my parents is more forthcoming with the truth than the one who supposedly loves me?"

Papalotl—

"No! You don't get to call me that anymore! You've lost the right!" I strode out of the temple, my anger shaking the ground under me with each step.

Quetzalcoatl suddenly materialized in front of me in a swirl of white smoke, blocking my way down the stairs. *It's not what you think—*

"I was foolish enough to believe your lies once; the second time I was ignorant of how you really are, but I remember now, and I won't be fooled again." ·

But please, I must explain—

"I don't need more of your lies; in fact, if I never saw you ever again, that would be the first good thing to happen to me in this life!"

His jaw quivered. *I never meant to hurt you, Mayahuel. I love you.*

"And I loathe you."

I didn't want to be there anymore, didn't want to look on his face lest his betrayal transfer to Little Reed. I closed my eyes and willed myself to leave the Divine Dream; but when I felt the hold loosening, I took one last furious stab at him. "Your son would be a far better god than you could ever be."

When I opened my eyes, I was back on the stairs of the pyramid, Citlallotoc still between my legs, fast asleep. I peered up at the sky once more but then climbed aside and sat with my knees jammed to my chest, tears of disappointment and heartache muddying my vision. I doubted Citlallotoc could hear me cry, for he didn't stir when I moved off him. I'd done this hoping to feel better but instead I'd only made myself feel worse.

I couldn't sit naked out here all night, so I dried my eyes and put my clothes back on. Picking up Citlallotoc's loincloth, I went to wake him.

It had always been challenging waking Black Otter after sex, so Citlallotoc's unresponsiveness didn't surprise me. I shook his shoulder, starting gently and working up to full intensity, until his head flopped to and fro. When he didn't rouse, I gave his cheek a small smack, gritting my teeth as I did it, but still, no response.

Leaning closer, I noticed he was barely breathing. I peeled back one of his eyelids to find his eyes unmoving and his pupils dilated. A quick check of his pulse found it as weak as his breathing. "Citlallotoc?" I slapped his cheeks again, rougher this time, but still nothing.

My own heart racing, I wrestled him off the steps and laid him on the ground on his back, trying various techniques Nimilitzli had taught me long ago to revive someone who had passed out or stopped breathing. But all I could think about was how nothing had saved Yamehecatl, and the rising panic soon paralyzed me. I screamed for help as loud as I could.

◻

Within moments, several guards arrived, and when they saw Citlallotoc's condition, one ran back to camp to fetch the surgeon while the others tried to revive him. I stayed out of the way, huddled up like a terrified child. *What did I do to him?* My brain barely registered it when one of the guards announced that Citlallotoc was finally awake; but when they helped him sit up, I burst into tears.

The surgeon arrived a few moments later and checked Citlallotoc over, making him drink some water from a skin and swallow some medicine. He instructed the men to help Citlallotoc back to camp. "And one of you remain with him until I get there." He then came to me. "What happened?"

I fumbled for an answer, my cheeks ablaze, but now wasn't the time to hold back the truth because it embarrassed me. Citlalltoc's life might depend on it. "We were...we had sex, and I thought he'd fallen asleep, but I couldn't wake him."

If the surgeon was scandalized by my confession, he did a fantastic job of hiding it. "Then he was awake when he finished?" he asked, his tone completely professional.

I shook my head, trying to swallow the panic. "I don't know." I'd been swept up in the flood of memories and the Divine Dream; I might as well have not even been there. "Is he going to be all right?"

"He's severely dehydrated, but he should be fine with some rest and plenty of water."

"Thank the gods," I whispered. When I realized what I'd said, I almost started chuckling at the absurdity of praising the likes of Quetzalcoatl and Smoking Mirror—and myself—for this mercy.

The women's camp was alive with activity when I returned, and many of the novices cast me curious looks as I hurried to my tent, desperate to be away from their prying gazes. *I never should have listened to the desire,* I thought, crawling into my bed. *Bad things always happen when I listen to the desire.*

You are so whiny, the desire growled. *How are you going to feed if you continue to cling to those weak human morals?*

I hadn't noticed until now how full and glutted I felt, as if I'd finished a celebratory feast. "I feed through sex?" I whispered, repulsed, but I couldn't deny it. My hunger and desire always went hand-in-hand, and Black Otter had become weaker and sicker the more we were intimate. I had been devouring him one night at a time.

And I'd fed on Citlallotoc and nearly killed him in the process. If I bedded Little Reed...?

A guard came to my tent flap. "Lord Citlallotoc asked for you."

The stares were worse in the men's camp. Had rumor already spread about what

467

Citlallotoc and I had been doing out on the sacred precinct? I held my head high, determined not to blush or crumble under their gazes, but relief washed over me when I finally ducked into Citlallotoc's tent.

As a high-ranking nobleman, Citlallotoc could have used one of the large, multi-room tents that Little Reed and I used when traveling, but he always opted for a small, one-person tent, the same one he'd used back in his army days; he wasn't the kind of man to indulge in luxury for luxury's sake. The surgeon had to leave to make room for me, but not without first imploring Citlallotoc to keep resting; the man gave me a pointed look on his way out. I couldn't stop the burning blush.

Citlallotoc looked tired but he still smiled, taking my hand with his. "I'm sorry about what happened out there, on the precinct. Did I scare you?"

"You...definitely worried me," I admitted, not meeting his gaze.

His cheeks flared. "That's never happened to me before; at least not while doing...that. It must mean it was really good."

Or really, really bad for you, I thought, but bit my tongue.

He rolled on his side so he could lie closer to me. The look of adoration and happiness on his face made my chest hurt. "When we get back to Tollan, if we both go to Topiltzin and tell him how we feel about each other, he can't go on telling us no, right? He'll see we're in love, and he'll have to bend."

All this talk of love turned my mouth dry. "Citlallotoc, about tonight...it was a mistake, and we can't let it happen again."

His grip tightened on my hand, tense and possessive. "What do you mean?"

"Let go of my hand, Citlallotoc," I said, trying to keep my voice even and non-threatening. I'd seen that same look in Black Otter's eyes more than once.

And for a moment I thought I would have to call my guards to make him, but he finally let me go, looking as if I'd stuck him in the back with my sacrificial blade. "You don't love me?"

"I do; you're one of my dearest friends, but it's not like that—"

"You mean not like you feel for Topiltzin," he interjected.

I bit my lip.

Growing agitated, he said, "But you kissed me. If you didn't feel that way about me, why did you do that? Why did you let it go as far as it did?"

I shook my head. "I'm sorry. I was upset—"

"Oh dear gods!" He sat up, bewildered. "How am I ever going to face Topiltzin again when I took advantage of his sister?"

"You didn't take advantage of me—"

"If you hadn't been upset, would we still have done what we did?"

After a guilty pause, I admitted, "Probably not."

"What will Topiltzin say when he hears of this?"

"He doesn't have to know. I can tell the surgeon—"

"Of course he has to know! I can't lie to my best friend!"

I pushed him back down on his bed, fearing his rising agitation would worsen his illness. He set his hand over mine again, that possessiveness back. "I'd still make a good husband, Quetzalpetlatl. I will devote my life to you, to making you happy; I will give you my heart, with no conditions attached—"

"Citlallotoc—"

"We can take care of each other when we're old. I owe you that much at least."

"You don't owe me anything," I protested.

But he shook his head, tears in his eyes. "I cost you your son—"

"No, you didn't."

"I didn't protect him well enough." He let go of my hand and looked away as the tears broke free. "So why should you expect me to be able to protect you, to care for you either? So of course Topiltzin wouldn't let me marry you. He would want someone worthy and strong marrying you."

"Please stop this," I choked, my own tears running sudden and thick. "You are strong, and worthy, and any woman would be lucky to have you."

"But you don't want me."

I don't want to hurt you the way I hurt Black Otter, I almost said, but the cotton in my throat blocked it. The desperation in his voice was impossible to miss. Within a few months I would strip him of everything he was, everything he cared about in this world, except me; he wouldn't care about honor or duty, or Little Reed.

But Citlallotoc wasn't the only one displaying alarming behavior. Little Reed and I had never consummated and yet he'd refused to bed Anacoana, and used his friendship with Citlallotoc to keep him from pursuing me. He was as singularly focused on me as anyone, and if Citlallotoc became real competition, might he resort to murder as Black Otter had? I didn't want to think Little Reed capable of such things, but I never would have thought Black Otter was either.

And what if I rejected Citlallotoc for Little Reed? What would Citlallotoc do?

You can't ever go back to Tollan, I realized. *If you do, eventually, you'll destroy them both.*

Citlallotoc pulled my hand to his lips and gave it a gentle kiss. "But maybe, with time, you could learn to love me?"

I pulled my hand slowly away from him, every fiber of my being yelling at me to run. "I think you should rest, and we can talk about this later. We've been through a lot tonight."

"We should sleep on it," he agreed, a hopeful smile on his face.

"Exactly."

"If you want, you can sleep here tonight." He pulled open his blanket, showing that he was naked—and ready—under his waist-length xicolli.

I averted my gaze, the desire growling. I hated that voice so much. "You heard the surgeon," I scolded him with a smile as I went to the tent flap, itching to leave. "I'll talk to you tomorrow."

"I'm looking forward to it."

And finally I escaped out into the night air, my heart hammering painfully against my ribs.

Mazatzin came over from his tent, looking weary but concerned. "Is he going to be all right?"

"He'll be fine," I assured him. *Especially once I'm gone from his life. And from Little Reed's.* I glared when my personal guards pressed close to me, determined not to let me out of their sight again. I wouldn't get far with them following me everywhere.

To Mazatzin, I said, "Would you mind escorting me to the Temple of the Feathered Serpent? I feel the need to make prayers for Citlallotoc's recovery."

Mazatzin nodded, and after fetching his robe, we went to the sacred precinct, the guards following at a discreet distance. We walked in silence most of the way before Mazatzin asked, "Something is weighing on you, and I wish you'd talk to me about it."

Laughing, I said, "I'm surprised you don't already know."

"About you and Citlallotoc? That's not what I'm talking about. Something else is bothering you; you've been secretive since we left Tollan, and you sneaked away in the middle of the night and ended up at the Temple of the Moon with Citlallotoc. And now you're asking me to go and pray with you—"

"It's not what you think," I assured him, holding my hands up.

"And I'm not thinking you're going to seduce me, if that's what you're worried about," he replied. "I don't see you that way, and I trust you to respect that."

Maybe you shouldn't, I thought. If he'd been the one to find me instead of Citlallotoc, might things have still gone as they had? And if he'd resisted more vehemently than Citlallotoc had, what might the desire have done? I shivered to even consider that I might have something in common with Ahexotl. "I wish I could tell you, Mazatzin."

"Why can't you?"

"Because it would change everything between us, and I'm dealing with too much of that already with too many other people. I need the stability of our friendship, just as it is."

He nodded. "I'm honored to be a rock for you to cling to in your time of need."

We reached the Pyramid of the Feathered Serpent with its many statues of Quetzalcoatl and Tlaloc the rain god. As Mazatzin started up the stairs, he asked, "Have you given any thought to which story you want to tell at the vision ceremony tonight?" He stopped when I didn't follow him.

"I won't be here for the vision ceremony."

"Are you not feeling well?"

I shook my head. "I'm not going back to Tollan either."

He came back down the stairs, his expression confused. "What do you mean?"

"Everything I touch...I destroy it."

"How can you say such a thing?"

"Because it's true. I can't be around other people."

He stammered a moment before asking, "But where would you go?"

A good question. And I knew the answer: if I couldn't be around humans without hurting them, I needed to be around other gods instead. I knew so little about how to be a goddess, how to do any of the things gods did—for Tzitzimitl and Quetzalcoatl had kept me ignorant of these things—and I needed guidance. But could I really trust Mextli? I stared at the grinning feathered serpent heads decorating the temple's walls in rows, interspersed with heads of the goggle-wearing Tlaloc. *I certainly can't trust you.*

When I looked at the embroidered feathered serpents on the front of my robe, my anger boiled over. I stripped the robe off and threw it at the temple. "You can keep your damn priesthood and pick someone else to be your foolish high priestess, because I'm done!" I shouted.

Mazatzin stared at me, agape. "Why would you...what has happened, Quetzalpetlatl?"

Tears leaked down my cheeks. "I've finally seen the truth: Quetzalcoatl is a liar who paints beautiful pictures of the future but doesn't warn you of the price it demands until it's too late. He doesn't tell you that your parents will die, and that you won't know any happiness for it; he'll make you believe he loves you when in fact he's waiting for the next opportunity to unleash the Earth Monster on you!"

I tore the sacrificial blade from my belt and started to throw it too, but when I saw the stag horn handle in the shape of the Feathered Serpent, I paused, my gut clenching. This wasn't my mother's sacrificial blade, for I'd lost that for good long ago, but I'd paid someone to make one exactly like it in shape and design, and I'd spent days adding the wear marks and dents myself, all from my last memory of holding it. While this wasn't my mother's blade, it was the closest thing I had to having anything of hers, of the woman who had loved and cared for me with no expectation or judgment, and I couldn't bring myself to throw it away.

I returned the blade to my belt and held the handle tight, taking deep, calming breaths before continuing, "All I can say is that everything has changed, and I can't be Quetzalcoatl's high priestess anymore; nor can I go back to Tollan where I'm surrounded by reminders of the god."

"But what about Topiltzin?" Mazatzin asked. "How will he go on without you?"

"He has a new wife and child, and he deserves the happiness that brings. If I'm there, he'll never find that. Promise me that if he talks of coming to find me, you will talk him out of it. Promise!"

He hesitated, then nodded. "I won't pretend to understand all this, but I will do as you ask."

"And you must tell Malinalli goodbye for me. Please tell her I'm sorry I didn't come to say it myself, but that I know she will do well as the new high priestess. But warn her to beware of gods making outrageous promises."

"I will tell her." He frowned deeply. "Will I ever see you again?"

I took his hand between mine and tried to smile, but instead it came out as a frown. "As much as I'd like that, my friend, it would be better if you didn't." My jaw quivering, I turned and walked off past the pyramid, into the open field beyond it, into the rising sun.

My guards shouted for me to wait for them, but when I looked back, Mazatzin held them back. He still stood next to the temple, a slump to his shoulders, but he was letting me go, and I silently thanked him for that.

Once away, I didn't look back again. The past held only pain and disappointment, and I couldn't afford to live there anymore. I knew my real name now, but I still needed to find myself, and find my future. And if I'd been able to come back from the dead—twice now—maybe I could bring my son back too. The thought gave me the first joy I'd felt in months.

And hopefully Mextli could help me on that journey.

If I could find him; if I could trust him.

T. L. MORGANFIELD

THE BONE FLOWER GODDESS

PART ONE
THE YEAR THREE REED

CHAPTER ONE

I didn't see the giant hole in the ground until just before I fell into it. I tried to stop my sprint, but my worn sandals slipped in the damp grass and I went over head-first, arms flailing, tumbling like a rubber ball falling back to earth after having been kicked by the gods. My stomach dropped for only a breath before I hit the water.

Instinct made me gasp for air after the impact, but when water gushed into my lungs, those same instincts brought visceral panic. But after a few desperate gasps, my rationality set in: I didn't need to breathe. I wasn't human, so I couldn't drown or bleed to death anymore. I didn't even need to breathe at all. But thirty-five years of conditioning was hard even for a reborn goddess to overcome.

I swam to the edge of the pool and pulled myself out onto the sandy bank, my dress clinging to me. Shouts echoed above and I looked up to see a handful of warriors peering down from the lip of the cenote I'd fallen into. A big man wearing a leather and bone headdress pushed his way through the others and grimaced down at me. "Why do you run?" he called, indignant. "Have I not been kind to you?"

I tried to answer, but the water in my lungs rendered me silent. I coughed it up then called back, "It's for your own good." My voice sounded raw.

He scrunched his nose. "Ungrateful! I give you food, I give you a bed, I give you protection, and this is how you repay me?"

He *had* given me all of that, in exchange for sharing my body with him, but if he knew that was the true food he gave me, I doubted he'd be so eager to have me back.

Human men have no sense of self-preservation, my desire whispered in my head. *All they care about is the pleasure of the moment.*

I'd spent much of my adult life teaching myself to ignore that other voice, fearing her power and actions when I let her have her say; I still thought daily about that fateful night when I'd nearly killed Citlallotoc because I hadn't been strong enough to hold her back. She scared me, but there were precious few others to talk to anymore now that I tried to avoid humans while I searched for more of my own kind.

Yet sometimes circumstances drove me back to them. I limited my feeding habits to no more than twice with any single person, for any more than that had horrific consequences. But often the men were reluctant to let me go, which is why I'd snuck away from this one's camp in the middle of the night. It didn't surprise me that he'd tracked me down—he wasn't the first—but I'd hoped he wouldn't make me expend magic to escape. The more magic I used, the more I had to feed. It was a vicious circle I was incapable of escaping.

I scraped the wet hair back from my face. "This is the only time I'm going to tell you to go back home and forget about me."

The man scowled. "Bring the ropes!" he barked at the men next to him, but then he shouted down at me, "No one makes a fool of me, woman!" The men unrolled a maguey rope over the cenote's grassy lip and he grabbed onto it, preparing to rappel down after me.

I looked for a way out, but the walls angled over the jade-colored water. There was a tunnel though, directly across the water from me. I looked up to see the man shimmying down the rope, clenching his obsidian blade between his teeth. *It's now or use magic.* I dove back into the water.

I wasn't a strong swimmer—I'd had little reason to be, either as a priestess or the Queen of Tollan, since I rarely left the sanctuary of the city—but without the threat of drowning, I didn't worry. I stayed submerged; if the man wanted me, he would have to work for it.

But when something brushed against me, I stopped mid-stroke. The water was startlingly clear with sunbeams stabbing through from the surface, but I could make out little beyond the cloud of my own dark hair floating around me. Something crashed into the water to my left though, followed by a watery surge of sound pounding against my eardrums. *Is that screaming?* I turned and pushed my hair out of the way.

The man was in the water now, tangling with a monstrous beast. Red bubbles gushed as the creature flashed its claws back and forth. I froze, but when I saw the grasping hand on the end of the creature's tail, I made for the shore as fast as I could, my heart thudding. *He's found me again!* I expected the slimy grip of a clawed hand on my ankle at any moment.

I pulled myself ashore and pushed my tangled hair away from my eyes, desperate to know if the creature had followed me. I was alone on the bank, with the tunnel entrance still on the opposite side of the cavern; I'd gotten turned around in my panic.

And now the water lay eerily still. Above me, the men peered down in absolute silence, waiting for their leader to resurface.

Eventually he did, bobbing like a gassy corpse. All of his fingers were gone, chewed off at the knuckles and floating as flotsam in the ripples around him. He stared up into the sky with empty eye sockets as a cloud of red bled through the water from his body. Something large circled the grisly display, its sleek, furry back cresting the water like a serpent.

My heart still didn't slow. I'd take being pursued by humans over who was waiting for me in that water. I hadn't seen Black Otter—my former husband—since the night he'd forced me to kill him after he'd confessed to murdering my son in some disgusting plan to win me back. Drowning him had given me a moment's satisfaction, until I realized that it had been my own divine nature that had poisoned his mind.

Yet even then death couldn't stop his obsession; moments after I'd killed him, he'd risen from the dead as a monster under the thrall of the river goddess Jade Skirt. He'd sold away everything human in himself in hopes of possessing me again.

I glanced again at the tunnel. It seemed even further away now.

Black Otter ceased his circling and came towards me, swimming fast.

I gathered my magic in my hands, my whole body vibrating with anticipation and fear.

The water rose up and a huge otter-like creature leaped out, dagger-shaped fangs flashing, claws outspread. "Mine!"

I released, hitting him squarely in the chest with my magic, and he flew backwards into the water again, sending the waves washing up over my feet. The sandy mud sucked at my sandals as I made my way along the narrow bank, glancing over my shoulder as I went. Black Otter still thrashed around, disoriented by my octli magic.

But when I reached the tunnel, the muddy ground gave way under my left foot, sending me sliding down into the water. I scrambled and clawed my way back ashore and into the opening of the tunnel just as Black Otter popped up right where I'd fallen in. I scurried deeper into the dark, expecting him to lunge after me.

But he remained submerged to his waist, gripping the muddy bank with his clawed fingers. He bared his teeth, droplets of water dangling from his whiskers, his ink-black eyes vacant. "Mine!"

"Leave me alone!"

He bristled and growled. "Mine!" But when I didn't respond, he set into a keening cry that sounded terrifyingly like a baby calling for its mother.

My son had never cried as an infant—no doubt a side effect of being divine like me— but still the taunting sound set my heart racing with fury. I ripped off a muddy sandal and pelted him in the nose with it.

He scratched at his face, startled, but then he roared and lunged out of the water at me. I shuffled backwards on all fours.

Yet he stopped short. The hand on his long, sleek tail gripped onto the bank; my only saving grace, that he couldn't completely separate himself from water. "Mine!"

I threw my other sandal at him, setting him into a pawing frenzy, but then I pressed further into the tunnel, leaving him shrieking and crying.

Eventually the light faded, giving way to complete darkness. My skin gave off a soft orange glow; not real light, just my divine essence, and when I tripped over a rock, I crawled instead, to make sure I didn't walk off a cliff. I couldn't even see the ground under my glowing hands. I followed the trickle of water in the distance, hoping that would lead to another cenote. It might mean facing off against Black Otter again, but what else could I do?

A dim glow grew in the distance and I picked up the pace, eager to be free of the darkness. The light grew brighter, but not as much as I would expect for a cenote. And it had a strange blue hue more akin to moonlight. Surely I hadn't been underground so long that night had fallen?

The tunnel opened onto a cavernous room lit by blue-flame torches mounted along the shimmering walls. A trail of black water wound among the stalagmites, leading to a cliff. I eyed the water as I walked by, keeping at a distance.

I wondered why I didn't hear the sounds of a waterfall, but my arrival at the edge answered that. The water became a fat rope that snaked along the edge of a set of stone stairs that descended into the bowels of the earth to a landing. The right side of the staircase opened onto a sheer drop, and when I peered over the edge, darkness shrouded the bottom. Halfway down the stairs stood a gate.

My stomach constricted. *This all seems familiar.*

Hissing brought me whirling around. Black Otter slunk out of the water nearest the stairs, fangs bared. "Mine!" He lunged at me.

I stepped to the left, narrowly avoiding being knocked over the edge. He caught my arm with his claws though, shredding my dress sleeve and laying open the flesh beneath. I collided with the wall but then fell, and the world became a jumble of sound, light, and pain as I rolled head over feet. It didn't stop even when I did.

I blinked, dazed. The stairs now rose ahead of me, and Black Otter clung to the edge of the cliff above, his tail-hand thrashing around, trying to get extra purchase.

I looked behind me; the gate had stopped me from rolling all the way down the steps to the landing below. I sat on the cliff-side though, and with an endless drop just a breath away, I scrambled and pressed up against the wall, clutching my knees to my chest, my heart hammering. Glowing gold stardust spewed from multiple cuts on my body.

Black Otter finally clawed his way up onto the ledge then limped out of sight. The sound of splashing echoed through the cavern, but then he reappeared, glaring down at me from the top step. "Mine!" He started down the stairs, the hand on his tail dragging along the rope of water pouring down the corner of the stairs.

I looked behind me again, through the white bars of the gate. The stairs continued at least another hundred steps before leveling off onto the platform. Black Otter was nearly upon me, fangs bared, his inky black eyes flashing....

There's only one place left to run. I pushed the gate open and crawled through.

But when I slammed it shut behind me, Black Otter skidded to a stop, confused. He pressed closer, nostrils flaring as he sniffed. He also peered over the cliff edge. "Mine!" His cry echoed into the nothingness. He turned his glare upon the gate and after a tense silence, he pounded his paws on the stone steps. "Mine! Mine! Mine! Mine!"

I watched, as confused as he, but then I realized, *He can't see me anymore.* I turned my attention to the gate between us.

Arm and leg bones bundled together with sinew formed the bars, and numerous skulls crowned the top—bears, jaguars, deer, rabbits, rodents, even some birds. They stared down at me with empty eye sockets, grinning at a private joke. *I've seen this before*—

Suddenly the gate swung open again.

I pushed back on it, fearing this would break whatever fragile magic kept me hidden from Black Otter, but no matter how hard I pushed, the gate wouldn't be denied. I fled down the steps, expecting to hear claws scraping the stone as he scrambled after me.

But instead his voice grew fainter. I paused to glance back.

He paced and prowled on the other side of the open gate, but now a man walked down the stairs with a small brown dog leading the way. I stepped aside for them— they passed me without so much as a glance—then watched them descend to the platform. The man followed the dog to the left and disappeared. After a quick check that the gate had closed, I continued down the stairs.

A corbelled arch formed a doorway in the wall along the side of the landing, opening into another cavern. The trickle of water wound over the threshold to a broad black river bordering the cavern's right side. A small house of stone and bones sat opposite it, shrouded by a skeletal tree where orbs of blue light bobbed among its branches like monstrous fireflies. One of them broke from the others and floated towards the man and the dog standing next to the river.

It circled them a few times then spiraled down and was absorbed into the dog's body. The dog in turn doubled in size, and when it looked up at the man, its once black eyes glowed with the orb's light. *For your sacrifice, I shall lead you through Lord Death's trials,* a voice whispered in the air. *Come, so you may find your eternal rest.* It turned to the river and waded in, the man following.

Ayya! This is the underworld! I backed away from the doorway, overcome by nightmarish memories. I *had* been here before, after Quetzalcoatl betrayed me to the Earth Monster. I'd stood on the banks of this very river, the wounds from my grandmother's murderous claws still fresh on my body, but they weren't the cause of the pain in my heart. Even now Quetzalcoatl's last words continued to haunt me: *Death is your true gift, my love.*

I must get out of here! I rushed back to the stairs.

But when I tried to take the first step up, I bounced back like a rubber ball hitting a wall. I landed on my rump and blinked in surprise. I tried again, but still failed to pass beyond the landing, as if an invisible force blocked my way. Further up, Black Otter had finally given up, but I waited until he disappeared from sight before launching myself at the stairs, firing magic ahead of me.

But the barrier tossed me back even harder. I skidded all the way across the platform and over the edge, but I caught myself on the lip. I hung, my legs dangling heavy and arm muscles shaking, before managing to pull myself back up, legs scrambling against the rock face. Back on solid ground, I curled up into a ball against the wall, far from the edge. "I can't face the trials of the underworld again! I can't! I can't!"

Get a hold of yourself, the desire growled.

"I can't do it again!"

More people—both men and women—walked by with their guide dogs, completely oblivious to me huddled on the floor.

Do they look terrified? the desire scolded. *Do you see any of them blubbering like a mewling child?*

"They don't know what awaits them," I fired back.

And you do, which means you have an advantage they don't. You're a goddess, for pity's sake! Act like one!

She successfully shamed me, but it still took at least two dozen more calming breaths to get me to my feet again, and even then I lurked in the doorway, rubbing my arms for comfort. *Perhaps Xolotl can raise the barrier, so I can go back.* Determined, I headed for the dilapidated house.

I pulled aside the tattered cloth curtain covering the house's doorway. The inside was empty, and judging from the thick layer of dust everywhere, no one had been there for many bundles of years. I let the curtain drop along with my stomach. What now?

Last time, Xolotl had been waiting to guide me through the trials that all the dead had to conquer to reach Mictlan. There had been no orbs, but there also hadn't been a steady stream of dead coming from the platform; there had been far fewer people in the world back then. I looked up at the bobbing orbs. "I need to speak with Xolotl."

But they continued floating serenely, new ones emerging from the dead tree's spindly branches as others left to join with the dogs—the sacrifices to Xolotl that humans buried with their dead. If they had any awareness that I was there, they didn't show it.

"Nantli?" a small voice squeaked from behind the house.

My heart stopped. *I know that voice.* I stepped toward the edge of the house.

At the back corner, a small boy of no more than seven peered back at me. He wore a tattered rabbit costume with lacquered maize leaves for ears, and though the eyes gazing back at me were as dead as any I'd ever seen, joy brought my heart jumping back to life. "Yamehecatl?"

CHAPTER TWO

Yamehecatl's chalk-pale cheeks turned up in a broad smile, showing off his missing front teeth, and he raced to me, his arms spread wide. "It is you, Nantli!"

He knocked me over backwards when he leaped into my own outspread arms but I didn't care. I never really thought I'd ever get to hold my son again. I clutched him, tears drenching my cheeks. He felt so very cold in my arms, but I didn't dare let go of him.

"I told Xolotl you would come for me, but he didn't believe me! I knew you and Tatli would come eventually!" He leaned to look around me. "Where's Tatli?"

I shook my head. "It's just me, my darling."

"Oh?" The confusion in his eyes broke my heart. "You're not dead, are you?"

I smiled, tears clouding my vision. "No. I'm quite alive, my darling breeze."

Yamehecatl embraced me again.

"I haven't the words to tell you how happy I am to hold you again, but why haven't you started on the trials yet?"

He dried his own cold tears away. "Xolotl was here for a little while and tried to get me to swim the river, but I wasn't going anywhere without you, Nantli. Eventually he just left. There were times when I started doubting—when the voice in my head said you and Tatli were never coming for me, but I knew better."

Guilt bubbled up inside me; I'd been looking for other gods, not my son; I was only here now by accident.

But really, what did it matter? "Well, I'm here now."

"And I finally get to leave this place." He pulled at my arm, eager to go.

I looked over my shoulder at the doorway I'd come through. "We can't go back that way."

"No, that way's blocked," he acknowledged. "Xolotl said you can only go one direction on the road into Mictlan." He looked too before admitting, "And I already tried, just to see if he was telling the truth."

"Which means we have to cross the river."

Yamehecatl shook his head, alarmed. "Xolotl warned me not to try it without him or I'll get pulled under and never surface. I saw some people try it and it happened just as he said it would."

"Where is Xolotl anyway? He's supposed to be leading you through these trials—"

"He stayed with me for a long time, but then one day he wasn't here anymore and I haven't seen him since."

"After we paid him with a dog? Ayya! He's going to get an earful when I see him again." I glared at the river, wondering what to do next.

A woman came through the archway, accompanied by a dog. One of the orbs broke off from the others circling the spindly tree and made for the river, where the woman and the dog waited. It joined with the dog then the two waded out into the river. *Maybe the orbs are Xolotl's nahuals.* I hurried to the river bank. "Xolotl! I need to speak with you!"

But the dog ignored me, as did the woman. I shouted a few more times and even waved my hands around when the dog reached the opposite shore, but still no response.

"Xolotl told me that the dead can't see each other," Yamehecatl said. "At least not the mortal dead."

I turned to him, about to ask how he could see her, but then the truth hit me. "How long have you known that you're not mortal?"

He flashed his gap-tooth smile. "Night Wind told me, a few weeks before I died, but he made me promise not to say anything to anyone about it, especially to you."

"Why not me?"

"Because you're a priestess, and you would say I was being blasphemous."

I knelt and held him by both hands. "I wouldn't ever call you blasphemous, my darling. I love you too much to do that."

"I know. But Nantli, why didn't you tell me?"

"I didn't know. If I had...I definitely wouldn't keep that secret from you. It's too important. If Night Wind hadn't told you the truth, you would have died a mortal and there would be no chance for you to come back to life again."

His face lit up. "I can live again?"

I nodded. "And you will, I promise. We just need to find a way out of here." I returned to studying the river and wondering how I might get one of Xolotl's nahuals to help us when I had no dog to entice it.

"Nantli?"

"Yes, my darling breeze?" But when he started crying, I pulled him into my arms to comfort him. "What's wrong?"

"I'm sorry."

"For what?"

"For not telling you that I knew...about you."

I frowned, confused. "What do you mean?"

"I knew you were a goddess and I didn't say anything."

"You knew? But what...how...how did you know?"

Yamehecatl wiped his nose with his wrist. "I figured it out. I mean, it wasn't difficult, really. You can use magic, and we both remember everything, so what else could it be? I told Night Wind and he said you were but that I couldn't say anything to you about it."

"Why not?"

"He said if I did, you would get hurt, and that if I loved you, I would keep my mouth shut about it. I'm sorry, Nantli."

As he broke into still more tears, I hugged him tight. He felt so cold, but the anger boiling inside me would surely warm his dead flesh. "There is nothing to forgive, dear. Night Wind is a callous liar who just wants to hurt us. I know this may be difficult to hear, but he isn't your friend."

"What do you mean?"

"Night Wind is really the Smoking Mirror, and as a god of lies, you can't trust anything he says." *Though if not for him, you wouldn't know your true identity, would you?*

"But why would Smoking Mirror want to hurt us, Nantli? What did we do to him?"

I sighed. "You, my darling, did absolutely nothing. Smoking Mirror just hates Quetzalcoatl, and since you're Quetzalcoatl's son...."

"He hates me too." Yamehecatl frowned.

"I'm sorry. None of this is your fault."

"But why does he hate you?"

"Because I kept him from taking over the valley, and I killed his chosen high priest."

"Then it's true what everyone says? That you unleashed Quetzalcoatl on the false king?"

I nodded. "I let the Feathered Serpent take control of my body so we could battle Smoking Mirror, who was trying to kill your Tatli, and that's...how you came to be."

"Wow!" He gazed at me with wide, wondering eyes. "You're a really powerful goddess,

Nantli!"

I laughed. "Not really, dear, but thank you."

He shook his head. "I bet Xolotl left because he knew you were coming and he wouldn't be able to stop you from saving me! He was scared!"

"I doubt that."

I took another look at the river. Mortals couldn't walk the road into Mictlan alone, but perhaps a goddess could?

But when I started towards the water, Yamehecatl grabbed onto my wrist. "Where are you going?"

"I must test a theory." When he didn't let go, I gently pried his fingers from my arm then knelt in front of him again. "There is only one way out of the underworld, and it's over that river and through the other trials. I think I can be Xolotl for you, but I must test my hunch before letting you try to cross. I thought I lost you forever once already; I won't risk it again."

Yamehecatl pursed his lips but nodded. "Xolotl did say that anyone living must walk the road too, but if they take too long, they will be dead when they reach Mictlan."

"Then time is urgent." I rose but made sure he was calm before heading for the river again. At the bank I paused, breathed deeply, then stepped into the water.

Icy cold drilled into my feet, bringing with it needles of fear. I continued on, one slow step at a time, until the water reached my waist. My heart hammered as I waited for my nightmarish memories to come to fruition.

I jolted when boney fingers closed around my ankle and began pulling. Instinct told me to kick and flee—and I almost did—but then I remembered what Xolotl had told me so many bundles of years ago: *One must overcome the fear of the unknown to cross the river. To not do so is to drown in fear.* I squeezed my eyes shut and strove for calm, and soon the tugging and clawing ceased.

I waded back to shore, my heart light with excitement.

Yamehecatl rushed to the river bank. "Is it safe, Nantli?"

"Perfectly, my dear." I held my hand out.

"But Xolotl said those without a guide get lost forever."

"Xolotl isn't the only one who knows the way. This isn't my first time in the underworld, remember?"

Yamehecatl thought on that then he smiled brightly. "Oh, because the Earth Monster—" He didn't go on though, looking acutely distressed.

"She killed me," I finished for him. "So yes, I've walked the road before, and I know what to expect. Don't worry, we'll get to Mictlan together."

He smiled as he took my hand. "I love you, Nantli."

I bent to kiss his cold forehead. "And I missed you so very much, my darling."

He wiped it away with the back of his hand, just as he used to when he was still alive. "We just have to swim the river?"

"This is just the first trial. There will be eight more after that."

"I'm not a strong swimmer, Nantli." He eyed the water with trepidation.

"You will ride on my back. I need you to remember one thing though."

"What's that?"

"No matter what you feel, none of it is real and it can't hurt you. Understand?"

He nodded, but fear still shone in his eyes.

I gave his hand a squeeze. "It will be all right."

He climbed onto my back when I knelt on the bank to let him up. "Arms around my neck." I supported his legs with my arms as I waded out into the river, walking slow and methodical as not to let the fast-moving water knock me over. Yamehecatl squealed when the water reached his feet—"So cold!"—then I eased down into the current and swam out into the middle of the river, paddling hard.

Yamehecatl did all right for the first minute—shivering but not complaining—but suddenly he buried his face in the back of my head. "Something's touching me, Nantli! Something's touching my leg!"

"Just remember...it's not real," I panted between waves hitting my mouth. "It can't...hurt you...unless you...let it." Bony fingers brushed against my legs and feet, but I focused on keeping the fear at bay.

"It's not real. It's not real," he sputtered into my wet hair, his grip so tight he would have strangled me if I were still mortal. He repeated it over and over, like a prayer, but his shivering grew worse. "They're trying to pull me down, Nantli! Sing me a song! Please!"

The only ones I could think of were praises for Quetzalcoatl, and he was the last god I wished to say anything nice about, but with Yamehecatl shaking violently, now wasn't the time for the anger. Singing songs about the Feathered Serpent always put him at ease.

With the water slapping into my mouth and his strangling grip around my neck, I had to sputter and gasp the words out. But it started working right away. His grip loosened and his breathing slowed, and soon he joined in. For a moment, even I forgot we were fording the black river instead of sitting in my bed in Tollan, singing together as we so often had. I hadn't felt so happy in over a year now and I desperately wanted to hold onto that.

Soon I felt mud under my feet again and once I was able to stand upright, Yamehecatl jumped down and ran ashore, ecstatic. "We made it! We made it, Nantli!"

I trudged ashore, surprisingly tired. I hadn't felt fatigued since rediscovering my divinity—it seemed gods required no rest—but now my muscles protested just as they used to after a brisk walk up and down the temple steps in Tollan. *An ominous portent?* I wondered, but I shook it off. The sooner we moved on, the sooner we'd be done.

￮

An archway in the wall led into a short tunnel that opened into another vast cavern, but when we stopped at the entrance, all of Yamehecatl's excitement fled. Obsidian arrow and spear heads rained from the darkened cavern ceiling. He tightened his grip on my hand. "How do we get past this?"

"We have to run."

"But it's so far!"

"There's no way around it. You have to run, and not stop. It only gets worse if you stop. Just remember that the arrows can't kill you; you're already dead, after all."

"But what about you? You're not."

The sound of shattering obsidian made my stomach clench, but the longer we waited, the harder the downpour became.

But then I remembered how the blades had bounced off of Xolotl when he'd led me through the cavern, as if he had an invisible shield protecting him—his magic, undoubtedly. Maybe my own would do the same for me?

I reached out into the open, but within a couple breaths, an arrowhead sliced deep into the muscle of my forearm. I yanked my arm to my chest with a yelp, holding the wound with my other hand as golden star dust bled through my fingers. So much for my magic protecting me.

I clenched my teeth and pulled the blade out. "Don't worry about me." I tried to sound unconcerned despite the dread growing in the pit of my stomach.

"But I *am* worried about you, Nantli," he insisted. He thought a moment then asked, "Do you remember how Tatli always told this part of the story, of Quetzalcoatl's journey into the underworld?"

I nodded. "The Feathered Serpent carried Xolotl on his shoulders, to cloak himself from the blades."

"I could do that for you." When I opened my mouth to tell him "absolutely not!" he pointed out, "Like you said, I'm already dead, so it can't kill me."

"It still hurts like nothing you've ever known," I warned. "We'll just run—"

"But what if it kills you?"

And if that happens, who's going to guide him to Mictlan. I wasn't sure how matters worked when one died on the road; would I have to start the journey all over again, and would Xolotl take mercy on me and guide me despite the lack of a sacrifice? *He skipped out on guiding Yamehecatl. That's a far cry from mercy.*

"Please, Nantli. I want to help you," Yamehecatl said, holding my hand between both of his. "I know I'm just a little boy, but I can be brave, because I love you and you're my nantli. If Tatli were here, he would do this for you, but since he's not...." He looked ready to cry.

That was enough to set my own tears threatening. "No, he's not, and I know you're brave, my darling. I just can't stand the thought of you hurt—"

"And Tatli always says there's nothing more honorable than making sacrifices for the ones we love." He squeezed my hand, suddenly seeming so much older than his mere seven years. "You made many for me, so please let me make this one for you."

I wiped away the tears that had broken free and I went to my knees and pulled him into a fierce hug. "You are the bravest boy I've ever known, Yamehecatl."

"I learned it from you, Nantli," he whispered back.

After a brief discussion on how to proceed, we decided I'd get the best cover by putting him upon my shoulders; that would expose the least amount of both of our bodies to the arrow-storm. He was quite heavy and I had to lever myself up using the wall for support, but soon I stood facing the cavern with Yamehecatl hunched over upon my shoulders. The storm had grown nastier, with twice as many obsidian blades raining down as before. Memories of the pain made me hesitate, but if we remained here much longer, the storm might become impassable. "Ready?" I asked Yamehecatl.

"Ready!" he called.

With a deep breath, I dove out into the cavern.

I didn't make it any further than a single step before Yamehecatl squealed in pain, and for half a breath, I stopped, overcome by the need to make sure he was all right, but then my good sense won out. Stopping would only bring him more pain. I gripped his legs tightly with both hands and ran.

Yamehecatl's awkward hunch over the top of me had me leaning forward more than I would have liked, so I felt off balance and on the verge of crashing over every step I took. My world became the sound of his cries—each one more agonized than the last—and blurs of black and grey streaking all around me. I wasn't even sure if I was going in the right direction but I kept moving, even when a blade got past Yamehecatl and caught my calf in stride. I hardly noticed the pain though; I was a blubbering mess, thinking of my son taking the brunt of the attack.

When I finally reached the next archway, I couldn't get to my knees fast enough. Yamehecatl clung to me with a petrified grip and it took a full minute of coaxing to get him to finally let go and slide down my back. I wept when I saw the mess of arrow and spearheads all over his back and arms; I'd told him to shield his head, and he looked like a porcupine on his upper body.

"You were so very brave, my love," I whispered, tears flooding down my cheeks as I carefully worked the blades from his body. He shuddered each time, but he made no noise as I worked. Like a drained corpse, he didn't bleed from his wounds, but the blades left his rabbit suit in tatters. When I pulled the last one from him, I drew him onto my lap and held him close, stroking his head while I rocked him.

We sat that way a very long time before Yamehecatl came back to himself. "We made it through all right?" he asked, his voice still distant, but I was glad he'd finally spoken again.

"We did," I whispered.

"You didn't take the blade out of your leg."

I'd been so wrapped up in caring for him that I hadn't even noticed my own wound. It didn't throb as I would expect, but it burned when I yanked it out. Shimmering gold dust oozed out thick, like sap, and the wound showed no signs of sealing on its own, as it normally would, so I tore off the hem of my dress and tied it around it. "Don't worry about me, my dear. I'll be all right. How are you feeling?"

He shrugged. "It doesn't hurt much anymore."

"You're so brave, my love," I whispered, returning to stroking his head. He sighed and snuggled against my breast, holding me tight.

We sat like that for a long time, but I didn't have forever to wait. I made sure Yamehecatl was physically ready to go though before insisting we move onto the next cavern. My own wounded leg had grown stiff and I had to hobble around before being able to put weight on it.

"I told him he was wrong about you," Yamehecatl said as he took my hand when I held it out to him.

"Who?"

"The voice in my head. He always said you didn't love me."

My stomach clenched. "I love you more than anything, Yamehecatl."

"I know you do, Nantli. He always said mean things, like that you wanted me to stay a baby forever, and that's why you kept calling me Yamehecatl instead of Ehecacone."

"I'm sorry. It's just, for so long you were Yamehecatl to me...but I understand. I will make sure to always call you Ehecacone for now on."

He smiled brightly. "Thank you, Nantli."

"What else does he say?"

"Just nonsense, really. He claims you wanted to get rid of me before I was even born."

My son had never brought this subject up when he was in a rational state of mind; the accusation always came when the drunkenness had taken over, when he became someone so completely unlike the sweet little boy I knew, and for a very long time, I'd dreaded having to answer that. And though it really wasn't a question this time, I couldn't baldly lie to him. It was time we had the discussion.

I took both of his hands in mine and knelt in front of him. "I don't ever want to keep the truth from you, no matter how much it pains me...but...it's true that I thought of ending my pregnancy."

He furrowed his brow. "What do you mean?"

I took a deep breath. "For a few weeks, when I first learned that I was going to be a mother, I didn't want to be one, and I was planning to take some medicine that would make it so I wouldn't be."

He stared at me, devastated, and it took all my willpower to not turn away in shame. "But why?"

"I was very scared," I admitted, my voice catching as the tears came on. "I knew you were the god's son, and...." I paused to collect myself then went on, "You know how your Tatli is the god's son too? Well, my mother—your grandmother—she died giving birth to him because, while it's already dangerous business giving birth to a normal mortal child, it's especially dangerous for a mortal woman to give birth to the child of a god. I was at your grandmother's side when she gave birth to your Tatli, and...and I saw what it did to her. It's one of the worst memories of my life. And I was afraid that I too would die if I carried you to birth."

"But you're not mortal, Nantli," Ehecacone pointed out.

"But I didn't know that back then; that's something I only found out recently. At the time, I very much thought I would die."

"And so you really planned to get rid of me?"

I pursed my lips, trying not to burst into guilty tears as I admitted, "I did."

He looked uncertain and didn't respond right away, but eventually he said, "But you didn't do it." When I shook my head, he asked, "Why not?"

"Because I finally started listening to my heart," I said. "And she loves you so much she would risk everything for you. I've never once regretted my decision to keep you, not even when Black Otter took you from me."

"Black Otter?" he asked, confused.

I wiped away tears and nodded. "I would have given my life to stop him, and I wouldn't have thought twice about it."

Ehecacone sniffled, trying to hold back his own tears. "I'm so sorry, Nantli...all those things I used to say when the other voice took over...."

I pulled him into a tight hug and whispered, "You have nothing to be sorry about, my dear sweet breeze. I'm the one who should being saying sorry to you. Can you ever forgive me?"

His tears wetted my shoulder. "Can you forgive me for ever saying that you hated me?"

"Of course, my love. It's all right."

He kissed my cheek then pulled away to wipe his runny nose with his wrist. "I would do anything for you too, Nantli."

Looking at the plethora of holes in his rabbit suit left by the obsidian blades, my heart swelled painfully with pride and thankfulness. "I know you would, dear."

CHAPTER THREE

 Based on my own memories, I estimated it would take us only a handful of hours to finish the journey, but for the first time in my life, my perfect memory proved imperfect.

After the cavern of arrowheads, the tunnel opened into a gorge surrounded by steep, jagged rock walls. The temperature plummeted and as we hiked further in, snow began drifting down from above. We followed a winding creek, trying to avoid crossing it and possibly wetting our feet, especially as the storm picked up and the wind began howling through the canyon, but the longer we walked, the narrower the gorge became until we had no choice but to walk in the middle of the creek. My feet went numb long before the water finally froze hard enough for us to walk on without falling through. All the while we clutched each other for warmth; futile since Ehecacone's dead body gave off only more cold.

"How much further, Nantli?" he asked as we shuffled through the frozen wasteland.

"Not far now," I told him, though I didn't entirely trust my memory anymore in that regard.

And I felt as if I were growing weaker the further along I went. My feet were numb and my legs felt heavy, each step more difficult than the one before. The wind cut like knives across my exposed skin, and not even shivering did much to help it. The monotony of the swirling whiteness lulled my brain and increasingly I thought of curling up in the snow and just going to sleep. I hadn't slept in over six months, not since that fateful night when Smoking Mirror changed the entire course of my life. There'd been a few times when I'd wished I still didn't know the truth—that I wished I was back in Tollan with Little Reed, celebrating the birth of the next heir to the throne. I wished I didn't know the child was actually Citlallotoc's because Little Reed was so wrapped up in the poison I cast over all mortals that he couldn't bring himself to bed another woman. I wished I didn't know that that same poison had driven Black Otter to murder my son. As an immortal that never slept anymore, I never got any peace from the questions and regrets that constantly plagued me since that night.

I flinched when someone suddenly shook my shoulder, and to my confusion, I realized I was lying on the ground. Ehecacone gazed down at me with wide, concerned eyes. "What happened?" I asked, sitting up, disoriented.

"You were walking and all of a sudden you just fell over, like you passed out," he sputtered, shivering in his thin rabbit suit. "Are you all right?"

I looked around, still confused and trying to get my bearings. "Yes, I'm fine. I'm just...feeling tired." And what did that mean for me?

"Maybe you should rest for a while," he suggested.

But I shook my head. "It's much too cold here, and there's no shelter. We must press on." I stumbled to my feet with his help and we continued on into the blinding storm. I felt more alert now, but the cold started really sinking its teeth into me. I worried for my numb toes directly exposed to the snow, but I had nothing to protect them with; I'd lost my shoes to Black Otter, and because it was summer up in the living world, I was dressed in nothing more than a thin dress. What I wouldn't do right now for a fur-lined cloak, or some leathers to cover my feet!

Soon the exhaustion hit hard and my mind started drifting again in the maddening whiteness. Back to that final time I'd spoken with Quetzalcoatl in the Divine Dream, how he'd lied so shamelessly, how he tried to convince me to give him the chance to fill my head with more lies to cover for his treachery, lies such as that he loved me and hadn't meant to hurt me. *Death is your real gift*, he'd told me so long ago, and even now I could still hear his laughter in my head.

"Are we almost there, Nantli?" Ehecacone asked, clutching my hand tightly with his own ice-cold one.

"I don't know," I admitted. I hoped so, for I wasn't sure how much more of this cold and swirling snow and memories of betrayal I could handle. "Will you sing me a song, my sweet breeze, to help us pass the time?"

"Of course, Nantli." He then set into one of the prayer songs we always sang.

"Not one about Quetzalcoatl!" I snapped, the fury overcoming me. It came on like a brush fire and my skin seemed to burn. "Never sing of that deceitful snake again!"

Ehecacone stared up at me with scared eyes, and he started pulling his hand from mine, but I tightened my grip.

"I'm sorry. I didn't mean to snap at you, my dear," I said.

He gave me a wary look before finally letting me pull him along.

I don't know how much longer we walked, but eventually I saw the faint outline of a tunnel in the side of a mountain right ahead of us. Ehecacone hooted when he too saw it, and he pulled me along faster. We stumbled over the icy rocks, the wind tearing at us, and it still followed us when we ran into the tunnel, out of the elements. I hobbled along, trying to remember what came next, but my mind was crying for sleep. The wind only followed us so far, and I noticed a marked temperature increase the further in we went.

"You should rest for a while, Nantli," Ehecacone suggested. I couldn't see him in the dark, but he pulled on my arm, motioning me to sit down. I followed his instructions without argument and leaned against the tunnel wall, thankful to be off my feet. He climbed onto my lap and I held him close, not minding how chilly he was, for the air had grown quite hot by now. I rested my head on his, holding my breath against the musty smell of decay seeping off of him; instead, I tried to remember how he used to smell when he was alive; like papayas and fresh flowers, and love....

"Nantli?" Ehecacone's words seemed to come from a dream, but I realized I was awake again, my body aching and my toes burning badly. I tried to move them but the effort only sent shocks of pain through my feet.

I gritted my teeth then asked, "Yes, my dear?"

"You've stopped glowing."

I looked down at my hands to find them completely lost in the darkness. Did this mean I was turning mortal? I had started sleeping again, and I feared my toes were deeply frostbitten. At the very least, my magic was so low I couldn't heal myself anymore. Xolotl's warnings about taking too long to walk the road repeated in my head, but it still wasn't enough to convince my muscles to wake up.

Ehecacone snuggled against my chest. "Why can't we sing about Quetzalcoatl anymore?"

I stroked his head in the dark. "You can sing about the Feathered Serpent if you like. I had no right to tell you that, and I'm sorry."

He remained quiet before tentatively asking, "But you don't want to sing about him anymore?"

I didn't want to talk about this; I'd spent his whole life teaching him to love and honor the Feathered Serpent—to honor his father—but in my exhaustion, I'd opened the door to the conversation. I sighed. "No, I don't."

"Why not?"

My voice broke as I replied, "Because he's not who I thought he was."

"What do you mean?"

"You remember the story I told you, about Quetzalcoatl and Mayahuel?"

"Of course."

"Well...it's all true, and you were right about Quetzalcoatl; he wasn't very heroic at all. In fact, he was treacherous; he lured me down from Heaven, claimed he loved me, but when the Earth Monster came, he abandoned me and let her tear me apart. He didn't even try to help me." I hadn't wanted to cry, but the tears had their own ideas. "He told me my real gift to humanity wasn't love; he intended me to die all along so humanity could have the maguey, to make octli and commune with the rest of the gods."

"Oh Nantli!" Ehecacone whispered, reaching up to wipe my tears away with his cold fingers.

"I never should have listened to him...never should have left the garden...." But as I hugged my son tighter, I had to admit, "Though then again, he gave me you, so I can't say it was all terrible and horrible." Though given that Quetzalcoatl never said a word to me about our son nor showed any evidence he cared that Ehecacone had died, I had to believe that our son hadn't been part of his grand scheme against me, but a happy accident. The only one I could really claim, since Little Reed was just as much a source of torment for me as one of happiness.

"I will never sing about him again either," Ehecacone said, anger in his voice.

"He has much to answer for," I whispered, wiping away my own tears. "But I won't tell you that you must shun your father—"

"No one is allowed to hurt you, Mother. No one."

"No," I agreed.

"You were right. Tatli is my father, and nobody else matters."

I choked on more tears as I said, "And I know for a fact that you were as important to Topiltzin as any child he might have put in my belly himself, had circumstances been different."

"When we get out of here, can we go back to Tollan and see Father?" Ehecacone asked as he helped me to my feet. "I want to tell him that I love him."

I gritted my teeth against the sharp pain in my toes. "He already knows you love him, but yes, absolutely. We'll go back and see him. But now, let's get going or we'll never get to see anyone again."

◻

Once we reached the light streaming in from the other end of the tunnel, I saw that my toes had blistered and turned black. Every step was like walking on obsidian shards. I focused on meditation techniques I'd learned in the priesthood to keep my mind off the pain, but with minimal success.

The next cavern consisted of a bridge over a deep chasm, and flaming flags dangled from poles along the edges. Ehecacone started walking out, seemingly unconcerned, but I pulled him back. "We're going to have to run," I warned him. "I want you to go on ahead without me, because I'm hobbled and I'll just slow you down. Wait for me at the other end, all right?"

"But what about you?" he asked.

"There's nothing you can do to help me on this one. I just have to face the fire and make it to the other side. If for some reason, I don't make it...remember you're brave, and you can go on without me. You have to. For me. Understand?"

The boy who stood before me looked only seven summers old physically, but something had changed in his eyes since we'd started this journey together. He looked back at me with the gaze of someone older, someone wiser. "All right."

I hugged him firmly then pointed to the bridge. "Go as fast as you can, and try to stay to the middle. The flames have to reach far to get you there, so they are thinner and do less damage to your body."

He nodded then walked to the head of the bridge. He paused to give me an encouraging smile, then he sprinted, keeping to the middle as I'd told him.

As soon as he stepped out onto the bridge, the flaming flags sprung to life, snapping out at him. But to my astonishment, when he reached the first flame, he took to all fours and instead of running through it, he leaped over it. After that first one, he skittered

491

under the next and dodged the third. He traversed the obstacle course of flaming flags with the skill of a crafty old rabbit outrunning ocelots and sneaking past hunters' traps—an image only reinforced by his ratty rabbit suit. I held my breath as he skipped past the last two flaming flags then slid to a stop on the other side of the bridge. He looked back at me and leaped into the air, pumping his fist. "Did you see me, Mother? Not a single scratch!"

"You were amazing, my darling!" I called back, my heart overcome with pride and joy. "I knew you could do it!"

"Now it's your turn," he called back.

But when I took my first limping step forward, I knew I would have a much harder time of it. I stopped at the mouth of the bridge, breathing deeply to calm my frayed nerves.

"You can do it!" Ehecacone hollered to me.

I nodded then started across.

The flaming flags sprang to life again and whipped out at me. I took it slowly, thinking maybe I could maneuver my way past them as they snapped back and forth, but I was too slow; the one to my right kissed my cheek with its blistering tongue, making me step closer to the left side where the other one lashed me across the back. Panicked, I ran, screaming each time the flames sliced into my skin. I wasn't even sure which direction I was going anymore; I just ran, pain surrounding me from every direction. I vaguely felt one of my frostbitten toes snap off in my scramble, but I kept going, stumbling forward like a drunk. I heard Ehecacone yelling, but I couldn't find him. I plunged through another set of flaming flags, and I felt myself falling, but I blacked out before the crash.

¤

I woke up sprawled out, my entire body stiff and crusty and oozing. I tried to move, but the shocks of fresh pain rendered me paralyzed. I panted, the air hot and dry in my lungs, and my tongue felt like a piece of dried leather in my mouth. "Ehecacone?" I croaked, making myself turn my head to search for him.

He sat just inside the mouth of the tunnel, staring at me with sunken, haunted eyes, as if he couldn't believe what he was seeing. He soon shook it off and rushed over to me though, tears streaming down his face. "I thought for sure you'd died," he whispered, hovering over me, the uncertainty and fear plain in his eyes.

I'm not going to survive this ordeal, I suddenly thought, but before the fatalism could fully seep in, the voice of my desire—so absent until now—suddenly spoke up. *Stop giving up. If you give up, Quetzalcoatl wins. And who's going to guide Ehecacone? You told him to go on without you, but he's shown he hasn't the fortitude to do so. Xolotl isn't going to help him, and Quetzalcoatl doesn't give a damn about him. So stop laying here and get up already.*

As much as I despised that voice, sometimes I was grateful that it knew exactly what to say to shame me into action. I fought past the shocks of pain to make myself sit up, and Ehecacone rushed to help me, being careful not to touch my burns. *This must be how Citlallotoc felt after the surgeon cauterized his arm,* I thought, struggling to my feet. I glanced down to see I'd lost not just one toe on my blackened feet, but three. If I made it through this, I wondered if they would be permanently gone, like the fingers I cut off when I was mortal.

Not if, the desire scolded me. *When.*

"We should get moving again," I said, and together Ehecacone and I limped down the hallway to the next trial.

But there I stopped again, my heart sinking. The next cavern was small, no more than twenty paces across, but between us and the next tunnel were the jagged walls of two mountains smashing against each other every few breaths. My earlier doubts now turned to certainty: I was going to die.

Ehecacone looked expectantly up at me. "How do we get through this one?"

I motioned him to follow me and I went to the far left side of the tunnel, just outside the reach of the clashing mountains. "See that?" I pointed to a small alcove cut out from the side of the right-hand mountain just before the two came crashing together again.

He nodded.

"There are three of those along the way; two on that side, one on the opposite. To make it to the other side, you have to make it to each before the mountains come together and crush you."

"What happens if we don't make it in time?"

"You'll get mangled, and it will make the remaining trials more difficult for you, but otherwise you'll be all right."

"But what about you?"

I took a deep breath. "Ehecacone. I can't go on."

"Then I'm not either!"

"You can't stay here because of me—"

"But if you stay here, you'll run out of time—"

"It doesn't matter, my dear breeze—"

"But you promised to guide me to Mictlan! You told me good people don't break their promises; you don't break promises, Mother!"

I gritted my teeth. Such arguing used to annoy me when he was still alive, but now it just made me ashamed. "All right," I choked, terrified and trying to hold back tears. "But we must go separately because I'll just slow you down and you'll get injured."

"And you promise you will come right after me?"

"I promise."

He nodded then turned back towards the walls. He flinched when they crashed together, sending shards of rock and clouds of dust flying into the air. While he crouched, timing the number of breaths between each collision, I massaged my leg muscles and stretched, making sure I was as loose and ready to move as possible. "Two long breaths once they stop moving," he murmured as he stood again.

"I'd go as soon as they separate enough for you fit between them," I suggested. "The first one is pretty close, but the other two are further apart. You shouldn't have much trouble, since you're small, but make sure you can see where the next one is before attempting to go to it."

Ehecacone nodded and set himself up at the edge of the walls, pointed towards the first alcove. I leaned over him, making some last moment timings of my own, then said, "Go!"

He sprinted at full speed between the parting walls and made it to the first alcove even before the walls stopped moving. He looked ahead for the next, but I shouted, "Stay there until after they crash together!" At the last moment, he pulled back inside, avoiding being crushed as the walls slammed together, raining dirt and stone into the air. I held my breath as I waited for the walls to part so I could see him again.

I breathed in agonized relief when I saw my son tucked in the alcove, unharmed. "Let it go again, then go when they start parting again!"

The walls crashed again but this time when they parted, the alcove was empty.

"I made it!" Ehecacone called from beyond my sight.

I lined myself up, my heart thudding. I let the walls crash together again then I made a dash for the alcove.

I felt as if I were moving in slow motion, every muscle protesting and my burnt skin screaming, but I made it to the alcove a hair before the walls slammed in around me. The crash was deafening and I clamped my eyes shut against the storm of dust spinning around me. When the walls parted, I turned around and rubbed the dust from my eyes, searching for Ehecacone in the next niche.

But he wasn't there. "Are you all right?" I called, but before anyone could answer, the walls smashed together again. I pressed myself hard against the walls of the alcove, cringing away from the dust and rock showering over me.

But when the walls parted again, he called back to me. "I'm fine. I'm in the third alcove!"

"I'm heading to the second one soon," I called back. "Don't wait for me!"

The walls clashed again and this time I made myself keep my eyes open, so I could see the next alcove as soon as possible, and when I spotted it, I dashed again, my heart pounding. I didn't even notice my protesting muscles this time. The second niche scooped me up as the walls jerked together, encasing me in darkness and dust. As the walls slid back, I retreated with the niche and pinned myself against the back, my heart pounding so hard it hurt. I checked the next niche to see Ehecacone still there—making sure I made it to mine—but the next time I looked, he was gone. It looked so far away and this time I hesitated to go until the walls came together and parted another four times.

I made it, but just barely. The walls caught the tail of my dress and ground it together hard, pulling me against the joint between the walls and the alcove. I tore my dress up the front trying to pull away, then I fell forward when the walls finally parted. I had to scramble to my feet to avoid being brained when they came crashing back again. When I glanced ahead, in the direction out of the walls, I briefly spotted Ehecacone waiting for me, peering back anxiously. The gap was even longer than the last. There was no way I was going to make it.

I couldn't wait here forever, but I didn't want Ehecacone to see the walls crush me either. "I want you to keep your back turned," I called to him.

But he shook his head vehemently. "You're going to make it, Mother." He had that same wild look in his eyes as he used to get when the drunkenness took over. "You're going to make it." He held his hands out to me.

I waited another three crashes, working up the courage to make that last dash, then as soon as the walls started creaking apart, I started squeezing my way out. I tried to banish all thoughts of what it must feel like to be full-body crushed but it kept creeping in as I ran, blood thudding in my ears. I felt as if I was moving in slow motion, but I kept my gaze focused on the absolute certainty on my son's face directly ahead of me.

The walls crashed behind me, and for a breath I stopped short, something holding me back, but then a sickening ripping sound brought me tumbling to the ground. I didn't feel any pain, but then I was so numb and dizzy I probably wouldn't have felt it if the walls had crushed me to a pulp. I just hoped the damage wasn't so bad I couldn't go on. I took a few deep breaths then turned over.

But to my surprise, my dress lay in tatters on the ground and I was naked save for my cotton undergarment. The ripping had been my dress coming apart when the walls caught it again and I'd literally fallen out of it. I laid back and laughed, my whole body shaking.

Ehecacone gathered up the remains of my dress and knelt next to me. "I knew you would make it," he said, his voice startlingly calm. "It takes more than mountains to kill you, Mother."

CHAPTER FOUR

Making it unscathed through the clashing mountains gave me the boost of confidence I needed to believe I wasn't destined to die again. From there, we came to another river, this one guarded by giant serpents, but they proved little challenge; they swam near us when we tried to cross, but they always turned away when they came close. *That's because like you, they are earth monsters,* Xolotl had told me long ago. *And despite what your grandmother did to you, most earth monsters feel a kinship with each other.* One of them did take a snap at Ehecacone, but when I punched it in the nose, it snorted and retreated.

When we climbed back ashore and I wrung out the remains of my dress before tying it back around myself, Ehecacone glared into the water. "You'd think they could at least respect the fact that I'm a fellow snake," he grumbled.

I chuckled. "While Quetzalcoatl is your father, you're not very much like him, my dear." Remembering how like a rabbit he'd looked when dodging the flaming flags, it was obvious he took more after me; I was the one whose nahuals were rabbits, and who had been born into the mortal world on the day Tochtli.

"Good," he grumbled as we turned away from the river and stood facing the next challenge.

We didn't have to pass through any more tunnels, for we'd reached the lowest—and largest—cavern of the underworld, and just beyond this mountain lay the plains of Mictlan, where Lord Death ruled.

We both scrutinized the path winding up the mountain in front of us. The whole side was made of countless obsidian blades, jutting in all directions, leaving only a very narrow foot path that had to be taken single file, placing one foot in front of the other. It was impossible to make it to the top without cutting oneself on the blades, but one could at least mitigate the damage.

"When we get out of here, I'm going to make Quetzalcoatl answer for what he did to you," Ehecacone said, holding my hand as we started up the path.

"Don't even think about rushing off to confront him," I said. "He's a very powerful god, and you...well, we don't even know what your real powers are yet. And I won't have you sacrificing yourself in the name of revenge."

"He can't just get away with this though, Mother!"

"He won't. I promise. But in the meantime, patience, my dear."

The going was long and at times difficult, especially when the path narrowed so much that one couldn't even place one foot in front of the other without blades slicing into our ankles and feet. Ehecacone seemed unaffected by the wounds, but my own feet had become a bloody mess—my golden stardust had not only thickened to bloodlike consistency, but it had turned red as well. I stopped halfway up and tore up more of my dress, to tie around my feet for protection. Two more of my toes came off as I wrapped, and I suspected I would lose at least a couple more before this was all over.

It took several more hours, but eventually we reached the summit. From there the plain of Mictlan spread out below us, obscured by a mask of fog. "I thought we were almost there!" Ehecacone exclaimed, frustration coloring his voice.

"There are only two more trials left, and the next one is probably the easiest of them all. We just need to descend the mountain."

"Over more obsidian blades?"

"No, it's all dirt on this side."

"Then let's go!" He made to start down, but I caught his arm.

"I know it looks innocent, but you must go carefully, and slowly."

"Why?"

"Because one false step and you tumble to the bottom, and it's a long way down."

Ehecacone contemplated the slope then took my hand. "We'll go slowly then."

That worked for a while. The slope was steep; at every step it felt as though my body were becoming heavier and heavier, and sharp pains radiated up through my shins. The more exhausted I became, the harder it was to focus on my steps and my speed, and several times I nearly went down, taking Ehecacone with me. Eventually I let go of him, if only because it was just a matter of time before my attention wandered enough that I would pitch over.

And no sooner had I done so than the ground shifted under me like water and I went down, rump-first. I tried to grab onto a nearby rock, but my fingers slipped over it as if it were slick with ice and I rolled down the hill. Ehecacone's scream was drowned in the noisy avalanche of dirt and debris, and the crash of trees snapping.

I suddenly stopped, sprawled out on dry, dusty ground, my teeth tingling in my head. I closed my eyes, a burning pain radiating up my right leg. When I dared look down, no bones jutted out, but my leg was bent at an unnatural angle.

Ehecacone shouted that he was coming to help me but it still took a while for him to navigate his way down. "Are you all right?" he panted, dropping to his knees next to me.

"I'm pretty sure my leg's broken." I tried to sit up but the pain shooting up my leg made me dizzy. I lay down again, trying to keep my wits as Ehecacone looked down on me with growing panic. I set a supportive hand on his arm. "Don't worry, we'll get through the last trial; I promise."

"But can you even walk?"

Gritting my teeth, I rolled over onto my belly then dragged myself to a nearby spindly, dead tree anchored into the hard, cracked earth. I wailed and wept as I pulled myself up, and though I was dizzy and sweating profusely, eventually I got up onto my good leg. I hugged onto the tree, drawing in deep, calming breaths. When I opened my eyes, Ehecacone stood next to me, his dirty face even paler than normal. "It will be very slow going, but we'll make it," I said, my voice thick with pain. "I'll need to lean on you though, all right?"

"What if I'm not strong enough?"

"You're strong enough. Trust in yourself."

Ehecacone nodded then looked into the fog stretching across the plain. "Is it far?"

"Under normal circumstances, not really; with my leg as it is, it will take a while."

In fact, it took longer than crossing the gorge in the snow. Even without putting any weight on my bad leg, every movement brought a cry of pain to my lips; at first I tried biting them back, but it felt better to let them go. Still, after a while, my head swam too much for the pain to register except on the periphery of my attention.

The fog swallowed us as soon as we started across the plain and we couldn't see much beyond a dozen paces around us. When we first headed into the fog, there was silence, save for our shuffling feet and my agonized cries, but as we went further in, a buzzing began to fill the air, and it grew in intensity with each passing moment; the volume didn't increase, but the sheer number of sounds did, like bees coming together at a hive. I didn't remember hearing this the last time I'd been here.

Ehecacone looked around anxiously. "What is that sound, Mother?"

"I don't know." My own anxiety began building.

Suddenly a man appeared from the fog, dressed like a warrior. Both Ehecacone and I stopped, startled. He stood facing to the side away from us, staring blankly at the ground, but when I called out to him, he looked up and the buzzing intensified. He gazed at us with haunted eyes, and when he turned towards us, I saw he bled from a gaping gash just below his ribcage on the right side. I immediately recognized it as a sacrificial wound. He said nothing and soon went back to staring at the ground, and as we pressed on, more like him appeared from the fog, all with that same hopeless look about them and a hole in their chests where someone had torn their hearts out.

Ehecacone gripped my hand even tighter, his breath growing rapidly. "Who are all these people, Mother?"

"I don't know." We'd seen hundreds so far, mostly clustered in small groups at the edge of our field of view, so there were likely thousands more out in the fog, unseen. They all watched us pass with forlorn gazes, and I choked a bit when I thought I spotted Ozomatli among them, dressed in his black high priest robes, the front untied and hanging open to show off his wounded chest. I looked away, overwrought with guilt, but when I looked back, the fog had consumed him again.

But when I saw my father standing ahead of us, by himself, my heart flopped. He didn't wear his royal regalia; instead he wore only a tattered night xicolli ripped open in the front, and his gruesome, ruined chest peered out at me, a grisly reminder of what I'd found when I came to his room that night that seemed so very long ago now.

I didn't realize I'd picked up my limping pace until I was within a few steps of him. "Tatli!" I cried, flinging my arms around him and hugging him tight. His jagged rib bones stuck me in the chest but I was just grateful to finally hold him again. In my memories, he had been a giant, and now that I held him again as a fully grown woman, he seemed larger than ever; I couldn't even reach all the way around him.

He didn't hug me back though. He stared down at me with a hollowness, so I gave up hugging him and instead held his face between my hands and looked up at him. His cheeks were so cold. "It's me, Father. Quetzalpetlatl."

There was still no recognition in his distant eyes; he looked confused and irritated. Disappointment punched me in the chest, and I let my hands drop back to my sides.

Ehecacone edged closer to me. "That's your father, Mother?"

I nodded, the tears coming fast. "My mortal father...your grandfather."

He eyed the gaping hole in Mixcoatl's chest. "What happened to him?"

"My uncle sacrificed him...." I looked around at the other men gathered around—I hadn't seen a single woman among them this entire time—and the truth of what I saw hit me. "These are all the Smoking Mirror's sacrifices!"

"Very good, Mayahuel!" a screechy voice spoke up behind us and I nearly fell over in fright.

But when we turned to find the skeletal figure dressed in a robe of brown and gray owl feathers looming over us, we both shrieked and went over backwards in a heap.

The creature chuckled, his transparent skin stretching thin over his skull. He wore a necklace of extruded eyeballs, but his own orbital sockets contained glowing blue orbs similar to those that swam around the tree outside Xolotl's house. Insects writhed up from beneath his bone-feet jutting out from under the hem of his robe, scattering in all directions.

Once I overcame my revulsion at the sight, my memory provided a name for the face. "Lord Death."

He bowed slightly, acknowledging my greeting.

A one-eyed, hunched-shouldered man lurked behind his robe, crouched close to the ground. "Xolotl," I said, my pulse rising again, this time in anger.

Ehecacone eyed both gods and clung to my arm like a monkey as I struggled back to my feet.

"My, you're looking quite the shambles, my dear," Lord Death said. "I confess myself surprised you would come back here again so soon, but I'm impressed that you took the difficult path."

"It wasn't by choice," I said. "I had no desire to ever come here again."

Xolotl shuffled out from behind him. "You should move beyond the sacrificial stone soon, My Lady, otherwise you'll die—"

"And I told you not to talk!" Lord Death made to slap Xolotl across the head with the back of his bone-hand, but Xolotl cowered and clamped both hands over his mouth. Appeased, Lord Death turned back to me and put his creepy smile back on. "He's of course right. Your time is nearly up."

I sneered at him. "And I'm sure that just slipped your mind until Xolotl mentioned it."

He kept smiling but now stepped aside, his arm held up to point the way for me. "Do hurry, my dear."

With a final glare, I shuffled forward again, Ehecacone still clinging to me. We soon exited the fog bank, coming out next to a large stone table.

The surface was slick with blood and a flint knife sat ready. I paused to look at it before Xolotl came up next to me and took my hand with his and led me on further.

Once we passed the table, I felt magic bubble up inside me, starting down in my toes. Such a sweet relief! As I'd hoped, my body started healing itself—my missing toes re-grew, my broken leg mended, and my burns disappeared. Magic pulsed in my fingertips; not strong, but enough to make the desire purr.

But Ehecacone's grip on my hand suddenly broke, making me stumble. I turned back to see him lying face-down on the ground, his body completely still, eyes staring blankly into the dust.

"Ehecacone!" I rushed to pick him up, but as soon as I touched him, flaming pain raged through my hands and arms. I tried to hold onto him through it, but soon the skin of my hands started blistering and the flesh swelled, threatening to burst. I had to let him go.

As soon as I did, my hands returned to normal and the pain disappeared, leaving me breathing heavily but unscathed.

"We mustn't touch what isn't ours anymore," Lord Death said with a gruesome grin.

The rage rose like a jaguar inside me and I flung myself at him. "Give me back my son!"

But Xolotl stepped between us, keeping me from colliding with Lord Death. I still flailed, swinging my fists at the grinning skeleton, but he held me back firmly.

"I'm tempted to tell him to let you go, Mayahuel," Lord Death said. "It would be amusing to see the look on your face when you realize that to touch the lord of death is to know death itself."

As his words sunk in, I stopped struggling against Xolotl and finally stepped away, pacing and feeling foolish for what I'd nearly done to myself. "I want my son back," I panted.

"Then you and I have business to discuss, don't we?"

Finally catching my breath and reclaiming my calm, I answered, "Indeed we do."

Lord Death motioned to Ehecacone. "Xolotl, gather him up and bring him along." He then started down the dusty path through the field of reeds leading to his palace of black glass in the distance. "Come along, my little thorny one," he told me.

I gritted my teeth at the name, but I followed behind Xolotl as he lugged Ehecacone upon his shoulder like a sack of masa, following his master's bony footsteps.

◻

Even though I'd spent eons in Mictlan, I'd never been inside Lord Death's palace. I wondered what new terrors awaited me in there. He led the way down a dusty stone path lined with gnarled, white leafless trees, with me and Xolotl following a few steps behind.

I stared at Xolotl's twisted back with contempt. "I can't believe Topiltzin and I wasted a perfectly good dog on you, you wretch," I hissed. "I should have known you'd take our sacrifice and then abandon my son to walk the road on his own."

Xolotl eyed me over his shoulder, looking as if he wanted to say something, but he didn't.

"And still nothing to say for yourself. How unsurprising, the one who once touted Quetzalcoatl's goodness turns out to be as two-faced as he is."

Xolotl flinched, but Lord Death broke into muted laughter. "There is a reason the humans fear both snakes and dogs: both are evil and strike without warning."

The palace's walls were made of bones pressed between thin sheets of obsidian, and the front doors resembled the gate on the stairs, except these were crowned with human skulls. I stared up at them as I passed through, unnerved that their empty gazes followed me.

The inside wasn't much better; skeletons of large predatory animals decorated the long main hallway, each articulated by way of Lord Death's glowing blue magic. I stared up at the huge lizard-creature with dagger-like fangs that formed the archway for the great hall—obviously the bones of an earth monster—and wondered if I was related to it in some way. Perhaps the mother or father missing from my recollections?

Xolotl loped ahead of his master and held open the great hall's large owl-feathered curtain with his free hand, my son still dangling over his gnarled shoulder. I stepped inside after Lord Death, but stopped to gawk at the floor-to-ceiling pane of obsidian glass forming the back wall, providing a dark view of the Black Lake and the foggy plain beyond.

A throne of bones plated in light green jade sat alone upon the dais before the window, and Lord Death alighted upon it with the grace of a bird of prey. He smoothed the owl-feather gown over his knobby knees. Where his feet touched the ground, insects burst from the stone floor, as if fleeing a coming flood. He reclined to the left side, resting his elbow against the only armrest—there wasn't one on the throne's right side.

I looked for somewhere to sit too, but apparently Lord Death didn't entertain guests. Xolotl propped Ehecacone against the obsidian pane then returned to the dais's step and sat there. I could have followed his example, but the thought of sitting so close to either of them gave me chills.

"So, my little thorny goddess, what brings you back home again?" Lord Death asked.

"This isn't my home," I snapped.

Lord Death chuckled. "And yet you've come back—"

"I didn't realize I was entering the underworld when I went past the gate."

"Then there are still holes in your memory? Understandable; you were dead a very long time. Regardless, Xolotl and I welcome you back."

"I don't intend to stay."

"Then we shall start by discussing the toll you intend to pay to leave again." Lord Death stared at me expectantly.

"Toll?"

"Everyone pays to pass through Mictlan, my dear. The dead must pay with their hearts, so it's only fair that the living offer me something too, am I right?"

I chewed my lip before saying, "I have nothing to give you."

He grinned wide, his blue glowing eyes intensifying. "If you were anyone else, Mayahuel, I would scold you for claiming you have nothing to barter with, for all gods have very high currency. But when you've been a goddess for so little time, I must excuse your ignorance of our ways. Come look." He rose and went to the pane overlooking the Black Lake. Once I joined him, he pointed out. "Your payment, my dear, resides out there."

I followed his gesture, beyond the Black Lake to the plain covered in fog. "I don't see anything."

"Why your sacrifices, of course."

"I don't have any sacrifices—"

"Oh, but there will be. Unless you're planning on dying again soon." He arched his hairless eyebrow ridge at me.

"Of course not."

"The longer you're alive, the more sacrifices you will accumulate, and they will all come here to linger in the mist, crowding the plain of Mictlan with their vacant stares and incessant buzzing." He grated his teeth but then put on a smile again. "I do not mind storing your sacrifices for you...for a price."

"But people only make offerings of octli and maguey spines to honor me."

"For now. But times change. Not all that long ago, Smoking Mirror settled for burnt tobacco, but now look at his collection of souls—"

"I'm nothing like Smoking Mirror," I shot back. "I'm happy with what the people give me."

"They all say that. But gods cannot live on devotion alone, not even the Feathered Serpent. Why else offer blood at all?"

I narrowed my eyes at him. "What exactly do you want from me?"

"You haven't a heaven to send your sacrifices to, so I hold them for you, and all I ask is a modest fee for my generosity."

I crossed my arms. "And what would that fee be, exactly?"

He stood taller, a broad smile on his face. "A portion of the magic you siphon off from your human sacrifices, of course."

That sounded reasonable. "How much do you want?"

"For every twenty sacrifices you accumulate, fourteen of those go directly to me."

"Fourteen?" I wanted to laugh, but given the meaningful look Xolotl gave me, I decided this was merely the opening offer. After scrutinizing Lord Death's robes a long moment, I countered, "One of twenty."

Now he laughed. "You insult me, child, but again, I will excuse your ignorance—for now. Twelve out of twenty."

"Three."

"Twelve."

"Eight."

"Twelve," he repeated, his smile stretching thinner with amusement.

"Ten?" I offered.

He raised his pale lips with derision. "Fourteen of twenty, Mayahuel. Or remain here forever."

I glared out at the Black Lake. I doubted he'd demanded such insulting terms of Smoking Mirror.

"Well?" Lord Death asked.

I turned the glare upon him. "Let me think about it."

He bowed his head. "Take your time." He looked highly pleased with himself. He shooed Xolotl out of his way as he stepped down off the dais.

It's ridiculous that he should get more magic from our sacrifices than we do! the desire hissed. *If only we didn't have to store them down here....*

"What must I do to get a heaven of my own, so you don't have to store sacrifices for me?"

He laughed. "You will never get a heaven of your own, my dear. Smoking Mirror has millions of sacrifices and yet even he has yet to earn his own heaven. And as you've pointed out already, you don't even have any yet."

"So one gets their own heaven for their sacrifices by having enough people sacrificed to them?"

"Yes. And as you no doubt saw while venturing through the fog, that number can be uncountable." Lord Death crossed his arms. "I'm growing impatient, Mayahuel."

His demands weren't fair, but what choice did I have? I couldn't stay in the underworld for eternity. I may have descended from earth monsters, but I didn't share their love of the darkness. I craved the warmth of the sunlight, and if I had to agree to such an uneven split to get that back....

Maybe, but if we're not careful, we'll bargain away everything we have before we can negotiate for our son. My gaze fell to Ehecacone sitting slumped against the glass, oblivious. *Let me make a counter proposal while we still can.* "Fourteen out of twenty, but you also raise my son from the dead and he comes back to earth with me."

Lord Death shook his head, chuckling. "You ask so much but offer so little. No, the son of the Feathered Serpent is much more valuable than that."

"Then take fifteen out of twenty of my sacrifices."

"Not even all of your sacrifices will buy his life, Mayahuel, so don't waste your breath. He is valuable enough as he is right now."

I clenched my fists. "Name your price then."

With a grotesque grin, he answered, "Nothing short of giving me the Feathered Serpent himself would make me release your son."

"Then you shall have the Feathered Serpent," the desire growled for me.

My heart thudded. *Revenge won't bring Ehecacone back—*

Of course it will, you idiot, the desire snapped. *You heard Lord Death. And turning Quetzalcoatl over to him is no more than the snake deserves after what he's done to us.*

Lord Death stared back at me, intense. "Do not fool with me, Mayahuel."

I stood taller. "If I bring you Quetzalcoatl, will you give me back my son, alive and well?"

"And how exactly would you do that? The Feathered Serpent is the most powerful god in Omeyocan, and you...you're little more than a wisp of magic in the wind."

"That's for me to worry about, not you. If I fail, you're out nothing, right?"

Lord Death pondered before conceding, "That much is true."

"Ehecacone isn't the one you want sitting on the banks of the Black Lake; he's not the one who embarrassed you, who tricked you into surrendering what was rightfully yours." I pointed to the missing armrest on his throne, the bone the Feathered Serpent had taken to restore humanity long ago.

Lord Death hissed through his teeth. "Indeed not."

"You will finally have your revenge, and all it will cost you is a fledgling god."

The grin returned and Lord Death rubbed his bone-hands together. "I have waited so long for this...."

"Then we have a deal?" I held my hand out to him.

He looked at it with an amused smile. "I don't think you want to do that, my dear. To touch death is to know death, remember?"

I withdrew, embarrassed by my mistake, but pressed on. "Well?"

"Bring me Quetzalcoatl and I will return your son to you. Those are the terms."

"And you open the way out of here, so I can fetch your prize," I added.

"Done." He looked around, seemingly lost in his own scheming, and as an afterthought, he added, "Xolotl will escort you out."

I took one last look at Ehecacone, feeling resolute. *I will see you again very soon, my little Warm Breeze.* I then followed Xolotl—now in dog form—out of the great hall.

But when we reached the front doorway, Lord Death materialized, blocking my way. "You're right that I lose nothing by accepting this deal," he said, "but should you fail to deliver as promised, remember that I have your son and I can raise him from the dead at any time, for any reason—including making him pay for your failures. Don't fail me, Mayahuel."

The desire bristled, but I kept a calm demeanor. "I won't fail you, My Lord."

"And don't take forever," he warned. "I'm not a patient god."

"Neither am I." I then followed Xolotl out the doorway.

CHAPTER FIVE

 Xolotl kept up his silence as we climbed the steep stone stairs out of the underworld; he didn't even look back when I asked him if he knew where I could find Mextli, since I hadn't found any sign nor heard any whisper of the war god since our last meeting in Teotihuacan. Mextli had offered me his assistance back then and now I needed that help more than ever.

Seeing the sun again brought such joy I nearly cried. "It feels like years since I've stood in sunlight," I said as I stopped in a beam shooting down from the opening of the cenote. It wasn't the same one I'd entered the underworld from; here the air was dry and hot, and the pool of water was shallow and brackish. I couldn't see any trees or bushes around the lip of the cenote, and there wasn't a cloud to be seen.

Xolotl said nothing, just vanished. For a moment I thought he'd left me, but then I saw him at the lip of the cenote, peering back down at me over the edge.

"How do you do that?" I called up to him. "Be here one breath and suddenly up there the next?"

Xolotl merely snorted.

I looked around until I found a place to climb out, but even then it took me a long time to finally pull myself up over the lip of the cenote.

The bare ground was blistering under my hands and the sun shone blindingly down on me, so I had to shield my eyes when I looked around. A vast desert stretched around us for as far as I could see in any direction. "Why did you bring me here?" When he just stared at me, a frown on his ugly, mangled dog face, I sneered back at him. "Fine. I don't need your help anymore, so along with you."

He sighed and turned to leave, but then he stopped. He turned back into his deformed human body and knelt to scribble something in the dirt. I watched him, but the symbols he drew made no sense to me. He looked up at me and pointed at them, an eager expression in his black eyes. When I shook my head, he pointed to my eyes and then back at the writing, more vehemently this time.

"If you want to say something to me, just say it!" I cried, annoyed.

He opened his mouth as if to speak, but then grimaced, as if suddenly gripped with pain. He swallowed then pointed to the drawings once more, a sad expression on his face. When I shook my head, exasperated, he turned back into the black dog and jogged away. He jumped down into the cenote, but I heard no splash, and when I went to look inside, he was gone.

I returned to the writing in the sand and stood staring at it, growing increasingly vexed.

But the longer I stared at it, the more meaning crept into my brain. First one word, then another, as if I were reading a language I had known as a young child but forgot from lack of use. Eventually the meaning came to me.

Mind whom you put your trust and faith in.

"I've learned that the hard way," I muttered, sweeping the words away with my bare foot, disgusted. "I don't need reminders."

ロ

Unsure what else to do, I sought shelter from the sun by heading for a large rock formation to the north. A single spindly mesquite tree grew in the shade, but there wasn't much else to be found once I got there. I sat down to survey the desert and decide what to do next. There had to be some way I could find Mextli.

At first glance, the land seemed dead, but the wildlife slowly made its presence known. Fluffy white clouds trooped across the sky, providing a good canvas for the hawks, buzzards, and eagles soaring overhead. A multitude of biting flies buzzed around me, though they quickly dropped to the ground in death throes after sampling my golden blood. A brown lizard watched me from the side of the rock formation, his black eyes shimmering like obsidian in the sunlight, and a tan rattlesnake slithered out of the shade to bask in the sunlight. All harsh creatures for a harsh environment. I couldn't imagine any humans surviving out here. I sat watching the animals and insects go about their routines for an hour or more, until suddenly I heard scraping behind me.

I looked over my shoulder to see a group of men standing at the corner of the rock formation. They wore little clothing; mostly deer skin breeches that went to their knees, though some also had vests, but they all wore gnarled leather sandals. They'd smeared mud over all their exposed skin—to protect their skin from the blistering sun?—and a few wore headdresses of hawk or eagle feathers fanned over their foreheads, to shield their eyes from the harsh light. Every man carried a weapon —flint-headed spears and knives, thick wooden clubs, and the occasional bow.

I didn't move as they scrutinized me, but when I heard more noise, I turned to see more of them in front of me, surrounding me. In response, a surge of desire slithered through me. *Lucky us! We need something to replenish our magic.*

The lead man—who had painted the left side of his mud-covered face blue—spoke to the man next to him, and that man in turn motioned to the others, who then pressed slowly in towards me, weapons held loose but ready. I held my hands up, signaling my surrender.

They took me around to the other side of the rocks where still more people stood—twenty-three in all: three guards and twenty men bound together by a long length of leather rope tied around their necks. Many of the wounded had been carefully patched up, but they all looked upon me with dead eyes. The guards however regarded me with expressions of dreamy longing, but they soon broke it off when the leader barked and cuffed each. They hurried for an extra length of rope from a deerskin bag one of them held.

"You needn't tie me up," I tried to assure the leader. "I'll come willingly."

He seemed to understand me, for he held his hand up to the man with the rope, but when he spoke to me next, I had no idea what he said. The language wasn't like the dialects spoken back in the valley, or even Tollan. "I'm sorry, but I don't understand," I told him and he looked at me in puzzlement. He spoke again, slower this time, but still I couldn't make much of it, so I held my hands up and shook my head.

He took the rope but instead of tying it around my neck—like the others—he tied it loosely around my waist. He looked up at me expectantly and I nodded my agreement. Whatever would make him comfortable. Hopefully we could develop enough trust that by the time night fell, he wouldn't feel the need to bind me when he brought me to his bed, making my escape easier once I'd replenished my magic from him.

But to my surprise, we walked no more than an hour before I spotted a large encampment on the horizon. The warriors hooted and smiled, and they prodded the group of prisoners to go faster. The leader kept hold of my rope the whole time, remaining silent and stoic as an example to his men, though when women came running from the tents to greet us, he finally cracked a smile and embraced a woman who ran to him. She looked a few years younger than me, and was round with child. Three small children rushed to greet him too, the eldest no more than six or seven, and the youngest—the only boy—no more than a year old, judging from how tightly he held his sisters' hands as they helped him. The woman gave me a cursory glance but then returned her smiling attention to the man—*Her husband,* I concluded. He handed my rope off to one of the other men then hefted his son up onto his shoulders and took his wife by the hand. He walked the rest of the way into camp with his family.

The sight left me feeling melancholy; not all that long ago, that had been me and Little Reed and Ehecacone. *But it will be again, soon,* I reassured myself. *Or at the very least you'll have your son back.*

More women and children hurried from the tents to see their husbands and fathers. I garnered just as much attention as the warriors paraded us through the encampment to the central area where several shamans awaited us.

Their faces were painted black with gold stripes across their cheeks. The hairs on my nape stood up. *Priests of Smoking Mirror?*

They looked us over one by one, nodding at each prisoner in turn, but when they came to me, they conferred in whispers until the head priest nodded. They hurried me from the line as a third priest started flicking his blood-soaked fingers at each man in a purifying ceremony. A woman handed out bits of plant for them to eat.

A tall, pointy-nosed man dressed in bones and a feathered headdress came from across camp to examine the line of prisoners. *Not the chief, but maybe his son,* I concluded, given his youthful arrogance and the guards hovering nearby. His gaze clouded when he saw me, then he turned to talk to the priests. Much discussion ensued, but when he pointed at me, the priests' words turned heated. The man grew increasingly agitated, but when the head priest pointed to another tent not far beyond us—sitting in front of a sacrificial stone—the young man frowned and snapped something, but turned and walked away. The priests grinned at each other but then wrenched me over to the tent overlooking the altar.

I'd hoped they would leave me there alone, so I might sneak off, but one of them remained, holding my rope while the other returned to the line of sacrifices.

A crowd began gathering in the center of the encampment and the priests took to chanting and laying out baskets and flint blades. They waited until the first man in the prisoner line started swaying on his feet, then the head priest made a speech in front of the crowd. The men and women listened with rapt attention; even the children stood silent and reverent. I listened carefully too, but I couldn't make anything out of it.

When the head priest gave the signal, his assistants cut the first prisoner loose from the ropes and dragged him towards the sacrificial stone. He didn't fight; he stared around with wide, awestruck eyes, drooling from the side of his mouth. He didn't resist when they laid him over the stone, his chest puffed out, and he didn't scream when the head priest cut him open and pulled his heart out with the quickness of a seasoned professional; he just slowly drifted away as the other priests hoisted his body off the stone. They tossed it aside, where a small group of women relieved it of the head and slashed the wrists before stringing the body up by the ankles from a tree growing behind the tent. There they collected the blood in a large clay jar; a curiously bulky item for a nomadic people to keep. Before that first one was even fully hung, the priests had hustled the second man to the stone and the head priest extracted his heart too. With this efficiency, they would make it through all the prisoners in less than an hour.

I managed to observe the first full process without losing my composure, but with sickening heat rising up inside me at the sight of so much gore, I took to staring at the side of the tent I stood next to. My heart thudded painfully loud in my ears as memories of my human father swept upon me. I only looked up again when the flap on the tent swished open to my left.

Given the priests' decorations, I'd expected they were Smoking Mirror worshippers, but instead a giant of a man came out. He wore only a loincloth, showing off the fact that the entire left side of his body was painted blue, and when he stood straight, he towered over everyone. I couldn't fathom how he'd ever fit into that tiny tent, but like myself he glowed, with a soft turquoise color. *Mextli!* It seemed Xolotl had been listening after all.

The people chanted but lay prostrate upon the ground, trembling in terror as he settled onto the mat in front of his tent and pulled one of the dripping baskets of hearts over in front of him. The head priest approached, prostrating himself, but then hurried forward when Mextli motioned him to stand up straight. The priest whispered to him, pointing at me, but Mextli thundered, "War prizes go out after I've eaten my fill." He then started shoveling handfuls of hearts from the basket into his broad mouth.

I moved towards him, but the priest holding my rope pulled me back. I yanked in response, but my strength wasn't a match, so I shouted, "Mextli!"

PART TWO
THE YEAR EIGHT FLINT

CHAPTER SIX

"Mextli!" I cried as the priest nearly yanked me off my feet. "It's me! Mayahuel!"

But Mextli was so engrossed in the hearts that he either ignored me or didn't hear me. Given his insistence that I had a friend in him, I chose to believe it was the latter, and so pulled what magic I could muster to my hands and unleashed it on the priest.

The attack took the priest by surprise and he went over with a yelp. This drew the attention of the warriors guarding the sacrifices and they rushed towards me, but I sent them tumbling with another shot of magic. It only disoriented them though—I'd have to dig very deep into my magic stores to incapacitate them, and I didn't dare let myself become completely helpless. Instead I took off running, heading for Mextli.

The head priest stopped with the bloody blade poised above his head when he saw me. He shouted, and the other two priests dropped the dead body they'd been carrying then moved to cut me off. I ran into them full-speed and we went down in a heap right in front of Mextli, tipping over the baskets of hearts. I rolled over and landed right in Mextli's lap.

But he dumped me unceremoniously on the ground when he rose to his feet, roaring in displeasure. Wetness soaked through my tattered dress where I landed and an unpleasant liquid squish accompanied it when I moved to sit up. Mextli grabbed me one-handed, his giant fingers encircling both my neck and right shoulder as he hauled me up, a wild, alien look churning in his wide eyes. He flexed his free hand and a flint blade materialized in it.

"Mextli! It's me! Mayahuel!" I gasped. "Surely you remember me?"

He glared at me with hard, implacable eyes, but slowly the expression softened into recognition. "Mayahuel?" Embarrassment lit his fleshy cheek as he lowered me gently to the ground. "It is you!"

I finally breathed again, but when I looked down to see I'd reduced most of the hearts to a juicy, dirt-coated pulp, I cringed. "Forgive me...about your meal."

He looked down at the mess under my feet and frowned, annoyed, but when he looked up at me again, he looked contrite. "Never mind that; the humans will bring me more. Forgive me for not recognizing you and...manhandling you so."

"No harm done." Though the memory of that focused anger and dispassion troubled me. As did the words Xolotl had written in the dust only a few hours ago.

The priests had scrambled away when Mextli lunged to his feet, but now all three crawled back, crying and scraping at his feet. He waved them away, disgusted. "Never mind the mess. Bring me what's left and next time you will make up for the loss."

They bowed deeply as they backed away, groveling. The rest of the crowd stood in terrified silence, so Mextli whispered, "Let us talk where we have no audience." And he ducked inside the tiny tent, leaving the flap swaying in the hot evening air.

I glanced back at the watching crowd, not entirely trusting the priests or soldiers to not come at me again, but everyone just stared, so I too ducked inside the tent.

I expected to run into Mextli immediately upon entry, but to my amazement, I now stood in the entrance of a great hall similar to the one in any palace. An icpalli throne made of rushes and eagle feathers sat at one end, though it was massive compared to my throne back in Tollan. It creaked and strained under Mextli's weight as he sat down. "Please, come sit." He picked up two clay cups and dipped them into a large vat sitting next to the throne.

When I came forward and accepted a cup, I found it was filled with blood. So this was what the women were doing out there with the remains of the sacrifices. My heart rebelled at the thought of drinking it, but I was so low on magic.... *Forgive me*, I thought and drained the cup in one mighty swig. I wasn't even sure who I was begging forgiveness from, but it felt like the right thing to do.

Euphoria filled my veins as the magic surged, and I swallowed down a second cup after Mextli refilled it for me. "Thank you," I whispered, feeling half-drunk from the pulsing magic beneath my skin. Not as powerful as the aftermath of taking a man to bed, but good enough for now. I settled down on the floor next to the throne, unsure if I could keep my feet much longer.

"My pleasure." Mextli drained his own cup then set it aside. "You looked as if you needed it."

I gazed around the room, taking in the murals of bloody battle decorating the walls, and the sunlight leaking in through the exposed windows. "What is this place?"

"My house, of course."

"But the tent...it's so small!"

"Makes it very easy for the humans to transport it when they move, as they often do."

"But how...can it be so big inside?"

Mextli chuckled. "We are gods, Mayahuel; what do such human concepts mean to us? We can exist inside a grain of sand if we wish, or within one of the countless grains within that single grain." He shook his head. "The Feathered Serpent truly taught you nothing, did he?"

Mention of Quetzalcoatl made me surly, and again reminded me of why I was here. "Indeed not."

Mextli nodded. "I'm glad you sought me out, though I'd hoped you would do so much sooner than this."

"I found you as soon as I could. It's only been a few months."

"Have you become so lost you cannot keep track of time anymore? It's been five years, Mayahuel."

"Five years!" But then, I had been in Mictlan a long time, and it was said that time didn't move in the same way there as it did on the mortal plane.

I wasn't sure I wanted to tell him yet about my trip into Mictlan or my deal with Lord Death—especially in light of Xolotl's warning—so I opted for, "I guess I have been quite lost since that night in Teotihuacan, and you didn't tell me where to find you."

"I didn't," he conceded. "I just assumed...well, I assumed wrong, and I apologize."

Someone cleared their throat and I looked towards the entrance to see the high priest on his knees, bent in supplication over a basket of hearts. The other two priests carried the large jar of blood upon their shoulders, but they kept their eyes downcast. A pool of crimson gathered on the floor under the basket. The head priest said something and bowed deeply.

Mextli rose, looking deadly serious. "Bring your offerings forward then."

The three men hurried to deposit the blood jar next to the one already there and they placed the basket of hearts at Mextli's feet. They slashed their palms with their flint knives and babbled reverently in their foreign tongue as they squeezed their wounded hands over the hearts, continuing the litany until Mextli interrupted them, irritated. "Yes yes, and keep the darkness from overcoming the day. I accept your offering and promise to rise again tomorrow in the east, and see the Mexica forward on their journey to greatness."

The priests muttered in gratitude and backed slowly down the hall and out the tent flap on the other side of the arched stone doorway.

Mextli sat and pulled the basket between his feet. He started to take a bite out of one of the hearts but then he held it out to me. "Hungry?" The look on his face reminded me of a petulant child who'd been told he must share his toys.

The blood oozed off the organ, painting Mextli's bare hand red, making my heart race. Panicked heat rose in my gut. I'd only ever held an actual human heart twice in my short life—first my father's when my uncle had cut it from him, and then that poor man Black Otter murdered on the pretense of summoning Smoking Mirror. I had no desire to ever hold another. "Thank you, but no." I didn't catch the grimace in time though.

He chuckled like a coyote, that sharp, cruel look in his eyes again. "We all have our particular appetites. Tell me what yours is and I'll order the priests to bring it for you right away, and we can share our first meal in friendship." He popped the heart into his mouth as if it were a small nut.

What a ridiculous scene that would be—Mextli chewing hearts on his throne while I ravaged someone on the floor in front of him—yet the desire purred like an interested jaguar. "Blood is all I need," I assured him with a feigned smile.

"Nonsense! I pride myself on being a good host, so come, tell me what I can get for you."

"Truly, the blood is enough."

"Enough? Of course it's enough, when there's nothing else available. No one lives on blood alone, Mayahuel; that would be like...like the humans eating nothing but cactus—it keeps them alive during famine, but they don't ignore all the other things they can eat—things that make them healthier and stronger—"

"Blood is just fine!" My cheeks lit with heat; I hadn't intended to yell.

Mextli scrutinized me then said, "Those humans you lived with...they made you ashamed about how you feed, didn't they? Probably told you it was evil. You don't have to be embarrassed anymore, Mayahuel. You're among your own kind now." When I didn't answer, he sighed but asked, "Would you like more blood then?"

I handed my cup to him and when he returned it refilled, I stared into it instead of drinking. "Forgive my snappishness. These last five years have been difficult...and trying. I thought I would never find you."

"Forgive my not telling you where I would be. I just assumed you'd know how to find me."

"I'm afraid my knowledge of everyday living as a goddess is poor at best."

"Then our first order of business shall be to fix that. What kinds of things can you do already?" When I hesitated, he added, "So I know where to focus our efforts."

When I still resisted answering, the desire growled, *If we aren't going to accept his help, why in Mictlan did we seek him out at all?*

"Well, I can't do much; there's the maguey plants, as you know—I can make them do things for me, like attack enemies with their roots and spines. I can also talk to rabbits."

"Your nahual, maybe?"

"I think so, but I haven't worked as much with them as with the maguey."

"But that's not your most potent magic. I saw what you did on that temple top in Chimalhuacan."

I'd rendered half the city intoxicated with a good stiff push of magic, and even poisoned King Toxtli when he stabbed me. "It is very powerful magic, but I don't have control over it." An understatement, considering I'd nearly killed Little Reed with it.

Mextli waved me off. "Our most powerful magic always takes the longest to properly cultivate. What else?"

I shrugged. "That's it."

"What about using the teoyoh?" When I squinted at him, not understanding, he went on, "Moving from place to place with magic?" When I shook my head, he looked taken aback. "How do you travel around?"

"I walk, of course."

"Walk!" Mextli leaned forward, muttering under his breath.

"I don't mind walking," I assured him. "I had to do it all the time when I was a human being—"

"You're not a human being, Mayahuel; you're a goddess, and a goddess who can't use the teoyoh...how can you ever go to Omeyocan, or travel safely into Mictlan if you haven't that one simple, most important skill? A god who can't use the teoyoh is hardly a god at all!"

I hadn't even considered that I could go to Omeyocan now that I was a goddess again, and to my shame, the thought terrified me. What if I came upon my grandmother? What would she do? She'd already killed me once, so why not again?

"The Feathered Serpent had no right to keep these things from you," Mextli grumbled.

"No, but then my grandmother didn't teach me much of anything either."

"I will teach you everything you need to know to get along," Mextli said, returning to his hearts.

Good. I was one step closer to getting Ehecacone back then.

I sipped at the blood in my cup while Mextli ate with increasing fervor. When he finished, he tossed the empty basket aside then lounged back against his icpalli, a blood-drunk haze to his eyes. When I finally spoke again, he didn't look at me, lost in his own thoughts, but eventually he turned to me. "What?"

"Who taught you? About being a god?"

"Smoking Mirror," he said with a nostalgic smile, though it soon slipped away. "Most of it, anyway. Some things you have to learn about on your own. But I will teach you everything I know."

I gave him a grateful smile. "Thank you, Mextli."

He started to smile back, but stopped suddenly. "Enough talk. Let's get started. First lesson: how to locate other gods." He sat straighter on his icpalli, reminding me of when my foster mother Nimilitzli gave lectures to her new students at the calmecac. "First, you do know what teotl is, right?"

"Never heard of it," I admitted.

He shook his head, grumbling, but then replied, "Teotl is the essence of everything; it's the very nature of the gods: we are beings of energy at our most basic, and that energy permeates everything and can manipulate both the visual and invisible world." He set both of his hands against his bare chest. "I created this body to house my teotl, just as you created yours, but...this is where it gets tricky. You see, everything living has its own teotl—trees, animals, even humans—but those are different than divine teotl; whereas ours can manipulate and change the world at will, for humans, their teotl is trapped in their bodies until death frees it. That's why we are immortal and they are not. They...taste different than us."

I raised a dubious eyebrow. "Taste?"

Mextli chuckled. "Humans are quite tasty, don't you think? We cannot help but crave their teotl—"

"And that's why we drink their blood, and eat their...." I motioned to the basket lying on the floor.

"Exactly. Divine teotl tastes different; it tastes like...power."

"I don't know what power tastes like."

"I couldn't describe it to you, but I can say that it tingles the senses, and it doesn't trigger the hunger the way human teotl does. When you finally learn to taste it, you will know it immediately."

Now I was thoroughly intrigued. "So how do I learn to taste it?"

"Close your eyes and clear your mind. Focus on your senses. Since you're surrounded by my teotl here in my house, it shouldn't take you long to detect it."

I did as he told me, using my priestly training to focus my mind.

Soon my skin started tingling and a smell began permeating my nose, spreading to my sinuses and filling my mouth—a sweet nectar smell, like honeysuckle in full-bloom. I imagined a garden filled with flowers, teeming with ruby-throated hummingbirds zipping from blossom to blossom. A pleasant feeling—like being wrapped in a warm blanket—swept over me. "I'm not tasting anything but...you smell like flowers! Do we all smell like this?"

"Each god's teotl is unique, and every god experiences divine teotl differently, so perhaps you don't taste it as such," Mextli said.

"The smell is very potent—not unpleasant, mind you—but it's very all-encompassing."

"That's because you're sitting in a bubble of my magic; you are literally surrounded by my teotl."

It sounded so intimate, almost sexual, but given the nonchalance he said it with, I doubted he meant it that way. I finally opened my eyes again. "What do I smell like?"

Mextli shrugged. "I don't experience the world in such a manner, so I wouldn't know how to describe it to you."

"Then what do I taste like?" The desire cackled in my head and my cheeks heated with embarrassment.

But Mextli didn't miss a beat. "Like pain; a victim."

I furrowed my brows. "I'm no victim, thank you. Maybe at one time someone took advantage of my innocence, but that's not who I am."

"Of course not. But whether we like it or not, our pasts leave their mark on us, often in ways we're completely unaware of. It is not a criticism, Mayahuel, just a truth. But you didn't let me finish. Yes, you taste of pain and having been betrayed, but you also taste of ambition and confidence. It is an intriguing mix."

"Then we can change our teotl? You said our pasts mark us, so the present can do the same, changing the way we taste or smell?"

"It never fundamentally changes, if that's what you're asking. The past will always be a part of you, but new experiences will join them, creating a different overall impression. The older the god, the more nuanced the teotl."

I smelled the air again, intrigued. Mextli's scent seemed rather straightforward at first, but the longer I studied it, the more different impressions popped out at me; sunlight, decomposition, water, an unidentified animal smell. *He's quite complicated,* I thought, wondering what it all meant. *And I bet Quetzalcoatl smells like snakes and lies.*

Mextli rose from his throne. "You'll understand more once you meet more gods and goddesses, and once you learn a specific god's teotl, you can find them anywhere on earth or in Heaven. In your case, you would just let your nose lead the way."

"You mean I can smell all the others right now?"

"Of course, but until you know whom you're smelling, it does little good. Come. I'm supposed to address my humans after the meal, to assure them that I'm happy with their offering, and that they need not fear my wrath tonight."

CHAPTER SEVEN

I was startled to see night had fallen when we stepped out of the tent. I hadn't thought we'd been inside for all that long. The humans still gathered in the center of camp, clustered around bonfires eating and laughing, but when Mextli strode out into the middle of the crowd, the priests scrambled forward, prostrating themselves until Mextli motioned them back to their feet. Everyone else looked on with anxiety.

"I thank every one of you for tonight's feast. The Mexica are truly a great and strong people, and all tremble before their might!" When Mextli raised his feathered fist to the sky, the men hooted and raised their fists too. But there wasn't a smile to be found among the crowd. "I know life in the desert is hard and everyone suffers, but continue to invest your faith in me and I will see you and your children elevated to greatness. The day will come when you will finally see the eagle's shadow and look up to see it carrying the sign, and it will lead you home. This I promise you."

The priests said something and the rest of the crowd repeated it, bowing their heads in prayer. Mextli stood silent, listening to the litany, but eventually he told everyone to rise again. "I must also thank you for an unexpected gift." He turned and motioned to me.

After a hesitation, I joined him at the center of camp.

"This is Lady Mayahuel, Goddess of the Maguey. She will be staying with us."

A murmur traveled through the crowd—and I noticed several of the warriors who'd captured me looking like they'd swallowed a leech.

The priests though flung themselves on the ground at my feet, groveling, and though I didn't understand a word they said, the cadence of their voices spoke of fear. Perhaps because they'd planned to give me away as a war prize? "It's quite all right," I assured them, reaching down to help them back to their feet.

But when I touched the nearest one, he shrieked as if I'd burned him. I jumped back, startled.

But he rose to his feet, a look of ecstasy on his face. He babbled incoherently, tears streaming down his face even as he smiled.

"What did I do?" I murmured, backing away still more.

Mextli chuckled. "Humans believe a simple touch from a god means the universe."

I watched the man, feeling foolish. I'd spent much of my mortal life believing myself god-touched because Quetzalcoatl's nahual had bitten me, so why hadn't I anticipated such a reaction? *I need to be more careful interacting with these humans.*

The man stepped toward Mextli but kept his eyes downcast as he spoke. Mextli listened, nodding, but then replied, "She'll need her own tent, and from now on, you will see to her needs. I relieve you of your duties to me."

The priest bowed deeper, his smile nearly reaching his ears. He then spoke to me, keeping his eyes downcast too as he did. When he stopped, waiting expectantly, I looked at Mextli. "I don't understand a word your people say."

"That's because you're still thinking in human language," Mextli said with a gentle ribbing. "Once you relearn the language of the gods, you'll be able to understand anyone who speaks to you, regardless of what language they use."

"How can that be?"

"Because our language is the source of all other languages. I know it probably makes no sense right now, but once you start learning and remembering...it will."

I looked at the man again, who was still waiting on my answer. "What did he say?"

"He asked where you would like your tent set up, and what he can bring you to eat."

"I don't need anything to eat, thank you. As for the tent...?" I looked around before turning to Mextli for guidance.

"Next to my own will be sufficient for now," Mextli told the man. Once the man bowed and shuffled backwards from us, Mextli told me, "You really should eat some more. We have much work to do tomorrow, so you should be fully nourished."

"What kind of work?"

"I will teach you how to use the teoyoh. It is the most important magic a god needs to master in order to get along in life, so that's our top priority. We'll start at dawn."

"Why not tonight?"

"I have other engagements. And you need time to feed; learning to use the teoyoh takes a lot of energy, so don't think that blood alone will suffice. Eat as much as you can and we'll meet up again in the morning."

A couple of warriors came forward with the makings of a tent and the priests directed them where to set it up. Once they finished, my new head priest held the flap open and bowed. I peered inside to find it was just an ordinary tent, like the ones soldiers used while on the march. It would be a tight fit for two people, and there was no way Mextli could come inside. "Kind of small for a goddess, isn't it?" I asked Mextli with a crooked grin.

He waved me off. "I'll teach you how to expand it later, but will it do for tonight?"

"It will be fine."

"I must go then."

"You're leaving?" When he arched an eyebrow at the panic in my voice, I swallowed and added, "Sorry. It's just...I don't know these people—"

"You have nothing to fear, Mayahuel. They will treat you like the goddess you are; they will worship you the way you should have been worshipped all along."

I nodded then added, "Thank you for your kindness, and understanding."

My words seemed to startle him, but once he recovered, he bowed his head. "It is my pleasure." He vanished with a snapping sound.

Everyone was watching, waiting for me to speak. After an uncomfortably long pause, I announced, "Everyone, please, go back to your feast." I had to repeat myself a couple times before the sounds of conversation and music filled the air again.

The priests remained standing in front of me, expectant expressions on their faces. My high priest bowed again as he spoke, but I couldn't hear him over the noise. "I would like to speak with you alone, if possible," I told him. When he motioned to my tent, I shook my head. "Somewhere else; some place quiet, so we can better hear each other."

His face lit and he started towards the north, motioning me to follow him with a sweeping bow. I did so.

The camp was surprisingly large, with many tents; Lord Ten Spines's tribe had consisted of less than fifty people, but this one was easily several hundred strong. The priest wound through the field of tents, leaving the celebratory noise behind.

Eventually we came out the other side of camp, onto a moon-drenched plain dotted with maguey plants. I couldn't help but smile. I reached out with a thread of magic in greeting and the magueys answered in silent excitement, making my chest swell with joy. That feeling only grew brighter when I noticed a few rabbits poking their heads out from holes near the bases of the maguey. "This is perfect!" I whispered.

The priest asked me something, but it sounded like nonsense to my ears. I motioned him to sit down, and once he did, I sat opposite him. I opened my mouth to explain that I didn't understand him, but the desire piped up, *We can't reveal our shortcomings. He must think we are all-powerful and all-knowing, to keep his respect.*

But how can I learn his language if I keep making him repeat everything he says? I protested. But before the desire could growl out a response, the answer came to me. "Do you know any of my prayers, priest?"

He shook his head and muttered a word I assumed meant "no". Perfect.

"I'm going to teach you all the prayers," I told him then started doing so, one line at a time and making him repeat them after me. By the time he'd memorized the first prayer, the fog around my understanding began lifting and when we finished an hour later, I'd taught him twelve different prayers and I could understand everything he spoke, even when I asked him to teach me some of the prayers they said to honor Mextli. I'd always been very good with language—I'd been able to speak in complex sentences before my second year alive, and I'd learned to speak several of the Chichimec tongues fluently within a few months of first hearing them when I was human—but as a goddess, that talent had more than quadrupled. "You've done a wonderful job," I told the priest once we'd finished with the language lesson.

"You honor me, My Most Great Lady of the Maguey," he said, prostrating himself on the ground in front of me. "I will endeavor to serve you with the utmost loyalty and effectiveness."

"I don't doubt it."

He beamed but then turned serious again. "Now that I have learned the sacred prayers, I wish to instruct the people in honoring you. We know His Lord from the South requires the hearts of warriors, but what sacrifices should we make to please you, My Lady?"

Lie down and let me show you, priest, the desire growled, hungry and eager; just imagining it brought a shiver of anticipation. But when I forced the desire back, it snarled, *Mextli said to feed in preparation for tomorrow.*

We have but one priest, and we both know what kind of man he'll become after we bring him to our bed, I reminded her. *We can't feed on him.*

Fine, the desire hissed, petulant, but it argued no further.

"I don't want sacrifices," I told the priest. "But there are a few things you can do to honor me."

"My life is to please you, My Lady. Tell me what you require."

"The normal ritual bloodlettings with thorns are good. But please, *please* don't paint yourself with the blood." I tried not to wrinkle my nose at his blood-smeared appearance but failed. "Just...provide it in a cup for me to drink."

"No wearing the blood," the priest confirmed.

"I'd also prefer you be clean, and wear fresh clothing."

"Then you wish me to make a pilgrimage to the cenote to wash my old life away?"

"No. Just use some of the water from the rain jars and that will be sufficient." He looked puzzled and a bit unsure, so I said, "You have a question?"

"No. It is not important. What the goddess asks shall be done."

I furrowed my brow. "No. Tell me."

"No one uses the water for anything but drinking. Lord Tlaloc seldom pours his jars upon us here, and it is a long journey to the cenote, especially carrying the water jars—"

"Of course," I muttered, embarrassed to not have thought of it myself. "I've changed my mind; no more blood, but no wasting the camp's water. I will bring you water myself." After all, the cenote wasn't far at all if I could use the teoyoh.

The priest nodded, relieved. "What else do you require of me, Most Great Lady of the Maguey?"

Bring me a man to soothe my hunger, priest! the desire growled, but I pushed it aside again. I couldn't think of any way to broach the subject without my intent becoming embarrassingly transparent.

Embarrassing? We don't answer to humans, you fool!

"That's all for now," I replied, feeling flushed and bothered despite my attempts to muzzle the rising desire. "Now, if you don't mind, I'd rather be alone for the rest of the evening."

He bowed. "Of course, My Lady." He started backing away, but before turning to leave, he asked, "Do you wish me to have the men set up your temple out here?"

"Perhaps in the morning." I gazed up into the night sky with a smile. "For now, the stars and the heavens are shelter enough." Especially after so long trapped in the underworld.

¤

Time passed much quicker when I was still human; as a goddess, I didn't sleep, which meant having to find ways to fill the time, and each moment felt like counting the grains of sand upon an infinite beach.

After the priest left, I walked among the maguey, running my hands over their giant, fleshy leaves, pausing to tap my fingertip on the sharp spines and feel the plants' contented energy seep through my skin. It was almost like being home.

Except Little Reed wasn't here with me. Not a day went by where I didn't regret that decision to not see him one last time, to explain to him the truth about myself and why I had to leave. I'd often thought to go back, just to say goodbye to him, but I knew it would be a mistake. Without my love magic distracting him from his wife, I imagined Little would finally have gotten over his aversion to bedding her and that they would now have a handful of beautiful children to carry on the royal legacy in Tollan. I also imagined that Citlallotoc and Little Reed had mended their differences over me, and that Citlallotoc had finally found someone who made him happy and appreciated the man he was. Tollan was no doubt thriving like never before now that her leaders weren't so distracted by silly things.

I tried to feel happy that so many would prosper with me out of the way, but at the same time, to feel thus would be to admit that I deserved no happiness myself, or that others could only be happy in the wake of my own misery. Maybe things could be different here? I was still surrounded by humans, but I was also among my own kind, and I didn't have to hide my true nature anymore. I could embrace it the way I never could back in Tollan. And getting Ehecacone back would go a long way to improving my happiness.

Still, a part of me longed to see Little Reed at least once more....

Footsteps drew me from my thoughts and I looked back toward camp to see a man heading my direction. At first I thought it was my priest, but as he came closer, I recognized him as the young man who'd spoken to the priests earlier, about me. Now that I understood the Mexicas' language, t my once again perfect memory provide the content of that discussion to me; he'd asked them for me, to honor his position as the future chief, but the priests had scoffed and said I belonged to the god, and so Mextli would give me to whomever he deemed worthy, which was highly unlikely to be him.

"You call yourself a warrior and yet you've claimed no prisoners," my priest had told him. "First you dare shave your youth-lock without cause, and now you call yourself the most worthy warrior among us? We would give the god your heart in sacrifice, but the taste of your cowardice would insult him." The young man had huffed away after that. I hadn't seen him when Mextli addressed the crowd later, and given his slippery grin and nonchalant demeanor, I doubted he'd heard the announcement of my godhood.

Dinner finally, the desire purred.

But when he pressed too close, I stepped back toward the maguey. He grinned, perhaps enjoying my discomfort—reminding me sharply of Ahexotl. He let me have my space now though, instead pacing like an anxious jaguar. "It's customary for one as lowly as yourself to bow before her new master," he said.

I was about to say the same thing about you, boy, the desire hissed, a sneer sliding onto my lips.

He laughed at my expression. "Are you not honored that the war god gave you to me?"

He reminded me too much of Ahexotl, and how helpless—and ashamed—he'd made me feel; the desire remembered too and immediately supplanted me, laughing with a perfect mixture of derision and seduction. "Maybe he gave you to me instead."

He looked taken aback, but when I stepped up to him, he swallowed hard, his bravado fleeing.

I traced my fingertips over the contours of his lips. "You like to serve the gods?" He stared at me, befuddled and flustered, and the desire chuckled. She loved the opening volleys more than the game itself, loved bringing men to their knees with the slightest touch and a well-considered word. She loved the control.

Resistance, on the other hand, irritated her. Not many men cared to resist, but increasingly I thought of Citlallotoc—clinging to his honor with all his might—pitted against this hungry power determined to make him turn his back on it.

And finally succeeding through sheer relentlessness....

My son had no chance against you, Ihuitimal had told me with his last breath. *No man does.*

I wanted to think he was wrong, but I had yet to meet that man.

With this particular one, all the desire had to do was pull loose the knot holding my tattered dress in place at my shoulder and let the rag pool around my ankles, and she had him.

CHAPTER EIGHT

I went back to my tent, leaving the man to sleep off our encounter among the maguey. My rational side felt I should care about him, given what we'd done; prior to taking off on my own, I'd never been intimate with anyone I hadn't cared about on some level. But in the months following my revelation, necessity had forced me to be less discerning. This man was a complete stranger, and nothing about our moments together had convinced me that I wanted anything to do with him beyond that.

Most of the people had retired to their tents as well, the feast finally winding down in the early hours of the morning; only the priests remained awake, overseeing the cleaning-up duties.

When my priest saw me, he hurried over, bowing. "Is there anything I can do for you, My Lady?"

"No, I'm just going to be in my tent until Mextli returns."

"Red Hawk did not disturb you out among the maguey, did he?"

I paused with my hand on the tent flap. "Red Hawk?"

"The chief's youngest son. His brothers are upstanding warriors, but I'm afraid Red Hawk's disposition is one of...entitlement?" He thought on this a moment before adding, "Even his own mother thinks everyone would have been better served if she'd left him in the desert when he was a babe."

Then no one will miss him if we use him up, the desire growled, and I felt sick to my stomach.

"Is something the matter, My Lady?" my priest asked, no doubt seeing the frown on my face.

She's just unused to thinking of your kind as food, the desire cackled. *She'll unlearn her weak human ways of thinking eventually.*

I shook my head. "No, I'm fine, I'm just...I'll be in my tent, and I don't want to be disturbed until Mextli returns. Understand?"

"Of course, My Lady." He bowed as he backed away and I retreated into the quiet of my tent, glad to be alone again.

Except the desire wasn't about to leave me in peace. *We're going to have to tell him eventually how we feed. He must know how to honor us.*

We're not taking our priest to bed!

Of course not. One doesn't slaughter a big male turkey before he's sired his share of chicks to carry on the next generation.

I cringed. "Humans are not turkeys," I muttered.

Oh but they are. Just as the humans raise the birds for their dinner table, we raise them for ours. Do the humans agonize over the moral repercussions of their eating habits even half as much as you do? Even Quetzalcoatl—the self-professed savior of humanity—admitted that no god can survive without blood, and it is folly to even try.

As much as I despised the Feathered Serpent, perhaps he'd shown me the answer to my doubts. He lived exclusively off the blood of his priests, given in earnest devotion, so why couldn't I as well?

Because we have one priest whereas he has thousands. And that one's devotion is up for debate.

"It's one right now, but with some work, I will bring in more," I countered, sitting down.

Why should we emulate the Feathered Serpent anyway? He loves his precious humans so much that he was willing to murder us for their benefit.

"And it's time I return that favor." I lay down and stretched out, staring up at the ceiling of the tent. "And with him gone, someone will need to fill that void in the hearts of humanity, so why not me?"

Now you're thinking like the goddess we are, the desire said with a chuckle.

□

I spent the rest of the night daydreaming about where Ehecacone and I would go once I had him back, and how I would help him uncover his own magical abilities, so when I heard the telltale crack of Mextli's return, it startled me. I hurried out of my tent just in time to see him duck into his own.

I paused at the flap of his tent, wondering what the appropriate protocol was. There weren't any bells on the hem to attract his attention. I'd never had to worry about such things when I went to visit Quetzalcoatl in the Divine Dream. After a moment of waffling, I called out, "Mextli?" My voice sounded painfully loud in the silence.

"Come in," he answered, so I ducked inside.

He lounged on his throne, quaffing a cup of blood. "You're looking significantly brighter today," he noted. "I trust your priest took care of your needs?"

"He will serve me well." The heat rushed to my cheeks and I had to force myself not to look away lest he taunt me for acting too human. I cleared my throat before saying, "I'm ready whenever you are."

"Eager, I see. Good, because today will be strenuous but rewarding." He drained his own cup then rose. Let's go." He held his feathered hand out to me.

I stared at it instead of taking it though. He'd been nothing but hospitable since I'd arrived in camp, but he hadn't been so in the past; he once put me in bodily jeopardy to satisfy his own curiosity, and then he attacked Little Reed with the intent of killing him—something I didn't think I could ever quite forgive him for.

He didn't attack you though, even when you attacked him, the desire reminded me.

Mextli's face remained neutral as we stared each other down. "I understand your mistrust, Mayahuel, and perhaps it's too soon to ask you to reconsider any judgments you've made, but there are some things I cannot teach you without your trust. Using the teoyoh is one of them. But if you're more comfortable starting with something else, that is fine as well."

Who but Mextli do we know who could possibly teach us what we need to know to defeat Quetzalcoatl? Still, I eyed his hand before taking hold of it. Mine looked so tiny against it, and the feel of his hummingbird feathers reminded me of those intimate moments Quetzalcoatl and I had shared together in the Divine Dream. To my surprise, my heart raced instead of recoiled.

He closed his fist around my hand, but kept his grip loose. "Are you all right?" His tone was a puzzling mix of concern and disinterest. How did he do that?

"I'm fine." I cleared my throat again, uncomfortable at how often I found myself disarmed around him. "So, what now?"

"I will go with you first, so you can experience the magic, and know what it feels like, so you can do it on your own."

"Go?"

His half-blue lips stretched into a smile. "You'll see. This is how Smoking Mirror taught me."

I cocked my head. "That seems a bit...fatherly for him."

"If you truly knew him, you'd see he is a god of unexpected depth."

All I knew was that anytime Smoking Mirror came around, I ended up in pain.

"These first few times, focus your attention on the pulse of my magic, how it builds, and how it dissipates," Mextli said.

"All right."

"Ready?"

I took a deep breath to calm the sudden flutter of anxiety in my chest. "Ready."

And then all I knew was a throbbing pulse, like the flash of a falling star just before it disappeared in the blackness of night. My own magic surged—

But it all disappeared and I found myself standing out in the desert, clutching Mextli's hand with both of mine while my heart raced. I nearly went to my knees in my light-headedness.

Mextli tightened his grip to keep me from falling over. "The first time is intense."

"Where are we?"

"Not far from the Mexica camp."

After a dazed look around, I spotted the outline of the tents in the distance. "Intense indeed," I muttered, my wits finally returning to me.

Mextli nodded. "When you're ready, we'll go again."

With a couple calming breaths, I said, "I'm ready."

Now that I knew what to expect, I was better able to process the bombardment of sensations and magic encapsulating me. I let it flow over me, making my own magic pulse and throb. Spectral blue hummingbirds played across my vision, crashing into each other and shattering into beams of light that flew away, crashing into other beams and re-coalescing into birds of energy and heat. I landed better this time, and felt my magic shifting and flowing in my blood as it never had before. "Again!" I panted, clamping even harder onto his feathered hand.

His magic coiled around me like a lover's hands, and my own mimicked its every pulse in an intricate dance. Bright balls of light and heat in the shape of rabbits burst from my own glowing aura. They dashed off among the brilliant blue hummingbirds circling me. I looked for Mextli, wondering if he was seeing this too, but before I could find him, my feet hit the ground and we stood surrounded by endless desert. A familiar, pleasant tingle radiated through my body; not the heavy, demanding hunger of my desire, but desire nonetheless; like when I looked at Little Reed. Heat rose in my cheeks and I carefully extracted my hand from Mextli's, unnerved by my unexpected reaction. "I think I'm ready to try this on my own."

Mextli nodded but said, "There is still more you need to know first though. The feel of the magic alone isn't enough. You must believe."

"Believe?"

He nodded. "Faith is an absolute must. To enter the teoyoh, you must *think* yourself a god—teotoca—and to return, you must *know* you're a god—teoti. I find thinking the words themselves makes it easier. Give it a try."

I closed my eyes, letting the magic rise up inside me.

"Say the words in your head," he reminded me.

Teotoca teoti! My magic lurched in my chest, but suddenly the air gushed from my lungs and I found myself lying on the ground, on my back, dazed. "What happened?"

He chuckled. "You came back sideways." He offered his hand to help me up. "Keep your eyes open, so your mind is properly oriented for the landing."

I dusted myself off and nearly launched my tattered dress off my shoulder in the effort. I hurried to right it, glancing at Mextli as I did so, but he had no reaction, making me feel foolish. *He might look like a man, but he isn't one,* I reminded myself. "Let me try again," I suggested, trying not to look too obvious in my learned embarrassment.

"Whenever you're ready."

I took a deep breath—another of those learned human responses I found so difficult to let go of—then let the magic build again. *Teotoca teoti!*

When I rematerialized this time, I landed on my feet, but still stumbled a few steps.

"Better," Mextli said. "But you're saying both of the words together, aren't you? Don't. Say the teotoca to enter the teoyoh then say teoti when you want to come out. Try again."

Indeed when I held back the second word, I remained in the pulsing flames of the teoyoh, letting it flow over me. Saying teoti promptly returned me to the material world. I did it again and again and again, disappearing and reappearing in the same spot, but I quickly got the hang of it. "How do I rematerialize somewhere else?" I pointed to a cactus a few dozen paces from us. "Say I wanted to land over there."

"That is a bit trickier. Come." He strode over to the cactus in five steps whereas it took me at least fifteen. "As I said yesterday, everything around us has its own teotl; it flows all around us like a river, and it's upon the currents of that river—the teoyoh—that we move from one place to another. And just as each of us has a signature energy, so does every material object in the world, and we use that unique energy to know where to rematerialize." He spread his hands in the air above the cactus as if warming them over a fire.

I followed his lead and focused my attention. My magic ebbed and flowed through me, changing yet again.

"Feel it?"

"I don't know,"

Mextli moved over to a rock a few steps away. "Feel over here, so you'll know the difference."

I did so, and my own magic changed yet again. "I feel differently over here," I noted.

He nodded. "That's because your teotl is committing the new signatures to memory, building a map of sorts that you will use to move around the world. You probably weren't aware of it, but you have been building this map all of your life, with every place you've ever walked."

I blinked. "So if I wanted to visit Xochicalco...?"

Mextli smiled. "Go ahead."

"But you still haven't told me how."

"Just will it."

I started to close my eyes but caught myself. I pictured the cistern outside the calmecac, where Little Reed and I had sat next to each other that fateful morning before the ritual ballgame to determine the next king of Xochicalco; how he'd held my hand and told me, "Whatever happens, just remember that I love you, and I always have." I didn't see him for two years after that. The memory brought a bittersweet joy into my heart.

Teotoca! The magic rushed over me, a blur of orange fire dancing across my vision.

When I left the teoyoh, I stood before the crumbling remains of a cistern outside dilapidated stone buildings. Tall grasses and wild flowers thrived between the cracks in the plastered stone ground, and when I turned around, I saw the burnt remains of the Temple of Quetzalcoatl, looking so small in the overgrown precinct. The last time I'd been here, smoke had covered everything in a gray, depressing mist, but today, the sun shone bright and hot, and butterflies bobbed among the flowers while birdsong and monkey-chatter filled the air.

Mextli materialized with a sharp crack and looked around too. "Rather easy, right?"

I nodded, taking in the scene with a heart that vacillated between heaviness and joy. I wished the city still looked as it did when I'd lived here; I wished I'd see Mazatzin coming up the main staircase; see Nimilitzli standing at the door of the great temple, ringing the bell for the afternoon service; see the novice priests and priestesses hurrying through the calmecac's courtyard in their white robes; see the youngest ones carrying brooms to the temple or dragging bags of laundry to the storerooms. But it was all gone.

I walked to the temple and stared at the friezes on the sides—the feathered serpents, the noblemen, the calendar symbols. Only flakes of the colorful paint remained now that no one maintained the art. I ran my fingers over the stone facade that bore Quetzalcoatl's face, remembering how it had peeled off the temple, alive and fierce in protecting me and Little Reed—*no, just Little Reed*, I thought, withdrawing my hand. *That was who the servant had come to kill, after all. I was unimportant, and no one would have bothered with me if not for Little Reed.*

Mextli came over, a frown on his face. "This place has some kind of meaning to you?"

"I lived most of my life here. But then the king burned it down because I wouldn't...." The next thought punched me in the gut. *Because I'd driven him mad. If not for my being here, Xochicalco might still be standing.* "What does it matter?" I muttered, turning away to look down the hillside to the ruins below us. "I destroy everything I touch."

"Whatever happened here, it could have been avoided if Quetzalcoatl hadn't kept secrets from you," Mextli countered. "Our teotls have powerful influence over human minds, so the responsibility rests with him, not you, Mayahuel."

"But your humans don't act so crazy. How do you keep them from doing dangerous things, to themselves and others?"

"Because they know who I am, and what kind of power I'm capable of, and because of that, they avoid contact with me; except my priests, of course, but they are a special breed, willing and able to give themselves over to my power and influence, and so they can speak for me to the people. That is the sole purpose of the priesthood, to act as the safe mediator between the mortal and the divine. The kings and chieftains fancy themselves the most powerful among their people, but they rule only by our grace. The truly powerful humans are the priests, for they speak our will to those who cannot surrender themselves to us without madness."

That explained much about Mazatzin's seeming imperviousness to my magic. "It must be lonely, having to separate yourself from your people."

"Hardly. Humans and I have nothing in common, so they are not *my people* in that sense. I interact often with other gods, both here on earth and in Omeyocan." He sobered as he went on, "Though it will be nice having a fellow god around. We younger ones aren't powerful enough to rule from a distance the way the old gods do, and that often means living separate from our own kind for large swathes of time while we build our own following here on earth." Mextli looked down over the hillside as well, contemplative. "May I suggest a game?"

Now was my turn to chuckle. "Gods play games?"

"Some of us are quite fond of games, like Tlachtli."

"I don't like Tlachtli at all."

"Someday I'd like to play Quetzalcoatl, if he would accept my challenge," Mextli said, standing tall, his hands folded behind him. "I suspect I would be very good at it. But I'm not suggesting we play Tlachtli. I'm thinking something that will help you practice your seeking skills."

"Tell me more."

"I will go somewhere through the teoyoh, and you will attempt to find me." Before I could accept his challenge, he disappeared with a crack, the sound sending the monkeys into startled shrieks in the distance.

I looked around, unsure what to do, but then pulled my thoughts together. *I know his energy, so this shouldn't be too hard.* I let my magic build, and when I thought, *Teotoca!* the orange flames engulfed my senses. I lingered in the teoyoh a moment, smelling for Mextli, and when I finally found it, I thought *teoti!* and the world snapped back into place around me.

I stood in the Mexica camp, at the central fire pit in front of Mextli's tent. The women skittered away at my sudden appearance while the men clutched their weapons, looking nervous.

Mextli chuckled behind me. "Too easy." Before I could turn around though, the crack resounded through camp.

I reached out again with my magic and welcomed the flames of divine energy when they came. I landed this time in a place I didn't recognize—a forest surrounded by trees casting a heavy darkness in the daylight. I looked up to see Mextli's bulky form perched on a large branch above me.

"Not bad," he said, amusement in his voice. "But slow. I could have visited three different places in the same time it took you to get here. Let's try again." He disappeared.

I didn't hesitate this time. I barked the divine word in my head, letting loose the flood of magic, and I registered the barest glimpse of the energy flames before I landed again.

This time I arrived in the market of a bustling city, and shrieks rose as the people around me hurried away, some shouting about witches. I couldn't see Mextli but I felt his presence nearby.

"Better," his voice boomed. "Again!"

We played this game over and over, me getting faster and more accurate with each leap. Soon we were coming in and out of the teoyoh so fast that I caught only glimpses of the places we landed; a mountain pass with snow swirling through the air; a thick, humid jungle; atop the Temple of the Sun in Teotihuacan; at the bottom of a lake; small seaside villages; the fields outside Culhuacan. We even dashed through Tollan, landing near the treasure houses—where I caught the faint smell of birds and snakes, from the feather and serpent houses nearby.

Eventually I caught up with him though, tackling him as I came out of the teoyoh. He roared in surprise as we rolled through the tall wild grasses, churning up dirt in our wake, and when we finally tumbled to a stop, he tossed me off and I landed with an *umph!*

He laughed as he lay on his back a few paces away from me. "Nicely done, Mayahuel! You're very good at this!"

I rolled over, laughing even as I cringed in pain. "Yes well, I had a very good teacher." The sun hung low. "Have we really been at this for hours?"

Mextli shrugged. "So what if we have? It's not as if time has any meaning to us."

I suppose not. I sat up to find we were in the middle of a field of golden grass with a small city in the distance. "Where are we?"

Mextli sat up too. "Aztlan."

"Where's that?"

"North of the great desert, in the homeland of the Mexica. I was born here."

"Really?"

He nodded. "The Smoking Mirror descended from Omeyocan as a spider and placed a ball of feathers under the idol of Tlaloc in the city's temple. My mother found it, and when she tucked it between her breasts, she became pregnant with me."

Kind of like Little Reed. The thought itched at the back of my mind. "Then you grew up here?"

He cracked a smirk. "In a manner of speaking. My mother—her name is Coatlicue—she had a daughter named Coyolxauhqui, who was a horrible sorceress who terrorized the city, and when she heard that her mother was pregnant with me, she sent the Tzitzimime to murder us both."

"Tzitzimime?"

Mextli pointed to the sky that was turning purple in the dusk. "The Demons Descending from Above. The stars come down to earth to hunt in the darkest hours of the night."

I cast a wary glance towards the sky. "Should we be sitting out here?"

He chuckled. "You needn't worry. They know better than to come anywhere near me. When my sister sent them to kill our mother, I sprang from Coatlicue's womb fully-grown, and fully-armed, and I slew them and sent my sister fleeing into the mountains." He pointed to the dark outlines of peaks to the north of us. "I pursued her up there, to a cave, and for her crimes, I cut her head off and threw her body down into the valley, for all to walk upon." He had the same malevolent gleam in his eyes that I saw when he'd wrenched me off my feet for ruining his basket of hearts. "After that, I led the Mexica out of Aztlan, away from this place."

"Too many bad memories?" I didn't want to even think of the mess he'd left behind after he'd sprang fully-grown and fully-armed from that poor woman's body.

Mextli shrugged. "The Mexica's future is in the south, where someday they will rule all. This I have promised them."

"That's a very big promise."

"I am a very big god," Mextli said with a grin.

I chuckled, surprisingly charmed by his brazen confidence. Pulling my knees to my chest, I said, "So, Smoking Mirror is your father then."

His face turned sober. "He is my brother."

"Whose feathers were they then?"

"Smoking Mirror's, as I told you already. He formed them from his war god essence and placed it under the idol."

I stared at him, puzzled. "But that means he made you from himself, which makes him your father."

Mextli turned his hardened gaze upon me, and I saw nothing of the god I'd spent all day with in those eyes. "As I said, he is my brother."

The acid in his voice made me fidget. "He's your brother." Hopefully that would calm the storm brewing in his eyes. Was this how I looked when the desire took over?

Just as suddenly as it had left, his smile returned. "This was indeed a good day. You did very well, Mayahuel. I'm most impressed."

"Thank you." I still hugged my knees to my chest, watching him carefully.

"We should get back to the camp. You expended a good deal of energy and should replenish before we continue tomorrow."

CHAPTER NINE

When we returned to the Mexica camp, the smell of cooking food permeated the air. All of the women were gathered around the fires, a scene reminiscent of those early days in Tollan when Little Reed and I had lived out of our tent, and Bitter Rabbit and Mitotia would cook our meals under the dark night skies. *I wonder how Mitotia's doing. Are she and Malinalli still together? And has Malinalli adjusted to being the High Priestess of Quetzalcoatl? She never wanted the job to begin with, but I'm sure she's taken to it just fine. She's brilliant and tough, after all.*

Yet I couldn't suppress the guilt for having thrust such a responsibility upon her without explanation, or even saying goodbye.

We can go to Tollan and see how she's doing, the desire said. *We could be there in a blink.*

The thought was so appealing—and I started working over plans in my head—but reality soon dampened my enthusiasm. If I was seen, word would surely get back to Little Reed that I'd been there, and what would he think if I didn't go see him?

Then go see him too!

Except how could I explain to him that everything he felt for me was a lie? My showing up there could seriously undermine whatever happiness he'd finally found with Anacoana, and I'd done enough damage there already. *I can't ever go back to Tollan,* I realized, heaviness settling over me. *I have to let it go; I have to let Little Reed go, for both of us.*

And what about your promise to Ehecacone, to take him to see Little Reed? the desire asked.

I'll have to tell him I can't go with him. The thought felt like a blow to the chest.

"Do you wish to come inside for some blood?" Mextli asked, holding open his tent flap.

I smiled wanly. "Actually, I think I want to go back to my own tent for the night. I'm very drained and...and...."

"And you need to feed." He nodded. "I shall see you tomorrow then." He ducked into his tent.

Looking forward to some alone time, I turned to my own tent.

But it was gone. I looked around, but when I didn't spot it, I went to one of the women tending a nearby fire. "Excuse me, but do you know what happened to my tent?"

She stared up at me, her mouth hanging open. The women behind her—who were mending animal skins—all gasped then scurried away. She remained frozen though, a bewildered look on her face.

I watched, puzzled as the others disappear into nearby tents. "Did I say something wrong?"

The woman clutched her chest, a strange look on her face. "The goddess has spoken to me!" she whispered, breathless. "The goddess has chosen to talk to me!" Her expression shifted to nausea. "What will Yaotl say?"

The memory of Mextli's words from this afternoon came back to me. *Stupid! I mustn't talk to anyone but my priest.* "It's all right," I said, backing away. "I'll find it myself."

But she sprang to her feet, nearly knocking over the cooking pot. She hurried around the fire and prostrated herself on the ground at my feet. "I live only to serve you, My Lady."

"No, really, that's not necessary—"

"Xihuitl moved your temple, My Lady, to the maguey field outside of camp."

"Xihuitl?"

"Your chosen shaman, My Lady."

My cheeks blazed. *I didn't even ask my own priest his name. Seems I'm becoming more god-like every day.* I cleared my throat before replying, "Thank you," then I headed for the north end of camp.

As the woman had said, my tent was set up among the maguey plants. Xihuitl sat outside of it, in front of a small fire where he was burning incense and meditating, but when I entered the clearing, he hurried to his feet then prostrated himself before me too. "Does your new sacred location please you, My Lady?"

"Yes. Thank you."

"If it pleases you, I have moved my own tent to the edge of camp, so I will always be close at hand to serve you." He pointed behind me and I turned to see a new tent erected at the edge of the clearing, along the footpath back to the camp.

And the woman stood next to it, watching us anxiously.

"Why are you lurking back there, Xochitl? It's a grave crime to spy on the gods!" Xihuitl called to her, coming to his feet and lumbering toward her.

"But she spoke to me!" Xochitl called, backing away.

"Lies!"

I rushed to cut him off. "No, I indeed spoke to her. It's all right."

He stared at me with confused eyes but then dropped his gaze. He went to his hands and knees again. "Forgive my outburst, My Lady. I did not know I had failed you."

"Failed me? You haven't failed me."

"Is that not why you've granted Xochitl your grace? You're not disappointed in my service?"

"Omeyocan no! You've been a very good priest," I assured him. "Please rise. I don't like you groveling in the dirt at my feet."

He stood again, looking chastened. "Forgive my displeasing behavior, My Lady."

"Please stop chastising yourself. You've done nothing to deserve it." I looked back at Xochitl and beckoned her over.

She hurried, keeping her own gaze downcast.

"I spoke to Xochitl because...." But the desire stopped me. *We can't admit it was a mistake; gods are supposed to be perfect, otherwise why else would they worship us?*

I floundered a breath longer but then said, "I've decided I need both a priest and priestess. A woman can serve me in ways that a man cannot, just as you serve me in ways that she cannot," I told Xihuitl.

Xihuitl looked at Xochitl—skeptical—then he told me, "But My Lady, she is not unblemished."

"Unblemished?"

"She is not pure of the flesh, as a shaman should be. She has a husband...and she's with child!"

I looked over at Xochitl. It was difficult to see her body under her buckskins, but her cheeks were blazing bright.

I turned back to Xihuitl, my own head swimming with warnings about admitting my own mistakes. "Such things don't matter to me; I'm a mother myself, and it's nonsense to say that being a mother precludes one from being able to serve the gods." *And in my experience, those most concerned about the purity of priestesses are those who are trying to cover for their own lack of bodily purity,* the desire almost growled, but Xihuitl was already looking thoroughly scolded.

I turned to Xochitl. "If you do not wish to serve, I understand and release you of that obligation with no ill feelings."

Xochitl hurried forward, fervor on her face. "It would be the greatest honor of my life to serve you, My Lady. I promise I won't let you down!"

"I know you won't," I said with a smile.

She bowed. "Tell me how to best serve you, My Lady."

"Well, I *am* a bit hungry," I admitted.

"Tell us what you require and we shall fetch it immediately."

The desire started rising up inside me but I pushed it back. *Not yet. I want to try something different.*

Different?

You're not afraid, are you?

The desire bristled but retreated.

Both Xochitl and Xihuitl were waiting with infinite patience, so I said, "Each of you will give me a little of your own blood each day. Not too much, for I don't want either of you becoming ill." I motioned them to follow me over to one of the maguey plants.

I took hold of one of the thorns and bent it back and forth until it broke loose, but when I pulled it off, it brought long, stringy fibers with it. "Take a maguey thorn and put it through your tongue, like this...." I opened my mouth and demonstrated on myself.

It had been so long since last I'd done this that the shock of the pain took me by surprise. And to think there'd been a time when I'd found such sensations comforting. I dragged the damp maguey fibers through my fresh wound then choked back the throbbing sensation in my mouth. "The threads should be dry though, and braided together," I said once I found the will to make my tongue work again. "It soaks up the blood better."

Xihuitl fingered the thorns on another maguey plant. "Then we should not use the thorns tonight?"

"Just use your blade to bleed your earlobes and dribble it into a cup, and that will do for tonight," I said.

Xochitl pulled one of the thorns loose and smiled with pride as the threads came out in multiple long strands. "I will make the ropes and thorns for us," she told Xihuitl. "You get the cup and blade."

He scowled at her orders but hurried away to his tent.

◻

After my priests bled their ears into a small clay cup for me, I gave Xihuitl orders to start training Xochitl in the stories of the Mexica gods, so she would have the appropriate priestly knowledge. The real reason though was so I could listen in as they sat outside my tent and learn all I could about Mexica theology, to know which gods they worshipped and how they told their stories; all knowledge I needed to be an effective goddess for them. I sat drinking the little bit of blood and listened in silence, committing everything to memory the same way I used to in calmecac so long ago.

But the blood was gone all too soon and the hunger still burned bright and petulant. I stared into the empty cup, wondering if I should do something so uncouth as to try the lick the remainder off the sides.

To Mictlan with blood, the desire growled. *We can't live on so little. When we have countless followers giving a little to us every day, like Quetzalcoatl does, then we can live on blood alone. But until then, we need to feed naturally.*

I sighed. I'd hoped this would prove enough, but the desire was right. *But I hate feeding off them...like that.*

The desire hissed, annoyed. *Did you ever give this much thought to the animals you ate when you were still mortal? Did you weep for the turkeys or dogs raised for the slaughter? Did you say a prayer for the soul of the deer filling your tamales? Or did you thank the gods for giving you that food? This is what Omeyocan has given us, and we should be thankful, for without it, we die.*

I set the cup aside to put my head in my hands. *I don't want to kill anyone.*

We needn't kill them. Black Otter lived for many years after.

I wouldn't call that 'living'.

We limit the number of times we take each to bed, just as we have been, but when we're done with them, we banish them. It's the perfect arrangement: we get to eat, they get the pleasure, and no one dies.

I looked up at the tent flap, hesitating. *And what happens when we go through every man in camp?*

We can't do that, of course, for we'd have no one left to worship us. The humans bring Mextli war prisoners; they'll just need to bring some for us as well. When I still hesitated, the desire asked, *Do you wish me to go out there and speak with the priest about our needs?*

"No, I'll do it," I grumbled, crawling out the flap finally.

My emergence startled both of them and they rose to bow to me. "Is there something we can do for you, My Lady?" Xihuitl asked.

"It's getting late and both of you need your sleep. Xochitl, please go home to your husband and get a good night's rest."

Xochitl bowed again then headed back to camp.

"Shall I retire as well, My Lady?" Xihuitl looked ragged and eager for his bed.

"Of course, but first...Red Hawk...."

"The chief's son?"

I nodded. "Tell him I wish to see him, right away."

"Immediately, My Lady." And without a backward glance, he hurried back into camp.

I waited outside my tent, pacing and working over what I'd say to Red Hawk when he came.

He and Xihuitl arrived shortly, and I thanked my priest for all his service and sent him home for the night. Both Red Hawk and I watched him until he disappeared into his tent.

Then Red Hawk turned ardent eyes upon me and drew me into a groping hug. "Then last night was as good for you as it was for me?" he asked, kissing my neck.

His very touch made my skin crawl, so I welcomed the desire when it supplanted me. "If you thought last night was good, you're in for a treat tonight," it purred, pulling him toward the tent.

CHAPTER TEN

 The night's activities left me energized and fidgety, reminding me of that time long ago when Citlallotoc had convinced me to smoke tobacco to keep me moving through my exhaustion. I sat among the maguey, practicing manipulating the plants while Red Hawk snored loudly in my tent, but long before dawn, I couldn't take sitting still anymore. I went back into camp, to see if Mextli wanted to get an early start on the day's lessons.

But when I peeked inside his tent, I found it empty; no Mextli, no throne, no vast hall, just a small, empty tent. I stared at it, confused, but then returned to my own.

With Red Hawk sprawled out, there was no room for me inside my tent, so I sat out front, watching a scorpion hunting among the nearby rocks.

A bit before sunrise, Mextli appeared next to me with a snap, making me flinch. "You should have sensed me coming," he chided, a wicked grin on his face. "One mustn't get so distracted by the beauty of the world that one doesn't see danger when it's coming."

I raised an eyebrow. "You're a danger to me?"

He chuckled. "No."

When Red Hawk suddenly started snoring, I cut him off by asking loudly, "Will you show me how to make my tent bigger? Like yours?" I held my breath when I ran out of things to say, but thankfully Red Hawk had fallen silent again.

Mextli glanced back at my tent, but then said, "Very well. Come along." He vanished with a crack and I followed closely behind him.

We materialized out in the desert, next to a rock outcropping. Mextli flexed his left hand and a deerskin tent materialized out of thin air in front of us, already set up.

"How did you do that?" I asked.

"Do what?"

"Make that appear? Did you bring it from the camp?"

He shook his head. "Every god has a special power unique to themselves alone, a power not shared by others. In my case, I can create weapons and military supplies from my thoughts."

"So that's how you summoned knives out of seemingly nowhere?"

"Exactly."

"And every god has a special power that none of the others have? What's Smoking Mirror's?"

Mextli gave me a sideways glance, suspicion on his face, but he answered, "He can see the future."

"Really?" When Mextli nodded, I cocked my head and asked, "Then he must have known he would lose against me at the battle for Culhuacan, so why did he face off with me?"

"The actions of gods are seldom predictable," Mextli answered. "He can see the future as it pertains to mortals, whose behaviors are extremely predictable. Surely you've noticed this?"

I chuckled. "Well, obviously prediction is not my special power, because human behavior is as mysterious to me as that of my fellow gods."

"Experience will teach you otherwise."

"What about Quetzalcoatl? What's his special power?" Such information could come in handy.

Mextli cast his gaze at the sun rising in the east. "He can instill unwavering faith and devotion in the hearts of humans. That is why he has so many followers."

"That is powerful." All of Quetzalcoatl's talk of earning the devotion of his followers felt so very hollow now, and the bitterness welled up anew. He hadn't just lied to me; he was lying to everyone, and growing powerful off that lie.

And you don't? I wondered. *How many men have convinced themselves that they are in love with you and it's all a lie?*

Yes, but we don't reinforce their delusion by telling them that what they feel is real, the desire retorted. *There's a difference.*

"I wonder what my own special power is," I muttered. I invited the desire to give its opinion, but it remained silent, so I said, "I do have that octli magic."

"From what Smoking Mirror tells me, your son possesses that as well, so it is not unique to you," Mextli answered.

That must be why he often fell into spontaneous intoxication, though it seemed that where I could direct it outward, he tended to direct it inward. After a moment's thought, I said, "Well...I can make humans fall in love with me just by being near them."

"A fairly typical ability for a love goddess, Mayahuel," Mextli chided me with a chuckle. "And you aren't the only one around."

"I guess not," I admitted, thinking of Xochiquetzal. "I guess I'll figure out my uniqueness eventually."

"We all do," Mextli agreed.

"So, about making the inside of the tent bigger...."

Mextli nodded. "You create a pocket of the Divine Dream. You're familiar with what the Divine Dream is?" When I nodded, he went on, "Once you've built the pocket, you can then shape it however you like. Very simple, really."

"But how does one build pockets of the Divine Dream?" I asked. "My experience...well, it always manipulated me, not the other way around. And even then, I could only see it with the help of the Teonanacatl." *Or when you have sex,* the desire reminded me but I bit my tongue.

Mextli crinkled his eyebrows. "You can't see it now?"

"Well, I can *see* it, but I can't interact with it. It's more like...a wash of color over reality. The way you talk about it...you make it seem as if it's a physical thing."

"You're thinking like a human again, Mayahuel."

I creased my brow. "Meaning what?"

"That you think of the physical and mental world as two separate things, unrelated to each other, that there's a clear line between them. The Divine Dream is all around us, in everything, all the time. Humans can perceive both worlds, but they cannot exist in the Divine Dream the way we do. That is how Quetzalcoatl created them—limited. But we gods exist simultaneously in both and so can manipulate both with ease. This is so very basic, Mayahuel." Mextli sighed. "Forgive my criticism, but it frustrates me how unprepared the Feathered Serpent kept you."

"It frustrates me even more than it does you," I said.

"But you shall be ignorant no more. I will make sure of it." He beckoned me to follow him up onto the rock outcrop. "You said you've only ever been able to see into the Divine Dream with the sacred mushrooms?"

"Well, that's not entirely true," I admitted. "When I'd do certain things...things I do now to feed, I could see into the Divine Dream. But now that I'm a goddess, I can see it all of the time, but I have no idea how to interact with it."

"Then you've never changed your form?"

I blinked at him. "I can change my form?"

"Of course. You're not limited to that human body you were reborn into; you can re-fashion it in any manner you wish. If you want to be a rock, then you can be a rock; if you wish to be a bird and fly over the earth, you can do that too. You can even be elemental; sometimes I like to be the sun, at least when Nanauatzin isn't already being it. Quetzalcoatl liked being the wind, and Smoking Mirror plays at being wildfire."

"And I could be any of that too?" When Mextli nodded, I asked, "How?"

"Just do it."

I frowned: "What?"

"So much of being divine, Mayahuel, is believing all things are possible. The only thing that keeps your thoughts from becoming reality is that you don't believe. You must let go of all that human behavioral training and know that you can do whatever you want—you can *be* whatever you want."

I laughed. "You make it sound easy."

"It *is* easy." He suddenly morphed into a tiny emerald-blue hummingbird, his wings beating so fast they were mere blurs as he hovered before me. "You just must believe." His deep, booming voice sounded comical coming from such a small creature's mouth.

"So if I wanted to become a rabbit—?"

"Don't want; just do it."

I sighed and closed my eyes.

Stop clinging to your own limitations and believe in your potential, the desire chided. *You are a goddess, capable of anything, and more.*

I thought of Ehecacone when he was young, asking me if I ever dreamt of becoming a rabbit, and I imagined the glee on his face as I changed into one right in front of him. As a child, I'd often wanted to be a rabbit, hopping around on all fours, mimicking the rabbits I saw creeping among the bushes in the main garden. Black Otter would play a jaguar, stalking me through the palace halls, and he'd try to pin me in corners or on the floor, but I was better at such games and always eluded him. But now I really could be one, and it would be fabulous to be so fast, so sleek, so fuzzy....

"Not hard at all," Mextli said.

I opened my eyes to find my human hands gone, replaced with delicate, triangular paws covered in brown fur. I pulled them up against my soft white belly to find I now rested on powerful haunches, and the newly-rising sun stretched a long-eared shadow across the desert floor in front of me. I'd done it! I was in the body of a rabbit!

But when I tried to take a step, I went over the edge of the rock outcropping and landed on my back on the ground. My body didn't work at all like I was used to.

Because it's not a human body, silly, the desire laughed. *The joints are all in different places.*

And when I tried to speak, it came out only as high-pitched squeals. How did Mextli manage to speak? I tried again and again, but finally gave up and instead returned to my human form.

Mextli alighted on the edge of the rock outcropping. "Not to your liking?"

"How are you able to speak in that form?" I asked, sitting up and brushing the dust off myself. "When I try, nothing but nonsense comes out."

"Because you're trying to use the limitations of the form," Mextli said. "You really think this tiny body could produce the same deep timbre as my pseudo-human body can? Its mouth can't form speech at all. I speak by projecting my divine voice while moving my mouth in a kind of mimicry; I can simply project if I wish, but I've found that humans have difficulty figuring out where I am without that cue, even if I'm directly in front of them."

I changed back into my rabbit form and tried again. "Like this?" I finally blurted out after manipulating my new mouth a few times.

"You're out of sync. Don't make it difficult. Let your mind move your mouth unconsciously, just as it would if you were in your human form."

"How about now?" I asked, trying not to think about it.

Mextli bobbed his tiny head. "Very nice."

I spent a few moments testing out my new body, figuring out the mechanics, and soon I was loping around in circles. I splayed my claws across the ground and scratched a couple of times, laughing as I did. "This is fun!" Oh how I wished Ehecacone could see me!

Soon he will, and I'll get to teach him all of this!

Mextli turned back into his hulking, half-feathered form and stepped down off the outcropping. "Let's move on to the tent."

I hopped over and sat in front of the flap. "So, how do I start?"

"However you wish."

"Must I be inside?"

He shrugged. "Since this is your first time, it will help."

I nudged my way past the hide flap and sat in the middle. The tent had looked so small before, but from a rabbit-eye view it looked so much bigger.

"Now imagine what you want, and let the Divine Dream build it around you," Mextli said from outside.

I hadn't thought this far ahead, so after a handful of frustrated breaths while I tried to come up with some image in my head, my mind went back to the familiar. With a tickling of magic, the tent melted away.

My old quarters in Tollan slowly formed around me. The curtain leading to the bath yard was half-open, letting the afternoon sunlight drape across my bed of reed mats and animal skins. My wooden idol of the Feathered Serpent stood between it and the next doorway, this one covered with a blue curtain embroidered with rabbits playing drums and reed flutes—the side entrance into Ehecacone's room next door. Just as the first time I'd seen it in the Divine Dream before my son was born, the patterns on the curtain's hem danced about as if alive.

From there I turned to the main doorway into my quarters which was closed off by a curtain. Beyond it, I heard the quetzals calling, and Little Reed's voice, and Citlallotoc's. I returned to my human form then stepped slowly forward, my heart hammering in my ears. Were they really here? Could I talk to Little Reed—interact with him—the way Quetzalcoatl always did with me? The thought sent my heart racing even faster.

But when I parted the curtain, I found the family garden deserted. The pink and orange skies of the Divine Dream were full of fluffy clouds, and fat flakes of Love floated down from above, coating everything in a layer of shimmer. The shapes of birds soared through the air, but they moved with a dreaminess that told me they weren't real. When my gaze found the statue of Quetzalcoatl, I watched it with a growing apprehension that it would start moving and uncoiling, just as the one at the temple had in that long ago visit with the Feathered Serpent in the Divine Dream.

It didn't move, but the face changed; the feathered scales and neck feathers melted away until only a cylindrical pillar remained. *So I can indeed change the Divine Dream however I want.* I switched my gaze over to the light blue curtain covering the doorway on the portico opposite my own, the one emblazoned with Little Reed's royal sigil—a green and white feathered serpent. I imagined Little Reed parting the curtain and rushing to me, to embrace and kiss me. I imagined him weeping as he asked why I'd left and pleaded with me to never leave again. The image left me feeling guilty—for both hurting him so, and for secretly hoping my departure had done just that.

The curtain to his quarters remained completely still. So there were still some things I couldn't make happen here.

I blinked away the disappointment then looked around, sure that Mextli was standing behind me, watching. He wasn't though. I noticed though that the curtain over the door to my quarters had a symbol on it now, a sigil of sorts: a maguey plant with a naked woman crouched before it, holding up a bowl of octli in one hand and clutching a nursing infant to her breast with the other. I recognized my face in the painting, but I'd never imagined I could look so magnificent, so...godlike.

I scrutinized the curtain for a moment until I heard Mextli say, "How are you doing?" His voice sounded distant, as if he were beyond the rooms surrounding the garden.

"Mextli?" I called out, walking around the garden, looking for him.

"Yes?"

I furrowed my brows. "Where are you?"

"Outside the tent. You must invite me in before I can enter your newly-formed pocket of the Divine Dream."

Was that why I couldn't find him last night, and why his tent had appeared empty? "You can come on in," I called back.

He pushed aside the curtain to my quarters and hunched over as he stepped into the garden, to keep from hitting his head on the corbelled arch. As he looked around with curiosity, I was suddenly very glad that the feathered serpent statue had changed to a plain pillar. "Interesting choice," he said. "I wouldn't think you'd like gardens."

I raised an eyebrow. "Why not?"

"The Earth Monster kept you locked up in the one in Omeyocan for eons, and then the Feathered Serpent murdered you in Tamoachan. I'd think you'd have an aversion to such places after all that."

With that in mind, I expected to feel differently as I looked around again, but nothing changed in my heart. "I don't know. Most gardens have been good places for me; even the one in Omeyocan was peaceful, and beautiful, and as for Tamoachan...." *For a while it was wonderful in ways I couldn't even begin to explain,* I wanted to say, but it felt foolish; it had all been a lie. "Aside from Tamoachan, I've always felt at home in them." I smiled. "I used to sit out here on this patio and weave cloth and watch Ehecacone play with his toys—"

"This is Tollan?"

There wasn't any detectable sharpness to Mextli's tone, but I still felt stabbed by the question. "It's the first place I thought of, and it seemed easy to recreate...."

"Understandable," Mextli conceded. "The first few times I made my pockets after Smoking Mirror first taught me, they were just recreations of my mother's—" He stopped, suddenly looking uncomfortable, as if he'd just about divulged something embarrassing. He cleared his throat, resting his gaze everywhere but on me before continuing, "The familiar is always a good place to start, but with practice, you can build completely fresh places that don't exist in the real world. The possibilities are endless."

"I'm beginning to see that." I sat on the patio stones by the pillar and gazed up into the sky where Omeyocan nestled among the clouds. "The other gods...can they see us down here? Right now?"

Mextli looked up too. "They cannot see into your private bubble. You would have to invite them in the same as you invited me in."

"And I have to re-invite you in each time?"

"Every time you form a new pocket, yes. I could leave right now and return on my own, so long as you didn't allow the Divine Dream to reabsorb itself, and so long as you don't rescind my invitation."

"So you form a new pocket every time you retire to your tent?"

"Gods like Quetzalcoatl or Tlaloc keep theirs permanent, but I find it to be an unnecessary expenditure of energy. You and I don't have an endless supply of followers keeping us constantly glutted on sacrifices."

"I definitely don't have that. But we can also invite humans into our private space, right? After all, your priests came into your tent that first night."

Mextli nodded. "Humans can enter and interact with you under the influence of peyotl or the sacred mushrooms. Humans can't *physically* enter the Divine Dream though; they are bound to the physical plane. When you saw my priests inside my pocket of Divine Dream, that was their mental projection of themselves."

"So, if I wanted to interact with my own priest inside my personal space here, he would have to be under the influence of peyotl or the Teonanacatl?"

"And you'd have to invite him in, just as you would with a god," he confirmed.

An itch of excitement rose inside me. I'd sworn off ever going back to Tollan, but I could see Little Reed in my private Divine Dream space the way I used to with Quetzalcoatl long ago. But how did I let him know I wanted to meet him here? "Must a person be under the influence for me to invite them in? I've heard of our kind speaking to humans in their dreams. That could be a good way for me to garner more followers, so how do I do that?"

He laughed. "I'm glad to see you embracing your godhood so eagerly."

The appreciation in his eyes made the desire flare and growl in my chest. A strange contrast to my dreamy thoughts of Little Reed earlier.

"Communicating with humans through dreams is a very powerful tool; they believe the dream world is full of meaning and they take those interactions very seriously. Smoking Mirror came to my sister in her dreams and warned her that her own death was close at hand, driving her to try to kill our mother, and thus releasing me upon herself."

"So how do I do this?"

Mextli sat next to me, taking up the rest of the patio. "It's not very easy, unless you already have a relationship with the person whose mind you're trying to enter. It's best to practice on priests, for they are most open to visions, and they can even have waking ones. Let's try it. Think of a message you want to give to your priest."

"Like what?"

"I don't know, but it should be something you consider worthy of a vision, because once he receives it, he's going to interpret it as such, and it could end up becoming a fixture of your worship."

I frowned. "Maybe this isn't something I should do on an impulse then."

He shook his head. "Just think of something simple but important you want him to do for you. Perhaps you want him to decorate your tent with flowers, or do something related to your feeding needs. Don't over-think it."

After a moment's thought, I came up with something. "All right, what next?"

"Locate him in the same way you would locate me if you couldn't find me."

I reached out with my divine senses. It took only a breath to find Xihuitl's familiar musky smell, almost as if he stood next to me. "Found him."

"When you feel the currents of his thoughts, ride them into his head."

At first I wasn't sure what Mextli meant, but suddenly my own mind became swept up in a gush of images, light, and sound. I saw through Xihuitl's eyes: he was knapping a piece of flint for a blade but he suddenly stopped, as if frozen. "My Lady," he whispered, his voice growing soft and slurred.

"Now deliver your message," Mextli's voice continued from a distance.

Xihuitl, I spoke into the ether, letting the desire's powerful cadence take over. *Bring Lord Red Hawk to my tent each night until I tell you to remove him from the camp. Do you understand?*

"I do, My Lady," he whispered.

And once I'm through with him, you will ensure he is replaced with a new man—or woman, it doesn't matter—to see to the health of your goddess.

"I shall not fail you, My Lady!"

I opened my own eyes, snapping back to myself. "You're right; it wasn't that difficult."

Mextli nodded. "But onto other things now. Let us return to the real world."

I looked around at the garden, searching for an exit. "How?"

"Just dissipate the bubble." When I cocked my head at him, he added, "Tell it to go away."

I gave the silent command and the garden dissolved around me until it was all replaced with the inside of the small tent. When I poked my head out of the flap, Mextli stood outside waiting for me. After I exited the tent, he made it disappear with a flick of his fingers.

"That was rather easy," I said.

"Most things are," he replied. "But other things take quite a bit of practice; like controlling elemental forces. Observe." He stretched his broad arms out and raised his chin towards the sky.

Suddenly, a gentle breeze blew in from the south, rustling the dry leaves of the nearby mizquitl tree. It slithered around me like a lover's caress, and again the desire took to growling plaintively. When he lowered his arms, the breeze died down to hot stillness.

"You...you mean I can control the wind?" I asked, my insides a torrent of lust and excitement.

"All gods can manipulate and control the elements of the world," Mextli said. "I can whip up the wind, make it rain, create brush fires, and make the sun blaze hotter, and so can you."

"You can make rain? But I thought only Tlaloc could do that, and that's why he's the Rain God."

Mextli shook his head. "Tlaloc is the Rain God because he's the best at that skill; I could make it rain here, right now, but I'm not very good at it; I'm still learning to control water. But Tlaloc is a master. He can make it rain anywhere, at any time. And Nanahautzin is the Sun God because he can make the heat of the sun so hot it would destroy all life on earth in less than the blink of an eye, and Quetzalcoatl can make the wind wipe out the entire countryside. But they can be deposed from their lofty position."

"How?"

"If another god—or goddess—becomes more skilled at controlling and manipulating an element, that god can then vie for their title. If I practice and work enough—and get more humans to worship me as the Sun God, then I could depose Nanahuatzin."

"And if I became better at controlling the wind than Quetzalcoatl...then I'd become the Wind Goddess?"

He nodded. "But you also must be worshipped as the Wind Goddess. That is key."

Had I perhaps found my means of fulfilling my deal with Lord Death? "And what would happen to Quetzalcoatl if I deposed him as the Wind God?"

"He would lose his place in Heaven and become earthbound until he regained his position from you."

"It's perfect!" I murmured.

"The perfect what?"

I hesitated a breath before settling for, "Revenge, for him killing me so long ago."

Mextli chuckled. "Your ambition is admirable, Mayahuel, and we all should have goals, but I must warn you that Smoking Mirror has been trying to depose Quetzalcoatl as the Wind God for thousands of years now. You haven't even learned the very basics of controlling *any* element yet."

When Lord Death said not to take too long, I doubted he meant that he'd wait thousands of years for me to deliver. Still, right now it seemed the best option. "Let's get started, for I think I will be a much better student than Smoking Mirror."

Mextli uttered a deep rumbling laugh and shook his head. "Very well. And since you seem set upon challenging the Feathered Serpent for supremacy of the wind, that's where we'll start."

CHAPTER ELEVEN

 "Don't be discouraged, Mayahuel," Mextli said as we walked through camp. "Like I said, controlling elements is one of the most difficult things we do."

"But I destroyed the camp!"

"You did, but they will clean it up."

I watched the women pick through what remained of their homes after I'd accidentally unleashed a massive sandstorm on the camp. Several warriors were hurrying around, directing the re-erection of the tents. "They shouldn't have to clean up after me though."

"It's their job to do it, Mayahuel. We give them things, and they return the favor."

Except I felt like I was only giving them work rather than anything useful.

Shouting drew my attention to the south end of camp, but when women started screaming, the hairs on my neck bristled. Children fled towards us, crying and shrieking as a handful of warriors poured around the lines of tents, brandishing wooden clubs and flint axes, shouting and beating down any Mexica warrior who got in their path.

Mextli roared something before charging into the growing mayhem while I stood frozen.

But when I saw Xochitl fall as the warrior she fled smacked her with his fist, fury rose up inside me like a ball of deadly flame.

"That's my priestess, human!" the desire bellowed, my own heartbeat growing distant in my ears. I didn't resist as my arms rose of their own accord, magic building in my fingertips, nor did I hold back when the throb became a burn, demanding release.

Not that long ago, whenever I used my magic, it sprayed everywhere, hitting more than my intended target, but while teaching me to manipulate the wind, Mextli had taught me how to focus it into a tight stream, the better to avoid damaging my own allies. I'd struggled with it when we practiced out in the desert, but now, in the heat of the moment, I didn't even think about it.

My magic slammed Xochitl's attacker in the chest like a fist and catapulted him backwards into a tent ten paces behind him. I didn't wait to see if he was still alive; every time I laid eyes upon a warrior attacking one of Mextli's men or trying to drag off more women, I unleashed again, sending bodies flying through the air and our own warriors scrambling for cover. The anger in my chest soon gave way to grim satisfaction.

But when I sent one of the now retreating warriors sprawling into the stabbing spear points of our own warriors, that satisfaction turned into intoxicating glee. I laughed as I watched Mextli dispatch two warriors with one swipe of his sword, but when he met my gaze—his own dark and hungry and intense—a desirous shudder rang through me. *He really is a sight to see,* the desire breathed, letting a simmering smile slide to my lips.

He held my gaze for a long moment that left me breathless, but his expression remained unchanged until he turned to survey the mayhem we'd created. I saw it only for a flash, but the subtle smile was burned in my mind. I wasn't sure what to make of it. *Let's find out,* the desire suggested but I shook her away.

I slowly returned to my body to find my skin tingled and my heart raced painfully. Sobbing filled the air. Xochitl still lay on the ground, curled up into a ball, but a man now knelt over her, stroking her hair and whispering to her. *Her husband,* I concluded, and when I came closer, he started to back away, sickening terror in his eyes. But before he could move far, I whispered, "Take care of your wife." The power of my own voice startled me, given how close to shaking apart I felt.

As he returned to tending to her, I approached the man I'd sent flying into the tent. He laid dead, eyes open, milky-white fluid dribbling from the corners of his mouth and out of his nostrils. *As if I'd filled him completely full of octli,* I thought. I looked around, taking in the destruction I'd wrought; unlike the Mexica warriors wrestling their few captives together with ropes, I'd taken no prisoners.

When Mextli came up next to me, he wore a broad grin on his half-feathered face. "You're a most formidable warrior, Mayahuel."

I answered the compliment with a wan smile.

The same darkness still lingered in his gaze, but whereas before I'd thought it viewed me as little more than a buzzing insect when it took him, there was appreciation in there now. "Like I told you that day in Tollan, when you let the inner monster out, you're magnificent."

The desire tried to rear up again, eager to turn that remark into some of the sexually-charged banter she so enjoyed, but his word choice struck me like an arrow. As I looked back down at the dead man lying in the remains of the tent, I felt sick. Monster indeed; I hadn't needed to kill him, or the others, but I'd done it without hesitation.

One of the Mexica warriors came over and prostrated himself before Mextli. "We captured three of the raiders, My Lord, and two escaped into the desert. The rest are dead."

A priest came forward too. "We will begin processing the bodies for you immediately."

"They are Mayahuel's," Mextli answered. "She killed them, so that makes them her sacrifices."

"I don't want them," I sputtered. When he arched his one eyebrow at me, I quickly added, "They're little use to me dead."

He watched me, making me feel intensely scrutinized, but eventually he turned back to his priest. "Do it quickly. I want to eat before I leave with the men."

The priest bowed and backed away, and the warrior hurried away too, barking orders at the other men.

"You're leaving?" I asked.

Mextli nodded. "This was a retaliatory raid, so it must be answered swiftly, especially since some of them escaped."

Mextli shifted into a feathered xicolli over cotton armor and a black feathered headdress appeared on his head. "Do you wish to come along? You'd be a very useful asset."

I shook my head. "No, thank you. War's not to my taste. Besides, I blew down half the camp with that wind gust, so I will stay behind and help the women put it back together."

He nodded, thoughtful. "And with you here to protect them, I can take all the men with me, so we can bring back even more prisoners. This will be good for you; a chance to lead on your own." He flexed his left hand and a flint-bladed spear materialized in his fist. "When I get back, we'll celebrate with a grand feast."

While Mextli ate the hearts of the men I'd killed, I wandered around the camp, seeing if I could lend a hand. But my divine status foiled my every attempt at helpful interaction. People scrambled out of my way, mothers hurried their children into their tents, and the men gibbered in incoherent terror when I tried to help them right a tent pole or asked after the wounded. I wanted to appear unfazed by it all, but when Mextli and the men finally marched out of camp and into the growing dusk, it was a relief to finally duck into my tent and let the built-up emotions pour out.

I sat on my bed in the Divine Dream and wept. Was I becoming exactly the kind of god I despised? I loathed taking human life—I loathed taking anything of them—and yet how could I survive if I didn't?

I had no one I could talk to about this. The humans avoided me out of fear, and even if Mextli were still here, he wouldn't understand; that much was clear from his reaction to my murdering those men today. He probably wouldn't call it murder.

When one plays at war, sometimes one ends up dead, the desire reminded me.

But in my heart it felt little different.

¤

Within a few hours of Mextli leaving, I already started missing him. I'd been alone for much of the time after leaving Teotihuacan, and hadn't minded it much, but ever since my journey into Mictlan with Ehecacone, I'd come to realize just how unhappy I'd been on my own. I liked being around others, particularly those I didn't have to worry about hiding my true nature from. And while I didn't need to hide my divinity from the Mexica, they were poor company compared to Mextli; they mostly avoided me, and the one human who didn't—Xochitl—was all too eager to play servant to me. I could no more talk to her about my troubles or regrets than I could control the wind.

Not that I didn't try working on the latter. I remained at camp during the night hours, to stand guard while the women and children slept, but come morning, I went out into the desert and practiced and practiced, trying to control the wind.

But it seemed the more I tried, the worse I failed. I would have been pleased if I could make the air move just slightly, but every effort produced winds that knocked me over backwards or ripped the gnarled desert trees from the ground.

And when I blew over the camp a second time, I concluded that controlling the wind wasn't my strong suit. Imagining Quetzalcoatl sitting among the clouds, watching me and laughing at my efforts made me rage enough that by the third day Mextli was gone, I decided to give up any notion of becoming the Wind Goddess. I would have to find some other way to make good on my deal with Lord Death.

To pass the time, and keep my mind off my failures, I took to making thread from the maguey for weaving; my dress was little more than scrap cloth anymore, and I might as well have been walking around naked. Once I had enough thread to start, I fashioned a loom from sticks, and fished a smooth bone from the trash heap to use for my shuttle. I then sat in the shade of one of my magueys and worked day and night.

On the afternoon after I started, I looked up from my work to notice Xochitl watching me from the corner of my tent, a curious look on her face. When she noticed my gaze, she straightened but then knelt in supplication. "Forgive my uncouth stare, My Lady."

I waved her off. "Is there something you need?"

She shook her head as she kept it downcast. "No, My Lady. I was just…wondering what you are doing."

"I'm weaving." When she didn't immediately leave me to it, I added, "Do you wish to join me?"

She stammered a moment before blurting, "I would never presume to impose upon the Maguey Goddess."

"You're hardly imposing. I have enough thread for both of us, though we'll have to find some more sticks to make the loom." I beckoned her to come over.

She obeyed, but then hesitated to sit down. When I asked her what was wrong, she finally admitted, "I do not know how to weave, My Lady."

"At all?" When she nodded, her admission struck me dumb; I'd never known any woman who didn't have at least a rudimentary knowledge of weaving—learning to weave was something every young girl had to do, regardless of her social standing. Even Mitotia had learned to weave, and her people had been nomads like the Mexica for many generations before settling in Tollan. I'd always dismissed the claims that Chichimecs knew nothing about weaving as tired prejudice, but perhaps there was something to it. "Your mother never taught you?"

Xochitl shook her head. "My mother didn't know how either, so she couldn't teach me, of course. My grandmother knew a bit about weaving, since she was a girl when the Southern Hummingbird freed us from our servitude, but out in the desert, there is not cotton to make thread, so she never taught my mother how. The story is the same for many of us, so I suppose that's why the art has become lost." She peered down at my loom with intense interest, as if she were looking upon magic.

This was the perfect opportunity to give back to the Mexica for their worship. Xochitl was punctual in her daily offerings, and I'd felt terrible for taking it when I was doing nothing for her in return, but finally I could repay her loyalty, and do something useful for the rest of her people. "Well, that settles it. I'm going to teach you, and the rest of the women how to weave, and how to make thread from the maguey."

Xochitl looked up at me in excitement, momentarily forgetting propriety. "Truly?"

"Absolutely. First though, I need you to gather the best teachers among you, and have them meet us back here. In the meantime, I will go gather sticks to make the looms."

When I returned from the remains of the mizquitl tree I'd blown down the day before, where I'd foraged my own sticks, Xochitl was waiting for me with seven other women ranging in age from barely out of adolescence to one who looked twice as old as Nimilitzli had been when she'd died. They all looked anxious and a little scared, but once I got them gathered in a circle and demonstrated how to form the loom, the work seemed to put them at ease.

And they all proved excellent pupils. Within the hour, everyone sat working and talking as if they weren't sitting in the presence of a feared goddess, and the next morning, they all showed up before dawn, eager to learn how to make the thread.

I took them through the somewhat arduous process that involved beating the maguey leaves with wooden clubs until they split then scraping out all of the pulp until only the coarse fibers remained. We then dried them in the hot desert sun before twisting the individual strands together into thread. I also showed them how to dye the thread with the cochineal bugs found on the magueys and under the broad, paddle-like leaves of the prickly pear. As we all sat around weaving and the women talked loudly amongst themselves, it felt pleasantly like being back in the women's hall in Culhuacan with my mother. Who needed to be the Wind God anyway? I hadn't felt this contented since becoming a goddess.

Chapter Twelve

Mextli and his men returned before sunset on the sixth day, and they brought with them a line of many prisoners, both male and female. The Mexica women rushed out into the desert to greet their husbands and sons while the children ran up and down the line, gawking at the prisoners.

My own impulse was to hurry out there with them, to greet Mextli, and I was halfway to doing so when I stopped myself. What would I say to him? The women were hugging and kissing their loved ones and telling them how much they missed them, and while I'd indeed missed Mextli these last six days, I was sure he would chastise me for acting so human. So I remained back by the central fire, letting him come to me.

He nodded when he saw me, but he waited to speak until he came to stand next to me. "I trust all was well in my absence?" He didn't look at me as he spoke; instead, he surveyed the camp from his tremendous height.

"Everything was fine." I folded my arms behind my back, trying to match his indifference. "And how was your expedition?"

"Victorious." He pointed to the line of prisoners being paraded into the center of camp. "We burned their camp to the ground."

I blinked. "You wiped it out completely?" When he nodded, I choked, "What about the children?"

He shrugged. "Tlaloc ate well that night."

I thought I might become ill. "Was that really necessary?"

Mextli raised an eyebrow at me. "Our people struggle to feed their own children. We can't afford to take on more burdens."

"Then why bring the women? Why not just kill them too?"

"As the Mexica look out for my needs, I look out for theirs," Mextli said, giving me a curious look. "Children are a burden at the best of times, and taking in their enemy's children would take food from the mouths of their own children. Besides, boys become men who wish to avenge their parents. This is the way of war, Mayahuel. These people don't live in cities, surrounded by safety and plenty; their reality is a harsh one, of death and despair. Many of the men will be dragged off to the sacrifice, but most of the women will perish trying to bring more humans into this world. If the tribe is to survive and fulfill its destiny, more women must take their place. This is reality."

I almost snapped off at him, but even in my own head I understood his logic. Which made it all the worse to me; it was that same logic that had driven Black Otter to murder my son.

"Forgive me," I mumbled, desperate to be alone as tears started stinging my eyes. "I'm tired, so I'm going back to my tent." And without waiting for his answer to my ludicrous claim, I hurried away.

I threw aside the flap and immediately summoned the Divine Dream, surrounding myself in the familiar sight of my old quarters back in Tollan. Its familiarity comforted me; I could even hear Ehecacone making animal noises out on the portico while he played, as he often had; I knew he wasn't really there, but it didn't matter. The memory brought joy to squelch the terrible pain swelling in my chest. Someday soon I would have my son back and that awful hole in my heart would finally heal.

And yet seeing the mural of Quetzalcoatl on the wall before my bed reminded me of just how far off I was from my dreams. My rage grew, and I wished the painting would just go away.

And as if had been commanded, the image slowly faded away until only the white plaster remained. When I looked around, everything that had been imagery of Quetzalcoatl was gone now; no wooden idol, no blankets woven with serpent patterns. Even the obsidian mirror that hung on the wall near the doorway out into the family garden had lost the silver snakes encircling it. The room now was blank and cold.

Let's fix that, the desire suggested, and a painting started forming on the wall opposite my bed, bleeding outward from the center like watered ink on fig-bark paper. I watched with fascination as the colors and lines slowly coalesced into the same image as on my door curtain. All around me, the room transformed in richness and color; stylized rabbits and butterflies danced across the walls, leaving trails of painted landscapes, plants, and animals in their wake; a giant maguey blossom pattern slowly wove into the blankets under me, and a wooden idol of myself sprouted out of the stone floor, the bowl in my hands slowly filling with octli.

But the more images of myself appeared, the more uncomfortable I grew with the self-absorbedness of it all.

This is our temple, the desire chided me. *The humans will expect it to be decorated as such.*

That was true enough.

I lay on my bed, just listening to my son out in the garden for what felt forever before Mextli's voice drifted in from beyond the Divine Dream, asking permission to come inside. It was on the tip of my tongue to tell him to go away, but the desire stopped me. *If we ever want to get Ehecacone back—especially since our other plan is a complete failure— we need help.*

I sat up, pulling my knees to my chest. "Come in."

Mextli pushed aside the curtain from the garden and stepped inside, taking in my Divine Dream with stoic eyes. "Forgive my intrusion...and my earlier insensitivity. I should have realized it would be a painful topic for you."

I smiled wanly, glad for his words. "No, I'm sorry. It was just...difficult to hear...."

"Well, you have spent most of your life drowning in the black-and-white philosophy of the Feathered Serpent, but once you meet the other gods, you'll see his way isn't the only right and just one."

I'd never thought of Quetzalcoatl's ways as being so strident, but perhaps that was why I'd had such difficulty living up to them. "I suppose so."

"Can you forgive me?"

"For what?"

"For never extending my condolences, about your son. I'm sure you know this already but...he won't be dead forever. Gods never really die, not the way humans do."

I nodded.

"He'll come back someday."

"He will, and much sooner than someday." When Mextli cocked his head, I said, "I made a deal, with Lord Death."

Mextli furrowed his brow. "It's never a good idea to make deals with Lord Death."

"I know, but he has Ehecacone, and I want him back—more than I want anything."

"What must you do to fulfill your end of the bargain?"

I sucked in a deep breath then exhaled loudly. "I have to bring him Quetzalcoatl, to trade for my son."

Mextli shook his head, a frown on his face. "Mayahuel, you've taken on a task beyond your ilk."

"I know, but he wouldn't accept anything less, and I can't renegotiate—I either deliver the Feathered Serpent, or Lord Death keeps Ehecacone forever. He's threatened to take his revenge against Quetzalcoatl on my son if I don't—" My throat constricted, cutting off my words.

Mextli's expression darkened. "Dishonorable."

I nodded. "I thought maybe if I could depose Quetzalcoatl as the Wind God, that would make it easier to capture him, but I'm really quite useless with controlling the wind—"

"Element control takes much practice, but yes, your plan was foolhardy. The Feathered Serpent's mastery of the wind element is legendary."

I looked away, feeling foolish. "You're right, of course, but I have no other plan now, and I thought perhaps with your help—"

"Even the two of us working together can't take on the Feathered Serpent. For all of our power, we are but small gods in comparison. Smoking Mirror, on the other hand, has magic neither of us could ever hope to possess."

The hair on my nape stood on end. "Surely one of the other gods would be willing—"

"And why should they care about Lord Death holding the son of the Feathered Serpent hostage? Quetzalcoatl has taken much from us. If anything, letting Lord Death keep Ehecacone would be a bonus, for then he can't seek revenge for his father losing this war."

"Ehecacone doesn't care about his father. He knows the kind of god he is; he knows what he did to me, and that he didn't care enough to protect him. My son is no threat to anyone."

"Who we are changes over time, along with our experiences, Mayahuel. You—of all people—know that."

I bit my lip. "Then you won't help me?"

"I will help you, but like I said, we can't do this alone."

"But not Smoking Mirror," I insisted.

He sighed. "Very well. We can speak to the other gods, but don't expect anything. Regardless though, I will help you in any way I can."

I smiled, growing warm inside. "Thank you. You're a good friend."

He blinked at me, startled.

"Haven't you any friends?" When he hesitated, I asked, "Not even Smoking Mirror?"

"Smoking Mirror is solitary in nature, and while he did give me his time when he first created me, as you've pointed out before, he never does anything out of kindness, or just to do it; there is a purpose behind every action, every word he utters, which is why it's very wise to not rush into dealing with him. Nor have I had much interaction with the other gods. Being so young and untested, I don't even have a place in Omeyocan to call my own."

"Well, neither do I."

"That's not true. Everyone calls the garden where you were kept the Earth Monster's garden, but in fact it is yours."

"Really?"

He nodded. "You built it with your teotl, so that makes it yours. The Earth Monster was your guest."

I looked up to see the ceiling of my room had become transparent and I could look up at Omeyocan floating among the clouds. "I have a home!"

"Indeed." He looked up too, but with a frown.

"I'm sure you'll get your own place up there soon," I assured him.

"Not likely."

"Why not?"

"Because I would have to depose one of the gods, or marry one of them."

"Marry?"

He nodded. "Among the gods, marriage is a formal sharing of power, but it is an alliance never to be entered into lightly."

"Why not?"

"Because while you inherit the power of your partner, your power is no longer yours alone."

"Sounds more equitable than most human marriages," I said. "But how is it that I have a place up in Heaven and you don't? You're more powerful than me."

"I know I've called you young before, but in truth, you're a very old goddess. You were born before the humans came, when the world was still primordial and going through its first throes of life. You were there from the beginning, in the garden, waiting for that fateful day when the Feathered Serpent liberated you for his own nefarious purposes. I, on the other hand, have been around barely two bundles of years yet."

I turned to study the feathers on the side of his face. "I'm sorry."

He met my gaze. "For what?"

"That things should be so unfair."

He shrugged. "I'm content with my lot; my humans are dedicated and loyal, I have the respect of most of the gods, and now I have a friend." He smiled, proud.

I smiled back. "Indeed you do."

He broke into a grin. "I must admit you had me concerned when you left. When gods speak of sleeping, they mean death, and they don't return from it for hundreds of bundles of years."

"Sometimes I feel like it," I admitted.

"Why ever would you want to do that? You're doing so well here. I noticed you've been teaching the women new skills, and they seem rather happy about it."

"That's one of the admirable things about humans; they're always thirsty for new knowledge."

"And that is why we're here, to give them the things they couldn't get on their own."

His wording gave me pause though. I'd seen both men and women create and destroy of their own free will, and it seemed arrogant to believe that these people couldn't figure out something like weaving if not for me. After all, I'd learned the skill from my own human mother, who had learned it from her mother, generation after generation. Funny, it was humanity who had taught a goddess such an important art form.

"I'd invite you to tonight's feast, but I realize that the accompanying activities will make you uncomfortable, so I won't begrudge you remaining here instead," Mextli said. "I will give your priest your share of the prisoners, and be sure to feed well tonight."

"Why?"

"Because tomorrow I'm taking you to Omeyocan, to meet the other gods."

◻

Once Mextli left, I stepped outside to see Xihuitl hovering nearby with five other men, watching my tent anxiously. When I met his gaze, he hurried forward and prostrated himself upon the ground at my feet. "My Lady, it is so good to see you again!"

"It's good to see you too," I replied, uncomfortable; not so much that he was bowing and scraping to me; as the Queen of Tollan, I'd been accustomed to such behavior, but he exuded anxiety as if he were facing judgment rather than greeting me. "Please, rise and speak your mind," I insisted.

He hurried to his feet again, but kept his gaze downcast. "I'm pleased to inform you that my expedition with the other men went well, and I captured a sacrifice for you." He beckoned to the others—two of them Mexica warriors, one holding a rope tied around the necks of two ratty-dressed warriors with their hands bound while the second man hustled the third prisoner forward until they stood directly behind Xihuitl, so my priest could present his gift with a sweep of his arms.

I looked the prisoner over, the desire slithering up on me. He was larger than Xihuitl, and much more muscular; I couldn't imagine my scrawny priest taking on this man, even bound as he was. He regarded me with wary eyes—one of them blackened—and a hint of distaste. "And you captured him yourself?" the desire asked Xihuitl as an amused smile slid to my lips.

Xihuitl face lit with unabashed pride. "I did, My Lady. Not that he was by any means an easy mark, and he nearly took my head off with his bare hands, but sometimes being small and smart has its advantages." When I didn't reply, he watched me examining his prize with a critical eye for a moment before blurting out, "Does he please you, My Lady?"

"We'll find out soon enough," the desire growled, baring my teeth. "And these other two?"

"Gifts from Lord Mextli."

"Good. I'll start with yours." I stepped aside and held the tent flap open.

The warrior shoved his prisoner roughly inside then retreated quickly back to the edge of the clearing, as if being so close to me scared him. It made the desire chuckle. "When I'm finished with him, bring me another one." Without waiting for an answer, I ducked inside.

From his kneeling position, the man looked up at me with a mixture of loathing and fear, but when I knelt to stroke his cheek lovingly, his resistance melted slowly away. "Don't worry. I'm not going to hurt you; if anything, you're going to feel the greatest pleasure you've ever known." He met my mouth hungrily when I leaned in to kiss him.

When I reemerged from my tent a handful of moments later, hunger still whispered plaintively in my belly and the desire was already thinking about who to have Xihuitl bring next. But then I looked up to see Red Hawk pacing at the entrance to the clearing, looking agitated as Xihuitl kept blocking his way. When he saw me, the frown on his face deepened and his complexion darkened. "What are you doing?"

The desire sneered. "And why would that be any of your business, you insolent little man?"

This time when Xihuitl tried to block him, Red Hawk punched him in the gut, sending him to his knees in surprise. Red Hawk closed the gap between us in a bounding jog but he stopped in front of me, his shoulders heaving as if he were holding back an animal. "You were not in my tent when I returned, as you should be.

That is unacceptable. Perhaps men in your old village tolerated such disrespectful behavior from their wives, but we Mexica do not!"

I laughed. "You think I'm your wife?"

"I've taken you to bed; that makes you my wife."

"Then I must be married to the man in my tent, for he's pleasured me too. And he was much better at it than you."

Red Hawk stared at me aghast, but then he grabbed me by the arm. Jealousy oozed off him like a pungent odor, but it only riled the desire more. "I shall have him killed," he hissed between clenched teeth. "You are mine! You hear me?"

Behind Red Hawk, Xihuitl had regained his feet and drew his knife, but I smiled at him, a deadly calm coursing through me. "It's quite alright, Xihuitl," I assured him. "I can handle him myself."

Red Hawk snarled a laugh. "Handle me, will you?" He yanked me by the arm, heading back into camp. "We'll see who gets handled, woman."

Xihuitl lunged forward a step, ready to attack Red Hawk, but I shot him a cold look that stopped him short just before Red Hawk hustled me by.

As we wound through camp, to the tents pitched around the central fire, people stopped their work to watch Red Hawk hurry me along. The desire kept the smile locked on my lips despite the shocked stares and scandalized whispers. When we reached Red Hawk's tent, he thrashed the flap aside and manhandled me inside.

Now alone, he hissed, "How dare you humiliate me in front of another man?" He maintained his stony grip on my arm. "Have you no idea who I am, woman?"

"I know exactly who you are," the desire said with a sultry smirk that gave him pause. I traced my fingers down his chest, sending a shudder through him until he let me go, then I shoved him over backwards onto the ground.

He gasped, appalled, but when I banished my clothing with a flick of my fingers then straddled him, the objections left his eyes. As I started riding him with increasing speed, the desire added, "You're a sacrifice, of course."

Before he could respond, the wave of pleasure and energy surged over me. He gasped in ecstasy too, but as the desire drew more and more out of him, he started writhing and pushing at me, trying to get me off him.

But the desire bared my teeth and drew harder from him, digging my fingernails into his muscular shoulders as I continued holding him down. "Don't close your eyes, human," she hissed. "You *will* look upon the face of the power you disrespected!"

Red Hawk opened his eyes again and when he beheld my terrible glory, the abject horror in his eyes stoked the desire to new heights—especially when I thought of those dreams about draining King Red Flint to nothing. It was intoxicating.

And yet a terrible fear rose in my heart as I watched Red Hawk dying. What was I doing? *Stop!*

The desire only drew harder, and Red Hawk cried out for mercy, his voice weaker with each breath.

I said stop! When she still didn't let go of him, I tried wrestling control of my own body back from her.

She fought me, but only long enough to draw the last gasping breath from Red Hawk, then I snapped back into control. The feel of his cooling flesh between my legs sent a spike of disgust and despair through me and I couldn't scramble away quickly enough. I huddled at the flap, staring at him as he lay deathly still, his skin a sickly pale color. "How could you...?" I whispered.

He manhandled us, the desire spat. *We've put up with enough of that in our mortal life, and I won't let us spend eternity accepting more of it. You have no spine. He got what he deserved, and my only regret is that I didn't do it in front of the whole village, so everyone will know what happens to those who disrespect us.*

"This is not who I am!" The desire growled, annoyed, but before she could say anything more, I added, "You are nothing but a scream in the night, trying to manipulate everyone with fear and threats. And I have no need of you! The world has no need of you!"

If not for me, you would have died a mortal long ago. Intellect is nothing without the primal; men can build great cities and write beautiful poetry, but without the primal to create new life, to protect it, in a generation the earth would swallow it all back, gone and forgotten. For having wasted so much time studying the dualistic nature of existence in that human school, you certainly didn't listen to its lessons, did you?

"You're the reason humans harm each other," I snarled. "You're the reason women live every day in fear for their safety! You're the reason men like Red Flint and Red Hawk think they can do whatever they want, whenever they want, to whomever they want. You are no better than Smoking Mirror!"

The desire bristled. *How dare you—*

"How dare *you* even think you're anything worthwhile when all you do is damage everything you touch. I don't need you; I don't want *you* inside my head, and the world would be better off without you. So be gone already!"

Have it your way. And we'll see just how long you last.

"I will survive just fine," I fired back, but she didn't answer.

I felt strangely empty inside, as if something had sucked the very energy out of me. Much like I'd felt after losing Ehecacone. It left me unnerved, and yet relieved too. So long I'd just wanted her gone, had wanted to be left in peace from her sarcastic taunts and self-serving rapacity, and now finally I was free.

CHAPTER THIRTEEN

 When I met with Mextli outside his tent the next morning before dawn, I must have looked as anxious as I felt, for he asked, "Are you all right?"

"I'm fine." My voice cracked a bit though; I was nervous about meeting the other gods, and my anxiety about it only increased now that the time was upon me.

He raised his eye brow at me. "And you fed properly?"

My face flushed with guilt as memories of last night resurfaced. "Sufficiently."

I could tell by the look on his face that he knew I was hiding something, but he let it go. He held his hand out to me. "This first time, I will guide you. Like with using the teoyoh, you need to feel the stream of energy to know where to go."

Logic told me I could trust Mextli—I'd even declared him my friend last night—and yet when I went to take his hand, an inexplicable fear gripped me.

"You're sure nothing is wrong?"

"I'm just nervous…about going to Omeyocan. What if we run into Quetzalcoatl? I'm not ready to face him yet."

"You needn't worry about that happening."

"Why not?"

"The Feathered Serpent has been absent from Omeyocan for a while now, tending to his schemes here on earth, so you needn't worry about encountering him today."

Quetzalcoatl had said we couldn't be together outside the Divine Dream until he'd finished certain business, and the last time I'd seen him, he'd said nothing to suggest that business was complete. Surely he would have come to see me "in the flesh" if he had.

"Don't worry, Mayahuel. The Feathered Serpent can't hurt you anymore." Mextli gave me a confident smile.

I returned the gesture, though without the same confidence. And when I took his hand, that desirous reaction I'd had the first time was completely absent now; his feathers were itchy, and the thought of him touching more of my body with it left me disgusted rather than making my heart race. What did it mean?

"Shall we go now?" Mextli asked, a hint of impatience to his voice.

"I'm ready." As ready as I was likely to ever be, anyway.

◻

Traveling to Omeyocan wasn't much different than traveling anywhere else, except that it took a great deal more energy. The currents of the teoyoh were strong here, reminding me of lazy summer days spent watching the clouds crawl across the blue sky. The whole landscape felt suspended in time; the water ran over falls slow as honey, and bees and butterflies bobbed through the air as if they hadn't a care in the world.

The place resembled earth and yet looked nothing like it at the same time: there were temples, but they weren't perched atop pyramids, and some were constructed of ridiculous building materials, such as feathers and clouds and smoke. Plants both familiar and alien grew everywhere, sometimes so thick that the buildings were mere flashes of color and light between the trunks of giant trees.

Because my grandmother had kept me locked in the garden, I'd seen none of this when I'd lived here; even when I'd scaled the garden's wall to escape, I'd not bothered to look back at my home when I reached the top. I'd been far more concerned with seeing the face of the mysterious voice that had asked me to leave with him. The familiar energy buzzing in this alien environment piqued my anxiety and I tightened my grip on Mextli's hand.

"Don't worry, I won't let you go," he said, a serious expression on his face. "It takes practice to learn to hold oneself on the divine plane."

"So if I let go of you—?"

"You would fall back to earth."

I blinked. "So we aren't just here in our heads?"

"Omeyocan is the nexus of the material and the spiritual, where the two meet. It is the gateway to the Divine Dream in one direction, and the gateway to the human world from the other. It is the place where we are at our truest divine manifestation, but until you can accept that without the slightest question, you cannot remain here. By holding onto me, my faith will shield you from that."

I looked around, not quite understanding, but tightened my grip on him further. "Would the fall kill me?"

"No, but it isn't fun."

"You fell?"

The feathers on his arm ruffled a bit as he admitted, "Smoking Mirror let me fall the first time he brought me to Omeyocan."

I stared at him, gape-jawed. "He *let you*?"

"He told me the fastest way to gain faith is through fear."

That sounded like Smoking Mirror.

"And he was right; after that I never questioned, I just accepted. Come, let me show you around. Everyone is eager to meet you."

The ground felt solid under my feet as we walked, but when I looked down, the stones dissolved into clouds, and the earth looked so vast and distant below. The sight made my magic tingle unpleasantly, so I resolved to not look down again.

The path wound through a forest of trees painted unnatural blues, reds, and yellows; some even shined with a light all their own. We climbed a flight of winding stone stairs and emerged above a second set of cloud banks. Spread out before us was a village, each house different and all surrounded by gardens. In the distance I spotted the tall stone walls of my garden.

Another house sat near it, perched upon a high hill of rocks and swirling clouds. I couldn't distinguish many details from this distance, but judging from the way the sun hit it, the walls were one continuous curve rather than flat and angular.

It was on the tip of my tongue to ask whose house that was when a woman leaped out of the trees next to the path and landed gracefully in front of us, like a puma springing from a branch. Flowers of every color covered her like a dress, and their aromatic perfume wafted off in visible trails as she moved. Her skin pulsed orange, like my own, and her long black hair swirled around her as if caught in a perpetual soft breeze.

Mextli stopped short, looking annoyed. She smiled coyly and looked around him, searching. "Where's Smoking Mirror?" Her voice was a curious mix of innocent and sultry.

"Not here," Mextli replied, an edge to his voice.

"Pity." Her gaze finally came to me and her pout instantly turned into a smile. "And who's this?"

"Mayahuel, of course." Mextli turned to me to add, "And this is Xochiquetzal."

I opened my mouth to give a greeting, but Xochiquetzal broke into an ecstatic dance and clapped her hands. "Mayahuel! Oh my! You're a love goddess too, aren't you? Oh, what am I saying; you are *the* love goddess!" Her bright smile and gushing admiration irritated me, but I smiled back, as was expected. "We have *so* much to talk about!"

"We do?" I finally managed, polite but confused.

But before Xochiquetzal could answer, Mextli pulled me along. "We haven't time for distractions today, Xochiquetzal. Mayahuel hasn't been back in many years and she's just relearning how to be here, so we can't stay long and we have many people to see."

She skipped to keep up with us. "Then you want to see Xochipilli too?" A swirl of pollen and fragrance enveloped us, making my nose itch, and I suddenly understood Mextli's annoyance.

Mextli swatted it away as if it were a swarm of pesky insects. "Eventually, yes, but not today. I'm taking her to see Nanahuatzin. We have business."

She giggled. "What kind of business?"

"Business that doesn't concern you."

"When is Smoking Mirror coming back?"

"When he feels like it. Now along with you!"

Xochiquetzal twirled like a young girl, her face glowing so bright it hurt my eyes. "You will tell him I asked after him, won't you?"

"He cares not."

"You always say that, you feathery giant, but we both know better. I've seen how he looks at me." She pranced up and took hold of my free arm. "I'll come see you down in the desert, when your dear hummingbird isn't quite so agitated. We have *much* to talk about." She kissed my cheek—a soft, sensual touch that left my stomach churning—then she vanished, leaving behind a shower of flower petals and perfume.

Mextli sighed and walked faster, the better to leave the fragrant precipitation behind us.

"Is she always so...excitable?" I asked.

"Annoyingly so. I don't know how Xochipilli puts up with her."

"Xochipilli?"

"Her brother, the Flower Prince. He's annoying too, what with his dancing and playing music all the time, but he's at least rational. There's no talking to her."

"Meaning?"

"You heard her. She talks about nothing, and does it with near insanity."

"She doesn't strike me as insane," I replied. "Flighty, yes, but not insane. Not everyone is interested in war."

"Nor is everyone interested in the banality of physical attraction and sex."

And one can hardly make judgments without having tried it to begin with, the desire would have said, but without her around anymore, I found myself silently agreeing with him. I was suddenly very aware of the unpleasant itchiness of his feathered hand against mine and had to suppress the overwhelming urge to wrench my hand away.

The path climbed a gentle slope of clouds, up to a temple built on a mountaintop. Up here the sun blazed hot—far hotter than a mortal could stand—and I had to shield my eyes from the glare with my free hand. Mextli seemed unperturbed by the heat and light; if anything, his feathers shimmered all the brighter, and a contented smile tugged at his half-blue lips. Thankfully we soon stepped into the shade of the temple entrance, whose ceiling was held aloft upon giant pillars bearing carvings in the likeness of Tonatiuh the Sun.

Inside, a god nearly as big as Mextli himself sat up on a golden throne, swigging from a gold cup. He glowed pale red, nearly matching the skin that hung in tatters from his body. The room smelled of heat and sickness; not wholly unexpected, given he was a leper.

Mextli knelt, sweeping the fingers of his free hand across the stone floor. "It is a great pleasure to see you again, Lord Nanahuatzin."

Nanahuatzin sniffed and took another drink, but once he swallowed, he peered down at me with contempt. "Well, if it isn't the meddlesome Maguey Goddess. And she doesn't even bow for me."

I looked at Mextli, confused, but when he cast me a chastising glare, I went to my knees too. "My apologies, My Lord. I'm still learning our ways."

"I thought you were teaching her, Mextli," Nanahuatzin said.

"I am, but the process is slow. The gaps in her knowledge aren't always readily apparent," Mextli replied.

Nanahuatzin snapped his fingers and a tiny skeleton scurried out from behind the throne, carrying a golden jug, which he used to refill the Sun God's cup. "Pour for our guests as well, Paynal," the Sun God ordered then returned to swigging.

Paynal hurried down off the dais to us. He summoned two cups and filled them one at a time as they floated in the air between us. He then sent them to our hands with a flick of his bony finger. Without a word, he scampered back to his master's throne and disappeared behind it.

I looked down into the cup, thinking it was blood, but in fact it was xocolatl, with a bit of blood mixed in, to give it a deeper red color. I really didn't want it, but didn't want to be rude either—especially given my earlier mistake—so I sipped it politely.

I loved xocolatl, and wasn't sure what to expect with the blood added to it, but I didn't expect to feel as indifferent as I did now. Surely xocolatl made by the gods themselves wasn't so tasteless and uninteresting? And yet each drink had less impact than the last.

"Allow me to be the first to extend you a warm welcome back home, Mayahuel," Nanahuatzin said. "You were kept in Mictlan far too long."

I bowed my head. "Thank you, My Lord."

"Mextli tells me you have a matter to discuss with me."

I glanced at Mextli, confused, but when he mouthed *Ehecacone*, I felt foolish. Of course. That was the entire reason we'd come here today. "I do indeed, and thank you for taking my audience, My Lord," I started, the nervousness swelling again. "I...well, as you might know, I have a son—"

"The one sired by the Feathered Serpent, yes, I'm aware of him."

"Yes, Quetzalcoatl is his father, and...his name is Ehecacone, and...well, right now he's in Mictlan, being held by Lord Death—"

"I'm aware of that as well," Nanahuatzin cut in. "I'm also aware that Mictlantecuhtli is refusing to revive him."

"Well...he's not so much refusing as demanding an exchange to do so. And that's why I've come to speak with you today."

Nanahuatzin chuckled. "I may be the leader of the gods, Mayahuel, but I have no power over Lord Death or his realm, no more than he has power over the living realm." He raised his free hand to gesture around him. "I'm sorry, but I cannot make him resurrect your son for you."

"I understand that, which is why I came to ask your help with fulfilling his demand."

"And what would that be?"

"He will only accept the Feathered Serpent in trade for my son's life."

"And how exactly am I to help you with that?"

The question left me speechless for a moment before I finally admitted, "I don't really know, My Lord. I was hoping you might have some ideas of your own."

Nanahuatzin swigged down more xocolatl then lounged back on his golden icpalli, looking thoughtful. "I'm not unsympathetic to your plight, Mayahuel, but I'm afraid that I cannot help you with this. As the leader of our kind, I must display a certain amount of magnanimousness, and I simply cannot inject myself in a dispute that will see one god imprisoned in order to set another free, especially when that god did nothing to facilitate the other's imprisonment."

I furrowed my brow. "You mean since Quetzalcoatl didn't kill Ehecacone, you won't help me?"

"Precisely."

I stammered a moment before blurting out, "What about what he did to me?"

"I don't know what you mean."

"He fed me to the earth monster!"

Nanahuatzin chuckled. "The earth monster killed you, not the Feathered Serpent. After all, you willingly went to earth with him, so if anyone spurred Tzitzimitl on, it was you."

Rationally I knew I should feel outraged at him blaming me for my own death, but the emotion never came. I felt only guilt and shame, and a further swelling of the fear.

"For her crimes, Tzitzimitl has been Lord Death's guest for thousands of bundles of years, so justice was done. Are you not thankful for that?"

Tears stung at my eyes but I held them back, afraid he would laugh at me further if I broke down. "I am, My Lord."

He set his cup on the floor next to his icpalli then leaned towards me, elbows on his knees. "It is not that I don't believe the Feathered Serpent is beyond reproach; his actions of late make it very clear that he does a poor job of thinking about his fellow gods, about their needs and the grand traditions that our worship among the humans is built upon. Personally, I begrudge his telling me how humans should worship me, as if his way is the only right one. But if I step up and help you with this, I would be thumbing my nose at those who came before you requesting my help with his selfish ways. You are far from the first god to request that I do something about him. I, however, by necessity must stay out of such disputes."

"Even when he's being treasonous against all of the gods?"

Nanahuatzin chuckled then said to Mextli, "I see you've been whispering Smoking Mirror's words in her ears. Perhaps she should ask him for help."

The thought sent a shudder through me. "I don't want his help."

"And I can understand why," Nanahuatzin said, leaning back against his throne. "Do you have any further business to discuss with me?"

I looked to Mextli, but he shook his head. "I guess not, My Lord."

"Then, if you'll excuse me, I have other matters to attend to." Nanahuatzin vanished with a snap.

I sighed. "That hardly went well."

Mextli shrugged. "Nanahuatzin is a politician, so his response is hardly surprising. It was worth a try though." As we walked back outside, into the blinding sun, he added, "A point in your favor though is that he didn't forbid you from pursuing the matter, which means he believes your case has some merit to it. We are then free to continue trying to find others who are willing to help."

"Who else can we ask?"

"There are a few of the older gods we can perhaps sway, like Xipe Totec, or Tlaloc. Though I have reservations about involving the Rain God."

"Why?"

"Because he's flighty at the best of times. His loyalties are easily swayed by whatever will benefit him at the moment."

"An opportunist?" I offered.

"Of the worst variety. He served Quetzalcoatl's plots so long as it suited him, but as soon as support for Smoking Mirror's opposition to this power-grab increased, Tlaloc changed his position. His only interest is in making sure he's on the winning side."

We followed the path down off the mountain, to where it ran parallel to a river, but when we reached the junction, the water suddenly rose up, forming a throne upon which sat a woman in a blue dress that matched her icy glow. She smiled with regal confidence, her back straight and her dress cascading over her shoulders in waterfalls that formed a foaming pool in her lap. "Back again so soon, Mextli? Shame on you! Tlaloc is going to get suspicious of us!"

Mextli glared at her. "There's hardly anything to be suspicious of."

"Always so coy, aren't you?" She laughed then slid off her watery throne. Her smile evaporated when she turned her cool gaze upon me. "This is her then? The Feathered Serpent's little...woman?" Without waiting for an answer, she went on, "You probably know me as Jade Skirt, Goddess of Rivers, Lakes, and the Seas." She held her hand out to me as if expecting me to kiss it.

I stared at it, consumed by inexplicable dread. She smelled of brine and the algae skimmed off Lake Metzliapan that merchants made into cakes to sell in the market. Just being near her set my flesh crawling.

Her smile broadened but she withdrew her hand. "So, what brings you back so soon then?" she asked Mextli while still scrutinizing me like a caiman hunting a small deer drinking at the banks of a lake.

"We had business to discuss with Nanahuatzin, and now we're going to go speak with Xipe Totec."

"And what business would that be?"

Mextli looked at me, as if asking if I wanted to make my case for aid to Jade Skirt, but her piercing stare unsettled me to my very core. I wanted to get away from her as quickly as possible.

When I failed to speak, Mextli replied, "Mayahuel requires some assistance retrieving her son from Lord Death."

"The one her dearest Black Otter killed?" She smiled wide.

Behind her, Black Otter suddenly slunk out of the water and walked towards me, but he stopped next to Jade Skirt and pressed his long body against her leg like a dog seeking attention. His shiny black eyes remained fixed on me though, his lips pulled back in a silent snarl.

To me, Jade Skirt said, "Do you like what I did to your former husband, Mayahuel? His name is so very fitting now, isn't it? He always wanted to be king, and now he is—of all other otters."

Mextli glared at Black Otter as he hissed "Mine" softly.

"And how do you like the hand on the tail addition? As I understand it, he was always a very *grabby* man." Jade Skirt broke into cackling laughter.

Her amusement should have infuriated me, but I felt oddly hollow. "You should have just let him die in the lake."

She pressed on as if I hadn't spoken at all. "I think I shall make more of him. I'm not as famous as my husband, so I don't get very many sacrifices, but with more Black Otters in the lakes and streams—all pulling fishermen from their boats and drowning them in my name—that is most certainly something to consider."

"Can we please go?" I muttered to Mextli, tightening my grip on his hand in my growing anxiety.

He hesitated but then said, "Forgive us, but we must be going. This is Mayahuel's first time back, and so the visit should be short." We then continued on, though when I glanced back at Jade Skirt, she blew a kiss that squirted water into my face.

Once we were far enough away that she couldn't hear us anymore, I asked, "What did I do to her, to deserve that kind of treatment?"

"One doesn't have to do anything," Mextli replied. "It just amuses her to confound the other gods."

"So that's what the whole making Tlaloc suspicious of you bit is about? You two aren't...?" I looked at him questioningly.

He frowned, puzzled. "We aren't what?"

I thought to explain, but in truth I had no feelings whatsoever about it, even if they were a couple. Strange, given my earlier enamored thoughts about him. "Never mind."

"Then let us hurry. Xipe Totec's house isn't far now."

□

In fact, Xipe Totec's house wasn't really a house at all; it was a maize field that stretched for hundreds of paces, butting up right next to the tall stone walls of my hidden garden. When I again spotted the round house on the mountain overlooking it, Mextli informed me that was Quetzalcoatl's house. He glared at it as we walked, adding to my sense of dread that grew oddly stronger the closer we came to it and my garden. We stopped a ways down the road from them though.

"Before you meet Xipe Totec, there are some things you should know," Mextli said. "Like Tlaloc, he initially supported Quetzalcoatl's reforms on earth, but he's since changed his allegiance. I think he might be amenable to helping you because he left Quetzalcoatl's cause out of disillusionment rather than cowardice. He in particular took a significant hit to his power under the Feathered Serpent's reforms."

I supposed that made sense. The cult of Xipe Totec had started to decline in power once Little Reed and I had moved to Tollan, mainly out of a lack of volunteers for the sacrifices. Seems very few people wanted to be driven through with arrows and then have their bodies flayed to honor the God of Agriculture.

We'd stopped halfway up the maize field, and now Mextli stepped down into the ditch where he held the vibrant green stocks aside like a door curtain, inviting me to step into the shaded row. The air was pungent with the smell of peat, and my bare toes sunk a bit into the spongy earth as we made our way towards the center of the field.

Xipe Totec sat upon the ground in a small clearing, bent over a maize seedling like a doting father. He wore a bloody human skin draped over his golden glowing shoulders like a cape, and he whispered cooingly as he let blood from it drip upon the seedling. A smell of fertile earth and water lingered about him. He only looked up when Mextli called out to him, but even then, he showed only mild interest in us. "And what brings you here today, Southern Hummingbird?" he asked as he returned to caring for his plant.

"Someone has come to meet with you." He pulled me forward a bit, so I stood in front of him, and for a moment I thought perhaps I was expected to bow. "May I present Mayahuel, the Maguey Goddess."

"I know who she is," Xipe Totec said without looking up. "Nonetheless, a pleasure to finally officially meet you, My Lady."

After a hesitation, I answered, "Likewise."

Xipe Totec scooped up a handful of dirt and rubbed it between his palms then dusted it away on his thighs as he stood up. He wasn't much taller than me, and under that cape of skin he looked completely human. And though I recognized that he was handsome, I felt nothing about it; not even a slight interest.

"It must feel good to be back home after so long," he said with a smile. He cast his gaze towards the walls of my garden visible above the tall maize stalks around us.

I looked too, but that lack of caring continued. "I suppose."

When no one spoke next, Mextli nudged me.

"What?"

With a pointed look, he asked, "Don't you have some business to discuss with him?"

The thought of having to go through the story all over again—especially knowing it would likely do me no good—annoyed me, but I pressed on anyway. I recapped my dilemma with Lord Death, doing my best to not drag the explanations out, even as Xipe Totec listened patiently, the look on his face as indifferent as I felt inside. Once I finished, I sighed, glad to have that over with.

Xipe Totec scraped the dirt with the big toe of his right foot. "You have my sympathies for your troubles, Mayahuel, but I'm afraid I wouldn't be much help. Because of the reforms you and Quetzalcoatl instituted in Tollan—which have since filtered out into the rest of the Tolteca cities—my power reserves are precarious; it will take years for me to regain what I lost. Not that I'm complaining: I made the ill-advised decision to support Quetzalcoatl's reforms, so now I must reap the crop I planted. However, I'm in no position to go head-to-head with a god as powerful as Quetzalcoatl, particularly when the aim is to give him over to the one god who has the power to trap him indefinitely. I know you wish for your son's return, but I hope you will heed my warning when I say perhaps that isn't worth getting yourself killed by the Feathered Serpent all over again."

He has a point, I thought, but didn't say it aloud. It felt mildly wrong to think like that.

"If you must pursue this, you should seek Smoking Mirror's aid. I think you will find he is the only one who is willing—and able—to take on Quetzalcoatl at this point."

"How would he be able to do anything, really?" I asked, annoyed. "He doesn't even have a place up here in Omeyocan."

Xipe Totec shrugged. "When one has nothing to lose.... And Mayahuel, only fools underestimate Smoking Mirror."

I harrumphed. "May we go?" I asked Mextli.

The darkness crossed Mextli's face—momentarily replacing my indifference with a hint of fear—but then he said, "I suppose that's enough visits for today." To Xipe Totec, he added, "This is her first time back."

Xipe Totec nodded. "I'm sorry I can't be of more help, Mayahuel."

I shrugged, eager to be on my way.

Mextli tightened his grip on my hand enough that it might have crushed it had I been mortal still. "Thank you for your time, Lord Flayed One." Then without another word, he pulled us into the teoyoh.

A blink later we came out back in the Mexica camp and to my relief he immediately let me go. My hand felt unpleasantly itchy from his feathers, and I took to rubbing it against my thigh, as if trying to wipe off the sensation.

"Is everything all right with you?" he asked, watching me with his dark gaze.

"Everything is fine," I replied. I added a bright smile to it to appease the suspicious look on his face.

He scrutinized me a moment more before finally saying, "I'm sorry things didn't go better with the others. At least no one is furious with you; I was concerned that might happen, given your role in the Feathered Serpent's power-grab."

I shrugged.

"Tomorrow we'll go back and see a few more of our kin, but I must warn you that I haven't high hopes that we'll fare any better than today. I thought Xipe Totec and Nanahuatzin were our best chance of success."

"Then perhaps we shouldn't even bother."

"I wouldn't say that. Someone might surprise us. In the meantime, you should go feed, because tomorrow you're going to hold yourself up while in Omeyocan."

Good. Then I won't have to hold his feathered hand anymore, I thought as I walked back to my tent. Rationally I knew the thought was completely out of character given my earlier attraction to him—and that it should worry me—but even that realization produced no emotional reaction from me. Instead I crawled inside and lay staring up at the ceiling, watching the sun's glow travel across the buckskin. I didn't summon the Divine Dream, or even think about the day's events; I just lay staring, letting the time wash over me like hot bath water.

Eventually though, Xihuitl's voice drew me out of my contentedness and dragged me back into the world of annoyance. "What?"

"I've brought you your evening offering, My Lady!"

I sighed. "I suppose I must eat something," I grumbled, then announced, "Bring him in."

Xihuitl open the flap of my tent and the man I'd taken to bed last night—before the incident with Red Hawk—hurried inside. He twitched his head a bit, like those people who sometimes abused the Teonanactl for personal pleasure—and he stared down at me with an eagerness that made my stomach churn.

"Do you need anything further from me tonight?" Xihuitl asked, peering at me around the man.

The growing dread and disgust at the idea of being alone with this man made me want to make up some excuse to keep Xihuitl here, but I could think of none. With a sigh, I said, "No. You're free to go about your business for the evening."

He bowed then left.

I then turned my gaze up at the man he left behind. He had to hunch over as not to tear my tent off its riggings. He didn't say anything, but animal desire oozed off him like a stench. I knew he was waiting for my instructions, so I said, "Well, let's get this over with then." With a thought, I banished my clothing.

He pawed his way out of his own and practically tripped onto me in his eagerness. The feel of his hands on my skin, his groping, licking, biting, sweating—it all repulsed me, and it only became worse once he was panting and grunting and thrusting into me. How had I ever liked this? It was just discomfort and violation; my body didn't want him inside it either, and that made each movement more painful than the next.

Trying to escape the unpleasantness of the moment, I thought about Little Reed, of all of those wonderful intimate moments we'd shared, but to my growing horror, the disgust bloomed even more. My heart didn't palpitate the way it used to when I thought of him, and rather than the memories of his caresses and kisses making me flush with longing, I felt disgusted at myself for even thinking about him like that.

This definitely should have worried me; I'd built so much of my life around my feelings for Little Reed—but the emotions remained absent, as if I couldn't even bring myself to care anymore. I should be fighting to uncover them, but it felt easier to just let them lay buried....

There was no pleasure, but eventually reality bled away and the Divine Dream pulsed and vibrated around me, swallowing me into contentedness. I could stay here forever, unconcerned about the world, about Little Reed, about Mextli or Smoking Mirror. Here I didn't even have to worry about how I was going to get Ehecacone back. I hadn't felt this calm since I'd been dead.

Eventually it faded away though, and I had to shove the man off me. He was cold with death, but this revelation didn't move me one way or the other. He was taking up space in my tent though, so I silently asked the maguey to take him into the earth. Being the loyal servants they are, they obeyed without question, and the world was once again calm.

CHAPTER FOURTEEN

Mextli arrived at my tent early as usual and called out to me, "Are you ready to go?"

The thought of even moving annoyed me, but not as much as the thought of having to go talk to more gods who wouldn't help me with some useless mission that I knew was a complete waste of time. For a moment, I thought to just not even answer, but I knew Mextli wouldn't let that go, so I made myself get up and step out of my tent. "I don't want to go back," I said, walking past him to survey the clearing, if only to look like I cared.

"Why not?"

"Because I'm not going to convince anyone of anything, so what's the use?"

"That's not entirely true, Mayahuel. Smoking Mirror will help you, if you just ask."

I started to laugh, but then sighed, deciding it was too much effort. "Whatever you say."

Mextli came around to look me in the face. "Is something the matter, Mayahuel?"

"Actually, for the first time in a long time, nothing is the matter, and I'm feeling rather content about that."

An expression of puzzlement played over his face, but then he asked, "Do you wish to go talk to Smoking Mirror?"

"Not really," I admitted.

My answer seemed to baffle him. "Do you wish me to bring him here to talk to you?"

"Whatever. I don't care."

He stared at me for a long moment before speaking again. "I shall go fetch him then." He still didn't leave though, an indecisive look on his half-feathered face. "You're sure nothing is wrong?"

"I've never been more sure of anything in my life." I smiled, to make him stop questioning me.

He nodded then vanished with a loud snap that rankled me, but once the morning silence returned, the tension washed away and I thought of crawling back into my tent to lie there, not thinking.

"I thought he'd never leave!" a familiar voice spoke up behind me, and I turned to see Xochiquetzal lurking among the maguey. She hurried over, bits of her dress peeling off her like flower petals in the breeze.

"Why are you here?"

"Like I said, we have much to talk about."

I couldn't imagine what.

Xihuitl—who had been sitting nearby, meditating—hurried to his feet for a better look, and already that annoying glaze seeped into his eyes. He usually didn't become distracted by me, but perhaps the close proximity of two love goddesses was too much for even him. And when I looked around to the women working on their weaving where we usually met by the maguey, they too were watching with dreamy looks on their faces.

Xochiquetzal noticed too and giggled. "Humans are so amusing, don't you think?" She cast Xihuitl a sultry smile but then suggested, "Shall we go somewhere where we won't be distracting them?

I shrugged but then followed her out of camp, into the desert.

Once we were out of sight of any people, I thought perhaps I should say something.

"It's good to see you again."

"Is it truly? For you seem rather indifferent to my being here. Anyway, I've been trying to come see you for hours now, but I wanted to wait until Mextli wasn't around. He finds me annoying."

Before I could think better of it, I said, "Indeed he does."

It didn't seem to bother her though. "He just doesn't *get* us love goddesses; most of the gods don't, which is why I'm so excited to finally meet you. As I said before, we have *so* much to talk about."

"Like what?"

"Quetzalcoatl, of course."

"Why?"

"You're not the only one with a painful past with him, Mayahuel."

I sighed. I had nothing to say about Quetzalcoatl—I'd already wasted enough of my life and energy on him—but I could see she was desperate to talk about him. And besides, maybe if I played along, she would leave me alone sooner. "What happened?"

"He abandoned me, when I needed him most."

When she didn't offer more, I repeated, "And why did you need him so?"

"Well, everyone needs their father, don't they?"

"He's your father?"

"I don't generally call him such," she said. "And I suspect he doesn't call me his daughter either, which is just as well. Someday I will be powerful enough to write my own history and he will be no part of it."

"He has a habit of making children and then not being there for them." I should have felt anger—even irritation at the mildest—for the truth of the statement, and yet I couldn't have cared less.

And it was achingly freeing to feel so.

"I disappointed him," she admitted. "I imagine he thought I would be more like you."

"Why would he think you'd be more like me?"

"Because he took a flower and spilled his teotl upon it, and from that I bloomed."

"Spilled his teotl?"

"Stroked his tepolli until he climaxed, of course."

I grimaced, disgusted.

She cocked her head. "Having lived among humans, surely you're familiar with the practice? Human males do it a lot; the women do it often too, though it looks nothing like what the men do. Both kinds are fun to watch though, don't you think?"

"Can't say I've ever really...watched anyone." The thought made my divine flesh crawl.

She gasped. "Are you serious? Oh! We simply must correct this! We'll go back to camp and we'll have one of the men do it for us. That one near your tent looked more than willing—"

"Heavens no!" When she gave me a startled look, I pressed, "We were talking, remember?" She was far too easily distracted.

"Of course! Forgive me. Where were we?"

I suppressed the urge to snap impatiently at her. "You said that you thought he was disappointed that you weren't more like me." When she nodded but didn't say anything, I asked, "Why would you think that?"

"Because he took the flower from the maguey plant that grew from your bones."

I felt a flash of something—surprise, or perhaps confusion, and a phantom question—*Does that make me her mother?*—floated up from the back of my mind, but it soon flitted away too. *So what if I am?* I thought.

"Perhaps it was just as well that he and I were never close," Xochiquetzal went on, oblivious. "Seeing how he betrayed you to your death. That could have been me!"

"I suppose."

"I'm so very glad you've come to our side in all this nonsense. I was really hoping you would; I mean, I don't care about all the warring stuff—that's nonsense, of course—but the others were talking about putting you back on the Black Lake in Mictlan if you didn't abandon the Feathered Serpent, and quite frankly I'm glad that won't happen now. It's lonely being the only love goddess."

She gazed expectantly when I didn't respond, so I said, "I'm glad too."

"The others just don't understand."

I nodded. "I have difficulty understanding it myself."

"It's not so difficult. War gods think about war and battle all the time, and we think about love and sex. It's who we are, and why should we change that? Especially for the comfort of others? It's not as if our love magic works on other gods, so what do they care?"

"I suppose not." Though given that I had so little interest in sex now—repulsive, disgusting sex—what did that make me? "Is sex the only way we can feed?"

"Well, there's always blood—all gods can subsist on such offerings, but it's nothing compared to a vigorous lovemaking session with a couple of willing men, or even a single woman; women are particularly filling, don't you think?"

I wrinkled my nose. "I've never tried."

She gaped at me. "Oh, how those humans have tainted you! Women are the best, but you must be careful. Unlike men, they can climax multiple times over a short period of time and so it's very easy to drain them to death without much effort."

"So it's blood or sex, or nothing?"

"Well, for me, but Xochipilli doesn't really care for sex. He has different tastes."

I perked up at that. "Xochipilli is your brother, right?"

She nodded. "Do you want to meet him?"

"Of course." Hopefully he would have some alternative suggestions to my having to subject myself to tedious, unappealing physical contact to keep myself alive.

I expected her to disappear into the teoyoh and then for someone else to appear, but instead, a cyclone of wind started whipping around her, sending her hair fluttering above her. Her flower-bedecked body came apart a bit at a time until all that remained was a swirling torrent of petals.

Then they started coming back together again. Her delicate body reformed, except the petals didn't coalesce into a dress; they formed a loincloth and a broad, male chest, and when the face reformed, it was a man's. Once the wind died down, he opened his eyes and looked around in wonderment.

But then he fixed his gaze on me. "Mayahuel, right?" His voice was rich and deep, the exact opposite of Xochiquetzal's. He was lean but muscular, and he wore a crown of feathers woven into his hair, which in turn was tied up in an elaborate knot on the top of his head.

"Xochiquetzal?" I asked, confused.

He shook his head. "I'm Xochipilli, her brother. She said you wished to meet me."

"I did, but...where did she go?"

He smiled, patient. "She is still here, just as I am always wherever she is. We are different aspects of a single divine being, and this is how we express that."

"Then you're a *love god*?"

"Most everyone calls me the god of music and flowers, but, in a manner of speaking, you're right. I'm a god of passion." He spread his fingers and a flute of reeds materialized in his hands. "Passion for music, for art, for anything, really." He put the flute to his lips.

To my surprise, the music that came out was beautifully sweet and yet sad. The sound carried on the wind, ringing through the heavens, painting swaths of color across the desert landscape.

My magic vibrated and danced with every note. It had been a long time since last I'd felt so mesmerized by anything; the last time had probably been that night with Little Reed, when we'd nearly disregarded that sacrifice I'd made to save him and let the beans fall where they may, all so we might know each other's love at least once in our lives. I'd so desperately wanted it—so much it pained me now, raw and unfettered and wonderful. I wanted to stay in this moment forever.

When I looked around, I noticed we were no longer alone; Xihuitl stood a little ways off, between me and the camp, a dreamy look on his face, holding his chest as it rose and fell rapidly. Several of the women stood with him, some of them crying, some of them looking more determined than I'd ever seen them. Other people stood still further back from them, watching us in breathless silence.

Xihuitl finally dropped his hand from his chest and, muttering under his breath, he turned and headed back to camp at a swift walk. One at a time, the others followed his example until it was just me and Xochipilli left.

But as soon as Xochipilli lowered the flute from his lips, the feelings of warmth and longing and love faded away again, leaving me empty and incomplete. *What have I done to myself?* I wondered just before the fatalistic indifference sank its fangs into me again, even deeper now than before. I wanted to just curl into a ball on the ground and fall asleep, never to wake again.

Xochipilli smiled then pressed the flute between his palms until it disappeared. "Xochiquetzal creates romantic love, but I stoke the heart's passions for everything else. Without that, there would be no temples, no houses, no statues. Sons wouldn't love their mothers, nor would friendship even be possible."

Xochiquetzal is the primal, and Xochipilli is the rational, I realized. Just as I was once two natures, very much like theirs.

But now I was nothing.

▢

Xochipilli/Xochiquetzal left after that, and I soon learned why; within a few breaths of their departure, a loud snap resounded through the still air, and Mextli and an old man dressed in a tattered feathered cloak appeared out of the teoyoh.

"Apologies for taking so long," Mextli said. He then gestured to the old man. "As promised, the Lord of the Smoking Mirror, Tezcatlipoca."

The last time I'd seen Smoking Mirror, he'd been a child—specifically my nephew Night Wind. He'd changed much in the last five years, and I wouldn't have recognized him if not for Mextli's introduction.

Smoking Mirror wobbled towards me with the aid of a twisty walking stick, grimacing and wheezing. "So here we all are, together again at last," he panted when he finally stopped in front of me. The faint odor of burning tobacco hung around him. "Mextli has informed me of the unfortunate situation with my nephew."

The old me would have raised her hackles at him mentioning Ehecacone with his fetid tongue, but I just said, "What about it?"

He gazed upon me with appraising eyes. "I've come to offer you my help, in exchange for an alliance between us against Quetzalcoatl."

I grimaced. "Sounds like a lot of work."

Smoking Mirror chuckled. "Yes, it will require some effort from you, but then your request requires effort from me."

I lifted my gaze to the clouds crawling lazily across the blue sky and scratched my chin. "I appreciate your offer, My Lord, but I'm going to decline."

Now he outright laughed. "Without me, you will never get your son back."

I shrugged. "It hardly matters anyway."

Mextli stepped closer too. "What do you mean it doesn't matter?"

"Nothing matters, really," I said. "Not you, not him—" I pointed at Smoking Mirror—"not Quetzalcoatl, not even Ehecacone. No one—nor anything—matters, when you really think about it."

"It sounds more like you're just not thinking at all," Mextli said, the darkness rearing up in his eyes. He curled his lip, disgusted.

I waved him off.

Now even Smoking Mirror was scowling. "Take me back, Mextli. You've wasted too much of my time here already."

Mextli set his jaw stubbornly but then he took Smoking Mirror by the arm and they disappeared with a resounding snap.

The fresh quiet brought back the intoxicating calm and I returned to my tent to lie upon the ground and stare up at the ceiling.

After considerable debate, I summoned a bubble of the Divine Dream, so I could lie in absolute silence instead of having to listen to the distant noises of the camp, but after a while, that too felt like too much effort to keep going. Eventually I would have to replenish my magic, which meant allowing one of the humans to debase my body for their own pleasure. I craved peace and silence without effort.

I had that when I was dead, I realized. *But that will take so much effort. It's not as if we gods die easily.*

But then it would be the last effort I ever have to make, so it would be worth it, I thought. *Quetzalcoatl killed me once; perhaps I could convince him to do it again.* But then I had no idea where to find him.

An angry snap interrupted my beloved calm. *Mextli. Yes, I'll get him to do it.*

"Come out here now, Mayahuel!" he rumbled.

I sighed, not wanting to move, but then I reminded myself that I wouldn't have to make any more efforts before too long.

I came outside to find Mextli standing there, scowling down at me. "What has gotten into you?" he demanded.

"What does it matter?"

"I put myself out on a limb for you with Smoking Mirror, and now he thinks I'm some kind of fool!"

"Maybe you are."

He flinched. "What did you say?" he hissed.

I tried to think of how the desire would have responded at that moment. "Are you a deaf fool too?"

Mextli flexed his hand, bringing a macuahuitl sword to his grip. "Do you want to die, little goddess?" he snarled.

"If you wouldn't mind," I said and raised my chin to expose my neck for the sword swipe.

But to my disappointment, he didn't accept the invitation. Instead he stared back at me with ill-tempered confusion, but slowly the darkness leaked away. "Why would you say that?"

"Because nothing matters."

He tossed aside the sword, and stepping up to me, he took hold of me by my arms. "What is going on, Mayahuel? Why are you acting like this? This isn't you at all!"

"What does it matter?"

He gripped me a little tighter. "What happened?"

I shrugged. "I told her to go away, and she obliged me."

"Told who?"

"The part of me that revels in performing disgusting, demeaning acts with humans; the part that takes pleasure in striking fear into hearts and takes joy in killing."

He sighed. "Why would you do that?"

"What does it matter, really?"

The darkness crept back in as he said, "Because without her, you're unbalanced. Yes, she's extreme, but then so are you; you just tried to get me to kill you, for Mictlan's sake! But together, you create one stable, balanced being. You need her, and she needs you."

"She's gone, so what does it matter?"

"She isn't gone. Let me talk to her."

"You can't."

"I can, and *I will*."

I scrutinized him, wondering if I could use this to get him to give me the death I wanted, but then he added,

"If you don't let me talk to her, then I'll make sure you never find that peace you're looking for." And judging from the look in his eyes, he was determined to carry out his threat.

I resisted some more, but I knew this standoff wouldn't end until I gave him what he wanted.

"I will speak with her now," he growled.

A familiar heat grew inside me, bringing with it a slew of emotions, just like when Xochipilli had played his flute, but more raw and unfettered. Thoughts of Little Reed rushed into my head, bringing with them tingling feelings of love and desire and devotion. And relief.

But next came memories of Ehecacone, wrapped in a bittersweet blanket of warmth and guilt—I'd turned my back on him, nearly left him to Lord Death's non-existent mercy. I hadn't thought at all of how my death would affect him and his chances of ever getting his life back. My own selfishness horrified me.

A bright ball of rage in my gut soon pushed that aside as the desire rose up powerful and unabashed. She curled my lip into a sultry smile at Mextli. "You are indeed an arrogant little hummingbird boy, thinking you can order me around like that," she said. "You think very much of yourself, don't you?"

He smiled back, sharp and dangerous, sending a mix of anxiety and longing through me. "I have no reason not to."

She laughed heartily but then admitted, "Indeed not."

"It's time to stop playing games."

I leaned in closer and whispered, "Who said anything about playing games?"

"No more telling your other half that they aren't necessary—either of you. This isn't the time for an identity crisis; Smoking Mirror is on the verge of completely dismissing you, and without his help, you'll never get Ehecacone back." When I opened my mouth to protest, he cut in, "And don't try to say that you don't need him, for then who are you to call me arrogant?"

The desire finally started backing down and I put on a stiff smile. "So, we need him. Agreed."

"Then you must make peace with yourself and stop battling over stupid things. You need to be Mayahuel, full and complete, empowered by the passion, and wiser for the rationality. You must find that balance we all find in ourselves, because if you don't...bad things happen."

Fear tickled my gut. "What kind of things?"

"Chaos, and pain. Haven't you had enough of that in your life?"

I nodded.

The color shifted in his eyes, and when he spoke again, his voice had returned to normal. "I will leave you to work this out tonight."

I swallowed the distaste as I asked, "Shouldn't we go speak with Smoking Mirror?"

"He is not in a charitable mood right now," Mextli said. "He was pretty hot with me when we last spoke, so hopefully we haven't completely blown our chances of getting his help. I would give him a few days to cool off before approaching him again."

"I'm sorry if I've made this all the harder."

Mextli sighed. "No, I understand. You're hardly the first of our kind to contend with conflicts of your dualistic nature; we all face that time and again. Every one of us is capable of great extremes and it can be a struggle to maintain the middle ground. Spend some time in the Divine Dream, working this all out. No matter how much either side annoys you, just remember that they are you and you are them, and the sooner you accept yourself—extremes and all—the sooner you'll be able to focus on the truly important things, like getting your son back."

I nodded, but as he started to walk back into camp, I said, "Thank you!"

"For what?"

"For not killing me, for starters. But mostly for being a good friend."

A smile quirked at his lips. "It was my pleasure."

The desire and longing flared up but I just watched him go, a bit of a smile on my own face.

CHAPTER FIFTEEN

 When I returned to the tent, I immediately formed a bubble of the Divine Dream and I stood in the calming familiarity of my quarters in Tollan. I settled down on the bed and sat listening to the birdsongs and monkey chatter from out in the garden. When my thoughts wandered to Little Reed, the desire simmered and purred. *I'm sorry I told you that you were worthless,* I thought to her. *I was wrong.*

I shouldn't have let things go so far as they did, she admitted. *I should have stepped back in when you started thinking about death. Stubbornness is one of my faults.*

We both have our share, but we can manage them. Can we agree to work together for now on? For the sake of those we care about, and ourselves?

We can. And we'll embrace who we really are? All of it?
Yes, but will you still berate me as "too human" when I trip?
No.
I smiled. *Thank you.*
One more matter.
Yes?
Mextli. Let's pursue something more serious with him.
Like what? But when images of his feathery hand caressing the bare skin of my belly flashed through my head, my cheeks heated. *He's not interested in such things.*

The desire scoffed. *So he claims, but he just doesn't know it yet. There was a time before we were interested in such things, remember? We just have to teach him.*

It was on the tip of my tongue to ask how I would do that, but it felt too much like our same old arguments. *All right. We'll try. I have a request too though.*
I'm listening.
I want to see Little Reed again.
So do I.
My cheeks flared. *Then it isn't just me?*
The desire chuckled. *No, it's definitely not just you.*
But then how can we want Mextli too?
We are a love goddess; it's in our nature to love, and to do so broadly.
I suppose, I conceded.
Let's go see Little Reed, the desire suggested. When I hesitated, she asked, *Why not?*
I couldn't form into words the fear that the idea brought over me.

But she found them for me almost immediately. *You really think I would hurt him?*
I've had reason for concern, I replied, thinking about Black Otter.

She sighed. *It concerns me too, but Little Reed is different; we've loved him since before he was born, deep in our divine essence. You remember the dream when we were seven. We can't be with him the way we want, but that doesn't change the truth of our love for him, and his love for us.*
But what if his love for us isn't real?
A wave of anxiety and doubt flooded through me. *Let's deal with that when and if it becomes necessary.*

I took a deep breath and nodded. "Yes, let's go see him."

◻

My visit to Tollan required a bit of planning; I couldn't just appear in the palace unannounced, not after being gone for so long. Besides, where would I appear where someone wouldn't see me suddenly emerge from the teoyoh? For all I knew, my quarters were no longer mine, and it wouldn't do to startle someone, be it a servant, a guard, or maybe even Lady Anacoana; after all, my room was the only one that had direct access to the royal nursery.

In the end, I decided on a two-step approach. There were hundreds of rabbits living in the priestly gardens, and their underground burrows would provide the perfect cover for my arrival. I'd need to come out of the teoyoh as a rabbit myself, but then I could find somewhere to change back into my human form unseen.

Not that my sudden appearance among the rabbits in the burrows went unnoticed. The one I appeared next to scurried away, but once I sent out waves of calming magic, it came back and pressed closer in greeting, nose wiggling. As I moved through the tunnels and into the open areas, more of them gathered to greet me, some even rubbing up against my side in affection. I nuzzled each back in turn but then continued up to the surface, eager to be on my way. The thought of finally seeing Little Reed again had my heart pounding.

But when I reached the mouth of the burrows, I smelled humans. I peered cautiously towards the pond in the distance, and immediately recognized Mitotia sitting on the bank, exactly where she and Malinalli had been sitting that day when I'd figured out the truth about them. The stench of anxiety and fear hung in the air, but after a momentary hesitation, I left the burrow and crawled my way through the grass towards the pond. I loped up to the edge of the field grass, but stopped, hiding among the thick patches while still being able to see her.

She looked much as I remembered her: as serious and contemplative as the faded black tattoo of the Feathered serpent on the side of her face, following her jawline.

Another woman came from the direction of the flagstone path from the gate, and Mitotia sprang to her feet. I recognized Malinalli's scent immediately. She wore the high priestess of Quetzalcoatl robes, and her long black hair was tied back in a tidy knot at the back of her head.

"Thank the gods you're finally here," Mitotia whispered as she flung herself into Malinalli's arms, hugging her tight.

Malinalli returned the hug, her sudden anxiety like a miasma in the air. "What's wrong? You're trembling." She took Mitotia's face between her hands. "What's happened?"

"He saw us." Mitotia's voice broke and she began to cry.

"Who?"

"That guard, the one we keep running into in the halls at the palace. He's been following us!"

"You spoke to him?" When Mitotia nodded, Malinalli went on, "Why is he following us?"

"To report about our loyalties."

"What did you tell him?

"That we're loyal to the King and to the God, of course. But then he told me what he'd seen...." Mitotia started sobbing and Malinalli pulled her into a hug again. "He was watching us, not just in the hallways, but in our quarters, and he's threatening to reveal us to the entire city!"

"Then this guard wants something from you, to keep quiet?"

Mitotia pulled away and stood with her back to her, gripping her own arms with both hands. "I think you already know what he wants, but I can't do that—I won't do that. I'll run away from Tollan before I'll stoop to such...such blackmail." She turned back to Malinalli, pleading in her voice as she said, "That's what we should do anyway. We should just leave—"

"And go where?" Malinalli shook her head. "I love you, Mitotia, but I'm the god's high priestess, and I made a promise to Quetzalpetlatl—"

"You owe her nothing! She skipped out on us, with no explanation, with no regard for what it would do to all of us, especially to the King. And Citlallotoc."

Her mention of them in such dire terms made my heart quicken unpleasantly.

"She must have had her reasons," Malinalli fired back. "She wouldn't just up and leave for no good reason at all."

"She could have at least given us those reasons," Mitotia replied. "You've been her best friend all her life, so that was the least she could have done to honor that."

The whole exchange and Mitotia's bitterness poured acid in my stomach.

"You're just saying that to wound me," Malinalli said.

Mitotia sighed and reached out to take Malinalli's hand, but Malinalli withdrew from her reach. "I'm saying it because I'm tired of *her* wounding you. You deserve better than that." When she again tried to press closer and Malinalli again backed away, she sighed. "I'm sorry. I shouldn't have said it. Please forgive me."

Malinalli set her jaw but then said, "I will not let anyone drive me out of my own home—out of the city I helped found."

"What are you going to do?"

"Whatever's necessary."

"I would rather we left than you be killed." She fell silent when a couple of priests walked down the flagstone path, towards the priestly retreat, but once they were out of sight, she said, "I have to go. My temple duties start very soon."

Malinalli nodded but said nothing more as Mitotia hurried away. She stared into the pond for a long moment before heading to the priestly retreat.

I watched her, my heart heavy. My illusions that everything had turned cheerful and bright with my departure were shattered, and all I felt now was intense guilt. Mitotia was right; I had owed them better than to just up and leave with no explanation. And now some unscrupulous palace guard was trying to blackmail them.... *Maybe this isn't such a good idea, coming here and trying to find Little Reed.*

But the desire was adamant. *We've come this far. We can't back out now.*

After a moment more of internal debate, I relented. I hopped closer to the path, to check for more priests or priestess, but the path was clear. I changed back into my human shape, then looked back at the priestly sanctuary again. *Little Reed might be in his meditation room instead of at the palace,* the desire said.

It would be better to announce our arrival at the palace first. We're not the queen anymore, after all.

Little Reed declared us the Queen of Tollan until the day we die.

He did, I conceded. *But let's not be sneaking around any more than necessary.*

We don't need to sneak around at all. Let's just appear and no one will dare question us.

I don't want to reveal our divine nature to anyone here.

Why not?

Because we don't want to ruin the friendships we have. You've seen how people react when they find out we're not mortal.

The desire grumbled a bit but then admitted, *Indeed, we don't want that with our friends. Your way is the better way.*

As the calmecac's noontime bell rang in the distance, I headed up the deserted path, to the gate.

The courtyard beyond was far from empty; novices in their white robes hurried about or lounged on the stone benches around the cistern. No one paid me any attention as I closed the garden gate then wove my way through the crowd. Still, I looked around with anxiety, noticing how different I looked wrapped in the length of plain cloth I'd made for myself while the women and girls wore robes or colorful dresses. Surely someone would recognize me.

But by the time I'd worked my way halfway across the precinct, I realized that no one did, so I strode forward with purpose. I looked around, taking in the buildings and flowers that I'd missed so terribly. Seeing it again in the bright sunlight brought joy to my heart.

The palace looked much as I remembered it. Statues of the gods still held up the ceiling in the Hall of the Gods and the scent of flowers hung heavy in the dry air. There were more guards though than when I'd lived there; they were everywhere, watching everyone with suspicious vigilance, and when one of them caught sight of me headed for the stairs leading into the main foyer, he hurried over to intercept me. "All visitors must be approved by the chief of security," he said, a chill to his voice.

"I'm here to see the king," I replied, matching his tone. The desire growled, restless, but she kept herself at bay. "Anyone may request audience with the king at any time."

The man narrowed his eyes at me. "You can either follow the rules, or you will be escorted off the palace grounds."

"Fine then. I demand to see the Justice of the Peace immediately," I snapped. Citlallotoc would clear this up right quickly.

"If he has time available for you, he will see you," the guard replied. "However, that doesn't change the fact that you must check in with palace security."

"Then take me there already," I hissed.

He hesitated a breath—no doubt debating whether or not to forcibly remove me from the palace—but then he led the way over to a long line of men and women waiting on the opposite side of the vestibule. "Wait your turn and the chief of security will get to you in turn."

The desire sneered in disgust that we should be made to wait—*We're the damn Queen, for Mictlan's sake!*—but I said nothing and kept my place in the queue of people waiting to speak with the security guard twenty people ahead of me.

It took a while, but eventually my turn came. A large man dressed in cotton armor and a feathered xicolli motioned me forward while a scribe sat poised to record my information in a large book of pressed fig bark paper. "Your name, and the reason for your visit," the man rumbled.

I sighed. Earlier I'd been concerned that I would be recognized, but now the fact that no one did had become downright irritating. "Lady Quetzalpetlatl, Queen of Tollan, former high priestess of Quetzalcoatl, sister and former wife to Revered Speaker Topiltzin, and daughter of King Mixcoatl of Culhuacan. And as for my purpose here...I live here, or at least did so five years ago, and I've returned to see my brother."

The scribe stared at me in astonishment, but the chief of security frowned, irritated. "So you're claiming to be the king's sister?"

"I'm not claiming; I *am*," I retorted.

He laughed. "Dressed in that rag? Try again, Chichimec."

The desire wanted to rail back with outrage at being mistaken for a Chichimec, but she agreed that would hardly be productive right now. Besides, now that I listened to myself, I had taken on a northern accent since joining the Mexica. I cleared my throat before speaking again. "If you allow me to see Topiltzin, he will verify my identity."

"We don't allow unidentified people to see the king."

"Then take me before Citlallotoc. He will recognize me as well." When he chuckled dismissively, I asked, "And what is so funny?"

"Citlallotoc is no longer the Justice of the Peace of Tollan."

He wasn't? Citlallotoc had vowed to serve me and Little Reed for the rest of his days, so the fact he was gone made my stomach sink. Was it because of what happened between us at Teotihuacan? "What about Mazatzin, the god's fire priest? Or Malinalli? Either of them would recognize me—"

"I don't have time to continue listening to lies and manipulation—" the chief of security started, but he looked back in irritation when the scribe cleared his throat loudly. "What?"

"The king's standing orders, My Lord?" the scribe offered. "Anyone claiming to be Lady Quetzalpetlatl is to be brought before him—"

"I'm aware of his orders," the man barked back. He scrutinized me a moment longer but then beckoned to the guard who'd brought me here to begin with. When the other man arrived, he said, "Take her to the great hall to see the king. And make sure you stay with her."

The guard bowed then took me by the arm.

"I can walk just fine on my own," I snapped then followed him up the stairs into the Hall of the Gods. We soon passed through the corbelled archway of the great hall.

There were a number of people inside, some sitting on the reed mats reserved for the city's council members, others standing in a line along the wall by the entrance, waiting for their turn to approach the dais. There was only one reed icpalli there—mine was missing—and a man dressed in the royal robes sat upon it.

I couldn't confirm that it was Little Reed though, for he wore a mask. It was a deep ruddy color, the shade of dried blood, and shaped like a beak, the way the god Ehecatl's mouth was often drawn in art. He also wore a tall quetzal-feather headdress. He didn't look up from the man kneeling on the floor before the dais when we entered.

"You'll have to wait for your turn." The guard pointed to the other people waiting for their audience.

But I ignored him. Instead I stared at the eyes of the man behind the mask, willing him to look up at me. Surely when Little Reed saw me, all of this ridiculousness would end.

Yet when he finally did look in my direction, I knew it wasn't Little Reed. They weren't the eyes I'd loved gazing into, and they held no recognition for me either. Who was this man posing as him?

A second man stood next to him, dressed in the mantle of the Justice of the Peace and holding a folding codex for writing in. I didn't recognize him either. The man in the mask never spoke; when he had something to say, he motioned to the other man, who then leaned down and listened at the mask's mouth, then the justice of the peace reported what he'd been told.

I headed for the dais, irresistibly drawn. I had to know who the man behind the mask was.

A hand grabbed me. "Where do you think you're going?" the guard hissed.

How dare you touch me? I let loose a tiny burst of magic and he yelped, releasing me to shake his hand as if I'd burned him. I resumed my journey towards the throne.

Soon enough, the man in Citlallotoc's mantle noticed my advance. Perhaps it was the rage seeping off me, but he started shouting, "Someone stop that woman!"

The council members rose to their feet, making to intercept me, but suddenly Mazatzin broke through the crowd. "My Lady?" he gasped, a disbelieving look on his face. His hair was streaked with silver, and years of worry and stress had creased the corners of his eyes. He rushed to me and pulled me into a desperate, crushing hug. "I was sure you were never coming back," he murmured. "Not after all you said before you left."

"I didn't think I would either," I admitted, tears clogging my throat.

"What is the meaning of this?" the Justice of the Peace demanded, shoving past the man on his knees below the dais. "Who is this insolent woman?"

"The king should know," Mazatzin fired back. He turned to glare at the man in the mask. "Surely you recognize her, Your Majesty?"

I stepped up again, inviting the angry desire to come forward. "Indeed. I was only your wife for seven years, and your sister for seventeen before that." I spread my arms before me. "What's the matter, Topiltzin? Why no hug for the woman you loved?"

The man in the mask rose slowly from the throne, our eyes locked. There was fear and indecision in his.

The Justice of the Peace blocked my line of sight to the other man. "Get this imposter out of here immediately! To the prison yard with her!"

Mazatzin came forward, blocking the guards who'd come to take me. "Enough of this nonsense! Surely you recognize your own sister, Your Grace; she's hardly changed in appearance since last any of us saw her. I recognized her immediately, and at best I can only claim friendship with her. You were her husband, for Mictlan's sake!"

The man in the mask stood stock still before motioning to the guards again, and this time they began clearing the room. It took a few moments before it was only me, Mazatzin, the Justice of the Peace, and the man in the mask. The guards lingered just outside the great hall's entrance, keeping watch.

"What is the meaning of all of this?" the Justice of the Peace demanded, still furious.

"I would ask the same thing." I went around him to step up on the dais. The man in the mask stepped away from me, nearly falling over onto the throne. I glared at him. "You're not Topiltzin."

Mazatzin folded his arms, grim satisfaction on his face while the other two men exchanged looks. "This works on the average citizen, Matlacxochitl, but you can't fool the one person who knows Topiltzin better than anyone in Tollan."

I bared my teeth. "Matlacxochitl! Posing as the king? How dare you?"

His shoulders dropped but then he carefully removed the mask and headdress. I gasped when I beheld his face, not out of outrage, but shock.

I hadn't seen Matlacxochitl since he'd left Tollan to govern Chimalhuacan after Tollan's construction was finished, but even back then he'd worn a mask to cover his facial disfigurement. Rebels had cut off his nose and one of his ears, and for the first time I saw the result: the twisted, puckered skin around the hole of his eardrum and the shriveled pit that was all that remained of his nose. I shuddered to think of what it must have been like to be cut up like that.

"Forgive me for not hiding my hideousness, My Lady." He fumbled with the mask in his hands. "I usually only take the mask off in the privacy of my quarters."

I peeled my horrified gaze away from him. "What happened to your other mask? The one that covers the upper portion of your face?"

"I stopped wearing it since this one covers everything as well."

I suppressed the shudder creeping up on me. "You still haven't answered my other question: why are you posing as Topiltzin?"

"Because the king left me in charge when he himself became incapable of ruling any longer."

Mazatzin glowered. "He left you in charge, but that doesn't give you license to impersonate him."

"We've already been over this, Lord Mazatzin; to admit that the king is on his deathbed with no heir ready to take—"

"Deathbed?" I cut in, my heart jolting. "What do you mean he's on his deathbed?"

Mazatzin set his hand on my shoulder. "Topiltzin hasn't left his bed for almost a year now."

"What happened to him?"

"His accelerated aging...it's finally caught up with him. We expect that he will pass on into Mictlan at any time now."

A pain spread through my chest, so similar to the feeling of not being able to breathe, and for a moment I thought I might faint. I grabbed onto Mazatzin's shoulders to keep it from happening, breathing rapidly. *No! He can't be really dying! Gods, please no! Why didn't anyone warn me?*

But then, what did any of my kind care about the mortal son of their enemy?

"I must see him," I panted. "Right away."

CHAPTER SIXTEEN

 As Mazatzin led the way out of the great hall, Malinalli came into the vestibule from the priestly quarters, and when she saw me, she stopped short. We locked gazes for a breath before she rushed to me and flung her arms around my neck. "Dear gods, is it really you?" she whispered through tears.

I hesitated to return the hug but then I let go of the fear of what my aura might do to her and embraced her fiercely. Her conversation with Mitotia came back to me as my own tears began winding down my cheeks. "I'm sorry, Malinalli," I murmured. "I'm so sorry!"

She was all smiles when we finally separated though. "It doesn't matter. You're back!"

I cringed inside. She was so happy, I didn't have the heart to tell her I wasn't staying. Instead, I said, "Mazatzin is taking me to see Topiltzin."

"May I come along too?" she asked, hopeful. When I nodded, she put her arm around my shoulder and we continued on our way. "Has Mazatzin told you about the King's condition?" she asked, her voice turning sober.

I nodded but said nothing more as we headed down the hallway to the royal quarters.

How often had I walked this path, so carefree and without the trepidation that plagued me now? On the surface, nothing about the place had changed in the years I'd been gone, but underneath it all, I felt something sinister and alien lurking about. I looked in every shadow for signs of Xolotl, come to take Little Reed away from me forever.

Anger rolled through me though when we entered the family garden and my eyes found the column statue of Quetzalcoatl on the patio. It grinned at me, enjoying my pain. *His supposedly favored son lies dying and yet he still does nothing. Just more proof he doesn't care about anything but his own power.*

Malinalli escorted me to the light blue curtain emblazoned with a white and green feathered serpent. I hesitated, part of me afraid that I'd step inside and find that in my own self-absorption and fear I'd waited too long and he was already dead. Even the desire shivered inside me, equally afraid.

But I had to see him. I pushed the curtain open, took a deep breath, and stepped inside.

The smell of urine and decay met my nose, bringing forth memories of those couple of days when my mother took me to see my human grandmother where she'd laid abed coughing and wheezing. I hadn't understood any of it back then, why I had to not only tolerate the smell, but had to hold my breath as I had to kiss her sunken cheeks. I hadn't understood why my mother made me sit in there so still while I could hear all my friends' playful shouting from the gardens, and I hadn't understood why my mother had spent most of the visit smiling cheerfully only to burst into sobs once we left the room. I hadn't taken the need to say goodbye seriously and didn't even realize that I wouldn't get the chance to say it again until several days after.

And in the days following Nimilitzli's death, I'd spent a good deal of my bed time thinking about how once again I'd failed to say goodbye properly.

All of this raced through my mind as I stared down at the man lying in Little Reed's bed. I barely recognized him behind the shaggy beard and stringy silver hair. His chest rose slow and shallow under the blankets and furs, his breath rattling. *Still alive.* I sank to my knees next to him, some of the weight lifting from my shoulders. I wasn't too late. I found his skin clammy when I set my hand on his forehead, but he didn't stir.

"He rarely wakes up anymore," Malinalli whispered behind me. "And when he does, he's incoherent and doesn't recognize anyone."

Another daydream shattered; he wouldn't wake up and smile when he saw me again. A hot tear wound down the side of my nose and fell, to soak into the blanket lying over him. "He's made his confession to Tlazotlteotl?" I choked on the words.

"He didn't want to see her," Malinalli answered. "He told Mazatzin that she wouldn't see him anyway, and she's not the one he needs forgiveness from."

What had he meant by that? I couldn't imagine Little Reed needing forgiveness for anything, except perhaps his blindness to his father's true character, but that was hardly his fault.

I took his cool hand in mine and pulled it to my lips for a kiss. *If I did this to you with grief, Little Reed, I'm so very sorry. Please forgive me!* Tinkling bells drew my attention to the doorway.

Anacoana stood there with a bowl in her hand and a look of shock on her face. "Quetzalpetlatl?" She almost dropped the bowl but fumbled it back under control, sloshing watery atole over her hands. "What are you doing here?" She stared in my direction with venom in her eyes, but not directly at me. When I looked down at Little Reed again, I realized she was reacting to my holding his hand.

My first impulse was to release my grip and apologize, but the desire growled like a cornered jaguar. *We loved him first. We have every right to hold him.* So I didn't let his hand go. "I came to see Topiltzin," I finally replied. "To see how he's been doing."

"Not very well, as you can see," she spat. "His mind has fallen down a dark shaft and he doesn't even recognize his own wife anymore. I fear I shall wake a widow any day now."

Malinalli glared at Anacoana. "That's hardly the appropriate tone to take with Tollan's queen, My Lady."

The color in Anacoana's face flared bright.

I held up my hand to cut off any further arguing though. "I wish I had arrived sooner, My Lady, but I'm here now, ready to pay my respects to Tollan's king...and her queen." I bowed to her.

Anacoana's furious expression softened and her jaw quivered. "You...you honor me, My Lady," she stammered.

To Malinalli, I said, "Would you give us a moment to speak alone?"

"Of course." She cast a hard glare at Anacoana before leaving.

Anacoana stared at the floor, trembling, so I began instead. "I'm sorry I upset you, My Lady. That wasn't my intension in coming here."

She shook her head. "No, please, forgive my harsh words. These last few years have been very difficult, watching the king slowly slip away—not just from me, but from everyone. I try not to be bitter, about being left to care for him on my own, but often it feels like more than I can handle."

I looked down at Little Reed again, my insides aching. "If I'd known this was what would happen to him so soon...."

Guilt now showed in her eyes. "Would you think me evil and spiteful if I admitted that I was relieved when you didn't return from Teotihuacan?"

"I understand why you would have been. I left because...I hoped it would finally let you and Topiltzin be happy together, in the way that seemed impossible so long as I was around."

Anacoana knelt beside the bed next to me, and looked down at Little Reed with a frown. "I thought surely he'd finally start noticing me, but instead he fell into a deep depression and barely spoke to me at all. Before you left, he at least made a perfunctory effort to honor our marriage, if only for appearances' sake, and to keep you from chastising him, but after you left.... I should have known it wouldn't make anything better." She stirred the atole in the bowl, looking on the verge of tears. "I should have known, on our very wedding night, that this marriage wasn't going to be everything I dreamed it would be." She cleared her throat before saying, "The child I was carrying...it wasn't Topiltzin's."

I nodded. "Citlallotoc told me as much."

She squeezed her eyes shut. "I thought maybe he did it out of pity for me—sending Citlallotoc to our wedding bed instead of coming himself—but after you left, it became obvious that I repulsed him."

"Surely not—"

"He still would not bed me, not even to ensure himself an heir after I delivered a stillborn child. I even told him—" She set the back of her hand to her mouth to stifle a sob, the tears coming now. "I even told him that he was obligated by the marriage contract to give me children, and that he was breaking his oath by refusing to do his husbandly duties to me, but do you know what he said to me? 'Then go find one of the guards that sparks your interest, and I'll say nothing about it.' Like I was a common whore!"

I stared down at Little Reed, taken aback. I tried imagining him being so indifferent, so callous, and though I couldn't hear him speak such words in my head, I doubted Anacoana was lying. I'd thought I knew Black Otter well, but he'd hidden his true character exceedingly well. And it cost me my son. "I'm so sorry, My Lady. No one deserves such cruelty."

She wiped away her tears with her wrist. "I might not have taken it so badly had Citlallotoc still been here; after all, for a little while, he and I had been happy with our arrangement. But as you can probably guess, he's too honorable to continue cuckolding his king, even with Topiltzin's permission. I resented him for that, but in my heart I still longed for him, and when he left too...." She shook her head.

When she didn't go on, I cautiously asked, "Why did he leave?"

"I don't know. He never spoke a word to me again after I accused him of turning his back on me when he found I was with child." She sniffled then sat straighter. "Forgive me, but I really must feed the king. Would you help me sit him up?"

I worked Little Reed slowly to a sitting position against the wall while he grumbled and coughed. He opened his eyes, but they were octli-colored, and staring, oblivious.

"Topiltzin, it's me," I whispered near his ear, hoping for a reaction, but he just wheezed and tried to slouch again. I sat against the wall next to him, holding him upright while Anacoana patiently spoon-fed him the atole. Half of it went directly from his lips down into his scraggly beard, and she wiped it away with a cloth, as if he were a drooling infant. Once the bowl was empty, I laid him back down and he drifted off again in a matter of breaths.

I watched Anacoana dab at the mess of atole in his whiskers, making sure he was cleaned up. "If he'd treated me the way he treated you...I don't know that I'd be here now taking care of him, as you are," I admitted.

"It's my duty." She tossed the dirty cloth into the corner where other laundry lay piled. "And for once, I'm actually the most important person in his life."

Indeed. I couldn't look her in the eye though. Instead I focused my blurry gaze down at him. "He doesn't even recognize me anymore."

Anacoana folded her hands in her lap. "I'm sorry, My Lady. This must be terrible for you, seeing him like this."

I wiped my knuckles across my eyes. "Thank you for taking care of him...making him comfortable in his final days. And I'm sorry I wasn't here to alleviate some of the burden for you."

She reached over and grasped my hand. When I looked up at her, she smiled. "You're here now."

The hope in her eyes was too much to bear. "If you'll excuse me, I must speak with Malinalli and Mazatzin." I rose and hurried outside into the garden, welcoming the fresh air after the stifling smell of sickness.

Both Malinalli and Mazatzin stood near the hallway back into the palace. Malinalli hurried over when I stepped out. "I'm sorry about Lady Anacoana's harshness—"

"She's entitled to it," I said. "I left a mess for her to look after."

"Everything has been tough since you left," Mazatzin said as he stepped up too. "For everyone."

"I imagine so. And Topiltzin has been like this for a year, you said?"

Mazatzin nodded. "He's deteriorated a great deal more in the last month or so; he used to respond to our voices, but now...."

"The end is close." I choked on the words and had to clear my throat to go on. "It's a good thing I came when I did."

"Indeed," Malinalli said. "Good both for the king, and the kingdom. We need our queen back more than ever." She gave Mazatzin a pointed look.

He nodded again. "The future of Tollan is in question, My Lady, and much needs your attention."

I bit my lip. "I don't know how much help I can be—"

Mazatzin looked back into the hallway but then took my arm and led me across the garden, to the far side. "Matlacxochitl is poised to seize the throne once the Black Dog comes for Topiltzin," he whispered once we were on the portico.

"He impersonated Topiltzin so he could name himself the next king, since there is no blood heir," Malinalli added. "But now that you're back, you can dispute that claim."

"I don't understand. How has he even been able to impersonate Topiltzin? They look nothing alike," I pointed out.

"After you left, Topiltzin started wearing the mask," Malinalli said. "The one you saw Matlacxochitl wearing earlier."

"Why?"

She glanced at Mazatzin before answering, "He was so depressed...about you leaving...that he didn't want anyone to see his face when he appeared in public."

I snapped my mouth shut.

"Though I'm sure Citlallotoc's departure contributed too," she added. "He didn't leave his quarters for a week after that."

Wonderful. I'd made it easy for Matlacxochitl to step right onto Little Reed's throne.

"But maybe this is all for the best. Matlacxochitl was a good governor in Chimalhuacan—"

"He's begun undoing everything you and Topiltzin built," Mazatzin said. "He's removed many of the restrictions on sacrifices, including the requirement that all willing victims register their consent with the royal court. And he's defacing the Feathered Serpent's temple."

I creased my brow. "Defacing it?"

"He's having the columns re-carved, in the likeness of warriors. He claims Topiltzin told him to do this, under orders from the god himself, but Tollan is a city of peace, so why would we place warriors directly inside the temple?"

It was a good question, and my instincts told me this was a bad sign, but the desire growled, *Why should we care if someone is undermining Quetzalcoatl? How is that any different from what we're planning to do?*

I'm not worried about him, I countered. *I'm worried about Malinalli and Mazatzin, and the citizens of Tollan. They don't deserve to get hurt.*

Indeed not, the desire conceded. *And how dare anyone impersonate Little Reed?*

I stood taller. I'd created this mess, and the least I could do for my friends was try to fix it. "I will speak with the Council, and with Matlacxochitl. Immediately."

CHAPTER SEVENTEEN

While Mazatzin went to call the meeting in the great hall, Malinalli came to my old quarters with me, to help me change out of my dull, plain wrapper and into my royal regalia.

"Topiltzin wouldn't let anyone take over your quarters after you left, not even when Anacoana told him she would need its easier access to the royal nursery. He kept it all exactly the way you left it," she told me as she led me inside.

He indeed had; even the cloak I'd abandoned on the bed the morning I'd left for Teotihuacan still lay undisturbed. Surprisingly, there wasn't a layer of dust on everything; apparently the servants still came in and cleaned regularly, if only to keep away the decay. I picked up the cloak, taking me back to that day when I'd looked around with a heaviness born of the knowledge that I might very possibly never see it again, since I was heading into a confrontation with an evil sorcerer god. It felt surprisingly right to be here again, in the actual room rather than in a divine facsimile. I closed my eyes and breathed in the smell of bone flowers drifting in from my own private garden beyond the bath yard patio. It calmed the buzzing anxiety my visit with Little Reed had left me with.

"Do you want to bathe first?" Malinalli asked as she disappeared into my dressing room.

After so many years on the move, the thought of a luxurious hot bath was tempting, but I didn't have time for frivolities. I needed to set things right, and I still had to get Little Reed alone, so I could finally tell him the truth and say my goodbyes. The longer I remained here, the more likely Mextli would notice my absence and question me about it. "Perhaps later," I answered.

She hurried back with a dress and two robes. "So which one do you want? Your royal robe, or your high priestess one?" She held up the latter, as if to encourage me to choose it.

But seeing the gold and silver feathered serpents sown on the front brought an unpleasant heat in my gut. "No, you're the high priestess now. I will wear the other one."

Once I'd changed into the dress and donned my robe, Malinalli brought out my jewelry box for me to pick pieces out. Among the gold and turquoise necklaces and bangles, I spotted the silver feathered serpent bracelet Citlallotoc had given me. I stared at it a moment, a flux of guilt and self-loathing fighting in my stomach before I settled for the feather and turquoise necklace that had once been my mother's. Malinalli then fixed my white heron-feather headdress on my head.

"I swear, it looks like you haven't aged a day since I last saw you," she commented as she examined her work. "Wish I could say the same about myself."

"There's nothing shameful in growing older. Besides, I think it looks very good on you, and I bet Mitotia thinks so too."

Her lips twitched, making me wonder if I'd hit a tender nerve, but she then smiled. "You're all ready."

꙳

Most of the Council was already in the great hall when I arrived. Some of them recognized me and came forward in greeting, but at least half of them were unknown to me. Those ones kept their distance, whispering amongst themselves. Curiously there were no women on the council as there had been when I had still been Tollan's queen. Matlacxochitl had indeed been switching the pieces around on the patolli board.

With the greetings finished, I crested the step onto the dais and looked down at the reed-woven icpalli throne before me. "I would like to know where my throne is," I announced, turning back to the crowd.

Matlacxochitl's older brother Blood Wolf stepped forward, looking very grizzled and frail, a far cry from that fiery-tempered young man who had whisked my mother and I off to safety in Xochicalco so long ago. "The King had it put away in storage a few months ago, My Lady. He'd given up hope of your return and it pained him too much to have it sitting empty next to him every time he held court."

I scrutinized Blood Wolf, wondering if he didn't know of his brother's machinations, or if he took me for an ignorant fool. Until I learned the truth, I decided it best to play the part of the fool. "I suppose this will do for now." I sat down, which brought a wave of confused—and hostile—whispers among the men.

I took my time settling in then looked around. Not seeing Matlacxochitl, I sighed. "Oh, where is my dearest brother? Surely someone told him I wished him to be here for this meeting?"

"I informed him myself, My Lady," Mazatzin answered from where he stood next to the doorway. "I assured him that you very much wanted to speak with him."

Just then the Justice of the Peace strode through the doorway, followed by Matlacxochitl dressed as himself in his old half-mask.

When Blood Wolf saw his brother, he started and rose to his feet again. "Brother? When did you come to Tollan?"

"He's been here for several years now," Mazatzin answered.

"Several years?" The surprise and hurt on Blood Wolf's face told me all I needed to know.

Without answering his brother, Matlacxochitl approached the dais and bowed, sweeping his fingers across the ground at my feet. "Forgive my tardiness, My Lady, but I had to change clothing before the meeting."

"Indeed. I certainly would have been displeased if you'd shown up dressed *inappropriately.*" When he started rising, I snapped, "I did not dismiss you yet."

"I beg your pardon, My Lady."

"You should be begging more than my pardon, Lord Matlacxochitl, considering your crimes against the Crown."

The color drained from Blood Wolf's face. "Crimes, My Lady? What has my brother done?"

I sat straighter, watching Matlacxochitl with intense eyes. "Yes, Lord Matlacxochitl. Please tell everyone what you've been doing for the last few years since your arrival in Tollan."

This time he looked up to meet my arrow-like gaze. "I was doing my duty to the Kingdom, and Lord Topiltzin, My Lady," he retorted.

"And what duty requires you to pose as my brother and fool not only Tollan's citizens, but the city's own Council?"

Blood Wolf started coughing in distress. "What is she talking about, Brother?" he choked out.

I stood, letting the rage and indignation carry me to my feet. "Lord Matlacxochitl has been pretending to be the king while Topiltzin has lain bedridden and dying, all with the intent of naming himself Tollan's heir once my brother passed on to Mictlan."

Matlacxochitl shot to his own feet, fists clenched. "It wouldn't have been necessary if Tollan's queen hadn't run out on her own responsibilities, and if the king had been of sound enough mind to think to name an heir after his wife miscarried. Someone had to think about the people and their future."

"A future that turns its back on everything Topiltzin and I built here? How dare you undo the founding principles of Tollan, and do it in Topiltzin's name!"

"The changes you and Lord Topiltzin made are admirable in theory, My Lady, but they are impractical in practice—"

"*Do not trifle with me, human,*" the desire snarled but I caught myself before I could say more. I breathed deeply and stood straighter, smoothing my hands down the front of my robe. "It doesn't matter what you think, because you will not be king once my brother passes on to Mictlan; in fact, you will leave Tollan tonight, and you will never return."

Matlacxochitl pursed his lips, his face darkening. "You're exiling me?"

"Would you rather I hand down a death sentence? After all, what you've done could be considered high treason."

My words brought a confused murmur to the crowd. Matlacxochitl set his jaw and didn't respond.

Maybe we should kill him anyway, the desire growled, but I held firm. There was no capital punishment in Tollan, and no matter how much I thirsted for Matlacxochitl's blood in the name of justice, I would follow the law, out of respect for Little Reed. My disregarding it in the past hadn't turned out well.

I motioned to the guards, who stepped forward. "You will escort Lord Matlacxochitl from the city."

They hesitated, looking at each other and then the Council.

"You heard your queen," Blood Wolf barked. His jaw quivered as if he might break into tears under his furrowed brows. "Now carry out your orders."

The guards took Matlacxochitl by the arms and escorted him from the great hall. He held my gaze while I lanced my own angry one right back at him, daring him to say anything. But he left without protest or resistance.

Blood Wolf came forward and knelt on the floor before me. "I must apologize for my brother's conduct, My Lady. As his blood relation, I share in his shame."

"Of course you don't, Lord Blood Wolf. I have known you to always be an honorable, loyal man, and whatever your brother chose to do, he alone bears the burden of that guilt," I insisted. "Please rise."

He didn't stand, but he did raise his head to meet my gaze. "Then let me take this moment to renew my fealty to you, as Tollan's queen."

"And I gladly accept it. Please rise, Lord Blood Wolf."

He finally came to his feet, slowly, matching his frail appearance. "Is it indeed true that Lord Topiltzin is dying?"

I nodded. "I have seen him myself, and he is indeed expecting the Black Dog any time now."

Blood Wolf looked around at the others. "Why were none of us told of this?"

Mazatzin stepped forward. "Both Lady Malinalli and I were sworn to secrecy under the threat of death, as was the king's wife. The guards who were privy were loyal to Matlacxochitl, and so kept his secrets." He cast his glare at the Justice of the Peace, who had imperceptibly moved towards the doorway out before then. "As was Lord Timaltzin."

Timaltzin froze, his distressed gaze locked with mine.

I glared at him, my fists clenching. "Guards, seize him as well."

"I had no choice, My Lady!" Timaltzin cried, struggling against the guards. "Lord Matlacxochitl threatened my family if I didn't go along with him!"

My gut was to distrust him—he'd been rather snappy with me when I'd arrived—but I didn't know him at all, had never even met him, so maybe he was telling the truth. "Your involvement will be investigated and put to trial. In the meantime, you will reside in the prison yard."

He wept as the guards removed him from the great hall.

"Lord Blood Wolf." When he turned to me again, I stood and motioned him up onto the dais. "As a loyal subject of Tollan, and a man I know personally to be of high character, I wish to offer you the position of Justice of the Peace. I beg you accept this honor."

He bowed. "I am both pleased and humbled by your faith in me, My Lady. Thank you." When I sat again, he took the position at my right, where Citlallotoc had always stood when that rank had belonged to him.

"Your first duty as Justice of the Peace will be to identify who is still loyal to Topiltzin and bring those who have turned their back on him to account before the throne." I looked around at the other Council members as I spoke, taking in the diversity of reactions, ranging from stern nods of agreement to darting gazes and stiff frowns. I addressed the crowd. "I know that I have been missing from Tollan for a number of years, and many of you have doubts and fears about where we all go from here. But know this: I will personally see to Tollan's future and ensure that there is no struggle or unrest when the time comes for Topiltzin to leave us. There will be peaceful transition from one king to the next, and that king will carry on the important works that Topiltzin and I started here."

Many of the men nodded and hooted their approval. I made note of who remained silent, for Blood Wolf to question later.

"Let us feast to honor your return, My Lady," Blood Wolf suggested. "It will not be a grand feast, given the short notice, but we can still celebrate in good order."

I nodded. "You will see to it for me?"

"Absolutely. And perhaps tomorrow we can prepare something much larger and invite all of the nobles?"

"A good idea. The citizenry should know of the situation, so they too can rest easy knowing their future is being looked after with utmost care."

Blood Wolf bowed and stepped down from the dais to address the crowd. "Let us adjourn until nightfall, so we might prepare ourselves and our spouses for tonight's festivities. If you wish to renew your pledge of fealty, please arrive an hour prior to the feasting."

As the crowd dispersed in a flurry of conversation, I motioned Malinalli to me. "Please bring Mitotia tonight. I'm looking forward to seeing her again."

She nodded and turned to leave too, but then stopped to ask, "Should I invite Amoxtli too?"

"He's here in Tollan?" The last I'd heard he was the fire priest of Quetzalcoatl back in Culhuacan.

"He returned shortly after you left, to assume guardianship of his niece when Lord Black Otter and Night Wind went missing." She frowned. "Such a tragedy for her; she's lost so much of her family."

I gritted my teeth against the guilt grinding in my gut. "Tragic indeed. Yes, I would like him to attend, and Cuicatl as well."

She bowed then finally left.

By then, only Mazatzin remained behind, smiling at me with brotherly affection. "I cannot tell you how relieved I am that you've returned home, Quetzalpetlatl."

"It is so very good to see you again, my friend." I hugged my arms against my chest as I looked around. "So much has changed."

"As have you as well."

I started. "How have I changed?"

He shrugged. "I cannot put it into words, but your presence feels very different than it used to. Have you come to terms with whatever it was that made you leave in the first place?"

Now was my turn to shrug. "Come to an acceptance, perhaps, but some things can't be moved beyond...at least not just yet."

He nodded. "I must admit that...after all you said that morning, about the god and being through...this was the last place I ever expected to see you again."

"I hesitated for a long time, but in the end, I had to see Topiltzin one last time. And I had to make sure that you and Malinalli were all right. Seeing what Matlacxochitl was doing...I'm very glad I did come back. He would have returned us to the days of Ihuitimal, which is why finding the right successor for Topiltzin is a top priority."

"Do you have someone in mind?"

I smiled at him. "Well, you would make a very fine king."

But he shook his head. "And it is a job I would not accept. There are leaders, and then there are servants, and I'm afraid that in my heart, I am the latter."

"One can be both," I corrected him.

"Yes, one can. Both you and Topiltzin exemplify that. I, however, am not that kind of man."

I chuckled. "Always so modest. But don't worry, I know the temperature of your heart when it comes to ruling. I have someone else in mind."

"Who?"

"Citlallotoc, of course. He is Topiltzin's best friend, and best man, and he was an integral part of Tollan's founding and keeping the law. What better candidate could there be?"

Mazatzin frowned. "While I agree he is the best man for the throne, I don't know that you could convince him of it. He and Topiltzin haven't spoken in five years. I don't believe they parted on good terms."

"That may be, but surely he wouldn't deny his queen's summons?"

"Probably not, but he might well deny your more important request."

"We won't know until we ask him, will we? I need you to journey to Acolman and bring him here, so I may convince him that there is no better man for this job. And tell him that I won't accept *no* for an answer." I cringed almost as soon as I said it; I hadn't accepted his repeated *no*'s that night on the sacred precinct in Teotihuacan either, and now look at how things were. "Tell him I would be eternally grateful to him if he would come see me to discuss this important business."

He nodded. "Should I leave right away? If I hurry, I could likely get passage with a trade caravan heading out tonight."

"It would be for the best. We can't let disorder in the throne's succession continue much longer. Your having to leave so abruptly won't cause trouble with anyone close to you? A wife or a lover?"

Smiling bashfully, Mazatzin replied, "My devotions rest only with the god, and my king and queen. As always, my house is otherwise empty."

I smiled back, wistful. "I suppose not all of us are made for that kind of life, are we?" *And yet some of us feel incomplete without it.* I gave him a hug, taking in the solid, muscular bulk of his body, and the presence of the hump on his shoulder; he was so like his father physically and yet so very different in every other way. "Be sure to hurry back."

"If all goes well, I should be back within the week, with Citlallotoc."

"Thank you."

As I watched him go, I indeed felt grateful that I'd finally found the courage to come back.

CHAPTER EIGHTEEN

 Most of the Council came early to renew their vows of fealty to me, and a few more showed up late, as the servants brought the food out. They apologized for their tardiness and promised to make their pledges on the morrow, when it wouldn't interrupt the feasting and celebrating. I noticed five of the men who had been at the earlier council meeting didn't show up for the feast at all, and when I mentioned this to Blood Wolf, he promised to investigate their whereabouts after the meal.

I didn't give much more thought to it though. As an immortal, I didn't worry about things like assassins or kidnappers plotting against me anymore. I could set any attacker to rights with a mere flick of my finger. I'd seldom thought myself fearful when I was still a mortal queen, but that had been an illusion created by the constant presence of armed guards protecting me. Blood Wolf had assigned me guards but I found their presence more annoying than anything.

But I would let that go for everyone else's sake. It was best to play my role and not let it known that I was anyone but the woman they all remembered.

The high priests and priestesses of the various religious orders came as well, and though I was unfamiliar with the new high priest of the Smoking Mirror, the Chichimec woman Yaretzi was still his high priestess. She greeted me with an unsettlingly amused smile, though perhaps my reaction had more to do with the faint odor of guano that lingered around her. I didn't recall her ever smelling so repugnant, but maybe she'd been sacrificing bats to her dark god. It was a relief when she finally moved off to join the other priests in conversation; though I had the distinct feeling she was still watching me from afar.

Mitotia smiled politely when she came into the great hall at Malinalli's side and I embraced her heartily, squeezing her tight. The tattoo of the feathered serpent along her jawline looked newly freshened with ink and I tried to avoid looking at it if only to keep from letting a distasteful frown find its way onto my own face. Another reminder that my feud with Quetzalcoatl had nothing to do with those who worshipped him in blissful ignorance of his true character. Still, like always, my eye was drawn to it whenever I looked at her face.

"You're looking very well," I remarked as I escorted her to the two mats near the throne, which I'd reserved for her and Malinalli. "The fire priestess robes suit you."

"Thank you, My Lady. And you're looking very well too." When we stopped at the mats, she looked me over, a puzzled look on her face. "In fact...I could have sworn you used to have silver in your hair."

"I've been pulling them out whenever I find them," I lied. I hadn't given much thought to my own appearance for a while now, and in my mind's eye, I didn't have silver hairs. Given how many times I reformed my body from my teotl each day, it made sense that I'd unconsciously changed how I looked.

Malinalli smiled, accepting my explanation, but Mitotia continued studying my face with a suspicious eye. I smiled back, unsure what more to say.

Malinalli cleared her throat, finally distracting Mitotia. "Some people age more gracefully than others. There's no need to stare so, Mitotia."

"It's all right," I assured her. "I have been gone a while."

"Where were you?" Mitotia asked.

"Travelling. I never stayed in one place for long."

"And you found what you were looking for?"

I furrowed my brows. "Why do you think I was looking for anything?"

"Why else would you leave? If not to look for something you were missing?"

My face heated with a mixture of discomfort and anger. Why was she interrogating me so?

"That's quite enough, don't you think, Mitotia?" Malinalli cast me an apologetic glance. "What matters is she's back."

"Are you?" Mitotia asked, not letting me off that easily.

Thankfully I saw Amoxtli enter the great hall, saving me. "If you'll excuse me, my cousin has arrived and I really should go greet him." Without waiting for an answer, I hurried over to the entrance where Amoxtli stood, looking around.

A misty-eyed smile broke out on his face when I called out to him as I cut through the crush of men and women. He hurried to me and pulled me into a crushing hug. "Dear gods, I was sure you were gone for good," he murmured, tears in his voice. It was strange to see him so emotionally vulnerable; he was a plumper version of his father Ihuitimal, but he had a weary, weathered look about him. It was readily apparent these last five years had taken a heavy toll on him.

"It's so good to see you again, cousin," I whispered, unable to stop my own tears. "How have you been?"

"Busy. Always busy." He wiped at his cheeks then turned to a young woman standing behind him. "You remember Cuicatl?"

Cuicatl stepped up, an ill-tempered boredom hanging about her. She looked a good deal like her mother Jade Flower, but she had Black Otter's intense eyes. Standing next to Amoxtli, they looked very much like a troubled family.

"I do remember." The look on her face said that touching was off-limits, so I gave her a bow. "I suppose you often hear that you look like your mother."

She cast me an annoyed glance but then looked away before saying, "Sometimes."

"You're what...seventeen summers now?"

She sniffed in the affirmative.

"Did you take the trials to become a priestess?"

"She decided the priestly life isn't for her," Amoxtli answered. "Right now she's apprenticing with the feather worker who provides all of the king's banners."

"You enjoy it?" I asked Cuicatl.

She shrugged. "I suppose."

As we walked towards the head of the great hall, Amoxtli whispered, "Please pardon her, cousin. She's had a rough time: first she lost her mother, and then her father walked out on her, taking her brother with him."

Was that what they thought? "That's...horrible. No wonder she's so surly."

"I tried to do right by her, being that I'm all that's left of her immediate family, but I'm afraid I know little about children. I undoubtedly made mistakes along the way. She barely talks to me either."

"I'm so sorry."

"Perhaps I did the wrong thing by pushing her to embrace faith in the Feathered Serpent to help get through her losses, but I guess, after losing so many people, doubt feels a little more useful than faith."

I glanced back at Cuicatl as I climbed the dais. She was me; bitter and disenchanted and angry at having been a chisel others used to transfer blows. It soured my gut to know that I'd been a part of making her that way.

¤

After the feast, Malinalli escorted me back to my quarters. When we turned down the hallway from the vestibule, I noticed Mitotia watching us, a conflicted look on her face. She quickly turned and disappeared down the hallway to the priestly quarters when she realized I'd seen her.

"Is all well with you and Mitotia?" I asked as we walked.

"Of course." Malinalli didn't look at me though.

"I hope my being here isn't causing problems—"

"Why ever would you think that?"

I snapped my mouth shut. I couldn't admit that I'd overheard their conversation earlier today. Eventually I said, "I don't know. She didn't seem entirely comfortable when we talked, as if she doesn't trust me or something." When Malinalli didn't answer, I added, "It's understandable. I have been gone a long time, so naturally she'd be skeptical of why I've come back."

This time Malinalli smiled. "It's her skepticism that will make her a very strong high priestess when I step down."

"You're not going to stay the high priestess?"

She shook her head. "As much as I enjoy the work, she's the one you were grooming to take your place, and I bow to your superior knowledge of the matter, as the god's chosen high priestess."

"Mitotia will make a good high priestess someday, but my choice was just as political as anything else, Malinalli. Don't throw away your future because of a decision I made long ago in order to appease an offended ally."

"You know it's a position I never aspired to."

I sighed. "I know."

When we reached my room, she turned down the blankets for me and asked if I wanted to take a bath before bed. I told her I was fine, and so she bade me good night and started to leave. But she stopped at the curtain, hesitating.

I was eager to return to the Mexica camp; I'd stayed later than I thought prudent, but seeing her indecision now, I couldn't just send her away. "Do you want to talk?"

After a tense pause, she finally said, "I wish I could say Mitotia and I were happy, but...things that must happen in secrecy rarely ever remain good for long."

"Indeed not. It often becomes a burden difficult to bear."

"I love her as much as ever, but I've started to think that's just not enough, especially when it could cost us everything."

"Is someone threatening you?"

Malinalli fumbled with her hands as she turned to look at me. "Let's just say that the royal court isn't as let-live as it once was. Matlacxochitl's methods of rule weren't your brother's, and he surrounded himself with people who think just like him. He instituted an outright ban on relationships like mine and Mitotia's, and one of the guards found out about us and has threatened to expose us before the entire council...." She started shaking, tears flooding down her cheeks.

I hurried over to embrace her. "You don't have to worry about that anymore. Matlacxochitl isn't the law in Tollan, and I won't let anyone like him take the throne. In fact, I've already sent Mazatzin to Acolman to bring Citlallotoc back, so I can name him Tollan's heir."

She wiped her tears away. "Then what everyone says about you and Citlallotoc...it's true?"

I furrowed my brows. "What is everyone saying?"

"That you two were in love, but Topiltzin couldn't stand his best friend taking you to wife, and he forbade it, so you ran away, and Citlallotoc did the same a few weeks later, to be with you."

"I haven't seen Citlallotoc in five years."

She nodded. "It's just...the guards who went with you to Teotihuacan told stories, about you and Citlallotoc...on the steps of the Temple of the Moon."

A heated flush crept up my neck and I withdrew back to the bed. "Well, that much is true."

She sat next to me on the blankets. "Is that why you left?"

I didn't answer, but I couldn't meet her eyes.

"But if the two of you didn't run off to be together...then where have you been?"

"It's not important. What matters is that I'm going to fix all the messes I made, and then I will leave everyone in peace again, hopefully for good this time."

"You're not staying?" When I nodded, she sputtered, "But...but we need you! Tollan needs her queen, now more than ever!"

I shook my head. "I set this life aside five years ago, Malinalli. I can't come back to it."

"Of course you can!"

"You don't understand; I'm not the woman I was back then."

"Why not?"

"Because too much has happened; too much has changed for me, and I can't ever be that...that woman again."

Malinalli set a hand on my shoulder. "What really happened to you in Teotihuacan? Mazatzin said you cursed the Feathered Serpent and warned me not to trust him."

I shook my head, the words caught in my throat and the threat of tears stinging my eyes.

"Please tell me what went wrong, Quetzalpetlatl."

"I found out the truth, and it was more than I could handle," I finally sputtered.

"The truth about what?"

I shook my head. "If I told you, it would change everything between us."

"Surely not—"

"No, truly. If you knew the truth about me...we wouldn't be able to sit here talking like friends anymore."

"What could you have possibly done that would make me turn so absolutely against you?" she asked, worry in her eyes.

I laughed. She'd read that completely wrong. "Well, I did execute Black Otter, for murdering my son."

She stared at me, her mouth agape. "Black Otter killed Ehecacone?"

"In a jealous rage over Topiltzin. He just couldn't let go...."

"I'm so sorry, Quetzalpetlatl." She pulled me into a fierce hug.

I hadn't wanted the contact—in fact I was so strung up that the thought of anyone touching me made my magic pulse angrily—but as soon as her arms closed around me, the cloak of rage and fear slid away, replaced with a calm heat of gratefulness and safety. I hugged her back, burying my face in her shoulder. She stroked my hair, not saying anything, just being there.

But when I finally looked up at her again, the warmth grew into a pulsing heat. We were leaned in so close together that her breasts pressed against mine, soft and enticing in a way I'd never allowed myself to consider. Pain and longing lurked in her dark eyes, bringing a hitch to my chest and a throb to my ears. I thought of that time long ago when I'd nearly asked her to join me and Black Otter in my bed; of all of the times I'd seen her body when we'd shared a steam bath when we were just priestesses; the feel of her fingers dragging through my hair when she'd brushed and fixed my hair for me. *Women are the best*, Xochiquetzal had told me, and in that moment, finding out if she was right seemed eminently important.

I didn't have to make the first move though. Malinalli closed the small gap between us, but unlike the countless men I'd known, she didn't try to devour my mouth with hers, imposing her will. Instead she brushed her lips against my own, as if begging permission, and only when I moved mine against hers did she commit. She enveloped me in the sweet fragrance of jaguar flowers, making my mind drift, but my blood pulsed with raw, joyous desire, drowning out the sorrows plaguing my heart. She slid her hands up to my neck, to my cheeks, kind and comforting—something I hadn't felt in so very long and missed so very badly.

My hands wandered down her sides, taking in the softness of not just the robe's fabric, but of her body underneath. My own shivered, and she deepened the kiss. When my hands reached her hips, I bunched the cloth in my fists, kneading and pulling at it with increasing desperation. And growing hunger.

But you must be careful. It's very easy to drain them without much effort.

Xochiquetzal's warning broke through the fog in my head and I tore myself away from Malinalli, my heart thudding. She stared back at me with a worried look, almost as if she couldn't see me anymore but sensed my presence, like an apparition. As the haziness faded from her eyes, replaced by bewilderment, I turned away, gulping down fear and guilt. What in Mictlan was I doing?

"Quetzalpetlatl—"

"I'm sorry. I shouldn't have...we can't...."

"Why—?"

"I don't want to hurt you, Malinalli...or Mitotia."

She squeezed her eyes shut, balling her fists at her side. "Dear gods, what have I done?"

"You didn't do anything. I did it—"

But she shook her head. "I have to go. I'm sorry, but...I have to go." She hurried out into the garden, tearing aside the door curtain in her hurry.

I ran after her. "It's not your fault, Malinalli! Please! Come back! There's something I must tell you!" What did it matter now if I told her the truth of my nature? I'd already irrevocably changed everything for us.

But by the time I reached the portico outside my door, I saw only the tail of her robe just before she vanished down the corridor back into the palace. When Anacoana appeared at her own door curtain, blurry-eyed, I ducked back inside my room.

When I looked up to see the Feathered Serpent mural grinning back at me, I scooped up a small wooden idol next to my bed and threw it at it. The hollow idol split neatly in half but the plaster in the middle of Quetzalcoatl's face broke off all over the ground. "You must find it so funny, watching me fail at not hurting those I love," I panted.

The bells on my door curtain jingled. "Quetzalpetlatl?" Anacoana called. "Are you all right?"

Anguish stoked the plaintive pulse of hunger in my gut. I couldn't stay here and risk causing more trouble, so I jumped into the teoyoh without answering.

CHAPTER NINETEEN

When I returned to the Mexica camp, I slumped on the floor inside my tent, heavy with dread. "Why do I wreck everything I touch?" I muttered, sniffling back tears. Was I making a huge mistake involving myself in the succession issue in Tollan? Was I just helping Quetzalcoatl continue his lies? And would Mextli see my actions as a betrayal?

We can't go back, the desire agreed, even more surly than usual. *We'll only make things worse if we do.*

But we promised—

Let them work it out on their own. We've exposed Matlacxochitl, and Citlallotoc will come back and take the throne. They don't need us; humans are resilient in ways we never will be.

But what about what happened with Malinalli? Don't we owe her an explanation? But I felt only defensiveness when I thought of what happened.

It doesn't matter, the desire scolded me. *We can't change what happened. We need to stop hemming. Ehecacone is waiting for us to rescue him, so let's get on with this. We must convince Mextli to take us to see Smoking Mirror and we'll finally be done with the Feathered Serpent, once and for all.*

On that I could agree without hesitation. It was time to put aside my distaste for Smoking Mirror for the good of my son.

But when I reached Mextli's tent, he wasn't there, nor was he hiding out in a private bubble of the Divine Dream—or if he was, he wasn't answering me. I reached out with my divine senses.

I smelled his presence in the streams of magic coursing everywhere, but I hesitated to follow it. What if he didn't want to be bothered right now? Privacy was just as important to gods as it was to mortals, and it would be intrusive to show up unannounced.

Then let's go somewhere nearby, so we can at least know where he is, the desire suggested.

I reached out with my divine senses and a blink later I stood at the mouth of a path leading into a moonlit forest. Mextli must have been somewhere up the path, but where exactly was I?

It wasn't until I looked around and saw the tall stone walls of my garden outlined against the sky behind me that I realized I was in Omeyocan. A second path—this one of jagged stone steps—wound up a nearby mountainside to a circular building with clouds swirling serenely around it. Off to my right a third path led to the fields where Xipe Totec lived among his rows of maize.

I stared down the wooded path before me, but soon my gaze wandered back to the building on the mountain. It was Quetzalcoatl's house, as Mextli had told me. I didn't want to go up there.

And yet an irresistible impulse drew me towards the stairs. It wasn't as if Mextli was expecting me, after all, and he had said that Quetzalcoatl hadn't been back to Omeyocan for years. Part of me needed to go up there, almost as if seeing where he lived would somehow explain why the god I'd once loved so deeply could betray me.

After another glance towards the woods, I instead trekked slowly up the ragged steps carved out of the boulders and dirt.

I reached the top with surprising speed. Even though it was the middle of the night, the clouds were startlingly bright, and they slithered like snakes across the ground, coiling around my feet, encouraging me forward to the plain white door curtain hanging in tatters. I pulled it aside and peered within, my heart pounding.

I half expected to see Quetzalcoatl coiled up in his feathered serpent form, shaking the rattle on his tail just before striking me with his silver fangs, but the interior was completely empty. There was no hearth, no water jars, no blankets. The white walls were smooth, interrupted only by curtainless windows every few paces. The inside was massively large—much larger than I would have thought, given the size of the exterior. I stood in the center of the room and looked around, my hair ruffling in the gentle breezes twisting in through the unobstructed windows. It was a surprisingly calming place.

Feeling less apprehensive now, I went to one of the windows and looked out, over the buildings and fields below me. The path through the woods wasn't visible in the dark, but a glow of light filtered up through the forest canopy a ways into it. I spotted Xipe Totec tending his patch of maize and beans by the light of a bonfire in the clearing where we'd talked, dressed in his ragged old cape of human skin. Next to his field came the tall walls of my own garden. If it had been daylight out, I probably could have seen into my garden from this high vantage point, but it was shrouded in cold darkness now.

"It's really a very spectacular view, isn't it?" an unfamiliar voice spoke up behind me, and I jumped. I whirled around to see an old woman in the doorway, a halo of faint white light pulsing off her. Her eyes crinkled when she smiled at me. "My apologies. I didn't mean to startle you."

"Who are you?" I asked, taking deep breaths to slow my throbbing pulse.

"I'm just a very old creator goddess," she replied, coming inside. She didn't have a staff, but she walked with a slight hunch. "The humans call me the Snake Woman."

"Cihuacoatl," I whispered, awed. She was one of the very oldest of the gods, *the* mother goddess of all mother goddesses.

She nodded. "Then you're familiar with me?"

"I learned all about you in calmecac—that's the humans' priestly school—"

"I know. It was I who suggested to Quetzalcoatl to inspire the humans to create the schools to teach future priests and priestesses our stories." She shuffled over to my side and she too looked out over the fields and gardens below. "I'm also the one who taught him the secrets of creation; the same knowledge he in turn taught to you. You've done some very interesting things with it."

I furrowed my brow. "What do you mean?"

She chuckled. "Before you and Ehecatl formed that tree in Tamoachan, sex was no different than eating or drinking; a bodily necessity, but nothing more. But you took that knowledge and you stirred it around in your own nature and turned it into something completely new, something the world had never seen before. And it changed everyone. It changed civilization itself."

I shrugged. "It just happened. It's not as if I set out to change anything."

"It's the ones no one intended that end up mattering the most," Cihuacoatl replied. "Even we gods cannot fully comprehend how our choices can change the world, and even ourselves." She scrutinized me for a moment then said, "I hear you've been trying to recruit other gods to help you in some conflict with the Feathered Serpent."

I returned the considering gaze. "I was. And everyone but Smoking Mirror seems to want to stay out of it."

Cihuacoatl laughed. "When it comes to Quetzalcoatl, of course Smoking Mirror can't help himself. That conflict started at the dawn of time and it will continue long after humanity has disappeared. Listen to an old goddess, Mayahuel: you'd do best to stay out of that yourself."

"I can't. My son's life depends on it."

She shook her head. "My poor dear. One of the things they don't teach in the calmecac is that when it comes to the gods, it is our greatest gifts that are also our greatest weaknesses."

"Meaning?"

"Your love for your son is a means to an end for ambitious gods looking to increase their own power."

My temper flared. "Am I just supposed to abandon him, then?"

"Of course not. Just know that whatever choice you make, you will have regrets, so make sure they are ones you—and humanity—can live with." She then shuffled back out the way she came in.

I stared after her, both furious and baffled. What was I supposed to do with such vague advice?

When I returned to looking out the window, the sun had started creeping above the horizon, painting swathes of orange across the heavens.

"I didn't imagine I'd ever find you up here," Xochiquetzal suddenly spoke up. I jumped, startled yet again, but before I could turn around this time, she stood next to me at the window sill. The sensual scent of her flowers carried on the gentle breeze flowing by me.

"I was just…curious," I said.

"What did Cihuacoatl have to say to you?"

I glanced back at the door curtain again before replying, "I can't quite figure it out, to be honest."

"She's a weird old woman, isn't she?"

"Actually, she reminds me of the woman who raised me when I was a human being, and she turned out to be mostly right about everything."

"Then you're not going to accept Smoking Mirror's help, to get your son back?"

I frowned. "I think at this point, since no one else is willing to help me, I have very little choice but to go to him."

"Why haven't you asked me to help you?"

I blinked at her before admitting, "I don't know. I guess I just assumed that, since I have very limited powers…."

"That I would too?" She giggled. "I'll admit that I probably don't have much to offer, but I want to help however I can. Individually, we might not be as powerful as the old gods, but with enough of us working together, that's an entirely different matter."

I smiled. "You're absolutely right. Thank you."

The last time we'd talked, I'd been so deep into my depressive state that I hadn't given much thought to Xochiquetzal—and Xochipilli—nor really internalized that they were my children as much as Ehecacone was. But the thought sent a mix of joy and terror through me now. I wondered what she would want, or expect from me given this truth, and was I ready for it?

Xochiquetzal leaned her delicate elbows against the sill and uttered a contented sigh. "Isn't Omeyocan just beautiful?

"It is." I leaned against the sill too, taking in the fresh colors revealed by the rising sun. "And the view from up here is exceptional."

"It's the most magnificent one in all of Omeyocan."

"You come up here often?"

She shrugged. "When the Feathered Serpent isn't here, which has been a whole lot lately. I don't like to talk to him when he is here. Not that he would talk to me anyway." She frowned.

I frowned too. "He's not worth fretting about. Believe me; I know."

"It's just so unfair; he gets to have the most beautiful view of the world and yet he doesn't even care enough to be here to enjoy it. Nor does he share it. Do you know that he set up magic to keep Smoking Mirror out of here?"

I shook my head.

"Smoking Mirror is just as entitled to this beauty as him, and yet he denies him. He's awful!"

This wasn't the first time she'd mentioned Smoking Mirror with the dreaminess of a young girl in the thrall of infatuation, but still I raised an eyebrow in surprise. How could anyone feel anything but contempt for Smoking Mirror? He was beyond self-absorbed, and took great joy in hurting others, both humans and gods alike. I suspected she didn't know the real him at all. Still, it seemed rude to start lecturing her. "You really like him, don't you?"

She smiled. "Someday I'm going to make him my husband."

I couldn't imagine Smoking Mirror marrying anyone and having to share his powers, least of all with a good-hearted daughter of his nemesis. "Well, he'd be a fool if he refused you."

"Indeed he would be."

With the daylight growing, I could finally see down into my walled garden. There was the copal tree I once spent years and years sitting next to, watching the hummingbirds and the bees, and the top of the cave where my grandmother spent her time sleeping. Had Quetzalcoatl stood here watching me, plotting and scheming to steal me away from my grandmother, or had it just been a whim?

"Why haven't you gone back into your garden yet?" Xochiquetzal asked.

"I don't know. I guess I just didn't feel the need."

"If I had a house in Omeyocan, I would never leave it. That's why I want to be Smoking Mirror's wife. It's one of the only ways for us younger gods to have a place here in Omeyocan, since the old gods have scooped it all up and claimed it for themselves."

"But Mextli said that Smoking Mirror doesn't have a house here in Omeyocan either."

"He doesn't," Mextli suddenly answered from the doorway behind us.

"Well, Mictlan!" Xochiquetzal whispered under her breath, vexed. "Now he's going to make me leave." But then she switched on the smile and asked him, "Have you asked Smoking Mirror about my proposal yet?"

He frowned. "Of course I haven't. He hasn't time for such nonsense."

"It isn't nonsense!"

"He has much on his thoughts right now, and much to accomplish before he can even think about forming such alliances. Your time would be better spent offering your powers to service his plans. He will not forget those who stood with him when this is all over."

Xochiquetzal bunched her shoulders and smiled like a shy young girl. "He won't?"

Mextli's frown deepened in annoyance. "Of course not. And why are you doing that?"

"Doing what?" She batted her eyes at him in mock ignorance. I stifled a grin.

He harrumphed. "Both of you are love goddesses, and yet you don't see Mayahuel acting so ridiculously childish, do you?"

"That's because the best parts of love aren't for children," I said, the desire seizing my tongue. Heat already smoldered in my chest, and began pulsing throughout my body when he locked gazes with me. I couldn't tell if he was befuddled by my words or disgusted—for his hard, darker-self lurked in his gaze—but the desire didn't care; she just smiled back at him, sultry and daring.

"Indeed not." Xochiquetzal giggled but then told me, "I should go. I'm sure you two have much to...talk about." She flicked a trail of flower petals across Mextli's cheek as she strolled past him out the door. She laughed when he swatted it away, annoyed, then she disappeared down the stairs.

"If she thinks Smoking Mirror will have anything to do with her, she's fooling herself," Mextli muttered, scratching his cheek as if the petals had irritated his feathers. "He has even less patience for nonsense than I do."

The desire narrowed my eyes. "So we love goddesses are nothing but nonsense?"

He laughed. "Of course you're not, Mayahuel. Xochiquetzal, on the other hand, is pushy and impulsive and annoying. And completely predictable. You, however, are a mystery...and a challenge."

This time the desire purred, the heat building again. "And you like challenges, don't you?"

He pinned me with his gaze—leaving me even hotter and breathless—but instead of answering the question, he said, "There is someone I wish you to meet."

"Who?"

"It's a surprise." He gave me a secretive smile.

We walked back down the mountain, to the crossroads, and from there he turned down the path leading into the woods.

"I'm pleased to see that you're back to yourself," Mextli noted as we walked. "I was worried about you."

My face heated at the admission. "Thank you, for helping pull me out of my own stupidity."

"I suppose it can be difficult living with such stark duality when you not only don't understand why you're that way, but you've been told to view that part of yourself as evil."

"No one ever told me that it was evil," I said. "Quite to the contrary, it was an important part of life, to be taken seriously and nurtured. It just...made things difficult when I chose a life that was supposed to forsake it, as a sign of my devotion to Quetzalcoatl."

"It doesn't surprise me that the Feathered Serpent would demand such nonsense. He would reduce all of us to half-beings if he could. But you needn't forsake anything anymore. You are free to be yourself, unabashed and unashamed."

His words made my heart race.

The path soon led us to a small stone house tucked among the trees. "Wait here, while I make sure it's a good time to visit." He pulled aside the curtain and stepped inside, letting it fall behind him. The sound of sweeping came from within.

As I looked around, I noticed a man standing at the corner of the house farthest from me, a pipe clenched between his yellowed teeth. He wasn't giant, like Mextli, but he had the same hard look about him. Red and white stripes decorated his aura, and he wore a feathered cloak over his left shoulder. His stare was piercing.

I cleared my throat, swallowing back the strange anxiety and discomfort his mere presence instilled in me. He smelled of blood and lightning. "Hello."

He chewed his thick pipe stem before answering, "Mayahuel."

I looked at the curtain again, hoping Mextli would come out soon, but I jumped back when I returned my gaze to the man to find him standing closer to me, almost within arm's reach. "What are you doing?" I demanded.

He studied me with cold, calculating eyes. "Do I scare you?"

I stood taller, both put-out and embarrassed. "Of course not."

"You're twitchy, like a deer...no, like a rabbit." He smelled the air. "Yes...definitely a rabbit."

The curtain turned aside and Mextli stepped outside again. He too started when he saw the other man. "Mixcoatl. Coatlicue said you were out hunting."

Mixcoatl flashed a clever grin at him. "I'm always hunting." He turned his appraising gaze back on me. "Yes...most definitely a skittish little rabbit."

I couldn't help staring back at him. This god had my human father's name, but thankfully the resemblance ended there. After all of the stories Mitotia had told me about her people's patron god—how he'd raped his way into power, and maintained that control through a ritual reenactment of that first violation year after year—if this Mixcoatl had looked like my mortal father, it would have been more than I could stand.

Mextli frowned. "You've met Mayahuel, Goddess of the Maguey?"

"I've acquainted myself with the Feathered Serpent's collaborator."

Before I could say anything, Mextli stepped right up to Mixcoatl, hulking over him like a bear, his feathers puffed. "Watch your forked tongue, Cloud Serpent. Funny you should throw around accusations of treachery given your own children's collaborations with my sorceress sister."

"And yet your mother still became my wife." Mixcoatl grinned as he returned the pipe stem to his mouth.

That made Mextli's feathers ruffle even more, but before he could retort, the curtain came aside and a woman stepped out between them. "There will be no battles outside my door curtain."

I would have expected Mextli's mother to be a giant, like her son, but in fact she was slight of build. Nor did she resemble her son in the ways that human children often took after their parents. Her skin was smooth and colored a hue typical of humans, and she wore her long hair tied back in a tidy knot. No feathers grew from her body like they did on Mextli; she looked completely human, even dressed in a plain dress that resembled the robes worn by novice priests and priestesses. She had no divine glow to her, but she smelled like the serpent house in Tollan.

"I was just leaving anyway." Mixcoatl tapped out his pipe against the corner of the house and the ashes turned to clouds as they fell. He then tucked the pipe into his jaguar-skin belt.

"Why don't you make yourself useful and go hunt the Feathered Serpent?" Mextli barked.

Mixcoatl grinned at him. "Now that would hardly be sporting, would it?" He darted a glance at me but said nothing as he walked away, down the path back the way we'd come just moments before.

Mextli watched him, eyes narrowed, but then he turned to the woman. "Mother, this is Mayahuel."

When she turned her gaze upon me, I felt a strange dread, like she was a snake and I was a mouse she was watching. "A pleasure to meet you at last," she said, bowing her head to me. "I'm Coatlicue."

With her name being Snake Skirt, perhaps her smell wasn't so strange after all. "It's very nice to meet you as well." I returned the bow.

Her appraising gaze swept over me a breath before she announced, "Let us go inside. I'm eager to hear all about you, Mayahuel." Without waiting for an answer, she went past the curtain.

I looked up at Mextli but he only smiled and held the door curtain open for me.

The interior of the house resembled the inside of a temple. A wooden idol that was a pretty good representation of Mextli sat against the back wall, clutching a sword in one hand and a serpent scepter in the other. Several reed mats sat in front of it, and Coatlicue sat upon one of them. She motioned Mextli and me to take the other two. "Can I offer you something to eat?" The water jar sitting in the corner floated over to her outstretched hand.

"Thank you," I murmured when she handed me a clay cup filled with blood. Mextli accepted one as well and downed it in one swallow while I nursed mine politely.

"Mextli tells me my people have welcomed you into their community," Coatlicue said, sipping from her own cup. When I nodded, she went on, "They were always a very devoted people, very respectful of their gods. It's such an honor that they have accepted my son as their leader. Treat them well, and they will always return the favor. I understand that you too were a priestess."

I tensed a little at her words but nodded. "For most of my life, yes."

"Me as well, as you can probably tell." Coatlicue motioned at our surroundings. "Did you enjoy it?"

"For the most part, yes."

She nodded. "I loved it; a much better life than most slaves could claim, and then for the Smoking Mirror to choose me to bear Mextli...." She sighed longingly. "I was truly a blessed mortal."

I blinked. "You were fully human?"

"As mortal as any Mexica."

Mextli answered, "Smoking Mirror turned her immortal moments before my birth, and later I brought her back from Mictlan."

Both my rational side and the desire gasped simultaneously, and it was all I could do to not blurt my thoughts out loud. *It's possible to turn mortals into gods? What if we could turn Little Reed immortal?* I had to make myself listen to the conversation again.

"And he avenged me against my wretched daughter." Coatlicue beamed. "No mother could ever hope for a more perfect son."

"Mextli's impressive on multiple fronts," I said, hoping my distraction hadn't been obvious. "He's taught me much, and I owe him a great deal."

"As do we all," she said, her smile careful again. "I understand you have a house here in Omeyocan."

I nodded. "It's the garden back at the crossroads, next to Xipe Totec's fields."

"You're so lucky. I had to marry Mixcoatl to gain a place here in Omeyocan."

"You could have remained with the Mexica, Mother," Mextli said. "You are welcome among them."

She waved him off. "I know I complain about Mixcoatl and his ways, but I am quite content, my fierce hummingbird. It isn't as if he demands much of me; he has no mortal cravings, and so in that regard, we are well-matched. Besides, the nomadic life is not to my liking; I much prefer high stone temples to meager tents. But someday, when you've settled them somewhere and they can build me a permanent temple, I'll come stay with you on earth again."

He nodded, seemingly disappointed.

"Besides, you have much on your plate right now, with the war with Quetzalcoatl and other political matters. I'd just as soon stay out of it, and I can't really do that if I'm down there right now." She shifted her gaze to me again. "If I might ask, Mayahuel, where do you stand in the current conflict?"

"She is with us, Mother," Mextli said before I could answer.

When she raised an appraising eyebrow at me, I said, "In fact, Smoking Mirror and I are close to an agreement. I'm most definitely not on the Feathered Serpent's side anymore. I learned from my mistakes."

"We all make them." Coatlicue held up the blood jar. "Would you like a refill?"

"Actually, I think we'll be on our way, Mother," Mextli said, rising to his feet. He had to hunch over to keep from striking his head on the ceiling. "Mayahuel was going to show me her garden today."

That was news to me, but since he seemed eager to leave, I declined another cup of blood and thanked her for her hospitality. "It was very nice to meet you."

"Likewise." She watched me all the way to the door curtain—which Mextli was holding open for me—and again I felt like a mouse being stalked by a snake. It was a relief to be out into the open again, away from her.

CHAPTER TWENTY

As Mextli and I proceeded back down the path, I said, "Your mother seems...nice."

He laughed. "You needn't mince words, Mayahuel. I know she's intense. Even I find it difficult to be around her for more than a few moments at a time. And I sensed you were becoming uneasy with her questions."

Then it wasn't just me. "Regardless, she thinks the world of you."

"She does."

We walked in silence for a moment before I finally mustered up the courage to say, "So...I didn't know we can change mortals into immortals."

"Technically speaking, only three of us can," Mextli corrected me. "Lord Death has the ability, of course, as does Smoking Mirror."

"And who's the third one?"

"Quetzalcoatl."

My newfound hope fell back to earth. "And it's not something that can be learned?"

He gave me a curious look as he answered, "It's a power that you either have or don't. It cannot be taught."

"But how do you know if you have it or not?"

"You just do." He cast me a curious look. "Why?"

I couldn't admit that I would use such a power to save Little Reed's life, so I shrugged and answered, "It just sounds like a really nice power to have."

"I suppose it could be useful under the right circumstances."

After a moment of walking silently, I asked, "Was there a particular reason you wanted me to meet your mother?"

He shrugged. "She heard I was helping you, and she was curious. She asked to meet you, and so I obliged her."

"Like the obedient son," I said with a laugh. "Do you think I passed her test?"

"Test?"

I laughed some more but waved him off. "Never mind. Are we really going to my garden?"

"It was an excuse to bow out gracefully but...you haven't been back in thousands of years. Don't you think it's time you looked in on it?"

By then we'd reached the crossroads again and the massive walls stood before us. There was no door anywhere in sight, so I peered up at the top, squinting against the sun shining bright in the sky. "Any idea how we get inside?"

"The same way you got out?" he suggested.

Back then, strange magic had tried to convince me that I'd never reach the top, and I didn't relish battling it again. It had taken days for me to reach the top—and my freedom. There had to be an easier way....

I approached the wall and ran my fingers over the gaps in the stones, searching for signs of a hidden doorway. As I'd predicted, the magic that had tried to keep me inside still pulsed in the walls, but this time it lit up my own in all new ways. The wall magic shrank away from me like a leech from a flame. I pushed harder, forcing it back, and my fingers started sinking into the wall as if it were blocks of honey rather than stone. Once I'd submerged myself to my elbows, I pushed outward, like parting a curtain.

The walls gave way, revealing a tunnel leading to the garden within. I stood holding the walls open, taking in the strange perspective.

Mextli gazed over my shoulder. "Well, aren't you going to go in?"

Indeed, what was I waiting for? The tunnel was empty and the only life visible beyond it was the bees, butterflies, and hummingbirds puttering around the flowers and trees. Mextli had said that the Earth Monster had been exiled from Omeyocan, and the garden's stillness reflected that.

I finally stepped inside and went to the mouth of the tunnel, where the hard dirt gave way to lush grass and beds of vibrant flowers in black, fertile soil. The air smelled like summer in the gardens back in Tollan, and it should have made my heart swell, but there was another odor here, one of foreign yet familiar magic. And it was everywhere.

Unlike Quetzalcoatl's house—which was bigger on the inside than the outside—mine was smaller on the inside than I thought it would be. The patch of garden was maybe twenty paces across at its longest side, and the copal tree took up most of that space. The rest of the garden was dominated by the tunnel, which I now recognized as the cave where my grandmother had always slept. I'd never found the garden exit because she'd been guarding it all along, keeping me inside.

And it had been her magic that had tried to deter me from climbing the walls—that tried to convince me that attempting to leave was futile. None of the magic around me was my own. This garden wasn't mine; it was built completely from my grandmother's jealousy and anger.

And I wanted it gone.

As if I'd given a silent order, the walls began melting away. The flowers shriveled in on themselves, regressing slowly back into their seeds and the cave vanished. The ground turned to clouds and now Xipe Totec's fields were clearly visible, as was the crossroads and the path into the woods. Xipe Totec emerged from the rows of maize, and leaned on his digging stick, looking like a human farmer in spite of his blood-red face and cape of skin. He didn't say anything as he chewed a stick of grass and watched me intently.

Mextli looked around at my blank clouds with mild interest. "Not to your liking?"

"It wasn't mine," I said. "I didn't build it, and it's just a reminder of things I'd rather forget. I'd rather start over fresh."

"A good idea. What are you going to build?"

"I don't know. What would you build, if this was your house?"

He raised an eyebrow as he looked around. "I've never really given it any thought. I suppose it would have to be someplace that makes me feel safe. Xipe Totec has his field of vegetables, and Tlaloc submerges himself in water, and my mother lives in the temple where she served Nanahuatzin during her mortal life."

I nodded. "You make your tent look like a palace hall."

But he shook his head. "That is not where I feel safest." When I cocked an eyebrow at him, he went on, "My priests and warriors have certain expectations of me and who I am; that is reflected in what I choose to show them when they enter my temple. Where I spend my own time...that is a different matter."

"Where do you go?" When he hesitated to answer, I said, "I promise not to judge, no matter what it is."

Mextli gave me an earnest look before admitting, "My mother's womb."

His answer shocked me, but I trained my face to not show it. I had been certain it would be something like an army camp, surrounded by soldiers and weapons—all of the things he ruled as a god—and yet instead he longed to return to the cramped quarters of a human woman's womb? It seemed so strange.

"It's the only place I have ever felt truly safe," he said, the earnest expression set in stone upon his face. "Ever since I was born, I've been in a constant state of vigilance, never able to relax my defenses. I wish I could find that kind of peace again."

Every time I spent any time at all with Mextli, I found myself surprised by the new depths he revealed to me. *And here I promised not to judge him, and yet I did it anyway,* I thought, ashamed.

"So, where do you feel safest?" he asked me.

I turned my attention back to my empty space. I always chose my quarters in Tollan for the Divine Dream, but after yesterday, that didn't feel quite so safe and happy anymore. But the area outside the Mexica camp hardly felt like home either.

But there is one place that's always felt like home to me. I closed my eyes, imagining the sacred precinct where I'd spent so many years of my life—far more than anywhere else I'd ever lived since being reborn. I thought of all those evenings sitting in Nimilitzli's house, eating dinner and discussing religious philosophy with her. It was one of the few memories I could look back upon without regrets.

When I opened my eyes, the blank clouds had been replaced with a dreamy replica of Xochicalco's sacred precinct, complete with temples, priestly houses, calmecac, and the vast staircases. Mextli and I stood in front of the doorway to Nimilitzli's house, in the shelter of the side of Quetzalcoatl's temple.

Seeing the painted bas relief of the feathered serpent on the side used to fill me with joy and purpose, but now I felt only a sad sense of loss. I moved my hand across it in my field of vision and the carvings disappeared, replaced with a flat plaster surface, waiting for new decoration. For now I left it blank.

Mextli gazed around with interest. "You have very powerful magic, Mayahuel."

I chuckled. "Hardly."

But he shook his head. "Only the most powerful gods create such elaborate magical renderings, so yes, you're definitely quite powerful."

"This isn't elaborate; I just copied that place we visited, when you taught me to use the teoyoh."

"Still...to be able to not just create this, but to hold it together so flawlessly.... That's not something most gods can do. Very impressive!"

I looked around some more, not sure how to take this compliment. I was hardly powerful compared to the likes of Quetzalcoatl or Smoking Mirror. Even Mextli's magic seemed to dwarf my own. But I was just beginning to learn, and it often surprised me what I was capable of. Maybe I was underestimating myself.

And wasn't that what Quetzalcoatl said, that people tended to underestimate me?

And since when should we believe a word that comes from his split tongue? the desire hissed.

Mextli walked across the precinct, towards the calmecac, taking in everything with an unnervingly awestruck expression. I followed but sat on the stone ring of the cistern, remembering all those afternoons when Malinalli and I would eat our lunches there between teaching classes. Back then I never would have thought of doing anything like what happened last night, but I wondered if even back when we used to sit here sharing lunches, had she felt that tickly feeling in her stomach whenever she looked at me? I felt it a bit myself now when I thought of her, remembering the softness of her robe and the curve of her hips, the taste of her tongue....

"That's Quetzalcoatl's temple, isn't it?" Mextli was staring back at the temple now, a contemplative look on his face.

"It was, but I stripped all of the carvings from it, so now it's just a temple. I haven't yet decided how to redecorate it."

He nodded then turned back to me. "I can't say I'm surprised that you chose this place. It was obvious when we visited the earthly site that it meant a great deal to you."

"It's the only place I've ever truly felt at home."

He knelt in front of the cistern and set his unfeathered hand on the stone. He didn't say anything, as if feeling the heat left behind by the sun blazing overhead.

But strangely I felt as if he were touching me instead; it wasn't a tactile sensation, but rather a caress of energy deep inside of me, and it only intensified when he ran his hand back and forth over the stone surface, feeling the contours and texture.

"Your magic...it's...so very strong, Mayahuel," he murmured, admiration in his voice.

When he looked up at me, his eyes intense, it was more than the desire could take. Throwing all caution aside, I leaned forward and put my lips to his, desperate to have him close to me. I even bunched my fists in the front of his feathered xicolli and tried to pull him to me, but he was so immovable that I ended up pulling myself to him instead.

And yet he didn't return my gesture in the least; in fact, he seemed completely unaffected by my attempt to kiss him and when I pulled away, confused—and not without an angry flame of frustration—he stared back at me, puzzled. And a bit suspicious. "What are you doing?" His voice was a whisper yet it sounded like a booming shout to my ears.

I withdrew from him, swallowing back embarrassment. I couldn't find words that wouldn't sound ridiculous.

But he set his hand on my arm, keeping me from scooting further away. "I meant...what does it mean?"

I gaped at him before finally saying, "Well, it doesn't have to mean anything—"

"Then why did you do it?"

"Because...I don't know." And it was the truth. "It's just one of those nonsense things we love goddesses do, I guess," I stammered.

He frowned, skeptical. "You're angry at me for what I said about Xochiquetzal."

I shook my head. "I'm not angry at you. It's just...I don't know how to explain it to you so you would understand."

"Perhaps you should try anyway."

A flush crept up my neck. *Get back here and help me!* I scolded the desire. She was so much better at this than my rational side. But she remained aloof, and Mextli was watching me expectantly, so I pressed on as best I could. "You've...you've been very good to me...and...and I like having you around, and...you make me feel...."

When my words stalled, he raised his one eyebrow. "I make you feel what?"

"Lots of things; dizzy, hot, a bit fluttery in my stomach—"

"I'm sorry."

I laughed. "It's not unpleasant. If anything, it's quite wonderful."

"I'll have to take your word for it because it sounds disturbing to me."

"Then the kiss...it was unpleasant for you?"

"No. But frankly, I don't understand why the humans do it so much."

Now the desire butted me aside, indignant. "That's because you did it completely wrong! You sat there like a stone statue!"

Mextli cracked a smile. "What was I supposed to do?"

I scooted closer again, right up to him, the desire pulsing defiantly through me. "Just do what I do, and you'll see." I then leaned in and kissed him again.

This time he mimicked my every move, parting his lips when I did, setting his hands on my shoulders when I put mine on his, and offering his tongue when I offered him mine—

"Oh!" I pulled back, startled.

He looked at me with uncertain eyes. "What did I do? You told me to follow your lead—"

"You have feathers on your tongue!"

He frowned. "Of course I do. The entire left side of my material body consists of feathers."

"The entire?" My gaze started wandering down to his loincloth but I caught myself. "I guess I just wasn't expecting them, that's all."

"If they bother you, I can make them go away—"

"No, no, it's all right." I pressed closer again, the desire calming the nervous thudding of my heart. "I think they're...interesting." I took his mouth to mine again, greeting his half-feathered tongue with enthusiasm.

I'd expected a distinct—even unpleasant—taste, thanks to the feathers, but in fact he had none at all, except perhaps a trace of heat and sunlight. When I deepened the kiss, he followed suit, his hand movements copying my own as I let my fingers venture lazily down the contour of his chest. When he started massaging my left breast through my dress because I did the same to him, I knew I could easily get him to do whatever I wanted him to. I needed only to move my hand on him wherever I wanted him to touch me. *Just think of the wonderful purposes we could put that half-feathered tongue of his to,* the desire purred, sending a shiver through me—a motion he mimicked as well.

But the more closely he copied me, the more my enthusiasm waned. While the pleasure he was giving me was wonderful—and disturbingly reminiscent of my more intimate moments with Quetzalcoatl—it all felt hollow when I considered that I wasn't giving him the same. With humans, it was always readily apparent that they were enjoying themselves as much as I was, but by all appearances, Mextli was merely going through the motions and not feeling anything himself. There was no passion in his kiss, no longing in his touch. I might as well have been touching myself for all the good this was doing either of us. I didn't even know how to react to him being so completely unaffected by me. I'd never encountered such a reaction.

He just needs to learn, the desire chided, a hint of desperation to her voice. *What did we know of such things before the Feathered Serpent taught us the secrets of creation? We just need to teach Mextli too.*

The thought wasn't without appeal. And really, wasn't this what I'd wanted all along? Someone that I knew my magic didn't affect, so I'd know his or her feelings for me were genuine?

But what about Little Reed?

Little Reed is dead, the desire growled.

No, he isn't.

He might as well be, for all the help we can give him.

The truth of her words sent a spike of anguish roaring through me. I didn't want to believe that it was truly over for good, but I suspected I was just deluding myself.

Mextli pulled away, worry in his eyes. "Something's wrong."

I shook my head. "No, nothing is wrong. Absolutely nothing." I just hoped it didn't sound like the lie it was.

"You're sure?" When I nodded, he said, "There is something I wish to ask you."

"What would that be?"

He looked charmingly nervous now as he rubbed the back of his neck. "Would you be interested in an alliance...with me?"

I smirked, puzzled yet amused by his nervousness. "An alliance? But I thought we already had one, of sorts."

"I mean an *official* alliance, before the other gods, and before the Mexica."

I still wasn't sure what exactly he meant, but then it dawned on me. "Are you proposing marriage to me?"

He sat up stiffly. "If that is how you wish to think about it, then yes, I am asking you to be my wife."

I raised an eyebrow, unsure what to say. "This is rather sudden, isn't it?"

He furrowed his brow. "I'm not sure what timing has to do with anything. It's readily apparent that we complement each other quite well, and as you said, we've already agreed to an unofficial alliance."

"I suppose."

He looked nervous again as he added, "Besides, you know things about me that I've never told anyone...not even Smoking Mirror. And I believe I've proven my good intentions, have I not? We are friends, right?"

"We are," I agreed. "And you did save me from myself the other day. I could never thank you enough for that."

He smiled, pleased. "See? It seems only rational that we take this to the next step, by solidifying it into an official alliance recognized by both gods and men."

"I suppose it does, but Mextli...." Too flustered to know what to say, I finally settled on, "I need time to think about it. This is a big step...a huge step, really."

Mextli nodded. "I understand. I do not wish to rush you to a decision, so please, take whatever time you need."

An awkward silence fell between us, and after a few moments of looking around, Mextli said, "I should go back to the camp. I haven't spoken to my warriors yet today, and I'm sure they're waiting for my daily address."

I nodded. "I'm going to stay here a little while longer, do some more work around my new house."

"I shall see you later today then?" he asked.

I nodded, but when he rose to leave, I asked, "This alliance...is that why you wanted me to meet your mother?" I couldn't keep the grin from quirking at my lips.

"That is standard practice, isn't it? To introduce a potential new spouse to the rest of one's family?" he asked.

I laughed. "It is. I just never took you for the...traditional type. At least not when it comes to these kinds of things."

He smiled back at me. "You're not the only one who can surprise, Mayahuel." He then leaned down and gave me another kiss, this one completely his own, and startlingly wonderful. It left me feeling pleasantly numb and floating, as if we were standing on a cloud—which I suppose we were. I hadn't felt this disconnected from pain and sorrow and worry since....

Well, since that first time that Little Reed had kissed me next to the temple the night before he left for the army.

CHAPTER TWENTY-ONE

Once Mextli left, I wandered around my recreation of Xochicalco, trying to focus on how I wanted to rework the little details, but my mind kept wandering back to those moments next to the cistern. This new development was exciting, for sure, but all the same, it felt a bit like a betrayal of everything Little Reed and I had.

We can't keep clinging to what never was—and never can be. It's time to move on, the desire chided me.

But he's not even dead yet! How can we just jump into anything more serious than friendship with Mextli while Little Reed is still living? Don't we at least owe it to him to wait until he's passed on to Mictlan?

No, we don't. We owe nothing to anyone but ourselves. We've spent all of our life catering to the needs of others; it's time to give some thought to our own happiness, and take some action towards achieving that.

It just...feels so wrong.

The desire sighed. *I feel it too, but what if we hem too long and we lose our chance with Mextli?*

It feels like we're trying to replace Little Reed.

No one could ever replace him. We both know that. But Mextli could be very good for us too, if we just give him the chance. We could finally be happy.

Or we might not be, I countered. *He finds our physical needs ridiculous.*

But with a little time and effort, we can change that, the desire replied. *He's already taken to the little bit we've taught him about love.*

I stared wistfully at the cistern across the precinct from where I sat on the bottom step of the temple. *He has. But what if he finds our need for sex repulsive and disgusting?*

Then we know he's not worth our time. But if he isn't...?

"Then it could be something very good," I murmured, the courage and sense of purpose building.

All this thinking is just wasted time until we know whether or not he's willing to meet our needs, so let's go talk to him.

"Agreed."

◻

When I arrived back in camp, I found several priests standing outside Mextli's tent with the morning offering of two hearts in a reed basket. They started at my sudden appearance, but they soon bowed. "Good day, Lady Mayahuel."

"I realize it's offering time, but I have important business with your master and it will require some privacy. I need you to come back later." I didn't want Mextli distracted by his stomach.

The priests exchanged nervous glances before the lead one replied, "His Grace becomes very...edgy when his offerings aren't delivered on time."

"I will make sure he knows that it was I who told you to wait, and I promise that he won't take any frustrations out on you."

He bowed. "Thank you, My Lady. We shall wait over by the fire." He and the other two priests retreated.

I faced the tent flap but hesitated, nervous now that the moment was upon me. *I want you to do the talking for us. You're better at this.*

The desire grabbed control of my tongue and some of the anxiety melted away. "Mextli! May I come in?"

"Of course," Mextli called, so I stepped inside.

Mextli sat on his icpalli throne, but he'd turned it around and sat staring into a garden off a patio behind the dais. It hadn't been there the other times I'd visited him, nor had he ever struck me as the kind who appreciated flowers and gardens.

But as I approached, I realized he was watching a swarm of hummingbirds dueling each other with their pointy beaks, their movements a carefully choreographed dance of violence and blood. I stood at his side, watching it too, fascinated. "Are they your nahuals?" I asked after a while.

He nodded. "Very fierce, aren't they?"

"Most definitely. One wouldn't think so to look at them, as tiny as they are."

"Size has little to do with one's fierceness. After all, you stood up to me multiple times in the past."

I chuckled. "I suppose I did."

"And I hear your nahuals are not to be taken lightly either," he said with a grin. "As individuals, they might not look like much, but as a group, driven to protect their mistress, even the fiercest of nahuals wouldn't stand their ground against them."

"They are a force to be reckoned with," I replied, the smile falling from my face at the memory of all those rabbits swarming over Smoking Mirror's nahual, trying to save Ehecacone. And I'd rewarded their efforts by killing them under a flood of octli magic. Even now, the memory of that jaguar grinning at me set my heart thudding and the magic tingling in my fingers. "And yet it still wasn't enough."

Mextli set his hand on mine and gave it a warm squeeze. "We will get your son back, Mayahuel. And soon. I promise."

The determination in his eyes made my heart race even faster, but pleasantly so. Just another reason to give serious consideration to a formal alliance with him.

I'd only ever imagined myself married to one person—Little Reed, of course; even when I'd stupidly pursued matters with Red Flint, I hadn't thought at all of what our marriage would be like but rather how it would wound Little Reed. And though I'd tried to make myself embrace my marriage to Black Otter, my heart knew all along that Little Reed wasn't really dead and so had refused.

But now things were different. I'd had the marriage to Little Reed, and though it hadn't been everything I'd always dreamed it would be, my heart finally accepted the inevitable. That dream was over, and it was time to find new ones. I could see a future with Mextli, the two of us together leading the Mexica into a bright future, with him continuing to teach me how to be a goddess while I taught him how to be more than just a war god. I'd settled for much before and came to resent it, but with Mextli, there would be none of that. He would accept the whole me, or we would just be friends.

Mextli leaned towards me, his elbow against his knee, his hand still on mine. "Do you wish to talk about something?"

I nodded. "Very much so."

He summoned a second reed throne, next to his own. "Then let us talk." He motioned for me to sit too.

I did so, the nervousness creeping up on me again, but this time I was determined. "I want to accept your proposal."

"I'm glad to hear it."

"But I must make certain that we're in agreement about expectations and...needs, on both sides." I withdrew my hand from his to smooth my dress across my knees. "In the past, I've given up things I wanted, and I cannot do that again."

"I do not wish you to give up anything on my account. I wish for this alliance...this marriage to be mutually beneficial."

"What would be your expectations of me in this?"

"Loyalty, of course. That would be paramount. As is support for my decisions, though I would also want your input on matters, such as how we deal with our humans, our enemies, and our allies. I won't expect absolute agreement in matters of war, but I would expect that if there were disagreement, you will respect my decision and not undermine me with your own actions."

"I would expect the same of you," I said. "I imagine there will be things we both feel strongly about and that we can respect each other enough to come to a consensus about how to proceed."

"I imagine so as well. Other than that...." He thought for a moment before saying, "I won't expect you to be friends with Smoking Mirror, but I must ask that you understand that my relationship with him is important, and I will not abandon it, not even for you."

"I understand, and I request the same of you regarding the people of Tollan. They may live in the Feathered Serpent's sacred city, but they must be left alone. And that includes Topiltzin."

Mextli looked at me with sad, pitying eyes. "Mayahuel—"

"This is not negotiable. Without that promise, there will be no alliance."

Looking annoyed, he opened his mouth to argue more, but then he sighed and nodded. "You have my word. Is there anything else?"

I nodded and took a deep breath. *I can do this.* "As gods, we both have our own special needs, things that are just part of who we are. You're a war god, so it's only natural that you should need to wage war, both offensive and defensive, right?"

"On that we can agree."

With the desire in charge, I'd expected a bit more confidence in all this, but she was surprisingly nervous as she spoke. "As a love goddess, I have...certain interests...certain *needs* that are just part of who I am. It's as inescapable for me as your need for war, and any meaningful relationship we're to have...it must include it. I can get some of what I need from humans, but I want it with you as well."

Mextli stared at me, confused. "Perhaps you should just state what it is you require of me."

My mouth felt dry, making it so easy to stay silent and stall by trying to find the perfect words to say.

He sighed then took my hand in his again, his grip warm and calming. "Is this something the humans taught you to be embarrassed about? Like your feeding habits?"

"Yes. No. Yes, maybe, I don't know. But...they are one in the same." When he wrinkled his brow at me, I said, "When I have sex with humans, it nourishes me, the way that eating hearts nourishes you. I was never taught that my appetites were shameful—not systemically, anyway—but I figured out early on that my desires and urges were not like other women's, and trying to live my life as a celibate priestess in the face of my divine nature was...soul-wrecking in ways that it wasn't for humans. It was a relief to finally understand why I am the way I am, and to not wonder anymore if I was crazy."

"Then why all of the evasiveness about your feeding habits? Why did you hide it from me?"

"Because you kept saying I was acting so human, like that was a bad thing, so why should I think you would react any other way to this?"

Mextli's grip tightened a bit. "My apologies for making you think that," he murmured. "It wasn't my intention to make you feel it necessary to hide your true self from me."

"If we're to be husband and wife, I want to share everything with you." I reached up to touch his feathered cheek with my free hand. "Everything."

But the look on Mextli's face was mystifyingly unreadable. "I'm honored that you think so highly of me, Mayahuel, but...you feed through sex and yet you wish to have sex with me; that would be like me wishing to eat your heart, if you had one."

It was on the tip of the desire's tongue to tell him I did have a heart, but I held the words back for her. *He seems so sure that we don't have one. Are hearts something most gods don't have?*

And if so, what did my having one mean?

Let's not share everything all at once, the desire agreed, cautious. *One step at a time.*

"I realize it sounds strange, but I don't believe it works the same way with gods," I finally answered. "The first person I was ever intimate with was Quetzalcoatl, and he didn't suffer any ill effects. He's the one who taught me the art of creation."

Uncertainty lurked in his eyes, along with hints of that darkness. "Will you be teaching it to me then, if we do this?"

The desire grinned. "Does that frighten you?"

The darkness supplanted him and he bared his teeth in a careful grin. "Nothing scares me."

"I didn't think so." My smile melted to seriousness though. "But let's be clear on one thing: in the past, I've put my own needs aside for the sake of convenience, but I won't do that again. I require not only consummation of our marriage, but also regular intimacy after that. If these are things you don't wish to provide then let us dismiss any notion of an official bound alliance."

Mextli leaned back in his icpalli, a thoughtful look on his face. "This sex you wish for us to engage in...is it like what we did this afternoon, in your house in Omeyocan?"

"It's even better," the desire purred.

He smiled back, a predatory look in his eyes. "I'm definitely interested."

I set my three-fingered hand on his feathered one. "It would be wise for you to try it first before making a decision, for it just won't do for us to bind ourselves before the other gods only to find out afterwards that sex is not to your liking."

He turned his hand so he gripped mine. "That would be wise."

Now that I knew we were in agreement, all of the nervousness slipped away, fueling my growing courage—and libido. I abandoned my throne to straddle him on his, and I ran my fingers through the feathers of his xicolli, imagining they were the ones hidden beneath. "There's no time like now to give it a try."

He answered with a deep kiss. A quick learner indeed.

I pressed myself against him, luxuriating in the passion. It wasn't the slow, lazy kind Quetzalcoatl and I had always practiced in the Divine Dream, but it also wasn't the desperate, animal longing that took over humans when I let them touch me. It was a pleasant in-between, especially with his feathery hand rubbing my arm, sending chills through me.

But now that we were entwined, something felt wrong. He barely had to shift his hand at all to move from my shoulder to my elbow, and though I wanted to sit in his lap, I had to stand upon my knees, but even then, he hunched over to reach me. We were so disproportionate in size, I worried that the situation would become not just uncomfortable but painful once matters progressed far enough.

You worry too much, the desire chided.

I feel like a child in his lap, I fired back, and even the desire couldn't rumble past that thought. In response, my teotl began building beneath my skin, expanding outward, and my body grew to accommodate it. Once it ended, Mextli was still larger than me, but the size difference felt more natural now. *Is that better?*

Much. At least now he wouldn't crush me when he lay atop me.

We continued wrestling tongues, the desire growing increasingly impatient with his constant mimicry rather than taking command. I tore my lips away long enough to growl, "Undress me," before savaging his mouth with mine again.

And though he took my enthusiasm as a challenge of tongue strength, he still didn't heed my command. Eventually I pulled away, flustered.

"What is the matter?" he asked, puzzled.

"I asked you to undress me, but—"

"I cannot do that, Mayahuel."

The desire bared my teeth. "Why not?"

He furrowed his brow at me, as if he didn't comprehend the question.

"Why are you looking at me that way?"

"You do realize that your clothing is a part of your physical manifestation, and it's no different than your fingers and ears?"

I stared back at him. "Why would I know that?"

He opened his mouth to answer, but then thought better of it.

I laughed. "You mean I didn't have to make myself a new dress? I just needed to summon a change of clothing?"

"I thought you just preferred to wear that rag you came here in."

I drew back enough to look down at myself and with a thought, my simple white dress was transformed into a delicate feather-woven one, similar to the one I'd worn to my wedding to Black Otter when I was just a girl. I changed it again, this time so I wore a warrior's xicolli—just to see if I could make one. "And you can do the same?" I asked, astounded.

In answer, he made his own xicolli disappear, and a black feathered headdress appeared upon his head.

My gaze was drawn immediately to the neat seam of feathers running straight down the middle of his chest and down his stomach. I set my hands against him, one on his fleshy pectoral, the other on the feathered one, then slowly drew them down his chest, tracing the contours of his muscles. As I pushed my fingers further down, my gaze wandered to his loincloth. "And the feathers...they go all the way down?" When he nodded, the desire said, "Show me." I slipped off his lap and knelt on the floor, waiting.

He grinned as he rose, that intense darkness engulfing his eyes. Once he stood fully upright, he banished his loincloth just as he had the xicolli, and my wonderings about whether that part was in proportion to the rest of him was finally answered. A flush of longing crept up my neck as I stared. "Why feathers anyway?"

He shrugged. "Why do you choose a clothed human form? It's not as if we must wear clothing."

"I don't like people staring at me; I don't like them seeing only my body and not me." I tilted my head to look up at his face finally. "Why do you wear clothing?"

His grin grew darker. "One must be able to hide some weapons from their opponents."

I furrowed my brow. What did he mean by that?

He settled on the ground next to me. "If your clothing will interfere, just make it go away."

Initially I balked at the idea, but eventually I made all of my clothing just disappear. My memories of Little Reed undressing me in the throes of passion were some of my most erotic, but Quetzalcoatl and I had almost always skipped over the whole undressing part, so maybe this was just how we gods did this.

Mextli scrutinized me, but as if assessing my magic skills rather than as a man admiring my feminine beauty. There was no lust in his eyes, no signs of arousal at the sight of my nakedness. I'd said I'd wanted people to notice me, not my body, but now it felt strange and wrong, and not even the desire knew what to do.

He took my right hand and gazed upon it as if it were an interesting stone he'd found in the bottom of a brook. "You can grow your fingers back now, you know?"

"But I gave them up in sacrifice—"

"In your mortal life. That life is over, and you can change anything you want now, remold, re-fashion it all. You can even leave this completely human body behind if you so choose."

I had been a caiman-like creature in my previous incarnation, but I had no desire to go back to that. Yet I couldn't imagine abandoning this body I'd spent all of my mortal life in. *It would be nice to have my fingers back though....*

Two small buds sprouted from the empty space next to my middle finger on my right hand, slowly expanding outward into the ones I'd cut off long ago. A sob stuck in my throat when I started wiggling them. *I can feel them! Actually feel them again for the first time in so many years!*

"And the scars, they needn't stay either," Mextli murmured, rubbing his thumbs over the faint streaks on my hips and belly.

I stared down at them. For years after having Ehecacone, I'd mourned the loss of my skin's flawlessness, but now they were the only evidence that I'd once been a mother. And if I never got my son back, they would be all I had left of his existence. "No, I want to keep those. Someone dear gave them to me."

Though now that I looked at my fingers again, it felt so wrong to keep them. I'd given them up to save Little Reed, and though I'd often seen their absence as a bitter reminder that we could never be together, now they had become symbolic of my love for him. Even knowing what I would have to give up by making that sacrifice now, I wouldn't hesitate to do it again; he was worth it. So I made the fingers disappear again, and when Mextli raised his eyebrow, I said, "I don't need to change anything about myself. This is who I am."

He smiled. "You are very wise, Mayahuel."

I pulled myself onto Mextli's lap again and took his mouth with mine. I moved his hands across my bare skin, along my ribs, over my breasts, and back down to cradle my rear. It never took more than a mere touch to get mortal men ready, but Mextli remained unaffected even by my firm strokes on his half-feathered tepolli. "You need to be harder," the desire whispered in his ear as I stroked him still more firmly. The feathers themselves felt intriguingly smooth no matter which direction I stroked them.

"Why?" But when I whispered the details in his ear, he pulled back to give me a puzzled look. "You really wish me to do such things to you?"

A hot mixture of desire and embarrassment lit my cheeks. "It's not as painful as it sounds, really."

"You're sure?"

"Of course."

Within a blink, the darkness lurking in his eyes took over, and his gentle grip on my arms turned crushing. He pushed me over backwards, pinning me to the ground, but when he turned that stone grip onto my legs, pushing them apart, the desire fled, leaving only the fear to take the brunt of his hard thrust into me.

I reacted only with surprise on the second one, but when the third brought pain blooming in my abdomen, I finally reacted in self defense; I let loose a blast of magic against his chest, singeing some of his feathers and flesh.

It stopped him, but the darkness intensified. "What did you do that for?"

"Why are you suddenly being so rough with me?" I fired back. "That hurts!"

He narrowed his eyes, irritated. "You said this is what you wanted...that it doesn't hurt as much as it seems...." But then the darkness fled his eyes, replaced with concern, regret, and confusion. "I'm sorry. I should have known...."

"Known what?"

"That it was crazy to use a weapon of war on you for your enjoyment."

Now was my turn to feel stupid. "Forgive me for not being more precise; it didn't occur to me that you'd be...familiar with some of sex's unpleasant uses."

"I should have asked for more clarification."

An uncomfortable silence settled between us as an even more unpleasant question rose in my head. "You haven't...used this weapon against anyone, have you?" His answer could very well change everything between us.

He shook his head. "Other options are more effective at achieving my goals."

"Thank goodness," I murmured. When he cast me a puzzled look, I said, "When I was mortal, I had some...bad experiences involving that."

"I am sorry."

I waved him off. "I'd rather not talk about it."

"What should we talk about then?"

Growing brave again, I took his hand. "The proper way to make love."

He still looked uncertain though. "Make love?"

"It's called that because it brings people closer to each other, on an emotional level." I drew closer to him again. "It sows love and affection."

"I don't experience such feelings."

I straddled his lap, pressing my body against his. "Just because you haven't yet doesn't mean you can't." I kissed him again.

He hesitated before carefully wrapping his arms around me. When we finally parted lips, he whispered, "Teach me, Mayahuel."

I sunk slowly down onto him, luxuriating in the sensation of flesh and feathers, delightfully familiar and yet also disturbingly reminiscent of someone else. I moved methodically, making sure to keep my gaze locked with his, the better to chase away the thoughts of Quetzalcoatl. "The basics are the same, but you move with a different purpose."

"And what is the purpose?" he asked, watching me intently.

"To give pleasure." I kissed him, the desire overcoming me.

He tipped me onto my back, laying me gently on the stone. "Like this?" He moved carefully inside me, a stark contrast to earlier.

"Perfect." Everything was coming together so well, and the pleasure began blossoming in my abdomen.

But opening my eyes again chased away all notions of perfection. I was used to seeing pleasure-induced disorientation in the eyes of my lovers, but Mextli might as well have been doing some menial but necessary task for all the passion in his eyes. *He's not enjoying this at all.*

But he does not dislike it either, the desire argued. *You were indifferent the first time too, remember? Quetzalcoatl had to teach us to feel pleasure. We just have to teach Mextli.*

But I had no idea how Quetzalcoatl had done any of that....

There will be time enough for that. Let's just enjoy this for now.

The pleasure rose in a wave over me, making me gasp, but when Mextli stopped moving, I panted, "No, don't stop!"

"But I'm hurting you again—"

"You're not. Don't stop." He picked up the pace even more when I begged him to. I clung to him, a tense storm roiling inside me, waiting for the first lightning strike to start everything. My magic pulsed and throbbed, and my body felt on the verge of flying apart and unleashing my raw, unfettered teotl out over the world. Like I had when those raiders attacked our camp. For that thought alone, I resisted the growing urge to let go and let the pleasure overtake me.

Nothing bad will happen, the desire whispered, a pleading to her tone. *We've done this before, remember? And no one got hurt.*

I gazed up at Mextli. He looked like a man focused on a task requiring great mental concentration. *If only I could share with him what I'm feeling right now, so he can understand....*

I couldn't hold back forever though. The wave of pleasure finally crashed over me, and the Divine Dream flexed around us before everything became blinding light. Even Mextli glowed, as if I was gazing upon his uncontained teotl. He pulsed bright turquoise, and his magic swirled around him in a flurry of glowing hummingbirds. I'd never seen anything more breath-taking, more beautiful.

My own body had given way to an intense, burning orange, and my magic reached out in tendrils, forming leaping rabbits. They danced around the birds, which darted away, uncertain, and the streams of our magic mingled together, sliding and twisting around each other. This all felt very familiar.

Yes, this is just like when Quetzalcoatl and I came together in Tamoachan. His magic had been the softest purple, almost white, and it spectral serpents had speckled feathers, and eyes that were a deep—almost black—purple. My own magic hadn't formed anything recognizable from its tendrils, but when the serpents had coiled themselves around the tips, time seemed to slow and pulses of pleasure and contentment took over everything; Quetzalcoatl's thoughts and emotions had flowed over and through me, like he was an ocean I was swimming in. I'd wanted to stay there forever. I couldn't wait to feel like that again.

Overcome with anticipation, my glowing magic rabbits bounded after Mextli's skittish hummingbirds. The birds darted and flitted among our entangled tendrils as if playing a chase game, but when one of my rabbits pounced upon one, the bird burst into a spray of light. A heavy pulse of magic throbbed up my orange tendrils, bringing with it a strange, sudden flash of memory.

I was somewhere dark and warm, and safe, huddled like a sleeping infant, but then suddenly everything turned to light and wetness. I wiped liquid from my eyes to see beastly creatures with dog-like faces, needle-like fangs and glowing red eyes surrounding me, hissing as they pressed forward, thick spines raised upon their backs. But I had macuahuitl swords in both of my hands—one of them covered in countless tiny blue hummingbird feathers.

These are Mextli's memories! Of his birth, perhaps?

The ebb of magic grew in intensity as more of my rabbits caught the birds, and more of Mextli's memories flowed into me with it. I chased his sister Coyolxauhqui into a cave in the mountains until I'd trapped her and she huddled against a wall, a look of utter hatred on her face. The copper bells on her cheeks tinkled preternaturally loud when my sword took her head from her neck. Then there was the adoration and devotion on Coatlicue's face when she first saw me after rising from the dead; it warmed my empty chest. But then came the stinging pain when Smoking Mirror glared at me and hissed, *Don't ever call me Father again, Mextli.*

I was overflowing with power now, and Mextli's magic shifted hues with growing rapidity. His birds took frightened flight in every direction, pulses of fear ebbing like icy water through me. This was nothing like with Quetzalcoatl, and I had no idea what was happening.

What do we do? I shot off at the desire, my own panic rising.

I don't know. Her voice was uncharacteristically anxious.

I dug through my memories, trying to find the answer. With Quetzalcoatl, the magic had flowed like a whirlpool between us, but what was happening now felt more like a one-way flood. Would I kill Mextli if I kept at it much longer?

When I have too much magic, I get rid of the excess, so I pushed magic back up my tendrils. Maybe I could start the perpetual flow.

But Mextli resisted. He tried to retract his tendrils, but my own pursued him even more aggressively, latching onto them as if they had actual physical substance. More of his magic flooded in and I started to truly panic. I couldn't control my own magic and didn't even know how to break this bond we'd created. *Let him go!* I shouted, not knowing what else to do.

The rabbits paused their pursuit of the birds as if suddenly frozen, but then they joined the tendrils in a slow retreat. The influx of magic abated but I was still flooded. Even as my physical body re-coalesced to contain my teotl again, it oozed out of me like slime from a salamander's skin.

The world reformed around me to reveal Mextli's tent was gone. I lay on the ground, completely naked while many men and women stood at a distance, watching me. Mextli, however, stood staring down at me, his chest heaving, a confused, almost terrified expression on his face.

Dear gods, I'm sorry, Mextli! was on the tip of my tongue, but as soon as I stumbled to my feet, he struck me full-force in the chest with his fist, returning me to the ground. The shock of the raw pain made me gasp as I clutched my sternum, my mind reeling.

But when I heard his first heavy footstep towards me, instinct took over. I sprang back to my feet, magic pouring from my hands, ready to throw it at him if necessary.

The angry, vengeful darkness dominated his eyes, but he suddenly stopped, an air of uncertainty hanging over him. When I followed his gaze, my heart started racing.

I held a lightweight macuahuitl sword in each hand. Where did these come from?

But when I flexed my right-hand grip, the sword changed into an obsidian-headed spear. *How am I doing this? I'm not a war goddess; I've never created such things before.*

The humans whispered, and Mextli bared his teeth. "Thief," he growled, low and dangerous.

I tightened my grip on both weapons. "I don't know what's happening."

"Liar!" His voice shook the ground and everyone looked around as if deciding whether to run away.

"You're scaring me, Mextli!" Tears clogged my throat. "Please stop."

"Don't play coy with me, Mayahuel. You knew exactly what you were doing, didn't you?"

"What are you talking about?"

"It was all a lie, wasn't it? You not knowing how to use your magic and having me teach you...." He looked around, as if suddenly realizing that we weren't alone, and when he returned his glare to me, shrewdness had replaced the anger.

"Listen well, everyone," he announced, his voice booming over the silent camp. "Mayahuel is leaving us."

My heart dropped into my stomach.

"Every one of you has been trustworthy, loyal servants, both to me and her, but she's chosen to betray what trust you've put in her. So she is leaving us now. And henceforth, anyone found worshipping her—whether it is by praying or offering sacrifices—shall be put to the eagle stone in my name."

Trading out his predatory posture, Mextli stood straighter, as if he dared me to attack him. "Run on back to your precious Topiltzin, Mayahuel. He's going to need your protection more than ever now."

My magic thrummed hot at the threat, but when I spotted Xochitl standing next to her husband with a look of utter confusion on her face—and both hands gripping her round belly—the anger cooled. Whatever was transpiring between me and Mextli had nothing to do with the Mexica, and the best thing I could do for her—for all of them—was leave.

I slowly lowered my weapons. "I'll go, but you owe me an explanation, Mextli. Once you've had a chance to calm down."

"Oh, we *will* see each other again soon, but I won't be any calmer than now," he replied. The image of his hateful glare followed me as I disappeared into the teoyoh.

PART THREE
THE YEAR NINE HOUSE

CHAPTER TWENTY-TWO

I didn't think about where to go; I just wanted to be somewhere safe, away from Mextli and the new threat he posed. But it didn't surprise me when I materialized in my private quarters in Tollan, fully dressed in my royal robes and neatly groomed. Inside though, I was a complete wreck. I sunk down on the bed and tears I didn't even realize I was holding back came flowing down my cheeks. My head was a muddle of confusion and embarrassment. Things had definitely gotten out of hand, and I'd done nothing to help it.

Not true! the desire insisted. *We tried to break the bond when we realized we were hurting him.*

I stared down at the spear in my left hand, watching it change to a dagger, then to an axe each time I flexed my grip on the handle. *Actually, we only made it worse,* I realized when it dawned on me how I was suddenly able to make weapons of war. *All of those power surges when we were bound together, filling me up to the point of bursting...it was his war magic. We were pulling it out of him!* Feeling sick, I let the weapons drop to the ground, my hands now sweating. No wonder he called me a thief.

I'm sorry, the desire said, her voice small and shaking in my head. *This is my fault.*

Hardly, I replied. *We both agreed to pursue this with him.*

But you were right, to be concerned about him accepting us. I should have known that he wouldn't, especially after how he talked about Xochiquetzal. I was just...just so desperate...I'm sorry. Fresh tears rolled down my cheeks and a terrible ache reverberated through my chest as the desire took over my tongue. "I just wanted to not feel this terrible pain anymore," she whispered. "Very soon, the time will come where we can't ever see or speak to Little Reed again, for eternity, and when I think about it—"

I blinked back the tears and nodded.

"I let our hopes get up when we found out that Coatlicue had once been mortal," she went on while I wiped the tears from my cheek with my fist. "And seeing that dashed yet again...I'm sorry. I thought moving on into a new relationship would help soften the blow, for both of us."

"I don't think we need to soften the blow," I replied, taking my own turn to speak aloud. "I think we need to feel it, and always remember it."

"But it hurts so much!"

"I'd rather feel that than nothing at all. At least then I know I'm still alive and there's the potential to feel happiness again."

The desire sniffled. "What are we going to do about Ehecacone now? We can't take on Quetzalcoatl on our own."

I finished drying my tears then looked around my empty quarters. "I don't know. I haven't thought that far ahead yet. But I'm not sure that we should stay here. When Mextli comes for us...."

"No one will be safe," the desire finished.

"But we made a promise, and we haven't finished it."

You're right, the desire agreed, retreating back into my head. *And we can't just up and disappear again, knowing how many people we hurt doing so last time.*

"We stay to help install a new king, then we go again, and this time we explain our reasons, so the people understand and accept."

We're going to tell them the truth about us?

"Eventually. We owe them that much."

The bells on my door curtain rang. I scooped the spear and sword under the blankets on my bed before asking, "Who is it?"

"It's me, My Lady." Anacoana's voice. She poked her head past the curtain when I told her to enter, but the smile fell from her face. "You've been crying?"

"It's nothing." I took another swipe at my cheeks, to wipe away what I'd missed. "I was just...thinking about Topiltzin."

"Sometimes I cannot help my own tears. But I imagine this is very tough for you, seeing him like he is after so long."

"It is."

"I came looking for you earlier, to ask if you wanted to take over some of the duties of caring for him—I know you were closer in his heart than I could ever hope to be—but I couldn't find you. I even had the guards search for you, but no one knew where you were."

I faltered before replying, "I'm sorry for sneaking off as I did. I was in the priestly gardens, meditating. I should have told my guards where I was going, but I've grown used to coming and going as I please."

She nodded, appeased.

"I thank you for your offer, and I'm happy to take over your duties to the king, if it would please you. I know it's been a burden on you, shouldering so much, but I'm happy to give you a much needed break from such matters."

She stiffened, and after a brief struggle for words, she said, "You're most kind, My Lady, but it wouldn't feel right for me to completely burden you with his full-time care. You have other important obligations to the kingdom whereas I only have my obligations to the king himself."

I sensed it was more of a defense of her usefulness than any sense of obligation, perhaps fearing I'd take away whatever value she had for Little Reed. But then I'd felt that same way when he would ask me to relinquish some of my priestly duties to others so as to lighten my own burden.

I smiled reassuringly at her. "I understand, My Lady. I'm at your disposal should you need me for anything. You look exhausted, so perhaps I can take the night shift for you, so you can catch up on your sleep? I don't mind in the least."

"I am tired," she admitted, letting some of the tension roll off her shoulders as they sagged a bit again. "I thank you."

"I'm happy to help. Sleep well."

She smiled and started to leave, but then she turned back again, embarrassment on her face. "Forgive me, My Lady, but the reason I came to speak with you in the first place...Lord Citlallotoc has arrived from Acolman and is with the king as we speak."

I blinked. "But I just sent Mazatzin out last night!"

Anacoana nodded. "They both arrived no more than a few moments ago."

When I departed my quarters, Anacoana at my heels, I found Mazatzin leaning against the wall outside Little Reed's quarters. He stood straighter then bowed when I approached.

"What is this I hear about Lord Citlallotoc having arrived already?" I asked, my voice barely above a whisper in the silent garden.

He nodded. "I got a few hours down the road when I came upon him, headed for Tollan."

"He was already on his way here?"

"He told me he received a summons a week ago, saying he needed to appear before Lord Topiltzin as soon as possible."

Someone sent for Citlallotoc before I arrived? Surely Malinalli would have told me if she'd done so, and it seemed unlikely Matlacxochitl would have—for Citlallotoc would have immediately known he wasn't Little Reed. "He's in there with Topiltzin?" I pointed to Little Reed's quarters.

Mazatzin nodded. "He insisted on seeing the king right away."

I paused at the door curtain, wondering if I should wait, but decided it would be best to speak with him in private. Taking a deep breath, I parted the curtain and stepped inside.

Citlallotoc knelt on the floor next to the bed, holding Little Reed's frail hand in his one remaining one. He looked up when I entered. "Quetzalpetlatl!" He started to his feet, but I motioned him to stay put. After a hesitation, he settled again. "Mazatzin said you just came back yesterday."

I nodded as I sat opposite him. "I thought I'd been away long enough."

His gaze lingered on mine, his jaw tightening a fraction, but then he returned his attention to Little Reed. "You're looking quite well, My Lady."

"As do you." It was just a politeness though; while he might not have changed much physically, there was tiredness in his eyes and posture, and not just from the journey from Acolman. "I'm glad you came back."

"When my king calls for me, I try to be there."

"He needs you now more than ever; as do I."

This time he did look up at me.

"As you can see, Topiltzin hasn't long before beginning his journey to Mictlan, and he left no heir for the throne. The future of Tollan is in question."

"But you're back now."

"I'm only here to make sure that my brother's interests are looked after properly, and to ensure that someone of dedication and integrity takes the throne upon his death."

"And then you're going to leave again?" When I nodded, he asked, "Why?"

I hesitated before saying, "I'm not capable of being Tollan's queen anymore, so it's time I moved on, for the good of her people."

I wasn't sure if he accepted my vague explanation, but he didn't argue. "Who do you have in mind to replace Topiltzin?"

"You, of course."

Citlallotoc shook his head. "I cannot accept that honor, My Lady."

"You must."

"Surely there is someone else, someone the King trusts—"

"I don't trust Topiltzin's judgment in this matter," I replied. "The man he entrusted with the care of the city went on to deceive the Council and her citizens, and overturned many of our most sacred laws. I don't believe Topiltzin was in a well state of mind when he chose him, and he's even less so now."

Citlallotoc furrowed his brow. "Whom did he name?"

"Matlacxochitl. Until yesterday, he'd spent the last three years impersonating Topiltzin with the intent of naming himself Tollan's heir. He forced me to send him into exile for treason."

He frowned. "Blood Wolf always said his brother was ambitious, but I doubt even he had any idea of its extent."

"I had just sent Mazatzin to Acolman to ask you to come take Matlacxochitl's place here in Tollan, so I'm relieved that you arrived so soon. Topiltzin could leave us any day now."

He sighed. "I am honored by your faith in me, My Lady, but I am not the right man for the throne."

"Why not?"

"Because I betrayed Topiltzin's friendship. I betrayed his trust."

I cast my gaze down at Little Reed lying on the bed between us. "He said as much to you?"

"He didn't have to. I know what I did, and it was dishonorable."

"And it was a request that he had no business making of you in the first place, Citlallotoc. Our lives and happiness were not his to bargain with. What happened in Teotihuacan...it is a matter between you and me, and only you and me."

"I promised him—"

"And he promised *me* that he would never treat me as a commodity to be traded upon, the way so many other noblemen have treated their wives and sisters and daughters. He broke that promise when he made you promise to not pursue me, and you are not a man to abide false promises, so your honor is clean."

He hung his head, flummoxed. "I don't even know how to respond to that, My Lady," he finally said.

"My brother isn't perfect, and I can forgive his flaws. Just as I wish you would forgive yourself for this one little thing. He loved you, and I know that if he could, he would tell you as much, to set your heart at ease. If my brother's friendship meant anything to you—"

"It was everything to me," he cut in, an edge to his voice.

I nodded. "Then you will honor it by embracing this responsibility."

"I did swear my fealty to him for the remainder of my life." A pained expression crossed his face as he stared down at Little Reed's sleeping form. "Very well, My Lady. I will do this, for both you and Topiltzin."

"Thank you." I wanted to reach out and squeeze his hand in mine, but I fought the impulse. After what I'd done to him in Teotihuacan...that was a privilege I'd thrown away. Instead I brushed Little Reed's hair off his forehead with a gentle sweep of my fingers.

Citlallotoc watched me. "I can't believe he's really leaving us."

I bit my lip before saying, "Neither can I, and so soon. His aging seemed to slow down there for a number of years...."

He nodded, his jaw quivering. "Do you think...our leaving...do you think it did this to him?"

"I don't know." When my voice broke, I paused to collect myself. "Maybe...or perhaps it's just his time."

Citlallotoc nodded, fighting back tears. "I'll do my very best to give justice to your legacy, my friend, and I promise I'll stay true to your laws, philosophies, and your chosen god." He kissed Little Reed's hand then got to his feet. "I suppose I should meet with the Council. I'm sure they have many questions for me."

"A good idea. The sooner everything is settled, the better."

To my surprise, he offered me his hand to help me up. I hesitated before accepting, but I let go of him as soon as was polite. "Thank you."

"My pleasure, My Lady," he murmured, avoiding my gaze.

▢

Citlallotoc's arrival in the great hall was greeted with much enthusiasm from those members who'd served while he'd still been Justice of the Peace. Those who were newer hung off to the sides, watching the laughing and heartfelt greetings with uncertainty. I, in turn, watched them closely from the dais, my discussion with Blood Wolf from the night before lingering forward on my mind. Purging the Council of Matlacxochitl's supporters would need to be a top priority.

Citlallotoc finally made it to the dais and I invited him to stand next to me. A hush fell as I turned to address the crowd. "Thank you all for coming to council in this most mournful time for Tollan. As many of you are aware, Revered Speaker Topiltzin didn't name an heir prior to his falling ill, so the task of deciding who should rule Tollan once he leaves us has fallen to me, as his closest living blood relative. And I've chosen someone whom I think that, if Topiltzin were still with us now, he'd heartily approve of. I speak of course of Tollan's former war chief, Justice of the Peace, and my brother's best man, Lord Citlallotoc of Acolman."

Hoots and whistles rose in the crowd.

Last night I'd ordered my old icpalli brought out of storage and it now sat next to Little Reed's; the servants had even decorated the back of it with stalks of bone flowers, as they used to. I settled onto my throne, silently rejoicing at the familiar contours the years of council meetings had molded into it. I motioned Citlallotoc to take Little Reed's throne.

He looked at it, uncertain, but when he went to sit down, a voice shouted out, "Halt!" He did so and turned to look out into the crowd.

I saw red when Matlacxochitl strode up the middle of the great hall towards the dais, the crowd parting for him and murmuring in confusion. A handful of soldiers came with him, clutching spears in their hands.

My guards exchanged unsure looks, but when they saw the deep-set frown on my face, they rushed forward to block Matlacxochitl's way. Tension mounted in the room.

But Matlacxochitl stopped well before the dais, and glared back at me behind his half-mask, his mouth matching my own frown.

"What in Mictlan are you doing here?" I growled, rising to my feet. "I sentenced you to exile!"

"And I don't recognize your authority," he fired back.

"I am the Queen of Tollan—"

"Anacoana is the Queen of Tollan. You forfeited your crown when you left Tollan five years ago, vowing never to return."

Blood Wolf stepped from the crowd. "Enough of this foolishness, brother! Topiltzin never revoked Lady Quetzalpetlatl's claim to the throne! You know that!"

"It wounds me that my own brother doesn't stand with me. She left a mess for the rest of us to clean up, and now she swoops in here as if nothing happened and names a traitor as heir to the throne!"

I laughed. "Ironic words coming from the mouth of an actual traitor."

"The king himself kicked *him* out of Tollan five years ago for disloyalty." He jabbed a finger at Citlallotoc.

Citlallotoc stiffened. "Topiltzin didn't kick me out. I left of my own volition."

"And would you care to tell everyone why?"

Citlallotoc set his jaw.

Matlacxochitl flourished his cape as he turned to the crowd. "Was it because the King discovered that you were sleeping with his wife and he couldn't be sure the child she carried was truly his?"

Confused murmurs spilled through the crowd.

"Very reliable sources tell me that you were paying late-night visits to Lady Anacoana's quarters on a regular basis for months after she married Topiltzin—"

"You imply deception where none existed," I said. "Topiltzin was fully aware of the situation, and in fact, he not only encouraged it, he suggested it. The sad truth is that my brother couldn't bear any more children of his own. He and I were lucky to be blessed with Prince Ehecacone, but that is the only blood offspring the gods saw fit to grant us. Tollan needed an heir, and Topiltzin couldn't produce one himself, so he asked his best friend to father a child for him, for the good of the kingdom." It felt dishonorable to blatantly lie, but the truth would not only damage Little Reed's reputation and legacy, but also humiliate Anacoana in front of the entire court.

Matlacxochitl glared at me. "I thought Topiltzin sought a divorce from you because *you* were the barren one."

"Our reasons are none of your business, nor do they have any bearing on the situation at hand."

"But if the affair had nothing to do with anything, then why did Lord Citlallotoc leave?"

"To make sure Tollan's future was safe and secure, of course."

"Meaning?"

"Already Prince Ehecacone had been murdered, and rather than risk another tragedy, Topiltzin planned to send his new child to Acolman, to be raised there in King Huemac's household. And to be blunt, he had good reason to be concerned, considering the lengths you went through to slither your way onto the throne. And your defying my orders now suggests you've made a concerted effort to fill the Council and the king's guard with your own little loyal, yipping dogs."

He smiled, smug. "If you had seen to your duties in the first place, it wouldn't have been necessary for me to step in. But I will not just step away now. I earned the throne with my loyalty—"

"You have a very warped definition of loyalty," I fired back. "You've overturned the very laws the god handed down through myself and Topiltzin—"

"And Quetzalcoatl isn't the only god in the heavens."

I narrowed my eyes. "Smoking Mirror put you up to this, didn't he?"

Matlacxochitl turned to the crowd again. "For twelve years, Topiltzin has turned his back on the other gods, creating laws to weaken the other cults while elevating the Feathered Serpent. He attempted to name Quetzalcoatl *the only god*, but that is a lie, and we forget that at our peril. Already we've seen evidence of the other gods' discontent— the mudslides last autumn, followed by the almost complete lack of rain this year. We're living on the stored grain thanks to drought devastating our crops. The gods have abandoned us because we've turned our backs on them!"

An angry murmur rolled through the crowd.

"Citlallotoc will continue Topiltzin's disastrous policies—*her disastrous policies*—" He pointed at me—"and it will lead to Tollan's destruction!"

"Will you continue Lord Topiltzin's policies, Lord Citlallotoc?" a voice asked from the crowd.

Citlallotoc stepped up to the edge of the dais. "Topiltzin's laws have seen peace reign in Tolteca lands for the first time in many bundles of years, so yes, my intention is to continue them, for the health and well-being of Tollan's people."

"And what about your allies? How do you intend to run this empire that Topiltzin built?" This voice I recognized as Lord Mozauhqui, the son of the king of Tepanec. He turned a glare onto Matlacxochitl. "In the last few years, while impersonating the king, Lord Matlacxochitl had grown increasingly demanding of his allies, exacting tribute where Topiltzin expected nothing of us but peace."

"I intend to continue respecting our allies' sovereignty."

"And when the food is gone and the people are starving in the streets?" Matlacxochitl demanded. "When the poor are tussling at your palace gates, what will you do then?"

"I will ask our allies for their assistance, not demand it," Citlallotoc growled.

"And we would gladly give it," Mozauhqui replied, defiant.

"The empire was built upon mutual trust and respect, not power plays and fear," Citlallotoc told Matlacxochitl. "Your way would see the empire crumble and the cities fall into constant war again."

"And your way would have it fall into war with the gods. These last few years were just the beginning. And curiously Quetzalcoatl has done nothing to stop it."

"As if you'd know anything about the ways of the gods, little man," I snarled.

Matlacxochitl frowned. "Then by all means educate us, My Lady. You are, after all, a high priestess of the Feathered Serpent."

"I am not anymore. Nor would I claim to know anything about Quetzalcoatl's motivations, but just because one side appears to be winning doesn't mean the other side is doing nothing. Only a small-minded individual would think so, and small minds have no place on thrones."

His shoulders rose like a bristling jaguar, but then he turned away to address the crowd again. "In the end, it doesn't matter what she thinks; what matters if what the Council thinks. She can name whomever she wishes to the throne, but without the support of the Council, that man would have no power. The Council should decide who will take the throne."

"That would be fair if you hadn't loaded it with a majority of your supporters," Mozauhqui replied. "And who knows what you've done with the king's guard."

Matlacxochitl smirked. "Then perhaps it would be best for everyone if Lord Citlallotoc stood aside, to avoid unnecessary conflict."

I glared at Matlacxochitl while the desire growled deep in my chest. "And perhaps it would be best if you don't forget what I did at the battle for Culhuacan."

His smirk dropped and a worried whisper raced through the crowd. Even Matlacxochitl's guards looked ill-at-ease.

I reclined, grinning. "The Council will not determine who rules next. And while it is my birthright to name the heir myself, I too will stand aside in this matter. Instead, the citizens of Tollan herself will determine whom to entrust their future to. Let there be public debates between the candidates, so each can make their case for why they should rule Tollan, and then let the people cast their lots. At this juncture, it's the only truly fair way to determine the throne's future."

"I will agree to that," Citlallotoc said.

Matlacxochitl mulled a moment before replying, "I have no objections either." To Citlallotoc, he added, "Though perhaps you should reconsider, My Lord, lest your transgressions with the Queen become revealed to the entire city."

"And I would be forced to divulge your treason," I cut in, narrowing my eyes at him. "Which one do you think will cause the most stir among the citizenry? Are you sure you wish to remain a contender?"

Matlacxochitl nodded stiffly, returning my glare. "I trust that you will extend your royal hospitality without my having to fear for my safety, the same as you're giving to Lord Citlallotoc?"

Now was my turn to mull. I didn't like him having such easy access to his rival, given his treachery.

Smirking, Matlacxochitl told Citlallotoc, "Surely you're not afraid of me, My Lord?"

Citlallotoc laughed. "Hardly. I have no fear of you remaining here in the palace. I trust in Quetzalcoatl to protect me from whatever evil you might be plotting against me."

It was on the tip of my tongue to warn him not to place faith in the goodness of the Feathered Serpent, but with everyone listening, now wasn't the time to cast doubts on the city's patron god. I didn't want to give Matlacxochitl credibility in anyone's eyes. "You shall be assigned quarters in the western wing, but you are not allowed into the royal quarters for any reason. And I shall assign my own guards to watch over you, for the sake of the palace's other residents."

"Are *you* afraid of me then, My Lady?"

"Don't attempt to shame me into foolishness, Matlacxochitl. I make a habit of not underestimating the cunning of my enemies. And yes, you are my enemy."

Matlacxochitl bowed. "It's good to know where I stand with you."

"It is lucky for you that both Citlallotoc and I are more honorable than you. I doubt we would be as lucky as you if our positions were reversed."

He sneered. "I don't need deception to win this competition. I am the better man for the throne, and the people will see that in the end."

"Then let us reconvene this business tomorrow morning, when everyone is rested. Dinner is growing cold while we duel over words that make no difference today. Forgive me for not inviting you to join the feast though; this is in honor of Citlallotoc and your very presence is an affront."

"I will eat in my own quarters, My Lady." Matlacxochitl gave me a mock bow then stormed from the great hall, his guards following, bringing a rush of conversation.

"And anyone else who doesn't wish to honor Lord Citlallotoc's return," I called over the noise, bringing a hush, "you are free to join your chosen leader. No one will harass you for doing so."

The crowd remained silent as everyone looked around, waiting to see who would leave. No one did, though several councilmen looked distinctly uncomfortable as everyone took to the reed mats spread about the floor.

As the servants filled our dishes, Citlallotoc searched the room from Little Reed's icpalli. "Where's Anacoana?"

"No doubt sleeping," I said. "She needed to catch up on her rest."

He let out a ragged breath. "At least she wasn't here for Matlacxochitl dragging her name through the muck. She deserves better than that." He shook his head. "I never should have agreed to Topiltzin's request."

"He asked it out of loyalty to you. Flame Tongue put him in an impossible situation but he still felt guilty for getting between you and Anacoana. Undoubtedly he thought it the best reparation he could make to you."

Citlallotoc nodded. "My feelings for her clouded my judgment in that regard."

Lowering my voice, I said, "Things didn't go well for you two in the past, but...Anacoana will be widowed soon—"

But he shook his head. "It is much too late for that."

"You're already married?"

"No." He picked at his food. "Too much has passed between us since then."

"The past can be forgiven."

"Perhaps." He still wouldn't look at me though as he started to eat.

I ate a few bites myself, letting the silence linger until it became too much to bear. "We need to talk."

"About what?"

"About what happened between us...in Teotihuacan."

He stopped mid-chew but made no move to look at me.

"I know this isn't the right time or place, but...it could be beneficial, for both of us."

"And if I don't wish to talk about it?"

"I won't force you to." As soon as I said it, my choice of words tasted terrible in my mouth. "I understand the...awkwardness of all of this, and if you feel the need to...excise some of that, I will listen to whatever you need to say."

He chuckled guardedly. "Maybe you have some words in need of saying to me as well?"

"There is only one thing I can possibly say, and that is I'm sorry for all of the damage I have caused you."

"Am I damaged now, since you rejected me?"

"That's not what I meant."

"It is all right, My Lady. I have much practice with rejection, so you haven't hurt me anymore than anyone else has."

I'm not so sure about that, I almost said, but instead frowned. "Still, if there's anything you wish to talk about, come find me, at any time." I handed my plate off to one of the servants and rose.

Citlallotoc raised an eyebrow. "You're done eating already?"

"I'm not hungry, but I should feed Topiltzin. The servants will ready your old quarters for you; I'm sure you're tired from your journey." I nodded and left the dais.

But he called back to me, "Wait." He handed his own plate off to a servant then came over to me to whisper, "I'm not ready to talk about that night yet, but perhaps tomorrow, after I've rested...."

"Then I shall see you at breakfast?"

"Yes." He looked as if he wanted to say more, but then lowered his head into a bow. "Sleep well, My Lady."

CHAPTER TWENTY-THREE

 The halls were quiet at this late hour, and only a few guards lingered at their posts. I stopped by the royal kitchens and brewed up a small bowl of atole for Little Reed before continuing on to the royal living quarters. I checked on Anacoana, who was sleeping soundly, and ordered the idle servants to fix Citlallotoc's old room for him.

Little Reed was sound asleep in his bed, his breath wheezing and rattling. He muttered and grumbled when I struggled to sit him up, but eventually I propped him up against his Feathered Serpent idol. I shot scathing glares at it between spooning the watery atole into his mouth.

Once I'd emptied the bowl, I wiped his messy beard. He looked so unkempt and rumpled, and a feculent odor grew stronger around him. "You need a good bath and some grooming, my love." I kissed his cheek then went to the bath yard to fill his wash tub.

I set the first pot of water on the brazier, and was about to return to the room to fetch a stick of fire from the hearth, but then I thought of that first battle between Mextli and I long ago now, how he'd set my maguey roots on fire to escape. Now that I had his magic, could I too make fire myself? I bent next to the bundle of sticks under the tripod and flicked my fingers at it.

To my delight, tongues of blue flames sprang from my fingertips, igniting the lumber faster than normal flames. "I could get used to this," I murmured as I watched the water begin to steam. Once I'd filled the tub with water and heated it with the hot water from the fire, I went to fetch Little Reed.

He was much heavier than he looked, and I struggled to lift his frail body out of bed. There wasn't any way I could carry him to the bath yard myself.

How easily you forget you're a goddess. My face heated with embarrassment. Draping Little Reed's arm over my shoulder, I took us both into the teoyoh then into the bath yard.

In that brief instance in the fires of the teoyoh, strange white wisps of unidentified magic curled among mine, and I had the unsettled feeling that I wasn't the only one of my kind in the stream. Was Smoking Mirror spying on me? "Teoti," I murmured aloud, eager to be back in the material world. I filed the feeling away for future reference then laid Little Reed on the mats to undress him.

Under his robes he was wasted away, everything shriveled and sagging. He lay completely limp while I worked, oblivious even when I wrestled his naked, bony body into the tub then rubbed copal soap over his loose, spotted skin. *And to think he's only lived thirty-five years. The curse of being only half divine, perhaps? How can there be nothing beneficial about having one divine parent? No special abilities or magic, just a shortened lifespan?*

One of the few reasons to be thankful for Quetzalcoatl being Ehecacone's father rather than Black Otter, the desire said, uncharacteristically sober.

I trimmed Little Reed's shaggy beard so it wasn't so unruly, and contemplated shaving it off, but when I nicked his jowls with his obsidian shaving blade, I decided it best to leave it be. I combed the tangles from his long silver hair and trimmed it a too, so it looked well-kept. *At least he'll look kingly and dignified when Xolotl comes for him.*

But as I leaned over to scoop him up under his arms, I noticed he was staring at me.

"Little Reed?"

He didn't respond, but continued staring.

I waved a hand in front of his face, and though he didn't blink, I was certain he was looking at me. I searched for the right words to say, but I knew they would never come if I didn't just start talking.

"I don't know how much longer you have, Little Reed, and I don't even know if you can hear or understand anything I'm saying, but I may not get another chance to tell you any of this, and...you have the right to know the truth." I took a deep breath, committing. "I'm not who you think I am, Little Reed. I'm not even who *I* thought I was. You see...oh, where to start? With what happened at Teotihuacan five years ago, I guess.

"I was very angry about what happened to our son—so angry I summoned Smoking Mirror, so I could confront him, but it turned out it wasn't his doing." Pain rose in my chest. "I was wrong about Black Otter. I should have known...I shouldn't have trusted him...." I wiped hot tears from my eyes. "He murdered Ehecacone, Little Reed. He tried to drive a wedge between you and me, and in that regard, he succeeded, since everything fell apart for us after that. But even that's not the worst of it. He sold his soul to the lake goddess and turned himself into a hideous monster, so he could continue pursuing me; even now, after I killed him for his crimes, he's still after me.

"But I can blame him only so much, for I caused his insanity, just as I caused Red Flint's." I stared down into the dingy water, dreading most what I had to say next. "And I fear I've caused it in you too."

When I looked up at him again, there was still no change in his expression, so I went on.

"During my confrontation with the Smoking Mirror, I discovered something so...devastating that I couldn't come home again, not with knowing what damage I was doing to everyone around me."

I took a deep breath. The moment was finally upon me. "There's no easy way to put this, so I'll just say it: I'm not a human being, Little Reed. I'm the goddess Mayahuel. I feel so foolish, for when I think about it, I should have known long ago, but then who would believe it was anything but ego? I was sure it was just in my head, but now that I know the truth, everything makes sense. Just being around me drove both Red Flint and Black Otter insane.

"And it kills me to say this, because I love you so much...." I choked but made myself go on. "What you feel for me isn't real, Little Reed. I made you waste your life on me when you could have been happy with someone else, and I'm so very sorry for that. If I'd known what I was doing to you, maybe I could have spared you...."

I balled my fists, rage flooding over me. "But I didn't find out until it was too late, and I know this will be even more difficult to hear, but your father knew the truth but he kept it from me, out of spite. I had to find out from Smoking Mirror, of all gods!"

I rested my forehead on the edge of the tub, the anger boiling away until I felt only grief. "That's why I didn't come back from Teotihuacan. I had to leave because I loved you too much to continue poisoning your mind. The one good thing that will come of you passing on into Mictlan will be that I won't have this hold over you anymore. You'll finally have peace again."

When I looked up again, Little Reed was slumped against the lip of the tub, asleep again. A strand of drool wound down the corner of his mouth onto his chin. I wiped it away with a rag. "I want you to know though that my love for you is very much real and having you in my life has meant so much. No matter what your father did, you are the one thing I cannot thank him enough for."

Once I returned him to his bed, I dressed him in a clean sleep xicolli and tucked him under his blankets. He didn't rouse during any of it. I bent to kiss his forehead and whisper good night, but stopped. For all I knew, just touching him strengthened those false bonds between us. *I should avoid touching him unless absolutely necessary.* Instead I patted the blanket over his hands. "Sleep well, Little Reed." I then left his quarters.

But when I stepped out on the portico, I heard sandals scraping on flagstone followed by the rustling of bushes. Beyond the torches on the portico, I couldn't make out anything in the moonless night. "Who's there?" When no one answered, my tension rose. Fearing an assassination attempt against Little Reed was eminent, I flexed my hand, bringing an obsidian-bladed dagger to it. The handle felt just like the buckhorn one of my mother's sacrificial blade, bringing with it deadly confidence. "Come out, now! I am not defenseless!"

The silence continued for a breath, but then came movement in the bushes. I tightened my grip on the knife as a shadow moved to the flagstone patio in the middle of the yard, but I relaxed it when the figure moved into the dim torchlight. "Malinalli? What are you doing lurking out there?"

She stared at me with a frightening dead look, her face ashen.

I stepped towards her. "Are you all right?"

But she sprang away like I was a hissing jaguar. Her shoulders heaved with heavy breath.

I stopped. "We should talk, about what happened when I saw you last—"

"Did you make me this way?" she asked, her voice barely above a whisper.

Make her what way? "What are you talking about?"

"Did you make me an abomination before the eyes of the gods?"

"Why...what...why would you think—"

"I heard you talking to Topiltzin."

My heart thudded painfully in my ears. "Malinalli—"

"Is this why I am the way I am?" she fired at me, anger supplanting the fear.

After a hesitation, I admitted, "I don't know."

"All these years I could have been normal, if not for you," she muttered, looking bewildered.

"You're not abnormal, Malinalli. Please don't say that about yourself!"

"What else can I possibly be? Why else would I choose to live a life of lies, a life of shame where I can't show my true self outside the privacy of my own quarters? If I was normal, I wouldn't have to hide anything from anyone; I wouldn't have to worry that I will be killed if anyone found out whom I share my bed with. Why would any normal person choose to live under such conditions?"

Her words alarmed me. "I don't have answers right now, Malinalli, but if we just talk about it, rationally—"

"I can't be rational, not right now. I mean, you're a...a...." She backed away, shaking her head vigorously.

"I know this is a lot to take in, but deep inside, I'm still the woman you've always known. In my heart you're still my best friend, but if I've lost that...." I choked, tears finally breaking free. "Please, Malinalli. It was never my intention to hurt you and I'm so very sorry that I did. Please forgive me."

But Malinalli continued shaking her head. "I don't know that I can. At least not right now; I need to think, and pray for guidance." Now she switched to nods. "Yes, I'll seek the guidance of the Feathered Serpent. He will know what to do."

You can't trust anything Quetzalcoatl tells you. But before I could say anything, she ran off into the dark. "Malinalli!" I came down onto the flagstone patio, but she was already gone. I slumped to the ground, holding my head in my hands as I wept.

"My, my," a creaky voice cackled. "For a creator goddess, you're sure good at destroying things, aren't you?"

I looked up to see Smoking Mirror standing on the portico outside Anacoana's room, leaning his frail, shriveled body against his gnarled staff. He grinned at me.

Anger dragged me to my feet. "How did you get in here?"

"I have a standing invitation. I'm the royal chemist."

"Why are you here?"

"The queen often has trouble sleeping, and suffers head pains. I provide medicines as needed."

"And what about to Topiltzin?"

"I *am* the royal chemist, my dear."

Magic roiled in my fingertips. "Then you did this to him? You made him into an invalid with your evil medicines?"

Smoking Mirror laughed, a rickety sound that didn't carry far in the still night. "You think so little of me, Mayahuel. But no, I didn't do any of that to him. If you're looking for someone to blame, that rests squarely with the Feathered Serpent. You should take up your complaints with him."

"If I knew where he was, I would," I snarled.

He hobbled down off the portico. "I'm pleased to see that you're back to your normal temperamental self."

I stared at him, suspicious. Had he not yet spoken to Mextli about what happened earlier today? Maybe it wasn't too late to strike a deal with him. "I have...regained my balance."

"An unbalanced god is a dangerous god," Smoking Mirror replied.

"What brings you here?"

"It's come to my attention that you are meddling in affairs with the humans here."

"You mean the royal succession?"

"Precisely! I'm sure it wasn't your intention to step on my toes, but you're meddling in things you shouldn't."

"So Matlacxochitl is your man?" Just as I'd figured.

"The healing process after Quetzalcoatl's treachery will be a long and difficult process for the humans. Matlacxochitl will return them to the correct path quickly, with far less pain than the alternative."

I narrowed my eyes. "Is that a threat?"

"What do you care of the humans anyway? You're not one of them."

"I have friends among them, people I care about; people whom Matlacxochitl would harm."

"And so long as they stand with the Feathered Serpent, they are my enemy, and I will show them as much mercy as they showed my followers in Culhuacan."

I shook my head. "He will harm people I love."

"As will you if you stay. In fact, you will end up with much more blood on your hands if you don't walk away."

I stood straighter, my indignation rising. "You underestimate me, Smoking Mirror."

He grinned wide. "And you think too highly of your own abilities."

"I will help them, and they will thank me for it," the desire snarled.

Chuckling, Smoking Mirror started down the path towards the hallway back into the palace. "Let's just hope you come to your senses before it's too late, Mayahuel. Come see me again when you're ready to put your ego aside and deal in reality."

I followed him to the hallway but stopped where my guards were posted. I watched him shuffle down to the main hallway then disappear around the corner.

"No one but myself, Anacoana, Citlallotoc, Malinalli or Mazatzin are allowed in the royal quarters without my express permission. Understand?" I told the guards. "And make sure the daytime guards know as well."

I returned to Little Reed's quarters, anxious. I didn't trust Smoking Mirror's claims of innocence concerning Little Reed's current state; having unfettered access to his enemy's mortal son, why wouldn't he try something? It gave me chills to think of that sorcerer plotting over my beloved's bed while he lay unaware. *The royal quarters aren't safe for him anymore.*

But where could I take him?

The priestly retreat, the desire suggested. Nobody but priests had access to it, so Smoking Mirror couldn't just walk in there without an escort in his current form. It wasn't perfect, especially since it relied on the Feathered Serpent's mood as to whether or not he would extend his protection, but if I told only a few trusted people and one of us always stayed with him, I would feel much better.

I gathered as much of Little Reed and his bedding into my arms as I could then moved him through the teoyoh to the private mediation room he and I used to share at the priestly sanctuary. My anxiety rose when those same white wisps of magic infiltrated the stream with me, along with a faint reptilian smell. Was Coatlicue nearby? If our enemies were indeed monitoring my movements through the teoyoh, I couldn't risk taking Little Reed through it anymore. I didn't know how to defend him if Mextli or one of Smoking Mirror's other allies attacked us in there.

We arrived to pitch blackness, but I recognized the soothing odor of the copalli incense Little Reed and I always burned on the plate in our meditation room. I had to fetch wood from the store rooms, but once I had the fire burning bright in the hearth, I found the room looked much like I remembered it; murals of Quetzalcoatl on the walls, and a large stone idol sitting against the garden-side. But unlike my quarters, there was a thick layer of dust over everything; no one ever came in here anymore, it seemed. I swept the area in front of the hearth clean and set up Little Reed's bed there, then spent the rest of the night turning the room into a livable space for him to pass his remaining days.

At dawn, I fixed a warm bowl of atole for his breakfast in the priestly kitchens, but when I heard footsteps out in the main garden, I peeked out from behind the closed curtain.

Mitotia headed to one of the meditation rooms opposite mine.

I gathered up the bowl and hurried out after her. "Mitotia!" When she started, I added, "I'm sorry. I didn't mean to frighten you."

She smoothed her dress, looking distinctly uncomfortable. "It's all right. I'm just used to there being no one here this early."

"Are you busy?"

"Do you need my help with something?"

I nodded and motioned her to follow me. "I've moved Topiltzin out of the palace for safety's sake."

"Has someone threatened him?"

"Not directly, but with the conflict over the throne, I'd rather he be somewhere I know to be safe." When we reached the door to my meditation room, I pulled aside the curtain for us.

Mitotia looked around when we stopped next to the bed. "However I can help, you can count on me."

"Thank you." I knelt next to Little Reed to sit him up for his meal. "It's vitally important that only trusted individuals know he's here. My intention is to only inform you, Malinalli, and Mazatzin."

She knelt to help me. "What about Anacoana?"

"I'll tell her, but she's not permitted in here anyway, since she's not a member of the priesthood."

"But Mazatzin said you quit the priesthood when you left."

"I quit Quetzalcoatl's priesthood. I don't think that in my heart I could ever really stop being a priestess. It's in my nature to serve."

"Whom do you serve now then?"

"The people of Tollan, regardless of their spiritual hearts."

I wasn't sure if my answer appeased her, but she didn't say anymore.

"I must attend the public debates today, so I need someone to watch over Topiltzin while I'm gone," I said. "Would you do this favor for me?"

"Of course, My Lady."

I handed her the bowl. "Thank you. I should get going before I'm late." When I reached the door curtain though, I said, "I'll talk to Mazatzin, but if you could tell Malinalli for me, I'd greatly appreciate it."

"I will."

"And please let her know that whenever she's ready to talk, I'm willing to sit down and listen."

Mitotia cocked her head, confused. "Is something the matter?"

"We just had a misunderstanding last night, that's all. I upset her, and I want to make it up to her anyway I can." Feeling the intensity of her gaze, I added, "I realize I betrayed our friendship when I left as I did, and she has every right to be angry, but I will do my very best to be a better friend—to be a better person this time."

After mulling on my words for a breath, Mitotia asked, "Are you going to leave again?"

"I will likely have to," I admitted. "But I promise a full explanation when the time comes. No sneaking away this time."

Mitotia nodded, but her expression was guarded. "I will speak with Malinalli when I see her next."

"Thank you. I will return at lunch time."

It was a relief when I finally stepped out into the garden.

But when I left the retreat and started crossing over the bridge, splashing in the river below caught my attention. I stopped to gaze over the wooden railing, expecting a fish.

Instead, inky black eyes peered back at me from the water.

I backed slowly towards the middle of the bridge.

"Mine!" Black Otter hissed below.

My heart hammered steadily as I glanced to shore. It wasn't far but Black Otter was fast, and long when he stretched himself out. Hearing clicking on the wood, I darted my attention back to the river.

Black Otter was climbing up onto the bridge, water cascading off his fur in rivulets. When we locked gazes, he bared his teeth into a grotesque grin. "Mine!" he hissed softly.

I ran.

He lunged after me, stretching out to rake his claws at me, but he missed as I cleared the bridge for the mainland. But with the next bound, he tackled me by the legs, tripping me to the ground. To my horror, when I looked back, he was completely out of the water, not a bit of him touching it. How could that be?

There was no time to dwell on that though. I flexed my right hand, to bring a dagger to it, but nothing materialized. Mextli's magic still tingled in my hands, but it felt weak compared to what I had become accustomed to. I flexed my fingers over and over again, cursing each time nothing happened.

But just when I was sure I would have to rely on my own octli magic, the blade appeared in my palm. I rammed it down between Black Otter's shoulder blades and twisted.

He cried out and let me go then retreated back to the water at a painful limp. He eased himself into the river then disappeared from sight. I stared at the water, waiting for Mitotia to come running from the retreat to ask what all of the noise was, but no one came out. Black Otter resurfaced though and glared at me, a petulant look on his monstrous face. "Mine!" he whined.

I hurried to my feet and scrambled further into the garden, almost tripping as I looked over my shoulder as I ran. He came up onto the shore, and the dagger was missing from his back, but he didn't pursue me. I would have to be careful coming and going from the retreat from now on.

I'll just have to use the teoyoh to get in and out, I decided, then with a final glare at him, I vanished into thin air.

CHAPTER TWENTY-FOUR

Anacoana was still sleeping when I returned to the palace, so I let her be and left a message with the guards to let her know to come find me when she woke up. From there, I ate breakfast with most of the council—including Matlacxochitl—but then we all adjourned to the sacred precinct for a day of debating.

Workmen had built a platform at the base of the Feathered Serpent's temple with a canopy to shield us from the sun, and by the time we'd arrived in the precinct, a very large crowd of citizens had already gathered to hear the debates. Blood Wolf had done a wonderfully efficient job of setting this up on such short notice.

An icpalli had been set out for me while everyone else was given a reed mat to sit upon. Mazatzin greeted me with a bow when I came up onto the platform, but I noticed Malinalli wasn't there. She hadn't been at breakfast either. "She's feeling ill this morning," Mazatzin informed me when I asked. "Do you wish me to send someone to fetch Mitotia in her stead?"

"No, I have her doing other things for me today. We'll just proceed as is."

Once the rest of the council and the two candidates had taken their mats upon the dais, I rose from my icpalli and addressed the crowd, which had grown twice as large since our arrival. "I cannot put into words just how happy it makes me to be here in Tollan again, back among the countless good people who have made this city the greatest in the empire. Nor can I adequately express just how much I have missed my home city; missed the sounds of her market, the smell of her citizens feeding their families every night, and the joy her people take in living within her loving embrace.

"Many of you no doubt wonder as to my whereabouts these past five years. All I can say is that I embarked on a much-needed journey of personal discovery, so I might better serve the needs of each of you. When I left, I was not fit to be your queen."

A murmur of confusion swept through the crowd.

"And when I left, Tollan was in good hands; the king was well and strong, both physically and mentally. But that has changed. It saddens me to announce that Topiltzin, King of Tollan and Emperor of the Tolteca, has fallen gravely ill and will pass on into Mictlan very soon."

The confusion turned into a tide of distress. "He didn't look ill when I went before him yesterday!" one voice called out, and another cried, "But there is no heir! What are we to do?"

I raised my hands for calm and slowly the noise level in the precinct fell low enough so I could be heard again. "It is true there is no blood heir to carry on his legacy—"

"But what about you, My Lady?" a woman shouted. "You carry the king's blood."

"That is true, but I've come to understand that I am not worthy of ruling you." As the noise rose again, I called out over it, "But it is my duty to make sure that someone of grace and character takes up the mantle of rule in my absence, and that is why we are here today.

"Two contenders have stepped forward, willing to take on the tremendous responsibility of overseeing Tollan's future, and as her citizens, you will choose who will lead you next. They will each make their case for why you should name them your next king and when all the debates have been heard, each adult citizen—both male and female—will cast their lot in favor of their desired candidate, and the winner will be crowned Tollan's new king upon Topiltzin's death."

An interested whisper passed through the crowd, but no one shouted any questions or objections, so I went on. "Let me introduce the candidates. First—" I motioned to Matlacxochitl— "I present Lord Matlacxochitl, the younger brother of our own Lord Blood Wolf. He's served a good number of years as the governor of Chimalhuacan."

Matlacxochitl stepped forward and raised a hand in greeting, which was met with a healthy round of hooting and cheering.

Once the crowd calmed down, I motioned him back to his mat then summoned Citlallotoc. "And second—and more familiar to most of you, undoubtedly—Lord Citlallotoc, brother to King Huemac of Acolman, former Justice of the Peace in Tollan, and Topiltzin's most trusted advisor."

When Citlallotoc stepped up, the hoots and shouts were louder, and they lasted long after I'd retired back to my icpalli to let the debates begin.

The speeches and arguments didn't hold my attention though. I'd heard most of it already, and soon my mind drifted back to the conversation between me and Smoking Mirror last night. Would he try to disrupt the debates today? I scanned the crowd for signs of him—or his allies—but I saw nothing to give me pause.

I did notice that both Citlallotoc and Matlacxochitl avoided criticizing each other during this opening volley. They discussed their policy plans, what they would change and what they would maintain. Matlacxochitl was downright respectful compared to last night.

I wondered how long that would last.

The crowd dispersed for the afternoon at lunch time and I returned to the palace to check on Anacoana before bringing Little Reed his meal. When I came to her room, she was awake but still in her bed, looking bedraggled.

"I'm so exhausted," she complained as she struggled to sit up. "How late is it?"

"Lunch time."

"It is? Did the king get his breakfast?"

"I took care of it. You needn't worry."

She laid back again, letting out an exhausted breath. "I'm sorry to set so much at your feet like this. You already have so much to deal with as it is."

"I don't begrudge it at all. You've been doing it for much longer, and it's time you had a break from it, to look after yourself." When she started to protest, I set a gentle hand on her shoulder, to keep her from trying to sit up again. "You've been so busy caring for Topiltzin that you haven't taken care of yourself. I insist you rest now, for you still look as if you need more sleep."

"That does sound wonderful," she replied, rather dreamily. "You're sure it's all right? You don't think Topiltzin will mind?"

"I think he would want you to rest," I said as I helped her slide back under her blankets. She sighed as she settled in.

A gourd pitcher half-full of dark liquid sat next to her bed. The sleep tonic Smoking Mirror had mentioned last night? Suspicious of his intentions, I smelled it, and while it did have a pungent aroma and a bitter taste, I didn't detect any magic in it.

"Can you pour me a little tonic?" she asked, her voice already sluggish.

"Are you sure you need it?"

"I can hardly sleep without it anymore."

So I poured a cup for her. Soon after she finished it, she was snoring softly.

I retreated into my own quarters before jumping into the teoyoh and I came out in the store room at the priestly retreat. I materialized behind the stack of copal wood, to hide my arrival if anyone was in there, but I found myself alone. After a quick trip into the kitchens for some atole, I went to relieve Mitotia.

When I parted the curtain, she wasn't alone. Mitotia worked on her weaving while Malinalli read through a priestly codex. They both looked up when I cleared my throat.

"I've brought Topiltzin's lunch," I announced as I stepped inside and pulled the curtain closed behind me. I glanced at Malinalli—who didn't meet my gaze—before addressing Mitotia. "Any trouble while I was gone?"

Mitotia shook her head. "After his breakfast, he slept peacefully." She too glanced at Malinalli before saying, "I have some things I must do back at the calmecac, so if you don't need me further right now...."

"Yes, of course you may go. And thank you for your help."

She hurried from the room, leaving me alone with Malinalli and Little Reed.

Malinalli said nothing, and though she'd bowed her head as if to return to her reading, I could tell she wasn't. I wondered if I should say anything, but I decided it was best to let her start the conversation, so I knelt next to Little Reed and sat him up for his meal.

But as I struggled to pull him upright, Malinalli came over to help, kneeling across from me. Once he was sitting up, I murmured, "Thank you."

She nodded but remained kneeling, a determined expression on her face. Still, it took a handful of breaths for her to finally speak. "I have questions."

"And I will provide all of the answers I can."

"So you're Mayahuel?" When I nodded, she asked, "Can you prove it?"

"I can perform feats of magic, if that's what you mean."

"I already knew about the magic. How do I know you're really who you're claiming to be?"

I thought about it while I spooned atole into Little Reed's mouth. "I don't have any way of proving it definitively to anyone but myself. What we were taught in calmecac doesn't mesh with what I remember of events before my death."

Malinalli furrowed her brow. "But you're not dead."

"I was, for many hundreds of bundles of years, but Quetzalcoatl brought me back."

"Why?"

So many bitter thoughts raced through my head that I had to take a moment to compose myself. "I don't really know. I wish I understood it myself; sometimes I wish he hadn't, if only so I wouldn't feel so lost and betrayed." I choked on the words, and Malinalli waited patiently for me to continue. "Long ago, the Feathered Serpent orchestrated my death so humanity would have octli to commune with the gods." I was shaking so badly I had to put the bowl down.

After a long pause, she said, "You were in love with him." There was pity in her voice.

I nodded. "I thought he felt the same way about me, but I was foolishly wrong."

"But if he didn't care, why would he bring you back from the dead? That doesn't make sense."

"Probably because it serves his needs to have me here now. But he never loved me; for thirty-five years he kept my true identity secret from me, and any number of times I could have died a mortal and been gone forever; he gave me a son but then did nothing to save his life; and he's condemned Topiltzin to an early death." I gazed at Little Reed with teary eyes. "We're all nothing but beans for him to roll while he plays his grand patolli game."

Silence fell between us while I dried my tears and resumed feeding Little Reed. Most of the atole went into his beard, but I pressed on anyway.

"Is that why you left?" Malinalli finally asked. "Why you didn't come home from Teotihuacan?"

I shook my head. "If that was all, I could have seen fit to continue on as the queen of Tollan, but...my own divine nature...." I closed my eyes against the sting of fresh tears. "My divine nature was poisoning Topiltzin's mind, driving him slowly crazy, just as I'd driven Red Flint and Black Otter to madness. I couldn't stand the thought that I was hurting him so much—or that I was hurting you or Mazatzin, or Citlallotoc. Every one of you means everything to me; I couldn't continue doing that, so I decided I couldn't come home. I'm sorry I didn't share my reasons with you, Malinalli. I thought everyone would be better off not knowing the truth about me."

She nodded. "We need to talk about what happened in your quarters the other night."

"I do owe you an explanation," I conceded.

"Do you have...feelings for me?"

I hesitated before saying, "You are extremely important to me, Malinalli; so important that I've resisted certain impulses out of fear of ruining our friendship. But yes, I love you, and my life is richer for having known you. Maybe it could have been more than that, but...." I looked down at Little Reed. "I've loved Topiltzin my whole life, even before he was born. I had a vision of him before my mother became pregnant with him, and even then he made my heart dance as no one else ever has."

"Like it was destiny?" Malinalli offered.

"Perhaps." I wiped the dribbled atole from Little Reed's lips. "But it feels immensely cruel of Heaven to let me so completely love someone I cannot even be intimate with without killing him."

"You and Topiltzin never—?"

I shook my head.

"But what about Ehecacone?"

"He's Quetzalcoatl's son. I became pregnant when he possessed me on the battlefield at Culhuacan. Topiltzin married me so he could claim Ehecacone as his own son, since we could never be intimate after I pledged my body and heart to the Feathered Serpent to save his life." I sighed. "And to think that I used to curse that sacrifice I made, when in fact it probably saved him from me." Seeing Malinalli's puzzled expression, I added, "I feed by having sex."

A weird look came to her face. "Only with men?"

"I can feed on anyone," I admitted. "Which makes what happened between us all the more...regrettable."

Malinalli stared at me, the color drained from her face. "You were intending to feed upon me?"

"That's what stopped me. I don't want to hurt you."

"Then why would you even let it start?"

The betrayal in her voice stung me. "I don't know," I whispered. "Topiltzin is on his deathbed, and despite all of my powers, there's nothing I can do to save him. I...I wanted to feel something other than pain and hopelessness...I'm sorry, Malinalli. I should have been stronger." I covered my eyes with the back of my hand. "I should have been stronger for Citlallotoc too. I was careless and I almost killed him. And my actions only exacerbated an already tense issue between him and Topiltzin. It's my fault he left; if I'd respected his wishes, if I hadn't pressured him to forget his honor...." Seeing her staring at me with wide eyes, I bowed my head in shame. "It's something I can never be forgiven for."

"That's his decision, not yours," she said.

I nodded. "But I have much to answer for."

"Is that why you came back?"

I chuckled dejectedly. "It didn't start that way; I wanted to see Topiltzin one last time, but finding what a mess I created here in Tollan...I must make amends for my past misdeeds and ensure Tollan's future."

"And when all of this succession business is over?"

"I will leave again, for the good of everyone. I still have so much to learn about being a goddess and controlling my divine nature, and I can't risk exposing Tollan to my mistakes along the way. Until I learn to use my powers without hurting anyone, I need to keep a distance from humans."

"That is understandable," Malinalli conceded.

Neither of us said anything while we situated Little Reed back down in his bed, but once the uncomfortable silence took over, I said, "You asked me last night if I made you the way you are—"

"You didn't," she said. When I looked up at her, she hung her head this time. "I've thought a great deal about it, and I've realized that in all of my years, I've never felt for any man what I've felt for Mitotia...or you. The one time I was with a man...it felt completely unnatural. But with Mitotia...I don't have to even try. It doesn't matter; this is who I am, and I feel at peace with that."

I smiled, relieved. "I'm happy for you. Learning to accept ourselves fully is often a long and difficult task, with many setbacks and mistakes."

She returned the smile but without as much enthusiasm as I'd hoped. "Do you wish me to watch after Topiltzin while you're at the debates tonight?"

"That would be helpful, but tomorrow you should come while Mazatzin watches the king. It's important that you, as the high priestess of Tollan, be present for at least some of it." After passing another moment in tense silence, I said, "I should go. The debates will start up again soon."

She nodded, but when I stood, she said, "Thank you for answering my questions, My Lady."

"Thank you for giving me the opportunity to explain," I said.

"I'd hoped that talking to you would give me a sense of where to go from here, but…I feel even more befuddled than before."

"As do I." After a pause, I asked, "Did you tell Mitotia…about me?"

"No, and I don't know that I will. At least not before I know how I feel about all of this. Though since she's going to be the next high priestess, perhaps she ought to know regardless."

I bowed my head and nodded.

In the distance, the copper gong on the temple of the Feathered Serpent rang, signaling the beginning of the new hour. "You should go," Malinalli said. "You're probably already late and it's a long walk back to the palace."

"Distance doesn't matter anymore," I said. "I can be anywhere I want in the blink of an eye, but yes, I should go, so I don't keep anyone waiting. I'll be back at dinner time."

She nodded.

I fumbled my hands together as I said, "Thank you for everything you've done for me, Malinalli." Then I muttered "teotoca" and disappeared into the flames of the teoyoh.

CHAPTER TWENTY-FIVE

For the next two days, I spent my days sitting on the reed icpalli in the sacred precinct, thinking about my conversation with Malinalli and paying very little attention while Citlallotoc and Matlacxochitl argued over policy. Both men were still careful not to fling accusations of treason and disloyalty, but it became increasingly obvious that Citlallotoc's arguments were winning. Even the recent drought and food shortages couldn't dampen the memory of so much prosperity under Little Reed's rule, and when the time finally came for the casting of lots, the number of jars containing Citlallotoc's chips grew faster than Matlacxochitl's. Even Matlacxochitl knew he'd lost long before the final lot was cast, for he'd looked bewildered most of the day while we sat watching the citizens toss their painted stones into the jars for their chosen candidate. I left before the final voting was done, confident that Citlallotoc would be crowned king, and my work here in Tollan would soon be over. I decided it called for a nice hot bath, my first in years.

As I walked into the palace trailed by my guards, I saw Mitotia walk into the Hall of the Gods, heading out from her own quarters for her priestly duties. We really hadn't spoken much since my return, and even now we passed each other with only a silent nod for a greeting.

But as I turned down the corridor leading to the royal quarters, I glanced over to see that the guards at the entrance to the foyer had stopped her. I backed up, my own guards following me.

One of the men—the guard who'd escorted me into the great hall the day I arrived back in Tollan—was talking to Mitotia. I couldn't hear his words, but the slimy smile on his face raised the hairs on my neck. I headed back down the stairs towards them.

Before I could reach them, Mitotia shouldered her way past him and continued on her way at a brisk walk, her head down and fists clenched. He laughed to his compatriot. "Pretty soon I'll have both of them in my bed."

When he saw me coming, he dropped the smile and went to his knees. His friend followed suit. "My Lady."

"What is your name?" I demanded.

"Patli, My Lady."

"You weren't a palace guard five years ago, were you?"

He shook his head.

"And you're no longer one now."

He looked up at me with wide eyes. "My Lady?"

"You will leave this palace this very moment and never cast your shadow upon its floors ever again."

"I don't understand—"

"Do not play coy with me, Patli. I'm well aware of the nature of your discussions with Ladies Mitotia and Malinalli, and frankly, men like you are disgusting, vile excuses for human beings. It's indicative of what kind of king Matlacxochitl would have been that he allowed men like you to not only operate under his rule but flourish."

His face now flushed, Patli said, "You're obviously unaware of the abominable behavior those two engage in—"

"The only abominable behavior is being displayed by you," I shot back, and on the wave of rage rising inside me, the desire took hold of my tongue. "If I weren't trying to be a better person, I would devour you one screaming, begging breath at a time, just to see the look on your face when the reality of your foolishness hit you just before the Black Dog dragged his cold tongue over your eyes."

That flush turned pale and I smelled fear oozing off of him. The scent was unnervingly enticing.

The desire receded slowly, leaving me feeling jittery. "Fortunately your resignation will suffice," I said. "You will make a better farmer than a guard."

He returned to his bowed position, hunched all the way over. "Yes, My Lady."

"But if I hear of you so much as speaking to either Mitotia or Malinalli, I will not be as merciful anymore." I then turned and swept away to my quarters.

◻

"Many congratulations on your victory," Lord Mozauhqui told Citlallotoc with a hearty clap on the shoulder.

The council was gathered in the great hall for breakfast, and though the voting results hadn't yet been publicly announced, word of Citlallotoc's definitive triumph had already spread through the noble ranks.

Matlacxochitl was there too, watching sullenly from the corner while the others gathered around Citlallotoc, alliances already shifting. He stiffened when I approached him, a cup of xocolatl in my hand.

"My condolences on your defeat," I said. "I must commend you on not running a dirty campaign; perhaps you are not as treacherous as I originally thought."

"Thank you for your generosity, My Lady." He said it with acid in his voice.

I smirked. "There is perhaps a lesson to be learned in all of this. We cannot return to a past where most people suffered under the ambitions of the elite. Tollan's citizens have made it clear that they will not accept anything less than a king who will move them into the future instead of returning them to the past."

"The people know not what is good for them," he muttered.

Is Smoking Mirror now speaking with your tongue too? I almost asked. "I was going to suggest that we let the last two years be bygones and that you return to your position as governor of Chimalhuacan, but I think perhaps you're not made for political office. You've been listening to all the wrong people."

"Those are big words coming from the mouth of the woman who helped Topiltzin turn humanity down the dangerous path of opposing the gods, and you'll regret it all when the gods bring you to justice for your sacrilege."

"As if you'd know anything about the gods, you mealy-mouth—"

But before I could finish, Citlallotoc came over and extended his hand out to Matlacxochitl. "I wanted to congratulate you on a hard fought battle, My Lord."

Matlacxochitl contemplated the gesture before slowly taking it, clasping Citlallotoc's forearm with his own hand. "Congratulations on your ascension. It must be a tremendous relief knowing that now you can fuck not only the king's sister but his wife as well without the burden of conscience."

An outraged gasp rose in the crowd gathered around.

Citlallotoc narrowed his eyes, and judging from the bulge of his arm muscles, he tightened his grip on Matlacxochitl's arm. "Do not mistake my congeniality for weakness. Speak one more disrespectful word about Lady Anacoana or the Queen, and I'll remove your tongue, as those rebels should have when they cut off your nose and your ear."

Matlacxochitl stared back, defiant, but the strain in his own arm told the real story.

Citlallotoc finally let him go, practically pushing him away. "You would do well to listen to your queen and leave Tollan now, for I will not be so forgiving of your behavior once the throne and its powers have passed to me."

After a brief glare at everyone standing around, Matlacxochitl retreated from the room.

"I know the law in Tollan is exile, but my arm longs to divide him in half with a sword," Citlallotoc admitted, watching him leave.

I didn't want to talk about Matlacxochitl anymore, so I looked around. "Have you and Lady Anacoana had a chance to talk since your return?"

He shook his head. "Every time I've tried to call upon her, she's been resting. Her servants tell me she's been ill the last few days."

I hadn't seen much of her either, and I'd hoped she might have recovered from her exhaustion by now. Citlallotoc might believe the past was too much to contend with, but I suspected they could repair their fractured relationship if they just sat down and talked. I would have to look in on her after breakfast.

Yet when I returned to the royal quarters, I found Anacoana's bed empty. I was just about to ask the guards if they'd seen her, but as I started down the portico, I heard girlish giggling coming from Citlallotoc's room.

I pulled the door curtain aside to find Anacoana sprawled out on the bed, looking unusually provocative and sensual. She giggled like a young girl, whispering under her breath, and even when I cleared my throat, she merely glanced at me, uninterested.

"Are you feeling all right, My Lady?" I asked, stepping up to the bed.

"I'm just wonderful, thank you." She hid her smile behind the back of her hand when she started giggling again. "Oh Quetzalpetlatl! I've never felt better!"

I raised an eyebrow before saying, "I'm glad to hear it."

She stroked her hair with one hand, my own presence seemingly forgotten again.

"I'd hoped you would come to breakfast this morning," I said. "Much has happened since yesterday."

She just shrugged and still didn't look at me. She stared into the far corner of the room, as if someone were standing there talking to her, but when I looked, the area was empty.

"Citlallotoc wants to talk to you," I offered.

Anacoana laughed. "As if I don't know. Why do you think I'm lying here?" She sat up and began sliding her dress off her shoulders. "Why didn't you bring him with you?"

Taken aback, I grabbed her hand before she could expose more than just her shoulders. "Are you crazy? You're Topiltzin's wife and he's not even dead yet!"

"Topiltzin gave me permission long ago to seek out other men, so what does he care?" She let me push the dress back into place though. "In fact, he gave both Citlallotoc and I permission to carry on to our hearts' content."

"Yes, but discretion is necessary, My Lady—"

"To Mictlan with discretion!" she snapped. "Citlallotoc couldn't abide the secrecy, so no more of that nonsense. I will take him in front of the whole city! Mark him as mine now and forever, so everyone knows he's off limits!" She gave me a pointed look.

"A queen doesn't behave so lewdly," I chided her. "What would your father think?"

She laughed. "Where on earth have you been? My father is dead, thank the gods. My mother put a knife through his skull for hitting her one too many times. The priests garroted her for it, but my brother said she refused to show any remorse, even when they showed her the flowery garland."

I stammered before settling on, "I understand your wanting to move on with your life, but I really think you should wait until Topiltzin passes on to Mictlan."

"Why?"

"Because it's the honorable thing to do."

"I don't care a wit about honor."

"But Citlallotoc does."

Anacoana pushed past me to pace in front of the hearth. "Blast it, you're right! But I've waited so long, and Topiltzin just isn't dying quick enough!"

I suddenly felt like she was squeezing my heart. "Don't say that."

"We should poison him, to speed things up."

"Maybe I should poison you, you little—" the desire roared, but I pushed it back. I felt dizzy with rage, but managed to keep my tone calm as I said, "You're suggesting treason, Anacoana."

She laughed. "Don't tell me you don't want him gone just as much as I do. I see it in your eyes: it tortures you to see him rotting away like a corpse. You wish he'd just die so you can move on with your life too. Don't deny it."

I snapped my mouth shut. Yes, I'd thought it, but not for the reasons she accused me of. The selfish part of me didn't want him to ever die; if I could turn him immortal, I would, without hesitation, even if it meant I still couldn't have him. The thought of losing him forever was like a swarm of ants trying to eat its way out of my insides.

"I've loved him all my life, so don't even suggest that I would want him dead," I snarled. "He's everything to me: my family, my best friend, and my husband. I'm sorry he was never any of that for you, but that gives you no right to say something so horrible."

To my chagrin, Anacoana laughed. "You're so funny, Quetzalpetlatl."

Now I was thankful that I hadn't yet told her where I'd moved Little Reed. "There's nothing funny about any of this. Frankly, I'm appalled that you'd behave like a defiant, selfish little girl. This is completely unlike you."

"What would you know about me?"

"Quite a bit."

Anacoana narrowed her eyes at me. "I know what this is about." She jabbed me in the chest with her finger. "You want Citlallotoc for yourself!"

"Stop this nonsense—"

"First you stole away Black Otter, then you made sure Topiltzin would never love me, and now you're trying to keep Citlallotoc from me too!"

"You couldn't be further from the truth—"

"He's mine! And if you try to take him from me, I swear to the gods I will kill you!"

She had such a wild look in her eyes that I stepped away, but her yelling brought my guards into the room. While one of them stood in front of me, the other one held Anacoana back with both hands.

"I see exactly what you're up to, you shameless whore!" Anacoana shouted, drawing the other guards into the room too. "All this time I thought you were my friend, but now I see the truth: you're an evil witch, plying innocent men with love potions to turn their hearts against all other women! But I will stop you!" Two of the guards grabbed her by the arms and she thrashed against them. "Let me go! You should be arresting her, not me!"

"You're not under arrest," I assured her. "But you're obviously not well."

The guards took her back to her quarters, and after some more struggling, they forced more of the sleep tonic down her. In a matter of minutes, she lay motionless on her bed, fast asleep. There were many of the medicine gourds lying scattered around her room.

"Has the royal chemist been back to see her?" I asked the guards.

"Not that we know of, My Lady," one of them said. "We've kept most people out of the royal quarters in accordance with your orders."

"I think My Lady sent her servants to fetch her medicines for her though," the other guard added.

I had little doubt that Smoking Mirror was behind Anacoana's sudden strange behavior. His seeming lack of action since last I saw him had indeed been too good to be true. "Watch her very closely. Don't let her leave her room," I told the guards then I left, my own guards following closely behind.

□

My guards led me to the house of the royal chemist in the jaguar neighborhood, and to my shock, when I rang the copper bells, Xochiquetzal answered the door curtain. I immediately sensed my guards' growing distraction, so I ordered them to remain outside then I pushed my way past her and yanked the curtain closed behind us. "What in Mictlan are you doing here?" I hissed.

She glared at me. "Smoking Mirror had need of a love goddess's talents, so I offered him my services."

"You're working for Smoking Mirror now?"

"Don't complain; you had your chance and instead you chose the Feathered Serpent over the rest of us."

"I didn't choose Quetzalcoatl!"

"You betrayed Mextli!"

I snapped my mouth shut, my face flushed. Seems what happened was no longer a secret. "What happened between me and Mextli...that was an accident. I didn't know that would happen."

"He's very mad at you," she warned. "And so am I! Do you realize that now Smoking Mirror will never trust me?"

"Why shouldn't he trust you?"

"Because of you and Quetzalcoatl, of course! He was willing to forgive me one parent, but both?"

Hearing her acknowledge my being her mother brought a hitch to my throat. I tried to speak, but nothing could get past it.

"I'm having to work really hard to show him that I'm not treacherous like you." She gestured to the row of gourd bottles lined up on the shelf next to the hearth. "I've been working day and night trying to make sure we have enough love potion for Topiltzin's wife."

I blinked. "You've been drugging Lady Anacoana?" When she nodded, I demanded, "Why?"

She folded her arms. "Wouldn't you like to know?"

"Xochiquetzal, you can't trust anything Smoking Mirror promises you—"

"You have never given him a chance! You've already forgotten that without him you wouldn't even know you are a goddess, and you'd still be under Quetzalcoatl's thumb."

"I haven't forgotten anything, including all the terrible things Smoking Mirror did to me. He's no more innocent than Quetzalcoatl is, and I'd be a fool to believe he is."

"Mextli is right. All you care about is yourself."

Standing straighter, I replied, "And you should care more about yourself than you do."

She gasped but then said, "What does it matter to you what I do and don't do?"

"I am your mother."

"And you're terrible at it."

Now was my turn to feel slapped. "It's not as if I've had much of a chance to prove myself to you."

She pushed past me to stand glaring into the hearth. "I don't owe you anything. I got along just fine on my own all of these many years, and I'll continue to do just fine for many more to come."

Irritated that I'd let her draw me into childish arguing, I sighed. "All I'm saying is that you deserve someone who won't use you for their own selfish purposes, someone who won't hold things over you that you have no control over." When she still wouldn't look at me, I hung my head. "You have much to be angry at me about; I haven't been there for you anymore than Quetzalcoatl has, but in my defense, I didn't know I had a daughter—and a second son—until just a few days ago, but even then, I didn't know how you felt about my being your mother, and I don't know if you wish to acknowledge it, but regardless, I am here now and I'd like to build on that, for both of us, if it's possible. I'm willing to try, if you wish."

She finally looked at me, an arch to her eyebrows. "Would you be willing to support me where it concerns Smoking Mirror?"

I pursed my lips, mulling before replying, "I am, but please, please, go into it with open eyes. It's his nature to exploit innocence and invoke fear in the name of power, and I don't want to see you become just another tool in his quest for more of it."

Xochiquetzal sniffed, frowning, then turned away from me again. "Xochipilli and I will give it thought. In the meantime, I believe we're done talking, so go."

I nodded but as I started to turn back to the door, I again spotted the gourd pitchers lining the shelf on the wall. "You should know that I won't let Lady Anacoana consume anymore of your love potion."

She shrugged. "My job is to make the potion, not to make sure anyone drinks it."

"If you ever need to talk, about what we've discussed here today, or anything else, just send word to the palace and I'll come meet you."

She harrumphed in reply, so I ducked back out onto the street, a brand new regret weighing me down. I had far too many of them these days.

CHAPTER TWENTY-SIX

At midday, the Council and the high priests of all of the orders met upon the wooden dais in the sacred precinct. A considerable crowd of men and women had gathered, all eager to hear the election results, and when I came to the front of the dais, the crowd took to cheering. I let them go for a moment before raising my hands for silence.

"I'm pleased to announce that the people have spoken and a new heir to Tollan's throne has been selected by an overwhelming majority. Thank you everyone who participated in this most unusual but important duty to your kingdom. Everyone should be proud of their contribution to Tollan's continued success.

"But now, without further ado, I present the next king of Tollan." I stepped aside and motioned Citlallotoc forward.

He stepped up from behind the dais and raised his arm in greeting as the crowd burst into cheers. The applause and cheering continued for a long time before he was finally able to calm the crowd enough to address them.

"I thank each and every one of you for placing your trust in me to see us all into the future. I promise to serve Tollan to the best of my ability, and continue the traditions lay down by both Lord Topiltzin and Lady Quetzalpetlatl. While the circumstances of my ascension leave me with a heavy heart, we shall make it through these unfortunate times and come out the other side stronger than ever!"

More cheering erupted.

"And to those who didn't cast their lots for me, I will work extra hard to earn your respect and trust. Your concerns and wishes for the future are as important to me as any, and together we will make sure Tollan remains on the forefront of the Tolteca Empire."

"Big words for a one-armed mortal!" a familiar voice shouted from the crowd.

My joy at hearing Citlallotoc's impassioned speech died in my chest. I scanned the crowd, and it didn't take long to locate Mextli standing near the very back of the crowd. He stood twice as tall as anyone, and it amazed me that I hadn't noticed him before. He was dressed for war, but he held no weapons in his large hands.

I glared at him. "What are you doing here?"

"I think you already know, My Lady." He gave me a malicious smile.

"You!" Citlallotoc grabbed his sword from his belt. "One would think that having been handed defeat twice at the hands of Tollan's queen you'd know better than to darken this city's stones with your shadow!"

"And one would think that after having to be saved twice by a woman, you'd keep your mouth shut," Mextli fired back.

Citlallotoc made to leave the dais, but I grabbed his arm. "He's baiting you."

"You were warned to stay out of matters of royal succession," Mextli said. "But you didn't listen, and now it's time to pay the price."

He turned to the crowd. "The days of Quetzalcoatl's rule are at an end, and the time of the Smoking Mirror is beginning, and those who stand in his way will be trampled under the feet of change. For twenty years, Tollan's king and queen have blasphemed the other gods, have changed the laws passed down on earth by Heaven itself, and have led you all astray.

"The Smoking Mirror is merciful though. He recognizes that you all are just humans, easily manipulated and fooled into acting against your own interests. It isn't too late to redeem yourselves and spare Tollan from ruin. Forsake Topiltzin and his ways, and refuse to accept his successor, who shares all of his fatal flaws. You will only be given this one chance!"

A murmur of confusion spilled through the crowd, but eventually that turned to shouts of, "Who are you to tell us what to do?" and "Treason against the crown!"

"Calm down everyone!" I called, trying to be heard over the shouts, but the rumble from the crowd only grew in intensity. The people nearest Mextli had stepped away from him, and most of the faces in the crowd were frowning or twisted in anger. Many shook their fists at him as they shouted. The guards around the precinct readied their spears, looking around with unease but making no move to control the crowd.

"Let them tear him apart," Citlallotoc muttered, a stiff sneer on his face. "It's what he deserves."

Magic tingled nervously in my finger tips. "It could well be our men who get torn apart."

Suddenly the shouts turned to cries of surprise as Mextli's hands turned to blue fire balls. He grinned at the people shrinking away from him. "You humans like to learn the hard way, don't you?" He launched the fireballs into the crowd.

Screams echoed through the precinct and people ran in every direction. Those closest to Mextli burst into flames, and those fires jumped into the fleeing crowd like men doing acrobatics.

Cut off from escape by the fire and the crowd, the people nearest the temple flooded the dais, knocking Council members and priests aside. The flow separated me from Citlallotoc and surrounded me with screaming and cursing.

But a hand clamped down on my arm and I turned to see Malinalli. "We must get out of here!" she shouted. Mazatzin stood with her, looking harried.

"But what about Citlallotoc?" I shouted back, but then I saw several guards hustling him through the crowd, knocking over anyone who got in their way.

"Let's go!" Mazatzin shouted.

But someone ran into me, knocking both me and Malinalli over. Someone stepped on my hand and Malinalli cried out in pain as more and more people stepped upon us. Fearing she would be trampled to death, I let loose a concentrated burst of magic at those nearest us, knocking them backwards. Mazatzin hustled Malinalli—bruised and tender— to her feet, and I hurried after them, letting off a few more bursts of magic to make sure the way was clear.

But just as I laid out the last man heading for me, the blue flame warriors jumped up onto the dais. They thrust and jabbed flaming swords and spears at us, and the wood beneath their feet caught fire with preternatural speed. I brought the magic pounding up into my fingers as they ran in circles, building a growing ring of fire around us.

Malinalli looked around with wild eyes, and Mazatzin yelped when one of the flaming warriors jabbed his neck with its spear, searing his skin.

I blasted magic at the flame warriors, but instead of quelling them, the fire flared high and hot, as if I'd thrown fuel onto them. Mazatzin shrieked as flames engulfed his left hand and started eating up the sleeve of his robe. Malinalli pounded at it with her hands, trying to put it out, but the smell of burning flesh grew heavier with each breath.

With the wall of flames completely encasing us now, I had no choice but to flee. I swept my arms over both Malinalli and Mazatzin and yelled, "Teotoca!" over the roar of the flames.

ㅁ

The air was deliciously cooler when we emerged from the teoyoh, but I had no time to feel relief. We were greeted by a gasp and the sound of something breaking, but I didn't bother looking away from Mazatzin. The jump had extinguished the flames eating up his robe, but the flesh on his hand was blistered and red.

"The water jar!" I shouted as I rolled his scorched robe sleeve up, checking the skin underneath. The hairs were burnt and the skin irritated, but nothing like his hand.

It took a second shout for someone to finally get the jar. I caught Mitotia's stunned gaze for only a breath before pouring some of the water over Mazatzin's hand, to stop his flesh from continuing to cook. He howled in agony.

"Get me some clean rags," I panted. "We'll need to wrap his hand."

Mitotia hesitated again but this time went before I could snap at her.

Malinalli stared down at Mazatzin with wild eyes. "Can't you...can't you just heal him?"

I shook my head. "I wish I had healing powers, but I don't." I smoothed Mazatzin's graying hair from his forehead as he lay panting after the dousing.

Mitotia hurried back into the room bearing bandages. I wet the first one quickly and started wrapping it around Mazatzin's hand. "Get the next one ready for me." And for the next endless minutes, Mitotia kept the wet bandages coming while I wrapped them around Mazatzin's hand. By the time I'd finished, he was delirious with pain, so I gave him a small dose of my octli magic through my fingertips to put him to sleep.

Mitotia looked bewildered but she said nothing as she knelt next to him, Malinalli across from her. I took the water jar back to the corner and remained there, trying to gather my thoughts in the face of overwhelming guilt. I should have gotten Malinalli and Mazatzin out of there instead of trying to stop the flames. I'd been an arrogant fool, and now Mazatzin's hand would never be the same, and I couldn't stop thinking about Smoking Mirror's warnings.

"How did you—how did you suddenly appear, out of nowhere?" Mitotia finally spoke, her voice shaking

"It's how we...gods travel from place to place."

"Gods?" The color drained from her face as she looked at me.

I nodded.

"She's the goddess Mayahuel," Malinalli provided.

Mitotia stared at her, a look of utter shock on her face. And hurt. "You knew?"

"She found out just a few days ago," I said. "I imagine the news was too shocking to talk about with anyone right away."

After a hesitation, she asked, "Is that why you left?"

"I had to. I can't stay among humans for long without causing them harm. Already things are going sour, and I haven't even been back a week. Maybe I should have stayed away. It might be best for everyone if I just left again now—"

"But you said you would stay and help us," Malinalli said.

"I did, but I fear I'm doing more harm than good."

She stood up, her posture defiant. "You promised. You can't just up and leave again, especially now. You heard that…that creature in the sacred precinct; we need you now more than ever."

Mitotia looked at me expectantly.

"And what if my staying makes everything worse?" I asked. "Besides, I'm but one goddess, here on my own, and Smoking Mirror has allies. I'm no match for that."

"One goddess on our side is better than none," Malinalli countered. "None of us have any reason to believe Quetzalcoatl cares anymore. You can't abandon us too."

Her words filled me with shame. "Very well, I'll stay." It cut me to be compared to Quetzalcoatl, but I truly hoped I wouldn't come to regret this decision.

I looked to the door. "I really should go make sure Citlallotoc got out safe."

Malinalli nodded stiffly. "And I'll fetch the royal chemist to see Mazatzin—"

"Absolutely not!" When both women gaped at me, I rushed to add, "The royal chemist is Smoking Mirror."

"How can that be?" Mitotia asked.

"He took over the body of Black Otter's son and used him to infiltrate the royal court. He's also been plying Lady Anacoana with love potion."

"For what reason?"

"I don't know," I admitted, though I suspected that I would find out before long.

"I'll walk back with you," Malinalli offered, but I held a hand up.

"It would be better if you stayed here and helped Mitotia watch after Topiltzin and Mazatzin. Until I know what's going on, I think both of you will be safer here."

"All right, but let me walk you out." She wasn't taking no for an answer this time, and without waiting for my response, she walked out of the curtain into the garden. I cast a hesitant glance at Mitotia before following her out.

Malinalli was waiting for me a dozen steps away from the door, where we wouldn't be overheard if we whispered. "I must say thank you," she said. "You saved my life back there."

"Your welcome, but surely you know it's not something I'd ever hesitate to do, Malinalli. You're my best friend."

She nodded. "I know that. It's just…I was pretty tough on you in there."

"You had every right to be. I'm trying not to mess up things, and yet everything I touch…."

"Everything will be fine."

"I should have acted quicker back there in the precinct."

"Mazatzin's alive, and I'm sure he's grateful for that. At least it didn't burn his dominant hand."

I shook my head. "I never should have set my magic on the fire."

"What did you do?"

"I shot it with my octli—" I slapped my forehead, feeling stupid. "By Mictlan, I actually poured fuel on it! I'm an idiot!"

"Anyone could have made the same mistake," Malinalli said, setting a supportive hand on my shoulder. It was the first time she'd touched me since that night in my quarters, and though I wondered if she realized what she was doing, I felt on the verge of tears. Such a small gesture, but for that moment, it was as if we were still best friends and nothing had changed between us. "I'll do my best to get us safely out of this," I said past the tears clogging my throat.

"I trust you will."

"I'll be back soon with news," I said, finally pulling away, to make sure I didn't pull her into the teoyoh with me.

She gave me an encouraging smile and I held onto the hope it gave me as I vanished into the flames of the teoyoh.

□

"One hundred and fifty-three dead, all burned to death," Blood Wolf informed me when I reached the great hall. "And hundreds more are wounded. When I couldn't find you in the melee, I was sure you were dead too."

"Malinalli and Mazatzin got me out," I told him.

He exhaled a ragged breath. "Thank the gods! The last thing we need right now is for the queen to be killed, for that would surely instill panic among the people."

I nodded. "Citlallotoc is all right?"

"His guards removed him very quickly, but I'm furious how your own guards didn't do the same for you. I will immediately assign a new set to protect you, My Lady."

"That won't be necessary. I'm sure they just became disoriented in the commotion." And it wasn't as if mortal guards could protect me from Mextli; he would get at me if he truly wanted to.

"I would feel more comfortable if you'd indulge me on this, My Lady."

I shrugged. "Whatever makes you feel better. Where's Citlallotoc?"

"He went to check on Lady Anacoana. He was very worried that she might have been out in the crowd, but I assured him that she had been abed all day. Still he insisted on going to see her."

I tapped my fingers on my knee as I sat on my icpalli, debating whether I should go check on her too. The love potion had made her sleep almost all day, so she was probably all right....

"I've sent warriors out into the city to hunt down the man who started all this rubbish," Blood Wolf went on. "I aim to have him and that treacherous Matlacxochitl standing here in front of the throne by tomorrow, answering for their heinous crimes against Tollan. This I swear to you."

I shook my head, alarmed. "No, call them all back. That will only make matters worse, and more lives will be lost."

"But My Lady, we can't just let them—"

"Trust me, all the soldiers in Tollan couldn't bring Mextli in. I don't want more bloodshed."

"Then what are we to do?"

"I don't know yet, but I'm thinking about it."

Blood Wolf motioned one of the guards over and issued orders to bring the rest of the guards back in from the city. He then returned to his spot next to my throne. "You're probably right. The fire that man set...it moved with unnatural swiftness."

"We are dealing with magic now, and only more magic can answer it."

"You will call on the god, like you did in Culhuacan?"

"I will do what's necessary." The words haunted me though; the last time I'd said that, I'd hesitated, and Nimilitzli ended up dead and Little Reed very nearly joined her.

A servant suddenly clamored towards the dais, panting as if he'd run far. "My Lady! My Lady! Come quickly!"

"What is the meaning of this?" Blood Wolf demanded.

"Lord Citlallotoc—he's been stabbed!"

I shot to my feet and pushed my way past Blood Wolf. "Stabbed? By who?"
"Lady Anacoana!"

CHAPTER TWENTY-SEVEN

I arrived in the royal quarters to the sounds of screaming and cursing coming from Anacoana's quarters, but a number of guards were gathered around the doorway to Citallotoc's quarters. They blocked my entrance, but once Citallotoc heard me calling to him, he ordered they let me by.

He sat upon his bed, his personal physician tending to wounds on his arm, hand, and his chest. The one on his chest was a glancing blow, leaving a shallow cut, but the ones on his arm were deeper, with the worst of them on his palm; one looked as if the blade had gone completely through. "What on earth happened?"

"Lady Anacoana attacked me with a knife," Citlallotoc replied, his face stoic as he watched his physician started winding a bandage around his wounded hand.

"Why?"

After some hesitation, he finally looked up at me, and though he said nothing, the message was clear in his eyes; he didn't want to talk about it in front of his men. I nodded then retreated to the corner, staying out of the way while the doctor finished his work, and when it was done, Citlallotoc announced, "I would like a private moment with Lady Quetzalpetlatl."

He remained on the bed while everyone filed out, but once the room was clear, he went to the curtain and told his guards to step out into the garden, away from the door. He then closed the curtain but remained standing there, holding the seam together with his bandaged hand.

"What we discuss here...you must promise you will tell no one," he said, his voice lowered.

"Why?"

"Because it would ruin me in the eyes of the Council, and destroy my reputation among my guards and warriors."

"What happened?"

He finally moved back towards the bed, but he didn't sit down. "I went to make sure that Anacoana was all right. I was worried that she might have gone to the precinct to see the announcement. But she was awake in her room, and so I stayed to talk to her...." He turned his back to me, distress seeping off of him like a choking smoke.

I sat down on the bed and waited for him to continue, my own anxiety elevated.

After a handful of deep breaths, he said, "We were just talking, and it was going very well—better than it had in years—but she...she became...." He sucked in a nervous breath and set the back of his wounded hand against his forehead. He turned to face me again, slowly, and the look on his face was one of shame and fear. "She became very aggressive...sexually. She climbed on my lap and made me...she made me touch her—" He looked ill. "I told her we couldn't act like this, no matter what Topiltzin might have allowed in the past, but she kept insisting, and demanding...."

"It's not your fault, Citlallotoc."

He laughed, uneasy. "I must have said something, or done something to provoke

642

her—"

"You did nothing."

"You weren't there—"

"I know you well enough to say with certainty that you would never be anything but honorable with another man's wife, no matter how close to death her husband might be."

Citlallotoc turned away again. "I told her I don't feel the way I used to, but that I would always take care of her, out of respect for Topiltzin. That's when she pulled out the knife." He stared down at his bandaged hand. "If I hadn't seen her move for it when I did, she might have stabbed me right in the throat. Instead, she impaled me through the hand when I tried to shove her away. Then she was on me like a jaguar, ripping at me with her fingernails...." He dropped his hand to peer at me over his shoulder. "Is this what I did to her, Quetzalpetlatl? Did she become like this because of what happened between us?"

I stood, shaking to hear him bearing the blame for any of this. "She's not in her right mind, Citlallotoc, and you didn't cause it. Smoking Mirror has been plying her with love potion."

Citlallotoc turned to me, the fear deep on his face now. "The Smoking Mirror is here, in Tollan? He's actually here, in the flesh?"

"I'm afraid so."

He looked ready to pass out, so I grabbed onto him and helped him settle down onto the bed. "Mextli was telling the truth!" Bewilderment on his face, he panted, "The gods *have* turned against us!"

"Only some of them."

"And Mextli...he's one too?"

I nodded. "He's a war god."

"Dear gods, and I've tried to fight him—twice!"

"And you survived him twice. That's nothing to sniff at," I said.

He brayed with manic laughter. "Yes, but I only survived because...." His strained smile dropped as he turned to look at me. "You...you're one of them too, aren't you?"

Given the desperation in his eyes, I wondered if he could handle the truth right now, but eventually I said, "For many years I didn't know it, but...yes, I am."

He turned away, that sick look on his face again. "And Topiltzin?"

I shook my head. "Regrettably, no. He's mortal as any human."

He nodded slowly. "But you are....are you Xochiquetzal?"

"Actually, I'm Mayahuel."

"I thought surely you were a love goddess."

"I am. I've just never been worshipped as one."

"No wonder Topiltzin didn't want to let you go."

"I'd like to hope it was because he truly loved me as I love him, not because I made him feel something that wasn't real," I said.

Citlallotoc tightened his jaw. "I feel so foolish now, about those things I said to you in Teotihuacan. No wonder you ran away."

I started reaching for his hand but stopped. Those days were over. "We must talk, about what happened that night in the sacred precinct."

"You mean when I was weak and betrayed my best friend?"

"You weren't weak. You were exceedingly loyal and strong, and I...." The desire slithered up to take my tongue, a strange spike of regret coming with her. "If anyone is to blame, it's me. You said no, but I continued pushing...and arguing with you."

"We didn't do anything I didn't want to. I'd wanted it for a long time."

"Except maybe it was my divine essence that made you want it."

He shook his head and stood, putting distance between us. "I don't want to go down that path, Quetzalpetlatl."

"Citlallotoc—"

"No! I know what you're getting at, and I won't even entertain it. I mean, think about it. I'm twice your size!"

"My power is not in my size, Citlallotoc—"

"Enough! This is ridiculous, and if my guards overheard this nonsense.... I've suffered enough indignity answering for my conduct with Anacoana years ago, but if they thought for a moment that I couldn't defend myself against a woman—"

I shot to my feet. "We both know I'm no mere woman. That's mitigating."

"It doesn't matter; either way I come out looking weak. You asked me here to be Tollan's next ruler, so I beg you to not undermine me with this."

"I don't want to undermine you, but that doesn't change the fact that I owe you an apology for my own conduct, and...and for nearly killing you in my carelessness. I know that no apology will ever be enough—"

"If it will make you stop pressing the issue, I accept your apology. And now we'll never speak of it again."

I looked away, cursing myself for making him feel pressured yet again. "As you wish."

"I do," he said, curt.

After another pause, I asked, "And what about Anacoana? If there's a trial, the truth will come out."

He stared into the hearth, his voice stiff. "As the queen, that decision rests with you."

"She is under the influence of dark magic and I'd just as soon let her recover from that before deciding what to do about all of this."

He nodded, an air of relief coming over him. "Now if you'll excuse me, I wish to rest." He held the curtain open.

Without further argument, I headed for the door, but when I neared, Citlallotoc whispered, "Where is Quetzalcoatl in all of this? With so many gods here in Tollan now, surely he's here as well, so why didn't he stop Mextli? Why has he let any of this happen? Has he abandoned us? In our time of greatest need?"

It was on the tip of my tongue to rip into Quetzalcoatl, to say that he was no friend to anyone, but in these trying times, sometimes hope was better than bitter truth. "I don't know about the Feathered Serpent, but the people of Tollan have at least one goddess on their side."

◻

After I left Citlallotoc's room, I crossed the garden to Anacoana's quarters. Eerie silence had replaced the cursing and screaming, and when I peeked inside, she was asleep again.

"We gave her some more sleep tonic," one of her guards told me. "It was the only way to calm her down."

I snatched up the remainder of the love potion and threw it out into the flowerbeds in her private garden. "She is not to be given any more sleep tonics or other medicines," I said. "Nor is she to eat anything that isn't brought to her by me. Is that clear?"

The guards snapped straighter and nodded. "Yes, My Lady," they said in unison.

"And I want anything that could be used as a weapon removed from her quarters immediately. If she becomes unruly again, bind her. She is not to leave her quarters, and one of you will stand guard at the doorway into the back passage, so she cannot slip out that way. I'll be back later to check on her."

CHAPTER TWENTY-EIGHT

 With the Council, I visited the sacred precinct to assess the damage left by Mextli's attack, then we went around to the homes of some of the victims, to deliver my condolences and supplies of food and clothing to those left behind. Women and men alike cried and wailed for their lost loved ones, imploring me for answers as to why this happened and why I hadn't called on Quetzalcoatl to protect them. By the time we returned to the palace, all I wanted was to leave Tollan and go into hiding far from everything, but I'd made my promise and no matter how much it pained me, I would keep it.

I sat on my throne and listened while the Council members discussed what to do now. A small number of them—mostly those who had supported Matlacxochitl—said this was a sure sign that the elections had been a mistake and that the high priests should consult with the gods to name the next king. Most people scoffed at that notion though and called those who said it traitors to the crown. I let them argue and instead focused my own thoughts on what I could do myself. *Smoking Mirror warned me, and I didn't listen. Maybe it's not too late to go back to him and try to make a deal.*

"I don't understand why the search for the culprit in this morning's tragedy was called off," an unfamiliar councilman piped up. "What if this barbarian does this same thing in the noble quarters, or in the Chichimec quarters—"

"He wouldn't do it in the Chichimec quarters," another man rebutted. "No doubt he's one of them!"

"We will not turn upon each other now," Citlallotoc said. "That is exactly what the enemies of Tollan want: for us to tear ourselves apart from the inside. We can't make their ambitions so easily achieved."

"And perhaps we shouldn't make it so easy for our enemies to justify our destruction!" another man called. "We should listen to the warning given us today!"

"Topiltzin built this city on faith, not fear—"

"To Mictlan with Topiltzin!"

An outraged rumble carried through the room, and Citlallotoc rose to his feet, hand poised to take his sword, but then he cringed in pain. Gritting his teeth, he hissed, "Anyone who is so bold as to slander the king has no place in this hall, or this city."

"And you should listen to his warnings, little man," a deep, familiar voice spoke up. Everyone turned and many gasped to see Mextli standing in the great hall's entrance, palace guards holding him by the arms as if they'd taken him into custody.

Citlallotoc strode to the edge of the dais, this time putting aside the pain to take his sword in hand. "So, the villain has been brought in for justice after all!"

My divine instincts told me Mextli wasn't here against his will. I launched to my feet too and barked at the guards, "Do not touch him!"

Mextli grinned. "Oh, never fear, My Lady. I have indeed come to face justice for my crimes against you and the future king. I will not harm these innocent men who are merely doing their jobs." He looked over his shoulder at the guard to his right. "Aren't you going to march me before the Queen for judgment?"

"They will do no such thing!" I said, stepping down off the dais. "You will come no closer."

"You aren't afraid of me, are you?" He started walking up the center of the great hall towards me.

I retreated back up onto the dais, and the guards rushed to stop him, but when they reached him, my warnings to not touch him must have re-entered their heads. They didn't grab hold of him but walked the rest of the way with him, their spears at the ready.

Mextli stopped before the dais and dropped to his knees. He gazed imploringly up at both Citlallotoc and I, a smile on his face, but the darkness lurked in his eyes, staring me down. "So, what is my punishment, My Lady?"

"In Tollan, exile is the proscribed sentence for your heinous crime," Citlallotoc said.

"That is no punishment at all, for I will just come back and do it again," Mextli said. "For the safety of your city, the Queen must put me to death."

"I am more than happy to oblige you." Citlallotoc started to step down, his sword ready.

But I grabbed his arm. He stiffened at the touch, but didn't move to free himself. However, the sour odor of his discomfort compelled me to let him go.

"What's the matter, My Lady? Don't you want justice for those I murdered?" Mextli asked.

I glared at him. "You're too eager for us to kill you."

"Perhaps I'm contrite and believe I should pay for my evil deeds."

I laughed. "Or maybe you're inviting all of us onto your web."

He grinned wider. "I guess you'll just have to find out, won't you?"

I looked to Citlallotoc, but he appeared just as frustrated as I felt. A tense unease emanated from the crowd before us.

To Mextli, I said, "We will not be rushed to a decision, so you will spend the night in the prison yard while the Council discusses what to do about this situation."

Mextli grinned. "As you wish, My Lady."

"Guards, escort him to the prison yard." I then moved to return to my icpalli.

Citlallotoc did the same, but before he'd gone more than two steps, Mextli asked, "Did you enjoy Smoking Mirror's gift, little man?"

Citlallotoc froze.

"Though I wonder what kind of man—or future king, for that matter—refuses a beautiful woman when she offers herself so freely? Perhaps you just don't like women, what with all your talk about how much you 'loved' your king."

Citlallotoc's face burned deep red.

"Ignore him," I warned Citlallotoc, then to the guards, "Get him out of here already."

The guards grabbed onto Mextli's arms, but he ignored them. "But that's not really the problem at all, is it, My Lord?" He closed his eyes and drew in a deep breath between his clenched teeth, as if tasting the air for something. "It was fear, and shame; the same things that drove you from Tollan five years ago. It was happening all over again, but this time, the Council would find out the truth: that you are so weak that you can't keep a woman half your size from having her way with you, like when the Queen ignored your pleas of honor and instead ravaged you on the steps of the Temple of the Moon in Teotihuacan. They'd finally see that you're no man at all, but rather a scared little boy crying in the corner of his mother's room—"

Before I could say anything more, Citlallotoc whirled around and buried his sword between Mextli's neck and shoulder blade.

Mextli stared down at it then broke out laughing. "A nice blow, for a one-armed man." Golden dust began oozing down the feathered half of his chest.

"Give my regards to Lord Death, you Chichimec dog," Citlallotoc hissed, and he yanked on the sword handle with all his strength, making the dust gush out like a blizzard.

"You can tell him yourself." Mextli fell over backwards, a cloud of shimmering dust floating in the air around him.

The guards backed away, expressions of horror on their faces. "What is this...sorcery?" one of them asked, his voice shaking.

Citlallotoc waved the dust away as he looked back at me, no doubt expecting me to answer.

But the dust's golden hue shifted to moldy-green, and he began coughing and gagging, his eyes bulging. The guards started folding over with hacking coughs as the smell of putrefying flesh swelled. Even my own eyes started stinging.

The green dust soon spread all over the great hall, sending people into coughing and vomiting fits. A strange buzzing noise rose and a black cloud of flying insects swarmed out of Mextli's dead body, attacking the crowd. Terrified screams joined the already chaotic noise. The concentration of insects and dust soon grew so thick I couldn't see more than an arm's length in front of me.

I clambered about, calling for Citlallotoc, but after only a few steps, I fell over the edge of the dais, crashing to the floor. I found Mextli and the bodies of the guards, both dead. I crawled until I found Citlallotoc; he lay face down, his eyes bulging and bloodshot, his final gasp for air still locked on his purple face like a ghastly scream. The sight was a punch to my chest.

I never should have brought him here. What was I thinking? He was happy back home in Acolman, but I brought him here to die!

The cries soon fell quiet—evidence of the swiftness of Mextli's toxic death—but still more rose from out in the Hall of the Gods. I looked down at Citlallotoc again, my heart heavy and my fear ramping up.

There's nothing you can do for him now, the desire reminded me. *He's already gone, but that doesn't mean you can't still save others.*

Yes. Now wasn't the time to dwell on my own shortcomings. The palace needed to be evacuated.

I stumbled through the cloud of dust and insects, tripping over bodies strewn upon the floor, but eventually I found the entryway and clamored out into the Hall of the Gods.

The pestilence had infiltrated the vestibule, but I soon emerged from the cloud to find people fleeing through the public gardens while others sat on the steps, trying to catch their breaths and coughing the noxious dust from their lungs. The guards shouted in the confusion, herding as many people out as they could, but when one of them saw me, he hurried over, looking beleaguered. "Are you all right, My Lady?"

"I'm fine, but the people in the living quarters need to be evacuated. Take a couple of your men and go to the east wing, and take anyone you find out through the emergency corridor. Be sure to cover your nose and mouth before venturing into the green mist." I then turned and started back into the cloud myself.

But the guard grabbed my arm. "Where are you going? You must evacuate with everyone else!"

"I'm going to the royal quarters to get Lady Anacoana, and then we'll leave together through the passage to the priestly gardens."

"I can send some men to do that—"

"No, there's more people needing your help in the east wing. I will take care of Lady Anacoana. Now go!" I slipped his hold then plunged back into the cloud of dust and whirling insects. I heard him shouting for me to come back, but now that I was concealed from view, I jumped into the teoyoh.

I materialized in the hallway to the royal quarters. The guards that usually stood watch were gone—no doubt drawn away by the sounds of commotion deeper in the palace—but when I stepped out into the garden, one of Anacoana's guards still maintained his watch at her doorway. In his harried state, he forgot to bow when I approached. "What is going on, My Lady?"

"Is Lady Anacoana awake?"

"She wasn't when I last checked on her." He opened the curtain to let me inside.

We both stopped short when we found the bed empty. "Perhaps she's in the water yard," he suggested, and hurried towards the private garden ahead of me.

But she wasn't there either. And when we went through the doorway leading out into the back passageway, we found the other guard lying on the ground. A makeshift garrote made from a dress was still wound around his neck.

"I'll mount a search for her immediately, My Lady," the guard said, looking exceptionally pale.

I shook my head. "No. Go help evacuate the palace, and be sure to wear a cloth over your nose and mouth before you go."

"But what about you, My Lady?"

"I'm going to the priestly gardens."

He fidgeted a breath before saying, "I would be negligent in my oath to the crown if I left you unattended as you are. Where are your guards?"

"I don't have time for this. Follow my orders or I will relieve you of your duties!"

He hesitated only a moment more before bowing and heading back into the palace at a jog. Once he was out of sight, I leaped into the teoyoh, following the sweet fragrance of Anacoana's mortal teotl.

□

I rematerialized in my meditation room in the priestly retreat, in almost complete darkness; someone had quelled the fire in the hearth. I saw a shadow knelt next to Little Reed's bed, but when my divine eyes adjusted, I saw it was Anacoana. She held a dagger, poised to stab Little Reed as he slept.

I dove over him and tackled her, knocking the blade from her hands. She grunted but clawed at my face with both hands. I pushed back, pinning her arms to the ground at her sides.

"Get off me!" she shrieked. "I want him dead, and you're not going to stop me!"

Magic tingled in my fingertips but I resisted releasing it. "I don't want to hurt you, Anacoana!"

But she kneed me in the stomach and wiggled away. When she reached for the blade on the floor, I shot a blast of magic at it, sending it skating across the room to hit the far wall.

She jumped after it, but I grabbed her ankle and she crashed to the ground with a grunt. But then she kicked me in the face, breaking my nose, and I let her go. My magic mended my wound quickly, but the pain-induced tears still clouded my eyes. I brushed

648

them aside and blinked to bring my vision back into focus.

Anacoana had grabbed up the knife again and came around the other side, the blade held aloft to deal the killing blow to Little Reed. I reached out my hand, ready to blast her over backwards with my octli magic.

But someone came up behind her and slid a blade across her throat. The action itself was silent, but Anacoana choked. She dropped the blade to clutch her throat, gasping and sputtering before falling to her knees, blood gushing over her fingers. She slumped over, her breath rattling as her blood flowed out onto the floor.

The door curtain stood open now, and at first I couldn't make out the figure standing there, set against the early evening light pouring in from outside, but as my eyes adjusted, her features came into shape. "Yaretzi?" The high priestess of Smoking Mirror.

She turned her cold gaze upon me. "Are you all right, My Lady?" Her voice lacked surprise or anxiety, almost as if she were asking me my breakfast order instead of inquiring about my health after a deadly struggle.

"I'm fine, but...." I moved around to Anacoana, to feel for a pulse on her neck. It was thready and fading, and her pooled blood soaked into the reed matting of Little Reed's bedding. Her pulse ceased before I pulled my fingers away. "You didn't have to kill her," I panted.

"Of course I did," Yaretzi replied, dispassionate. "She was poised to kill Topiltzin."

"You could have disarmed her."

Before she could answer, Malinalli rushed into the room and slid to a stop with a gasp. "Omeyocan save me, what happened?"

"Lady Anacoana attempted to murder her husband," Yaretzi replied. "But I stopped her, and now the Queen is upset with me."

I glared at Yaretzi, but Malinalli hurried to me and fell to her knees. "Forgive my negligence, My Lady! I left for only a few moments, to go to the water yard, but I shouldn't have left the king alone. I beg your forgiveness!"

The way Malinalli prostrated herself unnerved me, and Yaretzi was watching with a curious smirk on her face. "Would you please give us a moment alone, Lady Yaretzi?" I asked.

Her smirk stretched further. "Of course."

"But wait out by the store room, for I wish to speak with you further," the desire hissed.

She bowed her head, still amused, then she disappeared out the curtain, closing it behind her.

"Malinalli," I started, but when she didn't move from her prostrated stance, I nudged her shoulders with both hands. "Please, sit up and look at me."

She finally did so, gazing at me with watery eyes.

"This isn't your fault."

"I shouldn't have left him alone! Dear gods! What if you hadn't come back—"

"He's all right."

"I let you down."

"Not at all. It wasn't fair of me to leave so much on your shoulders. I'm sorry."

Malinalli cast her forlorn gaze down at Anacoana. "I can't believe all of this. Everything has turned to madness!"

I hesitated to say more, but she had to know the full situation. "Citlallotoc and the entire Council are dead."

She covered her mouth with both hands, fresh tears welling in her eyes. "How?"

"Poison. You musn't go back to the palace; it's completely uninhabitable."

She blinked, a lost look on her face. "What are we going to do?"

"For now, we stay here until it's safe to go back, so please, go get some sleep in your meditation room. You very much look like you could use the rest. I've asked too much of you these last few days."

"But what about Anacoana?"

"I'll take care of her." I stood and held my hand out to her. "I'll take care of everything, but right now I want you to take care of yourself."

She accepted my offered hand and I helped her to her feet. "You're right. I need some sleep. I'm useless if I'm exhausted."

I walked her across the garden to the meditation room she and Mazatzin shared, then I went to where Yaretzi stood by the store rooms. Her smug smirk made my magic roil.

"You didn't have to kill her," I hissed.

"Topiltzin would be dead if I hadn't."

"I was taking care of the situation—"

She laughed.

I squeezed my fists and set my jaw hard. "Have you something you wish to say to me?"

"You're like a dog that doesn't realize it's actually a jaguar and can't understand why it keeps eating its companions, Mayahuel, and frankly, it's amusing."

I stared at her, my mouth hanging open. "What...why did you call me that?"

Her grin stretched sharply up her cheeks, and when she spoke again, her voice had changed to a high-pitched, shrill sound, like a bat squeal. "I've been watching you for a long time, She of the Maguey."

I drew in a sharp breath. "Who are you?"

In answer, wings of obsidian blades sprang from her back, shredding her human flesh. As more of her bladed body tore loose of its fleshy prison, her skin and flesh dropped around her clawed feet. "You know me as Itzpapalotl, the Obsidian Butterfly," she hissed, her eyes glowing green like the rest of her newly-revealed aura.

I backed away, bewildered. "You...you possessed Yaretzi?"

"And limit myself and my magic? I wouldn't be so foolish."

"Then you've....you've always been here?"

"Among the tasty morsels? Of course. Smoking Mirror needed eyes inside the priestly orders, and I've served him well."

I looked back at the doorway to my meditation room. "But then why did you save Topiltzin? He's Quetzalcoatl's son."

"It's not his time yet."

The matter-of-fact way she said it raised the hairs on my neck. "What's that to mean?"

She smiled smoothly. "Just that it isn't his turn."

"His turn for the same terror and death Mextli's been wreaking over the people of Tollan?"

"And there's that puppy whine again. Why should anyone care about the humans?"

"The dispute is with Quetzalcoatl, not with the humans."

"When it comes to the Feathered Serpent, they are good bait."

"Really? Because I don't see him anywhere."

Itzpapalotl smiled but said nothing.

"Leave these people alone!" I insisted

She shook her head. "They must see what happens when they blindly follow charlatans like the Feathered Serpent, so they will know never to make that same mistake again. They must realize that they will be held accountable with their blood and very lives. We must imprint the penalty on their consciousness, so they will teach their children the sad tale of their misstep, and their children will teach the lesson to their children, generation after generation, so we never again have to come to such crossroads.

"And Topiltzin must be there to the bitter end, so his name will become the warning echoing through time: this is the consequence of defying the gods."

Her words made my magic sizzle in my limbs. "Enough already! Smoking Mirror has won; Quetzalcoatl fled the battlefield and continuing this is just cruel."

"It is, isn't it?" Itzpapalotl cooed. She disappeared with a crack.

CHAPTER TWENTY-NINE

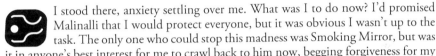 I stood there, anxiety settling over me. What was I to do now? I'd promised Malinalli that I would protect everyone, but it was obvious I wasn't up to the task. The only one who could stop this madness was Smoking Mirror, but was it in anyone's best interest for me to crawl back to him now, begging forgiveness for my foolishness?

We could lead everyone away from Tollan, I thought, but the desire rebelled.

We built this city; it's ours, and it's cowardly to just hand it over to Smoking Mirror's sycophants—

A strange music drifted in from above, soft at first but growing in intensity. I looked up, half expecting to see its source floating above me, but I saw only the sunset streaking orange and red across the sky. It sounded like a bone flute, sweet and trilling like a quetzal bird. If I weren't feeling so anxious, I might have sat down and listened to its haunting melody. I closed my eyes though as the tempo picked up, relishing the sudden distraction from my worries.

Hearing curtain bells tinkling, I turned to see Malinalli glide out of her meditation room, twirling and stepping in time to the music. The sight brought a lazy smile to my face.

But while her movement was fluid and graceful, the anxiety and fear was plain on her face.

My growing concern shattered my mysterious contentment, and I immediately moved to intercept her. But when I reached out to grab her, she twirled out of my reach, heading for the bridge leading out into the main priestly gardens. "Quetzalpetlatl! Help me! Please!"

I ran after her and this time grabbed onto her arm, but she yanked me around with her, not missing a beat. I almost lost my grip but instead matched her steps to keep my balance and stay with her. "Stop dancing!"

"I can't!" she cried. "No matter how hard I try, my legs just won't stop moving!"

I dug my heels into the ground, hoping to slow her momentum, but there was no stopping her. She wrenched free, flinging me backwards into one of the walls. I hit with such force that the white plaster crumbled off behind me.

"Help me!"

I looked back to see Mazatzin dancing out of my meditation room, his face looking as if he was barely awake in spite of his body moving with strength and precision. He too swung around in time with the strange music playing on the wind. "What dark magic is this?"

I looked back at Malinalli; she was nearing the retreat's entrance, with just the gate and the bridge standing between her and the gardens beyond. If I couldn't stop her with physical force, my only alternative was magical force. Perhaps a little burst of octli magic could incapacitate her.

But dear gods, what if I killed her in the process?

Just be extra careful in how much you shoot at her. Taking a deep breath, I fired a small burst of magic.

I hit her square in the back, and her head lolled down against her chest, but her body kept moving, completely unaffected. I thought to increase the dosage, to overpower the music magic, but my fear of accidentally killing her stayed my hand.

Bind her, the desire suggested. *There's ropes in the store room.*

I ran up behind her and jumped on her back. The moment I wrapped my arms around her, I leaped through the fires of the teoyoh into the store room. When we rematerialized, she danced us right into the wall, knocking us both over, but as she started struggling to her feet again, I grabbed a length of rope from a nearby shelf and wrapped it around her legs. They kicked, trying to stop me, but I bound them together so all she could do was fishtail back and forth. I also bound her wrists together behind her then stood back to check my handiwork.

She wiggled around on the floor, but couldn't go anywhere.

I rushed back into the garden to see Mazatzin heading out to the bridge, but I grabbed him from behind too. We landed in the store room in the same manner, but Mazatzin kept his balance and I had to trip him with the ropes to make him go over.

"What is going on?" he cried, terrified. "How did I get in here?"

I finished binding him then rolled him over to lie next to Malinalli. "I'm sorry about this, Mazatzin, but it's for your own safety."

His legs flailed around as he asked, "Am I hallucinating?"

I shook my head. "No, you're awake, and I will explain everything to you, I promise, but first I must make this music stop. If it's affecting you and Malinalli like this, it could be affecting everyone else the same way."

Mazatzin still looked panicked but he nodded. "Do what you must."

"I promise I will be back to free you as soon as it's safe. All right?"

"Yes. Please hurry," he panted, his body thrashing around.

□

I arrived in the sacred precinct to mayhem. Some people stood watching while other people danced frantically, screaming for help. City guards shouted for everyone to return to their homes and tried to stop some of the dancers, but just as with Malinalli and Mazatzin, the dancers tossed them around and aside as if they were nothing. I climbed up the steps of the temple of Quetzalcoatl to get a better look at the scene, and to my horror, I realized that it was only the white-robed priests of the Feathered Serpent's order who were affected by the enchanted music.

I rushed to a group of priests of Tlaloc who were watching the whole scene in befuddlement. "Go to the storerooms and bring as many ropes as you can carry," I shouted over the din. "The only way to stop them is to tie their legs together so they can't move anymore." When they stared at me, even more dumbfounded, I added, "Hurry up and do as your queen commands!" Only then did they run for the calmecac.

I went from group to group and gave them the same instructions, but soon I realized

652

that this was taking too much time; people were already dancing beyond the sacred precinct. I cut through the milling and dancing crowd, following those leaving the precinct and out into the city.

Eventually the line of dancers wove outside the city walls, out among the canals. I stared up the path between the fields, following the line of people dancing up into the hills where the turquoise and silver mines were.

"Mine!"

Before I could move, hairy arms with clawed hands snapped around me, and I went over backwards into a nearby canal. I thrashed, but a strong, coil-like appendage wrapped around my legs, binding me the same as I'd bound Mazatzin and Malinalli. The world grew dimmer as we sank deeper into the canal, the day's dying sunlight now only splashes of color at the water's surface.

Unable to break free by physical means, I jumped into the teoyoh, taking my captor with me.

I came back on dry land, but he still clung to me, hissing and howling in my ear. I jumped back into the teoyoh again then came out midair, so I knocked the breath from him when we hit the ground. He still didn't let go though, so I did it again, dropping from an even higher height. This time he unlatched his limbs from me when we hit the ground. I rolled away, dizzy.

But I fell back into the water again. I clung to the bank once I resurfaced and looked around, blinking the water away from my eyes.

Black Otter lay on the ground away from the water, thrashing around in pain. The hand on his tail clawed towards the canal, dragging the rest of him with it. I hurried back ashore as he slipped tail-first back into the water, cutting off his pained cries. I sprang into the teoyoh, intending to take myself up the path, safely out of his reach.

But a bolt of magic knocked me back out of the stream, dropping me back where I was. As Black Otter popped his head out of the water to snarl at me, I tried again, but with the same results, except this time I fell into the next canal, at the opposite side of the maize field.

"Mine!" Black Otter shrieked then disappeared from sight. I jumped into the teoyoh again but when I landed, I was all the way back at the beginning of the fields. What in Mictlan—?

Laugher filled the air, and a geyser of water rose up from the nearest canal. The goddess Jade Skirt sat upon it as if it were a throne. "Oh my, you *are* amusing to watch, Mayahuel!" She slapped her knee as she broke into even louder laughter.

"You're the one blocking me?"

"As if I would waste my precious time with such trivialities," she replied, her mirth now forgotten. "I'm not afraid of you!"

"I never said you were."

"Because I'm not." She bent forward and the water of her geyser shifted to form a shelf for her to lean upon. "Though I wish I could say the same about Mextli. Seems you gave him quite the scare."

The desire flared with pride.

"Besides, if we were to battle, I have my own army that serves my every whim," Jade Skirt went on.

Black Otter popped up in the water in front of her geyser, showing me his silvery fangs. "Mine!" he hissed.

I laughed in spite of myself. "He's you're army?"

She grinned caiman-like back at me. "No. This is my army."

As she stretched her arms out, more creatures just like Black Otter began popping up in the waters of the canals; hundreds of them, all with otter-like heads, and shrieking and hissing in a terrible cacophony. Some slunk up onto the bank, keeping the fingers of the hands on their tails dipped in the water while still others swam up and down the canals.

Jade Skirt lounged back on her throne of water. "I think they turned out quite well, don't you?"

"They're lovely," I replied, dryly.

She glared at me. "How very rude you are. I think you need a lesson in politeness." She flicked her fingers.

Suddenly the water in the canals started rising and the creatures' frenzy grew louder. I darted a quick glare at Jade Skirt but then ran as fast as I could, heading for the hills. The creatures shrieked and lunged from both sides, but the road was wide enough to keep them from reaching me.

But as the water seeped over the banks, running out onto the road, I lost that advantage. I wove back and forth between the dancing priests, dodging slashing claws and snapping fangs. Behind me cries rose then fell to gurgling, but I couldn't stop. I had to reach the end of the fields, where the ground was higher. Only when I reached the incline did I look back.

The fields of half-dead maize were flooded and the creatures dragged the dancers and farmers into the canals. They vanished under water to gushing bubbles, but then re-emerged not as humans anymore but rather as more of the beasts, all of them covered in slick fur and staring with ink-black eyes.

As I stood staring in horrified silence, the water crept closer and closer to the hills, bringing the creatures with it. They would reach me any moment, and swallow up all those people I'd ran past.

In that instant, I made a decision.

I rushed back towards the water, firing small bursts octli magic to knock back the creatures at the head of the advancing water. Already I was feeling my magic waning from overuse, so once the water ran over my sandaled feet, I knelt, submerging my hands, and I pushed a hefty dose of magic out of my fingers, hoping it would finally stop Jade Skirt and her army of monsters.

It took a few breaths, but soon the creatures began shrieking in pain and confusion rather than excitement. A milky cloud of white spread out from me, and the further it went, the faster it infiltrated the water, overrunning the canals and the fields. The creatures thrashed around in the water-turned-octli, gurgling and crying, and they began collapsing by the dozens, their bodies twitching in their death throes.

"You...you...you treacherous serpent!" Jade Skirt shrieked, standing atop her geyser. Black Otter stood at her feet, pressed against her legs like a frightened child. I felt her magic pushing back through the octli, trying to keep it from infiltrating her geyser.

Fearing she would overpower my magic, I fled up the path into the hills, cutting in between the dancing priests. Her curses and screams echoed up the canyon after me.

I didn't run more than a few moments before I found the source of the music.

Xochipilli sat on a tall outcrop of rocks and Mextli stood next to the edge of the road, overlooking the quarry below. When a priest danced within reach of him, Mextli grabbed them by the front of the robe and hurled them over the edge where they crashed to the rocks below. The pile of bodies at the bottom was already significant, and the line of remaining priests was alarmingly short.

To my horror, I spotted Mitotia and Amoxtli among the dancers heading to their deaths. I sprinted to the head of the line, and just as Mextli reached for Mitotia, I hit his hands with a burst of magic, making him snap them back to his chest with a muffled yelp. Next I unleased a strike against Xochipilli, who howled in surprise and dropped his flute, ending the enchanted dance. The line of dancers collapsed to the ground, panting and crying in exhaustion.

When Xochipilli made to retrieve his flute, I held my hands out and warned him, "Don't make me hit you again, son." I doubted I had enough magic left to disarm him again, but to my relief he stopped, staring at me in amazement.

"I wondered how long it would take you to get here." Mextli shook his hands as if they still stung.

When Mitotia looked up at me, I said, "Get the others, and lead them back down to the city."

She nodded then crawled to the others lying sprawled upon the ground.

"And what makes you think I'll let them leave?" Mextli asked.

I turned my hands on him, and he winced ever so slightly. "Let's end this. I wish to speak to Smoking Mirror."

"For what purpose?"

Hearing the priests hurry back down the path behind me, I waited until they were out of earshot before speaking. "He said when I was ready to accept an agreement that I should come see him, and well…I'm ready to talk."

"And what makes you think he'd be interested?"

After a hesitation, I said, "I could still be useful to him."

I expected laughter, but instead Mextli studied me with a hint of appreciation.

A sudden wave of water hit me from behind, and when I turned around, another hit me in the chest, nearly taking me off my feet. I stumbled backwards until I ran into something, and when I looked up I saw it was Mextli.

"Jade Skirt, enough already," Mextli snarled.

The river goddess stood in the middle of the path, a puddle of water spreading out under her feet. Black Otter stood with her, his handed-tail thrashing back and forth as he crouched to spring. "Hand her over, Mextli!" Jade Skirt roared. "She destroyed my servants!"

To my surprise—and utter unease—Mextli wrapped his feathered arm around me, clutching me to his chest. "No."

Jade Skirt narrowed her eyes at him, and as if that were a silent order, Black Otter lunged at us.

But Mextli grabbed him by the neck and dangled him out over the ravine. Black Otter choked and thrashed, slashing open wounds on Mextli's arm, but the war god maintained his grip.

Jade Skirt's eyes bulged. "How dare you—?" But when Mextli squeezed harder, making Black Otter gag and writhe, she shouted, "No! Please! He's the only one I have left!"

"Then you will listen when I speak," Mextli replied. "Otherwise I will dash his brains out on the rocks below."

She held her hands up. "Fine. She's yours. Just don't hurt him."

With a hint of amusement, Mextli said, "She's Smoking Mirror's, not mine."

"She's Smoking Mirror's and I promise not to touch her. Now please, give me back my servant!"

Mextli threw Black Otter back at Jade Skirt, knocking her over. "Off with you then. The treacherous thorn bush goddess and I have business to discuss."

She glowered at him, but then wrapped her arms around Black Otter's neck before disappearing into the teoyoh.

Mextli shoved me away. "I'm declaring a temporary truce while you negotiate with Smoking Mirror. I suggest you hurry." He then too disappeared with a snap.

Only Xochipilli and I remained, but when he reached for his flute again, I scrambled to my feet. He held his hands up in surrender though. "I won't play it. There's a truce, remember?"

I slowly lowered my own hands to my sides. "I had to be sure."

"I understand." He picked up his flute and pressed it lengthwise between his palms until it disappeared.

"I must admit...you were the last person I expected to find helping Smoking Mirror," I said, disappointment blooming in my chest.

"I don't have much choice in the matter. Xochiquetzal was adamant about joining the cause, and I couldn't really stop her, so here I am."

"Enchanting the Feathered Serpent's priests with your music," I finished.

"It's all I have to offer the cause. Frankly, I'm glad you showed up and finally stopped me. Killing isn't one of my preferred art forms." He jumped down from the rocks. "Did you mean it, when you called me your son?"

"Of course I did."

He smiled, boyishly charming. In some ways he reminded me of Ehecacone. And it made my heart sting.

"I know Xochiquetzal is really mad at you, but I...I'd rather let the past be the past, and move on into the future. Nothing good ever comes of dwelling on things we can't change."

"I hope we can move forward too," I said.

He started to say something more, but suddenly the cyclone of flowers started whipping around him. Within a moment, he was gone and Xochiquetzal stood in his place. "Don't count on it, Mayahuel," she spat, but she then too disappeared in a burst of flowers.

CHAPTER THIRTY

I stood outside the door curtain to the royal chemist's house for a long time, hesitating to jingle the bells. Going inside was admitting defeat, and I feared that even then it was too late. I imagined Smoking Mirror laughing when I told him I wanted peace; laughing so hard his frail human body couldn't stand it and he keeled over dead. But what choice did I have? I was practically powerless in the face of so many gods working against me, and Quetzalcoatl hadn't even the decency to stay and protect the people of Tollan.

I reached to tug on the curtain, but before I could touch it, Mextli yanked it open from the inside. "For someone who claims to have had enough of war, you sure take your time making it to your meetings," he rumbled.

"I couldn't go through the teoyoh like you did, since you didn't lift the magical barrier before you left," I replied, glaring at him. "And even then, I can't sense where Smoking Mirror is."

He smiled smoothly. "Of course not. In his current state, he's highly vulnerable to his enemies, so we took measures to protect him." He stepped aside, inviting me in with a silent gesture.

The house felt overcrowded even with just me and Mextli—who was hunched under the low ceiling—but Smoking Mirror wasn't there.

"Get any silly ideas and I will scatter your teotl to the corners of the universe," Mextli said.

Before I could ask what he meant, he put his stony grip on my shoulder and we disappeared.

The familiar sensation of rushing energy swallowed me, and Mextli's magic twined around and through me for half a breath before we landed, each of us returned to our physical forms. My heart thudded drunkenly, with a twinge of loss and yearning.

We stood in a cavern lit by a single bonfire in the middle. Itzpapalotl crouched next to it, the firelight reflecting off her angled obsidian body, and Xochiquetzal sat off by herself at the edge of the fire light. Jade Skirt was there as well, pacing the back wall as she glared at me.

Smoking Mirror sat with his back to us, but when Mextli went to him, he turned to look at me over his shoulder. Mextli whispered before moving off, letting Smoking Mirror ease himself to his feet with the aid of his knobby walking stick. I remained standing beyond the firelight, too nervous to approach, so he came to me, hobbling slowly.

He looked little better than Little Reed; octli-whiteness had engulfed one of his eyes, and several more of his teeth were missing now. "So, you've come to your senses," he said, his spirit as fiery as ever.

I didn't answer until he stopped a few paces from me, and even then, I kept my voice low. "You warned me, and I've seen the error of my thinking."

"I know how difficult it is for any god to admit their mistakes, so I commend your humility now. Please, come join me at the fire. You're most welcome among us here."

I looked over at the others—and judging from the frosty looks all around, I knew it was a lie—but I doubted any of them would dare countermand him, so I followed him.

Smoking Mirror returned to his spot in front of the fire and held his hands out to warm them. "This body...its blood doesn't circulate very well anymore; too much stress on the heart inside of it, I'd guess. Luckily I need only put up with these tiring inconveniences for a few more days at best." When he noticed me still standing, he patted the ground with his gnarled hand. "Sit down, so we may talk."

I obeyed but kept at an arm's length.

Once I sat down, Mextli did too, on Smoking Mirror's other side.

"I'm pleased that you've finally joined us," Smoking Mirror said.

"I don't know that I'm at that particular juncture just yet," I replied, not looking at him.

"What is it now that's still holding you back?"

"I don't like what the others are doing, specifically to the people of Tollan."

The other gods chuckled, except Xochiquetzal, who harrumphed and stared into the fire.

Smoking Mirror cleared his throat for silence. "I understand. You spent many years among these humans, living as one of them. It's difficult to completely sever those ties of brotherhood so quickly. But the events of the past day were absolutely necessary, for the future of the city."

"I understand your reasons, but please, enough is enough! You've made your point."

Mextli exhaled a laugh. "Those are big demands for someone who's on the losing side."

"Yes, you've won," I went on. "Anything more is completely pointless, and likely will work against your endgame anyway. If you continue killing off all of the humans in Tollan, who's going to be left to pass on the lesson?"

Smoking Mirror nodded. "There is certainly logic to your argument, Mayahuel, and I'm not a god to disregard good sense. But you're rushing ahead of yourself. I haven't in fact won yet; Quetzalcoatl is still out there, not answering for his treachery. So long as he is free to contaminate yet another human community with his mutinous reforms, the war is far from over. And—" He held up a shaky finger— "Your son—my nephew—will continue languishing down in Mictlan. That is why you're here, really. Am I right?"

I hadn't even had time to think about Ehecacone these last few days since everything started falling apart, but now that I thought of him trapped in Mictlan forever, waiting for a rescue that might never come.... "Then it's not too late? You'll still help me?"

"Of course I will, but in return, you must help me."

"What can I do?"

Pressing his fingers together as if praying, Smoking Mirror said, "I want Quetzalcoatl's teotl."

I furrowed my eyebrows. "What do you mean?"

"His magic, I want it, and you will deliver it to me. I will tell you where to find him, and you will take his magic from him, and then you will give it to me."

That didn't clear anything up. "And how exactly am I supposed to do that?"

Smoking Mirror grinned wide. "Mextli told me about your...special ability."

I turned to glare at Mextli. "I don't know what you're talking about."

"Come now, Mayahuel," Smoking Mirror said. "You should be thankful; if not for that, you and I would have nothing to discuss right now and I might in fact have decided to deal with you permanently. But instead you're useful to me."

"Let's not speak in puzzles," I said. "Just tell me exactly what you expect me to do."

"I expect you to seduce the Feathered Serpent into your bed where you will use your special ability to extract all of his teotl and then you will transfer it to me, through the same method."

The hairs on my neck bristled. "You want me to have sex with you?"

Xochiquetzal looked up from the fire, a panicked look on her face.

"Precisely," Smoking Mirror said, his own face eerily neutral.

Even the desire recoiled, and my magic pulsed most unpleasantly. "And for doing this, I get what?"

"Quetzalcoatl, of course. Once you've drained him of all of his magic, he's yours to do with as you please. I presume you'll take him to Mictlan to trade for your son's life, but that is entirely up to you."

"That's hardly good enough. You're asking me to do something I find physically repulsive, and expose myself to you and your magic at my most vulnerable. You haven't exactly been trustworthy in the past."

Smoking Mirror chuckled. "Indeed not. But you can rest easy; any deals we make will be sealed with a vow before Heaven, to protect both of our interests against treachery."

"I still need more than just Quetzalcoatl."

"Then tell me, Mayahuel, what unfulfilled desire can I offer you to make this deal acceptable to you?"

Little Reed, the desire purred, desperate, and my pulse jumped. Yes, if I could have anything, it would be him, with me forever, the husband at my side in Omeyocan. I couldn't turn him immortal myself, but Smoking Mirror had the power. I was suddenly too excited and hopeful to speak.

But surely Smoking Mirror won't agree to give his mortal enemy's son immortality and magic that he could someday use to avenge his father; magic he might use against me if he found out about my part in it.

He will understand our reasons, the desire said.

And if he doesn't?

He will.

"Well?" Smoking Mirror pressed.

The thought of letting Little Reed disappear into oblivion outweighed the thought of any potential risks. I drew in a deep breath, preparing for battle. "You will make Topiltzin immortal, the way you made Coatlicue a goddess."

Jade Skirt burst into hysterical laughter. "Omeyocan save us, you're such a fool—" But she snapped her mouth shut when Smoking Mirror cast a scolding glare at her.

After clearing his throat, Smoking Mirror returned his attention to me. "I must admit that such a thing doesn't sit well with me."

"No better than the idea of what you wish me to do with you does for me," I replied. "One compromise begets another."

"And if I say no?"

"Then we have nothing more to discuss. This point is not negotiable."

Smoking Mirror scrutinized the fire, deep in thought.

Across from him, Xochiquetzal looked devastated. *Perhaps this isn't such a good idea, especially if we want a relationship with her and Xochipilli in the future.*

But we're so close to everything we've ever wanted, the desire warned. *What do we owe her, really? It's not as if we knew about her, and she doesn't even want to be our daughter.*

That could change.

We're not throwing away our one opportunity for true happiness because she can't see what a lout Smoking Mirror is.

Smoking Mirror finally turned from the fire. "Fine. I accept your terms." He held his hand out to me.

But I eyed it warily. "Let's be absolutely clear about the details. When you turn Topiltzin immortal, he's not going to be the way he is right now. He will be clear-headed and healthy."

"Of course he will."

"Nor will you enslave him to me or you or anyone else. He will be his own god, bound to nobody."

Sighing, Smoking Mirror said, "Agreed."

"And you and your supporters will allow him to take his supporters and leave Tollan, unharrassed and unharmed."

Mextli frowned, but Smoking Mirror answered, "Very well. No harm shall come to any of your precious humans by my hand, or anyone else's here."

"Or your human allies," I insisted.

"Or my human allies," he agreed.

"And to show your good faith in this agreement, you will deliver Topiltzin's immortality immediately, before anything else."

Smoking Mirror narrowed his eyes at me. "Now you're just becoming demanding."

"Take it or leave it," the desire hissed.

"Very well. You get Topiltzin, then I will deliver Quetzalcoatl's location, upon which time you will then bed him, either willingly or through force, draining him of all of his teotl, then you will initiate the transfer of his teotl to me. Once that is complete, I will give you what's left of Quetzalcoatl and we will go our separate ways." He held his hand out to me again. "Now let us make the vow before Heaven, to solidify our deal."

Deep inside I felt as if I was missing something important, but the desire scoffed. *I've got all contingencies covered. Let's do this now, before Smoking Mirror changes his mind.*

I took Smoking Mirror's frail hand and clasped it. His skin was papery and cold.

"I promise to make Topiltzin immortal, to deliver Quetzalcoatl to Mayahuel, and to protect those humans loyal to Topiltzin from physical harm," he said, his voice raspy with exhaustion. His hand grew warm with magic though. When I didn't say anything, he said, "Now state your promise."

"I promise to deliver Quetzalcoatl's teotl to Smoking Mirror." My own hand grew hot too as my magic surged.

"Now state what the penalty will be for me if I break my end of the bargain," Smoking Mirror said.

"If Smoking Mirror fails to deliver on any of his promises, this deal will be broken and I don't have to deliver on any of my promises to him."

Smoking Mirror tightened his grip on my hand. "And if Mayahuel breaks her promise, she shall be forever bound in servitude to me, using her magic to serve my needs." He then dropped my hand as if it were a snake that might bite him if he held it any longer.

"That's not fair!" I said.

"Are you intending on not fulfilling your end of the bargain?"

"Of course not."

"Then stop your complaining. The vow is made, so let us get started." He motioned to Xochiquetzal. "Take your mother back to the house. I will join you once I've relieved my infernal bladder."

Xochiquetzal glared at me but rose to her feet. "Let's go already," she growled when I stood to join her. She grabbed my hand and before I could get in my next breath, we stood in the middle of the small chemist's house.

She tossed my hand away and stood facing the hearth, arms folded across her chest.

"Xochiquetzal, I'm sorry I must do this—"

"You didn't have to do it at all!" she fired back.

"Was I supposed to just let Ehecacone linger forever in Mictlan? Lord Death threatened to torture him if I don't bring Quetzalcoatl to trade for him. And while I know this isn't ideal, you must know that I'm not looking forward to doing this with Smoking Mirror. The entire notion makes me sick to my stomach."

"I don't care! You know how I feel about him!"

"Yes, I do, but he knows too, and yet he still insists on doing this. It just shows he doesn't care. You deserve better than that!"

She whirled on me. "What I deserve is a better mother!" She shouldered me aside and disappeared out the curtain, leaving the bells tinkling.

□

I walked back to the priestly retreat, so I could see the state of the city and the sacred precinct, but also because I didn't have enough magic left to use the teoyoh. Every human I looked at made the desire simmer and growl, but luckily most people seemed to be hiding in their houses, afraid to come out. Not even the guards were present at the palace gates, and by all appearances, the inside was dark and uninhabited. It reminded me of the Empty Days before the beginning of the new bundle of years, like the night

Little Reed was born in Xochicalco.

The sacred precinct looked much the same, though when I went by the calmecac, it looked as if it had been ransacked and the classrooms' contents strewn about the courtyard. Someone had locked the gates into the priestly gardens, forcing me to jump to the other side through the teoyoh, but at least the gardens themselves had been spared from the chaos. Still I hurried to the retreat at a run, and dashed across the bridge when I saw Black Otter lurking in the water of the canal. He didn't try to pursue me though.

Inside I found Mazatzin and Malinalli had already been freed by Mitotia and Amoxtli and they were all gathered around the basalt slab outside the kitchens, eating and looking bedraggled. Malinalli hurried over. "Thank Omeyocan you're all right!"

"I'm sorry I had to tie you up like that."

"If you hadn't, I might be dead. Mitotia and Amoxtli told us what happened at the quarry."

Seeing both of the men watching me, I approached the table. To Mazatzin, I said, "I promised that I would explain everything to you when I returned—"

"It's all right," he said. "Malinalli told us while you were gone."

I nodded, unsure what to say then. Eventually though I said, "Smoking Mirror has agreed to a ceasefire for now, so we need not fear further attacks tonight."

"And you trust his word?" Amoxtli asked, incredulous.

"In this case, yes. There are consequences if he breaks it."

"Does Citlallotoc know of this?" Mitotia asked.

After a hesitation, I said, "Citlallotoc is dead."

She gasped. "Oh my gods! This is all my fault!"

"Mextli killed him in the attack on the palace. You had nothing to do with it."

Tears welled in her eyes. "But I called him here, before you came back. I sent him a message in Acolman, asking him to come see Topiltzin. I was hoping he'd see what was going on with Matlacxochitl and he'd intervene for all of us."

"That still doesn't make you responsible. If you hadn't called him here, he would have received my summons. But in the end, it was Mextli that took his life, not you, and trying to take blame upon ourselves isn't useful right now."

She nodded, wiping the tears away. "My apologies."

"It's all right," I said with what I hoped was a comforting smile.

"So how dire is the situation right now?" Mazatzin asked.

"The entire Council is dead, as are a good number of Quetzalcoatl's priests. Most of the city's population appears to have gone into hiding. For all intents and purposes, Tollan has fallen to Smoking Mirror."

A shocked silence settled over the garden. Malinalli looked especially stunned.

"I need each of you to go out into the city and find all of the remaining priests of Quetzalcoatl and bring them back here, packed and ready to march. Tomorrow we're all leaving Tollan."

"Leaving?" Mitotia asked, astonished.

I nodded. "I won't make anyone go who wishes to stay, but I have every reason to believe that Smoking Mirror's followers will execute anyone who doesn't leave."

"I don't understand," Amoxtli stammered. "Where is the god? He aided Topiltzin in Culhuacan, so why not now?"

"I don't know," I said. "Perhaps he's abandoned us. I tried to protect the city in his absence, but…I failed you all, and I am sorry. It pains me to lose everything Topiltzin and I built here, but cities can be rebuilt while lives lost cannot be replaced."

I'd hoped my words might fortify their resolve, but both Amoxtli and Mazatzin still looked befuddled and distressed. Even Mitotia looked troubled.

"We should hurry," Malinalli suggested, putting on her leader voice. "Morning isn't all that far off now."

The others nodded but as they went out the main entrance, she hung back. "Are we taking Topiltzin with us?" The others nodded but as they went out the main entrance, she hung back. "We're taking Topiltzin with us, right?" When I nodded, she asked, "Do you need help putting the litter together?"

I shook my head. "I can do it on my own."

She nodded and turned to leave.

"I'm sorry I let you down, Malinalli," I called after her.

She paused, resting her hand on the archway leading out to the bridge.

"I thought...I thought too highly of my own abilities, and now Tollan is in ruins—" I choked back tears.

"You didn't let me down," she said, not looking at me. "You tried, which is more than Quetzalcoatl can claim. This is his city, but he hasn't even bothered to defend it."

"The people of Tollan deserve better gods than any of us," I whispered.

Malinalli looked back at me, tears in her eyes too. "That may be, but I'm still hopeful that my faith will pay off in the end," she said and walked out.

I stared at the archway a long time, mulling over her words before turning my gaze to the doorway to the meditation room where Little Reed was waiting for me to turn him immortal. "Yes, your faith will pay off in the end, Malinalli," I whispered. "Humanity will finally get the god they deserve."

CHAPTER THIRTY-ONE

I needed to replenish my magic before proceeding, but I didn't have time to find someone to appease the desire. It was already dark and sunrise would come all too soon, so instead I went to each of the meditation rooms and pilfered what blood I could find from the various idols. I must have been a monstrous sight, sucking dried blood from the maguey thorns and their rough ropes, and eating the dried grass balls. It was hardly filling, but it took the edge off my hunger and the magic simmered in my fingertips again. I'd take care of filling myself up once Little Reed was safe and immortal.

After that, I fetched a fresh jug of water from the river, watching Black Otter carefully. He glared at me as he swam back and forth, but he kept his distance, abiding by the ceasefire. Still, I filled it quickly then went to my meditation room where Little Reed was.

I paused to touch his neck, my heart dancing nervously while I checked to make sure he hadn't passed away while I'd been gone, but his pulse was strong as usual. I pulled over the tray with his gold-plated pitcher and cup.

He must drink every bit of the potion, Smoking Mirror had told me. *So mix it in a container that it won't stick to.*

I pulled the leather pouch of powder he'd given me from the pocket of my dress and poured it into the pitcher.

Next, add water and mix it well.

I poured the water slowly into the pitcher then stirred it with a lacquered xocolatl stirring stick, being sure to tap it clean afterwards.

Finally—and this is most important—change the water mixture to octli with your own magic. That way you can control how young the potion will make him. Picture him as you'd like to see him, and so it shall be.

I set my hand over the opening of the pitcher and let a slow dribble of magic ooze off my fingers. I then stirred it again, for good measure.

The potion to make Little Reed immortal was now ready.

I poured the first cup but hesitated. By feeding this to him, I was fully committing to the deal with Smoking Mirror, no backing out no matter what. *Are we absolutely sure this is the right thing to do?*

Little Reed will be twice the god his father ever was, the desire chided me. *We're doing humanity a favor by revealing Quetzalcoatl for the fraud he truly is. No longer will he lead them down the path to destruction for his own selfish purposes. Little Reed is the god humanity deserves. He's the god they* need *now more than ever.*

My mind set, I put the cup aside so I could sit him up. "Wake up, Little Reed. It's time for some drink."

He roused enough to take a swallow, but he cringed and tried to push the cup away. I held his hand down and gave him some more, against which he struggled vehemently. I was stronger than him though. It was slow going, but eventually he drank the entire cup of the potion. He grumbled while I refilled the cup.

"I know you don't like octli, but it will make you feel much better," I said as I put the next cup to his lips. He struggled again and tried to move his head away, but eventually he relented. Once he finished off the last of it, I laid him back down and he went to sleep.

I wonder how long it will take. Smoking Mirror hadn't said, but he wasn't coming to see me again until daybreak, so it should do its work by then. *It better,* the desire rumbled.

I gathered some rags and used the remainder of the water from the jar to make sure Little Reed was fresh and clean when he woke up, and I changed his clothing. I'd hoped I would start seeing signs of him changing by the time I finished, but he still looked exactly the same, and he breathed with the same rattle as normal.

Unsure what else to do, I settled against the wall between the bed and the hearth, and waited. No one was ringing the hourly bells tonight, so I had no idea what time it was, but the sky beyond the half-open curtain was the deep bluish-purple of night. Malinalli came by after a few hours, to update me on their progress fulfilling my orders, then she retired to her meditation room to get some sleep. I spent the rest of the night watching the stars crawl maddeningly slow across the heavens.

The first sign that something was different came when the rasp in Little Reed's breath faded away to the sound of healthy, steady breathing. I watched him closely then, my magic dancing joyfully under my skin.

As still more time passed, the age spots on his hands and face faded away and the wrinkled skin around his eyes smoothed out. His silver hair steadily reverted to brown, his whiskers retreated back into his chin, and his withered muscles grew in volume. Seeing him returning to health overwhelmed me, but I couldn't look away. I didn't want to miss a single moment of his transformation.

By the time roundness replaced the skeletal thinness of his face, the first signs of the approaching dawn had turned the sky gray. I hadn't seen Little Reed in those years between his leaving for the army and when treachery had forced him to come back to

Xochicalco, but I'd always imagined that he had looked this vital and strong.

And when he finally opened his eyes and I saw they were clear and focused again, I had to hold back a sob. There was only one question left now: was his love for me true, or had it all been a painful illusion?

Little Reed looked around, confused, but when his gaze met mine, a heartbreaking expression of disbelief crossed his face. "Papalotl?" he whispered, his voice shaking.

I couldn't hold the tears back any longer. "Yes, Little Reed. It's me," I choked, holding my arms open in welcome.

Without hesitation, he sat up and accepted my embrace, almost crushing me. He buried his face in my neck. "Dear gods, I thought I'd lost you forever," he whispered, tears muddling his voice.

I returned his hug with just as much ferocity. It hadn't been a lie at all; he really did love me. I wept as a wave of relief and regret and guilt washed over me. How could I ever have doubted his true feelings for me?

He pulled back to touch my face. Anguish plagued his dark eyes. "I'm so sorry, Papalotl—"

"No, it's me who owes you an apology, leaving like I did, without talking to you. I promise I'll never do that again, ever."

"Then you forgive me?"

"There is nothing you need to beg my forgiveness for; not even for demanding Citlallotoc to stay away from me. It was for his own good anyway." I stroked his cheek. "Besides, I couldn't have married him, not given how much I've always loved you."

He squeezed his eyes shut. "You truly still love me?"

"Forever and always, Little Reed."

He pulled me into a passionate kiss that sent the desire soaring so high that I felt intoxicated. It had been a long time since it had affected me so; not since I was a young woman and gave little thought to the truth behind my own intense reactions. And just like back then, I let it flow over me.

He trailed his lips over my chin, down to my neck, his hands on my back urging me closer still, so I climbed onto his lap. When his lips neared the collar of my dress, I made it melt away, making way for his achingly wonderful progression down my body. I remolded my clothing to give way as he slid his hands under my dress and kneaded my divine flesh with his strong fingers. Under his night xicolli, his already firm tepolli pressed against my thigh.

I understood now why the desire never took over when I was with Little Reed: we were always of the same mind when it came to him. And we both decided we'd held back long enough.

"Make love to me, Little Reed," I panted, desperate.

"Now?"

"Yes. Now. Please." I pulled his night xicolli up, to keep it from blocking him from me, and as soon as he'd properly positioned himself, I joined us together with a plaintive gasp.

My whole body tensed, but my magic was so primed and ready for what promised to come next that the pleasure built of its own accord, rushing to it without either of us moving. I tried to resist but it was beyond my control.

Warnings of what happened with Mextli flooded my mind. Omeyocan save me, what had I been thinking? I hadn't even told Little Reed what he was now, and I knew nothing about controlling my power; I could kill him without any effort. "Little Reed!" I gasped in panic as the pleasure roared up on me, unstoppable.

But he only held me tighter. "It will be all right, Papalotl," he whispered. "Just don't resist." He thrust hard into me, his own body shuddering in time with mine, but then the world melted away into blinding light.

I saw my own orange teotl first, but there was no other glow to give any indication of where Little Reed was. Had Smoking Mirror lied to me and hadn't turned him immortal at all? I should have known better than to trust anything he promised.

But then I noticed a shifting of shadows, forming what I realized was the barely visible outline of tendrils. They slithered among mine, my teotl rabbits watching them with cautious curiosity. It was only when the tendrils crossed paths with my own that I could see they were the purest white I'd ever seen, and shaped like serpents. *Like his father,* I thought.

Until I saw they each had a familiar ring of wispy feathers around their necks. Like Quetzalcoatl had.

It can't be! Quetzalcoatl's teotl had been purplish, and the serpents had dark, almost black eyes. The eyes on these were only discernible when they passed over one of my rabbits, when my orange teotl shown clearly through them, as if they were empty. *Little Reed is the son of the god, not Quetzalcoatl himself—*

But when one of my curious rabbits jumped up and clasped one of the feathered serpents between its paws, a flash of memory unfurled around me; of me—not human me, but the earth monster I once was—lying on my back on a grassy bank, gazing longingly up at me, as if I were watching myself through someone else's eyes. My coils—no, not mine—slid and caressed my scaly body, making me laugh with a toothy smile that filled the headspace around me with a desperate heart-like thudding.

Every god gives at least one gift to the world, I whispered, my pulse humming in my belly. *Isn't it time you shared yours?*

Earth monster me gazed back at me in earnest. *But how do I do that?* In my own head, my voice back then had been harsh and snarly, but through ears not my own, the sound was sweet like honey.

Close your eyes and I will show you.

Omeyocan save me, Little Reed is Quetzalcoatl!

And he'd captured me again, wrapped me up in his divine coils and would crush me, just like last time. I'd been so worried about harming Little Reed, but here I was, the fish trapped in that very same net. I was such a fool, *again*! And would I end up on the banks of the Black Lake in Mictlan all over *again*? My panic soared.

But instead of attacking my rabbits, the feathered serpents retreated. The throb of magic all around me waned and the material world slowly leaked back in its place. I was once again on Little Reed's lap—*no, Quetzalcoatl's!*—his body still inside mine, but neither of us moved.

I stared at him, rage and devastation sparring in my gut while I struggled to find the right words.

Quetzalcoatl saved me the trouble though. "Papalotl—"

I shoved him away, finally separating us and I retreated beyond the second bed where Mazatzin had slept. The rage choked me before I blurted, "Don't you dare call me that! You have no right! How dare you?"

"But I thought you knew." He started moving towards me but he froze when I raised my hands as if to throw magic at him. "When you said I didn't need your forgiveness, I thought—"

"You thought I could ever forgive you? When all you've ever done is lie to me?"

"Please, Mayahuel, let me explain. It isn't what you think."

I shook my head, tears flowing down my cheeks as the devastation finally won out. "It was bad enough that you refused to tell me who I was, and that you fed me to my grandmother, but to then hide yourself from me like this...to make me believe you were someone else—someone I loved so much it hurt.... How could you do that to me?"

"It wasn't my intention to hide from you, you must believe me. I tried to tell you, in a letter, but Ihuitimal intercepted it and you never—"

"That was one time—one! What about the other twenty-odd years we lived together?"

"I should have. I'm sorry." He hung his head.

I seized the opportunity to leave. I didn't want to talk about any of this. I slashed aside the curtain and stumbled into the garden.

Luckily I was alone, for I'd forgotten my nakedness. I reformed my dress with an errant thought, unsure of even where I was going now.

I wasn't alone for long though. Quetzalcoatl hurried out after me. "If I had it all to do over again, I would have had my nahual tell you that I had incarnated into this world as Chimalma's only son. My vision was always the two of us leading humanity into a new future, side by side not as humans but as the gods we really are."

I was striding toward the entrance, but at his words I whirled on him. "And this was somehow going to be accomplished by keeping me ignorant of my own divine nature?"

He stopped a few paces from me, a contrite look on his face. "I wasn't allowed to tell you the truth about yourself. You had to figure it out on your own."

"What is that even supposed to mean?"

"When I made the deal with Lord Death to resurrect you, part of the bargain was that I couldn't tell you who you really were."

"Why?"

"Because he despises me; he's never forgiven me for winning the bones of humanity from him. And since there was a good chance that you would never figure out you were a goddess and you'd die a mortal death...what better revenge than making me suffer losing you forever?"

An unexpected twinge of guilt rose inside me. "And what would happen if you told me?"

"You would return to the Black Lake and I would be enslaved to Lord Death for eternity. Though I don't understand...how did Smoking Mirror tell you when the deal prohibited anyone from telling you, lest you return to the Black Lake as if the deal never took place?"

"He didn't actually tell me," I admitted. "I figured it out on my own; he just confirmed it."

"That does explain why you're still alive."

I folded my arms. "So you weren't withholding that information out of malice. But why didn't you just tell me who *you* really were all along?"

He hesitated, looking uncomfortable, but then said, "Because I thought if you knew from the start that I was a god that we couldn't have the close relationship I wanted. I thought it would add a barrier between us that you might not be able to overcome."

"But we were lovers, in the Divine Dream—"

"The Divine Dream isn't reality for humans, and by the time that happened, you'd thought of me as your brother for ten full years. After that...the fear of losing what we already had...it all just accumulated and grew, especially when you told me why you stopped coming to see me in the Divine Dream."

I swallowed a wad of guilt building in my throat. "I can see how that would present difficulties."

He nodded. "But in the end...I was just cowardly. I should have told you and accepted the beans as they fell, and for that I am sorry, Mayahuel. The last thing I wanted to do was hurt you all over again."

The *all over again* part re-hardened my heart. "And now we come to the matter of Tamoachan, and my *gift to humanity*."

Quetzalcoatl bowed his head. "Indeed."

"You let Tzitzimitl kill me!"

"I did," he admitted.

His words struck an arrow through my heart. "But...how could you? After everything we shared...?""

"The why is hardly relevant," Smoking Mirror suddenly spoke up behind me.

I turned to see Mextli leading his decrepit form by the arm across the bridge from the gardens. Itzpapalotl, Jade Skirt, and Xochiquetzal followed behind, the first two looking rather smug while the latter looked distressed.

"Brother?" Quetzalcoatl walked closer, but then he stopped short. "What is going on?"

Smoking Mirror smiled wide. "Your coup is over, and you've lost. Tollan has fallen and the humans have turned against you; even as we speak, packs of people are roaming the streets in search of captives, and soon the blood will run freely down the temple steps. Things are finally back to how they should be."

Quetzalcoatl turned his incredulous gaze to me. "Is this true?"

"I couldn't stop them," I said. "I tried, and it cost a lot of people their lives." After a tense pause, I added, "Including Anacoana and Citlallotoc."

The distress on his face deepened. "No!"

"Yes, many, many lives, all because you wouldn't come out and face me, brother," Smoking Mirror wheezed. He and Mextli finally stopped a dozen paces from us. "When the game became contentious, you ran away like a coward."

"I didn't run anywhere," Quetzalcoatl replied. "My mortal body broke down, temporarily trapping me between worlds, but I was always here."

Smoking Mirror grinned. "Here, yes, but completely useless when it really counted." He turned his cold gaze upon me. "I confess surprise that you haven't yet upheld your end of our bargain, Mayahuel."

"Bargain?" Quetzalcoatl asked me, confused.

The panic welling up inside of me rendered me mute.

"She's going to use her special magic—you know the one I'm talking about—to drain you of all of your teotl and give it to me," Smoking Mirror answered for me.

Quetzalcoatl stared at me, incredulous and wounded. "Is this true?"

"I...I didn't—" I choked on tears.

"Why?"

"Because you killed her in Tamoachan, of course," Smoking Mirror said. "You told her that her death was her gift to humanity!"

Quetzalcoatl took a step closer to Smoking Mirror, but Mextli moved to stand between them. "Funny how you leave out your part in it, *Brother*," Quetzalcoatl said.

I switched my gaze back and forth between them. "What does that mean?"

"Since we're all revealing truths today, I believe it's your turn." Quetzalcoatl motioned to Smoking Mirror.

Smoking Mirror's smile broadened. "The truth hardly matters at this point. The deal has been struck."

"Tell her **how** you know about her special power."

"Mextli told him," I said. The shocked expression on Quetzalcoatl's face brought heat to my cheeks.

"Yes, he indeed shared with me what you two did—and for now on I think he will heed my warnings when I tell him not to do something, won't you?" He cast a spear-like glare at Mextli, who bowed his head, looking embarrassed.

"He knew about your ability long before that," Quetzalcoatl said.

"How?"

"Because you've been with him before."

I snapped a glare at him, taken aback. How dare he accuse me of something so...distasteful? "I have not! The very thought...."

Though we'll have to do it soon enough, the desire reminded me. Even she shuddered.

Quetzalcoatl nodded. "You have, when he and I were still Ehecatl."

"That doesn't make sense. Ehecatl is just one of your many names."

"No, it was my very first name; before there was the Feathered Serpent and the Smoking Mirror, there was one god who was both the darkness and the light, and he was called the Wind.

"But he lived in constant internal conflict; he went to the underworld to steal humanity's bones because he wanted to be important and worshipped by all humanity, but he ended up learning what it meant to be human." He reached out and gently took my hand in his. "And he brought you from Heaven to bring Love to the people, who were living in constant fear and violence. But you also brought Love to his heart, and you changed him forever."

The look of adoration in his eyes overwhelmed me. It was the same look that had confused my heart about the god and Little Reed, and now the reason why seemed so glaringly obvious that I felt a fool for not having realized the truth before.

"Yes, and it was all just sickening," Smoking Mirror spat. "Ehecatl could have been the most powerful of all the gods—he wanted it so very badly—but then came Love; his one big mistake. Every time the darkness moved to fulfill his destiny, the light—with its infernal sense of conscience and fairness—ruined everything, and Love was making it even worse. There was only one possible course of action." He focused his hard, hate-filled gaze squarely on me. "You had to die and be made to serve the darkness—to serve me."

I stared back at him, a feeling of clarity flowing over me. "I remember you now," I whispered. "When my grandmother came, Ehecatl...he changed. He turned cold and disappeared, and I was all alone...." Rage bubbled up inside me. "It was *you* who buried my bones so the maguey would grow, and the humans could brew octli. *You're* the one who said my real gift was my death!"

Smoking Mirror smiled smugly.

I looked at Quetzalcoatl again, my rage dwindling away. "It wasn't you at all."

Tears shone in his eyes. "I'm just as culpable. I didn't stop him."

"Why not?"

"Because I was weaker than him; so much weaker that he nearly consumed me entirely. I'm only here now because of an act of faith by my first priestess. Her sacrifice severed Ehecatl into his two halves, and I became Quetzalcoatl—"

"And he became the Smoking Mirror," I finished.

The hatred flamed in Smoking Mirror's eyes. "That priestess cost me everything; she gave the Feathered Serpent all of Ehecatl's strongest magic and left me with practically nothing. I spend hundreds of bundles of years starving on the fringes of human civilization, gathering my own followers when and where I could while he sat here in the midst of so much adoration, so many offerings. It should have been me!

"But I've reaped my revenge, Brother. All of that magic is coming back to me, delivered with delicious irony by the very goddess who started this whole sorry ordeal with us." To me, he smiled wide. "Time to deliver, my dear."

"And if she doesn't?" Quetzalcoatl asked, challengingly.

"Then she becomes enslaved to me for the rest of her existence, and I use her to take what I want from you anyway."

When I saw Mextli glaring hatefully at me, a new angle came to me. "It's not going to work, Smoking Mirror. The magic I take from others, it fades away, so even if you get your paws on Quetzalcoatl's teotl, it won't last."

Smoking Mirror laughed. "Perhaps if you were trying to give me any other god's magic, but Quetzalcoatl's teotl is the same as my own, so it will just be coming home in a new body." He stepped closer to me. "Time to make your decision, Mayahuel."

Chapter Thirty-Two

I stepped away from Quetzalcoatl, overwhelmed and panicking. "Omeyocan save me, what have I done?"

"Assured victory for me no matter what you do," Smoking Mirror replied, delight painting his wrinkled face.

Quetzalcoatl took me by the shoulders. "You can't listen to him, Mayahuel. He lies."

I shook my head. "No, he's right. No matter what I do, I can't stop him from hurting you!"

"There's always an out on these deals—"

"There is," Smoking Mirror admitted. "But it will do her no good because I've upheld my end; all of her precious humans remain unharmed, and I gave you to her, just as she wanted."

I whirled on him. "This is hardly how I wanted anything!"

"And it's my fault that you were too dense to realize that Topiltzin was already immortal?"

"So the potion was all just for show then?"

Chuckling, Smoking Mirror said, "Actually, that's my favorite part. It was indeed a magic elixir, one that when activated with your magic will bind whatever god consumes it into human flesh."

My heart skipped a beat. "You turned him human?"

"Of course not. That would break our bargain; after all, I promised you immortality, and he's indeed still immortal. Mextli, give Mayahuel a demonstration."

Mextli summoned a knife to his feathered hand and advanced on Quetzalcoatl.

I flung myself in front of him. "What are you doing?" When he didn't slow, I threw a burst of magic at him.

But he slashed the knife at it, bouncing it back at me. It hit me in the chest, knocking me over backwards, dazed. I looked up just in time to see him plunge the blade into Quetzalcoatl's neck. "No!"

Quetzalcoatl clutched at Mextli's hand on the blade jutting out of his neck, but when Mextli yanked it out, sending a geyser of blood spraying across his feathered xicolli, Quetzalcoatl collapsed into a heap. I sobbed as I crawled to him. He twitched, his eyes wide and staring, but when I set my hand on him, he fell still, his final breath escaping him with a rattle. I stared at him, my breath stuck in my throat.

But suddenly he gasped as if emerging from a very deep lake. He stared around in terror, but he clutched onto me with both hands when he saw me. He was still covered in blood, but when I checked for his wound, it was gone.

Smoking Mirror grinned. "See? He's still immortal. But he feels everything the same way he always did as a human being, but he'll never die from any of it. I'm sure Lord Death will find this an added bonus when you trade him for your son."

I stared down at Quetzalcoatl, my insides curling. "I can't do this to you!" I whispered.

"Are you refusing to uphold your end of our bargain, Mayahuel?" When Smoking Mirror spoke, a tightness formed around my throat, as if someone was placing a slave collar on it.

I started reaching for my throat, but Quetzalcoatl grabbed my hand, holding it tight. "Just do it," he whispered, his voice raspy.

"What?"

"It's going to happen either way, but don't enslave yourself to him for me. If you're still free, at least there will be someone who can oppose him."

"But I'm so weak, and when he has your teotl too—"

He squeezed my hand. "You're stronger than you know, Papalotl. Have faith."

A sob escaped me.

"Time to make your decision, Mayahuel," Smoking Mirror said, impatient.

I turned to glare at him.

And found Malinalli standing behind his hunched form. All of the shouting must have woken her. I drew in a startled breath when she raised her sacrificial blade aloft.

She brought it down in what seemed like slow motion, burying it between Smoking Mirror's shoulder blades, then yanked it out and stuck him again, this time from the side, under the ribs. She gritted her teeth as she twisted the weapon.

Smoking Mirror's gasping cry brought the other gods whirling around. Xochiquetzal shrieked as if she were the one being stabbed, and Mextli knocked Malinalli aside as he moved to shield his master from further attacks. Smoking Mirror crumbled to his knees, cringing in pain as he pawed at the knife handle with his gnarled hands. "Who in Mictlan dares?" he choked, blood dribbling from his frail lips.

Itzpapalotl bared her wings of obsidian blades with a loud clacking. "Treacherous human!"

"Stop!" Mextli boomed.

But too late. Itzpapalotl drove the end of her wing through Malinalli's back, impaling her all the way through.

Malinalli gagged, but when Itzpapalotl withdrew her blades, she stumbled away to lean against the copal tree, clutching her bleeding chest.

"Dear gods no!" I rushed to her, arriving just in time to catch her as she fell over backwards. "No! No! No!" I heard other hysterical screaming, but I focused on lowering her gently to the ground and resting her head in my lap. *Omeyocan please, don't let it be as bad as I fear it is!*

"You idiots!" Smoking Mirror roared between wet coughs. "I had everything...exactly as I...wanted it!"

I smoothed the damp hair from Malinalli's forehead. "Why on earth did you do that?" I cried.

She gazed up at me with pained eyes, her chest heaving with each difficult breath.

"Now he has nothing to force your hand with."

Indeed, the tight feeling around my neck had gone away completely. The deal was broken. "Oh Malinalli!" The tears came thick.

In the midst of the growing commotion in the garden, Mitotia collapsed to her knees next to Malinalli and clutched her hand to her chest. "Just stay still. If we can get a doctor here quickly—"

But Malinalli shook her head. "It's too late for that, my love." She reached up to caress Mitotia's tattooed cheek, tracing the feathered serpent there with her fingertips.

"Don't say that!" Mitotia said, tears winding down her cheeks.

"I'm not afraid," Malinalli assured her. But when she looked up at me again, her eyes widened. "Oh my! Have you any idea how...glorious you are to behold?" When Quetzalcoatl crouched next to me and looked down at her too, she whispered, "My Lord!"

He touched her hand. "Faith will see you on from here, my friend."

"I know it will," she said with conviction. "It's always led me."

I couldn't hold in the sobs anymore. "Why did you do this?"

She wrapped her hand around mine where it clutched her shoulder. "Because you're the goddess the people need right now. You just need a little help to prove it to yourself."

"Get your hands off of me!" Smoking Mirror shouted, and Xochiquetzal shrank away from him. "You're all idiots!"

"Death is my gift, to all of you." Malinalli shifted her anxious gaze to each of us in turn, but when she came back to me, she whispered, "You can do this, Quetzalpetlatl. I have faith in you. Take my gift, and find that faith within yourself." Her chest then fell still.

Feeling empty and numb, I looked up to see Smoking Mirror watching me, a sneer on his face. "Mextli," he said. "I'm done with this body."

Without a word, Mextli drew his macuahuitl sword from the air and took Smoking Mirror's head off with a single hack. He and the others then hurried away, taking shelter under the archway entrance of the priestly retreat.

The sight made my magic jitter, but it turned into hysterical pulses when smoke began swirling out of Smoking Mirror's headless body.

Quetzalcoatl rested his hand on my shoulder and gave it a gentle squeeze. "Remember faith. Trust in it."

The ground started rumbling under me, and the billowing smoke formed a gigantic black cloud, obscuring the body. It twisted and roiled into the form of a giant wildcat, and when it opened its eyes, they burned like hot embers. It opened its flame-filled mouth with a scream that rattled the stone bricks of the building, sending cracks snaking across the plaster walls.

I stared up at the smoke-jaguar with wide eyes, my mind racing. What should I do now?

Suddenly my magic surged; the world bent around me and I could see the teotl flowing through everything and everyone. My own whipped around me, just like in those moments with Mextli and Quetzalcoatl, the tendrils reaching out, orange spectral rabbits bursting forth to dash around the garden. They bounded among the other gods, Mextli with his turquoise hummingbirds, Itzpapalotl's green bats, Jade Skirt's blue fish, and Xochiquetzal's yellow quetzals. Smoking Mirror's were jaguars, dark purple, almost black, and they swatted their paws and hissed at my rabbits when they came close.

Does this work the same way as before? Deciding to find out, I targeted Itzpapalotl first. For Malinalli.

My rabbits changed direction and ambushed the goddess's gliding bats, pouncing on them or snatching them out of midair with their long teeth. She screamed. Her magic pulsed up my tendrils, but it wasn't very powerful; she had even less magic than I did. All I could do was change my hands into obsidian swords; perhaps useful in a physical altercation with an army, but hardly so in a battle of magic. I let her go and she disappeared with a snap of green light, taking her petrified cries with her.

Jade Skirt wasn't much better. Her little fishes tried fighting back by flipping their tails at my rabbits' faces, but they were quickly subdued. She tried throwing water at me to break the connection, but I blocked it with hardly a thought. I made the water in the canal beyond the retreat's walls rise up, but flooding the garden would only endanger Mitotia. I let Jade Skirt go too, and just like Itzpapalotl, she fled.

My rabbits moved towards Xochiquetzal's birds, but I called them off with a silent command. She was my daughter, and I still hoped that someday that we might be able to put the past behind us and have a relationship. "Leave, Xochiquetzal," I said. "This situation isn't about you."

She looked from me to Smoking Mirror, seemingly unsure, but then she said, "I'm sorry, Smoking Mirror," and she too vanished.

"You're completely useless anyway!" Smoking Mirror roared, churning up more smoke as he pawed the ground. He kept his distance though.

Mextli still remained, watching me warily.

"You should leave too," I said. "Despite everything that's happened, I haven't forgotten the kindness you showed me."

I'd hoped to see the compassionate side in his eyes again, the side that I could have fallen in love with under the right circumstances, but the darkness refused to yield. "I don't flee from battles, and I won't abandon my brother. I pledged my very existence to him."

"Just know that I won't hesitate to drain you of every bit of your teotl if necessary," I said. "Don't make the mistake of forcing my hand."

He sneered but remained where he was, his hummingbirds hovering close to him.

I turned to Smoking Mirror finally. "You can still leave—"

"I will see you in Mictlan before I will leave!" His teotl jaguars attacked my rabbits, and his smoke rushed at me, its fangs bared.

We collided with a crash that blasted the plaster from the walls around us, and we both lost physical form. I pulled in as much magic as I could, intending to throw it back at him, but as soon as it flowed into me, it flowed back out. The more I tried and failed, the more my rage grew, and soon we were caught in a whirlpool of flowing magic, his jaguars tangling with my rabbits while my rabbits bit and scratched madly.

I know all of your tricks, Mayahuel, Smoking Mirror hissed. *You can't win this battle!*

And neither can you! I tried to pull still more of his magic, determined to kill him with a sneak attack, but the flow's intensity only increased. We were deadlocked, and the only way out was death, for both of us. *Good! I'd rather be dead than let him win!* I thought with a suffocating ferocity.

Death is my gift, to all of you, Malinalli's voice echoed in my head, and for a moment it calmed the uncontrolled rage. *Surely this isn't what she made this sacrifice for,* I thought. Nothing I tried did any good; he was more than equal to my most powerful magic—

Rage and hate isn't my most powerful magic, I thought. All of my mistakes of the past, all of my missteps, they came back to me now, from Red Flint, to Black Otter, even Quetzalcoatl. All of it had been born of anger and the need for revenge. *I am a goddess of love, not hate.*

And yet all this time, I'd been fighting hatred and anger with more of the same, dragging Smoking Mirror's dark, sinister magic through me, whipping my own negativity and loathing to new heights. And it only seemed to make him stronger.

Let's give him a dose of what he came here to destroy.

The desire hesitated, but only for a breath before I let my own love magic leak into the flow, and I stopped fighting back.

Smoking Mirror shrieked loud, his voice a mixture of jaguar yell and human scream. *Oh no you don't!* He tried pushing more of his dark magic back at me, but it just opened the flood gate on my own. Smoking Mirror hissed and gurgled, waves of hatred and fear coursing through us, but I countered it with memories of everyone I'd ever loved: my father, my mother, my aunt Eloxochitl, my uncle Nochuatl, Nimilitzli. Black Otter, Jade Flower, Citlallotoc, Mazatzin, Amoxtli. Even Mextli. But most especially Malinalli, and Little Reed, and Ehecacone, who'd all given me so much and made me who I was. Who proved the transformative nature of my greatest gift.

Maybe I can change Smoking Mirror too.

My rabbits had disappeared, but his teotl jaguars now glowed with a hint of orange, and they pawed at themselves as if something had captured them by their heads. Smoking Mirror howled. *Never!* His teotl writhed as if in pain, but he made no attempt to withdraw. *You won't defeat me! You aren't powerful enough!*

I don't want to defeat you, I said. *I just want you to see that there's more to life than hate.*

I am the Darkness! Smoking Mirror screamed. *You cannot change me!* His teotl grew to new, reality-bending levels, bent on destroying us both.

Have it your way. I released one last blast of love magic into the flow then immediately severed the connection between us. I vaguely heard him roar as my teotl reformed my physical body, but then a blast of wind knocked me over backwards. Loud crashing and chaos filled the air, but then everything fell still and silent. When I looked up, gold dust fell from the sky like snowflakes.

The garden had been wiped out, the trees uprooted and the bushes bared of leaves. The buildings had been leveled to the ground too. Mextli stood where the entrance had once been, looking stunned.

Beyond him, out in the priestly gardens, Mazatzin and Amoxtli stood at the head of a large group of priests and priestesses and their families. They too stared at the rubble agape.

Mextli reached out so the glittery dust gathered on his feathered hand. He rubbed a pinch of it between his fingers before putting it to his tongue. He gagged then shook the dust from his hands, a bewildered look on his face. "Smoking Mirror?" he whispered. He looked up at me, his eyes wide. "You killed him?" He backed away a couple steps, as if I might come after him next, but then just like the other gods, he disappeared with a snap.

CHAPTER THIRTY-THREE

With Mazatzin's help, I found Quetzalcoatl and Mitotia under the remains of the copal tree. They'd been saved by virtue of one of the walls not fully crumbling when the tree hit it, though Quetzalcoatl had been impaled through the shoulder by a branch while he'd shielded Mitotia when the tree came over.

The branch had to be cut from the tree and it took both Mazatzin and Amoxtli to pull the branch out of his chest. They stared in amazement—and fear—when they witnessed the sucking chest wound heal by magic.

"I think it's time we told everyone the truth, about both of us," I told Quetzalcoatl once we were alone while the rest of the priests were combing through the wreckage for whatever they could scavenge.

He nodded. "I will address the crowd in a few minutes." He gritted his teeth in pain as he raised his arms to let me slip a new xicolli one of the priests had given him on over his head.

I cringed. "Not fully healed yet?"

"I'm all right," he assured me.

When an uneasy silence fell between us, I whispered, "I'm so sorry. You have every right to hate me—"

"I don't hate you. I understand why you did what you did."

"But you're trapped in that body thanks to me."

Smiling, he said, "So it'll just be like the last thirty years, except I won't grow old anymore. I definitely won't miss the aching bones."

I tried to smile but it came out as a frown.

He set a hand on my shoulder. "Everything is going to be all right."

Nothing will ever be all right again, I almost said, but it was too painful to admit aloud. I'd done all of this to get my son back, but I didn't even have that as a consolation in this disaster. How would I ever get him back now? "You're far too easy on me."

"You're tough enough on yourself for both of us."

Mazatzin and Amoxtli gathered everyone in the field beyond the river, where long ago I used to take Ehecacone to play and where I'd practice my magic with Malinalli; bittersweet memories of everything this war with Smoking Mirror had cost not just me, but everyone.

The chatter of conversation was already muted, but when Quetzalcoatl and I approached, the crowd fell silent, waiting.

"Thank you for coming here today," he began. "I know many of you have questions, the least of all being why I stand before you right now rejuvenated as I am. And that is as good a place to start as any.

He took a deep breath before continuing, "For years, you've been told that I am the only legitimate son of Mixcoatl, the former king of the city of Culhuacan, and many of you fought at my side to help me reclaim that throne after Ihuitimal murdered him. But I have to tell you today that that is not the truth. I have no blood relationship to Culhuacan's former king."

A confused murmur built in the crowd but fell silent when he raised his hand.

"And still others of you were told that though I wasn't Mixcoatl's blood son, I was instead the mortal son of the god Quetzalcoatl, placed by the god himself in the belly of a mortal woman so I could see the Feathered Serpent's reforms actualized here on earth. But again, this is not the truth. I am not the son of Quetzalcoatl."

"Then who are you?" someone shouted.

He looked at me, the anxiety plain in his eyes; it wasn't the supreme confidence he'd always shown me in the Divine Dream, but rather the very human look of doubt I'd sometimes see in Little Reed's eyes. I'd always seen Little Reed and Quetzalcoatl as separate beings, but now I realized they were just like me: different masks joined by their shared teotl, and that I'd always loved each of them equally, and I always would. I took his hand in a show of support.

He gave me a grateful smile then said, "The truth is…I *am* Quetzalcoatl himself. I bore myself into the mortal world as a human being so I could live among you and show you a new path of worship that would see an end to human sacrifice."

The people in the crowd looked at each other in confusion, and some in outrage.

"I know many of you will question this claim," Quetzalcoatl went on. "And no doubt believe me sacrilegious for making it, but I've lived a lie for the last thirty-five years, not just to all of you who put your faith in me as the god you chose to commit your lives to, or the people who put their faith in me as their king, but also to those who loved me as a friend—" He motioned to Mazatzin, who had a bewildered look on his face. Quetzalcoatl then turned to me. "And the one who loved me first as her god, and then her brother, and later as her husband. I deeply regret how my deception has hurt everyone around me, and, in the wake of what has transpired here over the last day, how I failed every last citizen of Tollan when they needed me most. I am so very sorry."

The tempo of conversation picked up, quickly growing to a dull roar. "How do we know you're not lying now?" someone shouted, and still another person asked, "Can you prove that you're truly who you claim?"

"Yes! Where's the proof? If you're truly the god, you can prove it!"

"Show us your divine form!"

He held his hands up for silence, and though the crowd didn't completely quiet, he was able to say, "I understand your reticence, but unfortunately I can't—"

The rise of angry shouting cut him off, and no amount of calling for quiet could convince them.

Mazatzin stepped up and shouted, "I've known this man almost my entire life, and I've served the god almost as long, and as one of the Feathered Serpent's highest servants, I believe—" But the crowd only grew more insistent.

I leaned in to whisper to Quetzalcoatl, "Raise your hands to the sky."

He cast a doubtful look at me but then did as I said.

I reached into him with my tendrils of magic and pulled a strand of his wind magic out, letting it filter out around me into the air. In response, the breeze picked up and flowed through the crowd, whipping people's hair around their faces.

After all of my failed attempts at controlling the wind, I expected the same difficulties, but with Quetzalcoatl's wind magic came a distinct sense of genius born of countless years of experience. I suddenly could move a single particle of air at a time, or, if I wanted to, I could send them all rushing like water over the land, reducing everything to dust. The breadth of his knowledge and magic was staggering, and humbling.

Calming the thrill, I whispered, "Move your arms around," and when he did, I made the wind move in the same direction.

The people watched in awe, and many cried in joy as the wind caressed across their faces.

I could have played with the air currents for days, churning up the pollen and flower petals in intricate patterns, but I was only borrowing this wonderful magic, and I needed to return it home again. I reduced the pull on Quetzalcoatl's teotl until the wind disappeared, returning the air to stillness.

"He *is* the god!" someone shouted and still more cried their agreement. Many took to their knees in supplication.

"Thank you," Quetzalcoatl whispered with a hint of breathlessness.

I answered with a smile.

"Is the queen a god too?" one of the younger priestesses asked, clamoring to the front of the crowd.

I knew the time would come when I had to finally tell everyone the truth, but I hadn't yet given any thought to actually announcing it. I looked to Quetzalcoatl, and he gave me an encouraging smile of his own. I cleared my throat before telling the priestess, "I am the goddess Mayahuel."

Her face lit with pride and excitement, and a gasp of awe passed among the crowd. "We have two gods leading us!" she shouted. "We are truly a blessed people!"

Movement off to my left drew my attention away from the crowd.

A massive group of men armed with weapons and farming implements moved down the path from the sacred precinct, headed towards us. Matlacxochitl walked at the lead, surrounded by soldiers in padded armor and carrying macuahuitl swords. I tapped Quetzalcoatl's arm to get his attention.

Matlacxochitl stopped at a distance and stared us down. "You're looking remarkably better today, Lord Topiltzin."

The crowd of priests pressed closer to us, an anxious murmur passing through them as Quetzalcoatl stepped up. "And you're looking well as usual, Lord Matlacxochitl." His gaze wandered to the armed crowd behind him. "I'm sure this is merely an oversight, but only members of the priestly orders are allowed inside these gardens."

"Much has changed since this time yesterday."

"Indeed."

Matlacxochitl looked over our crowd of priests. "There are important matters that we must discuss, Topiltzin. About the future of Tollan."

"Very well." Quetzalcoatl motioned to the ruins of the priestly retreat. "Shall we speak over here?"

Matlacxochitl nodded, but when I moved to follow them, he stopped. "With all due respect, Lady Quetzalpetlatl, I've already dealt with you as much as I care to, and we all know how your negotiations ended for the city. I will speak with Topiltzin alone."

Quetzalcoatl narrowed his eyes. "She is Tollan's queen—"

"Then we have nothing to discuss. We can instead deal with this matter through military might."

I set a hand on Quetzalcoatl's shoulder. "It's all right. I will stay here with the people and make sure they are kept safe from treachery." I cast a challenging glare at Matlacxochitl.

Matlacxochitl sneered in answer.

"You're sure?" Quetzalcoatl whispered.

"Of course."

They walked off and I remained back with Mazatzin, watching the gathered army. Still more people entered the garden behind them, filling it back to the sacred precinct.

"Amoxtli and I gathered everyone we could find who was still loyal to the god or Topiltzin," Mazatzin whispered as we watched. "We are vastly out-manned."

"That may be, but we have the gods on our side," Amoxtli noted.

I turned to look at the families who had gathered to leave with us. "Where's Cuicatl?"

He sighed. "She's decided to remain behind. I believe her exact words were, 'I'm not leaving home yet again for the sake of any good-for-nothing gods.'"

I set my hand on his shoulder. "She is a woman now, so she will make her own choices."

He nodded, but still looked ready to cry. "I know she's not my daughter, but still...I feel like I failed her."

I wanted to say something to comfort him, but I knew all too well what he felt, and that no words could fix it. I'd failed Ehecacone too.

Quetzalcoatl and Matlacxochitl were talking peaceably, but Quetzalcoatl was also watching the gathering crowd. Their discussion went on for several more minutes before both men returned. Matlacxochitl went to his ranks while Quetzalcoatl took his place before our crowd. He looked pained as he stood there, perhaps thinking about what to say, but eventually he found his voice.

"I want to thank each and every one of you for your loyalty and support, particularly in this most trying of times. It was good people such as yourselves that moved me to make these reforms, which makes what I must say all the more painful. In the interests of the safety of her citizens, I am stepping down as Tollan's king."

A gasp travelled through the crowd, but a blustery cheer rose behind us.

"But you're the god!" a man yelled from the crowd before us. "You could easily crush anyone who opposes you!" Those behind us were being too loud to hear the declaration over their own cheers.

Quetzalcoatl shook his head. "There has been enough unnecessary bloodshed already, and the majority of Tollan's citizens are in favor of me stepping aside. I will respect the wishes of the majority, and I will leave."

"But what about the Queen?"

"I'm stepping down as well," I said.

"And what about us?" one of the priests asked.

Quetzalcoatl nodded. "The decision is yours alone. You may choose to stay, but know that the new king requires an oath of fealty from each and every citizen, and all priests will have to renounce their worship of the Feathered Serpent."

That garnered angry shouts, but when he raised his hands for silence, they immediately fell quiet.

"The other choice is to leave Tollan, either on your own, or you may come with me and Lady Mayahuel as we attempt to find a new land to settle. It is starting over with no civil support or allies—and we'll likely have many enemies to contend with—but we will be free to live as we wish, and every man and woman will have a voice."

A discontented murmur ran through the crowd as everyone looked at their neighbor.

"You needn't make a decision this moment. Take today to discuss it with your family, and in the morning, those who wish to join us can gather here."

□

Quetzalcoatl, Mazatzin, and Amoxtli spent the rest of the afternoon building a pyre in the remains of the priestly retreat while Mitotia and I prepared Malinalli's body for the funeral. We spoke little to each other as we cleaned her up and wrapped her in the traditional paper bandages; the process reminded me of preparing Ehecacone for his burial, complete with the dull ache that wouldn't go away. I would never get to see her again; we'd never again discuss our day or listen to each other's troubles, and I'd never have the chance to thank her for her faith in me when I needed it most.

But I also knew in my heart that my own pain and loss was nothing compared to what Mitotia must be going through. And I was the cause of it. I had no idea how to bridge this new gap between us.

But as we sat waiting for the men to finish building the pyre, I knew I couldn't maintain the silence between us forever. "I'm so sorry for your loss, Mitotia." Though even then I couldn't speak louder than a whisper.

Mitotia gave me a wan smile, but said nothing.

"You should know...I knew her a very long time, and in all of those years, I never saw her happier than when she was with you. You were everything to her, and her sacrifice…it was more for you than anyone else."

Mitotia sniffled. "I keep thinking I should hate you, for bringing us all to this juncture, but…but I'm so proud of her, giving everything she had to save us all. It's a debt I can never repay." She squeezed her eyes shut against fresh tears. "Forgive me, My Lady, but I fear it will be a while before I'm able to reconcile my feelings on this."

"I'm struggling with it myself…and whether I can ever be worthy of such a precious gift, given the choices I've made."

She opened her eyes and took a deep breath, as if she'd just set down a heavy load. "The thing about the future is that there's always new choices to make, new opportunities to either repeat our mistakes, or commit to a new path."

□

As the sun set, everyone gathered around the funeral pyre where Mazatzin and Quetzalcoatl had set up Malinalli's body for the ceremony. In accordance with custom, she sat upright, cross-legged and wrapped from head to foot in paper bandages, over which we'd dressed her in the robes and white heron-feathered headdress of the high priestess. Mitotia tied a little brown dog to the pyre—our offering for Xolotl.

Quetzalcoatl gave a stirring speech about faith and love and sacrifice, but it couldn't keep me from dwelling on what awaited Malinalli in the afterlife. Thanks to my not having a heaven for my sacrifices, she would wander the mists of Mictlan just as my father did. Such a travesty that she'd given so much and I couldn't repay that with paradise or even eternal rest.

Once Quetzalcoatl finished his speech, he called me forward. "Would you like to say the prayer?"

I nodded then took my place where he'd stood.

"Lord of the Final Road,
Hear my prayers and accept my sacrifice.
Lend your guidance to this woman
On the treacherous road ahead.
Calm her fear in crossing the Black River,
Shield her in the cavern of arrows,
Teach her the words to sooth the savage snakes,
Bandage her feet as she summits the bladed mountain,
And stand with her when she faces the eternal mists.
She made the ultimate sacrifice for the people she loved and served,
So show her your mercy."

I slit the little dog's throat and laid its body upon Malinalli's lap. "Goodbye, my friend." I gave her bandaged hand a final squeeze before stepping away to rejoin Quetzalcoatl, Mazatzin, and Mitotia at the clay brazier.

We lit pine-pitch torches then gathered at the four corners of the pyre, lighting one side at a time: first the east side, where the sun rose, giving birth to the new day, then to the north where the sun rose to the height of its life, then the west where it slowly died on the horizon, having lived all day long, and then finally the south, where the sun made its journey into the underworld. As with the sun, so went humans, except their journey lasted many, many years rather than a single day.

The pyre burned deep into the night, and only a handful of us remained awake to watch it. A makeshift camp had sprung up in the field outside the remains of the retreat, and judging from the number of tents, no one seemed to have decided to stay behind, and in fact, as the hours passed, a small scattering of new people arrived to join our group. It was heartening to see we hadn't lost the faith of all of the people of Tollan.

I spent hours staring into the flames, thinking first about Malinalli wandering the mists of Mictlan, but then about Ehecacone. I'd promised I would come back for him, but I'd failed. When Lord Death grew tired of waiting, would he make good on his threats to torture my son? What if he already knew I wasn't coming with Quetzalcoatl? Perhaps he'd already started taking his frustration out on Ehecacone.

Someone cleared their throat behind me, and I looked over my shoulder to see Quetzalcoatl standing there, head bowed. "May I sit with you for a while, Mayahuel?"

I moved aside to make room for him on the stone rubble I was using as a bench. Sitting this close to me, I could just make out the subtle glow of his aura, like dawn's soft light squeezing past a curtain's edge, and he smelled faintly of reptiles and feathers—that same smell I'd detected in the teoyoh when I'd taken him to the priestly retreat. My orange rabbits hopped closer to him, curious, their own glow illuminating the outlines of his spectral feathered serpents curled into tight coils as if they were sleeping.

Once he was settled, I said, "I must admit, it feels weird to hear you call me that, but then it also feels strange calling you Quetzalcoatl."

"It feels the same to me, but I suppose it will get easier for us with time."

I felt a twinge of resentment; I'd hoped he would ask if he could still call me Papalotl, so I could continue calling him Little Reed, but perhaps some things just couldn't be anymore. I nodded though, accepting it.

We sat in awkward silence a moment before he said, "I know I told everyone you were leaving with us, but if you'd rather be on your own...I understand."

"No, I want to come along...if that's all right."

"Of course it's all right. The people will be glad you're coming along."

I chuckled. "From what I've heard around camp today, everyone's leaving to follow you, not me, but...they find it weird—and unfair—that we won and yet we're the ones leaving."

"That's because we didn't really win."

I gaped at him. "But I defeated Smoking Mirror—not just beat him, but sent him to Mictlan. How can you say we have lost?"

"I misspoke; *we* didn't lose anything. *I* lost it for us, a long time ago. Back during the battle for Culhuacan."

Frowning, I said, "That doesn't make sense at all."

He shifted on the stone, as if he was about to confess something embarrassing. "You already know that I offered up my own mortal life to bring you back from the dead that day, but by doing so, I was also sacrificing the success of my plans to end human sacrifice."

A ball of guilt and anger formed in my stomach. "You sacrificed humanity's future...to save me?"

"It was a spur-of-the-moment decision that I didn't think through very well because I couldn't bear the thought of losing you forever...."

"But then why didn't it just end that day?"

"Because you made your sacrifice, which meant I wouldn't have to face the consequences of my thoughtlessness just yet. Instead, I would have to live on not knowing the precise moment Heaven would collect on my debt."

I stared at the bonfire. "I don't understand…if there was no hope for success in ending human sacrifice, why didn't you just give up? Why go through with building Tollan and passing all of those laws if it was all for naught?"

Quetzalcoatl shook his head. "It wasn't all for naught, Mayahuel. While I was lying abed recovering from my wounds from the battle, I realized the true consequence of my sacrifice, but I also realized I owed my friends and followers better than to just abandon them to the growing power of darkness and fear that Smoking Mirror would bring. I couldn't hand them the safe future I'd promised, but I could show them what the future could be, and grow hope and courage in their hearts so that some day they might stand up to their oppressors and accept nothing less than a future free of fear."

"That seems to have failed too though," I said, glum. "Most of Tollan's citizens have rejected us and our reforms."

"But look how many haven't." He motioned to the tents and cooking fires spread out over the field beyond the remains of the retreat. "These men and women carry on the hope of a better future, and so long as that continues in their children and their children's children, Smoking Mirror will not ever win completely."

"That is true, but…must they really leave? This is their city, built on the blood and sweat of the faithful. It should be Matlacxochitl and his lot that is marching out tomorrow."

Quetzalcoatl looked further into the gardens, beyond the field, to where the flag stone path led to the sacred precinct. Several patrols of Matlacxochitl's men were keeping watch there, making sure we didn't attempt to sneak back into the city proper. "If our numbers were reversed, that might be feasible, but we both know that our people would just be throwing their lives away."

I laughed. "Yes, our numbers are few, but that hardly matters. I could take the city on my own—"

"Yes, but do you truly want to just be the next Smoking Mirror?"

I snapped my mouth shut, my face growing hot with embarrassment. "Maybe some day I will learn to stop feeling so bloodthirsty."

He set his hand on mine. "Don't be down on yourself, Mayahuel. Your heart is in the right place, but the easy answer is often the wrong one, for it demands little effort from us."

The silence fell between us again as we both stared into the fire, but eventually I said, "Can I ask you some questions?"

"Of course."

"I understand why you forbade Citlallotoc from pursuing me—I would have driven him crazy with my love magic, just as I did to Black Otter and Red Flint—"

"You aren't to blame for what those two did," Quetzalcoatl said. "You didn't make them feel or think anything they weren't already capable of; you just made them show their true natures for everyone to see. That's how love magic works; it intensifies what is already there. Red Flint was already paranoid, and Black Otter was an obsessive personality."

"And a murderer," I muttered. When Quetzalcoatl cast me a puzzled look, I said, "He tried to murder both his father and his brother, and he succeeded in murdering our son, because he was jealous of our marriage."

Anguish descended upon his eyes and he turned to stare at the ground.

"You can understand then why I wouldn't want to visit such chances upon Citlallotoc," I said.

He shook his head. "Citlallotoc would have been unquestioningly loyal to you to his dying breath, for that was his nature, but that wasn't my concern. There's always deadly consequences for humans engaging in physical intimacy with the gods; in your case, you consume their life force, but in my case…I would impregnate anyone I was intimate with, and giving birth to a divine being is always fatal to a human."

"Is that why you refused to consummate your marriage to Anacoana?"

He nodded. "You saw first hand what happened to Chimalma when she gave birth to my mortal incarnation. I couldn't do that to yet another woman, not even to ensure an heir to Tollan." He stared at his hands as he said, "I didn't give any thought to what my request would do to Chimalma, and it never occurred to me that it might affect you so…. I think back on what kind of a god I was before all this, and I hardly even recognize myself. Being a human being, and an everyday part of others' lives as a friend, a leader, a brother, and a father…I realized just how selfish and thoughtless I was. I had no business calling myself the benefactor of humanity when I treated their lives as expendable as any of the other gods did. Knowing people like Citlallotoc, and Mazatzin, and Malinalli…and Nimilitzli…. The hardest thing I ever had to do in my life was go to ask Nimilitzli to take on the burden of fulfilling your sacrifice to make sure Red Flint won that ball game against Obsidian Eagle."

I gaped at him. "You asked her to sacrifice herself, for me?"

"I didn't have to; when I told her you were struggling to make a fitting sacrifice, she stepped up without hesitation, much like Malinalli did today. I've benefited greatly from such sacrifices throughout my existence but I've never actually sat at someone's side while they made that ultimate sacrifice, and I…." His voice broke, but eventually he went on, "I'm humbled by the selflessness the human heart is capable of."

I hadn't realized I was crying until I felt the tears on my cheeks. "I often think our kind is unworthy of such selfless devotion."

He nodded. "That doesn't mean we can't strive to earn it going forward." He sniffled a bit but then stood up. "I should really get some sleep." He then bade me goodnight and headed back to his tent set up in the rubble of what used to be our meditation room.

I watched him go, but just before he ducked inside, I called out to him, "You know why they're capable of such selflessness, don't you? It's because they came from Ehecatl's blood, and while Ehecatl had much darkness in him, he also had a great deal of light, and you're proof of that."

He smiled stiffly, as if he might cry, but he nodded then retreated into his tent.

CHAPTER THIRTY-FOUR

 After Quetzalcoatl retired, I went back to staring at the fire, but soon movement by the far right side of the pyre drew me out of my thoughts. My stomach leaped when I noticed the tall, shaggy black dog watching me.

But my concerns that it was a wolf were quickly extinguished; the firelight didn't reflect upon it, and a faint dark green glow surrounded it. Spectral dogs bounded around it, dragging its tendrils of magic behind them.

The wolf-dog jogged over to me. When it stopped, I greeted it with wariness. "Xolotl."

He inclined his head. "Mayahuel."

"I see you've come to collect my friend."

He shook his head. "No, I came for her earlier today. I saw what she did for you; that's quite a selfless gift."

"Then why are you here?"

"Lord Death wishes to see you."

My stomach clenched. "I'm sure he does."

"He was quite surprised to find that you'd sent Smoking Mirror to him instead of Quetzalcoatl."

I smiled. "Well, he was Ehecatl too at one point, so I figured he was just as good as the Feathered Serpent for payment of our agreement."

Xolotl showed off his fangs as he smiled. "While that is true, I'm afraid that the master wasn't impressed. He's already raised Smoking Mirror from the dead."

"Then he's upset that I killed his friend?"

"They are not friends, and Lord Death doesn't raise anyone from the dead for free. Both Xochiquetzal and Mextli paid a formidable sum of magic for Smoking Mirror's return. He was, however, disturbed to learn that you have the Feathered Serpent in your possession, and yet have made no efforts to bring him to Mictlan."

I laughed. "Quetzalcoatl isn't *in my possession*, but yes, I have no intention of handing him over to Lord Death. Not even for my son."

"He'll be disappointed to hear that."

"I'm sure he will be."

Xolotl sat down, looking contemplative.

"Aren't you going to go tell your master that I'm reneging on our deal? I'm sure the two of you are looking forward to making my son's afterlife miserable."

"I have no desire to harm your son, Mayahuel—"

"And yet you abandoned him to walk the road himself."

"That wasn't my choice. You have no idea what is like to be a slave to another god; I have very little will of my own and must do things I despise because I am bound to Lord Death for eternity. I feel guilty for leaving Ehecacone at my house after accepting your sacrifice, but when my master said I must, I had no choice."

"Why would he do that?"

"To lure either you or the Feathered Serpent into walking the road with your son, of course. A living god that walks the road can die a mortal death if they do not reach Mictlan in time, and that's one of Lord Death's favorite bargaining chips to play against his enemies."

"So, if you'd already taken Ehecacone to Mictlan?"

"You could have just left at any time. By making you take the road, he could exact tolls and favors from you, not only on behalf of your son, but yourself as well. And if it had been Quetzalcoatl who had walked the road with your son...Lord Death could have held him indefinitely."

"Then it was a good thing it was me who went down there rather than him."

"Indeed. And Lord Death can't trap you down there now. You needn't fear that."

"That's not my fear; what I'm afraid of is telling him that I can't give him Quetzalcoatl, and he repays that by making me watch him raise my son from the dead so he can torture him. He's already threatened it."

Xolotl nodded. "That is absolutely what he intends to do, but there is one thing you should know. He's not aware of the nature of your magic."

I narrowed my eyes at him. "What do *you* know about the nature of my magic?"

"I see everything my nahuals see, and as we both know, a human died when you confronted Smoking Mirror. So yes, I know how your magic works. I haven't, however, told my master."

"Why not?"

"Because information is the most powerful currency. If Lord Death had told you that Quetzalcoatl had withheld knowledge of your divine nature out of necessity rather than malice, would you have made that deal with him?"

"Probably not," I admitted. "That's why he wouldn't let you talk to me that day in Mictlan, isn't it? Because you might tell me something he didn't want me knowing." When he nodded, I said, "But why wouldn't you tell him about what you saw this morning?"

Xolotl looked around but then whispered, "Because Quetzalcoatl is the only god who has ever been kind to me. All of the others have always treated me worse than dirt, and my master is the worst of them. But the Feathered Serpent treats me like a thinking, feeling being, and I will do anything to help him. My being Lord Death's servant sometimes makes that difficult, but I do what I can."

"But what does that have to do with me?"

"Because the Feathered Serpent loves you, and he loves his son too, so I will help both of you when I can. That's why I helped him convince Lord Death to resurrect you, and why I was going to tell you who you really were when you died in Culhuacan."

Memories of that day washed over me. He had in fact started to tell me something.... "But I thought no one could tell me the truth—"

"When you were still alive, yes," Xolotl corrected me. "But once you were dead, the rule no longer applied. And because you had not yet crossed through the gate into the underworld, you could still reclaim your godhood; like I said, information is powerful. Unfortunately, Quetzalcoatl made his sacrifice before I could actually tell you, meaning the deal came back into force."

My mind reeled. "But...but what if Lord Death found out you told me?"

He shrugged. "He would have punished me severely. But it's hardly fair that you should face oblivion because my master hates the Feathered Serpent. Besides, he'd never actually kill me; he needs me to be his eyes here on earth."

I stared at him, guilt welling up inside me. "I'm so sorry, Xolotl, for treating you so badly. I owe you better than that."

"I would hardly consider your treatment bad, Mayahuel. If anything, appearances justified your suspicion, and I'm sorry I couldn't be more forthright with you the last time we spoke."

"I still feel horrible. Please accept my apologies."

"Very well. I accept."

I stared into the burning pyre. "So you really didn't tell Lord Death about my being able to pull magic out of other gods?"

Xolotl nodded. "If he did know, he wouldn't have sent me to bring you to Mictlan to speak with him. He would quietly go about his plans and hope you didn't think to come see him on your own."

"But surely Smoking Mirror or Mextli told him?"

"Smoking Mirror would never admit a weakness that someone might use to exploit him, and Mextli is loyal to him. And as for Xochiquetzal, she's far too desperate to gain Smoking Mirror's affections to dare say anything he might disapprove of."

"But surely Lord Death knows I'm powerful enough to have killed Smoking Mirror, and so will be on the lookout for treachery?"

Xolotl chuckled. "You do not understand Lord Death very well, Mayahuel. The rules

THE BONE FLOWER TRILOGY

of normal gods do not apply to death gods; he cannot be killed by anyone or anything, so he doesn't fear things the rest of us do. What concerns him is being made a fool of in the eyes of the other gods, hence his loathing of Quetzalcoatl. But he doesn't worry about you; to him, you're a minor goddess whom he fooled into agreeing to deliver the god she loves to him. It doesn't even bother him that you didn't fulfill your end of the bargain, for he will take joy in your pain when he exercises his cruel power over those dearest to you. He cannot even fathom that you can use his own magic against him."

"Quetzalcoatl is always saying everyone underestimates me," I said. I doubted Smoking Mirror would ever make that mistake again. *And if I succeed in getting Ehecacone back, Lord Death won't either, so I had better make sure I do this right.*

◻

I thought to tell Quetzalcoatl that I was leaving for Mictlan with Xolotl, but decided against it; he might try to talk me out of it, but I had to do this. Ehecacone couldn't be left to suffer down there.

I never thought I'd ever look forward to returning to the cold mistiness of Mictlan, but when Xolotl and I materialized at the doors to Lord Death's palace, I was brimming with excitement.

Xolotl changed into his limping human form. "There are a few things you should be aware of before facing the master," he whispered. "Lord Death's magic is some of the most powerful there is, but because of that power, he's incapable of leaving the underworld. That means that so long as you have any of his magic inside you, you can't leave either. You must get rid of all of it if you're to leave."

"All right." I then followed him inside.

He loped down the long hallway of articulated bones, to the curtain of brown owl feathers. He gave me a final pointed look before pulling the curtain aside for me. I thanked him with a nod then stepped into the great hall.

Lord Death sat upon his throne of jade bones, Ehecacone sitting upon his lap, seemingly asleep. He watched me as I approached the dais, a pleased smile on his skeletal face. His magic glowed light blue, like his ghostlit eyes, but the tendrils formed claws and grinning skulls.

Once Xolotl announced me, Lord Death said, "So wonderful to see you again, Mayahuel. I'd started wondering if I ever would."

"It took a bit longer than I thought it would," I said.

"Then you've brought me a gift?"

"I indeed have."

He leaned forward to look around me. "Funny, but I don't see Quetzalcoatl with you."

"My gift is your chance to renegotiate our deal."

He stared at me for a bewildered moment before bursting into screechy laughter. "My dear little thorny one, you forget to whom you're speaking!"

"I'm well aware, and that's why I'm giving you this opportunity. I know you're a god with an eye for a good bargain, so I'm making you an even better offer."

He laughed louder, clutching his sides. "I fear you've scrambled something in your head. But I confess curiosity: what is this better deal?"

"A healthy portion of any sacrifice I receive—say a full half—as tribute from this day forward. In return, you give me back my son."

He narrowed his ghost light eyes at me. "Now you just insult. No one sacrifices anything to you."

"Not true. I already have a small collection of restless souls wandering through the mists on the plain, and while it's true that not many sacrifice to me now, the power of my sacrifices is more than a hundred of Smoking Mirror's or Mextli's. You're getting an excellent deal."

"And you're asking for your son to suffer for your insolence." He squeezed Ehecacone's arm with his bony fingers.

My temper flared, but I kept my voice even as I asked, "Then you're turning down my generous offer?"

Lord Death bared his skeletal teeth. "I spit at your pathetic offer."

"Very well then." I crested the step up onto the dais and reached for Ehecacone.

"Need I remind you that you're being foolhardy?" Lord Death asked.

In answer, I set my rabbits loose on his wispy claws and skulls and yanked the magic out of him. In the brief moment he sat stock still in bewilderment as he tried to figure out what was happening to him, I snatched my son off his lap and cradled him in my arms. When Lord Death launched to his feet to stop me, I knocked him back into his throne with a blast of his own magic. He stared at me agape. "How—?"

In answer, I let his death-god magic flow into Ehecacone, sparking awake my son's own divinity. My boy's teotl—rich chocolate in color and smelling like fresh octli—burst to life and his eyes snapped open. He blinked a few times before focusing on me. The look in his eyes reminded me of the first time he had recognized me when he was an infant, and I thought my heart might break from sheer joy. "Mother!" he cried and wrapped his arms around my neck. I hugged him back, tears in my eyes.

"How in Mictlan is this even possible?" Lord Death muttered, an expression of utter befuddlement on his skeletal face.

I started backing towards the doorway. "I'm sorry, but I can't let you use my son to harm Quetzalcoatl. I meant it when I said that I would share my sacrifices with you, but now you've forced my hand, so I get my son and you get nothing."

Lord Death sprang to his feet again and fired a blast of magic at me, his teeth gritted, but I swiped it aside. His ghost lights grew brighter with surprise, then glowing blue wisps started streaming in through the obsidian window overlooking the Black Lake, coming from the misty plain where the heavenless sacrifices wandered. He was pulling extra magic from them. It would do him little good though; I could match him no matter what, but I didn't like the idea of Ehecacone possibly getting in the way of a battle.

When I reached the doorway, I set my son down and pushed him behind me. I set my hand on his, but didn't take my eyes off of Lord Death. "Can you feel my magic, darling?"

"I can," he whispered.

"Feel what I'm doing with it?"

"Yes."

"Do the same thing, but think about becoming something else—something fast. An animal of some kind."

Ehecacone turned into a very large brown rabbit. He sat upon his haunches, looking at his furry front paws with wonder.

"Now, follow the hall to the front door, and go outside. Wait for me there."

"But Mother—"

"I won't be long. I promise."

After another hesitation, he dashed off down the hall, his claws clicking on the obsidian floor.

"You're wasting your time, fool." Lord Death's ghostlit eyes glowed painfully bright. "You've cheated the wrong god." He threw his full load of magic at me.

I braced myself, unsure exactly what to expect, but I really hoped Xolotl was right about death-god magic.

The blast hit me, and I immediately knew it was intended to kill. I felt no pain though, no stripping of my own magic. My hair blew away from my face, but otherwise I remained unaffected. Lord Death gaped at me, disbelieving.

"Don't you know you can't kill a death god?" I asked.

"You're no death god!"

"No, but I've got your death-god magic, and I'm not above using it." And just to demonstrate, I swiped my hand across the room, letting loose a wave of magic that penetrated the palace walls and spread over Mictlan and out onto the misty plain beyond. Suddenly, the constant buzz that had once been a staple of the atmosphere ceased.

Lord Death's eyes visibly dimmed and he stumbled back until he fell onto his throne. "What have you done?" he whispered.

"I gave all those trapped on the plain of Mictlan their eternal rest," I answered with a smile. "Surely you don't mind? After all, you complained bitterly about how annoying their constant buzzing was, but now you don't have to listen to them anymore."

Lord Death clenched his bone-fingers in fury. "You will regret this treachery, Mayahuel."

"Perhaps, but not today." I too transformed into a rabbit and dashed off after Ehecacone. Behind me, Lord Death shouted at Xolotl to bring me back immediately.

I burst through the front doors of the palace to find my son crouched among the bone-dry reeds, watching the doorway with anxious eyes. He bounded out to meet me.

"This way!" I called, not slowing down. He leaped after me, catching up easily. Hearing the door creak open behind us, I chanced a glance over my shoulder.

Xolotl bolted out into the palace's courtyard in his wolf form, and he took off after us at full speed.

"Faster, my darling!" As we came down the road, heading back towards the plain of Mictlan, I said, "Do you see that doorway ahead? The one in the cavern wall to our left?"

"Yes!" Ehecacone panted as we ran.

"Go there, and get out to the other side. And whatever you do, don't wait for me. Climb the stairs and get out of the underworld!"

"You're coming with me, aren't you?"

"I will, but I want to make sure you make it first. Understood?"

"I guess."

"Now go!"

He took off even faster, turning up clouds of grey dust under his broad feet. I, however, slid to a stop and turned to face Xolotl as he bore down on me.

I'm sorry, Xolotl. I know you're only doing what your master ordered you to, but I've come too far to let him win.

Half a breath before he ran into me, I turned into a large wolf-dog too, so while the blow took me over, my sheer size was enough to knock him over. We tumbled across the dusty ground, our legs tangled, and after slashing our fangs at each other, we separated, both of us limping.

Except his wounds looked worse. I hadn't bitten him very much, but he was gushing golden dust and strange iridescent insects from numerous wounds. He looked down at the bugs then lapped them up with his lolling tongue, and his wounds healed. "You're not fully drained yet," he whispered as he moved towards me again, hackles raised and fangs bared. "You won't be able to leave the underworld until you rid yourself of every last drop of his magic."

I backed away, changing back into my human form. "I don't want to hurt you, Xolotl."

"We all do what we must." A growl rose in his throat. "There is no other way."

I glanced over my shoulder to see Ehecacone waiting for me on the other side of the door way, an anxious expression on his face.

"It's now, or you stay in Mictlan forever, Mayahuel." Xolotl lunged at me.

I didn't think; I just blasted everything I had left of Lord Death's magic at him. Hopefully it would shield me from his fangs.

The blast knocked him backwards and he rolled a few times before coming to a stop. Though even then, I noticed his fur moving like boiling water. He screamed as his skin split open and insects began pouring out.

"Dear gods, Xolotl!" I hurried to him. My impulse was to set a soothing hand on him, but the streaming bugs left none of his fur exposed. Only his wide, panicked eye was visible. "Oh no! What have I done to you?"

"Go," he croaked. "The master is coming."

I looked up to see Lord Death gliding down the path from the palace. He hadn't seen us yet, but he would soon if I didn't run. "I'm so sorry, Xolotl," I whispered then turned and ran. I changed back into a rabbit midstride and bounded through the doorway to the stairs out of the underworld. I slid to a stop as Ehecacone bounced up and down in front of me in excitement.

"I almost thought you weren't going to make it, Mother! I was sure he was going to get you!"

I gazed back at Xolotl. Lord Death now knelt next to his body, staring at the mess with disgust. He cast me a hot glare. I had little doubt at that moment that he hated me just as much as he hated Quetzalcoatl. "I'm not proud of what I did, but we should always remember Xolotl in our prayers, for I doubt either of us would be leaving right now if not for him." I nudged Ehecacone's bottom to get him moving and we headed up the stairs.

□

I expected the stairs to open onto the same cenote in the desert where Xolotl had brought me out before, but to my surprise, we emerged into a cave dimly lit by a single kettle brazier. I recognized the stacks of octli jars near the ladder leading up; we were in the vision cavern below the priestly gardens in Tollan, where we stored all of the octli, and initiates made their first foray into the Divine Dream before becoming priests and priestesses. We would be back at the temporary camp in a matter of minutes.

"Change back into your human form," I told Ehecacone as I did the same myself. He managed it after a few failed tries, but he still wore his tatty rabbit costume, complete with the holes and rips he'd gained during our journey into Mictlan. He started climbing up the ladder, but I grabbed his arm. "We need to talk about a few things first."

"All right." He climbed atop the jars of octli and sat.

I took his hands in mine. "Do you remember the talk we had on the road, about Quetzalcoatl?"

He furrowed his eyebrows deep. "Oh, I remember."

I nodded. "I said a lot of things about him...things that I thought were true at the time, but I've since discovered are false. I was so very wrong about him, Ehecacone, and I made a mistake in holding a grudge against him."

"Then he didn't kill you long ago?"

"The truth is complicated, but now that I know what really happened, I don't hold him responsible. And I found out that since my first death, he had been working hard and making sacrifices to bring me back, and I'm so very grateful for that."

Ehecacone smiled. "So am I."

"I want you to have a good relationship with your father, so please, don't hold anything I said against him. Get to know him and form your own opinion about what kind of god he is."

Perking up, Ehecacone asked, "Then he's here and I can actually talk to him?"

I nodded. "Remember the other conversation we had, when you asked if the king was Quetzalcoatl?"

"He is, isn't he?" He jumped down off the jars. "I just knew it!"

"You did indeed, my darling," I said with a smile.

"Can we go see him now?" He hooted in excitement when I nodded.

"But one last thing before we go, and this is very important. No using your magic around other people."

He frowned. "But why not?"

"Because you're new to it, and it's very easy to hurt people when we don't know what we're doing. I will teach you how to properly use your magic, but until then, pretend you're still a human boy, all right?"

Once Ehecacone agreed, we both headed up the ladder and came out through a trap door in the floor of the initiation building. He skipped and ran the entire way to the camp, and it made my heart swell to see him so happy.

A few people who had known Ehecacone when he was still alive stared at him agape when we came into camp, but he hurried through the crowd, calling, "Father! Where are you? Father?"

Quetzalcoatl stepped out of his tent, a disbelieving look on his face, but his eyes widened when he saw Ehecacone running towards him. "Ehecacone?" he gasped but then scooped his son up into his arms, hugging him tight. Tears clogged his voice as he whispered, "But how can this be?"

"Mother rescued me!" When he looked at his father, he furrowed his brow, cross. "What happened to your hair? Where's all the silver?"

"I've been rejuvenated," Quetzalcoatl said with a smile. An edge of worry tainted it though when I came to stand next to them. "You really went to the underworld again?"

I nodded and Ehecacone piped up, "You should have been there! She was so brave! She brought me back to life, then showed me how to change into a rabbit, and Xolotl came after us, but then she changed into a giant wolf, just like him, and they fought, but then she threw magic at him and all these bugs came scurrying out from under his skin!" He paused to take a gasping breath. "I couldn't believe it!"

Quetzalcoatl raised an eyebrow at me. "You took Lord Death's magic?"

"He wanted something I wasn't willing to give him, and was going to hurt our son because of it, so I did the only thing I could. Are you disappointed in me?"

"Hardly. You could have told me what you were going to do though."

"I didn't want you worrying about me. We have a lot of marching to do today."

He nodded. "It would have kept me up all night." I wasn't sure what to make of the cross look on his face, though he let it slip away once he returned his attention to Ehecacone and listened to our son regale him in detail with the tale of our journey into

Mictlan.

CHAPTER THIRTY-FIVE

We left Tollan without incident. Matlacxochitl's men lined the streets with weapons ready, in case anything went amiss, but our long caravan trudged out of the city without raising a fuss. As we came to the hillside where I'd first laid eyes upon the land where the Feathered Serpent's temple would be built, I stopped to look back, wondering if I'd ever see it again. The city looked much the same as I always remembered it, except perhaps the lack of greenness, but in my heart, it had changed.

Just like all the other dear things in my life.

But other changes were for the good. Every day, Ehecacone and I wandered away from the rest of the group for a few hours, and I would teach him how to use his magic and about the responsibilities that came with being a god. He was an eager learner, and I was always the proud teacher, especially as the weeks passed and his abilities grew by leaps and bounds.

Not that everything between us was perfect; as when he was still human, small things would trigger his darker side, but now that he wasn't flesh and blood anymore, the drunkenness didn't make him fall asleep. Instead he'd rant and rave at me for my mistakes or past choices then storm away into the forest. I always followed at a distance, to make sure he didn't hurt himself, or anyone else, but mostly he sat alone and wept. Some wounds would take time and patience to heal, and I intended to give him both.

Quetzalcoatl and I spoke little that first month after we left Tollan. When we did, it was about Ehecacone or logistics of the march or setting up camp. We each kept our own tents, though I used mine for escaping into the Divine Dream. Often I wished he would use the Teonanacatl to join me in there, but he never did, and I grew increasingly anxious that despite our cordial relationship, we were no longer friends as we'd once been.

My other friendships were going strong though. Mazatzin was always there with a smile and an ear, should I need it, and even Mitotia and I had grown closer since Malinalli's death. We never talked about her, nor about the conversation we'd shared before the funeral, so it caught me off guard when she asked me to bless her as my very own high priestess.

"I want to serve love, in all its varied and wondrous forms, and how better can I do that than devote my life to the goddess who gave it to us to begin with?"

Yet it felt so wrong that her personal pain was my source of power. Even a month after that fateful day in Tollan, my new powers had yet to wane as I thought they would with time. That troubling feeling only grew when Ehecacone and I found her sitting alone in the woods late one night, knelt over a burnt bone and muttering prayers of thanks not only to me, but Malinalli as well. When Ehecacone asked her about it the next morning, she admitted to taking the bone from the funeral pyre after the fire went out, so she'd have something of Malinalli to keep with her always.

"It's tradition among my people, to keep a bone of our loved ones who die in service to the gods, so we never forget the sacrifice they made for us. And so their memory lives on."

Oh how much I wished I had one too, not just from Malinalli, but my father, my mother, and from Nimilitzli. All I had now was memories, and often it felt that those weren't enough.

◻

"When are you going to take me to Omeyocan, Mother?" Ehecacone asked when we came back to camp after a night away in the woods practicing our shapeshifting skills. He was still in his giant rabbit form, and I suspected that someday soon he would leave his human one behind completely and stay a rabbit permanently. I tried not to feel a loss at the thought, for I wanted him to choose his own self image as much as I chose mine, but I couldn't help it.

In truth I hadn't mentioned Omeyocan to him at all because I was a little anxious about going back myself. It was difficult to say how my actions in Tollan were playing among the gods who'd remained uninvolved, and a part of me worried that I might put Ehecacone in danger by taking him there.

But if I could kill another god with such little effort, I doubted anyone would dare try anything—especially Smoking Mirror or Mextli. "I suppose there's no good reason not to take you there."

"Can we go now then? Yesterday, Father told me about his house and I really want to see it."

I glanced up at the puffy clouds drifting serenely overhead in the growing dawn. "All right. I should probably check in on my own house while we're there."

"You have a house too?" When I nodded, he asked, "Can I see it too?"

"Of course. Now change back into your human form, so we can go."

"Why?"

"Because I need to hold your hand during this first trip, so you don't fall."

Ehecacone morphed into his human form—a lanky boy of thirteen who looked eerily like Night Wind had the last time I'd seen him, before Smoking Mirror's magic ate his vitality away. I wondered if he knew he'd chosen such a self-image. Even though the resemblance sent a shiver of hostility through me, I wouldn't lecture him about it. He would choose his form and I would accept it no matter what. I took his hand in mine and together we jumped into the teoyoh.

We landed at the crossroads, at the foot of the steps leading up the mountain to Quetzalcoatl's house. Ehecacone stared up into the swirling clouds with an awestruck gasp then pulled me along up the winding staircase. When we reached the top, he stood staring, his mouth hanging open as he gawked at the round building.

But disappointment replaced his awe when we walked inside. "It's empty?" he asked, looking around. Nothing had changed since the last time I'd been there. "But…he said there was a great city, and in the middle was a grand garden bigger than any found on earth. He told me he fashioned Tollan itself from it."

"He said that?" I too stared at the empty room, puzzled.

"You don't think he lied to me, do you?" Ehecacone asked with a pang of hurt.

"Your father doesn't lie. You'll just have to ask him about it when we go back."

Ehecacone's shoulders sagged. "I was so looking forward to seeing it."

I gave his hand a gentle squeeze. "I'm sure you will, someday."

We went to the window and looked out over Omeyocan, and that seemed to alleviate his disappointment. "Wow! You can see everything from up here!"

"Indeed."

"Where's your house, Mother?"

I pointed at the temple precinct below. "That's it right there."

His eyes widened. "Yours is so much more interesting! Can we go down and look at it?"

"Of course we can—" But I paused when I noticed someone sitting on the stone ring of the cistern. It was too far away to make out who it was, but I could tell the person was female. Could it be Xochiquetzal? I hadn't thought to set up any kind of magic barrier to keep the other gods out the last time I'd been here, but maybe it would be a good idea to do so, to make sure my enemies weren't snooping around my house.

Though I cringed at the thought of calling my only daughter my enemy. She had chosen Smoking Mirror over me and Quetzalcoatl, but it seemed unnecessarily harsh to ban her from my house. Still, who knew what poison Smoking Mirror was whispering in her ear these days?

I didn't tell Ehecacone any of this as we walked down the stone stairs, back to the crossroads, but I hesitated when we reached the tall, broad staircase that led up the hill to the sacred precinct.

"What's wrong, Mother?" Ehecacone asked.

I took a deep breath then said, "Someone is in my house, and I don't know who it is."

He swallowed, a worried look on his face. "There is?"

I nodded. "I saw her, from the window up there in your father's house."

"Do you think she'll try to hurt us?"

"I will protect you, so you needn't worry. I just want you to do one thing for me, all right?"

"Anything."

"Don't let go of my hand, no matter what. I don't want you to fall. Understand?"

He nodded then added his other hand to his grip of mine.

We walked cautiously up the stairs and emerged onto the precinct. With the stairs emptying near my replica of Xochicalco' calmecac, the cistern was in plain view now.

I stopped short, my heart skipping. It wasn't Xochiquetzal sitting on the stone ring. It was Malinalli.

My feet carried me forward at a jog, but when she looked up at me, I stopped short. I waited to see recognition in her eyes, but she looked right through me as if I weren't there at all.

"Are you all right, Mother?" Ehecacone asked when I said nothing.

I nodded slowly, but to Malinalli, I said, "Hello."

She sighed then returned her attention to the cistern, staring into the water.

"Who are you talking to?" Ehecacone asked, puzzled.

"Malinalli." I gestured to her with my free hand. "Can't you see her?"

He looked right at Malinalli but shook his head. "I don't see anyone."

How could he not see her? She was just as close to him as she was to me.

A familiar voice spoke up behind me, "Others can't see into your heaven, Mayahuel." I turned to see Cihuacoatl shuffling towards us from the stairs.

Ehecacone brightened upon seeing her. "I can see *her* though, Mother."

Cihuacoatl chuckled and came to stand next to us. "Of course you can see me, Son of the Wind. We're practically family, you and I. If I hadn't taught your father the secrets of creation, he never would have taught them to your mother, and you would have never been born."

"Does that make you my grandmother?" he asked, a hint of hope in his voice.

She laughed louder. "I am everyone's grandmother, so yes."

I looked at Malinalli again, confused. "But...I don't have a heaven for my sacrifices, and that's why they were collecting in Mictlan. I was told I would need a great deal more sacrifices than I have."

"Or just one very meaningful one."

"You mean...her sacrifice...she gave me a heaven?"

Cihuacoatl nodded. "Such a powerful one; we all felt it when it happened. It's not every day that a new heaven forms unexpectedly."

Was there any end to the gifts Malinalli's friendship and love could grant me? I stifled a sob with the back of my hand as I watched her sit there gazing forlornly into the water. "So my sacrifices will come here for now on?" When Cihuacoatl nodded, I looked around expectantly. "But where are the others? The ones Lord Death was keeping in Mictlan?"

"From what Xolotl tells me, you granted them their eternal rest, along with all the other sacrifices Lord Death was holding. They've disappeared into the ether, never to be seen again. You've made it necessary for both Smoking Mirror and Mextli to start over from scratch."

I raised an eyebrow. I hadn't thought about that possibility at all. "They're probably very upset with me now, aren't they?"

"I wouldn't go seeking them to find out if I were you," Cihuacoatl said with a grin.

I turned to Malinalli again, a hollowness growing in my chest. "Why can't she see me though?"

"She's dead, and you are not. When others join your heaven, she will be able to see them. That's how it works."

"So she'll be alone here until more people offer their lives to me...or until people start sacrificing people to me?" When Cihuacoatl nodded, I said, "But I don't want lives. And...she doesn't look happy."

"Humans have always needed the company of others. They inherited that trait from their father."

Ehecacone tilted his head, thoughtful. "We were taught in calmecac that Quetzalcoatl is the father of mankind. Is that what you mean?"

She nodded, a patient smile on her face. "He created them from his blood, so they are his children, just as much as you are."

"So I have countless brothers and sisters!"

I wanted to smile at Ehecacone's newfound excitement, but I couldn't turn my mind away from Malinalli's situation. We'd always been taught as humans that sacrificing ourselves led to paradise, but now that I saw the truth...this was hardly it. I bit my lip.

"You have a question, my dear?" Cihuacoatl asked me.

I sighed, trying to find the right words. "This just...it's not fair. She gave everything she had—for me, for Quetzalcoatl, for the people of Tollan—and her reward is to spend years—maybe even bundles of years—alone here with no one to talk to? I know what that's like, and I wouldn't wish that on anyone. Least of all my best friend."

Cihuacoatl's face turned sober. "Well, you could always give her eternal rest, or you could turn her immortal."

"I don't have the power to turn humans into immortals."

"Of course you do. You're a creator goddess, the same as me, the same as Ehecatl."

"But Mextli said—"

"Mextli knows nothing about creation. He knows only how to sow war."

"But what about Smoking Mirror? He turned Coatlicue immortal."

"Because he too is a creator god, of course. He's the destructive element of the cycle. Creation often involves destroying the old to make way for the new."

I cast my gaze back to Malinalli again, indecisive.

"You should know though that doing anything other than just leaving her be has consequences for you. You will no longer be able to draw magic from the sacrifice she made, and while your heaven will remain regardless, for you it will be as if she didn't make the sacrifice at all. You're quite powerful now thanks to her, so keep that in mind."

"I don't really care about the power. She gave it to me to do one specific thing, and I did it, so it's only right to let it go now, for her."

Cihuacoatl bowed her head. "Do whatever you think best. Just be sure to hold onto her if you do; there's no ruder introduction to one's new divinity than to find yourself falling from Heaven." She patted Ehecacone on the head with a smile then she turned and headed back towards the stairs, walking leisurely.

Ehecacone watched her too, smiling, but then he turned to me. "So what are you going to do, Mother?"

"The only right thing to do," I said.

Together we walked over to Malinalli and I took hold of her arm. She looked around, confused—and a bit frightened. My magic flexed and pulsed, and with each wave, my power waned. She tried to pull away from me, but I held her firmly, making sure she didn't break free and fall through the clouds beneath us.

After what felt like an eternity, the pulsing finally ceased. And Malinalli looked up at me again. This time she saw me. "Quetzalpetlatl?"

I smiled, my insides aching with joy.

She looked at Ehecacone standing next to me, and furrowed her brow. "Night Wind?"

Ehecacone screwed his face into a frown. "I'm not him!" He looked to me. "I don't look like him, do I?"

"Maybe a little, dear," I said.

He gasped, but then changed his features a bit, so he looked more like Little Reed had at that age. "How's this?"

I smiled. "Whatever makes you happy, my love."

"Ehecacone?" Malinalli asked with a gasp. "You're alive?"

He nodded. "And so are you!"

She looked to me, struggling for words.

I squeezed her hand. "Let's go."

"Where?"

"Home."

CHAPTER THIRTY-SIX

When we came out of the teoyoh, we were in my tent, which someone had set up in my absence. Ehecacone rushed outside ahead of me, letting in the smell of salty air and a streak of bright sunlight. The cries of strange birds filled the air, as well as the crashing of waves. Ehecacone shouted a greeting to someone and told them I was inside, but his voice quickly faded away.

A moment later, Mitotia parted the tent flap and stepped inside, holding a cup of blood for me. "My morning offering for—" But she froze when she saw Malinalli standing next to me.

Malinalli was still holding my hand from the journey, but when I nodded to her encouragingly, she finally let me go and rushed to Mitotia, practically knocking the cup from her hand when she embraced her. "My love," Malinalli whispered, burying her face in Mitotia's hair.

Mitotia gripped her tight. "But…but how?"

"One sacrifice begets another." When Malinalli looked at back at me, I said, "I realize this will be difficult to reconcile, but I promise to be there for you, to help you cope with it. You're immortal now."

Her eyes bulged. "I am?"

I nodded. "Knowing your true nature is the important part, and as for the rest…we'll figure it out as we go along."

Malinalli looked about ready to faint but she held onto Mitotia tighter. "But why?"

"To thank you for your faith in me, when I needed it most. Every one of us owes you a deep debt of gratitude, and I hope this makes a start at paying back my portion of it."

She wiped tears from her eyes. "Then everything turned out all right?"

"We had to leave Tollan, but we're all doing well," I assured her.

"And Quetzalcoatl?"

"He's alive and well, and he's leading us into the future."

"As is My Lady," Mitotia added, smiling through joyful tears. "They're doing it together, as they've always done."

It was time to find out if that was even possible anymore.

◻

I left Mitotia and Malinalli in my tent to talk and went to find Quetzalcoatl. The salty breeze was warm and many of the men were out in the surf with nets, bringing in dinner. As I walked along the sand, searching, Ehecacone appeared next to me.

"You shouldn't be using the teoyoh unless absolutely necessary, dear," I warned him. "The blood offering supply is limited." We had yet to figure out his primary means of gathering magic, and I'd been giving him all of my blood offerings, since I hadn't needed them when I had Malinalli's sacrifice to live on, but having given that up, I would have to go back to my old feeding habits; a thought I didn't relish, but for Malinalli, I would make do.

"Sorry," he murmured. "It's just so much easier than walking."

"I know. Have you seen your father yet?"

"He's out fishing with the men."

I scoured the line as we walked until I spotted Quetzalcoatl. He wore only a white loincloth, and I marveled at how much bigger his muscles had become in the last month. Sweat shone on his dark brown skin, but he smiled and laughed with the other men. The sight of him made my heart quicken.

Ehecacone and I sat in the sand and I watched Quetzalcoatl for a long time while Ehecacone built palaces and temples in the hot sand. Eventually boring of the game, he knocked down everything then sat next to me again. "Mother?"

"Yes."

"Why doesn't Father have magic, like us?"

"He does, but he can't use it anymore."

"Why not?"

I sighed. "Because in my ignorance and shortsightedness, I let Smoking Mirror trick me into trapping him inside a mortal body."

Ehecacone gasped. "Can he die forever now?"

"No, he's still immortal."

"Why would you say it's your fault?"

I sighed. "I'm the reason your father is trapped in his human body. In my ignorance, I bound him to flesh, and I don't know if it's possible to ever reverse that."

"Oh." He sighed too, but wiggled his nose like a rabbit. "I'm sure he still loves you, Mother."

"I'm hoping he does."

"Maybe you should ask him about it."

"I'm going to, as soon as he's done fishing."

"Good!" Ehecacone took hold of my hand and smiled.

After a while, the men dragged their nets in and Quetzalcoatl came ashore. When he saw us and waved, Ehecacone waved back. When he reached us, he ruffled our son's tassel of black hair. "You wouldn't believe all of the fish we caught!"

"I'm glad I don't eat anymore, because I always hated fish," Ehecacone said, and Quetzalcoatl laughed.

His smile became formal when he turned to me. "You two were gone for quite a while."

"We were?" I asked, puzzled.

"About a week."

My face heated with guilt. "I'm sorry. I didn't know we were gone that long."

"Mother took me to Omeyocan," Ehecacone added.

Quetzalcoatl raised an eyebrow. "Oh you did?"

"I'm sorry," I said. "If I'd known we'd be gone that long, I would have told you where we were going."

"I got to see the inside of your house, Father," Ehecacone went on. "It looked nothing like how you described it."

Quetzalcoatl chuckled. "It does look very different to me than to anyone else."

"And I got to see Mother's house too. It looks like a sacred precinct."

"I fashioned it after Xochicalco," I said.

With a smile, Quetzalcoatl said, "I'd very much like to see it someday."

Guilt—for him being incapable of going there now, or possibly ever again—halted my tongue, but Ehecacone was more than willing to fill the silence. "And Mother has a heaven of her own, and she brought Malinalli back from the dead!"

Quetzalcoatl blinked at me. "You did?"

I shrugged. "I couldn't just leave her there. The place was empty, and since I don't approve of human sacrifice in my worship, it's my intention that it will remain so for a very long time to come. She gave all of us so much…it seemed cruel to condemn her to an eternity alone. I wouldn't even have a heaven if not for her." Embarrassment lit my cheeks as I asked, "Should I have left her there?"

"That's hardly my call," he said. "I'm sure Mitotia is happy to see her again."

"She is."

Mazatzin came down from the camp, holding Quetzalcoatl's high priest robe over his arm. He bowed when he reached us then he helped Quetzalcoatl shrug himself into his robe. "Will you be doing a service tonight, My Lord? It's been several weeks since the last one, and the people are anxious to hear you speak again."

"I will." Quetzalcoatl tied his robe shut. "Let us discuss it over lunch."

Swallowing my anxiety, I said, "Can we talk for a moment, My Lord? In private?"

Quetzalcoatl cast me a questioning glance but nodded. To Mazatzin, he said, "We'll discuss it when I get back. My Lady and I are going to walk down the beach a ways, so can you see to it that we're not disturbed?"

"I'll make sure everyone knows to give you privacy, My Lord." Mazatzin gave me a smile and a bow before turning to Ehecacone. "Perhaps you could help me catch some butterflies for this afternoon's prayers?"

"You bet!" Ehecacone gave me an encouraging smile then he hurried up the embankment, back into camp. Mazatzin followed.

Quetzalcoatl and I headed south along the sand, keeping an arm's length between us as we walked. I didn't want to barge into the topic right away, so I started off with something else. "Are we staying here through the winter?"

He nodded. "It will be warm here, and there's plenty to eat, though I'm sure by spring we'll all be tired of fish." He chuckled.

"Sometimes I miss eating. I have such good memories of food and meals with friends and family."

"You're welcome to eat at the meals with everyone at any time."

"I know, but I would be wasting the food. We don't have an unlimited supply anymore."

"True, but you're still welcome to sit with us."

"I think I will start doing that. Thank you."

With the sounds of the camp now distant, we fell into awkward silence. Eventually though, Quetzalcoatl said, "Ehecacone is progressing very nicely with his magic. You've been a most excellent teacher."

"Thank you."

"I'm sorry that I haven't been much help with any of it—"

"You've been teaching him a great deal," I countered

"It's just...he's very interested in the physical aspects of being a god, and that's not something I can help him with."

"The novelty of physical magic will wear off, but he'll always need to know more about what it means to be a god, and you're very good at teaching him that. You're still teaching me a great deal."

He smiled. "Yes, I can help him with that." He sighed then added, "I must admit, I never thought something as simple as being a parent could be so overwhelming. I don't know how humans have more than one child at a time!"

I folded my hands behind my back. "Speaking of children, I wanted to ask you something, about our other child."

He furrowed his brow. "Our other child?"

"Well, children, to be more precise. I'm talking about Xochiquetzal and Xochipilli."

Quetzalcoatl stopped, a look of utter puzzlement on his face. "I don't understand."

"When I met Xochiquetzal, she said you were her father—that you made her from a flower on the plant that grew from my bones."

"I made her?"

My cheeks flushed as I said, "She claimed you...released your essence on one of my flowers and she grew from that."

At first his face was unchanged, but then a slow creep of realization changed it. "Oh my. Well, I suppose it's possible...."

I raised an eyebrow.

Lowering his voice, he said, "After you...died...I thought your essence might still be inside the plant, so I...bonded with it, hoping to find you inside. Instead, I found only disappointment."

Chuckling, I said, "I'd say you found more than that."

His face darkened with embarrassment.

"You should know that Xochiquetzal thinks that you abandoned her."

"I didn't even know about her." Quetzalcoatl went to the water's edge and stared out onto the horizon. "You said children?"

"Well, there's also Xochipilli, but he and Xochiquetzal aren't exactly separate beings. Like Ehecatl's darkness and light, they are separate aspects of a single god, but those aspects manifest as different gods depending upon which one is in control."

"Smoking Mirror and I used to do that, when we were still Ehecatl." He sighed, looking run-down. "Are you disgusted with me?"

"Of course not. Though if we're to have any more children, I do ask that you don't spring them on me as a surprise."

I meant it as a quip, hoping to lighten the mood, but it had the opposite effect. He covered his face with both hands and groaned. "I owe you an apology, Mayahuel. I should have been more careful, and I should have foreseen what would happen when I possessed your human body in Culhuacan."

"I don't need any apologies. I was surprised to find out about Xochiquetzal and Xochipilli, and Xochiquetzal doesn't like me any more than she likes you, but as for Ehecacone...I have no regrets, only gratefulness. Thank you for our son."

Tears shone in his eyes. "I'm grateful for him too." He looked back up towards camp, as if expecting to see Ehecacone running down the beach to us. When he turned back to me, he said, "About Malinalli...I'm sorry if I sounded like I was questioning your decision. I do understand your reasons; I think if I had the chance...I would bring Citlallotoc back too. If only because there's so much I wish I could tell him now...so much I would not only thank him for, but also apologize for."

"I too wish I would have gotten the chance to say goodbye to him," I admitted.

"How did he die, exactly?"

"Mextli poisoned him."

He clenched his fist. "Then he's down in Mictlan with the rest of Mextli's sacrifices, giving that feathered menace more power."

"Actually...I sent both Mextli's and Smoking Mirror's sacrifices to their eternal rest when I confronted Lord Death for Ehecacone."

Quetzalcoatl stared at me with a mixture of fear and awe. "Well, that's one way to make sure Smoking Mirror doesn't come back looking for revenge right away."

I hadn't even thought of that possibility. Now I was more grateful than ever that I'd wiped out their sacrifices.

"What about Anacoana? How did she die?"

"Yaretzi slit her throat when she tried to murder you."

He blinked. "Anacoana tried to murder me?"

"She was under the influence of a heavy love potion, courtesy of our daughter, so she certainly wasn't in her sanest mind. But ironically, if she'd finished you, you wouldn't be trapped now as you are." I frowned; Itzpapalotl's suspicious rescue made frustrating sense now. I shook my head.

"I'm sorry I left you to deal with such a mess on your own," he said, guilt and sadness invading his voice. "I didn't think I would linger in the inbetween as long as I did."

"I'm pretty sure that Smoking Mirror was plying you with medicines to keep your mortal body hanging on long enough to bring his plans to fruition."

We stood in long silence again, but I knew if I waited much longer, I might let the fear win and I'd just stay exactly where I was, never moving forward. Whatever his answer, I had to know the truth. "The reason I wanted to talk to you...."

"Yes?"

"It's about our future."

"What about it troubles you?"

"I'm not necessarily troubled, but...." I stepped closer to him, and with a deep breath, I said, "I know it might be too much to hope for, given what I did, but...is it at all possible that our relationship can be what it once was?"

A glimmer of hope came to his eyes. "Do you mean like when we were married?"

"I nodded. "Or maybe even more than just husband and wife...for political purposes?"

"You mean lovers?"

"Yes?" I said, daring to let the hope grow.

In answer, he bridged the gap between us and kissed me. My teotl felt as if it would burst out everywhere, but once we separated again, I could barely stand. "I'd hoped you would ask me that," he whispered, leaning his head against mine. "And I must admit that I started worrying that you hadn't yet."

"I'm sorry, Little Reed, for everything—"

"It's the past, and let's not speak of it again." His next kiss brought the desire dancing joyously in my belly. When we separated again, he whispered, "I so missed you calling me Little Reed, Papalotl."

"And I will always be your precious Butterfly," I promised then kissed him again.

He pulled his robe off and took my hand. "Over here," and we retreated to the shade beside an outcrop of red lava rocks, where we were unlikely to be seen from a distance. He laid the robe on the sand for us, and I stretched out on it, leaving space for him to join me.

But when he made to untie his loincloth, I grabbed his hand. "That's my job," the desire purred. I pulled the knot loose slowly, watching the joy and anticipation play across his face. I marveled at how clear and open his gaze was; none of the usual drunken haze, but also none of the indifference I'd seen in Mextli's eyes. I saw only love and devotion of the kind I'd craved my entire life; the kind that mirrored my own feelings for him.

Little Reed couldn't undress me, but I played to the illusion by making my dress melt away under his hands, much like he'd done that first time we were intimate in the Divine Dream, when he'd promised that someday we would be together in the real world. It had taken far longer than either of us had thought, but that day was finally here. "Now?" I whispered, digging my fingernails into his nape with desperation.

He smiled. "Now."

Unlike our desperate coupling in our meditation room back in Tollan, he eased himself into me with infinite patience. There was no reason to hurry and we both took our time, testing our bodies against each other, figuring out what worked and what didn't. Unlike with human men, I couldn't automatically read Little Reed's desires and preferences, but I preferred it this way. It had never lasted so long in the real world, so I'd never known the joys of the slow, steady build outside the Divine Dream. Until now. And I never again wanted it to be any other way.

But that was all just foreplay; the real pleasure came after the climax, when the world melted away into blinding white light, and our tendrils of magic coiled around each other, his white feathered serpents swimming in a joyous, intimate dance with my vibrant orange rabbits. As the flow between us began, his consciousness mingled with mine and we held no more secrets.

I saw his meeting in Mictlan with Lord Death and the sure odds that one of us would end up back there—never to return—but the chance at redemption, for us to fall in love all over again and find the future together that Smoking Mirror had ended for us so many years ago, it was all worth the risk.

But because I had to be reborn as a human being, he made the decision to bear himself into the human world as well, so we could be equals and bring changes to humanity together. It meant sacrificing his ability to use his own magic until his trapped divine essence finally devoured its fleshy prison, but it was the only way to bring about the reforms the world needed.

Without his magic to defend himself against Smoking Mirror, everything would fail before it could even start, but it was Xolotl who pointed out the workaround. *Entrust Mayahuel with the ability to release your divinity for brief moments, in exchange for a sacrifice. Your mortal body will be at its most vulnerable during those moments, for your consciousness cannot be in two places at once, but if love is as strong as you claim, then it will keep you safe and ensure your plan's success.*

And in those early years, love indeed protected him, whether it was me shielding him with my own body against an assassin's knife, or Mazatzin standing in defense of his unconscious body while Chichimecs ambushed our camp in Teotihuacan, or Citlallotoc carrying him nearly dead from the limestone quarry after Red Flint's men had slit his throat.

But it was also love that prompted him to sacrifice everything he'd worked for in order to bring me back from the brink of death. From that day forward, he was destined to fail in his reforms, and I felt all of his pain and guilt in knowing there was nothing he could do to stop it.

But he never turned from the path; we built Tollan and made our reforms, and we tried to show everyone that love was more powerful than fear. Yes, we'd failed in Tollan, but our journey was far from over. We'd shown humanity that things didn't have to be as they always had been; we'd given them hope, and that was something as precious as love itself.

As in Tamoachan so long ago, awash in each other's memories and thoughts and emotions, we became one again: one consciousness, one body, one destiny. I wanted it to last forever.

Eventually though, reality brought us back to ourselves. The magic I'd used to bind him to flesh exerted itself and I felt him slipping away from me again. I tried to counter it, hoping since it was my own magic, I could control it or even take it back and free him, but no matter what I did, it continued pulling him away from me.

Our bodies re-solidified and the dull ache of guilt and loss filled the new emptiness left by his departure.

When I opened my eyes, I found him crying as I held him. The sight crushed me. "Little Reed...."

"Thank you," he whispered.

I blinked through my own tears, confused. "For what?"

"For helping me feel like a god again."

ロ

That evening, Little Reed, Ehecacone, and I gathered around the massive central bonfire set up on the beach. Someone had made a set of crude reed thrones for me and Little Reed to sit upon, and Mitotia had even found wild bone flowers to decorate mine with. The familiar sweet scent mixed with the briny smell of the ocean was oddly comforting.

There were too many people to fit everyone around the fire at once, so the meal went in shifts, giving every person the chance to sit and eat with us. It reminded me of the communal meals in the priesthood in Xochicalco, before my taking the mantle of queen had kept me from participating anymore.

Once the final meal shift completed, the night had fallen into the late hours, but everyone remained on the beach, waiting to hear Little Reed speak. Once he rose to his feet, everyone piled in closer to the fire, standing to make sure everyone had a spot within the firelight.

"I know I usually do the services, but tonight, Lady Mayahuel will share wisdom with us." Little Reed gestured to me to stand.

The crowd turned their attention upon me as I stepped up to the fire. "I'm sure everyone is tired after a long, hard day, and the many that came before as we left Tollan, so I will make this speech short. Lord Topiltzin-Quetzalcoatl and I thank each and every one of you for your contribution and hard work, and for your continued faith in our leadership. Many of you no doubt still feel the keen pain of having to leave Tollan, but know this: Tollan has not left you! Tollan is not buildings or gardens or even laws: it is the notion that everyone gets back what they give, and that goes most especially for the gods. So long as we all continue living by this principle, Tollan will continue to flourish, in the hearts and minds of each and every one of you, and there will come a day when it is the philosophy of self-sacrifice rather than fear that will rule the hearts of mankind, and Tollan will return to the people once again. As will her king, and her queen!"

A cheer rose over the beach, and many prayers were said and dances performed. In the celebrating crowd, I spotted Malinalli and Mitotia dancing together with eyes only for each other, and Ehecacone bounded about as a large rabbit, beating his paws on a drum slung over his neck with a jaguar hide strap and regaling everyone with all the songs I'd taught him as a boy.

The festivities finally wrapped up near the midnight hour, but as the crowd dispersed back to their tents, Little Reed and I went out onto the empty beach with Mazatzin, and like before, he bound us together in marriage. We didn't bother with the usual religious rituals; I doubted many of the gods would bless our marriage, nor did we need their approval. It was enough that we had each other. I retired to Little Reed's tent with him, to celebrate our renewed partnership, then I lay at his side while he slept, thinking of the future ahead, surrounded by my husband, my son, and all of those friends dearest to me.

For the first time in countless bundles of years, my heart was finally content.

◻

In the morning, as we sat around the fire eating breakfast, a group of men and women came up the beach from the south of camp carrying baskets of food—maize, beans, and dried deer meat. They bowed as they approached and Little Reed rose to greet them.

"Our king sent us to welcome you," the big warrior leading the group told us. Red designs decorated his body, and his head was shaved and his earlobes hung low with heavy wooden spools. "Our shaman had a vision that you were coming, and that you'd lead us out of the misery that has claimed our village." As the others with him set the baskets down in the sand before us, he went on, "We bring you gifts and ask that you come back to our village and listen to our king and consider his plea."

Little Reed smiled. "We'd be honored to do what we can to help your people." He then held out his hand to help me up. "Won't we, my love?"

"Absolutely," I agreed, and squeezed his hand in mine.

◻   ◻   ◻

Author's Note

 Ce Acatl Topiltzin Quetzalcoatl is often thought of as the "King Arthur" of Mesoamerica: he was the great uniter, the father of Toltec civilization, and the champion against human sacrifice.

Given the Aztec preoccupation with blood sacrifice, it's easy to see why his story was so compelling to them. The importance of the Topiltzin myth in Mesoamerican thought and history cannot be overstated: some stories of the Spanish Conquest point to Emperor Moctezuma the Younger becoming frozen with fear and indecision because he thought Hernan Cortes was the fulfillment of Topiltzin's promise to return and reclaim his throne. The Mexica (Aztecs) derived their right to rule through connecting their own royal families with the bloodlines of the legendary Toltec priest-king, and they considered themselves the beneficiaries of the culture he created for the Toltecs. He is so inextricably intertwined with the god from whom he took his name that often the lines between history and mythology become so blurred as to be indistinguishable from each other.

The legends of Topiltzin Quetzalcoatl are many and diverse. Practically every area of central Mexico had its own version. Who his father and mother were varied with the telling, as did the name and number of his uncles, where he was born, and how he spent his formative years; but one element remains firm through all the stories: he outlawed human sacrifice in defiance of the gods, and for that he and his followers were driven from Tollan through cruel—and often magical—trickery. Some versions have him disappearing into the southern jungles to build new cities, while others say he immolated himself upon a raft of serpents, rising into the sky as the planet Venus. Often these tales promised he would return someday in the future to reclaim his throne.

But what do we know of the woman Quetzalpetlatl? Very little. Her name appears in only one rendition of the stories, recorded in the Anales de Cuauhtitlan, a collection of Nahuatl narratives from the basin of Mexico and Puebla. She is called Topiltzin's "sister", though it's unclear whether she's an actual blood relative or merely a priestess under his authority. Regardless, through the dark influence of the sorcerer god Tezcatlipoca, Topiltzin committed transgressions—religious and/or sexual—with Quetzalpetlatl, and left Tollan in shame. But what became of Quetzalpetlatl, whom the gods used to destroy Topiltzin's reputation and power? She's never mentioned again.

These books set out to posit answers to these mysteries: who was Quetzalpetlatl, what was her relationship to Topiltzin, what role did she play in his greatest accomplishments, and, eventually, what became of her once the gods finished using her to destroy Mesoamerica's most famous hero?

◻

The goddess Mayahuel's origin story appeared in *Histoyre du Mechique*, a French translation of a much older, incomplete Spanish missionary text detailing the exploits of the god Quetzalcoatl, both on earth and in the heavens. The story is detailed as such:

With the rebirth of humanity in the wake of the end of the Fourth Sun, the gods wish to give their creations something to provide them with pleasure and happiness. It is Quetzalcoatl, in the guise of Ehecatl, who thinks of the virgin goddess Mayahuel, who is kept prisoner by her fierce grandmother, the goddess Tzitzimitl. He abducts her while her grandmother sleeps, and he takes her to earth, carrying her upon his shoulders, and once there, they come together to form a tree.

But when Tzitzimitl wakes to find her granddaughter gone, she enlists the help of the tzitzimime—star demons—to hunt her down. They search all over the earth for her, but they are only able to find her when the tree's two branches inexplicably split away from each other, making Mayahuel recognizable. The star demons descend on her and devour her, leaving only her bones behind.

Meanwhile, Ehecatl has survived the attack unscathed and he gathers Mayahuel's bones and buries them. From that sacred ground, the metl tree—the maguey or the agave—grows, and from its milky-white sap, humans learn to ferment the sacred wine called octli—or now commonly known as pulque.

As many Central American gods are want to do, Mayahuel doesn't stay dead forever. She becomes the wife of the medicine god Patecatl and gives birth to the Centzontotochtin—the Four Hundred Rabbits; the god Tepoztecatl—otherwise known as Ehecacone (Son of the Wind)—being among them. She becomes a symbol of fecundity and fertility, and she's often portrayed as suckling a baby at one of her four-hundred breasts.

While the mythology doesn't support a conflation of the goddess with the mysterious mythical figure of Quetzalpetlatl, there are enough interesting details to form a tangible "what if" story. After all, both Mayahuel and Quetzalpetlatl are little more than pawns in the machinations of the gods—Quetzalpetlatl is used by Tezcatlipoca to religiously—and sexually—discredit Topiltzin, and Ehecatl exploits Mayahuel's innocence to lure her to her death, all to give humanity the gift of octli. Both women's stories are incomplete and dissatisfying on their own, but together, they make for something interesting, not just for themselves, but for those around them as well.

List of Characters

Ahexotl – high priest of Quetzalcoatl in Xochicalco

Amoxtli – son of Ihuitimal, brother to Black Otter, cousin to Quetzalpetlatl and Topiltzin

Anacoana – daughter of King Flame Tongue of Xico

Atzi – concubine of Cuitlapanton, mother of Obsidian Eagle and Pochotzin.

Bitter Rabbit – Ten Spine's wife, mother of Mitotia

Black Otter - son of Ihuitimal

Blood Wolf - friend of Nochuatl, Justice of the Peace of Tollan under Quetzalpetlatl

Camaxtli – brother to Red Flint

Chimalma – wife of Mixcoatl, mother of Quetzalpetlatl and Topiltzin

Cihuacoatl (Snake Woman) – very old creator goddess

Citlallotoc – Topiltzin's best friend and war chief

Coatlicue (Snake Skirt) – mother of Mextli, former human turned immortal

Corn Flower – concubine of Black Otter

Coyolxauhqui – sorceress sister of Mextli

Cuicatl – daughter of Black Otter and Jade Flower

Cuitlapanton – king of Xochicalco

Ehecacone (Yamehecatl) – son of Quetzalcoatl and Quetzalpetlatl

Eloxochitl – Ihuitimal's wife, Black Otter's mother, sister to Chimalma

Emerald – sister and legitimate wife of Cuitlapanton, mother of Red Flint

Eztetl – a fire priest of Quetzalcoatl

Flame Tongue – King of Xico, father of Anacoana

Growling Monkey – king of Xochimilco

Huemac – younger brother to Citlallotoc, King of Acolman

Ihuitimal – brother of Mixcoatl, father of Black Otter and Amoxtli, high priest of the Smoking Mirror

Iczoxochitl – novice priestess

Itzpapalotl (the Obsidian Butterfly) – minor goddess, ally of Smoking Mirror

Ixchell – priestess of Quetzalcoatl

Jade Flower – Quetzalpetlatl's half-sister, mother of Cuicatl and Night Wind

Jade Skirt (Chalchiuhtlicue) – Goddess of Rivers, Streams, and the Seas.

Lord Death (Mictlantecuhtli) – God of Death, Lord of Mictlan

Malinalli – priestess of Quetzalcoatl, Quetzalpetlatl's best friend

Mayahuel – Goddess of the Maguey

Matlacxochitl – younger brother of Blood Wolf

Mazatzin – priest of Quetzalcoatl, brother of Red Flint

Meconetzin – king of Chalco

Mextli (Huitzilopochtli) – god of war, leader of the Mexica, brother to Smoking Mirror

Mitotia – priestess of Quetzalcoatl

Mixcoatl – king of Culhuacan, father of Quetzalpetlatl

Mixcoatl (the Cloud Serpent) – god of the hunt, husband of Coatlicue

Mocneltzin – son of Cuitlapanton

Mothotli – fire priestess of Quetzalcoatl in Xochicalco

Mozauhqui – son of the king of Tepanec

Nahuacatl – King Toztli's son, heir of Chimalhuacan

Necalli – lord on Cuitlapanton's war council

Night Wind – son of Black Otter and Jade Flower

Nimilitzli – high priestess of Quetzalcoatl in Xochicalco, foster mother to Quetzalpetlatl and Topiltzin,

Nanahuatzin (Tonatiuh) – the leper sun god

Nochuatl – brother of Ihuitimal and Mixcoatl

Obsidian Eagle – son of Cuitlapanton

Oquitzin – son of Cuitlapanton

Ozomatli – priest of the Smoking Mirror

Papantzin – concubine of Black Otter

Paper Flower – priestess of Quetzalcoatl

Patli – guard in Tollan

Pochotzin – son of Cuitlapanton

Quetzalcoatl (the Feathered Serpent) – god of civilization, father of mankind. Also known as Ehecatl, god of the wind.

Quetzalpetlatl (Papalotl) – legitimate daughter of King Mixcoatl, sister of Topiltzin

Red Flint – prince of Xochicalco

Red Hawk – son of the chief of the Mexica

Spear Fish – Cuitlapanton's war chief

Stargazer – son of Cuitlapanton

Storm House – a captain in Culhuacan's army

Talking Serpent – novice priest

Tayanna – priestess of Quetzalcoatl

Tecuciztecatl – god of the moon

Ten Spines – chieftain of the Tollan Chichimecs

Tezcatlipoca (the Smoking Mirror) – Chichimec god of war and sorcerers, god of the night

Timaltzin – Justice of the Peace of Tollan under Matlacxochitl

Tlaloc – god of rain

Tlanextli – priest of Tlaloc, husband of Ixchell

Topiltzin (Little Reed) – son of Quetzalcoatl, brother to Quetzalpetlatl

Tototl – lord on Cuitlapanton's war council

Toztli – king of Chimalhuacan

Turquoise Bells – sister and wife of Red Flint

Tzitzimime (Monsters Descending from Above) - celestial monsters

Tzitzimitl (the Earth Monster) – grandmother to Mayahuel

Ueman – shaman of the god Mixcoatl

Xihuitl – high priest of Mayahuel

Xipe Totec (The Flayed Lord) – god of the harvest

Xipil – lord on Cuitlapanton's war council

Xochipilli (Flower Prince) – god of music and dance, brother of Xochiquetzal

Xochiquetzal (Precious Flower) – love goddess, sister of Xochipilli

Xochitl – high priestess of Mayahuel

Xolotl (the Black Dog) – servant god to Mictlantecuhtli and the guide of the dead

Yaretzi – high priestess of the Smoking Mirror

Zeltzin – concubine to Mixcoatl, mother of Jade Flower

FURTHER READING

Richard Blanton, Stephen A. Kowalewski, Gary Feinman, and Jill Appel, *Ancient Mesoamerica: A Comparison of Change in Three Regions*, Cambridge University Press, 1981.

Burr Cartwright Brundage, *The Phoenix of the Western World: Quetzalcoatl and the Sky Religion*, University of Oklahoma Press, 1981.

David Carrasco, *Quetzalcoatl and the Irony of Empire: Myths and Prophecies in the Aztec Tradition*, University Press of Colorado, 2001.

Sophie Coe, *America's First Cuisines*, University of Texas Press, 1994.

Nigel Davies, *The Toltecs Until the Fall of Tula*, University of Oklahoma Press, 1977.

Richard A. Diehl, *Tula: The Toltec Capital of Ancient Mexico*, Thames and Hudson, 1983.

William Gates, *An Aztec Herbal: The Classic Codex of 1552*, Dover Publications, Inc, 2000.

Rich Holmer, *The Aztec Book of Destiny*, BookSurge, LLC, 2005.

Miguel León-Portilla, *Aztec Thought and Culture*, University of Oklahoma Press, 1963.

Roberta H. Markman and Peter T Markman, *The Flayed God: The Mythology of Mesoamerica*, Harper San Francisco, 1992.

Mary Miller and Karl Taube, *An Illustrated Dictionary of the Gods and Symbols of Ancient Mexico and the Maya*, Thames and Hudson, 1993.

H. B. Nicholson, *Topiltzin Quetzalcoatl: The Once and Future Lord of the Toltecs*, University Press of Colorado, 2001.

Guilhem Olivier, *Mockeries and Metamorphoses of an Aztec God: Tezcatlipoca, "Lord of the Smoking Mirror"*, University Press of Colorado, 2003.

John M. D. Pohl, *Aztec, Mixtec and Zapotec Armies*, Osprey Publishing, 1991.

John Pohl, PhD and Adam Hook, *Aztec Warrior, A.D. 1325-1521*, Osprey Military, 2001.

Fray Bernardino de Sahagún, *The Florentine Codex: The General History of the Things of New Spain*, translated by Arthur J. O. Anderson and Charles E. Dibble, The School of American Research and The University of Utah, 1975.

Jacques Soustelle, *Daily Life of the Aztecs*, Dover Publications, Inc., 2002.

ABOUT THE AUTHOR

T. L. Morganfield lives in Colorado with her husband and children. She's an alumna of the Clarion West Workshop and she graduated from Metropolitan State University with dual degrees in English and History. She reads and writes way too much about Aztec history and mythology, but it keeps her muse happy, which makes for a happy writer, so she has no plans of changing her ways.

You can join her mailing list at www.tlmorganfield.com to receive updates on her latest work.